I0819997

Collected Novels and Short Stories

By

Nathaniel Hawthorne

Cover Photograph: sariykotik1970

ISBN: 978-1-78139-380-2

© 2013 Benediction Classics, Oxford.

Contents

THE SCARLET LETTER

THE HOUSE OF THE SEVEN GABLES

THE BLITHEDALE ROMANCE

MOSSES FROM AN OLD MANSE AND OTHER STORIES

TWICE-TOLD TALES.

TANGLEWOOD TALES

THE SCARLET LETTER

EDITOR'S NOTE

Nathaniel Hawthorne was already a man of forty-six, and a tale writer of some twenty-four years' standing, when "The Scarlet Letter" appeared. He was born at Salem, Mass., on July 4th, 1804, son of a sea-captain. He led there a shy and rather sombre life; of few artistic encouragements, yet not wholly uncongenial, his moody, intensely meditative temperament being considered. Its colours and shadows are marvelously reflected in his "Twice-Told Tales" and other short stories, the product of his first literary period. Even his college days at Bowdoin did not quite break through his acquired and inherited reserve; but beneath it all, his faculty of divining men and women was exercised with almost uncanny prescience and subtlety. "The Scarlet Letter," which explains as much of this unique imaginative art, as is to be gathered from reading his highest single achievement, yet needs to be ranged with his other writings, early and late, to have its last effect. In the year that saw it published, he began "The House of the Seven Gables," a later romance or prose-tragedy of the Puritan-American community as he had himself known it— defrauded of art and the joy of life, "starving for symbols" as Emerson has it. Nathaniel Hawthorne died at Plymouth, New Hampshire, on May 18th, 1864.

THE CUSTOM-HOUSE

INTRODUCTORY TO "THE SCARLET LETTER"

It is a little remarkable, that—though disinclined to talk overmuch of myself and my affairs at the fireside, and to my personal friends—an autobiographical impulse should twice in my life have taken possession of me, in addressing the public. The first time was three or four years since, when I favoured the reader—inexcusably, and for no earthly reason that either the indulgent reader or the intrusive author could imagine—with a description of my way of life in the deep quietude of an Old Manse. And now—because, beyond my deserts, I was happy enough to find a listener or two on the former occasion—I again seize the public by the button, and talk of my three years' experience in a Custom-House. The example of the famous "P. P., Clerk of this Parish," was never more faithfully followed. The truth seems to be, however, that when he casts his leaves forth upon the wind, the author addresses, not the many who will fling aside his volume, or never take it up, but the few who will understand him better than most of his schoolmates or lifemates. Some authors, indeed, do far more than this, and indulge themselves in such confidential depths of revelation as could fittingly be addressed only and exclusively to the one heart and mind of perfect sympathy; as if the printed book, thrown at large on the wide world, were certain to find out the divided segment of the writer's own nature, and complete his circle of existence by bringing him into communion with it. It is scarcely decorous, however, to speak all, even where we speak impersonally. But, as thoughts are frozen and utterance benumbed, unless the speaker stand in some true relation with his audience, it may be pardonable to imagine that a friend, a kind and apprehensive, though not the closest friend, is listening to our talk; and then, a native reserve being thawed by this genial consciousness, we may prate of the circumstances that lie around us, and even of ourself, but still keep the inmost Me behind its veil. To this extent, and within these limits, an author, methinks, may be autobiographical, without violating either the reader's rights or his own.

It will be seen, likewise, that this Custom-House sketch has a certain propriety, of a kind always recognised in literature, as explaining how a large portion of the following pages came into my possession, and as offering proofs of the authenticity of a narrative therein contained. This, in fact—a desire to put myself in my true position as editor, or very little more, of the most prolix among the tales that make up my volume—this, and no other, is my true reason for assuming a personal relation with the public. In accomplishing the main purpose, it has appeared allowable, by a few extra touches, to give a faint representation of a mode of life not heretofore described, together with some of the characters that move in it, among whom the author happened to make one.

In my native town of Salem, at the head of what, half a century ago, in the days of old King Derby, was a bustling wharf—but which is now burdened with decayed wooden warehouses, and exhibits few or no symptoms of commercial life; except, perhaps, a bark or brig, half-way down its melancholy length, discharging hides; or, nearer at hand, a Nova Scotia schooner, pitching out her cargo of firewood—at the head, I say, of this dilapidated wharf, which the tide often overflows, and along which, at the base and in the rear of the row of buildings, the track of many languid years is seen in a border of unthrifty grass—here, with a view from its front windows adown this not very enlivening prospect, and thence across the harbour, stands a spacious edifice of brick. From the loftiest point of its roof, during precisely three and a half hours of each forenoon, floats or droops, in breeze or calm, the banner of the republic; but with the thirteen stripes turned vertically, instead of horizontally, and thus indicating that a civil, and not a military, post of Uncle Sam's government is here established. Its front is ornamented with a portico of half-a-dozen wooden pillars, supporting a balcony, beneath which a flight of wide granite steps descends towards the street. Over the entrance hovers an enormous specimen of the American eagle, with outspread wings, a shield before her breast, and, if I recollect aright, a bunch of intermingled thunderbolts and barbed arrows in each claw. With the customary infirmity of temper that characterizes this unhappy fowl, she appears by the fierceness of her beak and eye, and the general truculency of her attitude, to threaten mischief to the inoffensive community; and especially to warn all citizens careful of their safety against intruding on the premises which she overshadows with her wings. Nevertheless, vixenly as she looks, many people are seeking at this very moment to shelter themselves under the wing of the federal eagle; imagining, I presume, that her bosom has all the softness and snugness of an eiderdown pillow. But she has no great tenderness even in her best of moods, and, sooner or later—oftener soon than late—is apt to fling off her nestlings with a scratch of her claw, a dab of her beak, or a rankling wound from her barbed arrows.

The pavement round about the above-described edifice—which we may as well name at once as the Custom-House of the port—has grass enough growing in its chinks to show that it has not, of late days, been worn by any multitudinous resort of business. In some months of the year, however, there often chances a forenoon when affairs move onward with a livelier tread. Such occasions might remind the elderly citizen of that period, before the last war with England, when Salem was a port by itself; not scorned, as she is now, by her own merchants and ship-owners, who permit her wharves to crumble to ruin while their ventures go to swell, needlessly and imperceptibly, the mighty flood of commerce at New York or Boston. On some such morning, when three or four vessels happen to have arrived at once usually from Africa or South America—or to be on the verge of their departure thitherward, there is a sound of frequent feet passing briskly up and down the granite steps. Here, before his own wife has greeted him, you may greet the sea-flushed ship-master, just in port, with his vessel's papers under his arm in a tarnished tin box. Here, too, comes his owner, cheerful, sombre, gracious or in the sulks, accordingly as his scheme of the now accomplished voyage has been realized in merchandise that will readily be turned to gold, or has buried him under a bulk of incommodities such as nobody will care to rid him of. Here, likewise—the germ of the wrinkle-browed, grizzly-bearded, careworn merchant—we have the smart young clerk, who gets the taste of traffic as a wolf-cub does of blood, and already sends adventures in his master's ships, when he had better be sailing mimic boats upon a mill-pond. Another figure in the scene is the outward-bound sailor, in quest of a protection; or the recently arrived one, pale and feeble, seeking a passport to the hospital. Nor must we forget the captains of the rusty little schooners that bring firewood from the British provinces; a rough-looking set of tarpaulins, without the alertness of the Yankee aspect, but contributing an item of no slight importance to our decaying trade.

Cluster all these individuals together, as they sometimes were, with other miscellaneous ones to diversify the group, and, for the time being, it made the Custom-House a stirring scene. More frequently, however, on ascending the steps, you would discern— in the entry if it were summer time, or in their appropriate rooms if wintry or inclement weathers—a row of venerable figures, sitting in old-fashioned chairs, which were tipped on their hind legs back against the wall. Oftentimes they were asleep, but occasionally might be heard talking together, in voices between a speech and a snore, and with that lack of energy that distinguishes the occupants of alms-houses, and all other human beings who depend for subsistence on charity, on monopolized labour, or anything else but their own independent exertions. These old gentlemen—seated, like Matthew at the receipt of custom, but not very liable to be summoned thence, like him, for apostolic errands—were Custom-House officers.

Furthermore, on the left hand as you enter the front door, is a certain room or office, about fifteen feet square, and of a lofty height, with two of its arched windows commanding a view of the aforesaid dilapidated wharf, and the third looking across a narrow lane, and along a portion of Derby Street. All three give glimpses of the shops of grocers, block-makers, slop-sellers, and ship-chandlers, around the doors of which are generally to be seen, laughing and gossiping, clusters of old salts, and such other wharf-rats as haunt the Wapping of a seaport. The room itself is cobwebbed, and dingy with old paint; its floor is strewn with grey sand, in a fashion that has elsewhere fallen into long disuse; and it is easy to conclude, from the general slovenliness of the place, that this is a sanctuary into which womankind, with her tools of magic, the broom and mop, has very infrequent access. In the way of furniture, there is a stove with a voluminous funnel;

an old pine desk with a three-legged stool beside it; two or three wooden-bottom chairs, exceedingly decrepit and infirm; and—not to forget the library—on some shelves, a score or two of volumes of the Acts of Congress, and a bulky Digest of the Revenue laws. A tin pipe ascends through the ceiling, and forms a medium of vocal communication with other parts of the edifice. And here, some six months ago—pacing from corner to corner, or lounging on the long-legged stool, with his elbow on the desk, and his eyes wandering up and down the columns of the morning newspaper—you might have recognised, honoured reader, the same individual who welcomed you into his cheery little study, where the sunshine glimmered so pleasantly through the willow branches on the western side of the Old Manse. But now, should you go thither to seek him, you would inquire in vain for the Locofoco Surveyor. The besom of reform hath swept him out of office, and a worthier successor wears his dignity and pockets his emoluments.

This old town of Salem—my native place, though I have dwelt much away from it both in boyhood and maturer years—possesses, or did possess, a hold on my affection, the force of which I have never realized during my seasons of actual residence here. Indeed, so far as its physical aspect is concerned, with its flat, unvaried surface, covered chiefly with wooden houses, few or none of which pretend to architectural beauty—its irregularity, which is neither picturesque nor quaint, but only tame—its long and lazy street, lounging wearisomely through the whole extent of the peninsula, with Gallows Hill and New Guinea at one end, and a view of the alms-house at the other—such being the features of my native town, it would be quite as reasonable to form a sentimental attachment to a disarranged checker-board. And yet, though invariably happiest elsewhere, there is within me a feeling for Old Salem, which, in lack of a better phrase, I must be content to call affection. The sentiment is probably assignable to the deep and aged roots which my family has stuck into the soil. It is now nearly two centuries and a quarter since the original Briton, the earliest emigrant of my name, made his appearance in the wild and forest-bordered settlement which has since become a city. And here his descendants have been born and died, and have mingled their earthly substance with the soil, until no small portion of it must necessarily be akin to the mortal frame wherewith, for a little while, I walk the streets. In part, therefore, the attachment which I speak of is the mere sensuous sympathy of dust for dust. Few of my countrymen can know what it is; nor, as frequent transplantation is perhaps better for the stock, need they consider it desirable to know.

But the sentiment has likewise its moral quality. The figure of that first ancestor, invested by family tradition with a dim and dusky grandeur, was present to my boyish imagination as far back as I can remember. It still haunts me, and induces a sort of home-feeling with the past, which I scarcely claim in reference to the present phase of the town. I seem to have a stronger claim to a residence here on account of this grave, bearded, sable-cloaked, and steeple-crowned progenitor—who came so early, with his Bible and his sword, and trode the unworn street with such a stately port, and made so large a figure, as a man of war and peace—a stronger claim than for myself, whose name is seldom heard and my face hardly known. He was a soldier, legislator, judge; he was a ruler in the Church; he had all the Puritanic traits, both good and evil. He was likewise a bitter persecutor; as witness the Quakers, who have remembered him in their histories, and relate an incident of his hard severity towards a woman of their sect, which will last longer, it is to be feared, than any record of his better deeds, although these were many. His son, too, inherited the persecuting spirit, and made himself so conspicuous in the martyrdom of the witches, that their blood may fairly be said to have left a stain upon him. So deep a stain, indeed, that his dry old bones, in the Charter-street burial-ground, must still retain it, if they have not crumbled utterly to dust! I know not whether these ancestors of mine bethought themselves to repent, and ask pardon of Heaven for their cruelties; or whether they are now groaning under the heavy consequences of them in another state of being. At all events, I, the present writer, as their representative, hereby take shame upon myself for their sakes, and pray that any curse incurred by them—as I have heard, and as the dreary and unprosperous condition of the race, for many a long year back, would argue to exist—may be now and henceforth removed.

Doubtless, however, either of these stern and black-browed Puritans would have thought it quite a sufficient retribution for his sins that, after so long a lapse of years, the old trunk of the family tree, with so much venerable moss upon it, should have borne, as its topmost bough, an idler like myself. No aim that I have ever cherished would they recognise as laudable; no success of mine—if my life, beyond its domestic scope, had ever been brightened by success—would they deem otherwise than worthless, if not positively disgraceful. "What is he?" murmurs one grey shadow of my forefathers to the other. "A writer of story books! What kind of business in life—what mode of glorifying God, or being serviceable to mankind in his day and generation—may that be? Why, the degenerate fellow might as well have been a fiddler!" Such are the compliments bandied between my great grandsires and myself, across the gulf of time! And yet, let them scorn me as they will, strong traits of their nature have intertwined themselves with mine.

Planted deep, in the town's earliest infancy and childhood, by these two earnest and energetic men, the race has ever since subsisted here; always, too, in respectability; never, so far as I have known, disgraced by a single unworthy member; but seldom or never, on the other hand, after the first two generations, performing any memorable deed, or so much as putting forward a claim to public notice. Gradually, they have sunk almost out of sight; as old houses, here and there about the streets, get covered half-way to the eaves by the accumulation of new soil. From father to son, for above a hundred years, they followed the sea; a grey-headed shipmaster, in each generation, retiring from the quarter-deck to the homestead, while a boy of fourteen took the hereditary place before the mast, confronting the salt spray and the gale which had blustered against his sire and grandsire. The boy, also in due time, passed from the forecastle to the cabin, spent a tempestuous manhood, and returned from his world-wanderings, to grow old, and die, and mingle his dust with the natal earth. This long connexion of a family with one spot, as its place of birth and burial, creates a kindred between the human being and the locality, quite independent of any charm in the scenery or moral circumstances that surround him. It is not love but instinct. The new inhabitant—who came himself from a foreign land, or whose father or grandfather came—has little claim to be called a Salemite; he has no conception of the oyster-like tenacity with which an old settler, over whom his third century is creeping, clings to the spot where his successive generations have been embedded. It is no matter that the place is joyless for him; that he is weary of the old wooden houses, the mud and dust, the dead level of site and sentiment, the chill east wind, and the chillest of social atmospheres;—all these, and whatever faults besides he may see or imagine, are nothing to the purpose. The spell survives, and just as powerfully as if the natal spot were an earthly paradise. So has it been in my case. I felt it almost as a destiny to make Salem my home; so that the mould of features and cast of character which had all along been familiar here—ever, as one representative of the race lay down in the grave, another assuming, as it were, his sentry-march along the main street—might still in my little day be seen and recognised in the old town. Nevertheless, this very sentiment is an evidence that the connexion, which has become an unhealthy one, should at last be severed. Human nature will not flourish, any more than a potato, if it be planted and re-planted, for too long a series of generations, in the same worn-out soil. My children have had other birth-places, and, so far as their fortunes may be within my control, shall strike their roots into unaccustomed earth.

On emerging from the Old Manse, it was chiefly this strange, indolent, unjoyous attachment for my native town that brought me to fill a place in Uncle Sam's brick edifice, when I might as well, or better, have gone somewhere else. My doom was on me. It was not the first time, nor the second, that I had gone away—as it seemed, permanently—but yet returned, like the bad halfpenny, or as if Salem were for me the inevitable centre of the universe. So, one fine morning I ascended the flight of granite steps, with the President's commission in my pocket, and was introduced to the corps of gentlemen who were to aid me in my weighty responsibility as chief executive officer of the Custom-House.

I doubt greatly—or, rather, I do not doubt at all—whether any public functionary of the United States, either in the civil or military line, has ever had such a patriarchal body of veterans under his orders as myself. The whereabouts of the Oldest Inhabitant was at once settled when I looked at them. For upwards of twenty years before this epoch, the independent position of the Collector had kept the Salem Custom-House out of the whirlpool of political vicissitude, which makes the tenure of office generally so fragile. A soldier—New England's most distinguished soldier—he stood firmly on the pedestal of his gallant services; and, himself secure in the wise liberality of the successive administrations through which he had held office, he had been the safety of his subordinates in many an hour of danger and heart-quake. General Miller was radically conservative; a man over whose kindly nature habit had no slight influence; attaching himself strongly to familiar faces, and with difficulty moved to change, even when change might have brought unquestionable improvement. Thus, on taking charge of my department, I found few but aged men. They were ancient sea-captains, for the most part, who, after being tossed on every sea, and standing up sturdily against life's tempestuous blast, had finally drifted into this quiet nook, where, with little to disturb them, except the periodical terrors of a Presidential election, they one and all acquired a new lease of existence. Though by no means less liable than their fellow-men to age and infirmity, they had evidently some talisman or other that kept death at bay. Two or three of their number, as I was assured, being gouty and rheumatic, or perhaps bed-ridden, never dreamed of making their appearance at the Custom-House during a large part of the year; but, after a torpid winter, would creep out into the warm sunshine of May or June, go lazily about what they termed duty, and, at their own leisure and convenience, betake themselves to bed again. I must plead guilty to the charge of abbreviating the official breath of more than one of these venerable servants of the republic. They were allowed, on my representation, to rest from their arduous labours, and soon afterwards—as if their sole principle of life had been zeal for their country's service—as I verily believe it was—withdrew to a better world. It is a pious consolation to me that, through my interference, a sufficient space was allowed them for repentance of the evil and corrupt practices into which, as a matter of course, every Custom-House officer must be supposed to fall. Neither the front nor the back entrance of the Custom-House opens on the road to Paradise.

The greater part of my officers were Whigs. It was well for their venerable brotherhood that the new Surveyor was not a politician, and though a faithful Democrat in principle, neither received nor held his office with any reference to political services. Had it been otherwise—had an active politician been put into this influential post, to assume the easy task of making head against a Whig Collector, whose infirmities withheld him from the personal administration of his office—hardly a man of the old corps would have drawn the breath of official life within a month after the exterminating angel had come up the Custom-House steps. According to the received code in such matters, it would have been nothing short of duty, in a politician, to bring every one of those white heads under the axe of the guillotine. It was plain enough to discern that the old fellows dreaded some such discourtesy at my hands. It pained, and at the same time amused me, to behold the terrors that attended my advent, to see a furrowed cheek, weather-beaten by half a century of storm, turn ashy pale at the glance of so harmless an individual as myself; to detect, as one or another addressed me, the tremor of a voice which, in long-past days, had been wont to bellow through a speaking-trumpet, hoarsely enough to frighten Boreas himself to silence. They knew, these excellent old persons, that, by all established rule—and, as regarded some of them, weighed by their own lack of efficiency for business—they ought to have given place to younger men, more orthodox in politics, and altogether fitter than themselves to serve our common Uncle. I knew it, too, but could never quite find in my heart to act upon the knowledge. Much and deservedly to my own discredit, therefore, and considerably to the detriment of my official conscience, they continued, during my incumbency, to creep about the wharves, and loiter up and down the Custom-House steps. They spent a good deal of time, also, asleep in their accustomed corners, with their chairs tilted back against the walls; awaking, however, once or twice in the forenoon, to bore one another with the several thousandth repetition of old sea-stories and mouldy jokes, that had grown to be passwords and countersigns among them.

The discovery was soon made, I imagine, that the new Surveyor had no great harm in him. So, with lightsome hearts and the happy consciousness of being usefully employed—in their own behalf at least, if not for our beloved country—these good old gentlemen went through the various formalities of office. Sagaciously under their spectacles, did they peep into the holds of vessels. Mighty was their fuss about little matters, and marvellous, sometimes, the obtuseness that allowed greater ones to slip between their fingers Whenever such a mischance occurred—when a waggon-load of valuable merchandise had been smuggled ashore, at noonday, perhaps, and directly beneath their unsuspicious noses—nothing could exceed the vigilance and alacrity with which they proceeded to lock, and double-lock, and secure with tape and sealing-wax, all the avenues of the delinquent vessel. Instead of a reprimand for their previous negligence, the case seemed rather to require an eulogium on their praiseworthy caution after the mischief had happened; a grateful recognition of the promptitude of their zeal the moment that there was no longer any remedy.

Unless people are more than commonly disagreeable, it is my foolish habit to contract a kindness for them. The better part of my companion's character, if it have a better part, is that which usually comes uppermost in my regard, and forms the type whereby I recognise the man. As most of these old Custom-House officers had good traits, and as my position in reference to them, being paternal and protective, was favourable to the growth of friendly sentiments, I soon grew to like them all. It was pleasant in the summer forenoons—when the fervent heat, that almost liquefied the rest of the human family, merely communicated a genial warmth to their half torpid systems—it was pleasant to hear them chatting in the back entry, a row of them all tipped against the wall, as usual; while the frozen witticisms of past generations were thawed out, and came bubbling with laughter from their lips. Externally, the jollity of aged men has much in common with the mirth of children; the intellect, any more than a deep sense of humour, has little to do with the matter; it is, with both, a gleam that plays upon the surface, and imparts a sunny and cheery aspect alike to the green branch and grey, mouldering trunk. In one case, however, it is real sunshine; in the other, it more resembles the phosphorescent glow of decaying wood.

It would be sad injustice, the reader must understand, to represent all my excellent old friends as in their dotage. In the first place, my coadjutors were not invariably old; there were men among them in their strength and prime, of marked ability and energy, and altogether superior to the sluggish and dependent mode of life on which their evil stars had cast them. Then, moreover, the white locks of age were sometimes found to be the thatch of an intellectual tenement in good repair. But, as respects the majority of my corps of veterans, there will be no wrong done if I characterize them generally as a set of wearisome old souls, who had gathered nothing worth preservation from their varied experience of life. They seemed to have flung away all the golden grain of practical wisdom, which they had enjoyed so many opportunities of harvesting, and most carefully to have stored their memory with the husks. They spoke with far more interest and unction of their morning's breakfast, or yesterday's, to-day's, or tomorrow's dinner, than of the shipwreck of forty or fifty years ago, and all the world's wonders which they had witnessed with their youthful eyes.

The father of the Custom-House—the patriarch, not only of this little squad of officials, but, I am bold to say, of the respectable body of tide-waiters all over the United States—was a certain permanent Inspector. He might truly be termed a legitimate son of the revenue system, dyed in the wool, or rather born in the purple; since his sire, a Revolutionary colonel, and formerly collector of the port, had created an office for him, and appointed him to fill it, at a period of the early ages which few living men can now remember. This Inspector, when I first knew him, was a man of fourscore years, or thereabouts, and certainly one of the most wonderful specimens of winter-green that you would be likely to discover in a lifetime's search. With his florid cheek, his compact figure smartly arrayed in a bright-buttoned blue coat, his brisk and vigorous step, and his hale and hearty aspect, altogether he seemed—not young, indeed—but a kind of new contrivance of Mother Nature in the shape of man, whom age and infirmity had no business to touch. His voice and laugh, which perpetually re-echoed through the Custom-House, had nothing of the tremulous quaver and cackle of an old man's utterance; they came strutting out of his lungs, like the crow of a cock, or the blast of a clarion. Looking at him merely as an animal—and there was very little else to look at—he was a most satisfactory object, from the thorough healthfulness and wholesomeness of his system, and his capacity, at that extreme age, to enjoy all, or nearly all, the delights which he had ever aimed at or conceived of. The careless security of his life in the Custom-House, on a regular income, and with but slight and infrequent apprehensions of removal, had no doubt contributed to make time pass lightly over him. The original and more potent causes, however, lay in the rare perfection of his animal nature, the moderate proportion of intellect, and the very trifling admixture of moral and spiritual ingredients; these latter qualities, indeed, being in barely enough measure to keep the old gentleman from walking on all-fours. He possessed no power of thought, no depth of feeling, no troublesome sensibilities: nothing, in short, but a few commonplace instincts, which, aided by the cheerful temper which grew inevitably out of his physical well-being, did duty very respectably, and to general acceptance, in lieu of a heart. He had been the husband of three wives, all long since dead; the father of twenty children, most of whom, at every age of childhood or maturity, had likewise returned to dust. Here, one would suppose, might have been sorrow enough to imbue the sunniest disposition through and through with a sable tinge. Not so with our old Inspector. One brief sigh sufficed to carry off the entire burden of these dismal reminiscences. The next moment he was as ready for sport as any unbreeched infant: far readier than the Collector's junior clerk, who at nineteen years was much the elder and graver man of the two.

I used to watch and study this patriarchal personage with, I think, livelier curiosity than any other form of humanity there presented to my notice. He was, in truth, a rare phenomenon; so perfect, in one point of view; so shallow, so delusive, so impalpable such an absolute nonentity, in every other. My conclusion was that he had no soul, no heart, no mind; nothing, as I have already said, but instincts; and yet, withal, so cunningly had the few materials of his character been put together that there was no painful perception of deficiency, but, on my part, an entire contentment with what I found in him. It might be difficult—and it was so—to conceive how he should exist hereafter, so earthly and sensuous did he seem; but surely his existence here, admitting that it was to terminate with his last breath, had been not unkindly given; with no higher moral responsibilities than the beasts of the field, but with a larger scope of enjoyment than theirs, and with all their blessed immunity from the dreariness and duskiness of age.

One point in which he had vastly the advantage over his four-footed brethren was his ability to recollect the good dinners which it had made no small portion of the happiness of his life to eat. His gourmandism was a highly agreeable trait; and to hear him talk of roast meat was as appetizing as a pickle or an oyster. As he possessed no higher attribute, and neither sacrificed nor vitiated any spiritual endowment by devoting all his energies and ingenuities to subserve the delight and profit of his maw, it always pleased and satisfied me to hear him expatiate on fish, poultry, and butcher's meat, and the most eligible methods of preparing them for the table. His reminiscences of good cheer, however ancient the date of the actual banquet, seemed to bring the savour of pig or turkey under one's very nostrils. There were flavours on his palate that had lingered there not less than sixty or seventy years, and were still apparently as fresh as that of the mutton chop which he had just devoured for his breakfast. I have heard him smack his lips over dinners, every guest at which, except himself, had long been food for worms. It was marvellous to observe how the ghosts of bygone meals were continually rising up before him—not in anger or retribution, but as if grateful for his former appreciation, and seeking to reduplicate an endless series of enjoyment, at once shadowy and sensual: a tenderloin of beef, a hind-quarter of veal, a spare-rib of pork, a particular chicken, or a remarkably praiseworthy turkey, which had perhaps adorned his board in the days of the elder Adams, would be remembered; while all the subsequent experience of our race, and all the events that brightened or darkened his individual career, had gone over him with as little permanent effect as the passing breeze. The chief tragic event of the old man's life, so far as I could judge, was his mishap with a certain goose, which lived and died some twenty or forty years ago: a goose of most promising figure, but which, at table, proved so inveterately tough, that the carving-knife would make no impression on its carcase, and it could only be divided with an axe and handsaw.

But it is time to quit this sketch; on which, however, I should be glad to dwell at considerably more length, because of all men whom I have ever known, this individual was fittest to be a Custom-House officer. Most persons, owing to causes which I may not have space to hint at, suffer moral detriment from this peculiar mode of life. The old Inspector was incapable of it; and, were he to continue in office to the end of time, would be just as good as he was then, and sit down to dinner with just as good an appetite.

There is one likeness, without which my gallery of Custom-House portraits would be strangely incomplete, but which my comparatively few opportunities for observation enable me to sketch only in the merest outline. It is that of the Collector, our gallant old General, who, after his brilliant military service, subsequently to which he had ruled over a wild Western territory, had come hither, twenty years before, to spend the decline of his varied and honourable life.

The brave soldier had already numbered, nearly or quite, his three-score years and ten, and was pursuing the remainder of his earthly march, burdened with infirmities which even the martial music of his own spirit-stirring recollections could do little towards lightening. The step was palsied now, that had been foremost in the charge. It was only with the assistance of a servant, and by leaning his hand heavily on the iron balustrade, that he could slowly and painfully ascend the Custom-House steps, and, with a toilsome progress across the floor, attain his customary chair beside the fireplace. There he used to sit, gazing with a somewhat dim serenity of aspect at the figures that came and went, amid the rustle of papers, the administering of oaths, the discussion of business, and the casual talk of the office; all which sounds and circumstances seemed but indistinctly to impress his senses, and hardly to make their way into his inner sphere of contemplation. His countenance, in this repose, was mild and kindly. If his notice was sought, an expression of courtesy and interest gleamed out upon his features, proving that there was light within him, and that it was only the outward medium of the intellectual lamp that obstructed the rays in their passage. The closer you penetrated to the substance of his mind, the sounder it appeared. When no longer called upon to speak or listen—either of which operations cost him an evident effort—his face would briefly subside into its former not uncheerful quietude. It was not painful to behold this look; for, though dim, it had not the imbecility of decaying age. The framework of his nature, originally strong and massive, was not yet crumpled into ruin.

To observe and define his character, however, under such disadvantages, was as difficult a task as to trace out and build up anew, in imagination, an old fortress, like Ticonderoga, from a view of its grey and broken ruins. Here and there, perchance, the walls may remain almost complete; but elsewhere may be only a shapeless mound, cumbrous with its very strength, and overgrown, through long years of peace and neglect, with grass and alien weeds.

Nevertheless, looking at the old warrior with affection—for, slight as was the communication between us, my feeling towards him, like that of all bipeds and quadrupeds who knew him, might not improperly be termed so,—I could discern the main points of his portrait. It was marked with the noble and heroic qualities which showed it to be not a mere accident, but of good right, that he had won a distinguished name. His spirit could never, I conceive, have been characterized by an uneasy activity; it must, at any period of his life, have required an impulse to set him in motion; but once stirred up, with obstacles to overcome, and an adequate object to be attained, it was not in the man to give out or fail. The heat that had formerly pervaded his nature, and which was not yet extinct, was never of the kind that flashes and flickers in a blaze; but rather a deep red glow, as of iron in a furnace. Weight, solidity, firmness—this was the expression of his repose, even in such decay as had crept untimely over him at the period of which I speak. But I could imagine, even then, that, under some excitement which should go deeply into his consciousness—roused by a trumpet's peal, loud enough to awaken all of his energies that were not dead, but only slumbering—he was yet capable of flinging off his infirmities like a sick man's gown, dropping the staff of age to seize a battle-sword, and starting up once more a warrior. And, in so intense a moment his demeanour would have still been calm. Such an exhibition, however, was but to be pictured in fancy; not to be anticipated, nor desired. What I saw in him—as evidently as the indestructible ramparts of Old Ticonderoga, already cited as the most appropriate simile—was the features of stubborn and ponderous endurance, which might well have amounted to obstinacy in his earlier days; of integrity, that, like most of his other endowments, lay in a somewhat heavy mass, and was just as unmalleable or unmanageable as a ton of iron ore; and of benevolence which, fiercely as he led the bayonets on at Chippewa or Fort Erie, I take to be of quite as genuine a stamp as what actuates any or all the polemical philanthropists of the age. He had slain men with his own hand, for aught I know—certainly, they had fallen like blades of grass at the sweep of the scythe before the charge to which his spirit imparted its triumphant energy—but, be that as it might, there was never in his heart so much cruelty as would have brushed the down off a butterfly's wing. I have not known the man to whose innate kindliness I would more confidently make an appeal.

Many characteristics—and those, too, which contribute not the least forcibly to impart resemblance in a sketch—must have vanished, or been obscured, before I met the General. All merely graceful attributes are usually the most evanescent; nor does nature adorn the human ruin with blossoms of new beauty, that have their roots and proper nutriment only in the chinks and crevices of decay, as she sows wall-flowers over the ruined fortress of Ticonderoga. Still, even in respect of grace and beauty, there were points well worth noting. A ray of humour, now and then, would make its way through the veil of dim obstruction, and glimmer pleasantly upon our faces. A trait of native elegance, seldom seen in the masculine character after childhood or early youth, was shown in the General's fondness for the sight and fragrance of flowers. An old soldier might be supposed to prize only the bloody laurel on his brow; but here was one who seemed to have a young girl's appreciation of the floral tribe.

There, beside the fireplace, the brave old General used to sit; while the Surveyor—though seldom, when it could be avoided, taking upon himself the difficult task of engaging him in conversation—was fond of standing at a distance, and watching his quiet and almost slumberous countenance. He seemed away from us, although we saw him but a few yards off; remote, though we passed close beside his chair; unattainable, though we might have stretched forth our hands and touched his own. It might be that he lived a more real life within his thoughts than amid the unappropriate environment of the Collector's office. The evolutions of the parade; the tumult of the battle; the flourish of old heroic music, heard thirty years before—such scenes and sounds, perhaps, were all alive before his intellectual sense. Meanwhile, the merchants and ship-masters, the spruce clerks and uncouth sailors, entered and departed; the bustle of his commercial and Custom-House life kept up its little murmur round about him; and neither with the men nor their affairs did the General appear to sustain the most distant relation. He was as much out of place as an old sword—now rusty, but which had flashed once in the battle's front, and showed still a bright gleam along its blade—would have been among the inkstands, paper-folders, and mahogany rulers on the Deputy Collector's desk.

There was one thing that much aided me in renewing and re-creating the stalwart soldier of the Niagara frontier—the man of true and simple energy. It was the recollection of those memorable words of his—"I'll try, Sir"—spoken on the very verge of a desperate and heroic enterprise, and breathing the soul and spirit of New England hardihood, comprehending all perils, and encountering all. If, in our country, valour were rewarded by heraldic honour, this phrase—which it seems so easy to speak, but which only he, with such a task of danger and glory before him, has ever spoken—would be the best and fittest of all mottoes for the General's shield of arms.

It contributes greatly towards a man's moral and intellectual health to be brought into habits of companionship with individuals unlike himself, who care little for his pursuits, and whose sphere and abilities he must go out of himself to appreciate. The accidents of my life have often afforded me this advantage, but never with more fulness and variety than during my continuance in office. There was one man, especially, the observation of whose character gave me a new idea of talent. His gifts were emphatically those of a man of business; prompt, acute, clear-minded; with an eye that saw through all perplexities, and a faculty of arrangement that made them vanish as by the waving of an enchanter's wand. Bred up from boyhood in the Custom-House, it was his proper field of activity; and the many intricacies of business, so harassing to the interloper, presented themselves before him with the regularity of a perfectly comprehended system. In my contemplation, he stood as the ideal of his class. He was, indeed, the Custom-House in himself; or, at all events, the mainspring that kept its variously revolving wheels in motion; for, in an institution like this, where its officers are appointed to subserve their own profit and convenience, and seldom with a leading reference to their fitness for the duty to be performed, they must perforce seek elsewhere the dexterity which is not in them. Thus, by an inevitable necessity, as a magnet attracts steel-filings, so did our man of business draw to himself the difficulties which everybody met with. With an easy condescension, and kind forbearance towards our stupidity—which, to his order of mind, must have seemed little short of crime—would he forth-with, by the merest touch of his finger, make the incomprehensible as clear as daylight. The merchants valued him not less than we, his esoteric friends. His integrity was perfect; it was a law of nature with him, rather than a choice or a principle; nor can it be otherwise than the main condition of an intellect so remarkably clear and accurate as his to be honest and regular in the administration of affairs. A stain on his conscience, as to anything that came within the range of his vocation, would trouble such a man very much in the same way, though to a far greater degree, than an error in the balance of an account, or an ink-blot on the fair page of a book of record. Here, in a word—and it is a rare instance in my life—I had met with a person thoroughly adapted to the situation which he held.

Such were some of the people with whom I now found myself connected. I took it in good part, at the hands of Providence, that I was thrown into a position so little akin to my past habits; and set myself seriously to gather from it whatever profit was to be had. After my fellowship of toil and impracticable schemes with the dreamy brethren of Brook Farm; after living for three years within the subtle influence of an intellect like Emerson's; after those wild, free days on the Assabeth, indulging fantastic speculations, beside our fire of fallen boughs, with Ellery Channing; after talking with Thoreau about pine-trees and Indian relics in his hermitage at Walden; after growing fastidious by sympathy with the classic refinement of Hillard's culture; after becoming imbued with poetic sentiment at Longfellow's hearthstone—it was time, at length, that I should exercise other faculties of my nature, and nourish myself with food for which I had hitherto had little appetite. Even the old Inspector was desirable, as a change of diet, to a man who had known Alcott. I looked upon it as an evidence, in some measure, of a system naturally well balanced, and lacking no essential part of a thorough organization, that, with such associates to remember, I could mingle at once with men of altogether different qualities, and never murmur at the change.

Literature, its exertions and objects, were now of little moment in my regard. I cared not at this period for books; they were apart from me. Nature—except it were human nature—the nature that is developed in earth and sky, was, in one sense, hidden from me; and all the imaginative delight wherewith it had been spiritualized passed away out of my mind. A gift, a faculty, if it had not been departed, was suspended and inanimate within me. There would have been something sad, unutterably dreary, in all this, had I not been conscious that it lay at my own option to recall whatever was valuable in the past. It might be true, indeed, that this was a life which could not, with impunity, be lived too long; else, it might make me permanently other than I had been, without transforming me into any shape which it would be worth my while to take. But I never considered it as other than a transitory life. There was always a prophetic instinct, a low whisper in my ear, that within no long period, and whenever a new change of custom should be essential to my good, change would come.

Meanwhile, there I was, a Surveyor of the Revenue and, so far as I have been able to understand, as good a Surveyor as need be. A man of thought, fancy, and sensibility (had he ten times the Surveyor's proportion of those qualities), may, at any time, be a man of affairs, if he will only choose to give himself the trouble. My fellow-officers, and the merchants and sea-captains with whom my official duties brought me into any manner of connection, viewed me in no other light, and probably knew me in no other character. None of them, I presume, had ever read a page of my inditing, or would have cared a fig the more for me if they had read them all; nor would it have mended the matter, in the least, had those same unprofitable pages been written with a pen like that of Burns or of Chaucer, each of whom was a Custom-House officer in his day, as well as I. It is a good lesson—though it may often be a hard one—for a man who has dreamed of literary fame, and of making for himself a rank among the world's dignitaries by such means, to step aside out of the narrow circle in which his claims are recognized and to find how utterly devoid of significance, beyond that circle, is all that he achieves, and all he aims at. I know not that I especially needed the lesson, either in the way of warning or rebuke; but at any rate, I learned it thoroughly: nor, it gives me pleasure to reflect, did the truth, as it came home to my perception, ever cost me a pang, or require to be thrown off in a sigh. In the way of literary talk, it is true, the Naval Officer—an excellent fellow, who came into the office with me, and went out only a little later—would often engage me in a discussion about one or the other of his favourite topics, Napoleon or Shakespeare. The Collector's junior clerk, too a young gentleman who, it was whispered occasionally covered a sheet of Uncle Sam's letter paper with what (at the distance of a few yards) looked very much like poetry—used now and then to speak to me of books, as matters with which I might possibly be conversant. This was my all of lettered intercourse; and it was quite sufficient for my necessities.

No longer seeking nor caring that my name should be blasoned abroad on title-pages, I smiled to think that it had now another kind of vogue. The Custom-House marker imprinted it, with a stencil and black paint, on pepper-bags, and baskets of anatto, and cigar-boxes, and bales of all kinds of dutiable merchandise, in testimony that these commodities had paid the impost, and gone regularly through the office. Borne on such queer vehicle of fame, a knowledge of my existence, so far as a name conveys it, was carried where it had never been before, and, I hope, will never go again.

But the past was not dead. Once in a great while, the thoughts that had seemed so vital and so active, yet had been put to rest so quietly, revived again. One of the most remarkable occasions, when the habit of bygone days awoke in me, was that which brings it within the law of literary propriety to offer the public the sketch which I am now writing.

In the second storey of the Custom-House there is a large room, in which the brick-work and naked rafters have never been covered with panelling and plaster.

The edifice—originally projected on a scale adapted to the old commercial enterprise of the port, and with an idea of subsequent prosperity destined never to be realized—contains far more space than its occupants know what to do with. This airy hall, therefore, over the Collector's apartments, remains unfinished to this day, and, in spite of the aged cobwebs that festoon its dusky beams, appears still to await the labour of the carpenter and mason. At one end of the room, in a recess, were a number of barrels piled one upon another, containing bundles of official documents. Large quantities of similar rubbish lay lumbering the floor. It was sorrowful to think how many days, and weeks, and months, and years of toil had been wasted on these musty papers, which were now only an encumbrance on earth, and were hidden away in this forgotten corner, never more to be glanced at by human eyes. But then, what reams of other manuscripts—filled, not with the dulness of official formalities, but with the thought of inventive brains and the rich effusion of deep hearts—had gone equally to oblivion; and that, moreover, without serving a purpose in their day, as these heaped-up papers had, and—saddest of all—without purchasing for their writers the comfortable livelihood which the clerks of the Custom-House had gained by these worthless scratchings of the pen. Yet not altogether worthless, perhaps, as materials of local history. Here, no doubt, statistics of the former commerce of Salem might be discovered, and memorials of her princely merchants—old King Derby—old Billy Gray—old Simon Forrester—and many another magnate in his day, whose powdered head, however, was scarcely in the tomb before his mountain pile of wealth began to dwindle. The founders of the greater part of the families which now compose the aristocracy of Salem might here be traced, from the petty and obscure beginnings of their traffic, at periods generally much posterior to the Revolution, upward to what their children look upon as long-established rank.

Prior to the Revolution there is a dearth of records; the earlier documents and archives of the Custom-House having, probably, been carried off to Halifax, when all the king's officials accompanied the British army in its flight from Boston. It has often been a matter of regret with me; for, going back, perhaps, to the days of the Protectorate, those papers must have contained many references to forgotten or remembered men, and to antique customs, which would have affected me with the same pleasure as when I used to pick up Indian arrow-heads in the field near the Old Manse.

But, one idle and rainy day, it was my fortune to make a discovery of some little interest. Poking and burrowing into the heaped-up rubbish in the corner, unfolding one and another document, and reading the names of vessels that had long ago foundered at sea or rotted at the wharves, and those of merchants never heard of now on 'Change, nor very readily decipherable on their mossy tombstones; glancing at such matters with the saddened, weary, half-reluctant interest which we bestow on the corpse of dead activity—and exerting my fancy, sluggish with little use, to raise up from these dry bones an image of the old town's brighter aspect, when India was a new region, and only Salem knew the way thither—I chanced to lay my hand on a small package, carefully done up in a piece of ancient yellow parchment. This envelope had the air of an official record of some period long past, when clerks engrossed their stiff and formal chirography on more substantial materials than at present. There was something about it that quickened an instinctive curiosity, and made me undo the faded red tape that tied up the package, with the sense that a treasure would here be brought to light. Unbending the rigid folds of the parchment cover, I found it to be a commission, under the hand and seal of Governor Shirley, in favour of one Jonathan Pue, as Surveyor of His Majesty's Customs for the Port of Salem, in the Province of Massachusetts Bay. I remembered to have read (probably in Felt's "Annals") a notice of the decease of Mr. Surveyor Pue, about fourscore years ago; and likewise, in a newspaper of recent times, an account of the digging up of his remains in the little graveyard of St. Peter's Church, during the renewal of that edifice. Nothing, if I rightly call to mind, was left of my respected predecessor, save an imperfect skeleton, and some fragments of apparel, and a wig of majestic frizzle, which, unlike the head that it once adorned, was in very satisfactory preservation. But, on examining the papers which the parchment commission served to envelop, I found more traces of Mr. Pue's mental part, and the internal operations of his head, than the frizzled wig had contained of the venerable skull itself.

They were documents, in short, not official, but of a private nature, or, at least, written in his private capacity, and apparently with his own hand. I could account for their being included in the heap of Custom-House lumber only by the fact that Mr. Pue's death had happened suddenly, and that these papers, which he probably kept in his official desk, had never come to the knowledge of his heirs, or were supposed to relate to the business of the revenue. On the transfer of the archives to Halifax, this package, proving to be of no public concern, was left behind, and had remained ever since unopened.

The ancient Surveyor—being little molested, I suppose, at that early day with business pertaining to his office—seems to have devoted some of his many leisure hours to researches as a local antiquarian, and other inquisitions of a similar nature. These supplied material for petty activity to a mind that would otherwise have been eaten up with rust.

A portion of his facts, by-the-by, did me good service in the preparation of the article entitled "MAIN STREET," included in the present volume. The remainder may perhaps be applied to purposes equally valuable hereafter, or not impossibly may be worked up, so far as they go, into a regular history of Salem, should my veneration for the natal soil ever impel me to so pious a task. Meanwhile, they shall be at the command of any gentleman, inclined and competent, to take the unprofitable labour off my hands. As a final disposition I contemplate depositing them with the Essex Historical Society. But the object that most drew my attention to the mysterious package was a certain affair of fine red cloth, much worn and faded, There were traces about it of gold embroidery, which, however, was greatly frayed and defaced, so that none, or very little, of the glitter was left. It had been wrought, as was easy to perceive, with wonderful skill of needlework; and the stitch (as I am assured by ladies conversant with such mysteries) gives evidence of a now forgotten art, not to be discovered even by the process of picking out the threads. This rag of scarlet cloth—for time, and wear, and a sacrilegious moth had reduced it to little other than a rag—on careful examination, assumed the shape of a letter.

It was the capital letter A. By an accurate measurement, each limb proved to be precisely three inches and a quarter in length. It had been intended, there could be no doubt, as an ornamental article of dress; but how it was to be worn, or what rank, honour, and dignity, in by-past times, were signified by it, was a riddle which (so evanescent are the fashions of the world in these particulars) I saw little hope of solving. And yet it strangely interested me. My eyes fastened themselves upon the old scarlet letter, and would not be turned aside. Certainly there was some deep meaning in it most worthy of interpretation, and which, as it were, streamed forth from the mystic symbol, subtly communicating itself to my sensibilities, but evading the analysis of my mind.

When thus perplexed—and cogitating, among other hypotheses, whether the letter might not have been one of those decorations which the white men used to contrive in order to take the eyes of Indians—I happened to place it on my breast. It seemed to me—the reader may smile, but must not doubt my word—it seemed to me, then, that I experienced a sensation not altogether physical, yet almost so, as of burning heat, and as if the letter were not of red cloth, but red-hot iron. I shuddered, and involuntarily let it fall upon the floor.

In the absorbing contemplation of the scarlet letter, I had hitherto neglected to examine a small roll of dingy paper, around which it had been twisted. This I now opened, and had the satisfaction to find recorded by the old Surveyor's pen, a reasonably complete explanation of the whole affair. There were several foolscap sheets, containing many particulars respecting the life and conversation of one Hester Prynne, who appeared to have been rather a noteworthy personage in the view of our ancestors. She had flourished during the period between the early days of Massachusetts and the close of the seventeenth century. Aged persons, alive in the time of Mr. Surveyor Pue, and from whose oral testimony he had made up his narrative, remembered her, in their youth, as a very old, but not decrepit woman, of a stately and solemn aspect. It had been her habit, from an almost immemorial date, to go about the country as a kind of voluntary nurse, and doing whatever miscellaneous good she might; taking upon herself, likewise, to give advice in all matters, especially those of the heart, by which means—as a person of such propensities inevitably must—she gained from many people the reverence due to an angel, but, I should imagine, was looked upon by others as an intruder and a nuisance. Prying further into the manuscript, I found the record of other doings and sufferings of this singular woman, for most of which the reader is referred to the story entitled "THE SCARLET LETTER"; and it should be borne carefully in mind that the main facts of that story are authorized and authenticated by the document of Mr. Surveyor Pue. The original papers, together with the scarlet letter itself—a most curious relic—are still in my possession, and shall be freely exhibited to whomsoever, induced by the great interest of the narrative, may desire a sight of them. I must not be understood affirming that, in the dressing up of the tale, and imagining the motives and modes of passion that influenced the characters who figure in it, I have invariably confined myself within the limits of the old Surveyor's half-a-dozen sheets of foolscap. On the contrary, I have allowed myself, as to such points, nearly, or altogether, as much license as if the facts had been entirely of my own invention. What I contend for is the authenticity of the outline.

This incident recalled my mind, in some degree, to its old track. There seemed to be here the groundwork of a tale. It impressed me as if the ancient Surveyor, in his garb of a hundred years gone by, and wearing his immortal wig—which was buried with him, but did not perish in the grave—had met me in the deserted chamber of the Custom-House. In his port was the dignity of one who had borne His Majesty's commission, and who was therefore illuminated by a ray of the splendour that shone so dazzlingly about the throne. How unlike alas the hangdog look of a republican official, who, as the servant of the people, feels himself less than the least, and below the lowest of his masters. With his own ghostly hand, the obscurely seen, but majestic, figure had imparted to me the scarlet symbol and the little roll of explanatory manuscript. With his own ghostly voice he had exhorted me, on the sacred consideration of my filial duty and reverence towards him—who might reasonably regard himself as my official ancestor—to bring his mouldy and moth-eaten lucubrations before the public. "Do this," said the ghost of Mr. Surveyor Pue, emphatically nodding the head that looked so imposing within its memorable wig; "do this, and the profit shall be all your own. You will shortly need it; for it is not in your days as it was in mine, when a man's office was a life-lease, and oftentimes an heirloom. But I charge you, in this matter of old Mistress Prynne, give to your predecessor's memory the credit which will be rightfully due" And I said to the ghost of Mr. Surveyor Pue—"I will".

On Hester Prynne's story, therefore, I bestowed much thought. It was the subject of my meditations for many an hour, while pacing to and fro across my room, or traversing, with a hundredfold repetition, the long extent from the front door of the Custom-House to the side entrance, and back again. Great were the weariness and annoyance of the old Inspector and the Weighers and Gaugers, whose slumbers were disturbed by the unmercifully lengthened tramp of my passing and returning footsteps. Remembering their own former habits, they used to say that the Surveyor was walking the quarter-deck. They probably fancied that my sole object—and, indeed, the sole object for which a sane man could ever put himself into voluntary motion—was to get an appetite for dinner. And, to say the truth, an appetite, sharpened by the east wind that generally blew along the passage, was the only valuable result of so much indefatigable exercise. So little adapted is the atmosphere of a Custom-house to the delicate harvest of fancy and sensibility, that, had I remained there through ten Presidencies yet to come, I doubt whether the tale of "The Scarlet Letter" would ever have been brought before the public eye. My imagination was a tarnished mirror. It would not reflect, or only with miserable dimness, the figures with which I did my best to people it. The characters of the narrative would not be warmed and rendered malleable by any heat that I could kindle at my intellectual forge. They would take neither the glow of passion nor the tenderness of sentiment, but retained all the rigidity of dead corpses, and stared me in the face with a fixed and ghastly grin of contemptuous defiance. "What have you to do with us?" that expression seemed to say. "The little power you might have once possessed over the tribe of unrealities is gone! You have bartered it for a pittance of the public gold. Go then, and earn your wages!" In short, the almost torpid creatures of my own fancy twitted me with imbecility, and not without fair occasion.

It was not merely during the three hours and a half which Uncle Sam claimed as his share of my daily life that this wretched numbness held possession of me. It went with me on my sea-shore walks and rambles into the country, whenever—which was seldom and reluctantly—I bestirred myself to seek that invigorating charm of Nature which used to give me such freshness and activity of thought, the moment that I stepped across the threshold of the Old Manse. The same torpor, as regarded the capacity for intellectual effort, accompanied me home, and weighed upon me in the chamber which I most absurdly termed my study. Nor did it quit me when, late at night, I sat in the deserted parlour, lighted only by the glimmering coal-fire and the moon, striving to picture forth imaginary scenes, which, the next day, might flow out on the brightening page in many-hued description.

If the imaginative faculty refused to act at such an hour, it might well be deemed a hopeless case. Moonlight, in a familiar room, falling so white upon the carpet, and showing all its figures so distinctly—making every object so minutely visible, yet so unlike a morning or noontide visibility—is a medium the most suitable for a romance-writer to get acquainted with his illusive guests. There is the little domestic scenery of the well-known apartment; the chairs, with each its separate individuality; the centre-table, sustaining a work-basket, a volume or two, and an extinguished lamp; the sofa; the book-case; the picture on the wall—all these details, so completely seen, are so spiritualised by the unusual light, that they seem to lose their actual substance, and become things of intellect. Nothing is too small or too trifling to undergo this change, and acquire dignity thereby. A child's shoe; the doll, seated in her little wicker carriage; the hobby-horse—whatever, in a word, has been used or played with during the day is now invested with a quality of strangeness and remoteness, though still almost as vividly present as by daylight. Thus, therefore, the floor of our familiar room has become a neutral territory, somewhere between the real world and fairy-land, where the Actual and the Imaginary may meet, and each imbue itself with the nature of the other. Ghosts might enter here without affrighting us. It would be too much in keeping with the scene to excite surprise, were we to look about us and discover a form, beloved, but gone hence, now sitting quietly in a streak of this magic moonshine, with an aspect that would make us doubt whether it had returned from afar, or had never once stirred from our fireside.

The somewhat dim coal fire has an essential Influence in producing the effect which I would describe. It throws its unobtrusive tinge throughout the room, with a faint ruddiness upon the walls and ceiling, and a reflected gleam upon the polish of the furniture. This warmer light mingles itself with the cold spirituality of the moon-beams, and communicates, as it were, a heart and sensibilities of human tenderness to the forms which fancy summons up. It converts them from snow-images into men and women. Glancing at the looking-glass, we behold—deep within its haunted verge—the smouldering glow of the half-extinguished anthracite, the white moon-beams on the floor, and a repetition of all the gleam and shadow of the picture, with one remove further from the actual, and nearer to the imaginative. Then, at such an hour, and with this scene before him, if a man, sitting all alone, cannot dream strange things, and make them look like truth, he need never try to write romances.

But, for myself, during the whole of my Custom-House experience, moonlight and sunshine, and the glow of firelight, were just alike in my regard; and neither of them was of one whit more avail than the twinkle of a tallow-candle. An entire class of susceptibilities, and a gift connected with them—of no great richness or value, but the best I had—was gone from me.

It is my belief, however, that had I attempted a different order of composition, my faculties would not have been found so pointless and inefficacious. I might, for instance, have contented myself with writing out the narratives of a veteran shipmaster, one of the Inspectors, whom I should be most ungrateful not to mention, since scarcely a day passed that he did not stir me to laughter and admiration by his marvelous gifts as a story-teller. Could I have preserved the picturesque force of his style, and the humourous colouring which nature taught him how to throw over his descriptions, the result, I honestly believe, would have been something new in literature. Or I might readily have found a more serious task. It was a folly, with the materiality of this daily life pressing so intrusively upon me, to attempt to fling myself back into another age, or to insist on creating the semblance of a world out of airy matter, when, at every moment, the impalpable beauty of my soap-bubble was broken by the rude contact of some actual circumstance. The wiser effort would have been to diffuse thought and imagination through the opaque substance of to-day, and thus to make it a bright transparency; to spiritualise the burden that began to weigh so heavily; to seek, resolutely, the true and indestructible value that lay hidden in the petty and wearisome incidents, and ordinary characters with which I was now conversant. The fault was mine. The page of life that was spread out before me seemed dull and commonplace only because I had not fathomed its deeper import. A better book than I shall ever write was there; leaf after leaf presenting itself to me, just as it was written out by the reality of the flitting hour, and vanishing as fast as written, only because my brain wanted the insight, and my hand the cunning, to transcribe it. At some future day, it may be, I shall remember a few scattered fragments and broken paragraphs, and write them down, and find the letters turn to gold upon the page.

These perceptions had come too late. At the Instant, I was only conscious that what would have been a pleasure once was now a hopeless toil. There was no occasion to make much moan about this state of affairs. I had ceased to be a writer of tolerably poor tales and essays, and had become a tolerably good Surveyor of the Customs. That was all. But, nevertheless, it is anything but agreeable to be haunted by a suspicion that one's intellect is dwindling away, or exhaling, without your consciousness, like ether out of a phial; so that, at every glance, you find a smaller and less volatile residuum. Of the fact there could be no doubt and, examining myself and others, I was led to conclusions, in reference to the effect of public office on the character, not very favourable to the mode of life in question. In some other form, perhaps, I may hereafter develop these effects. Suffice it here to say that a Custom-House officer of long continuance can hardly be a very praiseworthy or respectable personage, for many reasons; one of them, the tenure by which he holds his situation, and another, the very nature of his business, which—though, I trust, an honest one—is of such a sort that he does not share in the united effort of mankind.

An effect—which I believe to be observable, more or less, in every individual who has occupied the position—is, that while he leans on the mighty arm of the Republic, his own proper strength departs from him. He loses, in an extent proportioned to the weakness or force of his original nature, the capability of self-support. If he possesses an unusual share of native energy, or the enervating magic of place do not operate too long upon him, his forfeited powers may be redeemable. The ejected officer—fortunate in the unkindly shove that sends him forth betimes, to struggle amid a struggling world—may return to himself, and become all that he has ever been. But this seldom happens. He usually keeps his ground just long enough for his own ruin, and is then thrust out, with sinews all unstrung, to totter along the difficult footpath of life as he best may. Conscious of his own infirmity—that his tempered steel and elasticity are lost—he for ever afterwards looks wistfully about him in quest of support external to himself. His pervading and continual hope—a hallucination, which, in the face of all discouragement, and making light of impossibilities, haunts him while he lives, and, I fancy, like the convulsive throes of the cholera, torments him for a brief space after death—is, that finally, and in no long time, by some happy coincidence of circumstances, he shall be restored to office. This faith, more than anything else, steals the pith and availability out of whatever enterprise he may dream of undertaking. Why should he toil and moil, and be at so much trouble to pick himself up out of the mud, when, in a little while hence, the strong arm of his Uncle will raise and support him? Why should he work for his living here, or go to dig gold in California, when he is so soon to be made happy, at monthly intervals, with a little pile of glittering coin out of his Uncle's pocket? It is sadly curious to observe how slight a taste of office suffices to infect a poor fellow with this singular disease. Uncle Sam's gold—meaning no disrespect to the worthy old gentleman—has, in this respect, a quality of enchantment like that of the devil's wages. Whoever touches it should look well to himself, or he may find the bargain to go hard against him, involving, if not his soul, yet many of its better attributes; its sturdy force, its courage and constancy, its truth, its self-reliance, and all that gives the emphasis to manly character.

Here was a fine prospect in the distance. Not that the Surveyor brought the lesson home to himself, or admitted that he could be so utterly undone, either by continuance in office or ejectment. Yet my reflections were not the most comfortable. I began to grow melancholy and restless; continually prying into my mind, to discover which of its poor properties were gone, and what degree of detriment had already accrued to the remainder. I endeavoured to calculate how much longer I could stay in the Custom-House, and yet go forth a man. To confess the truth, it was my greatest apprehension—as it would never be a measure of policy to turn out so quiet an individual as myself; and it being hardly in the nature of a public officer to resign—it was my chief trouble, therefore, that I was likely to grow grey and decrepit in the Surveyorship, and become much such another animal as the old Inspector. Might it not, in the tedious lapse of official life that lay before me, finally be with me as it was with this venerable friend—to make the dinner-hour the nucleus of the day, and to spend the rest of it, as an old dog spends it, asleep in the sunshine or in the shade? A dreary look-forward, this, for a man who felt it to be the best definition of happiness to live throughout the whole range of his faculties and sensibilities. But, all this while, I was giving myself very unnecessary alarm. Providence had meditated better things for me than I could possibly imagine for myself.

A remarkable event of the third year of my Surveyorship—to adopt the tone of "P. P. "—was the election of General Taylor to the Presidency. It is essential, in order to form a complete estimate of the advantages of official life, to view the incumbent at the in-coming of a hostile administration. His position is then one of the most singularly irksome, and, in every contingency, disagreeable, that a wretched mortal can possibly occupy; with seldom an alternative of good on either hand, although what presents itself to him as the worst event may very probably be the best. But it is a strange experience, to a man of pride and sensibility, to know that his interests are within the control of individuals who neither love nor understand him, and by whom, since one or the other must needs happen, he would rather be injured than obliged. Strange, too, for one who has kept his calmness throughout the contest, to observe the bloodthirstiness that is developed in the hour of triumph, and to be conscious that he is himself among its objects! There are few uglier traits of human nature than this tendency—which I now witnessed in men no worse than their neighbours—to grow cruel, merely because they possessed the power of inflicting harm. If the guillotine, as applied to office-holders, were a literal fact, instead of one of the most apt of metaphors, it is my sincere belief that the active members of the victorious party were sufficiently excited to have chopped off all our heads, and have thanked Heaven for the opportunity! It appears to me—who have been a calm and curious observer, as well in victory as defeat—that this fierce and bitter spirit of malice and revenge has never distinguished the many triumphs of my own party as it now did that of the Whigs. The Democrats take the offices, as a general rule, because they need them, and because the practice of many years has made it the law of political warfare, which unless a different system be proclaimed, it was weakness and cowardice to murmur at. But the long habit of victory has made them generous. They know how to spare when they see occasion; and when they strike, the axe may be sharp indeed, but its edge is seldom poisoned with ill-will; nor is it their custom ignominiously to kick the head which they have just struck off.

In short, unpleasant as was my predicament, at best, I saw much reason to congratulate myself that I was on the losing side rather than the triumphant one. If, heretofore, I had been none of the warmest of partisans I began now, at this season of peril and adversity, to be pretty acutely sensible with which party my predilections lay; nor was it without something like regret and shame that, according to a reasonable calculation of chances, I saw my own prospect of retaining office to be better than those of my democratic brethren. But who can see an inch into futurity beyond his nose? My own head was the first that fell.

The moment when a man's head drops off is seldom or never, I am inclined to think, precisely the most agreeable of his life. Nevertheless, like the greater part of our misfortunes, even so serious a contingency brings its remedy and consolation with it, if the sufferer will but make the best rather than the worst, of the accident which has befallen him. In my particular case the consolatory topics were close at hand, and, indeed, had suggested themselves to my meditations a considerable time before it was requisite to use them. In view of my previous weariness of office, and vague thoughts of resignation, my fortune somewhat resembled that of a person who should entertain an idea of committing suicide, and although beyond his hopes, meet with the good hap to be murdered. In the Custom-House, as before in the Old Manse, I had spent three years—a term long enough to rest a weary brain: long enough to break off old intellectual habits, and make room for new ones: long enough, and too long, to have lived in an unnatural state, doing what was really of no advantage nor delight to any human being, and withholding myself from toil that would, at least, have stilled an unquiet impulse in me. Then, moreover, as regarded his unceremonious ejectment, the late Surveyor was not altogether ill-pleased to be recognised by the Whigs as an enemy; since his inactivity in political affairs—his tendency to roam, at will, in that broad and quiet field where all mankind may meet, rather than confine himself to those narrow paths where brethren of the same household must diverge from one another—had sometimes made it questionable with his brother Democrats whether he was a friend. Now, after he had won the crown of martyrdom (though with no longer a head to wear it on), the point might be looked upon as settled. Finally, little heroic as he was, it seemed more decorous to be overthrown in the downfall of the party with which he had been content to stand than to remain a forlorn survivor, when so many worthier men were falling: and at last, after subsisting for four years on the mercy of a hostile administration, to be compelled then to define his position anew, and claim the yet more humiliating mercy of a friendly one.

Meanwhile, the press had taken up my affair, and kept me for a week or two careering through the public prints, in my decapitated state, like Irving's Headless Horseman, ghastly and grim, and longing to be buried, as a political dead man ought. So much for my figurative self. The real human being all this time, with his head safely on his shoulders, had brought himself to the comfortable conclusion that everything was for the best; and making an investment in ink, paper, and steel pens, had opened his long-disused writing desk, and was again a literary man.

Now it was that the lucubrations of my ancient predecessor, Mr. Surveyor Pue, came into play. Rusty through long idleness, some little space was requisite before my intellectual machinery could be brought to work upon the tale with an effect in any degree satisfactory. Even yet, though my thoughts were ultimately much absorbed in the task, it wears, to my eye, a stern and sombre aspect: too much ungladdened by genial sunshine; too little relieved by the tender and familiar influences which soften almost every scene of nature and real life, and undoubtedly should soften every picture of them. This uncaptivating effect is perhaps due to the period of hardly accomplished revolution, and still seething turmoil, in which the story shaped itself. It is no indication, however, of a lack of cheerfulness in the writer's mind: for he was happier while straying through the gloom of these sunless fantasies than at any time since he had quitted the Old Manse. Some of the briefer articles, which contribute to make up the volume, have likewise been written since my involuntary withdrawal from the toils and honours of public life, and the remainder are gleaned from annuals and magazines, of such antique date, that they have gone round the circle, and come back to novelty again. Keeping up the metaphor of the political guillotine, the whole may be considered as the POSTHUMOUS PAPERS OF A DECAPITATED SURVEYOR: and the sketch which I am now bringing to a close, if too autobiographical for a modest person to publish in his lifetime, will readily be excused in a gentleman who writes from beyond the grave. Peace be with all the world! My blessing on my friends! My forgiveness to my enemies! For I am in the realm of quiet!

The life of the Custom-House lies like a dream behind me. The old Inspector—who, by-the-bye, I regret to say, was overthrown and killed by a horse some time ago, else he would certainly have lived for ever—he, and all those other venerable personages who sat with him at the receipt of custom, are but shadows in my view: white-headed and wrinkled images, which my fancy used to sport with, and has now flung aside for ever. The merchants—Pingree, Phillips, Shepard, Upton, Kimball, Bertram, Hunt—these and many other names, which had such classic familiarity for my ear six months ago,—these men of traffic, who seemed to occupy so important a position in the world—how little time has it required to disconnect me from them all, not merely in act, but recollection! It is with an effort that I recall the figures and appellations of these few. Soon, likewise, my old native town will loom upon me through the haze of memory, a mist brooding over and around it; as if it were no portion of the real earth, but an overgrown village in cloud-land, with only imaginary inhabitants to people its wooden houses and walk its homely lanes, and the unpicturesque prolixity of its main street. Henceforth it ceases to be a reality of my life; I am a citizen of somewhere else. My good townspeople will not much regret me, for—though it has been as dear an object as any, in my literary efforts, to be of some importance in their eyes, and to win myself a pleasant memory in this abode and burial-place of so many of my forefathers—there has never been, for me, the genial atmosphere which a literary man requires in order to ripen the best harvest of his mind. I shall do better amongst other faces; and these familiar ones, it need hardly be said, will do just as well without me.

It may be, however—oh, transporting and triumphant thought—that the great-grandchildren of the present race may sometimes think kindly of the scribbler of bygone days, when the antiquary of days to come, among the sites memorable in the town's history, shall point out the locality of THE TOWN PUMP.

I. THE PRISON DOOR

A throng of bearded men, in sad-coloured garments and grey steeple-crowned hats, inter-mixed with women, some wearing hoods, and others bareheaded, was assembled in front of a wooden edifice, the door of which was heavily timbered with oak, and studded with iron spikes.

The founders of a new colony, whatever Utopia of human virtue and happiness they might originally project, have invariably recognised it among their earliest practical necessities to allot a portion of the virgin soil as a cemetery, and another portion as the site of a prison. In accordance with this rule it may safely be assumed that the forefathers of Boston had built the first prison-house somewhere in the Vicinity of Cornhill, almost as seasonably as they marked out the first burial-ground, on Isaac Johnson's lot, and round about his grave, which subsequently became the nucleus of all the congregated sepulchres in the old churchyard of King's Chapel. Certain it is that, some fifteen or twenty years after the settlement of the town, the wooden jail was already marked with weather-stains and other indications of age, which gave a yet darker aspect to its beetle-browed and gloomy front. The rust on the ponderous iron-work of its oaken door looked more antique than anything else in the New World. Like all that pertains to crime, it seemed never to have known a youthful era. Before this ugly edifice, and between it and the wheel-track of the street, was a grass-plot, much overgrown with burdock, pig-weed, apple-pern, and such unsightly vegetation, which evidently found something congenial in the soil that had so early borne the black flower of civilised society, a prison. But on one side of the portal, and rooted almost at the threshold, was a wild rose bush, covered, in this month of June, with its delicate gems, which might be imagined to offer their fragrance and fragile beauty to the prisoner as he went in, and to the condemned criminal as he came forth to his doom, in token that the deep heart of Nature could pity and be kind to him.

This rose-bush, by a strange chance, has been kept alive in history; but whether it had merely survived out of the stern old wilderness, so long after the fall of the gigantic pines and oaks that originally overshadowed it, or whether, as there is fair authority for believing, it had sprung up under the footsteps of the sainted Ann Hutchinson as she entered the prison-door, we shall not take upon us to determine. Finding it so directly on the threshold of our narrative, which is now about to issue from that inauspicious portal, we could hardly do otherwise than pluck one of its flowers, and present it to the reader. It may serve, let us hope, to symbolise some sweet moral blossom that may be found along the track, or relieve the darkening close of a tale of human frailty and sorrow.

II. THE MARKET-PLACE

The grass-plot before the jail, in Prison Lane, on a certain summer morning, not less than two centuries ago, was occupied by a pretty large number of the inhabitants of Boston, all with their eyes intently fastened on the iron-clamped oaken door. Amongst any other population, or at a later period in the history of New England, the grim rigidity that petrified the bearded physiognomies of these good people would have augured some awful business in hand. It could have betokened nothing short of the anticipated execution of some noted culprit, on whom the sentence of a legal tribunal had but confirmed the verdict of public sentiment. But, in that early severity of the Puritan character, an inference of this kind could not so indubitably be drawn. It might be that a sluggish bond-servant, or an undutiful child, whom his parents had given over to the civil authority, was to be corrected at the whipping-post. It might be that an Antinomian, a Quaker, or other heterodox religionist, was to be scourged out of the town, or an idle or vagrant Indian, whom the white man's firewater had made riotous about the streets, was to be driven with stripes into the shadow of the forest. It might be, too, that a witch, like old Mistress Hibbins, the bitter-tempered widow of the magistrate, was to die upon the gallows. In either case, there was very much the same solemnity of demeanour on the part of the spectators, as befitted a people among whom religion and law were almost identical, and in whose character both were so thoroughly interfused, that the mildest and severest acts of public discipline were alike made venerable and awful. Meagre, indeed, and cold, was the sympathy that a transgressor might look for, from such bystanders, at the scaffold. On the other hand, a penalty which, in our days, would infer a degree of mocking infamy and ridicule, might then be invested with almost as stern a dignity as the punishment of death itself.

It was a circumstance to be noted on the summer morning when our story begins its course, that the women, of whom there were several in the crowd, appeared to take a peculiar interest in whatever penal infliction might be expected to ensue. The age had not so much refinement, that any sense of impropriety restrained the wearers of petticoat and farthingale from stepping forth into the public ways, and wedging their not unsubstantial persons, if occasion were, into the throng nearest to the scaffold at an execution. Morally, as well as materially, there was a coarser fibre in those wives and maidens of old English birth and breeding than in their fair descendants, separated from them by a series of six or seven generations; for, throughout that chain of ancestry, every successive mother had transmitted to her child a fainter bloom, a more delicate and briefer beauty, and a slighter physical frame, if not character of less force and solidity than her own. The women who were now standing about the prison-door stood within less than half a century of the period when the man-like Elizabeth had been the not altogether unsuitable representative of the sex. They were her countrywomen: and the beef and ale of their native land, with a moral diet not a whit more refined, entered largely into their composition. The bright morning sun, therefore, shone on broad shoulders and well-developed busts, and on round and ruddy cheeks, that had ripened in the far-off island, and had hardly yet grown paler or thinner in the atmosphere of New England. There was, moreover, a boldness and rotundity of speech among these matrons, as most of them seemed to be, that would startle us at the present day, whether in respect to its purport or its volume of tone.

"Goodwives," said a hard-featured dame of fifty, "I'll tell ye a piece of my mind. It would be greatly for the public behoof if we women, being of mature age and church-members in good repute, should have the handling of such malefactresses as this Hester Prynne. What think ye, gossips? If the hussy stood up for judgment before us five, that are now here in a knot together, would she come off with such a sentence as the worshipful magistrates have awarded? Marry, I trow not."

"People say," said another, "that the Reverend Master Dimmesdale, her godly pastor, takes it very grievously to heart that such a scandal should have come upon his congregation."

"The magistrates are God-fearing gentlemen, but merciful overmuch—that is a truth," added a third autumnal matron. "At the very least, they should have put the brand of a hot iron on Hester Prynne's forehead. Madame Hester would have winced at that, I warrant me. But she—the naughty baggage—little will she care what they put upon the bodice of her gown! Why, look you, she may cover it with a brooch, or such like heathenish adornment, and so walk the streets as brave as ever!"

"Ah, but," interposed, more softly, a young wife, holding a child by the hand, "let her cover the mark as she will, the pang of it will be always in her heart."

"What do we talk of marks and brands, whether on the bodice of her gown or the flesh of her forehead?" cried another female, the ugliest as well as the most pitiless of these self-constituted judges. "This woman has brought shame upon us all, and ought to die; is there not law for it? Truly there is, both in the Scripture and the statute-book. Then let the magistrates, who have made it of no effect, thank themselves if their own wives and daughters go astray."

"Mercy on us, goodwife!" exclaimed a man in the crowd, "is there no virtue in woman, save what springs from a wholesome fear of the gallows? That is the hardest word yet! Hush now, gossips for the lock is turning in the prison-door, and here comes Mistress Prynne herself."

II. THE MARKET-PLACE

The door of the jail being flung open from within there appeared, in the first place, like a black shadow emerging into sunshine, the grim and gristly presence of the town-beadle, with a sword by his side, and his staff of office in his hand. This personage prefigured and represented in his aspect the whole dismal severity of the Puritanic code of law, which it was his business to administer in its final and closest application to the offender. Stretching forth the official staff in his left hand, he laid his right upon the shoulder of a young woman, whom he thus drew forward, until, on the threshold of the prison-door, she repelled him, by an action marked with natural dignity and force of character, and stepped into the open air as if by her own free will. She bore in her arms a child, a baby of some three months old, who winked and turned aside its little face from the too vivid light of day; because its existence, heretofore, had brought it acquaintance only with the grey twilight of a dungeon, or other darksome apartment of the prison.

When the young woman—the mother of this child—stood fully revealed before the crowd, it seemed to be her first impulse to clasp the infant closely to her bosom; not so much by an impulse of motherly affection, as that she might thereby conceal a certain token, which was wrought or fastened into her dress. In a moment, however, wisely judging that one token of her shame would but poorly serve to hide another, she took the baby on her arm, and with a burning blush, and yet a haughty smile, and a glance that would not be abashed, looked around at her townspeople and neighbours. On the breast of her gown, in fine red cloth, surrounded with an elaborate embroidery and fantastic flourishes of gold thread, appeared the letter A. It was so artistically done, and with so much fertility and gorgeous luxuriance of fancy, that it had all the effect of a last and fitting decoration to the apparel which she wore, and which was of a splendour in accordance with the taste of the age, but greatly beyond what was allowed by the sumptuary regulations of the colony.

The young woman was tall, with a figure of perfect elegance on a large scale. She had dark and abundant hair, so glossy that it threw off the sunshine with a gleam; and a face which, besides being beautiful from regularity of feature and richness of complexion, had the impressiveness belonging to a marked brow and deep black eyes. She was ladylike, too, after the manner of the feminine gentility of those days; characterised by a certain state and dignity, rather than by the delicate, evanescent, and indescribable grace which is now recognised as its indication. And never had Hester Prynne appeared more ladylike, in the antique interpretation of the term, than as she issued from the prison. Those who had before known her, and had expected to behold her dimmed and obscured by a disastrous cloud, were astonished, and even startled, to perceive how her beauty shone out, and made a halo of the misfortune and ignominy in which she was enveloped. It may be true that, to a sensitive observer, there was some thing exquisitely painful in it. Her attire, which indeed, she had wrought for the occasion in prison, and had modelled much after her own fancy, seemed to express the attitude of her spirit, the desperate recklessness of her mood, by its wild and picturesque peculiarity. But the point which drew all eyes, and, as it were, transfigured the wearer—so that both men and women who had been familiarly acquainted with Hester Prynne were now impressed as if they beheld her for the first time—was that SCARLET LETTER, so fantastically embroidered and illuminated upon her bosom. It had the effect of a spell, taking her out of the ordinary relations with humanity, and enclosing her in a sphere by herself.

"She hath good skill at her needle, that's certain," remarked one of her female spectators; "but did ever a woman, before this brazen hussy, contrive such a way of showing it? Why, gossips, what is it but to laugh in the faces of our godly magistrates, and make a pride out of what they, worthy gentlemen, meant for a punishment?"

"It were well," muttered the most iron-visaged of the old dames, "if we stripped Madame Hester's rich gown off her dainty shoulders; and as for the red letter which she hath stitched so curiously, I'll bestow a rag of mine own rheumatic flannel to make a fitter one!"

"Oh, peace, neighbours—peace!" whispered their youngest companion; "do not let her hear you! Not a stitch in that embroidered letter but she has felt it in her heart."

The grim beadle now made a gesture with his staff. "Make way, good people—make way, in the King's name!" cried he. "Open a passage; and I promise ye, Mistress Prynne shall be set where man, woman, and child may have a fair sight of her brave apparel from this time till an hour past meridian. A blessing on the righteous colony of the Massachusetts, where iniquity is dragged out into the sunshine! Come along, Madame Hester, and show your scarlet letter in the market-place!"

A lane was forthwith opened through the crowd of spectators. Preceded by the beadle, and attended by an irregular procession of stern-browed men and unkindly visaged women, Hester Prynne set forth towards the place appointed for her punishment. A crowd of eager and curious schoolboys, understanding little of the matter in hand, except that it gave them a half-holiday, ran before her progress, turning their heads continually to stare into her face and at the winking baby in her arms, and at the ignominious letter on her breast. It was no great distance, in those days, from the prison door to the market-place. Measured by the prisoner's experience, however, it might be reckoned a journey of some length; for haughty as her demeanour was, she perchance underwent an agony from every footstep of those that thronged to see her, as if her heart had been flung into the street for them all to spurn and trample upon. In our nature, however, there is a provision, alike marvellous and merciful, that the sufferer should never know the intensity of what he endures by its present torture, but chiefly by the pang that rankles after it. With almost a serene deportment, therefore, Hester Prynne passed through this portion of her ordeal, and came to a sort of scaffold, at the western extremity of the market-place. It stood nearly beneath the eaves of Boston's earliest church, and appeared to be a fixture there.

In fact, this scaffold constituted a portion of a penal machine, which now, for two or three generations past, has been merely historical and traditionary among us, but was held, in the old time, to be as effectual an agent, in the promotion of good citizenship, as ever was the guillotine among the terrorists of France. It was, in short, the platform of the pillory; and above it rose the framework of that instrument of discipline, so fashioned as to confine the human head in its tight grasp, and thus hold it up to the public gaze. The very ideal of ignominy was embodied and made manifest in this contrivance of wood and iron. There can be no outrage, methinks, against our common nature—whatever be the delinquencies of the individual—no outrage more flagrant than to forbid the culprit to hide his face for shame; as it was the essence of this punishment to do. In Hester Prynne's instance, however, as not unfrequently in other cases, her sentence bore that she should stand a certain time upon the platform, but without undergoing that gripe about the neck and confinement of the head, the proneness to which was the most devilish characteristic of this ugly engine. Knowing well her part, she ascended a flight of wooden steps, and was thus displayed to the surrounding multitude, at about the height of a man's shoulders above the street.

Had there been a Papist among the crowd of Puritans, he might have seen in this beautiful woman, so picturesque in her attire and mien, and with the infant at her bosom, an object to remind him of the image of Divine Maternity, which so many illustrious painters have vied with one another to represent; something which should remind him, indeed, but only by contrast, of that sacred image of sinless motherhood, whose infant was to redeem the world. Here, there was the taint of deepest sin in the most sacred quality of human life, working such effect, that the world was only the darker for this woman's beauty, and the more lost for the infant that she had borne.

The scene was not without a mixture of awe, such as must always invest the spectacle of guilt and shame in a fellow-creature, before society shall have grown corrupt enough to smile, instead of shuddering at it. The witnesses of Hester Prynne's disgrace had not yet passed beyond their simplicity. They were stern enough to look upon her death, had that been the sentence, without a murmur at its severity, but had none of the heartlessness of another social state, which would find only a theme for jest in an exhibition like the present. Even had there been a disposition to turn the matter into ridicule, it must have been repressed and overpowered by the solemn presence of men no less dignified than the governor, and several of his counsellors, a judge, a general, and the ministers of the town, all of whom sat or stood in a balcony of the meeting-house, looking down upon the platform. When such personages could constitute a part of the spectacle, without risking the majesty, or reverence of rank and office, it was safely to be inferred that the infliction of a legal sentence would have an earnest and effectual meaning. Accordingly, the crowd was sombre and grave. The unhappy culprit sustained herself as best a woman might, under the heavy weight of a thousand unrelenting eyes, all fastened upon her, and concentrated at her bosom. It was almost intolerable to be borne. Of an impulsive and passionate nature, she had fortified herself to encounter the stings and venomous stabs of public contumely, wreaking itself in every variety of insult; but there was a quality so much more terrible in the solemn mood of the popular mind, that she longed rather to behold all those rigid countenances contorted with scornful merriment, and herself the object. Had a roar of laughter burst from the multitude—each man, each woman, each little shrill-voiced child, contributing their individual parts—Hester Prynne might have repaid them all with a bitter and disdainful smile. But, under the leaden infliction which it was her doom to endure, she felt, at moments, as if she must needs shriek out with the full power of her lungs, and cast herself from the scaffold down upon the ground, or else go mad at once.

Yet there were intervals when the whole scene, in which she was the most conspicuous object, seemed to vanish from her eyes, or, at least, glimmered indistinctly before them, like a mass of imperfectly shaped and spectral images. Her mind, and especially her memory, was preternaturally active, and kept bringing up other scenes than this roughly hewn street of a little town, on the edge of the western wilderness: other faces than were lowering upon her from beneath the brims of those steeple-crowned hats. Reminiscences, the most trifling and immaterial, passages of infancy and school-days, sports, childish quarrels, and the little domestic traits of her maiden years, came swarming back upon her, intermingled with recollections of whatever was gravest in her subsequent life; one picture precisely as vivid as another; as if all were of similar importance, or all alike a play. Possibly, it was an instinctive device of her spirit to relieve itself by the exhibition of these phantasmagoric forms, from the cruel weight and hardness of the reality.

Be that as it might, the scaffold of the pillory was a point of view that revealed to Hester Prynne the entire track along which she had been treading, since her happy infancy. Standing on that miserable eminence, she saw again her native village, in Old England, and her paternal home: a decayed house of grey stone, with a poverty-stricken aspect, but retaining a half obliterated shield of arms over the portal, in token of antique gentility. She saw her father's face, with its bold brow, and reverend white beard that flowed over the old-fashioned Elizabethan ruff; her mother's, too, with the look of heedful and anxious love which it always wore in her remembrance, and which, even since her death, had so often laid the impediment of a gentle remonstrance in her daughter's pathway. She saw her own face, glowing with girlish beauty, and illuminating all the interior of the dusky mirror in which she had been wont to gaze at it. There she beheld another countenance, of a man well stricken in years, a pale, thin, scholar-like visage, with eyes dim and bleared by the lamp-light that had served them to pore over many ponderous books. Yet those same bleared optics had a strange, penetrating power, when it was their owner's purpose to read the human soul. This figure of the study and the cloister, as Hester Prynne's womanly fancy failed not to recall, was slightly deformed, with the left shoulder a trifle higher than the right. Next rose before her in memory's picture-gallery, the intricate and narrow thoroughfares, the tall, grey houses, the huge cathedrals, and the public edifices, ancient in date and quaint in architecture, of a continental city; where new life had awaited her, still in connexion with the misshapen scholar: a new life, but feeding itself on time-worn materials, like a tuft of green moss on a crumbling wall. Lastly, in lieu of these shifting scenes, came back the rude market-place of the Puritan, settlement, with all the townspeople assembled, and levelling their stern regards at Hester Prynne—yes, at herself—who stood on the scaffold of the pillory, an infant on her arm, and the letter A, in scarlet, fantastically embroidered with gold thread, upon her bosom.

Could it be true? She clutched the child so fiercely to her breast that it sent forth a cry; she turned her eyes downward at the scarlet letter, and even touched it with her finger, to assure herself that the infant and the shame were real. Yes these were her realities—all else had vanished!

III. THE RECOGNITION

From this intense consciousness of being the object of severe and universal observation, the wearer of the scarlet letter was at length relieved, by discerning, on the outskirts of the crowd, a figure which irresistibly took possession of her thoughts. An Indian in his native garb was standing there; but the red men were not so infrequent visitors of the English settlements that one of them would have attracted any notice from Hester Prynne at such a time; much less would he have excluded all other objects and ideas from her mind. By the Indian's side, and evidently sustaining a companionship with him, stood a white man, clad in a strange disarray of civilized and savage costume.

He was small in stature, with a furrowed visage, which as yet could hardly be termed aged. There was a remarkable intelligence in his features, as of a person who had so cultivated his mental part that it could not fail to mould the physical to itself and become manifest by unmistakable tokens. Although, by a seemingly careless arrangement of his heterogeneous garb, he had endeavoured to conceal or abate the peculiarity, it was sufficiently evident to Hester Prynne that one of this man's shoulders rose higher than the other. Again, at the first instant of perceiving that thin visage, and the slight deformity of the figure, she pressed her infant to her bosom with so convulsive a force that the poor babe uttered another cry of pain. But the mother did not seem to hear it.

At his arrival in the market-place, and some time before she saw him, the stranger had bent his eyes on Hester Prynne. It was carelessly at first, like a man chiefly accustomed to look inward, and to whom external matters are of little value and import, unless they bear relation to something within his mind. Very soon, however, his look became keen and penetrative. A writhing horror twisted itself across his features, like a snake gliding swiftly over them, and making one little pause, with all its wreathed intervolutions in open sight. His face darkened with some powerful emotion, which, nevertheless, he so instantaneously controlled by an effort of his will, that, save at a single moment, its expression might have passed for calmness. After a brief space, the convulsion grew almost imperceptible, and finally subsided into the depths of his nature. When he found the eyes of Hester Prynne fastened on his own, and saw that she appeared to recognize him, he slowly and calmly raised his finger, made a gesture with it in the air, and laid it on his lips.

Then touching the shoulder of a townsman who stood near to him, he addressed him in a formal and courteous manner:

"I pray you, good Sir," said he, "who is this woman?—and wherefore is she here set up to public shame?"

"You must needs be a stranger in this region, friend," answered the townsman, looking curiously at the questioner and his savage companion, "else you would surely have heard of Mistress Hester Prynne and her evil doings. She hath raised a great scandal, I promise you, in godly Master Dimmesdale's church."

"You say truly," replied the other; "I am a stranger, and have been a wanderer, sorely against my will. I have met with grievous mishaps by sea and land, and have been long held in bonds among the heathen-folk to the southward; and am now brought hither by this Indian to be redeemed out of my captivity. Will it please you, therefore, to tell me of Hester Prynne's—have I her name rightly?—of this woman's offences, and what has brought her to yonder scaffold?"

"Truly, friend; and methinks it must gladden your heart, after your troubles and sojourn in the wilderness," said the townsman, "to find yourself at length in a land where iniquity is searched out and punished in the sight of rulers and people, as here in our godly New England. Yonder woman, Sir, you must know, was the wife of a certain learned man, English by birth, but who had long ago dwelt in Amsterdam, whence some good time agone he was minded to cross over and cast in his lot with us of the Massachusetts. To this purpose he sent his wife before him, remaining himself to look after some necessary affairs. Marry, good Sir, in some two years, or less, that the woman has been a dweller here in Boston, no tidings have come of this learned gentleman, Master Prynne; and his young wife, look you, being left to her own misguidance—"

"Ah!—aha!—I conceive you," said the stranger with a bitter smile. "So learned a man as you speak of should have learned this too in his books. And who, by your favour, Sir, may be the father of yonder babe—it is some three or four months old, I should judge—which Mistress Prynne is holding in her arms?"

"Of a truth, friend, that matter remaineth a riddle; and the Daniel who shall expound it is yet a-wanting," answered the townsman. "Madame Hester absolutely refuseth to speak, and the magistrates have laid their heads together in vain. Peradventure the guilty one stands looking on at this sad spectacle, unknown of man, and forgetting that God sees him."

"The learned man," observed the stranger with another smile, "should come himself to look into the mystery."

"It behoves him well if he be still in life," responded the townsman. "Now, good Sir, our Massachusetts magistracy, bethinking themselves that this woman is youthful and fair, and doubtless was strongly tempted to her fall, and that, moreover, as is most likely, her husband may be at the bottom of the sea, they have not been bold to put in force the extremity of our righteous law against her. The penalty thereof is death. But in their great mercy and tenderness of heart they have doomed Mistress Prynne to stand only a space of three hours on the platform of the pillory, and then and thereafter, for the remainder of her natural life to wear a mark of shame upon her bosom."

"A wise sentence," remarked the stranger, gravely, bowing his head. "Thus she will be a living sermon against sin, until the ignominious letter be engraved upon her tombstone. It irks me, nevertheless, that the partner of her iniquity should not at least, stand on the scaffold by her side. But he will be known—he will be known!—he will be known!"

He bowed courteously to the communicative townsman, and whispering a few words to his Indian attendant, they both made their way through the crowd.

While this passed, Hester Prynne had been standing on her pedestal, still with a fixed gaze towards the stranger—so fixed a gaze that, at moments of intense absorption, all other objects in the visible world seemed to vanish, leaving only him and her. Such an interview, perhaps, would have been more terrible than even to meet him as she now did, with the hot mid-day sun burning down upon her face, and lighting up its shame; with the scarlet token of infamy on her breast; with the sin-born infant in her arms; with a whole people, drawn forth as to a festival, staring at the features that should have been seen only in the quiet gleam of the fireside, in the happy shadow of a home, or beneath a matronly veil at church. Dreadful as it was, she was conscious of a shelter in the presence of these thousand witnesses. It was better to stand thus, with so many betwixt him and her, than to greet him face to face—they two alone. She fled for refuge, as it were, to the public exposure, and dreaded the moment when its protection should be withdrawn from her. Involved in these thoughts, she scarcely heard a voice behind her until it had repeated her name more than once, in a loud and solemn tone, audible to the whole multitude.

"Hearken unto me, Hester Prynne!" said the voice.

It has already been noticed that directly over the platform on which Hester Prynne stood was a kind of balcony, or open gallery, appended to the meeting-house. It was the place whence proclamations were wont to be made, amidst an assemblage of the magistracy, with all the ceremonial that attended such public observances in those days. Here, to witness the scene which we are describing, sat Governor Bellingham himself with four sergeants about his chair, bearing halberds, as a guard of honour. He wore a dark feather in his hat, a border of embroidery on his cloak, and a black velvet tunic beneath—a gentleman advanced in years, with a hard experience written in his wrinkles. He was not ill-fitted to be the head and representative of a community which owed its origin and progress, and its present state of development, not to the impulses of youth, but to the stern and tempered energies of manhood and the sombre sagacity of age; accomplishing so much, precisely because it imagined and hoped so little. The other eminent characters by whom the chief ruler was surrounded were distinguished by a dignity of mien, belonging to a period when the forms of authority were felt to possess the sacredness of Divine institutions. They were, doubtless, good men, just and sage. But, out of the whole human family, it would not have been easy to select the same number of wise and virtuous persons, who should be less capable of sitting in judgment on an erring woman's heart, and disentangling its mesh of good and evil, than the sages of rigid aspect towards whom Hester Prynne now turned her face. She seemed conscious, indeed, that whatever sympathy she might expect lay in the larger and warmer heart of the multitude; for, as she lifted her eyes towards the balcony, the unhappy woman grew pale, and trembled.

The voice which had called her attention was that of the reverend and famous John Wilson, the eldest clergyman of Boston, a great scholar, like most of his contemporaries in the profession, and withal a man of kind and genial spirit. This last attribute, however, had been less carefully developed than his intellectual gifts, and was, in truth, rather a matter of shame than self-congratulation with him. There he stood, with a border of grizzled locks beneath his skull-cap, while his grey eyes, accustomed to the shaded light of his study, were winking, like those of Hester's infant, in the unadulterated sunshine. He looked like the darkly engraved portraits which we see prefixed to old volumes of sermons, and had no more right than one of those portraits would have to step forth, as he now did, and meddle with a question of human guilt, passion, and anguish.

"Hester Prynne," said the clergyman, "I have striven with my young brother here, under whose preaching of the Word you have been privileged to sit"—here Mr. Wilson laid his hand on the shoulder of a pale young man beside him—"I have sought, I say, to persuade this godly youth, that he should deal with you, here in the face of Heaven, and before these wise and upright rulers, and in hearing of all the people, as touching the vileness and blackness of your sin. Knowing your natural temper better than I, he could the better judge what arguments to use, whether of tenderness or terror, such as might prevail over your hardness and obstinacy, insomuch that you should no longer hide the name of him who tempted you to this grievous fall. But he opposes to me—with a young man's oversoftness, albeit wise beyond his years—that it were wronging the very nature of woman to force her to lay open her heart's secrets in such broad daylight, and in presence of so great a multitude. Truly, as I sought to convince him, the shame lay in the commission of the sin, and not in the showing of it forth. What say you to it, once again, brother Dimmesdale? Must it be thou, or I, that shall deal with this poor sinner's soul?"

There was a murmur among the dignified and reverend occupants of the balcony; and Governor Bellingham gave expression to its purport, speaking in an authoritative voice, although tempered with respect towards the youthful clergyman whom he addressed:

"Good Master Dimmesdale," said he, "the responsibility of this woman's soul lies greatly with you. It behoves you; therefore, to exhort her to repentance and to confession, as a proof and consequence thereof."

The directness of this appeal drew the eyes of the whole crowd upon the Reverend Mr. Dimmesdale—young clergyman, who had come from one of the great English universities, bringing all the learning of the age into our wild forest land. His eloquence and religious fervour had already given the earnest of high eminence in his profession. He was a person of very striking aspect, with a white, lofty, and impending brow; large, brown, melancholy eyes, and a mouth which, unless when he forcibly compressed it, was apt to be tremulous, expressing both nervous sensibility and a vast power of self restraint. Notwithstanding his high native gifts and scholar-like attainments, there was an air about this young minister—an apprehensive, a startled, a half-frightened look—as of a being who felt himself quite astray, and at a loss in the pathway of human existence, and could only be at ease in some seclusion of his own. Therefore, so far as his duties would permit, he trod in the shadowy by-paths, and thus kept himself simple and childlike, coming forth, when occasion was, with a freshness, and fragrance, and dewy purity of thought, which, as many people said, affected them like the speech of an angel.

Such was the young man whom the Reverend Mr. Wilson and the Governor had introduced so openly to the public notice, bidding him speak, in the hearing of all men, to that mystery of a woman's soul, so sacred even in its pollution. The trying nature of his position drove the blood from his cheek, and made his lips tremulous.

"Speak to the woman, my brother," said Mr. Wilson. "It is of moment to her soul, and, therefore, as the worshipful Governor says, momentous to thine own, in whose charge hers is. Exhort her to confess the truth!"

The Reverend Mr. Dimmesdale bent his head, in silent prayer, as it seemed, and then came forward.

"Hester Prynne," said he, leaning over the balcony and looking down steadfastly into her eyes, "thou hearest what this good man says, and seest the accountability under which I labour. If thou feelest it to be for thy soul's peace, and that thy earthly punishment will thereby be made more effectual to salvation, I charge thee to speak out the name of thy fellow-sinner and fellow-sufferer! Be not silent from any mistaken pity and tenderness for him; for, believe me, Hester, though he were to step down from a high place, and stand there beside thee, on thy pedestal of shame, yet better were it so than to hide a guilty heart through life. What can thy silence do for him, except it tempt him—yea, compel him, as it were—to add hypocrisy to sin? Heaven hath granted thee an open ignominy, that thereby thou mayest work out an open triumph over the evil within thee and the sorrow without. Take heed how thou deniest to him—who, perchance, hath not the courage to grasp it for himself—the bitter, but wholesome, cup that is now presented to thy lips!"

The young pastor's voice was tremulously sweet, rich, deep, and broken. The feeling that it so evidently manifested, rather than the direct purport of the words, caused it to vibrate within all hearts, and brought the listeners into one accord of sympathy. Even the poor baby at Hester's bosom was affected by the same influence, for it directed its hitherto vacant gaze towards Mr. Dimmesdale, and held up its little arms with a half-pleased, half-plaintive murmur. So powerful seemed the minister's appeal that the people could not believe but that Hester Prynne would speak out the guilty name, or else that the guilty one himself in whatever high or lowly place he stood, would be drawn forth by an inward and inevitable necessity, and compelled to ascend the scaffold.

Hester shook her head.

"Woman, transgress not beyond the limits of Heaven's mercy!" cried the Reverend Mr. Wilson, more harshly than before. "That little babe hath been gifted with a voice, to second and confirm the counsel which thou hast heard. Speak out the name! That, and thy repentance, may avail to take the scarlet letter off thy breast."

"Never," replied Hester Prynne, looking, not at Mr. Wilson, but into the deep and troubled eyes of the younger clergyman. "It is too deeply branded. Ye cannot take it off. And would that I might endure his agony as well as mine!"

"Speak, woman!" said another voice, coldly and sternly, proceeding from the crowd about the scaffold, "Speak; and give your child a father!"

"I will not speak!" answered Hester, turning pale as death, but responding to this voice, which she too surely recognised. "And my child must seek a heavenly father; she shall never know an earthly one!"

"She will not speak!" murmured Mr. Dimmesdale, who, leaning over the balcony, with his hand upon his heart, had awaited the result of his appeal. He now drew back with a long respiration. "Wondrous strength and generosity of a woman's heart! She will not speak!"

Discerning the impracticable state of the poor culprit's mind, the elder clergyman, who had carefully prepared himself for the occasion, addressed to the multitude a discourse on sin, in all its branches, but with continual reference to the ignominious letter. So forcibly did he dwell upon this symbol, for the hour or more during which his periods were rolling over the people's heads, that it assumed new terrors in their imagination, and seemed to derive its scarlet hue from the flames of the infernal pit. Hester Prynne, meanwhile, kept her place upon the pedestal of shame, with glazed eyes, and an air of weary indifference. She had borne that morning all that nature could endure; and as her temperament was not of the order that escapes from too intense suffering by a swoon, her spirit could only shelter itself beneath a stony crust of insensibility, while the faculties of animal life remained entire. In this state, the voice of the preacher thundered remorselessly, but unavailingly, upon her ears. The infant, during the latter portion of her ordeal, pierced the air with its wailings and screams; she strove to hush it mechanically, but seemed scarcely to sympathise with its trouble. With the same hard demeanour, she was led back to prison, and vanished from the public gaze within its iron-clamped portal. It was whispered by those who peered after her that the scarlet letter threw a lurid gleam along the dark passage-way of the interior.

IV. THE INTERVIEW

After her return to the prison, Hester Prynne was found to be in a state of nervous excitement, that demanded constant watchfulness, lest she should perpetrate violence on herself, or do some half-frenzied mischief to the poor babe. As night approached, it proving impossible to quell her insubordination by rebuke or threats of punishment, Master Brackett, the jailer, thought fit to introduce a physician. He described him as a man of skill in all Christian modes of physical science, and likewise familiar with whatever the savage people could teach in respect to medicinal herbs and roots that grew in the forest. To say the truth, there was much need of professional assistance, not merely for Hester herself, but still more urgently for the child—who, drawing its sustenance from the maternal bosom, seemed to have drank in with it all the turmoil, the anguish and despair, which pervaded the mother's system. It now writhed in convulsions of pain, and was a forcible type, in its little frame, of the moral agony which Hester Prynne had borne throughout the day.

Closely following the jailer into the dismal apartment, appeared that individual, of singular aspect whose presence in the crowd had been of such deep interest to the wearer of the scarlet letter. He was lodged in the prison, not as suspected of any offence, but as the most convenient and suitable mode of disposing of him, until the magistrates should have conferred with the Indian sagamores respecting his ransom. His name was announced as Roger Chillingworth. The jailer, after ushering him into the room, remained a moment, marvelling at the comparative quiet that followed his entrance; for Hester Prynne had immediately become as still as death, although the child continued to moan.

"Prithee, friend, leave me alone with my patient," said the practitioner. "Trust me, good jailer, you shall briefly have peace in your house; and, I promise you, Mistress Prynne shall hereafter be more amenable to just authority than you may have found her heretofore."

"Nay, if your worship can accomplish that," answered Master Brackett, "I shall own you for a man of skill, indeed! Verily, the woman hath been like a possessed one; and there lacks little that I should take in hand, to drive Satan out of her with stripes."

The stranger had entered the room with the characteristic quietude of the profession to which he announced himself as belonging. Nor did his demeanour change when the withdrawal of the prison keeper left him face to face with the woman, whose absorbed notice of him, in the crowd, had intimated so close a relation between himself and her. His first care was given to the child, whose cries, indeed, as she lay writhing on the trundle-bed, made it of peremptory necessity to postpone all other business to the task of soothing her. He examined the infant carefully, and then proceeded to unclasp a leathern case, which he took from beneath his dress. It appeared to contain medical preparations, one of which he mingled with a cup of water.

"My old studies in alchemy," observed he, "and my sojourn, for above a year past, among a people well versed in the kindly properties of simples, have made a better physician of me than many that claim the medical degree. Here, woman! The child is yours—she is none of mine—neither will she recognise my voice or aspect as a father's. Administer this draught, therefore, with thine own hand."

Hester repelled the offered medicine, at the same time gazing with strongly marked apprehension into his face. "Wouldst thou avenge thyself on the innocent babe?" whispered she.

"Foolish woman!" responded the physician, half coldly, half soothingly. "What should ail me to harm this misbegotten and miserable babe? The medicine is potent for good, and were it my child—yea, mine own, as well as thine! I could do no better for it."

As she still hesitated, being, in fact, in no reasonable state of mind, he took the infant in his arms, and himself administered the draught. It soon proved its efficacy, and redeemed the leech's pledge. The moans of the little patient subsided; its convulsive tossings gradually ceased; and in a few moments, as is the custom of young children after relief from pain, it sank into a profound and dewy slumber. The physician, as he had a fair right to be termed, next bestowed his attention on the mother. With calm and intent scrutiny, he felt her pulse, looked into her eyes—a gaze that made her heart shrink and shudder, because so familiar, and yet so strange and cold—and, finally, satisfied with his investigation, proceeded to mingle another draught.

"I know not Lethe nor Nepenthe," remarked he; "but I have learned many new secrets in the wilderness, and here is one of them—a recipe that an Indian taught me, in requital of some lessons of my own, that were as old as Paracelsus. Drink it! It may be less soothing than a sinless conscience. That I cannot give thee. But it will calm the swell and heaving of thy passion, like oil thrown on the waves of a tempestuous sea."

He presented the cup to Hester, who received it with a slow, earnest look into his face; not precisely a look of fear, yet full of doubt and questioning as to what his purposes might be. She looked also at her slumbering child.

"I have thought of death," said she—"have wished for it—would even have prayed for it, were it fit that such as I should pray for anything. Yet, if death be in this cup, I bid thee think again, ere thou beholdest me quaff it. See! it is even now at my lips."

"Drink, then," replied he, still with the same cold composure. "Dost thou know me so little, Hester Prynne? Are my purposes wont to be so shallow? Even if I imagine a scheme of vengeance, what could I do better for my object than to let thee live—than to give thee medicines against all harm and peril of life—so that this burning shame may still blaze upon thy bosom?" As he spoke, he laid his long fore-finger on the scarlet letter, which forthwith seemed to scorch into Hester's breast, as if it had been red hot. He noticed her involuntary gesture, and smiled. "Live, therefore, and bear about thy doom with thee, in the eyes of men and women—in the eyes of him whom thou didst call thy husband—in the eyes of yonder child! And, that thou mayest live, take off this draught."

Without further expostulation or delay, Hester Prynne drained the cup, and, at the motion of the man of skill, seated herself on the bed, where the child was sleeping; while he drew the only chair which the room afforded, and took his own seat beside her. She could not but tremble at these preparations; for she felt that—having now done all that humanity, or principle, or, if so it were, a refined cruelty, impelled him to do for the relief of physical suffering—he was next to treat with her as the man whom she had most deeply and irreparably injured.

"Hester," said he, "I ask not wherefore, nor how thou hast fallen into the pit, or say, rather, thou hast ascended to the pedestal of infamy on which I found thee. The reason is not far to seek. It was my folly, and thy weakness. I—a man of thought—the book-worm of great libraries—a man already in decay, having given my best years to feed the hungry dream of knowledge—what had I to do with youth and beauty like thine own? Misshapen from my birth-hour, how could I delude myself with the idea that intellectual gifts might veil physical deformity in a young girl's fantasy? Men call me wise. If sages were ever wise in their own behoof, I might have foreseen all this. I might have known that, as I came out of the vast and dismal forest, and entered this settlement of Christian men, the very first object to meet my eyes would be thyself, Hester Prynne, standing up, a statue of ignominy, before the people. Nay, from the moment when we came down the old church-steps together, a married pair, I might have beheld the bale-fire of that scarlet letter blazing at the end of our path!"

"Thou knowest," said Hester—for, depressed as she was, she could not endure this last quiet stab at the token of her shame—"thou knowest that I was frank with thee. I felt no love, nor feigned any."

"True," replied he. "It was my folly! I have said it. But, up to that epoch of my life, I had lived in vain. The world had been so cheerless! My heart was a habitation large enough for many guests, but lonely and chill, and without a household fire. I longed to kindle one! It seemed not so wild a dream—old as I was, and sombre as I was, and misshapen as I was—that the simple bliss, which is scattered far and wide, for all mankind to gather up, might yet be mine. And so, Hester, I drew thee into my heart, into its innermost chamber, and sought to warm thee by the warmth which thy presence made there!"

"I have greatly wronged thee," murmured Hester.

"We have wronged each other," answered he. "Mine was the first wrong, when I betrayed thy budding youth into a false and unnatural relation with my decay. Therefore, as a man who has not thought and philosophised in vain, I seek no vengeance, plot no evil against thee. Between thee and me, the scale hangs fairly balanced. But, Hester, the man lives who has wronged us both! Who is he?"

"Ask me not!" replied Hester Prynne, looking firmly into his face. "That thou shalt never know!"

"Never, sayest thou?" rejoined he, with a smile of dark and self-relying intelligence. "Never know him! Believe me, Hester, there are few things whether in the outward world, or, to a certain depth, in the invisible sphere of thought—few things hidden from the man who devotes himself earnestly and unreservedly to the solution of a mystery. Thou mayest cover up thy secret from the prying multitude. Thou mayest conceal it, too, from the ministers and magistrates, even as thou didst this day, when they sought to wrench the name out of thy heart, and give thee a partner on thy pedestal. But, as for me, I come to the inquest with other senses than they possess. I shall seek this man, as I have sought truth in books: as I have sought gold in alchemy. There is a sympathy that will make me conscious of him. I shall see him tremble. I shall feel myself shudder, suddenly and unawares. Sooner or later, he must needs be mine."

The eyes of the wrinkled scholar glowed so intensely upon her, that Hester Prynne clasped her hand over her heart, dreading lest he should read the secret there at once.

"Thou wilt not reveal his name? Not the less he is mine," resumed he, with a look of confidence, as if destiny were at one with him. "He bears no letter of infamy wrought into his garment, as thou dost, but I shall read it on his heart. Yet fear not for him! Think not that I shall interfere with Heaven's own method of retribution, or, to my own loss, betray him to the gripe of human law. Neither do thou imagine that I shall contrive aught against his life; no, nor against his fame, if as I judge, he be a man of fair repute. Let him live! Let him hide himself in outward honour, if he may! Not the less he shall be mine!"

"Thy acts are like mercy," said Hester, bewildered and appalled; "but thy words interpret thee as a terror!"

"One thing, thou that wast my wife, I would enjoin upon thee," continued the scholar. "Thou hast kept the secret of thy paramour. Keep, likewise, mine! There are none in this land that know me. Breathe not to any human soul that thou didst ever call me husband! Here, on this wild outskirt of the earth, I shall pitch my tent; for, elsewhere a wanderer, and isolated from human interests, I find here a woman, a man, a child, amongst whom and myself there exist the closest ligaments. No matter whether of love or hate: no matter whether of right or wrong! Thou and thine, Hester Prynne, belong to me. My home is where thou art and where he is. But betray me not!"

"Wherefore dost thou desire it?" inquired Hester, shrinking, she hardly knew why, from this secret bond. "Why not announce thyself openly, and cast me off at once?"

"It may be," he replied, "because I will not encounter the dishonour that besmirches the husband of a faithless woman. It may be for other reasons. Enough, it is my purpose to live and die unknown. Let, therefore, thy husband be to the world as one already dead, and of whom no tidings shall ever come. Recognise me not, by word, by sign, by look! Breathe not the secret, above all, to the man thou wottest of. Shouldst thou fail me in this, beware! His fame, his position, his life will be in my hands. Beware!"

"I will keep thy secret, as I have his," said Hester.

"Swear it!" rejoined he.

And she took the oath.

"And now, Mistress Prynne," said old Roger Chillingworth, as he was hereafter to be named, "I leave thee alone: alone with thy infant and the scarlet letter! How is it, Hester? Doth thy sentence bind thee to wear the token in thy sleep? Art thou not afraid of nightmares and hideous dreams?"

"Why dost thou smile so at me?" inquired Hester, troubled at the expression of his eyes. "Art thou like the Black Man that haunts the forest round about us? Hast thou enticed me into a bond that will prove the ruin of my soul?"

"Not thy soul," he answered, with another smile. "No, not thine!"

V. HESTER AT HER NEEDLE

Hester Prynne's term of confinement was now at an end. Her prison-door was thrown open, and she came forth into the sunshine, which, falling on all alike, seemed, to her sick and morbid heart, as if meant for no other purpose than to reveal the scarlet letter on her breast. Perhaps there was a more real torture in her first unattended footsteps from the threshold of the prison than even in the procession and spectacle that have been described, where she was made the common infamy, at which all mankind was summoned to point its finger. Then, she was supported by an unnatural tension of the nerves, and by all the combative energy of her character, which enabled her to convert the scene into a kind of lurid triumph. It was, moreover, a separate and insulated event, to occur but once in her lifetime, and to meet which, therefore, reckless of economy, she might call up the vital strength that would have sufficed for many quiet years. The very law that condemned her—a giant of stern features but with vigour to support, as well as to annihilate, in his iron arm—had held her up through the terrible ordeal of her ignominy. But now, with this unattended walk from her prison door, began the daily custom; and she must either sustain and carry it forward by the ordinary resources of her nature, or sink beneath it. She could no longer borrow from the future to help her through the present grief. Tomorrow would bring its own trial with it; so would the next day, and so would the next: each its own trial, and yet the very same that was now so unutterably grievous to be borne. The days of the far-off future would toil onward, still with the same burden for her to take up, and bear along with her, but never to fling down; for the accumulating days and added years would pile up their misery upon the heap of shame. Throughout them all, giving up her individuality, she would become the general symbol at which the preacher and moralist might point, and in which they might vivify and embody their images of woman's frailty and sinful passion. Thus the young and pure would be taught to look at her, with the scarlet letter flaming on her breast—at her, the child of honourable parents—at her, the mother of a babe that would hereafter be a woman—at her, who had once been innocent—as the figure, the body, the reality of sin. And over her grave, the infamy that she must carry thither would be her only monument.

It may seem marvellous that, with the world before her—kept by no restrictive clause of her condemnation within the limits of the Puritan settlement, so remote and so obscure—free to return to her birth-place, or to any other European land, and there hide her character and identity under a new exterior, as completely as if emerging into another state of being—and having also the passes of the dark, inscrutable forest open to her, where the wildness of her nature might assimilate itself with a people whose customs and life were alien from the law that had condemned her—it may seem marvellous that this woman should still call that place her home, where, and where only, she must needs be the type of shame. But there is a fatality, a feeling so irresistible and inevitable that it has the force of doom, which almost invariably compels human beings to linger around and haunt, ghost-like, the spot where some great and marked event has given the colour to their lifetime; and, still the more irresistibly, the darker the tinge that saddens it. Her sin, her ignominy, were the roots which she had struck into the soil. It was as if a new birth, with stronger assimilations than the first, had converted the forest-land, still so uncongenial to every other pilgrim and wanderer, into Hester Prynne's wild and dreary, but life-long home. All other scenes of earth—even that village of rural England, where happy infancy and stainless maidenhood seemed yet to be in her mother's keeping, like garments put off long ago—were foreign to her, in comparison. The chain that bound her here was of iron links, and galling to her inmost soul, but could never be broken.

It might be, too—doubtless it was so, although she hid the secret from herself, and grew pale whenever it struggled out of her heart, like a serpent from its hole—it might be that another feeling kept her within the scene and pathway that had been so fatal. There dwelt, there trode, the feet of one with whom she deemed herself connected in a union that, unrecognised on earth, would bring them together before the bar of final judgment, and make that their marriage-altar, for a joint futurity of endless retribution. Over and over again, the tempter of souls had thrust this idea upon Hester's contemplation, and laughed at the passionate and desperate joy with which she seized, and then strove to cast it from her. She barely looked the idea in the face, and hastened to bar it in its dungeon. What she compelled herself to believe—what, finally, she reasoned upon as her motive for continuing a resident of New England—was half a truth, and half a self-delusion. Here, she said to herself had been the scene of her guilt, and here should be the scene of her earthly punishment; and so, perchance, the torture of her daily shame would at length purge her soul, and work out another purity than that which she had lost: more saint-like, because the result of martyrdom.

Hester Prynne, therefore, did not flee. On the outskirts of the town, within the verge of the peninsula, but not in close vicinity to any other habitation, there was a small thatched cottage. It had been built by an earlier settler, and abandoned, because the soil about it was too sterile for cultivation, while its comparative remoteness put it out of the sphere of that social activity which already marked the habits of the emigrants. It stood on the shore, looking across a basin of the sea at the forest-covered hills, towards the west. A clump of scrubby trees, such as alone grew on the peninsula, did not so much conceal the cottage from view, as seem to denote that here was some object which would fain have been, or at least ought to be, concealed. In this little lonesome dwelling, with some slender means that she possessed, and by the licence of the magistrates, who still kept an inquisitorial watch over her, Hester established herself, with her infant child. A mystic shadow of suspicion immediately attached itself to the spot. Children, too young to comprehend wherefore this woman should be shut out from the sphere of human charities, would creep nigh enough to behold her plying her needle at the cottage-window, or standing in the doorway, or labouring in her little garden, or coming forth along the pathway that led townward, and, discerning the scarlet letter on her breast, would scamper off with a strange contagious fear.

Lonely as was Hester's situation, and without a friend on earth who dared to show himself, she, however, incurred no risk of want. She possessed an art that sufficed, even in a land that afforded comparatively little scope for its exercise, to supply food for her thriving infant and herself. It was the art, then, as now, almost the only one within a woman's grasp—of needle-work. She bore on her breast, in the curiously embroidered letter, a specimen of her delicate and imaginative skill, of which the dames of a court might gladly have availed themselves, to add the richer and more spiritual adornment of human ingenuity to their fabrics of silk and gold. Here, indeed, in the sable simplicity that generally characterised the Puritanic modes of dress, there might be an infrequent call for the finer productions of her handiwork. Yet the taste of the age, demanding whatever was elaborate in compositions of this kind, did not fail to extend its influence over our stern progenitors, who had cast behind them so many fashions which it might seem harder to dispense with.

Public ceremonies, such as ordinations, the installation of magistrates, and all that could give majesty to the forms in which a new government manifested itself to the people, were, as a matter of policy, marked by a stately and well-conducted ceremonial, and a sombre, but yet a studied magnificence. Deep ruffs, painfully wrought bands, and gorgeously embroidered gloves, were all deemed necessary to the official state of men assuming the reins of power, and were readily allowed to individuals dignified by rank or wealth, even while sumptuary laws forbade these and similar extravagances to the plebeian order. In the array of funerals, too—whether for the apparel of the dead body, or to typify, by manifold emblematic devices of sable cloth and snowy lawn, the sorrow of the survivors—there was a frequent and characteristic demand for such labour as Hester Prynne could supply. Baby-linen—for babies then wore robes of state—afforded still another possibility of toil and emolument.

By degrees, not very slowly, her handiwork became what would now be termed the fashion. Whether from commiseration for a woman of so miserable a destiny; or from the morbid curiosity that gives a fictitious value even to common or worthless things; or by whatever other intangible circumstance was then, as now, sufficient to bestow, on some persons, what others might seek in vain; or because Hester really filled a gap which must otherwise have remained vacant; it is certain that she had ready and fairly requited employment for as many hours as she saw fit to occupy with her needle. Vanity, it may be, chose to mortify itself, by putting on, for ceremonials of pomp and state, the garments that had been wrought by her sinful hands. Her needle-work was seen on the ruff of the Governor; military men wore it on their scarfs, and the minister on his band; it decked the baby's little cap; it was shut up, to be mildewed and moulder away, in the coffins of the dead. But it is not recorded that, in a single instance, her skill was called in to embroider the white veil which was to cover the pure blushes of a bride. The exception indicated the ever relentless vigour with which society frowned upon her sin.

Hester sought not to acquire anything beyond a subsistence, of the plainest and most ascetic description, for herself, and a simple abundance for her child. Her own dress was of the coarsest materials and the most sombre hue, with only that one ornament—the scarlet letter—which it was her doom to wear. The child's attire, on the other hand, was distinguished by a fanciful, or, we may rather say, a fantastic ingenuity, which served, indeed, to heighten the airy charm that early began to develop itself in the little girl, but which appeared to have also a deeper meaning. We may speak further of it hereafter. Except for that small expenditure in the decoration of her infant, Hester bestowed all her superfluous means in charity, on wretches less miserable than herself, and who not unfrequently insulted the hand that fed them. Much of the time, which she might readily have applied to the better efforts of her art, she employed in making coarse garments for the poor. It is probable that there was an idea of penance in this mode of occupation, and that she offered up a real sacrifice of enjoyment in devoting so many hours to such rude handiwork. She had in her nature a rich, voluptuous, Oriental characteristic—a taste for the gorgeously beautiful, which, save in the exquisite productions of her needle, found nothing else, in all the possibilities of her life, to exercise itself upon. Women derive a pleasure, incomprehensible to the other sex, from the delicate toil of the needle. To Hester Prynne it might have been a mode of expressing, and therefore soothing, the passion of her life. Like all other joys, she rejected it as sin. This morbid meddling of conscience with an immaterial matter betokened, it is to be feared, no genuine and steadfast penitence, but something doubtful, something that might be deeply wrong beneath.

In this manner, Hester Prynne came to have a part to perform in the world. With her native energy of character and rare capacity, it could not entirely cast her off, although it had set a mark upon her, more intolerable to a woman's heart than that which branded the brow of Cain. In all her intercourse with society, however, there was nothing that made her feel as if she belonged to it. Every gesture, every word, and even the silence of those with whom she came in contact, implied, and often expressed, that she was banished, and as much alone as if she inhabited another sphere, or communicated with the common nature by other organs and senses than the rest of human kind. She stood apart from mortal interests, yet close beside them, like a ghost that revisits the familiar fireside, and can no longer make itself seen or felt; no more smile with the household joy, nor mourn with the kindred sorrow; or, should it succeed in manifesting its forbidden sympathy, awakening only terror and horrible repugnance. These emotions, in fact, and its bitterest scorn besides, seemed to be the sole portion that she retained in the universal heart. It was not an age of delicacy; and her position, although she understood it well, and was in little danger of forgetting it, was often brought before her vivid self-perception, like a new anguish, by the rudest touch upon the tenderest spot. The poor, as we have already said, whom she sought out to be the objects of her bounty, often reviled the hand that was stretched forth to succour them. Dames of elevated rank, likewise, whose doors she entered in the way of her occupation, were accustomed to distil drops of bitterness into her heart; sometimes through that alchemy of quiet malice, by which women can concoct a subtle poison from ordinary trifles; and sometimes, also, by a coarser expression, that fell upon the sufferer's defenceless breast like a rough blow upon an ulcerated wound. Hester had schooled herself long and well; and she never responded to these attacks, save by a flush of crimson that rose irrepressibly over her pale cheek, and again subsided into the depths of her bosom. She was patient—a martyr, indeed but she forebore to pray for enemies, lest, in spite of her forgiving aspirations, the words of the blessing should stubbornly twist themselves into a curse.

Continually, and in a thousand other ways, did she feel the innumerable throbs of anguish that had been so cunningly contrived for her by the undying, the ever-active sentence of the Puritan tribunal. Clergymen paused in the streets, to address words of exhortation, that brought a crowd, with its mingled grin and frown, around the poor, sinful woman. If she entered a church, trusting to share the Sabbath smile of the Universal Father, it was often her mishap to find herself the text of the discourse. She grew to have a dread of children; for they had imbibed from their parents a vague idea of something horrible in this dreary woman gliding silently through the town, with never any companion but one only child. Therefore, first allowing her to pass, they pursued her at a distance with shrill cries, and the utterances of a word that had no distinct purport to their own minds, but was none the less terrible to her, as proceeding from lips that babbled it unconsciously. It seemed to argue so wide a diffusion of her shame, that all nature knew of it; it could have caused her no deeper pang had the leaves of the trees whispered the dark story among themselves—had the summer breeze murmured about it—had the wintry blast shrieked it aloud! Another peculiar torture was felt in the gaze of a new eye. When strangers looked curiously at the scarlet letter and none ever failed to do so—they branded it afresh in Hester's soul; so that, oftentimes, she could scarcely refrain, yet always did refrain, from covering the symbol with her hand. But then, again, an accustomed eye had likewise its own anguish to inflict. Its cool stare of familiarity was intolerable. From first to last, in short, Hester Prynne had always this dreadful agony in feeling a human eye upon the token; the spot never grew callous; it seemed, on the contrary, to grow more sensitive with daily torture.

But sometimes, once in many days, or perchance in many months, she felt an eye—a human eye—upon the ignominious brand, that seemed to give a momentary relief, as if half of her agony were shared. The next instant, back it all rushed again, with still a deeper throb of pain; for, in that brief interval, she had sinned anew. (Had Hester sinned alone?)

Her imagination was somewhat affected, and, had she been of a softer moral and intellectual fibre would have been still more so, by the strange and solitary anguish of her life. Walking to and fro, with those lonely footsteps, in the little world with which she was outwardly connected, it now and then appeared to Hester—if altogether fancy, it was nevertheless too potent to be resisted—she felt or fancied, then, that the scarlet letter had endowed her with a new sense. She shuddered to believe, yet could not help believing, that it gave her a sympathetic knowledge of the hidden sin in other hearts. She was terror-stricken by the revelations that were thus made. What were they? Could they be other than the insidious whispers of the bad angel, who would fain have persuaded the struggling woman, as yet only half his victim, that the outward guise of purity was but a lie, and that, if truth were everywhere to be shown, a scarlet letter would blaze forth on many a bosom besides Hester Prynne's? Or, must she receive those intimations—so obscure, yet so distinct—as truth? In all her miserable experience, there was nothing else so awful and so loathsome as this sense. It perplexed, as well as shocked her, by the irreverent inopportuneness of the occasions that brought it into vivid action. Sometimes the red infamy upon her breast would give a sympathetic throb, as she passed near a venerable minister or magistrate, the model of piety and justice, to whom that age of antique reverence looked up, as to a mortal man in fellowship with angels. "What evil thing is at hand?" would Hester say to herself. Lifting her reluctant eyes, there would be nothing human within the scope of view, save the form of this earthly saint! Again a mystic sisterhood would contumaciously assert itself, as she met the sanctified frown of some matron, who, according to the rumour of all tongues, had kept cold snow within her bosom throughout life. That unsunned snow in the matron's bosom, and the burning shame on Hester Prynne's—what had the two in common? Or, once more, the electric thrill would give her warning—"Behold Hester, here is a companion!" and, looking up, she would detect the eyes of a young maiden glancing at the scarlet letter, shyly and aside, and quickly averted, with a faint, chill crimson in her cheeks as if her purity were somewhat sullied by that momentary glance. O Fiend, whose talisman was that fatal symbol, wouldst thou leave nothing, whether in youth or age, for this poor sinner to revere?—such loss of faith is ever one of the saddest results of sin. Be it accepted as a proof that all was not corrupt in this poor victim of her own frailty, and man's hard law, that Hester Prynne yet struggled to believe that no fellow-mortal was guilty like herself.

The vulgar, who, in those dreary old times, were always contributing a grotesque horror to what interested their imaginations, had a story about the scarlet letter which we might readily work up into a terrific legend. They averred that the symbol was not mere scarlet cloth, tinged in an earthly dye-pot, but was red-hot with infernal fire, and could be seen glowing all alight whenever Hester Prynne walked abroad in the night-time. And we must needs say it seared Hester's bosom so deeply, that perhaps there was more truth in the rumour than our modern incredulity may be inclined to admit.

VI. PEARL

We have as yet hardly spoken of the infant; that little creature, whose innocent life had sprung, by the inscrutable decree of Providence, a lovely and immortal flower, out of the rank luxuriance of a guilty passion. How strange it seemed to the sad woman, as she watched the growth, and the beauty that became every day more brilliant, and the intelligence that threw its quivering sunshine over the tiny features of this child! Her Pearl—for so had Hester called her; not as a name expressive of her aspect, which had nothing of the calm, white, unimpassioned lustre that would be indicated by the comparison. But she named the infant "Pearl," as being of great price—purchased with all she had—her mother's only treasure! How strange, indeed! Man had marked this woman's sin by a scarlet letter, which had such potent and disastrous efficacy that no human sympathy could reach her, save it were sinful like herself. God, as a direct consequence of the sin which man thus punished, had given her a lovely child, whose place was on that same dishonoured bosom, to connect her parent for ever with the race and descent of mortals, and to be finally a blessed soul in heaven! Yet these thoughts affected Hester Prynne less with hope than apprehension. She knew that her deed had been evil; she could have no faith, therefore, that its result would be good. Day after day she looked fearfully into the child's expanding nature, ever dreading to detect some dark and wild peculiarity that should correspond with the guiltiness to which she owed her being.

Certainly there was no physical defect. By its perfect shape, its vigour, and its natural dexterity in the use of all its untried limbs, the infant was worthy to have been brought forth in Eden: worthy to have been left there to be the plaything of the angels after the world's first parents were driven out. The child had a native grace which does not invariably co-exist with faultless beauty; its attire, however simple, always impressed the beholder as if it were the very garb that precisely became it best. But little Pearl was not clad in rustic weeds. Her mother, with a morbid purpose that may be better understood hereafter, had bought the richest tissues that could be procured, and allowed her imaginative faculty its full play in the arrangement and decoration of the dresses which the child wore before the public eye. So magnificent was the small figure when thus arrayed, and such was the splendour of Pearl's own proper beauty, shining through the gorgeous robes which might have extinguished a paler loveliness, that there was an absolute circle of radiance around her on the darksome cottage floor. And yet a russet gown, torn and soiled with the child's rude play, made a picture of her just as perfect. Pearl's aspect was imbued with a spell of infinite variety; in this one child there were many children, comprehending the full scope between the wild-flower prettiness of a peasant-baby, and the pomp, in little, of an infant princess. Throughout all, however, there was a trait of passion, a certain depth of hue, which she never lost; and if in any of her changes, she had grown fainter or paler, she would have ceased to be herself—it would have been no longer Pearl!

This outward mutability indicated, and did not more than fairly express, the various properties of her inner life. Her nature appeared to possess depth, too, as well as variety; but—or else Hester's fears deceived her—it lacked reference and adaptation to the world into which she was born. The child could not be made amenable to rules. In giving her existence a great law had been broken; and the result was a being whose elements were perhaps beautiful and brilliant, but all in disorder, or with an order peculiar to themselves, amidst which the point of variety and arrangement was difficult or impossible to be discovered. Hester could only account for the child's character—and even then most vaguely and imperfectly—by recalling what she herself had been during that momentous period while Pearl was imbibing her soul from the spiritual world, and her bodily frame from its material of earth. The mother's impassioned state had been the medium through which were transmitted to the unborn infant the rays of its moral life; and, however white and clear originally, they had taken the deep stains of crimson and gold, the fiery lustre, the black shadow, and the untempered light of the intervening substance. Above all, the warfare of Hester's spirit at that epoch was perpetuated in Pearl. She could recognize her wild, desperate, defiant mood, the flightiness of her temper, and even some of the very cloud-shapes of gloom and despondency that had brooded in her heart. They were now illuminated by the morning radiance of a young child's disposition, but, later in the day of earthly existence, might be prolific of the storm and whirlwind.

The discipline of the family in those days was of a far more rigid kind than now. The frown, the harsh rebuke, the frequent application of the rod, enjoined by Scriptural authority, were used, not merely in the way of punishment for actual offences, but as a wholesome regimen for the growth and promotion of all childish virtues. Hester Prynne, nevertheless, the loving mother of this one child, ran little risk of erring on the side of undue severity. Mindful, however, of her own errors and misfortunes, she early sought to impose a tender but strict control over the infant immortality that was committed to her charge. But the task was beyond her skill. After testing both smiles and frowns, and proving that neither mode of treatment possessed any calculable influence, Hester was ultimately compelled to stand aside and permit the child to be swayed by her own impulses. Physical compulsion or restraint was effectual, of course, while it lasted. As to any other kind of discipline, whether addressed to her mind or heart, little Pearl might or might not be within its reach, in accordance with the caprice that ruled the moment. Her mother, while Pearl was yet an infant, grew acquainted with a certain peculiar look, that warned her when it would be labour thrown away to insist, persuade or plead.

It was a look so intelligent, yet inexplicable, perverse, sometimes so malicious, but generally accompanied by a wild flow of spirits, that Hester could not help questioning at such moments whether Pearl was a human child. She seemed rather an airy sprite, which, after playing its fantastic sports for a little while upon the cottage floor, would flit away with a mocking smile. Whenever that look appeared in her wild, bright, deeply black eyes, it invested her with a strange remoteness and intangibility: it was as if she were hovering in the air, and might vanish, like a glimmering light that comes we know not whence and goes we know not whither. Beholding it, Hester was constrained to rush towards the child—to pursue the little elf in the flight which she invariably began—to snatch her to her bosom with a close pressure and earnest kisses—not so much from overflowing love as to assure herself that Pearl was flesh and blood, and not utterly delusive. But Pearl's laugh, when she was caught, though full of merriment and music, made her mother more doubtful than before.

Heart-smitten at this bewildering and baffling spell, that so often came between herself and her sole treasure, whom she had bought so dear, and who was all her world, Hester sometimes burst into passionate tears. Then, perhaps—for there was no foreseeing how it might affect her—Pearl would frown, and clench her little fist, and harden her small features into a stern, unsympathising look of discontent. Not seldom she would laugh anew, and louder than before, like a thing incapable and unintelligent of human sorrow. Or—but this more rarely happened—she would be convulsed with rage of grief and sob out her love for her mother in broken words, and seem intent on proving that she had a heart by breaking it. Yet Hester was hardly safe in confiding herself to that gusty tenderness: it passed as suddenly as it came. Brooding over all these matters, the mother felt like one who has evoked a spirit, but, by some irregularity in the process of conjuration, has failed to win the master-word that should control this new and incomprehensible intelligence. Her only real comfort was when the child lay in the placidity of sleep. Then she was sure of her, and tasted hours of quiet, sad, delicious happiness; until—perhaps with that perverse expression glimmering from beneath her opening lids—little Pearl awoke!

How soon—with what strange rapidity, indeed did Pearl arrive at an age that was capable of social intercourse beyond the mother's ever-ready smile and nonsense-words! And then what a happiness would it have been could Hester Prynne have heard her clear, bird-like voice mingling with the uproar of other childish voices, and have distinguished and unravelled her own darling's tones, amid all the entangled outcry of a group of sportive children. But this could never be. Pearl was a born outcast of the infantile world. An imp of evil, emblem and product of sin, she had no right among christened infants. Nothing was more remarkable than the instinct, as it seemed, with which the child comprehended her loneliness: the destiny that had drawn an inviolable circle round about her: the whole peculiarity, in short, of her position in respect to other children. Never since her release from prison had Hester met the public gaze without her. In all her walks about the town, Pearl, too, was there: first as the babe in arms, and afterwards as the little girl, small companion of her mother, holding a forefinger with her whole grasp, and tripping along at the rate of three or four footsteps to one of Hester's. She saw the children of the settlement on the grassy margin of the street, or at the domestic thresholds, disporting themselves in such grim fashions as the Puritanic nurture would permit; playing at going to church, perchance, or at scourging Quakers; or taking scalps in a sham fight with the Indians, or scaring one another with freaks of imitative witchcraft. Pearl saw, and gazed intently, but never sought to make acquaintance. If spoken to, she would not speak again. If the children gathered about her, as they sometimes did, Pearl would grow positively terrible in her puny wrath, snatching up stones to fling at them, with shrill, incoherent exclamations, that made her mother tremble, because they had so much the sound of a witch's anathemas in some unknown tongue.

The truth was, that the little Puritans, being of the most intolerant brood that ever lived, had got a vague idea of something outlandish, unearthly, or at variance with ordinary fashions, in the mother and child, and therefore scorned them in their hearts, and not unfrequently reviled them with their tongues. Pearl felt the sentiment, and requited it with the bitterest hatred that can be supposed to rankle in a childish bosom. These outbreaks of a fierce temper had a kind of value, and even comfort for the mother; because there was at least an intelligible earnestness in the mood, instead of the fitful caprice that so often thwarted her in the child's manifestations. It appalled her, nevertheless, to discern here, again, a shadowy reflection of the evil that had existed in herself. All this enmity and passion had Pearl inherited, by inalienable right, out of Hester's heart. Mother and daughter stood together in the same circle of seclusion from human society; and in the nature of the child seemed to be perpetuated those unquiet elements that had distracted Hester Prynne before Pearl's birth, but had since begun to be soothed away by the softening influences of maternity.

At home, within and around her mother's cottage, Pearl wanted not a wide and various circle of acquaintance. The spell of life went forth from her ever-creative spirit, and communicated itself to a thousand objects, as a torch kindles a flame wherever it may be applied. The unlikeliest materials—a stick, a bunch of rags, a flower—were the puppets of Pearl's witchcraft, and, without undergoing any outward change, became spiritually adapted to whatever drama occupied the stage of her inner world. Her one baby-voice served a multitude of imaginary personages, old and young, to talk withal. The pine-trees, aged, black, and solemn, and flinging groans and other melancholy utterances on the breeze, needed little transformation to figure as Puritan elders; the ugliest weeds of the garden were their children, whom Pearl smote down and uprooted most unmercifully. It was wonderful, the vast variety of forms into which she threw her intellect, with no continuity, indeed, but darting up and dancing, always in a state of preternatural activity—soon sinking down, as if exhausted by so rapid and feverish a tide of life—and succeeded by other shapes of a similar wild energy. It was like nothing so much as the phantasmagoric play of the northern lights. In the mere exercise of the fancy, however, and the sportiveness of a growing mind, there might be a little more than was observable in other children of bright faculties; except as Pearl, in the dearth of human playmates, was thrown more upon the visionary throng which she created. The singularity lay in the hostile feelings with which the child regarded all these offsprings of her own heart and mind. She never created a friend, but seemed always to be sowing broadcast the dragon's teeth, whence sprung a harvest of armed enemies, against whom she rushed to battle. It was inexpressibly sad—then what depth of sorrow to a mother, who felt in her own heart the cause—to observe, in one so young, this constant recognition of an adverse world, and so fierce a training of the energies that were to make good her cause in the contest that must ensue.

Gazing at Pearl, Hester Prynne often dropped her work upon her knees, and cried out with an agony which she would fain have hidden, but which made utterance for itself betwixt speech and a groan—"O Father in Heaven—if Thou art still my Father—what is this being which I have brought into the world?" And Pearl, overhearing the ejaculation, or aware through some more subtile channel, of those throbs of anguish, would turn her vivid and beautiful little face upon her mother, smile with sprite-like intelligence, and resume her play.

One peculiarity of the child's deportment remains yet to be told. The very first thing which she had noticed in her life, was—what?—not the mother's smile, responding to it, as other babies do, by that faint, embryo smile of the little mouth, remembered so doubtfully afterwards, and with such fond discussion whether it were indeed a smile. By no means! But that first object of which Pearl seemed to become aware was—shall we say it?—the scarlet letter on Hester's bosom! One day, as her mother stooped over the cradle, the infant's eyes had been caught by the glimmering of the gold embroidery about the letter; and putting up her little hand she grasped at it, smiling, not doubtfully, but with a decided gleam, that gave her face the look of a much older child. Then, gasping for breath, did Hester Prynne clutch the fatal token, instinctively endeavouring to tear it away, so infinite was the torture inflicted by the intelligent touch of Pearl's baby-hand. Again, as if her mother's agonised gesture were meant only to make sport for her, did little Pearl look into her eyes, and smile. From that epoch, except when the child was asleep, Hester had never felt a moment's safety: not a moment's calm enjoyment of her. Weeks, it is true, would sometimes elapse, during which Pearl's gaze might never once be fixed upon the scarlet letter; but then, again, it would come at unawares, like the stroke of sudden death, and always with that peculiar smile and odd expression of the eyes.

Once this freakish, elvish cast came into the child's eyes while Hester was looking at her own image in them, as mothers are fond of doing; and suddenly for women in solitude, and with troubled hearts, are pestered with unaccountable delusions she fancied that she beheld, not her own miniature portrait, but another face in the small black mirror of Pearl's eye. It was a face, fiend-like, full of smiling malice, yet bearing the semblance of features that she had known full well, though seldom with a smile, and never with malice in them. It was as if an evil spirit possessed the child, and had just then peeped forth in mockery. Many a time afterwards had Hester been tortured, though less vividly, by the same illusion.

In the afternoon of a certain summer's day, after Pearl grew big enough to run about, she amused herself with gathering handfuls of wild flowers, and flinging them, one by one, at her mother's bosom; dancing up and down like a little elf whenever she hit the scarlet letter. Hester's first motion had been to cover her bosom with her clasped hands. But whether from pride or resignation, or a feeling that her penance might best be wrought out by this unutterable pain, she resisted the impulse, and sat erect, pale as death, looking sadly into little Pearl's wild eyes. Still came the battery of flowers, almost invariably hitting the mark, and covering the mother's breast with hurts for which she could find no balm in this world, nor knew how to seek it in another. At last, her shot being all expended, the child stood still and gazed at Hester, with that little laughing image of a fiend peeping out—or, whether it peeped or no, her mother so imagined it—from the unsearchable abyss of her black eyes.

"Child, what art thou?" cried the mother.

"Oh, I am your little Pearl!" answered the child.

But while she said it, Pearl laughed, and began to dance up and down with the humoursome gesticulation of a little imp, whose next freak might be to fly up the chimney.

"Art thou my child, in very truth?" asked Hester.

Nor did she put the question altogether idly, but, for the moment, with a portion of genuine earnestness; for, such was Pearl's wonderful intelligence, that her mother half doubted whether she were not acquainted with the secret spell of her existence, and might not now reveal herself.

"Yes; I am little Pearl!" repeated the child, continuing her antics.

"Thou art not my child! Thou art no Pearl of mine!" said the mother half playfully; for it was often the case that a sportive impulse came over her in the midst of her deepest suffering. "Tell me, then, what thou art, and who sent thee hither?"

"Tell me, mother!" said the child, seriously, coming up to Hester, and pressing herself close to her knees. "Do thou tell me!"

"Thy Heavenly Father sent thee!" answered Hester Prynne.

But she said it with a hesitation that did not escape the acuteness of the child. Whether moved only by her ordinary freakishness, or because an evil spirit prompted her, she put up her small forefinger and touched the scarlet letter.

"He did not send me!" cried she, positively. "I have no

Heavenly Father!"

"Hush, Pearl, hush! Thou must not talk so!" answered the mother, suppressing a groan. "He sent us all into the world. He sent even me, thy mother. Then, much more thee! Or, if not, thou strange and elfish child, whence didst thou come?"

"Tell me! Tell me!" repeated Pearl, no longer seriously, but laughing and capering about the floor. "It is thou that must tell me!"

But Hester could not resolve the query, being herself in a dismal labyrinth of doubt. She remembered—betwixt a smile and a shudder—the talk of the neighbouring townspeople, who, seeking vainly elsewhere for the child's paternity, and observing some of her odd attributes, had given out that poor little Pearl was a demon offspring: such as, ever since old Catholic times, had occasionally been seen on earth, through the agency of their mother's sin, and to promote some foul and wicked purpose. Luther, according to the scandal of his monkish enemies, was a brat of that hellish breed; nor was Pearl the only child to whom this inauspicious origin was assigned among the New England Puritans.

VII. THE GOVERNOR'S HALL

Hester Prynne went one day to the mansion of Governor Bellingham, with a pair of gloves which she had fringed and embroidered to his order, and which were to be worn on some great occasion of state; for, though the chances of a popular election had caused this former ruler to descend a step or two from the highest rank, he still held an honourable and influential place among the colonial magistracy.

Another and far more important reason than the delivery of a pair of embroidered gloves, impelled Hester, at this time, to seek an interview with a personage of so much power and activity in the affairs of the settlement. It had reached her ears that there was a design on the part of some of the leading inhabitants, cherishing the more rigid order of principles in religion and government, to deprive her of her child. On the supposition that Pearl, as already hinted, was of demon origin, these good people not unreasonably argued that a Christian interest in the mother's soul required them to remove such a stumbling-block from her path. If the child, on the other hand, were really capable of moral and religious growth, and possessed the elements of ultimate salvation, then, surely, it would enjoy all the fairer prospect of these advantages by being transferred to wiser and better guardianship than Hester Prynne's. Among those who promoted the design, Governor Bellingham was said to be one of the most busy. It may appear singular, and, indeed, not a little ludicrous, that an affair of this kind, which in later days would have been referred to no higher jurisdiction than that of the select men of the town, should then have been a question publicly discussed, and on which statesmen of eminence took sides. At that epoch of pristine simplicity, however, matters of even slighter public interest, and of far less intrinsic weight than the welfare of Hester and her child, were strangely mixed up with the deliberations of legislators and acts of state. The period was hardly, if at all, earlier than that of our story, when a dispute concerning the right of property in a pig not only caused a fierce and bitter contest in the legislative body of the colony, but resulted in an important modification of the framework itself of the legislature.

Full of concern, therefore—but so conscious of her own right that it seemed scarcely an unequal match between the public on the one side, and a lonely woman, backed by the sympathies of nature, on the other—Hester Prynne set forth from her solitary cottage. Little Pearl, of course, was her companion. She was now of an age to run lightly along by her mother's side, and, constantly in motion from morn till sunset, could have accomplished a much longer journey than that before her. Often, nevertheless, more from caprice than necessity, she demanded to be taken up in arms; but was soon as imperious to be let down again, and frisked onward before Hester on the grassy pathway, with many a harmless trip and tumble. We have spoken of Pearl's rich and luxuriant beauty—a beauty that shone with deep and vivid tints, a bright complexion, eyes possessing intensity both of depth and glow, and hair already of a deep, glossy brown, and which, in after years, would be nearly akin to black. There was fire in her and throughout her: she seemed the unpremeditated offshoot of a passionate moment. Her mother, in contriving the child's garb, had allowed the gorgeous tendencies of her imagination their full play, arraying her in a crimson velvet tunic of a peculiar cut, abundantly embroidered in fantasies and flourishes of gold thread. So much strength of colouring, which must have given a wan and pallid aspect to cheeks of a fainter bloom, was admirably adapted to Pearl's beauty, and made her the very brightest little jet of flame that ever danced upon the earth.

But it was a remarkable attribute of this garb, and indeed, of the child's whole appearance, that it irresistibly and inevitably reminded the beholder of the token which Hester Prynne was doomed to wear upon her bosom. It was the scarlet letter in another form: the scarlet letter endowed with life! The mother herself—as if the red ignominy were so deeply scorched into her brain that all her conceptions assumed its form—had carefully wrought out the similitude, lavishing many hours of morbid ingenuity to create an analogy between the object of her affection and the emblem of her guilt and torture. But, in truth, Pearl was the one as well as the other; and only in consequence of that identity had Hester contrived so perfectly to represent the scarlet letter in her appearance.

As the two wayfarers came within the precincts of the town, the children of the Puritans looked up from their play,—or what passed for play with those sombre little urchins—and spoke gravely one to another.

"Behold, verily, there is the woman of the scarlet letter: and of a truth, moreover, there is the likeness of the scarlet letter running along by her side! Come, therefore, and let us fling mud at them!"

But Pearl, who was a dauntless child, after frowning, stamping her foot, and shaking her little hand with a variety of threatening gestures, suddenly made a rush at the knot of her enemies, and put them all to flight. She resembled, in her fierce pursuit of them, an infant pestilence—the scarlet fever, or some such half-fledged angel of judgment—whose mission was to punish the sins of the rising generation. She screamed and shouted, too, with a terrific volume of sound, which, doubtless, caused the hearts of the fugitives to quake within them. The victory accomplished, Pearl returned quietly to her mother, and looked up, smiling, into her face.

Without further adventure, they reached the dwelling of Governor Bellingham. This was a large wooden house, built in a fashion of which there are specimens still extant in the streets of our older towns now moss-grown, crumbling to decay, and melancholy at heart with the many sorrowful or joyful occurrences, remembered or forgotten, that have happened and passed away within their dusky chambers. Then, however, there was the freshness of the passing year on its exterior, and the cheerfulness, gleaming forth from the sunny windows, of a human habitation, into which death had never entered. It had, indeed, a very cheery aspect, the walls being overspread with a kind of stucco, in which fragments of broken glass were plentifully intermixed; so that, when the sunshine fell aslantwise over the front of the edifice, it glittered and sparkled as if diamonds had been flung against it by the double handful. The brilliancy might have be fitted Aladdin's palace rather than the mansion of a grave old Puritan ruler. It was further decorated with strange and seemingly cabalistic figures and diagrams, suitable to the quaint taste of the age which had been drawn in the stucco, when newly laid on, and had now grown hard and durable, for the admiration of after times.

Pearl, looking at this bright wonder of a house began to caper and dance, and imperatively required that the whole breadth of sunshine should be stripped off its front, and given her to play with.

"No, my little Pearl!" said her mother; "thou must gather thine own sunshine. I have none to give thee!"

They approached the door, which was of an arched form, and flanked on each side by a narrow tower or projection of the edifice, in both of which were lattice-windows, the wooden shutters to close over them at need. Lifting the iron hammer that hung at the portal, Hester Prynne gave a summons, which was answered by one of the Governor's bond servant—a free-born Englishman, but now a seven years' slave. During that term he was to be the property of his master, and as much a commodity of bargain and sale as an ox, or a joint-stool. The serf wore the customary garb of serving-men at that period, and long before, in the old hereditary halls of England.

"Is the worshipful Governor Bellingham within?" inquired Hester.

"Yea, forsooth," replied the bond-servant, staring with wide-open eyes at the scarlet letter, which, being a new-comer in the country, he had never before seen. "Yea, his honourable worship is within. But he hath a godly minister or two with him, and likewise a leech. Ye may not see his worship now."

"Nevertheless, I will enter," answered Hester Prynne; and the bond-servant, perhaps judging from the decision of her air, and the glittering symbol in her bosom, that she was a great lady in the land, offered no opposition.

So the mother and little Pearl were admitted into the hall of entrance. With many variations, suggested by the nature of his building materials, diversity of climate, and a different mode of social life, Governor Bellingham had planned his new habitation after the residences of gentlemen of fair estate in his native land. Here, then, was a wide and reasonably lofty hall, extending through the whole depth of the house, and forming a medium of general communication, more or less directly, with all the other apartments. At one extremity, this spacious room was lighted by the windows of the two towers, which formed a small recess on either side of the portal. At the other end, though partly muffled by a curtain, it was more powerfully illuminated by one of those embowed hall windows which we read of in old books, and which was provided with a deep and cushioned seat. Here, on the cushion, lay a folio tome, probably of the Chronicles of England, or other such substantial literature; even as, in our own days, we scatter gilded volumes on the centre table, to be turned over by the casual guest. The furniture of the hall consisted of some ponderous chairs, the backs of which were elaborately carved with wreaths of oaken flowers; and likewise a table in the same taste, the whole being of the Elizabethan age, or perhaps earlier, and heirlooms, transferred hither from the Governor's paternal home. On the table—in token that the sentiment of old English hospitality had not been left behind—stood a large pewter tankard, at the bottom of which, had Hester or Pearl peeped into it, they might have seen the frothy remnant of a recent draught of ale.

On the wall hung a row of portraits, representing the forefathers of the Bellingham lineage, some with armour on their breasts, and others with stately ruffs and robes of peace. All were characterised by the sternness and severity which old portraits so invariably put on, as if they were the ghosts, rather than the pictures, of departed worthies, and were gazing with harsh and intolerant criticism at the pursuits and enjoyments of living men.

At about the centre of the oaken panels that lined the hall was suspended a suit of mail, not, like the pictures, an ancestral relic, but of the most modern date; for it had been manufactured by a skilful armourer in London, the same year in which Governor Bellingham came over to New England. There was a steel head-piece, a cuirass, a gorget and greaves, with a pair of gauntlets and a sword hanging beneath; all, and especially the helmet and breastplate, so highly burnished as to glow with white radiance, and scatter an illumination everywhere about upon the floor. This bright panoply was not meant for mere idle show, but had been worn by the Governor on many a solemn muster and training field, and had glittered, moreover, at the head of a regiment in the Pequod war. For, though bred a lawyer, and accustomed to speak of Bacon, Coke, Noye, and Finch, as his professional associates, the exigencies of this new country had transformed Governor Bellingham into a soldier, as well as a statesman and ruler.

Little Pearl, who was as greatly pleased with the gleaming armour as she had been with the glittering frontispiece of the house, spent some time looking into the polished mirror of the breastplate.

"Mother," cried she, "I see you here. Look! Look!"

Hester looked by way of humouring the child; and she saw that, owing to the peculiar effect of this convex mirror, the scarlet letter was represented in exaggerated and gigantic proportions, so as to be greatly the most prominent feature of her appearance. In truth, she seemed absolutely hidden behind it. Pearl pointed upwards also, at a similar picture in the head-piece; smiling at her mother, with the elfish intelligence that was so familiar an expression on her small physiognomy. That look of naughty merriment was likewise reflected in the mirror, with so much breadth and intensity of effect, that it made Hester Prynne feel as if it could not be the image of her own child, but of an imp who was seeking to mould itself into Pearl's shape.

"Come along, Pearl," said she, drawing her away, "Come and look into this fair garden. It may be we shall see flowers there; more beautiful ones than we find in the woods."

Pearl accordingly ran to the bow-window, at the further end of the hall, and looked along the vista of a garden walk, carpeted with closely-shaven grass, and bordered with some rude and immature attempt at shrubbery. But the proprietor appeared already to have relinquished as hopeless, the effort to perpetuate on this side of the Atlantic, in a hard soil, and amid the close struggle for subsistence, the native English taste for ornamental gardening. Cabbages grew in plain sight; and a pumpkin-vine, rooted at some distance, had run across the intervening space, and deposited one of its gigantic products directly beneath the hall window, as if to warn the Governor that this great lump of vegetable gold was as rich an ornament as New England earth would offer him. There were a few rose-bushes, however, and a number of apple-trees, probably the descendants of those planted by the Reverend Mr. Blackstone, the first settler of the peninsula; that half mythological personage who rides through our early annals, seated on the back of a bull.

Pearl, seeing the rose-bushes, began to cry for a red rose, and would not be pacified.

"Hush, child—hush!" said her mother, earnestly. "Do not cry, dear little Pearl! I hear voices in the garden. The Governor is coming, and gentlemen along with him."

In fact, adown the vista of the garden avenue, a number of persons were seen approaching towards the house. Pearl, in utter scorn of her mother's attempt to quiet her, gave an eldritch scream, and then became silent, not from any notion of obedience, but because the quick and mobile curiosity of her disposition was excited by the appearance of those new personages.

VIII. THE ELF-CHILD AND THE MINISTER

Governor Bellingham, in a loose gown and easy cap—such as elderly gentlemen loved to endue themselves with, in their domestic privacy—walked foremost, and appeared to be showing off his estate, and expatiating on his projected improvements. The wide circumference of an elaborate ruff, beneath his grey beard, in the antiquated fashion of King James's reign, caused his head to look not a little like that of John the Baptist in a charger. The impression made by his aspect, so rigid and severe, and frost-bitten with more than autumnal age, was hardly in keeping with the appliances of worldly enjoyment wherewith he had evidently done his utmost to surround himself. But it is an error to suppose that our great forefathers—though accustomed to speak and think of human existence as a state merely of trial and warfare, and though unfeignedly prepared to sacrifice goods and life at the behest of duty—made it a matter of conscience to reject such means of comfort, or even luxury, as lay fairly within their grasp. This creed was never taught, for instance, by the venerable pastor, John Wilson, whose beard, white as a snow-drift, was seen over Governor Bellingham's shoulders, while its wearer suggested that pears and peaches might yet be naturalised in the New England climate, and that purple grapes might possibly be compelled to flourish against the sunny garden-wall. The old clergyman, nurtured at the rich bosom of the English Church, had a long established and legitimate taste for all good and comfortable things, and however stern he might show himself in the pulpit, or in his public reproof of such transgressions as that of Hester Prynne, still, the genial benevolence of his private life had won him warmer affection than was accorded to any of his professional contemporaries.

Behind the Governor and Mr. Wilson came two other guests—one, the Reverend Arthur Dimmesdale, whom the reader may remember as having taken a brief and reluctant part in the scene of Hester Prynne's disgrace; and, in close companionship with him, old Roger Chillingworth, a person of great skill in physic, who for two or three years past had been settled in the town. It was understood that this learned man was the physician as well as friend of the young minister, whose health had severely suffered of late by his too unreserved self-sacrifice to the labours and duties of the pastoral relation.

The Governor, in advance of his visitors, ascended one or two steps, and, throwing open the leaves of the great hall window, found himself close to little

Pearl. The shadow of the curtain fell on Hester Prynne, and partially concealed her.

"What have we here?" said Governor Bellingham, looking with surprise at the scarlet little figure before him. "I profess, I have never seen the like since my days of vanity, in old King James's time, when I was wont to esteem it a high favour to be admitted to a court mask! There used to be a swarm of these small apparitions in holiday time, and we called them children of the Lord of Misrule. But how gat such a guest into my hall?"

"Ay, indeed!" cried good old Mr. Wilson. "What little bird of scarlet plumage may this be? Methinks I have seen just such figures when the sun has been shining through a richly painted window, and tracing out the golden and crimson images across the floor. But that was in the old land. Prithee, young one, who art thou, and what has ailed thy mother to bedizen thee in this strange fashion? Art thou a Christian child—ha? Dost know thy catechism? Or art thou one of those naughty elfs or fairies whom we thought to have left behind us, with other relics of Papistry, in merry old England?"

"I am mother's child," answered the scarlet vision, "and my name is Pearl!"

"Pearl?—Ruby, rather—or Coral!—or Red Rose, at the very least, judging from thy hue!" responded the old minister, putting forth his hand in a vain attempt to pat little Pearl on the cheek. "But where is this mother of thine? Ah! I see," he added; and, turning to Governor Bellingham, whispered, "This is the selfsame child of whom we have held speech together; and behold here the unhappy woman, Hester Prynne, her mother!"

"Sayest thou so?" cried the Governor. "Nay, we might have judged that such a child's mother must needs be a scarlet woman, and a worthy type of her of Babylon! But she comes at a good time, and we will look into this matter forthwith."

Governor Bellingham stepped through the window into the hall, followed by his three guests.

"Hester Prynne," said he, fixing his naturally stern regard on the wearer of the scarlet letter, "there hath been much question concerning thee of late. The point hath been weightily discussed, whether we, that are of authority and influence, do well discharge our consciences by trusting an immortal soul, such as there is in yonder child, to the guidance of one who hath stumbled and fallen amid the pitfalls of this world. Speak thou, the child's own mother! Were it not, thinkest thou, for thy little one's temporal and eternal welfare that she be taken out of thy charge, and clad soberly, and disciplined strictly, and instructed in the truths of heaven and earth? What canst thou do for the child in this kind?"

"I can teach my little Pearl what I have learned from this!" answered Hester Prynne, laying her finger on the red token.

"Woman, it is thy badge of shame!" replied the stern magistrate. "It is because of the stain which that letter indicates that we would transfer thy child to other hands."

"Nevertheless," said the mother, calmly, though growing more pale, "this badge hath taught me—it daily teaches me—it is teaching me at this moment—

lessons whereof my child may be the wiser and better, albeit they can profit nothing to myself."

"We will judge warily," said Bellingham, "and look well what we are about to do. Good Master Wilson, I pray you, examine this Pearl—since that is her name—and see whether she hath had such Christian nurture as befits a child of her age."

The old minister seated himself in an arm-chair and made an effort to draw Pearl betwixt his knees. But the child, unaccustomed to the touch or familiarity of any but her mother, escaped through the open window, and stood on the upper step, looking like a wild tropical bird of rich plumage, ready to take flight into the upper air. Mr. Wilson, not a little astonished at this outbreak—for he was a grandfatherly sort of personage, and usually a vast favourite with children—essayed, however, to proceed with the examination.

"Pearl," said he, with great solemnity, "thou must take heed to instruction, that so, in due season, thou mayest wear in thy bosom the pearl of great price. Canst thou tell me, my child, who made thee?"

Now Pearl knew well enough who made her, for Hester Prynne, the daughter of a pious home, very soon after her talk with the child about her Heavenly Father, had begun to inform her of those truths which the human spirit, at whatever stage of immaturity, imbibes with such eager interest. Pearl, therefore—so large were the attainments of her three years' lifetime—could have borne a fair examination in the New England Primer, or the first column of the Westminster Catechisms, although unacquainted with the outward form of either of those celebrated works. But that perversity, which all children have more or less of, and of which little Pearl had a tenfold portion, now, at the most inopportune moment, took thorough possession of her, and closed her lips, or impelled her to speak words amiss. After putting her finger in her mouth, with many ungracious refusals to answer good Mr. Wilson's question, the child finally announced that she had not been made at all, but had been plucked by her mother off the bush of wild roses that grew by the prison-door.

This phantasy was probably suggested by the near proximity of the Governor's red roses, as Pearl stood outside of the window, together with her recollection of the prison rose-bush, which she had passed in coming hither.

Old Roger Chillingworth, with a smile on his face, whispered something in the young clergyman's ear. Hester Prynne looked at the man of skill, and even then, with her fate hanging in the balance, was startled to perceive what a change had come over his features—how much uglier they were, how his dark complexion seemed to have grown duskier, and his figure more misshapen—since the days when she had familiarly known him. She met his eyes for an instant, but was immediately constrained to give all her attention to the scene now going forward.

"This is awful!" cried the Governor, slowly recovering from the astonishment into which Pearl's response had thrown him. "Here is a child of three years old, and she cannot tell who made her! Without question, she is equally in the dark as to her soul, its present depravity, and future destiny! Methinks, gentlemen, we need inquire no further."

Hester caught hold of Pearl, and drew her forcibly into her arms, confronting the old Puritan magistrate with almost a fierce expression. Alone in the world, cast off by it, and with this sole treasure to keep her heart alive, she felt that she possessed indefeasible rights against the world, and was ready to defend them to the death.

"God gave me the child!" cried she. "He gave her in requital of all things else which ye had taken from me. She is my happiness—she is my torture, none the less! Pearl keeps me here in life! Pearl punishes me, too! See ye not, she is the scarlet letter, only capable of being loved, and so endowed with a millionfold the power of retribution for my sin? Ye shall not take her! I will die first!"

"My poor woman," said the not unkind old minister, "the child shall be well cared for—far better than thou canst do for it."

"God gave her into my keeping!" repeated Hester Prynne, raising her voice almost to a shriek. "I will not give her up!" And here by a sudden impulse, she turned to the young clergyman, Mr. Dimmesdale, at whom, up to this moment, she had seemed hardly so much as once to direct her eyes. "Speak thou for me!" cried she. "Thou wast my pastor, and hadst charge of my soul, and knowest me better than these men can. I will not lose the child! Speak for me! Thou knowest—for thou hast sympathies which these men lack—thou knowest what is in my heart, and what are a mother's rights, and how much the stronger they are when that mother has but her child and the scarlet letter! Look thou to it! I will not lose the child! Look to it!"

At this wild and singular appeal, which indicated that Hester Prynne's situation had provoked her to little less than madness, the young minister at once came forward, pale, and holding his hand over his heart, as was his custom whenever his peculiarly nervous temperament was thrown into agitation. He looked now more careworn and emaciated than as we described him at the scene of Hester's public ignominy; and whether it were his failing health, or whatever the cause might be, his large dark eyes had a world of pain in their troubled and melancholy depth.

"There is truth in what she says," began the minister, with a voice sweet, tremulous, but powerful, insomuch that the hall re-echoed and the hollow armour rang with it—"truth in what Hester says, and in the feeling which inspires her! God gave her the child, and gave her, too, an instinctive knowledge of its nature and requirements—both seemingly so peculiar—which no other mortal being can possess. And, moreover, is there not a quality of awful sacredness in the relation between this mother and this child?"

"Ay—how is that, good Master Dimmesdale?" interrupted the
Governor. "Make that plain, I pray you!"

"It must be even so," resumed the minister. "For, if we deem it otherwise, do we not thereby say that the Heavenly Father, the creator of all flesh, hath lightly recognised a deed of sin, and made of no account the distinction between unhallowed lust and holy love? This child of its father's guilt and its mother's shame has come from the hand of God, to work in many ways upon her heart, who pleads so earnestly and with such bitterness of spirit the right to keep her. It was meant for a blessing—for the one blessing of her life! It was meant, doubtless, the mother herself hath told us, for a retribution, too; a torture to be felt at many an unthought-of moment; a pang, a sting, an ever-recurring agony, in the midst of a troubled joy! Hath she not expressed this thought in the garb of the poor child, so forcibly reminding us of that red symbol which sears her bosom?"

"Well said again!" cried good Mr. Wilson. "I feared the woman had no better thought than to make a mountebank of her child!"

"Oh, not so!—not so!" continued Mr. Dimmesdale. "She recognises, believe me, the solemn miracle which God hath wrought in the existence of that child. And may she feel, too—what, methinks, is the very truth—that this boon was meant, above all things else, to keep the mother's soul alive, and to preserve her from blacker depths of sin into which Satan might else have sought to plunge her! Therefore it is good for this poor, sinful woman, that she hath an infant immortality, a being capable of eternal joy or sorrow, confided to her care—to be trained up by her to righteousness, to remind her, at every moment, of her fall, but yet to teach her, as if it were by the Creator's sacred pledge, that, if she bring the child to heaven, the child also will bring its parents thither! Herein is the sinful mother happier than the sinful father. For Hester Prynne's sake, then, and no less for the poor child's sake, let us leave them as Providence hath seen fit to place them!"

"You speak, my friend, with a strange earnestness," said old

Roger Chillingworth, smiling at him.

"And there is a weighty import in what my young brother hath spoken," added the Rey. Mr. Wilson.

"What say you, worshipful Master Bellingham? Hath he not pleaded well for the poor woman?"

"Indeed hath he," answered the magistrate; "and hath adduced such arguments, that we will even leave the matter as it now stands; so long, at least, as there shall be no further scandal in the woman. Care must be had nevertheless, to put the child to due and stated examination in the catechism, at thy hands or Master Dimmesdale's. Moreover, at a proper season, the tithing-men must take heed that she go both to school and to meeting."

The young minister, on ceasing to speak had withdrawn a few steps from the group, and stood with his face partially concealed in the heavy folds of the window-curtain; while the shadow of his figure, which the sunlight cast upon the floor, was tremulous with the vehemence of his appeal. Pearl, that wild and flighty little elf stole softly towards him, and taking his hand in the grasp of both her own, laid her cheek against it; a caress so tender, and withal so unobtrusive, that her mother, who was looking on, asked herself—"Is that my Pearl?" Yet she knew that there was love in the child's heart, although it mostly revealed itself in passion, and hardly twice in her lifetime had been softened by such gentleness as now. The minister—for, save the long-sought regards of woman, nothing is sweeter than these marks of childish preference, accorded spontaneously by a spiritual instinct, and therefore seeming to imply in us something truly worthy to be loved—the minister looked round, laid his hand on the child's head, hesitated an instant, and then kissed her brow. Little Pearl's unwonted mood of sentiment lasted no longer; she laughed, and went capering down the hall so airily, that old Mr. Wilson raised a question whether even her tiptoes touched the floor.

"The little baggage hath witchcraft in her, I profess," said he to Mr. Dimmesdale. "She needs no old woman's broomstick to fly withal!"

"A strange child!" remarked old Roger Chillingworth. "It is easy to see the mother's part in her. Would it be beyond a philosopher's research, think ye, gentlemen, to analyse that child's nature, and, from it make a mould, to give a shrewd guess at the father?"

"Nay; it would be sinful, in such a question, to follow the clue of profane philosophy," said Mr. Wilson. "Better to fast and pray upon it; and still better, it may be, to leave the mystery as we find it, unless Providence reveal it of its own accord. Thereby, every good Christian man hath a title to show a father's kindness towards the poor, deserted babe."

The affair being so satisfactorily concluded, Hester Prynne, with Pearl, departed from the house. As they descended the steps, it is averred that the lattice of a chamber-window was thrown open, and forth into the sunny day was thrust the face of Mistress Hibbins, Governor Bellingham's bitter-tempered sister, and the same who, a few years later, was executed as a witch.

"Hist, hist!" said she, while her ill-omened physiognomy seemed to cast a shadow over the cheerful newness of the house. "Wilt thou go with us to-night? There will be a merry company in the forest; and I well-nigh promised the Black Man that comely Hester Prynne should make one."

"Make my excuse to him, so please you!" answered Hester, with a triumphant smile. "I must tarry at home, and keep watch over my little Pearl. Had they taken her from me, I would willingly have gone with thee into the forest, and signed my name in the Black Man's book too, and that with mine own blood!"

"We shall have thee there anon!" said the witch-lady, frowning, as she drew back her head.

But here—if we suppose this interview betwixt Mistress Hibbins and Hester Prynne to be authentic, and not a parable—was already an illustration of the young minister's argument against sundering the relation of a fallen mother to the offspring of her frailty. Even thus early had the child saved her from Satan's snare.

IX. THE LEECH

Under the appellation of Roger Chillingworth, the reader will remember, was hidden another name, which its former wearer had resolved should never more be spoken. It has been related, how, in the crowd that witnessed Hester Prynne's ignominious exposure, stood a man, elderly, travel-worn, who, just emerging from the perilous wilderness, beheld the woman, in whom he hoped to find embodied the warmth and cheerfulness of home, set up as a type of sin before the people. Her matronly fame was trodden under all men's feet. Infamy was babbling around her in the public market-place. For her kindred, should the tidings ever reach them, and for the companions of her unspotted life, there remained nothing but the contagion of her dishonour; which would not fail to be distributed in strict accordance and proportion with the intimacy and sacredness of their previous relationship. Then why—since the choice was with himself—should the individual, whose connexion with the fallen woman had been the most intimate and sacred of them all, come forward to vindicate his claim to an inheritance so little desirable? He resolved not to be pilloried beside her on her pedestal of shame. Unknown to all but Hester Prynne, and possessing the lock and key of her silence, he chose to withdraw his name from the roll of mankind, and, as regarded his former ties and interest, to vanish out of life as completely as if he indeed lay at the bottom of the ocean, whither rumour had long ago consigned him. This purpose once effected, new interests would immediately spring up, and likewise a new purpose; dark, it is true, if not guilty, but of force enough to engage the full strength of his faculties.

In pursuance of this resolve, he took up his residence in the Puritan town as Roger Chillingworth, without other introduction than the learning and intelligence of which he possessed more than a common measure. As his studies, at a previous period of his life, had made him extensively acquainted with the medical science of the day, it was as a physician that he presented himself and as such was cordially received. Skilful men, of the medical and chirurgical profession, were of rare occurrence in the colony. They seldom, it would appear, partook of the religious zeal that brought other emigrants across the Atlantic. In their researches into the human frame, it may be that the higher and more subtle faculties of such men were materialised, and that they lost the spiritual view of existence amid the intricacies of that wondrous mechanism, which seemed to involve art enough to comprise all of life within itself. At all events, the health of the good town of Boston, so far as medicine had aught to do with it, had hitherto lain in the guardianship of an aged deacon and apothecary, whose piety and godly deportment were stronger testimonials in his favour than any that he could have produced in the shape of a diploma. The only surgeon was one who combined the occasional exercise of that noble art with the daily and habitual flourish of a razor. To such a professional body Roger Chillingworth was a brilliant acquisition. He soon manifested his familiarity with the ponderous and imposing machinery of antique physic; in which every remedy contained a multitude of far-fetched and heterogeneous ingredients, as elaborately compounded as if the proposed result had been the Elixir of Life. In his Indian captivity, moreover, he had gained much knowledge of the properties of native herbs and roots; nor did he conceal from his patients that these simple medicines, Nature's boon to the untutored savage, had quite as large a share of his own confidence as the European Pharmacopoeia, which so many learned doctors had spent centuries in elaborating.

This learned stranger was exemplary as regarded at least the outward forms of a religious life; and early after his arrival, had chosen for his spiritual guide the Reverend Mr. Dimmesdale. The young divine, whose scholar-like renown still lived in Oxford, was considered by his more fervent admirers as little less than a heavenly ordained apostle, destined, should he live and labour for the ordinary term of life, to do as great deeds, for the now feeble New England Church, as the early Fathers had achieved for the infancy of the Christian faith. About this period, however, the health of Mr. Dimmesdale had evidently begun to fail. By those best acquainted with his habits, the paleness of the young minister's cheek was accounted for by his too earnest devotion to study, his scrupulous fulfilment of parochial duty, and more than all, to the fasts and vigils of which he made a frequent practice, in order to keep the grossness of this earthly state from clogging and obscuring his spiritual lamp. Some declared, that if Mr. Dimmesdale were really going to die, it was cause enough that the world was not worthy to be any longer trodden by his feet. He himself, on the other hand, with characteristic humility, avowed his belief that if Providence should see fit to remove him, it would be because of his own unworthiness to perform its humblest mission here on earth. With all this difference of opinion as to the cause of his decline, there could be no question of the fact. His form grew emaciated; his voice, though still rich and sweet, had a certain melancholy prophecy of decay in it; he was often observed, on any slight alarm or other sudden accident, to put his hand over his heart with first a flush and then a paleness, indicative of pain.

Such was the young clergyman's condition, and so imminent the prospect that his dawning light would be extinguished, all untimely, when Roger Chillingworth made his advent to the town. His first entry on the scene, few people could tell whence, dropping down as it were out of the sky or starting from the nether earth, had an aspect of mystery, which was easily heightened to the miraculous. He was now known to be a man of skill; it was observed that he gathered herbs and the blossoms of wild-flowers, and dug up roots and plucked off twigs from the forest-trees like one acquainted with hidden virtues in what was valueless to common eyes. He was heard to speak of Sir Kenelm Digby and other famous men—whose scientific attainments were esteemed hardly less than supernatural—as having been his correspondents or associates. Why, with such rank in the learned world, had he come hither? What, could he, whose sphere was in great cities, be seeking in the wilderness? In answer to this query, a rumour gained ground—and however absurd, was entertained by some very sensible people—that Heaven had wrought an absolute miracle, by transporting an eminent Doctor of Physic from a German university bodily through the air and setting him down at the door of Mr. Dimmesdale's study! Individuals of wiser faith, indeed, who knew that Heaven promotes its purposes without aiming at the stage-effect of what is called miraculous interposition, were inclined to see a providential hand in Roger Chillingworth's so opportune arrival.

This idea was countenanced by the strong interest which the physician ever manifested in the young clergyman; he attached himself to him as a parishioner, and sought to win a friendly regard and confidence from his naturally reserved sensibility. He expressed great alarm at his pastor's state of health, but was anxious to attempt the cure, and, if early undertaken, seemed not despondent of a favourable result. The elders, the deacons, the motherly dames, and the young and fair maidens of Mr. Dimmesdale's flock, were alike importunate that he should make trial of the physician's frankly offered skill. Mr. Dimmesdale gently repelled their entreaties.

"I need no medicine," said he.

But how could the young minister say so, when, with every successive Sabbath, his cheek was paler and thinner, and his voice more tremulous than before—when it had now become a constant habit, rather than a casual gesture, to press his hand over his heart? Was he weary of his labours? Did he wish to die? These questions were solemnly propounded to Mr. Dimmesdale by the elder ministers of Boston, and the deacons of his church, who, to use their own phrase, "dealt with him," on the sin of rejecting the aid which Providence so manifestly held out. He listened in silence, and finally promised to confer with the physician.

"Were it God's will," said the Reverend Mr. Dimmesdale, when, in fulfilment of this pledge, he requested old Roger Chillingworth's professional advice, "I could be well content that my labours, and my sorrows, and my sins, and my pains, should shortly end with me, and what is earthly of them be buried in my grave, and the spiritual go with me to my eternal state, rather than that you should put your skill to the proof in my behalf."

"Ah," replied Roger Chillingworth, with that quietness, which, whether imposed or natural, marked all his deportment, "it is thus that a young clergyman is apt to speak. Youthful men, not having taken a deep root, give up their hold of life so easily! And saintly men, who walk with God on earth, would fain be away, to walk with him on the golden pavements of the New Jerusalem."

"Nay," rejoined the young minister, putting his hand to his heart, with a flush of pain flitting over his brow, "were I worthier to walk there, I could be better content to toil here."

"Good men ever interpret themselves too meanly," said the physician.

In this manner, the mysterious old Roger Chillingworth became the medical adviser of the Reverend Mr. Dimmesdale. As not only the disease interested the physician, but he was strongly moved to look into the character and qualities of the patient, these two men, so different in age, came gradually to spend much time together. For the sake of the minister's health, and to enable the leech to gather plants with healing balm in them, they took long walks on the sea-shore, or in the forest; mingling various walks with the splash and murmur of the waves, and the solemn wind-anthem among the tree-tops. Often, likewise, one was the guest of the other in his place of study and retirement. There was a fascination for the minister in the company of the man of science, in whom he recognised an intellectual cultivation of no moderate depth or scope; together with a range and freedom of ideas, that he would have vainly looked for among the members of his own profession. In truth, he was startled, if not shocked, to find this attribute in the physician. Mr. Dimmesdale was a true priest, a true religionist, with the reverential sentiment largely developed, and an order of mind that impelled itself powerfully along the track of a creed, and wore its passage continually deeper with the lapse of time. In no state of society would he have been what is called a man of liberal views; it would always be essential to his peace to feel the pressure of a faith about him, supporting, while it confined him within its iron framework. Not the less, however, though with a tremulous enjoyment, did he feel the occasional relief of looking at the universe through the medium of another kind of intellect than those with which he habitually held converse. It was as if a window were thrown open, admitting a freer atmosphere into the close and stifled study, where his life was wasting itself away, amid lamp-light, or obstructed day-beams, and the musty fragrance, be it sensual or moral, that exhales from books. But the air was too fresh and chill to be long breathed with comfort. So the minister, and the physician with him, withdrew again within the limits of what their Church defined as orthodox.

Thus Roger Chillingworth scrutinised his patient carefully, both as he saw him in his ordinary life, keeping an accustomed pathway in the range of thoughts familiar to him, and as he appeared when thrown amidst other moral scenery, the novelty of which might call out something new to the surface of his character. He deemed it essential, it would seem, to know the man, before attempting to do him good. Wherever there is a heart and an intellect, the diseases of the physical frame are tinged with the peculiarities of these. In Arthur Dimmesdale, thought and imagination were so active, and sensibility so intense, that the bodily infirmity would be likely to have its groundwork there. So Roger Chillingworth—the man of skill, the kind and friendly physician—strove to go deep into his patient's bosom, delving among his principles, prying into his recollections, and probing everything with a cautious touch, like a treasure-seeker in a dark cavern. Few secrets can escape an investigator, who has opportunity and licence to undertake such a quest, and skill to follow it up. A man burdened with a secret should especially avoid the intimacy of his physician. If the latter possess native sagacity, and a nameless something more,—let us call it intuition; if he show no intrusive egotism, nor disagreeable prominent characteristics of his own; if he have the power, which must be born with him, to bring his mind into such affinity with his patient's, that this last shall unawares have spoken what he imagines himself only to have thought; if such revelations be received without tumult, and acknowledged not so often by an uttered sympathy as by silence, an inarticulate breath, and here and there a word to indicate that all is understood; if to these qualifications of a confidant be joined the advantages afforded by his recognised character as a physician;—then, at some inevitable moment, will the soul of the sufferer be dissolved, and flow forth in a dark but transparent stream, bringing all its mysteries into the daylight.

Roger Chillingworth possessed all, or most, of the attributes above enumerated. Nevertheless, time went on; a kind of intimacy, as we have said, grew up between these two cultivated minds, which had as wide a field as the whole sphere of human thought and study to meet upon; they discussed every topic of ethics and religion, of public affairs, and private character; they talked much, on both sides, of matters that seemed personal to themselves; and yet no secret, such as the physician fancied must exist there, ever stole out of the minister's consciousness into his companion's ear. The latter had his suspicions, indeed, that even the nature of Mr. Dimmesdale's bodily disease had never fairly been revealed to him. It was a strange reserve!

After a time, at a hint from Roger Chillingworth, the friends of Mr. Dimmesdale effected an arrangement by which the two were lodged in the same house; so that every ebb and flow of the minister's life-tide might pass under the eye of his anxious and attached physician. There was much joy throughout the town when this greatly desirable object was attained. It was held to be the best possible measure for the young clergyman's welfare; unless, indeed, as often urged by such as felt authorised to do so, he had selected some one of the many blooming damsels, spiritually devoted to him, to become his devoted wife. This latter step, however, there was no present prospect that Arthur Dimmesdale would be prevailed upon to take; he rejected all suggestions of the kind, as if priestly celibacy were one of his articles of Church discipline. Doomed by his own choice, therefore, as Mr. Dimmesdale so evidently was, to eat his unsavoury morsel always at another's board, and endure the life-long chill which must be his lot who seeks to warm himself only at another's fireside, it truly seemed that this sagacious, experienced, benevolent old physician, with his concord of paternal and reverential love for the young pastor, was the very man, of all mankind, to be constantly within reach of his voice.

The new abode of the two friends was with a pious widow, of good social rank, who dwelt in a house covering pretty nearly the site on which the venerable structure of King's Chapel has since been built. It had the graveyard, originally

Isaac Johnson's home-field, on one side, and so was well adapted to call up serious reflections, suited to their respective employments, in both minister and man of physic. The motherly care of the good widow assigned to Mr. Dimmesdale a front apartment, with a sunny exposure, and heavy window-curtains, to create a noontide shadow when desirable. The walls were hung round with tapestry, said to be from the Gobelin looms, and, at all events, representing the Scriptural story of David and Bathsheba, and Nathan the Prophet, in colours still unfaded, but which made the fair woman of the scene almost as grimly picturesque as the woe-denouncing seer. Here the pale clergyman piled up his library, rich with parchment-bound folios of the Fathers, and the lore of Rabbis, and monkish erudition, of which the Protestant divines, even while they vilified and decried that class of writers, were yet constrained often to avail themselves. On the other side of the house, old Roger Chillingworth arranged his study and laboratory: not such as a modern man of science would reckon even tolerably complete, but provided with a distilling apparatus and the means of compounding drugs and chemicals, which the practised alchemist knew well how to turn to purpose. With such commodiousness of situation, these two learned persons sat themselves down, each in his own domain, yet familiarly passing from one apartment to the other, and bestowing a mutual and not incurious inspection into one another's business.

And the Reverend Arthur Dimmesdale's best discerning friends, as we have intimated, very reasonably imagined that the hand of Providence had done all this for the purpose—besought in so many public and domestic and secret prayers—of restoring the young minister to health. But, it must now be said, another portion of the community had latterly begun to take its own view of the relation betwixt Mr. Dimmesdale and the mysterious old physician. When an uninstructed multitude attempts to see with its eyes, it is exceedingly apt to be deceived. When, however, it forms its judgment, as it usually does, on the intuitions of its great and warm heart, the conclusions thus attained are often so profound and so unerring as to possess the character of truth supernaturally revealed. The people, in the case of which we speak, could justify its prejudice against Roger Chillingworth by no fact or argument worthy of serious refutation. There was an aged handicraftsman, it is true, who had been a citizen of London at the period of Sir Thomas Overbury's murder, now some thirty years agone; he testified to having seen the physician, under some other name, which the narrator of the story had now forgotten, in company with Dr. Forman, the famous old conjurer, who was implicated in the affair of Overbury. Two or three individuals hinted that the man of skill, during his Indian captivity, had enlarged his medical attainments by joining in the incantations of the savage priests, who were universally acknowledged to be powerful enchanters, often performing seemingly miraculous cures by their skill in the black art. A large number—and many of these were persons of such sober sense and practical observation that their opinions would have been valuable in other matters—affirmed that Roger Chillingworth's aspect had undergone a remarkable change while he had dwelt in town, and especially since his abode with Mr. Dimmesdale. At first, his expression had been calm, meditative, scholar-like. Now there was something ugly and evil in his face, which they had not previously noticed, and which grew still the more obvious to sight the oftener they looked upon him. According to the vulgar idea, the fire in his laboratory had been brought from the lower regions, and was fed with infernal fuel; and so, as might be expected, his visage was getting sooty with the smoke.

To sum up the matter, it grew to be a widely diffused opinion that the Rev. Arthur Dimmesdale, like many other personages of special sanctity, in all ages of the Christian world, was haunted either by Satan himself or Satan's emissary, in the guise of old Roger Chillingworth. This diabolical agent had the Divine permission, for a season, to burrow into the clergyman's intimacy, and plot against his soul. No sensible man, it was confessed, could doubt on which side the victory would turn. The people looked, with an unshaken hope, to see the minister come forth out of the conflict transfigured with the glory which he would unquestionably win. Meanwhile, nevertheless, it was sad to think of the perchance mortal agony through which he must struggle towards his triumph.

Alas! to judge from the gloom and terror in the depth of the poor minister's eyes, the battle was a sore one, and the victory anything but secure.

X. THE LEECH AND HIS PATIENT

Old Roger Chillingworth, throughout life, had been calm in temperament, kindly, though not of warm affections, but ever, and in all his relations with the world, a pure and upright man. He had begun an investigation, as he imagined, with the severe and equal integrity of a judge, desirous only of truth, even as if the question involved no more than the air-drawn lines and figures of a geometrical problem, instead of human passions, and wrongs inflicted on himself. But, as he proceeded, a terrible fascination, a kind of fierce, though still calm, necessity, seized the old man within its gripe, and never set him free again until he had done all its bidding. He now dug into the poor clergyman's heart, like a miner searching for gold; or, rather, like a sexton delving into a grave, possibly in quest of a jewel that had been buried on the dead man's bosom, but likely to find nothing save mortality and corruption. Alas, for his own soul, if these were what he sought!

Sometimes a light glimmered out of the physician's eyes, burning blue and ominous, like the reflection of a furnace, or, let us say, like one of those gleams of ghastly fire that darted from Bunyan's awful doorway in the hillside, and quivered on the pilgrim's face. The soil where this dark miner was working had perchance shown indications that encouraged him.

"This man," said he, at one such moment, to himself, "pure as they deem him—all spiritual as he seems—hath inherited a strong animal nature from his father or his mother. Let us dig a little further in the direction of this vein!"

Then after long search into the minister's dim interior, and turning over many precious materials, in the shape of high aspirations for the welfare of his race, warm love of souls, pure sentiments, natural piety, strengthened by thought and study, and illuminated by revelation—all of which invaluable gold was perhaps no better than rubbish to the seeker—he would turn back, discouraged, and begin his quest towards another point. He groped along as stealthily, with as cautious a tread, and as wary an outlook, as a thief entering a chamber where a man lies only half asleep—or, it may be, broad awake—with purpose to steal the very treasure which this man guards as the apple of his eye. In spite of his premeditated carefulness, the floor would now and then creak; his garments would rustle; the shadow of his presence, in a forbidden proximity, would be thrown across his victim. In other words, Mr. Dimmesdale, whose sensibility of nerve often produced the effect of spiritual intuition, would become vaguely aware that something inimical to his peace had thrust itself into relation with him. But Old Roger Chillingworth, too, had perceptions that were almost intuitive; and when the minister threw his startled eyes towards him, there the physician sat; his kind, watchful, sympathising, but never intrusive friend.

Yet Mr. Dimmesdale would perhaps have seen this individual's character more perfectly, if a certain morbidness, to which sick hearts are liable, had not rendered him suspicious of all mankind. Trusting no man as his friend, he could not recognize his enemy when the latter actually appeared. He therefore still kept up a fa-familiar intercourse with him, daily receiving the old physician in his study, or visiting the laboratory, and, for recreation's sake, watching the processes by which weeds were converted into drugs of potency.

One day, leaning his forehead on his hand, and his elbow on the sill of the open window, that looked towards the grave-yard, he talked with Roger Chillingworth, while the old man was examining a bundle of unsightly plants.

"Where," asked he, with a look askance at them—for it was the clergyman's peculiarity that he seldom, now-a-days, looked straight forth at any object, whether human or inanimate, "where, my kind doctor, did you gather those herbs, with such a dark, flabby leaf?"

"Even in the graveyard here at hand," answered the physician, continuing his employment. "They are new to me. I found them growing on a grave, which bore no tombstone, no other memorial of the dead man, save these ugly weeds, that have taken upon themselves to keep him in remembrance. They grew out of his heart, and typify, it may be, some hideous secret that was buried with him, and which he had done better to confess during his lifetime."

"Perchance," said Mr. Dimmesdale, "he earnestly desired it, but could not."

"And wherefore?" rejoined the physician.

"Wherefore not; since all the powers of nature call so earnestly for the confession of sin, that these black weeds have sprung up out of a buried heart, to make manifest, an outspoken crime?"

"That, good sir, is but a phantasy of yours," replied the minister. "There can be, if I forbode aright, no power, short of the Divine mercy, to disclose, whether by uttered words, or by type or emblem, the secrets that may be buried in the human heart. The heart, making itself guilty of such secrets, must perforce hold them, until the day when all hidden things shall be revealed. Nor have I so read or interpreted Holy Writ, as to understand that the disclosure of human thoughts and deeds, then to be made, is intended as a part of the retribution. That, surely, were a shallow view of it. No; these revelations, unless I greatly err, are meant merely to promote the intellectual satisfaction of all intelligent beings, who will stand waiting, on that day, to see the dark problem of this life made plain. A knowledge of men's hearts will be needful to the completest solution of that problem. And, I conceive moreover, that the hearts holding such miserable secrets as you speak of, will yield them up, at that last day, not with reluctance, but with a joy unutterable."

"Then why not reveal it here?" asked Roger Chillingworth, glancing quietly aside at the minister. "Why should not the guilty ones sooner avail themselves of this unutterable solace?"

"They mostly do," said the clergyman, griping hard at his breast, as if afflicted with an importunate throb of pain. "Many, many a poor soul hath given its confidence to me, not only on the death-bed, but while strong in life, and fair in reputation. And ever, after such an outpouring, oh, what a relief have I witnessed in those sinful brethren! even as in one who at last draws free air, after a long stifling with his own polluted breath. How can it be otherwise? Why should a wretched man—guilty, we will say, of murder—prefer to keep the dead corpse buried in his own heart, rather than fling it forth at once, and let the universe take care of it!"

"Yet some men bury their secrets thus," observed the calm physician.

"True; there are such men," answered Mr. Dimmesdale. "But not to suggest more obvious reasons, it may be that they are kept silent by the very constitution of their nature. Or—can we not suppose it?—guilty as they may be, retaining, nevertheless, a zeal for God's glory and man's welfare, they shrink from displaying themselves black and filthy in the view of men; because, thenceforward, no good can be achieved by them; no evil of the past be redeemed by better service. So, to their own unutterable torment, they go about among their fellow-creatures, looking pure as new-fallen snow, while their hearts are all speckled and spotted with iniquity of which they cannot rid themselves."

"These men deceive themselves," said Roger Chillingworth, with somewhat more emphasis than usual, and making a slight gesture with his forefinger. "They fear to take up the shame that rightfully belongs to them. Their love for man, their zeal for God's service—these holy impulses may or may not coexist in their hearts with the evil inmates to which their guilt has unbarred the door, and which must needs propagate a hellish breed within them. But, if they seek to glorify God, let them not lift heavenward their unclean hands! If they would serve their fellowmen, let them do it by making manifest the power and reality of conscience, in constraining them to penitential self-abasement! Would thou have me to believe, O wise and pious friend, that a false show can be better—can be more for God's glory, or man' welfare—than God's own truth? Trust me, such men deceive themselves!"

"It may be so," said the young clergyman, indifferently, as waiving a discussion that he considered irrelevant or unseasonable. He had a ready faculty, indeed, of escaping from any topic that agitated his too sensitive and nervous temperament.—"But, now, I would ask of my well-skilled physician, whether, in good sooth, he deems me to have profited by his kindly care of this weak frame of mine?"

Before Roger Chillingworth could answer, they heard the clear, wild laughter of a young child's voice, proceeding from the adjacent burial-ground. Looking instinctively from the open window—for it was summer-time—the minister beheld Hester Prynne and little Pearl passing along the footpath that traversed the enclosure. Pearl looked as beautiful as the day, but was in one of those moods of perverse merriment which, whenever they occurred, seemed to remove her entirely out of the sphere of sympathy or human contact. She now skipped irreverently from one grave to another; until coming to the broad, flat, armorial tombstone of a departed worthy—perhaps of Isaac Johnson himself—she began to dance upon it. In reply to her mother's command and entreaty that she would behave more decorously, little Pearl paused to gather the prickly burrs from a tall burdock which grew beside the tomb. Taking a handful of these, she arranged them along the lines of the scarlet letter that decorated the maternal bosom, to which the burrs, as their nature was, tenaciously adhered. Hester did not pluck them off.

Roger Chillingworth had by this time approached the window and smiled grimly down.

"There is no law, nor reverence for authority, no regard for human ordinances or opinions, right or wrong, mixed up with that child's composition," remarked he, as much to himself as to his companion. "I saw her, the other day, bespatter the Governor himself with water at the cattle-trough in Spring Lane. What, in heaven's name, is she? Is the imp altogether evil? Hath she affections? Hath she any discoverable principle of being?"

"None, save the freedom of a broken law," answered Mr. Dimmesdale, in a quiet way, as if he had been discussing the point within himself, "Whether capable of good, I know not."

The child probably overheard their voices, for, looking up to the window with a bright, but naughty smile of mirth and intelligence, she threw one of the prickly burrs at the Rev. Mr. Dimmesdale. The sensitive clergyman shrank, with nervous dread, from the light missile. Detecting his emotion, Pearl clapped her little hands in the most extravagant ecstacy. Hester Prynne, likewise, had involuntarily looked up, and all these four persons, old and young, regarded one another in silence, till the child laughed aloud, and shouted—"Come away, mother! Come away, or yonder old black man will catch you! He hath got hold of the minister already. Come away, mother or he will catch you! But he cannot catch little Pearl!"

So she drew her mother away, skipping, dancing, and frisking fantastically among the hillocks of the dead people, like a creature that had nothing in common with a bygone and buried generation, nor owned herself akin to it. It was as if she had been made afresh out of new elements, and must perforce be permitted to live her own life, and be a law unto herself without her eccentricities being reckoned to her for a crime.

"There goes a woman," resumed Roger Chillingworth, after a pause, "who, be her demerits what they may, hath none of that mystery of hidden sinfulness which you deem so grievous to be borne. Is Hester Prynne the less miserable, think you, for that scarlet letter on her breast?"

"I do verily believe it," answered the clergyman. "Nevertheless, I cannot answer for her. There was a look of pain in her face which I would gladly have been spared the sight of. But still, methinks, it must needs be better for the sufferer to be free to show his pain, as this poor woman Hester is, than to cover it up in his heart."

There was another pause, and the physician began anew to examine and arrange the plants which he had gathered.

"You inquired of me, a little time agone," said he, at length, "my judgment as touching your health."

"I did," answered the clergyman, "and would gladly learn it.

Speak frankly, I pray you, be it for life or death."

"Freely then, and plainly," said the physician, still busy with his plants, but keeping a wary eye on Mr. Dimmesdale, "the disorder is a strange one; not so much in itself nor as outwardly manifested,—in so far, at least as the symptoms have been laid open to my observation. Looking daily at you, my good sir, and watching the tokens of your aspect now for months gone by, I should deem you a man sore sick, it may be, yet not so sick but that an instructed and watchful physician might well hope to cure you. But I know not what to say, the disease is what I seem to know, yet know it not."

"You speak in riddles, learned sir," said the pale minister, glancing aside out of the window.

"Then, to speak more plainly," continued the physician, "and I crave pardon, sir, should it seem to require pardon, for this needful plainness of my speech. Let me ask as your friend, as one having charge, under Providence, of your life and physical well being, hath all the operations of this disorder been fairly laid open and recounted to me?"

"How can you question it?" asked the minister. "Surely it were child's play to call in a physician and then hide the sore!"

"You would tell me, then, that I know all?" said Roger Chillingworth, deliberately, and fixing an eye, bright with intense and concentrated intelligence, on the minister's face. "Be it so! But again! He to whom only the outward and physical evil is laid open, knoweth, oftentimes, but half the evil which he is called upon to cure. A bodily disease, which we look upon as whole and entire within itself, may, after all, be but a symptom of some ailment in the spiritual part. Your pardon once again, good sir, if my speech give the shadow of offence. You, sir, of all men whom I have known, are he whose body is the closest conjoined, and imbued, and identified, so to speak, with the spirit whereof it is the instrument."

"Then I need ask no further," said the clergyman, somewhat hastily rising from his chair. "You deal not, I take it, in medicine for the soul!"

"Thus, a sickness," continued Roger Chillingworth, going on, in an unaltered tone, without heeding the interruption, but standing up and confronting the emaciated and white-cheeked minister, with his low, dark, and misshapen figure,—"a sickness, a sore place, if we may so call it, in your spirit hath immediately its appropriate manifestation in your bodily frame. Would you, therefore, that your physician heal the bodily evil? How may this be unless you first lay open to him the wound or trouble in your soul?"

"No, not to thee! not to an earthly physician!" cried Mr. Dimmesdale, passionately, and turning his eyes, full and bright, and with a kind of fierceness, on old Roger Chillingworth. "Not to thee! But, if it be the soul's disease, then do I commit myself to the one Physician of the soul! He, if it stand with His good pleasure, can cure, or he can kill. Let Him do with me as, in His justice and wisdom, He shall see good. But who art thou, that meddlest in this matter? that dares thrust himself between the sufferer and his God?"

With a frantic gesture he rushed out of the room.

"It is as well to have made this step," said Roger Chillingworth to himself, looking after the minister, with a grave smile. "There is nothing lost. We shall be friends again anon. But see, now, how passion takes hold upon this man, and hurrieth him out of himself! As with one passion so with another. He hath done a wild thing ere now, this pious Master Dimmesdale, in the hot passion of his heart."

It proved not difficult to re-establish the intimacy of the two companions, on the same footing and in the same degree as heretofore. The young clergyman, after a few hours of privacy, was sensible that the disorder of his nerves had hurried him into an unseemly outbreak of temper, which there had been nothing in the physician's words to excuse or palliate. He marvelled, indeed, at the violence with which he had thrust back the kind old man, when merely proffering the advice which it was his duty to bestow, and which the minister himself had expressly sought. With these remorseful feelings, he lost no time in making the amplest apologies, and besought his friend still to continue the care which, if not successful in restoring him to health, had, in all probability, been the means of prolonging his feeble existence to that hour. Roger Chillingworth readily assented, and went on with his medical supervision of the minister; doing his best for him, in all good faith, but always quitting the patient's apartment, at the close of the professional interview, with a mysterious and puzzled smile upon his lips. This expression was invisible in Mr. Dimmesdale's presence, but grew strongly evident as the physician crossed the threshold.

"A rare case," he muttered. "I must needs look deeper into it. A strange sympathy betwixt soul and body! Were it only for the art's sake, I must search this matter to the bottom."

It came to pass, not long after the scene above recorded, that the Reverend Mr. Dimmesdale, noon-day, and entirely unawares, fell into a deep, deep slumber, sitting in his chair, with a large black-letter volume open before him on the table. It must have been a work of vast ability in the somniferous school of literature. The profound depth of the minister's repose was the more remarkable, inasmuch as he was one of those persons whose sleep ordinarily is as light as fitful, and as easily scared away, as a small bird hopping on a twig. To such an unwonted remoteness, however, had his spirit now withdrawn into itself that he stirred not in his chair when old Roger Chillingworth, without any extraordinary precaution, came into the room. The physician advanced directly in front of his patient, laid his hand upon his bosom, and thrust aside the vestment, that hitherto had always covered it even from the professional eye.

Then, indeed, Mr. Dimmesdale shuddered, and slightly stirred.

After a brief pause, the physician turned away.

But with what a wild look of wonder, joy, and horror! With what a ghastly rapture, as it were, too mighty to be expressed only by the eye and features, and therefore bursting forth through the whole ugliness of his figure, and making itself even riotously manifest by the extravagant gestures with which he threw up his arms towards the ceiling, and stamped his foot upon the floor! Had a man seen old Roger Chillingworth, at that moment of his ecstasy, he would have had no need to ask how Satan comports himself when a precious human soul is lost to heaven, and won into his kingdom.

But what distinguished the physician's ecstasy from Satan's was the trait of wonder in it!

XI. THE INTERIOR OF A HEART

After the incident last described, the intercourse between the clergyman and the physician, though externally the same, was really of another character than it had previously been. The intellect of Roger Chillingworth had now a sufficiently plain path before it. It was not, indeed, precisely that which he had laid out for himself to tread. Calm, gentle, passionless, as he appeared, there was yet, we fear, a quiet depth of malice, hitherto latent, but active now, in this unfortunate old man, which led him to imagine a more intimate revenge than any mortal had ever wreaked upon an enemy. To make himself the one trusted friend, to whom should be confided all the fear, the remorse, the agony, the ineffectual repentance, the backward rush of sinful thoughts, expelled in vain! All that guilty sorrow, hidden from the world, whose great heart would have pitied and forgiven, to be revealed to him, the Pitiless—to him, the Unforgiving! All that dark treasure to be lavished on the very man, to whom nothing else could so adequately pay the debt of vengeance!

The clergyman's shy and sensitive reserve had balked this scheme. Roger Chillingworth, however, was inclined to be hardly, if at all, less satisfied with the aspect of affairs, which Providence—using the avenger and his victim for its own purposes, and, perchance, pardoning, where it seemed most to punish—had substituted for his black devices. A revelation, he could almost say, had been granted to him. It mattered little for his object, whether celestial or from what other region. By its aid, in all the subsequent relations betwixt him and Mr. Dimmesdale, not merely the external presence, but the very inmost soul of the latter, seemed to be brought out before his eyes, so that he could see and comprehend its every movement. He became, thenceforth, not a spectator only, but a chief actor in the poor minister's interior world. He could play upon him as he chose. Would he arouse him with a throb of agony? The victim was for ever on the rack; it needed only to know the spring that controlled the engine: and the physician knew it well. Would he startle him with sudden fear? As at the waving of a magician's wand, up rose a grisly phantom—up rose a thousand phantoms—in many shapes, of death, or more awful shame, all flocking round about the clergyman, and pointing with their fingers at his breast!

All this was accomplished with a subtlety so perfect, that the minister, though he had constantly a dim perception of some evil influence watching over him, could never gain a knowledge of its actual nature. True, he looked doubtfully, fearfully—even, at times, with horror and the bitterness of hatred—at the deformed figure of the old physician. His gestures, his gait, his grizzled beard, his slightest and most indifferent acts, the very fashion of his garments, were odious in the clergyman's sight; a token implicitly to be relied on of a deeper antipathy in the breast of the latter than he was willing to acknowledge to himself. For, as it was impossible to assign a reason for such distrust and abhorrence, so Mr. Dimmesdale, conscious that the poison of one morbid spot was infecting his heart's entire substance, attributed all his presentiments to no other cause. He took himself to task for his bad sympathies in reference to Roger Chillingworth, disregarded the lesson that he should have drawn from them, and did his best to root them out. Unable to accomplish this, he nevertheless, as a matter of principle, continued his habits of social familiarity with the old man, and thus gave him constant opportunities for perfecting the purpose to which—poor forlorn creature that he was, and more wretched than his victim—the avenger had devoted himself.

While thus suffering under bodily disease, and gnawed and tortured by some black trouble of the soul, and given over to the machinations of his deadliest enemy, the Reverend Mr. Dimmesdale had achieved a brilliant popularity in his sacred office. He won it indeed, in great part, by his sorrows. His intellectual gifts, his moral perceptions, his power of experiencing and communicating emotion, were kept in a state of preternatural activity by the prick and anguish of his daily life. His fame, though still on its upward slope, already overshadowed the soberer reputations of his fellow-clergymen, eminent as several of them were. There are scholars among them, who had spent more years in acquiring abstruse lore, connected with the divine profession, than Mr. Dimmesdale had lived; and who might well, therefore, be more profoundly versed in such solid and valuable attainments than their youthful brother. There were men, too, of a sturdier texture of mind than his, and endowed with a far greater share of shrewd, hard iron, or granite understanding; which, duly mingled with a fair proportion of doctrinal ingredient, constitutes a highly respectable, efficacious, and unamiable variety of the clerical species. There were others again, true saintly fathers, whose faculties had been elaborated by weary toil among their books, and by patient thought, and etherealised, moreover, by spiritual communications with the better world, into which their purity of life had almost introduced these holy personages, with their garments of mortality still clinging to them. All that they lacked was, the gift that descended upon the chosen disciples at Pentecost, in tongues of flame; symbolising, it would seem, not the power of speech in foreign and unknown languages, but that of addressing the whole human brotherhood in the heart's native language. These fathers, otherwise so apostolic, lacked Heaven's last and rarest attestation of their office, the Tongue of Flame. They would have vainly sought—had they ever dreamed of seeking—to express the highest truths through the humblest medium of familiar words and images. Their voices came down, afar and indistinctly, from the upper heights where they habitually dwelt.

Not improbably, it was to this latter class of men that Mr. Dimmesdale, by many of his traits of character, naturally belonged. To the high mountain peaks of faith and sanctity he would have climbed, had not the tendency been thwarted by the burden, whatever it might be, of crime or anguish, beneath which it was his doom to totter. It kept him down on a level with the lowest; him, the man of ethereal attributes, whose voice the angels might else have listened to and answered! But this very burden it was that gave him sympathies so intimate with the sinful brotherhood of mankind; so that his heart vibrated in unison with theirs, and received their pain into itself and sent its own throb of pain through a thousand other hearts, in gushes of sad, persuasive eloquence. Oftenest persuasive, but sometimes terrible! The people knew not the power that moved them thus. They deemed the young clergyman a miracle of holiness. They fancied him the mouthpiece of Heaven's messages of wisdom, and rebuke, and love. In their eyes, the very ground on which he trod was sanctified. The virgins of his church grew pale around him, victims of a passion so imbued with religious sentiment, that they imagined it to be all religion, and brought it openly, in their white bosoms, as their most acceptable sacrifice before the altar. The aged members of his flock, beholding Mr. Dimmesdale's frame so feeble, while they were themselves so rugged in their infirmity, believed that he would go heavenward before them, and enjoined it upon their children that their old bones should be buried close to their young pastor's holy grave. And all this time, perchance, when poor Mr. Dimmesdale was thinking of his grave, he questioned with himself whether the grass would ever grow on it, because an accursed thing must there be buried!

It is inconceivable, the agony with which this public veneration tortured him. It was his genuine impulse to adore the truth, and to reckon all things shadow-like, and utterly devoid of weight or value, that had not its divine essence as the life within their life. Then what was he?—a substance?—or the dimmest of all shadows? He longed to speak out from his own pulpit at the full height of his voice, and tell the people what he was. "I, whom you behold in these black garments of the priesthood—I, who ascend the sacred desk, and turn my pale face heavenward, taking upon myself to hold communion in your behalf with the Most High Omniscience—I, in whose daily life you discern the sanctity of Enoch—I, whose footsteps, as you suppose, leave a gleam along my earthly track, whereby the Pilgrims that shall come after me may be guided to the regions of the blest—I, who have laid the hand of baptism upon your children—I, who have breathed the parting prayer over your dying friends, to whom the Amen sounded faintly from a world which they had quitted—I, your pastor, whom you so reverence and trust, am utterly a pollution and a lie!"

More than once, Mr. Dimmesdale had gone into the pulpit, with a purpose never to come down its steps until he should have spoken words like the above. More than once he had cleared his throat, and drawn in the long, deep, and tremulous breath, which, when sent forth again, would come burdened with the black secret of his soul. More than once—nay, more than a hundred times—he had actually spoken! Spoken! But how? He had told his hearers that he was altogether vile, a viler companion of the vilest, the worst of sinners, an abomination, a thing of unimaginable iniquity, and that the only wonder was that they did not see his wretched body shrivelled up before their eyes by the burning wrath of the Almighty! Could there be plainer speech than this? Would not the people start up in their seats, by a simultaneous impulse, and tear him down out of the pulpit which he defiled? Not so, indeed! They heard it all, and did but reverence him the more. They little guessed what deadly purport lurked in those self-condemning words. "The godly youth!" said they among themselves. "The saint on earth! Alas! if he discern such sinfulness in his own white soul, what horrid spectacle would he behold in thine or mine!" The minister well knew—subtle, but remorseful hypocrite that he was!—the light in which his vague confession would be viewed. He had striven to put a cheat upon himself by making the avowal of a guilty conscience, but had gained only one other sin, and a self-acknowledged shame, without the momentary relief of being self-deceived. He had spoken the very truth, and transformed it into the veriest falsehood. And yet, by the constitution of his nature, he loved the truth, and loathed the lie, as few men ever did. Therefore, above all things else, he loathed his miserable self!

His inward trouble drove him to practices more in accordance with the old, corrupted faith of Rome than with the better light of the church in which he had been born and bred. In Mr. Dimmesdale's secret closet, under lock and key, there was a bloody scourge. Oftentimes, this Protestant and Puritan divine had plied it on his own shoulders, laughing bitterly at himself the while, and smiting so much the more pitilessly because of that bitter laugh. It was his custom, too, as it has been that of many other pious Puritans, to fast—not however, like them, in order to purify the body, and render it the fitter medium of celestial illumination—but rigorously, and until his knees trembled beneath him, as an act of penance. He kept vigils, likewise, night after night, sometimes in utter darkness, sometimes with a glimmering lamp, and sometimes, viewing his own face in a looking-glass, by the most powerful light which he could throw upon it. He thus typified the constant introspection wherewith he tortured, but could not purify himself. In these lengthened vigils, his brain often reeled, and visions seemed to flit before him; perhaps seen doubtfully, and by a faint light of their own, in the remote dimness of the chamber, or more vividly and close beside him, within the looking-glass. Now it was a herd of diabolic shapes, that grinned and mocked at the pale minister, and beckoned him away with them; now a group of shining angels, who flew upward heavily, as sorrow-laden, but grew more ethereal as they rose. Now came the dead friends of his youth, and his white-bearded father, with a saint-like frown, and his mother turning her face away as she passed by. Ghost of a mother—thinnest fantasy of a mother—methinks she might yet have thrown a pitying glance towards her son! And now, through the chamber which these spectral thoughts had made so ghastly, glided Hester Prynne leading along little Pearl, in her scarlet garb, and pointing her forefinger, first at the scarlet letter on her bosom, and then at the clergyman's own breast.

None of these visions ever quite deluded him. At any moment, by an effort of his will, he could discern substances through their misty lack of substance, and convince himself that they were not solid in their nature, like yonder table of carved oak, or that big, square, leather-bound and brazen-clasped volume of divinity. But, for all that, they were, in one sense, the truest and most substantial things which the poor minister now dealt with. It is the unspeakable misery of a life so false as his, that it steals the pith and substance out of whatever realities there are around us, and which were meant by Heaven to be the spirit's joy and nutriment. To the untrue man, the whole universe is false—it is impalpable—it shrinks to nothing within his grasp. And he himself in so far as he shows himself in a false light, becomes a shadow, or, indeed, ceases to exist. The only truth that continued to give Mr. Dimmesdale a real existence on this earth was the anguish in his inmost soul, and the undissembled expression of it in his aspect. Had he once found power to smile, and wear a face of gaiety, there would have been no such man!

On one of those ugly nights, which we have faintly hinted at, but forborne to picture forth, the minister started from his chair. A new thought had struck him. There might be a moment's peace in it. Attiring himself with as much care as if it had been for public worship, and precisely in the same manner, he stole softly down the staircase, undid the door, and issued forth.

XII. THE MINISTER'S VIGIL

Walking in the shadow of a dream, as it were, and perhaps actually under the influence of a species of somnambulism, Mr. Dimmesdale reached the spot where, now so long since, Hester Prynne had lived through her first hours of public ignominy. The same platform or scaffold, black and weather-stained with the storm or sunshine of seven long years, and foot-worn, too, with the tread of many culprits who had since ascended it, remained standing beneath the balcony of the meeting-house. The minister went up the steps.

It was an obscure night in early May. An unvaried pall of cloud muffled the whole expanse of sky from zenith to horizon. If the same multitude which had stood as eye-witnesses while Hester Prynne sustained her punishment could now have been summoned forth, they would have discerned no face above the platform nor hardly the outline of a human shape, in the dark grey of the midnight. But the town was all asleep. There was no peril of discovery. The minister might stand there, if it so pleased him, until morning should redden in the east, without other risk than that the dank and chill night air would creep into his frame, and stiffen his joints with rheumatism, and clog his throat with catarrh and cough; thereby defrauding the expectant audience of to-morrow's prayer and sermon. No eye could see him, save that ever-wakeful one which had seen him in his closet, wielding the bloody scourge. Why, then, had he come hither? Was it but the mockery of penitence? A mockery, indeed, but in which his soul trifled with itself! A mockery at which angels blushed and wept, while fiends rejoiced with jeering laughter! He had been driven hither by the impulse of that Remorse which dogged him everywhere, and whose own sister and closely linked companion was that Cowardice which invariably drew him back, with her tremulous gripe, just when the other impulse had hurried him to the verge of a disclosure. Poor, miserable man! what right had infirmity like his to burden itself with crime? Crime is for the iron-nerved, who have their choice either to endure it, or, if it press too hard, to exert their fierce and savage strength for a good purpose, and fling it off at once! This feeble and most sensitive of spirits could do neither, yet continually did one thing or another, which intertwined, in the same inextricable knot, the agony of heaven-defying guilt and vain repentance.

And thus, while standing on the scaffold, in this vain show of expiation, Mr. Dimmesdale was overcome with a great horror of mind, as if the universe were gazing at a scarlet token on his naked breast, right over his heart. On that spot, in very truth, there was, and there had long been, the gnawing and poisonous tooth of bodily pain. Without any effort of his will, or power to restrain himself, he shrieked aloud: an outcry that went pealing through the night, and was beaten back from one house to another, and reverberated from the hills in the background; as if a company of devils, detecting so much misery and terror in it, had made a plaything of the sound, and were bandying it to and fro.

"It is done!" muttered the minister, covering his face with his hands. "The whole town will awake and hurry forth, and find me here!"

But it was not so. The shriek had perhaps sounded with a far greater power, to his own startled ears, than it actually possessed. The town did not awake; or, if it did, the drowsy slumberers mistook the cry either for something frightful in a dream, or for the noise of witches, whose voices, at that period, were often heard to pass over the settlements or lonely cottages, as they rode with Satan through the air. The clergyman, therefore, hearing no symptoms of disturbance, uncovered his eyes and looked about him. At one of the chamber-windows of Governor Bellingham's mansion, which stood at some distance, on the line of another street, he beheld the appearance of the old magistrate himself with a lamp in his hand a white night-cap on his head, and a long white gown enveloping his figure. He looked like a ghost evoked unseasonably from the grave. The cry had evidently startled him. At another window of the same house, moreover appeared old Mistress Hibbins, the Governor's sister, also with a lamp, which even thus far off revealed the expression of her sour and discontented face. She thrust forth her head from the lattice, and looked anxiously upward. Beyond the shadow of a doubt, this venerable witch-lady had heard Mr. Dimmesdale's outcry, and interpreted it, with its multitudinous echoes and reverberations, as the clamour of the fiends and night-hags, with whom she was well known to make excursions in the forest.

Detecting the gleam of Governor Bellingham's lamp, the old lady quickly extinguished her own, and vanished. Possibly, she went up among the clouds. The minister saw nothing further of her motions. The magistrate, after a wary observation of the darkness—into which, nevertheless, he could see but little further than he might into a mill-stone—retired from the window.

The minister grew comparatively calm. His eyes, however, were soon greeted by a little glimmering light, which, at first a long way off was approaching up the street. It threw a gleam of recognition, on here a post, and there a garden fence, and here a latticed window-pane, and there a pump, with its full trough of water, and here again an arched door of oak, with an iron knocker, and a rough log for the door-step. The Reverend Mr. Dimmesdale noted all these minute particulars, even while firmly convinced that the doom of his existence was stealing onward, in the footsteps which he now heard; and that the gleam of the lantern would fall upon him in a few moments more, and reveal his long-hidden secret. As the light drew nearer, he beheld, within its illuminated circle, his brother clergyman—or, to speak more accurately, his professional father, as well as highly valued friend—the Reverend Mr. Wilson, who, as Mr. Dimmesdale now conjectured, had been praying at the bedside of some dying man. And so he had. The good old minister came freshly from the death-chamber of Governor Winthrop, who had passed from earth to heaven within that very hour. And now surrounded, like the saint-like personage of olden times, with a radiant halo, that glorified him amid this gloomy night of sin—as if the departed Governor had left him an inheritance of his glory, or as if he had caught upon himself the distant shine of the celestial city, while looking thitherward to see the triumphant pilgrim pass within its gates—now, in short, good Father Wilson was moving homeward, aiding his footsteps with a lighted lantern! The glimmer of this luminary suggested the above conceits to Mr. Dimmesdale, who smiled—nay, almost laughed at them—and then wondered if he was going mad.

As the Reverend Mr. Wilson passed beside the scaffold, closely muffling his Geneva cloak about him with one arm, and holding the lantern before his breast with the other, the minister could hardly restrain himself from speaking—

"A good evening to you, venerable Father Wilson. Come up hither, I pray you, and pass a pleasant hour with me!"

Good Heavens! Had Mr. Dimmesdale actually spoken? For one instant he believed that these words had passed his lips. But they were uttered only within his imagination. The venerable Father Wilson continued to step slowly onward, looking carefully at the muddy pathway before his feet, and never once turning his head towards the guilty platform. When the light of the glimmering lantern had faded quite away, the minister discovered, by the faintness which came over him, that the last few moments had been a crisis of terrible anxiety, although his mind had made an involuntary effort to relieve itself by a kind of lurid playfulness.

Shortly afterwards, the like grisly sense of the humorous again stole in among the solemn phantoms of his thought. He felt his limbs growing stiff with the unaccustomed chilliness of the night, and doubted whether he should be able to descend the steps of the scaffold. Morning would break and find him there. The neighbourhood would begin to rouse itself. The earliest riser, coming forth in the dim twilight, would perceive a vaguely-defined figure aloft on the place of shame; and half-crazed betwixt alarm and curiosity, would go knocking from door to door, summoning all the people to behold the ghost—as he needs must think it—of some defunct transgressor. A dusky tumult would flap its wings from one house to another. Then—the morning light still waxing stronger—old patriarchs would rise up in great haste, each in his flannel gown, and matronly dames, without pausing to put off their night-gear. The whole tribe of decorous personages, who had never heretofore been seen with a single hair of their heads awry, would start into public view with the disorder of a nightmare in their aspects. Old Governor Bellingham would come grimly forth, with his King James' ruff fastened askew, and Mistress Hibbins, with some twigs of the forest clinging to her skirts, and looking sourer than ever, as having hardly got a wink of sleep after her night ride; and good Father Wilson too, after spending half the night at a death-bed, and liking ill to be disturbed, thus early, out of his dreams about the glorified saints. Hither, likewise, would come the elders and deacons of Mr. Dimmesdale's church, and the young virgins who so idolized their minister, and had made a shrine for him in their white bosoms, which now, by-the-bye, in their hurry and confusion, they would scantly have given themselves time to cover with their kerchiefs. All people, in a word, would come stumbling over their thresholds, and turning up their amazed and horror-stricken visages around the scaffold. Whom would they discern there, with the red eastern light upon his brow? Whom, but the Reverend Arthur Dimmesdale, half-frozen to death, overwhelmed with shame, and standing where Hester Prynne had stood!

Carried away by the grotesque horror of this picture, the minister, unawares, and to his own infinite alarm, burst into a great peal of laughter. It was immediately responded to by a light, airy, childish laugh, in which, with a thrill of the heart—but he knew not whether of exquisite pain, or pleasure as acute—he recognised the tones of little Pearl.

"Pearl! Little Pearl!" cried he, after a moment's pause; then, suppressing his voice—"Hester! Hester Prynne! Are you there?"

"Yes; it is Hester Prynne!" she replied, in a tone of surprise; and the minister heard her footsteps approaching from the side-walk, along which she had been passing. "It is I, and my little Pearl."

"Whence come you, Hester?" asked the minister. "What sent you hither?"

"I have been watching at a death-bed," answered Hester Prynne "at Governor Winthrop's death-bed, and have taken his measure for a robe, and am now going homeward to my dwelling."

"Come up hither, Hester, thou and little Pearl," said the Reverend Mr. Dimmesdale. "Ye have both been here before, but I was not with you. Come up hither once again, and we will stand all three together."

She silently ascended the steps, and stood on the platform, holding little Pearl by the hand. The minister felt for the child's other hand, and took it. The moment that he did so, there came what seemed a tumultuous rush of new life, other life than his own pouring like a torrent into his heart, and hurrying through all his veins, as if the mother and the child were communicating their vital warmth to his half-torpid system. The three formed an electric chain.

"Minister!" whispered little Pearl.

"What wouldst thou say, child?" asked Mr. Dimmesdale.

"Wilt thou stand here with mother and me, to-morrow noontide?" inquired Pearl.

"Nay; not so, my little Pearl," answered the minister; for, with the new energy of the moment, all the dread of public exposure, that had so long been the anguish of his life, had returned upon him; and he was already trembling at the conjunction in which—with a strange joy, nevertheless—he now found himself—"not so, my child. I shall, indeed, stand with thy mother and thee one other day, but not to-morrow."

Pearl laughed, and attempted to pull away her hand. But the minister held it fast.

"A moment longer, my child!" said he.

"But wilt thou promise," asked Pearl, "to take my hand, and mother's hand, to-morrow noontide?"

"Not then, Pearl," said the minister; "but another time."

"And what other time?" persisted the child.

"At the great judgment day," whispered the minister; and, strangely enough, the sense that he was a professional teacher of the truth impelled him to answer the child so. "Then, and there, before the judgment-seat, thy mother, and thou, and I must stand together. But the daylight of this world shall not see our meeting!"

Pearl laughed again.

But before Mr. Dimmesdale had done speaking, a light gleamed far and wide over all the muffled sky. It was doubtless caused by one of those meteors, which the night-watcher may so often observe burning out to waste, in the vacant regions of the atmosphere. So powerful was its radiance, that it thoroughly illuminated the dense medium of cloud betwixt the sky and earth. The great vault brightened, like the dome of an immense lamp. It showed the familiar scene of the street with the distinctness of mid-day, but also with the awfulness that is always imparted to familiar objects by an unaccustomed light. The wooden houses, with their jutting storeys and quaint gable-peaks; the doorsteps and thresholds with the early grass springing up about them; the garden-plots, black with freshly-turned earth; the wheel-track, little worn, and even in the market-place margined with green on either side—all were visible, but with a singularity of aspect that seemed to give another moral interpretation to the things of this world than they had ever borne before. And there stood the minister, with his hand over his heart; and Hester Prynne, with the embroidered letter glimmering on her bosom; and little Pearl, herself a symbol, and the connecting link between those two. They stood in the noon of that strange and solemn splendour, as if it were the light that is to reveal all secrets, and the daybreak that shall unite all who belong to one another.

There was witchcraft in little Pearl's eyes; and her face, as she glanced upward at the minister, wore that naughty smile which made its expression frequently so elvish. She withdrew her hand from Mr. Dimmesdale's, and pointed across the street. But he clasped both his hands over his breast, and cast his eyes towards the zenith.

Nothing was more common, in those days, than to interpret all meteoric appearances, and other natural phenomena that occurred with less regularity than the rise and set of sun and moon, as so many revelations from a supernatural source. Thus, a blazing spear, a sword of flame, a bow, or a sheaf of arrows seen in the midnight sky, prefigured Indian warfare. Pestilence was known to have been foreboded by a shower of crimson light. We doubt whether any marked event, for good or evil, ever befell New England, from its settlement down to revolutionary times, of which the inhabitants had not been previously warned by some spectacle of its nature. Not seldom, it had been seen by multitudes. Oftener, however, its credibility rested on the faith of some lonely eye-witness, who beheld the wonder through the coloured, magnifying, and distorted medium of his imagination, and shaped it more distinctly in his after-thought. It was, indeed, a majestic idea that the destiny of nations should be revealed, in these awful hieroglyphics, on the cope of heaven. A scroll so wide might not be deemed too expensive for Providence to write a people's doom upon. The belief was a favourite one with our forefathers, as betokening that their infant commonwealth was under a celestial guardianship of peculiar intimacy and strictness. But what shall we say, when an individual discovers a revelation addressed to himself alone, on the same vast sheet of record. In such a case, it could only be the symptom of a highly disordered mental state, when a man, rendered morbidly self-contemplative by long, intense, and secret pain, had extended his egotism over the whole expanse of nature, until the firmament itself should appear no more than a fitting page for his soul's history and fate.

We impute it, therefore, solely to the disease in his own eye and heart that the minister, looking upward to the zenith, beheld there the appearance of an immense letter—the letter A—marked out in lines of dull red light. Not but the meteor may have shown itself at that point, burning duskily through a veil of cloud, but with no such shape as his guilty imagination gave it, or, at least, with so little definiteness, that another's guilt might have seen another symbol in it.

There was a singular circumstance that characterised Mr. Dimmesdale's psychological state at this moment. All the time that he gazed upward to the zenith, he was, nevertheless, perfectly aware that little Pearl was pointing her finger towards old Roger Chillingworth, who stood at no great distance from the scaffold. The minister appeared to see him, with the same glance that discerned the miraculous letter. To his feature as to all other objects, the meteoric light imparted a new expression; or it might well be that the physician was not careful then, as at all other times, to hide the malevolence with which he looked upon his victim. Certainly, if the meteor kindled up the sky, and disclosed the earth, with an awfulness that admonished Hester Prynne and the clergyman of the day of judgment, then might Roger Chillingworth have passed with them for the arch-fiend, standing there with a smile and scowl, to claim his own. So vivid was the expression, or so intense the minister's perception of it, that it seemed still to remain painted on the darkness after the meteor had vanished, with an effect as if the street and all things else were at once annihilated.

"Who is that man, Hester?" gasped Mr. Dimmesdale, overcome with terror. "I shiver at him! Dost thou know the man? I hate him, Hester!"

She remembered her oath, and was silent.

"I tell thee, my soul shivers at him!" muttered the minister again. "Who is he? Who is he? Canst thou do nothing for me? I have a nameless horror of the man!"

"Minister," said little Pearl, "I can tell thee who he is!"

"Quickly, then, child!" said the minister, bending his ear close to her lips. "Quickly, and as low as thou canst whisper."

Pearl mumbled something into his ear that sounded, indeed, like human language, but was only such gibberish as children may be heard amusing themselves with by the hour together. At all events, if it involved any secret information in regard to old Roger Chillingworth, it was in a tongue unknown to the erudite clergyman, and did but increase the bewilderment of his mind. The elvish child then laughed aloud.

"Dost thou mock me now?" said the minister.

"Thou wast not bold!—thou wast not true!" answered the child. "Thou wouldst not promise to take my hand, and mother's hand, to-morrow noon-tide!"

"Worthy sir," answered the physician, who had now advanced to the foot of the platform—"pious Master Dimmesdale! can this be you? Well, well, indeed! We men of study, whose heads are in our books, have need to be straitly looked after! We dream in our waking moments, and walk in our sleep. Come, good sir, and my dear friend, I pray you let me lead you home!"

"How knewest thou that I was here?" asked the minister, fearfully.

"Verily, and in good faith," answered Roger Chillingworth, "I knew nothing of the matter. I had spent the better part of the night at the bedside of the worshipful Governor Winthrop, doing what my poor skill might to give him ease. He, going home to a better world, I, likewise, was on my way homeward, when this light shone out. Come with me, I beseech you, Reverend sir, else you will be poorly able to do Sabbath duty to-morrow. Aha! see now how they trouble the brain—these books!—these books! You should study less, good sir, and take a little pastime, or these night whimsies will grow upon you."

"I will go home with you," said Mr. Dimmesdale.

With a chill despondency, like one awakening, all nerveless, from an ugly dream, he yielded himself to the physician, and was led away.

The next day, however, being the Sabbath, he preached a discourse which was held to be the richest and most powerful, and the most replete with heavenly influences, that had ever proceeded from his lips. Souls, it is said, more souls than one, were brought to the truth by the efficacy of that sermon, and vowed within themselves to cherish a holy gratitude towards Mr. Dimmesdale throughout the long hereafter. But as he came down the pulpit steps, the grey-bearded sexton met him, holding up a black glove, which the minister recognised as his own.

"It was found," said the Sexton, "this morning on the scaffold where evil-doers are set up to public shame. Satan dropped it there, I take it, intending a scurrilous jest against your reverence. But, indeed, he was blind and foolish, as he ever and always is. A pure hand needs no glove to cover it!"

"Thank you, my good friend," said the minister, gravely, but startled at heart; for so confused was his remembrance, that he had almost brought himself to look at the events of the past night as visionary.

"Yes, it seems to be my glove, indeed!"

"And, since Satan saw fit to steal it, your reverence must needs handle him without gloves henceforward," remarked the old sexton, grimly smiling. "But did your reverence hear of the portent that was seen last night? a great red letter in the sky—the letter A, which we interpret to stand for Angel. For, as our good Governor Winthrop was made an angel this past night, it was doubtless held fit that there should be some notice thereof!"

"No," answered the minister; "I had not heard of it."

XIII. ANOTHER VIEW OF HESTER

In her late singular interview with Mr. Dimmesdale, Hester Prynne was shocked at the condition to which she found the clergyman reduced. His nerve seemed absolutely destroyed. His moral force was abased into more than childish weakness. It grovelled helpless on the ground, even while his intellectual faculties retained their pristine strength, or had perhaps acquired a morbid energy, which disease only could have given them. With her knowledge of a train of circumstances hidden from all others, she could readily infer that, besides the legitimate action of his own conscience, a terrible machinery had been brought to bear, and was still operating, on Mr. Dimmesdale's well-being and repose. Knowing what this poor fallen man had once been, her whole soul was moved by the shuddering terror with which he had appealed to her—the outcast woman—for support against his instinctively discovered enemy. She decided, moreover, that he had a right to her utmost aid. Little accustomed, in her long seclusion from society, to measure her ideas of right and wrong by any standard external to herself, Hester saw—or seemed to see—that there lay a responsibility upon her in reference to the clergyman, which she owned to no other, nor to the whole world besides. The links that united her to the rest of humankind—links of flowers, or silk, or gold, or whatever the material—had all been broken. Here was the iron link of mutual crime, which neither he nor she could break. Like all other ties, it brought along with it its obligations.

Hester Prynne did not now occupy precisely the same position in which we beheld her during the earlier periods of her ignominy. Years had come and gone. Pearl was now seven years old. Her mother, with the scarlet letter on her breast, glittering in its fantastic embroidery, had long been a familiar object to the townspeople. As is apt to be the case when a person stands out in any prominence before the community, and, at the same time, interferes neither with public nor individual interests and convenience, a species of general regard had ultimately grown up in reference to Hester Prynne. It is to the credit of human nature that, except where its selfishness is brought into play, it loves more readily than it hates. Hatred, by a gradual and quiet process, will even be transformed to love, unless the change be impeded by a continually new irritation of the original feeling of hostility. In this matter of Hester Prynne there was neither irritation nor irksomeness. She never battled with the public, but submitted uncomplainingly to its worst usage; she made no claim upon it in requital for what she suffered; she did not weigh upon its sympathies. Then, also, the blameless purity of her life during all these years in which she had been set apart to infamy was reckoned largely in her favour. With nothing now to lose, in the sight of mankind, and with no hope, and seemingly no wish, of gaining anything, it could only be a genuine regard for virtue that had brought back the poor wanderer to its paths.

It was perceived, too, that while Hester never put forward even the humblest title to share in the world's privileges—further than to breathe the common air and earn daily bread for little Pearl and herself by the faithful labour of her hands—she was quick to acknowledge her sisterhood with the race of man whenever benefits were to be conferred. None so ready as she to give of her little substance to every demand of poverty, even though the bitter-hearted pauper threw back a gibe in requital of the food brought regularly to his door, or the garments wrought for him by the fingers that could have embroidered a monarch's robe. None so self-devoted as Hester when pestilence stalked through the town. In all seasons of calamity, indeed, whether general or of individuals, the outcast of society at once found her place. She came, not as a guest, but as a rightful inmate, into the household that was darkened by trouble, as if its gloomy twilight were a medium in which she was entitled to hold intercourse with her fellow-creature. There glimmered the embroidered letter, with comfort in its unearthly ray. Elsewhere the token of sin, it was the taper of the sick chamber. It had even thrown its gleam, in the sufferer's bard extremity, across the verge of time. It had shown him where to set his foot, while the light of earth was fast becoming dim, and ere the light of futurity could reach him. In such emergencies Hester's nature showed itself warm and rich—a well-spring of human tenderness, unfailing to every real demand, and inexhaustible by the largest. Her breast, with its badge of shame, was but the softer pillow for the head that needed one. She was self-ordained a Sister of Mercy, or, we may rather say, the world's heavy hand had so ordained her, when neither the world nor she looked forward to this result. The letter was the symbol of her calling. Such helpfulness was found in her—so much power to do, and power to sympathise—that many people refused to interpret the scarlet A by its original signification. They said that it meant Abel, so strong was Hester Prynne, with a woman's strength.

It was only the darkened house that could contain her. When sunshine came again, she was not there. Her shadow had faded across the threshold. The helpful inmate had departed, without one backward glance to gather up the meed of gratitude, if any were in the hearts of those whom she had served so zealously. Meeting them in the street, she never raised her head to receive their greeting. If they were resolute to accost her, she laid her finger on the scarlet letter, and passed on. This might be pride, but was so like humility, that it produced all the softening influence of the latter quality on the public mind. The public is despotic in its temper; it is capable of denying common justice when too strenuously demanded as a right; but quite as frequently it awards more than justice, when the appeal is made, as despots love to have it made, entirely to its generosity. Interpreting Hester Prynne's deportment as an appeal of this nature, society was inclined to show its former victim a more benign countenance than she cared to be favoured with, or, perchance, than she deserved.

The rulers, and the wise and learned men of the community, were longer in acknowledging the influence of Hester's good qualities than the people. The prejudices which they shared in common with the latter were fortified in themselves by an iron frame-work of reasoning, that made it a far tougher labour to expel them. Day by day, nevertheless, their sour and rigid wrinkles were relaxing into something which, in the due course of years, might grow to be an expression of almost benevolence. Thus it was with the men of rank, on whom their eminent position imposed the guardianship of the public morals. Individuals in private life, meanwhile, had quite forgiven Hester Prynne for her frailty; nay, more, they had begun to look upon the scarlet letter as the token, not of that one sin for which she had borne so long and dreary a penance, but of her many good deeds since. "Do you see that woman with the embroidered badge?" they would say to strangers. "It is our Hester—the town's own Hester—who is so kind to the poor, so helpful to the sick, so comfortable to the afflicted!" Then, it is true, the propensity of human nature to tell the very worst of itself, when embodied in the person of another, would constrain them to whisper the black scandal of bygone years. It was none the less a fact, however, that in the eyes of the very men who spoke thus, the scarlet letter had the effect of the cross on a nun's bosom. It imparted to the wearer a kind of sacredness, which enabled her to walk securely amid all peril. Had she fallen among thieves, it would have kept her safe. It was reported, and believed by many, that an Indian had drawn his arrow against the badge, and that the missile struck it, and fell harmless to the ground.

The effect of the symbol—or rather, of the position in respect to society that was indicated by it—on the mind of Hester Prynne herself was powerful and peculiar. All the light and graceful foliage of her character had been withered up by this red-hot brand, and had long ago fallen away, leaving a bare and harsh outline, which might have been repulsive had she possessed friends or companions to be repelled by it. Even the attractiveness of her person had undergone a similar change. It might be partly owing to the studied austerity of her dress, and partly to the lack of demonstration in her manners. It was a sad transformation, too, that her rich and luxuriant hair had either been cut off, or was so completely hidden by a cap, that not a shining lock of it ever once gushed into the sunshine. It was due in part to all these causes, but still more to something else, that there seemed to be no longer anything in Hester's face for Love to dwell upon; nothing in Hester's form, though majestic and statue like, that Passion would ever dream of clasping in its embrace; nothing in Hester's bosom to make it ever again the pillow of Affection. Some attribute had departed from her, the permanence of which had been essential to keep her a woman. Such is frequently the fate, and such the stern development, of the feminine character and person, when the woman has encountered, and lived through, an experience of peculiar severity. If she be all tenderness, she will die. If she survive, the tenderness will either be crushed out of her, or—and the outward semblance is the same—crushed so deeply into her heart that it can never show itself more. The latter is perhaps the truest theory. She who has once been a woman, and ceased to be so, might at any moment become a woman again, if there were only the magic touch to effect the transformation. We shall see whether Hester Prynne were ever afterwards so touched and so transfigured.

Much of the marble coldness of Hester's impression was to be attributed to the circumstance that her life had turned, in a great measure, from passion and feeling to thought. Standing alone in the world—alone, as to any dependence on society, and with little Pearl to be guided and protected—alone, and hopeless of retrieving her position, even had she not scorned to consider it desirable—she cast away the fragment of a broken chain. The world's law was no law for her mind. It was an age in which the human intellect, newly emancipated, had taken a more active and a wider range than for many centuries before. Men of the sword had overthrown nobles and kings. Men bolder than these had overthrown and rearranged—not actually, but within the sphere of theory, which was their most real abode—the whole system of ancient prejudice, wherewith was linked much of ancient principle. Hester Prynne imbibed this spirit. She assumed a freedom of speculation, then common enough on the other side of the Atlantic, but which our forefathers, had they known it, would have held to be a deadlier crime than that stigmatised by the scarlet letter. In her lonesome cottage, by the seashore, thoughts visited her such as dared to enter no other dwelling in New England; shadowy guests, that would have been as perilous as demons to their entertainer, could they have been seen so much as knocking at her door.

It is remarkable that persons who speculate the most boldly often conform with the most perfect quietude to the external regulations of society. The thought suffices them, without investing itself in the flesh and blood of action. So it seemed to be with Hester. Yet, had little Pearl never come to her from the spiritual world, it might have been far otherwise. Then she might have come down to us in history, hand in hand with Ann Hutchinson, as the foundress of a religious sect. She might, in one of her phases, have been a prophetess. She might, and not improbably would, have suffered death from the stern tribunals of the period, for attempting to undermine the foundations of the Puritan establishment. But, in the education of her child, the mother's enthusiasm of thought had something to wreak itself upon. Providence, in the person of this little girl, had assigned to Hester's charge, the germ and blossom of womanhood, to be cherished and developed amid a host of difficulties. Everything was against her. The world was hostile. The child's own nature had something wrong in it which continually betokened that she had been born amiss—the effluence of her mother's lawless passion—and often impelled Hester to ask, in bitterness of heart, whether it were for ill or good that the poor little creature had been born at all.

Indeed, the same dark question often rose into her mind with reference to the whole race of womanhood. Was existence worth accepting even to the happiest among them? As concerned her own individual existence, she had long ago decided in the negative, and dismissed the point as settled. A tendency to speculation, though it may keep women quiet, as it does man, yet makes her sad. She discerns, it may be, such a hopeless task before her. As a first step, the whole system of society is to be torn down and built up anew. Then the very nature of the opposite sex, or its long hereditary habit, which has become like nature, is to be essentially modified before woman can be allowed to assume what seems a fair and suitable position. Finally, all other difficulties being obviated, woman cannot take advantage of these preliminary reforms until she herself shall have undergone a still mightier change, in which, perhaps, the ethereal essence, wherein she has her truest life, will be found to have evaporated. A woman never overcomes these problems by any exercise of thought. They are not to be solved, or only in one way. If her heart chance to come uppermost, they vanish. Thus Hester Prynne, whose heart had lost its regular and healthy throb, wandered without a clue in the dark labyrinth of mind; now turned aside by an insurmountable precipice; now starting back from a deep chasm. There was wild and ghastly scenery all around her, and a home and comfort nowhere. At times a fearful doubt strove to possess her soul, whether it were not better to send Pearl at once to Heaven, and go herself to such futurity as Eternal Justice should provide.

The scarlet letter had not done its office. Now, however, her interview with the Reverend Mr. Dimmesdale, on the night of his vigil, had given her a new theme of reflection, and held up to her an object that appeared worthy of any exertion and sacrifice for its attainment. She had witnessed the intense misery beneath which the minister struggled, or, to speak more accurately, had ceased to struggle. She saw that he stood on the verge of lunacy, if he had not already stepped across it. It was impossible to doubt that, whatever painful efficacy there might be in the secret sting of remorse, a deadlier venom had been infused into it by the hand that proffered relief. A secret enemy had been continually by his side, under the semblance of a friend and helper, and had availed himself of the opportunities thus afforded for tampering with the delicate springs of Mr. Dimmesdale's nature. Hester could not but ask herself whether there had not originally been a defect of truth, courage, and loyalty on her own part, in allowing the minister to be thrown into a position where so much evil was to be foreboded and nothing auspicious to be hoped. Her only justification lay in the fact that she had been able to discern no method of rescuing him from a blacker ruin than had overwhelmed herself except by acquiescing in Roger Chillingworth's scheme of disguise. Under that impulse she had made her choice, and had chosen, as it now appeared, the more wretched alternative of the two. She determined to redeem her error so far as it might yet be possible. Strengthened by years of hard and solemn trial, she felt herself no longer so inadequate to cope with Roger Chillingworth as on that night, abased by sin and half-maddened by the ignominy that was still new, when they had talked together in the prison-chamber. She had climbed her way since then to a higher point. The old man, on the other hand, had brought himself nearer to her level, or, perhaps, below it, by the revenge which he had stooped for.

In fine, Hester Prynne resolved to meet her former husband, and do what might be in her power for the rescue of the victim on whom he had so evidently set his gripe. The occasion was not long to seek. One afternoon, walking with Pearl in a retired part of the peninsula, she beheld the old physician with a basket on one arm and a staff in the other hand, stooping along the ground in quest of roots and herbs to concoct his medicine withal.

XIV. HESTER AND THE PHYSICIAN

Hester bade little Pearl run down to the margin of the water, and play with the shells and tangled sea-weed, until she should have talked awhile with yonder gatherer of herbs. So the child flew away like a bird, and, making bare her small white feet went pattering along the moist margin of the sea. Here and there she came to a full stop, and peeped curiously into a pool, left by the retiring tide as a mirror for Pearl to see her face in. Forth peeped at her, out of the pool, with dark, glistening curls around her head, and an elf-smile in her eyes, the image of a little maid whom Pearl, having no other playmate, invited to take her hand and run a race with her. But the visionary little maid on her part, beckoned likewise, as if to say—"This is a better place; come thou into the pool." And Pearl, stepping in mid-leg deep, beheld her own white feet at the bottom; while, out of a still lower depth, came the gleam of a kind of fragmentary smile, floating to and fro in the agitated water.

Meanwhile her mother had accosted the physician. "I would speak a word with you," said she—"a word that concerns us much."

"Aha! and is it Mistress Hester that has a word for old Roger Chillingworth?" answered he, raising himself from his stooping posture. "With all my heart! Why, mistress, I hear good tidings of you on all hands! No longer ago than yes-ter-eve, a magistrate, a wise and godly man, was discoursing of your affairs, Mistress Hester, and whispered me that there had been question concerning you in the council. It was debated whether or no, with safety to the commonweal, yon-der scarlet letter might be taken off your bosom. On my life, Hester, I made my intreaty to the worshipful magistrate that it might be done forthwith."

"It lies not in the pleasure of the magistrates to take off the badge," calmly re-plied Hester. "Were I worthy to be quit of it, it would fall away of its own nature, or be transformed into something that should speak a different purport."

"Nay, then, wear it, if it suit you better," rejoined he, "A woman must needs follow her own fancy touching the adornment of her person. The letter is gaily embroidered, and shows right bravely on your bosom!"

All this while Hester had been looking steadily at the old man, and was shocked, as well as wonder-smitten, to discern what a change had been wrought upon him within the past seven years. It was not so much that he had grown old-er; for though the traces of advancing life were visible he bore his age well, and seemed to retain a wiry vigour and alertness. But the former aspect of an intellectual and studious man, calm and quiet, which was what she best remembered in him, had altogether vanished, and been succeeded by an eager, searching, almost fierce, yet carefully guarded look. It seemed to be his wish and purpose to mask this expression with a smile, but the latter played him false, and flickered over his visage so derisively that the spectator could see his blackness all the better for it. Ever and anon, too, there came a glare of red light out of his eyes, as if the old man's soul were on fire and kept on smouldering duskily within his breast, until by some casual puff of passion it was blown into a momentary flame. This he repressed as speedily as possible, and strove to look as if nothing of the kind had happened.

In a word, old Roger Chillingworth was a striking evidence of man's faculty of transforming himself into a devil, if he will only, for a reasonable space of time, undertake a devil's office. This unhappy person had effected such a transformation by devoting himself for seven years to the constant analysis of a heart full of torture, and deriving his enjoyment thence, and adding fuel to those fiery tortures which he analysed and gloated over.

The scarlet letter burned on Hester Prynne's bosom. Here was another ruin, the responsibility of which came partly home to her.

"What see you in my face," asked the physician, "that you look at it so earnestly?"

"Something that would make me weep, if there were any tears bitter enough for it," answered she. "But let it pass! It is of yonder miserable man that I would speak."

"And what of him?" cried Roger Chillingworth, eagerly, as if he loved the topic, and were glad of an opportunity to discuss it with the only person of whom he could make a confidant. "Not to hide the truth, Mistress Hester, my thoughts happen just now to be busy with the gentleman. So speak freely and I will make answer."

"When we last spake together," said Hester, "now seven years ago, it was your pleasure to extort a promise of secrecy as touching the former relation betwixt yourself and me. As the life and good fame of yonder man were in your hands there seemed no choice to me, save to be silent in accordance with your behest. Yet it was not without heavy misgivings that I thus bound myself, for, having cast off all duty towards other human beings, there remained a duty towards him, and something whispered me that I was betraying it in pledging myself to keep your counsel. Since that day no man is so near to him as you. You tread behind his every footstep. You are beside him, sleeping and waking. You search his thoughts. You burrow and rankle in his heart! Your clutch is on his life, and you cause him to die daily a living death, and still he knows you not. In permitting this I have surely acted a false part by the only man to whom the power was left me to be true!"

"What choice had you?" asked Roger Chillingworth. "My finger, pointed at this man, would have hurled him from his pulpit into a dungeon, thence, peradventure, to the gallows!"

"It had been better so!" said Hester Prynne.

"What evil have I done the man?" asked Roger Chillingworth again. "I tell thee, Hester Prynne, the richest fee that ever physician earned from monarch could not have bought such care as I have wasted on this miserable priest! But for my aid his life would have burned away in torments within the first two years after the perpetration of his crime and thine. For, Hester, his spirit lacked the strength that could have borne up, as thine has, beneath a burden like thy scarlet letter. Oh, I could reveal a goodly secret! But enough. What art can do, I have exhausted on him. That he now breathes and creeps about on earth is owing all to me!"

"Better he had died at once!" said Hester Prynne.

"Yea, woman, thou sayest truly!" cried old Roger Chillingworth, letting the lurid fire of his heart blaze out before her eyes. "Better had he died at once! Never did mortal suffer what this man has suffered. And all, all, in the sight of his worst enemy! He has been conscious of me. He has felt an influence dwelling always upon him like a curse. He knew, by some spiritual sense—for the Creator never made another being so sensitive as this—he knew that no friendly hand was pulling at his heartstrings, and that an eye was looking curiously into him, which sought only evil, and found it. But he knew not that the eye and hand were mine! With the superstition common to his brotherhood, he fancied himself given over to a fiend, to be tortured with frightful dreams and desperate thoughts, the sting of remorse and despair of pardon, as a foretaste of what awaits him beyond the grave. But it was the constant shadow of my presence, the closest propinquity of the man whom he had most vilely wronged, and who had grown to exist only by this perpetual poison of the direst revenge! Yea, indeed, he did not err, there was a fiend at his elbow! A mortal man, with once a human heart, has become a fiend for his especial torment."

The unfortunate physician, while uttering these words, lifted his hands with a look of horror, as if he had beheld some frightful shape, which he could not recognise, usurping the place of his own image in a glass. It was one of those moments—which sometimes occur only at the interval of years—when a man's moral aspect is faithfully revealed to his mind's eye. Not improbably he had never before viewed himself as he did now.

"Hast thou not tortured him enough?" said Hester, noticing the old man's look. "Has he not paid thee all?"

"No, no! He has but increased the debt!" answered the physician, and as he proceeded, his manner lost its fiercer characteristics, and subsided into gloom. "Dost thou remember me, Hester, as I was nine years agone? Even then I was in the autumn of my days, nor was it the early autumn. But all my life had been made up of earnest, studious, thoughtful, quiet years, bestowed faithfully for the increase of mine own knowledge, and faithfully, too, though this latter object was but casual to the other—faithfully for the advancement of human welfare. No life had been more peaceful and innocent than mine; few lives so rich with benefits conferred. Dost thou remember me? Was I not, though you might deem me cold, nevertheless a man thoughtful for others, craving little for himself—kind, true, just and of constant, if not warm affections? Was I not all this?"

"All this, and more," said Hester.

"And what am I now?" demanded he, looking into her face, and permitting the whole evil within him to be written on his features. "I have already told thee what I am—a fiend! Who made me so?"

"It was myself," cried Hester, shuddering. "It was I, not less than he. Why hast thou not avenged thyself on me?"

"I have left thee to the scarlet letter," replied Roger

Chillingworth. "If that has not avenged me, I can do no more!"

He laid his finger on it with a smile.

"It has avenged thee," answered Hester Prynne.

"I judged no less," said the physician. "And now what wouldst thou with me touching this man?"

"I must reveal the secret," answered Hester, firmly. "He must discern thee in thy true character. What may be the result I know not. But this long debt of confidence, due from me to him, whose bane and ruin I have been, shall at length be paid. So far as concerns the overthrow or preservation of his fair fame and his earthly state, and perchance his life, he is in my hands. Nor do I—whom the scarlet letter has disciplined to truth, though it be the truth of red-hot iron entering into the soul—nor do I perceive such advantage in his living any longer a life of ghastly emptiness, that I shall stoop to implore thy mercy. Do with him as thou wilt! There is no good for him, no good for me, no good for thee. There is no good for little Pearl. There is no path to guide us out of this dismal maze."

"Woman, I could well-nigh pity thee," said Roger Chillingworth, unable to restrain a thrill of admiration too, for there was a quality almost majestic in the despair which she expressed. "Thou hadst great elements. Peradventure, hadst thou met earlier with a better love than mine, this evil had not been. I pity thee, for the good that has been wasted in thy nature."

"And I thee," answered Hester Prynne, "for the hatred that has transformed a wise and just man to a fiend! Wilt thou yet purge it out of thee, and be once more human? If not for his sake, then doubly for thine own! Forgive, and leave his further retribution to the Power that claims it! I said, but now, that there could be no good event for him, or thee, or me, who are here wandering together in this gloomy maze of evil, and stumbling at every step over the guilt wherewith we have strewn our path. It is not so! There might be good for thee, and thee alone, since thou hast been deeply wronged and hast it at thy will to pardon. Wilt thou give up that only privilege? Wilt thou reject that priceless benefit?"

"Peace, Hester—peace!" replied the old man, with gloomy sternness—"it is not granted me to pardon. I have no such power as thou tellest me of. My old faith, long forgotten, comes back to me, and explains all that we do, and all we suffer. By thy first step awry, thou didst plant the germ of evil; but since that moment it has all been a dark necessity. Ye that have wronged me are not sinful, save in a kind of typical illusion; neither am I fiend-like, who have snatched a fiend's office from his hands. It is our fate. Let the black flower blossom as it may! Now, go thy ways, and deal as thou wilt with yonder man."

He waved his hand, and betook himself again to his employment of gathering herbs.

XV. HESTER AND PEARL

So Roger Chillingworth—a deformed old figure with a face that haunted men's memories longer than they liked—took leave of Hester Prynne, and went stooping away along the earth. He gathered here and there a herb, or grubbed up a root and put it into the basket on his arm. His gray beard almost touched the ground as he crept onward. Hester gazed after him a little while, looking with a half fantastic curiosity to see whether the tender grass of early spring would not be blighted beneath him and show the wavering track of his footsteps, sere and brown, across its cheerful verdure. She wondered what sort of herbs they were which the old man was so sedulous to gather. Would not the earth, quickened to an evil purpose by the sympathy of his eye, greet him with poisonous shrubs of species hitherto unknown, that would start up under his fingers? Or might it suffice him that every wholesome growth should be converted into something deleterious and malignant at his touch? Did the sun, which shone so brightly everywhere else, really fall upon him? Or was there, as it rather seemed, a circle of ominous shadow moving along with his deformity whichever way he turned himself? And whither was he now going? Would he not suddenly sink into the earth, leaving a barren and blasted spot, where, in due course of time, would be seen deadly nightshade, dogwood, henbane, and whatever else of vegetable wickedness the climate could produce, all flourishing with hideous luxuriance? Or would he spread bat's wings and flee away, looking so much the uglier the higher he rose towards heaven?

"Be it sin or no," said Hester Prynne, bitterly, as still she gazed after him, "I hate the man!"

She upbraided herself for the sentiment, but could not overcome or lessen it. Attempting to do so, she thought of those long-past days in a distant land, when he used to emerge at eventide from the seclusion of his study and sit down in the firelight of their home, and in the light of her nuptial smile. He needed to bask himself in that smile, he said, in order that the chill of so many lonely hours among his books might be taken off the scholar's heart. Such scenes had once appeared not otherwise than happy, but now, as viewed through the dismal medium of her subsequent life, they classed themselves among her ugliest remembrances. She marvelled how such scenes could have been! She marvelled how she could ever have been wrought upon to marry him! She deemed it her crime most to be repented of, that she had ever endured and reciprocated the lukewarm grasp of his hand, and had suffered the smile of her lips and eyes to mingle and melt into his own. And it seemed a fouler offence committed by Roger Chillingworth than any which had since been done him, that, in the time when her heart knew no better, he had persuaded her to fancy herself happy by his side.

"Yes, I hate him!" repeated Hester more bitterly than before.

"He betrayed me! He has done me worse wrong than I did him!"

Let men tremble to win the hand of woman, unless they win along with it the utmost passion of her heart! Else it may be their miserable fortune, as it was Roger Chillingworth's, when some mightier touch than their own may have awakened all her sensibilities, to be reproached even for the calm content, the marble image of happiness, which they will have imposed upon her as the warm reality. But Hester ought long ago to have done with this injustice. What did it betoken? Had seven long years, under the torture of the scarlet letter, inflicted so much of misery and wrought out no repentance?

The emotion of that brief space, while she stood gazing after the crooked figure of old Roger Chillingworth, threw a dark light on Hester's state of mind, revealing much that she might not otherwise have acknowledged to herself.

He being gone, she summoned back her child.

"Pearl! Little Pearl! Where are you?"

Pearl, whose activity of spirit never flagged, had been at no loss for amusement while her mother talked with the old gatherer of herbs. At first, as already told, she had flirted fancifully with her own image in a pool of water, beckoning the phantom forth, and—as it declined to venture—seeking a passage for herself into its sphere of impalpable earth and unattainable sky. Soon finding, however, that either she or the image was unreal, she turned elsewhere for better pastime. She made little boats out of birch-bark, and freighted them with snailshells, and sent out more ventures on the mighty deep than any merchant in New England; but the larger part of them foundered near the shore. She seized a live horse-shoe by the tail, and made prize of several five-fingers, and laid out a jelly-fish to melt in the warm sun. Then she took up the white foam that streaked the line of the advancing tide, and threw it upon the breeze, scampering after it with winged footsteps to catch the great snowflakes ere they fell. Perceiving a flock of beach-birds that fed and fluttered along the shore, the naughty child picked up her apron full of pebbles, and, creeping from rock to rock after these small sea-fowl, displayed remarkable dexterity in pelting them. One little gray bird, with a white breast, Pearl was almost sure had been hit by a pebble, and fluttered away with a broken wing. But then the elf-child sighed, and gave up her sport, because it grieved her to have done harm to a little being that was as wild as the sea-breeze, or as wild as Pearl herself.

Her final employment was to gather seaweed of various kinds, and make herself a scarf or mantle, and a head-dress, and thus assume the aspect of a little mermaid. She inherited her mother's gift for devising drapery and costume. As the last touch to her mermaid's garb, Pearl took some eel-grass and imitated, as best she could, on her own bosom the decoration with which she was so familiar on her mother's. A letter—the letter A—but freshly green instead of scarlet. The child bent her chin upon her breast, and contemplated this device with strange interest, even as if the one only thing for which she had been sent into the world was to make out its hidden import.

"I wonder if mother will ask me what it means?" thought Pearl.

Just then she heard her mother's voice, and, flitting along as lightly as one of the little sea-birds, appeared before Hester Prynne dancing, laughing, and pointing her finger to the ornament upon her bosom.

"My little Pearl," said Hester, after a moment's silence, "the green letter, and on thy childish bosom, has no purport. But dost thou know, my child, what this letter means which thy mother is doomed to wear?"

"Yes, mother," said the child. "It is the great letter A. Thou hast taught me in the horn-book."

Hester looked steadily into her little face; but though there was that singular expression which she had so often remarked in her black eyes, she could not satisfy herself whether Pearl really attached any meaning to the symbol. She felt a morbid desire to ascertain the point.

"Dost thou know, child, wherefore thy mother wears this letter?"

"Truly do I!" answered Pearl, looking brightly into her mother's face. "It is for the same reason that the minister keeps his hand over his heart!"

"And what reason is that?" asked Hester, half smiling at the absurd incongruity of the child's observation; but on second thoughts turning pale.

"What has the letter to do with any heart save mine?"

"Nay, mother, I have told all I know," said Pearl, more seriously than she was wont to speak. "Ask yonder old man whom thou hast been talking with,—it may be he can tell. But in good earnest now, mother dear, what does this scarlet letter mean?—and why dost thou wear it on thy bosom?—and why does the minister keep his hand over his heart?"

She took her mother's hand in both her own, and gazed into her eyes with an earnestness that was seldom seen in her wild and capricious character. The thought occurred to Hester, that the child might really be seeking to approach her with childlike confidence, and doing what she could, and as intelligently as she knew how, to establish a meeting-point of sympathy. It showed Pearl in an unwonted aspect. Heretofore, the mother, while loving her child with the intensity of a sole affection, had schooled herself to hope for little other return than the waywardness of an April breeze, which spends its time in airy sport, and has its gusts of inexplicable passion, and is petulant in its best of moods, and chills oftener than caresses you, when you take it to your bosom; in requital of which misdemeanours it will sometimes, of its own vague purpose, kiss your cheek with a kind of doubtful tenderness, and play gently with your hair, and then be gone about its other idle business, leaving a dreamy pleasure at your heart. And this, moreover, was a mother's estimate of the child's disposition. Any other observer might have seen few but unamiable traits, and have given them a far darker colouring. But now the idea came strongly into Hester's mind, that Pearl, with her remarkable precocity and acuteness, might already have approached the age when she could have been made a friend, and intrusted with as much of her mother's sorrows as could be imparted, without irreverence either to the parent or the child. In the little chaos of Pearl's character there might be seen emerging and could have been from the very first—the steadfast principles of an unflinching courage—an uncontrollable will—sturdy pride, which might be disciplined into self-respect—and a bitter scorn of many things which, when examined, might be found to have the taint of falsehood in them. She possessed affections, too, though hitherto acrid and disagreeable, as are the richest flavours of unripe fruit. With all these sterling attributes, thought Hester, the evil which she inherited from her mother must be great indeed, if a noble woman do not grow out of this elfish child.

Pearl's inevitable tendency to hover about the enigma of the scarlet letter seemed an innate quality of her being. From the earliest epoch of her conscious life, she had entered upon this as her appointed mission. Hester had often fancied that Providence had a design of justice and retribution, in endowing the child with this marked propensity; but never, until now, had she bethought herself to ask, whether, linked with that design, there might not likewise be a purpose of mercy and beneficence. If little Pearl were entertained with faith and trust, as a spirit messenger no less than an earthly child, might it not be her errand to soothe away the sorrow that lay cold in her mother's heart, and converted it into a tomb?—and to help her to overcome the passion, once so wild, and even yet neither dead nor asleep, but only imprisoned within the same tomb-like heart?

Such were some of the thoughts that now stirred in Hester's mind, with as much vivacity of impression as if they had actually been whispered into her ear. And there was little Pearl, all this while, holding her mother's hand in both her own, and turning her face upward, while she put these searching questions, once and again, and still a third time.

"What does the letter mean, mother? and why dost thou wear it? and why does the minister keep his hand over his heart?"

"What shall I say?" thought Hester to herself. "No! if this be the price of the child's sympathy, I cannot pay it."

Then she spoke aloud—

"Silly Pearl," said she, "what questions are these? There are many things in this world that a child must not ask about. What know I of the minister's heart? And as for the scarlet letter, I wear it for the sake of its gold thread."

In all the seven bygone years, Hester Prynne had never before been false to the symbol on her bosom. It may be that it was the talisman of a stern and severe, but yet a guardian spirit, who now forsook her; as recognising that, in spite of his strict watch over her heart, some new evil had crept into it, or some old one had never been expelled. As for little Pearl, the earnestness soon passed out of her face.

But the child did not see fit to let the matter drop. Two or three times, as her mother and she went homeward, and as often at supper-time, and while Hester was putting her to bed, and once after she seemed to be fairly asleep, Pearl looked up, with mischief gleaming in her black eyes.

"Mother," said she, "what does the scarlet letter mean?"

And the next morning, the first indication the child gave of being awake was by popping up her head from the pillow, and making that other enquiry, which she had so unaccountably connected with her investigations about the scarlet letter—

"Mother!—Mother!—Why does the minister keep his hand over his heart?"

"Hold thy tongue, naughty child!" answered her mother, with an asperity that she had never permitted to herself before. "Do not tease me; else I shall put thee into the dark closet!"

XVI. A FOREST WALK

Hester Prynne remained constant in her resolve to make known to Mr. Dimmesdale, at whatever risk of present pain or ulterior consequences, the true character of the man who had crept into his intimacy. For several days, however, she vainly sought an opportunity of addressing him in some of the meditative walks which she knew him to be in the habit of taking along the shores of the Peninsula, or on the wooded hills of the neighbouring country. There would have been no scandal, indeed, nor peril to the holy whiteness of the clergyman's good fame, had she visited him in his own study, where many a penitent, ere now, had confessed sins of perhaps as deep a dye as the one betokened by the scarlet letter. But, partly that she dreaded the secret or undisguised interference of old Roger Chillingworth, and partly that her conscious heart imparted suspicion where none could have been felt, and partly that both the minister and she would need the whole wide world to breathe in, while they talked together—for all these reasons Hester never thought of meeting him in any narrower privacy than beneath the open sky.

At last, while attending a sick chamber, whither the Rev. Mr. Dimmesdale had been summoned to make a prayer, she learnt that he had gone, the day before, to visit the Apostle Eliot, among his Indian converts. He would probably return by a certain hour in the afternoon of the morrow. Betimes, therefore, the next day, Hester took little Pearl—who was necessarily the companion of all her mother's expeditions, however inconvenient her presence—and set forth.

The road, after the two wayfarers had crossed from the Peninsula to the mainland, was no other than a foot path. It straggled onward into the mystery of the primeval forest. This hemmed it in so narrowly, and stood so black and dense on either side, and disclosed such imperfect glimpses of the sky above, that, to Hester's mind, it imaged not amiss the moral wilderness in which she had so long been wandering. The day was chill and sombre. Overhead was a gray expanse of cloud, slightly stirred, however, by a breeze; so that a gleam of flickering sunshine might now and then be seen at its solitary play along the path. This flitting cheerfulness was always at the further extremity of some long vista through the forest. The sportive sunlight—feebly sportive, at best, in the predominant pensiveness of the day and scene—withdrew itself as they came nigh, and left the spots where it had danced the drearier, because they had hoped to find them bright.

"Mother," said little Pearl, "the sunshine does not love you.

It runs away and hides itself, because it is afraid of something

on your bosom. Now, see! There it is, playing a good way off.

Stand you here, and let me run and catch it. I am but a child.

It will not flee from me—for I wear nothing on my bosom yet!"

"Nor ever will, my child, I hope," said Hester.

"And why not, mother?" asked Pearl, stopping short, just at the beginning of her race. "Will not it come of its own accord when I am a woman grown?"

"Run away, child," answered her mother, "and catch the sunshine.

It will soon be gone."

Pearl set forth at a great pace, and as Hester smiled to perceive, did actually catch the sunshine, and stood laughing in the midst of it, all brightened by its splendour, and scintillating with the vivacity excited by rapid motion. The light lingered about the lonely child, as if glad of such a playmate, until her mother had drawn almost nigh enough to step into the magic circle too.

"It will go now," said Pearl, shaking her head.

"See!" answered Hester, smiling; "now I can stretch out my hand and grasp some of it."

As she attempted to do so, the sunshine vanished; or, to judge from the bright expression that was dancing on Pearl's features, her mother could have fancied that the child had absorbed it into herself, and would give it forth again, with a gleam about her path, as they should plunge into some gloomier shade. There was no other attribute that so much impressed her with a sense of new and untransmitted vigour in Pearl's nature, as this never failing vivacity of spirits: she had not the disease of sadness, which almost all children, in these latter days, inherit, with the scrofula, from the troubles of their ancestors. Perhaps this, too, was a disease, and but the reflex of the wild energy with which Hester had fought against her sorrows before Pearl's birth. It was certainly a doubtful charm, imparting a hard, metallic lustre to the child's character. She wanted—what some people want throughout life—a grief that should deeply touch her, and thus humanise and make her capable of sympathy. But there was time enough yet for little Pearl.

"Come, my child!" said Hester, looking about her from the spot where Pearl had stood still in the sunshine—"we will sit down a little way within the wood, and rest ourselves."

"I am not aweary, mother," replied the little girl. "But you may sit down, if you will tell me a story meanwhile."

"A story, child!" said Hester. "And about what?"

"Oh, a story about the Black Man," answered Pearl, taking hold of her mother's gown, and looking up, half earnestly, half mischievously, into her face.

"How he haunts this forest, and carries a book with him a big, heavy book, with iron clasps; and how this ugly Black Man offers his book and an iron pen to everybody that meets him here among the trees; and they are to write their names with their own blood; and then he sets his mark on their bosoms. Didst thou ever meet the Black Man, mother?"

"And who told you this story, Pearl," asked her mother, recognising a common superstition of the period.

"It was the old dame in the chimney corner, at the house where you watched last night," said the child. "But she fancied me asleep while she was talking of it. She said that a thousand and a thousand people had met him here, and had written in his book, and have his mark on them. And that ugly tempered lady, old Mistress Hibbins, was one. And, mother, the old dame said that this scarlet letter was the Black Man's mark on thee, and that it glows like a red flame when thou meetest him at midnight, here in the dark wood. Is it true, mother? And dost thou go to meet him in the nighttime?"

"Didst thou ever awake and find thy mother gone?" asked Hester. "Not that I remember," said the child. "If thou fearest to leave me in our cottage, thou mightest take me along with thee. I would very gladly go! But, mother, tell me now! Is there such a Black Man? And didst thou ever meet him? And is this his mark?"

"Wilt thou let me be at peace, if I once tell thee?" asked her mother.

"Yes, if thou tellest me all," answered Pearl.

"Once in my life I met the Black Man!" said her mother. "This scarlet letter is his mark!"

Thus conversing, they entered sufficiently deep into the wood to secure themselves from the observation of any casual passenger along the forest track. Here they sat down on a luxuriant heap of moss; which at some epoch of the preceding century, had been a gigantic pine, with its roots and trunk in the darksome shade, and its head aloft in the upper atmosphere. It was a little dell where they had seated themselves, with a leaf-strewn bank rising gently on either side, and a brook flowing through the midst, over a bed of fallen and drowned leaves. The trees impending over it had flung down great branches from time to time, which choked up the current, and compelled it to form eddies and black depths at some points; while, in its swifter and livelier passages there appeared a channel-way of pebbles, and brown, sparkling sand. Letting the eyes follow along the course of the stream, they could catch the reflected light from its water, at some short distance within the forest, but soon lost all traces of it amid the bewilderment of tree-trunks and underbrush, and here and there a huge rock covered over with gray lichens. All these giant trees and boulders of granite seemed intent on making a mystery of the course of this small brook; fearing, perhaps, that, with its never-ceasing loquacity, it should whisper tales out of the heart of the old forest whence it flowed, or mirror its revelations on the smooth surface of a pool. Continually, indeed, as it stole onward, the streamlet kept up a babble, kind, quiet, soothing, but melancholy, like the voice of a young child that was spending its infancy without playfulness, and knew not how to be merry among sad acquaintance and events of sombre hue.

"Oh, brook! Oh, foolish and tiresome little brook!" cried
Pearl, after listening awhile to its talk, "Why art thou so sad?
Pluck up a spirit, and do not be all the time sighing and
murmuring!"

But the brook, in the course of its little lifetime among the forest trees, had gone through so solemn an experience that it could not help talking about it, and seemed to have nothing else to say. Pearl resembled the brook, inasmuch as the current of her life gushed from a well-spring as mysterious, and had flowed through scenes shadowed as heavily with gloom. But, unlike the little stream, she danced and sparkled, and prattled airily along her course.

"What does this sad little brook say, mother?" inquired she.

"If thou hadst a sorrow of thine own, the brook might tell thee of it," answered her mother, "even as it is telling me of mine. But now, Pearl, I hear a footstep along the path, and the noise of one putting aside the branches. I would have thee betake thyself to play, and leave me to speak with him that comes yonder."

"Is it the Black Man?" asked Pearl.

"Wilt thou go and play, child?" repeated her mother, "But do not stray far into the wood. And take heed that thou come at my first call."

"Yes, mother," answered Pearl, "But if it be the Black Man, wilt thou not let me stay a moment, and look at him, with his big book under his arm?"

"Go, silly child!" said her mother impatiently. "It is no Black Man! Thou canst see him now, through the trees. It is the minister!"

"And so it is!" said the child. "And, mother, he has his hand over his heart! Is it because, when the minister wrote his name in the book, the Black Man set his mark in that place? But why does he not wear it outside his bosom, as thou dost, mother?"

"Go now, child, and thou shalt tease me as thou wilt another time," cried Hester Prynne. "But do not stray far. Keep where thou canst hear the babble of the brook."

The child went singing away, following up the current of the brook, and striving to mingle a more lightsome cadence with its melancholy voice. But the little stream would not be comforted, and still kept telling its unintelligible secret of some very mournful mystery that had happened—or making a prophetic lamentation about something that was yet to happen—within the verge of the dismal forest. So Pearl, who had enough of shadow in her own little life, chose to break off all acquaintance with this repining brook. She set herself, therefore, to gathering violets and wood-anemones, and some scarlet columbines that she found growing in the crevice of a high rock.

When her elf-child had departed, Hester Prynne made a step or two towards the track that led through the forest, but still remained under the deep shadow of the trees. She beheld the minister advancing along the path entirely alone, and leaning on a staff which he had cut by the wayside. He looked haggard and feeble, and betrayed a nerveless despondency in his air, which had never so remarkably characterised him in his walks about the settlement, nor in any other situation where he deemed himself liable to notice. Here it was wofully visible, in this intense seclusion of the forest, which of itself would have been a heavy trial to the spirits. There was a listlessness in his gait, as if he saw no reason for taking one step further, nor felt any desire to do so, but would have been glad, could he be glad of anything, to fling himself down at the root of the nearest tree, and lie there passive for evermore. The leaves might bestrew him, and the soil gradually accumulate and form a little hillock over his frame, no matter whether there were life in it or no. Death was too definite an object to be wished for or avoided.

To Hester's eye, the Reverend Mr. Dimmesdale exhibited no symptom of positive and vivacious suffering, except that, as little Pearl had remarked, he kept his hand over his heart.

XVII. THE PASTOR AND HIS PARISHIONER

Slowly as the minister walked, he had almost gone by before Hester Prynne could gather voice enough to attract his observation. At length she succeeded.

"Arthur Dimmesdale!" she said, faintly at first, then louder, but hoarsely—"Arthur Dimmesdale!"

"Who speaks?" answered the minister. Gathering himself quickly up, he stood more erect, like a man taken by surprise in a mood to which he was reluctant to have witnesses. Throwing his eyes anxiously in the direction of the voice, he indistinctly beheld a form under the trees, clad in garments so sombre, and so little relieved from the gray twilight into which the clouded sky and the heavy foliage had darkened the noontide, that he knew not whether it were a woman or a shadow. It may be that his pathway through life was haunted thus by a spectre that had stolen out from among his thoughts.

He made a step nigher, and discovered the scarlet letter.

"Hester! Hester Prynne!", said he; "is it thou? Art thou in life?"

"Even so." she answered. "In such life as has been mine these seven years past! And thou, Arthur Dimmesdale, dost thou yet live?"

It was no wonder that they thus questioned one another's actual and bodily existence, and even doubted of their own. So strangely did they meet in the dim wood that it was like the first encounter in the world beyond the grave of two spirits who had been intimately connected in their former life, but now stood coldly shuddering in mutual dread, as not yet familiar with their state, nor wonted to the companionship of disembodied beings. Each a ghost, and awe-stricken at the other ghost. They were awe-stricken likewise at themselves, because the crisis flung back to them their consciousness, and revealed to each heart its history and experience, as life never does, except at such breathless epochs. The soul beheld its features in the mirror of the passing moment. It was with fear, and tremulously, and, as it were, by a slow, reluctant necessity, that Arthur Dimmesdale put forth his hand, chill as death, and touched the chill hand of Hester Prynne. The grasp, cold as it was, took away what was dreariest in the interview. They now felt themselves, at least, inhabitants of the same sphere.

Without a word more spoken—neither he nor she assuming the guidance, but with an unexpressed consent—they glided back into the shadow of the woods whence Hester had emerged, and sat down on the heap of moss where she and

Pearl had before been sitting. When they found voice to speak, it was at first only to utter remarks and inquiries such as any two acquaintances might have made, about the gloomy sky, the threatening storm, and, next, the health of each. Thus they went onward, not boldly, but step by step, into the themes that were brooding deepest in their hearts. So long estranged by fate and circumstances, they needed something slight and casual to run before and throw open the doors of intercourse, so that their real thoughts might be led across the threshold.

After awhile, the minister fixed his eyes on Hester Prynne's.

"Hester," said he, "hast thou found peace?"

She smiled drearily, looking down upon her bosom.

"Hast thou?" she asked.

"None—nothing but despair!" he answered. "What else could I look for, being what I am, and leading such a life as mine? Were I an atheist—a man devoid of conscience—a wretch with coarse and brutal instincts—I might have found peace long ere now. Nay, I never should have lost it. But, as matters stand with my soul, whatever of good capacity there originally was in me, all of God's gifts that were the choicest have become the ministers of spiritual torment. Hester, I am most miserable!"

"The people reverence thee," said Hester. "And surely thou workest good among them! Doth this bring thee no comfort?"

"More misery, Hester!—Only the more misery!" answered the clergyman with a bitter smile. "As concerns the good which I may appear to do, I have no faith in it. It must needs be a delusion. What can a ruined soul like mine effect towards the redemption of other souls?—or a polluted soul towards their purification? And as for the people's reverence, would that it were turned to scorn and hatred! Canst thou deem it, Hester, a consolation that I must stand up in my pulpit, and meet so many eyes turned upward to my face, as if the light of heaven were beaming from it!—must see my flock hungry for the truth, and listening to my words as if a tongue of Pentecost were speaking!—and then look inward, and discern the black reality of what they idolise? I have laughed, in bitterness and agony of heart, at the contrast between what I seem and what I am! And Satan laughs at it!"

"You wrong yourself in this," said Hester gently. "You have deeply and sorely repented. Your sin is left behind you in the days long past. Your present life is not less holy, in very truth, than it seems in people's eyes. Is there no reality in the penitence thus sealed and witnessed by good works? And wherefore should it not bring you peace?"

"No, Hester—no!" replied the clergyman. "There is no substance in it! It is cold and dead, and can do nothing for me! Of penance, I have had enough! Of penitence, there has been none! Else, I should long ago have thrown off these garments of mock holiness, and have shown myself to mankind as they will see me at the judgment-seat. Happy are you, Hester, that wear the scarlet letter openly upon your bosom! Mine burns in secret! Thou little knowest what a relief it is, after the torment of a seven years' cheat, to look into an eye that recognises me for what I am! Had I one friend—or were it my worst enemy!—to whom, when sickened with the praises of all other men, I could daily betake myself, and be known as the vilest of all sinners, methinks my soul might keep itself alive thereby. Even thus much of truth would save me! But now, it is all falsehood!—all emptiness!—all death!"

Hester Prynne looked into his face, but hesitated to speak. Yet, uttering his long-restrained emotions so vehemently as he did, his words here offered her the very point of circumstances in which to interpose what she came to say. She conquered her fears, and spoke:

"Such a friend as thou hast even now wished for," said she, "with whom to weep over thy sin, thou hast in me, the partner of it!" Again she hesitated, but brought out the words with an effort.—"Thou hast long had such an enemy, and dwellest with him, under the same roof!"

The minister started to his feet, gasping for breath, and clutching at his heart, as if he would have torn it out of his bosom.

"Ha! What sayest thou?" cried he. "An enemy! And under mine own roof! What mean you?"

Hester Prynne was now fully sensible of the deep injury for which she was responsible to this unhappy man, in permitting him to lie for so many years, or, indeed, for a single moment, at the mercy of one whose purposes could not be other than malevolent. The very contiguity of his enemy, beneath whatever mask the latter might conceal himself, was enough to disturb the magnetic sphere of a being so sensitive as Arthur Dimmesdale. There had been a period when Hester was less alive to this consideration; or, perhaps, in the misanthropy of her own trouble, she left the minister to bear what she might picture to herself as a more tolerable doom. But of late, since the night of his vigil, all her sympathies towards him had been both softened and invigorated. She now read his heart more accurately. She doubted not that the continual presence of Roger Chillingworth—the secret poison of his malignity, infecting all the air about him—and his authorised interference, as a physician, with the minister's physical and spiritual infirmities—that these bad opportunities had been turned to a cruel purpose. By means of them, the sufferer's conscience had been kept in an irritated state, the tendency of which was, not to cure by wholesome pain, but to disorganize and corrupt his spiritual being. Its result, on earth, could hardly fail to be insanity, and hereafter, that eternal alienation from the Good and True, of which madness is perhaps the earthly type.

Such was the ruin to which she had brought the man, once—nay, why should we not speak it?—still so passionately loved! Hester felt that the sacrifice of the clergyman's good name, and death itself, as she had already told Roger Chillingworth, would have been infinitely preferable to the alternative which she had taken upon herself to choose. And now, rather than have had this grievous wrong to confess, she would gladly have laid down on the forest leaves, and died there, at Arthur Dimmesdale's feet.

"Oh, Arthur!" cried she, "forgive me! In all things else, I have striven to be true! Truth was the one virtue which I might have held fast, and did hold fast, through all extremity; save when thy good—thy life—thy fame—were put in question! Then I consented to a deception. But a lie is never good, even though death threaten on the other side! Dost thou not see what I would say? That old man!—the physician!—he whom they call Roger Chillingworth!—he was my husband!"

The minister looked at her for an instant, with all that violence of passion, which—intermixed in more shapes than one with his higher, purer, softer qualities—was, in fact, the portion of him which the devil claimed, and through which he sought to win the rest. Never was there a blacker or a fiercer frown than Hester now encountered. For the brief space that it lasted, it was a dark transfiguration. But his character had been so much enfeebled by suffering, that even its lower energies were incapable of more than a temporary struggle. He sank down on the ground, and buried his face in his hands.

"I might have known it," murmured he—"I did know it! Was not the secret told me, in the natural recoil of my heart at the first sight of him, and as often as I have seen him since? Why did I not understand? Oh, Hester Prynne, thou little, little knowest all the horror of this thing! And the shame!—the indelicacy!—the horrible ugliness of this exposure of a sick and guilty heart to the very eye that would gloat over it! Woman, woman, thou art accountable for this!—I cannot forgive thee!"

"Thou shalt forgive me!" cried Hester, flinging herself on the fallen leaves beside him. "Let God punish! Thou shalt forgive!"

With sudden and desperate tenderness she threw her arms around him, and pressed his head against her bosom, little caring though his cheek rested on the scarlet letter. He would have released himself, but strove in vain to do so. Hester would not set him free, lest he should look her sternly in the face. All the world had frowned on her—for seven long years had it frowned upon this lonely woman—and still she bore it all, nor ever once turned away her firm, sad eyes. Heaven, likewise, had frowned upon her, and she had not died. But the frown of this pale, weak, sinful, and sorrow-stricken man was what Hester could not bear, and live!

"Wilt thou yet forgive me?" she repeated, over and over again.

"Wilt thou not frown? Wilt thou forgive?"

"I do forgive you, Hester," replied the minister at length, with a deep utterance, out of an abyss of sadness, but no anger. "I freely forgive you now. May God forgive us both. We are not, Hester, the worst sinners in the world. There is one worse than even the polluted priest! That old man's revenge has been blacker than my sin. He has violated, in cold blood, the sanctity of a human heart. Thou and I, Hester, never did so!"

"Never, never!" whispered she. "What we did had a consecration of its own. We felt it so! We said so to each other. Hast thou forgotten it?"

"Hush, Hester!" said Arthur Dimmesdale, rising from the ground.

"No; I have not forgotten!"

They sat down again, side by side, and hand clasped in hand, on the mossy trunk of the fallen tree. Life had never brought them a gloomier hour; it was the point whither their pathway had so long been tending, and darkening ever, as it stole along—and yet it unclosed a charm that made them linger upon it, and claim another, and another, and, after all, another moment. The forest was obscure around them, and creaked with a blast that was passing through it. The boughs were tossing heavily above their heads; while one solemn old tree groaned dolefully to another, as if telling the sad story of the pair that sat beneath, or constrained to forbode evil to come.

And yet they lingered. How dreary looked the forest-track that led backward to the settlement, where Hester Prynne must take up again the burden of her ignominy and the minister the hollow mockery of his good name! So they lingered an instant longer. No golden light had ever been so precious as the gloom of this dark forest. Here seen only by his eyes, the scarlet letter need not burn into the bosom of the fallen woman! Here seen only by her eyes, Arthur Dimmesdale, false to God and man, might be, for one moment true!

He started at a thought that suddenly occurred to him.

"Hester!" cried he, "here is a new horror! Roger Chillingworth knows your purpose to reveal his true character. Will he continue, then, to keep our secret? What will now be the course of his revenge?"

"There is a strange secrecy in his nature," replied Hester, thoughtfully; "and it has grown upon him by the hidden practices of his revenge. I deem it not likely that he will betray the secret. He will doubtless seek other means of satiating his dark passion."

"And I!—how am I to live longer, breathing the same air with this deadly enemy?" exclaimed Arthur Dimmesdale, shrinking within himself, and pressing his hand nervously against his heart—a gesture that had grown involuntary with him. "Think for me, Hester! Thou art strong. Resolve for me!"

"Thou must dwell no longer with this man," said Hester, slowly and firmly. "Thy heart must be no longer under his evil eye!"

"It were far worse than death!" replied the minister. "But how to avoid it? What choice remains to me? Shall I lie down again on these withered leaves, where I cast myself when thou didst tell me what he was? Must I sink down there, and die at once?"

"Alas! what a ruin has befallen thee!" said Hester, with the tears gushing into her eyes. "Wilt thou die for very weakness? There is no other cause!"

"The judgment of God is on me," answered the conscience-stricken priest. "It is too mighty for me to struggle with!"

"Heaven would show mercy," rejoined Hester, "hadst thou but the strength to take advantage of it."

"Be thou strong for me!" answered he. "Advise me what to do."

"Is the world, then, so narrow?" exclaimed Hester Prynne, fixing her deep eyes on the minister's, and instinctively exercising a magnetic power over a spirit so shattered and subdued that it could hardly hold itself erect. "Doth the universe lie within the compass of yonder town, which only a little time ago was but a leaf-strewn desert, as lonely as this around us? Whither leads yonder forest-track? Backward to the settlement, thou sayest! Yes; but, onward, too! Deeper it goes, and deeper into the wilderness, less plainly to be seen at every step; until some few miles hence the yellow leaves will show no vestige of the white man's tread. There thou art free! So brief a journey would bring thee from a world where thou hast been most wretched, to one where thou mayest still be happy! Is there not shade enough in all this boundless forest to hide thy heart from the gaze of Roger Chillingworth?"

"Yes, Hester; but only under the fallen leaves!" replied the minister, with a sad smile.

"Then there is the broad pathway of the sea!" continued Hester. "It brought thee hither. If thou so choose, it will bear thee back again. In our native land, whether in some remote rural village, or in vast London—or, surely, in Germany, in France, in pleasant Italy—thou wouldst be beyond his power and knowledge! And what hast thou to do with all these iron men, and their opinions? They have kept thy better part in bondage too long already!"

"It cannot be!" answered the minister, listening as if he were called upon to realise a dream. "I am powerless to go. Wretched and sinful as I am, I have had no other thought than to drag on my earthly existence in the sphere where Providence hath placed me. Lost as my own soul is, I would still do what I may for other human souls! I dare not quit my post, though an unfaithful sentinel, whose sure reward is death and dishonour, when his dreary watch shall come to an end!"

"Thou art crushed under this seven years' weight of misery," replied Hester, fervently resolved to buoy him up with her own energy. "But thou shalt leave it all behind thee! It shall not cumber thy steps, as thou treadest along the forest-path: neither shalt thou freight the ship with it, if thou prefer to cross the sea. Leave this wreck and ruin here where it hath happened. Meddle no more with it! Begin all anew! Hast thou exhausted possibility in the failure of this one trial? Not so! The future is yet full of trial and success. There is happiness to be enjoyed! There is good to be done! Exchange this false life of thine for a true one. Be, if thy spirit summon thee to such a mission, the teacher and apostle of the red men. Or, as is more thy nature, be a scholar and a sage among the wisest and the most renowned of the cultivated world. Preach! Write! Act! Do anything, save to lie down and die! Give up this name of Arthur Dimmesdale, and make thyself another, and a high one, such as thou canst wear without fear or shame. Why shouldst thou tarry so much as one other day in the torments that have so gnawed into thy life? that have made thee feeble to will and to do? that will leave thee powerless even to repent? Up, and away!"

"Oh, Hester!" cried Arthur Dimmesdale, in whose eyes a fitful light, kindled by her enthusiasm, flashed up and died away, "thou tellest of running a race to a man whose knees are tottering beneath him! I must die here! There is not the strength or courage left me to venture into the wide, strange, difficult world alone!"

It was the last expression of the despondency of a broken spirit. He lacked energy to grasp the better fortune that seemed within his reach.

He repeated the word—"Alone, Hester!"

"Thou shall not go alone!" answered she, in a deep whisper.

Then, all was spoken!

XVIII. A FLOOD OF SUNSHINE

Arthur Dimmesdale gazed into Hester's face with a look in which hope and joy shone out, indeed, but with fear betwixt them, and a kind of horror at her boldness, who had spoken what he vaguely hinted at, but dared not speak.

But Hester Prynne, with a mind of native courage and activity, and for so long a period not merely estranged, but outlawed from society, had habituated herself to such latitude of speculation as was altogether foreign to the clergyman. She had wandered, without rule or guidance, in a moral wilderness, as vast, as intricate, and shadowy as the untamed forest, amid the gloom of which they were now holding a colloquy that was to decide their fate. Her intellect and heart had their home, as it were, in desert places, where she roamed as freely as the wild Indian in his woods. For years past she had looked from this estranged point of view at human institutions, and whatever priests or legislators had established; criticising all with hardly more reverence than the Indian would feel for the clerical band, the judicial robe, the pillory, the gallows, the fireside, or the church. The tendency of her fate and fortunes had been to set her free. The scarlet letter was her passport into regions where other women dared not tread. Shame, Despair, Solitude! These had been her teachers—stern and wild ones—and they had made her strong, but taught her much amiss.

The minister, on the other hand, had never gone through an experience calculated to lead him beyond the scope of generally received laws; although, in a single instance, he had so fearfully transgressed one of the most sacred of them. But this had been a sin of passion, not of principle, nor even purpose. Since that wretched epoch, he had watched with morbid zeal and minuteness, not his acts—for those it was easy to arrange—but each breath of emotion, and his every thought. At the head of the social system, as the clergymen of that day stood, he was only the more trammelled by its regulations, its principles, and even its prejudices. As a priest, the framework of his order inevitably hemmed him in. As a man who had once sinned, but who kept his conscience all alive and painfully sensitive by the fretting of an unhealed wound, he might have been supposed safer within the line of virtue than if he had never sinned at all.

Thus we seem to see that, as regarded Hester Prynne, the whole seven years of outlaw and ignominy had been little other than a preparation for this very hour. But Arthur Dimmesdale! Were such a man once more to fall, what plea could be urged in extenuation of his crime? None; unless it avail him somewhat that he was broken down by long and exquisite suffering; that his mind was darkened and confused by the very remorse which harrowed it; that, between fleeing as an avowed criminal, and remaining as a hypocrite, conscience might find it hard to strike the balance; that it was human to avoid the peril of death and infamy, and the inscrutable machinations of an enemy; that, finally, to this poor pilgrim, on his dreary and desert path, faint, sick, miserable, there appeared a glimpse of human affection and sympathy, a new life, and a true one, in exchange for the heavy doom which he was now expiating. And be the stern and sad truth spoken, that the breach which guilt has once made into the human soul is never, in this mortal state, repaired. It may be watched and guarded, so that the enemy shall not force his way again into the citadel, and might even in his subsequent assaults, select some other avenue, in preference to that where he had formerly succeeded. But there is still the ruined wall, and near it the stealthy tread of the foe that would win over again his unforgotten triumph.

The struggle, if there were one, need not be described. Let it suffice that the clergyman resolved to flee, and not alone.

"If in all these past seven years," thought he, "I could recall one instant of peace or hope, I would yet endure, for the sake of that earnest of Heaven's mercy. But now—since I am irrevocably doomed—wherefore should I not snatch the solace allowed to the condemned culprit before his execution? Or, if this be the path to a better life, as Hester would persuade me, I surely give up no fairer prospect by pursuing it! Neither can I any longer live without her companionship; so powerful is she to sustain—so tender to soothe! O Thou to whom I dare not lift mine eyes, wilt Thou yet pardon me?"

"Thou wilt go!" said Hester calmly, as he met her glance.

The decision once made, a glow of strange enjoyment threw its flickering brightness over the trouble of his breast. It was the exhilarating effect—upon a prisoner just escaped from the dungeon of his own heart—of breathing the wild, free atmosphere of an unredeemed, unchristianised, lawless region. His spirit rose, as it were, with a bound, and attained a nearer prospect of the sky, than throughout all the misery which had kept him grovelling on the earth. Of a deeply religious temperament, there was inevitably a tinge of the devotional in his mood.

"Do I feel joy again?" cried he, wondering at himself. "Methought the germ of it was dead in me! Oh, Hester, thou art my better angel! I seem to have flung myself—sick, sin-stained, and sorrow-blackened—down upon these forest leaves, and to have risen up all made anew, and with new powers to glorify Him that hath been merciful! This is already the better life! Why did we not find it sooner?"

"Let us not look back," answered Hester Prynne. "The past is gone! Wherefore should we linger upon it now? See! With this symbol I undo it all, and make it as if it had never been!"

So speaking, she undid the clasp that fastened the scarlet letter, and, taking it from her bosom, threw it to a distance among the withered leaves. The mystic token alighted on the hither verge of the stream. With a hand's-breadth further flight, it would have fallen into the water, and have given the little brook another woe to carry onward, besides the unintelligible tale which it still kept murmuring about. But there lay the embroidered letter, glittering like a lost jewel, which some ill-fated wanderer might pick up, and thenceforth be haunted by strange phantoms of guilt, sinkings of the heart, and unaccountable misfortune.

The stigma gone, Hester heaved a long, deep sigh, in which the burden of shame and anguish departed from her spirit. O exquisite relief! She had not known the weight until she felt the freedom! By another impulse, she took off the formal cap that confined her hair, and down it fell upon her shoulders, dark and rich, with at once a shadow and a light in its abundance, and imparting the charm of softness to her features. There played around her mouth, and beamed out of her eyes, a radiant and tender smile, that seemed gushing from the very heart of womanhood. A crimson flush was glowing on her cheek, that had been long so pale. Her sex, her youth, and the whole richness of her beauty, came back from what men call the irrevocable past, and clustered themselves with her maiden hope, and a happiness before unknown, within the magic circle of this hour. And, as if the gloom of the earth and sky had been but the effluence of these two mortal hearts, it vanished with their sorrow. All at once, as with a sudden smile of heaven, forth burst the sunshine, pouring a very flood into the obscure forest, gladdening each green leaf, transmuting the yellow fallen ones to gold, and gleaming adown the gray trunks of the solemn trees. The objects that had made a shadow hitherto, embodied the brightness now. The course of the little brook might be traced by its merry gleam afar into the wood's heart of mystery, which had become a mystery of joy.

Such was the sympathy of Nature—that wild, heathen Nature of the forest, never subjugated by human law, nor illumined by higher truth—with the bliss of these two spirits! Love, whether newly-born, or aroused from a death-like slumber, must always create a sunshine, filling the heart so full of radiance, that it overflows upon the outward world. Had the forest still kept its gloom, it would have been bright in Hester's eyes, and bright in Arthur Dimmesdale's!

Hester looked at him with a thrill of another joy.

"Thou must know Pearl!" said she. "Our little Pearl! Thou hast seen her—yes, I know it!—but thou wilt see her now with other eyes. She is a strange child! I hardly comprehend her! But thou wilt love her dearly, as I do, and wilt advise me how to deal with her!"

"Dost thou think the child will be glad to know me?" asked the minister, somewhat uneasily. "I have long shrunk from children, because they often show a distrust—a backwardness to be familiar with me. I have even been afraid of little Pearl!"

"Ah, that was sad!" answered the mother. "But she will love thee dearly, and thou her. She is not far off. I will call her. Pearl! Pearl!"

"I see the child," observed the minister. "Yonder she is, standing in a streak of sunshine, a good way off, on the other side of the brook. So thou thinkest the child will love me?"

Hester smiled, and again called to Pearl, who was visible at some distance, as the minister had described her, like a bright-apparelled vision in a sunbeam, which fell down upon her through an arch of boughs. The ray quivered to and fro, making her figure dim or distinct—now like a real child, now like a child's spirit—as the splendour went and came again. She heard her mother's voice, and approached slowly through the forest.

Pearl had not found the hour pass wearisomely while her mother sat talking with the clergyman. The great black forest—stern as it showed itself to those who brought the guilt and troubles of the world into its bosom—became the playmate of the lonely infant, as well as it knew how. Sombre as it was, it put on the kindest of its moods to welcome her. It offered her the partridge-berries, the growth of the preceding autumn, but ripening only in the spring, and now red as drops of blood upon the withered leaves. These Pearl gathered, and was pleased with their wild flavour. The small denizens of the wilderness hardly took pains to move out of her path. A partridge, indeed, with a brood of ten behind her, ran forward threateningly, but soon repented of her fierceness, and clucked to her young ones not to be afraid. A pigeon, alone on a low branch, allowed Pearl to come beneath, and uttered a sound as much of greeting as alarm. A squirrel, from the lofty depths of his domestic tree, chattered either in anger or merriment—for the squirrel is such a choleric and humorous little personage, that it is hard to distinguish between his moods—so he chattered at the child, and flung down a nut upon her head. It was a last year's nut, and already gnawed by his sharp tooth. A fox, startled from his sleep by her light footstep on the leaves, looked inquisitively at Pearl, as doubting whether it were better to steal off, or renew his nap on the same spot. A wolf, it is said—but here the tale has surely lapsed into the improbable—came up and smelt of Pearl's robe, and offered his savage head to be patted by her hand. The truth seems to be, however, that the mother-forest, and these wild things which it nourished, all recognised a kindred wilderness in the human child.

And she was gentler here than in the grassy-margined streets of the settlement, or in her mother's cottage. The Bowers appeared to know it, and one and another whispered as she passed, "Adorn thyself with me, thou beautiful child, adorn thyself with me!"—and, to please them, Pearl gathered the violets, and anemones, and columbines, and some twigs of the freshest green, which the old trees held down before her eyes. With these she decorated her hair and her young waist, and became a nymph child, or an infant dryad, or whatever else was in closest sympathy with the antique wood. In such guise had Pearl adorned herself, when she heard her mother's voice, and came slowly back.

Slowly—for she saw the clergyman!

XIX. THE CHILD AT THE BROOKSIDE

"Thou wilt love her dearly," repeated Hester Prynne, as she and the minister sat watching little Pearl. "Dost thou not think her beautiful? And see with what natural skill she has made those simple flowers adorn her! Had she gathered pearls, and diamonds, and rubies in the wood, they could not have become her better! She is a splendid child! But I know whose brow she has!"

"Dost thou know, Hester," said Arthur Dimmesdale, with an unquiet smile, "that this dear child, tripping about always at thy side, hath caused me many an alarm? Methought—oh, Hester, what a thought is that, and how terrible to dread it!—that my own features were partly repeated in her face, and so strikingly that the world might see them! But she is mostly thine!"

"No, no! Not mostly!" answered the mother, with a tender smile. "A little longer, and thou needest not to be afraid to trace whose child she is. But how strangely beautiful she looks with those wild flowers in her hair! It is as if one of the fairies, whom we left in dear old England, had decked her out to meet us."

It was with a feeling which neither of them had ever before experienced, that they sat and watched Pearl's slow advance. In her was visible the tie that united them. She had been offered to the world, these seven past years, as the living hieroglyphic, in which was revealed the secret they so darkly sought to hide—all written in this symbol—all plainly manifest—had there been a prophet or magician skilled to read the character of flame! And Pearl was the oneness of their being. Be the foregone evil what it might, how could they doubt that their earthly lives and future destinies were conjoined when they beheld at once the material union, and the spiritual idea, in whom they met, and were to dwell immortally together; thoughts like these—and perhaps other thoughts, which they did not acknowledge or define—threw an awe about the child as she came onward.

"Let her see nothing strange—no passion or eagerness—in thy way of accosting her," whispered Hester. "Our Pearl is a fitful and fantastic little elf sometimes. Especially she is generally intolerant of emotion, when she does not fully comprehend the why and wherefore. But the child hath strong affections! She loves me, and will love thee!"

"Thou canst not think," said the minister, glancing aside at Hester Prynne, "how my heart dreads this interview, and yearns for it! But, in truth, as I already told thee, children are not readily won to be familiar with me. They will not climb my knee, nor prattle in my ear, nor answer to my smile, but stand apart, and eye me strangely. Even little babes, when I take them in my arms, weep bitterly. Yet Pearl, twice in her little lifetime, hath been kind to me! The first time—thou knowest it well! The last was when thou ledst her with thee to the house of yonder stern old Governor."

"And thou didst plead so bravely in her behalf and mine!" answered the mother. "I remember it; and so shall little Pearl. Fear nothing. She may be strange and shy at first, but will soon learn to love thee!"

By this time Pearl had reached the margin of the brook, and stood on the further side, gazing silently at Hester and the clergyman, who still sat together on the mossy tree-trunk waiting to receive her. Just where she had paused, the brook chanced to form a pool so smooth and quiet that it reflected a perfect image of her little figure, with all the brilliant picturesqueness of her beauty, in its adornment of flowers and wreathed foliage, but more refined and spiritualized than the reality. This image, so nearly identical with the living Pearl, seemed to communicate somewhat of its own shadowy and intangible quality to the child herself. It was strange, the way in which Pearl stood, looking so steadfastly at them through the dim medium of the forest gloom, herself, meanwhile, all glorified with a ray of sunshine, that was attracted thitherward as by a certain sympathy. In the brook beneath stood another child—another and the same—with likewise its ray of golden light. Hester felt herself, in some indistinct and tantalizing manner, estranged from Pearl, as if the child, in her lonely ramble through the forest, had strayed out of the sphere in which she and her mother dwelt together, and was now vainly seeking to return to it.

There were both truth and error in the impression; the child and mother were estranged, but through Hester's fault, not Pearl's. Since the latter rambled from her side, another inmate had been admitted within the circle of the mother's feelings, and so modified the aspect of them all, that Pearl, the returning wanderer, could not find her wonted place, and hardly knew where she was.

"I have a strange fancy," observed the sensitive minister, "that this brook is the boundary between two worlds, and that thou canst never meet thy Pearl again. Or is she an elfish spirit, who, as the legends of our childhood taught us, is forbidden to cross a running stream? Pray hasten her, for this delay has already imparted a tremor to my nerves."

"Come, dearest child!" said Hester encouragingly, and stretching out both her arms. "How slow thou art! When hast thou been so sluggish before now? Here is a friend of mine, who must be thy friend also. Thou wilt have twice as much love henceforward as thy mother alone could give thee! Leap across the brook and come to us. Thou canst leap like a young deer!"

Pearl, without responding in any manner to these honey-sweet expressions, remained on the other side of the brook. Now she fixed her bright wild eyes on her mother, now on the minister, and now included them both in the same glance, as if to detect and explain to herself the relation which they bore to one another. For some unaccountable reason, as Arthur Dimmesdale felt the child's eyes upon himself, his hand—with that gesture so habitual as to have become involuntary—stole over his heart. At length, assuming a singular air of authority, Pearl stretched out her hand, with the small forefinger extended, and pointing evidently towards her mother's breast. And beneath, in the mirror of the brook, there was the flower-girdled and sunny image of little Pearl, pointing her small forefinger too.

"Thou strange child! why dost thou not come to me?" exclaimed Hester.

Pearl still pointed with her forefinger, and a frown gathered on her brow—the more impressive from the childish, the almost baby-like aspect of the features that conveyed it. As her mother still kept beckoning to her, and arraying her face in a holiday suit of unaccustomed smiles, the child stamped her foot with a yet more imperious look and gesture. In the brook, again, was the fantastic beauty of the image, with its reflected frown, its pointed finger, and imperious gesture, giving emphasis to the aspect of little Pearl.

"Hasten, Pearl, or I shall be angry with thee!" cried Hester Prynne, who, however, inured to such behaviour on the elf-child's part at other seasons, was naturally anxious for a more seemly deportment now. "Leap across the brook, naughty child, and run hither! Else I must come to thee!"

But Pearl, not a whit startled at her mother's threats any more than mollified by her entreaties, now suddenly burst into a fit of passion, gesticulating violently, and throwing her small figure into the most extravagant contortions. She accompanied this wild outbreak with piercing shrieks, which the woods reverberated on all sides, so that, alone as she was in her childish and unreasonable wrath, it seemed as if a hidden multitude were lending her their sympathy and encouragement. Seen in the brook once more was the shadowy wrath of Pearl's image, crowned and girdled with flowers, but stamping its foot, wildly gesticulating, and, in the midst of all, still pointing its small forefinger at Hester's bosom.

"I see what ails the child," whispered Hester to the clergyman, and turning pale in spite of a strong effort to conceal her trouble and annoyance, "Children will not abide any, the slightest, change in the accustomed aspect of things that are daily before their eyes. Pearl misses something that she has always seen me wear!"

"I pray you," answered the minister, "if thou hast any means of pacifying the child, do it forthwith! Save it were the cankered wrath of an old witch like Mistress Hibbins," added he, attempting to smile, "I know nothing that I would not sooner encounter than this passion in a child. In Pearl's young beauty, as in the wrinkled witch, it has a preternatural effect. Pacify her if thou lovest me!"

Hester turned again towards Pearl with a crimson blush upon her cheek, a conscious glance aside clergyman, and then a heavy sigh, while, even before she had time to speak, the blush yielded to a deadly pallor.

"Pearl," said she sadly, "look down at thy feet! There!—before thee!—on the hither side of the brook!"

The child turned her eyes to the point indicated, and there lay the scarlet letter so close upon the margin of the stream that the gold embroidery was reflected in it.

"Bring it hither!" said Hester.

"Come thou and take it up!" answered Pearl.

"Was ever such a child!" observed Hester aside to the minister. "Oh, I have much to tell thee about her! But, in very truth, she is right as regards this hateful token. I must bear its torture yet a little longer—only a few days longer—until we shall have left this region, and look back hither as to a land which we have dreamed of. The forest cannot hide it! The mid-ocean shall take it from my hand, and swallow it up for ever!"

With these words she advanced to the margin of the brook, took up the scarlet letter, and fastened it again into her bosom. Hopefully, but a moment ago, as Hester had spoken of drowning it in the deep sea, there was a sense of inevitable doom upon her as she thus received back this deadly symbol from the hand of fate. She had flung it into infinite space! she had drawn an hour's free breath! and here again was the scarlet misery glittering on the old spot! So it ever is, whether thus typified or no, that an evil deed invests itself with the character of doom. Hester next gathered up the heavy tresses of her hair and confined them beneath her cap. As if there were a withering spell in the sad letter, her beauty, the warmth and richness of her womanhood, departed like fading sunshine, and a gray shadow seemed to fall across her.

When the dreary change was wrought, she extended her hand to
Pearl.

"Dost thou know thy mother now, child?", asked she, reproachfully, but with a subdued tone. "Wilt thou come across the brook, and own thy mother, now that she has her shame upon her—now that she is sad?"

"Yes; now I will!" answered the child, bounding across the brook, and clasping Hester in her arms "Now thou art my mother indeed! and I am thy little Pearl!"

In a mood of tenderness that was not usual with her, she drew down her mother's head, and kissed her brow and both her cheeks. But then—by a kind of necessity that always impelled this child to alloy whatever comfort she might chance to give with a throb of anguish—Pearl put up her mouth and kissed the scarlet letter, too.

"That was not kind!" said Hester. "When thou hast shown me a little love, thou mockest me!"

"Why doth the minister sit yonder?" asked Pearl.

"He waits to welcome thee," replied her mother. "Come thou, and entreat his blessing! He loves thee, my little Pearl, and loves thy mother, too. Wilt thou not love him? Come he longs to greet thee!"

"Doth he love us?" said Pearl, looking up with acute intelligence into her mother's face. "Will he go back with us, hand in hand, we three together, into the town?"

"Not now, my child," answered Hester. "But in days to come he will walk hand in hand with us. We will have a home and fireside of our own; and thou shalt sit upon his knee; and he will teach thee many things, and love thee dearly. Thou wilt love him—wilt thou not?"

"And will he always keep his hand over his heart?" inquired

Pearl.

"Foolish child, what a question is that!" exclaimed her mother.

"Come, and ask his blessing!"

But, whether influenced by the jealousy that seems instinctive with every petted child towards a dangerous rival, or from whatever caprice of her freakish nature, Pearl would show no favour to the clergyman. It was only by an exertion of force that her mother brought her up to him, hanging back, and manifesting her reluctance by odd grimaces; of which, ever since her babyhood, she had possessed a singular variety, and could transform her mobile physiognomy into a series of different aspects, with a new mischief in them, each and all. The minister—painfully embarrassed, but hoping that a kiss might prove a talisman to admit him into the child's kindlier regards—bent forward, and impressed one on her brow. Hereupon, Pearl broke away from her mother, and, running to the brook, stooped over it, and bathed her forehead, until the unwelcome kiss was quite washed off and diffused through a long lapse of the gliding water. She then remained apart, silently watching Hester and the clergyman; while they talked together and made such arrangements as were suggested by their new position and the purposes soon to be fulfilled.

And now this fateful interview had come to a close. The dell was to be left in solitude among its dark, old trees, which, with their multitudinous tongues, would whisper long of what had passed there, and no mortal be the wiser. And the melancholy brook would add this other tale to the mystery with which its little heart was already overburdened, and whereof it still kept up a murmuring babble, with not a whit more cheerfulness of tone than for ages heretofore.

XX. THE MINISTER IN A MAZE

As the minister departed, in advance of Hester Prynne and little Pearl, he threw a backward glance, half expecting that he should discover only some faintly traced features or outline of the mother and the child, slowly fading into the twilight of the woods. So great a vicissitude in his life could not at once be received as real. But there was Hester, clad in her gray robe, still standing beside the tree-trunk, which some blast had overthrown a long antiquity ago, and which time had ever since been covering with moss, so that these two fated ones, with earth's heaviest burden on them, might there sit down together, and find a single hour's rest and solace. And there was Pearl, too, lightly dancing from the margin of the brook—now that the intrusive third person was gone—and taking her old place by her mother's side. So the minister had not fallen asleep and dreamed!

In order to free his mind from this indistinctness and duplicity of impression, which vexed it with a strange disquietude, he recalled and more thoroughly defined the plans which Hester and himself had sketched for their departure. It had been determined between them that the Old World, with its crowds and cities, offered them a more eligible shelter and concealment than the wilds of New England or all America, with its alternatives of an Indian wigwam, or the few settlements of Europeans scattered thinly along the sea-board. Not to speak of the clergyman's health, so inadequate to sustain the hardships of a forest life, his native gifts, his culture, and his entire development would secure him a home only in the midst of civilization and refinement; the higher the state the more delicately adapted to it the man. In furtherance of this choice, it so happened that a ship lay in the harbour; one of those unquestionable cruisers, frequent at that day, which, without being absolutely outlaws of the deep, yet roamed over its surface with a remarkable irresponsibility of character. This vessel had recently arrived from the Spanish Main, and within three days' time would sail for Bristol. Hester Prynne—whose vocation, as a self-enlisted Sister of Charity, had brought her acquainted with the captain and crew—could take upon herself to secure the passage of two individuals and a child with all the secrecy which circumstances rendered more than desirable.

The minister had inquired of Hester, with no little interest, the precise time at which the vessel might be expected to depart. It would probably be on the fourth day from the present. "This is most fortunate!" he had then said to himself. Now, why the Reverend Mr. Dimmesdale considered it so very fortunate we hesitate to reveal. Nevertheless—to hold nothing back from the reader—it was because, on the third day from the present, he was to preach the Election Sermon; and, as such an occasion formed an honourable epoch in the life of a New England Clergyman, he could not have chanced upon a more suitable mode and time of terminating his professional career. "At least, they shall say of me," thought this exemplary man, "that I leave no public duty unperformed or ill-performed!" Sad, indeed, that an introspection so profound and acute as this poor minister's should be so miserably deceived! We have had, and may still have, worse things to tell of him; but none, we apprehend, so pitiably weak; no evidence, at once so slight and irrefragable, of a subtle disease that had long since begun to eat into the real substance of his character. No man, for any considerable period, can wear one face to himself and another to the multitude, without finally getting bewildered as to which may be the true.

The excitement of Mr. Dimmesdale's feelings as he returned from his interview with Hester, lent him unaccustomed physical energy, and hurried him townward at a rapid pace. The pathway among the woods seemed wilder, more uncouth with its rude natural obstacles, and less trodden by the foot of man, than he remembered it on his outward journey. But he leaped across the plashy places, thrust himself through the clinging underbrush, climbed the ascent, plunged into the hollow, and overcame, in short, all the difficulties of the track, with an unweariable activity that astonished him. He could not but recall how feebly, and with what frequent pauses for breath he had toiled over the same ground, only two days before. As he drew near the town, he took an impression of change from the series of familiar objects that presented themselves. It seemed not yesterday, not one, not two, but many days, or even years ago, since he had quitted them. There, indeed, was each former trace of the street, as he remembered it, and all the peculiarities of the houses, with the due multitude of gable-peaks, and a weather-cock at every point where his memory suggested one. Not the less, however, came this importunately obtrusive sense of change. The same was true as regarded the acquaintances whom he met, and all the well-known shapes of human life, about the little town. They looked neither older nor younger now; the beards of the aged were no whiter, nor could the creeping babe of yesterday walk on his feet to-day; it was impossible to describe in what respect they differed from the individuals on whom he had so recently bestowed a parting glance; and yet the minister's deepest sense seemed to inform him of their mutability. A similar impression struck him most remarkably as he passed under the walls of his own church. The edifice had so very strange, and yet so familiar an aspect, that Mr. Dimmesdale's mind vibrated between two ideas; either that he had seen it only in a dream hitherto, or that he was merely dreaming about it now.

This phenomenon, in the various shapes which it assumed, indicated no external change, but so sudden and important a change in the spectator of the familiar scene, that the intervening space of a single day had operated on his consciousness like the lapse of years. The minister's own will, and Hester's will, and the fate that grew between them, had wrought this transformation. It was the same town as heretofore, but the same minister returned not from the forest. He might have said to the friends who greeted him—"I am not the man for whom you take me! I left him yonder in the forest, withdrawn into a secret dell, by a mossy tree trunk, and near a melancholy brook! Go, seek your minister, and see if his emaciated figure, his thin cheek, his white, heavy, pain-wrinkled brow, be not flung down there, like a cast-off garment!" His friends, no doubt, would still have insisted with him—"Thou art thyself the man!" but the error would have been their own, not his.

Before Mr. Dimmesdale reached home, his inner man gave him other evidences of a revolution in the sphere of thought and feeling. In truth, nothing short of a total change of dynasty and moral code, in that interior kingdom, was adequate to account for the impulses now communicated to the unfortunate and startled minister. At every step he was incited to do some strange, wild, wicked thing or other, with a sense that it would be at once involuntary and intentional, in spite of himself, yet growing out of a profounder self than that which opposed the impulse. For instance, he met one of his own deacons. The good old man addressed him with the paternal affection and patriarchal privilege which his venerable age, his upright and holy character, and his station in the church, entitled him to use and, conjoined with this, the deep, almost worshipping respect, which the minister's professional and private claims alike demanded. Never was there a more beautiful example of how the majesty of age and wisdom may comport with the obeisance and respect enjoined upon it, as from a lower social rank, and inferior order of endowment, towards a higher. Now, during a conversation of some two or three moments between the Reverend Mr. Dimmesdale and this excellent and hoary-bearded deacon, it was only by the most careful self-control that the former could refrain from uttering certain blasphemous suggestions that rose into his mind, respecting the communion-supper. He absolutely trembled and turned pale as ashes, lest his tongue should wag itself in utterance of these horrible matters, and plead his own consent for so doing, without his having fairly given it. And, even with this terror in his heart, he could hardly avoid laughing, to imagine how the sanctified old patriarchal deacon would have been petrified by his minister's impiety.

Again, another incident of the same nature. Hurrying along the street, the Reverend Mr. Dimmesdale encountered the eldest female member of his church, a most pious and exemplary old dame, poor, widowed, lonely, and with a heart as full of reminiscences about her dead husband and children, and her dead friends of long ago, as a burial-ground is full of storied gravestones. Yet all this, which would else have been such heavy sorrow, was made almost a solemn joy to her devout old soul, by religious consolations and the truths of Scripture, wherewith she had fed herself continually for more than thirty years. And since Mr. Dimmesdale had taken her in charge, the good grandam's chief earthly comfort—which, unless it had been likewise a heavenly comfort, could have been none at all—was to meet her pastor, whether casually, or of set purpose, and be refreshed with a word of warm, fragrant, heaven-breathing Gospel truth, from his beloved lips, into her dulled, but rapturously attentive ear. But, on this occasion, up to the moment of putting his lips to the old woman's ear, Mr. Dimmesdale, as the great enemy of souls would have it, could recall no text of Scripture, nor aught else, except a brief, pithy, and, as it then appeared to him, unanswerable argument against the immortality of the human soul. The instilment thereof into her mind would probably have caused this aged sister to drop down dead, at once, as by the effect of an intensely poisonous infusion. What he really did whisper, the minister could never afterwards recollect. There was, perhaps, a fortunate disorder in his utterance, which failed to impart any distinct idea to the good widows comprehension, or which Providence interpreted after a method of its own. Assuredly, as the minister looked back, he beheld an expression of divine gratitude and ecstasy that seemed like the shine of the celestial city on her face, so wrinkled and ashy pale.

Again, a third instance. After parting from the old church member, he met the youngest sister of them all. It was a maiden newly-won—and won by the Reverend Mr. Dimmesdale's own sermon, on the Sabbath after his vigil—to barter the transitory pleasures of the world for the heavenly hope that was to assume brighter substance as life grew dark around her, and which would gild the utter gloom with final glory. She was fair and pure as a lily that had bloomed in Paradise. The minister knew well that he was himself enshrined within the stainless sanctity of her heart, which hung its snowy curtains about his image, imparting to religion the warmth of love, and to love a religious purity. Satan, that afternoon, had surely led the poor young girl away from her mother's side, and thrown her into the pathway of this sorely tempted, or—shall we not rather say?—this lost and desperate man. As she drew nigh, the arch-fiend whispered him to condense into small compass, and drop into her tender bosom a germ of evil that would be sure to blossom darkly soon, and bear black fruit betimes. Such was his sense of power over this virgin soul, trusting him as she did, that the minister felt potent to blight all the field of innocence with but one wicked look, and develop all its opposite with but a word. So—with a mightier struggle than he had yet sustained—he held his Geneva cloak before his face, and hurried onward, making no sign of recognition, and leaving the young sister to digest his rudeness as she might. She ransacked her conscience—which was full of harmless little matters, like her pocket or her work-bag—and took herself to task, poor thing! for a thousand imaginary faults, and went about her household duties with swollen eyelids the next morning.

Before the minister had time to celebrate his victory over this last temptation, he was conscious of another impulse, more ludicrous, and almost as horrible. It was—we blush to tell it—it was to stop short in the road, and teach some very wicked words to a knot of little Puritan children who were playing there, and had but just begun to talk. Denying himself this freak, as unworthy of his cloth, he met a drunken seaman, one of the ship's crew from the Spanish Main. And here, since he had so valiantly forborne all other wickedness, poor Mr. Dimmesdale longed at least to shake hands with the tarry black-guard, and recreate himself with a few improper jests, such as dissolute sailors so abound with, and a volley of good, round, solid, satisfactory, and heaven-defying oaths! It was not so much a better principle, as partly his natural good taste, and still more his buckramed habit of clerical decorum, that carried him safely through the latter crisis.

"What is it that haunts and tempts me thus?" cried the minister to himself, at length, pausing in the street, and striking his hand against his forehead.

"Am I mad? or am I given over utterly to the fiend? Did I make a contract with him in the forest, and sign it with my blood? And does he now summon me to its fulfilment, by suggesting the performance of every wickedness which his most foul imagination can conceive?"

At the moment when the Reverend Mr. Dimmesdale thus communed with himself, and struck his forehead with his hand, old Mistress Hibbins, the reputed witch-lady, is said to have been passing by. She made a very grand appearance, having on a high head-dress, a rich gown of velvet, and a ruff done up with the famous yellow starch, of which Anne Turner, her especial friend, had taught her the secret, before this last good lady had been hanged for Sir Thomas Overbury's murder. Whether the witch had read the minister's thoughts or no, she came to a full stop, looked shrewdly into his face, smiled craftily, and—though little given to converse with clergymen—began a conversation.

"So, reverend sir, you have made a visit into the forest," observed the witch-lady, nodding her high head-dress at him. "The next time I pray you to allow me only a fair warning, and I shall be proud to bear you company. Without taking overmuch upon myself my good word will go far towards gaining any strange gentleman a fair reception from yonder potentate you wot of."

"I profess, madam," answered the clergyman, with a grave obeisance, such as the lady's rank demanded, and his own good breeding made imperative—"I profess, on my conscience and character, that I am utterly bewildered as touching the purport of your words! I went not into the forest to seek a potentate, neither do I, at any future time, design a visit thither, with a view to gaining the favour of such personage. My one sufficient object was to greet that pious friend of mine, the Apostle Eliot, and rejoice with him over the many precious souls he hath won from heathendom!"

"Ha, ha, ha!" cackled the old witch-lady, still nodding her high head-dress at the minister. "Well, well! we must needs talk thus in the daytime! You carry it off like an old hand! But at midnight, and in the forest, we shall have other talk together!"

She passed on with her aged stateliness, but often turning back her head and smiling at him, like one willing to recognise a secret intimacy of connexion.

"Have I then sold myself," thought the minister, "to the fiend whom, if men say true, this yellow-starched and velveted old hag has chosen for her prince and master?"

The wretched minister! He had made a bargain very like it! Tempted by a dream of happiness, he had yielded himself with deliberate choice, as he had never done before, to what he knew was deadly sin. And the infectious poison of that sin had been thus rapidly diffused throughout his moral system. It had stupefied all blessed impulses, and awakened into vivid life the whole brotherhood of bad ones. Scorn, bitterness, unprovoked malignity, gratuitous desire of ill, ridicule of whatever was good and holy, all awoke to tempt, even while they frightened him. And his encounter with old Mistress Hibbins, if it were a real incident, did but show its sympathy and fellowship with wicked mortals, and the world of perverted spirits.

He had by this time reached his dwelling on the edge of the burial ground, and, hastening up the stairs, took refuge in his study. The minister was glad to have reached this shelter, without first betraying himself to the world by any of those strange and wicked eccentricities to which he had been continually impelled while passing through the streets. He entered the accustomed room, and looked around him on its books, its windows, its fireplace, and the tapestried comfort of the walls, with the same perception of strangeness that had haunted him throughout his walk from the forest dell into the town and thitherward. Here he had studied and written; here gone through fast and vigil, and come forth half alive; here striven to pray; here borne a hundred thousand agonies! There was the Bible, in its rich old Hebrew, with Moses and the Prophets speaking to him, and God's voice through all.

There on the table, with the inky pen beside it, was an unfinished sermon, with a sentence broken in the midst, where his thoughts had ceased to gush out upon the page two days before. He knew that it was himself, the thin and white-cheeked minister, who had done and suffered these things, and written thus far into the Election Sermon! But he seemed to stand apart, and eye this former self with scornful pitying, but half-envious curiosity. That self was gone. Another man had returned out of the forest—a wiser one—with a knowledge of hidden mysteries which the simplicity of the former never could have reached. A bitter kind of knowledge that!

While occupied with these reflections, a knock came at the door of the study, and the minister said, "Come in!"—not wholly devoid of an idea that he might behold an evil spirit. And so he did! It was old Roger Chillingworth that entered. The minister stood white and speechless, with one hand on the Hebrew Scriptures, and the other spread upon his breast.

"Welcome home, reverend sir," said the physician "And how found you that godly man, the Apostle Eliot? But methinks, dear sir, you look pale, as if the travel through the wilderness had been too sore for you. Will not my aid be requisite to put you in heart and strength to preach your Election Sermon?"

"Nay, I think not so," rejoined the Reverend Mr. Dimmesdale. "My journey, and the sight of the holy Apostle yonder, and the free air which I have breathed have done me good, after so long confinement in my study. I think to need no more of your drugs, my kind physician, good though they be, and administered by a friendly hand."

All this time Roger Chillingworth was looking at the minister with the grave and intent regard of a physician towards his patient. But, in spite of this outward show, the latter was almost convinced of the old man's knowledge, or, at least, his confident suspicion, with respect to his own interview with Hester Prynne. The physician knew then that in the minister's regard he was no longer a trusted friend, but his bitterest enemy. So much being known, it would appear natural that a part of it should be expressed. It is singular, however, how long a time often passes before words embody things; and with what security two persons, who choose to avoid a certain subject, may approach its very verge, and retire without disturbing it. Thus the minister felt no apprehension that Roger Chillingworth would touch, in express words, upon the real position which they sustained towards one another. Yet did the physician, in his dark way, creep frightfully near the secret.

"Were it not better," said he, "that you use my poor skill tonight? Verily, dear sir, we must take pains to make you strong and vigorous for this occasion of the Election discourse. The people look for great things from you, apprehending that another year may come about and find their pastor gone."

"Yes, to another world," replied the minister with pious resignation. "Heaven grant it be a better one; for, in good sooth, I hardly think to tarry with my flock through the flitting seasons of another year! But touching your medicine, kind sir, in my present frame of body I need it not."

"I joy to hear it," answered the physician. "It may be that my remedies, so long administered in vain, begin now to take due effect. Happy man were I, and well deserving of New England's gratitude, could I achieve this cure!"

"I thank you from my heart, most watchful friend," said the Reverend Mr. Dimmesdale with a solemn smile. "I thank you, and can but requite your good deeds with my prayers."

"A good man's prayers are golden recompense!" rejoined old Roger Chillingworth, as he took his leave. "Yea, they are the current gold coin of the New Jerusalem, with the King's own mint mark on them!"

Left alone, the minister summoned a servant of the house, and requested food, which, being set before him, he ate with ravenous appetite. Then flinging the already written pages of the Election Sermon into the fire, he forthwith began another, which he wrote with such an impulsive flow of thought and emotion, that he fancied himself inspired; and only wondered that Heaven should see fit to transmit the grand and solemn music of its oracles through so foul an organ pipe as he. However, leaving that mystery to solve itself, or go unsolved for ever, he drove his task onward with earnest haste and ecstasy.

Thus the night fled away, as if it were a winged steed, and he careering on it; morning came, and peeped, blushing, through the curtains; and at last sunrise threw a golden beam into the study, and laid it right across the minister's bedazzled eyes. There he was, with the pen still between his fingers, and a vast, immeasurable tract of written space behind him!

XXI. THE NEW ENGLAND HOLIDAY

Betimes in the morning of the day on which the new Governor was to receive his office at the hands of the people, Hester Prynne and little Pearl came into the market-place. It was already thronged with the craftsmen and other plebeian inhabitants of the town, in considerable numbers, among whom, likewise, were many rough figures, whose attire of deer-skins marked them as belonging to some of the forest settlements, which surrounded the little metropolis of the colony.

On this public holiday, as on all other occasions for seven years past, Hester was clad in a garment of coarse gray cloth. Not more by its hue than by some indescribable peculiarity in its fashion, it had the effect of making her fade personally out of sight and outline; while again the scarlet letter brought her back from this twilight indistinctness, and revealed her under the moral aspect of its own illumination. Her face, so long familiar to the townspeople, showed the marble quietude which they were accustomed to behold there. It was like a mask; or, rather like the frozen calmness of a dead woman's features; owing this dreary resemblance to the fact that Hester was actually dead, in respect to any claim of sympathy, and had departed out of the world with which she still seemed to mingle.

It might be, on this one day, that there was an expression unseen before, nor, indeed, vivid enough to be detected now; unless some preternaturally gifted observer should have first read the heart, and have afterwards sought a corresponding development in the countenance and mien. Such a spiritual seer might have conceived, that, after sustaining the gaze of the multitude through several miserable years as a necessity, a penance, and something which it was a stern religion to endure, she now, for one last time more, encountered it freely and voluntarily, in order to convert what had so long been agony into a kind of triumph. "Look your last on the scarlet letter and its wearer!"—the people's victim and lifelong bond-slave, as they fancied her, might say to them. "Yet a little while, and she will be beyond your reach! A few hours longer and the deep, mysterious ocean will quench and hide for ever the symbol which ye have caused to burn on her bosom!" Nor were it an inconsistency too improbable to be assigned to human nature, should we suppose a feeling of regret in Hester's mind, at the moment when she was about to win her freedom from the pain which had been thus deeply incorporated with her being. Might there not be an irresistible desire to quaff a last, long, breathless draught of the cup of wormwood and aloes, with which nearly all her years of womanhood had been perpetually flavoured. The wine of life, henceforth to be presented to her lips, must be indeed rich, delicious, and exhilarating, in its chased and golden beaker, or else leave an inevitable and weary languor, after the lees of bitterness wherewith she had been drugged, as with a cordial of intensest potency.

Pearl was decked out with airy gaiety. It would have been impossible to guess that this bright and sunny apparition owed its existence to the shape of gloomy gray; or that a fancy, at once so gorgeous and so delicate as must have been requisite to contrive the child's apparel, was the same that had achieved a task perhaps more difficult, in imparting so distinct a peculiarity to Hester's simple robe. The dress, so proper was it to little Pearl, seemed an effluence, or inevitable development and outward manifestation of her character, no more to be separated from her than the many-hued brilliancy from a butterfly's wing, or the painted glory from the leaf of a bright flower. As with these, so with the child; her garb was all of one idea with her nature. On this eventful day, moreover, there was a certain singular inquietude and excitement in her mood, resembling nothing so much as the shimmer of a diamond, that sparkles and flashes with the varied throbbings of the breast on which it is displayed. Children have always a sympathy in the agitations of those connected with them: always, especially, a sense of any trouble or impending revolution, of whatever kind, in domestic circumstances; and therefore Pearl, who was the gem on her mother's unquiet bosom, betrayed, by the very dance of her spirits, the emotions which none could detect in the marble passiveness of Hester's brow.

This effervescence made her flit with a bird-like movement, rather than walk by her mother's side.

She broke continually into shouts of a wild, inarticulate, and sometimes piercing music. When they reached the market-place, she became still more restless, on perceiving the stir and bustle that enlivened the spot; for it was usually more like the broad and lonesome green before a village meeting-house, than the centre of a town's business.

"Why, what is this, mother?" cried she. "Wherefore have all the people left their work to-day? Is it a play-day for the whole world? See, there is the blacksmith! He has washed his sooty face, and put on his Sabbath-day clothes, and looks as if he would gladly be merry, if any kind body would only teach him how! And there is Master Brackett, the old jailer, nodding and smiling at me. Why does he do so, mother?"

"He remembers thee a little babe, my child," answered Hester.

"He should not nod and smile at me, for all that—the black, grim, ugly-eyed old man!" said Pearl. "He may nod at thee, if he will; for thou art clad in gray, and wearest the scarlet letter. But see, mother, how many faces of strange people, and Indians among them, and sailors! What have they all come to do, here in the market-place?"

"They wait to see the procession pass," said Hester. "For the Governor and the magistrates are to go by, and the ministers, and all the great people and good people, with the music and the soldiers marching before them."

"And will the minister be there?" asked Pearl. "And will he hold out both his hands to me, as when thou ledst me to him from the brook-side?"

"He will be there, child," answered her mother, "but he will not greet thee to-day, nor must thou greet him."

"What a strange, sad man is he!" said the child, as if speaking partly to herself. "In the dark nighttime he calls us to him, and holds thy hand and mine, as when we stood with him on the scaffold yonder! And in the deep forest, where only the old trees can hear, and the strip of sky see it, he talks with thee, sitting on a heap of moss! And he kisses my forehead, too, so that the little brook would hardly wash it off! But, here, in the sunny day, and among all the people, he knows us not; nor must we know him! A strange, sad man is he, with his hand always over his heart!"

"Be quiet, Pearl—thou understandest not these things," said her mother. "Think not now of the minister, but look about thee, and see how cheery is everybody's face to-day. The children have come from their schools, and the grown people from their workshops and their fields, on purpose to be happy, for, to-day, a new man is beginning to rule over them; and so—as has been the custom of mankind ever since a nation was first gathered—they make merry and rejoice: as if a good and golden year were at length to pass over the poor old world!"

It was as Hester said, in regard to the unwonted jollity that brightened the faces of the people. Into this festal season of the year—as it already was, and continued to be during the greater part of two centuries—the Puritans compressed whatever mirth and public joy they deemed allowable to human infirmity; thereby so far dispelling the customary cloud, that, for the space of a single holiday, they appeared scarcely more grave than most other communities at a period of general affliction.

But we perhaps exaggerate the gray or sable tinge, which undoubtedly characterized the mood and manners of the age. The persons now in the market-place of Boston had not been born to an inheritance of Puritanic gloom. They were native Englishmen, whose fathers had lived in the sunny richness of the Elizabethan epoch; a time when the life of England, viewed as one great mass, would appear to have been as stately, magnificent, and joyous, as the world has ever witnessed. Had they followed their hereditary taste, the New England settlers would have illustrated all events of public importance by bonfires, banquets, pageantries, and processions. Nor would it have been impracticable, in the observance of majestic ceremonies, to combine mirthful recreation with solemnity, and give, as it were, a grotesque and brilliant embroidery to the great robe of state, which a nation, at such festivals, puts on. There was some shadow of an attempt of this kind in the mode of celebrating the day on which the political year of the colony commenced. The dim reflection of a remembered splendour, a colourless and manifold diluted repetition of what they had beheld in proud old London—we will not say at a royal coronation, but at a Lord Mayor's show—might be traced in the customs which our forefathers instituted, with reference to the annual installation of magistrates. The fathers and founders of the commonwealth—the statesman, the priest, and the soldier—seemed it a duty then to assume the outward state and majesty, which, in accordance with antique style, was looked upon as the proper garb of public and social eminence. All came forth to move in procession before the people's eye, and thus impart a needed dignity to the simple framework of a government so newly constructed.

Then, too, the people were countenanced, if not encouraged, in relaxing the severe and close application to their various modes of rugged industry, which at all other times, seemed of the same piece and material with their religion. Here, it is true, were none of the appliances which popular merriment would so readily have found in the England of Elizabeth's time, or that of James—no rude shows of a theatrical kind; no minstrel, with his harp and legendary ballad, nor gleeman with an ape dancing to his music; no juggler, with his tricks of mimic witchcraft; no Merry Andrew, to stir up the multitude with jests, perhaps a hundred years old, but still effective, by their appeals to the very broadest sources of mirthful sympathy. All such professors of the several branches of jocularity would have been sternly repressed, not only by the rigid discipline of law, but by the general sentiment which give law its vitality. Not the less, however, the great, honest face of the people smiled—grimly, perhaps, but widely too. Nor were sports wanting, such as the colonists had witnessed, and shared in, long ago, at the country fairs and on the village-greens of England; and which it was thought well to keep alive on this new soil, for the sake of the courage and manliness that were essential in them. Wrestling matches, in the different fashions of Cornwall and Devonshire, were seen here and there about the market-place; in one corner, there was a friendly bout at quarterstaff; and—what attracted most interest of all—on the platform of the pillory, already so noted in our pages, two masters of defence were commencing an exhibition with the buckler and broadsword. But, much to the disappointment of the crowd, this latter business was broken off by the interposition of the town beadle, who had no idea of permitting the majesty of the law to be violated by such an abuse of one of its consecrated places.

It may not be too much to affirm, on the whole, (the people being then in the first stages of joyless deportment, and the offspring of sires who had known how to be merry, in their day), that they would compare favourably, in point of holiday keeping, with their descendants, even at so long an interval as ourselves. Their immediate posterity, the generation next to the early emigrants, wore the blackest shade of Puritanism, and so darkened the national visage with it, that all the subsequent years have not sufficed to clear it up. We have yet to learn again the forgotten art of gaiety.

The picture of human life in the market-place, though its general tint was the sad gray, brown, or black of the English emigrants, was yet enlivened by some diversity of hue. A party of Indians—in their savage finery of curiously embroidered deerskin robes, wampum-belts, red and yellow ochre, and feathers, and armed with the bow and arrow and stone-headed spear—stood apart with countenances of inflexible gravity, beyond what even the Puritan aspect could attain. Nor, wild as were these painted barbarians, were they the wildest feature of the scene. This distinction could more justly be claimed by some mariners—a part of the crew of the vessel from the Spanish Main—who had come ashore to see the humours of Election Day. They were rough-looking desperadoes, with sun-blackened faces, and an immensity of beard; their wide short trousers were confined about the waist by belts, often clasped with a rough plate of gold, and sustaining always a long knife, and in some instances, a sword. From beneath their broad-brimmed hats of palm-leaf, gleamed eyes which, even in good-nature and merriment, had a kind of animal ferocity. They transgressed without fear or scruple, the rules of behaviour that were binding on all others: smoking tobacco under the beadle's very nose, although each whiff would have cost a townsman a shilling; and quaffing at their pleasure, draughts of wine or aqua-vitae from pocket flasks, which they freely tendered to the gaping crowd around them. It remarkably characterised the incomplete morality of the age, rigid as we call it, that a licence was allowed the seafaring class, not merely for their freaks on shore, but for far more desperate deeds on their proper element. The sailor of that day would go near to be arraigned as a pirate in our own. There could be little doubt, for instance, that this very ship's crew, though no unfavourable specimens of the nautical brotherhood, had been guilty, as we should phrase it, of depredations on the Spanish commerce, such as would have perilled all their necks in a modern court of justice.

But the sea in those old times heaved, swelled, and foamed very much at its own will, or subject only to the tempestuous wind, with hardly any attempts at regulation by human law. The buccaneer on the wave might relinquish his calling and become at once if he chose, a man of probity and piety on land; nor, even in the full career of his reckless life, was he regarded as a personage with whom it was disreputable to traffic or casually associate. Thus the Puritan elders in their black cloaks, starched bands, and steeple-crowned hats, smiled not unbenignantly at the clamour and rude deportment of these jolly seafaring men; and it excited neither surprise nor animadversion when so reputable a citizen as old Roger Chillingworth, the physician, was seen to enter the market-place in close and familiar talk with the commander of the questionable vessel.

The latter was by far the most showy and gallant figure, so far as apparel went, anywhere to be seen among the multitude. He wore a profusion of ribbons on his garment, and gold lace on his hat, which was also encircled by a gold chain, and surmounted with a feather. There was a sword at his side and a sword-cut on his forehead, which, by the arrangement of his hair, he seemed anxious rather to display than hide. A landsman could hardly have worn this garb and shown this face, and worn and shown them both with such a galliard air, without undergoing stern question before a magistrate, and probably incurring a fine or imprisonment, or perhaps an exhibition in the stocks. As regarded the shipmaster, however, all was looked upon as pertaining to the character, as to a fish his glistening scales.

After parting from the physician, the commander of the Bristol ship strolled idly through the market-place; until happening to approach the spot where Hester Prynne was standing, he appeared to recognise, and did not hesitate to address her. As was usually the case wherever Hester stood, a small vacant area—a sort of magic circle—had formed itself about her, into which, though the people were elbowing one another at a little distance, none ventured or felt disposed to intrude. It was a forcible type of the moral solitude in which the scarlet letter enveloped its fated wearer; partly by her own reserve, and partly by the instinctive, though no longer so unkindly, withdrawal of her fellow-creatures. Now, if never before, it answered a good purpose by enabling Hester and the seaman to speak together without risk of being overheard; and so changed was Hester Prynne's repute before the public, that the matron in town, most eminent for rigid morality, could not have held such intercourse with less result of scandal than herself.

"So, mistress," said the mariner, "I must bid the steward make ready one more berth than you bargained for! No fear of scurvy or ship fever this voyage. What with the ship's surgeon and this other doctor, our only danger will be from drug or pill; more by token, as there is a lot of apothecary's stuff aboard, which I traded for with a Spanish vessel."

"What mean you?" inquired Hester, startled more than she permitted to appear. "Have you another passenger?"

"Why, know you not," cried the shipmaster, "that this physician here—Chillingworth he calls himself—is minded to try my cabin-fare with you? Ay, ay, you must have known it; for he tells me he is of your party, and a close friend to the gentleman you spoke of—he that is in peril from these sour old Puritan rulers."

"They know each other well, indeed," replied Hester, with a mien of calmness, though in the utmost consternation. "They have long dwelt together."

Nothing further passed between the mariner and Hester Prynne. But at that instant she beheld old Roger Chillingworth himself, standing in the remotest corner of the market-place and smiling on her; a smile which—across the wide and bustling square, and through all the talk and laughter, and various thoughts, moods, and interests of the crowd—conveyed secret and fearful meaning.

XXII. THE PROCESSION

Before Hester Prynne could call together her thoughts, and consider what was practicable to be done in this new and startling aspect of affairs, the sound of military music was heard approaching along a contiguous street. It denoted the advance of the procession of magistrates and citizens on its way towards the meeting-house: where, in compliance with a custom thus early established, and ever since observed, the Reverend Mr. Dimmesdale was to deliver an Election Sermon.

Soon the head of the procession showed itself, with a slow and stately march, turning a corner, and making its way across the market-place. First came the music. It comprised a variety of instruments, perhaps imperfectly adapted to one another, and played with no great skill; but yet attaining the great object for which the harmony of drum and clarion addresses itself to the multitude—that of imparting a higher and more heroic air to the scene of life that passes before the eye. Little Pearl at first clapped her hands, but then lost for an instant the restless agitation that had kept her in a continual effervescence throughout the morning; she gazed silently, and seemed to be borne upward like a floating sea-bird on the long heaves and swells of sound. But she was brought back to her former mood by the shimmer of the sunshine on the weapons and bright armour of the military company, which followed after the music, and formed the honorary escort of the procession. This body of soldiery—which still sustains a corporate existence, and marches down from past ages with an ancient and honourable fame—was composed of no mercenary materials. Its ranks were filled with gentlemen who felt the stirrings of martial impulse, and sought to establish a kind of College of Arms, where, as in an association of Knights Templars, they might learn the science, and, so far as peaceful exercise would teach them, the practices of war. The high estimation then placed upon the military character might be seen in the lofty port of each individual member of the company. Some of them, indeed, by their services in the Low Countries and on other fields of European warfare, had fairly won their title to assume the name and pomp of soldiership. The entire array, moreover, clad in burnished steel, and with plumage nodding over their bright morions, had a brilliancy of effect which no modern display can aspire to equal.

And yet the men of civil eminence, who came immediately behind the military escort, were better worth a thoughtful observer's eye. Even in outward demeanour they showed a stamp of majesty that made the warrior's haughty stride look vulgar, if not absurd. It was an age when what we call talent had far less consideration than now, but the massive materials which produce stability and dignity of character a great deal more. The people possessed by hereditary right the quality of reverence, which, in their descendants, if it survive at all, exists in smaller proportion, and with a vastly diminished force in the selection and estimate of public men. The change may be for good or ill, and is partly, perhaps, for both. In that old day the English settler on these rude shores—having left king, nobles, and all degrees of awful rank behind, while still the faculty and necessity of reverence was strong in him—bestowed it on the white hair and venerable brow of age—on long-tried integrity—on solid wisdom and sad-coloured experience—on endowments of that grave and weighty order which gave the idea of permanence, and comes under the general definition of respectability. These primitive statesmen, therefore—Bradstreet, Endicott, Dudley, Bellingham, and their compeers—who were elevated to power by the early choice of the people, seem to have been not often brilliant, but distinguished by a ponderous sobriety, rather than activity of intellect. They had fortitude and self-reliance, and in time of difficulty or peril stood up for the welfare of the state like a line of cliffs against a tempestuous tide. The traits of character here indicated were well represented in the square cast of countenance and large physical development of the new colonial magistrates. So far as a demeanour of natural authority was concerned, the mother country need not have been ashamed to see these foremost men of an actual democracy adopted into the House of Peers, or make the Privy Council of the Sovereign.

Next in order to the magistrates came the young and eminently distinguished divine, from whose lips the religious discourse of the anniversary was expected. His was the profession at that era in which intellectual ability displayed itself far more than in political life; for—leaving a higher motive out of the question it offered inducements powerful enough in the almost worshipping respect of the community, to win the most aspiring ambition into its service. Even political power—as in the case of Increase Mather—was within the grasp of a successful priest.

It was the observation of those who beheld him now, that never, since Mr. Dimmesdale first set his foot on the New England shore, had he exhibited such energy as was seen in the gait and air with which he kept his pace in the procession. There was no feebleness of step as at other times; his frame was not bent, nor did his hand rest ominously upon his heart. Yet, if the clergyman were rightly viewed, his strength seemed not of the body. It might be spiritual and imparted to him by angelical ministrations. It might be the exhilaration of that potent cordial which is distilled only in the furnace-glow of earnest and long-continued thought. Or perchance his sensitive temperament was invigorated by the loud and piercing music that swelled heaven-ward, and uplifted him on its ascending wave. Nevertheless, so abstracted was his look, it might be questioned whether Mr. Dimmesdale even heard the music. There was his body, moving onward, and with an unaccustomed force. But where was his mind? Far and deep in its own region, busying itself, with preternatural activity, to marshal a procession of stately thoughts that were soon to issue thence; and so he saw nothing, heard nothing, knew nothing of what was around him; but the spiritual element took up the feeble frame and carried it along, unconscious of the burden, and converting it to spirit like itself. Men of uncommon intellect, who have grown morbid, possess this occasional power of mighty effort, into which they throw the life of many days and then are lifeless for as many more.

Hester Prynne, gazing steadfastly at the clergyman, felt a dreary influence come over her, but wherefore or whence she knew not, unless that he seemed so remote from her own sphere, and utterly beyond her reach. One glance of recognition she had imagined must needs pass between them. She thought of the dim forest, with its little dell of solitude, and love, and anguish, and the mossy tree-trunk, where, sitting hand-in-hand, they had mingled their sad and passionate talk with the melancholy murmur of the brook. How deeply had they known each other then! And was this the man? She hardly knew him now! He, moving proudly past, enveloped as it were, in the rich music, with the procession of majestic and venerable fathers; he, so unattainable in his worldly position, and still more so in that far vista of his unsympathizing thoughts, through which she now beheld him! Her spirit sank with the idea that all must have been a delusion, and that, vividly as she had dreamed it, there could be no real bond betwixt the clergyman and herself. And thus much of woman was there in Hester, that she could scarcely forgive him—least of all now, when the heavy footstep of their approaching Fate might be heard, nearer, nearer, nearer!—for being able so completely to withdraw himself from their mutual world—while she groped darkly, and stretched forth her cold hands, and found him not.

Pearl either saw and responded to her mother's feelings, or herself felt the remoteness and intangibility that had fallen around the minister. While the procession passed, the child was uneasy, fluttering up and down, like a bird on the point of taking flight. When the whole had gone by, she looked up into Hester's face—

"Mother," said she, "was that the same minister that kissed me by the brook?"

"Hold thy peace, dear little Pearl!" whispered her mother. "We must not always talk in the marketplace of what happens to us in the forest."

"I could not be sure that it was he—so strange he looked," continued the child. "Else I would have run to him, and bid him kiss me now, before all the people, even as he did yonder among the dark old trees. What would the minister have said, mother? Would he have clapped his hand over his heart, and scowled on me, and bid me begone?"

"What should he say, Pearl," answered Hester, "save that it was no time to kiss, and that kisses are not to be given in the market-place? Well for thee, foolish child, that thou didst not speak to him!"

Another shade of the same sentiment, in reference to Mr. Dimmesdale, was expressed by a person whose eccentricities—insanity, as we should term it—led her to do what few of the townspeople would have ventured on—to begin a conversation with the wearer of the scarlet letter in public. It was Mistress Hibbins, who, arrayed in great magnificence, with a triple ruff, a broidered stomacher, a gown of rich velvet, and a gold-headed cane, had come forth to see the procession. As this ancient lady had the renown (which subsequently cost her no less a price than her life) of being a principal actor in all the works of necromancy that were continually going forward, the crowd gave way before her, and seemed to fear the touch of her garment, as if it carried the plague among its gorgeous folds. Seen in conjunction with Hester Prynne—kindly as so many now felt towards the latter—the dread inspired by Mistress Hibbins had doubled, and caused a general movement from that part of the market-place in which the two women stood.

"Now, what mortal imagination could conceive it?" whispered the old lady confidentially to Hester. "Yonder divine man! That saint on earth, as the people uphold him to be, and as—I must needs say—he really looks! Who, now, that saw him pass in the procession, would think how little while it is since he went forth out of his study—chewing a Hebrew text of Scripture in his mouth, I warrant—to take an airing in the forest! Aha! we know what that means, Hester Prynne! But truly, forsooth, I find it hard to believe him the same man. Many a church member saw I, walking behind the music, that has danced in the same measure with me, when Somebody was fiddler, and, it might be, an Indian powwow or a Lapland wizard changing hands with us! That is but a trifle, when a woman knows the world. But this minister. Couldst thou surely tell, Hester, whether he was the same man that encountered thee on the forest path?"

"Madam, I know not of what you speak," answered Hester Prynne, feeling Mistress Hibbins to be of infirm mind; yet strangely startled and awe-stricken by the confidence with which she affirmed a personal connexion between so many persons (herself among them) and the Evil One. "It is not for me to talk lightly of a learned and pious minister of the Word, like the Reverend Mr. Dimmesdale."

"Fie, woman—fie!" cried the old lady, shaking her finger at Hester. "Dost thou think I have been to the forest so many times, and have yet no skill to judge who else has been there? Yea, though no leaf of the wild garlands which they wore while they danced be left in their hair! I know thee, Hester, for I behold the token. We may all see it in the sunshine! and it glows like a red flame in the dark. Thou wearest it openly, so there need be no question about that. But this minister! Let me tell thee in thine ear! When the Black Man sees one of his own servants, signed and sealed, so shy of owning to the bond as is the Reverend Mr. Dimmesdale, he hath a way of ordering matters so that the mark shall be disclosed, in open daylight, to the eyes of all the world! What is that the minister seeks to hide, with his hand always over his heart? Ha, Hester Prynne?"

"What is it, good Mistress Hibbins?" eagerly asked little Pearl.

"Hast thou seen it?"

"No matter, darling!" responded Mistress Hibbins, making Pearl a profound reverence. "Thou thyself wilt see it, one time or another. They say, child, thou art of the lineage of the Prince of Air! Wilt thou ride with me some fine night to see thy father? Then thou shalt know wherefore the minister keeps his hand over his heart!"

Laughing so shrilly that all the market-place could hear her, the weird old gentlewoman took her departure.

By this time the preliminary prayer had been offered in the meeting-house, and the accents of the Reverend Mr. Dimmesdale were heard commencing his discourse. An irresistible feeling kept Hester near the spot. As the sacred edifice was too much thronged to admit another auditor, she took up her position close beside the scaffold of the pillory. It was in sufficient proximity to bring the whole sermon to her ears, in the shape of an indistinct but varied murmur and flow of the minister's very peculiar voice.

This vocal organ was in itself a rich endowment, insomuch that a listener, comprehending nothing of the language in which the preacher spoke, might still have been swayed to and fro by the mere tone and cadence. Like all other music, it breathed passion and pathos, and emotions high or tender, in a tongue native to the human heart, wherever educated. Muffled as the sound was by its passage through the church walls, Hester Prynne listened with such intenseness, and sympathized so intimately, that the sermon had throughout a meaning for her, entirely apart from its indistinguishable words. These, perhaps, if more distinctly heard, might have been only a grosser medium, and have clogged the spiritual sense. Now she caught the low undertone, as of the wind sinking down to repose itself; then ascended with it, as it rose through progressive gradations of sweetness and power, until its volume seemed to envelop her with an atmosphere of awe and solemn grandeur. And yet, majestic as the voice sometimes became, there was for ever in it an essential character of plaintiveness. A loud or low expression of anguish—the whisper, or the shriek, as it might be conceived, of suffering humanity, that touched a sensibility in every bosom! At times this deep strain of pathos was all that could be heard, and scarcely heard sighing amid a desolate silence. But even when the minister's voice grew high and commanding—when it gushed irrepressibly upward—when it assumed its utmost breadth and power, so overfilling the church as to burst its way through the solid walls, and diffuse itself in the open air—still, if the auditor listened intently, and for the purpose, he could detect the same cry of pain. What was it? The complaint of a human heart, sorrow-laden, perchance guilty, telling its secret, whether of guilt or sorrow, to the great heart of mankind; beseeching its sympathy or forgiveness,—at every moment,—in each accent,—and never in vain! It was this profound and continual undertone that gave the clergyman his most appropriate power.

During all this time, Hester stood, statue-like, at the foot of the scaffold. If the minister's voice had not kept her there, there would, nevertheless, have been an inevitable magnetism in that spot, whence she dated the first hour of her life of ignominy. There was a sense within her—too ill-defined to be made a thought, but weighing heavily on her mind—that her whole orb of life, both before and after, was connected with this spot, as with the one point that gave it unity.

Little Pearl, meanwhile, had quitted her mother's side, and was playing at her own will about the market-place. She made the sombre crowd cheerful by her erratic and glistening ray, even as a bird of bright plumage illuminates a whole tree of dusky foliage by darting to and fro, half seen and half concealed amid the twilight of the clustering leaves. She had an undulating, but oftentimes a sharp and irregular movement. It indicated the restless vivacity of her spirit, which to-day was doubly indefatigable in its tip-toe dance, because it was played upon and vibrated with her mother's disquietude. Whenever Pearl saw anything to excite her ever active and wandering curiosity, she flew thitherward, and, as we might say, seized upon that man or thing as her own property, so far as she desired it, but without yielding the minutest degree of control over her motions in requital. The Puritans looked on, and, if they smiled, were none the less inclined to pronounce the child a demon offspring, from the indescribable charm of beauty and eccentricity that shone through her little figure, and sparkled with its activity. She ran and looked the wild Indian in the face, and he grew conscious of a nature wilder than his own. Thence, with native audacity, but still with a reserve as characteristic, she flew into the midst of a group of mariners, the swarthy-cheeked wild men of the ocean, as the Indians were of the land; and they gazed wonderingly and admiringly at Pearl, as if a flake of the sea-foam had taken the shape of a little maid, and were gifted with a soul of the sea-fire, that flashes beneath the prow in the night-time.

One of these seafaring men the shipmaster, indeed, who had spoken to Hester Prynne was so smitten with Pearl's aspect, that he attempted to lay hands upon her, with purpose to snatch a kiss. Finding it as impossible to touch her as to catch a humming-bird in the air, he took from his hat the gold chain that was twisted about it, and threw it to the child. Pearl immediately twined it around her neck and waist with such happy skill, that, once seen there, it became a part of her, and it was difficult to imagine her without it.

"Thy mother is yonder woman with the scarlet letter," said the seaman, "Wilt thou carry her a message from me?"

"If the message pleases me, I will," answered Pearl.

"Then tell her," rejoined he, "that I spake again with the black-a-visaged, hump shouldered old doctor, and he engages to bring his friend, the gentleman she wots of, aboard with him. So let thy mother take no thought, save for herself and thee. Wilt thou tell her this, thou witch-baby?"

"Mistress Hibbins says my father is the Prince of the Air!" cried Pearl, with a naughty smile. "If thou callest me that ill-name, I shall tell him of thee, and he will chase thy ship with a tempest!"

Pursuing a zigzag course across the marketplace, the child returned to her mother, and communicated what the mariner had said. Hester's strong, calm steadfastly-enduring spirit almost sank, at last, on beholding this dark and grim countenance of an inevitable doom, which at the moment when a passage seemed to open for the minister and herself out of their labyrinth of misery—showed itself with an unrelenting smile, right in the midst of their path.

XXII. THE PROCESSION

With her mind harassed by the terrible perplexity in which the shipmaster's intelligence involved her, she was also subjected to another trial. There were many people present from the country round about, who had often heard of the scarlet letter, and to whom it had been made terrific by a hundred false or exaggerated rumours, but who had never beheld it with their own bodily eyes. These, after exhausting other modes of amusement, now thronged about Hester Prynne with rude and boorish intrusiveness. Unscrupulous as it was, however, it could not bring them nearer than a circuit of several yards. At that distance they accordingly stood, fixed there by the centrifugal force of the repugnance which the mystic symbol inspired. The whole gang of sailors, likewise, observing the press of spectators, and learning the purport of the scarlet letter, came and thrust their sunburnt and desperado-looking faces into the ring. Even the Indians were affected by a sort of cold shadow of the white man's curiosity and, gliding through the crowd, fastened their snake-like black eyes on Hester's bosom, conceiving, perhaps, that the wearer of this brilliantly embroidered badge must needs be a personage of high dignity among her people. Lastly, the inhabitants of the town (their own interest in this worn-out subject languidly reviving itself, by sympathy with what they saw others feel) lounged idly to the same quarter, and tormented Hester Prynne, perhaps more than all the rest, with their cool, well-acquainted gaze at her familiar shame. Hester saw and recognized the selfsame faces of that group of matrons, who had awaited her forthcoming from the prison-door seven years ago; all save one, the youngest and only compassionate among them, whose burial-robe she had since made. At the final hour, when she was so soon to fling aside the burning letter, it had strangely become the centre of more remark and excitement, and was thus made to sear her breast more painfully, than at any time since the first day she put it on.

While Hester stood in that magic circle of ignominy, where the cunning cruelty of her sentence seemed to have fixed her for ever, the admirable preacher was looking down from the sacred pulpit upon an audience whose very inmost spirits had yielded to his control. The sainted minister in the church! The woman of the scarlet letter in the marketplace! What imagination would have been irreverent enough to surmise that the same scorching stigma was on them both!

XXIII. THE REVELATION OF THE SCARLET LETTER

The eloquent voice, on which the souls of the listening audience had been borne aloft as on the swelling waves of the sea, at length came to a pause. There was a momentary silence, profound as what should follow the utterance of oracles. Then ensued a murmur and half-hushed tumult, as if the auditors, released from the high spell that had transported them into the region of another's mind, were returning into themselves, with all their awe and wonder still heavy on them. In a moment more the crowd began to gush forth from the doors of the church. Now that there was an end, they needed more breath, more fit to support the gross and earthly life into which they relapsed, than that atmosphere which the preacher had converted into words of flame, and had burdened with the rich fragrance of his thought.

In the open air their rapture broke into speech. The street and the market-place absolutely babbled, from side to side, with applauses of the minister. His hearers could not rest until they had told one another of what each knew better than he could tell or hear.

According to their united testimony, never had man spoken in so wise, so high, and so holy a spirit, as he that spake this day; nor had inspiration ever breathed through mortal lips more evidently than it did through his. Its influence could be seen, as it were, descending upon him, and possessing him, and continually lifting him out of the written discourse that lay before him, and filling him with ideas that must have been as marvellous to himself as to his audience. His subject, it appeared, had been the relation between the Deity and the communities of mankind, with a special reference to the New England which they were here planting in the wilderness. And, as he drew towards the close, a spirit as of prophecy had come upon him, constraining him to its purpose as mightily as the old prophets of Israel were constrained, only with this difference, that, whereas the Jewish seers had denounced judgments and ruin on their country, it was his mission to foretell a high and glorious destiny for the newly gathered people of the Lord. But, throughout it all, and through the whole discourse, there had been a certain deep, sad undertone of pathos, which could not be interpreted otherwise than as the natural regret of one soon to pass away. Yes; their minister whom they so loved—

and who so loved them all, that he could not depart heavenward without a sigh—had the foreboding of untimely death upon him, and would soon leave them in their tears. This idea of his transitory stay on earth gave the last emphasis to the effect which the preacher had produced; it was as if an angel, in his passage to the skies, had shaken his bright wings over the people for an instant—at once a shadow and a splendour—and had shed down a shower of golden truths upon them.

Thus, there had come to the Reverend Mr. Dimmesdale—as to most men, in their various spheres, though seldom recognised until they see it far behind them—an epoch of life more brilliant and full of triumph than any previous one, or than any which could hereafter be. He stood, at this moment, on the very proudest eminence of superiority, to which the gifts or intellect, rich lore, prevailing eloquence, and a reputation of whitest sanctity, could exalt a clergyman in New England's earliest days, when the professional character was of itself a lofty pedestal. Such was the position which the minister occupied, as he bowed his head forward on the cushions of the pulpit at the close of his Election Sermon. Meanwhile Hester Prynne was standing beside the scaffold of the pillory, with the scarlet letter still burning on her breast!

Now was heard again the clamour of the music, and the measured tramp of the military escort issuing from the church door. The procession was to be marshalled thence to the town hall, where a solemn banquet would complete the ceremonies of the day.

Once more, therefore, the train of venerable and majestic fathers were seen moving through a broad pathway of the people, who drew back reverently, on either side, as the Governor and magistrates, the old and wise men, the holy ministers, and all that were eminent and renowned, advanced into the midst of them. When they were fairly in the marketplace, their presence was greeted by a shout. This—though doubtless it might acquire additional force and volume from the child-like loyalty which the age awarded to its rulers—was felt to be an irrepressible outburst of enthusiasm kindled in the auditors by that high strain of eloquence which was yet reverberating in their ears. Each felt the impulse in himself, and in the same breath, caught it from his neighbour. Within the church, it had hardly been kept down; beneath the sky it pealed upward to the zenith. There were human beings enough, and enough of highly wrought and symphonious feeling to produce that more impressive sound than the organ tones of the blast, or the thunder, or the roar of the sea; even that mighty swell of many voices, blended into one great voice by the universal impulse which makes likewise one vast heart out of the many. Never, from the soil of New England had gone up such a shout! Never, on New England soil had stood the man so honoured by his mortal brethren as the preacher!

How fared it with him, then? Were there not the brilliant particles of a halo in the air about his head? So etherealised by spirit as he was, and so apotheosised by worshipping admirers, did his footsteps, in the procession, really tread upon the dust of earth?

As the ranks of military men and civil fathers moved onward, all eyes were turned towards the point where the minister was seen to approach among them. The shout died into a murmur, as one portion of the crowd after another obtained a glimpse of him. How feeble and pale he looked, amid all his triumph! The energy—or say, rather, the inspiration which had held him up, until he should have delivered the sacred message that had brought its own strength along with it from heaven—was withdrawn, now that it had so faithfully performed its office. The glow, which they had just before beheld burning on his cheek, was extinguished, like a flame that sinks down hopelessly among the late decaying embers. It seemed hardly the face of a man alive, with such a death-like hue: it was hardly a man with life in him, that tottered on his path so nervously, yet tottered, and did not fall!

One of his clerical brethren—it was the venerable John Wilson—observing the state in which Mr. Dimmesdale was left by the retiring wave of intellect and sensibility, stepped forward hastily to offer his support. The minister tremulously, but decidedly, repelled the old man's arm. He still walked onward, if that movement could be so described, which rather resembled the wavering effort of an infant, with its mother's arms in view, outstretched to tempt him forward. And now, almost imperceptible as were the latter steps of his progress, he had come opposite the well-remembered and weather-darkened scaffold, where, long since, with all that dreary lapse of time between, Hester Prynne had encountered the world's ignominious stare. There stood Hester, holding little Pearl by the hand! And there was the scarlet letter on her breast! The minister here made a pause; although the music still played the stately and rejoicing march to which the procession moved. It summoned him onward—inward to the festival!—but here he made a pause.

Bellingham, for the last few moments, had kept an anxious eye upon him. He now left his own place in the procession, and advanced to give assistance judging, from Mr. Dimmesdale's aspect that he must otherwise inevitably fall. But there was something in the latter's expression that warned back the magistrate, although a man not readily obeying the vague intimations that pass from one spirit to another. The crowd, meanwhile, looked on with awe and wonder. This earthly faintness, was, in their view, only another phase of the minister's celestial strength; nor would it have seemed a miracle too high to be wrought for one so holy, had he ascended before their eyes, waxing dimmer and brighter, and fading at last into the light of heaven!

He turned towards the scaffold, and stretched forth his arms.

"Hester," said he, "come hither! Come, my little Pearl!"

It was a ghastly look with which he regarded them; but there was something at once tender and strangely triumphant in it. The child, with the bird-like motion, which was one of her characteristics, flew to him, and clasped her arms about his knees. Hester Prynne—slowly, as if impelled by inevitable fate, and against her strongest will—likewise drew near, but paused before she reached him. At this instant old Roger Chillingworth thrust himself through the crowd—or, perhaps, so dark, disturbed, and evil was his look, he rose up out of some nether region—to snatch back his victim from what he sought to do! Be that as it might, the old man rushed forward, and caught the minister by the arm.

"Madman, hold! what is your purpose?" whispered he. "Wave back that woman! Cast off this child! All shall be well! Do not blacken your fame, and perish in dishonour! I can yet save you! Would you bring infamy on your sacred profession?"

"Ha, tempter! Methinks thou art too late!" answered the minister, encountering his eye, fearfully, but firmly. "Thy power is not what it was! With God's help, I shall escape thee now!"

He again extended his hand to the woman of the scarlet letter.

"Hester Prynne," cried he, with a piercing earnestness, "in the name of Him, so terrible and so merciful, who gives me grace, at this last moment, to do what—for my own heavy sin and miserable agony—I withheld myself from doing seven years ago, come hither now, and twine thy strength about me! Thy strength, Hester; but let it be guided by the will which God hath granted me! This wretched and wronged old man is opposing it with all his might!—with all his own might, and the fiend's! Come, Hester—come! Support me up yonder scaffold."

The crowd was in a tumult. The men of rank and dignity, who stood more immediately around the clergyman, were so taken by surprise, and so perplexed as to the purport of what they saw—unable to receive the explanation which most readily presented itself, or to imagine any other—that they remained silent and inactive spectators of the judgement which Providence seemed about to work. They beheld the minister, leaning on Hester's shoulder, and supported by her arm around him, approach the scaffold, and ascend its steps; while still the little hand of the sin-born child was clasped in his. Old Roger Chillingworth followed, as one intimately connected with the drama of guilt and sorrow in which they had all been actors, and well entitled, therefore to be present at its closing scene.

"Hadst thou sought the whole earth over," said he looking darkly at the clergyman, "there was no one place so secret—no high place nor lowly place, where thou couldst have escaped me—save on this very scaffold!"

"Thanks be to Him who hath led me hither!" answered the minister.

Yet he trembled, and turned to Hester, with an expression of doubt and anxiety in his eyes, not the less evidently betrayed, that there was a feeble smile upon his lips.

"Is not this better," murmured he, "than what we dreamed of in the forest?"

"I know not! I know not!" she hurriedly replied. "Better? Yea; so we may both die, and little Pearl die with us!"

"For thee and Pearl, be it as God shall order," said the minister; "and God is merciful! Let me now do the will which He hath made plain before my sight. For, Hester, I am a dying man. So let me make haste to take my shame upon me!"

Partly supported by Hester Prynne, and holding one hand of little Pearl's, the Reverend Mr. Dimmesdale turned to the dignified and venerable rulers; to the holy ministers, who were his brethren; to the people, whose great heart was thoroughly appalled yet overflowing with tearful sympathy, as knowing that some deep life-matter—which, if full of sin, was full of anguish and repentance likewise—was now to be laid open to them. The sun, but little past its meridian, shone down upon the clergyman, and gave a distinctness to his figure, as he stood out from all the earth, to put in his plea of guilty at the bar of Eternal Justice.

"People of New England!" cried he, with a voice that rose over them, high, solemn, and majestic—yet had always a tremor through it, and sometimes a shriek, struggling up out of a fathomless depth of remorse and woe—"ye, that have loved me!—ye, that have deemed me holy!—behold me here, the one sinner of the world! At last—at last!—I stand upon the spot where, seven years since, I should have stood, here, with this woman, whose arm, more than the little strength wherewith I have crept hitherward, sustains me at this dreadful moment, from grovelling down upon my face! Lo, the scarlet letter which Hester wears! Ye have all shuddered at it! Wherever her walk hath been—wherever, so miserably burdened, she may have hoped to find repose—it hath cast a lurid gleam of awe and horrible repugnance round about her. But there stood one in the midst of you, at whose brand of sin and infamy ye have not shuddered!"

It seemed, at this point, as if the minister must leave the remainder of his secret undisclosed. But he fought back the bodily weakness—and, still more, the faintness of heart—that was striving for the mastery with him. He threw off all assistance, and stepped passionately forward a pace before the woman and the children.

"It was on him!" he continued, with a kind of fierceness; so determined was he to speak out the whole. "God's eye beheld it! The angels were for ever pointing at it! (The Devil knew it well, and fretted it continually with the touch of his burning finger!) But he hid it cunningly from men, and walked among you with the mien of a spirit, mournful, because so pure in a sinful world!—and sad, because he missed his heavenly kindred! Now, at the death-hour, he stands up before you! He bids you look again at Hester's scarlet letter! He tells you, that, with all its mysterious horror, it is but the shadow of what he bears on his own breast, and that even this, his own red stigma, is no more than the type of what has seared his inmost heart! Stand any here that question God's judgment on a sinner! Behold! Behold, a dreadful witness of it!"

With a convulsive motion, he tore away the ministerial band from before his breast. It was revealed! But it were irreverent to describe that revelation. For an instant, the gaze of the horror-stricken multitude was concentrated on the ghastly miracle; while the minister stood, with a flush of triumph in his face, as one who, in the crisis of acutest pain, had won a victory. Then, down he sank upon the scaffold! Hester partly raised him, and supported his head against her bosom. Old Roger Chillingworth knelt down beside him, with a blank, dull countenance, out of which the life seemed to have departed.

"Thou hast escaped me!" he repeated more than once. "Thou hast escaped me!"

"May God forgive thee!" said the minister. "Thou, too, hast deeply sinned!"

He withdrew his dying eyes from the old man, and fixed them on the woman and the child.

"My little Pearl," said he, feebly and there was a sweet and gentle smile over his face, as of a spirit sinking into deep repose; nay, now that the burden was removed, it seemed almost as if he would be sportive with the child—"dear little Pearl, wilt thou kiss me now? Thou wouldst not, yonder, in the forest! But now thou wilt?"

Pearl kissed his lips. A spell was broken. The great scene of grief, in which the wild infant bore a part had developed all her sympathies; and as her tears fell upon her father's cheek, they were the pledge that she would grow up amid human joy and sorrow, nor forever do battle with the world, but be a woman in it. Towards her mother, too, Pearl's errand as a messenger of anguish was fulfilled.

"Hester," said the clergyman, "farewell!"

"Shall we not meet again?" whispered she, bending her face down
close to his. "Shall we not spend our immortal life together?
Surely, surely, we have ransomed one another, with all this woe!
Thou lookest far into eternity, with those bright dying eyes!
Then tell me what thou seest!"

"Hush, Hester—hush!" said he, with tremulous solemnity. "The law we broke!—the sin here awfully revealed!—let these alone be in thy thoughts! I fear! I fear! It may be, that, when we forgot our God—when we violated our reverence each for the other's soul—it was thenceforth vain to hope that we could meet hereafter, in an everlasting and pure reunion. God knows; and He is merciful! He hath proved his mercy, most of all, in my afflictions. By giving me this burning torture to bear upon my breast! By sending yonder dark and terrible old man, to keep the torture always at red-heat! By bringing me hither, to die this death of triumphant ignominy before the people! Had either of these agonies been wanting, I had been lost for ever! Praised be His name! His will be done! Farewell!"

That final word came forth with the minister's expiring breath. The multitude, silent till then, broke out in a strange, deep voice of awe and wonder, which could not as yet find utterance, save in this murmur that rolled so heavily after the departed spirit.

XXIV. CONCLUSION

After many days, when time sufficed for the people to arrange their thoughts in reference to the foregoing scene, there was more than one account of what had been witnessed on the scaffold.

Most of the spectators testified to having seen, on the breast of the unhappy minister, a SCARLET LETTER—the very semblance of that worn by Hester Prynne—imprinted in the flesh. As regarded its origin there were various explanations, all of which must necessarily have been conjectural. Some affirmed that the Reverend Mr. Dimmesdale, on the very day when Hester Prynne first wore her ignominious badge, had begun a course of penance—which he afterwards, in so many futile methods, followed out—by inflicting a hideous torture on himself. Others contended that the stigma had not been produced until a long time subsequent, when old Roger Chillingworth, being a potent necromancer, had caused it to appear, through the agency of magic and poisonous drugs. Others, again and those best able to appreciate the minister's peculiar sensibility, and the wonderful operation of his spirit upon the body—whispered their belief, that the awful symbol was the effect of the ever-active tooth of remorse, gnawing from the inmost heart outwardly, and at last manifesting Heaven's dreadful judgment by the visible presence of the letter. The reader may choose among these theories. We have thrown all the light we could acquire upon the portent, and would gladly, now that it has done its office, erase its deep print out of our own brain, where long meditation has fixed it in very undesirable distinctness.

It is singular, nevertheless, that certain persons, who were spectators of the whole scene, and professed never once to have removed their eyes from the Reverend Mr. Dimmesdale, denied that there was any mark whatever on his breast, more than on a new-born infant's. Neither, by their report, had his dying words acknowledged, nor even remotely implied, any—the slightest—connexion on his part, with the guilt for which Hester Prynne had so long worn the scarlet letter. According to these highly-respectable witnesses, the minister, conscious that he was dying—conscious, also, that the reverence of the multitude placed him already among saints and angels—had desired, by yielding up his breath in the arms of that fallen woman, to express to the world how utterly nugatory is the choicest of man's own righteousness. After exhausting life in his efforts for mankind's spiritual good, he had made the manner of his death a parable, in order to impress on his admirers the mighty and mournful lesson, that, in the view of Infinite Purity, we are sinners all alike. It was to teach them, that the holiest amongst us has but attained so far above his fellows as to discern more clearly the Mercy which looks down, and repudiate more utterly the phantom of human merit, which would look aspiringly upward. Without disputing a truth so momentous, we must be allowed to consider this version of Mr. Dimmesdale's story as only an instance of that stubborn fidelity with which a man's friends—and especially a clergyman's—will sometimes uphold his character, when proofs, clear as the mid-day sunshine on the scarlet letter, establish him a false and sin-stained creature of the dust.

The authority which we have chiefly followed—a manuscript of old date, drawn up from the verbal testimony of individuals, some of whom had known Hester Prynne, while others had heard the tale from contemporary witnesses fully confirms the view taken in the foregoing pages. Among many morals which press upon us from the poor minister's miserable experience, we put only this into a sentence:—"Be true! Be true! Be true! Show freely to the world, if not your worst, yet some trait whereby the worst may be inferred!"

Nothing was more remarkable than the change which took place, almost immediately after Mr. Dimmesdale's death, in the appearance and demeanour of the old man known as Roger Chillingworth. All his strength and energy—all his vital and intellectual force—seemed at once to desert him, insomuch that he positively withered up, shrivelled away and almost vanished from mortal sight, like an uprooted weed that lies wilting in the sun. This unhappy man had made the very principle of his life to consist in the pursuit and systematic exercise of revenge; and when, by its completest triumph consummation that evil principle was left with no further material to support it—when, in short, there was no more Devil's work on earth for him to do, it only remained for the unhumanised mortal to betake himself whither his master would find him tasks enough, and pay him his wages duly. But, to all these shadowy beings, so long our near acquaintances—as well Roger Chillingworth as his companions we would fain be merciful. It is a curious subject of observation and inquiry, whether hatred and love be not the same thing at bottom. Each, in its utmost development, supposes a high degree of intimacy and heart-knowledge; each renders one individual dependent for the food of his affections and spiritual fife upon another: each leaves the passionate lover, or the no less passionate hater, forlorn and desolate by the withdrawal of his subject. Philosophically considered, therefore, the two passions seem essentially the same, except that one happens to be seen in a celestial radiance, and the other in a dusky and lurid glow. In the spiritual world, the old physician and the minister—mutual victims as they have been—may, unawares, have found their earthly stock of hatred and antipathy transmuted into golden love.

Leaving this discussion apart, we have a matter of business to communicate to the reader. At old Roger Chillingworth's decease, (which took place within the year), and by his last will and testament, of which Governor Bellingham and the Reverend Mr. Wilson were executors, he bequeathed a very considerable amount of property, both here and in England to little Pearl, the daughter of Hester Prynne.

So Pearl—the elf child—the demon offspring, as some people up to that epoch persisted in considering her—became the richest heiress of her day in the New World. Not improbably this circumstance wrought a very material change in the public estimation; and had the mother and child remained here, little Pearl at a marriageable period of life might have mingled her wild blood with the lineage of the devoutest Puritan among them all. But, in no long time after the physician's death, the wearer of the scarlet letter disappeared, and Pearl along with her. For many years, though a vague report would now and then find its way across the sea—like a shapeless piece of driftwood tossed ashore with the initials of a name upon it—yet no tidings of them unquestionably authentic were received. The story of the scarlet letter grew into a legend. Its spell, however, was still potent, and kept the scaffold awful where the poor minister had died, and likewise the cottage by the sea-shore where Hester Prynne had dwelt. Near this latter spot, one afternoon some children were at play, when they beheld a tall woman in a gray robe approach the cottage-door. In all those years it had never once been opened; but either she unlocked it or the decaying wood and iron yielded to her hand, or she glided shadow-like through these impediments—and, at all events, went in.

On the threshold she paused—turned partly round—for perchance the idea of entering alone and all so changed, the home of so intense a former life, was more dreary and desolate than even she could bear. But her hesitation was only for an instant, though long enough to display a scarlet letter on her breast.

And Hester Prynne had returned, and taken up her long-forsaken shame! But where was little Pearl? If still alive she must now have been in the flush and bloom of early womanhood. None knew—nor ever learned with the fulness of perfect certainty—whether the elf-child had gone thus untimely to a maiden grave; or whether her wild, rich nature had been softened and subdued and made capable of a woman's gentle happiness. But through the remainder of Hester's life there were indications that the recluse of the scarlet letter was the object of love and interest with some inhabitant of another land. Letters came, with armorial seals upon them, though of bearings unknown to English heraldry. In the cottage there were articles of comfort and luxury such as Hester never cared to use, but which only wealth could have purchased and affection have imagined for her. There were trifles too, little ornaments, beautiful tokens of a continual remembrance, that must have been wrought by delicate fingers at the impulse of a fond heart. And once Hester was seen embroidering a baby-garment with such a lavish richness of golden fancy as would have raised a public tumult had any infant thus apparelled, been shown to our sober-hued community.

In fine, the gossips of that day believed—and Mr. Surveyor Pue, who made investigations a century later, believed—and one of his recent successors in office, moreover, faithfully believes—that Pearl was not only alive, but married, and happy, and mindful of her mother; and that she would most joyfully have entertained that sad and lonely mother at her fireside.

But there was a more real life for Hester Prynne, here, in New England, than in that unknown region where Pearl had found a home. Here had been her sin; here, her sorrow; and here was yet to be her penitence. She had returned, therefore, and resumed—of her own free will, for not the sternest magistrate of that iron period would have imposed it—resumed the symbol of which we have related so dark a tale. Never afterwards did it quit her bosom. But, in the lapse of the toilsome, thoughtful, and self-devoted years that made up Hester's life, the scarlet letter ceased to be a stigma which attracted the world's scorn and bitterness, and became a type of something to be sorrowed over, and looked upon with awe, yet with reverence too. And, as Hester Prynne had no selfish ends, nor lived in any measure for her own profit and enjoyment, people brought all their sorrows and perplexities, and besought her counsel, as one who had herself gone through a mighty trouble. Women, more especially—in the continually recurring trials of wounded, wasted, wronged, misplaced, or erring and sinful passion—or with the dreary burden of a heart unyielded, because unvalued and unsought came to Hester's cottage, demanding why they were so wretched, and what the remedy! Hester comforted and counselled them, as best she might. She assured them, too, of her firm belief that, at some brighter period, when the world should have grown ripe for it, in Heaven's own time, a new truth would be revealed, in order to establish the whole relation between man and woman on a surer ground of mutual happiness. Earlier in life, Hester had vainly imagined that she herself might be the destined prophetess, but had long since recognised the impossibility that any mission of divine and mysterious truth should be confided to a woman stained with sin, bowed down with shame, or even burdened with a life-long sorrow. The angel and apostle of the coming revelation must be a woman, indeed, but lofty, pure, and beautiful, and wise; moreover, not through dusky grief, but the ethereal medium of joy; and showing how sacred love should make us happy, by the truest test of a life successful to such an end.

So said Hester Prynne, and glanced her sad eyes downward at the scarlet letter. And, after many, many years, a new grave was delved, near an old and sunken one, in that burial-ground beside which King's Chapel has since been built. It was near that old and sunken grave, yet with a space between, as if the dust of the two sleepers had no right to mingle. Yet one tomb-stone served for both. All around, there were monuments carved with armorial bearings; and on this simple slab of slate—as the curious investigator may still discern, and perplex himself with the purport—there appeared the semblance of an engraved escutcheon. It bore a device, a herald's wording of which may serve for a motto and brief description of our now concluded legend; so sombre is it, and relieved only by one ever-glowing point of light gloomier than the shadow:—

"ON A FIELD, SABLE, THE LETTER A, GULES"

THE HOUSE OF THE SEVEN GABLES

INTRODUCTORY NOTE. THE HOUSE OF THE SEVEN GABLES.

IN September of the year during the February of which Hawthorne had completed "The Scarlet Letter," he began "The House of the Seven Gables." Meanwhile, he had removed from Salem to Lenox, in Berkshire County, Massachusetts, where he occupied with his family a small red wooden house, still standing at the date of this edition, near the Stockbridge Bowl.

"I sha'n't have the new story ready by November," he explained to his publisher, on the 1st of October, "for I am never good for anything in the literary way till after the first autumnal frost, which has somewhat such an effect on my imagination that it does on the foliage here about me-multiplying and brightening its hues." But by vigorous application he was able to complete the new work about the middle of the January following.

Since research has disclosed the manner in which the romance is interwoven with incidents from the history of the Hawthorne family, "The House of the Seven Gables" has acquired an interest apart from that by which it first appealed to the public. John Hathorne (as the name was then spelled), the great-grandfather of Nathaniel Hawthorne, was a magistrate at Salem in the latter part of the seventeenth century, and officiated at the famous trials for witchcraft held there. It is of record that he used peculiar severity towards a certain woman who was among the accused; and the husband of this woman prophesied that God would take revenge upon his wife's persecutors. This circumstance doubtless furnished a hint for that piece of tradition in the book which represents a Pyncheon of a former generation as having persecuted one Maule, who declared that God would give his enemy "blood to drink." It became a conviction with the Hawthorne family that a curse had been pronounced upon its members, which continued in force in the time of the romancer; a conviction perhaps derived from the recorded prophecy of the injured woman's husband, just mentioned; and, here again, we have a correspondence with Maule's malediction in the story. Furthermore, there occurs in the "American Note-Books" (August 27, 1837), a reminiscence of the author's family, to the following effect. Philip English, a character well-known in early Salem annals, was among those who suffered from John Hathorne's magisterial harshness, and he maintained in consequence a lasting feud with the old Puritan official. But at his death English left daughters, one of whom is said to have married the son of Justice John Hathorne, whom English had declared he would never forgive. It is scarcely necessary to point out how clearly this foreshadows the final union of those hereditary foes, the Pyncheons and Maules, through the marriage of Phoebe and Holgrave. The romance, however, describes the Maules as possessing some of the traits known to have been characteristic of the Hawthornes: for example, "so long as any of the race were to be found, they had been marked out from other men—not strikingly, nor as with a sharp line, but with an effect that was felt rather than spoken of—by an hereditary characteristic of reserve." Thus, while the general suggestion of the Hawthorne line and its fortunes was followed in the romance, the Pyncheons taking the place of the author's family, certain distinguishing marks of the Hawthornes were assigned to the imaginary Maule posterity.

There are one or two other points which indicate Hawthorne's method of basing his compositions, the result in the main of pure invention, on the solid ground of particular facts. Allusion is made, in the first chapter of the "Seven Gables," to a grant of lands in Waldo County, Maine, owned by the Pyncheon family. In the "American Note-Books" there is an entry, dated August 12, 1837, which speaks of the Revolutionary general, Knox, and his land-grant in Waldo County, by virtue of which the owner had hoped to establish an estate on the English plan, with a tenantry to make it profitable for him. An incident of much greater importance in the story is the supposed murder of one of the Pyncheons by his nephew, to whom we are introduced as Clifford Pyncheon. In all probability Hawthorne connected with this, in his mind, the murder of Mr. White, a wealthy gentleman of Salem, killed by a man whom his nephew had hired. This took place a few years after Hawthorne's graduation from college, and was one of the celebrated cases of the day, Daniel Webster taking part prominently in the trial. But it should be observed here that such resemblances as these between sundry elements in the work of Hawthorne's fancy and details of reality are only fragmentary, and are rearranged to suit the author's purposes.

In the same way he has made his description of Hepzibah Pyncheon's seven-gabled mansion conform so nearly to several old dwellings formerly or still extant in Salem, that strenuous efforts have been made to fix upon some one of them as the veritable edifice of the romance. A paragraph in the opening chapter has perhaps assisted this delusion that there must have been a single original House of the Seven Gables, framed by flesh-and-blood carpenters; for it runs thus:—

"Familiar as it stands in the writer's recollection—for it has been an object of curiosity with him from boyhood, both as a specimen of the best and stateliest architecture of a long-past epoch, and as the scene of events more full of interest perhaps than those of a gray feudal castle—familiar as it stands, in its rusty old age, it is therefore only the more difficult to imagine the bright novelty with which it first caught the sunshine."

Hundreds of pilgrims annually visit a house in Salem, belonging to one branch of the Ingersoll family of that place, which is stoutly maintained to have been the model for Hawthorne's visionary dwelling. Others have supposed that the now vanished house of the identical Philip English, whose blood, as we have already noticed, became mingled with that of the Hawthornes, supplied the pattern; and still a third building, known as the Curwen mansion, has been declared the only genuine establishment. Notwithstanding persistent popular belief, the authenticity of all these must positively be denied; although it is possible that isolated reminiscences of all three may have blended with the ideal image in the mind of Hawthorne. He, it will be seen, remarks in the Preface, alluding to himself in the third person, that he trusts not to be condemned for "laying out a street that infringes upon nobody's private rights... and building a house of materials long in use for constructing castles in the air." More than this, he stated to persons still living that the house of the romance was not copied from any actual edifice, but was simply a general reproduction of a style of architecture belonging to colonial days, examples of which survived into the period of his youth, but have since been radically modified or destroyed. Here, as elsewhere, he exercised the liberty of a creative mind to heighten the probability of his pictures without confining himself to a literal description of something he had seen.

While Hawthorne remained at Lenox, and during the composition of this romance, various other literary personages settled or stayed for a time in the vicinity; among them, Herman Melville, whose intercourse Hawthorne greatly enjoyed, Henry James, Sr., Doctor Holmes, J. T. Headley, James Russell Lowell, Edwin P. Whipple, Frederika Bremer, and J. T. Fields; so that there was no lack of intellectual society in the midst of the beautiful and inspiring mountain scenery of the place. "In the afternoons, nowadays," he records, shortly before beginning the work, "this valley in which I dwell seems like a vast basin filled with golden Sunshine as with wine;" and, happy in the companionship of his wife and their three children, he led a simple, refined, idyllic life, despite the restrictions of a scanty and uncertain income. A letter written by Mrs. Hawthorne, at this time, to a member of her family, gives incidentally a glimpse of the scene, which may properly find a place here. She says: "I delight to think that you also can look forth, as I do now, upon a broad valley and a fine amphitheater of hills, and are about to watch the stately ceremony of the sunset from your piazza. But you have not this lovely lake, nor, I suppose, the delicate purple mist which folds these slumbering mountains in airy veils. Mr. Hawthorne has been lying down in the sun shine, slightly fleckered with the shadows of a tree, and Una and Julian have been making him look like the mighty Pan, by covering his chin and breast with long grass-blades, that looked like a verdant and venerable beard." The pleasantness and peace of his surroundings and of his modest home, in Lenox, may be taken into account as harmonizing with the mellow serenity of the romance then produced. Of the work, when it appeared in the early spring of 1851, he wrote to Horatio Bridge these words, now published for the first time:—

"'The House of the Seven Gables' in my opinion, is better than 'The Scarlet Letter:' but I should not wonder if I had refined upon the principal character a little too much for popular appreciation, nor if the romance of the book should be somewhat at odds with the humble and familiar scenery in which I invest it. But I feel that portions of it are as good as anything I can hope to write, and the publisher speaks encouragingly of its success."

From England, especially, came many warm expressions of praise,—a fact which Mrs. Hawthorne, in a private letter, commented on as the fulfillment of a possibility which Hawthorne, writing in boyhood to his mother, had looked forward to. He had asked her if she would not like him to become an author and have his books read in England.

G. P. L.

PREFACE.

WHEN a writer calls his work a Romance, it need hardly be observed that he wishes to claim a certain latitude, both as to its fashion and material, which he would not have felt himself entitled to assume had he professed to be writing a Novel. The latter form of composition is presumed to aim at a very minute fidelity, not merely to the possible, but to the probable and ordinary course of man's experience. The former—while, as a work of art, it must rigidly subject itself to laws, and while it sins unpardonably so far as it may swerve aside from the truth of the human heart—has fairly a right to present that truth under circumstances, to a great extent, of the writer's own choosing or creation. If he think fit, also, he may so manage his atmospherical medium as to bring out or mellow the lights and deepen and enrich the shadows of the picture. He will be wise, no doubt, to make a very moderate use of the privileges here stated, and, especially, to mingle the Marvelous rather as a slight, delicate, and evanescent flavor, than as any portion of the actual substance of the dish offered to the public. He can hardly be said, however, to commit a literary crime even if he disregard this caution.

In the present work, the author has proposed to himself—but with what success, fortunately, it is not for him to judge—to keep undeviatingly within his immunities. The point of view in which this tale comes under the Romantic definition lies in the attempt to connect a bygone time with the very present that is flitting away from us. It is a legend prolonging itself, from an epoch now gray in the distance, down into our own broad daylight, and bringing along with it some of its legendary mist, which the reader, according to his pleasure, may either disregard, or allow it to float almost imperceptibly about the characters and events for the sake of a picturesque effect. The narrative, it may be, is woven of so humble a texture as to require this advantage, and, at the same time, to render it the more difficult of attainment.

Many writers lay very great stress upon some definite moral purpose, at which they profess to aim their works. Not to be deficient in this particular, the author has provided himself with a moral,—the truth, namely, that the wrong-doing of one generation lives into the successive ones, and, divesting itself of every temporary advantage, becomes a pure and uncontrollable mischief; and he would feel it a singular gratification if this romance might effectually convince mankind—or, indeed, any one man—of the folly of tumbling down an avalanche of ill-gotten gold, or real estate, on the heads of an unfortunate posterity, thereby to maim and crush them, until the accumulated mass shall be scattered abroad in its original atoms. In good faith, however, he is not sufficiently imaginative to flatter himself with the slightest hope of this kind. When romances do really teach anything, or produce any effective operation, it is usually through a far more subtile process than the ostensible one. The author has considered it hardly worth his while, therefore, relentlessly to impale the story with its moral as with an iron rod,—or, rather, as by sticking a pin through a butterfly,—thus at once depriving it of life, and causing it to stiffen in an ungainly and unnatural attitude. A high truth, indeed, fairly, finely, and skilfully wrought out, brightening at every step, and crowning the final development of a work of fiction, may add an artistic glory, but is never any truer, and seldom any more evident, at the last page than at the first.

The reader may perhaps choose to assign an actual locality to the imaginary events of this narrative. If permitted by the historical connection,—which, though slight, was essential to his plan,—the author would very willingly have avoided anything of this nature. Not to speak of other objections, it exposes the romance to an inflexible and exceedingly dangerous species of criticism, by bringing his fancy-pictures almost into positive contact with the realities of the moment. It has been no part of his object, however, to describe local manners, nor in any way to meddle with the characteristics of a community for whom he cherishes a proper respect and a natural regard. He trusts not to be considered as unpardonably offending by laying out a street that infringes upon nobody's private rights, and appropriating a lot of land which had no visible owner, and building a house of materials long in use for constructing castles in the air. The personages of the tale—though they give themselves out to be of ancient stability and considerable prominence—are really of the author's own making, or at all events, of his own mixing; their virtues can shed no lustre, nor their defects redound, in the remotest degree, to the discredit of the venerable town of which they profess to be inhabitants. He would be glad, therefore, if-especially in the quarter to which he alludes-the book may be read strictly as a Romance, having a great deal more to do with the clouds overhead than with any portion of the actual soil of the County of Essex.

LENOX, January 27, 1851.

I The Old Pyncheon Family

HALFWAY down a by-street of one of our New England towns stands a rusty wooden house, with seven acutely peaked gables, facing towards various points of the compass, and a huge, clustered chimney in the midst. The street is Pyncheon Street; the house is the old Pyncheon House; and an elm-tree, of wide circumference, rooted before the door, is familiar to every town-born child by the title of the Pyncheon Elm. On my occasional visits to the town aforesaid, I seldom failed to turn down Pyncheon Street, for the sake of passing through the shadow of these two antiquities,—the great elm-tree and the weather-beaten edifice.

The aspect of the venerable mansion has always affected me like a human countenance, bearing the traces not merely of outward storm and sunshine, but expressive also, of the long lapse of mortal life, and accompanying vicissitudes that have passed within. Were these to be worthily recounted, they would form a narrative of no small interest and instruction, and possessing, moreover, a certain remarkable unity, which might almost seem the result of artistic arrangement. But the story would include a chain of events extending over the better part of two centuries, and, written out with reasonable amplitude, would fill a bigger folio volume, or a longer series of duodecimos, than could prudently be appropriated to the annals of all New England during a similar period. It consequently becomes imperative to make short work with most of the traditionary lore of which the old Pyncheon House, otherwise known as the House of the Seven Gables, has been the theme. With a brief sketch, therefore, of the circumstances amid which the foundation of the house was laid, and a rapid glimpse at its quaint exterior, as it grew black in the prevalent east wind,—pointing, too, here and there, at some spot of more verdant mossiness on its roof and walls,—we shall commence the real action of our tale at an epoch not very remote from the present day. Still, there will be a connection with the long past—a reference to forgotten events and personages, and to manners, feelings, and opinions, almost or wholly obsolete—which, if adequately translated to the reader, would serve to illustrate how much of old material goes to make up the freshest novelty of human life. Hence, too, might be drawn a weighty lesson from the little-regarded truth, that the act of the passing generation is the germ which may and must produce good or evil fruit in a far-distant time; that, together with the seed of the merely temporary crop, which mortals term expediency, they inevitably sow the acorns of a more enduring growth, which may darkly overshadow their posterity.

The House of the Seven Gables, antique as it now looks, was not the first habitation erected by civilized man on precisely the same spot of ground. Pyncheon Street formerly bore the humbler appellation of Maule's Lane, from the name of the original occupant of the soil, before whose cottage-door it was a cow-path. A natural spring of soft and pleasant water—a rare treasure on the sea-girt peninsula where the Puritan settlement was made—had early induced Matthew Maule to build a hut, shaggy with thatch, at this point, although somewhat too remote from what was then the centre of the village. In the growth of the town, however, after some thirty or forty years, the site covered by this rude hovel had become exceedingly desirable in the eyes of a prominent and powerful personage, who asserted plausible claims to the proprietorship of this and a large adjacent tract of land, on the strength of a grant from the legislature. Colonel Pyncheon, the claimant, as we gather from whatever traits of him are preserved, was characterized by an iron energy of purpose. Matthew Maule, on the other hand, though an obscure man, was stubborn in the defence of what he considered his right; and, for several years, he succeeded in protecting the acre or two of earth which, with his own toil, he had hewn out of the primeval forest, to be his garden ground and homestead. No written record of this dispute is known to be in existence. Our acquaintance with the whole subject is derived chiefly from tradition. It would be bold, therefore, and possibly unjust, to venture a decisive opinion as to its merits; although it appears to have been at least a matter of doubt, whether Colonel Pyncheon's claim were not unduly stretched, in order to make it cover the small metes and bounds of Matthew Maule. What greatly strengthens such a suspicion is the fact that this controversy between two ill-matched antagonists—at a period, moreover, laud it as we may, when personal influence had far more weight than now—remained for years undecided, and came to a close only with the death of the party occupying the disputed soil. The mode of his death, too, affects the mind differently, in our day, from what it did a century and a half ago. It was a death that blasted with strange horror the humble name of the dweller in the cottage, and made it seem almost a religious act to drive the plough over the little area of his habitation, and obliterate his place and memory from among men.

Old Matthew Maule, in a word, was executed for the crime of witchcraft. He was one of the martyrs to that terrible delusion, which should teach us, among its other morals, that the influential classes, and those who take upon themselves to be leaders of the people, are fully liable to all the passionate error that has ever characterized the maddest mob. Clergymen, judges, statesmen,—the wisest, calmest, holiest persons of their day stood in the inner circle round about the gallows, loudest to applaud the work of blood, latest to confess themselves miserably deceived. If any one part of their proceedings can be said to deserve less blame than another, it was the singular indiscrimination with which they persecuted, not merely the poor and aged, as in former judicial massacres, but people of all ranks; their own equals, brethren, and wives. Amid the disorder of such various ruin, it is not strange that a man of inconsiderable note, like Maule, should have trodden the martyr's path to the hill of execution almost unremarked in the throng of his fellow sufferers. But, in after days, when the frenzy of that hideous epoch had subsided, it was remembered how loudly Colonel Pyncheon had joined in the general cry, to purge the land from witchcraft; nor did it fail to be whispered, that there was an invidious acrimony in the zeal with which he had sought the condemnation of Matthew Maule. It was well known that the victim had recognized the bitterness of personal enmity in his persecutor's conduct towards him, and that he declared himself hunted to death for his spoil. At the moment of execution—with the halter about his neck, and while Colonel Pyncheon sat on horseback, grimly gazing at the scene Maule had addressed him from the scaffold, and uttered a prophecy, of which history, as well as fireside tradition, has preserved the very words. "God," said the dying man, pointing his finger, with a ghastly look, at the undismayed countenance of his enemy,—"God will give him blood to drink!" After the reputed wizard's death, his humble homestead had fallen an easy spoil into Colonel Pyncheon's grasp. When it was understood, however, that the Colonel intended to erect a family mansion-spacious, ponderously framed of oaken timber, and calculated to endure for many generations of his posterity over the spot first covered by the log-built hut of Matthew Maule, there was much shaking of the head among the village gossips. Without absolutely expressing a doubt whether the stalwart Puritan had acted as a man of conscience and integrity throughout the proceedings which have been sketched, they, nevertheless, hinted that he was about to build his house over an unquiet grave. His home would include the home of the dead and buried wizard, and would thus afford the ghost of the latter a kind of privilege to haunt its new apartments, and the chambers into which future bridegrooms were to lead their brides, and where children of the Pyncheon blood were to be born. The terror and ugliness of Maule's crime, and the wretchedness of his punishment, would darken the freshly plastered walls, and infect them early with the scent of an old and melancholy house. Why, then,—while so much of the soil around him was bestrewn with the virgin forest leaves,—why should Colonel Pyncheon prefer a site that had already been accurst?

But the Puritan soldier and magistrate was not a man to be turned aside from his well-considered scheme, either by dread of the wizard's ghost, or by flimsy sentimentalities of any kind, however specious. Had he been told of a bad air, it might have moved him somewhat, but he was ready to encounter an evil spirit on his own ground. Endowed with commonsense, as massive and hard as blocks of granite, fastened together by stern rigidity of purpose, as with iron clamps, he followed out his original design, probably without so much as imagining an objection to it. On the score of delicacy, or any scrupulousness which a finer sensibility might have taught him, the Colonel, like most of his breed and generation, was impenetrable. He therefore dug his cellar, and laid the deep foundations of his mansion, on the square of earth whence Matthew Maule, forty years before, had first swept away the fallen leaves. It was a curious, and, as some people thought, an ominous fact, that, very soon after the workmen began their operations, the spring of water, above mentioned, entirely lost the deliciousness of its pristine quality. Whether its sources were disturbed by the depth of the new cellar, or whatever subtler cause might lurk at the bottom, it is certain that the water of Maule's Well, as it continued to be called, grew hard and brackish. Even such we find it now; and any old woman of the neighborhood will certify that it is productive of intestinal mischief to those who quench their thirst there.

The reader may deem it singular that the head carpenter of the new edifice was no other than the son of the very man from whose dead gripe the property of the soil had been wrested. Not improbably he was the best workman of his time; or, perhaps, the Colonel thought it expedient, or was impelled by some better feeling, thus openly to cast aside all animosity against the race of his fallen antagonist. Nor was it out of keeping with the general coarseness and matter-of-fact character of the age, that the son should be willing to earn an honest penny, or, rather, a weighty amount of sterling pounds, from the purse of his father's deadly enemy. At all events, Thomas Maule became the architect of the House of the Seven Gables, and performed his duty so faithfully that the timber framework fastened by his hands still holds together.

Thus the great house was built. Familiar as it stands in the writer's recollection,—for it has been an object of curiosity with him from boyhood, both as a specimen of the best and stateliest architecture of a longpast epoch, and as the scene of events more full of human interest, perhaps, than those of a gray feudal castle,—familiar as it stands, in its rusty old age, it is therefore only the more difficult to imagine the bright novelty with which it first caught the sunshine. The impression of its actual state, at this distance of a hundred and sixty years, darkens inevitably through the picture which we would fain give of its appearance on the morning when the Puritan magnate bade all the town to be his guests. A ceremony of consecration, festive as well as religious, was now to be performed. A prayer and discourse from the Rev. Mr. Higginson, and the outpouring of a psalm from the general throat of the community, was to be made acceptable to the grosser sense by ale, cider, wine, and brandy, in copious effusion, and, as some authorities aver, by an ox, roasted whole, or at least, by the weight and substance of an ox, in more manageable joints and sirloins. The carcass of a deer, shot within twenty miles, had supplied material for the vast circumference of a pasty. A codfish of sixty pounds, caught in the bay, had been dissolved into the rich liquid of a chowder. The chimney of the new house, in short, belching forth its kitchen smoke, impregnated the whole air with the scent of meats, fowls, and fishes, spicily concocted with odoriferous herbs, and onions in abundance. The mere smell of such festivity, making its way to everybody's nostrils, was at once an invitation and an appetite.

Maule's Lane, or Pyncheon Street, as it were now more decorous to call it, was thronged, at the appointed hour, as with a congregation on its way to church. All, as they approached, looked upward at the imposing edifice, which was henceforth to assume its rank among the habitations of mankind. There it rose, a little withdrawn from the line of the street, but in pride, not modesty. Its whole visible exterior was ornamented with quaint figures, conceived in the grotesqueness of a Gothic fancy, and drawn or stamped in the glittering plaster, composed of lime, pebbles, and bits of glass, with which the woodwork of the walls was overspread. On every side the seven gables pointed sharply towards the sky, and presented the aspect of a whole sisterhood of edifices, breathing through the spiracles of one great chimney. The many lattices, with their small, diamond-shaped panes, admitted the sunlight into hall and chamber, while, nevertheless, the second story, projecting far over the base, and itself retiring beneath the third, threw a shadowy and thoughtful gloom into the lower rooms. Carved globes of wood were affixed under the jutting stories. Little spiral rods of iron beautified each of the seven peaks. On the triangular portion of the gable, that fronted next the street, was a dial, put up that very morning, and on which the sun was still marking the passage of the first bright hour in a history that was not destined to be all so bright. All around were scattered shavings, chips, shingles, and broken halves of bricks; these, together with the lately turned earth, on which the grass had not begun to grow, contributed to the impression of strangeness and novelty proper to a house that had yet its place to make among men's daily interests.

The principal entrance, which had almost the breadth of a church-door, was in the angle between the two front gables, and was covered by an open porch, with benches beneath its shelter. Under this arched doorway, scraping their feet on the unworn threshold, now trod the clergymen, the elders, the magistrates, the deacons, and whatever of aristocracy there was in town or county. Thither, too, thronged the plebeian classes as freely as their betters, and in larger number. Just within the entrance, however, stood two serving-men, pointing some of the guests to the neighborhood of the kitchen and ushering others into the statelier rooms,—hospitable alike to all, but still with a scrutinizing regard to the high or low degree of each. Velvet garments sombre but rich, stiffly plaited ruffs and bands, embroidered gloves, venerable beards, the mien and countenance of authority, made it easy to distinguish the gentleman of worship, at that period, from the tradesman, with his plodding air, or the laborer, in his leathern jerkin, stealing awe-stricken into the house which he had perhaps helped to build.

One inauspicious circumstance there was, which awakened a hardly concealed displeasure in the breasts of a few of the more punctilious visitors. The founder of this stately mansion—a gentleman noted for the square and ponderous courtesy of his demeanor, ought surely to have stood in his own hall, and to have offered the first welcome to so many eminent personages as here presented themselves in honor of his solemn festival. He was as yet invisible; the most favored of the guests had not beheld him. This sluggishness on Colonel Pyncheon's part became still more unaccountable, when the second dignitary of the province made his appearance, and found no more ceremonious a reception. The lieutenant-governor, although his visit was one of the anticipated glories of the day, had alighted from his horse, and assisted his lady from her side-saddle, and crossed the Colonel's threshold, without other greeting than that of the principal domestic.

This person—a gray-headed man, of quiet and most respectful deportment—found it necessary to explain that his master still remained in his study, or private apartment; on entering which, an hour before, he had expressed a wish on no account to be disturbed.

"Do not you see, fellow," said the high-sheriff of the county, taking the servant aside, "that this is no less a man than the lieutenant-governor? Summon Colonel Pyncheon at once! I know that he received letters from England this morning; and, in the perusal and consideration of them, an hour may have passed away without his noticing it. But he will be ill-pleased, I judge, if you suffer him to neglect the courtesy due to one of our chief rulers, and who may be said to represent King William, in the absence of the governor himself. Call your master instantly."

"Nay, please your worship," answered the man, in much perplexity, but with a backwardness that strikingly indicated the hard and severe character of Colonel Pyncheon's domestic rule; "my master's orders were exceeding strict; and, as your worship knows, he permits of no discretion in the obedience of those who owe him service. Let who list open yonder door; I dare not, though the governor's own voice should bid me do it!"

"Pooh, pooh, master high sheriff!" cried the lieutenant-governor, who had overheard the foregoing discussion, and felt himself high enough in station to play a little with his dignity. "I will take the matter into my own hands. It is time that the good Colonel came forth to greet his friends; else we shall be apt to suspect that he has taken a sip too much of his Canary wine, in his extreme deliberation which cask it were best to broach in honor of the day! But since he is so much behindhand, I will give him a remembrancer myself!"

Accordingly, with such a tramp of his ponderous riding-boots as might of itself have been audible in the remotest of the seven gables, he advanced to the door, which the servant pointed out, and made its new panels reecho with a loud, free knock. Then, looking round, with a smile, to the spectators, he awaited a response. As none came, however, he knocked again, but with the same unsatisfactory result as at first. And now, being a trifle choleric in his temperament, the lieutenant-governor uplifted the heavy hilt of his sword, wherewith he so beat and banged upon the door, that, as some of the bystanders whispered, the racket might have disturbed the dead. Be that as it might, it seemed to produce no awakening effect on Colonel Pyncheon. When the sound subsided, the silence through the house was deep, dreary, and oppressive, notwithstanding that the tongues of many of the guests had already been loosened by a surreptitious cup or two of wine or spirits.

"Strange, forsooth!—very strange!" cried the lieutenant-governor, whose smile was changed to a frown. "But seeing that our host sets us the good example of forgetting ceremony, I shall likewise throw it aside, and make free to intrude on his privacy."

He tried the door, which yielded to his hand, and was flung wide open by a sudden gust of wind that passed, as with a loud sigh, from the outermost portal through all the passages and apartments of the new house. It rustled the silken garments of the ladies, and waved the long curls of the gentlemen's wigs, and shook the window-hangings and the curtains of the bedchambers; causing everywhere a singular stir, which yet was more like a hush. A shadow of awe and half-fearful anticipation—nobody knew wherefore, nor of what—had all at once fallen over the company.

They thronged, however, to the now open door, pressing the lieutenant-governor, in the eagerness of their curiosity, into the room in advance of them. At the first glimpse they beheld nothing extraordinary: a handsomely furnished room, of moderate size, somewhat darkened by curtains; books arranged on shelves; a large map on the wall, and likewise a portrait of Colonel Pyncheon, beneath which sat the original Colonel himself, in an oaken elbow-chair, with a pen in his hand. Letters, parchments, and blank sheets of paper were on the table before him. He appeared to gaze at the curious crowd, in front of which stood the lieutenant-governor; and there was a frown on his dark and massive countenance, as if sternly resentful of the boldness that had impelled them into his private retirement.

A little boy—the Colonel's grandchild, and the only human being that ever dared to be familiar with him—now made his way among the guests, and ran towards the seated figure; then pausing halfway, he began to shriek with terror. The company, tremulous as the leaves of a tree, when all are shaking together, drew nearer, and perceived that there was an unnatural distortion in the fixedness of Colonel Pyncheon's stare; that there was blood on his ruff, and that his hoary beard was saturated with it. It was too late to give assistance. The iron-hearted Puritan, the relentless persecutor, the grasping and strong-willed man was dead! Dead, in his new house! There is a tradition, only worth alluding to as lending a tinge of superstitious awe to a scene perhaps gloomy enough without it, that a voice spoke loudly among the guests, the tones of which were like those of old Matthew Maule, the executed wizard,—"God hath given him blood to drink!"

Thus early had that one guest,—the only guest who is certain, at one time or another, to find his way into every human dwelling,—thus early had Death stepped across the threshold of the House of the Seven Gables!

Colonel Pyncheon's sudden and mysterious end made a vast deal of noise in its day. There were many rumors, some of which have vaguely drifted down to the present time, how that appearances indicated violence; that there were the marks of fingers on his throat, and the print of a bloody hand on his plaited ruff; and that his peaked beard was dishevelled, as if it had been fiercely clutched and pulled. It was averred, likewise, that the lattice window, near the Colonel's chair, was open; and that, only a few minutes before the fatal occurrence, the figure of a man had been seen clambering over the garden fence, in the rear of the house. But it were folly to lay any stress on stories of this kind, which are sure to spring up around such an event as that now related, and which, as in the present case, sometimes prolong themselves for ages afterwards, like the toadstools that indicate where the fallen and buried trunk of a tree has long since mouldered into the earth. For our own part, we allow them just as little credence as to that other fable of the skeleton hand which the lieutenant-governor was said to have seen at the Colonel's throat, but which vanished away, as he advanced farther into the room. Certain it is, however, that there was a great consultation and dispute of doctors over the dead body. One,—John Swinnerton by name,—who appears to have been a man of eminence, upheld it, if we have rightly understood his terms of art, to be a case of apoplexy. His professional brethren, each for himself, adopted various hypotheses, more or less plausible, but all dressed out in a perplexing mystery of phrase, which, if it do not show a bewilderment of mind in these erudite physicians, certainly causes it in the unlearned peruser of their opinions. The coroner's jury sat upon the corpse, and, like sensible men, returned an unassailable verdict of "Sudden Death!"

It is indeed difficult to imagine that there could have been a serious suspicion of murder, or the slightest grounds for implicating any particular individual as the perpetrator. The rank, wealth, and eminent character of the deceased must have insured the strictest scrutiny into every ambiguous circumstance. As none such is on record, it is safe to assume that none existed. Tradition,—which sometimes brings down truth that history has let slip, but is oftener the wild babble of the time, such as was formerly spoken at the fireside and now congeals in newspapers,—tradition is responsible for all contrary averments. In Colonel Pyncheon's funeral sermon, which was printed, and is still extant, the Rev. Mr. Higginson enumerates, among the many felicities of his distinguished parishioner's earthly career, the happy seasonableness of his death. His duties all performed,—the highest prosperity attained,—his race and future generations fixed on a stable basis, and with a stately roof to shelter them for centuries to come,—what other upward step remained for this good man to take, save the final step from earth to the golden gate of heaven! The pious clergyman surely would not have uttered words like these had he in the least suspected that the Colonel had been thrust into the other world with the clutch of violence upon his throat.

The family of Colonel Pyncheon, at the epoch of his death, seemed destined to as fortunate a permanence as can anywise consist with the inherent instability of human affairs. It might fairly be anticipated that the progress of time would rather increase and ripen their prosperity, than wear away and destroy it. For, not only had his son and heir come into immediate enjoyment of a rich estate, but there was a claim through an Indian deed, confirmed by a subsequent grant of the General Court, to a vast and as yet unexplored and unmeasured tract of Eastern lands. These possessions—for as such they might almost certainly be reckoned—comprised the greater part of what is now known as Waldo County, in the state of Maine, and were more extensive than many a dukedom, or even a reigning prince's territory, on European soil. When the pathless forest that still covered this wild principality should give place—as it inevitably must, though perhaps not till ages hence—to the golden fertility of human culture, it would be the source of incalculable wealth to the Pyncheon blood. Had the Colonel survived only a few weeks longer, it is probable that his great political influence, and powerful connections at home and abroad, would have consummated all that was necessary to render the claim available. But, in spite of good Mr. Higginson's congratulatory eloquence, this appeared to be the one thing which Colonel Pyncheon, provident and sagacious as he was, had allowed to go at loose ends. So far as the prospective territory was concerned, he unquestionably died too soon. His son lacked not merely the father's eminent position, but the talent and force of character to achieve it: he could, therefore, effect nothing by dint of political interest; and the bare justice or legality of the claim was not so apparent, after the Colonel's decease, as it had been pronounced in his lifetime. Some connecting link had slipped out of the evidence, and could not anywhere be found.

Efforts, it is true, were made by the Pyncheons, not only then, but at various periods for nearly a hundred years afterwards, to obtain what they stubbornly persisted in deeming their right. But, in course of time, the territory was partly regranted to more favored individuals, and partly cleared and occupied by actual settlers. These last, if they ever heard of the Pyncheon title, would have laughed at the idea of any man's asserting a right—on the strength of mouldy parchments, signed with the faded autographs of governors and legislators long dead and forgotten—to the lands which they or their fathers had wrested from the wild hand of nature by their own sturdy toil. This impalpable claim, therefore, resulted in nothing more solid than to cherish, from generation to generation, an absurd delusion of family importance, which all along characterized the Pyncheons. It caused the poorest member of the race to feel as if he inherited a kind of nobility, and might yet come into the possession of princely wealth to support it. In the better specimens of the breed, this peculiarity threw an ideal grace over the hard material of human life, without stealing away any truly valuable quality. In the baser sort, its effect was to increase the liability to sluggishness and dependence, and induce the victim of a shadowy hope to remit all self-effort, while awaiting the realization of his dreams. Years and years after their claim had passed out of the public memory, the Pyncheons were accustomed to consult the Colonel's ancient map, which had been projected while Waldo County was still an unbroken wilderness. Where the old land surveyor had put down woods, lakes, and rivers, they marked out the cleared spaces, and dotted the villages and towns, and calculated the progressively increasing value of the territory, as if there were yet a prospect of its ultimately forming a princedom for themselves.

In almost every generation, nevertheless, there happened to be some one descendant of the family gifted with a portion of the hard, keen sense, and practical energy, that had so remarkably distinguished the original founder. His character, indeed, might be traced all the way down, as distinctly as if the Colonel himself, a little diluted, had been gifted with a sort of intermittent immortality on earth. At two or three epochs, when the fortunes of the family were low, this representative of hereditary qualities had made his appearance, and caused the traditionary gossips of the town to whisper among themselves, "Here is the old Pyncheon come again! Now the Seven Gables will be new-shingled!" From father to son, they clung to the ancestral house with singular tenacity of home attachment. For various reasons, however, and from impressions often too vaguely founded to be put on paper, the writer cherishes the belief that many, if not most, of the successive proprietors of this estate were troubled with doubts as to their moral right to hold it. Of their legal tenure there could be no question; but old Matthew Maule, it is to be feared, trode downward from his own age to a far later one, planting a heavy footstep, all the way, on the conscience of a Pyncheon. If so, we are left to dispose of the awful query, whether each inheritor of the property—conscious of wrong, and failing to rectify it—did not commit anew the great guilt of his ancestor, and incur all its original responsibilities. And supposing such to be the case, would it not be a far truer mode of expression to say of the Pyncheon family, that they inherited a great misfortune, than the reverse?

We have already hinted that it is not our purpose to trace down the history of the Pyncheon family, in its unbroken connection with the House of the Seven Gables; nor to show, as in a magic picture, how the rustiness and infirmity of age gathered over the venerable house itself. As regards its interior life, a large, dim looking-glass used to hang in one of the rooms, and was fabled to contain within its depths all the shapes that had ever been reflected there,—the old Colonel himself, and his many descendants, some in the garb of antique babyhood, and others in the bloom of feminine beauty or manly prime, or saddened with the wrinkles of frosty age. Had we the secret of that mirror, we would gladly sit down before it, and transfer its revelations to our page. But there was a story, for which it is difficult to conceive any foundation, that the posterity of Matthew Maule had some connection with the mystery of the looking-glass, and that, by what appears to have been a sort of mesmeric process, they could make its inner region all alive with the departed Pyncheons; not as they had shown themselves to the world, nor in their better and happier hours, but as doing over again some deed of sin, or in the crisis of life's bitterest sorrow. The popular imagination, indeed, long kept itself busy with the affair of the old Puritan Pyncheon and the wizard Maule; the curse which the latter flung from his scaffold was remembered, with the very important addition, that it had become a part of the Pyncheon inheritance. If one of the family did but gurgle in his throat, a bystander would be likely enough to whisper, between jest and earnest, "He has Maule's blood to drink!" The sudden death of a Pyncheon, about a hundred years ago, with circumstances very similar to what have been related of the Colonel's exit, was held as giving additional probability to the received opinion on this topic. It was considered, moreover, an ugly and ominous circumstance, that Colonel Pyncheon's picture—in obedience, it was said, to a provision of his will—remained affixed to the wall of the room in which he died. Those stern, immitigable features seemed to symbolize an evil influence, and so darkly to mingle the shadow of their presence with the sunshine of the passing hour, that no good thoughts or purposes could ever spring up and blossom there. To the thoughtful mind there will be no tinge of superstition in what we figuratively express, by affirming that the ghost of a dead progenitor—perhaps as a portion of his own punishment—is often doomed to become the Evil Genius of his family.

The Pyncheons, in brief, lived along, for the better part of two centuries, with perhaps less of outward vicissitude than has attended most other New England families during the same period of time. Possessing very distinctive traits of their own, they nevertheless took the general characteristics of the little community in which they dwelt; a town noted for its frugal, discreet, well-ordered, and home-loving inhabitants, as well as for the somewhat confined scope of its sympathies; but in which, be it said, there are odder individuals, and, now and then, stranger occurrences, than one meets with almost anywhere else. During the Revolution, the Pyncheon of that epoch, adopting the royal side, became a refugee; but repented, and made his reappearance, just at the point of time to preserve the House of the Seven Gables from confiscation. For the last seventy years the most noted event in the Pyncheon annals had been likewise the heaviest calamity that ever befell the race; no less than the violent death—for so it was adjudged—of one member of the family by the criminal act of another. Certain circumstances attending this fatal occurrence had brought the deed irresistibly home to a nephew of the deceased Pyncheon. The young man was tried and convicted of the crime; but either the circumstantial nature of the evidence, and possibly some lurking doubts in the breast of the executive, or, lastly—an argument of greater weight in a republic than it could have been under a monarchy,—the high respectability and political influence of the criminal's connections, had availed to mitigate his doom from death to perpetual imprisonment. This sad affair had chanced about thirty years before the action of our story commences. Latterly, there were rumors (which few believed, and only one or two felt greatly interested in) that this long-buried man was likely, for some reason or other, to be summoned forth from his living tomb.

It is essential to say a few words respecting the victim of this now almost forgotten murder. He was an old bachelor, and possessed of great wealth, in addition to the house and real estate which constituted what remained of the ancient Pyncheon property. Being of an eccentric and melancholy turn of mind, and greatly given to rummaging old records and hearkening to old traditions, he had brought himself, it is averred, to the conclusion that Matthew Maule, the wizard, had been foully wronged out of his homestead, if not out of his life. Such being the case, and he, the old bachelor, in possession of the ill-gotten spoil,—with the black stain of blood sunken deep into it, and still to be scented by conscientious nostrils,—the question occurred, whether it were not imperative upon him, even at this late hour, to make restitution to Maule's posterity. To a man living so much in the past, and so little in the present, as the secluded and antiquarian old bachelor, a century and a half seemed not so vast a period as to obviate the propriety of substituting right for wrong. It was the belief of those who knew him best, that he would positively have taken the very singular step of giving up the House of the Seven Gables to the representative of Matthew Maule, but for the unspeakable tumult which a suspicion of the old gentleman's project awakened among his Pyncheon relatives. Their exertions had the effect of suspending his purpose; but it was feared that he would perform, after death, by the operation of his last will, what he had so hardly been prevented from doing in his proper lifetime. But there is no one thing which men so rarely do, whatever the provocation or inducement, as to bequeath patrimonial property away from their own blood. They may love other individuals far better than their relatives,—they may even cherish dislike, or positive hatred, to the latter; but yet, in view of death, the strong prejudice of propinquity revives, and impels the testator to send down his estate in the line marked out by custom so immemorial that it looks like nature. In all the Pyncheons, this feeling had the energy of disease. It was too powerful for the conscientious scruples of the old bachelor; at whose death, accordingly, the mansion-house, together with most of his other riches, passed into the possession of his next legal representative.

This was a nephew, the cousin of the miserable young man who had been convicted of the uncle's murder. The new heir, up to the period of his accession, was reckoned rather a dissipated youth, but had at once reformed, and made himself an exceedingly respectable member of society. In fact, he showed more of the Pyncheon quality, and had won higher eminence in the world, than any of his race since the time of the original Puritan. Applying himself in earlier manhood to the study of the law, and having a natural tendency towards office, he had attained, many years ago, to a judicial situation in some inferior court, which gave him for life the very desirable and imposing title of judge. Later, he had engaged in politics, and served a part of two terms in Congress, besides making a considerable figure in both branches of the State legislature. Judge Pyncheon was unquestionably an honor to his race. He had built himself a country-seat within a few miles of his native town, and there spent such portions of his time as could be spared from public service in the display of every grace and virtue—as a newspaper phrased it, on the eve of an election—befitting the Christian, the good citizen, the horticulturist, and the gentleman.

There were few of the Pyncheons left to sun themselves in the glow of the Judge's prosperity. In respect to natural increase, the breed had not thriven; it appeared rather to be dying out. The only members of the family known to be extant were, first, the Judge himself, and a single surviving son, who was now travelling in Europe; next, the thirty years' prisoner, already alluded to, and a sister of the latter, who occupied, in an extremely retired manner, the House of the Seven Gables, in which she had a life-estate by the will of the old bachelor. She was understood to be wretchedly poor, and seemed to make it her choice to remain so; inasmuch as her affluent cousin, the Judge, had repeatedly offered her all the comforts of life, either in the old mansion or his own modern residence. The last and youngest Pyncheon was a little country-girl of seventeen, the daughter of another of the Judge's cousins, who had married a young woman of no family or property, and died early and in poor circumstances. His widow had recently taken another husband.

As for Matthew Maule's posterity, it was supposed now to be extinct. For a very long period after the witchcraft delusion, however, the Maules had continued to inhabit the town where their progenitor had suffered so unjust a death. To all appearance, they were a quiet, honest, well-meaning race of people, cherishing no malice against individuals or the public for the wrong which had been done them; or if, at their own fireside, they transmitted from father to child any hostile recollection of the wizard's fate and their lost patrimony, it was never acted upon, nor openly expressed. Nor would it have been singular had they ceased to remember that the House of the Seven Gables was resting its heavy framework on a foundation that was rightfully their own. There is something so massive, stable, and almost irresistibly imposing in the exterior presentment of established rank and great possessions, that their very existence seems to give them a right to exist; at least, so excellent a counterfeit of right, that few poor and humble men have moral force enough to question it, even in their secret minds. Such is the case now, after so many ancient prejudices have been overthrown; and it was far more so in ante-Revolutionary days, when the aristocracy could venture to be proud, and the low were content to be abased. Thus the Maules, at all events, kept their resentments within their own breasts. They were generally poverty-stricken; always plebeian and obscure; working with unsuccessful diligence at handicrafts; laboring on the wharves, or following the sea, as sailors before the mast; living here and there about the town, in hired tenements, and coming finally to the almshouse as the natural home of their old age. At last, after creeping, as it were, for such a length of time along the utmost verge of the opaque puddle of obscurity, they had taken that downright plunge which, sooner or later, is the destiny of all families, whether princely or plebeian. For thirty years past, neither town-record, nor gravestone, nor the directory, nor the knowledge or memory of man, bore any trace of Matthew Maule's descendants. His blood might possibly exist elsewhere; here, where its lowly current could be traced so far back, it had ceased to keep an onward course.

So long as any of the race were to be found, they had been marked out from other men—not strikingly, nor as with a sharp line, but with an effect that was felt rather than spoken of—by an hereditary character of reserve. Their companions, or those who endeavored to become such, grew conscious of a circle round about the Maules, within the sanctity or the spell of which, in spite of an exterior of sufficient frankness and good-fellowship, it was impossible for any man to step. It was this indefinable peculiarity, perhaps, that, by insulating them from human aid, kept them always so unfortunate in life. It certainly operated to prolong in their case, and to confirm to them as their only inheritance, those feelings of repugnance and superstitious terror with which the people of the town, even after awakening from their frenzy, continued to regard the memory of the reputed witches. The mantle, or rather the ragged cloak, of old Matthew Maule had fallen upon his children. They were half believed to inherit mysterious attributes; the family eye was said to possess strange power. Among other good-for-nothing properties and privileges, one was especially assigned them,—that of exercising an influence over people's dreams. The Pyncheons, if all stories were true, haughtily as they bore themselves in the noonday streets of their native town, were no better than bond-servants to these plebeian Maules, on entering the topsy-turvy commonwealth of sleep. Modern psychology, it may be, will endeavor to reduce these alleged necromancies within a system, instead of rejecting them as altogether fabulous.

A descriptive paragraph or two, treating of the seven-gabled mansion in its more recent aspect, will bring this preliminary chapter to a close. The street in which it upreared its venerable peaks has long ceased to be a fashionable quarter of the town; so that, though the old edifice was surrounded by habitations of modern date, they were mostly small, built entirely of wood, and typical of the most plodding uniformity of common life. Doubtless, however, the whole story of human existence may be latent in each of them, but with no picturesqueness, externally, that can attract the imagination or sympathy to seek it there. But as for the old structure of our story, its white-oak frame, and its boards, shingles, and crumbling plaster, and even the huge, clustered chimney in the midst, seemed to constitute only the least and meanest part of its reality. So much of mankind's varied experience had passed there,—so much had been suffered, and something, too, enjoyed,—that the very timbers were oozy, as with the moisture of a heart. It was itself like a great human heart, with a life of its own, and full of rich and sombre reminiscences.

The deep projection of the second story gave the house such a meditative look, that you could not pass it without the idea that it had secrets to keep, and an eventful history to moralize upon. In front, just on the edge of the unpaved sidewalk, grew the Pyncheon Elm, which, in reference to such trees as one usually meets with, might well be termed gigantic. It had been planted by a great-grandson of the first Pyncheon, and, though now four-score years of age, or perhaps nearer a hundred, was still in its strong and broad maturity, throwing its shadow from side to side of the street, overtopping the seven gables, and sweeping the whole black roof with its pendant foliage. It gave beauty to the old edifice, and seemed to make it a part of nature. The street having been widened about forty years ago, the front gable was now precisely on a line with it. On either side extended a ruinous wooden fence of open lattice-work, through which could be seen a grassy yard, and, especially in the angles of the building, an enormous fertility of burdocks, with leaves, it is hardly an exaggeration to say, two or three feet long. Behind the house there appeared to be a garden, which undoubtedly had once been extensive, but was now infringed upon by other enclosures, or shut in by habitations and outbuildings that stood on another street. It would be an omission, trifling, indeed, but unpardonable, were we to forget the green moss that had long since gathered over the projections of the windows, and on the slopes of the roof nor must we fail to direct the reader's eye to a crop, not of weeds, but flower-shrubs, which were growing aloft in the air, not a great way from the chimney, in the nook between two of the gables. They were called Alice's Posies. The tradition was, that a certain Alice Pyncheon had flung up the seeds, in sport, and that the dust of the street and the decay of the roof gradually formed a kind of soil for them, out of which they grew, when Alice had long been in her grave. However the flowers might have come there, it was both sad and sweet to observe how Nature adopted to herself this desolate, decaying, gusty, rusty old house of the Pyncheon family; and how the ever-returning Summer did her best to gladden it with tender beauty, and grew melancholy in the effort.

There is one other feature, very essential to be noticed, but which, we greatly fear, may damage any picturesque and romantic impression which we have been willing to throw over our sketch of this respectable edifice. In the front gable, under the impending brow of the second story, and contiguous to the street, was a shop-door, divided horizontally in the midst, and with a window for its upper segment, such as is often seen in dwellings of a somewhat ancient date. This same shop-door had been a subject of no slight mortification to the present occupant of the august Pyncheon House, as well as to some of her predecessors. The matter is disagreeably delicate to handle; but, since the reader must needs be let into the secret, he will please to understand, that, about a century ago, the head of the Pyncheons found himself involved in serious financial difficulties. The fellow (gentleman, as he styled himself) can hardly have been other than a spurious interloper; for, instead of seeking office from the king or the royal governor, or urging his hereditary claim to Eastern lands, he bethought himself of no better avenue to wealth than by cutting a shop-door through the side of his ancestral residence. It was the custom of the time, indeed, for merchants to store their goods and transact business in their own dwellings. But there was something pitifully small in this old Pyncheon's mode of setting about his commercial operations; it was whispered, that, with his own hands, all beruffled as they were, he used to give change for a shilling, and would turn a half-penny twice over, to make sure that it was a good one. Beyond all question, he had the blood of a petty huckster in his veins, through whatever channel it may have found its way there.

Immediately on his death, the shop-door had been locked, bolted, and barred, and, down to the period of our story, had probably never once been opened. The old counter, shelves, and other fixtures of the little shop remained just as he had left them. It used to be affirmed, that the dead shop-keeper, in a white wig, a faded velvet coat, an apron at his waist, and his ruffles carefully turned back from his wrists, might be seen through the chinks of the shutters, any night of the year, ransacking his till, or poring over the dingy pages of his day-book. From the look of unutterable woe upon his face, it appeared to be his doom to spend eternity in a vain effort to make his accounts balance.

And now—in a very humble way, as will be seen—we proceed to open our narrative.

II The Little Shop-Window

IT still lacked half an hour of sunrise, when Miss Hepzibah Pyncheon—we will not say awoke, it being doubtful whether the poor lady had so much as closed her eyes during the brief night of midsummer—but, at all events, arose from her solitary pillow, and began what it would be mockery to term the adornment of her person. Far from us be the indecorum of assisting, even in imagination, at a maiden lady's toilet! Our story must therefore await Miss Hepzibah at the threshold of her chamber; only presuming, meanwhile, to note some of the heavy sighs that labored from her bosom, with little restraint as to their lugubrious depth and volume of sound, inasmuch as they could be audible to nobody save a disembodied listener like ourself. The Old Maid was alone in the old house. Alone, except for a certain respectable and orderly young man, an artist in the daguerreotype line, who, for about three months back, had been a lodger in a remote gable,—quite a house by itself, indeed,—with locks, bolts, and oaken bars on all the intervening doors. Inaudible, consequently, were poor Miss Hepzibah's gusty sighs. Inaudible the creaking joints of her stiffened knees, as she knelt down by the bedside. And inaudible, too, by mortal ear, but heard with all-comprehending love and pity in the farthest heaven, that almost agony of prayer—now whispered, now a groan, now a struggling silence—wherewith she besought the Divine assistance through the day! Evidently, this is to be a day of more than ordinary trial to Miss Hepzibah, who, for above a quarter of a century gone by, has dwelt in strict seclusion, taking no part in the business of life, and just as little in its intercourse and pleasures. Not with such fervor prays the torpid recluse, looking forward to the cold, sunless, stagnant calm of a day that is to be like innumerable yesterdays.

The maiden lady's devotions are concluded. Will she now issue forth over the threshold of our story? Not yet, by many moments. First, every drawer in the tall, old-fashioned bureau is to be opened, with difficulty, and with a succession of spasmodic jerks then, all must close again, with the same fidgety reluctance. There is a rustling of stiff silks; a tread of backward and forward footsteps to and fro across the chamber. We suspect Miss Hepzibah, moreover, of taking a step upward into a chair, in order to give heedful regard to her appearance on all sides, and at full length, in the oval, dingy-framed toilet-glass, that hangs above her table. Truly! well, indeed! who would have thought it! Is all this precious time to be lavished on the matutinal repair and beautifying of an elderly person, who never goes abroad, whom nobody ever visits, and from whom, when she shall have done her utmost, it were the best charity to turn one's eyes another way?

Now she is almost ready. Let us pardon her one other pause; for it is given to the sole sentiment, or, we might better say,—heightened and rendered intense, as it has been, by sorrow and seclusion,—to the strong passion of her life. We heard the turning of a key in a small lock; she has opened a secret drawer of an escritoire, and is probably looking at a certain miniature, done in Malbone's most perfect style, and representing a face worthy of no less delicate a pencil. It was once our good fortune to see this picture. It is a likeness of a young man, in a silken dressing-gown of an old fashion, the soft richness of which is well adapted to the countenance of reverie, with its full, tender lips, and beautiful eyes, that seem to indicate not so much capacity of thought, as gentle and voluptuous emotion. Of the possessor of such features we shall have a right to ask nothing, except that he would take the rude world easily, and make himself happy in it. Can it have been an early lover of Miss Hepzibah? No; she never had a lover—poor thing, how could she?—nor ever knew, by her own experience, what love technically means. And yet, her undying faith and trust, her fresh remembrance, and continual devotedness towards the original of that miniature, have been the only substance for her heart to feed upon.

She seems to have put aside the miniature, and is standing again before the toilet-glass. There are tears to be wiped off. A few more footsteps to and fro; and here, at last,—with another pitiful sigh, like a gust of chill, damp wind out of a long-closed vault, the door of which has accidentally been set, ajar—here comes Miss Hepzibah Pyncheon! Forth she steps into the dusky, time-darkened passage; a tall figure, clad in black silk, with a long and shrunken waist, feeling her way towards the stairs like a near-sighted person, as in truth she is.

The sun, meanwhile, if not already above the horizon, was ascending nearer and nearer to its verge. A few clouds, floating high upward, caught some of the earliest light, and threw down its golden gleam on the windows of all the houses in the street, not forgetting the House of the Seven Gables, which—many such sunrises as it had witnessed—looked cheerfully at the present one. The reflected radiance served to show, pretty distinctly, the aspect and arrangement of the room which Hepzibah entered, after descending the stairs. It was a low-studded room, with a beam across the ceiling, panelled with dark wood, and having a large chimney-piece, set round with pictured tiles, but now closed by an iron fire-board, through which ran the funnel of a modern stove. There was a carpet on the floor, originally of rich texture, but so worn and faded in these latter years that its once brilliant figure had quite vanished into one indistinguishable hue. In the way of furniture, there were two tables: one, constructed with perplexing intricacy and exhibiting as many feet as a centipede; the other, most delicately wrought, with four long and slender legs, so apparently frail that it was almost incredible what a length of time the ancient tea-table had stood upon them. Half a dozen chairs stood about the room, straight and stiff, and so ingeniously contrived for the discomfort of the human person that they were irksome even to sight, and conveyed the ugliest possible idea of the state of society to which they could have been adapted. One exception there was, however, in a very antique elbow-chair, with a high back, carved elaborately in oak, and a roomy depth within its arms, that made up, by its spacious comprehensiveness, for the lack of any of those artistic curves which abound in a modern chair.

As for ornamental articles of furniture, we recollect but two, if such they may be called. One was a map of the Pyncheon territory at the eastward, not engraved, but the handiwork of some skilful old draughtsman, and grotesquely illuminated with pictures of Indians and wild beasts, among which was seen a lion; the natural history of the region being as little known as its geography, which was put down most fantastically awry. The other adornment was the portrait of old Colonel Pyncheon, at two thirds length, representing the stern features of a Puritanic-looking personage, in a skull-cap, with a laced band and a grizzly beard; holding a Bible with one hand, and in the other uplifting an iron sword-hilt. The latter object, being more successfully depicted by the artist, stood out in far greater prominence than the sacred volume. Face to face with this picture, on entering the apartment, Miss Hepzibah Pyncheon came to a pause; regarding it with a singular scowl, a strange contortion of the brow, which, by people who did not know her, would probably have been interpreted as an expression of bitter anger and ill-will. But it was no such thing. She, in fact, felt a reverence for the pictured visage, of which only a far-descended and time-stricken virgin could be susceptible; and this forbidding scowl was the innocent result of her near-sightedness, and an effort so to concentrate her powers of vision as to substitute a firm outline of the object instead of a vague one.

We must linger a moment on this unfortunate expression of poor Hepzibah's brow. Her scowl,—as the world, or such part of it as sometimes caught a transitory glimpse of her at the window, wickedly persisted in calling it,—her scowl had done Miss Hepzibah a very ill office, in establishing her character as an ill-tempered old maid; nor does it appear improbable that, by often gazing at herself in a dim looking-glass, and perpetually encountering her own frown with its ghostly sphere, she had been led to interpret the expression almost as unjustly as the world did. "How miserably cross I look!" she must often have whispered to herself; and ultimately have fancied herself so, by a sense of inevitable doom. But her heart never frowned. It was naturally tender, sensitive, and full of little tremors and palpitations; all of which weaknesses it retained, while her visage was growing so perversely stern, and even fierce. Nor had Hepzibah ever any hardihood, except what came from the very warmest nook in her affections.

All this time, however, we are loitering faintheartedly on the threshold of our story. In very truth, we have an invincible reluctance to disclose what Miss Hepzibah Pyncheon was about to do.

It has already been observed, that, in the basement story of the gable fronting on the street, an unworthy ancestor, nearly a century ago, had fitted up a shop. Ever since the old gentleman retired from trade, and fell asleep under his coffin-lid, not only the shop-door, but the inner arrangements, had been suffered to remain unchanged; while the dust of ages gathered inch-deep over the shelves and counter, and partly filled an old pair of scales, as if it were of value enough to be weighed. It treasured itself up, too, in the half-open till, where there still lingered a base sixpence, worth neither more nor less than the hereditary pride which had here been put to shame. Such had been the state and condition of the little shop in old Hepzibah's childhood, when she and her brother used to play at hide-and-seek in its forsaken precincts. So it had remained, until within a few days past.

But now, though the shop-window was still closely curtained from the public gaze, a remarkable change had taken place in its interior. The rich and heavy festoons of cobweb, which it had cost a long ancestral succession of spiders their life's labor to spin and weave, had been carefully brushed away from the ceiling. The counter, shelves, and floor had all been scoured, and the latter was overstrewn with fresh blue sand. The brown scales, too, had evidently undergone rigid discipline, in an unavailing effort to rub off the rust, which, alas! had eaten through and through their substance. Neither was the little old shop any longer empty of merchantable goods. A curious eye, privileged to take an account of stock and investigate behind the counter, would have discovered a barrel, yea, two or three barrels and half ditto,—one containing flour, another apples, and a third, perhaps, Indian meal. There was likewise a square box of pine-wood, full of soap in bars; also, another of the same size, in which were tallow candles, ten to the pound. A small stock of brown sugar, some white beans and split peas, and a few other commodities of low price, and such as are constantly in demand, made up the bulkier portion of the merchandise. It might have been taken for a ghostly or phantasmagoric reflection of the old shop-keeper Pyncheon's shabbily provided shelves, save that some of the articles were of a description and outward form which could hardly have been known in his day. For instance, there was a glass pickle-jar, filled with fragments of Gibraltar rock; not, indeed, splinters of the veritable stone foundation of the famous fortress, but bits of delectable candy, neatly done up in white paper. Jim Crow, moreover, was seen executing his world-renowned dance, in gingerbread. A party of leaden dragoons were galloping along one of the shelves, in equipments and uniform of modern cut; and there were some sugar figures, with no strong resemblance to the humanity of any epoch, but less unsatisfactorily representing our own fashions than those of a hundred years ago. Another phenomenon, still more strikingly modern, was a package of lucifer matches, which, in old times, would have been thought actually to borrow their instantaneous flame from the nether fires of Tophet.

In short, to bring the matter at once to a point, it was incontrovertibly evident that somebody had taken the shop and fixtures of the long-retired and forgotten Mr. Pyncheon, and was about to renew the enterprise of that departed worthy, with a different set of customers. Who could this bold adventurer be? And, of all places in the world, why had he chosen the House of the Seven Gables as the scene of his commercial speculations?

We return to the elderly maiden. She at length withdrew her eyes from the dark countenance of the Colonel's portrait, heaved a sigh,—indeed, her breast was a very cave of Aolus that morning,—and stept across the room on tiptoe, as is the customary gait of elderly women. Passing through an intervening passage, she opened a door that communicated with the shop, just now so elaborately described. Owing to the projection of the upper story—and still more to the thick shadow of the Pyncheon Elm, which stood almost directly in front of the gable—the twilight, here, was still as much akin to night as morning. Another heavy sigh from Miss Hepzibah! After a moment's pause on the threshold, peering towards the window with her near-sighted scowl, as if frowning down some bitter enemy, she suddenly projected herself into the shop. The haste, and, as it were, the galvanic impulse of the movement, were really quite startling.

Nervously—in a sort of frenzy, we might almost say—she began to busy herself in arranging some children's playthings, and other little wares, on the shelves and at the shop-window. In the aspect of this dark-arrayed, pale-faced, ladylike old figure there was a deeply tragic character that contrasted irreconcilably with the ludicrous pettiness of her employment. It seemed a queer anomaly, that so gaunt and dismal a personage should take a toy in hand; a miracle, that the toy did not vanish in her grasp; a miserably absurd idea, that she should go on perplexing her stiff and sombre intellect with the question how to tempt little boys into her premises! Yet such is undoubtedly her object. Now she places a gingerbread elephant against the window, but with so tremulous a touch that it tumbles upon the floor, with the dismemberment of three legs and its trunk; it has ceased to be an elephant, and has become a few bits of musty gingerbread. There, again, she has upset a tumbler of marbles, all of which roll different ways, and each individual marble, devil-directed, into the most difficult obscurity that it can find. Heaven help our poor old Hepzibah, and forgive us for taking a ludicrous view of her position! As her rigid and rusty frame goes down upon its hands and knees, in quest of the absconding marbles, we positively feel so much the more inclined to shed tears of sympathy, from the very fact that we must needs turn aside and laugh at her. For here,—and if we fail to impress it suitably upon the reader, it is our own fault, not that of the theme, here is one of the truest points of melancholy interest that occur in ordinary life. It was the final throe of what called itself old gentility. A lady—who had fed herself from childhood with the shadowy food of aristocratic reminiscences, and whose religion it was that a lady's hand soils itself irremediably by doing aught for bread,—this born lady, after sixty years of narrowing means, is fain to step down from her pedestal of imaginary rank. Poverty, treading closely at her heels for a lifetime, has come up with her at last. She must earn her own food, or starve! And we have stolen upon Miss Hepzibah Pyncheon, too irreverently, at the instant of time when the patrician lady is to be transformed into the plebeian woman.

In this republican country, amid the fluctuating waves of our social life, somebody is always at the drowning-point. The tragedy is enacted with as continual a repetition as that of a popular drama on a holiday, and, nevertheless, is felt as deeply, perhaps, as when an hereditary noble sinks below his order. More deeply; since, with us, rank is the grosser substance of wealth and a splendid establishment, and has no spiritual existence after the death of these, but dies hopelessly along with them. And, therefore, since we have been unfortunate enough to introduce our heroine at so inauspicious a juncture, we would entreat for a mood of due solemnity in the spectators of her fate. Let us behold, in poor Hepzibah, the immemorial, lady—two hundred years old, on this side of the water, and thrice as many on the other,—with her antique portraits, pedigrees, coats of arms, records and traditions, and her claim, as joint heiress, to that princely territory at the eastward, no longer a wilderness, but a populous fertility,—born, too, in Pyncheon Street, under the Pyncheon Elm, and in the Pyncheon House, where she has spent all her days,—reduced. Now, in that very house, to be the hucksteress of a cent-shop.

This business of setting up a petty shop is almost the only resource of women, in circumstances at all similar to those of our unfortunate recluse. With her near-sightedness, and those tremulous fingers of hers, at once inflexible and delicate, she could not be a seamstress; although her sampler, of fifty years gone by, exhibited some of the most recondite specimens of ornamental needlework. A school for little children had been often in her thoughts; and, at one time, she had begun a review of her early studies in the New England Primer, with a view to prepare herself for the office of instructress. But the love of children had never been quickened in Hepzibah's heart, and was now torpid, if not extinct; she watched the little people of the neighborhood from her chamber-window, and doubted whether she could tolerate a more intimate acquaintance with them. Besides, in our day, the very ABC has become a science greatly too abstruse to be any longer taught by pointing a pin from letter to letter. A modern child could teach old Hepzibah more than old Hepzibah could teach the child. So—with many a cold, deep heart-quake at the idea of at last coming into sordid contact with the world, from which she had so long kept aloof, while every added day of seclusion had rolled another stone against the cavern door of her hermitage—the poor thing bethought herself of the ancient shop-window, the rusty scales, and dusty till. She might have held back a little longer; but another circumstance, not yet hinted at, had somewhat hastened her decision. Her humble preparations, therefore, were duly made, and the enterprise was now to be commenced. Nor was she entitled to complain of any remarkable singularity in her fate; for, in the town of her nativity, we might point to several little shops of a similar description, some of them in houses as ancient as that of the Seven Gables; and one or two, it may be, where a decayed gentlewoman stands behind the counter, as grim an image of family pride as Miss Hepzibah Pyncheon herself.

It was overpoweringly ridiculous,—we must honestly confess it,—the deportment of the maiden lady while setting her shop in order for the public eye. She stole on tiptoe to the window, as cautiously as if she conceived some bloody-minded villain to be watching behind the elm-tree, with intent to take her life. Stretching out her long, lank arm, she put a paper of pearl-buttons, a jew's-harp, or whatever the small article might be, in its destined place, and straightway vanished back into the dusk, as if the world need never hope for another glimpse of her. It might have been fancied, indeed, that she expected to minister to the wants of the community unseen, like a disembodied divinity or enchantress, holding forth her bargains to the reverential and awe-stricken purchaser in an invisible hand. But Hepzibah had no such flattering dream. She was well aware that she must ultimately come forward, and stand revealed in her proper individuality; but, like other sensitive persons, she could not bear to be observed in the gradual process, and chose rather to flash forth on the world's astonished gaze at once.

The inevitable moment was not much longer to be delayed. The sunshine might now be seen stealing down the front of the opposite house, from the windows of which came a reflected gleam, struggling through the boughs of the elm-tree, and enlightening the interior of the shop more distinctly than heretofore. The town appeared to be waking up. A baker's cart had already rattled through the street, chasing away the latest vestige of night's sanctity with the jingle-jangle of its dissonant bells. A milkman was distributing the contents of his cans from door to door; and the harsh peal of a fisherman's conch shell was heard far off, around the corner. None of these tokens escaped Hepzibah's notice. The moment had arrived. To delay longer would be only to lengthen out her misery. Nothing remained, except to take down the bar from the shop-door, leaving the entrance free—more than free—welcome, as if all were household friends—to every passer-by, whose eyes might be attracted by the commodities at the window. This last act Hepzibah now performed, letting the bar fall with what smote upon her excited nerves as a most astounding clatter. Then—as if the only barrier betwixt herself and the world had been thrown down, and a flood of evil consequences would come tumbling through the gap—she fled into the inner parlor, threw herself into the ancestral elbow-chair, and wept.

Our miserable old Hepzibah! It is a heavy annoyance to a writer, who endeavors to represent nature, its various attitudes and circumstances, in a reasonably correct outline and true coloring, that so much of the mean and ludicrous should be hopelessly mixed up with the purest pathos which life anywhere supplies to him. What tragic dignity, for example, can be wrought into a scene like this! How can we elevate our history of retribution for the sin of long ago, when, as one of our most prominent figures, we are compelled to introduce—not a young and lovely woman, nor even the stately remains of beauty, storm-shattered by affliction—but a gaunt, sallow, rusty-jointed maiden, in a long-waisted silk gown, and with the strange horror of a turban on her head! Her visage is not even ugly. It is redeemed from insignificance only by the contraction of her eyebrows into a near-sighted scowl. And, finally, her great life-trial seems to be, that, after sixty years of idleness, she finds it convenient to earn comfortable bread by setting up a shop in a small way. Nevertheless, if we look through all the heroic fortunes of mankind, we shall find this same entanglement of something mean and trivial with whatever is noblest in joy or sorrow. Life is made up of marble and mud. And, without all the deeper trust in a comprehensive sympathy above us, we might hence be led to suspect the insult of a sneer, as well as an immitigable frown, on the iron countenance of fate. What is called poetic insight is the gift of discerning, in this sphere of strangely mingled elements, the beauty and the majesty which are compelled to assume a garb so sordid.

III The First Customer

MISS HEPZIBAH PYNCHEON sat in the oaken elbow-chair, with her hands over her face, giving way to that heavy down-sinking of the heart which most persons have experienced, when the image of hope itself seems ponderously moulded of lead, on the eve of an enterprise at once doubtful and momentous. She was suddenly startled by the tinkling alarum—high, sharp, and irregular—of a little bell. The maiden lady arose upon her feet, as pale as a ghost at cock-crow; for she was an enslaved spirit, and this the talisman to which she owed obedience. This little bell,—to speak in plainer terms,—being fastened over the shop-door, was so contrived as to vibrate by means of a steel spring, and thus convey notice to the inner regions of the house when any customer should cross the threshold. Its ugly and spiteful little din (heard now for the first time, perhaps, since Hepzibah's periwigged predecessor had retired from trade) at once set every nerve of her body in responsive and tumultuous vibration. The crisis was upon her! Her first customer was at the door!

Without giving herself time for a second thought, she rushed into the shop, pale, wild, desperate in gesture and expression, scowling portentously, and looking far better qualified to do fierce battle with a housebreaker than to stand smiling behind the counter, bartering small wares for a copper recompense. Any ordinary customer, indeed, would have turned his back and fled. And yet there was nothing fierce in Hepzibah's poor old heart; nor had she, at the moment, a single bitter thought against the world at large, or one individual man or woman. She wished them all well, but wished, too, that she herself were done with them, and in her quiet grave.

The applicant, by this time, stood within the doorway. Coming freshly, as he did, out of the morning light, he appeared to have brought some of its cheery influences into the shop along with him. It was a slender young man, not more than one or two and twenty years old, with rather a grave and thoughtful expression for his years, but likewise a springy alacrity and vigor. These qualities were not only perceptible, physically, in his make and motions, but made themselves felt almost immediately in his character. A brown beard, not too silken in its texture, fringed his chin, but as yet without completely hiding it; he wore a short mustache, too, and his dark, high-featured countenance looked all the better for these natural ornaments. As for his dress, it was of the simplest kind; a summer sack of cheap and ordinary material, thin checkered pantaloons, and a straw hat, by no means of the finest braid. Oak Hall might have supplied his entire equipment. He was chiefly marked as a gentleman—if such, indeed, he made any claim to be—by the rather remarkable whiteness and nicety of his clean linen.

He met the scowl of old Hepzibah without apparent alarm, as having heretofore encountered it and found it harmless.

"So, my dear Miss Pyncheon," said the daguerreotypist,—for it was that sole other occupant of the seven-gabled mansion,—"I am glad to see that you have not shrunk from your good purpose. I merely look in to offer my best wishes, and to ask if I can assist you any further in your preparations."

People in difficulty and distress, or in any manner at odds with the world, can endure a vast amount of harsh treatment, and perhaps be only the stronger for it; whereas they give way at once before the simplest expression of what they perceive to be genuine sympathy. So it proved with poor Hepzibah; for, when she saw the young man's smile,—looking so much the brighter on a thoughtful face,—and heard his kindly tone, she broke first into a hysteric giggle and then began to sob.

"Ah, Mr. Holgrave," cried she, as soon as she could speak, "I never can go through with it! Never, never, never! I wish I were dead, and in the old family tomb, with all my forefathers! With my father, and my mother, and my sister! Yes, and with my brother, who had far better find me there than here! The world is too chill and hard,—and I am too old, and too feeble, and too hopeless!"

"Oh, believe me, Miss Hepzibah," said the young man quietly, "these feelings will not trouble you any longer, after you are once fairly in the midst of your enterprise. They are unavoidable at this moment, standing, as you do, on the outer verge of your long seclusion, and peopling the world with ugly shapes, which you will soon find to be as unreal as the giants and ogres of a child's story-book. I find nothing so singular in life, as that everything appears to lose its substance the instant one actually grapples with it. So it will be with what you think so terrible."

"But I am a woman!" said Hepzibah piteously. "I was going to say, a lady,—but I consider that as past."

"Well; no matter if it be past!" answered the artist, a strange gleam of half-hidden sarcasm flashing through the kindliness of his manner. "Let it go! You are the better without it. I speak frankly, my dear Miss Pyncheon!—for are we not friends? I look upon this as one of the fortunate days of your life. It ends an epoch and begins one. Hitherto, the life-blood has been gradually chilling in your veins as you sat aloof, within your circle of gentility, while the rest of the world was fighting out its battle with one kind of necessity or another. Henceforth, you will at least have the sense of healthy and natural effort for a purpose, and of lending your strength be it great or small—to the united struggle of mankind. This is success,—all the success that anybody meets with!"

"It is natural enough, Mr. Holgrave, that you should have ideas like these," rejoined Hepzibah, drawing up her gaunt figure with slightly offended dignity.

"You are a man, a young man, and brought up, I suppose, as almost everybody is nowadays, with a view to seeking your fortune. But I was born a lady, and have always lived one; no matter in what narrowness of means, always a lady."

"But I was not born a gentleman; neither have I lived like one," said Holgrave, slightly smiling; "so, my dear madam, you will hardly expect me to sympathize with sensibilities of this kind; though, unless I deceive myself, I have some imperfect comprehension of them. These names of gentleman and lady had a meaning, in the past history of the world, and conferred privileges, desirable or otherwise, on those entitled to bear them. In the present—and still more in the future condition of society-they imply, not privilege, but restriction!"

"These are new notions," said the old gentlewoman, shaking her head. "I shall never understand them; neither do I wish it."

"We will cease to speak of them, then," replied the artist, with a friendlier smile than his last one, "and I will leave you to feel whether it is not better to be a true woman than a lady. Do you really think, Miss Hepzibah, that any lady of your family has ever done a more heroic thing, since this house was built, than you are performing in it to-day? Never; and if the Pyncheons had always acted so nobly, I doubt whether an old wizard Maule's anathema, of which you told me once, would have had much weight with Providence against them."

"Ah!—no, no!" said Hepzibah, not displeased at this allusion to the sombre dignity of an inherited curse. "If old Maule's ghost, or a descendant of his, could see me behind the counter to-day, he would call it the fulfillment of his worst wishes. But I thank you for your kindness, Mr. Holgrave, and will do my utmost to be a good shop-keeper."

"Pray do" said Holgrave, "and let me have the pleasure of being your first customer. I am about taking a walk to the seashore, before going to my rooms, where I misuse Heaven's blessed sunshine by tracing out human features through its agency. A few of those biscuits, dipt in sea-water, will be just what I need for breakfast. What is the price of half a dozen?"

"Let me be a lady a moment longer," replied Hepzibah, with a manner of antique stateliness to which a melancholy smile lent a kind of grace. She put the biscuits into his hand, but rejected the compensation. "A Pyncheon must not, at all events under her forefathers' roof, receive money for a morsel of bread from her only friend!"

Holgrave took his departure, leaving her, for the moment, with spirits not quite so much depressed. Soon, however, they had subsided nearly to their former dead level. With a beating heart, she listened to the footsteps of early passengers, which now began to be frequent along the street. Once or twice they seemed to linger; these strangers, or neighbors, as the case might be, were looking at the display of toys and petty commodities in Hepzibah's shop-window. She was doubly tortured; in part, with a sense of overwhelming shame that strange and unloving eyes should have the privilege of gazing, and partly because the idea occurred to her, with ridiculous importunity, that the window was not arranged so skilfully, nor nearly to so much advantage, as it might have been. It seemed as if the whole fortune or failure of her shop might depend on the display of a different set of articles, or substituting a fairer apple for one which appeared to be specked. So she made the change, and straightway fancied that everything was spoiled by it; not recognizing that it was the nervousness of the juncture, and her own native squeamishness as an old maid, that wrought all the seeming mischief.

Anon, there was an encounter, just at the door-step, betwixt two laboring men, as their rough voices denoted them to be. After some slight talk about their own affairs, one of them chanced to notice the shop-window, and directed the other's attention to it.

"See here!" cried he; "what do you think of this? Trade seems to be looking up in Pyncheon Street!"

"Well, well, this is a sight, to be sure!" exclaimed the other. "In the old Pyncheon House, and underneath the Pyncheon Elm! Who would have thought it? Old Maid Pyncheon is setting up a cent-shop!"

"Will she make it go, think you, Dixey?" said his friend. "I don't call it a very good stand. There's another shop just round the corner."

"Make it go!" cried Dixey, with a most contemptuous expression, as if the very idea were impossible to be conceived. "Not a bit of it! Why, her face—I've seen it, for I dug her garden for her one year—her face is enough to frighten the Old Nick himself, if he had ever so great a mind to trade with her. People can't stand it, I tell you! She scowls dreadfully, reason or none, out of pure ugliness of temper."

"Well, that's not so much matter," remarked the other man. "These sour-tempered folks are mostly handy at business, and know pretty well what they are about. But, as you say, I don't think she'll do much. This business of keeping cent-shops is overdone, like all other kinds of trade, handicraft, and bodily labor. I know it, to my cost! My wife kept a cent-shop three months, and lost five dollars on her outlay."

"Poor business!" responded Dixey, in a tone as if he were shaking his head,—"poor business."

For some reason or other, not very easy to analyze, there had hardly been so bitter a pang in all her previous misery about the matter as what thrilled Hepzibah's heart on overhearing the above conversation. The testimony in regard to her scowl was frightfully important; it seemed to hold up her image wholly relieved from the false light of her self-partialities, and so hideous that she dared not look at it. She was absurdly hurt, moreover, by the slight and idle effect that her setting up shop—an event of such breathless interest to herself—appeared to have upon the public, of which these two men were the nearest representatives. A glance; a passing word or two; a coarse laugh; and she was doubtless forgotten before they turned the corner. They cared nothing for her dignity, and just as little for her degradation. Then, also, the augury of ill-success, uttered from the sure wisdom of experience, fell upon her half-dead hope like a clod into a grave. The man's wife had already tried the same experiment, and failed! How could the born lady—the recluse of half a lifetime, utterly unpractised in the world, at sixty years of age,—how could she ever dream of succeeding, when the hard, vulgar, keen, busy, hackneyed New England woman had lost five dollars on her little outlay! Success presented itself as an impossibility, and the hope of it as a wild hallucination.

Some malevolent spirit, doing his utmost to drive Hepzibah mad, unrolled before her imagination a kind of panorama, representing the great thoroughfare of a city all astir with customers. So many and so magnificent shops as there were! Groceries, toy-shops, drygoods stores, with their immense panes of plate-glass, their gorgeous fixtures, their vast and complete assortments of merchandise, in which fortunes had been invested; and those noble mirrors at the farther end of each establishment, doubling all this wealth by a brightly burnished vista of unrealities! On one side of the street this splendid bazaar, with a multitude of perfumed and glossy salesmen, smirking, smiling, bowing, and measuring out the goods. On the other, the dusky old House of the Seven Gables, with the antiquated shop-window under its projecting story, and Hepzibah herself, in a gown of rusty black silk, behind the counter, scowling at the world as it went by! This mighty contrast thrust itself forward as a fair expression of the odds against which she was to begin her struggle for a subsistence. Success? Preposterous! She would never think of it again! The house might just as well be buried in an eternal fog while all other houses had the sunshine on them; for not a foot would ever cross the threshold, nor a hand so much as try the door!

But, at this instant, the shop-bell, right over her head, tinkled as if it were bewitched. The old gentlewoman's heart seemed to be attached to the same steel spring, for it went through a series of sharp jerks, in unison with the sound. The door was thrust open, although no human form was perceptible on the other side of the half-window. Hepzibah, nevertheless, stood at a gaze, with her hands clasped, looking very much as if she had summoned up an evil spirit, and were afraid, yet resolved, to hazard the encounter.

"Heaven help me!" she groaned mentally. "Now is my hour of need!"

The door, which moved with difficulty on its creaking and rusty hinges, being forced quite open, a square and sturdy little urchin became apparent, with cheeks as red as an apple. He was clad rather shabbily (but, as it seemed, more owing to his mother's carelessness than his father's poverty), in a blue apron, very wide and short trousers, shoes somewhat out at the toes, and a chip hat, with the frizzles of his curly hair sticking through its crevices. A book and a small slate, under his arm, indicated that he was on his way to school. He stared at Hepzibah a moment, as an elder customer than himself would have been likely enough to do, not knowing what to make of the tragic attitude and queer scowl wherewith she regarded him.

"Well, child," said she, taking heart at sight of a personage so little formidable,—"well, my child, what did you wish for?"

"That Jim Crow there in the window," answered the urchin, holding out a cent, and pointing to the gingerbread figure that had attracted his notice, as he loitered along to school; "the one that has not a broken foot."

So Hepzibah put forth her lank arm, and, taking the effigy from the shop-window, delivered it to her first customer.

"No matter for the money," said she, giving him a little push towards the door; for her old gentility was contumaciously squeamish at sight of the copper coin, and, besides, it seemed such pitiful meanness to take the child's pocket-money in exchange for a bit of stale gingerbread. "No matter for the cent. You are welcome to Jim Crow."

The child, staring with round eyes at this instance of liberality, wholly unprecedented in his large experience of cent-shops, took the man of gingerbread, and quitted the premises. No sooner had he reached the sidewalk (little cannibal that he was!) than Jim Crow's head was in his mouth. As he had not been careful to shut the door, Hepzibah was at the pains of closing it after him, with a pettish ejaculation or two about the troublesomeness of young people, and particularly of small boys. She had just placed another representative of the renowned Jim Crow at the window, when again the shop-bell tinkled clamorously, and again the door being thrust open, with its characteristic jerk and jar, disclosed the same sturdy little urchin who, precisely two minutes ago, had made his exit. The crumbs and discoloration of the cannibal feast, as yet hardly consummated, were exceedingly visible about his mouth.

"What is it now, child?" asked the maiden lady rather impatiently; "did you come back to shut the door?"

"No," answered the urchin, pointing to the figure that had just been put up; "I want that other Jim Crow."

"Well, here it is for you," said Hepzibah, reaching it down; but recognizing that this pertinacious customer would not quit her on any other terms, so long as she had a gingerbread figure in her shop, she partly drew back her extended hand, "Where is the cent?"

The little boy had the cent ready, but, like a true-born Yankee, would have preferred the better bargain to the worse. Looking somewhat chagrined, he put the coin into Hepzibah's hand, and departed, sending the second Jim Crow in quest of the former one. The new shop-keeper dropped the first solid result of her commercial enterprise into the till. It was done! The sordid stain of that copper coin could never be washed away from her palm. The little schoolboy, aided by the impish figure of the negro dancer, had wrought an irreparable ruin. The structure of ancient aristocracy had been demolished by him, even as if his childish gripe had torn down the seven-gabled mansion. Now let Hepzibah turn the old Pyncheon portraits with their faces to the wall, and take the map of her Eastern territory to kindle the kitchen fire, and blow up the flame with the empty breath of her ancestral traditions! What had she to do with ancestry? Nothing; no more than with posterity! No lady, now, but simply Hepzibah Pyncheon, a forlorn old maid, and keeper of a cent-shop!

Nevertheless, even while she paraded these ideas somewhat ostentatiously through her mind, it is altogether surprising what a calmness had come over her. The anxiety and misgivings which had tormented her, whether asleep or in melancholy day-dreams, ever since her project began to take an aspect of solidity, had now vanished quite away. She felt the novelty of her position, indeed, but no longer with disturbance or affright. Now and then, there came a thrill of almost youthful enjoyment. It was the invigorating breath of a fresh outward atmosphere, after the long torpor and monotonous seclusion of her life. So wholesome is effort! So miraculous the strength that we do not know of! The healthiest glow that Hepzibah had known for years had come now in the dreaded crisis, when, for the first time, she had put forth her hand to help herself. The little circlet of the schoolboy's copper coin—dim and lustreless though it was, with the small services which it had been doing here and there about the world—had proved a talisman, fragrant with good, and deserving to be set in gold and worn next her heart. It was as potent, and perhaps endowed with the same kind of efficacy, as a galvanic ring! Hepzibah, at all events, was indebted to its subtile operation both in body and spirit; so much the more, as it inspired her with energy to get some breakfast, at which, still the better to keep up her courage, she allowed herself an extra spoonful in her infusion of black tea.

Her introductory day of shop-keeping did not run on, however, without many and serious interruptions of this mood of cheerful vigor. As a general rule, Providence seldom vouchsafes to mortals any more than just that degree of encouragement which suffices to keep them at a reasonably full exertion of their powers. In the case of our old gentlewoman, after the excitement of new effort had subsided, the despondency of her whole life threatened, ever and anon, to return. It was like the heavy mass of clouds which we may often see obscuring the sky, and making a gray twilight everywhere, until, towards nightfall, it yields temporarily to a glimpse of sunshine. But, always, the envious cloud strives to gather again across the streak of celestial azure.

Customers came in, as the forenoon advanced, but rather slowly; in some cases, too, it must be owned, with little satisfaction either to themselves or Miss Hepzibah; nor, on the whole, with an aggregate of very rich emolument to the till. A little girl, sent by her mother to match a skein of cotton thread, of a peculiar hue, took one that the near-sighted old lady pronounced extremely like, but soon came running back, with a blunt and cross message, that it would not do, and, besides, was very rotten! Then, there was a pale, care-wrinkled woman, not old but haggard, and already with streaks of gray among her hair, like silver ribbons; one of those women, naturally delicate, whom you at once recognize as worn to death by a brute—probably a drunken brute—of a husband, and at least nine children. She wanted a few pounds of flour, and offered the money, which the decayed gentlewoman silently rejected, and gave the poor soul better measure than if she had taken it. Shortly afterwards, a man in a blue cotton frock, much soiled, came in and bought a pipe, filling the whole shop, meanwhile, with the hot odor of strong drink, not only exhaled in the torrid atmosphere of his breath, but oozing out of his entire system, like an inflammable gas. It was impressed on Hepzibah's mind that this was the husband of the care-wrinkled woman. He asked for a paper of tobacco; and as she had neglected to provide herself with the article, her brutal customer dashed down his newly-bought pipe and left the shop, muttering some unintelligible words, which had the tone and bitterness of a curse. Hereupon Hepzibah threw up her eyes, unintentionally scowling in the face of Providence!

No less than five persons, during the forenoon, inquired for ginger-beer, or root-beer, or any drink of a similar brewage, and, obtaining nothing of the kind, went off in an exceedingly bad humor. Three of them left the door open, and the other two pulled it so spitefully in going out that the little bell played the very deuce with Hepzibah's nerves. A round, bustling, fire-ruddy housewife of the neighborhood burst breathless into the shop, fiercely demanding yeast; and when the poor gentlewoman, with her cold shyness of manner, gave her hot customer to understand that she did not keep the article, this very capable housewife took upon herself to administer a regular rebuke.

"A cent-shop, and no yeast!" quoth she; "That will never do! Who ever heard of such a thing? Your loaf will never rise, no more than mine will to-day. You had better shut up shop at once."

"Well," said Hepzibah, heaving a deep sigh, "perhaps I had!"

Several times, moreover, besides the above instance, her lady-like sensibilities were seriously infringed upon by the familiar, if not rude, tone with which people addressed her. They evidently considered themselves not merely her equals, but her patrons and superiors. Now, Hepzibah had unconsciously flattered herself with the idea that there would be a gleam or halo, of some kind or other, about her person, which would insure an obeisance to her sterling gentility, or, at least, a tacit recognition of it. On the other hand, nothing tortured her more intolerably than when this recognition was too prominently expressed. To one or two rather officious offers of sympathy, her responses were little short of acrimonious; and, we regret to say, Hepzibah was thrown into a positively unchristian state of mind by the suspicion that one of her customers was drawn to the shop, not by any real need of the article which she pretended to seek, but by a wicked wish to stare at her. The vulgar creature was determined to see for herself what sort of a figure a mildewed piece of aristocracy, after wasting all the bloom and much of the decline of her life apart from the world, would cut behind a counter. In this particular case, however mechanical and innocuous it might be at other times, Hepzibah's contortion of brow served her in good stead.

"I never was so frightened in my life!" said the curious customer, in describing the incident to one of her acquaintances. "She's a real old vixen, take my word of it! She says little, to be sure; but if you could only see the mischief in her eye!"

On the whole, therefore, her new experience led our decayed gentlewoman to very disagreeable conclusions as to the temper and manners of what she termed the lower classes, whom heretofore she had looked down upon with a gentle and pitying complaisance, as herself occupying a sphere of unquestionable superiority. But, unfortunately, she had likewise to struggle against a bitter emotion of a directly opposite kind: a sentiment of virulence, we mean, towards the idle aristocracy to which it had so recently been her pride to belong. When a lady, in a delicate and costly summer garb, with a floating veil and gracefully swaying gown, and, altogether, an ethereal lightness that made you look at her beautifully slippered feet, to see whether she trod on the dust or floated in the air,—when such a vision happened to pass through this retired street, leaving it tenderly and delusively fragrant with her passage, as if a bouquet of tea-roses had been borne along,—then again, it is to be feared, old Hepzibah's scowl could no longer vindicate itself entirely on the plea of near-sightedness.

"For what end," thought she, giving vent to that feeling of hostility which is the only real abasement of the poor in presence of the rich,—"for what good end, in the wisdom of Providence, does that woman live? Must the whole world toil, that the palms of her hands may be kept white and delicate?"

Then, ashamed and penitent, she hid her face.

"May God forgive me!" said she.

Doubtless, God did forgive her. But, taking the inward and outward history of the first half-day into consideration, Hepzibah began to fear that the shop would prove her ruin in a moral and religious point of view, without contributing very essentially towards even her temporal welfare.

IV A Day Behind the Counter

TOWARDS noon, Hepzibah saw an elderly gentleman, large and portly, and of remarkably dignified demeanor, passing slowly along on the opposite side of the white and dusty street. On coming within the shadow of the Pyncheon Elm, he stopt, and (taking off his hat, meanwhile, to wipe the perspiration from his brow) seemed to scrutinize, with especial interest, the dilapidated and rusty-visaged House of the Seven Gables. He himself, in a very different style, was as well worth looking at as the house. No better model need be sought, nor could have been found, of a very high order of respectability, which, by some indescribable magic, not merely expressed itself in his looks and gestures, but even governed the fashion of his garments, and rendered them all proper and essential to the man. Without appearing to differ, in any tangible way, from other people's clothes, there was yet a wide and rich gravity about them that must have been a characteristic of the wearer, since it could not be defined as pertaining either to the cut or material. His gold-headed cane, too,—a serviceable staff, of dark polished wood,—had similar traits, and, had it chosen to take a walk by itself, would have been recognized anywhere as a tolerably adequate representative of its master. This character—which showed itself so strikingly in everything about him, and the effect of which we seek to convey to the reader—went no deeper than his station, habits of life, and external circumstances. One perceived him to be a personage of marked influence and authority; and, especially, you could feel just as certain that he was opulent as if he had exhibited his bank account, or as if you had seen him touching the twigs of the Pyncheon Elm, and, Midas-like, transmuting them to gold.

In his youth, he had probably been considered a handsome man; at his present age, his brow was too heavy, his temples too bare, his remaining hair too gray, his eye too cold, his lips too closely compressed, to bear any relation to mere personal beauty. He would have made a good and massive portrait; better now, perhaps, than at any previous period of his life, although his look might grow positively harsh in the process of being fixed upon the canvas. The artist would have found it desirable to study his face, and prove its capacity for varied expression; to darken it with a frown,—to kindle it up with a smile.

While the elderly gentleman stood looking at the Pyncheon House, both the frown and the smile passed successively over his countenance. His eye rested on the shop-window, and putting up a pair of gold-bowed spectacles, which he held in his hand, he minutely surveyed Hepzibah's little arrangement of toys and commodities. At first it seemed not to please him,—nay, to cause him exceeding displeasure,—and yet, the very next moment, he smiled. While the latter expression was yet on his lips, he caught a glimpse of Hepzibah, who had involuntarily bent forward to the window; and then the smile changed from acrid and disagreeable to the sunniest complacency and benevolence. He bowed, with a happy mixture of dignity and courteous kindliness, and pursued his way.

"There he is!" said Hepzibah to herself, gulping down a very bitter emotion, and, since she could not rid herself of it, trying to drive it back into her heart. "What does he think of it, I wonder? Does it please him? Ah! he is looking back!"

The gentleman had paused in the street, and turned himself half about, still with his eyes fixed on the shop-window. In fact, he wheeled wholly round, and commenced a step or two, as if designing to enter the shop; but, as it chanced, his purpose was anticipated by Hepzibah's first customer, the little cannibal of Jim Crow, who, staring up at the window, was irresistibly attracted by an elephant of gingerbread. What a grand appetite had this small urchin!—Two Jim Crows immediately after breakfast!—and now an elephant, as a preliminary whet before dinner. By the time this latter purchase was completed, the elderly gentleman had resumed his way, and turned the street corner.

"Take it as you like, Cousin Jaffrey," muttered the maiden lady, as she drew back, after cautiously thrusting out her head, and looking up and down the street,—"Take it as you like! You have seen my little shop-window. Well!—what have you to say?—is not the Pyncheon House my own, while I'm alive?"

After this incident, Hepzibah retreated to the back parlor, where she at first caught up a half-finished stocking, and began knitting at it with nervous and irregular jerks; but quickly finding herself at odds with the stitches, she threw it aside, and walked hurriedly about the room. At length she paused before the portrait of the stern old Puritan, her ancestor, and the founder of the house. In one sense, this picture had almost faded into the canvas, and hidden itself behind the duskiness of age; in another, she could not but fancy that it had been growing more prominent and strikingly expressive, ever since her earliest familiarity with it as a child. For, while the physical outline and substance were darkening away from the beholder's eye, the bold, hard, and, at the same time, indirect character of the man seemed to be brought out in a kind of spiritual relief. Such an effect may occasionally be observed in pictures of antique date. They acquire a look which an artist (if he have anything like the complacency of artists nowadays) would never dream of presenting to a patron as his own characteristic expression, but which, nevertheless, we at once recognize as reflecting the unlovely truth of a human soul. In such cases, the painter's deep conception of his subject's inward traits has wrought itself into the essence of the picture, and is seen after the superficial coloring has been rubbed off by time.

While gazing at the portrait, Hepzibah trembled under its eye. Her hereditary reverence made her afraid to judge the character of the original so harshly as a perception of the truth compelled her to do. But still she gazed, because the face of the picture enabled her—at least, she fancied so—to read more accurately, and to a greater depth, the face which she had just seen in the street.

"This is the very man!" murmured she to herself. "Let Jaffrey Pyncheon smile as he will, there is that look beneath! Put on him a skull-cap, and a band, and a black cloak, and a Bible in one hand and a sword in the other,—then let Jaffrey smile as he might,—nobody would doubt that it was the old Pyncheon come again. He has proved himself the very man to build up a new house! Perhaps, too, to draw down a new curse!"

Thus did Hepzibah bewilder herself with these fantasies of the old time. She had dwelt too much alone,—too long in the Pyncheon House,—until her very brain was impregnated with the dry-rot of its timbers. She needed a walk along the noonday street to keep her sane.

By the spell of contrast, another portrait rose up before her, painted with more daring flattery than any artist would have ventured upon, but yet so delicately touched that the likeness remained perfect. Malbone's miniature, though from the same original, was far inferior to Hepzibah's air-drawn picture, at which affection and sorrowful remembrance wrought together. Soft, mildly, and cheerfully contemplative, with full, red lips, just on the verge of a smile, which the eyes seemed to herald by a gentle kindling-up of their orbs! Feminine traits, moulded inseparably with those of the other sex! The miniature, likewise, had this last peculiarity; so that you inevitably thought of the original as resembling his mother, and she a lovely and lovable woman, with perhaps some beautiful infirmity of character, that made it all the pleasanter to know and easier to love her.

"Yes," thought Hepzibah, with grief of which it was only the more tolerable portion that welled up from her heart to her eyelids, "they persecuted his mother in him! He never was a Pyncheon!"

But here the shop-bell rang; it was like a sound from a remote distance,—so far had Hepzibah descended into the sepulchral depths of her reminiscences. On entering the shop, she found an old man there, a humble resident of Pyncheon Street, and whom, for a great many years past, she had suffered to be a kind of familiar of the house. He was an immemorial personage, who seemed always to have had a white head and wrinkles, and never to have possessed but a single tooth, and that a half-decayed one, in the front of the upper jaw. Well advanced as Hepzibah was, she could not remember when Uncle Venner, as the neighborhood called him, had not gone up and down the street, stooping a little and drawing his feet heavily over the gravel or pavement. But still there was something tough and vigorous about him, that not only kept him in daily breath, but enabled him to fill a place which would else have been vacant in the apparently crowded world. To go of errands with his slow and shuffling gait, which made you doubt how he ever was to arrive anywhere; to saw a small household's foot or two of firewood, or knock to pieces an old barrel, or split up a pine board for kindling-stuff; in summer, to dig the few yards of garden ground appertaining to a low-rented tenement, and share the produce of his labor at the halves; in winter, to shovel away the snow from the sidewalk, or open paths to the woodshed, or along the clothes-line; such were some of the essential offices which Uncle Venner performed among at least a score of families. Within that circle, he claimed the same sort of privilege, and probably felt as much warmth of interest, as a clergyman does in the range of his parishioners. Not that he laid claim to the tithe pig; but, as an analogous mode of reverence, he went his rounds, every morning, to gather up the crumbs of the table and overflowings of the dinner-pot, as food for a pig of his own.

In his younger days—for, after all, there was a dim tradition that he had been, not young, but younger—Uncle Venner was commonly regarded as rather deficient, than otherwise, in his wits. In truth he had virtually pleaded guilty to the charge, by scarcely aiming at such success as other men seek, and by taking only that humble and modest part in the intercourse of life which belongs to the alleged deficiency. But now, in his extreme old age,—whether it were that his long and hard experience had actually brightened him, or that his decaying judgment rendered him less capable of fairly measuring himself,—the venerable man made pretensions to no little wisdom, and really enjoyed the credit of it. There was likewise, at times, a vein of something like poetry in him; it was the moss or wall-flower of his mind in its small dilapidation, and gave a charm to what might have been vulgar and commonplace in his earlier and middle life. Hepzibah had a regard for him, because his name was ancient in the town and had formerly been respectable. It was a still better reason for awarding him a species of familiar reverence that Uncle Venner was himself the most ancient existence, whether of man or thing, in Pyncheon Street, except the House of the Seven Gables, and perhaps the elm that overshadowed it.

This patriarch now presented himself before Hepzibah, clad in an old blue coat, which had a fashionable air, and must have accrued to him from the cast-off wardrobe of some dashing clerk. As for his trousers, they were of tow-cloth, very short in the legs, and bagging down strangely in the rear, but yet having a suitableness to his figure which his other garment entirely lacked. His hat had relation to no other part of his dress, and but very little to the head that wore it. Thus Uncle Venner was a miscellaneous old gentleman, partly himself, but, in good measure, somebody else; patched together, too, of different epochs; an epitome of times and fashions.

"So, you have really begun trade," said he,—"really begun trade! Well, I'm glad to see it. Young people should never live idle in the world, nor old ones neither, unless when the rheumatize gets hold of them. It has given me warning already; and in two or three years longer, I shall think of putting aside business and retiring to my farm. That's yonder,—the great brick house, you know,—the workhouse, most folks call it; but I mean to do my work first, and go there to be idle and enjoy myself. And I'm glad to see you beginning to do your work, Miss Hepzibah!"

"Thank you, Uncle Venner" said Hepzibah, smiling; for she always felt kindly towards the simple and talkative old man. Had he been an old woman, she might probably have repelled the freedom, which she now took in good part. "It is time for me to begin work, indeed! Or, to speak the truth, I have just begun when I ought to be giving it up."

"Oh, never say that, Miss Hepzibah!" answered the old man. "You are a young woman yet. Why, I hardly thought myself younger than I am now, it seems so little while ago since I used to see you playing about the door of the old house, quite a small child! Oftener, though, you used to be sitting at the threshold, and looking gravely into the street; for you had always a grave kind of way with you,—a grown-up air, when you were only the height of my knee. It seems as if I saw you now; and your grandfather with his red cloak, and his white wig, and his cocked hat, and his cane, coming out of the house, and stepping so grandly up the street! Those old gentlemen that grew up before the Revolution used to put on grand airs. In my young days, the great man of the town was commonly called King; and his wife, not Queen to be sure, but Lady. Nowadays, a man would not dare to be called King; and if he feels himself a little above common folks, he only stoops so much the lower to them. I met your cousin, the Judge, ten minutes ago; and, in my old tow-cloth trousers, as you see, the Judge raised his hat to me, I do believe! At any rate, the Judge bowed and smiled!"

"Yes," said Hepzibah, with something bitter stealing unawares into her tone; "my cousin Jaffrey is thought to have a very pleasant smile!"

"And so he has" replied Uncle Venner. "And that's rather remarkable in a Pyncheon; for, begging your pardon, Miss Hepzibah, they never had the name of being an easy and agreeable set of folks. There was no getting close to them. But Now, Miss Hepzibah, if an old man may be bold to ask, why don't Judge Pyncheon, with his great means, step forward, and tell his cousin to shut up her little shop at once? It's for your credit to be doing something, but it's not for the Judge's credit to let you!"

"We won't talk of this, if you please, Uncle Venner," said Hepzibah coldly. "I ought to say, however, that, if I choose to earn bread for myself, it is not Judge Pyncheon's fault. Neither will he deserve the blame," added she more kindly, remembering Uncle Venner's privileges of age and humble familiarity, "if I should, by and by, find it convenient to retire with you to your farm."

"And it's no bad place, either, that farm of mine!" cried the old man cheerily, as if there were something positively delightful in the prospect. "No bad place is the great brick farm-house, especially for them that will find a good many old cronies there, as will be my case. I quite long to be among them, sometimes, of the winter evenings; for it is but dull business for a lonesome elderly man, like me, to be nodding, by the hour together, with no company but his air-tight stove. Summer or winter, there's a great deal to be said in favor of my farm! And, take it in the autumn, what can be pleasanter than to spend a whole day on the sunny side of a barn or a wood-pile, chatting with somebody as old as one's self; or, perhaps, idling away the time with a natural-born simpleton, who knows how to be idle, because even our busy Yankees never have found out how to put him to any use? Upon my word, Miss Hepzibah, I doubt whether I've ever been so comfortable as

I mean to be at my farm, which most folks call the workhouse. But you,—you're a young woman yet,—you never need go there! Something still better will turn up for you. I'm sure of it!"

Hepzibah fancied that there was something peculiar in her venerable friend's look and tone; insomuch, that she gazed into his face with considerable earnestness, endeavoring to discover what secret meaning, if any, might be lurking there. Individuals whose affairs have reached an utterly desperate crisis almost invariably keep themselves alive with hopes, so much the more airily magnificent as they have the less of solid matter within their grasp whereof to mould any judicious and moderate expectation of good. Thus, all the while Hepzibah was perfecting the scheme of her little shop, she had cherished an unacknowledged idea that some harlequin trick of fortune would intervene in her favor. For example, an uncle—who had sailed for India fifty years before, and never been heard of since—might yet return, and adopt her to be the comfort of his very extreme and decrepit age, and adorn her with pearls, diamonds, and Oriental shawls and turbans, and make her the ultimate heiress of his unreckonable riches. Or the member of Parliament, now at the head of the English branch of the family,—with which the elder stock, on this side of the Atlantic, had held little or no intercourse for the last two centuries,—this eminent gentleman might invite Hepzibah to quit the ruinous House of the Seven Gables, and come over to dwell with her kindred at Pyncheon Hall. But, for reasons the most imperative, she could not yield to his request. It was more probable, therefore, that the descendants of a Pyncheon who had emigrated to Virginia, in some past generation, and became a great planter there,—hearing of Hepzibah's destitution, and impelled by the splendid generosity of character with which their Virginian mixture must have enriched the New England blood,—would send her a remittance of a thousand dollars, with a hint of repeating the favor annually. Or,—and, surely, anything so undeniably just could not be beyond the limits of reasonable anticipation,—the great claim to the heritage of Waldo County might finally be decided in favor of the Pyncheons; so that, instead of keeping a cent-shop, Hepzibah would build a palace, and look down from its highest tower on hill, dale, forest, field, and town, as her own share of the ancestral territory.

These were some of the fantasies which she had long dreamed about; and, aided by these, Uncle Venner's casual attempt at encouragement kindled a strange festal glory in the poor, bare, melancholy chambers of her brain, as if that inner world were suddenly lighted up with gas. But either he knew nothing of her castles in the air,—as how should he?—or else her earnest scowl disturbed his recollection, as it might a more courageous man's. Instead of pursuing any weightier topic, Uncle Venner was pleased to favor Hepzibah with some sage counsel in her shop-keeping capacity.

"Give no credit!"—these were some of his golden maxims,—"Never take paper-money. Look well to your change! Ring the silver on the four-pound weight! Shove back all English half-pence and base copper tokens, such as are very plenty about town! At your leisure hours, knit children's woollen socks and mittens! Brew your own yeast, and make your own ginger-beer!"

And while Hepzibah was doing her utmost to digest the hard little pellets of his already uttered wisdom, he gave vent to his final, and what he declared to be his all-important advice, as follows:—

"Put on a bright face for your customers, and smile pleasantly as you hand them what they ask for! A stale article, if you dip it in a good, warm, sunny smile, will go off better than a fresh one that you've scowled upon."

To this last apothegm poor Hepzibah responded with a sigh so deep and heavy that it almost rustled Uncle Venner quite away, like a withered leaf,—as he was,—before an autumnal gale. Recovering himself, however, he bent forward, and, with a good deal of feeling in his ancient visage, beckoned her nearer to him.

"When do you expect him home?" whispered he.

"Whom do you mean?" asked Hepzibah, turning pale.

"Ah!—You don't love to talk about it," said Uncle Venner. "Well, well! we'll say no more, though there's word of it all over town. I remember him, Miss Hepzibah, before he could run alone!"

During the remainder of the day, poor Hepzibah acquitted herself even less creditably, as a shop-keeper, than in her earlier efforts. She appeared to be walking in a dream; or, more truly, the vivid life and reality assumed by her emotions made all outward occurrences unsubstantial, like the teasing phantasms of a half-conscious slumber. She still responded, mechanically, to the frequent summons of the shop-bell, and, at the demand of her customers, went prying with vague eyes about the shop, proffering them one article after another, and thrusting aside—perversely, as most of them supposed—the identical thing they asked for. There is sad confusion, indeed, when the spirit thus flits away into the past, or into the more awful future, or, in any manner, steps across the spaceless boundary betwixt its own region and the actual world; where the body remains to guide itself as best it may, with little more than the mechanism of animal life. It is like death, without death's quiet privilege,—its freedom from mortal care. Worst of all, when the actual duties are comprised in such petty details as now vexed the brooding soul of the old gentlewoman. As the animosity of fate would have it, there was a great influx of custom in the course of the afternoon. Hepzibah blundered to and fro about her small place of business, committing the most unheard-of errors: now stringing up twelve, and now seven, tallow-candles, instead of ten to the pound; selling ginger for Scotch snuff, pins for needles, and needles for pins; misreckoning her change, sometimes to the public detriment, and much oftener to her own; and thus she went on, doing her utmost to bring chaos back again, until, at the close of the day's labor, to her inexplicable astonishment, she found the money-drawer almost destitute of coin. After all her painful traffic, the whole proceeds were perhaps half a dozen coppers, and a questionable ninepence which ultimately proved to be copper likewise.

At this price, or at whatever price, she rejoiced that the day had reached its end. Never before had she had such a sense of the intolerable length of time that creeps between dawn and sunset, and of the miserable irksomeness of having aught to do, and of the better wisdom that it would be to lie down at once, in sullen resignation, and let life, and its toils and vexations, trample over one's prostrate body as they may! Hepzibah's final operation was with the little devourer of Jim Crow and the elephant, who now proposed to eat a camel. In her bewilderment, she offered him first a wooden dragoon, and next a handful of marbles; neither of which being adapted to his else omnivorous appetite, she hastily held out her whole remaining stock of natural history in gingerbread, and huddled the small customer out of the shop. She then muffled the bell in an unfinished stocking, and put up the oaken bar across the door.

During the latter process, an omnibus came to a stand-still under the branches of the elm-tree. Hepzibah's heart was in her mouth. Remote and dusky, and with no sunshine on all the intervening space, was that region of the Past whence her only guest might be expected to arrive! Was she to meet him now?

Somebody, at all events, was passing from the farthest interior of the omnibus towards its entrance. A gentleman alighted; but it was only to offer his hand to a young girl whose slender figure, nowise needing such assistance, now lightly descended the steps, and made an airy little jump from the final one to the sidewalk. She rewarded her cavalier with a smile, the cheery glow of which was seen reflected on his own face as he reentered the vehicle. The girl then turned towards the House of the Seven Gables, to the door of which, meanwhile,—not the shop-door, but the antique portal,—the omnibus-man had carried a light trunk and a bandbox. First giving a sharp rap of the old iron knocker, he left his passenger and her luggage at the door-step, and departed.

"Who can it be?" thought Hepzibah, who had been screwing her visual organs into the acutest focus of which they were capable. "The girl must have mistaken the house." She stole softly into the hall, and, herself invisible, gazed through the dusty side-lights of the portal at the young, blooming, and very cheerful face which presented itself for admittance into the gloomy old mansion. It was a face to which almost any door would have opened of its own accord.

The young girl, so fresh, so unconventional, and yet so orderly and obedient to common rules, as you at once recognized her to be, was widely in contrast, at that moment, with everything about her. The sordid and ugly luxuriance of gigantic weeds that grew in the angle of the house, and the heavy projection that overshadowed her, and the time-worn framework of the door,—none of these things belonged to her sphere. But, even as a ray of sunshine, fall into what dismal place it may, instantaneously creates for itself a propriety in being there, so did it seem altogether fit that the girl should be standing at the threshold. It was no less evidently proper that the door should swing open to admit her. The maiden lady herself, sternly inhospitable in her first purposes, soon began to feel that the door ought to be shoved back, and the rusty key be turned in the reluctant lock.

"Can it be Phoebe?" questioned she within herself. "It must be little Phoebe; for it can be nobody else,—and there is a look of her father about her, too! But what does she want here? And how like a country cousin, to come down upon a poor body in this way, without so much as a day's notice, or asking whether she would be welcome! Well; she must have a night's lodging, I suppose; and to-morrow the child shall go back to her mother."

Phoebe, it must be understood, was that one little offshoot of the Pyncheon race to whom we have already referred, as a native of a rural part of New England, where the old fashions and feelings of relationship are still partially kept up. In her own circle, it was regarded as by no means improper for kinsfolk to visit one another without invitation, or preliminary and ceremonious warning. Yet, in consideration of Miss Hepzibah's recluse way of life, a letter had actually been written and despatched, conveying information of Phoebe's projected visit. This epistle, for three or four days past, had been in the pocket of the penny-postman, who, happening to have no other business in Pyncheon Street, had not yet made it convenient to call at the House of the Seven Gables.

"No—she can stay only one night," said Hepzibah, unbolting the door. "If Clifford were to find her here, it might disturb him!"

V May and November

PHOEBE PYNCHEON slept, on the night of her arrival, in a chamber that looked down on the garden of the old house. It fronted towards the east, so that at a very seasonable hour a glow of crimson light came flooding through the window, and bathed the dingy ceiling and paper-hangings in its own hue. There were curtains to Phoebe's bed; a dark, antique canopy, and ponderous festoons of a stuff which had been rich, and even magnificent, in its time; but which now brooded over the girl like a cloud, making a night in that one corner, while elsewhere it was beginning to be day. The morning light, however, soon stole into the aperture at the foot of the bed, betwixt those faded curtains. Finding the new guest there,—with a bloom on her cheeks like the morning's own, and a gentle stir of departing slumber in her limbs, as when an early breeze moves the foliage,—the dawn kissed her brow. It was the caress which a dewy maiden—such as the Dawn is, immortally—gives to her sleeping sister, partly from the impulse of irresistible fondness, and partly as a pretty hint that it is time now to unclose her eyes.

At the touch of those lips of light, Phoebe quietly awoke, and, for a moment, did not recognize where she was, nor how those heavy curtains chanced to be festooned around her. Nothing, indeed, was absolutely plain to her, except that it was now early morning, and that, whatever might happen next, it was proper, first of all, to get up and say her prayers. She was the more inclined to devotion from the grim aspect of the chamber and its furniture, especially the tall, stiff chairs; one of which stood close by her bedside, and looked as if some old-fashioned personage had been sitting there all night, and had vanished only just in season to escape discovery.

When Phoebe was quite dressed, she peeped out of the window, and saw a rosebush in the garden. Being a very tall one, and of luxuriant growth, it had been propped up against the side of the house, and was literally covered with a rare and very beautiful species of white rose. A large portion of them, as the girl afterwards discovered, had blight or mildew at their hearts; but, viewed at a fair distance, the whole rosebush looked as if it had been brought from Eden that very summer, together with the mould in which it grew. The truth was, nevertheless, that it had been planted by Alice Pyncheon,—she was Phoebe's great-great-grand-aunt,—in soil which, reckoning only its cultivation as a garden-plat, was now unctuous with nearly two hundred years of vegetable decay. Growing as they did, however, out of the old earth, the flowers still sent a fresh and sweet incense up to their Creator; nor could it have been the less pure and acceptable because Phoebe's young breath mingled with it, as the fragrance floated past the window. Hastening down the creaking and carpetless staircase, she found her way into the garden, gathered some of the most perfect of the roses, and brought them to her chamber.

Little Phoebe was one of those persons who possess, as their exclusive patrimony, the gift of practical arrangement. It is a kind of natural magic that enables these favored ones to bring out the hidden capabilities of things around them; and particularly to give a look of comfort and habitableness to any place which, for however brief a period, may happen to be their home. A wild hut of underbrush, tossed together by wayfarers through the primitive forest, would acquire the home aspect by one night's lodging of such a woman, and would retain it long after her quiet figure had disappeared into the surrounding shade. No less a portion of such homely witchcraft was requisite to reclaim, as it were, Phoebe's waste, cheerless, and dusky chamber, which had been untenanted so long—except by spiders, and mice, and rats, and ghosts—that it was all overgrown with the desolation which watches to obliterate every trace of man's happier hours. What was precisely Phoebe's process we find it impossible to say. She appeared to have no preliminary design, but gave a touch here and another there; brought some articles of furniture to light and dragged others into the shadow; looped up or let down a window-curtain; and, in the course of half an hour, had fully succeeded in throwing a kindly and hospitable smile over the apartment. No longer ago than the night before, it had resembled nothing so much as the old maid's heart; for there was neither sunshine nor household fire in one nor the other, and, save for ghosts and ghostly reminiscences, not a guest, for many years gone by, had entered the heart or the chamber.

There was still another peculiarity of this inscrutable charm. The bedchamber, no doubt, was a chamber of very great and varied experience, as a scene of human life: the joy of bridal nights had throbbed itself away here; new immortals had first drawn earthly breath here; and here old people had died. But—whether it were the white roses, or whatever the subtile influence might be—a person of delicate instinct would have known at once that it was now a maiden's bedchamber, and had been purified of all former evil and sorrow by her sweet breath and happy thoughts. Her dreams of the past night, being such cheerful ones, had exorcised the gloom, and now haunted the chamber in its stead.

After arranging matters to her satisfaction, Phoebe emerged from her chamber, with a purpose to descend again into the garden. Besides the rosebush, she had observed several other species of flowers growing there in a wilderness of neglect, and obstructing one another's development (as is often the parallel case in human society) by their uneducated entanglement and confusion. At the head of the stairs, however, she met Hepzibah, who, it being still early, invited her into a room which she would probably have called her boudoir, had her education embraced any such French phrase. It was strewn about with a few old books, and a work-basket, and a dusty writing-desk; and had, on one side, a large black article of furniture, of very strange appearance, which the old gentlewoman told Phoebe was a harpsichord. It looked more like a coffin than anything else; and, indeed,—not having been played upon, or opened, for years,—there must have been a vast deal of dead music in it, stifled for want of air. Human finger was hardly known to have touched its chords since the days of Alice Pyncheon, who had learned the sweet accomplishment of melody in Europe.

Hepzibah bade her young guest sit down, and, herself taking a chair near by, looked as earnestly at Phoebe's trim little figure as if she expected to see right into its springs and motive secrets.

"Cousin Phoebe," said she, at last, "I really can't see my way clear to keep you with me."

These words, however, had not the inhospitable bluntness with which they may strike the reader; for the two relatives, in a talk before bedtime, had arrived at a certain degree of mutual understanding. Hepzibah knew enough to enable her to appreciate the circumstances (resulting from the second marriage of the girl's mother) which made it desirable for Phoebe to establish herself in another home. Nor did she misinterpret Phoebe's character, and the genial activity pervading it,—one of the most valuable traits of the true New England woman,—which had impelled her forth, as might be said, to seek her fortune, but with a self-respecting purpose to confer as much benefit as she could anywise receive. As one of her nearest kindred, she had naturally betaken herself to Hepzibah, with no idea of forcing herself on her cousin's protection, but only for a visit of a week or two, which might be indefinitely extended, should it prove for the happiness of both.

To Hepzibah's blunt observation, therefore, Phoebe replied as frankly, and more cheerfully.

"Dear cousin, I cannot tell how it will be," said she. "But I really think we may suit one another much better than you suppose."

"You are a nice girl,—I see it plainly," continued Hepzibah; "and it is not any question as to that point which makes me hesitate. But, Phoebe, this house of mine is but a melancholy place for a young person to be in. It lets in the wind and rain, and the snow, too, in the garret and upper chambers, in winter-time, but it never lets in the sunshine. And as for myself, you see what I am,—a dismal and lonesome old woman (for I begin to call myself old, Phoebe), whose temper, I am afraid, is none of the best, and whose spirits are as bad as can be! I cannot make your life pleasant, Cousin Phoebe, neither can I so much as give you bread to eat."

"You will find me a cheerful little body" answered Phoebe, smiling, and yet with a kind of gentle dignity, "and I mean to earn my bread. You know I have not been brought up a Pyncheon. A girl learns many things in a New England village."

"Ah! Phoebe," said Hepzibah, sighing, "your knowledge would do but little for you here! And then it is a wretched thought that you should fling away your young days in a place like this. Those cheeks would not be so rosy after a month or two. Look at my face!" and, indeed, the contrast was very striking,—"you see how pale I am! It is my idea that the dust and continual decay of these old houses are unwholesome for the lungs."

"There is the garden,—the flowers to be taken care of," observed Phoebe. "I should keep myself healthy with exercise in the open air."

"And, after all, child," exclaimed Hepzibah, suddenly rising, as if to dismiss the subject, "it is not for me to say who shall be a guest or inhabitant of the old Pyncheon House. Its master is coming."

"Do you mean Judge Pyncheon?" asked Phoebe in surprise.

"Judge Pyncheon!" answered her cousin angrily. "He will hardly cross the threshold while I live! No, no! But, Phoebe, you shall see the face of him I speak of."

She went in quest of the miniature already described, and returned with it in her hand. Giving it to Phoebe, she watched her features narrowly, and with a certain jealousy as to the mode in which the girl would show herself affected by the picture.

"How do you like the face?" asked Hepzibah.

"It is handsome!—it is very beautiful!" said Phoebe admiringly. "It is as sweet a face as a man's can be, or ought to be. It has something of a child's expression,—and yet not childish,—only one feels so very kindly towards him! He ought never to suffer anything. One would bear much for the sake of sparing him toil or sorrow. Who is it, Cousin Hepzibah?"

"Did you never hear," whispered her cousin, bending towards her, "of Clifford Pyncheon?"

"Never. I thought there were no Pyncheons left, except yourself and our cousin Jaffrey," answered Phoebe. "And yet I seem to have heard the name of Clifford Pyncheon. Yes!—from my father or my mother; but has he not been a long while dead?"

"Well, well, child, perhaps he has!" said Hepzibah with a sad, hollow laugh; "but, in old houses like this, you know, dead people are very apt to come back again! We shall see. And, Cousin Phoebe, since, after all that I have said, your courage does not fail you, we will not part so soon. You are welcome, my child, for the present, to such a home as your kinswoman can offer you."

With this measured, but not exactly cold assurance of a hospitable purpose, Hepzibah kissed her cheek.

They now went below stairs, where Phoebe—not so much assuming the office as attracting it to herself, by the magnetism of innate fitness—took the most active part in preparing breakfast. The mistress of the house, meanwhile, as is usual with persons of her stiff and unmalleable cast, stood mostly aside; willing to lend her aid, yet conscious that her natural inaptitude would be likely to impede the business in hand. Phoebe and the fire that boiled the teakettle were equally bright, cheerful, and efficient, in their respective offices. Hepzibah gazed forth from her habitual sluggishness, the necessary result of long solitude, as from another sphere. She could not help being interested, however, and even amused, at the readiness with which her new inmate adapted herself to the circumstances, and brought the house, moreover, and all its rusty old appliances, into a suitableness for her purposes. Whatever she did, too, was done without conscious effort, and with frequent outbreaks of song, which were exceedingly pleasant to the ear. This natural tunefulness made Phoebe seem like a bird in a shadowy tree; or conveyed the idea that the stream of life warbled through her heart as a brook sometimes warbles through a pleasant little dell. It betokened the cheeriness of an active temperament, finding joy in its activity, and, therefore, rendering it beautiful; it was a New England trait,—the stern old stuff of Puritanism with a gold thread in the web.

Hepzibah brought out some old silver spoons with the family crest upon them, and a china tea-set painted over with grotesque figures of man, bird, and beast, in as grotesque a landscape. These pictured people were odd humorists, in a world of their own,—a world of vivid brilliancy, so far as color went, and still unfaded, although the teapot and small cups were as ancient as the custom itself of tea-drinking.

"Your great-great-great-great-grandmother had these cups, when she was married," said Hepzibah to Phoebe. "She was a Davenport, of a good family. They were almost the first teacups ever seen in the colony; and if one of them were to be broken, my heart would break with it. But it is nonsense to speak so about a brittle teacup, when I remember what my heart has gone through without breaking."

The cups—not having been used, perhaps, since Hepzibah's youth—had contracted no small burden of dust, which Phoebe washed away with so much care and delicacy as to satisfy even the proprietor of this invaluable china.

"What a nice little housewife you are!" exclaimed the latter, smiling, and at the same time frowning so prodigiously that the smile was sunshine under a thunder-cloud. "Do you do other things as well? Are you as good at your book as you are at washing teacups?"

"Not quite, I am afraid," said Phoebe, laughing at the form of Hepzibah's question. "But I was schoolmistress for the little children in our district last summer, and might have been so still."

"Ah! 'tis all very well!" observed the maiden lady, drawing herself up. "But these things must have come to you with your mother's blood. I never knew a Pyncheon that had any turn for them."

It is very queer, but not the less true, that people are generally quite as vain, or even more so, of their deficiencies than of their available gifts; as was Hepzibah of this native inapplicability, so to speak, of the Pyncheons to any useful purpose. She regarded it as an hereditary trait; and so, perhaps, it was, but unfortunately a morbid one, such as is often generated in families that remain long above the surface of society.

Before they left the breakfast-table, the shop-bell rang sharply, and Hepzibah set down the remnant of her final cup of tea, with a look of sallow despair that was truly piteous to behold. In cases of distasteful occupation, the second day is generally worse than the first. We return to the rack with all the soreness of the preceding torture in our limbs. At all events, Hepzibah had fully satisfied herself of the impossibility of ever becoming wonted to this peevishly obstreperous little bell. Ring as often as it might, the sound always smote upon her nervous system rudely and suddenly. And especially now, while, with her crested teaspoons and antique china, she was flattering herself with ideas of gentility, she felt an unspeakable disinclination to confront a customer.

"Do not trouble yourself, dear cousin!" cried Phoebe, starting lightly up. "I am shop-keeper to-day."

"You, child!" exclaimed Hepzibah. "What can a little country girl know of such matters?"

"Oh, I have done all the shopping for the family at our village store," said Phoebe. "And I have had a table at a fancy fair, and made better sales than anybody. These things are not to be learnt; they depend upon a knack that comes, I suppose," added she, smiling, "with one's mother's blood. You shall see that I am as nice a little saleswoman as I am a housewife!"

The old gentlewoman stole behind Phoebe, and peeped from the passageway into the shop, to note how she would manage her undertaking. It was a case of some intricacy. A very ancient woman, in a white short gown and a green petticoat, with a string of gold beads about her neck, and what looked like a nightcap on her head, had brought a quantity of yarn to barter for the commodities of the shop. She was probably the very last person in town who still kept the time-honored spinning-wheel in constant revolution. It was worth while to hear the croaking and hollow tones of the old lady, and the pleasant voice of Phoebe, mingling in one twisted thread of talk; and still better to contrast their figures,—so light and bloomy,—so decrepit and dusky,—with only the counter betwixt them, in one sense, but more than threescore years, in another. As for the bargain, it was wrinkled slyness and craft pitted against native truth and sagacity.

"Was not that well done?" asked Phoebe, laughing, when the customer was gone.

"Nicely done, indeed, child!" answered Hepzibah. "I could not have gone through with it nearly so well. As you say, it must be a knack that belongs to you on the mother's side."

It is a very genuine admiration, that with which persons too shy or too awkward to take a due part in the bustling world regard the real actors in life's stirring scenes; so genuine, in fact, that the former are usually fain to make it palatable to their self-love, by assuming that these active and forcible qualities are incompatible with others, which they choose to deem higher and more important. Thus, Hepzibah was well content to acknowledge Phoebe's vastly superior gifts as a shop-keeper'—she listened, with compliant ear, to her suggestion of various methods whereby the influx of trade might be increased, and rendered profitable, without a hazardous outlay of capital. She consented that the village maiden should manufacture yeast, both liquid and in cakes; and should brew a certain kind of beer, nectareous to the palate, and of rare stomachic virtues; and, moreover, should bake and exhibit for sale some little spice-cakes, which whosoever tasted would longingly desire to taste again. All such proofs of a ready mind and skilful handiwork were highly acceptable to the aristocratic hucksteress, so long as she could murmur to herself with a grim smile, and a half-natural sigh, and a sentiment of mixed wonder, pity, and growing affection:—

"What a nice little body she is! If she only could be a lady; too—but that's impossible! Phoebe is no Pyncheon. She takes everything from her mother!"

As to Phoebe's not being a lady, or whether she were a lady or no, it was a point, perhaps, difficult to decide, but which could hardly have come up for judgment at all in any fair and healthy mind. Out of New England, it would be impossible to meet with a person combining so many ladylike attributes with so many others that form no necessary (if compatible) part of the character. She shocked no canon of taste; she was admirably in keeping with herself, and never jarred against surrounding circumstances. Her figure, to be sure,—so small as to be almost childlike, and so elastic that motion seemed as easy or easier to it than rest, would hardly have suited one's idea of a countess. Neither did her face—with the brown ringlets on either side, and the slightly piquant nose, and the wholesome bloom, and the clear shade of tan, and the half dozen freckles, friendly remembrances of the April sun and breeze—precisely give us a right to call her beautiful. But there was both lustre and depth in her eyes. She was very pretty; as graceful as a bird, and graceful much in the same way; as pleasant about the house as a gleam of sunshine falling on the floor through a shadow of twinkling leaves, or as a ray of firelight that dances on the wall while evening is drawing nigh. Instead of discussing her claim to rank among ladies, it would be preferable to regard Phoebe as the example of feminine grace and availability combined, in a state of society, if there were any such, where ladies did not exist. There it should be woman's office to move in the midst of practical affairs, and to gild them all, the very homeliest,—were it even the scouring of pots and kettles,—with an atmosphere of loveliness and joy.

Such was the sphere of Phoebe. To find the born and educated lady, on the other hand, we need look no farther than Hepzibah, our forlorn old maid, in her rustling and rusty silks, with her deeply cherished and ridiculous consciousness of long descent, her shadowy claims to princely territory, and, in the way of accomplishment, her recollections, it may be, of having formerly thrummed on a harpsichord, and walked a minuet, and worked an antique tapestry-stitch on her sampler. It was a fair parallel between new Plebeianism and old Gentility.

It really seemed as if the battered visage of the House of the Seven Gables, black and heavy-browed as it still certainly looked, must have shown a kind of cheerfulness glimmering through its dusky windows as Phoebe passed to and fro in the interior. Otherwise, it is impossible to explain how the people of the neighborhood so soon became aware of the girl's presence. There was a great run of custom, setting steadily in, from about ten o' clock until towards noon,—relaxing, somewhat, at dinner-time, but recommencing in the afternoon, and, finally, dying away a half an hour or so before the long day's sunset. One of the stanchest patrons was little Ned Higgins, the devourer of Jim Crow and the elephant, who to-day signalized his omnivorous prowess by swallowing two dromedaries and a locomotive. Phoebe laughed, as she summed up her aggregate of sales upon the slate; while Hepzibah, first drawing on a pair of silk gloves, reckoned over the sordid accumulation of copper coin, not without silver intermixed, that had jingled into the till.

"We must renew our stock, Cousin Hepzibah!" cried the little saleswoman. "The gingerbread figures are all gone, and so are those Dutch wooden milkmaids, and most of our other playthings. There has been constant inquiry for cheap raisins, and a great cry for whistles, and trumpets, and jew's-harps; and at least a dozen little boys have asked for molasses-candy. And we must contrive to get a peck of russet apples, late in the season as it is. But, dear cousin, what an enormous heap of copper! Positively a copper mountain!"

"Well done! well done! well done!" quoth Uncle Venner, who had taken occasion to shuffle in and out of the shop several times in the course of the day. "Here's a girl that will never end her days at my farm! Bless my eyes, what a brisk little soul!"

"Yes, Phoebe is a nice girl!" said Hepzibah, with a scowl of austere approbation. "But, Uncle Venner, you have known the family a great many years. Can you tell me whether there ever was a Pyncheon whom she takes after?"

"I don't believe there ever was," answered the venerable man. "At any rate, it never was my luck to see her like among them, nor, for that matter, anywhere else. I've seen a great deal of the world, not only in people's kitchens and back-yards but at the street-corners, and on the wharves, and in other places where my business calls me; and I'm free to say, Miss Hepzibah, that I never knew a human creature do her work so much like one of God's angels as this child Phoebe does!"

Uncle Venner's eulogium, if it appear rather too high-strained for the person and occasion, had, nevertheless, a sense in which it was both subtile and true. There was a spiritual quality in Phoebe's activity. The life of the long and busy day—spent in occupations that might so easily have taken a squalid and ugly aspect—had been made pleasant, and even lovely, by the spontaneous grace with which these homely duties seemed to bloom out of her character; so that labor, while she dealt with it, had the easy and flexible charm of play. Angels do not toil, but let their good works grow out of them; and so did Phoebe.

The two relatives—the young maid and the old one—found time before nightfall, in the intervals of trade, to make rapid advances towards affection and confidence. A recluse, like Hepzibah, usually displays remarkable frankness, and at least temporary affability, on being absolutely cornered, and brought to the point of personal intercourse; like the angel whom Jacob wrestled with, she is ready to bless you when once overcome.

The old gentlewoman took a dreary and proud satisfaction in leading Phoebe from room to room of the house, and recounting the traditions with which, as we may say, the walls were lugubriously frescoed. She showed the indentations made by the lieutenant-governor's sword-hilt in the door-panels of the apartment where old Colonel Pyncheon, a dead host, had received his affrighted visitors with an awful frown. The dusky terror of that frown, Hepzibah observed, was thought to be lingering ever since in the passageway. She bade Phoebe step into one of the tall chairs, and inspect the ancient map of the Pyncheon territory at the eastward. In a tract of land on which she laid her finger, there existed a silver mine, the locality of which was precisely pointed out in some memoranda of Colonel Pyncheon himself, but only to be made known when the family claim should be recognized by government. Thus it was for the interest of all New England that the Pyncheons should have justice done them. She told, too, how that there was undoubtedly an immense treasure of English guineas hidden somewhere about the house, or in the cellar, or possibly in the garden.

"If you should happen to find it, Phoebe," said Hepzibah, glancing aside at her with a grim yet kindly smile, "we will tie up the shop-bell for good and all!"

"Yes, dear cousin," answered Phoebe; "but, in the mean time, I hear somebody ringing it!"

When the customer was gone, Hepzibah talked rather vaguely, and at great length, about a certain Alice Pyncheon, who had been exceedingly beautiful and accomplished in her lifetime, a hundred years ago. The fragrance of her rich and delightful character still lingered about the place where she had lived, as a dried rose-bud scents the drawer where it has withered and perished. This lovely Alice had met with some great and mysterious calamity, and had grown thin and white, and gradually faded out of the world. But, even now, she was supposed to haunt the House of the Seven Gables, and, a great many times,—especially when one of the Pyncheons was to die,—she had been heard playing sadly and beautifully on the harpsichord. One of these tunes, just as it had sounded from her spiritual touch, had been written down by an amateur of music; it was so exquisitely mournful that nobody, to this day, could bear to hear it played, unless when a great sorrow had made them know the still profounder sweetness of it.

"Was it the same harpsichord that you showed me?" inquired Phoebe.

"The very same," said Hepzibah. "It was Alice Pyncheon's harpsichord. When I was learning music, my father would never let me open it. So, as I could only play on my teacher's instrument, I have forgotten all my music long ago."

Leaving these antique themes, the old lady began to talk about the daguerreotypist, whom, as he seemed to be a well-meaning and orderly young man, and in narrow circumstances, she had permitted to take up his residence in one of the seven gables. But, on seeing more of Mr. Holgrave, she hardly knew what to make of him. He had the strangest companions imaginable; men with long beards, and dressed in linen blouses, and other such new-fangled and ill-fitting garments; reformers, temperance lecturers, and all manner of cross-looking philanthropists; community-men, and come-outers, as Hepzibah believed, who acknowledged no law, and ate no solid food, but lived on the scent of other people's cookery, and turned up their noses at the fare. As for the daguerreotypist, she had read a paragraph in a penny paper, the other day, accusing him of making a speech full of wild and disorganizing matter, at a meeting of his banditti-like associates. For her own part, she had reason to believe that he practised animal magnetism, and, if such things were in fashion nowadays, should be apt to suspect him of studying the Black Art up there in his lonesome chamber.

"But, dear cousin," said Phoebe, "if the young man is so dangerous, why do you let him stay? If he does nothing worse, he may set the house on fire!"

"Why, sometimes," answered Hepzibah, "I have seriously made it a question, whether I ought not to send him away. But, with all his oddities, he is a quiet kind of a person, and has such a way of taking hold of one's mind, that, without exactly liking him (for I don't know enough of the young man), I should be sorry to lose sight of him entirely. A woman clings to slight acquaintances when she lives so much alone as I do."

"But if Mr. Holgrave is a lawless person!" remonstrated Phoebe, a part of whose essence it was to keep within the limits of law.

"Oh!" said Hepzibah carelessly,—for, formal as she was, still, in her life's experience, she had gnashed her teeth against human law,—"I suppose he has a law of his own!"

VI Maule's Well

AFTER an early tea, the little country-girl strayed into the garden. The enclosure had formerly been very extensive, but was now contracted within small compass, and hemmed about, partly by high wooden fences, and partly by the outbuildings of houses that stood on another street. In its centre was a grass-plat, surrounding a ruinous little structure, which showed just enough of its original design to indicate that it had once been a summer-house. A hop-vine, springing from last year's root, was beginning to clamber over it, but would be long in covering the roof with its green mantle. Three of the seven gables either fronted or looked sideways, with a dark solemnity of aspect, down into the garden.

The black, rich soil had fed itself with the decay of a long period of time; such as fallen leaves, the petals of flowers, and the stalks and seed—vessels of vagrant and lawless plants, more useful after their death than ever while flaunting in the sun. The evil of these departed years would naturally have sprung up again, in such rank weeds (symbolic of the transmitted vices of society) as are always prone to root themselves about human dwellings. Phoebe saw, however, that their growth must have been checked by a degree of careful labor, bestowed daily and systematically on the garden. The white double rosebush had evidently been propped up anew against the house since the commencement of the season; and a pear-tree and three damson-trees, which, except a row of currant-bushes, constituted the only varieties of fruit, bore marks of the recent amputation of several superfluous or defective limbs. There were also a few species of antique and hereditary flowers, in no very flourishing condition, but scrupulously weeded; as if some person, either out of love or curiosity, had been anxious to bring them to such perfection as they were capable of attaining. The remainder of the garden presented a well-selected assortment of esculent vegetables, in a praiseworthy state of advancement. Summer squashes almost in their golden blossom; cucumbers, now evincing a tendency to spread away from the main stock, and ramble far and wide; two or three rows of string-beans and as many more that were about to festoon themselves on poles; tomatoes, occupying a site so sheltered and sunny that the plants were already gigantic, and promised an early and abundant harvest.

Phoebe wondered whose care and toil it could have been that had planted these vegetables, and kept the soil so clean and orderly. Not surely her cousin Hepzibah's, who had no taste nor spirits for the lady-like employment of cultivating flowers, and—with her recluse habits, and tendency to shelter herself within the dismal shadow of the house—would hardly have come forth under the speck of open sky to weed and hoe among the fraternity of beans and squashes.

It being her first day of complete estrangement from rural objects, Phoebe found an unexpected charm in this little nook of grass, and foliage, and aristocratic flowers, and plebeian vegetables. The eye of Heaven seemed to look down into it pleasantly, and with a peculiar smile, as if glad to perceive that nature, elsewhere overwhelmed, and driven out of the dusty town, had here been able to retain a breathing-place. The spot acquired a somewhat wilder grace, and yet a very gentle one, from the fact that a pair of robins had built their nest in the pear-tree, and were making themselves exceedingly busy and happy in the dark intricacy of its boughs. Bees, too,—strange to say,—had thought it worth their while to come hither, possibly from the range of hives beside some farm-house miles away. How many aerial voyages might they have made, in quest of honey, or honey-laden, betwixt dawn and sunset! Yet, late as it now was, there still arose a pleasant hum out of one or two of the squash-blossoms, in the depths of which these bees were plying their golden labor. There was one other object in the garden which Nature might fairly claim as her inalienable property, in spite of whatever man could do to render it his own. This was a fountain, set round with a rim of old mossy stones, and paved, in its bed, with what appeared to be a sort of mosaic-work of variously colored pebbles. The play and slight agitation of the water, in its upward gush, wrought magically with these variegated pebbles, and made a continually shifting apparition of quaint figures, vanishing too suddenly to be definable. Thence, swelling over the rim of moss-grown stones, the water stole away under the fence, through what we regret to call a gutter, rather than a channel. Nor must we forget to mention a hen-coop of very reverend antiquity that stood in the farther corner of the garden, not a great way from the fountain. It now contained only Chanticleer, his two wives, and a solitary chicken. All of them were pure specimens of a breed which had been transmitted down as an heirloom in the Pyncheon family, and were said, while in their prime, to have attained almost the size of turkeys, and, on the score of delicate flesh, to be fit for a prince's table. In proof of the authenticity of this legendary renown, Hepzibah could have exhibited the shell of a great egg, which an ostrich need hardly have been ashamed of. Be that as it might, the hens were now scarcely larger than pigeons, and had a queer, rusty, withered aspect, and a gouty kind of movement, and a sleepy and melancholy tone throughout all the variations of their clucking and cackling. It was evident that the race had degenerated, like many a noble race besides, in consequence of too strict a watchfulness to keep it pure. These feathered people had existed too long in their distinct variety; a fact of which the present representatives, judging by their lugubrious deportment, seemed to be aware. They kept themselves alive, unquestionably, and laid now and then an egg, and hatched a chicken; not for any pleasure of their own, but that the world might not absolutely lose what had once been so admirable a breed of fowls. The distinguishing mark of the hens was a crest of lamentably scanty growth, in these latter days, but so oddly and wickedly analogous to Hepzibah's turban, that Phoebe—to the poignant distress of her conscience, but inevitably—was led to fancy a general resemblance betwixt these forlorn bipeds and her respectable relative.

The girl ran into the house to get some crumbs of bread, cold potatoes, and other such scraps as were suitable to the accommodating appetite of fowls. Returning, she gave a peculiar call, which they seemed to recognize. The chicken crept through the pales of the coop and ran, with some show of liveliness, to her feet; while Chanticleer and the ladies of his household regarded her with queer, sidelong glances, and then croaked one to another, as if communicating their sage opinions of her character. So wise, as well as antique, was their aspect, as to give color to the idea, not merely that they were the descendants of a time-honored race, but that they had existed, in their individual capacity, ever since the House of the Seven Gables was founded, and were somehow mixed up with its destiny. They were a species of tutelary sprite, or Banshee; although winged and feathered differently from most other guardian angels.

"Here, you odd little chicken!" said Phoebe; "here are some nice crumbs for you!"

The chicken, hereupon, though almost as venerable in appearance as its mother—possessing, indeed, the whole antiquity of its progenitors in miniature,—mustered vivacity enough to flutter upward and alight on Phoebe's shoulder.

"That little fowl pays you a high compliment!" said a voice behind Phoebe.

Turning quickly, she was surprised at sight of a young man, who had found access into the garden by a door opening out of another gable than that whence she had emerged. He held a hoe in his hand, and, while Phoebe was gone in quest of the crumbs, had begun to busy himself with drawing up fresh earth about the roots of the tomatoes.

"The chicken really treats you like an old acquaintance," continued he in a quiet way, while a smile made his face pleasanter than Phoebe at first fancied it. "Those venerable personages in the coop, too, seem very affably disposed. You are lucky to be in their good graces so soon! They have known me much longer, but never honor me with any familiarity, though hardly a day passes without my bringing them food. Miss Hepzibah, I suppose, will interweave the fact with her other traditions, and set it down that the fowls know you to be a Pyncheon!"

"The secret is," said Phoebe, smiling, "that I have learned how to talk with hens and chickens."

"Ah, but these hens," answered the young man,—"these hens of aristocratic lineage would scorn to understand the vulgar language of a barn-yard fowl. I prefer to think—and so would Miss Hepzibah—that they recognize the family tone. For you are a Pyncheon?"

"My name is Phoebe Pyncheon," said the girl, with a manner of some reserve; for she was aware that her new acquaintance could be no other than the daguerreotypist, of whose lawless propensities the old maid had given her a disagreeable idea. "I did not know that my cousin Hepzibah's garden was under another person's care."

"Yes," said Holgrave, "I dig, and hoe, and weed, in this black old earth, for the sake of refreshing myself with what little nature and simplicity may be left in it, after men have so long sown and reaped here. I turn up the earth by way of pastime. My sober occupation, so far as I have any, is with a lighter material. In short, I make pictures out of sunshine; and, not to be too much dazzled with my own trade, I have prevailed with Miss Hepzibah to let me lodge in one of these dusky gables. It is like a bandage over one's eyes, to come into it. But would you like to see a specimen of my productions?"

"A daguerreotype likeness, do you mean?" asked Phoebe with less reserve; for, in spite of prejudice, her own youthfulness sprang forward to meet his. "I don't much like pictures of that sort,—they are so hard and stern; besides dodging away from the eye, and trying to escape altogether. They are conscious of looking very unamiable, I suppose, and therefore hate to be seen."

"If you would permit me," said the artist, looking at Phoebe, "I should like to try whether the daguerreotype can bring out disagreeable traits on a perfectly amiable face. But there certainly is truth in what you have said. Most of my likenesses do look unamiable; but the very sufficient reason, I fancy, is, because the originals are so. There is a wonderful insight in Heaven's broad and simple sunshine. While we give it credit only for depicting the merest surface, it actually brings out the secret character with a truth that no painter would ever venture upon, even could he detect it. There is, at least, no flattery in my humble line of art. Now, here is a likeness which I have taken over and over again, and still with no better result. Yet the original wears, to common eyes, a very different expression. It would gratify me to have your judgment on this character."

He exhibited a daguerreotype miniature in a morocco case. Phoebe merely glanced at it, and gave it back.

"I know the face," she replied; "for its stern eye has been following me about all day. It is my Puritan ancestor, who hangs yonder in the parlor. To be sure, you have found some way of copying the portrait without its black velvet cap and gray beard, and have given him a modern coat and satin cravat, instead of his cloak and band. I don't think him improved by your alterations."

"You would have seen other differences had you looked a little longer," said Holgrave, laughing, yet apparently much struck. "I can assure you that this is a modern face, and one which you will very probably meet. Now, the remarkable point is, that the original wears, to the world's eye,—and, for aught I know, to his most intimate friends,—an exceedingly pleasant countenance, indicative of benevolence, openness of heart, sunny good-humor, and other praiseworthy qualities of that cast. The sun, as you see, tells quite another story, and will not be coaxed out of it, after half a dozen patient attempts on my part. Here we have the man, sly, subtle, hard, imperious, and, withal, cold as ice. Look at that eye! Would you like to be at its mercy? At that mouth! Could it ever smile? And yet, if you could only see the benign smile of the original! It is so much the more unfortunate, as he is a public character of some eminence, and the likeness was intended to be engraved."

"Well, I don't wish to see it any more," observed Phoebe, turning away her eyes. "It is certainly very like the old portrait. But my cousin Hepzibah has another picture,—a miniature. If the original is still in the world, I think he might defy the sun to make him look stern and hard."

"You have seen that picture, then!" exclaimed the artist, with an expression of much interest. "I never did, but have a great curiosity to do so. And you judge favorably of the face?"

"There never was a sweeter one," said Phoebe. "It is almost too soft and gentle for a man's."

"Is there nothing wild in the eye?" continued Holgrave, so earnestly that it embarrassed Phoebe, as did also the quiet freedom with which he presumed on their so recent acquaintance. "Is there nothing dark or sinister anywhere? Could you not conceive the original to have been guilty of a great crime?"

"It is nonsense," said Phoebe a little impatiently, "for us to talk about a picture which you have never seen. You mistake it for some other. A crime, indeed! Since you are a friend of my cousin Hepzibah's, you should ask her to show you the picture."

"It will suit my purpose still better to see the original," replied the daguerreotypist coolly. "As to his character, we need not discuss its points; they have already been settled by a competent tribunal, or one which called itself competent. But, stay! Do not go yet, if you please! I have a proposition to make you."

Phoebe was on the point of retreating, but turned back, with some hesitation; for she did not exactly comprehend his manner, although, on better observation, its feature seemed rather to be lack of ceremony than any approach to offensive rudeness. There was an odd kind of authority, too, in what he now proceeded to say, rather as if the garden were his own than a place to which he was admitted merely by Hepzibah's courtesy.

"If agreeable to you," he observed, "it would give me pleasure to turn over these flowers, and those ancient and respectable fowls, to your care. Coming fresh from country air and occupations, you will soon feel the need of some such out-of-door employment. My own sphere does not so much lie among flowers. You can trim and tend them, therefore, as you please; and I will ask only the least trifle of a blossom, now and then, in exchange for all the good, honest kitchen vegetables with which I propose to enrich Miss Hepzibah's table. So we will be fellow-laborers, somewhat on the community system."

Silently, and rather surprised at her own compliance, Phoebe accordingly betook herself to weeding a flower-bed, but busied herself still more with cogitations respecting this young man, with whom she so unexpectedly found herself on terms approaching to familiarity. She did not altogether like him. His character perplexed the little country-girl, as it might a more practised observer; for, while the tone of his conversation had generally been playful, the impression left on her mind was that of gravity, and, except as his youth modified it, almost sternness. She rebelled, as it were, against a certain magnetic element in the artist's nature, which he exercised towards her, possibly without being conscious of it.

After a little while, the twilight, deepened by the shadows of the fruit-trees and the surrounding buildings, threw an obscurity over the garden.

"There," said Holgrave, "it is time to give over work! That last stroke of the hoe has cut off a beanstalk. Good-night, Miss Phoebe Pyncheon! Any bright day, if you will put one of those rosebuds in your hair, and come to my rooms in Central Street, I will seize the purest ray of sunshine, and make a picture of the flower and its wearer." He retired towards his own solitary gable, but turned his head, on reaching the door, and called to Phoebe, with a tone which certainly had laughter in it, yet which seemed to be more than half in earnest.

"Be careful not to drink at Maule's well!" said he. "Neither drink nor bathe your face in it!"

"Maule's well!" answered Phoebe. "Is that it with the rim of mossy stones? I have no thought of drinking there,—but why not?"

"Oh," rejoined the daguerreotypist, "because, like an old lady's cup of tea, it is water bewitched!"

He vanished; and Phoebe, lingering a moment, saw a glimmering light, and then the steady beam of a lamp, in a chamber of the gable. On returning into Hepzibah's apartment of the house, she found the low-studded parlor so dim and dusky that her eyes could not penetrate the interior. She was indistinctly aware, however, that the gaunt figure of the old gentlewoman was sitting in one of the straight-backed chairs, a little withdrawn from the window, the faint gleam of which showed the blanched paleness of her cheek, turned sideways towards a corner.

"Shall I light a lamp, Cousin Hepzibah?" she asked.

"Do, if you please, my dear child," answered Hepzibah. "But put it on the table in the corner of the passage. My eyes are weak; and I can seldom bear the lamplight on them."

What an instrument is the human voice! How wonderfully responsive to every emotion of the human soul! In Hepzibah's tone, at that moment, there was a certain rich depth and moisture, as if the words, commonplace as they were, had been steeped in the warmth of her heart. Again, while lighting the lamp in the kitchen, Phoebe fancied that her cousin spoke to her.

"In a moment, cousin!" answered the girl. "These matches just glimmer, and go out."

But, instead of a response from Hepzibah, she seemed to hear the murmur of an unknown voice. It was strangely indistinct, however, and less like articulate words than an unshaped sound, such as would be the utterance of feeling and sympathy, rather than of the intellect. So vague was it, that its impression or echo in Phoebe's mind was that of unreality. She concluded that she must have mistaken some other sound for that of the human voice; or else that it was altogether in her fancy.

She set the lighted lamp in the passage, and again entered the parlor. Hepzibah's form, though its sable outline mingled with the dusk, was now less imperfectly visible. In the remoter parts of the room, however, its walls being so ill adapted to reflect light, there was nearly the same obscurity as before.

"Cousin," said Phoebe, "did you speak to me just now?"

"No, child!" replied Hepzibah.

Fewer words than before, but with the same mysterious music in them! Mellow, melancholy, yet not mournful, the tone seemed to gush up out of the deep well of Hepzibah's heart, all steeped in its profoundest emotion. There was a tremor in it, too, that—as all strong feeling is electric—partly communicated itself to Phoebe. The girl sat silently for a moment. But soon, her senses being very acute, she became conscious of an irregular respiration in an obscure corner of the room. Her physical organization, moreover, being at once delicate and healthy, gave her a perception, operating with almost the effect of a spiritual medium, that somebody was near at hand.

"My dear cousin," asked she, overcoming an indefinable reluctance, "is there not some one in the room with us?"

"Phoebe, my dear little girl," said Hepzibah, after a moment's pause, "you were up betimes, and have been busy all day. Pray go to bed; for I am sure you must need rest. I will sit in the parlor awhile, and collect my thoughts. It has been my custom for more years, child, than you have lived!" While thus dismissing her, the maiden lady stept forward, kissed Phoebe, and pressed her to her heart, which beat against the girl's bosom with a strong, high, and tumultuous swell. How came there to be so much love in this desolate old heart, that it could afford to well over thus abundantly?

"Goodnight, cousin," said Phoebe, strangely affected by Hepzibah's manner. "If you begin to love me, I am glad!"

She retired to her chamber, but did not soon fall asleep, nor then very profoundly. At some uncertain period in the depths of night, and, as it were, through the thin veil of a dream, she was conscious of a footstep mounting the stairs heavily, but not with force and decision. The voice of Hepzibah, with a hush through it, was going up along with the footsteps; and, again, responsive to her cousin's voice, Phoebe heard that strange, vague murmur, which might be likened to an indistinct shadow of human utterance.

VII The Guest

WHEN Phoebe awoke,—which she did with the early twittering of the conjugal couple of robins in the pear-tree,—she heard movements below stairs, and, hastening down, found Hepzibah already in the kitchen. She stood by a window, holding a book in close contiguity to her nose, as if with the hope of gaining an olfactory acquaintance with its contents, since her imperfect vision made it not very easy to read them. If any volume could have manifested its essential wisdom in the mode suggested, it would certainly have been the one now in Hepzibah's hand; and the kitchen, in such an event, would forthwith have streamed with the fragrance of venison, turkeys, capons, larded partridges, puddings, cakes, and Christmas pies, in all manner of elaborate mixture and concoction. It was a cookery book, full of innumerable old fashions of English dishes, and illustrated with engravings, which represented the arrangements of the table at such banquets as it might have befitted a nobleman to give in the great hall of his castle. And, amid these rich and potent devices of the culinary art (not one of which, probably, had been tested, within the memory of any man's grandfather), poor Hepzibah was seeking for some nimble little titbit, which, with what skill she had, and such materials as were at hand, she might toss up for breakfast.

Soon, with a deep sigh, she put aside the savory volume, and inquired of Phoebe whether old Speckle, as she called one of the hens, had laid an egg the preceding day. Phoebe ran to see, but returned without the expected treasure in her hand. At that instant, however, the blast of a fish-dealer's conch was heard, announcing his approach along the street. With energetic raps at the shop-window, Hepzibah summoned the man in, and made purchase of what he warranted as the finest mackerel in his cart, and as fat a one as ever he felt with his finger so early in the season. Requesting Phoebe to roast some coffee,—which she casually observed was the real Mocha, and so long kept that each of the small berries ought to be worth its weight in gold,—the maiden lady heaped fuel into the vast receptacle of the ancient fireplace in such quantity as soon to drive the lingering dusk out of the kitchen. The country-girl, willing to give her utmost assistance, proposed to make an Indian cake, after her mother's peculiar method, of easy manufacture, and which she could vouch for as possessing a richness, and, if rightly prepared, a delicacy, unequalled by any other mode of breakfast-cake. Hepzibah gladly assenting, the kitchen was soon the scene of savory preparation.

Perchance, amid their proper element of smoke, which eddied forth from the ill-constructed chimney, the ghosts of departed cook-maids looked wonderingly on, or peeped down the great breadth of the flue, despising the simplicity of the projected meal, yet ineffectually pining to thrust their shadowy hands into each inchoate dish. The half-starved rats, at any rate, stole visibly out of their hiding-places, and sat on their hind-legs, snuffing the fumy atmosphere, and wistfully awaiting an opportunity to nibble.

Hepzibah had no natural turn for cookery, and, to say the truth, had fairly incurred her present meagreness by often choosing to go without her dinner rather than be attendant on the rotation of the spit, or ebullition of the pot. Her zeal over the fire, therefore, was quite an heroic test of sentiment. It was touching, and positively worthy of tears (if Phoebe, the only spectator, except the rats and ghosts aforesaid, had not been better employed than in shedding them), to see her rake out a bed of fresh and glowing coals, and proceed to broil the mackerel. Her usually pale cheeks were all ablaze with heat and hurry. She watched the fish with as much tender care and minuteness of attention as if,—we know not how to express it otherwise,—as if her own heart were on the gridiron, and her immortal happiness were involved in its being done precisely to a turn!

Life, within doors, has few pleasanter prospects than a neatly arranged and well-provisioned breakfast-table. We come to it freshly, in the dewy youth of the day, and when our spiritual and sensual elements are in better accord than at a later period; so that the material delights of the morning meal are capable of being fully enjoyed, without any very grievous reproaches, whether gastric or conscientious, for yielding even a trifle overmuch to the animal department of our nature. The thoughts, too, that run around the ring of familiar guests have a piquancy and mirthfulness, and oftentimes a vivid truth, which more rarely find their way into the elaborate intercourse of dinner. Hepzibah's small and ancient table, supported on its slender and graceful legs, and covered with a cloth of the richest damask, looked worthy to be the scene and centre of one of the cheerfullest of parties. The vapor of the broiled fish arose like incense from the shrine of a barbarian idol, while the fragrance of the Mocha might have gratified the nostrils of a tutelary Lar, or whatever power has scope over a modern breakfast-table. Phoebe's Indian cakes were the sweetest offering of all,—in their hue befitting the rustic altars of the innocent and golden age,—or, so brightly yellow were they, resembling some of the bread which was changed to glistening gold when Midas tried to eat it. The butter must not be forgotten,—butter which Phoebe herself had churned, in her own rural home, and brought it to her cousin as a propitiatory gift,—smelling of clover-blossoms, and diffusing the charm of pastoral scenery through the dark-panelled parlor. All this, with the quaint gorgeousness of the old china cups and saucers, and the crested spoons, and a silver cream-jug (Hepzibah's only other article of plate, and shaped like the rudest porringer), set out a board at which the stateliest of old Colonel Pyncheon's guests need not have scorned to take his place. But the Puritan's face scowled down out of the picture, as if nothing on the table pleased his appetite.

By way of contributing what grace she could, Phoebe gathered some roses and a few other flowers, possessing either scent or beauty, and arranged them in a glass pitcher, which, having long ago lost its handle, was so much the fitter for a flower-vase. The early sunshine—as fresh as that which peeped into Eve's bower while she and Adam sat at breakfast there—came twinkling through the branches of the pear-tree, and fell quite across the table. All was now ready. There were chairs and plates for three. A chair and plate for Hepzibah,—the same for Phoebe,—but what other guest did her cousin look for?

Throughout this preparation there had been a constant tremor in Hepzibah's frame; an agitation so powerful that Phoebe could see the quivering of her gaunt shadow, as thrown by the firelight on the kitchen wall, or by the sunshine on the parlor floor. Its manifestations were so various, and agreed so little with one another, that the girl knew not what to make of it. Sometimes it seemed an ecstasy of delight and happiness. At such moments, Hepzibah would fling out her arms, and infold Phoebe in them, and kiss her cheek as tenderly as ever her mother had; she appeared to do so by an inevitable impulse, and as if her bosom were oppressed with tenderness, of which she must needs pour out a little, in order to gain breathing-room. The next moment, without any visible cause for the change, her unwonted joy shrank back, appalled, as it were, and clothed itself in mourning; or it ran and hid itself, so to speak, in the dungeon of her heart, where it had long lain chained, while a cold, spectral sorrow took the place of the imprisoned joy, that was afraid to be enfranchised,—a sorrow as black as that was bright. She often broke into a little, nervous, hysteric laugh, more touching than any tears could be; and forthwith, as if to try which was the most touching, a gush of tears would follow; or perhaps the laughter and tears came both at once, and surrounded our poor Hepzibah, in a moral sense, with a kind of pale, dim rainbow. Towards Phoebe, as we have said, she was affectionate,—far tenderer than ever before, in their brief acquaintance, except for that one kiss on the preceding night,—yet with a continually recurring pettishness and irritability. She would speak sharply to her; then, throwing aside all the starched reserve of her ordinary manner, ask pardon, and the next instant renew the just-forgiven injury.

At last, when their mutual labor was all finished, she took Phoebe's hand in her own trembling one.

"Bear with me, my dear child," she cried; "for truly my heart is full to the brim! Bear with me; for I love you, Phoebe, though I speak so roughly. Think nothing of it, dearest child! By and by, I shall be kind, and only kind!"

"My dearest cousin, cannot you tell me what has happened?" asked Phoebe, with a sunny and tearful sympathy. "What is it that moves you so?"

"Hush! hush! He is coming!" whispered Hepzibah, hastily wiping her eyes. "Let him see you first, Phoebe; for you are young and rosy, and cannot help letting a smile break out whether or no. He always liked bright faces! And mine is old now, and the tears are hardly dry on it. He never could abide tears. There; draw the curtain a little, so that the shadow may fall across his side of the table! But let there be a good deal of sunshine, too; for he never was fond of gloom, as some people are. He has had but little sunshine in his life,—poor Clifford,—and, oh, what a black shadow. Poor, poor Clifford!"

Thus murmuring in an undertone, as if speaking rather to her own heart than to Phoebe, the old gentlewoman stepped on tiptoe about the room, making such arrangements as suggested themselves at the crisis.

Meanwhile there was a step in the passage-way, above stairs. Phoebe recognized it as the same which had passed upward, as through her dream, in the night-time. The approaching guest, whoever it might be, appeared to pause at the head of the staircase; he paused twice or thrice in the descent; he paused again at the foot. Each time, the delay seemed to be without purpose, but rather from a forgetfulness of the purpose which had set him in motion, or as if the person's feet came involuntarily to a stand-still because the motive-power was too feeble to sustain his progress. Finally, he made a long pause at the threshold of the parlor. He took hold of the knob of the door; then loosened his grasp without opening it. Hepzibah, her hands convulsively clasped, stood gazing at the entrance.

"Dear Cousin Hepzibah, pray don't look so!" said Phoebe, trembling; for her cousin's emotion, and this mysteriously reluctant step, made her feel as if a ghost were coming into the room. "You really frighten me! Is something awful going to happen?"

"Hush!" whispered Hepzibah. "Be cheerful! whatever may happen, be nothing but cheerful!"

The final pause at the threshold proved so long, that Hepzibah, unable to endure the suspense, rushed forward, threw open the door, and led in the stranger by the hand. At the first glance, Phoebe saw an elderly personage, in an old-fashioned dressing-gown of faded damask, and wearing his gray or almost white hair of an unusual length. It quite overshadowed his forehead, except when he thrust it back, and stared vaguely about the room. After a very brief inspection of his face, it was easy to conceive that his footstep must necessarily be such an one as that which, slowly and with as indefinite an aim as a child's first journey across a floor, had just brought him hitherward. Yet there were no tokens that his physical strength might not have sufficed for a free and determined gait. It was the spirit of the man that could not walk. The expression of his countenance—while, notwithstanding it had the light of reason in it—seemed to waver, and glimmer, and nearly to die away, and feebly to recover itself again. It was like a flame which we see twinkling among half-extinguished embers; we gaze at it more intently than if it were a positive blaze, gushing vividly upward,—more intently, but with a certain impatience, as if it ought either to kindle itself into satisfactory splendor, or be at once extinguished.

For an instant after entering the room, the guest stood still, retaining Hepzibah's hand instinctively, as a child does that of the grown person who guides it. He saw Phoebe, however, and caught an illumination from her youthful and pleasant aspect, which, indeed, threw a cheerfulness about the parlor, like the circle of reflected brilliancy around the glass vase of flowers that was standing in the sunshine. He made a salutation, or, to speak nearer the truth, an ill-defined, abortive attempt at curtsy. Imperfect as it was, however, it conveyed an idea, or, at least, gave a hint, of indescribable grace, such as no practised art of external manners could have attained. It was too slight to seize upon at the instant; yet, as recollected afterwards, seemed to transfigure the whole man.

"Dear Clifford," said Hepzibah, in the tone with which one soothes a wayward infant, "this is our cousin Phoebe,—little Phoebe Pyncheon,—Arthur's only child, you know. She has come from the country to stay with us awhile; for our old house has grown to be very lonely now."

"Phoebe—Phoebe Pyncheon?—Phoebe?" repeated the guest, with a strange, sluggish, ill-defined utterance. "Arthur's child! Ah, I forget! No matter. She is very welcome!"

"Come, dear Clifford, take this chair," said Hepzibah, leading him to his place. "Pray, Phoebe, lower the curtain a very little more. Now let us begin breakfast."

The guest seated himself in the place assigned him, and looked strangely around. He was evidently trying to grapple with the present scene, and bring it home to his mind with a more satisfactory distinctness. He desired to be certain, at least, that he was here, in the low-studded, cross-beamed, oaken-panelled parlor, and not in some other spot, which had stereotyped itself into his senses. But the effort was too great to be sustained with more than a fragmentary success. Continually, as we may express it, he faded away out of his place; or, in other words, his mind and consciousness took their departure, leaving his wasted, gray, and melancholy figure—a substantial emptiness, a material ghost—to occupy his seat at table. Again, after a blank moment, there would be a flickering taper-gleam in his eyeballs. It betokened that his spiritual part had returned, and was doing its best to kindle the heart's household fire, and light up intellectual lamps in the dark and ruinous mansion, where it was doomed to be a forlorn inhabitant.

At one of these moments of less torpid, yet still imperfect animation, Phoebe became convinced of what she had at first rejected as too extravagant and startling an idea. She saw that the person before her must have been the original of the beautiful miniature in her cousin Hepzibah's possession. Indeed, with a feminine eye for costume, she had at once identified the damask dressing-gown, which enveloped him, as the same in figure, material, and fashion, with that so elaborately represented in the picture. This old, faded garment, with all its pristine brilliancy extinct, seemed, in some indescribable way, to translate the wearer's untold misfortune, and make it perceptible to the beholder's eye. It was the better to be discerned, by this exterior type, how worn and old were the soul's more immediate garments; that form and countenance, the beauty and grace of which had almost transcended the skill of the most exquisite of artists. It could the more adequately be known that the soul of the man must have suffered some miserable wrong, from its earthly experience. There he seemed to sit, with a dim veil of decay and ruin betwixt him and the world, but through which, at flitting intervals, might be caught the same expression, so refined, so softly imaginative, which Malbone—venturing a happy touch, with suspended breath—had imparted to the miniature! There had been something so innately characteristic in this look, that all the dusky years, and the burden of unfit calamity which had fallen upon him, did not suffice utterly to destroy it.

Hepzibah had now poured out a cup of deliciously fragrant coffee, and presented it to her guest. As his eyes met hers, he seemed bewildered and disquieted.

"Is this you, Hepzibah?" he murmured sadly; then, more apart, and perhaps unconscious that he was overheard, "How changed! how changed! And is she angry with me? Why does she bend her brow so?"

Poor Hepzibah! It was that wretched scowl which time and her nearsightedness, and the fret of inward discomfort, had rendered so habitual that any vehemence of mood invariably evoked it. But at the indistinct murmur of his words her whole face grew tender, and even lovely, with sorrowful affection; the harshness of her features disappeared, as it were, behind the warm and misty glow.

"Angry!" she repeated; "angry with you, Clifford!"

Her tone, as she uttered the exclamation, had a plaintive and really exquisite melody thrilling through it, yet without subduing a certain something which an obtuse auditor might still have mistaken for asperity. It was as if some transcendent musician should draw a soul-thrilling sweetness out of a cracked instrument, which makes its physical imperfection heard in the midst of ethereal harmony,—so deep was the sensibility that found an organ in Hepzibah's voice!

"There is nothing but love here, Clifford," she added,—"nothing but love! You are at home!"

The guest responded to her tone by a smile, which did not half light up his face. Feeble as it was, however, and gone in a moment, it had a charm of wonderful beauty. It was followed by a coarser expression; or one that had the effect of coarseness on the fine mould and outline of his countenance, because there was nothing intellectual to temper it. It was a look of appetite. He ate food with what might almost be termed voracity; and seemed to forget himself, Hepzibah, the young girl, and everything else around him, in the sensual enjoyment which the bountifully spread table afforded. In his natural system, though high-wrought and delicately refined, a sensibility to the delights of the palate was probably inherent. It would have been kept in check, however, and even converted into an accomplishment, and one of the thousand modes of intellectual culture, had his more ethereal characteristics retained their vigor. But as it existed now, the effect was painful and made Phoebe droop her eyes.

In a little while the guest became sensible of the fragrance of the yet untasted coffee. He quaffed it eagerly. The subtle essence acted on him like a charmed draught, and caused the opaque substance of his animal being to grow transparent, or, at least, translucent; so that a spiritual gleam was transmitted through it, with a clearer lustre than hitherto.

"More, more!" he cried, with nervous haste in his utterance, as if anxious to retain his grasp of what sought to escape him. "This is what I need! Give me more!"

Under this delicate and powerful influence he sat more erect, and looked out from his eyes with a glance that took note of what it rested on. It was not so much that his expression grew more intellectual; this, though it had its share, was not the most peculiar effect. Neither was what we call the moral nature so forcibly awakened as to present itself in remarkable prominence. But a certain fine temper of being was now not brought out in full relief, but changeably and imperfectly betrayed, of which it was the function to deal with all beautiful and enjoyable things. In a character where it should exist as the chief attribute, it would bestow on its possessor an exquisite taste, and an enviable susceptibility of happiness. Beauty would be his life; his aspirations would all tend toward it; and, allowing his frame and physical organs to be in consonance, his own developments would likewise be beautiful. Such a man should have nothing to do with sorrow; nothing with strife; nothing with the martyrdom which, in an infinite variety of shapes, awaits those who have the heart, and will, and conscience, to fight a battle with the world. To these heroic tempers, such martyrdom is the richest meed in the world's gift. To the individual before us, it could only be a grief, intense in due proportion with the severity of the infliction. He had no right to be a martyr; and, beholding him so fit to be happy and so feeble for all other purposes, a generous, strong, and noble spirit would, methinks, have been ready to sacrifice what little enjoyment it might have planned for itself,—it would have flung down the hopes, so paltry in its regard,—if thereby the wintry blasts of our rude sphere might come tempered to such a man.

Not to speak it harshly or scornfully, it seemed Clifford's nature to be a Sybarite. It was perceptible, even there, in the dark old parlor, in the inevitable polarity with which his eyes were attracted towards the quivering play of sunbeams through the shadowy foliage. It was seen in his appreciating notice of the vase of flowers, the scent of which he inhaled with a zest almost peculiar to a physical organization so refined that spiritual ingredients are moulded in with it. It was betrayed in the unconscious smile with which he regarded Phoebe, whose fresh and maidenly figure was both sunshine and flowers,—their essence, in a prettier and more agreeable mode of manifestation. Not less evident was this love and necessity for the Beautiful, in the instinctive caution with which, even so soon, his eyes turned away from his hostess, and wandered to any quarter rather than come back. It was Hepzibah's misfortune,—not Clifford's fault. How could he,—so yellow as she was, so wrinkled, so sad of mien, with that odd uncouthness of a turban on her head, and that most perverse of scowls contorting her brow,—how could he love to gaze at her? But, did he owe her no affection for so much as she had silently given? He owed her nothing. A nature like Clifford's can contract no debts of that kind. It is—we say it without censure, nor in diminution of the claim which it indefeasibly possesses on beings of another mould—it is always selfish in its essence; and we must give it leave to be so, and heap up our heroic and disinterested love upon it so much the more, without a recompense. Poor Hepzibah knew this truth, or, at least, acted on the instinct of it. So long estranged from what was lovely as Clifford had been, she rejoiced—rejoiced, though with a present sigh, and a secret purpose to shed tears in her own chamber that he had brighter objects now before his eyes than her aged and uncomely features. They never possessed a charm; and if they had, the canker of her grief for him would long since have destroyed it.

The guest leaned back in his chair. Mingled in his countenance with a dreamy delight, there was a troubled look of effort and unrest. He was seeking to make himself more fully sensible of the scene around him; or, perhaps, dreading it to be a dream, or a play of imagination, was vexing the fair moment with a struggle for some added brilliancy and more durable illusion.

"How pleasant!—How delightful!" he murmured, but not as if addressing any one. "Will it last? How balmy the atmosphere through that open window! An open window! How beautiful that play of sunshine! Those flowers, how very fragrant! That young girl's face, how cheerful, how blooming!—a flower with the dew on it, and sunbeams in the dew-drops! Ah! this must be all a dream! A dream! A dream! But it has quite hidden the four stone walls!"

Then his face darkened, as if the shadow of a cavern or a dungeon had come over it; there was no more light in its expression than might have come through the iron grates of a prison-window—still lessening, too, as if he were sinking farther into the depths. Phoebe (being of that quickness and activity of temperament that she seldom long refrained from taking a part, and generally a good one, in what was going forward) now felt herself moved to address the stranger.

"Here is a new kind of rose, which I found this morning in the garden," said she, choosing a small crimson one from among the flowers in the vase. "There will be but five or six on the bush this season. This is the most perfect of them all; not a speck of blight or mildew in it. And how sweet it is!—sweet like no other rose! One can never forget that scent!"

"Ah!—let me see!—let me hold it!" cried the guest, eagerly seizing the flower, which, by the spell peculiar to remembered odors, brought innumerable associations along with the fragrance that it exhaled. "Thank you! This has done me good. I remember how I used to prize this flower,—long ago, I suppose, very long ago!—or was it only yesterday? It makes me feel young again! Am I young? Either this remembrance is singularly distinct, or this consciousness strangely dim! But how kind of the fair young girl! Thank you! Thank you!"

The favorable excitement derived from this little crimson rose afforded Clifford the brightest moment which he enjoyed at the breakfast-table. It might have lasted longer, but that his eyes happened, soon afterwards, to rest on the face of the old Puritan, who, out of his dingy frame and lustreless canvas, was looking down on the scene like a ghost, and a most ill-tempered and ungenial one. The guest made an impatient gesture of the hand, and addressed Hepzibah with what might easily be recognized as the licensed irritability of a petted member of the family.

"Hepzibah!—Hepzibah!" cried he with no little force and distinctness, "why do you keep that odious picture on the wall? Yes, yes!—that is precisely your taste! I have told you, a thousand times, that it was the evil genius of the house!—my evil genius particularly! Take it down, at once!"

"Dear Clifford," said Hepzibah sadly, "you know it cannot be!"

"Then, at all events," continued he, still speaking with some energy, "pray cover it with a crimson curtain, broad enough to hang in folds, and with a golden border and tassels. I cannot bear it! It must not stare me in the face!"

"Yes, dear Clifford, the picture shall be covered," said Hepzibah soothingly. "There is a crimson curtain in a trunk above stairs,—a little faded and moth-eaten, I'm afraid,—but Phoebe and I will do wonders with it."

"This very day, remember" said he; and then added, in a low, self-communing voice, "Why should we live in this dismal house at all? Why not go to the South of France?—to Italy?—Paris, Naples, Venice, Rome? Hepzibah will say we have not the means. A droll idea that!"

He smiled to himself, and threw a glance of fine sarcastic meaning towards Hepzibah.

But the several moods of feeling, faintly as they were marked, through which he had passed, occurring in so brief an interval of time, had evidently wearied the stranger. He was probably accustomed to a sad monotony of life, not so much flowing in a stream, however sluggish, as stagnating in a pool around his feet. A slumberous veil diffused itself over his countenance, and had an effect, morally speaking, on its naturally delicate and elegant outline, like that which a brooding mist, with no sunshine in it, throws over the features of a landscape. He appeared to become grosser,—almost cloddish. If aught of interest or beauty—even ruined beauty—had heretofore been visible in this man, the beholder might now begin to doubt it, and to accuse his own imagination of deluding him with whatever grace had flickered over that visage, and whatever exquisite lustre had gleamed in those filmy eyes.

Before he had quite sunken away, however, the sharp and peevish tinkle of the shop-bell made itself audible. Striking most disagreeably on Clifford's auditory organs and the characteristic sensibility of his nerves, it caused him to start upright out of his chair.

"Good heavens, Hepzibah! what horrible disturbance have we now in the house?" cried he, wreaking his resentful impatience—as a matter of course, and a custom of old—on the one person in the world that loved him. "I have never heard such a hateful clamor! Why do you permit it? In the name of all dissonance, what can it be?"

It was very remarkable into what prominent relief—even as if a dim picture should leap suddenly from its canvas—Clifford's character was thrown by this apparently trifling annoyance. The secret was, that an individual of his temper can always be pricked more acutely through his sense of the beautiful and harmonious than through his heart. It is even possible—for similar cases have often happened—that if Clifford, in his foregoing life, had enjoyed the means of cultivating his taste to its utmost perfectibility, that subtile attribute might, before this period, have completely eaten out or filed away his affections. Shall we venture to pronounce, therefore, that his long and black calamity may not have had a redeeming drop of mercy at the bottom?

"Dear Clifford, I wish I could keep the sound from your ears," said Hepzibah, patiently, but reddening with a painful suffusion of shame. "It is very disagreeable even to me. But, do you know, Clifford, I have something to tell you? This ugly noise,—pray run, Phoebe, and see who is there!—this naughty little tinkle is nothing but our shop-bell!"

"Shop-bell!" repeated Clifford, with a bewildered stare.

"Yes, our shop-bell," said Hepzibah, a certain natural dignity, mingled with deep emotion, now asserting itself in her manner. "For you must know, dearest Clifford, that we are very poor. And there was no other resource, but either to accept assistance from a hand that I would push aside (and so would you!) were it to offer bread when we were dying for it,—no help, save from him, or else to earn our subsistence with my own hands! Alone, I might have been content to starve. But you were to be given back to me! Do you think, then, dear Clifford," added she, with a wretched smile, "that I have brought an irretrievable disgrace on the old house, by opening a little shop in the front gable? Our great-great-grandfather did the same, when there was far less need! Are you ashamed of me?"

"Shame! Disgrace! Do you speak these words to me, Hepzibah?" said Clifford,—not angrily, however; for when a man's spirit has been thoroughly crushed, he may be peevish at small offences, but never resentful of great ones. So he spoke with only a grieved emotion. "It was not kind to say so, Hepzibah! What shame can befall me now?"

And then the unnerved man—he that had been born for enjoyment, but had met a doom so very wretched—burst into a woman's passion of tears. It was but of brief continuance, however; soon leaving him in a quiescent, and, to judge by his countenance, not an uncomfortable state. From this mood, too, he partially rallied for an instant, and looked at Hepzibah with a smile, the keen, half-derisory purport of which was a puzzle to her.

"Are we so very poor, Hepzibah?" said he.

Finally, his chair being deep and softly cushioned, Clifford fell asleep. Hearing the more regular rise and fall of his breath (which, however, even then, instead of being strong and full, had a feeble kind of tremor, corresponding with the lack of vigor in his character),—hearing these tokens of settled slumber, Hepzibah seized the opportunity to peruse his face more attentively than she had yet dared to do. Her heart melted away in tears; her profoundest spirit sent forth a moaning voice, low, gentle, but inexpressibly sad. In this depth of grief and pity she felt that there was no irreverence in gazing at his altered, aged, faded, ruined face. But no sooner was she a little relieved than her conscience smote her for gazing curiously at him, now that he was so changed; and, turning hastily away, Hepzibah let down the curtain over the sunny window, and left Clifford to slumber there.

VIII The Pyncheon of To-day

PHOEBE, on entering the shop, beheld there the already familiar face of the little devourer—if we can reckon his mighty deeds aright—of Jim Crow, the elephant, the camel, the dromedaries, and the locomotive. Having expended his private fortune, on the two preceding days, in the purchase of the above unheard-of luxuries, the young gentleman's present errand was on the part of his mother, in quest of three eggs and half a pound of raisins. These articles Phoebe accordingly supplied, and, as a mark of gratitude for his previous patronage, and a slight super-added morsel after breakfast, put likewise into his hand a whale! The great fish, reversing his experience with the prophet of Nineveh, immediately began his progress down the same red pathway of fate whither so varied a caravan had preceded him. This remarkable urchin, in truth, was the very emblem of old Father Time, both in respect of his all-devouring appetite for men and things, and because he, as well as Time, after ingulfing thus much of creation, looked almost as youthful as if he had been just that moment made.

After partly closing the door, the child turned back, and mumbled something to Phoebe, which, as the whale was but half disposed of, she could not perfectly understand.

"What did you say, my little fellow?" asked she.

"Mother wants to know" repeated Ned Higgins more distinctly, "how Old Maid Pyncheon's brother does? Folks say he has got home."

"My cousin Hepzibah's brother?" exclaimed Phoebe, surprised at this sudden explanation of the relationship between Hepzibah and her guest. "Her brother! And where can he have been?"

The little boy only put his thumb to his broad snub-nose, with that look of shrewdness which a child, spending much of his time in the street, so soon learns to throw over his features, however unintelligent in themselves. Then as Phoebe continued to gaze at him, without answering his mother's message, he took his departure.

As the child went down the steps, a gentleman ascended them, and made his entrance into the shop. It was the portly, and, had it possessed the advantage of a little more height, would have been the stately figure of a man considerably in the decline of life, dressed in a black suit of some thin stuff, resembling broadcloth as closely as possible. A gold-headed cane, of rare Oriental wood, added materially to the high respectability of his aspect, as did also a neckcloth of the utmost snowy purity, and the conscientious polish of his boots. His dark, square countenance, with its almost shaggy depth of eyebrows, was naturally impressive, and would, perhaps, have been rather stern, had not the gentleman considerately taken upon himself to mitigate the harsh effect by a look of exceeding good-humor and benevolence. Owing, however, to a somewhat massive accumulation of animal substance about the lower region of his face, the look was, perhaps, unctuous rather than spiritual, and had, so to speak, a kind of fleshly effulgence, not altogether so satisfactory as he doubtless intended it to be. A susceptible observer, at any rate, might have regarded it as affording very little evidence of the general benignity of soul whereof it purported to be the outward reflection. And if the observer chanced to be ill-natured, as well as acute and susceptible, he would probably suspect that the smile on the gentleman's face was a good deal akin to the shine on his boots, and that each must have cost him and his bootblack, respectively, a good deal of hard labor to bring out and preserve them.

As the stranger entered the little shop, where the projection of the second story and the thick foliage of the elm-tree, as well as the commodities at the window, created a sort of gray medium, his smile grew as intense as if he had set his heart on counteracting the whole gloom of the atmosphere (besides any moral gloom pertaining to Hepzibah and her inmates) by the unassisted light of his countenance. On perceiving a young rose-bud of a girl, instead of the gaunt presence of the old maid, a look of surprise was manifest. He at first knit his brows; then smiled with more unctuous benignity than ever.

"Ah, I see how it is!" said he in a deep voice,—a voice which, had it come from the throat of an uncultivated man, would have been gruff, but, by dint of careful training, was now sufficiently agreeable,—"I was not aware that Miss Hepzibah Pyncheon had commenced business under such favorable auspices. You are her assistant, I suppose?"

"I certainly am," answered Phoebe, and added, with a little air of lady-like assumption (for, civil as the gentleman was, he evidently took her to be a young person serving for wages), "I am a cousin of Miss Hepzibah, on a visit to her."

"Her cousin?—and from the country? Pray pardon me, then," said the gentleman, bowing and smiling, as Phoebe never had been bowed to nor smiled on before; "in that case, we must be better acquainted; for, unless I am sadly mistaken, you are my own little kinswoman likewise! Let me see,—Mary?—Dolly?—Phoebe?—yes, Phoebe is the name! Is it possible that you are Phoebe Pyncheon, only child of my dear cousin and classmate, Arthur? Ah, I see your father now, about your mouth! Yes, yes! we must be better acquainted! I am your kinsman, my dear. Surely you must have heard of Judge Pyncheon?"

As Phoebe curtsied in reply, the Judge bent forward, with the pardonable and even praiseworthy purpose—considering the nearness of blood and the difference of age—of bestowing on his young relative a kiss of acknowledged kindred and natural affection. Unfortunately (without design, or only with such instinctive design as gives no account of itself to the intellect) Phoebe, just at the critical moment, drew back; so that her highly respectable kinsman, with his body bent over the counter and his lips protruded, was betrayed into the rather absurd predicament of kissing the empty air. It was a modern parallel to the case of Ixion embracing a cloud, and was so much the more ridiculous as the Judge prided himself on eschewing all airy matter, and never mistaking a shadow for a substance. The truth was,—and it is Phoebe's only excuse,—that, although Judge Pyncheon's glowing benignity might not be absolutely unpleasant to the feminine beholder, with the width of a street, or even an ordinary-sized room, interposed between, yet it became quite too intense, when this dark, full-fed physiognomy (so roughly bearded, too, that no razor could ever make it smooth) sought to bring itself into actual contact with the object of its regards. The man, the sex, somehow or other, was entirely too prominent in the Judge's demonstrations of that sort. Phoebe's eyes sank, and, without knowing why, she felt herself blushing deeply under his look. Yet she had been kissed before, and without any particular squeamishness, by perhaps half a dozen different cousins, younger as well as older than this dark-browned, grisly-bearded, white-neck-clothed, and unctuously-benevolent Judge! Then, why not by him?

On raising her eyes, Phoebe was startled by the change in Judge Pyncheon's face. It was quite as striking, allowing for the difference of scale, as that betwixt a landscape under a broad sunshine and just before a thunder-storm; not that it had the passionate intensity of the latter aspect, but was cold, hard, immitigable, like a day-long brooding cloud.

"Dear me! what is to be done now?" thought the country-girl to herself. "He looks as if there were nothing softer in him than a rock, nor milder than the east wind! I meant no harm! Since he is really my cousin, I would have let him kiss me, if I could!"

Then, all at once, it struck Phoebe that this very Judge Pyncheon was the original of the miniature which the daguerreotypist had shown her in the garden, and that the hard, stern, relentless look, now on his face, was the same that the sun had so inflexibly persisted in bringing out. Was it, therefore, no momentary mood, but, however skilfully concealed, the settled temper of his life? And not merely so, but was it hereditary in him, and transmitted down, as a precious heirloom, from that bearded ancestor, in whose picture both the expression and, to a singular degree, the features of the modern Judge were shown as by a kind of prophecy? A deeper philosopher than Phoebe might have found something very terrible in this idea. It implied that the weaknesses and defects, the bad passions, the mean tendencies, and the moral diseases which lead to crime are handed down from one generation to another, by a far surer process of transmission than human law has been able to establish in respect to the riches and honors which it seeks to entail upon posterity.

But, as it happened, scarcely had Phoebe's eyes rested again on the Judge's countenance than all its ugly sternness vanished; and she found herself quite overpowered by the sultry, dog-day heat, as it were, of benevolence, which this excellent man diffused out of his great heart into the surrounding atmosphere,—

very much like a serpent, which, as a preliminary to fascination, is said to fill the air with his peculiar odor.

"I like that, Cousin Phoebe!" cried he, with an emphatic nod of approbation. "I like it much, my little cousin! You are a good child, and know how to take care of yourself. A young girl—especially if she be a very pretty one—can never be too chary of her lips."

"Indeed, sir," said Phoebe, trying to laugh the matter off, "I did not mean to be unkind."

Nevertheless, whether or no it were entirely owing to the inauspicious commencement of their acquaintance, she still acted under a certain reserve, which was by no means customary to her frank and genial nature. The fantasy would not quit her, that the original Puritan, of whom she had heard so many sombre traditions,—the progenitor of the whole race of New England Pyncheons, the founder of the House of the Seven Gables, and who had died so strangely in it,—had now stept into the shop. In these days of off-hand equipment, the matter was easily enough arranged. On his arrival from the other world, he had merely found it necessary to spend a quarter of an hour at a barber's, who had trimmed down the Puritan's full beard into a pair of grizzled whiskers, then, patronizing a ready-made clothing establishment, he had exchanged his velvet doublet and sable cloak, with the richly worked band under his chin, for a white collar and cravat, coat, vest, and pantaloons; and lastly, putting aside his steel-hilted broadsword to take up a gold-headed cane, the Colonel Pyncheon of two centuries ago steps forward as the Judge of the passing moment!

Of course, Phoebe was far too sensible a girl to entertain this idea in any other way than as matter for a smile. Possibly, also, could the two personages have stood together before her eye, many points of difference would have been perceptible, and perhaps only a general resemblance. The long lapse of intervening years, in a climate so unlike that which had fostered the ancestral Englishman, must inevitably have wrought important changes in the physical system of his descendant. The Judge's volume of muscle could hardly be the same as the Colonel's; there was undoubtedly less beef in him. Though looked upon as a weighty man among his contemporaries in respect of animal substance, and as favored with a remarkable degree of fundamental development, well adapting him for the judicial bench, we conceive that the modern Judge Pyncheon, if weighed in the same balance with his ancestor, would have required at least an old-fashioned fifty-six to keep the scale in equilibrio. Then the Judge's face had lost the ruddy English hue that showed its warmth through all the duskiness of the Colonel's weather-beaten cheek, and had taken a sallow shade, the established complexion of his countrymen. If we mistake not, moreover, a certain quality of nervousness had become more or less manifest, even in so solid a specimen of Puritan descent as the gentleman now under discussion. As one of its effects, it bestowed on his countenance a quicker mobility than the old Englishman's had possessed, and keener vivacity, but at the expense of a sturdier something, on which these acute endowments seemed to act like dissolving acids. This process, for aught we know, may belong to the great system of human progress, which, with every ascending footstep, as it diminishes the necessity for animal force, may be destined gradually to spiritualize us, by refining away our grosser attributes of body. If so, Judge Pyncheon could endure a century or two more of such refinement as well as most other men.

The similarity, intellectual and moral, between the Judge and his ancestor appears to have been at least as strong as the resemblance of mien and feature would afford reason to anticipate. In old Colonel Pyncheon's funeral discourse the clergyman absolutely canonized his deceased parishioner, and opening, as it were, a vista through the roof of the church, and thence through the firmament above, showed him seated, harp in hand, among the crowned choristers of the spiritual world. On his tombstone, too, the record is highly eulogistic; nor does history, so far as he holds a place upon its page, assail the consistency and uprightness of his character. So also, as regards the Judge Pyncheon of to-day, neither clergyman, nor legal critic, nor inscriber of tombstones, nor historian of general or local politics, would venture a word against this eminent person's sincerity as a Christian, or respectability as a man, or integrity as a judge, or courage and faithfulness as the often-tried representative of his political party. But, besides these cold, formal, and empty words of the chisel that inscribes, the voice that speaks, and the pen that writes, for the public eye and for distant time,—and which inevitably lose much of their truth and freedom by the fatal consciousness of so doing,—there were traditions about the ancestor, and private diurnal gossip about the Judge, remarkably accordant in their testimony. It is often instructive to take the woman's, the private and domestic, view of a public man; nor can anything be more curious than the vast discrepancy between portraits intended for engraving and the pencil-sketches that pass from hand to hand behind the original's back.

For example: tradition affirmed that the Puritan had been greedy of wealth; the Judge, too, with all the show of liberal expenditure, was said to be as close-fisted as if his gripe were of iron. The ancestor had clothed himself in a grim assumption of kindliness, a rough heartiness of word and manner, which most people took to be the genuine warmth of nature, making its way through the thick and inflexible hide of a manly character. His descendant, in compliance with the requirements of a nicer age, had etherealized this rude benevolence into that broad benignity of smile wherewith he shone like a noonday sun along the streets, or glowed like a household fire in the drawing-rooms of his private acquaintance. The Puritan—if not belied by some singular stories, murmured, even at this day, under the narrator's breath—had fallen into certain transgressions to which men of his great animal development, whatever their faith or principles, must continue liable, until they put off impurity, along with the gross earthly substance that involves it. We must not stain our page with any contemporary scandal, to a similar purport, that may have been whispered against the Judge. The Puritan, again, an autocrat in his own household, had worn out three wives, and, merely by the remorseless weight and hardness of his character in the conjugal relation, had sent them, one after another, broken-hearted, to their graves. Here the parallel, in some sort, fails. The Judge had wedded but a single wife, and lost her in the third or fourth year of their marriage. There was a fable, however,—for such we choose to consider it, though, not impossibly, typical of Judge Pyncheon's marital deportment,—that the lady got her death-blow in the honeymoon, and never smiled again, because her husband compelled her to serve him with coffee every morning at his bedside, in token of fealty to her liege-lord and master.

But it is too fruitful a subject, this of hereditary resemblances,—the frequent recurrence of which, in a direct line, is truly unaccountable, when we consider how large an accumulation of ancestry lies behind every man at the distance of one or two centuries. We shall only add, therefore, that the Puritan—so, at least, says chimney-corner tradition, which often preserves traits of character with marvellous fidelity—was bold, imperious, relentless, crafty; laying his purposes deep, and following them out with an inveteracy of pursuit that knew neither rest nor conscience; trampling on the weak, and, when essential to his ends, doing his utmost to beat down the strong. Whether the Judge in any degree resembled him, the further progress of our narrative may show.

Scarcely any of the items in the above-drawn parallel occurred to Phoebe, whose country birth and residence, in truth, had left her pitifully ignorant of most of the family traditions, which lingered, like cobwebs and incrustations of smoke, about the rooms and chimney-corners of the House of the Seven Gables. Yet there was a circumstance, very trifling in itself, which impressed her with an odd degree of horror. She had heard of the anathema flung by Maule, the executed wizard, against Colonel Pyncheon and his posterity,—that God would give them blood to drink,—and likewise of the popular notion, that this miraculous blood might now and then be heard gurgling in their throats. The latter scandal—as became a person of sense, and, more especially, a member of the Pyncheon family—Phoebe had set down for the absurdity which it unquestionably was. But ancient superstitions, after being steeped in human hearts and embodied in human breath, and passing from lip to ear in manifold repetition, through a series of generations, become imbued with an effect of homely truth. The smoke of the domestic hearth has scented them through and through. By long transmission among household facts, they grow to look like them, and have such a familiar way of making themselves at home that their influence is usually greater than we suspect. Thus it happened, that when Phoebe heard a certain noise in Judge Pyncheon's throat,—rather habitual with him, not altogether voluntary, yet indicative of nothing, unless it were a slight bronchial complaint, or, as some people hinted, an apoplectic symptom,—when the girl heard this queer and awkward ingurgitation (which the writer never did hear, and therefore cannot describe), she very foolishly started, and clasped her hands.

Of course, it was exceedingly ridiculous in Phoebe to be discomposed by such a trifle, and still more unpardonable to show her discomposure to the individual most concerned in it. But the incident chimed in so oddly with her previous fancies about the Colonel and the Judge, that, for the moment, it seemed quite to mingle their identity.

"What is the matter with you, young woman?" said Judge Pyncheon, giving her one of his harsh looks. "Are you afraid of anything?"

"Oh, nothing, sir—nothing in the world!" answered Phoebe, with a little laugh of vexation at herself. "But perhaps you wish to speak with my cousin Hepzibah. Shall I call her?"

"Stay a moment, if you please," said the Judge, again beaming sunshine out of his face. "You seem to be a little nervous this morning. The town air, Cousin Phoebe, does not agree with your good, wholesome country habits. Or has anything happened to disturb you?—anything remarkable in Cousin Hepzibah's family?— An arrival, eh? I thought so! No wonder you are out of sorts, my little cousin. To be an inmate with such a guest may well startle an innocent young girl!"

"You quite puzzle me, sir," replied Phoebe, gazing inquiringly at the Judge. "There is no frightful guest in the house, but only a poor, gentle, childlike man, whom I believe to be Cousin Hepzibah's brother. I am afraid (but you, sir, will know better than I) that he is not quite in his sound senses; but so mild and quiet he seems to be, that a mother might trust her baby with him; and I think he would play with the baby as if he were only a few years older than itself. He startle me!—Oh, no indeed!"

"I rejoice to hear so favorable and so ingenuous an account of my cousin Clifford," said the benevolent Judge. "Many years ago, when we were boys and young men together, I had a great affection for him, and still feel a tender interest in all his concerns. You say, Cousin Phoebe, he appears to be weak minded. Heaven grant him at least enough of intellect to repent of his past sins!"

"Nobody, I fancy," observed Phoebe, "can have fewer to repent of."

"And is it possible, my dear," rejoined the Judge, with a commiserating look, "that you have never heard of Clifford Pyncheon?—that you know nothing of his history? Well, it is all right; and your mother has shown a very proper regard for the good name of the family with which she connected herself. Believe the best you can of this unfortunate person, and hope the best! It is a rule which Christians should always follow, in their judgments of one another; and especially is it right and wise among near relatives, whose characters have necessarily a degree of mutual dependence. But is Clifford in the parlor? I will just step in and see."

"Perhaps, sir, I had better call my cousin Hepzibah," said Phoebe; hardly knowing, however, whether she ought to obstruct the entrance of so affectionate a kinsman into the private regions of the house. "Her brother seemed to be just falling asleep after breakfast; and I am sure she would not like him to be disturbed. Pray, sir, let me give her notice!"

But the Judge showed a singular determination to enter unannounced; and as Phoebe, with the vivacity of a person whose movements unconsciously answer to her thoughts, had stepped towards the door, he used little or no ceremony in putting her aside.

"No, no, Miss Phoebe!" said Judge Pyncheon in a voice as deep as a thunder-growl, and with a frown as black as the cloud whence it issues. "Stay you here! I know the house, and know my cousin Hepzibah, and know her brother Clifford likewise.—nor need my little country cousin put herself to the trouble of announcing me!"—in these latter words, by the bye, there were symptoms of a change from his sudden harshness into his previous benignity of manner. "I am at home here, Phoebe, you must recollect, and you are the stranger. I will just step in, therefore, and see for myself how Clifford is, and assure him and Hepzibah of my kindly feelings and best wishes. It is right, at this juncture, that they should both hear from my own lips how much I desire to serve them. Ha! here is Hepzibah herself!"

Such was the case. The vibrations of the Judge's voice had reached the old gentlewoman in the parlor, where she sat, with face averted, waiting on her brother's slumber. She now issued forth, as would appear, to defend the entrance, looking, we must needs say, amazingly like the dragon which, in fairy tales, is wont to be the guardian over an enchanted beauty. The habitual scowl of her brow was undeniably too fierce, at this moment, to pass itself off on the innocent score of near-sightedness; and it was bent on Judge Pyncheon in a way that seemed to confound, if not alarm him, so inadequately had he estimated the moral force of a deeply grounded antipathy. She made a repelling gesture with her hand, and stood a perfect picture of prohibition, at full length, in the dark frame of the doorway. But we must betray Hepzibah's secret, and confess that the native timorousness of her character even now developed itself in a quick tremor, which, to her own perception, set each of her joints at variance with its fellows.

Possibly, the Judge was aware how little true hardihood lay behind Hepzibah's formidable front. At any rate, being a gentleman of steady nerves, he soon recovered himself, and failed not to approach his cousin with outstretched hand; adopting the sensible precaution, however, to cover his advance with a smile, so broad and sultry, that, had it been only half as warm as it looked, a trellis of grapes might at once have turned purple under its summer-like exposure. It may have been his purpose, indeed, to melt poor Hepzibah on the spot, as if she were a figure of yellow wax.

"Hepzibah, my beloved cousin, I am rejoiced!" exclaimed the Judge most emphatically. "Now, at length, you have something to live for. Yes, and all of us, let me say, your friends and kindred, have more to live for than we had yesterday. I have lost no time in hastening to offer any assistance in my power towards making Clifford comfortable. He belongs to us all. I know how much he requires,—how much he used to require,—with his delicate taste, and his love of the beautiful. Anything in my house,—pictures, books, wine, luxuries of the table,—he may command them all! It would afford me most heartfelt gratification to see him! Shall I step in, this moment?"

"No," replied Hepzibah, her voice quivering too painfully to allow of many words. "He cannot see visitors!"

"A visitor, my dear cousin!—do you call me so?" cried the Judge, whose sensibility, it seems, was hurt by the coldness of the phrase. "Nay, then, let me be Clifford's host, and your own likewise. Come at once to my house. The country air, and all the conveniences,—I may say luxuries,—that I have gathered about me, will do wonders for him. And you and I, dear Hepzibah, will consult together, and watch together, and labor together, to make our dear Clifford happy. Come! why should we make more words about what is both a duty and a pleasure on my part? Come to me at once!"

On hearing these so hospitable offers, and such generous recognition of the claims of kindred, Phoebe felt very much in the mood of running up to Judge Pyncheon, and giving him, of her own accord, the kiss from which she had so recently shrunk away. It was quite otherwise with Hepzibah; the Judge's smile seemed to operate on her acerbity of heart like sunshine upon vinegar, making it ten times sourer than ever.

"Clifford," said she,—still too agitated to utter more than an abrupt sentence,—"Clifford has a home here!"

"May Heaven forgive you, Hepzibah," said Judge Pyncheon,—reverently lifting his eyes towards that high court of equity to which he appealed,—"if you suffer any ancient prejudice or animosity to weigh with you in this matter. I stand here with an open heart, willing and anxious to receive yourself and Clifford into it. Do not refuse my good offices,—my earnest propositions for your welfare! They are such, in all respects, as it behooves your nearest kinsman to make. It will be a heavy responsibility, cousin, if you confine your brother to this dismal house and stifled air, when the delightful freedom of my country-seat is at his command."

"It would never suit Clifford," said Hepzibah, as briefly as before.

"Woman!" broke forth the Judge, giving way to his resentment, "what is the meaning of all this? Have you other resources? Nay, I suspected as much! Take care, Hepzibah, take care! Clifford is on the brink of as black a ruin as ever befell him yet! But why do I talk with you, woman as you are? Make way!—I must see Clifford!"

Hepzibah spread out her gaunt figure across the door, and seemed really to increase in bulk; looking the more terrible, also, because there was so much terror and agitation in her heart. But Judge Pyncheon's evident purpose of forcing a passage was interrupted by a voice from the inner room; a weak, tremulous, wailing voice, indicating helpless alarm, with no more energy for self-defence than belongs to a frightened infant.

"Hepzibah, Hepzibah!" cried the voice; "go down on your knees to him! Kiss his feet! Entreat him not to come in! Oh, let him have mercy on me! Mercy! mercy!"

For the instant, it appeared doubtful whether it were not the Judge's resolute purpose to set Hepzibah aside, and step across the threshold into the parlor, whence issued that broken and miserable murmur of entreaty. It was not pity that restrained him, for, at the first sound of the enfeebled voice, a red fire kindled in his eyes, and he made a quick pace forward, with something inexpressibly fierce and grim darkening forth, as it were, out of the whole man. To know Judge Pyncheon was to see him at that moment. After such a revelation, let him smile with what sultriness he would, he could much sooner turn grapes purple, or pumpkins yellow, than melt the iron-branded impression out of the beholder's memory. And it rendered his aspect not the less, but more frightful, that it seemed not to express wrath or hatred, but a certain hot fellness of purpose, which annihilated everything but itself.

Yet, after all, are we not slandering an excellent and amiable man? Look at the Judge now! He is apparently conscious of having erred, in too energetically pressing his deeds of loving-kindness on persons unable to appreciate them. He will await their better mood, and hold himself as ready to assist them then as at this moment. As he draws back from the door, an all-comprehensive benignity blazes from his visage, indicating that he gathers Hepzibah, little Phoebe, and the invisible Clifford, all three, together with the whole world besides, into his immense heart, and gives them a warm bath in its flood of affection.

"You do me great wrong, dear Cousin Hepzibah!" said he, first kindly offering her his hand, and then drawing on his glove preparatory to departure. "Very great wrong! But I forgive it, and will study to make you think better of me. Of course, our poor Clifford being in so unhappy a state of mind, I cannot think of urging an interview at present. But I shall watch over his welfare as if he were my own beloved brother; nor do I at all despair, my dear cousin, of constraining both him and you to acknowledge your injustice. When that shall happen, I desire no other revenge than your acceptance of the best offices in my power to do you."

With a bow to Hepzibah, and a degree of paternal benevolence in his parting nod to Phoebe, the Judge left the shop, and went smiling along the street. As is customary with the rich, when they aim at the honors of a republic, he apologized, as it were, to the people, for his wealth, prosperity, and elevated station, by a free and hearty manner towards those who knew him; putting off the more of his dignity in due proportion with the humbleness of the man whom he saluted, and thereby proving a haughty consciousness of his advantages as irrefragably as if he had marched forth preceded by a troop of lackeys to clear the way. On this particular forenoon, so excessive was the warmth of Judge Pyncheon's kindly aspect, that (such, at least, was the rumor about town) an extra passage of the water-carts was found essential, in order to lay the dust occasioned by so much extra sunshine!

No sooner had he disappeared than Hepzibah grew deadly white, and, staggering towards Phoebe, let her head fall on the young girl's shoulder.

"O Phoebe!" murmured she, "that man has been the horror of my life! Shall I never, never have the courage,—will my voice never cease from trembling long enough to let me tell him what he is?"

"Is he so very wicked?" asked Phoebe. "Yet his offers were surely kind!"

"Do not speak of them,—he has a heart of iron!" rejoined Hepzibah. "Go, now, and talk to Clifford! Amuse and keep him quiet! It would disturb him wretchedly to see me so agitated as I am. There, go, dear child, and I will try to look after the shop."

Phoebe went accordingly, but perplexed herself, meanwhile, with queries as to the purport of the scene which she had just witnessed, and also whether judges, clergymen, and other characters of that eminent stamp and respectability, could really, in any single instance, be otherwise than just and upright men. A doubt of this nature has a most disturbing influence, and, if shown to be a fact, comes with fearful and startling effect on minds of the trim, orderly, and limit-loving class, in which we find our little country-girl. Dispositions more boldly speculative may derive a stern enjoyment from the discovery, since there must be evil in the world, that a high man is as likely to grasp his share of it as a low one. A wider scope of view, and a deeper insight, may see rank, dignity, and station, all proved illusory, so far as regards their claim to human reverence, and yet not feel as if the universe were thereby tumbled headlong into chaos. But Phoebe, in order to keep the universe in its old place, was fain to smother, in some degree, her own intuitions as to Judge Pyncheon's character. And as for her cousin's testimony in disparagement of it, she concluded that Hepzibah's judgment was embittered by one of those family feuds which render hatred the more deadly by the dead and corrupted love that they intermingle with its native poison.

IX Clifford and Phoebe

TRULY was there something high, generous, and noble in the native composition of our poor old Hepzibah! Or else,—and it was quite as probably the case,—she had been enriched by poverty, developed by sorrow, elevated by the strong and solitary affection of her life, and thus endowed with heroism, which never could have characterized her in what are called happier circumstances. Through dreary years Hepzibah had looked forward—for the most part despairingly, never with any confidence of hope, but always with the feeling that it was her brightest possibility—to the very position in which she now found herself. In her own behalf, she had asked nothing of Providence but the opportunity of devoting herself to this brother, whom she had so loved,—so admired for what he was, or might have been,—and to whom she had kept her faith, alone of all the world, wholly, unfalteringly, at every instant, and throughout life. And here, in his late decline, the lost one had come back out of his long and strange misfortune, and was thrown on her sympathy, as it seemed, not merely for the bread of his physical existence, but for everything that should keep him morally alive. She had responded to the call. She had come forward,—our poor, gaunt Hepzibah, in her rusty silks, with her rigid joints, and the sad perversity of her scowl,—ready to do her utmost; and with affection enough, if that were all, to do a hundred times as much! There could be few more tearful sights,—and Heaven forgive us if a smile insist on mingling with our conception of it!—few sights with truer pathos in them, than Hepzibah presented on that first afternoon.

How patiently did she endeavor to wrap Clifford up in her great, warm love, and make it all the world to him, so that he should retain no torturing sense of the coldness and dreariness without! Her little efforts to amuse him! How pitiful, yet magnanimous, they were!

Remembering his early love of poetry and fiction, she unlocked a bookcase, and took down several books that had been excellent reading in their day. There was a volume of Pope, with the Rape of the Lock in it, and another of the Tatler, and an odd one of Dryden's Miscellanies, all with tarnished gilding on their covers, and thoughts of tarnished brilliancy inside. They had no success with Clifford. These, and all such writers of society, whose new works glow like the rich texture of a just-woven carpet, must be content to relinquish their charm, for every reader, after an age or two, and could hardly be supposed to retain any portion of it for a mind that had utterly lost its estimate of modes and manners. Hepzibah then took up Rasselas, and began to read of the Happy Valley, with a vague idea that some secret of a contented life had there been elaborated, which might at least serve Clifford and herself for this one day. But the Happy Valley had a cloud over it. Hepzibah troubled her auditor, moreover, by innumerable sins of emphasis, which he seemed to detect, without any reference to the meaning; nor, in fact, did he appear to take much note of the sense of what she read, but evidently felt the tedium of the lecture, without harvesting its profit. His sister's voice, too, naturally harsh, had, in the course of her sorrowful lifetime, concontracted a kind of croak, which, when it once gets into the human throat, is as ineradicable as sin. In both sexes, occasionally, this lifelong croak, accompanying each word of joy or sorrow, is one of the symptoms of a settled melancholy; and wherever it occurs, the whole history of misfortune is conveyed in its slightest accent. The effect is as if the voice had been dyed black; or,—if we must use a more moderate simile,—this miserable croak, running through all the variations of the voice, is like a black silken thread, on which the crystal beads of speech are strung, and whence they take their hue. Such voices have put on mourning for dead hopes; and they ought to die and be buried along with them!

Discerning that Clifford was not gladdened by her efforts, Hepzibah searched about the house for the means of more exhilarating pastime. At one time, her eyes chanced to rest on Alice Pyncheon's harpsichord. It was a moment of great peril; for,—despite the traditionary awe that had gathered over this instrument of music, and the dirges which spiritual fingers were said to play on it,—the devoted sister had solemn thoughts of thrumming on its chords for Clifford's benefit, and accompanying the performance with her voice. Poor Clifford! Poor Hepzibah! Poor harpsichord! All three would have been miserable together. By some good agency,—possibly, by the unrecognized interposition of the long-buried Alice herself,—the threatening calamity was averted.

But the worst of all—the hardest stroke of fate for Hepzibah to endure, and perhaps for Clifford, too was his invincible distaste for her appearance. Her features, never the most agreeable, and now harsh with age and grief, and resentment against the world for his sake; her dress, and especially her turban; the queer and quaint manners, which had unconsciously grown upon her in solitude,—such being the poor gentlewoman's outward characteristics, it is no great marvel, although the mournfullest of pities, that the instinctive lover of the Beautiful was fain to turn away his eyes. There was no help for it. It would be the latest impulse to die within him. In his last extremity, the expiring breath stealing faintly through Clifford's lips, he would doubtless press Hepzibah's hand, in fervent recognition of all her lavished love, and close his eyes,—but not so much to die, as to be constrained to look no longer on her face! Poor Hepzibah! She took counsel with herself what might be done, and thought of putting ribbons on her turban; but, by the instant rush of several guardian angels, was withheld from an experiment that could hardly have proved less than fatal to the beloved object of her anxiety.

To be brief, besides Hepzibah's disadvantages of person, there was an uncouthness pervading all her deeds; a clumsy something, that could but ill adapt itself for use, and not at all for ornament. She was a grief to Clifford, and she knew it. In this extremity, the antiquated virgin turned to Phoebe. No grovelling jealousy was in her heart. Had it pleased Heaven to crown the heroic fidelity of her life by making her personally the medium of Clifford's happiness, it would have rewarded her for all the past, by a joy with no bright tints, indeed, but deep and true, and worth a thousand gayer ecstasies. This could not be. She therefore turned to Phoebe, and resigned the task into the young girl's hands. The latter took it up cheerfully, as she did everything, but with no sense of a mission to perform, and succeeding all the better for that same simplicity.

By the involuntary effect of a genial temperament, Phoebe soon grew to be absolutely essential to the daily comfort, if not the daily life, of her two forlorn companions. The grime and sordidness of the House of the Seven Gables seemed to have vanished since her appearance there; the gnawing tooth of the dry-rot was stayed among the old timbers of its skeleton frame; the dust had ceased to settle down so densely, from the antique ceilings, upon the floors and furniture of the rooms below,—or, at any rate, there was a little housewife, as light-footed as the breeze that sweeps a garden walk, gliding hither and thither to brush it all away. The shadows of gloomy events that haunted the else lonely and desolate apartments; the heavy, breathless scent which death had left in more than one of the bedchambers, ever since his visits of long ago,—these were less powerful than the purifying influence scattered throughout the atmosphere of the household by the presence of one youthful, fresh, and thoroughly wholesome heart. There was no morbidness in Phoebe; if there had been, the old Pyncheon House was the very locality to ripen it into incurable disease. But now her spirit resembled, in its potency, a minute quantity of ottar of rose in one of Hepzibah's huge, iron-bound trunks, diffusing its fragrance through the various articles of linen and wrought-lace, kerchiefs, caps, stockings, folded dresses, gloves, and whatever else was treasured there. As every article in the great trunk was the sweeter for the rose-scent, so did all the thoughts and emotions of Hepzibah and Clifford, sombre as they might seem, acquire a subtle attribute of happiness from Phoebe's intermixture with them. Her activity of body, intellect, and heart impelled her continually to perform the ordinary little toils that offered themselves around her, and to think the thought proper for the moment, and to sympathize,—now with the twittering gayety of the robins in the pear-tree, and now to such a depth as she could with Hepzibah's dark anxiety, or the vague moan of her brother. This facile adaptation was at once the symptom of perfect health and its best preservative.

A nature like Phoebe's has invariably its due influence, but is seldom regarded with due honor. Its spiritual force, however, may be partially estimated by the fact of her having found a place for herself, amid circumstances so stern as those which surrounded the mistress of the house; and also by the effect which she produced on a character of so much more mass than her own. For the gaunt, bony frame and limbs of Hepzibah, as compared with the tiny lightsomeness of Phoebe's figure, were perhaps in some fit proportion with the moral weight and substance, respectively, of the woman and the girl.

To the guest,—to Hepzibah's brother,—or Cousin Clifford, as Phoebe now began to call him,—she was especially necessary. Not that he could ever be said to converse with her, or often manifest, in any other very definite mode, his sense of a charm in her society. But if she were a long while absent he became pettish and nervously restless, pacing the room to and fro with the uncertainty that characterized all his movements; or else would sit broodingly in his great chair, resting his head on his hands, and evincing life only by an electric sparkle of ill-humor, whenever Hepzibah endeavored to arouse him. Phoebe's presence, and the contiguity of her fresh life to his blighted one, was usually all that he required. Indeed, such was the native gush and play of her spirit, that she was seldom perfectly quiet and undemonstrative, any more than a fountain ever ceases to dimple and warble with its flow. She possessed the gift of song, and that, too, so naturally, that you would as little think of inquiring whence she had caught it, or what master had taught her, as of asking the same questions about a bird, in whose small strain of music we recognize the voice of the Creator as distinctly as in the loudest accents of his thunder. So long as Phoebe sang, she might stray at her own will about the house. Clifford was content, whether the sweet, airy homeliness of her tones came down from the upper chambers, or along the passageway from the shop, or was sprinkled through the foliage of the pear-tree, inward from the garden, with the twinkling sunbeams. He would sit quietly, with a gentle pleasure gleaming over his face, brighter now, and now a little dimmer, as the song happened to float near him, or was more remotely heard. It pleased him best, however, when she sat on a low footstool at his knee.

It is perhaps remarkable, considering her temperament, that Phoebe oftener chose a strain of pathos than of gayety. But the young and happy are not ill pleased to temper their life with a transparent shadow. The deepest pathos of Phoebe's voice and song, moreover, came sifted through the golden texture of a cheery spirit, and was somehow so interfused with the quality thence acquired, that one's heart felt all the lighter for having wept at it. Broad mirth, in the sacred presence of dark misfortune, would have jarred harshly and irreverently with the solemn symphony that rolled its undertone through Hepzibah's and her brother's life. Therefore, it was well that Phoebe so often chose sad themes, and not amiss that they ceased to be so sad while she was singing them.

Becoming habituated to her companionship, Clifford readily showed how capable of imbibing pleasant tints and gleams of cheerful light from all quarters his nature must originally have been. He grew youthful while she sat by him. A beauty,—not precisely real, even in its utmost manifestation, and which a painter would have watched long to seize and fix upon his canvas, and, after all, in vain,—beauty, nevertheless, that was not a mere dream, would sometimes play upon and illuminate his face. It did more than to illuminate; it transfigured him with an expression that could only be interpreted as the glow of an exquisite and happy spirit. That gray hair, and those furrows,—with their record of infinite sorrow so deeply written across his brow, and so compressed, as with a futile effort to crowd in all the tale, that the whole inscription was made illegible,—these, for the moment, vanished. An eye at once tender and acute might have beheld in the man some shadow of what he was meant to be. Anon, as age came stealing, like a sad twilight, back over his figure, you would have felt tempted to hold an argument with Destiny, and affirm, that either this being should not have been made mortal, or mortal existence should have been tempered to his qualities. There seemed no necessity for his having drawn breath at all; the world never wanted him; but, as he had breathed, it ought always to have been the balmiest of summer air. The same perplexity will invariably haunt us with regard to natures that tend to feed exclusively upon the Beautiful, let their earthly fate be as lenient as it may.

Phoebe, it is probable, had but a very imperfect comprehension of the character over which she had thrown so beneficent a spell. Nor was it necessary. The fire upon the hearth can gladden a whole semicircle of faces round about it, but need not know the individuality of one among them all. Indeed, there was something too fine and delicate in Clifford's traits to be perfectly appreciated by one whose sphere lay so much in the Actual as Phoebe's did. For Clifford, however, the reality, and simplicity, and thorough homeliness of the girl's nature were as powerful a charm as any that she possessed. Beauty, it is true, and beauty almost perfect in its own style, was indispensable. Had Phoebe been coarse in feature, shaped clumsily, of a harsh voice, and uncouthly mannered, she might have been rich with all good gifts, beneath this unfortunate exterior, and still, so long as she wore the guise of woman, she would have shocked Clifford, and depressed him by her lack of beauty. But nothing more beautiful—nothing prettier, at least—was ever made than Phoebe. And, therefore, to this man,—whose whole poor and impalpable enjoyment of existence heretofore, and until both his heart and fancy died within him, had been a dream,—whose images of women had more and more lost their warmth and substance, and been frozen, like the pictures of secluded artists, into the chillest ideality,—to him, this little figure of the cheeriest household life was just what he required to bring him back into the breathing world. Persons who have wandered, or been expelled, out of the common track of things, even were it for a better system, desire nothing so much as to be led back. They shiver in their loneliness, be it on a mountain-top or in a dungeon. Now, Phoebe's presence made a home about her,—that very sphere which the outcast, the prisoner, the potentate,—the wretch beneath mankind, the wretch aside from it, or the wretch above it,—instinctively pines after,—a home! She was real! Holding her hand, you felt something; a tender something; a substance, and a warm one: and so long as you should feel its grasp, soft as it was, you might be certain that your place was good in the whole sympathetic chain of human nature. The world was no longer a delusion.

By looking a little further in this direction, we might suggest an explanation of an often-suggested mystery. Why are poets so apt to choose their mates, not for any similarity of poetic endowment, but for qualities which might make the happiness of the rudest handicraftsman as well as that of the ideal craftsman of the spirit? Because, probably, at his highest elevation, the poet needs no human intercourse; but he finds it dreary to descend, and be a stranger.

There was something very beautiful in the relation that grew up between this pair, so closely and constantly linked together, yet with such a waste of gloomy and mysterious years from his birthday to hers. On Clifford's part it was the feeling of a man naturally endowed with the liveliest sensibility to feminine influence, but who had never quaffed the cup of passionate love, and knew that it was now too late. He knew it, with the instinctive delicacy that had survived his intellectual decay. Thus, his sentiment for Phoebe, without being paternal, was not less chaste than if she had been his daughter. He was a man, it is true, and recognized her as a woman. She was his only representative of womankind. He took unfailing note of every charm that appertained to her sex, and saw the ripeness of her lips, and the virginal development of her bosom. All her little womanly ways, budding out of her like blossoms on a young fruit-tree, had their effect on him, and sometimes caused his very heart to tingle with the keenest thrills of pleasure. At such moments,—for the effect was seldom more than momentary,—the half-torpid man would be full of harmonious life, just as a long-silent harp is full of sound, when the musician's fingers sweep across it. But, after all, it seemed rather a perception, or a sympathy, than a sentiment belonging to himself as an individual. He read Phoebe as he would a sweet and simple story; he listened to her as if she were a verse of household poetry, which God, in requital of his bleak and dismal lot, had permitted some angel, that most pitied him, to warble through the house. She was not an actual fact for him, but the interpretation of all that he lacked on earth brought warmly home to his conception; so that this mere symbol, or life-like picture, had almost the comfort of reality.

But we strive in vain to put the idea into words. No adequate expression of the beauty and profound pathos with which it impresses us is attainable. This being, made only for happiness, and heretofore so miserably failing to be happy,—his tendencies so hideously thwarted, that, some unknown time ago, the delicate springs of his character, never morally or intellectually strong, had given way, and he was now imbecile,—this poor, forlorn voyager from the Islands of the Blest, in a frail bark, on a tempestuous sea, had been flung, by the last mountain-wave of his shipwreck, into a quiet harbor. There, as he lay more than half lifeless on the strand, the fragrance of an earthly rose-bud had come to his nostrils, and, as odors will, had summoned up reminiscences or visions of all the living and breathing beauty amid which he should have had his home. With his native susceptibility of happy influences, he inhales the slight, ethereal rapture into his soul, and expires!

And how did Phoebe regard Clifford? The girl's was not one of those natures which are most attracted by what is strange and exceptional in human character. The path which would best have suited her was the well-worn track of ordinary life; the companions in whom she would most have delighted were such as one encounters at every turn. The mystery which enveloped Clifford, so far as it affected her at all, was an annoyance, rather than the piquant charm which many women might have found in it. Still, her native kindliness was brought strongly into play, not by what was darkly picturesque in his situation, nor so much, even, by the finer graces of his character, as by the simple appeal of a heart so forlorn as his to one so full of genuine sympathy as hers. She gave him an affectionate regard, because he needed so much love, and seemed to have received so little. With a ready tact, the result of ever-active and wholesome sensibility, she discerned what was good for him, and did it. Whatever was morbid in his mind and experience she ignored; and thereby kept their intercourse healthy, by the incautious, but, as it were, heaven-directed freedom of her whole conduct. The sick in mind, and, perhaps, in body, are rendered more darkly and hopelessly so by the manifold reflection of their disease, mirrored back from all quarters in the deportment of those about them; they are compelled to inhale the poison of their own breath, in infinite repetition. But Phoebe afforded her poor patient a supply of purer air. She impregnated it, too, not with a wild-flower scent,—for wildness was no trait of hers,—but with the perfume of garden-roses, pinks, and other blossoms of much sweetness, which nature and man have consented together in making grow from summer to summer, and from century to century. Such a flower was Phoebe in her relation with Clifford, and such the delight that he inhaled from her.

Yet, it must be said, her petals sometimes drooped a little, in consequence of the heavy atmosphere about her. She grew more thoughtful than heretofore. Looking aside at Clifford's face, and seeing the dim, unsatisfactory elegance and the intellect almost quenched, she would try to inquire what had been his life. Was he always thus? Had this veil been over him from his birth?—this veil, under which far more of his spirit was hidden than revealed, and through which he so imperfectly discerned the actual world,—or was its gray texture woven of some dark calamity? Phoebe loved no riddles, and would have been glad to escape the perplexity of this one. Nevertheless, there was so far a good result of her meditations on Clifford's character, that, when her involuntary conjectures, together with the tendency of every strange circumstance to tell its own story, had gradually taught her the fact, it had no terrible effect upon her. Let the world have done him what vast wrong it might, she knew Cousin Clifford too well—or fancied so—ever to shudder at the touch of his thin, delicate fingers.

Within a few days after the appearance of this remarkable inmate, the routine of life had established itself with a good deal of uniformity in the old house of our narrative. In the morning, very shortly after breakfast, it was Clifford's custom to fall asleep in his chair; nor, unless accidentally disturbed, would he emerge from a dense cloud of slumber or the thinner mists that flitted to and fro, until well towards noonday. These hours of drowsihead were the season of the old gentlewoman's attendance on her brother, while Phoebe took charge of the shop; an arrangement which the public speedily understood, and evinced their decided preference of the younger shopwoman by the multiplicity of their calls during her administration of affairs. Dinner over, Hepzibah took her knitting-work,—a long stocking of gray yarn, for her brother's winter wear,—and with a sigh, and a scowl of affectionate farewell to Clifford, and a gesture enjoining watchfulness on

Phoebe, went to take her seat behind the counter. It was now the young girl's turn to be the nurse,—the guardian, the playmate,—or whatever is the fitter phrase,—of the gray-haired man.

X The Pyncheon Garden

CLIFFORD, except for Phoebe's More active instigation would ordinarily have yielded to the torpor which had crept through all his modes of being, and which sluggishly counselled him to sit in his morning chair till eventide. But the girl seldom failed to propose a removal to the garden, where Uncle Venner and the daguerreotypist had made such repairs on the roof of the ruinous arbor, or summer-house, that it was now a sufficient shelter from sunshine and casual showers. The hop-vine, too, had begun to grow luxuriantly over the sides of the little edifice, and made an interior of verdant seclusion, with innumerable peeps and glimpses into the wider solitude of the garden.

Here, sometimes, in this green play-place of flickering light, Phoebe read to Clifford. Her acquaintance, the artist, who appeared to have a literary turn, had supplied her with works of fiction, in pamphlet form,—and a few volumes of poetry, in altogether a different style and taste from those which Hepzibah selected for his amusement. Small thanks were due to the books, however, if the girl's readings were in any degree more successful than her elderly cousin's. Phoebe's voice had always a pretty music in it, and could either enliven Clifford by its sparkle and gayety of tone, or soothe him by a continued flow of pebbly and brook-like cadences. But the fictions—in which the country-girl, unused to works of that nature, often became deeply absorbed—interested her strange auditor very little, or not at all. Pictures of life, scenes of passion or sentiment, wit, humor, and pathos, were all thrown away, or worse than thrown away, on Clifford; either because he lacked an experience by which to test their truth, or because his own griefs were a touch-stone of reality that few feigned emotions could withstand. When Phoebe broke into a peal of merry laughter at what she read, he would now and then laugh for sympathy, but oftener respond with a troubled, questioning look. If a tear—a maiden's sunshiny tear over imaginary woe—dropped upon some melancholy page, Clifford either took it as a token of actual calamity, or else grew peevish, and angrily motioned her to close the volume. And wisely too! Is not the world sad enough, in genuine earnest, without making a pastime of mock sorrows?

With poetry it was rather better. He delighted in the swell and subsidence of the rhythm, and the happily recurring rhyme. Nor was Clifford incapable of feeling the sentiment of poetry,—not, perhaps, where it was highest or deepest, but where it was most flitting and ethereal. It was impossible to foretell in what exquisite verse the awakening spell might lurk; but, on raising her eyes from the page to Clifford's face, Phoebe would be made aware, by the light breaking through it, that a more delicate intelligence than her own had caught a lambent flame from what she read. One glow of this kind, however, was often the precursor of gloom for many hours afterward; because, when the glow left him, he seemed conscious of a missing sense and power, and groped about for them, as if a blind man should go seeking his lost eyesight.

It pleased him more, and was better for his inward welfare, that Phoebe should talk, and make passing occurrences vivid to his mind by her accompanying description and remarks. The life of the garden offered topics enough for such discourse as suited Clifford best. He never failed to inquire what flowers had bloomed since yesterday. His feeling for flowers was very exquisite, and seemed not so much a taste as an emotion; he was fond of sitting with one in his hand, intently observing it, and looking from its petals into Phoebe's face, as if the garden flower were the sister of the household maiden. Not merely was there a delight in the flower's perfume, or pleasure in its beautiful form, and the delicacy or brightness of its hue; but Clifford's enjoyment was accompanied with a perception of life, character, and individuality, that made him love these blossoms of the garden, as if they were endowed with sentiment and intelligence. This affection and sympathy for flowers is almost exclusively a woman's trait. Men, if endowed with it by nature, soon lose, forget, and learn to despise it, in their contact with coarser things than flowers. Clifford, too, had long forgotten it; but found it again now, as he slowly revived from the chill torpor of his life.

It is wonderful how many pleasant incidents continually came to pass in that secluded garden-spot when once Phoebe had set herself to look for them. She had seen or heard a bee there, on the first day of her acquaintance with the place. And often,—almost continually, indeed,—since then, the bees kept coming thither, Heaven knows why, or by what pertinacious desire, for far-fetched sweets, when, no doubt, there were broad clover-fields, and all kinds of garden growth, much nearer home than this. Thither the bees came, however, and plunged into the squash-blossoms, as if there were no other squash-vines within a long day's flight, or as if the soil of Hepzibah's garden gave its productions just the very quality which these laborious little wizards wanted, in order to impart the Hymettus odor to their whole hive of New England honey. When Clifford heard their sunny, buzzing murmur, in the heart of the great yellow blossoms, he looked about him with a joyful sense of warmth, and blue sky, and green grass, and of God's free air in the whole height from earth to heaven. After all, there need be no question why the bees came to that one green nook in the dusty town. God sent them thither to gladden our poor Clifford. They brought the rich summer with them, in requital of a little honey.

When the bean-vines began to flower on the poles, there was one particular variety which bore a vivid scarlet blossom. The daguerreotypist had found these beans in a garret, over one of the seven gables, treasured up in an old chest of drawers by some horticultural Pyncheon of days gone by, who doubtless meant to sow them the next summer, but was himself first sown in Death's garden-ground. By way of testing whether there were still a living germ in such ancient seeds, Holgrave had planted some of them; and the result of his experiment was a splendid row of bean-vines, clambering, early, to the full height of the poles, and arraying them, from top to bottom, in a spiral profusion of red blossoms. And, ever since the unfolding of the first bud, a multitude of humming-birds had been attracted thither. At times, it seemed as if for every one of the hundred blossoms there was one of these tiniest fowls of the air,—a thumb's bigness of burnished plumage, hovering and vibrating about the bean-poles. It was with indescribable interest, and even more than childish delight, that Clifford watched the humming-birds. He used to thrust his head softly out of the arbor to see them the better; all the while, too, motioning Phoebe to be quiet, and snatching glimpses of the smile upon her face, so as to heap his enjoyment up the higher with her sympathy. He had not merely grown young;—he was a child again.

Hepzibah, whenever she happened to witness one of these fits of miniature enthusiasm, would shake her head, with a strange mingling of the mother and sister, and of pleasure and sadness, in her aspect. She said that it had always been thus with Clifford when the humming-birds came,—always, from his babyhood,—and that his delight in them had been one of the earliest tokens by which he showed his love for beautiful things. And it was a wonderful coincidence, the good lady thought, that the artist should have planted these scarlet-flowering beans—which the humming-birds sought far and wide, and which had not grown in the Pyncheon garden before for forty years—on the very summer of Clifford's return.

Then would the tears stand in poor Hepzibah's eyes, or overflow them with a too abundant gush, so that she was fain to betake herself into some corner, lest Clifford should espy her agitation. Indeed, all the enjoyments of this period were provocative of tears. Coming so late as it did, it was a kind of Indian summer, with a mist in its balmiest sunshine, and decay and death in its gaudiest delight. The more Clifford seemed to taste the happiness of a child, the sadder was the difference to be recognized. With a mysterious and terrible Past, which had annihilated his memory, and a blank Future before him, he had only this visionary and impalpable Now, which, if you once look closely at it, is nothing. He himself, as was perceptible by many symptoms, lay darkly behind his pleasure, and knew it to be a baby-play, which he was to toy and trifle with, instead of thoroughly believing. Clifford saw, it may be, in the mirror of his deeper consciousness, that he was an example and representative of that great class of people whom an inexplicable Providence is continually putting at cross-purposes with the world: breaking what seems its own promise in their nature; withholding their proper food, and setting poison before them for a banquet; and thus—when it might so easily, as one would think, have been adjusted otherwise—making their existence a strangeness, a solitude, and torment. All his life long, he had been learning how to be wretched, as one learns a foreign tongue; and now, with the lesson thoroughly by heart, he could with difficulty comprehend his little airy happiness.

Frequently there was a dim shadow of doubt in his eyes. "Take my hand, Phoebe," he would say, "and pinch it hard with your little fingers! Give me a rose, that I may press its thorns, and prove myself awake by the sharp touch of pain!" Evidently, he desired this prick of a trifling anguish, in order to assure himself, by that quality which he best knew to be real, that the garden, and the seven weather-beaten gables, and Hepzibah's scowl, and Phoebe's smile, were real likewise. Without this signet in his flesh, he could have attributed no more substance to them than to the empty confusion of imaginary scenes with which he had fed his spirit, until even that poor sustenance was exhausted.

The author needs great faith in his reader's sympathy; else he must hesitate to give details so minute, and incidents apparently so trifling, as are essential to make up the idea of this garden-life. It was the Eden of a thunder-smitten Adam, who had fled for refuge thither out of the same dreary and perilous wilderness into which the original Adam was expelled.

One of the available means of amusement, of which Phoebe made the most in Clifford's behalf, was that feathered society, the hens, a breed of whom, as we have already said, was an immemorial heirloom in the Pyncheon family. In compliance with a whim of Clifford, as it troubled him to see them in confinement, they had been set at liberty, and now roamed at will about the garden; doing some little mischief, but hindered from escape by buildings on three sides, and the difficult peaks of a wooden fence on the other. They spent much of their abundant leisure on the margin of Maule's well, which was haunted by a kind of snail, evidently a titbit to their palates; and the brackish water itself, however nauseous to the rest of the world, was so greatly esteemed by these fowls, that they might be seen tasting, turning up their heads, and smacking their bills, with precisely the air of wine-bibbers round a probationary cask. Their generally quiet, yet often brisk, and constantly diversified talk, one to another, or sometimes in soliloquy,—as they scratched worms out of the rich, black soil, or pecked at such plants as suited their taste,—had such a domestic tone, that it was almost a wonder why you could not establish a regular interchange of ideas about household matters, human and gallinaceous. All hens are well worth studying for the piquancy and rich variety of their manners; but by no possibility can there have been other fowls of such odd appearance and deportment as these ancestral ones. They probably embodied the traditionary peculiarities of their whole line of progenitors, derived through an unbroken succession of eggs; or else this individual Chanticleer and his two wives had grown to be humorists, and a little crack-brained withal, on account of their solitary way of life, and out of sympathy for Hepzibah, their lady-patroness.

Queer, indeed, they looked! Chanticleer himself, though stalking on two stilt-like legs, with the dignity of interminable descent in all his gestures, was hardly bigger than an ordinary partridge; his two wives were about the size of quails; and as for the one chicken, it looked small enough to be still in the egg, and, at the same time, sufficiently old, withered, wizened, and experienced, to have been founder of the antiquated race. Instead of being the youngest of the family, it rather seemed to have aggregated into itself the ages, not only of these living specimens of the breed, but of all its forefathers and foremothers, whose united excellences and oddities were squeezed into its little body. Its mother evidently regarded it as the one chicken of the world, and as necessary, in fact, to the world's continuance, or, at any rate, to the equilibrium of the present system of affairs, whether in church or state. No lesser sense of the infant fowl's importance could have justified, even in a mother's eyes, the perseverance with which she watched over its safety, ruffling her small person to twice its proper size, and flying in everybody's face that so much as looked towards her hopeful progeny. No lower estimate could have vindicated the indefatigable zeal with which she scratched, and her unscrupulousness in digging up the choicest flower or vegetable, for the sake of the fat earthworm at its root. Her nervous cluck, when the chicken happened to be hidden in the long grass or under the squash-leaves; her gentle croak of satisfaction, while sure of it beneath her wing; her note of ill-concealed fear and obstreperous defiance, when she saw her arch-enemy, a neighbor's cat, on the top of the high fence,—one or other of these sounds was to be heard at almost every moment of the day. By degrees, the observer came to feel nearly as much interest in this chicken of illustrious race as the mother-hen did.

Phoebe, after getting well acquainted with the old hen, was sometimes permitted to take the chicken in her hand, which was quite capable of grasping its cubic inch or two of body. While she curiously examined its hereditary marks,—the peculiar speckle of its plumage, the funny tuft on its head, and a knob on each of its legs,—the little biped, as she insisted, kept giving her a sagacious wink. The daguerreotypist once whispered her that these marks betokened the oddities of the Pyncheon family, and that the chicken itself was a symbol of the life of the old house, embodying its interpretation, likewise, although an unintelligible one, as such clews generally are. It was a feathered riddle; a mystery hatched out of an egg, and just as mysterious as if the egg had been addle!

The second of Chanticleer's two wives, ever since Phoebe's arrival, had been in a state of heavy despondency, caused, as it afterwards appeared, by her inability to lay an egg. One day, however, by her self-important gait, the sideways turn of her head, and the cock of her eye, as she pried into one and another nook of the garden,—croaking to herself, all the while, with inexpressible complacency,—it was made evident that this identical hen, much as mankind undervalued her, carried something about her person the worth of which was not to be estimated either in gold or precious stones. Shortly after, there was a prodigious cackling and gratulation of Chanticleer and all his family, including the wizened chicken, who appeared to understand the matter quite as well as did his sire, his mother, or his aunt. That afternoon Phoebe found a diminutive egg,—not in the regular nest, it was far too precious to be trusted there,—but cunningly hidden under the currant-bushes, on some dry stalks of last year's grass. Hepzibah, on learning the fact, took possession of the egg and appropriated it to Clifford's breakfast, on account of a certain delicacy of flavor, for which, as she affirmed, these eggs had always been famous. Thus unscrupulously did the old gentlewoman sacrifice the continuance, perhaps, of an ancient feathered race, with no better end than to supply her brother with a dainty that hardly filled the bowl of a tea-spoon! It must have been in reference to this outrage that Chanticleer, the next day, accompanied by the bereaved mother of the egg, took his post in front of Phoebe and Clifford, and delivered himself of a harangue that might have proved as long as his own pedigree, but for a fit of merriment on Phoebe's part. Hereupon, the offended fowl stalked away on his long stilts, and utterly withdrew his notice from Phoebe and the rest of human nature, until she made her peace with an offering of spice-cake, which, next to snails, was the delicacy most in favor with his aristocratic taste.

We linger too long, no doubt, beside this paltry rivulet of life that flowed through the garden of the Pyncheon House. But we deem it pardonable to record these mean incidents and poor delights, because they proved so greatly to Clifford's benefit. They had the earth-smell in them, and contributed to give him health and substance. Some of his occupations wrought less desirably upon him. He had a singular propensity, for example, to hang over Maule's well, and look at the constantly shifting phantasmagoria of figures produced by the agitation of the water over the mosaic-work of colored pebbles at the bottom. He said that faces looked upward to him there,—beautiful faces, arrayed in bewitching smiles,—each momentary face so fair and rosy, and every smile so sunny, that he felt wronged at its departure, until the same flitting witchcraft made a new one. But sometimes he would suddenly cry out, "The dark face gazes at me!" and be miserable the whole day afterwards. Phoebe, when she hung over the fountain by Clifford's side, could see nothing of all this,—neither the beauty nor the ugliness,—but only the colored pebbles, looking as if the gush of the waters shook and disarranged them. And the dark face, that so troubled Clifford, was no more than the shadow thrown from a branch of one of the damson-trees, and breaking the inner light of Maule's well. The truth was, however, that his fancy—reviving faster than his will and judgment, and always stronger than they—created shapes of loveliness that were symbolic of his native character, and now and then a stern and dreadful shape that typified his fate.

On Sundays, after Phoebe had been at church,—for the girl had a church-going conscience, and would hardly have been at ease had she missed either prayer, singing, sermon, or benediction,—after church-time, therefore, there was, ordinarily, a sober little festival in the garden. In addition to Clifford, Hepzibah, and Phoebe, two guests made up the company. One was the artist Holgrave, who, in spite of his consociation with reformers, and his other queer and questionable traits, continued to hold an elevated place in Hepzibah's regard. The other, we are almost ashamed to say, was the venerable Uncle Venner, in a clean shirt, and a broadcloth coat, more respectable than his ordinary wear, inasmuch as it was neatly patched on each elbow, and might be called an entire garment, except for a slight inequality in the length of its skirts. Clifford, on several occasions, had seemed to enjoy the old man's intercourse, for the sake of his mellow, cheerful vein, which was like the sweet flavor of a frost-bitten apple, such as one picks up under the tree in December. A man at the very lowest point of the social scale was easier and more agreeable for the fallen gentleman to encounter than a person at any of the intermediate degrees; and, moreover, as Clifford's young manhood had been lost, he was fond of feeling himself comparatively youthful, now, in apposition with the patriarchal age of Uncle Venner. In fact, it was sometimes ob-observable that Clifford half wilfully hid from himself the consciousness of being stricken in years, and cherished visions of an earthly future still before him; visions, however, too indistinctly drawn to be followed by disappointment—though, doubtless, by depression—when any casual incident or recollection made him sensible of the withered leaf.

So this oddly composed little social party used to assemble under the ruinous arbor. Hepzibah—stately as ever at heart, and yielding not an inch of her old gentility, but resting upon it so much the more, as justifying a princess-like condescension—exhibited a not ungraceful hospitality. She talked kindly to the vagrant artist, and took sage counsel—lady as she was—with the wood-sawyer, the messenger of everybody's petty errands, the patched philosopher. And Uncle Venner, who had studied the world at street-corners, and other posts equally well adapted for just observation, was as ready to give out his wisdom as a town-pump to give water.

"Miss Hepzibah, ma'am," said he once, after they had all been cheerful together, "I really enjoy these quiet little meetings of a Sabbath afternoon. They are very much like what I expect to have after I retire to my farm!"

"Uncle Venner" observed Clifford in a drowsy, inward tone, "is always talking about his farm. But I have a better scheme for him, by and by. We shall see!"

"Ah, Mr. Clifford Pyncheon!" said the man of patches, "you may scheme for me as much as you please; but I'm not going to give up this one scheme of my own, even if I never bring it really to pass. It does seem to me that men make a wonderful mistake in trying to heap up property upon property. If I had done so, I should feel as if Providence was not bound to take care of me; and, at all events, the city wouldn't be! I'm one of those people who think that infinity is big enough for us all—and eternity long enough."

"Why, so they are, Uncle Venner," remarked Phoebe after a pause; for she had been trying to fathom the profundity and appositeness of this concluding apothegm. "But for this short life of ours, one would like a house and a moderate garden-spot of one's own."

"It appears to me," said the daguerreotypist, smiling, "that Uncle Venner has the principles of Fourier at the bottom of his wisdom; only they have not quite so much distinctness in his mind as in that of the systematizing Frenchman."

"Come, Phoebe," said Hepzibah, "it is time to bring the currants."

And then, while the yellow richness of the declining sunshine still fell into the open space of the garden, Phoebe brought out a loaf of bread and a china bowl of currants, freshly gathered from the bushes, and crushed with sugar. These, with water,—but not from the fountain of ill omen, close at hand,—constituted all the entertainment. Meanwhile, Holgrave took some pains to establish an intercourse with Clifford, actuated, it might seem, entirely by an impulse of kindliness, in order that the present hour might be cheerfuller than most which the poor recluse had spent, or was destined yet to spend. Nevertheless, in the artist's deep, thoughtful, all-observant eyes, there was, now and then, an expression, not sinister, but questionable; as if he had some other interest in the scene than a stranger, a youthful and unconnected adventurer, might be supposed to have. With great mobility of outward mood, however, he applied himself to the task of enlivening the party; and with so much success, that even dark-hued Hepzibah threw off one tint of melancholy, and made what shift she could with the remaining portion. Phoebe said to herself,—"How pleasant he can be!" As for Uncle Venner, as a mark of friendship and approbation, he readily consented to afford the young man his countenance in the way of his profession,—not metaphorically, be it understood, but literally, by allowing a daguerreotype of his face, so familiar to the town, to be exhibited at the entrance of Holgrave's studio.

Clifford, as the company partook of their little banquet, grew to be the gayest of them all. Either it was one of those up-quivering flashes of the spirit, to which minds in an abnormal state are liable, or else the artist had subtly touched some chord that made musical vibration. Indeed, what with the pleasant summer evening, and the sympathy of this little circle of not unkindly souls, it was perhaps natural that a character so susceptible as Clifford's should become animated, and show itself readily responsive to what was said around him. But he gave out his own thoughts, likewise, with an airy and fanciful glow; so that they glistened, as it were, through the arbor, and made their escape among the interstices of the foliage. He had been as cheerful, no doubt, while alone with Phoebe, but never with such tokens of acute, although partial intelligence.

But, as the sunlight left the peaks of the Seven Gables, so did the excitement fade out of Clifford's eyes. He gazed vaguely and mournfully about him, as if he missed something precious, and missed it the more drearily for not knowing precisely what it was.

"I want my happiness!" at last he murmured hoarsely and indistinctly, hardly shaping out the words. "Many, many years have I waited for it! It is late! It is late! I want my happiness!"

Alas, poor Clifford! You are old, and worn with troubles that ought never to have befallen you. You are partly crazy and partly imbecile; a ruin, a failure, as almost everybody is,—though some in less degree, or less perceptibly, than their fellows. Fate has no happiness in store for you; unless your quiet home in the old family residence with the faithful Hepzibah, and your long summer afternoons with Phoebe, and these Sabbath festivals with Uncle Venner and the daguerreotypist, deserve to be called happiness! Why not? If not the thing itself, it is marvellously like it, and the more so for that ethereal and intangible quality which causes it all to vanish at too close an introspection. Take it, therefore, while you may. Murmur not,—question not,—but make the most of it!

XI The Arched Window

FROM the inertness, or what we may term the vegetative character, of his ordinary 'mood, Clifford would perhaps have been content to spend one day after another, interminably,—or, at least, throughout the summer-time,—in just the kind of life described in the preceding pages. Fancying, however, that it might be for his benefit occasionally to diversify the scene, Phoebe sometimes suggested that he should look out upon the life of the street. For this purpose, they used to mount the staircase together, to the second story of the house, where, at the termination of a wide entry, there was an arched window, of uncommonly large dimensions, shaded by a pair of curtains. It opened above the porch, where there had formerly been a balcony, the balustrade of which had long since gone to decay, and been removed. At this arched window, throwing it open, but keeping himself in comparative obscurity by means of the curtain, Clifford had an opportunity of witnessing such a portion of the great world's movement as might be supposed to roll through one of the retired streets of a not very populous city. But he and Phoebe made a sight as well worth seeing as any that the city could exhibit. The pale, gray, childish, aged, melancholy, yet often simply cheerful, and sometimes delicately intelligent aspect of Clifford, peering from behind the faded crimson of the curtain,—watching the monotony of every-day occurrences with a kind of inconsequential interest and earnestness, and, at every petty throb of his sensibility, turning for sympathy to the eyes of the bright young girl!

If once he were fairly seated at the window, even Pyncheon Street would hardly be so dull and lonely but that, somewhere or other along its extent, Clifford might discover matter to occupy his eye, and titillate, if not engross, his observation. Things familiar to the youngest child that had begun its outlook at existence seemed strange to him. A cab; an omnibus, with its populous interior, dropping here and there a passenger, and picking up another, and thus typifying that vast rolling vehicle, the world, the end of whose journey is everywhere and nowhere; these objects he followed eagerly with his eyes, but forgot them before the dust raised by the horses and wheels had settled along their track. As regarded novelties (among which cabs and omnibuses were to be reckoned), his mind appeared to have lost its proper gripe and retentiveness. Twice or thrice, for example, during the sunny hours of the day, a water-cart went along by the Pyncheon House, leaving a broad wake of moistened earth, instead of the white dust that had risen at a lady's lightest footfall; it was like a summer shower, which the city authorities had caught and tamed, and compelled it into the commonest routine of their convenience. With the water-cart Clifford could never grow familiar; it always affected him with just the same surprise as at first. His mind took an apparently sharp impression from it, but lost the recollection of this perambulatory shower, before its next reappearance, as completely as did the street itself, along which the heat so quickly strewed white dust again. It was the same with the railroad. Clifford could hear the obstreperous howl of the steam-devil, and, by leaning a little way from the arched window, could catch a glimpse of the trains of cars, flashing a brief transit across the extremity of the street. The idea of terrible energy thus forced upon him was new at every recurrence, and seemed to affect him as disagreeably, and with almost as much surprise, the hundredth time as the first.

Nothing gives a sadder sense of decay than this loss or suspension of the power to deal with unaccustomed things, and to keep up with the swiftness of the passing moment. It can merely be a suspended animation; for, were the power actually to perish, there would be little use of immortality. We are less than ghosts, for the time being, whenever this calamity befalls us.

Clifford was indeed the most inveterate of conservatives. All the antique fashions of the street were dear to him; even such as were characterized by a rudeness that would naturally have annoyed his fastidious senses. He loved the old rumbling and jolting carts, the former track of which he still found in his long-buried remembrance, as the observer of to-day finds the wheel-tracks of ancient vehicles in Herculaneum. The butcher's cart, with its snowy canopy, was an acceptable object; so was the fish-cart, heralded by its horn; so, likewise, was the countryman's cart of vegetables, plodding from door to door, with long pauses of the patient horse, while his owner drove a trade in turnips, carrots, summer-squashes, string-beans, green peas, and new potatoes, with half the housewives of the neighborhood. The baker's cart, with the harsh music of its bells, had a pleasant effect on Clifford, because, as few things else did, it jingled the very dissonance of yore. One afternoon a scissor-grinder chanced to set his wheel a-going under the Pyncheon Elm, and just in front of the arched window. Children came running with their mothers' scissors, or the carving-knife, or the paternal razor, or anything else that lacked an edge (except, indeed, poor Clifford's wits), that the grinder might apply the article to his magic wheel, and give it back as good as new. Round went the busily revolving machinery, kept in motion by the scissor-grinder's foot, and wore away the hard steel against the hard stone, whence issued an intense and spiteful prolongation of a hiss as fierce as those emitted by Satan and his compeers in Pandemonium, though squeezed into smaller compass. It was an ugly, little, venomous serpent of a noise, as ever did petty violence to human ears. But Clifford listened with rapturous delight. The sound, however disagreeable, had very brisk life in it, and, together with the circle of curious children watching the revolutions of the wheel, appeared to give him a more vivid sense of active, bustling, and sunshiny existence than he had attained in almost any other way. Nevertheless, its charm lay chiefly in the past; for the scissor-grinder's wheel had hissed in his childish ears.

He sometimes made doleful complaint that there were no stage-coaches nowadays. And he asked in an injured tone what had become of all those old square-topped chaises, with wings sticking out on either side, that used to be drawn by a plough-horse, and driven by a farmer's wife and daughter, peddling whortle-berries and blackberries about the town. Their disappearance made him doubt, he said, whether the berries had not left off growing in the broad pastures and along the shady country lanes.

But anything that appealed to the sense of beauty, in however humble a way, did not require to be recommended by these old associations. This was observable when one of those Italian boys (who are rather a modern feature of our streets) came along with his barrel-organ, and stopped under the wide and cool shadows of the elm. With his quick professional eye he took note of the two faces watching him from the arched window, and, opening his instrument, began to scatter its melodies abroad. He had a monkey on his shoulder, dressed in a Highland plaid; and, to complete the sum of splendid attractions wherewith he presented himself to the public, there was a company of little figures, whose sphere and habitation was in the mahogany case of his organ, and whose principle of life was the music which the Italian made it his business to grind out. In all their variety of occupation,—the cobbler, the blacksmith, the soldier, the lady with her fan, the toper with his bottle, the milk-maid sitting by her cow—this fortunate little society might truly be said to enjoy a harmonious existence, and to make life literally a dance. The Italian turned a crank; and, behold! every one of these small individuals started into the most curious vivacity. The cobbler wrought upon a shoe; the blacksmith hammered his iron, the soldier waved his glittering blade; the lady raised a tiny breeze with her fan; the jolly toper swigged lustily at his bottle; a scholar opened his book with eager thirst for knowledge, and turned his head to and fro along the page; the milkmaid energetically drained her cow; and a miser counted gold into his strong-box,—all at the same turning of a crank. Yes; and, moved by the self-same impulse, a lover saluted his mistress on her lips! Possibly some cynic, at once merry and bitter, had desired to signify, in this pantomimic scene, that we mortals, whatever our business or amusement,—however serious, however trifling,—all dance to one identical tune, and, in spite of our ridiculous activity, bring nothing finally to pass. For the most remarkable aspect of the affair was, that, at the cessation of the music, everybody was petrified at once, from the most extravagant life into a dead torpor. Neither was the cobbler's shoe finished, nor the blacksmith's iron shaped out; nor was there a drop less of brandy in the toper's bottle, nor a drop more of milk in the milkmaid's pail, nor one additional coin in the miser's strong-box, nor was the scholar a page deeper in his book. All were precisely in the same condition as before they made themselves so ridiculous by their haste to toil, to enjoy, to accumulate gold, and to become wise. Saddest of all, moreover, the lover was none the happier for the maiden's granted kiss! But, rather than swallow this last too acrid ingredient, we reject the whole moral of the show.

The monkey, meanwhile, with a thick tail curling out into preposterous prolixity from beneath his tartans, took his station at the Italian's feet. He turned a wrinkled and abominable little visage to every passer-by, and to the circle of children that soon gathered round, and to Hepzibah's shop-door, and upward to the arched window, whence Phoebe and Clifford were looking down. Every moment, also, he took off his Highland bonnet, and performed a bow and scrape. Sometimes, moreover, he made personal application to individuals, holding out his small black palm, and otherwise plainly signifying his excessive desire for whatever filthy lucre might happen to be in anybody's pocket. The mean and low, yet strangely man-like expression of his wilted countenance; the prying and crafty glance, that showed him ready to gripe at every miserable advantage; his enormous tail (too enormous to be decently concealed under his gabardine), and the deviltry of nature which it betokened,—take this monkey just as he was, in short, and you could desire no better image of the Mammon of copper coin, symbolizing the grossest form of the love of money. Neither was there any possibility of satisfying the covetous little devil. Phoebe threw down a whole handful of cents, which he picked up with joyless eagerness, handed them over to the Italian for safekeeping, and immediately recommenced a series of pantomimic petitions for more.

Doubtless, more than one New-Englander—or, let him be of what country he might, it is as likely to be the case—passed by, and threw a look at the monkey, and went on, without imagining how nearly his own moral condition was here exemplified. Clifford, however, was a being of another order. He had taken childish delight in the music, and smiled, too, at the figures which it set in motion. But, after looking awhile at the long-tailed imp, he was so shocked by his horrible ugliness, spiritual as well as physical, that he actually began to shed tears; a weakness which men of merely delicate endowments, and destitute of the fiercer, deeper, and more tragic power of laughter, can hardly avoid, when the worst and meanest aspect of life happens to be presented to them.

Pyncheon Street was sometimes enlivened by spectacles of more imposing pretensions than the above, and which brought the multitude along with them. With a shivering repugnance at the idea of personal contact with the world, a powerful impulse still seized on Clifford, whenever the rush and roar of the human tide grew strongly audible to him. This was made evident, one day, when a political procession, with hundreds of flaunting banners, and drums, fifes, clarions, and cymbals, reverberating between the rows of buildings, marched all through town, and trailed its length of trampling footsteps, and most infrequent uproar, past the ordinarily quiet House of the Seven Gables. As a mere object of sight, nothing is more deficient in picturesque features than a procession seen in its passage through narrow streets. The spectator feels it to be fool's play, when he can distinguish the tedious commonplace of each man's visage, with the perspiration and weary self-importance on it, and the very cut of his pantaloons, and the stiffness or laxity of his shirt-collar, and the dust on the back of his black coat. In order to become majestic, it should be viewed from some vantage point, as it rolls its slow and long array through the centre of a wide plain, or the stateliest public square of a city; for then, by its remoteness, it melts all the petty personalities, of which it is made up, into one broad mass of existence,—one great life,—one collected body of mankind, with a vast, homogeneous spirit animating it. But, on the other hand, if an impressible person, standing alone over the brink of one of these processions, should behold it, not in its atoms, but in its aggregate,—as a mighty river of life, massive in its tide, and black with mystery, and, out of its depths, calling to the kindred depth within him,—then the contiguity would add to the effect. It might so fascinate him that he would hardly be restrained from plunging into the surging stream of human sympathies.

So it proved with Clifford. He shuddered; he grew pale; he threw an appealing look at Hepzibah and Phoebe, who were with him at the window. They comprehended nothing of his emotions, and supposed him merely disturbed by the unaccustomed tumult. At last, with tremulous limbs, he started up, set his foot on the window-sill, and in an instant more would have been in the unguarded balcony. As it was, the whole procession might have seen him, a wild, haggard figure, his gray locks floating in the wind that waved their banners; a lonely being, estranged from his race, but now feeling himself man again, by virtue of the irrepressible instinct that possessed him. Had Clifford attained the balcony, he would probably have leaped into the street; but whether impelled by the species of terror that sometimes urges its victim over the very precipice which he shrinks from, or by a natural magnetism, tending towards the great centre of humanity, it were not easy to decide. Both impulses might have wrought on him at once.

But his companions, affrighted by his gesture,—which was that of a man hurried away in spite of himself,—seized Clifford's garment and held him back. Hepzibah shrieked. Phoebe, to whom all extravagance was a horror, burst into sobs and tears.

"Clifford, Clifford! are you crazy?" cried his sister.

"I hardly know, Hepzibah," said Clifford, drawing a long breath. "Fear nothing,—it is over now,—but had I taken that plunge, and survived it, methinks it would have made me another man!"

Possibly, in some sense, Clifford may have been right. He needed a shock; or perhaps he required to take a deep, deep plunge into the ocean of human life, and to sink down and be covered by its profoundness, and then to emerge, sobered, invigorated, restored to the world and to himself. Perhaps again, he required nothing less than the great final remedy—death!

A similar yearning to renew the broken links of brotherhood with his kind sometimes showed itself in a milder form; and once it was made beautiful by the religion that lay even deeper than itself. In the incident now to be sketched, there was a touching recognition, on Clifford's part, of God's care and love towards him,—towards this poor, forsaken man, who, if any mortal could, might have been pardoned for regarding himself as thrown aside, forgotten, and left to be the sport of some fiend, whose playfulness was an ecstasy of mischief.

It was the Sabbath morning; one of those bright, calm Sabbaths, with its own hallowed atmosphere, when Heaven seems to diffuse itself over the earth's face in a solemn smile, no less sweet than solemn. On such a Sabbath morn, were we pure enough to be its medium, we should be conscious of the earth's natural worship ascending through our frames, on whatever spot of ground we stood. The church-bells, with various tones, but all in harmony, were calling out and responding to one another,—"It is the Sabbath!—The Sabbath!—Yea; the Sabbath!"—and over the whole city the bells scattered the blessed sounds, now slowly, now with livelier joy, now one bell alone, now all the bells together, crying earnestly,—"It is the Sabbath!"—and flinging their accents afar off, to melt into the air and pervade it with the holy word. The air with God's sweetest and tenderest sunshine in it, was meet for mankind to breathe into their hearts, and send it forth again as the utterance of prayer.

Clifford sat at the window with Hepzibah, watching the neighbors as they stepped into the street. All of them, however unspiritual on other days, were transfigured by the Sabbath influence; so that their very garments—whether it were an old man's decent coat well brushed for the thousandth time, or a little boy's first sack and trousers finished yesterday by his mother's needle—had somewhat of the quality of ascension-robes. Forth, likewise, from the portal of the old house stepped Phoebe, putting up her small green sunshade, and throwing upward a glance and smile of parting kindness to the faces at the arched window. In her aspect there was a familiar gladness, and a holiness that you could play with, and yet reverence it as much as ever. She was like a prayer, offered up in the homeliest beauty of one's mother-tongue. Fresh was Phoebe, moreover, and airy and sweet in her apparel; as if nothing that she wore—neither her gown, nor her small straw bonnet, nor her little kerchief, any more than her snowy stockings—had ever been put on before; or, if worn, were all the fresher for it, and with a fragrance as if they had lain among the rosebuds.

The girl waved her hand to Hepzibah and Clifford, and went up the street; a religion in herself, warm, simple, true, with a substance that could walk on earth, and a spirit that was capable of heaven.

"Hepzibah," asked Clifford, after watching Phoebe to the corner, "do you never go to church?"

"No, Clifford!" she replied,—"not these many, many years!"

"Were I to be there," he rejoined, "it seems to me that I could pray once more, when so many human souls were praying all around me!"

She looked into Clifford's face, and beheld there a soft natural effusion; for his heart gushed out, as it were, and ran over at his eyes, in delightful reverence for God, and kindly affection for his human brethren. The emotion communicated itself to Hepzibah. She yearned to take him by the hand, and go and kneel down, they two together,—both so long separate from the world, and, as she now recognized, scarcely friends with Him above,—to kneel down among the people, and be reconciled to God and man at once.

"Dear brother," said she earnestly, "let us go! We belong nowhere. We have not a foot of space in any church to kneel upon; but let us go to some place of worship, even if we stand in the broad aisle. Poor and forsaken as we are, some pew-door will be opened to us!"

So Hepzibah and her brother made themselves, ready—as ready as they could in the best of their old-fashioned garments, which had hung on pegs, or been laid away in trunks, so long that the dampness and mouldy smell of the past was on them,—made themselves ready, in their faded bettermost, to go to church. They descended the staircase together,—gaunt, sallow Hepzibah, and pale, emaciated, age-stricken Clifford! They pulled open the front door, and stepped across the threshold, and felt, both of them, as if they were standing in the presence of the whole world, and with mankind's great and terrible eye on them alone. The eye of their Father seemed to be withdrawn, and gave them no encouragement. The warm sunny air of the street made them shiver. Their hearts quaked within them at the idea of taking one step farther.

"It cannot be, Hepzibah!—it is too late," said Clifford with deep sadness. "We are ghosts! We have no right among human beings,—no right anywhere but in this old house, which has a curse on it, and which, therefore, we are doomed to haunt! And, besides," he continued, with a fastidious sensibility, inalienably characteristic of the man, "it would not be fit nor beautiful to go! It is an ugly thought that I should be frightful to my fellow-beings, and that children would cling to their mothers' gowns at sight of me!"

They shrank back into the dusky passage-way, and closed the door. But, going up the staircase again, they found the whole interior of the house tenfold more dismal, and the air closer and heavier, for the glimpse and breath of freedom which they had just snatched. They could not flee; their jailer had but left the door ajar in mockery, and stood behind it to watch them stealing out. At the threshold, they felt his pitiless gripe upon them. For, what other dungeon is so dark as one's own heart! What jailer so inexorable as one's self!

But it would be no fair picture of Clifford's state of mind were we to represent him as continually or prevailingly wretched. On the contrary, there was no other man in the city, we are bold to affirm, of so much as half his years, who enjoyed so many lightsome and griefless moments as himself. He had no burden of care upon him; there were none of those questions and contingencies with the future to be settled which wear away all other lives, and render them not worth having by the very process of providing for their support. In this respect he was a child,—a child for the whole term of his existence, be it long or short. Indeed, his life seemed to be standing still at a period little in advance of childhood, and to cluster all his reminiscences about that epoch; just as, after the torpor of a heavy blow, the sufferer's reviving consciousness goes back to a moment considerably behind the accident that stupefied him. He sometimes told Phoebe and Hepzibah his dreams, in which he invariably played the part of a child, or a very young man.

So vivid were they, in his relation of them, that he once held a dispute with his sister as to the particular figure or print of a chintz morning-dress which he had seen their mother wear, in the dream of the preceding night. Hepzibah, piquing herself on a woman's accuracy in such matters, held it to be slightly different from what Clifford described; but, producing the very gown from an old trunk, it proved to be identical with his remembrance of it. Had Clifford, every time that he emerged out of dreams so lifelike, undergone the torture of transformation from a boy into an old and broken man, the daily recurrence of the shock would have been too much to bear. It would have caused an acute agony to thrill from the morning twilight, all the day through, until bedtime; and even then would have mingled a dull, inscrutable pain and pallid hue of misfortune with the visionary bloom and adolescence of his slumber. But the nightly moonshine interwove itself with the morning mist, and enveloped him as in a robe, which he hugged about his person, and seldom let realities pierce through; he was not often quite awake, but slept open-eyed, and perhaps fancied himself most dreaming then.

Thus, lingering always so near his childhood, he had sympathies with children, and kept his heart the fresher thereby, like a reservoir into which rivulets were pouring not far from the fountain-head. Though prevented, by a subtile sense of propriety, from desiring to associate with them, he loved few things better than to look out of the arched window and see a little girl driving her hoop along the sidewalk, or schoolboys at a game of ball. Their voices, also, were very pleasant to him, heard at a distance, all swarming and intermingling together as flies do in a sunny room.

Clifford would, doubtless, have been glad to share their sports. One afternoon he was seized with an irresistible desire to blow soap-bubbles; an amusement, as Hepzibah told Phoebe apart, that had been a favorite one with her brother when they were both children. Behold him, therefore, at the arched window, with an earthen pipe in his mouth! Behold him, with his gray hair, and a wan, unreal smile over his countenance, where still hovered a beautiful grace, which his worst enemy must have acknowledged to be spiritual and immortal, since it had survived so long! Behold him, scattering airy spheres abroad from the window into the street! Little impalpable worlds were those soap-bubbles, with the big world depicted, in hues bright as imagination, on the nothing of their surface. It was curious to see how the passers-by regarded these brilliant fantasies, as they came floating down, and made the dull atmosphere imaginative about them. Some stopped to gaze, and perhaps, carried a pleasant recollection of the bubbles onward as far as the street-corner; some looked angrily upward, as if poor Clifford wronged them by setting an image of beauty afloat so near their dusty pathway. A great many put out their fingers or their walking-sticks to touch, withal; and were perversely gratified, no doubt, when the bubble, with all its pictured earth and sky scene, vanished as if it had never been.

At length, just as an elderly gentleman of very dignified presence happened to be passing, a large bubble sailed majestically down, and burst right against his nose! He looked up,—at first with a stern, keen glance, which penetrated at once into the obscurity behind the arched window,—then with a smile which might be conceived as diffusing a dog-day sultriness for the space of several yards about him.

"Aha, Cousin Clifford!" cried Judge Pyncheon. "What! Still blowing soap-bubbles!"

The tone seemed as if meant to be kind and soothing, but yet had a bitterness of sarcasm in it. As for Clifford, an absolute palsy of fear came over him. Apart from any definite cause of dread which his past experience might have given him, he felt that native and original horror of the excellent Judge which is proper to a weak, delicate, and apprehensive character in the presence of massive strength. Strength is incomprehensible by weakness, and, therefore, the more terrible. There is no greater bugbear than a strong-willed relative in the circle of his own connections.

XII The Daguerreotypist

IT must not be supposed that the life of a personage naturally so active as Phoebe could be wholly confined within the precincts of the old Pyncheon House. Clifford's demands upon her time were usually satisfied, in those long days, considerably earlier than sunset. Quiet as his daily existence seemed, it nevertheless drained all the resources by which he lived. It was not physical exercise that overwearied him,—for except that he sometimes wrought a little with a hoe, or paced the garden-walk, or, in rainy weather, traversed a large unoccupied room,—it was his tendency to remain only too quiescent, as regarded any toil of the limbs and muscles. But, either there was a smouldering fire within him that consumed his vital energy, or the monotony that would have dragged itself with benumbing effect over a mind differently situated was no monotony to Clifford. Possibly, he was in a state of second growth and recovery, and was constantly assimilating nutriment for his spirit and intellect from sights, sounds, and events which passed as a perfect void to persons more practised with the world. As all is activity and vicissitude to the new mind of a child, so might it be, likewise, to a mind that had undergone a kind of new creation, after its long-suspended life.

Be the cause what it might, Clifford commonly retired to rest, thoroughly exhausted, while the sunbeams were still melting through his window-curtains, or were thrown with late lustre on the chamber wall. And while he thus slept early, as other children do, and dreamed of childhood, Phoebe was free to follow her own tastes for the remainder of the day and evening.

This was a freedom essential to the health even of a character so little susceptible of morbid influences as that of Phoebe. The old house, as we have already said, had both the dry-rot and the damp-rot in its walls; it was not good to breathe no other atmosphere than that. Hepzibah, though she had her valuable and redeeming traits, had grown to be a kind of lunatic by imprisoning herself so long in one place, with no other company than a single series of ideas, and but one affection, and one bitter sense of wrong. Clifford, the reader may perhaps imagine, was too inert to operate morally on his fellow-creatures, however intimate and exclusive their relations with him. But the sympathy or magnetism among human beings is more subtile and universal than we think; it exists, indeed, among different classes of organized life, and vibrates from one to another. A flower, for instance, as Phoebe herself observed, always began to droop sooner in Clifford's hand, or Hepzibah's, than in her own; and by the same law, converting her whole daily life into a flower fragrance for these two sickly spirits, the blooming girl must inevitably droop and fade much sooner than if worn on a younger and happier breast. Unless she had now and then indulged her brisk impulses, and breathed rural air in a suburban walk, or ocean breezes along the shore,—had occasionally obeyed the impulse of Nature, in New England girls, by attending a metaphysical or philosophical lecture, or viewing a seven-mile panorama, or listening to a concert,—had gone shopping about the city, ransacking entire depots of splendid merchandise, and bringing home a ribbon,—had employed, likewise, a little time to read the Bible in her chamber, and had stolen a little more to think of her mother and her native place—unless for such moral medicines as the above, we should soon have beheld our poor Phoebe grow thin and put on a bleached, unwholesome aspect, and assume strange, shy ways, prophetic of old-maidenhood and a cheerless future.

Even as it was, a change grew visible; a change partly to be regretted, although whatever charm it infringed upon was repaired by another, perhaps more precious. She was not so constantly gay, but had her moods of thought, which Clifford, on the whole, liked better than her former phase of unmingled cheerfulness; because now she understood him better and more delicately, and sometimes even interpreted him to himself. Her eyes looked larger, and darker, and deeper; so deep, at some silent moments, that they seemed like Artesian wells, down, down, into the infinite. She was less girlish than when we first beheld her alighting from the omnibus; less girlish, but more a woman.

The only youthful mind with which Phoebe had an opportunity of frequent intercourse was that of the daguerreotypist. Inevitably, by the pressure of the seclusion about them, they had been brought into habits of some familiarity. Had they met under different circumstances, neither of these young persons would have been likely to bestow much thought upon the other, unless, indeed, their extreme dissimilarity should have proved a principle of mutual attraction. Both, it is true, were characters proper to New England life, and possessing a common ground, therefore, in their more external developments; but as unlike, in their respective interiors, as if their native climes had been at world-wide distance. During the early part of their acquaintance, Phoebe had held back rather more than was customary with her frank and simple manners from Holgrave's not very marked advances. Nor was she yet satisfied that she knew him well, although they almost daily met and talked together, in a kind, friendly, and what seemed to be a familiar way.

The artist, in a desultory manner, had imparted to Phoebe something of his history. Young as he was, and had his career terminated at the point already attained, there had been enough of incident to fill, very creditably, an autobiographic volume. A romance on the plan of Gil Blas, adapted to American society and manners, would cease to be a romance. The experience of many individuals among us, who think it hardly worth the telling, would equal the vicissitudes of the Spaniard's earlier life; while their ultimate success, or the point whither they tend, may be incomparably higher than any that a novelist would imagine for his hero. Holgrave, as he told Phoebe somewhat proudly, could not boast of his origin, unless as being exceedingly humble, nor of his education, except that it had been the scantiest possible, and obtained by a few winter-months' attendance at a district school. Left early to his own guidance, he had begun to be self-dependent while yet a boy; and it was a condition aptly suited to his natural force of will. Though now but twenty-two years old (lacking some months, which are years in such a life), he had already been, first, a country schoolmaster; next, a salesman in a country store; and, either at the same time or afterwards, the political editor of a country newspaper. He had subsequently travelled New England and the Middle States, as a peddler, in the employment of a Connecticut manufactory of cologne-water and other essences. In an episodical way he had studied and practised dentistry, and with very flattering success, especially in many of the factory-towns along our inland streams. As a supernumerary official, of some kind or other, aboard a packet-ship, he had visited Europe, and found means, before his return, to see Italy, and part of France and Germany. At a later period he had spent some months in a community of Fourierists. Still more recently he had been a public lecturer on Mesmerism, for which science (as he assured Phoebe, and, indeed, satisfactorily proved, by putting Chanticleer, who happened to be scratching near by, to sleep) he had very remarkable endowments.

His present phase, as a daguerreotypist, was of no more importance in his own view, nor likely to be more permanent, than any of the preceding ones. It had been taken up with the careless alacrity of an adventurer, who had his bread to earn. It would be thrown aside as carelessly, whenever he should choose to earn his bread by some other equally digressive means. But what was most remarkable, and, perhaps, showed a more than common poise in the young man, was the fact that, amid all these personal vicissitudes, he had never lost his identity. Homeless as he had been,—continually changing his whereabout, and, therefore, responsible neither to public opinion nor to individuals,—putting off one exterior, and snatching up another, to be soon shifted for a third,—he had never violated the innermost man, but had carried his conscience along with him. It was impossible to know Holgrave without recognizing this to be the fact. Hepzibah had seen it. Phoebe soon saw it likewise, and gave him the sort of confidence which such a certainty inspires. She was startled, however, and sometimes repelled,—not by any doubt of his integrity to whatever law he acknowledged, but by a sense that his law differed from her own. He made her uneasy, and seemed to unsettle everything around her, by his lack of reverence for what was fixed, unless, at a moment's warning, it could establish its right to hold its ground.

Then, moreover, she scarcely thought him affectionate in his nature. He was too calm and cool an observer. Phoebe felt his eye, often; his heart, seldom or never. He took a certain kind of interest in Hepzibah and her brother, and Phoebe herself. He studied them attentively, and allowed no slightest circumstance of their individualities to escape him. He was ready to do them whatever good he might; but, after all, he never exactly made common cause with them, nor gave any reliable evidence that he loved them better in proportion as he knew them more. In his relations with them, he seemed to be in quest of mental food, not heart-sustenance. Phoebe could not conceive what interested him so much in her friends and herself, intellectually, since he cared nothing for them, or, comparatively, so little, as objects of human affection.

Always, in his interviews with Phoebe, the artist made especial inquiry as to the welfare of Clifford, whom, except at the Sunday festival, he seldom saw.

"Does he still seem happy?" he asked one day.

"As happy as a child," answered Phoebe; "but—like a child, too—very easily disturbed."

"How disturbed?" inquired Holgrave. "By things without, or by thoughts within?"

"I cannot see his thoughts! How should I?" replied Phoebe with simple piquancy. "Very often his humor changes without any reason that can be guessed at, just as a cloud comes over the sun. Latterly, since I have begun to know him better, I feel it to be not quite right to look closely into his moods. He has had such a great sorrow, that his heart is made all solemn and sacred by it. When he is cheerful,—when the sun shines into his mind,—then I venture to peep in, just as far as the light reaches, but no further. It is holy ground where the shadow falls!"

"How prettily you express this sentiment!" said the artist. "I can understand the feeling, without possessing it. Had I your opportunities, no scruples would prevent me from fathoming Clifford to the full depth of my plummet-line!"

"How strange that you should wish it!" remarked Phoebe involuntarily. "What is Cousin Clifford to you?"

"Oh, nothing,—of course, nothing!" answered Holgrave with a smile. "Only this is such an odd and incomprehensible world! The more I look at it, the more it puzzles me, and I begin to suspect that a man's bewilderment is the measure of his wisdom. Men and women, and children, too, are such strange creatures, that one never can be certain that he really knows them; nor ever guess what they have been from what he sees them to be now. Judge Pyncheon! Clifford! What a complex riddle—a complexity of complexities—do they present! It requires intuitive sympathy, like a young girl's, to solve it. A mere observer, like myself (who never have any intuitions, and am, at best, only subtile and acute), is pretty certain to go astray."

The artist now turned the conversation to themes less dark than that which they had touched upon. Phoebe and he were young together; nor had Holgrave, in his premature experience of life, wasted entirely that beautiful spirit of youth, which, gushing forth from one small heart and fancy, may diffuse itself over the universe, making it all as bright as on the first day of creation. Man's own youth is the world's youth; at least, he feels as if it were, and imagines that the earth's granite substance is something not yet hardened, and which he can mould into whatever shape he likes. So it was with Holgrave. He could talk sagely about the world's old age, but never actually believed what he said; he was a young man still, and therefore looked upon the world—that gray-bearded and wrinkled profligate, decrepit, without being venerable—as a tender stripling, capable of being improved into all that it ought to be, but scarcely yet had shown the remotest promise of becoming. He had that sense, or inward prophecy,—which a young man had better never have been born than not to have, and a mature man had better die at once than utterly to relinquish,—that we are not doomed to creep on forever in the old bad way, but that, this very now, there are the harbingers abroad of a golden era, to be accomplished in his own lifetime. It seemed to Holgrave,—as doubtless it has seemed to the hopeful of every century since the epoch of Adam's grandchildren,—that in this age, more than ever before, the moss-grown and rotten Past is to be torn down, and lifeless institutions to be thrust out of the way, and their dead corpses buried, and everything to begin anew.

As to the main point,—may we never live to doubt it!—as to the better centuries that are coming, the artist was surely right. His error lay in supposing that this age, more than any past or future one, is destined to see the tattered garments of Antiquity exchanged for a new suit, instead of gradually renewing themselves by patchwork; in applying his own little life-span as the measure of an interminable achievement; and, more than all, in fancying that it mattered anything to the great end in view whether he himself should contend for it or against it. Yet it was well for him to think so. This enthusiasm, infusing itself through the calmness of his character, and thus taking an aspect of settled thought and wisdom, would serve to keep his youth pure, and make his aspirations high. And when, with the years settling down more weightily upon him, his early faith should be modified by inevitable experience, it would be with no harsh and sudden revolution of his sentiments. He would still have faith in man's brightening destiny, and perhaps love him all the better, as he should recognize his helplessness in his own behalf; and the haughty faith, with which he began life, would be well bartered for a far humbler one at its close, in discerning that man's best directed effort accomplishes a kind of dream, while God is the sole worker of realities.

Holgrave had read very little, and that little in passing through the thoroughfare of life, where the mystic language of his books was necessarily mixed up with the babble of the multitude, so that both one and the other were apt to lose any sense that might have been properly their own. He considered himself a thinker, and was certainly of a thoughtful turn, but, with his own path to discover, had perhaps hardly yet reached the point where an educated man begins to think. The true value of his character lay in that deep consciousness of inward strength, which made all his past vicissitudes seem merely like a change of garments; in that enthusiasm, so quiet that he scarcely knew of its existence, but which gave a warmth to everything that he laid his hand on; in that personal ambition, hidden—from his own as well as other eyes—among his more generous impulses, but in which lurked a certain efficacy, that might solidify him from a theorist into the champion of some practicable cause. Altogether in his culture and want of culture,—in his crude, wild, and misty philosophy, and the practical experience that counteracted some of its tendencies; in his magnanimous zeal for man's welfare, and his recklessness of whatever the ages had established in man's behalf; in his faith, and in his infidelity; in what he had, and in what he lacked,—the artist might fitly enough stand forth as the representative of many compeers in his native land.

His career it would be difficult to prefigure. There appeared to be qualities in Holgrave, such as, in a country where everything is free to the hand that can grasp it, could hardly fail to put some of the world's prizes within his reach. But these matters are delightfully uncertain. At almost every step in life, we meet with young men of just about Holgrave's age, for whom we anticipate wonderful things, but of whom, even after much and careful inquiry, we never happen to hear another word. The effervescence of youth and passion, and the fresh gloss of the intellect and imagination, endow them with a false brilliancy, which makes fools of themselves and other people. Like certain chintzes, calicoes, and ginghams, they show finely in their first newness, but cannot stand the sun and rain, and assume a very sober aspect after washing-day.

But our business is with Holgrave as we find him on this particular afternoon, and in the arbor of the Pyncheon garden. In that point of view, it was a pleasant sight to behold this young man, with so much faith in himself, and so fair an appearance of admirable powers,—so little harmed, too, by the many tests that had tried his metal,—it was pleasant to see him in his kindly intercourse with Phoebe. Her thought had scarcely done him justice when it pronounced him cold; or, if so, he had grown warmer now. Without such purpose on her part, and unconsciously on his, she made the House of the Seven Gables like a home to him, and the garden a familiar precinct. With the insight on which he prided himself, he fancied that he could look through Phoebe, and all around her, and could read her off like a page of a child's story-book. But these transparent natures are often deceptive in their depth; those pebbles at the bottom of the fountain are farther from us than we think. Thus the artist, whatever he might judge of Phoebe's capacity, was beguiled, by some silent charm of hers, to talk freely of what he dreamed of doing in the world. He poured himself out as to another self. Very possibly, he forgot Phoebe while he talked to her, and was moved only by the inevitable tendency of thought, when rendered sympathetic by enthusiasm and emotion, to flow into the first safe reservoir which it finds. But, had you peeped at them through the chinks of the garden-fence, the young man's earnestness and heightened color might have led you to suppose that he was making love to the young girl!

At length, something was said by Holgrave that made it apposite for Phoebe to inquire what had first brought him acquainted with her cousin Hepzibah, and why he now chose to lodge in the desolate old Pyncheon House. Without directly answering her, he turned from the Future, which had heretofore been the theme of his discourse, and began to speak of the influences of the Past. One subject, indeed, is but the reverberation of the other.

"Shall we never, never get rid of this Past?" cried he, keeping up the earnest tone of his preceding conversation. "It lies upon the Present like a giant's dead body In fact, the case is just as if a young giant were compelled to waste all his strength in carrying about the corpse of the old giant, his grandfather, who died a long while ago, and only needs to be decently buried. Just think a moment, and it will startle you to see what slaves we are to bygone times,—to Death, if we give the matter the right word!"

"But I do not see it," observed Phoebe.

"For example, then," continued Holgrave: "a dead man, if he happens to have made a will, disposes of wealth no longer his own; or, if he die intestate, it is distributed in accordance with the notions of men much longer dead than he. A dead man sits on all our judgment-seats; and living judges do but search out and repeat his decisions. We read in dead men's books! We laugh at dead men's jokes, and cry at dead men's pathos! We are sick of dead men's diseases, physical and moral, and die of the same remedies with which dead doctors killed their patients! We worship the living Deity according to dead men's forms and creeds. Whatever we seek to do, of our own free motion, a dead man's icy hand obstructs us! Turn our eyes to what point we may, a dead man's white, immitigable face encounters them, and freezes our very heart! And we must be dead ourselves before we can begin to have our proper influence on our own world, which will then be no longer our world, but the world of another generation, with which we shall have no shadow of a right to interfere. I ought to have said, too, that we live in dead men's houses; as, for instance, in this of the Seven Gables!"

"And why not," said Phoebe, "so long as we can be comfortable in them?"

"But we shall live to see the day, I trust," went on the artist, "when no man shall build his house for posterity. Why should he? He might just as reasonably order a durable suit of clothes,—leather, or guttapercha, or whatever else lasts longest,—so that his great-grandchildren should have the benefit of them, and cut precisely the same figure in the world that he himself does. If each generation were allowed and expected to build its own houses, that single change, comparatively unimportant in itself, would imply almost every reform which society is now suffering for. I doubt whether even our public edifices—our capitols, statehouses, court-houses, city-hall, and churches,—ought to be built of such permanent materials as stone or brick. It were better that they should crumble to ruin once in twenty years, or thereabouts, as a hint to the people to examine into and reform the institutions which they symbolize."

"How you hate everything old!" said Phoebe in dismay. "It makes me dizzy to think of such a shifting world!"

"I certainly love nothing mouldy," answered Holgrave. "Now, this old Pyncheon House! Is it a wholesome place to live in, with its black shingles, and the green moss that shows how damp they are?—its dark, low-studded rooms—its grime and sordidness, which are the crystallization on its walls of the human breath, that has been drawn and exhaled here in discontent and anguish? The house ought to be purified with fire,—purified till only its ashes remain!"

"Then why do you live in it?" asked Phoebe, a little piqued.

"Oh, I am pursuing my studies here; not in books, however," replied Holgrave. "The house, in my view, is expressive of that odious and abominable Past, with all its bad influences, against which I have just been declaiming. I dwell in it for a while, that I may know the better how to hate it. By the bye, did you ever hear the story of Maule, the wizard, and what happened between him and your immeasurably great-grandfather?"

"Yes, indeed!" said Phoebe; "I heard it long ago, from my father, and two or three times from my cousin Hepzibah, in the month that I have been here. She seems to think that all the calamities of the Pyncheons began from that quarrel with the wizard, as you call him. And you, Mr. Holgrave look as if you thought so too! How singular that you should believe what is so very absurd, when you reject many things that are a great deal worthier of credit!"

"I do believe it," said the artist seriously; "not as a superstition, however, but as proved by unquestionable facts, and as exemplifying a theory. Now, see: under those seven gables, at which we now look up,—and which old Colonel Pyncheon meant to be the house of his descendants, in prosperity and happiness, down to an epoch far beyond the present,—under that roof, through a portion of three centuries, there has been perpetual remorse of conscience, a constantly defeated hope, strife amongst kindred, various misery, a strange form of death, dark suspicion, unspeakable disgrace,—all, or most of which calamity I have the means of tracing to the old Puritan's inordinate desire to plant and endow a family. To plant a family! This idea is at the bottom of most of the wrong and mischief which men do. The truth is, that, once in every half-century, at longest, a family should be merged into the great, obscure mass of humanity, and forget all about its ancestors. Human blood, in order to keep its freshness, should run in hidden streams, as the water of an aqueduct is conveyed in subterranean pipes. In the family existence of these Pyncheons, for instance,—forgive me Phoebe, but I cannot think of you as one of them,—in their brief New England pedigree, there has been time enough to infect them all with one kind of lunacy or another."

"You speak very unceremoniously of my kindred," said Phoebe, debating with herself whether she ought to take offence.

"I speak true thoughts to a true mind!" answered Holgrave, with a vehemence which Phoebe had not before witnessed in him. "The truth is as I say! Furthermore, the original perpetrator and father of this mischief appears to have perpetuated himself, and still walks the street,—at least, his very image, in mind and body,—with the fairest prospect of transmitting to posterity as rich and as wretched an inheritance as he has received! Do you remember the daguerreotype, and its resemblance to the old portrait?"

"How strangely in earnest you are!" exclaimed Phoebe, looking at him with surprise and perplexity; half alarmed and partly inclined to laugh. "You talk of the lunacy of the Pyncheons; is it contagious?"

"I understand you!" said the artist, coloring and laughing. "I believe I am a little mad. This subject has taken hold of my mind with the strangest tenacity of clutch since I have lodged in yonder old gable. As one method of throwing it off, I have put an incident of the Pyncheon family history, with which I happen to be acquainted, into the form of a legend, and mean to publish it in a magazine."

"Do you write for the magazines?" inquired Phoebe.

"Is it possible you did not know it?" cried Holgrave. "Well, such is literary fame! Yes. Miss Phoebe Pyncheon, among the multitude of my marvellous gifts I have that of writing stories; and my name has figured, I can assure you, on the covers of Graham and Godey, making as respectable an appearance, for aught I could see, as any of the canonized bead-roll with which it was associated. In the humorous line, I am thought to have a very pretty way with me; and as for pathos, I am as provocative of tears as an onion. But shall I read you my story?"

"Yes, if it is not very long," said Phoebe,—and added laughingly,—"nor very dull."

As this latter point was one which the daguerreotypist could not decide for himself, he forthwith produced his roll of manuscript, and, while the late sun-beams gilded the seven gables, began to read.

XIII Alice Pyncheon

THERE was a message brought, one day, from the worshipful Gervayse Pyncheon to young Matthew Maule, the carpenter, desiring his immediate presence at the House of the Seven Gables.

"And what does your master want with me?" said the carpenter to Mr. Pyncheon's black servant. "Does the house need any repair? Well it may, by this time; and no blame to my father who built it, neither! I was reading the old Colonel's tombstone, no longer ago than last Sabbath; and, reckoning from that date, the house has stood seven-and-thirty years. No wonder if there should be a job to do on the roof."

"Don't know what massa wants," answered Scipio. "The house is a berry good house, and old Colonel Pyncheon think so too, I reckon;—else why the old man haunt it so, and frighten a poor nigga, As he does?"

"Well, well, friend Scipio; let your master know that I'm coming," said the carpenter with a laugh. "For a fair, workmanlike job, he'll find me his man. And so the house is haunted, is it? It will take a tighter workman than I am to keep the spirits out of the Seven Gables. Even if the Colonel would be quiet," he added, muttering to himself, "my old grandfather, the wizard, will be pretty sure to stick to the Pyncheons as long as their walls hold together."

"What's that you mutter to yourself, Matthew Maule?" asked Scipio. "And what for do you look so black at me?"

"No matter, darky," said the carpenter. "Do you think nobody is to look black but yourself? Go tell your master I'm coming; and if you happen to see Mistress Alice, his daughter, give Matthew Maule's humble respects to her. She has brought a fair face from Italy,—fair, and gentle, and proud,—has that same Alice Pyncheon!"

"He talk of Mistress Alice!" cried Scipio, as he returned from his errand. "The low carpenter-man! He no business so much as to look at her a great way off!"

This young Matthew Maule, the carpenter, it must be observed, was a person little understood, and not very generally liked, in the town where he resided; not that anything could be alleged against his integrity, or his skill and diligence in the handicraft which he exercised. The aversion (as it might justly be called) with which many persons regarded him was partly the result of his own character and deportment, and partly an inheritance.

He was the grandson of a former Matthew Maule, one of the early settlers of the town, and who had been a famous and terrible wizard in his day. This old reprobate was one of the sufferers when Cotton Mather, and his brother ministers, and the learned judges, and other wise men, and Sir William Phipps, the sagacious governor, made such laudable efforts to weaken the great enemy of souls, by sending a multitude of his adherents up the rocky pathway of Gallows Hill. Since those days, no doubt, it had grown to be suspected that, in consequence of an unfortunate overdoing of a work praiseworthy in itself, the proceedings against the witches had proved far less acceptable to the Beneficent Father than to that very Arch Enemy whom they were intended to distress and utterly overwhelm. It is not the less certain, however, that awe and terror brooded over the memories of those who died for this horrible crime of witchcraft. Their graves, in the crevices of the rocks, were supposed to be incapable of retaining the occupants who had been so hastily thrust into them. Old Matthew Maule, especially, was known to have as little hesitation or difficulty in rising out of his grave as an ordinary man in getting out of bed, and was as often seen at midnight as living people at noonday. This pestilent wizard (in whom his just punishment seemed to have wrought no manner of amendment) had an inveterate habit of haunting a certain mansion, styled the House of the Seven Gables, against the owner of which he pretended to hold an unsettled claim for ground-rent. The ghost, it appears,—with the pertinacity which was one of his distinguishing characteristics while alive,—insisted that he was the rightful proprietor of the site upon which the house stood. His terms were, that either the aforesaid ground-rent, from the day when the cellar began to be dug, should be paid down, or the mansion itself given up; else he, the ghostly creditor, would have his finger in all the affairs of the Pyncheons, and make everything go wrong with them, though it should be a thousand years after his death. It was a wild story, perhaps, but seemed not altogether so incredible to those who could remember what an inflexibly obstinate old fellow this wizard Maule had been.

Now, the wizard's grandson, the young Matthew Maule of our story, was popularly supposed to have inherited some of his ancestor's questionable traits. It is wonderful how many absurdities were promulgated in reference to the young man. He was fabled, for example, to have a strange power of getting into people's dreams, and regulating matters there according to his own fancy, pretty much like the stage-manager of a theatre. There was a great deal of talk among the neighbors, particularly the petticoated ones, about what they called the witchcraft of Maule's eye. Some said that he could look into people's minds; others, that, by the marvellous power of this eye, he could draw people into his own mind, or send them, if he pleased, to do errands to his grandfather, in the spiritual world; others, again, that it was what is termed an Evil Eye, and possessed the valuable faculty of blighting corn, and drying children into mummies with the heartburn. But, after all, what worked most to the young carpenter's disadvantage was, first, the reserve and sternness of his natural disposition, and next, the fact of his not being a church-communicant, and the suspicion of his holding heretical tenets in matters of religion and polity.

After receiving Mr. Pyncheon's message, the carpenter merely tarried to finish a small job, which he happened to have in hand, and then took his way towards the House of the Seven Gables. This noted edifice, though its style might be getting a little out of fashion, was still as respectable a family residence as that of any gentleman in town. The present owner, Gervayse Pyncheon, was said to have contracted a dislike to the house, in consequence of a shock to his sensibility, in early childhood, from the sudden death of his grandfather. In the very act of running to climb Colonel Pyncheon's knee, the boy had discovered the old Puritan to be a corpse. On arriving at manhood, Mr. Pyncheon had visited England, where he married a lady of fortune, and had subsequently spent many years, partly in the mother country, and partly in various cities on the continent of Europe. During this period, the family mansion had been consigned to the charge of a kinsman, who was allowed to make it his home for the time being, in consideration of keeping the premises in thorough repair. So faithfully had this contract been fulfilled, that now, as the carpenter approached the house, his practised eye could detect nothing to criticise in its condition. The peaks of the seven gables rose up sharply; the shingled roof looked thoroughly water-tight; and the glittering plaster-work entirely covered the exterior walls, and sparkled in the October sun, as if it had been new only a week ago.

The house had that pleasant aspect of life which is like the cheery expression of comfortable activity in the human countenance. You could see, at once, that there was the stir of a large family within it. A huge load of oak-wood was passing through the gateway, towards the outbuildings in the rear; the fat cook—or probably it might be the housekeeper—stood at the side door, bargaining for some turkeys and poultry which a countryman had brought for sale. Now and then a maid-servant, neatly dressed, and now the shining sable face of a slave, might be seen bustling across the windows, in the lower part of the house. At an open window of a room in the second story, hanging over some pots of beautiful and delicate flowers,—exotics, but which had never known a more genial sunshine than that of the New England autumn,—was the figure of a young lady, an exotic, like the flowers, and beautiful and delicate as they. Her presence imparted an indescribable grace and faint witchery to the whole edifice. In other respects, it was a substantial, jolly-looking mansion, and seemed fit to be the residence of a patriarch, who might establish his own headquarters in the front gable and assign one of the remainder to each of his six children, while the great chimney in the centre should symbolize the old fellow's hospitable heart, which kept them all warm, and made a great whole of the seven smaller ones.

There was a vertical sundial on the front gable; and as the carpenter passed beneath it, he looked up and noted the hour.

"Three o'clock!" said he to himself. "My father told me that dial was put up only an hour before the old Colonel's death. How truly it has kept time these seven-and-thirty years past! The shadow creeps and creeps, and is always looking over the shoulder of the sunshine!"

It might have befitted a craftsman, like Matthew Maule, on being sent for to a gentleman's house, to go to the back door, where servants and work-people were usually admitted; or at least to the side entrance, where the better class of tradesmen made application. But the carpenter had a great deal of pride and stiffness in his nature; and, at this moment, moreover, his heart was bitter with the sense of hereditary wrong, because he considered the great Pyncheon House to be standing on soil which should have been his own. On this very site, beside a spring of delicious water, his grandfather had felled the pine-trees and built a cottage, in which children had been born to him; and it was only from a dead man's stiffened fingers that Colonel Pyncheon had wrested away the title-deeds. So young Maule went straight to the principal entrance, beneath a portal of carved oak, and gave such a peal of the iron knocker that you would have imagined the stern old wizard himself to be standing at the threshold.

Black Scipio answered the summons in a prodigious, hurry; but showed the whites of his eyes in amazement on beholding only the carpenter.

"Lord-a-mercy, what a great man he be, this carpenter fellow!" mumbled Scipio, down in his throat. "Anybody think he beat on the door with his biggest hammer!"

"Here I am!" said Maule sternly. "Show me the way to your master's parlor."

As he stept into the house, a note of sweet and melancholy music thrilled and vibrated along the passage-way, proceeding from one of the rooms above stairs. It was the harpsichord which Alice Pyncheon had brought with her from beyond the sea. The fair Alice bestowed most of her maiden leisure between flowers and music, although the former were apt to droop, and the melodies were often sad. She was of foreign education, and could not take kindly to the New England modes of life, in which nothing beautiful had ever been developed.

As Mr. Pyncheon had been impatiently awaiting Maule's arrival, black Scipio, of course, lost no time in ushering the carpenter into his master's presence. The room in which this gentleman sat was a parlor of moderate size, looking out upon the garden of the house, and having its windows partly shadowed by the foliage of fruit-trees. It was Mr. Pyncheon's peculiar apartment, and was provided with furniture, in an elegant and costly style, principally from Paris; the floor (which was unusual at that day) being covered with a carpet, so skilfully and richly wrought that it seemed to glow as with living flowers. In one corner stood a marble woman, to whom her own beauty was the sole and sufficient garment. Some pictures—that looked old, and had a mellow tinge diffused through all their artful splendor—hung on the walls. Near the fireplace was a large and very beautiful cabinet of ebony, inlaid with ivory; a piece of antique furniture, which Mr. Pyncheon had bought in Venice, and which he used as the treasure-place for medals, ancient coins, and whatever small and valuable curiosities he had picked up on his travels. Through all this variety of decoration, however, the room showed its original characteristics; its low stud, its cross-beam, its chimney-piece, with the old-fashioned Dutch tiles; so that it was the emblem of a mind industriously stored with foreign ideas, and elaborated into artificial refinement, but neither larger, nor, in its proper self, more elegant than before.

There were two objects that appeared rather out of place in this very handsomely furnished room. One was a large map, or surveyor's plan, of a tract of land, which looked as if it had been drawn a good many years ago, and was now dingy with smoke, and soiled, here and there, with the touch of fingers. The other was a portrait of a stern old man, in a Puritan garb, painted roughly, but with a bold effect, and a remarkably strong expression of character.

At a small table, before a fire of English sea-coal, sat Mr. Pyncheon, sipping coffee, which had grown to be a very favorite beverage with him in France. He was a middle-aged and really handsome man, with a wig flowing down upon his shoulders; his coat was of blue velvet, with lace on the borders and at the button-holes; and the firelight glistened on the spacious breadth of his waistcoat, which was flowered all over with gold. On the entrance of Scipio, ushering in the carpenter, Mr. Pyncheon turned partly round, but resumed his former position, and proceeded deliberately to finish his cup of coffee, without immediate notice of the guest whom he had summoned to his presence. It was not that he intended any rudeness or improper neglect,—which, indeed, he would have blushed to be guilty of,—but it never occurred to him that a person in Maule's station had a claim on his courtesy, or would trouble himself about it one way or the other.

The carpenter, however, stepped at once to the hearth, and turned himself about, so as to look Mr. Pyncheon in the face.

"You sent for me," said he. "Be pleased to explain your business, that I may go back to my own affairs."

"Ah! excuse me," said Mr. Pyncheon quietly. "I did not mean to tax your time without a recompense. Your name, I think, is Maule,—Thomas or Matthew Maule,—a son or grandson of the builder of this house?"

"Matthew Maule," replied the carpenter,—"son of him who built the house,—grandson of the rightful proprietor of the soil."

"I know the dispute to which you allude," observed Mr. Pyncheon with undisturbed equanimity. "I am well aware that my grandfather was compelled to resort to a suit at law, in order to establish his claim to the foundation-site of this edifice. We will not, if you please, renew the discussion. The matter was settled at the time, and by the competent authorities,—equitably, it is to be presumed,—and, at all events, irrevocably. Yet, singularly enough, there is an incidental reference to this very subject in what I am now about to say to you. And this same inveterate grudge,—excuse me, I mean no offence,—this irritability, which you have just shown, is not entirely aside from the matter."

"If you can find anything for your purpose, Mr. Pyncheon," said the carpenter, "in a man's natural resentment for the wrongs done to his blood, you are welcome to it."

"I take you at your word, Goodman Maule," said the owner of the Seven Gables, with a smile, "and will proceed to suggest a mode in which your hereditary resentments—justifiable or otherwise—may have had a bearing on my affairs. You have heard, I suppose, that the Pyncheon family, ever since my grandfather's days, have been prosecuting a still unsettled claim to a very large extent of territory at the Eastward?"

"Often," replied Maule,—and it is said that a smile came over his face,—"very often,—from my father!"

"This claim," continued Mr. Pyncheon, after pausing a moment, as if to consider what the carpenter's smile might mean, "appeared to be on the very verge of a settlement and full allowance, at the period of my grandfather's decease. It was well known, to those in his confidence, that he anticipated neither difficulty nor delay. Now, Colonel Pyncheon, I need hardly say, was a practical man, well acquainted with public and private business, and not at all the person to cherish ill-founded hopes, or to attempt the following out of an impracticable scheme. It is obvious to conclude, therefore, that he had grounds, not apparent to his heirs, for his confident anticipation of success in the matter of this Eastern claim. In a word, I believe,—and my legal advisers coincide in the belief, which, moreover, is authorized, to a certain extent, by the family traditions,—that my grandfather was in possession of some deed, or other document, essential to this claim, but which has since disappeared."

"Very likely," said Matthew Maule,—and again, it is said, there was a dark smile on his face,—"but what can a poor carpenter have to do with the grand affairs of the Pyncheon family?"

"Perhaps nothing," returned Mr. Pyncheon, "possibly much!"

Here ensued a great many words between Matthew Maule and the proprietor of the Seven Gables, on the subject which the latter had thus broached. It seems (although Mr. Pyncheon had some hesitation in referring to stories so exceedingly absurd in their aspect) that the popular belief pointed to some mysterious connection and dependence, existing between the family of the Maules and these vast unrealized possessions of the Pyncheons. It was an ordinary saying that the old wizard, hanged though he was, had obtained the best end of the bargain in his contest with Colonel Pyncheon; inasmuch as he had got possession of the great Eastern claim, in exchange for an acre or two of garden-ground. A very aged woman, recently dead, had often used the metaphorical expression, in her fireside talk, that miles and miles of the Pyncheon lands had been shovelled into Maule's grave; which, by the bye, was but a very shallow nook, between two rocks, near the summit of Gallows Hill. Again, when the lawyers were making inquiry for the missing document, it was a by-word that it would never be found, unless in the wizard's skeleton hand. So much weight had the shrewd lawyers assigned to these fables, that (but Mr. Pyncheon did not see fit to inform the carpenter of the fact) they had secretly caused the wizard's grave to be searched. Nothing was discovered, however, except that, unaccountably, the right hand of the skeleton was gone.

Now, what was unquestionably important, a portion of these popular rumors could be traced, though rather doubtfully and indistinctly, to chance words and obscure hints of the executed wizard's son, and the father of this present Matthew Maule. And here Mr. Pyncheon could bring an item of his own personal evidence into play. Though but a child at the time, he either remembered or fancied that Matthew's father had had some job to perform on the day before, or possibly the very morning of the Colonel's decease, in the private room where he and the carpenter were at this moment talking. Certain papers belonging to Colonel Pyncheon, as his grandson distinctly recollected, had been spread out on the table.

Matthew Maule understood the insinuated suspicion.

"My father," he said,—but still there was that dark smile, making a riddle of his countenance,—"my father was an honester man than the bloody old Colonel! Not to get his rights back again would he have carried off one of those papers!"

"I shall not bandy words with you," observed the foreign-bred Mr. Pyncheon, with haughty composure. "Nor will it become me to resent any rudeness towards either my grandfather or myself. A gentleman, before seeking intercourse with a person of your station and habits, will first consider whether the urgency of the end may compensate for the disagreeableness of the means. It does so in the present instance."

He then renewed the conversation, and made great pecuniary offers to the carpenter, in case the latter should give information leading to the discovery of the lost document, and the consequent success of the Eastern claim. For a long time Matthew Maule is said to have turned a cold ear to these propositions. At last, however, with a strange kind of laugh, he inquired whether Mr. Pyncheon would make over to him the old wizard's homestead-ground, together with the House of the Seven Gables, now standing on it, in requital of the documentary evidence so urgently required.

The wild, chimney-corner legend (which, without copying all its extravagances, my narrative essentially follows) here gives an account of some very strange behavior on the part of Colonel Pyncheon's portrait. This picture, it must be understood, was supposed to be so intimately connected with the fate of the house, and so magically built into its walls, that, if once it should be removed, that very instant the whole edifice would come thundering down in a heap of dusty ruin. All through the foregoing conversation between Mr. Pyncheon and the carpenter, the portrait had been frowning, clenching its fist, and giving many such proofs of excessive discomposure, but without attracting the notice of either of the two colloquists. And finally, at Matthew Maule's audacious suggestion of a transfer of the seven-gabled structure, the ghostly portrait is averred to have lost all patience, and to have shown itself on the point of descending bodily from its frame. But such incredible incidents are merely to be mentioned aside.

"Give up this house!" exclaimed Mr. Pyncheon, in amazement at the proposal. "Were I to do so, my grandfather would not rest quiet in his grave!"

"He never has, if all stories are true," remarked the carpenter composedly. "But that matter concerns his grandson more than it does Matthew Maule. I have no other terms to propose."

Impossible as he at first thought it to comply with Maule's conditions, still, on a second glance, Mr. Pyncheon was of opinion that they might at least be made matter of discussion. He himself had no personal attachment for the house, nor any pleasant associations connected with his childish residence in it. On the contrary, after seven-and-thirty years, the presence of his dead grandfather seemed still to pervade it, as on that morning when the affrighted boy had beheld him, with so ghastly an aspect, stiffening in his chair. His long abode in foreign parts, moreover, and familiarity with many of the castles and ancestral halls of England, and the marble palaces of Italy, had caused him to look contemptuously at the House of the Seven Gables, whether in point of splendor or convenience. It was a mansion exceedingly inadequate to the style of living which it would be incumbent on Mr. Pyncheon to support, after realizing his territorial rights. His steward might deign to occupy it, but never, certainly, the great landed proprietor himself. In the event of success, indeed, it was his purpose to return to England; nor, to say the truth, would he recently have quitted that more congenial home, had not his own fortune, as well as his deceased wife's, begun to give symptoms of exhaustion. The Eastern claim once fairly settled, and put upon the firm basis of actual possession, Mr. Pyncheon's property—to be measured by miles, not acres—would be worth an earldom, and would reasonably entitle him to solicit, or enable him to purchase, that elevated dignity from the British monarch. Lord Pyncheon!—or the Earl of Waldo!—how could such a magnate be expected to contract his grandeur within the pitiful compass of seven shingled gables?

In short, on an enlarged view of the business, the carpenter's terms appeared so ridiculously easy that Mr. Pyncheon could scarcely forbear laughing in his face. He was quite ashamed, after the foregoing reflections, to propose any diminution of so moderate a recompense for the immense service to be rendered.

"I consent to your proposition, Maule!" cried he. "Put me in possession of the document essential to establish my rights, and the House of the Seven Gables is your own!"

According to some versions of the story, a regular contract to the above effect was drawn up by a lawyer, and signed and sealed in the presence of witnesses. Others say that Matthew Maule was contented with a private written agreement, in which Mr. Pyncheon pledged his honor and integrity to the fulfillment of the terms concluded upon. The gentleman then ordered wine, which he and the carpenter drank together, in confirmation of their bargain. During the whole preceding discussion and subsequent formalities, the old Puritan's portrait seems to have persisted in its shadowy gestures of disapproval; but without effect, except that, as Mr. Pyncheon set down the emptied glass, he thought he beheld his grandfather frown.

"This sherry is too potent a wine for me; it has affected my brain already," he observed, after a somewhat startled look at the picture. "On returning to Europe, I shall confine myself to the more delicate vintages of Italy and France, the best of which will not bear transportation."

"My Lord Pyncheon may drink what wine he will, and wherever he pleases," replied the carpenter, as if he had been privy to Mr. Pyncheon's ambitious projects. "But first, sir, if you desire tidings of this lost document, I must crave the favor of a little talk with your fair daughter Alice."

"You are mad, Maule!" exclaimed Mr. Pyncheon haughtily; and now, at last, there was anger mixed up with his pride. "What can my daughter have to do with a business like this?"

Indeed, at this new demand on the carpenter's part, the proprietor of the Seven Gables was even more thunder-struck than at the cool proposition to surrender his house. There was, at least, an assignable motive for the first stipulation; there appeared to be none whatever for the last. Nevertheless, Matthew Maule sturdily insisted on the young lady being summoned, and even gave her father to understand, in a mysterious kind of explanation,—which made the matter considerably darker than it looked before,—that the only chance of acquiring the requisite knowledge was through the clear, crystal medium of a pure and virgin intelligence, like that of the fair Alice. Not to encumber our story with Mr. Pyncheon's scruples, whether of conscience, pride, or fatherly affection, he at length ordered his daughter to be called. He well knew that she was in her chamber, and engaged in no occupation that could not readily be laid aside; for, as it happened, ever since Alice's name had been spoken, both her father and the carpenter had heard the sad and sweet music of her harpsichord, and the airier melancholy of her accompanying voice.

So Alice Pyncheon was summoned, and appeared. A portrait of this young lady, painted by a Venetian artist, and left by her father in England, is said to have fallen into the hands of the present Duke of Devonshire, and to be now preserved at Chatsworth; not on account of any associations with the original, but for its value as a picture, and the high character of beauty in the countenance. If ever there was a lady born, and set apart from the world's vulgar mass by a certain gentle and cold stateliness, it was this very Alice Pyncheon. Yet there was the womanly mixture in her; the tenderness, or, at least, the tender capabilities. For the sake of that redeeming quality, a man of generous nature would have forgiven all her pride, and have been content, almost, to lie down in her path, and let Alice set her slender foot upon his heart. All that he would have required was simply the acknowledgment that he was indeed a man, and a fellow-being, moulded of the same elements as she.

As Alice came into the room, her eyes fell upon the carpenter, who was standing near its centre, clad in green woollen jacket, a pair of loose breeches, open at the knees, and with a long pocket for his rule, the end of which protruded; it was as proper a mark of the artisan's calling as Mr. Pyncheon's full-dress sword of that gentleman's aristocratic pretensions. A glow of artistic approval brightened over Alice Pyncheon's face; she was struck with admiration—which she made no attempt to conceal—of the remarkable comeliness, strength, and energy of Maule's figure. But that admiring glance (which most other men, perhaps, would have cherished as a sweet recollection all through life) the carpenter never forgave. It must have been the devil himself that made Maule so subtile in his preception.

"Does the girl look at me as if I were a brute beast?" thought he, setting his teeth. "She shall know whether I have a human spirit; and the worse for her, if it prove stronger than her own!"

"My father, you sent for me," said Alice, in her sweet and harp-like voice. "But, if you have business with this young man, pray let me go again. You know I do not love this room, in spite of that Claude, with which you try to bring back sunny recollections."

"Stay a moment, young lady, if you please!" said Matthew Maule. "My business with your father is over. With yourself, it is now to begin!"

Alice looked towards her father, in surprise and inquiry.

"Yes, Alice," said Mr. Pyncheon, with some disturbance and confusion. "This young man—his name is Matthew Maule—professes, so far as I can understand him, to be able to discover, through your means, a certain paper or parchment, which was missing long before your birth. The importance of the document in question renders it advisable to neglect no possible, even if improbable, method of regaining it. You will therefore oblige me, my dear Alice, by answering this person's inquiries, and complying with his lawful and reasonable requests, so far as they may appear to have the aforesaid object in view. As I shall remain in the room, you need apprehend no rude nor unbecoming deportment, on the young man's part; and, at your slightest wish, of course, the investigation, or whatever we may call it, shall immediately be broken off."

"Mistress Alice Pyncheon," remarked Matthew Maule, with the utmost deference, but yet a half-hidden sarcasm in his look and tone, "will no doubt feel herself quite safe in her father's presence, and under his all-sufficient protection."

"I certainly shall entertain no manner of apprehension, with my father at hand," said Alice with maidenly dignity. "Neither do I conceive that a lady, while true to herself, can have aught to fear from whomsoever, or in any circumstances!"

Poor Alice! By what unhappy impulse did she thus put herself at once on terms of defiance against a strength which she could not estimate?

"Then, Mistress Alice," said Matthew Maule, handing a chair,—gracefully enough, for a craftsman, "will it please you only to sit down, and do me the favor (though altogether beyond a poor carpenter's deserts) to fix your eyes on mine!"

Alice complied, She was very proud. Setting aside all advantages of rank, this fair girl deemed herself conscious of a power—combined of beauty, high, unsullied purity, and the preservative force of womanhood—that could make her sphere impenetrable, unless betrayed by treachery within. She instinctively knew, it may be, that some sinister or evil potency was now striving to pass her barriers; nor would she decline the contest. So Alice put woman's might against man's might; a match not often equal on the part of woman.

Her father meanwhile had turned away, and seemed absorbed in the contemplation of a landscape by Claude, where a shadowy and sun-streaked vista penetrated so remotely into an ancient wood, that it would have been no wonder if his fancy had lost itself in the picture's bewildering depths. But, in truth, the picture was no more to him at that moment than the blank wall against which it hung. His mind was haunted with the many and strange tales which he had heard, attributing mysterious if not supernatural endowments to these Maules, as well the grandson here present as his two immediate ancestors. Mr. Pyncheon's long residence abroad, and intercourse with men of wit and fashion,—courtiers, worldings, and free-thinkers,—had done much towards obliterating the grim Puritan superstitions, which no man of New England birth at that early period could entirely escape. But, on the other hand, had not a whole community believed Maule's grandfather to be a wizard? Had not the crime been proved? Had not the wizard died for it? Had he not bequeathed a legacy of hatred against the Pyncheons to this only grandson, who, as it appeared, was now about to exercise a subtle influence over the daughter of his enemy's house? Might not this influence be the same that was called witchcraft?

Turning half around, he caught a glimpse of Maule's figure in the looking-glass. At some paces from Alice, with his arms uplifted in the air, the carpenter made a gesture as if directing downward a slow, ponderous, and invisible weight upon the maiden.

"Stay, Maule!" exclaimed Mr. Pyncheon, stepping forward. "I forbid your proceeding further!"

"Pray, my dear father, do not interrupt the young man," said Alice, without changing her position. "His efforts, I assure you, will prove very harmless."

Again Mr. Pyncheon turned his eyes towards the Claude. It was then his daughter's will, in opposition to his own, that the experiment should be fully tried. Henceforth, therefore, he did but consent, not urge it. And was it not for her sake far more than for his own that he desired its success? That lost parchment once restored, the beautiful Alice Pyncheon, with the rich dowry which he could then bestow, might wed an English duke or a German reigning-prince, instead of some New England clergyman or lawyer! At the thought, the ambitious father almost consented, in his heart, that, if the devil's power were needed to the accomplishment of this great object, Maule might evoke him. Alice's own purity would be her safeguard.

With his mind full of imaginary magnificence, Mr. Pyncheon heard a half-uttered exclamation from his daughter. It was very faint and low; so indistinct that there seemed but half a will to shape out the words, and too undefined a purport to be intelligible. Yet it was a call for help!—his conscience never doubted it;—and, little more than a whisper to his ear, it was a dismal shriek, and long reechoed so, in the region round his heart! But this time the father did not turn.

After a further interval, Maule spoke.

"Behold your daughter," said he.

Mr. Pyncheon came hastily forward. The carpenter was standing erect in front of Alice's chair, and pointing his finger towards the maiden with an expression of triumphant power, the limits of which could not be defined, as, indeed, its scope stretched vaguely towards the unseen and the infinite. Alice sat in an attitude of profound repose, with the long brown lashes drooping over her eyes.

"There she is!" said the carpenter. "Speak to her!"

"Alice! My daughter!" exclaimed Mr. Pyncheon. "My own Alice!"

She did not stir.

"Louder!" said Maule, smiling.

"Alice! Awake!" cried her father. "It troubles me to see you thus! Awake!"

He spoke loudly, with terror in his voice, and close to that delicate ear which had always been so sensitive to every discord. But the sound evidently reached her not. It is indescribable what a sense of remote, dim, unattainable distance betwixt himself and Alice was impressed on the father by this impossibility of reaching her with his voice.

"Best touch her!" said Matthew Maule "Shake the girl, and roughly, too! My hands are hardened with too much use of axe, saw, and plane,—else I might help you!"

Mr. Pyncheon took her hand, and pressed it with the earnestness of startled emotion. He kissed her, with so great a heart-throb in the kiss, that he thought she must needs feel it. Then, in a gust of anger at her insensibility, he shook her maiden form with a violence which, the next moment, it affrighted him to remember. He withdrew his encircling arms, and Alice—whose figure, though flexible, had been wholly impassive—relapsed into the same attitude as before these attempts to arouse her. Maule having shifted his position, her face was turned towards him slightly, but with what seemed to be a reference of her very slumber to his guidance.

Then it was a strange sight to behold how the man of conventionalities shook the powder out of his periwig; how the reserved and stately gentleman forgot his dignity; how the gold-embroidered waistcoat flickered and glistened in the firelight with the convulsion of rage, terror, and sorrow in the human heart that was beating under it.

"Villain!" cried Mr. Pyncheon, shaking his clenched fist at Maule. "You and the fiend together have robbed me of my daughter. Give her back, spawn of the old wizard, or you shall climb Gallows Hill in your grandfather's footsteps!"

"Softly, Mr. Pyncheon!" said the carpenter with scornful composure. "Softly, an' it please your worship, else you will spoil those rich lace-ruffles at your wrists! Is it my crime if you have sold your daughter for the mere hope of getting a sheet of yellow parchment into your clutch? There sits Mistress Alice quietly asleep. Now let Matthew Maule try whether she be as proud as the carpenter found her awhile since."

He spoke, and Alice responded, with a soft, subdued, inward acquiescence, and a bending of her form towards him, like the flame of a torch when it indicates a gentle draught of air. He beckoned with his hand, and, rising from her chair,—blindly, but undoubtingly, as tending to her sure and inevitable centre,—the proud Alice approached him. He waved her back, and, retreating, Alice sank again into her seat.

"She is mine!" said Matthew Maule. "Mine, by the right of the strongest spirit!"

In the further progress of the legend, there is a long, grotesque, and occasionally awe-striking account of the carpenter's incantations (if so they are to be called), with a view of discovering the lost document. It appears to have been his object to convert the mind of Alice into a kind of telescopic medium, through which Mr. Pyncheon and himself might obtain a glimpse into the spiritual world. He succeeded, accordingly, in holding an imperfect sort of intercourse, at one remove, with the departed personages in whose custody the so much valued secret had been carried beyond the precincts of earth. During her trance, Alice described three figures as being present to her spiritualized perception. One was an aged, dignified, stern-looking gentleman, clad as for a solemn festival in grave and costly attire, but with a great blood-stain on his richly wrought band; the second, an aged man, meanly dressed, with a dark and malign countenance, and a broken halter about his neck; the third, a person not so advanced in life as the former two, but beyond the middle age, wearing a coarse woollen tunic and leather breeches, and with a carpenter's rule sticking out of his side pocket. These three visionary characters possessed a mutual knowledge of the missing document. One of them, in truth,—it was he with the blood-stain on his band,—seemed, unless his gestures were misunderstood, to hold the parchment in his immediate keeping, but was prevented by his two partners in the mystery from disburdening himself of the trust. Finally, when he showed a purpose of shouting forth the secret loudly enough to be heard from his own sphere into that of mortals, his companions struggled with him, and pressed their hands over his mouth; and forthwith—whether that he were choked by it, or that the secret itself was of a crimson hue—there was a fresh flow of blood upon his band. Upon this, the two meanly dressed figures mocked and jeered at the much-abashed old dignitary, and pointed their fingers at the stain.

At this juncture, Maule turned to Mr. Pyncheon.

"It will never be allowed," said he. "The custody of this secret, that would so enrich his heirs, makes part of your grandfather's retribution. He must choke with it until it is no longer of any value. And keep you the House of the Seven Gables! It is too dear bought an inheritance, and too heavy with the curse upon it, to be shifted yet awhile from the Colonel's posterity."

Mr. Pyncheon tried to speak, but—what with fear and passion—could make only a gurgling murmur in his throat. The carpenter smiled.

"Aha, worshipful sir!—so you have old Maule's blood to drink!" said he jeeringly.

"Fiend in man's shape! why dost thou keep dominion over my child?" cried Mr. Pyncheon, when his choked utterance could make way. "Give me back my daughter. Then go thy ways; and may we never meet again!"

"Your daughter!" said Matthew Maule. "Why, she is fairly mine! Nevertheless, not to be too hard with fair Mistress Alice, I will leave her in your keeping;

but I do not warrant you that she shall never have occasion to remember Maule, the carpenter."

He waved his hands with an upward motion; and, after a few repetitions of similar gestures, the beautiful Alice Pyncheon awoke from her strange trance. She awoke without the slightest recollection of her visionary experience; but as one losing herself in a momentary reverie, and returning to the consciousness of actual life, in almost as brief an interval as the down-sinking flame of the hearth should quiver again up the chimney. On recognizing Matthew Maule, she assumed an air of somewhat cold but gentle dignity, the rather, as there was a certain peculiar smile on the carpenter's visage that stirred the native pride of the fair Alice. So ended, for that time, the quest for the lost title-deed of the Pyncheon territory at the Eastward; nor, though often subsequently renewed, has it ever yet befallen a Pyncheon to set his eye upon that parchment.

But, alas for the beautiful, the gentle, yet too haughty Alice! A power that she little dreamed of had laid its grasp upon her maiden soul. A will, most unlike her own, constrained her to do its grotesque and fantastic bidding. Her father as it proved, had martyred his poor child to an inordinate desire for measuring his land by miles instead of acres. And, therefore, while Alice Pyncheon lived, she was Maule's slave, in a bondage more humiliating, a thousand-fold, than that which binds its chain around the body. Seated by his humble fireside, Maule had but to wave his hand; and, wherever the proud lady chanced to be,—whether in her chamber, or entertaining her father's stately guests, or worshipping at church,—whatever her place or occupation, her spirit passed from beneath her own control, and bowed itself to Maule. "Alice, laugh!"—the carpenter, beside his hearth, would say; or perhaps intensely will it, without a spoken word. And, even were it prayer-time, or at a funeral, Alice must break into wild laughter. "Alice, be sad!"—and, at the instant, down would come her tears, quenching all the mirth of those around her like sudden rain upon a bonfire. "Alice, dance."—and dance she would, not in such court-like measures as she had learned abroad, but some high-paced jig, or hop-skip rigadoon, befitting the brisk lasses at a rustic merry-making. It seemed to be Maule's impulse, not to ruin Alice, nor to visit her with any black or gigantic mischief, which would have crowned her sorrows with the grace of tragedy, but to wreak a low, ungenerous scorn upon her. Thus all the dignity of life was lost. She felt herself too much abased, and longed to change natures with some worm!

One evening, at a bridal party (but not her own; for, so lost from self-control, she would have deemed it sin to marry), poor Alice was beckoned forth by her unseen despot, and constrained, in her gossamer white dress and satin slippers, to hasten along the street to the mean dwelling of a laboring-man. There was laughter and good cheer within; for Matthew Maule, that night, was to wed the laborer's daughter, and had summoned proud Alice Pyncheon to wait upon his bride. And so she did; and when the twain were one, Alice awoke out of her enchanted sleep. Yet, no longer proud,—humbly, and with a smile all steeped in sadness,—she kissed Maule's wife, and went her way. It was an inclement night; the southeast wind drove the mingled snow and rain into her thinly sheltered bosom; her satin slippers were wet through and through, as she trod the muddy sidewalks. The next day a cold; soon, a settled cough; anon, a hectic cheek, a wasted form, that sat beside the harpsichord, and filled the house with music! Music in which a strain of the heavenly choristers was echoed! Oh; joy! For Alice had borne her last humiliation! Oh, greater joy! For Alice was penitent of her one earthly sin, and proud no more!

The Pyncheons made a great funeral for Alice. The kith and kin were there, and the whole respectability of the town besides. But, last in the procession, came Matthew Maule, gnashing his teeth, as if he would have bitten his own heart in twain,—the darkest and wofullest man that ever walked behind a corpse! He meant to humble Alice, not to kill her; but he had taken a woman's delicate soul into his rude gripe, to play with—and she was dead!

XIV Phoebe's Good-Bye

HOLGRAVE, plunging into his tale with the energy and absorption natural to a young author, had given a good deal of action to the parts capable of being developed and exemplified in that manner. He now observed that a certain remarkable drowsiness (wholly unlike that with which the reader possibly feels himself affected) had been flung over the senses of his auditress. It was the effect, unquestionably, of the mystic gesticulations by which he had sought to bring bodily before Phoebe's perception the figure of the mesmerizing carpenter. With the lids drooping over her eyes,—now lifted for an instant, and drawn down again as with leaden weights,—she leaned slightly towards him, and seemed almost to regulate her breath by his. Holgrave gazed at her, as he rolled up his manuscript, and recognized an incipient stage of that curious psychological condition which, as he had himself told Phoebe, he possessed more than an ordinary faculty of producing. A veil was beginning to be muffled about her, in which she could behold only him, and live only in his thoughts and emotions. His glance, as he fastened it on the young girl, grew involuntarily more concentrated; in his attitude there was the consciousness of power, investing his hardly mature figure with a dignity that did not belong to its physical manifestation. It was evident, that, with but one wave of his hand and a corresponding effort of his will, he could complete his mastery over Phoebe's yet free and virgin spirit: he could establish an influence over this good, pure, and simple child, as dangerous, and perhaps as disastrous, as that which the carpenter of his legend had acquired and exercised over the ill-fated Alice.

To a disposition like Holgrave's, at once speculative and active, there is no temptation so great as the opportunity of acquiring empire over the human spirit; nor any idea more seductive to a young man than to become the arbiter of a young girl's destiny. Let us, therefore,—whatever his defects of nature and education, and in spite of his scorn for creeds and institutions,—concede to the daguerreotypist the rare and high quality of reverence for another's individuality. Let us allow him integrity, also, forever after to be confided in; since he forbade himself to twine that one link more which might have rendered his spell over Phoebe indissoluble.

He made a slight gesture upward with his hand.

"You really mortify me, my dear Miss Phoebe!" he exclaimed, smiling half-sarcastically at her. "My poor story, it is but too evident, will never do for Godey or Graham! Only think of your falling asleep at what I hoped the newspaper critics would pronounce a most brilliant, powerful, imaginative, pathetic, and original winding up! Well, the manuscript must serve to light lamps with;—if, indeed, being so imbued with my gentle dulness, it is any longer capable of flame!"

"Me asleep! How can you say so?" answered Phoebe, as unconscious of the crisis through which she had passed as an infant of the precipice to the verge of which it has rolled. "No, no! I consider myself as having been very attentive; and, though I don't remember the incidents quite distinctly, yet I have an impression of a vast deal of trouble and calamity,—so, no doubt, the story will prove exceedingly attractive."

By this time the sun had gone down, and was tinting the clouds towards the zenith with those bright hues which are not seen there until some time after sunset, and when the horizon has quite lost its richer brilliancy. The moon, too, which had long been climbing overhead, and unobtrusively melting its disk into the azure,—like an ambitious demagogue, who hides his aspiring purpose by assuming the prevalent hue of popular sentiment,—now began to shine out, broad and oval, in its middle pathway. These silvery beams were already powerful enough to change the character of the lingering daylight. They softened and embellished the aspect of the old house; although the shadows fell deeper into the angles of its many gables, and lay brooding under the projecting story, and within the half-open door. With the lapse of every moment, the garden grew more picturesque; the fruit-trees, shrubbery, and flower-bushes had a dark obscurity among them. The commonplace characteristics—which, at noontide, it seemed to have taken a century of sordid life to accumulate—were now transfigured by a charm of romance. A hundred mysterious years were whispering among the leaves, whenever the slight sea-breeze found its way thither and stirred them. Through the foliage that roofed the little summer-house the moonlight flickered to and fro, and fell silvery white on the dark floor, the table, and the circular bench, with a continual shift and play, according as the chinks and wayward crevices among the twigs admitted or shut out the glimmer.

So sweetly cool was the atmosphere, after all the feverish day, that the summer eve might be fancied as sprinkling dews and liquid moonlight, with a dash of icy temper in them, out of a silver vase. Here and there, a few drops of this freshness were scattered on a human heart, and gave it youth again, and sympathy with the eternal youth of nature. The artist chanced to be one on whom the reviving influence fell. It made him feel—what he sometimes almost forgot, thrust so early as he had been into the rude struggle of man with man—how youthful he still was.

"It seems to me," he observed, "that I never watched the coming of so beautiful an eve, and never felt anything so very much like happiness as at this moment. After all, what a good world we live in! How good, and beautiful! How young it is, too, with nothing really rotten or age-worn in it! This old house, for example, which sometimes has positively oppressed my breath with its smell of decaying timber! And this garden, where the black mould always clings to my spade, as if I were a sexton delving in a graveyard! Could I keep the feeling that now possesses me, the garden would every day be virgin soil, with the earth's first freshness in the flavor of its beans and squashes; and the house!—it would be like a bower in Eden, blossoming with the earliest roses that God ever made. Moonlight, and the sentiment in man's heart responsive to it, are the greatest of renovators and reformers. And all other reform and renovation, I suppose, will prove to be no better than moonshine!"

"I have been happier than I am now; at least, much gayer," said Phoebe thoughtfully. "Yet I am sensible of a great charm in this brightening moonlight; and I love to watch how the day, tired as it is, lags away reluctantly, and hates to be called yesterday so soon. I never cared much about moonlight before. What is there, I wonder, so beautiful in it, to-night?"

"And you have never felt it before?" inquired the artist, looking earnestly at the girl through the twilight.

"Never," answered Phoebe; "and life does not look the same, now that I have felt it so. It seems as if I had looked at everything, hitherto, in broad daylight, or else in the ruddy light of a cheerful fire, glimmering and dancing through a room. Ah, poor me!" she added, with a half-melancholy laugh. "I shall never be so merry as before I knew Cousin Hepzibah and poor Cousin Clifford. I have grown a great deal older, in this little time. Older, and, I hope, wiser, and,—not exactly sadder,—but, certainly, with not half so much lightness in my spirits! I have given them my sunshine, and have been glad to give it; but, of course, I cannot both give and keep it. They are welcome, notwithstanding!"

"You have lost nothing, Phoebe, worth keeping, nor which it was possible to keep," said Holgrave after a pause. "Our first youth is of no value; for we are never conscious of it until after it is gone. But sometimes—always, I suspect, unless one is exceedingly unfortunate—there comes a sense of second youth, gushing out of the heart's joy at being in love; or, possibly, it may come to crown some other grand festival in life, if any other such there be. This bemoaning of one's self (as you do now) over the first, careless, shallow gayety of youth departed, and this profound happiness at youth regained,—so much deeper and richer than that we lost,—are essential to the soul's development. In some cases, the two states come almost simultaneously, and mingle the sadness and the rapture in one mysterious emotion."

"I hardly think I understand you," said Phoebe.

"No wonder," replied Holgrave, smiling; "for I have told you a secret which I hardly began to know before I found myself giving it utterance. Remember it, however; and when the truth becomes clear to you, then think of this moonlight scene!"

"It is entirely moonlight now, except only a little flush of faint crimson, upward from the west, between those buildings," remarked Phoebe. "I must go in. Cousin Hepzibah is not quick at figures, and will give herself a headache over the day's accounts, unless I help her."

But Holgrave detained her a little longer.

"Miss Hepzibah tells me," observed he, "that you return to the country in a few days."

"Yes, but only for a little while," answered Phoebe; "for I look upon this as my present home. I go to make a few arrangements, and to take a more deliberate leave of my mother and friends. It is pleasant to live where one is much desired and very useful; and I think I may have the satisfaction of feeling myself so here."

"You surely may, and more than you imagine," said the artist. "Whatever health, comfort, and natural life exists in the house is embodied in your person. These blessings came along with you, and will vanish when you leave the threshold. Miss Hepzibah, by secluding herself from society, has lost all true relation with it, and is, in fact, dead; although she galvanizes herself into a semblance of life, and stands behind her counter, afflicting the world with a greatly-to-be-deprecated scowl. Your poor cousin Clifford is another dead and long-buried person, on whom the governor and council have wrought a necromantic miracle. I should not wonder if he were to crumble away, some morning, after you are gone, and nothing be seen of him more, except a heap of dust. Miss Hepzibah, at any rate, will lose what little flexibility she has. They both exist by you."

"I should be very sorry to think so," answered Phoebe gravely. "But it is true that my small abilities were precisely what they needed; and I have a real interest in their welfare,—an odd kind of motherly sentiment,—which I wish you would not laugh at! And let me tell you frankly, Mr. Holgrave, I am sometimes puzzled to know whether you wish them well or ill."

"Undoubtedly," said the daguerreotypist, "I do feel an interest in this antiquated, poverty-stricken old maiden lady, and this degraded and shattered gentleman,—this abortive lover of the beautiful. A kindly interest, too, helpless old children that they are! But you have no conception what a different kind of heart mine is from your own. It is not my impulse, as regards these two individuals, either to help or hinder; but to look on, to analyze, to explain matters to myself, and to comprehend the drama which, for almost two hundred years, has been dragging its slow length over the ground where you and I now tread. If permitted to witness the close, I doubt not to derive a moral satisfaction from it, go matters how they may. There is a conviction within me that the end draws nigh. But, though Providence sent you hither to help, and sends me only as a privileged and meet spectator, I pledge myself to lend these unfortunate beings whatever aid I can!"

"I wish you would speak more plainly," cried Phoebe, perplexed and displeased; "and, above all, that you would feel more like a Christian and a human being! How is it possible to see people in distress without desiring, more than anything else, to help and comfort them? You talk as if this old house were a theatre; and you seem to look at Hepzibah's and Clifford's misfortunes, and those of generations before them, as a tragedy, such as I have seen acted in the hall of a country hotel, only the present one appears to be played exclusively for your amusement. I do not like this. The play costs the performers too much, and the audience is too cold-hearted."

"You are severe," said Holgrave, compelled to recognize a degree of truth in the piquant sketch of his own mood.

"And then," continued Phoebe, "what can you mean by your conviction, which you tell me of, that the end is drawing near? Do you know of any new trouble hanging over my poor relatives? If so, tell me at once, and I will not leave them!"

"Forgive me, Phoebe!" said the daguerreotypist, holding out his hand, to which the girl was constrained to yield her own. "I am somewhat of a mystic, it must be confessed. The tendency is in my blood, together with the faculty of mesmerism, which might have brought me to Gallows Hill, in the good old times of witch-craft. Believe me, if I were really aware of any secret, the disclosure of which would benefit your friends,—who are my own friends, likewise,—you should learn it before we part. But I have no such knowledge."

"You hold something back!" said Phoebe.

"Nothing,—no secrets but my own," answered Holgrave. "I can perceive, in-deed, that Judge Pyncheon still keeps his eye on Clifford, in whose ruin he had so large a share. His motives and intentions, however are a mystery to me. He is a determined and relentless man, with the genuine character of an inquisitor; and had he any object to gain by putting Clifford to the rack, I verily believe that he would wrench his joints from their sockets, in order to accomplish it. But, so wealthy and eminent as he is,—so powerful in his own strength, and in the sup-port of society on all sides,—what can Judge Pyncheon have to hope or fear from the imbecile, branded, half-torpid Clifford?"

"Yet," urged Phoebe, "you did speak as if misfortune were impending!"

"Oh, that was because I am morbid!" replied the artist. "My mind has a twist aside, like almost everybody's mind, except your own. Moreover, it is so strange to find myself an inmate of this old Pyncheon House, and sitting in this old gar-den—(hark, how Maule's well is murmuring!)—that, were it only for this one circumstance, I cannot help fancying that Destiny is arranging its fifth act for a catastrophe."

"There!" cried Phoebe with renewed vexation; for she was by nature as hostile to mystery as the sunshine to a dark corner. "You puzzle me more than ever!"

"Then let us part friends!" said Holgrave, pressing her hand. "Or, if not friends, let us part before you entirely hate me. You, who love everybody else in the world!"

"Good-by, then," said Phoebe frankly. "I do not mean to be angry a great while, and should be sorry to have you think so. There has Cousin Hepzibah been standing in the shadow of the doorway, this quarter of an hour past! She thinks I stay too long in the damp garden. So, good-night, and good-by."

On the second morning thereafter, Phoebe might have been seen, in her straw bonnet, with a shawl on one arm and a little carpet-bag on the other, bidding adieu to Hepzibah and Cousin Clifford. She was to take a seat in the next train of cars, which would transport her to within half a dozen miles of her country village.

The tears were in Phoebe's eyes; a smile, dewy with affectionate regret, was glimmering around her pleasant mouth. She wondered how it came to pass, that her life of a few weeks, here in this heavy-hearted old mansion, had taken such hold of her, and so melted into her associations, as now to seem a more important centre-point of remembrance than all which had gone before. How had Hepzibah—grim, silent, and irresponsive to her overflow of cordial sentiment—contrived to win so much love? And Clifford,—in his abortive decay, with the mystery of fearful crime upon him, and the close prison-atmosphere yet lurking in his breath,—how had he transformed himself into the simplest child, whom Phoebe felt bound to watch over, and be, as it were, the providence of his unconsidered hours! Everything, at that instant of farewell, stood out prominently to her view. Look where she would, lay her hand on what she might, the object responded to her consciousness, as if a moist human heart were in it.

She peeped from the window into the garden, and felt herself more regretful at leaving this spot of black earth, vitiated with such an age-long growth of weeds, than joyful at the idea of again scenting her pine forests and fresh clover-fields. She called Chanticleer, his two wives, and the venerable chicken, and threw them some crumbs of bread from the breakfast-table. These being hastily gobbled up, the chicken spread its wings, and alighted close by Phoebe on the window-sill, where it looked gravely into her face and vented its emotions in a croak. Phoebe bade it be a good old chicken during her absence, and promised to bring it a little bag of buckwheat.

"Ah, Phoebe!" remarked Hepzibah, "you do not smile so naturally as when you came to us! Then, the smile chose to shine out; now, you choose it should. It is well that you are going back, for a little while, into your native air. There has been too much weight on your spirits. The house is too gloomy and lonesome; the shop is full of vexations; and as for me, I have no faculty of making things look brighter than they are. Dear Clifford has been your only comfort!"

"Come hither, Phoebe," suddenly cried her cousin Clifford, who had said very little all the morning. "Close!—closer!—and look me in the face!"

Phoebe put one of her small hands on each elbow of his chair, and leaned her face towards him, so that he might peruse it as carefully as he would. It is probable that the latent emotions of this parting hour had revived, in some degree, his bedimmed and enfeebled faculties. At any rate, Phoebe soon felt that, if not the profound insight of a seer, yet a more than feminine delicacy of appreciation, was making her heart the subject of its regard. A moment before, she had known nothing which she would have sought to hide. Now, as if some secret were hinted to her own consciousness through the medium of another's perception, she was fain to let her eyelids droop beneath Clifford's gaze. A blush, too,—the redder, because she strove hard to keep it down,—ascended bigger and higher, in a tide of fitful progress, until even her brow was all suffused with it.

"It is enough, Phoebe," said Clifford, with a melancholy smile. "When I first saw you, you were the prettiest little maiden in the world; and now you have deepened into beauty. Girlhood has passed into womanhood; the bud is a bloom! Go, now—I feel lonelier than I did."

Phoebe took leave of the desolate couple, and passed through the shop, twinkling her eyelids to shake off a dew-drop; for—considering how brief her absence was to be, and therefore the folly of being cast down about it—she would not so far acknowledge her tears as to dry them with her handkerchief. On the doorstep, she met the little urchin whose marvellous feats of gastronomy have been recorded in the earlier pages of our narrative. She took from the window some specimen or other of natural history,—her eyes being too dim with moisture to inform her accurately whether it was a rabbit or a hippopotamus,—put it into the child's hand as a parting gift, and went her way. Old Uncle Venner was just coming out of his door, with a wood-horse and saw on his shoulder; and, trudging along the street, he scrupled not to keep company with Phoebe, so far as their paths lay together; nor, in spite of his patched coat and rusty beaver, and the curious fashion of his tow-cloth trousers, could she find it in her heart to outwalk him.

"We shall miss you, next Sabbath afternoon," observed the street philosopher. "It is unaccountable how little while it takes some folks to grow just as natural to a man as his own breath; and, begging your pardon, Miss Phoebe (though there can be no offence in an old man's saying it), that's just what you've grown to me! My years have been a great many, and your life is but just beginning; and yet, you are somehow as familiar to me as if I had found you at my mother's door, and you had blossomed, like a running vine, all along my pathway since. Come back soon, or I shall be gone to my farm; for I begin to find these wood-sawing jobs a little too tough for my back-ache."

"Very soon, Uncle Venner," replied Phoebe.

"And let it be all the sooner, Phoebe, for the sake of those poor souls yonder," continued her companion. "They can never do without you, now,—never, Phoebe; never—no more than if one of God's angels had been living with them, and making their dismal house pleasant and comfortable! Don't it seem to you they'd be in a sad case, if, some pleasant summer morning like this, the angel should spread his wings, and fly to the place he came from? Well, just so they feel, now that you're going home by the railroad! They can't bear it, Miss Phoebe; so be sure to come back!"

"I am no angel, Uncle Venner," said Phoebe, smiling, as she offered him her hand at the street-corner. "But, I suppose, people never feel so much like angels as when they are doing what little good they may. So I shall certainly come back!"

Thus parted the old man and the rosy girl; and Phoebe took the wings of the morning, and was soon flitting almost as rapidly away as if endowed with the aerial locomotion of the angels to whom Uncle Venner had so graciously compared her.

XV The Scowl and Smile

SEVERAL days passed over the Seven Gables, heavily and drearily enough. In fact (not to attribute the whole gloom of sky and earth to the one inauspicious circumstance of Phoebe's departure), an easterly storm had set in, and indefatigably apply itself to the task of making the black roof and walls of the old house look more cheerless than ever before. Yet was the outside not half so cheerless as the interior. Poor Clifford was cut off, at once, from all his scanty resources of enjoyment. Phoebe was not there; nor did the sunshine fall upon the floor. The garden, with its muddy walks, and the chill, dripping foliage of its summer-house, was an image to be shuddered at. Nothing flourished in the cold, moist, pitiless atmosphere, drifting with the brackish scud of sea-breezes, except the moss along the joints of the shingle-roof, and the great bunch of weeds, that had lately been suffering from drought, in the angle between the two front gables.

As for Hepzibah, she seemed not merely possessed with the east wind, but to be, in her very person, only another phase of this gray and sullen spell of weather; the East-Wind itself, grim and disconsolate, in a rusty black silk gown, and with a turban of cloud-wreaths on its head. The custom of the shop fell off, because a story got abroad that she soured her small beer and other damageable commodities, by scowling on them. It is, perhaps, true that the public had something reasonably to complain of in her deportment; but towards Clifford she was neither ill-tempered nor unkind, nor felt less warmth of heart than always, had it been possible to make it reach him. The inutility of her best efforts, however, palsied the poor old gentlewoman. She could do little else than sit silently in a corner of the room, when the wet pear-tree branches, sweeping across the small windows, created a noonday dusk, which Hepzibah unconsciously darkened with her woebegone aspect. It was no fault of Hepzibah's. Everything—even the old chairs and tables, that had known what weather was for three or four such lifetimes as her own—looked as damp and chill as if the present were their worst experience. The picture of the Puritan Colonel shivered on the wall. The house itself shivered, from every attic of its seven gables down to the great kitchen fireplace, which served all the better as an emblem of the mansion's heart, because, though built for warmth, it was now so comfortless and empty.

Hepzibah attempted to enliven matters by a fire in the parlor. But the storm demon kept watch above, and, whenever a flame was kindled, drove the smoke back again, choking the chimney's sooty throat with its own breath. Nevertheless, during four days of this miserable storm, Clifford wrapt himself in an old cloak, and occupied his customary chair. On the morning of the fifth, when summoned to breakfast, he responded only by a broken-hearted murmur, expressive of a determination not to leave his bed. His sister made no attempt to change his purpose. In fact, entirely as she loved him, Hepzibah could hardly have borne any longer the wretched duty—so impracticable by her few and rigid faculties—of seeking pastime for a still sensitive, but ruined mind, critical and fastidious, without force or volition. It was at least something short of positive despair, that today she might sit shivering alone, and not suffer continually a new grief, and unreasonable pang of remorse, at every fitful sigh of her fellow sufferer.

But Clifford, it seemed, though he did not make his appearance below stairs, had, after all, bestirred himself in quest of amusement. In the course of the forenoon, Hepzibah heard a note of music, which (there being no other tuneful contrivance in the House of the Seven Gables) she knew must proceed from Alice Pyncheon's harpsichord. She was aware that Clifford, in his youth, had possessed a cultivated taste for music, and a considerable degree of skill in its practice. It was difficult, however, to conceive of his retaining an accomplishment to which daily exercise is so essential, in the measure indicated by the sweet, airy, and delicate, though most melancholy strain, that now stole upon her ear. Nor was it less marvellous that the long-silent instrument should be capable of so much melody. Hepzibah involuntarily thought of the ghostly harmonies, prelusive of death in the family, which were attributed to the legendary Alice. But it was, perhaps, proof of the agency of other than spiritual fingers, that, after a few touches, the chords seemed to snap asunder with their own vibrations, and the music ceased.

But a harsher sound succeeded to the mysterious notes; nor was the easterly day fated to pass without an event sufficient in itself to poison, for Hepzibah and Clifford, the balmiest air that ever brought the humming-birds along with it. The final echoes of Alice Pyncheon's performance (or Clifford's, if his we must consider it) were driven away by no less vulgar a dissonance than the ringing of the shop-bell. A foot was heard scraping itself on the threshold, and thence somewhat ponderously stepping on the floor. Hepzibah delayed a moment, while muffling herself in a faded shawl, which had been her defensive armor in a forty years' warfare against the east wind. A characteristic sound, however,—neither a cough nor a hem, but a kind of rumbling and reverberating spasm in somebody's capacious depth of chest;—impelled her to hurry forward, with that aspect of fierce faint-heartedness so common to women in cases of perilous emergency. Few of her sex, on such occasions, have ever looked so terrible as our poor scowling Hepzibah. But the visitor quietly closed the shop-door behind him, stood up his umbrella against the counter, and turned a visage of composed benignity, to meet the alarm and anger which his appearance had excited.

Hepzibah's presentiment had not deceived her. It was no other than Judge Pyncheon, who, after in vain trying the front door, had now effected his entrance into the shop.

"How do you do, Cousin Hepzibah?—and how does this most inclement weather affect our poor Clifford?" began the Judge; and wonderful it seemed, indeed, that the easterly storm was not put to shame, or, at any rate, a little mollimollified, by the genial benevolence of his smile. "I could not rest without calling to ask, once more, whether I can in any manner promote his comfort, or your own."

"You can do nothing," said Hepzibah, controlling her agitation as well as she could. "I devote myself to Clifford. He has every comfort which his situation admits of."

"But allow me to suggest, dear cousin," rejoined the Judge, "you err,—in all affection and kindness, no doubt, and with the very best intentions,—but you do err, nevertheless, in keeping your brother so secluded. Why insulate him thus from all sympathy and kindness? Clifford, alas! has had too much of solitude. Now let him try society,—the society, that is to say, of kindred and old friends. Let me, for instance, but see Clifford, and I will answer for the good effect of the interview."

"You cannot see him," answered Hepzibah. "Clifford has kept his bed since yesterday."

"What! How! Is he ill?" exclaimed Judge Pyncheon, starting with what seemed to be angry alarm; for the very frown of the old Puritan darkened through the room as he spoke. "Nay, then, I must and will see him! What if he should die?"

"He is in no danger of death," said Hepzibah,—and added, with bitterness that she could repress no longer, "none; unless he shall be persecuted to death, now, by the same man who long ago attempted it!"

"Cousin Hepzibah," said the Judge, with an impressive earnestness of manner, which grew even to tearful pathos as he proceeded, "is it possible that you do not perceive how unjust, how unkind, how unchristian, is this constant, this long-continued bitterness against me, for a part which I was constrained by duty and conscience, by the force of law, and at my own peril, to act? What did I do, in detriment to Clifford, which it was possible to leave undone? How could you, his sister,—if, for your never-ending sorrow, as it has been for mine, you had known what I did,—have, shown greater tenderness? And do you think, cousin, that it has cost me no pang?—that it has left no anguish in my bosom, from that day to this, amidst all the prosperity with which Heaven has blessed me?—or that I do not now rejoice, when it is deemed consistent with the dues of public justice and the welfare of society that this dear kinsman, this early friend, this nature so delicately and beautifully constituted,—so unfortunate, let us pronounce him, and forbear to say, so guilty,—that our own Clifford, in fine, should be given back to life, and its possibilities of enjoyment? Ah, you little know me, Cousin Hepzibah! You little know this heart! It now throbs at the thought of meeting him! There lives not the human being (except yourself,—and you not more than I) who has shed so many tears for Clifford's calamity. You behold some of them now. There is none who would so delight to promote his happiness! Try me, Hepzibah!—try me, Cousin!—try the man whom you have treated as your enemy and

Clifford's!—try Jaffrey Pyncheon, and you shall find him true, to the heart's core!"

"In the name of Heaven," cried Hepzibah, provoked only to intenser indignation by this outgush of the inestimable tenderness of a stern nature,—"in God's name, whom you insult, and whose power I could almost question, since he hears you utter so many false words without palsying your tongue,—give over, I beseech you, this loathsome pretence of affection for your victim! You hate him! Say so, like a man! You cherish, at this moment, some black purpose against him in your heart! Speak it out, at once!—or, if you hope so to promote it better, hide it till you can triumph in its success! But never speak again of your love for my poor brother. I cannot bear it! It will drive me beyond a woman's decency! It will drive me mad! Forbear! Not another word! It will make me spurn you!"

For once, Hepzibah's wrath had given her courage. She had spoken. But, after all, was this unconquerable distrust of Judge Pyncheon's integrity, and this utter denial, apparently, of his claim to stand in the ring of human sympathies,—were they founded in any just perception of his character, or merely the offspring of a woman's unreasonable prejudice, deduced from nothing?

The Judge, beyond all question, was a man of eminent respectability. The church acknowledged it; the state acknowledged it. It was denied by nobody. In all the very extensive sphere of those who knew him, whether in his public or private capacities, there was not an individual—except Hepzibah, and some lawless mystic, like the daguerreotypist, and, possibly, a few political opponents—who would have dreamed of seriously disputing his claim to a high and honorable place in the world's regard. Nor (we must do him the further justice to say) did Judge Pyncheon himself, probably, entertain many or very frequent doubts, that his enviable reputation accorded with his deserts. His conscience, therefore, usually considered the surest witness to a man's integrity,—his conscience, unless it might be for the little space of five minutes in the twenty-four hours, or, now and then, some black day in the whole year's circle,—his conscience bore an accordant testimony with the world's laudatory voice. And yet, strong as this evidence may seem to be, we should hesitate to peril our own conscience on the assertion, that the Judge and the consenting world were right, and that poor Hepzibah with her solitary prejudice was wrong. Hidden from mankind,—forgotten by himself, or buried so deeply under a sculptured and ornamented pile of ostentatious deeds that his daily life could take no note of it,—there may have lurked some evil and unsightly thing. Nay, we could almost venture to say, further, that a daily guilt might have been acted by him, continually renewed, and reddening forth afresh, like the miraculous blood-stain of a murder, without his necessarily and at every moment being aware of it.

Men of strong minds, great force of character, and a hard texture of the sensibilities, are very capable of falling into mistakes of this kind. They are ordinarily men to whom forms are of paramount importance. Their field of action lies among the external phenomena of life. They possess vast ability in grasping, and arranging, and appropriating to themselves, the big, heavy, solid unrealities, such as gold, landed estate, offices of trust and emolument, and public honors. With these materials, and with deeds of goodly aspect, done in the public eye, an individual of this class builds up, as it were, a tall and stately edifice, which, in the view of other people, and ultimately in his own view, is no other than the man's character, or the man himself. Behold, therefore, a palace! Its splendid halls and suites of spacious apartments are floored with a mosaic-work of costly marbles; its windows, the whole height of each room, admit the sunshine through the most transparent of plate-glass; its high cornices are gilded, and its ceilings gorgeously painted; and a lofty dome—through which, from the central pavement, you may gaze up to the sky, as with no obstructing medium between—surmounts the whole. With what fairer and nobler emblem could any man desire to shadow forth his character? Ah! but in some low and obscure nook,—some narrow closet on the ground-floor, shut, locked and bolted, and the key flung away,—or beneath the marble pavement, in a stagnant water-puddle, with the richest pattern of mosaic-work above,—may lie a corpse, half decayed, and still decaying, and diffusing its death-scent all through the palace! The inhabitant will not be conscious of it, for it has long been his daily breath! Neither will the visitors, for they smell only the rich odors which the master sedulously scatters through the palace, and the incense which they bring, and delight to burn before him! Now and then, perchance, comes in a seer, before whose sadly gifted eye the whole structure melts into thin air, leaving only the hidden nook, the bolted closet, with the cobwebs festooned over its forgotten door, or the deadly hole under the pavement, and the decaying corpse within. Here, then, we are to seek the true emblem of the man's character, and of the deed that gives whatever reality it possesses to his life. And, beneath the show of a marble palace, that pool of stagnant water, foul with many impurities, and, perhaps, tinged with blood,—that secret abomination, above which, possibly, he may say his prayers, without remembering it,—is this man's miserable soul!

To apply this train of remark somewhat more closely to Judge Pyncheon. We might say (without in the least imputing crime to a personage of his eminent respectability) that there was enough of splendid rubbish in his life to cover up and paralyze a more active and subtile conscience than the Judge was ever troubled with. The purity of his judicial character, while on the bench; the faithfulness of his public service in subsequent capacities; his devotedness to his party, and the rigid consistency with which he had adhered to its principles, or, at all events, kept pace with its organized movements; his remarkable zeal as president of a Bible society; his unimpeachable integrity as treasurer of a widow's and orphan's fund; his benefits to horticulture, by producing two much esteemed varieties of the pear and to agriculture, through the agency of the famous Pyncheon bull; the cleanliness of his moral deportment, for a great many years past; the severity with which he had frowned upon, and finally cast off, an expensive and dissipated son, delaying forgiveness until within the final quarter of an hour of the young man's life; his prayers at morning and eventide, and graces at meal-time; his efforts in furtherance of the temperance cause; his confining himself, since the last attack of the gout, to five diurnal glasses of old sherry wine; the snowy whiteness of his linen, the polish of his boots, the handsomeness of his gold-headed cane, the square and roomy fashion of his coat, and the fineness of its material, and, in general, the studied propriety of his dress and equipment; the scrupulousness with which he paid public notice, in the street, by a bow, a lifting of the hat, a nod, or a motion of the hand, to all and sundry of his acquaintances, rich or poor; the smile of broad benevolence wherewith he made it a point to gladden the whole world,—what room could possibly be found for darker traits in a portrait made up of lineaments like these? This proper face was what he beheld in the looking-glass. This admirably arranged life was what he was conscious of in the progress of every day. Then might not he claim to be its result and sum, and say to himself and the community, "Behold Judge Pyncheon there"?

And allowing that, many, many years ago, in his early and reckless youth, he had committed some one wrong act,—or that, even now, the inevitable force of circumstances should occasionally make him do one questionable deed among a thousand praiseworthy, or, at least, blameless ones,—would you characterize the Judge by that one necessary deed, and that half-forgotten act, and let it overshadow the fair aspect of a lifetime? What is there so ponderous in evil, that a thumb's bigness of it should outweigh the mass of things not evil which were heaped into the other scale! This scale and balance system is a favorite one with people of Judge Pyncheon's brotherhood. A hard, cold man, thus unfortunately situated, seldom or never looking inward, and resolutely taking his idea of himself from what purports to be his image as reflected in the mirror of public opinion, can scarcely arrive at true self-knowledge, except through loss of property and reputation. Sickness will not always help him do it; not always the death-hour!

But our affair now is with Judge Pyncheon as he stood confronting the fierce outbreak of Hepzibah's wrath. Without premeditation, to her own surprise, and indeed terror, she had given vent, for once, to the inveteracy of her resentment, cherished against this kinsman for thirty years.

Thus far the Judge's countenance had expressed mild forbearance,—grave and almost gentle deprecation of his cousin's unbecoming violence,—free and Christian-like forgiveness of the wrong inflicted by her words. But when those words were irrevocably spoken, his look assumed sternness, the sense of power, and immitigable resolve; and this with so natural and imperceptible a change, that it seemed as if the iron man had stood there from the first, and the meek man not at all. The effect was as when the light, vapory clouds, with their soft coloring, suddenly vanish from the stony brow of a precipitous mountain, and leave there the frown which you at once feel to be eternal. Hepzibah almost adopted the insane belief that it was her old Puritan ancestor, and not the modern Judge, on whom she had just been wreaking the bitterness of her heart. Never did a man show stronger proof of the lineage attributed to him than Judge Pyncheon, at this crisis, by his unmistakable resemblance to the picture in the inner room.

"Cousin Hepzibah," said he very calmly, "it is time to have done with this."

"With all my heart!" answered she. "Then, why do you persecute us any longer? Leave poor Clifford and me in peace. Neither of us desires anything better!"

"It is my purpose to see Clifford before I leave this house," continued the Judge. "Do not act like a madwoman, Hepzibah! I am his only friend, and an all-powerful one. Has it never occurred to you,—are you so blind as not to have seen,—that, without not merely my consent, but my efforts, my representations, the exertion of my whole influence, political, official, personal, Clifford would never have been what you call free? Did you think his release a triumph over me? Not so, my good cousin; not so, by any means! The furthest possible from that! No; but it was the accomplishment of a purpose long entertained on my part. I set him free!"

"You!" answered Hepzibah. "I never will believe it! He owed his dungeon to you; his freedom to God's providence!"

"I set him free!" reaffirmed Judge Pyncheon, with the calmest composure. "And I came hither now to decide whether he shall retain his freedom. It will depend upon himself. For this purpose, I must see him."

"Never!—it would drive him mad!" exclaimed Hepzibah, but with an irresoluteness sufficiently perceptible to the keen eye of the Judge; for, without the slightest faith in his good intentions, she knew not whether there was most to dread in yielding or resistance. "And why should you wish to see this wretched, broken man, who retains hardly a fraction of his intellect, and will hide even that from an eye which has no love in it?"

"He shall see love enough in mine, if that be all!" said the Judge, with well-grounded confidence in the benignity of his aspect. "But, Cousin Hepzibah, you confess a great deal, and very much to the purpose. Now, listen, and I will frankly explain my reasons for insisting on this interview. At the death, thirty years since, of our uncle Jaffrey, it was found,—I know not whether the circumstance ever attracted much of your attention, among the sadder interests that clustered round that event,—but it was found that his visible estate, of every kind, fell far short of any estimate ever made of it. He was supposed to be immensely rich. Nobody doubted that he stood among the weightiest men of his day. It was one of his eccentricities, however,—and not altogether a folly, neither,—to conceal the amount of his property by making distant and foreign investments, perhaps under other names than his own, and by various means, familiar enough to capitalists, but unnecessary here to be specified. By Uncle Jaffrey's last will and testament, as you are aware, his entire property was bequeathed to me, with the single exception of a life interest to yourself in this old family mansion, and the strip of patrimonial estate remaining attached to it."

"And do you seek to deprive us of that?" asked Hepzibah, unable to restrain her bitter contempt. "Is this your price for ceasing to persecute poor Clifford?"

"Certainly not, my dear cousin!" answered the Judge, smiling benevolently. "On the contrary, as you must do me the justice to own, I have constantly expressed my readiness to double or treble your resources, whenever you should make up your mind to accept any kindness of that nature at the hands of your kinsman. No, no! But here lies the gist of the matter. Of my uncle's unquestionably great estate, as I have said, not the half—no, not one third, as I am fully convinced—was apparent after his death. Now, I have the best possible reasons for believing that your brother Clifford can give me a clew to the recovery of the remainder."

"Clifford!—Clifford know of any hidden wealth? Clifford have it in his power to make you rich?" cried the old gentlewoman, affected with a sense of something like ridicule at the idea. "Impossible! You deceive yourself! It is really a thing to laugh at!"

"It is as certain as that I stand here!" said Judge Pyncheon, striking his gold-headed cane on the floor, and at the same time stamping his foot, as if to express his conviction the more forcibly by the whole emphasis of his substantial person. "Clifford told me so himself!"

"No, no!" exclaimed Hepzibah incredulously. "You are dreaming, Cousin Jaffrey."

"I do not belong to the dreaming class of men," said the Judge quietly. "Some months before my uncle's death, Clifford boasted to me of the possession of the secret of incalculable wealth. His purpose was to taunt me, and excite my curiosity. I know it well. But, from a pretty distinct recollection of the particulars of our conversation, I am thoroughly convinced that there was truth in what he said. Clifford, at this moment, if he chooses,—and choose he must!—can inform me where to find the schedule, the documents, the evidences, in whatever shape they exist, of the vast amount of Uncle Jaffrey's missing property. He has the secret. His boast was no idle word. It had a directness, an emphasis, a particularity, that showed a backbone of solid meaning within the mystery of his expression."

"But what could have been Clifford's object," asked Hepzibah, "in concealing it so long?"

"It was one of the bad impulses of our fallen nature," replied the Judge, turning up his eyes. "He looked upon me as his enemy. He considered me as the cause of his overwhelming disgrace, his imminent peril of death, his irretrievable ruin. There was no great probability, therefore, of his volunteering information, out of his dungeon, that should elevate me still higher on the ladder of prosperity. But the moment has now come when he must give up his secret."

"And what if he should refuse?" inquired Hepzibah. "Or,—as I steadfastly believe,—what if he has no knowledge of this wealth?"

"My dear cousin," said Judge Pyncheon, with a quietude which he had the power of making more formidable than any violence, "since your brother's return, I have taken the precaution (a highly proper one in the near kinsman and natural guardian of an individual so situated) to have his deportment and habits constantly and carefully overlooked. Your neighbors have been eye-witnesses to whatever has passed in the garden. The butcher, the baker, the fish-monger, some of the customers of your shop, and many a prying old woman, have told me several of the secrets of your interior. A still larger circle—I myself, among the rest—can testify to his extravagances at the arched window. Thousands beheld him, a week or two ago, on the point of flinging himself thence into the street. From all this testimony, I am led to apprehend—reluctantly, and with deep grief—that Clifford's misfortunes have so affected his intellect, never very strong, that he cannot safely remain at large. The alternative, you must be aware,—and its adoption will depend entirely on the decision which I am now about to make,—the alternative is his confinement, probably for the remainder of his life, in a public asylum for persons in his unfortunate state of mind."

"You cannot mean it!" shrieked Hepzibah.

"Should my cousin Clifford," continued Judge Pyncheon, wholly undisturbed, "from mere malice, and hatred of one whose interests ought naturally to be dear to him,—a mode of passion that, as often as any other, indicates mental disease,—should he refuse me the information so important to myself, and which he assuredly possesses, I shall consider it the one needed jot of evidence to satisfy my mind of his insanity. And, once sure of the course pointed out by conscience, you know me too well, Cousin Hepzibah, to entertain a doubt that I shall pursue it."

"O Jaffrey,—Cousin Jaffrey," cried Hepzibah mournfully, not passionately, "it is you that are diseased in mind, not Clifford! You have forgotten that a woman was your mother!—that you have had sisters, brothers, children of your own!—or that there ever was affection between man and man, or pity from one man to another, in this miserable world! Else, how could you have dreamed of this? You are not young, Cousin Jaffrey!—no, nor middle-aged,—but already an old man! The hair is white upon your head! How many years have you to live? Are you not rich enough for that little time? Shall you be hungry,—shall you lack clothes, or a roof to shelter you,—between this point and the grave? No! but, with the half of what you now possess, you could revel in costly food and wines, and build a house twice as splendid as you now inhabit, and make a far greater show to the world,—and yet leave riches to your only son, to make him bless the hour of your death! Then, why should you do this cruel, cruel thing?—so mad a thing, that I know not whether to call it wicked! Alas, Cousin Jaffrey, this hard and grasping spirit has run in our blood these two hundred years. You are but doing over again, in another shape, what your ancestor before you did, and sending down to your posterity the curse inherited from him!"

"Talk sense, Hepzibah, for Heaven's sake!" exclaimed the Judge, with the impatience natural to a reasonable man, on hearing anything so utterly absurd as the above, in a discussion about matters of business. "I have told you my determination. I am not apt to change. Clifford must give up his secret, or take the consequences. And let him decide quickly; for I have several affairs to attend to this morning, and an important dinner engagement with some political friends."

"Clifford has no secret!" answered Hepzibah. "And God will not let you do the thing you meditate!"

"We shall see," said the unmoved Judge. "Meanwhile, choose whether you will summon Clifford, and allow this business to be amicably settled by an interview between two kinsmen, or drive me to harsher measures, which I should be most happy to feel myself justified in avoiding. The responsibility is altogether on your part."

"You are stronger than I," said Hepzibah, after a brief consideration; "and you have no pity in your strength! Clifford is not now insane; but the interview which you insist upon may go far to make him so. Nevertheless, knowing you as I do, I believe it to be my best course to allow you to judge for yourself as to the improbability of his possessing any valuable secret. I will call Clifford. Be merciful in your dealings with him!—be far more merciful than your heart bids you be!—for God is looking at you, Jaffrey Pyncheon!"

The Judge followed his cousin from the shop, where the foregoing conversation had passed, into the parlor, and flung himself heavily into the great ancestral chair. Many a former Pyncheon had found repose in its capacious arms: rosy children, after their sports; young men, dreamy with love; grown men, weary with cares; old men, burdened with winters,—they had mused, and slumbered, and departed to a yet profounder sleep. It had been a long tradition, though a doubtful one, that this was the very chair, seated in which the earliest of the Judge's New England forefathers—he whose picture still hung upon the wall—had given a dead man's silent and stern reception to the throng of distinguished guests. From that hour of evil omen until the present, it may be,—though we know not the secret of his heart,—but it may be that no wearier and sadder man had ever sunk into the chair than this same Judge Pyncheon, whom we have just beheld so immitigably hard and resolute. Surely, it must have been at no slight cost that he had thus fortified his soul with iron. Such calmness is a mightier effort than the violence of weaker men. And there was yet a heavy task for him to do. Was it a little matter—a trifle to be prepared for in a single moment, and to be rested from in another moment,—that he must now, after thirty years, encounter a kinsman risen from a living tomb, and wrench a secret from him, or else consign him to a living tomb again?

"Did you speak?" asked Hepzibah, looking in from the threshold of the parlor; for she imagined that the Judge had uttered some sound which she was anxious to interpret as a relenting impulse. "I thought you called me back."

"No, no" gruffly answered Judge Pyncheon with a harsh frown, while his brow grew almost a black purple, in the shadow of the room. "Why should I call you back? Time flies! Bid Clifford come to me!"

The Judge had taken his watch from his vest pocket and now held it in his hand, measuring the interval which was to ensue before the appearance of Clifford.

XVI Clifford's Chamber

NEVER had the old house appeared so dismal to poor Hepzibah as when she departed on that wretched errand. There was a strange aspect in it. As she trode along the foot-worn passages, and opened one crazy door after another, and ascended the creaking staircase, she gazed wistfully and fearfully around. It would have been no marvel, to her excited mind, if, behind or beside her, there had been the rustle of dead people's garments, or pale visages awaiting her on the landing-place above. Her nerves were set all ajar by the scene of passion and terror through which she had just struggled. Her colloquy with Judge Pyncheon, who so perfectly represented the person and attributes of the founder of the family, had called back the dreary past. It weighed upon her heart. Whatever she had heard, from legendary aunts and grandmothers, concerning the good or evil fortunes of the Pyncheons,—stories which had heretofore been kept warm in her remembrance by the chimney-corner glow that was associated with them,—now recurred to her, sombre, ghastly, cold, like most passages of family history, when brooded over in melancholy mood. The whole seemed little else but a series of calamity, reproducing itself in successive generations, with one general hue, and varying in little, save the outline. But Hepzibah now felt as if the Judge, and Clifford, and herself,—they three together,—were on the point of adding another incident to the annals of the house, with a bolder relief of wrong and sorrow, which would cause it to stand out from all the rest. Thus it is that the grief of the passing moment takes upon itself an individuality, and a character of climax, which it is destined to lose after a while, and to fade into the dark gray tissue common to the grave or glad events of many years ago. It is but for a moment, comparatively, that anything looks strange or startling,—a truth that has the bitter and the sweet in it.

But Hepzibah could not rid herself of the sense of something unprecedented at that instant passing and soon to be accomplished. Her nerves were in a shake. Instinctively she paused before the arched window, and looked out upon the street, in order to seize its permanent objects with her mental grasp, and thus to steady herself from the reel and vibration which affected her more immediate sphere. It brought her up, as we may say, with a kind of shock, when she beheld everything under the same appearance as the day before, and numberless preceding days, except for the difference between sunshine and sullen storm. Her eyes travelled along the street, from doorstep to doorstep, noting the wet sidewalks, with here and there a puddle in hollows that had been imperceptible until filled with water. She screwed her dim optics to their acutest point, in the hope of making out, with greater distinctness, a certain window, where she half saw, half guessed, that a tailor's seamstress was sitting at her work. Hepzibah flung herself upon that unknown woman's companionship, even thus far off. Then she was attracted by a chaise rapidly passing, and watched its moist and glistening top, and its splashing wheels, until it had turned the corner, and refused to carry any further her idly trifling, because appalled and overburdened, mind. When the vehicle had disappeared, she allowed herself still another loitering moment; for the patched figure of good Uncle Venner was now visible, coming slowly from the head of the street downward, with a rheumatic limp, because the east wind had got into his joints. Hepzibah wished that he would pass yet more slowly, and befriend her shivering solitude a little longer. Anything that would take her out of the grievous present, and interpose human beings betwixt herself and what was nearest to her,—whatever would defer for an instant the inevitable errand on which she was bound,—all such impediments were welcome. Next to the lightest heart, the heaviest is apt to be most playful.

Hepzibah had little hardihood for her own proper pain, and far less for what she must inflict on Clifford. Of so slight a nature, and so shattered by his previous calamities, it could not well be short of utter ruin to bring him face to face with the hard, relentless man who had been his evil destiny through life. Even had there been no bitter recollections, nor any hostile interest now at stake between them, the mere natural repugnance of the more sensitive system to the massive, weighty, and unimpressible one, must, in itself, have been disastrous to the former. It would be like flinging a porcelain vase, with already a crack in it, against a granite column. Never before had Hepzibah so adequately estimated the powerful character of her cousin Jaffrey,—powerful by intellect, energy of will, the long habit of acting among men, and, as she believed, by his unscrupulous pursuit of selfish ends through evil means. It did but increase the difficulty that Judge Pyncheon was under a delusion as to the secret which he supposed Clifford to possess. Men of his strength of purpose and customary sagacity, if they chance to adopt a mistaken opinion in practical matters, so wedge it and fasten it among things known to be true, that to wrench it out of their minds is hardly less difficult than pulling up an oak. Thus, as the Judge required an impossibility of Clifford, the latter, as he could not perform it, must needs perish. For what, in the grasp of a man like this, was to become of Clifford's soft poetic nature, that never should have had a task more stubborn than to set a life of beautiful enjoyment to the flow and rhythm of musical cadences! Indeed, what had become of it already? Broken! Blighted! All but annihilated! Soon to be wholly so!

For a moment, the thought crossed Hepzibah's mind, whether Clifford might not really have such knowledge of their deceased uncle's vanished estate as the Judge imputed to him. She remembered some vague intimations, on her brother's part, which—if the supposition were not essentially preposterous—might have been so interpreted. There had been schemes of travel and residence abroad, daydreams of brilliant life at home, and splendid castles in the air, which it would have required boundless wealth to build and realize. Had this wealth been in her power, how gladly would Hepzibah have bestowed it all upon her iron-hearted kinsman, to buy for Clifford the freedom and seclusion of the desolate old house! But she believed that her brother's schemes were as destitute of actual substance and purpose as a child's pictures of its future life, while sitting in a little chair by its mother's knee. Clifford had none but shadowy gold at his command; and it was not the stuff to satisfy Judge Pyncheon!

Was there no help in their extremity? It seemed strange that there should be none, with a city round about her. It would be so easy to throw up the window, and send forth a shriek, at the strange agony of which everybody would come hastening to the rescue, well understanding it to be the cry of a human soul, at some dreadful crisis! But how wild, how almost laughable, the fatality,—and yet how continually it comes to pass, thought Hepzibah, in this dull delirium of a world,—that whosoever, and with however kindly a purpose, should come to help, they would be sure to help the strongest side! Might and wrong combined, like iron magnetized, are endowed with irresistible attraction. There would be Judge Pyncheon,—a person eminent in the public view, of high station and great wealth, a philanthropist, a member of Congress and of the church, and intimately associated with whatever else bestows good name,—so imposing, in these advantageous lights, that Hepzibah herself could hardly help shrinking from her own conclusions as to his hollow integrity. The Judge, on one side! And who, on the other? The guilty Clifford! Once a byword! Now, an indistinctly remembered ignominy!

Nevertheless, in spite of this perception that the Judge would draw all human aid to his own behalf, Hepzibah was so unaccustomed to act for herself, that the least word of counsel would have swayed her to any mode of action. Little Phoebe Pyncheon would at once have lighted up the whole scene, if not by any available suggestion, yet simply by the warm vivacity of her character. The idea of the artist occurred to Hepzibah. Young and unknown, mere vagrant adventurer as he was, she had been conscious of a force in Holgrave which might well adapt him to be the champion of a crisis. With this thought in her mind, she unbolted a door, cobwebbed and long disused, but which had served as a former medium of communication between her own part of the house and the gable where the wandering daguerreotypist had now established his temporary home. He was not there. A book, face downward, on the table, a roll of manuscript, a half-written sheet, a newspaper, some tools of his present occupation, and several rejected daguerreotypes, conveyed an impression as if he were close at hand. But, at this period of the day, as Hepzibah might have anticipated, the artist was at his public rooms. With an impulse of idle curiosity, that flickered among her heavy thoughts, she looked at one of the daguerreotypes, and beheld Judge Pyncheon frowning at her. Fate stared her in the face. She turned back from her fruitless quest, with a heartsinking sense of disappointment. In all her years of seclusion, she had never felt, as now, what it was to be alone. It seemed as if the house stood in a desert, or, by some spell, was made invisible to those who dwelt around, or passed beside it; so that any mode of misfortune, miserable accident, or crime might happen in it without the possibility of aid. In her grief and wounded pride, Hepzibah had spent her life in divesting herself of friends; she had wilfully cast off the support which God has ordained his creatures to need from one another; and it was now her punishment, that Clifford and herself would fall the easier victims to their kindred enemy.

Returning to the arched window, she lifted her eyes,—scowling, poor, dim-sighted Hepzibah, in the face of Heaven!—and strove hard to send up a prayer through the dense gray pavement of clouds. Those mists had gathered, as if to symbolize a great, brooding mass of human trouble, doubt, confusion, and chill indifference, between earth and the better regions. Her faith was too weak; the prayer too heavy to be thus uplifted. It fell back, a lump of lead, upon her heart. It smote her with the wretched conviction that Providence intermeddled not in these petty wrongs of one individual to his fellow, nor had any balm for these little agonies of a solitary soul; but shed its justice, and its mercy, in a broad, sunlike sweep, over half the universe at once. Its vastness made it nothing. But Hepzibah did not see that, just as there comes a warm sunbeam into every cottage window, so comes a lovebeam of God's care and pity for every separate need.

At last, finding no other pretext for deferring the torture that she was to inflict on Clifford,—her reluctance to which was the true cause of her loitering at the window, her search for the artist, and even her abortive prayer,—dreading, also, to hear the stern voice of Judge Pyncheon from below stairs, chiding her delay,—she crept slowly, a pale, grief-stricken figure, a dismal shape of woman, with almost torpid limbs, slowly to her brother's door, and knocked!

There was no reply.

And how should there have been? Her hand, tremulous with the shrinking purpose which directed it, had smitten so feebly against the door that the sound could hardly have gone inward. She knocked again. Still no response! Nor was it to be wondered at. She had struck with the entire force of her heart's vibration, communicating, by some subtile magnetism, her own terror to the summons. Clifford would turn his face to the pillow, and cover his head beneath the bedclothes, like a startled child at midnight. She knocked a third time, three regular strokes, gentle, but perfectly distinct, and with meaning in them; for, modulate it with what cautious art we will, the hand cannot help playing some tune of what we feel upon the senseless wood.

Clifford returned no answer.

"Clifford! Dear brother!" said Hepzibah. "Shall I come in?"

A silence.

Two or three times, and more, Hepzibah repeated his name, without result; till, thinking her brother's sleep unwontedly profound, she undid the door, and entering, found the chamber vacant. How could he have come forth, and when, without her knowledge? Was it possible that, in spite of the stormy day, and worn out with the irksomeness within doors he had betaken himself to his customary haunt in the garden, and was now shivering under the cheerless shelter of the summer-house? She hastily threw up a window, thrust forth her turbaned head and the half of her gaunt figure, and searched the whole garden through, as completely as her dim vision would allow. She could see the interior of the summer-house, and its circular seat, kept moist by the droppings of the roof. It had no occupant. Clifford was not thereabouts; unless, indeed, he had crept for concealment (as, for a moment, Hepzibah fancied might be the case) into a great, wet mass of tangled and broad-leaved shadow, where the squash-vines were clambering tumultuously upon an old wooden framework, set casually aslant against the fence. This could not be, however; he was not there; for, while Hepzibah was looking, a strange grimalkin stole forth from the very spot, and picked his way across the garden. Twice he paused to snuff the air, and then anew directed his course towards the parlor window. Whether it was only on account of the stealthy, prying manner common to the race, or that this cat seemed to have more than ordinary mischief in his thoughts, the old gentlewoman, in spite of her much perplexity, felt an impulse to drive the animal away, and accordingly flung down a window stick. The cat stared up at her, like a detected thief or murderer, and, the next instant, took to flight. No other living creature was visible in the garden. Chanticleer and his family had either not left their roost, disheartened by the interminable rain, or had done the next wisest thing, by seasonably returning to it. Hepzibah closed the window.

But where was Clifford? Could it be that, aware of the presence of his Evil Destiny, he had crept silently down the staircase, while the Judge and Hepzibah stood talking in the shop, and had softly undone the fastenings of the outer door, and made his escape into the street? With that thought, she seemed to behold his gray, wrinkled, yet childlike aspect, in the old-fashioned garments which he wore about the house; a figure such as one sometimes imagines himself to be, with the world's eye upon him, in a troubled dream. This figure of her wretched brother would go wandering through the city, attracting all eyes, and everybody's wonder and repugnance, like a ghost, the more to be shuddered at because visible at noontide. To incur the ridicule of the younger crowd, that knew him not,—the harsher scorn and indignation of a few old men, who might recall his once familiar features! To be the sport of boys, who, when old enough to run about the streets, have no more reverence for what is beautiful and holy, nor pity for what is sad,—no more sense of sacred misery, sanctifying the human shape in which it embodies itself,—than if Satan were the father of them all! Goaded by their taunts, their loud, shrill cries, and cruel laughter,—insulted by the filth of the public ways, which they would fling upon him,—or, as it might well be, distracted by the mere strangeness of his situation, though nobody should afflict him with so much as a thoughtless word,—what wonder if Clifford were to break into some wild extravagance which was certain to be interpreted as lunacy? Thus Judge Pyncheon's fiendish scheme would be ready accomplished to his hands!

Then Hepzibah reflected that the town was almost completely water-girdled. The wharves stretched out towards the centre of the harbor, and, in this inclement weather, were deserted by the ordinary throng of merchants, laborers, and seafaring men; each wharf a solitude, with the vessels moored stem and stern, along its misty length. Should her brother's aimless footsteps stray thitherward, and he but bend, one moment, over the deep, black tide, would he not bethink himself that here was the sure refuge within his reach, and that, with a single step, or the slightest overbalance of his body, he might be forever beyond his kinsman's gripe? Oh, the temptation! To make of his ponderous sorrow a security! To sink, with its leaden weight upon him, and never rise again!

The horror of this last conception was too much for Hepzibah. Even Jaffrey Pyncheon must help her now She hastened down the staircase, shrieking as she went.

"Clifford is gone!" she cried. "I cannot find my brother. Help, Jaffrey Pyncheon! Some harm will happen to him!"

She threw open the parlor-door. But, what with the shade of branches across the windows, and the smoke-blackened ceiling, and the dark oak-panelling of the walls, there was hardly so much daylight in the room that Hepzibah's imperfect sight could accurately distinguish the Judge's figure. She was certain, however, that she saw him sitting in the ancestral arm-chair, near the centre of the floor, with his face somewhat averted, and looking towards a window. So firm and quiet is the nervous system of such men as Judge Pyncheon, that he had perhaps stirred not more than once since her departure, but, in the hard composure of his temperament, retained the position into which accident had thrown him.

"I tell you, Jaffrey," cried Hepzibah impatiently, as she turned from the parlor-door to search other rooms, "my brother is not in his chamber! You must help me seek him!"

But Judge Pyncheon was not the man to let himself be startled from an easy-chair with haste ill-befitting either the dignity of his character or his broad personal basis, by the alarm of an hysteric woman. Yet, considering his own interest in the matter, he might have bestirred himself with a little more alacrity.

"Do you hear me, Jaffrey Pyncheon?" screamed Hepzibah, as she again approached the parlor-door, after an ineffectual search elsewhere. "Clifford is gone."

At this instant, on the threshold of the parlor, emerging from within, appeared Clifford himself! His face was preternaturally pale; so deadly white, indeed, that, through all the glimmering indistinctness of the passageway, Hepzibah could discern his features, as if a light fell on them alone. Their vivid and wild expression seemed likewise sufficient to illuminate them; it was an expression of scorn and mockery, coinciding with the emotions indicated by his gesture. As Clifford stood on the threshold, partly turning back, he pointed his finger within the parlor, and shook it slowly as though he would have summoned, not Hepzibah alone, but the whole world, to gaze at some object inconceivably ridiculous. This action, so ill-timed and extravagant,—accompanied, too, with a look that showed more like joy than any other kind of excitement,—compelled Hepzibah to dread that her stern kinsman's ominous visit had driven her poor brother to absolute insanity. Nor could she otherwise account for the Judge's quiescent mood than by supposing him craftily on the watch, while Clifford developed these symptoms of a distracted mind.

"Be quiet, Clifford!" whispered his sister, raising her hand to impress caution. "Oh, for Heaven's sake, be quiet!"

"Let him be quiet! What can he do better?" answered Clifford, with a still wilder gesture, pointing into the room which he had just quitted. "As for us, Hepzibah, we can dance now!—we can sing, laugh, play, do what we will! The weight is gone, Hepzibah! It is gone off this weary old world, and we may be as light-hearted as little Phoebe herself."

And, in accordance with his words, he began to laugh, still pointing his finger at the object, invisible to Hepzibah, within the parlor. She was seized with a sudden intuition of some horrible thing. She thrust herself past Clifford, and disappeared into the room; but almost immediately returned, with a cry choking in her throat. Gazing at her brother with an affrighted glance of inquiry, she beheld him all in a tremor and a quake, from head to foot, while, amid these commoted elements of passion or alarm, still flickered his gusty mirth.

"My God! what is to become of us?" gasped Hepzibah.

"Come!" said Clifford in a tone of brief decision, most unlike what was usual with him. "We stay here too long! Let us leave the old house to our cousin Jaffrey! He will take good care of it!"

Hepzibah now noticed that Clifford had on a cloak,—a garment of long ago,—in which he had constantly muffled himself during these days of easterly storm. He beckoned with his hand, and intimated, so far as she could comprehend him, his purpose that they should go together from the house. There are chaotic, blind, or drunken moments, in the lives of persons who lack real force of character,—moments of test, in which courage would most assert itself,—but where these individuals, if left to themselves, stagger aimlessly along, or follow implicitly whatever guidance may befall them, even if it be a child's. No matter how preposterous or insane, a purpose is a Godsend to them. Hepzibah had reached this point. Unaccustomed to action or responsibility,—full of horror at what she had seen, and afraid to inquire, or almost to imagine, how it had come to pass,—affrighted at the fatality which seemed to pursue her brother,—stupefied by the dim, thick, stifling atmosphere of dread which filled the house as with a death-smell, and obliterated all definiteness of thought,—she yielded without a question, and on the instant, to the will which Clifford expressed. For herself, she was like a person in a dream, when the will always sleeps. Clifford, ordinarily so destitute of this faculty, had found it in the tension of the crisis.

"Why do you delay so?" cried he sharply. "Put on your cloak and hood, or whatever it pleases you to wear! No matter what; you cannot look beautiful nor brilliant, my poor Hepzibah! Take your purse, with money in it, and come along!"

Hepzibah obeyed these instructions, as if nothing else were to be done or thought of. She began to wonder, it is true, why she did not wake up, and at what still more intolerable pitch of dizzy trouble her spirit would struggle out of the maze, and make her conscious that nothing of all this had actually happened. Of course it was not real; no such black, easterly day as this had yet begun to be; Judge Pyncheon had not talked with, her. Clifford had not laughed, pointed, beckoned her away with him; but she had merely been afflicted—as lonely sleepers often are—with a great deal of unreasonable misery, in a morning dream!

"Now—now—I shall certainly awake!" thought Hepzibah, as she went to and fro, making her little preparations. "I can bear it no longer I must wake up now!"

But it came not, that awakening moment! It came not, even when, just before they left the house, Clifford stole to the parlor-door, and made a parting obeisance to the sole occupant of the room.

"What an absurd figure the old fellow cuts now!" whispered he to Hepzibah. "Just when he fancied he had me completely under his thumb! Come, come; make haste! or he will start up, like Giant Despair in pursuit of Christian and Hopeful, and catch us yet!"

As they passed into the street, Clifford directed Hepzibah's attention to something on one of the posts of the front door. It was merely the initials of his own name, which, with somewhat of his characteristic grace about the forms of the letters, he had cut there when a boy. The brother and sister departed, and left Judge Pyncheon sitting in the old home of his forefathers, all by himself; so heavy and lumpish that we can liken him to nothing better than a defunct nightmare, which had perished in the midst of its wickedness, and left its flabby corpse on the breast of the tormented one, to be gotten rid of as it might!

XVII The Flight of Two Owls

SUMMER as it was, the east wind set poor Hepzibah's few remaining teeth chattering in her head, as she and Clifford faced it, on their way up Pyncheon Street, and towards the centre of the town. Not merely was it the shiver which this pitiless blast brought to her frame (although her feet and hands, especially, had never seemed so death-a-cold as now), but there was a moral sensation, mingling itself with the physical chill, and causing her to shake more in spirit than in body. The world's broad, bleak atmosphere was all so comfortless! Such, indeed, is the impression which it makes on every new adventurer, even if he plunge into it while the warmest tide of life is bubbling through his veins. What, then, must it have been to Hepzibah and Clifford,—so time-stricken as they were, yet so like children in their inexperience,—as they left the doorstep, and passed from beneath the wide shelter of the Pyncheon Elm! They were wandering all abroad, on precisely such a pilgrimage as a child often meditates, to the world's end, with perhaps a sixpence and a biscuit in his pocket. In Hepzibah's mind, there was the wretched consciousness of being adrift. She had lost the faculty of self-guidance; but, in view of the difficulties around her, felt it hardly worth an effort to regain it, and was, moreover, incapable of making one.

As they proceeded on their strange expedition, she now and then cast a look sidelong at Clifford, and could not but observe that he was possessed and swayed by a powerful excitement. It was this, indeed, that gave him the control which he had at once, and so irresistibly, established over his movements. It not a little resembled the exhilaration of wine. Or, it might more fancifully be compared to a joyous piece of music, played with wild vivacity, but upon a disordered instrument. As the cracked jarring note might always be heard, and as it jarred loudest amidst the loftiest exultation of the melody, so was there a continual quake through Clifford, causing him most to quiver while he wore a triumphant smile, and seemed almost under a necessity to skip in his gait.

They met few people abroad, even on passing from the retired neighborhood of the House of the Seven Gables into what was ordinarily the more thronged and busier portion of the town. Glistening sidewalks, with little pools of rain, here and there, along their unequal surface; umbrellas displayed ostentatiously in the shop-windows, as if the life of trade had concentrated itself in that one article; wet leaves of the horse-chestnut or elm-trees, torn off untimely by the blast and scattered along the public way; an unsightly, accumulation of mud in the middle of the street, which perversely grew the more unclean for its long and laborious washing,—these were the more definable points of a very sombre picture. In the way of movement and human life, there was the hasty rattle of a cab or coach, its driver protected by a waterproof cap over his head and shoulders; the forlorn figure of an old man, who seemed to have crept out of some subterranean sewer, and was stooping along the kennel, and poking the wet rubbish with a stick, in quest of rusty nails; a merchant or two, at the door of the post-office, together with an editor and a miscellaneous politician, awaiting a dilatory mail; a few visages of retired sea-captains at the window of an insurance office, looking out vacantly at the vacant street, blaspheming at the weather, and fretting at the dearth as well of public news as local gossip. What a treasure-trove to these venerable quidnuncs, could they have guessed the secret which Hepzibah and Clifford were carrying along with them! But their two figures attracted hardly so much notice as that of a young girl, who passed at the same instant, and happened to raise her skirt a trifle too high above her ankles. Had it been a sunny and cheerful day, they could hardly have gone through the streets without making themselves obnoxious to remark. Now, probably, they were felt to be in keeping with the dismal and bitter weather, and therefore did not stand out in strong relief, as if the sun were shining on them, but melted into the gray gloom and were forgotten as soon as gone.

Poor Hepzibah! Could she have understood this fact, it would have brought her some little comfort; for, to all her other troubles,—strange to say!—there was added the womanish and old-maiden-like misery arising from a sense of unseemliness in her attire. Thus, she was fain to shrink deeper into herself, as it were, as if in the hope of making people suppose that here was only a cloak and hood, threadbare and woefully faded, taking an airing in the midst of the storm, without any wearer!

As they went on, the feeling of indistinctness and unreality kept dimly hovering round about her, and so diffusing itself into her system that one of her hands was hardly palpable to the touch of the other. Any certainty would have been preferable to this. She whispered to herself, again and again, "Am I awake?—Am I awake?" and sometimes exposed her face to the chill spatter of the wind, for the sake of its rude assurance that she was. Whether it was Clifford's purpose, or only chance, had led them thither, they now found themselves passing beneath the arched entrance of a large structure of gray stone. Within, there was a spacious breadth, and an airy height from floor to roof, now partially filled with smoke and steam, which eddied voluminously upward and formed a mimic cloud-region over their heads. A train of cars was just ready for a start; the locomotive was fretting and fuming, like a steed impatient for a headlong rush; and the bell rang out its hasty peal, so well expressing the brief summons which life vouchsafes to us in its hurried career. Without question or delay,—with the irresistible decision, if not rather to be called recklessness, which had so strangely taken possession of him, and through him of Hepzibah,—Clifford impelled her towards the cars, and assisted her to enter. The signal was given; the engine puffed forth its short, quick breaths; the train began its movement; and, along with a hundred other passengers, these two unwonted travellers sped onward like the wind.

At last, therefore, and after so long estrangement from everything that the world acted or enjoyed, they had been drawn into the great current of human life, and were swept away with it, as by the suction of fate itself.

Still haunted with the idea that not one of the past incidents, inclusive of Judge Pyncheon's visit, could be real, the recluse of the Seven Gables murmured in her brother's ear,—

"Clifford! Clifford! Is not this a dream?"

"A dream, Hepzibah!" repeated he, almost laughing in her face. "On the contrary, I have never been awake before!"

Meanwhile, looking from the window, they could see the world racing past them. At one moment, they were rattling through a solitude; the next, a village had grown up around them; a few breaths more, and it had vanished, as if swallowed by an earthquake. The spires of meeting-houses seemed set adrift from their foundations; the broad-based hills glided away. Everything was unfixed from its age-long rest, and moving at whirlwind speed in a direction opposite to their own.

Within the car there was the usual interior life of the railroad, offering little to the observation of other passengers, but full of novelty for this pair of strangely enfranchised prisoners. It was novelty enough, indeed, that there were fifty human beings in close relation with them, under one long and narrow roof, and drawn onward by the same mighty influence that had taken their two selves into its grasp. It seemed marvellous how all these people could remain so quietly in their seats, while so much noisy strength was at work in their behalf. Some, with tickets in their hats (long travellers these, before whom lay a hundred miles of railroad), had plunged into the English scenery and adventures of pamphlet novels, and were keeping company with dukes and earls. Others, whose briefer span forbade their devoting themselves to studies so abstruse, beguiled the little tedium of the way with penny-papers. A party of girls, and one young man, on opposite sides of the car, found huge amusement in a game of ball. They tossed it to and fro, with peals of laughter that might be measured by mile-lengths; for, faster than the nimble ball could fly, the merry players fled unconsciously along, leaving the trail of their mirth afar behind, and ending their game under another sky than had witnessed its commencement. Boys, with apples, cakes, candy, and rolls of variously tinctured lozenges,—merchandise that reminded Hepzibah of her deserted shop,—appeared at each momentary stopping-place, doing up their business in a hurry, or breaking it short off, lest the market should ravish them away with it. New people continually entered. Old acquaintances—for such they soon grew to be, in this rapid current of affairs—continually departed. Here and there, amid the rumble and the tumult, sat one asleep. Sleep; sport; business; graver or lighter study; and the common and inevitable movement onward! It was life itself!

Clifford's naturally poignant sympathies were all aroused. He caught the color of what was passing about him, and threw it back more vividly than he received it, but mixed, nevertheless, with a lurid and portentous hue. Hepzibah, on the other hand, felt herself more apart from human kind than even in the seclusion which she had just quitted.

"You are not happy, Hepzibah!" said Clifford apart, in a tone of approach. "You are thinking of that dismal old house, and of Cousin Jaffrey"—here came the quake through him,—"and of Cousin Jaffrey sitting there, all by himself! Take my advice,—follow my example,—and let such things slip aside. Here we are, in the world, Hepzibah!—in the midst of life!—in the throng of our fellow beings! Let you and I be happy! As happy as that youth and those pretty girls, at their game of ball!"

"Happy—" thought Hepzibah, bitterly conscious, at the word, of her dull and heavy heart, with the frozen pain in it,—"happy. He is mad already; and, if I could once feel myself broad awake, I should go mad too!"

If a fixed idea be madness, she was perhaps not remote from it. Fast and far as they had rattled and clattered along the iron track, they might just as well, as regarded Hepzibah's mental images, have been passing up and down Pyncheon Street. With miles and miles of varied scenery between, there was no scene for her save the seven old gable-peaks, with their moss, and the tuft of weeds in one of the angles, and the shop-window, and a customer shaking the door, and compelling the little bell to jingle fiercely, but without disturbing Judge Pyncheon! This one old house was everywhere! It transported its great, lumbering bulk with more than railroad speed, and set itself phlegmatically down on whatever spot she glanced at. The quality of Hepzibah's mind was too unmalleable to take new impressions so readily as Clifford's. He had a winged nature; she was rather of the vegetable kind, and could hardly be kept long alive, if drawn up by the roots. Thus it happened that the relation heretofore existing between her brother and herself was changed. At home, she was his guardian; here, Clifford had become hers, and seemed to comprehend whatever belonged to their new position with a singular rapidity of intelligence. He had been startled into manhood and intellectual vigor; or, at least, into a condition that resembled them, though it might be both diseased and transitory.

The conductor now applied for their tickets; and Clifford, who had made himself the purse-bearer, put a bank-note into his hand, as he had observed others do.

"For the lady and yourself?" asked the conductor. "And how far?"

"As far as that will carry us," said Clifford. "It is no great matter. We are riding for pleasure merely."

"You choose a strange day for it, sir!" remarked a gimlet-eyed old gentleman on the other side of the car, looking at Clifford and his companion, as if curious to make them out. "The best chance of pleasure, in an easterly rain, I take it, is in a man's own house, with a nice little fire in the chimney."

"I cannot precisely agree with you," said Clifford, courteously bowing to the old gentleman, and at once taking up the clew of conversation which the latter had proffered. "It had just occurred to me, on the contrary, that this admirable invention of the railroad—with the vast and inevitable improvements to be looked for, both as to speed and convenience—is destined to do away with those stale ideas of home and fireside, and substitute something better."

"In the name of common-sense," asked the old gentleman rather testily, "what can be better for a man than his own parlor and chimney-corner?"

"These things have not the merit which many good people attribute to them," replied Clifford. "They may be said, in few and pithy words, to have ill served a poor purpose. My impression is, that our wonderfully increased and still increasing facilities of locomotion are destined to bring us around again to the nomadic state. You are aware, my dear sir,—you must have observed it in your own experience,—that all human progress is in a circle; or, to use a more accurate and beautiful figure, in an ascending spiral curve. While we fancy ourselves going straight forward, and attaining, at every step, an entirely new position of affairs, we do actually return to something long ago tried and abandoned, but which we now find etherealized, refined, and perfected to its ideal. The past is but a coarse and sensual prophecy of the present and the future. To apply this truth to the topic now under discussion. In the early epochs of our race, men dwelt in temporary huts, of bowers of branches, as easily constructed as a bird's-nest, and which they built,—if it should be called building, when such sweet homes of a summer solstice rather grew than were made with hands,—which Nature, we will say, assisted them to rear where fruit abounded, where fish and game were plentiful, or, most especially, where the sense of beauty was to be gratified by a lovelier shade than elsewhere, and a more exquisite arrangement of lake, wood, and hill. This life possessed a charm which, ever since man quitted it, has vanished from existence. And it typified something better than itself. It had its drawbacks; such as hunger and thirst, inclement weather, hot sunshine, and weary and foot-blistering marches over barren and ugly tracts, that lay between the sites desirable for their fertility and beauty. But in our ascending spiral, we escape all this. These railroads—could but the whistle be made musical, and the rumble and the jar got rid of—are positively the greatest blessing that the ages have wrought out for us. They give us wings; they annihilate the toil and dust of pilgrimage; they spiritualize travel! Transition being so facile, what can be any man's inducement to tarry in one spot? Why, therefore, should he build a more cumbrous habitation than can readily be carried off with him? Why should he make himself a prisoner for life in brick, and stone, and old worm-eaten timber, when he may just as easily dwell, in one sense, nowhere,—in a better sense, wherever the fit and beautiful shall offer him a home?"

Clifford's countenance glowed, as he divulged this theory; a youthful character shone out from within, converting the wrinkles and pallid duskiness of age into an almost transparent mask. The merry girls let their ball drop upon the floor, and gazed at him. They said to themselves, perhaps, that, before his hair was gray and the crow's-feet tracked his temples, this now decaying man must have stamped the impress of his features on many a woman's heart. But, alas! no woman's eye had seen his face while it was beautiful.

"I should scarcely call it an improved state of things," observed Clifford's new acquaintance, "to live everywhere and nowhere!"

"Would you not?" exclaimed Clifford, with singular energy. "It is as clear to me as sunshine,—were there any in the sky,—that the greatest possible stumbling-blocks in the path of human happiness and improvement are these heaps of bricks and stones, consolidated with mortar, or hewn timber, fastened together with spike-nails, which men painfully contrive for their own torment, and call them house and home! The soul needs air; a wide sweep and frequent change of it. Morbid influences, in a thousand-fold variety, gather about hearths, and pollute the life of households. There is no such unwholesome atmosphere as that of an old home, rendered poisonous by one's defunct forefathers and relatives. I speak of what I know. There is a certain house within my familiar recollection,—one of those peaked-gable (there are seven of them), projecting-storied edifices, such as you occasionally see in our older towns,—a rusty, crazy, creaky, dry-rotted, dingy, dark, and miserable old dungeon, with an arched window over the porch, and a little shop-door on one side, and a great, melancholy elm before it! Now, sir, whenever my thoughts recur to this seven-gabled mansion (the fact is so very curious that I must needs mention it), immediately I have a vision or image of an elderly man, of remarkably stern countenance, sitting in an oaken elbow-chair, dead, stone-dead, with an ugly flow of blood upon his shirt-bosom! Dead, but with open eyes! He taints the whole house, as I remember it. I could never flourish there, nor be happy, nor do nor enjoy what God meant me to do and enjoy."

His face darkened, and seemed to contract, and shrivel itself up, and wither into age.

"Never, sir!" he repeated. "I could never draw cheerful breath there!"

"I should think not," said the old gentleman, eyeing Clifford earnestly, and rather apprehensively. "I should conceive not, sir, with that notion in your head!"

"Surely not," continued Clifford; "and it were a relief to me if that house could be torn down, or burnt up, and so the earth be rid of it, and grass be sown abundantly over its foundation. Not that I should ever visit its site again! for, sir, the farther I get away from it, the more does the joy, the lightsome freshness, the heart-leap, the intellectual dance, the youth, in short,—yes, my youth, my youth!—the more does it come back to me. No longer ago than this morning, I was old. I remember looking in the glass, and wondering at my own gray hair, and the wrinkles, many and deep, right across my brow, and the furrows down my cheeks, and the prodigious trampling of crow's-feet about my temples! It was too soon! I could not bear it! Age had no right to come! I had not lived! But now do I look old? If so, my aspect belies me strangely; for—a great weight being off my mind—I feel in the very heyday of my youth, with the world and my best days before me!"

"I trust you may find it so," said the old gentleman, who seemed rather embarrassed, and desirous of avoiding the observation which Clifford's wild talk drew on them both. "You have my best wishes for it."

"For Heaven's sake, dear Clifford, be quiet!" whispered his sister. "They think you mad."

"Be quiet yourself, Hepzibah!" returned her brother. "No matter what they think! I am not mad. For the first time in thirty years my thoughts gush up and find words ready for them. I must talk, and I will!"

He turned again towards the old gentleman, and renewed the conversation.

"Yes, my dear sir," said he, "it is my firm belief and hope that these terms of roof and hearth-stone, which have so long been held to embody something sacred, are soon to pass out of men's daily use, and be forgotten. Just imagine, for a moment, how much of human evil will crumble away, with this one change! What we call real estate—the solid ground to build a house on—is the broad foundation on which nearly all the guilt of this world rests. A man will commit almost any wrong,—he will heap up an immense pile of wickedness, as hard as granite, and which will weigh as heavily upon his soul, to eternal ages,—only to build a great, gloomy, dark-chambered mansion, for himself to die in, and for his posterity to be miserable in. He lays his own dead corpse beneath the underpinning, as one may say, and hangs his frowning picture on the wall, and, after thus converting himself into an evil destiny, expects his remotest great-grandchildren to be happy there. I do not speak wildly. I have just such a house in my mind's eye!"

"Then, sir," said the old gentleman, getting anxious to drop the subject, "you are not to blame for leaving it."

"Within the lifetime of the child already born," Clifford went on, "all this will be done away. The world is growing too ethereal and spiritual to bear these enormities a great while longer. To me, though, for a considerable period of time, I have lived chiefly in retirement, and know less of such things than most men,—even to me, the harbingers of a better era are unmistakable. Mesmerism, now! Will that effect nothing, think you, towards purging away the grossness out of human life?"

"All a humbug!" growled the old gentleman.

"These rapping spirits, that little Phoebe told us of, the other day," said Clifford,—"what are these but the messengers of the spiritual world, knocking at the door of substance? And it shall be flung wide open!"

"A humbug, again!" cried the old gentleman, growing more and more testy at these glimpses of Clifford's metaphysics. "I should like to rap with a good stick on the empty pates of the dolts who circulate such nonsense!"

"Then there is electricity,—the demon, the angel, the mighty physical power, the all-pervading intelligence!" exclaimed Clifford. "Is that a humbug, too? Is it a fact—or have I dreamt it—that, by means of electricity, the world of matter has become a great nerve, vibrating thousands of miles in a breathless point of time? Rather, the round globe is a vast head, a brain, instinct with intelligence! Or, shall we say, it is itself a thought, nothing but thought, and no longer the substance which we deemed it!"

"If you mean the telegraph," said the old gentleman, glancing his eye toward its wire, alongside the rail-track, "it is an excellent thing,—that is, of course, if the speculators in cotton and politics don't get possession of it. A great thing, indeed, sir, particularly as regards the detection of bank-robbers and murderers."

"I don't quite like it, in that point of view," replied Clifford. "A bank-robber, and what you call a murderer, likewise, has his rights, which men of enlightened humanity and conscience should regard in so much the more liberal spirit, because the bulk of society is prone to controvert their existence. An almost spiritual medium, like the electric telegraph, should be consecrated to high, deep, joyful, and holy missions. Lovers, day by, day—hour by hour, if so often moved to do it,—might send their heart-throbs from Maine to Florida, with some such words as these 'I love you forever!'—'My heart runs over with love!'—'I love you more than I can!' and, again, at the next message 'I have lived an hour longer, and love you twice as much!' Or, when a good man has departed, his distant friend should be conscious of an electric thrill, as from the world of happy spirits, telling him 'Your dear friend is in bliss!' Or, to an absent husband, should come tidings thus 'An immortal being, of whom you are the father, has this moment come from God!' and immediately its little voice would seem to have reached so far, and to be echoing in his heart. But for these poor rogues, the bank-robbers,—who, after all, are about as honest as nine people in ten, except that they disregard certain formalities, and prefer to transact business at midnight rather than 'Change-hours,—and for these murderers, as you phrase it, who are often excusable in the motives of their deed, and deserve to be ranked among public benefactors, if we consider only its result,—for unfortunate individuals like these, I really cannot applaud the enlistment of an immaterial and miraculous power in the universal world-hunt at their heels!"

"You can't, hey?" cried the old gentleman, with a hard look.

"Positively, no!" answered Clifford. "It puts them too miserably at disadvantage. For example, sir, in a dark, low, cross-beamed, panelled room of an old house, let us suppose a dead man, sitting in an arm-chair, with a blood-stain on his shirt-bosom,—and let us add to our hypothesis another man, issuing from the house, which he feels to be over-filled with the dead man's presence,—and let us lastly imagine him fleeing, Heaven knows whither, at the speed of a hurricane, by railroad! Now, sir, if the fugitive alight in some distant town, and find all the people babbling about that self-same dead man, whom he has fled so far to avoid the sight and thought of, will you not allow that his natural rights have been infringed? He has been deprived of his city of refuge, and, in my humble opinion, has suffered infinite wrong!"

"You are a strange man; Sir!" said the old gentleman, bringing his gimlet-eye to a point on Clifford, as if determined to bore right into him. "I can't see through you!"

"No, I'll be bound you can't!" cried Clifford, laughing. "And yet, my dear sir, I am as transparent as the water of Maule's well! But come, Hepzibah! We have flown far enough for once. Let us alight, as the birds do, and perch ourselves on the nearest twig, and consult wither we shall fly next!"

Just then, as it happened, the train reached a solitary way-station. Taking advantage of the brief pause, Clifford left the car, and drew Hepzibah along with him. A moment afterwards, the train—with all the life of its interior, amid which Clifford had made himself so conspicuous an object—was gliding away in the distance, and rapidly lessening to a point which, in another moment, vanished. The world had fled away from these two wanderers. They gazed drearily about them. At a little distance stood a wooden church, black with age, and in a dismal state of ruin and decay, with broken windows, a great rift through the main body of the edifice, and a rafter dangling from the top of the square tower. Farther off was a farm-house, in the old style, as venerably black as the church, with a roof sloping downward from the three-story peak, to within a man's height of the ground. It seemed uninhabited. There were the relics of a wood-pile, indeed, near the door, but with grass sprouting up among the chips and scattered logs. The small rain-drops came down aslant; the wind was not turbulent, but sullen, and full of chilly moisture.

Clifford shivered from head to foot. The wild effervescence of his mood—which had so readily supplied thoughts, fantasies, and a strange aptitude of words, and impelled him to talk from the mere necessity of giving vent to this bubbling-up gush of ideas had entirely subsided. A powerful excitement had given him energy and vivacity. Its operation over, he forthwith began to sink.

"You must take the lead now, Hepzibah!" murmured he, with a torpid and reluctant utterance. "Do with me as you will!" She knelt down upon the platform where they were standing and lifted her clasped hands to the sky. The dull, gray weight of clouds made it invisible; but it was no hour for disbelief,—no juncture this to question that there was a sky above, and an Almighty Father looking from it!

"O God!"—ejaculated poor, gaunt Hepzibah,—then paused a moment, to consider what her prayer should be,—"O God,—our Father,—are we not thy children? Have mercy on us!"

XVIII Governor Pyncheon

JUDGE PYNCHEON, while his two relatives have fled away with such ill-considered haste, still sits in the old parlor, keeping house, as the familiar phrase is, in the absence of its ordinary occupants. To him, and to the venerable House of the Seven Gables, does our story now betake itself, like an owl, bewildered in the daylight, and hastening back to his hollow tree.

The Judge has not shifted his position for a long while now. He has not stirred hand or foot, nor withdrawn his eyes so much as a hair's-breadth from their fixed gaze towards the corner of the room, since the footsteps of Hepzibah and Clifford creaked along the passage, and the outer door was closed cautiously behind their exit. He holds his watch in his left hand, but clutched in such a manner that you cannot see the dial-plate. How profound a fit of meditation! Or, supposing him asleep, how infantile a quietude of conscience, and what wholesome order in the gastric region, are betokened by slumber so entirely undisturbed with starts, cramp, twitches, muttered dreamtalk, trumpet-blasts through the nasal organ, or any slightest irregularity of breath! You must hold your own breath, to satisfy yourself whether he breathes at all. It is quite inaudible. You hear the ticking of his watch; his breath you do not hear. A most refreshing slumber, doubtless! And yet, the Judge cannot be asleep. His eyes are open! A veteran politician, such as he, would never fall asleep with wide-open eyes, lest some enemy or mischief-maker, taking him thus at unawares, should peep through these windows into his consciousness, and make strange discoveries among the reminiscences, projects, hopes, apprehensions, weaknesses, and strong points, which he has heretofore shared with nobody. A cautious man is proverbially said to sleep with one eye open. That may be wisdom. But not with both; for this were heedlessness! No, no! Judge Pyncheon cannot be asleep.

It is odd, however, that a gentleman so burdened with engagements,—and noted, too, for punctuality,—should linger thus in an old lonely mansion, which he has never seemed very fond of visiting. The oaken chair, to be sure, may tempt him with its roominess. It is, indeed, a spacious, and, allowing for the rude age that fashioned it, a moderately easy seat, with capacity enough, at all events, and offering no restraint to the Judge's breadth of beam. A bigger man might find ample accommodation in it. His ancestor, now pictured upon the wall, with all his English beef about him, used hardly to present a front extending from elbow to elbow of this chair, or a base that would cover its whole cushion. But there are better chairs than this,—mahogany, black walnut, rosewood, spring-seated and damask-cushioned, with varied slopes, and innumerable artifices to make them easy, and obviate the irksomeness of too tame an ease,—a score of such might be at Judge Pyncheon's service. Yes! in a score of drawing-rooms he would be more than welcome. Mamma would advance to meet him, with outstretched hand; the virgin daughter, elderly as he has now got to be,—an old widower, as he smilingly describes himself,—would shake up the cushion for the Judge, and do her pretty utmost to make him comfortable. For the Judge is a prosperous man. He cherishes his schemes, moreover, like other people, and reasonably brighter than most others; or did so, at least, as he lay abed this morning, in an agreeable half-drowse, planning the business of the day, and speculating on the probabilities of the next fifteen years. With his firm health, and the little inroad that age has made upon him, fifteen years or twenty—yes, or perhaps five-and-twenty!—are no more than he may fairly call his own. Five-and-twenty years for the enjoyment of his real estate in town and country, his railroad, bank, and insurance shares, his United States stock,—his wealth, in short, however invested, now in possession, or soon to be acquired; together with the public honors that have fallen upon him, and the weightier ones that are yet to fall! It is good! It is excellent! It is enough!

Still lingering in the old chair! If the Judge has a little time to throw away, why does not he visit the insurance office, as is his frequent custom, and sit awhile in one of their leathern-cushioned arm-chairs, listening to the gossip of the day, and dropping some deeply designed chance-word, which will be certain to become the gossip of to-morrow. And have not the bank directors a meeting at which it was the Judge's purpose to be present, and his office to preside? Indeed they have; and the hour is noted on a card, which is, or ought to be, in Judge Pyncheon's right vest-pocket. Let him go thither, and loll at ease upon his moneybags! He has lounged long enough in the old chair!

This was to have been such a busy day. In the first place, the interview with Clifford. Half an hour, by the Judge's reckoning, was to suffice for that; it would probably be less, but—taking into consideration that Hepzibah was first to be dealt with, and that these women are apt to make many words where a few would do much better—it might be safest to allow half an hour. Half an hour? Why, Judge, it is already two hours, by your own undeviatingly accurate chronometer. Glance your eye down at it and see! Ah; he will not give himself the trouble either to bend his head, or elevate his hand, so as to bring the faithful time-keeper within his range of vision! Time, all at once, appears to have become a matter of no moment with the Judge!

And has he forgotten all the other items of his memoranda? Clifford's affair arranged, he was to meet a State Street broker, who has undertaken to procure a heavy percentage, and the best of paper, for a few loose thousands which the Judge happens to have by him, uninvested. The wrinkled note-shaver will have taken his railroad trip in vain. Half an hour later, in the street next to this, there was to be an auction of real estate, including a portion of the old Pyncheon property, originally belonging to Maule's garden ground. It has been alienated from the Pyncheons these four-score years; but the Judge had kept it in his eye, and had set his heart on reannexing it to the small demesne still left around the Seven Gables; and now, during this odd fit of oblivion, the fatal hammer must have fallen, and transferred our ancient patrimony to some alien possessor. Possibly, indeed, the sale may have been postponed till fairer weather. If so, will the Judge make it convenient to be present, and favor the auctioneer with his bid, On the proximate occasion?

The next affair was to buy a horse for his own driving. The one heretofore his favorite stumbled, this very morning, on the road to town, and must be at once discarded. Judge Pyncheon's neck is too precious to be risked on such a contingency as a stumbling steed. Should all the above business be seasonably got through with, he might attend the meeting of a charitable society; the very name of which, however, in the multiplicity of his benevolence, is quite forgotten; so that this engagement may pass unfulfilled, and no great harm done. And if he have time, amid the press of more urgent matters, he must take measures for the renewal of Mrs. Pyncheon's tombstone, which, the sexton tells him, has fallen on its marble face, and is cracked quite in twain. She was a praiseworthy woman enough, thinks the Judge, in spite of her nervousness, and the tears that she was so oozy with, and her foolish behavior about the coffee; and as she took her departure so seasonably, he will not grudge the second tombstone. It is better, at least, than if she had never needed any! The next item on his list was to give orders for some fruit-trees, of a rare variety, to be deliverable at his country-seat in the ensuing autumn. Yes, buy them, by all means; and may the peaches be luscious in your mouth, Judge Pyncheon! After this comes something more important. A committee of his political party has besought him for a hundred or two of dollars, in addition to his previous disbursements, towards carrying on the fall campaign. The Judge is a patriot; the fate of the country is staked on the November election; and besides, as will be shadowed forth in another paragraph, he has no trifling stake of his own in the same great game. He will do what the committee asks; nay, he will be liberal beyond their expectations; they shall have a check for five hundred dollars, and more anon, if it be needed. What next? A decayed widow, whose husband was Judge Pyncheon's early friend, has laid her case of destitution before him, in a very moving letter. She and her fair daughter have scarcely bread to eat. He partly intends to call on her to-day,—perhaps so—perhaps not,—accordingly as he may happen to have leisure, and a small bank-note.

Another business, which, however, he puts no great weight on (it is well, you know, to be heedful, but not over-anxious, as respects one's personal health),—another business, then, was to consult his family physician. About what, for Heaven's sake? Why, it is rather difficult to describe the symptoms. A mere dimness of sight and dizziness of brain, was it?—or disagreeable choking, or stifling, or gurgling, or bubbling, in the region of the thorax, as the anatomists say?—or was it a pretty severe throbbing and kicking of the heart, rather creditable to him than otherwise, as showing that the organ had not been left out of the Judge's physical contrivance? No matter what it was. The doctor probably would smile at the statement of such trifles to his professional ear; the Judge would smile in his turn; and meeting one another's eyes, they would enjoy a hearty laugh together! But a fig for medical advice. The Judge will never need it.

Pray, pray, Judge Pyncheon, look at your watch, Now! What—not a glance! It is within ten minutes of the dinner hour! It surely cannot have slipped your memory that the dinner of to-day is to be the most important, in its consequences, of all the dinners you ever ate. Yes, precisely the most important; although, in the course of your somewhat eminent career, you have been placed high towards the head of the table, at splendid banquets, and have poured out your festive eloquence to ears yet echoing with Webster's mighty organ-tones. No public dinner this, however. It is merely a gathering of some dozen or so of friends from several districts of the State; men of distinguished character and influence, assembling, almost casually, at the house of a common friend, likewise distinguished, who will make them welcome to a little better than his ordinary fare. Nothing in the way of French cookery, but an excellent dinner, nevertheless. Real turtle, we understand, and salmon, tautog, canvas-backs, pig, English mutton, good roast beef, or dainties of that serious kind, fit for substantial country gentlemen, as these honorable persons mostly are. The delicacies of the season, in short, and flavored by a brand of old Madeira which has been the pride of many seasons. It is the Juno brand; a glorious wine, fragrant, and full of gentle might; a bottled-up happiness, put by for use; a golden liquid, worth more than liquid gold; so rare and admirable, that veteran wine-bibbers count it among their epochs to have tasted it! It drives away the heart-ache, and substitutes no head-ache! Could the Judge but quaff a glass, it might enable him to shake off the unaccountable lethargy which (for the ten intervening minutes, and five to boot, are already past) has made him such a laggard at this momentous dinner. It would all but revive a dead man! Would you like to sip it now, Judge Pyncheon?

Alas, this dinner. Have you really forgotten its true object? Then let us whisper it, that you may start at once out of the oaken chair, which really seems to be enchanted, like the one in Comus, or that in which Moll Pitcher imprisoned your own grandfather. But ambition is a talisman more powerful than witchcraft. Start up, then, and, hurrying through the streets, burst in upon the company, that they may begin before the fish is spoiled! They wait for you; and it is little for your interest that they should wait. These gentlemen—need you be told it?—have assembled, not without purpose, from every quarter of the State. They are practised politicians, every man of them, and skilled to adjust those preliminary measures which steal from the people, without its knowledge, the power of choosing its own rulers. The popular voice, at the next gubernatorial election, though loud as thunder, will be really but an echo of what these gentlemen shall speak, under their breath, at your friend's festive board. They meet to decide upon their candidate. This little knot of subtle schemers will control the convention, and, through it, dictate to the party. And what worthier candidate,—more wise and learned, more noted for philanthropic liberality, truer to safe principles, tried oftener by public trusts, more spotless in private character, with a larger stake in the common welfare, and deeper grounded, by hereditary descent, in the faith and practice of the Puritans,—what man can be presented for the suffrage of the people, so eminently combining all these claims to the chief-rulership as Judge Pyncheon here before us?

Make haste, then! Do your part! The meed for which you have toiled, and fought, and climbed, and crept, is ready for your grasp! Be present at this dinner!—drink a glass or two of that noble wine!—make your pledges in as low a whisper as you will!—and you rise up from table virtually governor of the glorious old State! Governor Pyncheon of Massachusetts!

And is there no potent and exhilarating cordial in a certainty like this? It has been the grand purpose of half your lifetime to obtain it. Now, when there needs little more than to signify your acceptance, why do you sit so lumpishly in your great-great-grandfather's oaken chair, as if preferring it to the gubernatorial one? We have all heard of King Log; but, in these jostling times, one of that royal kindred will hardly win the race for an elective chief-magistracy.

Well; it is absolutely too late for dinner! Turtle, salmon, tautog, woodcock, boiled turkey, South-Down mutton, pig, roast-beef, have vanished, or exist only in fragments, with lukewarm potatoes, and gravies crusted over with cold fat. The Judge, had he done nothing else, would have achieved wonders with his knife and fork. It was he, you know, of whom it used to be said, in reference to his ogre-like appetite, that his Creator made him a great animal, but that the dinner-hour made him a great beast. Persons of his large sensual endowments must claim indulgence, at their feeding-time. But, for once, the Judge is entirely too late for dinner! Too late, we fear, even to join the party at their wine! The guests are warm and merry; they have given up the Judge; and, concluding that the Free-Soilers have him, they will fix upon another candidate. Were our friend now to stalk in among them, with that wide-open stare, at once wild and stolid, his ungenial presence would be apt to change their cheer. Neither would it be seemly in Judge Pyncheon, generally so scrupulous in his attire, to show himself at a dinner-table with that crimson stain upon his shirt-bosom. By the bye, how came it there? It is an ugly sight, at any rate; and the wisest way for the Judge is to button his coat closely over his breast, and, taking his horse and chaise from the livery stable, to make all speed to his own house. There, after a glass of brandy and water, and a mutton-chop, a beefsteak, a broiled fowl, or some such hasty little dinner and supper all in one, he had better spend the evening by the fireside. He must toast his slippers a long while, in order to get rid of the chilliness which the air of this vile old house has sent curdling through his veins.

Up, therefore, Judge Pyncheon, up! You have lost a day. But to-morrow will be here anon. Will you rise, betimes, and make the most of it? To-morrow. To-morrow! To-morrow. We, that are alive, may rise betimes to-morrow. As for him that has died to-day, his morrow will be the resurrection morn.

Meanwhile the twilight is glooming upward out of the corners of the room. The shadows of the tall furniture grow deeper, and at first become more definite;

then, spreading wider, they lose their distinctness of outline in the dark gray tide of oblivion, as it were, that creeps slowly over the various objects, and the one human figure sitting in the midst of them. The gloom has not entered from without; it has brooded here all day, and now, taking its own inevitable time, will possess itself of everything. The Judge's face, indeed, rigid and singularly white, refuses to melt into this universal solvent. Fainter and fainter grows the light. It is as if another double-handful of darkness had been scattered through the air. Now it is no longer gray, but sable. There is still a faint appearance at the window; neither a glow, nor a gleam, nor a glimmer,—any phrase of light would express something far brighter than this doubtful perception, or sense, rather, that there is a window there. Has it yet vanished? No!—yes!—not quite! And there is still the swarthy whiteness,—we shall venture to marry these ill-agreeing words,—the swarthy whiteness of Judge Pyncheon's face. The features are all gone: there is only the paleness of them left. And how looks it now? There is no window! There is no face! An infinite, inscrutable blackness has annihilated sight! Where is our universe? All crumbled away from us; and we, adrift in chaos, may hearken to the gusts of homeless wind, that go sighing and murmuring about in quest of what was once a world!

Is there no other sound? One other, and a fearful one. It is the ticking of the Judge's watch, which, ever since Hepzibah left the room in search of Clifford, he has been holding in his hand. Be the cause what it may, this little, quiet, never-ceasing throb of Time's pulse, repeating its small strokes with such busy regularity, in Judge Pyncheon's motionless hand, has an effect of terror, which we do not find in any other accompaniment of the scene.

But', listen! That puff of the breeze was louder. It had a tone unlike the dreary and sullen one which has bemoaned itself, and afflicted all mankind with miserable sympathy, for five days past. The wind has veered about! It now comes boisterously from the northwest, and, taking hold of the aged framework of the Seven Gables, gives it a shake, like a wrestler that would try strength with his antagonist. Another and another sturdy tussle with the blast! The old house creaks again, and makes a vociferous but somewhat unintelligible bellowing in its sooty throat (the big flue, we mean, of its wide chimney), partly in complaint at the rude wind, but rather, as befits their century and a half of hostile intimacy, in tough defiance. A rumbling kind of a bluster roars behind the fire-board. A door has slammed above stairs. A window, perhaps, has been left open, or else is driven in by an unruly gust. It is not to be conceived, before-hand, what wonderful wind-instruments are these old timber mansions, and how haunted with the strangest noises, which immediately begin to sing, and sigh, and sob, and shriek,—and to smite with sledge-hammers, airy but ponderous, in some distant chamber,—and to tread along the entries as with stately footsteps, and rustle up and down the staircase, as with silks miraculously stiff,—whenever the gale catches the house with a window open, and gets fairly into it. Would that we were not an attendant spirit here! It is too awful! This clamor of the wind through the lonely house; the Judge's quietude, as he sits invisible; and that pertinacious ticking of his watch!

As regards Judge Pyncheon's invisibility, however, that matter will soon be remedied. The northwest wind has swept the sky clear. The window is distinctly seen. Through its panes, moreover, we dimly catch the sweep of the dark, clustering foliage outside, fluttering with a constant irregularity of movement, and letting in a peep of starlight, now here, now there. Oftener than any other object, these glimpses illuminate the Judge's face. But here comes more effectual light. Observe that silvery dance upon the upper branches of the pear-tree, and now a little lower, and now on the whole mass of boughs, while, through their shifting intricacies, the moonbeams fall aslant into the room. They play over the Judge's figure and show that he has not stirred throughout the hours of darkness. They follow the shadows, in changeful sport, across his unchanging features. They gleam upon his watch. His grasp conceals the dial-plate,—but we know that the faithful hands have met; for one of the city clocks tells midnight.

A man of sturdy understanding, like Judge Pyncheon, cares no more for twelve o'clock at night than for the corresponding hour of noon. However just the parallel drawn, in some of the preceding pages, between his Puritan ancestor and himself, it fails in this point. The Pyncheon of two centuries ago, in common with most of his contemporaries, professed his full belief in spiritual ministrations, although reckoning them chiefly of a malignant character. The Pyncheon of to-night, who sits in yonder arm-chair, believes in no such nonsense. Such, at least, was his creed, some few hours since. His hair will not bristle, therefore, at the stories which—in times when chimney-corners had benches in them, where old people sat poking into the ashes of the past, and raking out traditions like live coals—used to be told about this very room of his ancestral house. In fact, these tales are too absurd to bristle even childhood's hair. What sense, meaning, or moral, for example, such as even ghost-stories should be susceptible of, can be traced in the ridiculous legend, that, at midnight, all the dead Pyncheons are bound to assemble in this parlor? And, pray, for what? Why, to see whether the portrait of their ancestor still keeps its place upon the wall, in compliance with his testamentary directions! Is it worth while to come out of their graves for that?

We are tempted to make a little sport with the idea. Ghost-stories are hardly to be treated seriously any longer. The family-party of the defunct Pyncheons, we presume, goes off in this wise.

First comes the ancestor himself, in his black cloak, steeple-hat, and trunk-breeches, girt about the waist with a leathern belt, in which hangs his steel-hilted sword, he has a long staff in his hand, such as gentlemen in advanced life used to carry, as much for the dignity of the thing as for the support to be derived from it. He looks up at the portrait; a thing of no substance, gazing at its own painted image! All is safe. The picture is still there. The purpose of his brain has been kept sacred thus long after the man himself has sprouted up in graveyard grass. See! he lifts his ineffectual hand, and tries the frame. All safe! But is that a smile?—is it not, rather a frown of deadly import, that darkens over the shadow of his features? The stout Colonel is dissatisfied! So decided is his look of discontent as to impart additional distinctness to his features; through which, nevertheless, the moonlight passes, and flickers on the wall beyond. Something has strangely vexed the ancestor! With a grim shake of the head, he turns away. Here come other Pyncheons, the whole tribe, in their half a dozen generations, jostling and elbowing one another, to reach the picture. We behold aged men and grandames, a clergyman with the Puritanic stiffness still in his garb and mien, and a red-coated officer of the old French war; and there comes the shop-keeping Pyncheon of a century ago, with the ruffles turned back from his wrists; and there the periwigged and brocaded gentleman of the artist's legend, with the beautiful and pensive Alice, who brings no pride out of her virgin grave. All try the picture-frame. What do these ghostly people seek? A mother lifts her child, that his little hands may touch it! There is evidently a mystery about the picture, that perplexes these poor Pyncheons when they ought to be at rest. In a corner, meanwhile, stands the figure of an elderly man, in a leathern jerkin and breeches, with a carpenter's rule sticking out of his side pocket; he points his finger at the bearded Colonel and his descendants, nodding, jeering, mocking, and finally bursting into obstreperous, though inaudible laughter.

Indulging our fancy in this freak, we have partly lost the power of restraint and guidance. We distinguish an unlooked-for figure in our visionary scene. Among those ancestral people there is a young man, dressed in the very fashion of to-day: he wears a dark frock-coat, almost destitute of skirts, gray pantaloons, gaiter boots of patent leather, and has a finely wrought gold chain across his breast, and a little silver-headed whalebone stick in his hand. Were we to meet this figure at noon-day, we should greet him as young Jaffrey Pyncheon, the Judge's only surviving child, who has been spending the last two years in foreign travel. If still in life, how comes his shadow hither? If dead, what a misfortune! The old Pyncheon property, together with the great estate acquired by the young man's father, would devolve on whom? On poor, foolish Clifford, gaunt Hepzibah, and rustic little Phoebe! But another and a greater marvel greets us! Can we believe our eyes? A stout, elderly gentleman has made his appearance; he has an aspect of eminent respectability, wears a black coat and pantaloons, of roomy width, and might be pronounced scrupulously neat in his attire, but for a broad crimson stain across his snowy neckcloth and down his shirt-bosom. Is it the Judge, or no? How can it be Judge Pyncheon? We discern his figure, as plainly as the flickering moonbeams can show us anything, still seated in the oaken chair! Be the apparition whose it may, it advances to the picture, seems to seize the frame, tries to peep behind it, and turns away, with a frown as black as the ancestral one.

The fantastic scene just hinted at must by no means be considered as forming an actual portion of our story. We were betrayed into this brief extravagance by the quiver of the moonbeams; they dance hand-in-hand with shadows, and are reflected in the looking-glass, which, you are aware, is always a kind of window or doorway into the spiritual world. We needed relief, moreover, from our too long and exclusive contemplation of that figure in the chair. This wild wind, too, has tossed our thoughts into strange confusion, but without tearing them away from their one determined centre. Yonder leaden Judge sits immovably upon our soul. Will he never stir again? We shall go mad unless he stirs! You may the better estimate his quietude by the fearlessness of a little mouse, which sits on its hind legs, in a streak of moonlight, close by Judge Pyncheon's foot, and seems to meditate a journey of exploration over this great black bulk. Ha! what has startled the nimble little mouse? It is the visage of grimalkin, outside of the window, where he appears to have posted himself for a deliberate watch. This grimalkin has a very ugly look. Is it a cat watching for a mouse, or the devil for a human soul? Would we could scare him from the window!

Thank Heaven, the night is well-nigh past! The moonbeams have no longer so silvery a gleam, nor contrast so strongly with the blackness of the shadows among which they fall. They are paler now; the shadows look gray, not black. The boisterous wind is hushed. What is the hour? Ah! the watch has at last ceased to tick; for the Judge's forgetful fingers neglected to wind it up, as usual, at ten o'clock, being half an hour or so before his ordinary bedtime,—and it has run down, for the first time in five years. But the great world-clock of Time still keeps its beat. The dreary night—for, oh, how dreary seems its haunted waste, behind us!—gives place to a fresh, transparent, cloudless morn. Blessed, blessed radiance! The daybeam—even what little of it finds its way into this always dusky parlor—seems part of the universal benediction, annulling evil, and rendering all goodness possible, and happiness attainable. Will Judge Pyncheon now rise up from his chair? Will he go forth, and receive the early sunbeams on his brow? Will he begin this new day,—which God has smiled upon, and blessed, and given to mankind,—will he begin it with better purposes than the many that have been spent amiss? Or are all the deep-laid schemes of yesterday as stubborn in his heart, and as busy in his brain, as ever?

In this latter case, there is much to do. Will the Judge still insist with Hepzibah on the interview with Clifford? Will he buy a safe, elderly gentleman's horse? Will he persuade the purchaser of the old Pyncheon property to relinquish the bargain in his favor? Will he see his family physician, and obtain a medicine that shall preserve him, to be an honor and blessing to his race, until the utmost term of patriarchal longevity? Will Judge Pyncheon, above all, make due apologies to that company of honorable friends, and satisfy them that his absence from the festive board was unavoidable, and so fully retrieve himself in their good opinion that he shall yet be Governor of Massachusetts? And all these great purposes accomplished, will he walk the streets again, with that dog-day smile of elaborate benevolence, sultry enough to tempt flies to come and buzz in it? Or will he, after the tomb-like seclusion of the past day and night, go forth a humbled and repentant man, sorrowful, gentle, seeking no profit, shrinking from worldly honor, hardly daring to love God, but bold to love his fellow man, and to do him what good he may? Will he bear about with him,—no odious grin of feigned benignity, insolent in its pretence, and loathsome in its falsehood,—but the tender sadness of a contrite heart, broken, at last, beneath its own weight of sin? For it is our belief, whatever show of honor he may have piled upon it, that there was heavy sin at the base of this man's being.

Rise up, Judge Pyncheon! The morning sunshine glimmers through the foliage, and, beautiful and holy as it is, shuns not to kindle up your face. Rise up, thou subtle, worldly, selfish, iron-hearted hypocrite, and make thy choice whether still to be subtle, worldly, selfish, iron-hearted, and hypocritical, or to tear these sins out of thy nature, though they bring the lifeblood with them! The Avenger is upon thee! Rise up, before it be too late!

What! Thou art not stirred by this last appeal? No, not a jot! And there we see a fly,—one of your common house-flies, such as are always buzzing on the window-pane,—which has smelt out Governor Pyncheon, and alights, now on his forehead, now on his chin, and now, Heaven help us! is creeping over the bridge of his nose, towards the would-be chief-magistrate's wide-open eyes! Canst thou not brush the fly away? Art thou too sluggish? Thou man, that hadst so many busy projects yesterday! Art thou too weak, that wast so powerful? Not brush away a fly? Nay, then, we give thee up!

And hark! the shop-bell rings. After hours like these latter ones, through which we have borne our heavy tale, it is good to be made sensible that there is a living world, and that even this old, lonely mansion retains some manner of connection with it. We breathe more freely, emerging from Judge Pyncheon's presence into the street before the Seven Gables.

XIX Alice's Posies

UNCLE VENNER, trundling a wheelbarrow, was the earliest person stirring in the neighborhood the day after the storm.

Pyncheon Street, in front of the House of the Seven Gables, was a far pleasanter scene than a by-lane, confined by shabby fences, and bordered with wooden dwellings of the meaner class, could reasonably be expected to present. Nature made sweet amends, that morning, for the five unkindly days which had preceded it. It would have been enough to live for, merely to look up at the wide benediction of the sky, or as much of it as was visible between the houses, genial once more with sunshine. Every object was agreeable, whether to be gazed at in the breadth, or examined more minutely. Such, for example, were the well-washed pebbles and gravel of the sidewalk; even the sky-reflecting pools in the centre of the street; and the grass, now freshly verdant, that crept along the base of the fences, on the other side of which, if one peeped over, was seen the multifarious growth of gardens. Vegetable productions, of whatever kind, seemed more than negatively happy, in the juicy warmth and abundance of their life. The Pyncheon Elm, throughout its great circumference, was all alive, and full of the morning sun and a sweet-tempered little breeze, which lingered within this verdant sphere, and set a thousand leafy tongues a-whispering all at once. This aged tree appeared to have suffered nothing from the gale. It had kept its boughs unshattered, and its full complement of leaves; and the whole in perfect verdure, except a single branch, that, by the earlier change with which the elm-tree sometimes prophesies the autumn, had been transmuted to bright gold. It was like the golden branch that gained Aeneas and the Sibyl admittance into Hades.

This one mystic branch hung down before the main entrance of the Seven Gables, so nigh the ground that any passer-by might have stood on tiptoe and plucked it off. Presented at the door, it would have been a symbol of his right to enter, and be made acquainted with all the secrets of the house. So little faith is due to external appearance, that there was really an inviting aspect over the venerable edifice, conveying an idea that its history must be a decorous and happy one, and such as would be delightful for a fireside tale. Its windows gleamed cheerfully in the slanting sunlight. The lines and tufts of green moss, here and there, seemed pledges of familiarity and sisterhood with Nature; as if this human dwelling-place, being of such old date, had established its prescriptive title among primeval oaks and whatever other objects, by virtue of their long continuance, have acquired a gracious right to be. A person of imaginative temperament, while passing by the house, would turn, once and again, and peruse it well: its many peaks, consenting together in the clustered chimney; the deep projection over its basement-story; the arched window, imparting a look, if not of grandeur, yet of antique gentility, to the broken portal over which it opened; the luxuriance of gigantic burdocks, near the threshold; he would note all these characteristics, and be conscious of something deeper than he saw. He would conceive the mansion to have been the residence of the stubborn old Puritan, Integrity, who, dying in some forgotten generation, had left a blessing in all its rooms and chambers, the efficacy of which was to be seen in the religion, honesty, moderate competence, or upright poverty and solid happiness, of his descendants, to this day.

One object, above all others, would take root in the imaginative observer's memory. It was the great tuft of flowers,—weeds, you would have called them, only a week ago,—the tuft of crimson-spotted flowers, in the angle between the two front gables. The old people used to give them the name of Alice's Posies, in remembrance of fair Alice Pyncheon, who was believed to have brought their seeds from Italy. They were flaunting in rich beauty and full bloom to-day, and seemed, as it were, a mystic expression that something within the house was consummated.

It was but little after sunrise, when Uncle Venner made his appearance, as aforesaid, impelling a wheelbarrow along the street. He was going his matutinal rounds to collect cabbage-leaves, turnip-tops, potato-skins, and the miscellaneous refuse of the dinner-pot, which the thrifty housewives of the neighborhood were accustomed to put aside, as fit only to feed a pig. Uncle Venner's pig was fed entirely, and kept in prime order, on these eleemosynary contributions; insomuch that the patched philosopher used to promise that, before retiring to his farm, he would make a feast of the portly grunter, and invite all his neighbors to partake of the joints and spare-ribs which they had helped to fatten. Miss Hepzibah Pyncheon's housekeeping had so greatly improved, since Clifford became a member of the family, that her share of the banquet would have been no lean one; and Uncle Venner, accordingly, was a good deal disappointed not to find the large earthen pan, full of fragmentary eatables, that ordinarily awaited his coming at the back doorstep of the Seven Gables.

"I never knew Miss Hepzibah so forgetful before," said the patriarch to himself. "She must have had a dinner yesterday,—no question of that! She always has one, nowadays. So where's the pot-liquor and potato-skins, I ask? Shall I knock, and see if she's stirring yet? No, no,—'t won't do! If little Phoebe was about the house, I should not mind knocking; but Miss Hepzibah, likely as not, would scowl down at me out of the window, and look cross, even if she felt pleasantly. So, I'll come back at noon."

With these reflections, the old man was shutting the gate of the little backyard. Creaking on its hinges, however, like every other gate and door about the premises, the sound reached the ears of the occupant of the northern gable, one of the windows of which had a side-view towards the gate.

"Good-morning, Uncle Venner!" said the daguerreotypist, leaning out of the window. "Do you hear nobody stirring?"

"Not a soul," said the man of patches. "But that's no wonder. 'Tis barely half an hour past sunrise, yet. But I'm really glad to see you, Mr. Holgrave! There's a strange, lonesome look about this side of the house; so that my heart misgave me, somehow or other, and I felt as if there was nobody alive in it. The front of the house looks a good deal cheerier; and Alice's Posies are blooming there beautifully; and if I were a young man, Mr. Holgrave, my sweetheart should have one of those flowers in her bosom, though I risked my neck climbing for it! Well, and did the wind keep you awake last night?"

"It did, indeed!" answered the artist, smiling. "If I were a believer in ghosts,—and I don't quite know whether I am or not,—I should have concluded that all the old Pyncheons were running riot in the lower rooms, especially in Miss Hepzibah's part of the house. But it is very quiet now."

"Yes, Miss Hepzibah will be apt to over-sleep herself, after being disturbed, all night, with the racket," said Uncle Venner. "But it would be odd, now, wouldn't it, if the Judge had taken both his cousins into the country along with him? I saw him go into the shop yesterday."

"At what hour?" inquired Holgrave.

"Oh, along in the forenoon," said the old man. "Well, well! I must go my rounds, and so must my wheelbarrow. But I'll be back here at dinner-time; for my pig likes a dinner as well as a breakfast. No meal-time, and no sort of victuals, ever seems to come amiss to my pig. Good morning to you! And, Mr. Holgrave, if I were a young man, like you, I'd get one of Alice's Posies, and keep it in water till Phoebe comes back."

"I have heard," said the daguerreotypist, as he drew in his head, "that the water of Maule's well suits those flowers best."

Here the conversation ceased, and Uncle Venner went on his way. For half an hour longer, nothing disturbed the repose of the Seven Gables; nor was there any visitor, except a carrier-boy, who, as he passed the front doorstep, threw down one of his newspapers; for Hepzibah, of late, had regularly taken it in. After a while, there came a fat woman, making prodigious speed, and stumbling as she ran up the steps of the shop-door. Her face glowed with fire-heat, and, it being a pretty warm morning, she bubbled and hissed, as it were, as if all a-fry with chimney-warmth, and summer-warmth, and the warmth of her own corpulent velocity. She tried the shop-door; it was fast. She tried it again, with so angry a jar that the bell tinkled angrily back at her.

"The deuce take Old Maid Pyncheon!" muttered the irascible housewife. "Think of her pretending to set up a cent-shop, and then lying abed till noon! These are what she calls gentlefolk's airs, I suppose! But I'll either start her ladyship, or break the door down!"

She shook it accordingly, and the bell, having a spiteful little temper of its own, rang obstreperously, making its remonstrances heard,—not, indeed, by the ears for which they were intended,—but by a good lady on the opposite side of the street. She opened the window, and addressed the impatient applicant.

"You'll find nobody there, Mrs. Gubbins."

"But I must and will find somebody here!" cried Mrs. Gubbins, inflicting another outrage on the bell. "I want a half-pound of pork, to fry some first-rate flounders for Mr. Gubbins's breakfast; and, lady or not, Old Maid Pyncheon shall get up and serve me with it!"

"But do hear reason, Mrs. Gubbins!" responded the lady opposite. "She, and her brother too, have both gone to their cousin's, Judge Pyncheon's at his country-seat. There's not a soul in the house, but that young daguerreotype-man that sleeps in the north gable. I saw old Hepzibah and Clifford go away yesterday; and a queer couple of ducks they were, paddling through the mud-puddles! They're gone, I'll assure you."

"And how do you know they're gone to the Judge's?" asked Mrs. Gubbins. "He's a rich man; and there's been a quarrel between him and Hepzibah this many a day, because he won't give her a living. That's the main reason of her setting up a cent-shop."

"I know that well enough," said the neighbor. "But they're gone,—that's one thing certain. And who but a blood relation, that couldn't help himself, I ask you, would take in that awful-tempered old maid, and that dreadful Clifford? That's it, you may be sure."

Mrs. Gubbins took her departure, still brimming over with hot wrath against the absent Hepzibah. For another half-hour, or, perhaps, considerably more, there was almost as much quiet on the outside of the house as within. The elm, however, made a pleasant, cheerful, sunny sigh, responsive to the breeze that was elsewhere imperceptible; a swarm of insects buzzed merrily under its drooping shadow, and became specks of light whenever they darted into the sunshine; a locust sang, once or twice, in some inscrutable seclusion of the tree; and a solitary little bird, with plumage of pale gold, came and hovered about Alice's Posies.

At last our small acquaintance, Ned Higgins, trudged up the street, on his way to school; and happening, for the first time in a fortnight, to be the possessor of a cent, he could by no means get past the shop-door of the Seven Gables. But it would not open. Again and again, however, and half a dozen other agains, with the inexorable pertinacity of a child intent upon some object important to itself, did he renew his efforts for admittance. He had, doubtless, set his heart upon an elephant; or, possibly, with Hamlet, he meant to eat a crocodile. In response to his more violent attacks, the bell gave, now and then, a moderate tinkle, but could not be stirred into clamor by any exertion of the little fellow's childish and tiptoe strength. Holding by the door-handle, he peeped through a crevice of the curtain, and saw that the inner door, communicating with the passage towards the parlor, was closed.

"Miss Pyncheon!" screamed the child, rapping on the window-pane, "I want an elephant!"

There being no answer to several repetitions of the summons, Ned began to grow impatient; and his little pot of passion quickly boiling over, he picked up a stone, with a naughty purpose to fling it through the window; at the same time blubbering and sputtering with wrath. A man—one of two who happened to be passing by—caught the urchin's arm.

"What's the trouble, old gentleman?" he asked.

"I want old Hepzibah, or Phoebe, or any of them!" answered Ned, sobbing. "They won't open the door; and I can't get my elephant!"

"Go to school, you little scamp!" said the man. "There's another cent-shop round the corner. 'T is very strange, Dixey," added he to his companion, "what's become of all these Pyncheon's! Smith, the livery-stable keeper, tells me Judge Pyncheon put his horse up yesterday, to stand till after dinner, and has not taken him away yet. And one of the Judge's hired men has been in, this morning, to make inquiry about him. He's a kind of person, they say, that seldom breaks his habits, or stays out o' nights."

"Oh, he'll turn up safe enough!" said Dixey. "And as for Old Maid Pyncheon, take my word for it, she has run in debt, and gone off from her creditors. I foretold, you remember, the first morning she set up shop, that her devilish scowl would frighten away customers. They couldn't stand it!"

"I never thought she'd make it go," remarked his friend. "This business of cent-shops is overdone among the women-folks. My wife tried it, and lost five dollars on her outlay!"

"Poor business!" said Dixey, shaking his head. "Poor business!"

In the course of the morning, there were various other attempts to open a communication with the supposed inhabitants of this silent and impenetrable mansion. The man of root-beer came, in his neatly painted wagon, with a couple of dozen full bottles, to be exchanged for empty ones; the baker, with a lot of crackers which Hepzibah had ordered for her retail custom; the butcher, with a nice titbit which he fancied she would be eager to secure for Clifford. Had any observer of these proceedings been aware of the fearful secret hidden within the house, it would have affected him with a singular shape and modification of horror, to see the current of human life making this small eddy hereabouts,—whirling sticks, straws and all such trifles, round and round, right over the black depth where a dead corpse lay unseen!

The butcher was so much in earnest with his sweetbread of lamb, or whatever the dainty might be, that he tried every accessible door of the Seven Gables, and at length came round again to the shop, where he ordinarily found admittance.

"It's a nice article, and I know the old lady would jump at it," said he to himself. "She can't be gone away! In fifteen years that I have driven my cart through Pyncheon Street, I've never known her to be away from home; though often enough, to be sure, a man might knock all day without bringing her to the door. But that was when she'd only herself to provide for."

Peeping through the same crevice of the curtain where, only a little while before, the urchin of elephantine appetite had peeped, the butcher beheld the inner door, not closed, as the child had seen it, but ajar, and almost wide open. However it might have happened, it was the fact. Through the passage-way there was a dark vista into the lighter but still obscure interior of the parlor. It appeared to the butcher that he could pretty clearly discern what seemed to be the stalwart legs, clad in black pantaloons, of a man sitting in a large oaken chair, the back of which concealed all the remainder of his figure. This contemptuous tranquillity on the part of an occupant of the house, in response to the butcher's indefatigable efforts to attract notice, so piqued the man of flesh that he determined to withdraw.

"So," thought he, "there sits Old Maid Pyncheon's bloody brother, while I've been giving myself all this trouble! Why, if a hog hadn't more manners, I'd stick him! I call it demeaning a man's business to trade with such people; and from this time forth, if they want a sausage or an ounce of liver, they shall run after the cart for it!"

He tossed the titbit angrily into his cart, and drove off in a pet.

Not a great while afterwards there was a sound of music turning the corner and approaching down the street, with several intervals of silence, and then a renewed and nearer outbreak of brisk melody. A mob of children was seen moving onward, or stopping, in unison with the sound, which appeared to proceed from the centre of the throng; so that they were loosely bound together by slender strains of harmony, and drawn along captive; with ever and anon an accession of some little fellow in an apron and straw-hat, capering forth from door or gateway. Arriving under the shadow of the Pyncheon Elm, it proved to be the Italian boy, who, with his monkey and show of puppets, had once before played his hurdy-gurdy beneath the arched window. The pleasant face of Phoebe—and doubtless, too, the liberal recompense which she had flung him—still dwelt in his remembrance. His expressive features kindled up, as he recognized the spot where this trifling incident of his erratic life had chanced. He entered the neglected yard (now wilder than ever, with its growth of hog-weed and burdock), stationed himself on the doorstep of the main entrance, and, opening his show-box, began to play. Each individual of the automatic community forthwith set to work, according to his or her proper vocation: the monkey, taking off his Highland bonnet, bowed and scraped to the by-standers most obsequiously, with ever an observant eye to pick up a stray cent; and the young foreigner himself, as he turned the crank of his machine, glanced upward to the arched window, expectant of a presence that would make his music the livelier and sweeter. The throng of children stood near; some on the sidewalk; some within the yard; two or three establishing themselves on the very door-step; and one squatting on the threshold. Meanwhile, the locust kept singing in the great old Pyncheon Elm.

"I don't hear anybody in the house," said one of the children to another. "The monkey won't pick up anything here."

"There is somebody at home," affirmed the urchin on the threshold. "I heard a step!"

Still the young Italian's eye turned sidelong upward; and it really seemed as if the touch of genuine, though slight and almost playful, emotion communicated a juicier sweetness to the dry, mechanical process of his minstrelsy. These wanderers are readily responsive to any natural kindness—be it no more than a smile, or a word itself not understood, but only a warmth in it—which befalls them on the roadside of life. They remember these things, because they are the little enchantments which, for the instant,—for the space that reflects a landscape in a soap-bubble,—build up a home about them. Therefore, the Italian boy would not be discouraged by the heavy silence with which the old house seemed resolute to clog the vivacity of his instrument. He persisted in his melodious appeals; he still looked upward, trusting that his dark, alien countenance would soon be brightened by Phoebe's sunny aspect. Neither could he be willing to depart without again beholding Clifford, whose sensibility, like Phoebe's smile, had talked a kind of heart's language to the foreigner. He repeated all his music over and over again, until his auditors were getting weary. So were the little wooden people in his show-box, and the monkey most of all. There was no response, save the singing of the locust.

"No children live in this house," said a schoolboy, at last. "Nobody lives here but an old maid and an old man. You'll get nothing here! Why don't you go along?"

"You fool, you, why do you tell him?" whispered a shrewd little Yankee, caring nothing for the music, but a good deal for the cheap rate at which it was had. "Let him play as he likes! If there's nobody to pay him, that's his own lookout!"

Once more, however, the Italian ran over his round of melodies. To the common observer—who could understand nothing of the case, except the music and the sunshine on the hither side of the door—it might have been amusing to watch the pertinacity of the street-performer. Will he succeed at last? Will that stubborn door be suddenly flung open? Will a group of joyous children, the young ones of the house, come dancing, shouting, laughing, into the open air, and cluster round the show-box, looking with eager merriment at the puppets, and tossing each a copper for long-tailed Mammon, the monkey, to pick up?

But to us, who know the inner heart of the Seven Gables as well as its exterior face, there is a ghastly effect in this repetition of light popular tunes at its door-step. It would be an ugly business, indeed, if Judge Pyncheon (who would not have cared a fig for Paganini's fiddle in his most harmonious mood) should make his appearance at the door, with a bloody shirt-bosom, and a grim frown on his swarthily white visage, and motion the foreign vagabond away! Was ever before such a grinding out of jigs and waltzes, where nobody was in the cue to dance? Yes, very often. This contrast, or intermingling of tragedy with mirth, happens daily, hourly, momently. The gloomy and desolate old house, deserted of life, and with awful Death sitting sternly in its solitude, was the emblem of many a human heart, which, nevertheless, is compelled to hear the thrill and echo of the world's gayety around it.

Before the conclusion of the Italian's performance, a couple of men happened to be passing, On their way to dinner. "I say, you young French fellow!" called out one of them,—"come away from that doorstep, and go somewhere else with your nonsense! The Pyncheon family live there; and they are in great trouble, just about this time. They don't feel musical to-day. It is reported all over town that Judge Pyncheon, who owns the house, has been murdered; and the city marshal is going to look into the matter. So be off with you, at once!"

As the Italian shouldered his hurdy-gurdy, he saw on the doorstep a card, which had been covered, all the morning, by the newspaper that the carrier had flung upon it, but was now shuffled into sight. He picked it up, and perceiving something written in pencil, gave it to the man to read. In fact, it was an engraved card of Judge Pyncheon's with certain pencilled memoranda on the back, referring to various businesses which it had been his purpose to transact during the preceding day. It formed a prospective epitome of the day's history; only that affairs had not turned out altogether in accordance with the programme. The card must have been lost from the Judge's vest-pocket in his preliminary attempt to gain access by the main entrance of the house. Though well soaked with rain, it was still partially legible.

"Look here; Dixey!" cried the man. "This has something to do with Judge Pyncheon. See!—here's his name printed on it; and here, I suppose, is some of his handwriting."

"Let's go to the city marshal with it!" said Dixey. "It may give him just the clew he wants. After all," whispered he in his companion's ear, "it would be no wonder if the Judge has gone into that door and never come out again! A certain cousin of his may have been at his old tricks. And Old Maid Pyncheon having got herself in debt by the cent-shop,—and the Judge's pocket-book being well filled,—and bad blood amongst them already! Put all these things together and see what they make!"

"Hush, hush!" whispered the other. "It seems like a sin to be the first to speak of such a thing. But I think, with you, that we had better go to the city marshal."

"Yes, yes!" said Dixey. "Well!—I always said there was something devilish in that woman's scowl!"

The men wheeled about, accordingly, and retraced their steps up the street. The Italian, also, made the best of his way off, with a parting glance up at the arched window. As for the children, they took to their heels, with one accord, and scampered as if some giant or ogre were in pursuit, until, at a good distance from the house, they stopped as suddenly and simultaneously as they had set out. Their susceptible nerves took an indefinite alarm from what they had overheard. Looking back at the grotesque peaks and shadowy angles of the old mansion, they fancied a gloom diffused about it which no brightness of the sunshine could dispel. An imaginary Hepzibah scowled and shook her finger at them, from several windows at the same moment. An imaginary Clifford—for (and it would have deeply wounded him to know it) he had always been a horror to these small people—stood behind the unreal Hepzibah, making awful gestures, in a faded dressing-gown. Children are even more apt, if possible, than grown people, to catch the contagion of a panic terror. For the rest of the day, the more timid went whole streets about, for the sake of avoiding the Seven Gables; while the bolder signalized their hardihood by challenging their comrades to race past the mansion at full speed.

It could not have been more than half an hour after the disappearance of the Italian boy, with his unseasonable melodies, when a cab drove down the street. It stopped beneath the Pyncheon Elm; the cabman took a trunk, a canvas bag, and a bandbox, from the top of his vehicle, and deposited them on the doorstep of the old house; a straw bonnet, and then the pretty figure of a young girl, came into view from the interior of the cab. It was Phoebe! Though not altogether so blooming as when she first tripped into our story,—for, in the few intervening weeks, her experiences had made her graver, more womanly, and deeper-eyed, in token of a heart that had begun to suspect its depths,—still there was the quiet glow of natural sunshine over her. Neither had she forfeited her proper gift of making things look real, rather than fantastic, within her sphere. Yet we feel it to be a questionable venture, even for Phoebe, at this juncture, to cross the threshold of the Seven Gables. Is her healthful presence potent enough to chase away the crowd of pale, hideous, and sinful phantoms, that have gained admittance there since her departure? Or will she, likewise, fade, sicken, sadden, and grow into deformity, and be only another pallid phantom, to glide noiselessly up and down the stairs, and affright children as she pauses at the window?

At least, we would gladly forewarn the unsuspecting girl that there is nothing in human shape or substance to receive her, unless it be the figure of Judge Pyncheon, who—wretched spectacle that he is, and frightful in our remembrance, since our night-long vigil with him!—still keeps his place in the oaken chair.

Phoebe first tried the shop-door. It did not yield to her hand; and the white curtain, drawn across the window which formed the upper section of the door, struck her quick perceptive faculty as something unusual. Without making another effort to enter here, she betook herself to the great portal, under the arched window. Finding it fastened, she knocked. A reverberation came from the emptiness within. She knocked again, and a third time; and, listening intently, fancied that the floor creaked, as if Hepzibah were coming, with her ordinary tiptoe movement, to admit her. But so dead a silence ensued upon this imaginary sound, that she began to question whether she might not have mistaken the house, familiar as she thought herself with its exterior.

Her notice was now attracted by a child's voice, at some distance. It appeared to call her name. Looking in the direction whence it proceeded, Phoebe saw little Ned Higgins, a good way down the street, stamping, shaking his head violently, making deprecatory gestures with both hands, and shouting to her at mouth-wide screech.

"No, no, Phoebe!" he screamed. "Don't you go in! There's something wicked there! Don't—don't—don't go in!"

But, as the little personage could not be induced to approach near enough to explain himself, Phoebe concluded that he had been frightened, on some of his visits to the shop, by her cousin Hepzibah; for the good lady's manifestations, in truth, ran about an equal chance of scaring children out of their wits, or compelling them to unseemly laughter. Still, she felt the more, for this incident, how unaccountably silent and impenetrable the house had become. As her next resort, Phoebe made her way into the garden, where on so warm and bright a day as the present, she had little doubt of finding Clifford, and perhaps Hepzibah also, idling away the noontide in the shadow of the arbor. Immediately on her entering the garden gate, the family of hens half ran, half flew to meet her; while a strange grimalkin, which was prowling under the parlor window, took to his heels, clambered hastily over the fence, and vanished. The arbor was vacant, and its floor, table, and circular bench were still damp, and bestrewn with twigs and the disarray of the past storm. The growth of the garden seemed to have got quite out of bounds; the weeds had taken advantage of Phoebe's absence, and the long-continued rain, to run rampant over the flowers and kitchen-vegetables. Maule's well had overflowed its stone border, and made a pool of formidable breadth in that corner of the garden.

The impression of the whole scene was that of a spot where no human foot had left its print for many preceding days,—probably not since Phoebe's departure,—for she saw a side-comb of her own under the table of the arbor, where it must have fallen on the last afternoon when she and Clifford sat there.

The girl knew that her two relatives were capable of far greater oddities than that of shutting themselves up in their old house, as they appeared now to have done. Nevertheless, with indistinct misgivings of something amiss, and apprehensions to which she could not give shape, she approached the door that formed the customary communication between the house and garden. It was secured within, like the two which she had already tried. She knocked, however; and immediately, as if the application had been expected, the door was drawn open, by a considerable exertion of some unseen person's strength, not wide, but far enough to afford her a sidelong entrance. As Hepzibah, in order not to expose herself to inspection from without, invariably opened a door in this manner, Phoebe necessarily concluded that it was her cousin who now admitted her.

Without hesitation, therefore, she stepped across the threshold, and had no sooner entered than the door closed behind her.

XX The Flower of Eden

PHOEBE, coming so suddenly from the sunny daylight, was altogether bedimmed in such density of shadow as lurked in most of the passages of the old house. She was not at first aware by whom she had been admitted. Before her eyes had adapted themselves to the obscurity, a hand grasped her own with a firm but gentle and warm pressure, thus imparting a welcome which caused her heart to leap and thrill with an indefinable shiver of enjoyment. She felt herself drawn along, not towards the parlor, but into a large and unoccupied apartment, which had formerly been the grand reception-room of the Seven Gables. The sunshine came freely into all the uncurtained windows of this room, and fell upon the dusty floor; so that Phoebe now clearly saw—what, indeed, had been no secret, after the encounter of a warm hand with hers—that it was not Hepzibah nor Clifford, but Holgrave, to whom she owed her reception. The subtile, intuitive communication, or, rather, the vague and formless impression of something to be told, had made her yield unresistingly to his impulse. Without taking away her hand, she looked eagerly in his face, not quick to forebode evil, but unavoidably conscious that the state of the family had changed since her departure, and therefore anxious for an explanation.

The artist looked paler than ordinary; there was a thoughtful and severe contraction of his forehead, tracing a deep, vertical line between the eyebrows. His smile, however, was full of genuine warmth, and had in it a joy, by far the most vivid expression that Phoebe had ever witnessed, shining out of the New England reserve with which Holgrave habitually masked whatever lay near his heart. It was the look wherewith a man, brooding alone over some fearful object, in a dreary forest or illimitable desert, would recognize the familiar aspect of his dearest friend, bringing up all the peaceful ideas that belong to home, and the gentle current of every-day affairs. And yet, as he felt the necessity of responding to her look of inquiry, the smile disappeared.

"I ought not to rejoice that you have come, Phoebe," said he. "We meet at a strange moment!"

"What has happened!" she exclaimed. "Why is the house so deserted? Where are Hepzibah and Clifford?"

"Gone! I cannot imagine where they are!" answered Holgrave. "We are alone in the house!"

"Hepzibah and Clifford gone?" cried Phoebe. "It is not possible! And why have you brought me into this room, instead of the parlor? Ah, something terrible has happened! I must run and see!"

"No, no, Phoebe!" said Holgrave holding her back. "It is as I have told you. They are gone, and I know not whither. A terrible event has, indeed happened, but not to them, nor, as I undoubtingly believe, through any agency of theirs. If I read your character rightly, Phoebe," he continued, fixing his eyes on hers with stern anxiety, intermixed with tenderness, "gentle as you are, and seeming to have your sphere among common things, you yet possess remarkable strength. You have wonderful poise, and a faculty which, when tested, will prove itself capable of dealing with matters that fall far out of the ordinary rule."

"Oh, no, I am very weak!" replied Phoebe, trembling. "But tell me what has happened!"

"You are strong!" persisted Holgrave. "You must be both strong and wise; for I am all astray, and need your counsel. It may be you can suggest the one right thing to do!"

"Tell me!—tell me!" said Phoebe, all in a tremble. "It oppresses,—it terrifies me,—this mystery! Anything else I can bear!"

The artist hesitated. Notwithstanding what he had just said, and most sincerely, in regard to the self-balancing power with which Phoebe impressed him, it still seemed almost wicked to bring the awful secret of yesterday to her knowledge. It was like dragging a hideous shape of death into the cleanly and cheerful space before a household fire, where it would present all the uglier aspect, amid the decorousness of everything about it. Yet it could not be concealed from her; she must needs know it.

"Phoebe," said he, "do you remember this?" He put into her hand a daguerreotype; the same that he had shown her at their first interview in the garden, and which so strikingly brought out the hard and relentless traits of the original.

"What has this to do with Hepzibah and Clifford?" asked Phoebe, with impatient surprise that Holgrave should so trifle with her at such a moment. "It is Judge Pyncheon! You have shown it to me before!"

"But here is the same face, taken within this half-hour" said the artist, presenting her with another miniature. "I had just finished it when I heard you at the door."

"This is death!" shuddered Phoebe, turning very pale. "Judge Pyncheon dead!"

"Such as there represented," said Holgrave, "he sits in the next room. The Judge is dead, and Clifford and Hepzibah have vanished! I know no more. All beyond is conjecture. On returning to my solitary chamber, last evening, I noticed no light, either in the parlor, or Hepzibah's room, or Clifford's; no stir nor footstep about the house. This morning, there was the same death-like quiet. From my window, I overheard the testimony of a neighbor, that your relatives were seen leaving the house in the midst of yesterday's storm. A rumor reached me, too, of Judge Pyncheon being missed. A feeling which I cannot describe—an indefinite sense of some catastrophe, or consummation—impelled me to make my way into this part of the house, where I discovered what you see. As a point of evidence that may be useful to Clifford, and also as a memorial valuable to myself,—for, Phoebe, there are hereditary reasons that connect me strangely with that man's fate,—I used the means at my disposal to preserve this pictorial record of Judge Pyncheon's death."

Even in her agitation, Phoebe could not help remarking the calmness of Holgrave's demeanor. He appeared, it is true, to feel the whole awfulness of the Judge's death, yet had received the fact into his mind without any mixture of surprise, but as an event preordained, happening inevitably, and so fitting itself into past occurrences that it could almost have been prophesied.

"Why have you not thrown open the doors, and called in witnesses?" inquired she with a painful shudder. "It is terrible to be here alone!"

"But Clifford!" suggested the artist. "Clifford and Hepzibah! We must consider what is best to be done in their behalf. It is a wretched fatality that they should have disappeared! Their flight will throw the worst coloring over this event of which it is susceptible. Yet how easy is the explanation, to those who know them! Bewildered and terror-stricken by the similarity of this death to a former one, which was attended with such disastrous consequences to Clifford, they have had no idea but of removing themselves from the scene. How miserably unfortunate! Had Hepzibah but shrieked aloud,—had Clifford flung wide the door, and proclaimed Judge Pyncheon's death,—it would have been, however awful in itself, an event fruitful of good consequences to them. As I view it, it would have gone far towards obliterating the black stain on Clifford's character."

"And how," asked Phoebe, "could any good come from what is so very dreadful?"

"Because," said the artist, "if the matter can be fairly considered and candidly interpreted, it must be evident that Judge Pyncheon could not have come unfairly to his end. This mode of death had been an idiosyncrasy with his family, for generations past; not often occurring, indeed, but, when it does occur, usually attacking individuals about the Judge's time of life, and generally in the tension of some mental crisis, or, perhaps, in an access of wrath. Old Maule's prophecy was probably founded on a knowledge of this physical predisposition in the Pyncheon race. Now, there is a minute and almost exact similarity in the appearances connected with the death that occurred yesterday and those recorded of the death of Clifford's uncle thirty years ago. It is true, there was a certain arrangement of circumstances, unnecessary to be recounted, which made it possible nay, as men look at these things, probable, or even certain—that old Jaffrey Pyncheon came to a violent death, and by Clifford's hands."

"Whence came those circumstances?" exclaimed Phoebe. "He being innocent, as we know him to be!"

"They were arranged," said Holgrave,—"at least such has long been my conviction,—they were arranged after the uncle's death, and before it was made public, by the man who sits in yonder parlor. His own death, so like that former one, yet attended by none of those suspicious circumstances, seems the stroke of God upon him, at once a punishment for his wickedness, and making plain the innocence of Clifford. But this flight,—it distorts everything! He may be in concealment, near at hand. Could we but bring him back before the discovery of the Judge's death, the evil might be rectified."

"We must not hide this thing a moment longer!" said Phoebe. "It is dreadful to keep it so closely in our hearts. Clifford is innocent. God will make it manifest! Let us throw open the doors, and call all the neighborhood to see the truth!"

"You are right, Phoebe," rejoined Holgrave. "Doubtless you are right."

Yet the artist did not feel the horror, which was proper to Phoebe's sweet and order-loving character, at thus finding herself at issue with society, and brought in contact with an event that transcended ordinary rules. Neither was he in haste, like her, to betake himself within the precincts of common life. On the contrary, he gathered a wild enjoyment,—as it were, a flower of strange beauty, growing in a desolate spot, and blossoming in the wind,—such a flower of momentary happiness he gathered from his present position. It separated Phoebe and himself from the world, and bound them to each other, by their exclusive knowledge of Judge Pyncheon's mysterious death, and the counsel which they were forced to hold respecting it. The secret, so long as it should continue such, kept them within the circle of a spell, a solitude in the midst of men, a remoteness as entire as that of an island in mid-ocean; once divulged, the ocean would flow betwixt them, standing on its widely sundered shores. Meanwhile, all the circumstances of their situation seemed to draw them together; they were like two children who go hand in hand, pressing closely to one another's side, through a shadow-haunted passage. The image of awful Death, which filled the house, held them united by his stiffened grasp.

These influences hastened the development of emotions that might not otherwise have flowered so. Possibly, indeed, it had been Holgrave's purpose to let them die in their undeveloped germs. "Why do we delay so?" asked Phoebe. "This secret takes away my breath! Let us throw open the doors!"

"In all our lives there can never come another moment like this!" said Holgrave. "Phoebe, is it all terror?—nothing but terror? Are you conscious of no joy, as I am, that has made this the only point of life worth living for?"

"It seems a sin," replied Phoebe, trembling, "to think of joy at such a time!"

"Could you but know, Phoebe, how it was with me the hour before you came!" exclaimed the artist. "A dark, cold, miserable hour! The presence of yonder dead man threw a great black shadow over everything; he made the universe, so far as my perception could reach, a scene of guilt and of retribution more dreadful than the guilt. The sense of it took away my youth. I never hoped to feel young again! The world looked strange, wild, evil, hostile; my past life, so lonesome and dreary; my future, a shapeless gloom, which I must mould into gloomy shapes! But, Phoebe, you crossed the threshold; and hope, warmth, and joy came in with you! The black moment became at once a blissful one. It must not pass without the spoken word. I love you!"

"How can you love a simple girl like me?" asked Phoebe, compelled by his earnestness to speak. "You have many, many thoughts, with which I should try in vain to sympathize. And I,—I, too,—I have tendencies with which you would sympathize as little. That is less matter. But I have not scope enough to make you happy."

"You are my only possibility of happiness!" answered Holgrave. "I have no faith in it, except as you bestow it on me!"

"And then—I am afraid!" continued Phoebe, shrinking towards Holgrave, even while she told him so frankly the doubts with which he affected her. "You will lead me out of my own quiet path. You will make me strive to follow you where it is pathless. I cannot do so. It is not my nature. I shall sink down and perish!"

"Ah, Phoebe!" exclaimed Holgrave, with almost a sigh, and a smile that was burdened with thought.

"It will be far otherwise than as you forebode. The world owes all its onward impulses to men ill at ease. The happy man inevitably confines himself within ancient limits. I have a presentiment that, hereafter, it will be my lot to set out trees, to make fences,—perhaps, even, in due time, to build a house for another generation,—in a word, to conform myself to laws and the peaceful practice of society. Your poise will be more powerful than any oscillating tendency of mine."

"I would not have it so!" said Phoebe earnestly.

"Do you love me?" asked Holgrave. "If we love one another, the moment has room for nothing more. Let us pause upon it, and be satisfied. Do you love me, Phoebe?"

"You look into my heart," said she, letting her eyes drop. "You know I love you!"

And it was in this hour, so full of doubt and awe, that the one miracle was wrought, without which every human existence is a blank. The bliss which makes all things true, beautiful, and holy shone around this youth and maiden. They were conscious of nothing sad nor old. They transfigured the earth, and made it Eden again, and themselves the two first dwellers in it. The dead man, so close beside them, was forgotten. At such a crisis, there is no death; for immortality is revealed anew, and embraces everything in its hallowed atmosphere.

But how soon the heavy earth-dream settled down again!

"Hark!" whispered Phoebe. "Somebody is at the street door!"

"Now let us meet the world!" said Holgrave. "No doubt, the rumor of Judge Pyncheon's visit to this house, and the flight of Hepzibah and Clifford, is about to lead to the investigation of the premises. We have no way but to meet it. Let us open the door at once."

But, to their surprise, before they could reach the street door,—even before they quitted the room in which the foregoing interview had passed,—they heard footsteps in the farther passage. The door, therefore, which they supposed to be securely locked,—which Holgrave, indeed, had seen to be so, and at which Phoebe had vainly tried to enter,—must have been opened from without. The sound of footsteps was not harsh, bold, decided, and intrusive, as the gait of strangers would naturally be, making authoritative entrance into a dwelling where they knew themselves unwelcome. It was feeble, as of persons either weak or weary; there was the mingled murmur of two voices, familiar to both the listeners.

"Can it be?" whispered Holgrave.

"It is they!" answered Phoebe. "Thank God!—thank God!"

And then, as if in sympathy with Phoebe's whispered ejaculation, they heard Hepzibah's voice more distinctly.

"Thank God, my brother, we are at home!"

"Well!—Yes!—thank God!" responded Clifford. "A dreary home, Hepzibah! But you have done well to bring me hither! Stay! That parlor door is open. I cannot pass by it! Let me go and rest me in the arbor, where I used,—oh, very long ago, it seems to me, after what has befallen us,—where I used to be so happy with little Phoebe!"

But the house was not altogether so dreary as Clifford imagined it. They had not made many steps,—in truth, they were lingering in the entry, with the listlessness of an accomplished purpose, uncertain what to do next,—when Phoebe ran to meet them. On beholding her, Hepzibah burst into tears. With all her might, she had staggered onward beneath the burden of grief and responsibility, until now that it was safe to fling it down. Indeed, she had not energy to fling it down, but had ceased to uphold it, and suffered it to press her to the earth. Clifford appeared the stronger of the two.

"It is our own little Phoebe!—Ah! and Holgrave with, her" exclaimed he, with a glance of keen and delicate insight, and a smile, beautiful, kind, but melancholy. "I thought of you both, as we came down the street, and beheld Alice's Posies in full bloom. And so the flower of Eden has bloomed, likewise, in this old, darksome house to-day."

XXI The Departure

THE sudden death of so prominent a member of the social world as the Honorable Judge Jaffrey Pyncheon created a sensation (at least, in the circles more immediately connected with the deceased) which had hardly quite subsided in a fortnight.

It may be remarked, however, that, of all the events which constitute a person's biography, there is scarcely one—none, certainly, of anything like a similar importance—to which the world so easily reconciles itself as to his death. In most other cases and contingencies, the individual is present among us, mixed up with the daily revolution of affairs, and affording a definite point for observation. At his decease, there is only a vacancy, and a momentary eddy,—very small, as compared with the apparent magnitude of the ingurgitated object,—and a bubble or two, ascending out of the black depth and bursting at the surface. As regarded Judge Pyncheon, it seemed probable, at first blush, that the mode of his final departure might give him a larger and longer posthumous vogue than ordinarily attends the memory of a distinguished man. But when it came to be understood, on the highest professional authority, that the event was a natural, and—except for some unimportant particulars, denoting a slight idiosyncrasy—by no means an unusual form of death, the public, with its customary alacrity, proceeded to forget that he had ever lived. In short, the honorable Judge was beginning to be a stale subject before half the country newspapers had found time to put their columns in mourning, and publish his exceedingly eulogistic obituary.

Nevertheless, creeping darkly through the places which this excellent person had haunted in his lifetime, there was a hidden stream of private talk, such as it would have shocked all decency to speak loudly at the street-corners. It is very singular, how the fact of a man's death often seems to give people a truer idea of his character, whether for good or evil, than they have ever possessed while he was living and acting among them. Death is so genuine a fact that it excludes falsehood, or betrays its emptiness; it is a touchstone that proves the gold, and dishonors the baser metal. Could the departed, whoever he may be, return in a week after his decease, he would almost invariably find himself at a higher or lower point than he had formerly occupied, on the scale of public appreciation. But the talk, or scandal, to which we now allude, had reference to matters of no less old a date than the supposed murder, thirty or forty years ago, of the late

Judge Pyncheon's uncle. The medical opinion with regard to his own recent and regretted decease had almost entirely obviated the idea that a murder was committed in the former case. Yet, as the record showed, there were circumstances irrefragably indicating that some person had gained access to old Jaffrey Pyncheon's private apartments, at or near the moment of his death. His desk and private drawers, in a room contiguous to his bedchamber, had been ransacked; money and valuable articles were missing; there was a bloody hand-print on the old man's linen; and, by a powerfully welded chain of deductive evidence, the guilt of the robbery and apparent murder had been fixed on Clifford, then residing with his uncle in the House of the Seven Gables.

Whencesoever originating, there now arose a theory that undertook so to account for these circumstances as to exclude the idea of Clifford's agency. Many persons affirmed that the history and elucidation of the facts, long so mysterious, had been obtained by the daguerreotypist from one of those mesmerical seers who, nowadays, so strangely perplex the aspect of human affairs, and put everybody's natural vision to the blush, by the marvels which they see with their eyes shut.

According to this version of the story, Judge Pyncheon, exemplary as we have portrayed him in our narrative, was, in his youth, an apparently irreclaimable scapegrace. The brutish, the animal instincts, as is often the case, had been developed earlier than the intellectual qualities, and the force of character, for which he was afterwards remarkable. He had shown himself wild, dissipated, addicted to low pleasures, little short of ruffianly in his propensities, and recklessly expensive, with no other resources than the bounty of his uncle. This course of conduct had alienated the old bachelor's affection, once strongly fixed upon him. Now it is averred,—but whether on authority available in a court of justice, we do not pretend to have investigated,—that the young man was tempted by the devil, one night, to search his uncle's private drawers, to which he had unsuspected means of access. While thus criminally occupied, he was startled by the opening of the chamber-door. There stood old Jaffrey Pyncheon, in his nightclothes! The surprise of such a discovery, his agitation, alarm, and horror, brought on the crisis of a disorder to which the old bachelor had an hereditary liability; he seemed to choke with blood, and fell upon the floor, striking his temple a heavy blow against the corner of a table. What was to be done? The old man was surely dead! Assistance would come too late! What a misfortune, indeed, should it come too soon, since his reviving consciousness would bring the recollection of the ignominious offence which he had beheld his nephew in the very act of committing!

But he never did revive. With the cool hardihood that always pertained to him, the young man continued his search of the drawers, and found a will, of recent date, in favor of Clifford,—which he destroyed,—and an older one, in his own favor, which he suffered to remain. But before retiring, Jaffrey bethought himself of the evidence, in these ransacked drawers, that some one had visited the chamber with sinister purposes. Suspicion, unless averted, might fix upon the real offender. In the very presence of the dead man, therefore, he laid a scheme that should free himself at the expense of Clifford, his rival, for whose character he had at once a contempt and a repugnance. It is not probable, be it said, that he acted with any set purpose of involving Clifford in a charge of murder. Knowing that his uncle did not die by violence, it may not have occurred to him, in the hurry of the crisis, that such an inference might be drawn. But, when the affair took this darker aspect, Jaffrey's previous steps had already pledged him to those which remained. So craftily had he arranged the circumstances, that, at Clifford's trial, his cousin hardly found it necessary to swear to anything false, but only to withhold the one decisive explanation, by refraining to state what he had himself done and witnessed.

Thus Jaffrey Pyncheon's inward criminality, as regarded Clifford, was, indeed, black and damnable, while its mere outward show and positive commission was the smallest that could possibly consist with so great a sin. This is just the sort of guilt that a man of eminent respectability finds it easiest to dispose of. It was suffered to fade out of sight or be reckoned a venial matter, in the Honorable Judge Pyncheon's long subsequent survey of his own life. He shuffled it aside, among the forgotten and forgiven frailties of his youth, and seldom thought of it again.

We leave the Judge to his repose. He could not be styled fortunate at the hour of death. Unknowingly, he was a childless man, while striving to add more wealth to his only child's inheritance. Hardly a week after his decease, one of the Cunard steamers brought intelligence of the death, by cholera, of Judge Pyncheon's son, just at the point of embarkation for his native land. By this misfortune Clifford became rich; so did Hepzibah; so did our little village maiden, and, through her, that sworn foe of wealth and all manner of conservatism,—the wild reformer,—Holgrave!

It was now far too late in Clifford's life for the good opinion of society to be worth the trouble and anguish of a formal vindication. What he needed was the love of a very few; not the admiration, or even the respect, of the unknown many. The latter might probably have been won for him, had those on whom the guardianship of his welfare had fallen deemed it advisable to expose Clifford to a miserable resuscitation of past ideas, when the condition of whatever comfort he might expect lay in the calm of forgetfulness. After such wrong as he had suffered, there is no reparation. The pitiable mockery of it, which the world might have been ready enough to offer, coming so long after the agony had done its utmost work, would have been fit only to provoke bitterer laughter than poor Clifford was ever capable of. It is a truth (and it would be a very sad one but for the higher hopes which it suggests) that no great mistake, whether acted or endured, in our mortal sphere, is ever really set right. Time, the continual vicissitude of circumstances, and the invariable inopportunity of death, render it impossible. If, after long lapse of years, the right seems to be in our power, we find no niche to set it in. The better remedy is for the sufferer to pass on, and leave what he once thought his irreparable ruin far behind him.

The shock of Judge Pyncheon's death had a permanently invigorating and ultimately beneficial effect on Clifford. That strong and ponderous man had been

Clifford's nightmare. There was no free breath to be drawn, within the sphere of so malevolent an influence. The first effect of freedom, as we have witnessed in Clifford's aimless flight, was a tremulous exhilaration. Subsiding from it, he did not sink into his former intellectual apathy. He never, it is true, attained to nearly the full measure of what might have been his faculties. But he recovered enough of them partially to light up his character, to display some outline of the marvellous grace that was abortive in it, and to make him the object of no less deep, although less melancholy interest than heretofore. He was evidently happy. Could we pause to give another picture of his daily life, with all the appliances now at command to gratify his instinct for the Beautiful, the garden scenes, that seemed so sweet to him, would look mean and trivial in comparison.

Very soon after their change of fortune, Clifford, Hepzibah, and little Phoebe, with the approval of the artist, concluded to remove from the dismal old House of the Seven Gables, and take up their abode, for the present, at the elegant country-seat of the late Judge Pyncheon. Chanticleer and his family had already been transported thither, where the two hens had forthwith begun an indefatigable process of egg-laying, with an evident design, as a matter of duty and conscience, to continue their illustrious breed under better auspices than for a century past. On the day set for their departure, the principal personages of our story, including good Uncle Venner, were assembled in the parlor.

"The country-house is certainly a very fine one, so far as the plan goes," observed Holgrave, as the party were discussing their future arrangements. "But I wonder that the late Judge—being so opulent, and with a reasonable prospect of transmitting his wealth to descendants of his own—should not have felt the propriety of embodying so excellent a piece of domestic architecture in stone, rather than in wood. Then, every generation of the family might have altered the interior, to suit its own taste and convenience; while the exterior, through the lapse of years, might have been adding venerableness to its original beauty, and thus giving that impression of permanence which I consider essential to the happiness of any one moment."

"Why," cried Phoebe, gazing into the artist's face with infinite amazement, "how wonderfully your ideas are changed! A house of stone, indeed! It is but two or three weeks ago that you seemed to wish people to live in something as fragile and temporary as a bird's-nest!"

"Ah, Phoebe, I told you how it would be!" said the artist, with a half-melancholy laugh. "You find me a conservative already! Little did I think ever to become one. It is especially unpardonable in this dwelling of so much hereditary misfortune, and under the eye of yonder portrait of a model conservative, who, in that very character, rendered himself so long the evil destiny of his race."

"That picture!" said Clifford, seeming to shrink from its stern glance. "Whenever I look at it, there is an old dreamy recollection haunting me, but keeping just beyond the grasp of my mind. Wealth, it seems to say!—boundless wealth!—unimaginable wealth! I could fancy that, when I was a child, or a youth, that portrait had spoken, and told me a rich secret, or had held forth its hand, with the written record of hidden opulence. But those old matters are so dim with me, nowadays! What could this dream have been?"

"Perhaps I can recall it," answered Holgrave. "See! There are a hundred chances to one that no person, unacquainted with the secret, would ever touch this spring."

"A secret spring!" cried Clifford. "Ah, I remember now! I did discover it, one summer afternoon, when I was idling and dreaming about the house, long, long ago. But the mystery escapes me."

The artist put his finger on the contrivance to which he had referred. In former days, the effect would probably have been to cause the picture to start forward. But, in so long a period of concealment, the machinery had been eaten through with rust; so that at Holgrave's pressure, the portrait, frame and all, tumbled suddenly from its position, and lay face downward on the floor. A recess in the wall was thus brought to light, in which lay an object so covered with a century's dust that it could not immediately be recognized as a folded sheet of parchment. Holgrave opened it, and displayed an ancient deed, signed with the hieroglyphics of several Indian sagamores, and conveying to Colonel Pyncheon and his heirs, forever, a vast extent of territory at the Eastward.

"This is the very parchment, the attempt to recover which cost the beautiful Alice Pyncheon her happiness and life," said the artist, alluding to his legend. "It is what the Pyncheons sought in vain, while it was valuable; and now that they find the treasure, it has long been worthless."

"Poor Cousin Jaffrey! This is what deceived him," exclaimed Hepzibah. "When they were young together, Clifford probably made a kind of fairy-tale of this discovery. He was always dreaming hither and thither about the house, and lighting up its dark corners with beautiful stories. And poor Jaffrey, who took hold of everything as if it were real, thought my brother had found out his uncle's wealth. He died with this delusion in his mind!"

"But," said Phoebe, apart to Holgrave, "how came you to know the secret?"

"My dearest Phoebe," said Holgrave, "how will it please you to assume the name of Maule? As for the secret, it is the only inheritance that has come down to me from my ancestors. You should have known sooner (only that I was afraid of frightening you away) that, in this long drama of wrong and retribution, I represent the old wizard, and am probably as much a wizard as ever he was. The son of the executed Matthew Maule, while building this house, took the opportunity to construct that recess, and hide away the Indian deed, on which depended the immense land-claim of the Pyncheons. Thus they bartered their eastern territory for Maule's garden-ground."

"And now" said Uncle Venner "I suppose their whole claim is not worth one man's share in my farm yonder!"

"Uncle Venner," cried Phoebe, taking the patched philosopher's hand, "you must never talk any more about your farm! You shall never go there, as long as you live! There is a cottage in our new garden,—the prettiest little yellowish-brown cottage you ever saw; and the sweetest-looking place, for it looks just as if it were made of gingerbread,—and we are going to fit it up and furnish it, on purpose for you. And you shall do nothing but what you choose, and shall be as happy as the day is long, and shall keep Cousin Clifford in spirits with the wisdom and pleasantness which is always dropping from your lips!"

"Ah! my dear child," quoth good Uncle Venner, quite overcome, "if you were to speak to a young man as you do to an old one, his chance of keeping his heart another minute would not be worth one of the buttons on my waistcoat! And—soul alive!—that great sigh, which you made me heave, has burst off the very last of them! But, never mind! It was the happiest sigh I ever did heave; and it seems as if I must have drawn in a gulp of heavenly breath, to make it with. Well, well, Miss Phoebe! They'll miss me in the gardens hereabouts, and round by the back doors; and Pyncheon Street, I'm afraid, will hardly look the same without old Uncle Venner, who remembers it with a mowing field on one side, and the garden of the Seven Gables on the other. But either I must go to your country-seat, or you must come to my farm,—that's one of two things certain; and I leave you to choose which!"

"Oh, come with us, by all means, Uncle Venner!" said Clifford, who had a remarkable enjoyment of the old man's mellow, quiet, and simple spirit. "I want you always to be within five minutes, saunter of my chair. You are the only philosopher I ever knew of whose wisdom has not a drop of bitter essence at the bottom!"

"Dear me!" cried Uncle Venner, beginning partly to realize what manner of man he was. "And yet folks used to set me down among the simple ones, in my younger days! But I suppose I am like a Roxbury russet,—a great deal the better, the longer I can be kept. Yes; and my words of wisdom, that you and Phoebe tell me of, are like the golden dandelions, which never grow in the hot months, but may be seen glistening among the withered grass, and under the dry leaves, sometimes as late as December. And you are welcome, friends, to my mess of dandelions, if there were twice as many!"

A plain, but handsome, dark-green barouche had now drawn up in front of the ruinous portal of the old mansion-house. The party came forth, and (with the exception of good Uncle Venner, who was to follow in a few days) proceeded to take their places. They were chatting and laughing very pleasantly together; and—as proves to be often the case, at moments when we ought to palpitate with sensibility—Clifford and Hepzibah bade a final farewell to the abode of their forefathers, with hardly more emotion than if they had made it their arrangement to return thither at tea-time. Several children were drawn to the spot by so unusual a spectacle as the barouche and pair of gray horses. Recognizing little Ned Higgins among them, Hepzibah put her hand into her pocket, and presented the urchin, her earliest and staunchest customer, with silver enough to people the Domdaniel cavern of his interior with as various a procession of quadrupeds as passed into the ark.

Two men were passing, just as the barouche drove off.

"Well, Dixey," said one of them, "what do you think of this? My wife kept a cent-shop three months, and lost five dollars on her outlay. Old Maid Pyncheon has been in trade just about as long, and rides off in her carriage with a couple of hundred thousand,—reckoning her share, and Clifford's, and Phoebe's,—and some say twice as much! If you choose to call it luck, it is all very well; but if we are to take it as the will of Providence, why, I can't exactly fathom it!"

"Pretty good business!" quoth the sagacious Dixey,—"pretty good business!"

Maule's well, all this time, though left in solitude, was throwing up a succession of kaleidoscopic pictures, in which a gifted eye might have seen foreshadowed the coming fortunes of Hepzibah and Clifford, and the descendant of the legendary wizard, and the village maiden, over whom he had thrown love's web of sorcery. The Pyncheon Elm, moreover, with what foliage the September gale had spared to it, whispered unintelligible prophecies. And wise Uncle Venner, passing slowly from the ruinous porch, seemed to hear a strain of music, and fancied that sweet Alice Pyncheon—after witnessing these deeds, this bygone woe and this present happiness, of her kindred mortals—had given one farewell touch of a spirit's joy upon her harpsichord, as she floated heavenward from the HOUSE OF THE SEVEN GABLES!

THE BLITHEDALE ROMANCE

I. OLD MOODIE

The evening before my departure for Blithedale, I was returning to my bachelor apartments, after attending the wonderful exhibition of the Veiled Lady, when an elderly man of rather shabby appearance met me in an obscure part of the street.

"Mr. Coverdale," said he softly, "can I speak with you a moment?"

As I have casually alluded to the Veiled Lady, it may not be amiss to mention, for the benefit of such of my readers as are unacquainted with her now forgotten celebrity, that she was a phenomenon in the mesmeric line; one of the earliest that had indicated the birth of a new science, or the revival of an old humbug. Since those times her sisterhood have grown too numerous to attract much individual notice; nor, in fact, has any one of them come before the public under such skilfully contrived circumstances of stage effect as those which at once mystified and illuminated the remarkable performances of the lady in question. Nowadays, in the management of his "subject," "clairvoyant," or "medium," the exhibitor affects the simplicity and openness of scientific experiment; and even if he profess to tread a step or two across the boundaries of the spiritual world, yet carries with him the laws of our actual life and extends them over his preternatural conquests. Twelve or fifteen years ago, on the contrary, all the arts of mysterious arrangement, of picturesque disposition, and artistically contrasted light and shade, were made available, in order to set the apparent miracle in the strongest attitude of opposition to ordinary facts. In the case of the Veiled Lady, moreover, the interest of the spectator was further wrought up by the enigma of her identity, and an absurd rumor (probably set afloat by the exhibitor, and at one time very prevalent) that a beautiful young lady, of family and fortune, was enshrouded within the misty drapery of the veil. It was white, with somewhat of a subdued silver sheen, like the sunny side of a cloud; and, falling over the wearer from head to foot, was supposed to insulate her from the material world, from time and space, and to endow her with many of the privileges of a disembodied spirit.

Her pretensions, however, whether miraculous or otherwise, have little to do with the present narrative—except, indeed, that I had propounded, for the Veiled Lady's prophetic solution, a query as to the success of our Blithedale enterprise. The response, by the bye, was of the true Sibylline stamp,—nonsensical in its first aspect, yet on closer study unfolding a variety of interpretations, one of which has certainly accorded with the event. I was turning over this riddle in my mind, and trying to catch its slippery purport by the tail, when the old man above mentioned interrupted me.

"Mr. Coverdale!—Mr. Coverdale!" said he, repeating my name twice, in order to make up for the hesitating and ineffectual way in which he uttered it. "I ask your pardon, sir, but I hear you are going to Blithedale tomorrow."

I knew the pale, elderly face, with the red-tipt nose, and the patch over one eye; and likewise saw something characteristic in the old fellow's way of standing under the arch of a gate, only revealing enough of himself to make me recognize him as an acquaintance. He was a very shy personage, this Mr. Moodie; and the trait was the more singular, as his mode of getting his bread necessarily brought him into the stir and hubbub of the world more than the generality of men.

"Yes, Mr. Moodie," I answered, wondering what interest he could take in the fact, "it is my intention to go to Blithedale to-morrow. Can I be of any service to you before my departure?"

"If you pleased, Mr. Coverdale," said he, "you might do me a very great favor."

"A very great one?" repeated I, in a tone that must have expressed but little alacrity of beneficence, although I was ready to do the old man any amount of kindness involving no special trouble to myself. "A very great favor, do you say? My time is brief, Mr. Moodie, and I have a good many preparations to make. But be good enough to tell me what you wish."

"Ah, sir," replied Old Moodie, "I don't quite like to do that; and, on further thoughts, Mr. Coverdale, perhaps I had better apply to some older gentleman, or to some lady, if you would have the kindness to make me known to one, who may happen to be going to Blithedale. You are a young man, sir!"

"Does that fact lessen my availability for your purpose?" asked I. "However, if an older man will suit you better, there is Mr. Hollingsworth, who has three or four years the advantage of me in age, and is a much more solid character, and a philanthropist to boot. I am only a poet, and, so the critics tell me, no great affair at that! But what can this business be, Mr. Moodie? It begins to interest me; especially since your hint that a lady's influence might be found desirable. Come, I am really anxious to be of service to you."

But the old fellow, in his civil and demure manner, was both freakish and obstinate; and he had now taken some notion or other into his head that made him hesitate in his former design.

"I wonder, sir," said he, "whether you know a lady whom they call Zenobia?"

"Not personally," I answered, "although I expect that pleasure to-morrow, as she has got the start of the rest of us, and is already a resident at Blithedale. But have you a literary turn, Mr. Moodie? or have you taken up the advocacy of women's rights? or what else can have interested you in this lady? Zenobia, by the bye, as I suppose you know, is merely her public name; a sort of mask in which she comes before the world, retaining all the privileges of privacy,—a contrivance, in short, like the white drapery of the Veiled Lady, only a little more transparent. But it is late. Will you tell me what I can do for you?"

"Please to excuse me to-night, Mr. Coverdale," said Moodie. "You are very kind; but I am afraid I have troubled you, when, after all, there may be no need. Perhaps, with your good leave, I will come to your lodgings to-morrow morning, before you set out for Blithedale. I wish you a good-night, sir, and beg pardon for stopping you."

And so he slipt away; and, as he did not show himself the next morning, it was only through subsequent events that I ever arrived at a plausible conjecture as to what his business could have been. Arriving at my room, I threw a lump of cannel coal upon the grate, lighted a cigar, and spent an hour in musings of every hue, from the brightest to the most sombre; being, in truth, not so very confident as at some former periods that this final step, which would mix me up irrevocably with the Blithedale affair, was the wisest that could possibly be taken. It was nothing short of midnight when I went to bed, after drinking a glass of particularly fine sherry on which I used to pride myself in those days. It was the very last bottle; and I finished it, with a friend, the next forenoon, before setting out for Blithedale.

II. BLITHEDALE

There can hardly remain for me (who am really getting to be a frosty bachelor, with another white hair, every week or so, in my mustache), there can hardly flicker up again so cheery a blaze upon the hearth, as that which I remember, the next day, at Blithedale. It was a wood fire, in the parlor of an old farmhouse, on an April afternoon, but with the fitful gusts of a wintry snowstorm roaring in the chimney. Vividly does that fireside re-create itself, as I rake away the ashes from the embers in my memory, and blow them up with a sigh, for lack of more inspiring breath. Vividly for an instant, but anon, with the dimmest gleam, and with just as little fervency for my heart as for my finger-ends! The staunch oaken logs were long ago burnt out. Their genial glow must be represented, if at all, by the merest phosphoric glimmer, like that which exudes, rather than shines, from damp fragments of decayed trees, deluding the benighted wanderer through a forest. Around such chill mockery of a fire some few of us might sit on the withered leaves, spreading out each a palm towards the imaginary warmth, and talk over our exploded scheme for beginning the life of Paradise anew.

Paradise, indeed! Nobody else in the world, I am bold to affirm—nobody, at least, in our bleak little world of New England,—had dreamed of Paradise that day except as the pole suggests the tropic. Nor, with such materials as were at hand, could the most skilful architect have constructed any better imitation of Eve's bower than might be seen in the snow hut of an Esquimaux. But we made a summer of it, in spite of the wild drifts.

It was an April day, as already hinted, and well towards the middle of the month. When morning dawned upon me, in town, its temperature was mild enough to be pronounced even balmy, by a lodger, like myself, in one of the midmost houses of a brick block,—each house partaking of the warmth of all the rest, besides the sultriness of its individual furnace—heat. But towards noon there had come snow, driven along the street by a northeasterly blast, and whitening the roofs and sidewalks with a business-like perseverance that would have done credit to our severest January tempest. It set about its task apparently as much in earnest as if it had been guaranteed from a thaw for months to come. The greater, surely, was my heroism, when, puffing out a final whiff of cigar-smoke, I quitted my cosey pair of bachelor-rooms,—with a good fire burning in the grate, and a closet right at hand, where there was still a bottle or two in the champagne basket and a residuum of claret in a box,—quitted, I say, these comfortable quarters, and plunged into the heart of the pitiless snowstorm, in quest of a better life.

The better life! Possibly, it would hardly look so now; it is enough if it looked so then. The greatest obstacle to being heroic is the doubt whether one may not be going to prove one's self a fool; the truest heroism is to resist the doubt; and the profoundest wisdom to know when it ought to be resisted, and when to be obeyed.

Yet, after all, let us acknowledge it wiser, if not more sagacious, to follow out one's daydream to its natural consummation, although, if the vision have been worth the having, it is certain never to be consummated otherwise than by a failure. And what of that? Its airiest fragments, impalpable as they may be, will possess a value that lurks not in the most ponderous realities of any practicable scheme. They are not the rubbish of the mind. Whatever else I may repent of, therefore, let it be reckoned neither among my sins nor follies that I once had faith and force enough to form generous hopes of the world's destiny—yes!—and to do what in me lay for their accomplishment; even to the extent of quitting a warm fireside, flinging away a freshly lighted cigar, and travelling far beyond the strike of city clocks, through a drifting snowstorm.

There were four of us who rode together through the storm; and Hollingsworth, who had agreed to be of the number, was accidentally delayed, and set forth at a later hour alone. As we threaded the streets, I remember how the buildings on either side seemed to press too closely upon us, insomuch that our mighty hearts found barely room enough to throb between them. The snowfall, too, looked inexpressibly dreary (I had almost called it dingy), coming down through an atmosphere of city smoke, and alighting on the sidewalk only to be moulded into the impress of somebody's patched boot or overshoe. Thus the track of an old conventionalism was visible on what was freshest from the sky. But when we left the pavements, and our muffled hoof-tramps beat upon a desolate extent of country road, and were effaced by the unfettered blast as soon as stamped, then there was better air to breathe. Air that had not been breathed once and again! air that had not been spoken into words of falsehood, formality, and error, like all the air of the dusky city!

"How pleasant it is!" remarked I, while the snowflakes flew into my mouth the moment it was opened. "How very mild and balmy is this country air!"

"Ah, Coverdale, don't laugh at what little enthusiasm you have left!" said one of my companions. "I maintain that this nitrous atmosphere is really exhilarating; and, at any rate, we can never call ourselves regenerated men till a February northeaster shall be as grateful to us as the softest breeze of June!"

So we all of us took courage, riding fleetly and merrily along, by stone fences that were half buried in the wave-like drifts; and through patches of woodland, where the tree-trunks opposed a snow-incrusted side towards the northeast; and within ken of deserted villas, with no footprints in their avenues; and passed scattered dwellings, whence puffed the smoke of country fires, strongly impregnated with the pungent aroma of burning peat. Sometimes, encountering a traveller, we shouted a friendly greeting; and he, unmuffling his ears to the bluster and the snow-spray, and listening eagerly, appeared to think our courtesy worth less than the trouble which it cost him. The churl! He understood the shrill whistle of the blast, but had no intelligence for our blithe tones of brotherhood. This lack of faith in our cordial sympathy, on the traveller's part, was one among the innumerable tokens how difficult a task we had in hand for the reformation of the world. We rode on, however, with still unflagging spirits, and made such good companionship with the tempest that, at our journey's end, we professed ourselves almost loath to bid the rude blusterer good-by. But, to own the truth, I was little better than an icicle, and began to be suspicious that I had caught a fearful cold.

And now we were seated by the brisk fireside of the old farmhouse, the same fire that glimmers so faintly among my reminiscences at the beginning of this chapter. There we sat, with the snow melting out of our hair and beards, and our faces all ablaze, what with the past inclemency and present warmth. It was, indeed, a right good fire that we found awaiting us, built up of great, rough logs, and knotty limbs, and splintered fragments of an oak-tree, such as farmers are wont to keep for their own hearths, since these crooked and unmanageable boughs could never be measured into merchantable cords for the market. A family of the old Pilgrims might have swung their kettle over precisely such a fire as this, only, no doubt, a bigger one; and, contrasting it with my coal-grate, I felt so much the more that we had transported ourselves a world-wide distance from the system of society that shackled us at breakfast-time.

Good, comfortable Mrs. Foster (the wife of stout Silas Foster, who was to manage the farm at a fair stipend, and be our tutor in the art of husbandry) bade us a hearty welcome. At her back—a back of generous breadth—appeared two young women, smiling most hospitably, but looking rather awkward withal, as not well knowing what was to be their position in our new arrangement of the world. We shook hands affectionately all round, and congratulated ourselves that the blessed state of brotherhood and sisterhood, at which we aimed, might fairly be dated from this moment. Our greetings were hardly concluded when the door opened, and Zenobia—whom I had never before seen, important as was her place in our enterprise—Zenobia entered the parlor.

This (as the reader, if at all acquainted with our literary biography, need scarcely be told) was not her real name. She had assumed it, in the first instance, as her magazine signature; and, as it accorded well with something imperial which her friends attributed to this lady's figure and deportment, they half-laughingly adopted it in their familiar intercourse with her. She took the appellation in good part, and even encouraged its constant use; which, in fact, was thus far appropriate, that our Zenobia, however humble looked her new philosophy, had as much native pride as any queen would have known what to do with.

III. A KNOT OF DREAMERS

Zenobia bade us welcome, in a fine, frank, mellow voice, and gave each of us her hand, which was very soft and warm. She had something appropriate, I recollect, to say to every individual; and what she said to myself was this:—"I have long wished to know you, Mr. Coverdale, and to thank you for your beautiful poetry, some of which I have learned by heart; or rather it has stolen into my memory, without my exercising any choice or volition about the matter. Of course—permit me to say you do not think of relinquishing an occupation in which you have done yourself so much credit. I would almost rather give you up as an associate, than that the world should lose one of its true poets!"

"Ah, no; there will not be the slightest danger of that, especially after this inestimable praise from Zenobia," said I, smiling, and blushing, no doubt, with excess of pleasure. "I hope, on the contrary, now to produce something that shall really deserve to be called poetry,—true, strong, natural, and sweet, as is the life which we are going to lead,—something that shall have the notes of wild birds twittering through it, or a strain like the wind anthems in the woods, as the case may be."

"Is it irksome to you to hear your own verses sung?" asked Zenobia, with a gracious smile. "If so, I am very sorry, for you will certainly hear me singing them sometimes, in the summer evenings."

"Of all things," answered I, "that is what will delight me most."

While this passed, and while she spoke to my companions, I was taking note of Zenobia's aspect; and it impressed itself on me so distinctly, that I can now summon her up, like a ghost, a little wanner than the life but otherwise identical with it. She was dressed as simply as possible, in an American print (I think the dry-goods people call it so), but with a silken kerchief, between which and her gown there was one glimpse of a white shoulder. It struck me as a great piece of good fortune that there should be just that glimpse. Her hair, which was dark, glossy, and of singular abundance, was put up rather soberly and primly—without curls, or other ornament, except a single flower. It was an exotic of rare beauty, and as fresh as if the hothouse gardener had just clipt it from the stem. That flower has struck deep root into my memory. I can both see it and smell it, at this moment. So brilliant, so rare, so costly as it must have been, and yet enduring only for a day, it was more indicative of the pride and pomp which had a luxuriant growth in Zenobia's character than if a great diamond had sparkled among her hair.

Her hand, though very soft, was larger than most women would like to have, or than they could afford to have, though not a whit too large in proportion with the spacious plan of Zenobia's entire development. It did one good to see a fine intellect (as hers really was, although its natural tendency lay in another direction than towards literature) so fitly cased. She was, indeed, an admirable figure of a woman, just on the hither verge of her richest maturity, with a combination of features which it is safe to call remarkably beautiful, even if some fastidious persons might pronounce them a little deficient in softness and delicacy. But we find enough of those attributes everywhere. Preferable—by way of variety, at least—was Zenobia's bloom, health, and vigor, which she possessed in such overflow that a man might well have fallen in love with her for their sake only. In her quiet moods, she seemed rather indolent; but when really in earnest, particularly if there were a spice of bitter feeling, she grew all alive to her finger-tips.

"I am the first comer," Zenobia went on to say, while her smile beamed warmth upon us all; "so I take the part of hostess for to-day, and welcome you as if to my own fireside. You shall be my guests, too, at supper. Tomorrow, if you please, we will be brethren and sisters, and begin our new life from daybreak."

"Have we our various parts assigned?" asked some one.

"Oh, we of the softer sex," responded Zenobia, with her mellow, almost broad laugh,—most delectable to hear, but not in the least like an ordinary woman's laugh,—"we women (there are four of us here already) will take the domestic and indoor part of the business, as a matter of course. To bake, to boil, to roast, to fry, to stew,—to wash, and iron, and scrub, and sweep,—and, at our idler intervals, to repose ourselves on knitting and sewing,—these, I suppose, must be feminine occupations, for the present. By and by, perhaps, when our individual adaptations begin to develop themselves, it may be that some of us who wear the petticoat will go afield, and leave the weaker brethren to take our places in the kitchen."

"What a pity," I remarked, "that the kitchen, and the housework generally, cannot be left out of our system altogether! It is odd enough that the kind of labor which falls to the lot of women is just that which chiefly distinguishes artificial life—the life of degenerated mortals—from the life of Paradise. Eve had no dinner-pot, and no clothes to mend, and no washing-day."

"I am afraid," said Zenobia, with mirth gleaming out of her eyes, "we shall find some difficulty in adopting the paradisiacal system for at least a month to come. Look at that snowdrift sweeping past the window! Are there any figs ripe, do you think? Have the pineapples been gathered to-day? Would you like a bread-fruit, or a cocoanut? Shall I run out and pluck you some roses? No, no, Mr. Coverdale; the only flower hereabouts is the one in my hair, which I got out of a greenhouse this morning. As for the garb of Eden," added she, shivering playfully, "I shall not assume it till after May-day!"

Assuredly Zenobia could not have intended it,—the fault must have been entirely in my imagination. But these last words, together with something in her manner, irresistibly brought up a picture of that fine, perfectly developed figure, in Eve's earliest garment. Her free, careless, generous modes of expression often had this effect of creating images which, though pure, are hardly felt to be quite decorous when born of a thought that passes between man and woman. I imputed it, at that time, to Zenobia's noble courage, conscious of no harm, and scorning the petty restraints which take the life and color out of other women's conversation. There was another peculiarity about her. We seldom meet with women nowadays, and in this country, who impress us as being women at all,—their sex fades away and goes for nothing, in ordinary intercourse. Not so with Zenobia. One felt an influence breathing out of her such as we might suppose to come from Eve, when she was just made, and her Creator brought her to Adam, saying, "Behold! here is a woman!" Not that I would convey the idea of especial gentleness, grace, modesty, and shyness, but of a certain warm and rich characteristic, which seems, for the most part, to have been refined away out of the feminine system.

"And now," continued Zenobia, "I must go and help get supper. Do you think you can be content, instead of figs, pineapples, and all the other delicacies of Adam's supper-table, with tea and toast, and a certain modest supply of ham and tongue, which, with the instinct of a housewife, I brought hither in a basket? And there shall be bread and milk, too, if the innocence of your taste demands it."

The whole sisterhood now went about their domestic avocations, utterly declining our offers to assist, further than by bringing wood for the kitchen fire from a huge pile in the back yard. After heaping up more than a sufficient quantity, we returned to the sitting-room, drew our chairs close to the hearth, and began to talk over our prospects. Soon, with a tremendous stamping in the entry, appeared Silas Foster, lank, stalwart, uncouth, and grizzly-bearded. He came from foddering the cattle in the barn, and from the field, where he had been ploughing, until the depth of the snow rendered it impossible to draw a furrow. He greeted us in pretty much the same tone as if he were speaking to his oxen, took a quid from his iron tobacco-box, pulled off his wet cowhide boots, and sat down before the fire in his stocking-feet. The steam arose from his soaked garments, so that the stout yeoman looked vaporous and spectre-like.

"Well, folks," remarked Silas, "you'll be wishing yourselves back to town again, if this weather holds."

And, true enough, there was a look of gloom, as the twilight fell silently and sadly out of the sky, its gray or sable flakes intermingling themselves with the fast-descending snow. The storm, in its evening aspect, was decidedly dreary. It seemed to have arisen for our especial behoof,—a symbol of the cold, desolate, distrustful phantoms that invariably haunt the mind, on the eve of adventurous enterprises, to warn us back within the boundaries of ordinary life.

But our courage did not quail. We would not allow ourselves to be depressed by the snowdrift trailing past the window, any more than if it had been the sigh of a summer wind among rustling boughs. There have been few brighter seasons for us than that. If ever men might lawfully dream awake, and give utterance to their wildest visions without dread of laughter or scorn on the part of the audience,—

yes, and speak of earthly happiness, for themselves and mankind, as an object to be hopefully striven for, and probably attained, we who made that little semicircle round the blazing fire were those very men. We had left the rusty iron framework of society behind us; we had broken through many hindrances that are powerful enough to keep most people on the weary treadmill of the established system, even while they feel its irksomeness almost as intolerable as we did. We had stepped down from the pulpit; we had flung aside the pen; we had shut up the ledger; we had thrown off that sweet, bewitching, enervating indolence, which is better, after all, than most of the enjoyments within mortal grasp. It was our purpose—a generous one, certainly, and absurd, no doubt, in full proportion with its generosity—to give up whatever we had heretofore attained, for the sake of showing mankind the example of a life governed by other than the false and cruel principles on which human society has all along been based.

And, first of all, we had divorced ourselves from pride, and were striving to supply its place with familiar love. We meant to lessen the laboring man's great burden of toil, by performing our due share of it at the cost of our own thews and sinews. We sought our profit by mutual aid, instead of wresting it by the strong hand from an enemy, or filching it craftily from those less shrewd than ourselves (if, indeed, there were any such in New England), or winning it by selfish competition with a neighbor; in one or another of which fashions every son of woman both perpetrates and suffers his share of the common evil, whether he chooses it or no. And, as the basis of our institution, we purposed to offer up the earnest toil of our bodies, as a prayer no less than an effort for the advancement of our race.

Therefore, if we built splendid castles (phalansteries perhaps they might be more fitly called), and pictured beautiful scenes, among the fervid coals of the hearth around which we were clustering, and if all went to rack with the crumbling embers and have never since arisen out of the ashes, let us take to ourselves no shame. In my own behalf, I rejoice that I could once think better of the world's improvability than it deserved. It is a mistake into which men seldom fall twice in a lifetime; or, if so, the rarer and higher is the nature that can thus magnanimously persist in error.

Stout Silas Foster mingled little in our conversation; but when he did speak, it was very much to some practical purpose. For instance:—"Which man among you," quoth he, "is the best judge of swine? Some of us must go to the next Brighton fair, and buy half a dozen pigs."

Pigs! Good heavens! had we come out from among the swinish multitude for this? And again, in reference to some discussion about raising early vegetables for the market:—"We shall never make any hand at market gardening," said Silas Foster, "unless the women folks will undertake to do all the weeding. We haven't team enough for that and the regular farm-work, reckoning three of your city folks as worth one common field-hand. No, no; I tell you, we should have to get up a little too early in the morning, to compete with the market gardeners round Boston."

It struck me as rather odd, that one of the first questions raised, after our separation from the greedy, struggling, self-seeking world, should relate to the possibility of getting the advantage over the outside barbarians in their own field of labor. But, to own the truth, I very soon became sensible that, as regarded society at large, we stood in a position of new hostility, rather than new brotherhood. Nor could this fail to be the case, in some degree, until the bigger and better half of society should range itself on our side. Constituting so pitiful a minority as now, we were inevitably estranged from the rest of mankind in pretty fair proportion with the strictness of our mutual bond among ourselves.

This dawning idea, however, was driven back into my inner consciousness by the entrance of Zenobia. She came with the welcome intelligence that supper was on the table. Looking at herself in the glass, and perceiving that her one magnificent flower had grown rather languid (probably by being exposed to the fervency of the kitchen fire), she flung it on the floor, as unconcernedly as a village girl would throw away a faded violet. The action seemed proper to her character, although, methought, it would still more have befitted the bounteous nature of this beautiful woman to scatter fresh flowers from her hand, and to revive faded ones by her touch. Nevertheless, it was a singular but irresistible effect; the presence of Zenobia caused our heroic enterprise to show like an illusion, a masquerade, a pastoral, a counterfeit Arcadia, in which we grown-up men and women were making a play-day of the years that were given us to live in. I tried to analyze this impression, but not with much success.

"It really vexes me," observed Zenobia, as we left the room, "that Mr. Hollingsworth should be such a laggard. I should not have thought him at all the sort of person to be turned back by a puff of contrary wind, or a few snowflakes drifting into his face."

"Do you know Hollingsworth personally?" I inquired.

"No; only as an auditor—auditress, I mean—of some of his lectures," said she. "What a voice he has! and what a man he is! Yet not so much an intellectual man, I should say, as a great heart; at least, he moved me more deeply than I think myself capable of being moved, except by the stroke of a true, strong heart against my own. It is a sad pity that he should have devoted his glorious powers to such a grimy, unbeautiful, and positively hopeless object as this reformation of criminals, about which he makes himself and his wretchedly small audiences so very miserable. To tell you a secret, I never could tolerate a philanthropist before. Could you?"

"By no means," I answered; "neither can I now."

"They are, indeed, an odiously disagreeable set of mortals," continued Zenobia. "I should like Mr. Hollingsworth a great deal better if the philanthropy had been left out. At all events, as a mere matter of taste, I wish he would let the bad people alone, and try to benefit those who are not already past his help. Do you suppose he will be content to spend his life, or even a few months of it, among tolerably virtuous and comfortable individuals like ourselves?"

"Upon my word, I doubt it," said I. "If we wish to keep him with us, we must systematically commit at least one crime apiece! Mere peccadillos will not satisfy him."

Zenobia turned, sidelong, a strange kind of a glance upon me; but, before I could make out what it meant, we had entered the kitchen, where, in accordance with the rustic simplicity of our new life, the supper-table was spread.

IV. THE SUPPER-TABLE

The pleasant firelight! I must still keep harping on it. The kitchen hearth had an old-fashioned breadth, depth, and spaciousness, far within which lay what seemed the butt of a good-sized oak-tree, with the moisture bubbling merrily out at both ends. It was now half an hour beyond dusk. The blaze from an armful of substantial sticks, rendered more combustible by brushwood and pine, flickered powerfully on the smoke-blackened walls, and so cheered our spirits that we cared not what inclemency might rage and roar on the other side of our illuminated windows. A yet sultrier warmth was bestowed by a goodly quantity of peat, which was crumbling to white ashes among the burning brands, and incensed the kitchen with its not ungrateful fragrance. The exuberance of this household fire would alone have sufficed to bespeak us no true farmers; for the New England yeoman, if he have the misfortune to dwell within practicable distance of a wood-market, is as niggardly of each stick as if it were a bar of California gold.

But it was fortunate for us, on that wintry eve of our untried life, to enjoy the warm and radiant luxury of a somewhat too abundant fire. If it served no other purpose, it made the men look so full of youth, warm blood, and hope, and the women—such of them, at least, as were anywise convertible by its magic—so very beautiful, that I would cheerfully have spent my last dollar to prolong the blaze. As for Zenobia, there was a glow in her cheeks that made me think of Pandora, fresh from Vulcan's workshop, and full of the celestial warmth by dint of which he had tempered and moulded her.

"Take your places, my dear friends all," cried she; "seat yourselves without ceremony, and you shall be made happy with such tea as not many of the world's working-people, except yourselves, will find in their cups to-night. After this one supper, you may drink buttermilk, if you please. To-night we will quaff this nectar, which, I assure you, could not be bought with gold."

We all sat down,—grizzly Silas Foster, his rotund helpmate, and the two bouncing handmaidens, included,—and looked at one another in a friendly but rather awkward way. It was the first practical trial of our theories of equal brotherhood and sisterhood; and we people of superior cultivation and refinement (for as such, I presume, we unhesitatingly reckoned ourselves) felt as if something were already accomplished towards the millennium of love. The truth is, however, that the laboring oar was with our unpolished companions; it being far easier to condescend than to accept of condescension. Neither did I refrain from questioning, in secret, whether some of us—and Zenobia among the rest—would so quietly have taken our places among these good people, save for the cherished consciousness that it was not by necessity but choice. Though we saw fit to drink our tea out of earthen cups to-night, and in earthen company, it was at our own option to use pictured porcelain and handle silver forks again to-morrow. This same salvo, as to the power of regaining our former position, contributed much, I fear, to the equanimity with which we subsequently bore many of the hardships and humiliations of a life of toil. If ever I have deserved (which has not often been the case, and, I think, never), but if ever I did deserve to be soundly cuffed by a fellow mortal, for secretly putting weight upon some imaginary social advantage, it must have been while I was striving to prove myself ostentatiously his equal and no more. It was while I sat beside him on his cobbler's bench, or clinked my hoe against his own in the cornfield, or broke the same crust of bread, my earth-grimed hand to his, at our noontide lunch. The poor, proud man should look at both sides of sympathy like this.

The silence which followed upon our sitting down to table grew rather oppressive; indeed, it was hardly broken by a word, during the first round of Zenobia's fragrant tea.

"I hope," said I, at last, "that our blazing windows will be visible a great way off. There is nothing so pleasant and encouraging to a solitary traveller, on a stormy night, as a flood of firelight seen amid the gloom. These ruddy window panes cannot fail to cheer the hearts of all that look at them. Are they not warm with the beacon-fire which we have kindled for humanity?"

"The blaze of that brushwood will only last a minute or two longer," observed Silas Foster; but whether he meant to insinuate that our moral illumination would have as brief a term, I cannot say.

"Meantime," said Zenobia, "it may serve to guide some wayfarer to a shelter."

And, just as she said this, there came a knock at the house door.

"There is one of the world's wayfarers," said I. "Ay, ay, just so!" quoth Silas Foster. "Our firelight will draw stragglers, just as a candle draws dorbugs on a summer night."

Whether to enjoy a dramatic suspense, or that we were selfishly contrasting our own comfort with the chill and dreary situation of the unknown person at the threshold, or that some of us city folk felt a little startled at the knock which came so unseasonably, through night and storm, to the door of the lonely farmhouse,—so it happened that nobody, for an instant or two, arose to answer the summons. Pretty soon there came another knock. The first had been moderately loud; the second was smitten so forcibly that the knuckles of the applicant must have left their mark in the door panel.

"He knocks as if he had a right to come in," said Zenobia, laughing. "And what are we thinking of?—It must be Mr. Hollingsworth!"

Hereupon I went to the door, unbolted, and flung it wide open. There, sure enough, stood Hollingsworth, his shaggy greatcoat all covered with snow, so that he looked quite as much like a polar bear as a modern philanthropist.

"Sluggish hospitality this!" said he, in those deep tones of his, which seemed to come out of a chest as capacious as a barrel. "It would have served you right if I had lain down and spent the night on the doorstep, just for the sake of putting you to shame. But here is a guest who will need a warmer and softer bed."

And, stepping back to the wagon in which he had journeyed hither, Hollingsworth received into his arms and deposited on the doorstep a figure enveloped in a cloak. It was evidently a woman; or, rather,—judging from the ease with which he lifted her, and the little space which she seemed to fill in his arms, a slim and unsubstantial girl. As she showed some hesitation about entering the door, Hollingsworth, with his usual directness and lack of ceremony, urged her forward not merely within the entry, but into the warm and strongly lighted kitchen.

"Who is this?" whispered I, remaining behind with him, while he was taking off his greatcoat.

"Who? Really, I don't know," answered Hollingsworth, looking at me with some surprise. "It is a young person who belongs here, however; and no doubt she had been expected. Zenobia, or some of the women folks, can tell you all about it."

"I think not," said I, glancing towards the new-comer and the other occupants of the kitchen. "Nobody seems to welcome her. I should hardly judge that she was an expected guest."

"Well, well," said Hollingsworth quietly, "We'll make it right."

The stranger, or whatever she were, remained standing precisely on that spot of the kitchen floor to which Hollingsworth's kindly hand had impelled her. The cloak falling partly off, she was seen to be a very young woman dressed in a poor but decent gown, made high in the neck, and without any regard to fashion or smartness. Her brown hair fell down from beneath a hood, not in curls but with only a slight wave; her face was of a wan, almost sickly hue, betokening habitual seclusion from the sun and free atmosphere, like a flower-shrub that had done its best to blossom in too scanty light. To complete the pitiableness of her aspect, she shivered either with cold, or fear, or nervous excitement, so that you might have beheld her shadow vibrating on the fire-lighted wall. In short, there has seldom been seen so depressed and sad a figure as this young girl's; and it was hardly possible to help being angry with her, from mere despair of doing anything for her comfort. The fantasy occurred to me that she was some desolate kind of a creature, doomed to wander about in snowstorms; and that, though the ruddiness of our window panes had tempted her into a human dwelling, she would not remain long enough to melt the icicles out of her hair. Another conjecture likewise came into my mind. Recollecting Hollingsworth's sphere of philanthropic action, I deemed it possible that he might have brought one of his guilty patients, to be wrought upon and restored to spiritual health by the pure influences which our mode of life would create.

As yet the girl had not stirred. She stood near the door, fixing a pair of large, brown, melancholy eyes upon Zenobia—only upon Zenobia!—she evidently saw nothing else in the room save that bright, fair, rosy, beautiful woman. It was the strangest look I ever witnessed; long a mystery to me, and forever a memory. Once she seemed about to move forward and greet her,—I know not with what warmth or with what words,—but, finally, instead of doing so, she dropped down upon her knees, clasped her hands, and gazed piteously into Zenobia's face. Meeting no kindly reception, her head fell on her bosom.

I never thoroughly forgave Zenobia for her conduct on this occasion. But women are always more cautious in their casual hospitalities than men.

"What does the girl mean?" cried she in rather a sharp tone. "Is she crazy? Has she no tongue?"

And here Hollingsworth stepped forward.

"No wonder if the poor child's tongue is frozen in her mouth," said he; and I think he positively frowned at Zenobia. "The very heart will be frozen in her bosom, unless you women can warm it, among you, with the warmth that ought to be in your own!"

Hollingsworth's appearance was very striking at this moment. He was then about thirty years old, but looked several years older, with his great shaggy head, his heavy brow, his dark complexion, his abundant beard, and the rude strength with which his features seemed to have been hammered out of iron, rather than chiselled or moulded from any finer or softer material. His figure was not tall, but massive and brawny, and well befitting his original occupation; which as the reader probably knows—was that of a blacksmith. As for external polish, or mere courtesy of manner, he never possessed more than a tolerably educated bear; although, in his gentler moods, there was a tenderness in his voice, eyes, mouth, in his gesture, and in every indescribable manifestation, which few men could resist and no woman. But he now looked stern and reproachful; and it was with that inauspicious meaning in his glance that Hollingsworth first met Zenobia's eyes, and began his influence upon her life.

To my surprise, Zenobia—of whose haughty spirit I had been told so many examples—absolutely changed color, and seemed mortified and confused.

"You do not quite do me justice, Mr. Hollingsworth," said she almost humbly. "I am willing to be kind to the poor girl. Is she a protegee of yours? What can I do for her?"

"Have you anything to ask of this lady?" said Hollingsworth kindly to the girl. "I remember you mentioned her name before we left town."

"Only that she will shelter me," replied the girl tremulously. "Only that she will let me be always near her."

"Well, indeed," exclaimed Zenobia, recovering herself and laughing, "this is an adventure, and well-worthy to be the first incident in our life of love and free-heartedness! But I accept it, for the present, without further question, only," added she, "it would be a convenience if we knew your name."

"Priscilla," said the girl; and it appeared to me that she hesitated whether to add anything more, and decided in the negative. "Pray do not ask me my other name,—at least not yet,—if you will be so kind to a forlorn creature."

Priscilla!—Priscilla! I repeated the name to myself three or four times; and in that little space, this quaint and prim cognomen had so amalgamated itself with my idea of the girl, that it seemed as if no other name could have adhered to her for a moment. Heretofore the poor thing had not shed any tears; but now that she found herself received, and at least temporarily established, the big drops began to ooze out from beneath her eyelids as if she were full of them. Perhaps it showed the iron substance of my heart, that I could not help smiling at this odd scene of unknown and unaccountable calamity, into which our cheerful party had been entrapped without the liberty of choosing whether to sympathize or no. Hollingsworth's behavior was certainly a great deal more creditable than mine.

"Let us not pry further into her secrets," he said to Zenobia and the rest of us, apart; and his dark, shaggy face looked really beautiful with its expression of thoughtful benevolence. "Let us conclude that Providence has sent her to us, as the first-fruits of the world, which we have undertaken to make happier than we find it. Let us warm her poor, shivering body with this good fire, and her poor, shivering heart with our best kindness. Let us feed her, and make her one of us. As we do by this friendless girl, so shall we prosper. And, in good time, whatever is desirable for us to know will be melted out of her, as inevitably as those tears which we see now."

"At least," remarked I, "you may tell us how and where you met with her."

"An old man brought her to my lodgings," answered Hollingsworth, "and begged me to convey her to Blithedale, where—so I understood him—she had friends; and this is positively all I know about the matter."

Grim Silas Foster, all this while, had been busy at the supper-table, pouring out his own tea and gulping it down with no more sense of its exquisiteness than if it were a decoction of catnip; helping himself to pieces of dipt toast on the flat of his knife blade, and dropping half of it on the table-cloth; using the same serviceable implement to cut slice after slice of ham; perpetrating terrible enormities with the butter-plate; and in all other respects behaving less like a civilized Christian than the worst kind of an ogre. Being by this time fully gorged, he crowned his amiable exploits with a draught from the water pitcher, and then favored us with his opinion about the business in hand. And, certainly, though they proceeded out of an unwiped mouth, his expressions did him honor.

"Give the girl a hot cup of tea and a thick slice of this first-rate bacon," said Silas, like a sensible man as he was. "That's what she wants. Let her stay with us as long as she likes, and help in the kitchen, and take the cow-breath at milking time; and, in a week or two, she'll begin to look like a creature of this world."

So we sat down again to supper, and Priscilla along with us.

V. UNTIL BEDTIME

Silas Foster, by the time we concluded our meal, had stript off his coat, and planted himself on a low chair by the kitchen fire, with a lapstone, a hammer, a piece of sole leather, and some waxed-ends, in order to cobble an old pair of cow-hide boots; he being, in his own phrase, "something of a dab" (whatever degree of skill that may imply) at the shoemaking business. We heard the tap of his hammer at intervals for the rest of the evening. The remainder of the party adjourned to the sitting-room. Good Mrs. Foster took her knitting-work, and soon fell fast asleep, still keeping her needles in brisk movement, and, to the best of my observation, absolutely footing a stocking out of the texture of a dream. And a very substantial stocking it seemed to be. One of the two handmaidens hemmed a towel, and the other appeared to be making a ruffle, for her Sunday's wear, out of a little bit of embroidered muslin which Zenobia had probably given her.

It was curious to observe how trustingly, and yet how timidly, our poor Priscilla betook herself into the shadow of Zenobia's protection. She sat beside her on a stool, looking up every now and then with an expression of humble delight at her new friend's beauty. A brilliant woman is often an object of the devoted admiration—it might almost be termed worship, or idolatry—of some young girl, who perhaps beholds the cynosure only at an awful distance, and has as little hope of personal intercourse as of climbing among the stars of heaven. We men are too gross to comprehend it. Even a woman, of mature age, despises or laughs at such a passion. There occurred to me no mode of accounting for Priscilla's behavior, except by supposing that she had read some of Zenobia's stories (as such literature goes everywhere), or her tracts in defence of the sex, and had come hither with the one purpose of being her slave. There is nothing parallel to this, I believe,—nothing so foolishly disinterested, and hardly anything so beautiful,—in the masculine nature, at whatever epoch of life; or, if there be, a fine and rare development of character might reasonably be looked for from the youth who should prove himself capable of such self-forgetful affection.

Zenobia happening to change her seat, I took the opportunity, in an undertone, to suggest some such notion as the above.

"Since you see the young woman in so poetical a light," replied she in the same tone, "you had better turn the affair into a ballad. It is a grand subject, and worthy of supernatural machinery. The storm, the startling knock at the door, the entrance of the sable knight Hollingsworth and this shadowy snow-maiden, who, precisely at the stroke of midnight, shall melt away at my feet in a pool of ice-cold water and give me my death with a pair of wet slippers! And when the verses are written, and polished quite to your mind, I will favor you with my idea as to what the girl really is."

"Pray let me have it now," said I; "it shall be woven into the ballad."

"She is neither more nor less," answered Zenobia, "than a seamstress from the city; and she has probably no more transcendental purpose than to do my miscellaneous sewing, for I suppose she will hardly expect to make my dresses."

"How can you decide upon her so easily?" I inquired.

"Oh, we women judge one another by tokens that escape the obtuseness of masculine perceptions!" said Zenobia. "There is no proof which you would be likely to appreciate, except the needle marks on the tip of her forefinger. Then, my supposition perfectly accounts for her paleness, her nervousness, and her wretched fragility. Poor thing! She has been stifled with the heat of a salamander stove, in a small, close room, and has drunk coffee, and fed upon doughnuts, raisins, candy, and all such trash, till she is scarcely half alive; and so, as she has hardly any physique, a poet like Mr. Miles Coverdale may be allowed to think her spiritual."

"Look at her now!" whispered I.

Priscilla was gazing towards us with an inexpressible sorrow in her wan face and great tears running down her cheeks. It was difficult to resist the impression that, cautiously as we had lowered our voices, she must have overheard and been wounded by Zenobia's scornful estimate of her character and purposes.

"What ears the girl must have!" whispered Zenobia, with a look of vexation, partly comic and partly real. "I will confess to you that I cannot quite make her out. However, I am positively not an ill-natured person, unless when very grievously provoked,—and as you, and especially Mr. Hollingsworth, take so much interest in this odd creature, and as she knocks with a very slight tap against my own heart likewise,—why, I mean to let her in. From this moment I will be reasonably kind to her. There is no pleasure in tormenting a person of one's own sex, even if she do favor one with a little more love than one can conveniently dispose of; and that, let me say, Mr. Coverdale, is the most troublesome offence you can offer to a woman."

"Thank you," said I, smiling; "I don't mean to be guilty of it."

She went towards Priscilla, took her hand, and passed her own rosy finger-tips, with a pretty, caressing movement, over the girl's hair. The touch had a magical effect. So vivid a look of joy flushed up beneath those fingers, that it seemed as if the sad and wan Priscilla had been snatched away, and another kind of creature substituted in her place. This one caress, bestowed voluntarily by Zenobia, was evidently received as a pledge of all that the stranger sought from her, whatever the unuttered boon might be. From that instant, too, she melted in quietly amongst us, and was no longer a foreign element. Though always an object of peculiar interest, a riddle, and a theme of frequent discussion, her tenure at

Blithedale was thenceforth fixed. We no more thought of questioning it, than if Priscilla had been recognized as a domestic sprite, who had haunted the rustic fireside of old, before we had ever been warmed by its blaze.

She now produced, out of a work-bag that she had with her, some little wooden instruments (what they are called I never knew), and proceeded to knit, or net, an article which ultimately took the shape of a silk purse. As the work went on, I remembered to have seen just such purses before; indeed, I was the possessor of one. Their peculiar excellence, besides the great delicacy and beauty of the manufacture, lay in the almost impossibility that any uninitiated person should discover the aperture; although, to a practised touch, they would open as wide as charity or prodigality might wish. I wondered if it were not a symbol of Priscilla's own mystery.

Notwithstanding the new confidence with which Zenobia had inspired her, our guest showed herself disquieted by the storm. When the strong puffs of wind spattered the snow against the windows and made the oaken frame of the farmhouse creak, she looked at us apprehensively, as if to inquire whether these tempestuous outbreaks did not betoken some unusual mischief in the shrieking blast. She had been bred up, no doubt, in some close nook, some inauspiciously sheltered court of the city, where the uttermost rage of a tempest, though it might scatter down the slates of the roof into the bricked area, could not shake the casement of her little room. The sense of vast, undefined space, pressing from the outside against the black panes of our uncurtained windows, was fearful to the poor girl, heretofore accustomed to the narrowness of human limits, with the lamps of neighboring tenements glimmering across the street. The house probably seemed to her adrift on the great ocean of the night. A little parallelogram of sky was all that she had hitherto known of nature, so that she felt the awfulness that really exists in its limitless extent. Once, while the blast was bellowing, she caught hold of Zenobia's robe, with precisely the air of one who hears her own name spoken at a distance, but is unutterably reluctant to obey the call.

We spent rather an incommunicative evening. Hollingsworth hardly said a word, unless when repeatedly and pertinaciously addressed. Then, indeed, he would glare upon us from the thick shrubbery of his meditations like a tiger out of a jungle, make the briefest reply possible, and betake himself back into the solitude of his heart and mind. The poor fellow had contracted this ungracious habit from the intensity with which he contemplated his own ideas, and the infrequent sympathy which they met with from his auditors,—a circumstance that seemed only to strengthen the implicit confidence that he awarded to them. His heart, I imagine, was never really interested in our socialist scheme, but was forever busy with his strange, and, as most people thought it, impracticable plan, for the reformation of criminals through an appeal to their higher instincts.

Much as I liked Hollingsworth, it cost me many a groan to tolerate him on this point. He ought to have commenced his investigation of the subject by perpetrating some huge sin in his proper person, and examining the condition of his higher instincts afterwards.

V. UNTIL BEDTIME

The rest of us formed ourselves into a committee for providing our infant community with an appropriate name,—a matter of greatly more difficulty than the uninitiated reader would suppose. Blithedale was neither good nor bad. We should have resumed the old Indian name of the premises, had it possessed the oil-and-honey flow which the aborigines were so often happy in communicating to their local appellations; but it chanced to be a harsh, ill-connected, and interminable word, which seemed to fill the mouth with a mixture of very stiff clay and very crumbly pebbles. Zenobia suggested "Sunny Glimpse," as expressive of a vista into a better system of society. This we turned over and over for a while, acknowledging its prettiness, but concluded it to be rather too fine and sentimental a name (a fault inevitable by literary ladies in such attempts) for sunburnt men to work under. I ventured to whisper "Utopia," which, however, was unanimously scouted down, and the proposer very harshly maltreated, as if he had intended a latent satire. Some were for calling our institution "The Oasis," in view of its being the one green spot in the moral sand-waste of the world; but others insisted on a proviso for reconsidering the matter at a twelvemonths' end, when a final decision might be had, whether to name it "The Oasis" or "Sahara." So, at last, finding it impracticable to hammer out anything better, we resolved that the spot should still be Blithedale, as being of good augury enough.

The evening wore on, and the outer solitude looked in upon us through the windows, gloomy, wild, and vague, like another state of existence, close beside the little sphere of warmth and light in which we were the prattlers and bustlers of a moment. By and by the door was opened by Silas Foster, with a cotton handkerchief about his head, and a tallow candle in his hand.

"Take my advice, brother farmers," said he, with a great, broad, bottomless yawn, "and get to bed as soon as you can. I shall sound the horn at daybreak; and we've got the cattle to fodder, and nine cows to milk, and a dozen other things to do, before breakfast."

Thus ended the first evening at Blithedale. I went shivering to my fireless chamber, with the miserable consciousness (which had been growing upon me for several hours past) that I had caught a tremendous cold, and should probably awaken, at the blast of the horn, a fit subject for a hospital. The night proved a feverish one. During the greater part of it, I was in that vilest of states when a fixed idea remains in the mind, like the nail in Sisera's brain, while innumerable other ideas go and come, and flutter to and fro, combining constant transition with intolerable sameness. Had I made a record of that night's half-waking dreams, it is my belief that it would have anticipated several of the chief incidents of this narrative, including a dim shadow of its catastrophe. Starting up in bed at length, I saw that the storm was past, and the moon was shining on the snowy landscape, which looked like a lifeless copy of the world in marble.

From the bank of the distant river, which was shimmering in the moonlight, came the black shadow of the only cloud in heaven, driven swiftly by the wind, and passing over meadow and hillock, vanishing amid tufts of leafless trees, but reappearing on the hither side, until it swept across our doorstep.

How cold an Arcadia was this!

VI. COVERDALE'S SICK-CHAMBER

The horn sounded at daybreak, as Silas Foster had forewarned us, harsh, uproarious, inexorably drawn out, and as sleep-dispelling as if this hard-hearted old yeoman had got hold of the trump of doom.

On all sides I could hear the creaking of the bedsteads, as the brethren of Blithedale started from slumber, and thrust themselves into their habiliments, all awry, no doubt, in their haste to begin the reformation of the world. Zenobia put her head into the entry, and besought Silas Foster to cease his clamor, and to be kind enough to leave an armful of firewood and a pail of water at her chamber door. Of the whole household,—unless, indeed, it were Priscilla, for whose habits, in this particular, I cannot vouch,—of all our apostolic society, whose mission was to bless mankind, Hollingsworth, I apprehend, was the only one who began the enterprise with prayer. My sleeping-room being but thinly partitioned from his, the solemn murmur of his voice made its way to my ears, compelling me to be an auditor of his awful privacy with the Creator. It affected me with a deep reverence for Hollingsworth, which no familiarity then existing, or that afterwards grew more intimate between us,—no, nor my subsequent perception of his own great errors,—ever quite effaced. It is so rare, in these times, to meet with a man of prayerful habits (except, of course, in the pulpit), that such an one is decidedly marked out by the light of transfiguration, shed upon him in the divine interview from which he passes into his daily life.

As for me, I lay abed; and if I said my prayers, it was backward, cursing my day as bitterly as patient Job himself. The truth was, the hot-house warmth of a town residence, and the luxurious life in which I indulged myself, had taken much of the pith out of my physical system; and the wintry blast of the preceding day, together with the general chill of our airy old farmhouse, had got fairly into my heart and the marrow of my bones. In this predicament, I seriously wished—selfish as it may appear—that the reformation of society had been postponed about half a century, or, at all events, to such a date as should have put my intermeddling with it entirely out of the question.

What, in the name of common-sense, had I to do with any better society than I had always lived in? It had satisfied me well enough. My pleasant bachelor-parlor, sunny and shadowy, curtained and carpeted, with the bedchamber adjoining; my centre-table, strewn with books and periodicals; my writing-desk with a half-finished poem, in a stanza of my own contrivance; my morning lounge at the reading-room or picture gallery; my noontide walk along the cheery pavement, with the suggestive succession of human faces, and the brisk throb of human life in which I shared; my dinner at the Albion, where I had a hundred dishes at command, and could banquet as delicately as the wizard Michael Scott when the Devil fed him from the king of France's kitchen; my evening at the billiard club, the concert, the theatre, or at somebody's party, if I pleased,—what could be better than all this? Was it better to hoe, to mow, to toil and moil amidst the accumulations of a barnyard; to be the chambermaid of two yoke of oxen and a dozen cows; to eat salt beef, and earn it with the sweat of my brow, and thereby take the tough morsel out of some wretch's mouth, into whose vocation I had thrust myself? Above all, was it better to have a fever and die blaspheming, as I was like to do?

In this wretched plight, with a furnace in my heart and another in my head, by the heat of which I was kept constantly at the boiling point, yet shivering at the bare idea of extruding so much as a finger into the icy atmosphere of the room, I kept my bed until breakfast-time, when Hollingsworth knocked at the door, and entered.

"Well, Coverdale," cried he, "you bid fair to make an admirable farmer! Don't you mean to get up to-day?"

"Neither to-day nor to-morrow," said I hopelessly. "I doubt if I ever rise again!"

"What is the matter now?" he asked.

I told him my piteous case, and besought him to send me back to town in a close carriage.

"No, no!" said Hollingsworth with kindly seriousness. "If you are really sick, we must take care of you."

Accordingly he built a fire in my chamber, and, having little else to do while the snow lay on the ground, established himself as my nurse. A doctor was sent for, who, being homaeopathic, gave me as much medicine, in the course of a fortnight's attendance, as would have laid on the point of a needle. They fed me on water-gruel, and I speedily became a skeleton above ground. But, after all, I have many precious recollections connected with that fit of sickness.

Hollingsworth's more than brotherly attendance gave me inexpressible comfort. Most men—and certainly I could not always claim to be one of the exceptions—have a natural indifference, if not an absolutely hostile feeling, towards those whom disease, or weakness, or calamity of any kind causes to falter and faint amid the rude jostle of our selfish existence. The education of Christianity, it is true, the sympathy of a like experience and the example of women, may soften and, possibly, subvert this ugly characteristic of our sex; but it is originally there, and has likewise its analogy in the practice of our brute brethren, who hunt the sick or disabled member of the herd from among them, as an enemy. It is for this reason that the stricken deer goes apart, and the sick lion grimly withdraws himself into his den. Except in love, or the attachments of kindred, or other very long and habitual affection, we really have no tenderness. But there was something of the woman moulded into the great, stalwart frame of Hollingsworth; nor was he ashamed of it, as men often are of what is best in them, nor seemed ever to know that there was such a soft place in his heart. I knew it well, however, at that time, although afterwards it came nigh to be forgotten. Methought there could not be two such men alive as Hollingsworth. There never was any blaze of a fireside that warmed and cheered me, in the down-sinkings and shiverings of my spirit, so effectually as did the light out of those eyes, which lay so deep and dark under his shaggy brows.

Happy the man that has such a friend beside him when he comes to die! and unless a friend like Hollingsworth be at hand,—as most probably there will not,—he had better make up his mind to die alone. How many men, I wonder, does one meet with in a lifetime, whom he would choose for his deathbed companions! At the crisis of my fever I besought Hollingsworth to let nobody else enter the room, but continually to make me sensible of his own presence by a grasp of the hand, a word, a prayer, if he thought good to utter it; and that then he should be the witness how courageously I would encounter the worst. It still impresses me as almost a matter of regret that I did not die then, when I had tolerably made up my mind to it; for Hollingsworth would have gone with me to the hither verge of life, and have sent his friendly and hopeful accents far over on the other side, while I should be treading the unknown path. Now, were I to send for him, he would hardly come to my bedside, nor should I depart the easier for his presence.

"You are not going to die, this time," said he, gravely smiling. "You know nothing about sickness, and think your case a great deal more desperate than it is."

"Death should take me while I am in the mood," replied I, with a little of my customary levity.

"Have you nothing to do in life," asked Hollingsworth, "that you fancy yourself so ready to leave it?"

"Nothing," answered I; "nothing that I know of, unless to make pretty verses, and play a part, with Zenobia and the rest of the amateurs, in our pastoral. It seems but an unsubstantial sort of business, as viewed through a mist of fever. But, dear Hollingsworth, your own vocation is evidently to be a priest, and to spend your days and nights in helping your fellow creatures to draw peaceful dying breaths."

"And by which of my qualities," inquired he, "can you suppose me fitted for this awful ministry?"

"By your tenderness," I said. "It seems to me the reflection of God's own love."

"And you call me tender!" repeated Hollingsworth thoughtfully. "I should rather say that the most marked trait in my character is an inflexible severity of purpose. Mortal man has no right to be so inflexible as it is my nature and necessity to be."

"I do not believe it," I replied.

But, in due time, I remembered what he said.

Probably, as Hollingsworth suggested, my disorder was never so serious as, in my ignorance of such matters, I was inclined to consider it. After so much tragical preparation, it was positively rather mortifying to find myself on the mending hand.

All the other members of the Community showed me kindness, according to the full measure of their capacity. Zenobia brought me my gruel every day, made by her own hands (not very skilfully, if the truth must be told), and, whenever I seemed inclined to converse, would sit by my bedside, and talk with so much vivacity as to add several gratuitous throbs to my pulse. Her poor little stories and tracts never half did justice to her intellect. It was only the lack of a fitter avenue that drove her to seek development in literature. She was made (among a thousand other things that she might have been) for a stump oratress. I recognized no severe culture in Zenobia; her mind was full of weeds. It startled me sometimes, in my state of moral as well as bodily faint-heartedness, to observe the hardihood of her philosophy. She made no scruple of oversetting all human institutions, and scattering them as with a breeze from her fan. A female reformer, in her attacks upon society, has an instinctive sense of where the life lies, and is inclined to aim directly at that spot. Especially the relation between the sexes is naturally among the earliest to attract her notice.

Zenobia was truly a magnificent woman. The homely simplicity of her dress could not conceal, nor scarcely diminish, the queenliness of her presence. The image of her form and face should have been multiplied all over the earth. It was wronging the rest of mankind to retain her as the spectacle of only a few. The stage would have been her proper sphere. She should have made it a point of duty, moreover, to sit endlessly to painters and sculptors, and preferably to the latter; because the cold decorum of the marble would consist with the utmost scantiness of drapery, so that the eye might chastely be gladdened with her material perfection in its entireness. I know not well how to express that the native glow of coloring in her cheeks, and even the flesh-warmth over her round arms, and what was visible of her full bust,—in a word, her womanliness incarnated,—compelled me sometimes to close my eyes, as if it were not quite the privilege of modesty to gaze at her. Illness and exhaustion, no doubt, had made me morbidly sensitive.

I noticed—and wondered how Zenobia contrived it—that she had always a new flower in her hair. And still it was a hot-house flower,—an outlandish flower,—a flower of the tropics, such as appeared to have sprung passionately out of a soil the very weeds of which would be fervid and spicy. Unlike as was the flower of each successive day to the preceding one, it yet so assimilated its richness to the rich beauty of the woman, that I thought it the only flower fit to be worn; so fit, indeed, that Nature had evidently created this floral gem, in a happy exuberance, for the one purpose of worthily adorning Zenobia's head. It might be that my feverish fantasies clustered themselves about this peculiarity, and caused it to look more gorgeous and wonderful than if beheld with temperate eyes. In the height of my illness, as I well recollect, I went so far as to pronounce it preternatural.

"Zenobia is an enchantress!" whispered I once to Hollingsworth. "She is a sister of the Veiled Lady. That flower in her hair is a talisman. If you were to snatch it away, she would vanish, or be transformed into something else."

"What does he say?" asked Zenobia.

"Nothing that has an atom of sense in it," answered Hollingsworth. "He is a little beside himself, I believe, and talks about your being a witch, and of some magical property in the flower that you wear in your hair."

"It is an idea worthy of a feverish poet," said she, laughing rather compassionately, and taking out the flower. "I scorn to owe anything to magic. Here, Mr. Hollingsworth, you may keep the spell while it has any virtue in it; but I cannot promise you not to appear with a new one to-morrow. It is the one relic of my more brilliant, my happier days!"

The most curious part of the matter was that, long after my slight delirium had passed away,—as long, indeed, as I continued to know this remarkable woman,—her daily flower affected my imagination, though more slightly, yet in very much the same way. The reason must have been that, whether intentionally on her part or not, this favorite ornament was actually a subtile expression of Zenobia's character.

One subject, about which—very impertinently, moreover—I perplexed myself with a great many conjectures, was, whether Zenobia had ever been married. The idea, it must be understood, was unauthorized by any circumstance or suggestion that had made its way to my ears. So young as I beheld her, and the freshest and rosiest woman of a thousand, there was certainly no need of imputing to her a destiny already accomplished; the probability was far greater that her coming years had all life's richest gifts to bring. If the great event of a woman's existence had been consummated, the world knew nothing of it, although the world seemed to know Zenobia well. It was a ridiculous piece of romance, undoubtedly, to imagine that this beautiful personage, wealthy as she was, and holding a position that might fairly enough be called distinguished, could have given herself away so privately, but that some whisper and suspicion, and by degrees a full understanding of the fact, would eventually be blown abroad. But then, as I failed not to consider, her original home was at a distance of many hundred miles. Rumors might fill the social atmosphere, or might once have filled it, there, which would travel but slowly, against the wind, towards our Northeastern metropolis, and perhaps melt into thin air before reaching it.

There was not—and I distinctly repeat it—the slightest foundation in my knowledge for any surmise of the kind. But there is a species of intuition,—either a spiritual lie or the subtile recognition of a fact,—which comes to us in a reduced state of the corporeal system. The soul gets the better of the body, after wasting illness, or when a vegetable diet may have mingled too much ether in the blood. Vapors then rise up to the brain, and take shapes that often image falsehood, but sometimes truth. The spheres of our companions have, at such periods, a vastly greater influence upon our own than when robust health gives us a repellent and self-defensive energy. Zenobia's sphere, I imagine, impressed itself powerfully on mine, and transformed me, during this period of my weakness, into something like a mesmerical clairvoyant.

Then, also, as anybody could observe, the freedom of her deportment (though, to some tastes, it might commend itself as the utmost perfection of manner in a youthful widow or a blooming matron) was not exactly maiden-like. What girl had ever laughed as Zenobia did? What girl had ever spoken in her mellow tones? Her unconstrained and inevitable manifestation, I said often to myself, was that of a woman to whom wedlock had thrown wide the gates of mystery. Yet sometimes I strove to be ashamed of these conjectures. I acknowledged it as a masculine grossness—a sin of wicked interpretation, of which man is often guilty towards the other sex—thus to mistake the sweet, liberal, but womanly frankness of a noble and generous disposition. Still, it was of no avail to reason with myself nor to upbraid myself. Pertinaciously the thought, "Zenobia is a wife; Zenobia has lived and loved! There is no folded petal, no latent dewdrop, in this perfectly developed rose!"—irresistibly that thought drove out all other conclusions, as often as my mind reverted to the subject.

Zenobia was conscious of my observation, though not, I presume, of the point to which it led me.

"Mr. Coverdale," said she one day, as she saw me watching her, while she arranged my gruel on the table, "I have been exposed to a great deal of eye-shot in the few years of my mixing in the world, but never, I think, to precisely such glances as you are in the habit of favoring me with. I seem to interest you very much; and yet—or else a woman's instinct is for once deceived—I cannot reckon you as an admirer. What are you seeking to discover in me?"

"The mystery of your life," answered I, surprised into the truth by the unexpectedness of her attack. "And you will never tell me."

She bent her head towards me, and let me look into her eyes, as if challenging me to drop a plummet-line down into the depths of her consciousness.

"I see nothing now," said I, closing my own eyes, "unless it be the face of a sprite laughing at me from the bottom of a deep well."

A bachelor always feels himself defrauded, when he knows or suspects that any woman of his acquaintance has given herself away. Otherwise, the matter could have been no concern of mine. It was purely speculative, for I should not, under any circumstances, have fallen in love with Zenobia. The riddle made me so nervous, however, in my sensitive condition of mind and body, that I most ungratefully began to wish that she would let me alone. Then, too, her gruel was very wretched stuff, with almost invariably the smell of pine smoke upon it, like the evil taste that is said to mix itself up with a witch's best concocted dainties. Why could not she have allowed one of the other women to take the gruel in charge? Whatever else might be her gifts, Nature certainly never intended Zenobia for a cook. Or, if so, she should have meddled only with the richest and spiciest dishes, and such as are to be tasted at banquets, between draughts of intoxicating wine.

VII. THE CONVALESCENT

As soon as my incommodities allowed me to think of past occurrences, I failed not to inquire what had become of the odd little guest whom Hollingsworth had been the medium of introducing among us. It now appeared that poor Priscilla had not so literally fallen out of the clouds, as we were at first inclined to suppose. A letter, which should have introduced her, had since been received from one of the city missionaries, containing a certificate of character and an allusion to circumstances which, in the writer's judgment, made it especially desirable that she should find shelter in our Community. There was a hint, not very intelligible, implying either that Priscilla had recently escaped from some particular peril or irksomeness of position, or else that she was still liable to this danger or difficulty, whatever it might be. We should ill have deserved the reputation of a benevolent fraternity, had we hesitated to entertain a petitioner in such need, and so strongly recommended to our kindness; not to mention, moreover, that the strange maiden had set herself diligently to work, and was doing good service with her needle. But a slight mist of uncertainty still floated about Priscilla, and kept her, as yet, from taking a very decided place among creatures of flesh and blood.

The mysterious attraction, which, from her first entrance on our scene, she evinced for Zenobia, had lost nothing of its force. I often heard her footsteps, soft and low, accompanying the light but decided tread of the latter up the staircase, stealing along the passage-way by her new friend's side, and pausing while Zenobia entered my chamber. Occasionally Zenobia would be a little annoyed by Priscilla's too close attendance. In an authoritative and not very kindly tone, she would advise her to breathe the pleasant air in a walk, or to go with her work into the barn, holding out half a promise to come and sit on the hay with her, when at leisure. Evidently, Priscilla found but scanty requital for her love. Hollingsworth was likewise a great favorite with her. For several minutes together sometimes, while my auditory nerves retained the susceptibility of delicate health, I used to hear a low, pleasant murmur ascending from the room below; and at last ascertained it to be Priscilla's voice, babbling like a little brook to Hollingsworth. She talked more largely and freely with him than with Zenobia, towards whom, indeed, her feelings seemed not so much to be confidence as involuntary affection. I should have thought all the better of my own qualities had Priscilla marked me out for the third place in her regards. But, though she appeared to like me tolerably well, I could never flatter myself with being distinguished by her as Hollingsworth and Zenobia were.

Onę forenoon, during my convalescence, there came a gentle tap at my chamber door. I immediately said, "Come in, Priscilla!" with an acute sense of the applicant's identity. Nor was I deceived. It was really Priscilla,—a pale, large-eyed little woman (for she had gone far enough into her teens to be, at least, on the outer limit of girlhood), but much less wan than at my previous view of her, and far better conditioned both as to health and spirits. As I first saw her, she had reminded me of plants that one sometimes observes doing their best to vegetate among the bricks of an enclosed court, where there is scanty soil and never any sunshine. At present, though with no approach to bloom, there were indications that the girl had human blood in her veins.

Priscilla came softly to my bedside, and held out an article of snow-white linen, very carefully and smoothly ironed. She did not seem bashful, nor anywise embarrassed. My weakly condition, I suppose, supplied a medium in which she could approach me.

"Do not you need this?" asked she. "I have made it for you." It was a nightcap!

"My dear Priscilla," said I, smiling, "I never had on a nightcap in my life! But perhaps it will be better for me to wear one, now that I am a miserable invalid. How admirably you have done it! No, no; I never can think of wearing such an exquisitely wrought nightcap as this, unless it be in the daytime, when I sit up to receive company."

"It is for use, not beauty," answered Priscilla. "I could have embroidered it and made it much prettier, if I pleased."

While holding up the nightcap and admiring the fine needlework, I perceived that Priscilla had a sealed letter which she was waiting for me to take. It had arrived from the village post-office that morning. As I did not immediately offer to receive the letter, she drew it back, and held it against her bosom, with both hands clasped over it, in a way that had probably grown habitual to her. Now, on turning my eyes from the nightcap to Priscilla, it forcibly struck me that her air, though not her figure, and the expression of her face, but not its features, had a resemblance to what I had often seen in a friend of mine, one of the most gifted women of the age. I cannot describe it. The points easiest to convey to the reader were a certain curve of the shoulders and a partial closing of the eyes, which seemed to look more penetratingly into my own eyes, through the narrowed apertures, than if they had been open at full width. It was a singular anomaly of likeness coexisting with perfect dissimilitude.

"Will you give me the letter, Priscilla?" said I.

She started, put the letter into my hand, and quite lost the look that had drawn my notice.

"Priscilla," I inquired, "did you ever see Miss Margaret Fuller?"

"No," she answered.

"Because," said I, "you reminded me of her just now,—and it happens, strangely enough, that this very letter is from her."

Priscilla, for whatever reason, looked very much discomposed.

"I wish people would not fancy such odd things in me!" she said rather petulantly. "How could I possibly make myself resemble this lady merely by holding her letter in my hand?"

"Certainly, Priscilla, it would puzzle me to explain it," I replied; "nor do I suppose that the letter had anything to do with it. It was just a coincidence, nothing more."

She hastened out of the room, and this was the last that I saw of Priscilla until I ceased to be an invalid.

Being much alone during my recovery, I read interminably in Mr. Emerson's Essays, "The Dial," Carlyle's works, George Sand's romances (lent me by Zenobia), and other books which one or another of the brethren or sisterhood had brought with them. Agreeing in little else, most of these utterances were like the cry of some solitary sentinel, whose station was on the outposts of the advance guard of human progression; or sometimes the voice came sadly from among the shattered ruins of the past, but yet had a hopeful echo in the future. They were well adapted (better, at least, than any other intellectual products, the volatile essence of which had heretofore tinctured a printed page) to pilgrims like ourselves, whose present bivouac was considerably further into the waste of chaos than any mortal army of crusaders had ever marched before. Fourier's works, also, in a series of horribly tedious volumes, attracted a good deal of my attention, from the analogy which I could not but recognize between his system and our own. There was far less resemblance, it is true, than the world chose to imagine, inasmuch as the two theories differed, as widely as the zenith from the nadir, in their main principles.

I talked about Fourier to Hollingsworth, and translated, for his benefit, some of the passages that chiefly impressed me.

"When, as a consequence of human improvement," said I, "the globe shall arrive at its final perfection, the great ocean is to be converted into a particular kind of lemonade, such as was fashionable at Paris in Fourier's time. He calls it limonade a cedre. It is positively a fact! Just imagine the city docks filled, every day, with a flood tide of this delectable beverage!"

"Why did not the Frenchman make punch of it at once?" asked Hollingsworth. "The jack-tars would be delighted to go down in ships and do business in such an element."

I further proceeded to explain, as well as I modestly could, several points of Fourier's system, illustrating them with here and there a page or two, and asking Hollingsworth's opinion as to the expediency of introducing these beautiful peculiarities into our own practice.

"Let me hear no more of it!" cried he, in utter disgust. "I never will forgive this fellow! He has committed the unpardonable sin; for what more monstrous iniquity could the Devil himself contrive than to choose the selfish principle,—the principle of all human wrong, the very blackness of man's heart, the portion of ourselves which we shudder at, and which it is the whole aim of spiritual discipline to eradicate,—to choose it as the master workman of his system? To seize upon and foster whatever vile, petty, sordid, filthy, bestial, and abominable corruptions have cankered into our nature, to be the efficient instruments of his infernal regeneration! And his consummated Paradise, as he pictures it, would be worthy of the agency which he counts upon for establishing it. The nauseous villain!"

"Nevertheless," remarked I, "in consideration of the promised delights of his system,—so very proper, as they certainly are, to be appreciated by Fourier's countrymen,—I cannot but wonder that universal France did not adopt his theory at a moment's warning. But is there not something very characteristic of his nation in Fourier's manner of putting forth his views? He makes no claim to inspiration. He has not persuaded himself—as Swedenborg did, and as any other than a Frenchman would, with a mission of like importance to communicate—that he speaks with authority from above. He promulgates his system, so far as I can perceive, entirely on his own responsibility. He has searched out and discovered the whole counsel of the Almighty in respect to mankind, past, present, and for exactly seventy thousand years to come, by the mere force and cunning of his individual intellect!"

"Take the book out of my sight," said Hollingsworth with great virulence of expression, "or, I tell you fairly, I shall fling it in the fire! And as for Fourier, let him make a Paradise, if he can, of Gehenna, where, as I conscientiously believe, he is floundering at this moment!"

"And bellowing, I suppose," said I,—not that I felt any ill-will towards Fourier, but merely wanted to give the finishing touch to Hollingsworth's image, "bellowing for the least drop of his beloved limonade a cedre!"

There is but little profit to be expected in attempting to argue with a man who allows himself to declaim in this manner; so I dropt the subject, and never took it up again.

But had the system at which he was so enraged combined almost any amount of human wisdom, spiritual insight, and imaginative beauty, I question whether Hollingsworth's mind was in a fit condition to receive it. I began to discern that he had come among us actuated by no real sympathy with our feelings and our hopes, but chiefly because we were estranging ourselves from the world, with which his lonely and exclusive object in life had already put him at odds. Hollingsworth must have been originally endowed with a great spirit of benevolence, deep enough and warm enough to be the source of as much disinterested good as Providence often allows a human being the privilege of conferring upon his fellows. This native instinct yet lived within him. I myself had profited by it, in my necessity. It was seen, too, in his treatment of Priscilla. Such casual circumstances as were here involved would quicken his divine power of sympathy, and make him seem, while their influence lasted, the tenderest man and the truest friend on earth. But by and by you missed the tenderness of yesterday, and grew drearily conscious that Hollingsworth had a closer friend than ever you could be; and this friend was the cold, spectral monster which he had himself conjured up, and on which he was wasting all the warmth of his heart, and of which, at last,—as these men of a mighty purpose so invariably do,—he had grown to be the bond-slave. It was his philanthropic theory.

This was a result exceedingly sad to contemplate, considering that it had been mainly brought about by the very ardor and exuberance of his philanthropy. Sad, indeed, but by no means unusual: he had taught his benevolence to pour its warm tide exclusively through one channel; so that there was nothing to spare for other great manifestations of love to man, nor scarcely for the nutriment of individual attachments, unless they could minister in some way to the terrible egotism which he mistook for an angel of God. Had Hollingsworth's education been more enlarged, he might not so inevitably have stumbled into this pitfall. But this identical pursuit had educated him. He knew absolutely nothing, except in a single direction, where he had thought so energetically, and felt to such a depth, that no doubt the entire reason and justice of the universe appeared to be concentrated thitherward.

It is my private opinion that, at this period of his life, Hollingsworth was fast going mad; and, as with other crazy people (among whom I include humorists of every degree), it required all the constancy of friendship to restrain his associates from pronouncing him an intolerable bore. Such prolonged fiddling upon one string—such multiform presentation of one idea! His specific object (of which he made the public more than sufficiently aware, through the medium of lectures and pamphlets) was to obtain funds for the construction of an edifice, with a sort of collegiate endowment. On this foundation he purposed to devote himself and a few disciples to the reform and mental culture of our criminal brethren. His visionary edifice was Hollingsworth's one castle in the air; it was the material type in which his philanthropic dream strove to embody itself; and he made the scheme more definite, and caught hold of it the more strongly, and kept his clutch the more pertinaciously, by rendering it visible to the bodily eye. I have seen him, a hundred times, with a pencil and sheet of paper, sketching the facade, the side-view, or the rear of the structure, or planning the internal arrangements, as lovingly as another man might plan those of the projected home where he meant to be happy with his wife and children. I have known him to begin a model of the building with little stones, gathered at the brookside, whither we had gone to cool ourselves in the sultry noon of haying-time. Unlike all other ghosts, his spirit haunted an edifice, which, instead of being time-worn, and full of storied love, and joy, and sorrow, had never yet come into existence.

"Dear friend," said I once to Hollingsworth, before leaving my sick-chamber, "I heartily wish that I could make your schemes my schemes, because it would be so great a happiness to find myself treading the same path with you. But I am afraid there is not stuff in me stern enough for a philanthropist,—or not in this peculiar direction,—or, at all events, not solely in this. Can you bear with me, if such should prove to be the case?"

"I will at least wait awhile," answered Hollingsworth, gazing at me sternly and gloomily. "But how can you be my life-long friend, except you strive with me towards the great object of my life?"

Heaven forgive me! A horrible suspicion crept into my heart, and stung the very core of it as with the fangs of an adder. I wondered whether it were possible that Hollingsworth could have watched by my bedside, with all that devoted care, only for the ulterior purpose of making me a proselyte to his views!

VIII. A MODERN ARCADIA

May-day—I forget whether by Zenobia's sole decree, or by the unanimous vote of our community—had been declared a movable festival. It was deferred until the sun should have had a reasonable time to clear away the snowdrifts along the lee of the stone walls, and bring out a few of the readiest wild flowers. On the forenoon of the substituted day, after admitting some of the balmy air into my chamber, I decided that it was nonsense and effeminacy to keep myself a prisoner any longer. So I descended to the sitting-room, and finding nobody there, proceeded to the barn, whence I had already heard Zenobia's voice, and along with it a girlish laugh which was not so certainly recognizable. Arriving at the spot, it a little surprised me to discover that these merry outbreaks came from Priscilla.

The two had been a-maying together. They had found anemones in abundance, houstonias by the handful, some columbines, a few long-stalked violets, and a quantity of white everlasting flowers, and had filled up their basket with the delicate spray of shrubs and trees. None were prettier than the maple twigs, the leaf of which looks like a scarlet bud in May, and like a plate of vegetable gold in October. Zenobia, who showed no conscience in such matters, had also rifled a cherry-tree of one of its blossomed boughs, and, with all this variety of sylvan ornament, had been decking out Priscilla. Being done with a good deal of taste, it made her look more charming than I should have thought possible, with my recollection of the wan, frost-nipt girl, as heretofore described. Nevertheless, among those fragrant blossoms, and conspicuously, too, had been stuck a weed of evil odor and ugly aspect, which, as soon as I detected it, destroyed the effect of all the rest. There was a gleam of latent mischief—not to call it deviltry—in Zenobia's eye, which seemed to indicate a slightly malicious purpose in the arrangement.

As for herself, she scorned the rural buds and leaflets, and wore nothing but her invariable flower of the tropics.

"What do you think of Priscilla now, Mr. Coverdale?" asked she, surveying her as a child does its doll. "Is not she worth a verse or two?"

"There is only one thing amiss," answered I. Zenobia laughed, and flung the malignant weed away.

"Yes; she deserves some verses now," said I, "and from a better poet than myself. She is the very picture of the New England spring; subdued in tint and rather cool, but with a capacity of sunshine, and bringing us a few Alpine blossoms, as earnest of something richer, though hardly more beautiful, hereafter. The best type of her is one of those anemones."

"What I find most singular in Priscilla, as her health improves," observed Zenobia, "is her wildness. Such a quiet little body as she seemed, one would not have expected that. Why, as we strolled the woods together, I could hardly keep her from scrambling up the trees, like a squirrel. She has never before known what it is to live in the free air, and so it intoxicates her as if she were sipping wine. And she thinks it such a paradise here, and all of us, particularly Mr. Hollingsworth and myself, such angels! It is quite ridiculous, and provokes one's malice almost, to see a creature so happy, especially a feminine creature."

"They are always happier than male creatures," said I.

"You must correct that opinion, Mr. Coverdale," replied Zenobia contemptuously, "or I shall think you lack the poetic insight. Did you ever see a happy woman in your life? Of course, I do not mean a girl, like Priscilla and a thousand others,—for they are all alike, while on the sunny side of experience,—but a grown woman. How can she be happy, after discovering that fate has assigned her but one single event, which she must contrive to make the substance of her whole life? A man has his choice of innumerable events."

"A woman, I suppose," answered I, "by constant repetition of her one event, may compensate for the lack of variety."

"Indeed!" said Zenobia.

While we were talking, Priscilla caught sight of Hollingsworth at a distance, in a blue frock, and with a hoe over his shoulder, returning from the field. She immediately set out to meet him, running and skipping, with spirits as light as the breeze of the May morning, but with limbs too little exercised to be quite responsive; she clapped her hands, too, with great exuberance of gesture, as is the custom of young girls when their electricity overcharges them. But, all at once, midway to Hollingsworth, she paused, looked round about her, towards the river, the road, the woods, and back towards us, appearing to listen, as if she heard some one calling her name, and knew not precisely in what direction.

"Have you bewitched her?" I exclaimed.

"It is no sorcery of mine," said Zenobia; "but I have seen the girl do that identical thing once or twice before. Can you imagine what is the matter with her?"

"No; unless," said I, "she has the gift of hearing those 'airy tongues that syllable men's names,' which Milton tells about."

From whatever cause, Priscilla's animation seemed entirely to have deserted her. She seated herself on a rock, and remained there until Hollingsworth came up; and when he took her hand and led her back to us, she rather resembled my original image of the wan and spiritless Priscilla than the flowery May-queen of a few moments ago. These sudden transformations, only to be accounted for by an extreme nervous susceptibility, always continued to characterize the girl, though with diminished frequency as her health progressively grew more robust.

I was now on my legs again. My fit of illness had been an avenue between two existences; the low-arched and darksome doorway, through which I crept out of a life of old conventionalisms, on my hands and knees, as it were, and gained admittance into the freer region that lay beyond. In this respect, it was like death. And, as with death, too, it was good to have gone through it. No otherwise could I have rid myself of a thousand follies, fripperies, prejudices, habits, and other such worldly dust as inevitably settles upon the crowd along the broad highway, giving them all one sordid aspect before noon-time, however freshly they may have begun their pilgrimage in the dewy morning. The very substance upon my bones had not been fit to live with in any better, truer, or more energetic mode than that to which I was accustomed. So it was taken off me and flung aside, like any other worn-out or unseasonable garment; and, after shivering a little while in my skeleton, I began to be clothed anew, and much more satisfactorily than in my previous suit. In literal and physical truth, I was quite another man. I had a lively sense of the exultation with which the spirit will enter on the next stage of its eternal progress after leaving the heavy burden of its mortality in an early grave, with as little concern for what may become of it as now affected me for the flesh which I had lost.

Emerging into the genial sunshine, I half fancied that the labors of the brotherhood had already realized some of Fourier's predictions. Their enlightened culture of the soil, and the virtues with which they sanctified their life, had begun to produce an effect upon the material world and its climate. In my new enthusiasm, man looked strong and stately,—and woman, oh, how beautiful!—and the earth a green garden, blossoming with many-colored delights. Thus Nature, whose laws I had broken in various artificial ways, comported herself towards me as a strict but loving mother, who uses the rod upon her little boy for his naughtiness, and then gives him a smile, a kiss, and some pretty playthings to console the urchin for her severity.

In the interval of my seclusion, there had been a number of recruits to our little army of saints and martyrs. They were mostly individuals who had gone through such an experience as to disgust them with ordinary pursuits, but who were not yet so old, nor had suffered so deeply, as to lose their faith in the better time to come. On comparing their minds one with another they often discovered that this idea of a Community had been growing up, in silent and unknown sympathy, for years. Thoughtful, strongly lined faces were among them; sombre brows, but eyes that did not require spectacles, unless prematurely dimmed by the student's lamplight, and hair that seldom showed a thread of silver. Age, wedded to the past, incrusted over with a stony layer of habits, and retaining nothing fluid in its possibilities, would have been absurdly out of place in an enterprise like this. Youth, too, in its early dawn, was hardly more adapted to our purpose; for it would behold the morning radiance of its own spirit beaming over the very same spots of withered grass and barren sand whence most of us had seen it vanish. We had very young people with us, it is true,—downy lads, rosy girls in their first teens, and children of all heights above one's knee; but these had chiefly been sent hither for education, which it was one of the objects and methods of our institution to supply. Then we had boarders, from town and elsewhere, who lived with us in a familiar way, sympathized more or less in our theories, and sometimes shared in our labors.

On the whole, it was a society such as has seldom met together; nor, perhaps, could it reasonably be expected to hold together long. Persons of marked individuality—crooked sticks, as some of us might be called—are not exactly the easiest to bind up into a fagot. But, so long as our union should subsist, a man of intellect and feeling, with a free nature in him, might have sought far and near without finding so many points of attraction as would allure him hitherward. We were of all creeds and opinions, and generally tolerant of all, on every imaginable subject. Our bond, it seems to me, was not affirmative, but negative. We had individually found one thing or another to quarrel with in our past life, and were pretty well agreed as to the inexpediency of lumbering along with the old system any further. As to what should be substituted, there was much less unanimity. We did not greatly care—at least, I never did—for the written constitution under which our millennium had commenced. My hope was, that, between theory and practice, a true and available mode of life might be struck out; and that, even should we ultimately fail, the months or years spent in the trial would not have been wasted, either as regarded passing enjoyment, or the experience which makes men wise.

Arcadians though we were, our costume bore no resemblance to the beribboned doublets, silk breeches and stockings, and slippers fastened with artificial roses, that distinguish the pastoral people of poetry and the stage. In outward show, I humbly conceive, we looked rather like a gang of beggars, or banditti, than either a company of honest laboring-men, or a conclave of philosophers. Whatever might be our points of difference, we all of us seemed to have come to Blithedale with the one thrifty and laudable idea of wearing out our old clothes. Such garments as had an airing, whenever we strode afield! Coats with high collars and with no collars, broad-skirted or swallow-tailed, and with the waist at every point between the hip and arm-pit; pantaloons of a dozen successive epochs, and greatly defaced at the knees by the humiliations of the wearer before his lady-love,—in short, we were a living epitome of defunct fashions, and the very raggedest presentment of men who had seen better days. It was gentility in tatters. Often retaining a scholarlike or clerical air, you might have taken us for the denizens of Grub Street, intent on getting a comfortable livelihood by agricultural labor; or Coleridge's projected Pantisocracy in full experiment; or Candide and his motley associates at work in their cabbage garden; or anything else that was miserably out at elbows, and most clumsily patched in the rear. We might have been sworn comrades to Falstaff's ragged regiment. Little skill as we boasted in other points of husbandry, every mother's son of us would have served admirably to stick up for a scarecrow. And the worst of the matter was, that the first energetic movement essential to one downright stroke of real labor was sure to put a finish to these poor habiliments. So we gradually flung them all aside, and took to honest homespun and linsey-woolsey, as preferable, on the whole, to the plan recommended, I think, by Virgil,—"Ara nudus; sere nudus, "—which as

Silas Foster remarked, when I translated the maxim, would be apt to astonish the women-folks.

After a reasonable training, the yeoman life throve well with us. Our faces took the sunburn kindly; our chests gained in compass, and our shoulders in breadth and squareness; our great brown fists looked as if they had never been capable of kid gloves. The plough, the hoe, the scythe, and the hay-fork grew familiar to our grasp. The oxen responded to our voices. We could do almost as fair a day's work as Silas Foster himself, sleep dreamlessly after it, and awake at daybreak with only a little stiffness of the joints, which was usually quite gone by breakfast-time.

To be sure, our next neighbors pretended to be incredulous as to our real proficiency in the business which we had taken in hand. They told slanderous fables about our inability to yoke our own oxen, or to drive them afield when yoked, or to release the poor brutes from their conjugal bond at nightfall. They had the face to say, too, that the cows laughed at our awkwardness at milking-time, and invariably kicked over the pails; partly in consequence of our putting the stool on the wrong side, and partly because, taking offence at the whisking of their tails, we were in the habit of holding these natural fly-flappers with one hand and milking with the other. They further averred that we hoed up whole acres of Indian corn and other crops, and drew the earth carefully about the weeds; and that we raised five hundred tufts of burdock, mistaking them for cabbages; and that by dint of unskilful planting few of our seeds ever came up at all, or, if they did come up, it was stern-foremost; and that we spent the better part of the month of June in reversing a field of beans, which had thrust themselves out of the ground in this unseemly way. They quoted it as nothing more than an ordinary occurrence for one or other of us to crop off two or three fingers, of a morning, by our clumsy use of the hay-cutter. Finally, and as an ultimate catastrophe, these mendacious rogues circulated a report that we communitarians were exterminated, to the last man, by severing ourselves asunder with the sweep of our own scythes! and that the world had lost nothing by this little accident.

But this was pure envy and malice on the part of the neighboring farmers. The peril of our new way of life was not lest we should fail in becoming practical agriculturists, but that we should probably cease to be anything else. While our enterprise lay all in theory, we had pleased ourselves with delectable visions of the spiritualization of labor. It was to be our form of prayer and ceremonial of worship. Each stroke of the hoe was to uncover some aromatic root of wisdom, heretofore hidden from the sun. Pausing in the field, to let the wind exhale the moisture from our foreheads, we were to look upward, and catch glimpses into the far-off soul of truth. In this point of view, matters did not turn out quite so well as we anticipated. It is very true that, sometimes, gazing casually around me, out of the midst of my toil, I used to discern a richer picturesqueness in the visible scene of earth and sky. There was, at such moments, a novelty, an unwonted aspect, on the face of Nature, as if she had been taken by surprise and seen at unawares, with no opportunity to put off her real look, and assume the mask with which she mysteriously hides herself from mortals. But this was all. The clods of earth, which we so constantly belabored and turned over and over, were never etherealized into thought. Our thoughts, on the contrary, were fast becoming cloddish. Our labor symbolized nothing, and left us mentally sluggish in the dusk of the evening. Intellectual activity is incompatible with any large amount of bodily exercise. The yeoman and the scholar—the yeoman and the man of finest moral culture, though not the man of sturdiest sense and integrity—are two distinct individuals, and can never be melted or welded into one substance.

Zenobia soon saw this truth, and gibed me about it, one evening, as Hollingsworth and I lay on the grass, after a hard day's work.

"I am afraid you did not make a song today, while loading the hay-cart," said she, "as Burns did, when he was reaping barley."

"Burns never made a song in haying-time," I answered very positively. "He was no poet while a farmer, and no farmer while a poet."

"And on the whole, which of the two characters do you like best?" asked Zenobia. "For I have an idea that you cannot combine them any better than Burns did. Ah, I see, in my mind's eye, what sort of an individual you are to be, two or three years hence. Grim Silas Foster is your prototype, with his palm of sole-leather, and his joints of rusty iron (which all through summer keep the stiffness of what he calls his winter's rheumatize), and his brain of—I don't know what his brain is made of, unless it be a Savoy cabbage; but yours may be cauliflower, as a rather more delicate variety. Your physical man will be transmuted into salt beef and fried pork, at the rate, I should imagine, of a pound and a half a day; that being about the average which we find necessary in the kitchen. You will make your toilet for the day (still like this delightful Silas Foster) by rinsing your fingers and the front part of your face in a little tin pan of water at the doorstep, and teasing your hair with a wooden pocket-comb before a seven-by-nine-inch looking-glass. Your only pastime will be to smoke some very vile tobacco in the black stump of a pipe."

"Pray, spare me!" cried I. "But the pipe is not Silas's only mode of solacing himself with the weed."

"Your literature," continued Zenobia, apparently delighted with her description, "will be the 'Farmer's Almanac;' for I observe our friend Foster never gets so far as the newspaper. When you happen to sit down, at odd moments, you will fall asleep, and make nasal proclamation of the fact, as he does; and invariably you must be jogged out of a nap, after supper, by the future Mrs. Coverdale, and persuaded to go regularly to bed. And on Sundays, when you put on a blue coat with brass buttons, you will think of nothing else to do but to go and lounge over the stone walls and rail fences, and stare at the corn growing. And you will look with a knowing eye at oxen, and will have a tendency to clamber over into pig-sties, and feel of the hogs, and give a guess how much they will weigh after you shall have stuck and dressed them. Already I have noticed you begin to speak through your nose, and with a drawl. Pray, if you really did make any poetry today, let us hear it in that kind of utterance!"

"Coverdale has given up making verses now," said Hollingsworth, who never had the slightest appreciation of my poetry. "Just think of him penning a sonnet with a fist like that! There is at least this good in a life of toil, that it takes the nonsense and fancy-work out of a man, and leaves nothing but what truly belongs to him. If a farmer can make poetry at the plough-tail, it must be because his nature insists on it; and if that be the case, let him make it, in Heaven's name!"

"And how is it with you?" asked Zenobia, in a different voice; for she never laughed at Hollingsworth, as she often did at me. "You, I think, cannot have ceased to live a life of thought and feeling."

"I have always been in earnest," answered Hollingsworth. "I have hammered thought out of iron, after heating the iron in my heart! It matters little what my outward toil may be. Were I a slave, at the bottom of a mine, I should keep the same purpose, the same faith in its ultimate accomplishment, that I do now. Miles Coverdale is not in earnest, either as a poet or a laborer."

"You give me hard measure, Hollingsworth," said I, a little hurt. "I have kept pace with you in the field; and my bones feel as if I had been in earnest, whatever may be the case with my brain!"

"I cannot conceive," observed Zenobia with great emphasis,—and, no doubt, she spoke fairly the feeling of the moment,—"I cannot conceive of being so continually as Mr. Coverdale is within the sphere of a strong and noble nature, without being strengthened and ennobled by its influence!"

This amiable remark of the fair Zenobia confirmed me in what I had already begun to suspect, that Hollingsworth, like many other illustrious prophets, reformers, and philanthropists, was likely to make at least two proselytes among the women to one among the men. Zenobia and Priscilla! These, I believe (unless my unworthy self might be reckoned for a third), were the only disciples of his mission; and I spent a great deal of time, uselessly, in trying to conjecture what Hollingsworth meant to do with them—and they with him!

IX. HOLLINGSWORTH, ZENOBIA, PRISCILLA

It is not, I apprehend, a healthy kind of mental occupation to devote ourselves too exclusively to the study of individual men and women. If the person under examination be one's self, the result is pretty certain to be diseased action of the heart, almost before we can snatch a second glance. Or if we take the freedom to put a friend under our microscope, we thereby insulate him from many of his true relations, magnify his peculiarities, inevitably tear him into parts, and of course patch him very clumsily together again. What wonder, then, should we be frightened by the aspect of a monster, which, after all,—though we can point to every feature of his deformity in the real personage,—may be said to have been created mainly by ourselves.

Thus, as my conscience has often whispered me, I did Hollingsworth a great wrong by prying into his character; and am perhaps doing him as great a one, at this moment, by putting faith in the discoveries which I seemed to make. But I could not help it. Had I loved him less, I might have used him better. He and Zenobia and Priscilla—both for their own sakes and as connected with him—were separated from the rest of the Community, to my imagination, and stood forth as the indices of a problem which it was my business to solve. Other associates had a portion of my time; other matters amused me; passing occurrences carried me along with them, while they lasted. But here was the vortex of my meditations, around which they revolved, and whitherward they too continually tended. In the midst of cheerful society, I had often a feeling of loneliness. For it was impossible not to be sensible that, while these three characters figured so largely on my private theatre, I—though probably reckoned as a friend by all—was at best but a secondary or tertiary personage with either of them.

I loved Hollingsworth, as has already been enough expressed. But it impressed me, more and more, that there was a stern and dreadful peculiarity in this man, such as could not prove otherwise than pernicious to the happiness of those who should be drawn into too intimate a connection with him. He was not altogether human. There was something else in Hollingsworth besides flesh and blood, and sympathies and affections and celestial spirit.

This is always true of those men who have surrendered themselves to an overruling purpose. It does not so much impel them from without, nor even operate as a motive power within, but grows incorporate with all that they think and feel, and finally converts them into little else save that one principle. When such begins to be the predicament, it is not cowardice, but wisdom, to avoid these victims. They have no heart, no sympathy, no reason, no conscience. They will keep no friend, unless he make himself the mirror of their purpose; they will smite and slay you, and trample your dead corpse under foot, all the more readily, if you take the first step with them, and cannot take the second, and the third, and every other step of their terribly strait path. They have an idol to which they consecrate themselves high-priest, and deem it holy work to offer sacrifices of whatever is most precious; and never once seem to suspect—so cunning has the Devil been with them—that this false deity, in whose iron features, immitigable to all the rest of mankind, they see only benignity and love, is but a spectrum of the very priest himself, projected upon the surrounding darkness. And the higher and purer the original object, and the more unselfishly it may have been taken up, the slighter is the probability that they can be led to recognize the process by which godlike benevolence has been debased into all-devouring egotism.

Of course I am perfectly aware that the above statement is exaggerated, in the attempt to make it adequate. Professed philanthropists have gone far; but no originally good man, I presume, ever went quite so far as this. Let the reader abate whatever he deems fit. The paragraph may remain, however, both for its truth and its exaggeration, as strongly expressive of the tendencies which were really operative in Hollingsworth, and as exemplifying the kind of error into which my mode of observation was calculated to lead me. The issue was, that in solitude I often shuddered at my friend. In my recollection of his dark and impressive countenance, the features grew more sternly prominent than the reality, duskier in their depth and shadow, and more lurid in their light; the frown, that had merely flitted across his brow, seemed to have contorted it with an adamantine wrinkle. On meeting him again, I was often filled with remorse, when his deep eyes beamed kindly upon me, as with the glow of a household fire that was burning in a cave. "He is a man after all," thought I; "his Maker's own truest image, a philanthropic man!—not that steel engine of the Devil's contrivance, a philanthropist!" But in my wood-walks, and in my silent chamber, the dark face frowned at me again.

When a young girl comes within the sphere of such a man, she is as perilously situated as the maiden whom, in the old classical myths, the people used to expose to a dragon. If I had any duty whatever, in reference to Hollingsworth, it was to endeavor to save Priscilla from that kind of personal worship which her sex is generally prone to lavish upon saints and heroes. It often requires but one smile out of the hero's eyes into the girl's or woman's heart, to transform this devotion, from a sentiment of the highest approval and confidence, into passionate love. Now, Hollingsworth smiled much upon Priscilla,—more than upon any other person. If she thought him beautiful, it was no wonder. I often thought him so, with the expression of tender human care and gentlest sympathy which she alone seemed to have power to call out upon his features. Zenobia, I suspect, would have given her eyes, bright as they were, for such a look; it was the least that our poor Priscilla could do, to give her heart for a great many of them. There was the more danger of this, inasmuch as the footing on which we all associated at Blithedale was widely different from that of conventional society. While inclining us to the soft affections of the golden age, it seemed to authorize any indi-individual, of either sex, to fall in love with any other, regardless of what would elsewhere be judged suitable and prudent. Accordingly the tender passion was very rife among us, in various degrees of mildness or virulence, but mostly passing away with the state of things that had given it origin. This was all well enough; but, for a girl like Priscilla and a woman like Zenobia to jostle one another in their love of a man like Hollingsworth, was likely to be no child's play.

Had I been as cold-hearted as I sometimes thought myself, nothing would have interested me more than to witness the play of passions that must thus have been evolved. But, in honest truth, I would really have gone far to save Priscilla, at least, from the catastrophe in which such a drama would be apt to terminate.

Priscilla had now grown to be a very pretty girl, and still kept budding and blossoming, and daily putting on some new charm, which you no sooner became sensible of than you thought it worth all that she had previously possessed. So unformed, vague, and without substance, as she had come to us, it seemed as if we could see Nature shaping out a woman before our very eyes, and yet had only a more reverential sense of the mystery of a woman's soul and frame. Yesterday, her cheek was pale, to-day, it had a bloom. Priscilla's smile, like a baby's first one, was a wondrous novelty. Her imperfections and shortcomings affected me with a kind of playful pathos, which was as absolutely bewitching a sensation as ever I experienced. After she had been a month or two at Blithedale, her animal spirits waxed high, and kept her pretty constantly in a state of bubble and ferment, impelling her to far more bodily activity than she had yet strength to endure. She was very fond of playing with the other girls out of doors. There is hardly another sight in the world so pretty as that of a company of young girls, almost women grown, at play, and so giving themselves up to their airy impulse that their tiptoes barely touch the ground.

Girls are incomparably wilder and more effervescent than boys, more untamable and regardless of rule and limit, with an ever-shifting variety, breaking continually into new modes of fun, yet with a harmonious propriety through all. Their steps, their voices, appear free as the wind, but keep consonance with a strain of music inaudible to us. Young men and boys, on the other hand, play, according to recognized law, old, traditionary games, permitting no caprioles of fancy, but with scope enough for the outbreak of savage instincts. For, young or old, in play or in earnest, man is prone to be a brute.

Especially is it delightful to see a vigorous young girl run a race, with her head thrown back, her limbs moving more friskily than they need, and an air between that of a bird and a young colt. But Priscilla's peculiar charm, in a foot-race, was the weakness and irregularity with which she ran. Growing up without exercise, except to her poor little fingers, she had never yet acquired the perfect use of her legs. Setting buoyantly forth, therefore, as if no rival less swift than Atalanta could compete with her, she ran falteringly, and often tumbled on the grass. Such an incident—though it seems too slight to think of—was a thing to laugh at, but which brought the water into one's eyes, and lingered in the memory after far greater joys and sorrows were wept out of it, as antiquated trash. Priscilla's life, as I beheld it, was full of trifles that affected me in just this way.

When she had come to be quite at home among us, I used to fancy that Priscilla played more pranks, and perpetrated more mischief, than any other girl in the Community. For example, I once heard Silas Foster, in a very gruff voice, threatening to rivet three horseshoes round Priscilla's neck and chain her to a post, because she, with some other young people, had clambered upon a load of hay, and caused it to slide off the cart. How she made her peace I never knew; but very soon afterwards I saw old Silas, with his brawny hands round Priscilla's waist, swinging her to and fro, and finally depositing her on one of the oxen, to take her first lessons in riding. She met with terrible mishaps in her efforts to milk a cow; she let the poultry into the garden; she generally spoilt whatever part of the dinner she took in charge; she broke crockery; she dropt our biggest water pitcher into the well; and—except with her needle, and those little wooden instruments for purse-making—was as unserviceable a member of society as any young lady in the land. There was no other sort of efficiency about her. Yet everybody was kind to Priscilla; everybody loved her and laughed at her to her face, and did not laugh behind her back; everybody would have given her half of his last crust, or the bigger share of his plum-cake. These were pretty certain indications that we were all conscious of a pleasant weakness in the girl, and considered her not quite able to look after her own interests or fight her battle with the world. And Hollingsworth—perhaps because he had been the means of introducing Priscilla to her new abode—appeared to recognize her as his own especial charge.

Her simple, careless, childish flow of spirits often made me sad. She seemed to me like a butterfly at play in a flickering bit of sunshine, and mistaking it for a broad and eternal summer. We sometimes hold mirth to a stricter accountability than sorrow; it must show good cause, or the echo of its laughter comes back drearily. Priscilla's gayety, moreover, was of a nature that showed me how delicate an instrument she was, and what fragile harp-strings were her nerves. As they made sweet music at the airiest touch, it would require but a stronger one to burst them all asunder. Absurd as it might be, I tried to reason with her, and persuade her not to be so joyous, thinking that, if she would draw less lavishly upon her fund of happiness, it would last the longer. I remember doing so, one summer evening, when we tired laborers sat looking on, like Goldsmith's old folks under the village thorn-tree, while the young people were at their sports.

"What is the use or sense of being so very gay?" I said to Priscilla, while she was taking breath, after a great frolic. "I love to see a sufficient cause for everything, and I can see none for this. Pray tell me, now, what kind of a world you imagine this to be, which you are so merry in."

"I never think about it at all," answered Priscilla, laughing. "But this I am sure of, that it is a world where everybody is kind to me, and where I love everybody. My heart keeps dancing within me, and all the foolish things which you see me do are only the motions of my heart. How can I be dismal, if my heart will not let me?"

"Have you nothing dismal to remember?" I suggested. "If not, then, indeed, you are very fortunate!"

"Ah!" said Priscilla slowly.

And then came that unintelligible gesture, when she seemed to be listening to a distant voice.

"For my part," I continued, beneficently seeking to overshadow her with my own sombre humor, "my past life has been a tiresome one enough; yet I would rather look backward ten times than forward once. For, little as we know of our life to come, we may be very sure, for one thing, that the good we aim at will not be attained. People never do get just the good they seek. If it come at all, it is something else, which they never dreamed of, and did not particularly want. Then, again, we may rest certain that our friends of to-day will not be our friends of a few years hence; but, if we keep one of them, it will be at the expense of the others; and most probably we shall keep none. To be sure, there are more to be had; but who cares about making a new set of friends, even should they be better than those around us?"

"Not I!" said Priscilla. "I will live and die with these!"

"Well; but let the future go," resumed I. "As for the present moment, if we could look into the hearts where we wish to be most valued, what should you expect to see? One's own likeness, in the innermost, holiest niche? Ah! I don't know! It may not be there at all. It may be a dusty image, thrust aside into a corner, and by and by to be flung out of doors, where any foot may trample upon it. If not to-day, then to-morrow! And so, Priscilla, I do not see much wisdom in being so very merry in this kind of a world."

It had taken me nearly seven years of worldly life to hive up the bitter honey which I here offered to Priscilla. And she rejected it!

"I don't believe one word of what you say!" she replied, laughing anew. "You made me sad, for a minute, by talking about the past; but the past never comes back again. Do we dream the same dream twice? There is nothing else that I am afraid of."

So away she ran, and fell down on the green grass, as it was often her luck to do, but got up again, without any harm.

"Priscilla, Priscilla!" cried Hollingsworth, who was sitting on the doorstep; "you had better not run any more to-night. You will weary yourself too much. And do not sit down out of doors, for there is a heavy dew beginning to fall."

At his first word, she went and sat down under the porch, at Hollingsworth's feet, entirely contented and happy. What charm was there in his rude massiveness that so attracted and soothed this shadow-like girl? It appeared to me, who have always been curious in such matters, that Priscilla's vague and seemingly causeless flow of felicitous feeling was that with which love blesses inexperienced hearts, before they begin to suspect what is going on within them. It transports them to the seventh heaven; and if you ask what brought them thither, they neither can tell nor care to learn, but cherish an ecstatic faith that there they shall abide forever.

Zenobia was in the doorway, not far from Hollingsworth. She gazed at Priscilla in a very singular way. Indeed, it was a sight worth gazing at, and a beautiful sight, too, as the fair girl sat at the feet of that dark, powerful figure. Her air, while perfectly modest, delicate, and virgin-like, denoted her as swayed by Hollingsworth, attracted to him, and unconsciously seeking to rest upon his strength. I could not turn away my own eyes, but hoped that nobody, save Zenobia and myself, was witnessing this picture. It is before me now, with the evening twilight a little deepened by the dusk of memory.

"Come hither, Priscilla," said Zenobia. "I have something to say to you."

She spoke in little more than a whisper. But it is strange how expressive of moods a whisper may often be. Priscilla felt at once that something had gone wrong.

"Are you angry with me?" she asked, rising slowly, and standing before Zenobia in a drooping attitude. "What have I done? I hope you are not angry!"

"No, no, Priscilla!" said Hollingsworth, smiling. "I will answer for it, she is not. You are the one little person in the world with whom nobody can be angry!"

"Angry with you, child? What a silly idea!" exclaimed Zenobia, laughing. "No, indeed! But, my dear Priscilla, you are getting to be so very pretty that you absolutely need a duenna; and, as I am older than you, and have had my own little experience of life, and think myself exceedingly sage, I intend to fill the place of a maiden aunt. Every day, I shall give you a lecture, a quarter of an hour in length, on the morals, manners, and proprieties of social life. When our pastoral shall be quite played out, Priscilla, my worldly wisdom may stand you in good stead."

"I am afraid you are angry with me!" repeated Priscilla sadly; for, while she seemed as impressible as wax, the girl often showed a persistency in her own ideas as stubborn as it was gentle.

"Dear me, what can I say to the child!" cried Zenobia in a tone of humorous vexation. "Well, well; since you insist on my being angry, come to my room this moment, and let me beat you!"

Zenobia bade Hollingsworth good-night very sweetly, and nodded to me with a smile. But, just as she turned aside with Priscilla into the dimness of the porch, I caught another glance at her countenance. It would have made the fortune of a tragic actress, could she have borrowed it for the moment when she fumbles in her bosom for the concealed dagger, or the exceedingly sharp bodkin, or mingles the ratsbane in her lover's bowl of wine or her rival's cup of tea. Not that I in the least anticipated any such catastrophe,—it being a remarkable truth that custom has in no one point a greater sway than over our modes of wreaking our wild passions. And besides, had we been in Italy, instead of New England, it was hardly yet a crisis for the dagger or the bowl.

It often amazed me, however, that Hollingsworth should show himself so recklessly tender towards Priscilla, and never once seem to think of the effect which it might have upon her heart. But the man, as I have endeavored to explain, was thrown completely off his moral balance, and quite bewildered as to his personal relations, by his great excrescence of a philanthropic scheme. I used to see, or fancy, indications that he was not altogether obtuse to Zenobia's influence as a woman. No doubt, however, he had a still more exquisite enjoyment of Priscilla's silent sympathy with his purposes, so unalloyed with criticism, and therefore more grateful than any intellectual approbation, which always involves a possible reserve of latent censure. A man—poet, prophet, or whatever he may be—readily persuades himself of his right to all the worship that is voluntarily tendered. In requital of so rich benefits as he was to confer upon mankind, it would have been hard to deny Hollingsworth the simple solace of a young girl's heart, which he held in his hand, and smelled too, like a rosebud. But what if, while pressing out its fragrance, he should crush the tender rosebud in his grasp!

As for Zenobia, I saw no occasion to give myself any trouble. With her native strength, and her experience of the world, she could not be supposed to need any help of mine. Nevertheless, I was really generous enough to feel some little interest likewise for Zenobia. With all her faults (which might have been a great many besides the abundance that I knew of), she possessed noble traits, and a heart which must, at least, have been valuable while new. And she seemed ready to fling it away as uncalculatingly as Priscilla herself. I could not but suspect that, if merely at play with Hollingsworth, she was sporting with a power which she did not fully estimate. Or if in earnest, it might chance, between Zenobia's passionate force and his dark, self-delusive egotism, to turn out such earnest as would develop itself in some sufficiently tragic catastrophe, though the dagger and the bowl should go for nothing in it.

Meantime, the gossip of the Community set them down as a pair of lovers. They took walks together, and were not seldom encountered in the wood-paths: Hollingsworth deeply discoursing, in tones solemn and sternly pathetic; Zenobia, with a rich glow on her cheeks, and her eyes softened from their ordinary brightness, looked so beautiful, that had her companion been ten times a philanthropist, it seemed impossible but that one glance should melt him back into a man. Oftener than anywhere else, they went to a certain point on the slope of a pasture, commanding nearly the whole of our own domain, besides a view of the river, and an airy prospect of many distant hills. The bond of our Community was such, that the members had the privilege of building cottages for their own residence within our precincts, thus laying a hearthstone and fencing in a home private and peculiar to all desirable extent, while yet the inhabitants should continue to share the advantages of an associated life. It was inferred that Hollingsworth and Zenobia intended to rear their dwelling on this favorite spot.

I mentioned these rumors to Hollingsworth in a playful way.

"Had you consulted me," I went on to observe, "I should have recommended a site farther to the left, just a little withdrawn into the wood, with two or three peeps at the prospect among the trees. You will be in the shady vale of years long before you can raise any better kind of shade around your cottage, if you build it on this bare slope."

"But I offer my edifice as a spectacle to the world," said Hollingsworth, "that it may take example and build many another like it. Therefore, I mean to set it on the open hillside."

Twist these words how I might, they offered no very satisfactory import. It seemed hardly probable that Hollingsworth should care about educating the public taste in the department of cottage architecture, desirable as such improvement certainly was.

X. A VISITOR FROM TOWN

Hollingsworth and I—we had been hoeing potatoes, that forenoon, while the rest of the fraternity were engaged in a distant quarter of the farm—sat under a clump of maples, eating our eleven o'clock lunch, when we saw a stranger approaching along the edge of the field. He had admitted himself from the roadside through a turnstile, and seemed to have a purpose of speaking with us.

And, by the bye, we were favored with many visits at Blithedale, especially from people who sympathized with our theories, and perhaps held themselves ready to unite in our actual experiment as soon as there should appear a reliable promise of its success. It was rather ludicrous, indeed (to me, at least, whose enthusiasm had insensibly been exhaled together with the perspiration of many a hard day's toil), it was absolutely funny, therefore, to observe what a glory was shed about our life and labors, in the imaginations of these longing proselytes. In their view, we were as poetical as Arcadians, besides being as practical as the hardest-fisted husbandmen in Massachusetts. We did not, it is true, spend much time in piping to our sheep, or warbling our innocent loves to the sisterhood. But they gave us credit for imbuing the ordinary rustic occupations with a kind of religious poetry, insomuch that our very cow-yards and pig-sties were as delightfully fragrant as a flower garden. Nothing used to please me more than to see one of these lay enthusiasts snatch up a hoe, as they were very prone to do, and set to work with a vigor that perhaps carried him through about a dozen ill-directed strokes. Men are wonderfully soon satisfied, in this day of shameful bodily enervation, when, from one end of life to the other, such multitudes never taste the sweet weariness that follows accustomed toil. I seldom saw the new enthusiasm that did not grow as flimsy and flaccid as the proselyte's moistened shirt-collar, with a quarter of an hour's active labor under a July sun.

But the person now at hand had not at all the air of one of these amiable visionaries. He was an elderly man, dressed rather shabbily, yet decently enough, in a gray frock-coat, faded towards a brown hue, and wore a broad-brimmed white hat, of the fashion of several years gone by. His hair was perfect silver, without a dark thread in the whole of it; his nose, though it had a scarlet tip, by no means indicated the jollity of which a red nose is the generally admitted symbol. He was a subdued, undemonstrative old man, who would doubtless drink a glass of liquor, now and then, and probably more than was good for him,—not, however, with a purpose of undue exhilaration, but in the hope of bringing his spirits up to the ordinary level of the world's cheerfulness. Drawing nearer, there was a shy look about him, as if he were ashamed of his poverty, or, at any rate, for some reason or other, would rather have us glance at him sidelong than take a full front view. He had a queer appearance of hiding himself behind the patch on his left eye.

"I know this old gentleman," said I to Hollingsworth, as we sat observing him; "that is, I have met him a hundred times in town, and have often amused my fancy with wondering what he was before he came to be what he is. He haunts restaurants and such places, and has an odd way of lurking in corners or getting behind a door whenever practicable, and holding out his hand with some little article in it which he wishes you to buy. The eye of the world seems to trouble him, although he necessarily lives so much in it. I never expected to see him in an open field."

"Have you learned anything of his history?" asked Hollingsworth.

"Not a circumstance," I answered; "but there must be something curious in it. I take him to be a harmless sort of a person, and a tolerably honest one; but his manners, being so furtive, remind me of those of a rat,—a rat without the mischief, the fierce eye, the teeth to bite with, or the desire to bite. See, now! He means to skulk along that fringe of bushes, and approach us on the other side of our clump of maples."

We soon heard the old man's velvet tread on the grass, indicating that he had arrived within a few feet of where we Sat.

"Good-morning, Mr. Moodie," said Hollingsworth, addressing the stranger as an acquaintance; "you must have had a hot and tiresome walk from the city. Sit down, and take a morsel of our bread and cheese."

The visitor made a grateful little murmur of acquiescence, and sat down in a spot somewhat removed; so that, glancing round, I could see his gray pantaloons and dusty shoes, while his upper part was mostly hidden behind the shrubbery. Nor did he come forth from this retirement during the whole of the interview that followed. We handed him such food as we had, together with a brown jug of molasses and water (would that it had been brandy, or some thing better, for the sake of his chill old heart!), like priests offering dainty sacrifice to an enshrined and invisible idol. I have no idea that he really lacked sustenance; but it was quite touching, nevertheless, to hear him nibbling away at our crusts.

"Mr. Moodie," said I, "do you remember selling me one of those very pretty little silk purses, of which you seem to have a monopoly in the market? I keep it to this day, I can assure you."

"Ah, thank you," said our guest. "Yes, Mr. Coverdale, I used to sell a good many of those little purses."

He spoke languidly, and only those few words, like a watch with an inelastic spring, that just ticks a moment or two and stops again. He seemed a very forlorn old man. In the wantonness of youth, strength, and comfortable condition,—making my prey of people's individualities, as my custom was,—I tried to identify my mind with the old fellow's, and take his view of the world, as if looking through a smoke-blackened glass at the sun. It robbed the landscape of all its life. Those pleasantly swelling slopes of our farm, descending towards the wide meadows, through which sluggishly circled the brimful tide of the Charles, bathing the long sedges on its hither and farther shores; the broad, sunny gleam over the winding water; that peculiar picturesqueness of the scene where capes and headlands put themselves boldly forth upon the perfect level of the meadow, as into a green lake, with inlets between the promontories; the shadowy woodland, with twinkling showers of light falling into its depths; the sultry heat-vapor, which rose everywhere like incense, and in which my soul delighted, as indicating so rich a fervor in the passionate day, and in the earth that was burning with its love,—I beheld all these things as through old Moodie's eyes. When my eyes are dimmer than they have yet come to be, I will go thither again, and see if I did not catch the tone of his mind aright, and if the cold and lifeless tint of his perceptions be not then repeated in my own.

Yet it was unaccountable to myself, the interest that I felt in him.

"Have you any objection," said I, "to telling me who made those little purses?"

"Gentlemen have often asked me that," said Moodie slowly; "but I shake my head, and say little or nothing, and creep out of the way as well as I can. I am a man of few words; and if gentlemen were to be told one thing, they would be very apt, I suppose, to ask me another. But it happens just now, Mr. Coverdale, that you can tell me more about the maker of those little purses than I can tell you."

"Why do you trouble him with needless questions, Coverdale?" interrupted Hollingsworth. "You must have known, long ago, that it was Priscilla. And so, my good friend, you have come to see her? Well, I am glad of it. You will find her altered very much for the better, since that winter evening when you put her into my charge. Why, Priscilla has a bloom in her cheeks, now!"

"Has my pale little girl a bloom?" repeated Moodie with a kind of slow wonder. "Priscilla with a bloom in her cheeks! Ah, I am afraid I shall not know my little girl. And is she happy?"

"Just as happy as a bird," answered Hollingsworth.

"Then, gentlemen," said our guest apprehensively, "I don't think it well for me to go any farther. I crept hitherward only to ask about Priscilla; and now that you have told me such good news, perhaps I can do no better than to creep back again. If she were to see this old face of mine, the child would remember some very sad times which we have spent together. Some very sad times, indeed! She has forgotten them, I know,—them and me,—else she could not be so happy, nor have a bloom in her cheeks. Yes—yes—yes," continued he, still with the same torpid utterance; "with many thanks to you, Mr. Hollingsworth, I will creep back to town again."

"You shall do no such thing, Mr. Moodie," said Hollingsworth bluffly. "Priscilla often speaks of you; and if there lacks anything to make her cheeks bloom like two damask roses, I'll venture to say it is just the sight of your face. Come,—we will go and find her."

"Mr. Hollingsworth!" said the old man in his hesitating way.

"Well," answered Hollingsworth.

"Has there been any call for Priscilla?" asked Moodie; and though his face was hidden from us, his tone gave a sure indication of the mysterious nod and wink with which he put the question. "You know, I think, sir, what I mean."

"I have not the remotest suspicion what you mean, Mr. Moodie," replied Hollingsworth; "nobody, to my knowledge, has called for Priscilla, except yourself. But come; we are losing time, and I have several things to say to you by the way."

"And, Mr. Hollingsworth!" repeated Moodie.

"Well, again!" cried my friend rather impatiently. "What now?"

"There is a lady here," said the old man; and his voice lost some of its wearisome hesitation. "You will account it a very strange matter for me to talk about; but I chanced to know this lady when she was but a little child. If I am rightly informed, she has grown to be a very fine woman, and makes a brilliant figure in the world, with her beauty, and her talents, and her noble way of spending her riches. I should recognize this lady, so people tell me, by a magnificent flower in her hair."

"What a rich tinge it gives to his colorless ideas, when he speaks of Zenobia!" I whispered to Hollingsworth. "But how can there possibly be any interest or connecting link between him and her?"

"The old man, for years past," whispered Hollingsworth, "has been a little out of his right mind, as you probably see."

"What I would inquire," resumed Moodie, "is whether this beautiful lady is kind to my poor Priscilla."

"Very kind," said Hollingsworth.

"Does she love her?" asked Moodie.

"It should seem so," answered my friend. "They are always together."

"Like a gentlewoman and her maid-servant, I fancy?" suggested the old man.

There was something so singular in his way of saying this, that I could not resist the impulse to turn quite round, so as to catch a glimpse of his face, almost imagining that I should see another person than old Moodie. But there he sat, with the patched side of his face towards me.

"Like an elder and younger sister, rather," replied Hollingsworth.

"Ah!" said Moodie more complacently, for his latter tones had harshness and acidity in them,—"it would gladden my old heart to witness that. If one thing would make me happier than another, Mr. Hollingsworth, it would be to see that beautiful lady holding my little girl by the hand."

"Come along," said Hollingsworth, "and perhaps you may."

After a little more delay on the part of our freakish visitor, they set forth together, old Moodie keeping a step or two behind Hollingsworth, so that the latter could not very conveniently look him in the face. I remained under the tuft of maples, doing my utmost to draw an inference from the scene that had just passed. In spite of Hollingsworth's off-hand explanation, it did not strike me that our strange guest was really beside himself, but only that his mind needed screwing up, like an instrument long out of tune, the strings of which have ceased to vibrate smartly and sharply. Methought it would be profitable for us, projectors of a happy life, to welcome this old gray shadow, and cherish him as one of us, and let him creep about our domain, in order that he might be a little merrier for our sakes, and we, sometimes, a little sadder for his. Human destinies look ominous without some perceptible intermixture of the sable or the gray. And then, too, should any of our fraternity grow feverish with an over-exulting sense of prosperity, it would be a sort of cooling regimen to slink off into the woods, and spend an hour, or a day, or as many days as might be requisite to the cure, in uninterrupted communion with this deplorable old Moodie!

Going homeward to dinner, I had a glimpse of him, behind the trunk of a tree, gazing earnestly towards a particular window of the farmhouse; and by and by Priscilla appeared at this window, playfully drawing along Zenobia, who looked as bright as the very day that was blazing down upon us, only not, by many degrees, so well advanced towards her noon. I was convinced that this pretty sight must have been purposely arranged by Priscilla for the old man to see. But either the girl held her too long, or her fondness was resented as too great a freedom; for Zenobia suddenly put Priscilla decidedly away, and gave her a haughty look, as from a mistress to a dependant. Old Moodie shook his head; and again and again I saw him shake it, as he withdrew along the road; and at the last point whence the farmhouse was visible, he turned and shook his uplifted staff.

XI. THE WOOD-PATH

Not long after the preceding incident, in order to get the ache of too constant labor out of my bones, and to relieve my spirit of the irksomeness of a settled routine, I took a holiday. It was my purpose to spend it all alone, from breakfast-time till twilight, in the deepest wood-seclusion that lay anywhere around us. Though fond of society, I was so constituted as to need these occasional retirements, even in a life like that of Blithedale, which was itself characterized by a remoteness from the world. Unless renewed by a yet further withdrawal towards the inner circle of self-communion, I lost the better part of my individuality. My thoughts became of little worth, and my sensibilities grew as arid as a tuft of moss (a thing whose life is in the shade, the rain, or the noontide dew), crumbling in the sunshine after long expectance of a shower. So, with my heart full of a drowsy pleasure, and cautious not to dissipate my mood by previous intercourse with any one, I hurried away, and was soon pacing a wood-path, arched overhead with boughs, and dusky-brown beneath my feet.

At first I walked very swiftly, as if the heavy flood tide of social life were roaring at my heels, and would outstrip and overwhelm me, without all the better diligence in my escape. But, threading the more distant windings of the track, I abated my pace, and looked about me for some side-aisle, that should admit me into the innermost sanctuary of this green cathedral, just as, in human acquaintanceship, a casual opening sometimes lets us, all of a sudden, into the long-sought intimacy of a mysterious heart. So much was I absorbed in my reflections,—or, rather, in my mood, the substance of which was as yet too shapeless to be called thought,—that footsteps rustled on the leaves, and a figure passed me by, almost without impressing either the sound or sight upon my consciousness.

A moment afterwards, I heard a voice at a little distance behind me, speaking so sharply and impertinently that it made a complete discord with my spiritual state, and caused the latter to vanish as abruptly as when you thrust a finger into a soap-bubble.

"Halloo, friend!" cried this most unseasonable voice. "Stop a moment, I say! I must have a word with you!"

I turned about, in a humor ludicrously irate. In the first place, the interruption, at any rate, was a grievous injury; then, the tone displeased me. And finally, unless there be real affection in his heart, a man cannot,—such is the bad state to which the world has brought itself,—cannot more effectually show his contempt for a brother mortal, nor more gallingly assume a position of superiority, than by addressing him as "friend." Especially does the misapplication of this phrase bring out that latent hostility which is sure to animate peculiar sects, and those who, with however generous a purpose, have sequestered themselves from the crowd; a feeling, it is true, which may be hidden in some dog-kennel of the heart, grumbling there in the darkness, but is never quite extinct, until the dissenting party have gained power and scope enough to treat the world generously. For my part, I should have taken it as far less an insult to be styled "fellow," "clown," or "bumpkin." To either of these appellations my rustic garb (it was a linen blouse, with checked shirt and striped pantaloons, a chip hat on my head, and a rough hickory stick in my hand) very fairly entitled me. As the case stood, my temper darted at once to the opposite pole; not friend, but enemy!

"What do you want with me?" said I, facing about.

"Come a little nearer, friend," said the stranger, beckoning.

"No," answered I. "If I can do anything for you without too much trouble to myself, say so. But recollect, if you please, that you are not speaking to an acquaintance, much less a friend!"

"Upon my word, I believe not!" retorted he, looking at me with some curiosity; and, lifting his hat, he made me a salute which had enough of sarcasm to be offensive, and just enough of doubtful courtesy to render any resentment of it absurd. "But I ask your pardon! I recognize a little mistake. If I may take the liberty to suppose it, you, sir, are probably one of the aesthetic—or shall I rather say ecstatic?—laborers, who have planted themselves hereabouts. This is your forest of Arden; and you are either the banished Duke in person, or one of the chief nobles in his train. The melancholy Jacques, perhaps? Be it so. In that case, you can probably do me a favor."

I never, in my life, felt less inclined to confer a favor on any man.

"I am busy," said I.

So unexpectedly had the stranger made me sensible of his presence, that he had almost the effect of an apparition; and certainly a less appropriate one (taking into view the dim woodland solitude about us) than if the salvage man of antiquity, hirsute and cinctured with a leafy girdle, had started out of a thicket. He was still young, seemingly a little under thirty, of a tall and well-developed figure, and as handsome a man as ever I beheld. The style of his beauty, however, though a masculine style, did not at all commend itself to my taste. His countenance—I hardly know how to describe the peculiarity—had an indecorum in it, a kind of rudeness, a hard, coarse, forth-putting freedom of expression, which no degree of external polish could have abated one single jot. Not that it was vulgar. But he had no fineness of nature; there was in his eyes (although they might have artifice enough of another sort) the naked exposure of something that ought not to be left prominent. With these vague allusions to what I have seen in other faces as well as his, I leave the quality to be comprehended best—because with an intuitive repugnance—by those who possess least of it.

His hair, as well as his beard and mustache, was coal-black; his eyes, too, were black and sparkling, and his teeth remarkably brilliant. He was rather carelessly but well and fashionably dressed, in a summer-morning costume. There was a gold chain, exquisitely wrought, across his vest. I never saw a smoother or whiter gloss than that upon his shirt-bosom, which had a pin in it, set with a gem that glimmered, in the leafy shadow where he stood, like a living tip of fire. He carried a stick with a wooden head, carved in vivid imitation of that of a serpent. I hated him, partly, I do believe, from a comparison of my own homely garb with his well-ordered foppishness.

"Well, sir," said I, a little ashamed of my first irritation, but still with no waste of civility, "be pleased to speak at once, as I have my own business in hand."

"I regret that my mode of addressing you was a little unfortunate," said the stranger, smiling; for he seemed a very acute sort of person, and saw, in some degree, how I stood affected towards him. "I intended no offence, and shall certainly comport myself with due ceremony hereafter. I merely wish to make a few inquiries respecting a lady, formerly of my acquaintance, who is now resident in your Community, and, I believe, largely concerned in your social enterprise. You call her, I think, Zenobia."

"That is her name in literature," observed I; "a name, too, which possibly she may permit her private friends to know and address her by,—but not one which they feel at liberty to recognize when used of her personally by a stranger or casual acquaintance."

"Indeed!" answered this disagreeable person; and he turned aside his face for an instant with a brief laugh, which struck me as a noteworthy expression of his character. "Perhaps I might put forward a claim, on your own grounds, to call the lady by a name so appropriate to her splendid qualities. But I am willing to know her by any cognomen that you may suggest."

Heartily wishing that he would be either a little more offensive, or a good deal less so, or break off our intercourse altogether, I mentioned Zenobia's real name.

"True," said he; "and in general society I have never heard her called otherwise. And, after all, our discussion of the point has been gratuitous. My object is only to inquire when, where, and how this lady may most conveniently be seen."

"At her present residence, of course," I replied. "You have but to go thither and ask for her. This very path will lead you within sight of the house; so I wish you good-morning."

"One moment, if you please," said the stranger. "The course you indicate would certainly be the proper one, in an ordinary morning call. But my business is private, personal, and somewhat peculiar. Now, in a community like this, I should judge that any little occurrence is likely to be discussed rather more minutely than would quite suit my views. I refer solely to myself, you understand, and without intimating that it would be other than a matter of entire indifference to the lady. In short, I especially desire to see her in private. If her habits are such as I have known them, she is probably often to be met with in the woods, or by the river-side; and I think you could do me the favor to point out some favorite walk, where, about this hour, I might be fortunate enough to gain an interview."

I reflected that it would be quite a supererogatory piece of Quixotism in me to undertake the guardianship of Zenobia, who, for my pains, would only make me the butt of endless ridicule, should the fact ever come to her knowledge. I therefore described a spot which, as often as any other, was Zenobia's resort at this period of the day; nor was it so remote from the farmhouse as to leave her in much peril, whatever might be the stranger's character.

"A single word more," said he; and his black eyes sparkled at me, whether with fun or malice I knew not, but certainly as if the Devil were peeping out of them. "Among your fraternity, I understand, there is a certain holy and benevolent blacksmith; a man of iron, in more senses than one; a rough, cross-grained, well-meaning individual, rather boorish in his manners, as might be expected, and by no means of the highest intellectual cultivation. He is a philanthropical lecturer, with two or three disciples, and a scheme of his own, the preliminary step in which involves a large purchase of land, and the erection of a spacious edifice, at an expense considerably beyond his means; inasmuch as these are to be reckoned in copper or old iron much more conveniently than in gold or silver. He hammers away upon his one topic as lustily as ever he did upon a horseshoe! Do you know such a person?" I shook my head, and was turning away. "Our friend," he continued, "is described to me as a brawny, shaggy, grim, and ill-favored personage, not particularly well calculated, one would say, to insinuate himself with the softer sex. Yet, so far has this honest fellow succeeded with one lady whom we wot of, that he anticipates, from her abundant resources, the necessary funds for realizing his plan in brick and mortar!"

Here the stranger seemed to be so much amused with his sketch of Hollingsworth's character and purposes, that he burst into a fit of merriment, of the same nature as the brief, metallic laugh already alluded to, but immensely prolonged and enlarged. In the excess of his delight, he opened his mouth wide, and disclosed a gold band around the upper part of his teeth, thereby making it apparent that every one of his brilliant grinders and incisors was a sham. This discovery affected me very oddly.

I felt as if the whole man were a moral and physical humbug; his wonderful beauty of face, for aught I knew, might be removable like a mask; and, tall and comely as his figure looked, he was perhaps but a wizened little elf, gray and decrepit, with nothing genuine about him save the wicked expression of his grin. The fantasy of his spectral character so wrought upon me, together with the contagion of his strange mirth on my sympathies, that I soon began to laugh as loudly as himself.

By and by, he paused all at once; so suddenly, indeed, that my own cachinnation lasted a moment longer.

"Ah, excuse me!" said he. "Our interview seems to proceed more merrily than it began."

"It ends here," answered I. "And I take shame to myself that my folly has lost me the right of resenting your ridicule of a friend."

"Pray allow me," said the stranger, approaching a step nearer, and laying his gloved hand on my sleeve. "One other favor I must ask of you. You have a young person here at Blithedale, of whom I have heard,—whom, perhaps, I have known,—and in whom, at all events, I take a peculiar interest. She is one of those delicate, nervous young creatures, not uncommon in New England, and whom I suppose to have become what we find them by the gradual refining away of the physical system among your women. Some philosophers choose to glorify this habit of body by terming it spiritual; but, in my opinion, it is rather the effect of unwholesome food, bad air, lack of outdoor exercise, and neglect of bathing, on the part of these damsels and their female progenitors, all resulting in a kind of hereditary dyspepsia. Zenobia, even with her uncomfortable surplus of vitality, is far the better model of womanhood. But—to revert again to this young person—she goes among you by the name of Priscilla. Could you possibly afford me the means of speaking with her?"

"You have made so many inquiries of me," I observed, "that I may at least trouble you with one. What is your name?"

He offered me a card, with "Professor Westervelt" engraved on it. At the same time, as if to vindicate his claim to the professorial dignity, so often assumed on very questionable grounds, he put on a pair of spectacles, which so altered the character of his face that I hardly knew him again. But I liked the present aspect no better than the former one.

"I must decline any further connection with your affairs," said I, drawing back. "I have told you where to find Zenobia. As for Priscilla, she has closer friends than myself, through whom, if they see fit, you can gain access to her."

"In that case," returned the Professor, ceremoniously raising his hat, "good-morning to you."

He took his departure, and was soon out of sight among the windings of the wood-path. But after a little reflection, I could not help regretting that I had so peremptorily broken off the interview, while the stranger seemed inclined to continue it. His evident knowledge of matters affecting my three friends might have led to disclosures or inferences that would perhaps have been serviceable. I was particularly struck with the fact that, ever since the appearance of Priscilla, it had been the tendency of events to suggest and establish a connection between Zenobia and her. She had come, in the first instance, as if with the sole purpose of claiming Zenobia's protection. Old Moodie's visit, it appeared, was chiefly to ascertain whether this object had been accomplished. And here, to-day, was the questionable Professor, linking one with the other in his inquiries, and seeking communication with both.

Meanwhile, my inclination for a ramble having been balked, I lingered in the vicinity of the farm, with perhaps a vague idea that some new event would grow out of Westervelt's proposed interview with Zenobia. My own part in these transactions was singularly subordinate. It resembled that of the Chorus in a classic play, which seems to be set aloof from the possibility of personal concernment, and bestows the whole measure of its hope or fear, its exultation or sorrow, on the fortunes of others, between whom and itself this sympathy is the only bond. Destiny, it may be,—the most skilful of stage managers,—seldom chooses to arrange its scenes, and carry forward its drama, without securing the presence of at least one calm observer. It is his office to give applause when due, and sometimes an inevitable tear, to detect the final fitness of incident to character, and distil in his long-brooding thought the whole morality of the performance.

Not to be out of the way in case there were need of me in my vocation, and, at the same time, to avoid thrusting myself where neither destiny nor mortals might desire my presence, I remained pretty near the verge of the woodlands. My position was off the track of Zenobia's customary walk, yet not so remote but that a recognized occasion might speedily have brought me thither.

XII. COVERDALE'S HERMITAGE

Long since, in this part of our circumjacent wood, I had found out for myself a little hermitage. It was a kind of leafy cave, high upward into the air, among the midmost branches of a white-pine tree. A wild grapevine, of unusual size and luxuriance, had twined and twisted itself up into the tree, and, after wreathing the entanglement of its tendrils around almost every bough, had caught hold of three or four neighboring trees, and married the whole clump with a perfectly inextricable knot of polygamy. Once, while sheltering myself from a summer shower, the fancy had taken me to clamber up into this seemingly impervious mass of foliage. The branches yielded me a passage, and closed again beneath, as if only a squirrel or a bird had passed. Far aloft, around the stem of the central pine, behold a perfect nest for Robinson Crusoe or King Charles! A hollow chamber of rare seclusion had been formed by the decay of some of the pine branches, which the vine had lovingly strangled with its embrace, burying them from the light of day in an aerial sepulchre of its own leaves. It cost me but little ingenuity to enlarge the interior, and open loopholes through the verdant walls. Had it ever been my fortune to spend a honeymoon, I should have thought seriously of inviting my bride up thither, where our next neighbors would have been two orioles in another part of the clump.

It was an admirable place to make verses, tuning the rhythm to the breezy symphony that so often stirred among the vine leaves; or to meditate an essay for "The Dial," in which the many tongues of Nature whispered mysteries, and seemed to ask only a little stronger puff of wind to speak out the solution of its riddle. Being so pervious to air-currents, it was just the nook, too, for the enjoyment of a cigar. This hermitage was my one exclusive possession while I counted myself a brother of the socialists. It symbolized my individuality, and aided me in keeping it inviolate. None ever found me out in it, except, once, a squirrel. I brought thither no guest, because, after Hollingsworth failed me, there was no longer the man alive with whom I could think of sharing all. So there I used to sit, owl-like, yet not without liberal and hospitable thoughts. I counted the innumerable clusters of my vine, and fore-reckoned the abundance of my vintage. It gladdened me to anticipate the surprise of the Community, when, like an allegorical figure of rich October, I should make my appearance, with shoulders bent beneath the burden of ripe grapes, and some of the crushed ones crimsoning my brow as with a bloodstain.

Ascending into this natural turret, I peeped in turn out of several of its small windows. The pine-tree, being ancient, rose high above the rest of the wood, which was of comparatively recent growth. Even where I sat, about midway between the root and the topmost bough, my position was lofty enough to serve as an observatory, not for starry investigations, but for those sublunary matters in which lay a lore as infinite as that of the planets. Through one loophole I saw the river lapsing calmly onward, while in the meadow, near its brink, a few of the brethren were digging peat for our winter's fuel. On the interior cart-road of our farm I discerned Hollingsworth, with a yoke of oxen hitched to a drag of stones, that were to be piled into a fence, on which we employed ourselves at the odd intervals of other labor. The harsh tones of his voice, shouting to the sluggish steers, made me sensible, even at such a distance, that he was ill at ease, and that the balked philanthropist had the battle-spirit in his heart.

"Haw, Buck!" quoth he. "Come along there, ye lazy ones! What are ye about, now? Gee!"

"Mankind, in Hollingsworth's opinion," thought I, "is but another yoke of oxen, as stubborn, stupid, and sluggish as our old Brown and Bright. He vituperates us aloud, and curses us in his heart, and will begin to prick us with the goad-stick, by and by. But are we his oxen? And what right has he to be the driver? And why, when there is enough else to do, should we waste our strength in dragging home the ponderous load of his philanthropic absurdities? At my height above the earth, the whole matter looks ridiculous!"

Turning towards the farmhouse, I saw Priscilla (for, though a great way off, the eye of faith assured me that it was she) sitting at Zenobia's window, and making little purses, I suppose; or, perhaps, mending the Community's old linen. A bird flew past my tree; and, as it clove its way onward into the sunny atmosphere, I flung it a message for Priscilla.

"Tell her," said I, "that her fragile thread of life has inextricably knotted itself with other and tougher threads, and most likely it will be broken. Tell her that Zenobia will not be long her friend. Say that Hollingsworth's heart is on fire with his own purpose, but icy for all human affection; and that, if she has given him her love, it is like casting a flower into a sepulchre. And say that if any mortal really cares for her, it is myself; and not even I for her realities,—poor little seamstress, as Zenobia rightly called her!—but for the fancy-work with which I have idly decked her out!"

The pleasant scent of the wood, evolved by the hot sun, stole up to my nostrils, as if I had been an idol in its niche. Many trees mingled their fragrance into a thousand-fold odor. Possibly there was a sensual influence in the broad light of noon that lay beneath me. It may have been the cause, in part, that I suddenly found myself possessed by a mood of disbelief in moral beauty or heroism, and a conviction of the folly of attempting to benefit the world. Our especial scheme of reform, which, from my observatory, I could take in with the bodily eye, looked so ridiculous that it was impossible not to laugh aloud.

"But the joke is a little too heavy," thought I. "If I were wise, I should get out of the scrape with all diligence, and then laugh at my companions for remaining in it."

While thus musing, I heard with perfect distinctness, somewhere in the wood beneath, the peculiar laugh which I have described as one of the disagreeable characteristics of Professor Westervelt. It brought my thoughts back to our recent interview. I recognized as chiefly due to this man's influence the sceptical and sneering view which just now had filled my mental vision in regard to all life's better purposes. And it was through his eyes, more than my own, that I was looking at Hollingsworth, with his glorious if impracticable dream, and at the noble earthliness of Zenobia's character, and even at Priscilla, whose impalpable grace lay so singularly between disease and beauty. The essential charm of each had vanished. There are some spheres the contact with which inevitably degrades the high, debases the pure, deforms the beautiful. It must be a mind of uncommon strength, and little impressibility, that can permit itself the habit of such intercourse, and not be permanently deteriorated; and yet the Professor's tone represented that of worldly society at large, where a cold scepticism smothers what it can of our spiritual aspirations, and makes the rest ridiculous. I detested this kind of man; and all the more because a part of my own nature showed itself responsive to him.

Voices were now approaching through the region of the wood which lay in the vicinity of my tree. Soon I caught glimpses of two figures—a woman and a man—Zenobia and the stranger—earnestly talking together as they advanced.

Zenobia had a rich though varying color. It was, most of the while, a flame, and anon a sudden paleness. Her eyes glowed, so that their light sometimes flashed upward to me, as when the sun throws a dazzle from some bright object on the ground. Her gestures were free, and strikingly impressive. The whole woman was alive with a passionate intensity, which I now perceived to be the phase in which her beauty culminated. Any passion would have become her well; and passionate love, perhaps, the best of all. This was not love, but anger, largely intermixed with scorn. Yet the idea strangely forced itself upon me, that there was a sort of familiarity between these two companions, necessarily the result of an intimate love,—on Zenobia's part, at least,—in days gone by, but which had prolonged itself into as intimate a hatred, for all futurity. As they passed among the trees, reckless as her movement was, she took good heed that even the hem of her garment should not brush against the stranger's person. I wondered whether there had always been a chasm, guarded so religiously, betwixt these two.

As for Westervelt, he was not a whit more warmed by Zenobia's passion than a salamander by the heat of its native furnace. He would have been absolutely statuesque, save for a look of slight perplexity, tinctured strongly with derision. It was a crisis in which his intellectual perceptions could not altogether help him out. He failed to comprehend, and cared but little for comprehending, why Zenobia should put herself into such a fume; but satisfied his mind that it was all folly, and only another shape of a woman's manifold absurdity, which men can never understand. How many a woman's evil fate has yoked her with a man like this! Nature thrusts some of us into the world miserably incomplete on the emotional side, with hardly any sensibilities except what pertain to us as animals. No passion, save of the senses; no holy tenderness, nor the delicacy that results from this. Externally they bear a close resemblance to other men, and have perhaps all save the finest grace; but when a woman wrecks herself on such a being, she ultimately finds that the real womanhood within her has no corresponding part in him. Her deepest voice lacks a response; the deeper her cry, the more dead his silence. The fault may be none of his; he cannot give her what never lived within his soul. But the wretchedness on her side, and the moral deterioration attendant on a false and shallow life, without strength enough to keep itself sweet, are among the most pitiable wrongs that mortals suffer.

Now, as I looked down from my upper region at this man and woman,—outwardly so fair a sight, and wandering like two lovers in the wood,—I imagined that Zenobia, at an earlier period of youth, might have fallen into the misfortune above indicated. And when her passionate womanhood, as was inevitable, had discovered its mistake, here had ensued the character of eccentricity and defiance which distinguished the more public portion of her life.

Seeing how aptly matters had chanced thus far, I began to think it the design of fate to let me into all Zenobia's secrets, and that therefore the couple would sit down beneath my tree, and carry on a conversation which would leave me nothing to inquire. No doubt, however, had it so happened, I should have deemed myself honorably bound to warn them of a listener's presence by flinging down a handful of unripe grapes, or by sending an unearthly groan out of my hiding-place, as if this were one of the trees of Dante's ghostly forest. But real life never arranges itself exactly like a romance. In the first place, they did not sit down at all. Secondly, even while they passed beneath the tree, Zenobia's utterance was so hasty and broken, and Westervelt's so cool and low, that I hardly could make out an intelligible sentence on either side. What I seem to remember, I yet suspect, may have been patched together by my fancy, in brooding over the matter afterwards.

"Why not fling the girl off," said Westervelt, "and let her go?"

"She clung to me from the first," replied Zenobia. "I neither know nor care what it is in me that so attaches her. But she loves me, and I will not fail her."

"She will plague you, then," said he, "in more ways than one."

"The poor child!" exclaimed Zenobia. "She can do me neither good nor harm. How should she?"

I know not what reply Westervelt whispered; nor did Zenobia's subsequent exclamation give me any clew, except that it evidently inspired her with horror and disgust.

"With what kind of a being am I linked?" cried she. "If my Creator cares aught for my soul, let him release me from this miserable bond!"

"I did not think it weighed so heavily," said her companion..

"Nevertheless," answered Zenobia, "it will strangle me at last!"

And then I heard her utter a helpless sort of moan; a sound which, struggling out of the heart of a person of her pride and strength, affected me more than if she had made the wood dolorously vocal with a thousand shrieks and wails.

Other mysterious words, besides what are above written, they spoke together; but I understood no more, and even question whether I fairly understood so much as this. By long brooding over our recollections, we subtilize them into something akin to imaginary stuff, and hardly capable of being distinguished from it. In a few moments they were completely beyond ear-shot. A breeze stirred after them, and awoke the leafy tongues of the surrounding trees, which forthwith began to babble, as if innumerable gossips had all at once got wind of Zenobia's secret. But, as the breeze grew stronger, its voice among the branches was as if it said, "Hush! Hush!" and I resolved that to no mortal would I disclose what I had heard. And, though there might be room for casuistry, such, I conceive, is the most equitable rule in all similar conjunctures.

XIII. ZENOBIA'S LEGEND

The illustrious Society of Blithedale, though it toiled in downright earnest for the good of mankind, yet not unfrequently illuminated its laborious life with an afternoon or evening of pastime. Picnics under the trees were considerably in vogue; and, within doors, fragmentary bits of theatrical performance, such as single acts of tragedy or comedy, or dramatic proverbs and charades. Zenobia, besides, was fond of giving us readings from Shakespeare, and often with a depth of tragic power, or breadth of comic effect, that made one feel it an intolerable wrong to the world that she did not at once go upon the stage. Tableaux vivants were another of our occasional modes of amusement, in which scarlet shawls, old silken robes, ruffs, velvets, furs, and all kinds of miscellaneous trumpery converted our familiar companions into the people of a pictorial world. We had been thus engaged on the evening after the incident narrated in the last chapter. Several splendid works of art—either arranged after engravings from the old masters, or original illustrations of scenes in history or romance—had been presented, and we were earnestly entreating Zenobia for more.

She stood with a meditative air, holding a large piece of gauze, or some such ethereal stuff, as if considering what picture should next occupy the frame; while at her feet lay a heap of many-colored garments, which her quick fancy and magic skill could so easily convert into gorgeous draperies for heroes and princesses.

"I am getting weary of this," said she, after a moment's thought. "Our own features, and our own figures and airs, show a little too intrusively through all the characters we assume. We have so much familiarity with one another's realities, that we cannot remove ourselves, at pleasure, into an imaginary sphere. Let us have no more pictures to-night; but, to make you what poor amends I can, how would you like to have me trump up a wild, spectral legend, on the spur of the moment?"

Zenobia had the gift of telling a fanciful little story, off-hand, in a way that made it greatly more effective than it was usually found to be when she afterwards elaborated the same production with her pen. Her proposal, therefore, was greeted with acclamation.

"Oh, a story, a story, by all means!" cried the young girls. "No matter how marvellous; we will believe it, every word. And let it be a ghost story, if you please."

"No, not exactly a ghost story," answered Zenobia; "but something so nearly like it that you shall hardly tell the difference. And, Priscilla, stand you before me, where I may look at you, and get my inspiration out of your eyes. They are very deep and dreamy to-night."

I know not whether the following version of her story will retain any portion of its pristine character; but, as Zenobia told it wildly and rapidly, hesitating at no extravagance, and dashing at absurdities which I am too timorous to repeat,—giving it the varied emphasis of her inimitable voice, and the pictorial illustration of her mobile face, while through it all we caught the freshest aroma of the thoughts, as they came bubbling out of her mind,—thus narrated, and thus heard, the legend seemed quite a remarkable affair. I scarcely knew, at the time, whether she intended us to laugh or be more seriously impressed. From beginning to end, it was undeniable nonsense, but not necessarily the worse for that.

THE SILVERY VEIL

You have heard, my dear friends, of the Veiled Lady, who grew suddenly so very famous, a few months ago. And have you never thought how remarkable it was that this marvellous creature should vanish, all at once, while her renown was on the increase, before the public had grown weary of her, and when the enigma of her character, instead of being solved, presented itself more mystically at every exhibition? Her last appearance, as you know, was before a crowded audience. The next evening,—although the bills had announced her, at the corner of every street, in red letters of a gigantic size,—there was no Veiled Lady to be seen! Now, listen to my simple little tale, and you shall hear the very latest incident in the known life—(if life it may be called, which seemed to have no more reality than the candle-light image of one's self which peeps at us outside of a dark windowpane)—the life of this shadowy phenomenon.

A party of young gentlemen, you are to understand, were enjoying themselves, one afternoon,—as young gentlemen are sometimes fond of doing,—over a bottle or two of champagne; and, among other ladies less mysterious, the subject of the Veiled Lady, as was very natural, happened to come up before them for discussion. She rose, as it were, with the sparkling effervescence of their wine, and appeared in a more airy and fantastic light on account of the medium through which they saw her. They repeated to one another, between jest and earnest, all the wild stories that were in vogue; nor, I presume, did they hesitate to add any small circumstance that the inventive whim of the moment might suggest, to heighten the marvellousness of their theme.

"But what an audacious report was that," observed one, "which pretended to assert the identity of this strange creature with a young lady,"—and here he mentioned her name,—"the daughter of one of our most distinguished families!"

"Ah, there is more in that story than can well be accounted for," remarked another. "I have it on good authority, that the young lady in question is invariably out of sight, and not to be traced, even by her own family, at the hours when the

Veiled Lady is before the public; nor can any satisfactory explanation be given of her disappearance. And just look at the thing: Her brother is a young fellow of spirit. He cannot but be aware of these rumors in reference to his sister. Why, then, does he not come forward to defend her character, unless he is conscious that an investigation would only make the matter worse?"

It is essential to the purposes of my legend to distinguish one of these young gentlemen from his companions; so, for the sake of a soft and pretty name (such as we of the literary sisterhood invariably bestow upon our heroes), I deem it fit to call him Theodore.

"Pshaw!" exclaimed Theodore; "her brother is no such fool! Nobody, unless his brain be as full of bubbles as this wine, can seriously think of crediting that ridiculous rumor. Why, if my senses did not play me false (which never was the case yet), I affirm that I saw that very lady, last evening, at the exhibition, while this veiled phenomenon was playing off her juggling tricks! What can you say to that?"

"Oh, it was a spectral illusion that you saw!" replied his friends, with a general laugh. "The Veiled Lady is quite up to such a thing."

However, as the above-mentioned fable could not hold its ground against Theodore's downright refutation, they went on to speak of other stories which the wild babble of the town had set afloat. Some upheld that the veil covered the most beautiful countenance in the world; others,—and certainly with more reason, considering the sex of the Veiled Lady,—that the face was the most hideous and horrible, and that this was her sole motive for hiding it. It was the face of a corpse; it was the head of a skeleton; it was a monstrous visage, with snaky locks, like Medusa's, and one great red eye in the centre of the forehead. Again, it was affirmed that there was no single and unchangeable set of features beneath the veil; but that whosoever should be bold enough to lift it would behold the features of that person, in all the world, who was destined to be his fate; perhaps he would be greeted by the tender smile of the woman whom he loved, or, quite as probably, the deadly scowl of his bitterest enemy would throw a blight over his life. They quoted, moreover, this startling explanation of the whole affair: that the magician who exhibited the Veiled Lady—and who, by the bye, was the handsomest man in the whole world—had bartered his own soul for seven years' possession of a familiar fiend, and that the last year of the contract was wearing towards its close.

If it were worth our while, I could keep you till an hour beyond midnight listening to a thousand such absurdities as these. But finally our friend Theodore, who prided himself upon his common-sense, found the matter getting quite beyond his patience.

"I offer any wager you like," cried he, setting down his glass so forcibly as to break the stem of it, "that this very evening I find out the mystery of the Veiled Lady!"

Young men, I am told, boggle at nothing over their wine; so, after a little more talk, a wager of considerable amount was actually laid, the money staked, and Theodore left to choose his own method of settling the dispute.

How he managed it I know not, nor is it of any great importance to this veracious legend. The most natural way, to be sure, was by bribing the doorkeeper,—or possibly he preferred clambering in at the window. But, at any rate, that very evening, while the exhibition was going forward in the hall, Theodore contrived to gain admittance into the private withdrawing-room whither the Veiled Lady was accustomed to retire at the close of her performances. There he waited, listening, I suppose, to the stifled hum of the great audience; and no doubt he could distinguish the deep tones of the magician, causing the wonders that he wrought to appear more dark and intricate, by his mystic pretence of an explanation. Perhaps, too, in the intervals of the wild breezy music which accompanied the exhibition, he might hear the low voice of the Veiled Lady, conveying her sibylline responses. Firm as Theodore's nerves might be, and much as he prided himself on his sturdy perception of realities, I should not be surprised if his heart throbbed at a little more than its ordinary rate.

Theodore concealed himself behind a screen. In due time the performance was brought to a close, and whether the door was softly opened, or whether her bodiless presence came through the wall, is more than I can say, but, all at once, without the young man's knowing how it happened, a veiled figure stood in the centre of the room. It was one thing to be in presence of this mystery in the hall of exhibition, where the warm, dense life of hundreds of other mortals kept up the beholder's courage, and distributed her influence among so many; it was another thing to be quite alone with her, and that, too, with a hostile, or, at least, an unauthorized and unjustifiable purpose. I further imagine that Theodore now began to be sensible of something more serious in his enterprise than he had been quite aware of while he sat with his boon-companions over their sparkling wine.

Very strange, it must be confessed, was the movement with which the figure floated to and fro over the carpet, with the silvery veil covering her from head to foot; so impalpable, so ethereal, so without substance, as the texture seemed, yet hiding her every outline in an impenetrability like that of midnight. Surely, she did not walk! She floated, and flitted, and hovered about the room; no sound of a footstep, no perceptible motion of a limb; it was as if a wandering breeze wafted her before it, at its own wild and gentle pleasure. But, by and by, a purpose began to be discernible, throughout the seeming vagueness of her unrest. She was in quest of something. Could it be that a subtile presentiment had informed her of the young man's presence? And if so, did the Veiled Lady seek or did she shun him? The doubt in Theodore's mind was speedily resolved; for, after a moment or two of these erratic flutterings, she advanced more decidedly, and stood motionless before the screen.

"Thou art here!" said a soft, low voice. "Come forth, Theodore!" Thus summoned by his name, Theodore, as a man of courage, had no choice. He emerged from his concealment, and presented himself before the Veiled Lady, with the wine-flush, it may be, quite gone out of his cheeks.

"What wouldst thou with me?" she inquired, with the same gentle composure that was in her former utterance.

"Mysterious creature," replied Theodore, "I would know who and what you are!"

"My lips are forbidden to betray the secret," said the Veiled Lady.

"At whatever risk, I must discover it," rejoined Theodore.

"Then," said the Mystery, "there is no way save to lift my veil."

And Theodore, partly recovering his audacity, stept forward on the instant, to do as the Veiled Lady had suggested. But she floated backward to the opposite side of the room, as if the young man's breath had possessed power enough to waft her away.

"Pause, one little instant," said the soft, low voice, "and learn the conditions of what thou art so bold to undertake. Thou canst go hence, and think of me no more; or, at thy option, thou canst lift this mysterious veil, beneath which I am a sad and lonely prisoner, in a bondage which is worse to me than death. But, before raising it, I entreat thee, in all maiden modesty, to bend forward and impress a kiss where my breath stirs the veil; and my virgin lips shall come forward to meet thy lips; and from that instant, Theodore, thou shalt be mine, and I thine, with never more a veil between us. And all the felicity of earth and of the future world shall be thine and mine together. So much may a maiden say behind the veil. If thou shrinkest from this, there is yet another way." "And what is that?" asked Theodore. "Dost thou hesitate," said the Veiled Lady, "to pledge thyself to me, by meeting these lips of mine, while the veil yet hides my face? Has not thy heart recognized me? Dost thou come hither, not in holy faith, nor with a pure and generous purpose, but in scornful scepticism and idle curiosity? Still, thou mayest lift the veil! But, from that instant, Theodore, I am doomed to be thy evil fate; nor wilt thou ever taste another breath of happiness!"

There was a shade of inexpressible sadness in the utterance of these last words. But Theodore, whose natural tendency was towards scepticism, felt himself almost injured and insulted by the Veiled Lady's proposal that he should pledge himself, for life and eternity, to so questionable a creature as herself; or even that she should suggest an inconsequential kiss, taking into view the probability that her face was none of the most bewitching. A delightful idea, truly, that he should salute the lips of a dead girl, or the jaws of a skeleton, or the grinning cavity of a monster's mouth! Even should she prove a comely maiden enough in other respects, the odds were ten to one that her teeth were defective; a terrible drawback on the delectableness of a kiss

"Excuse me, fair lady," said Theodore, and I think he nearly burst into a laugh, "if I prefer to lift the veil first; and for this affair of the kiss, we may decide upon it afterwards."

"Thou hast made thy choice," said the sweet, sad voice behind the veil; and there seemed a tender but unresentful sense of wrong done to womanhood by the young man's contemptuous interpretation of her offer. "I must not counsel thee to pause, although thy fate is still in thine own hand!"

Grasping at the veil, he flung it upward, and caught a glimpse of a pale, lovely face beneath; just one momentary glimpse, and then the apparition vanished, and the silvery veil fluttered slowly down and lay upon the floor. Theodore was alone. Our legend leaves him there. His retribution was, to pine forever and ever for another sight of that dim, mournful face,—which might have been his life-long household fireside joy,—to desire, and waste life in a feverish quest, and never meet it more.

But what, in good sooth, had become of the Veiled Lady? Had all her existence been comprehended within that mysterious veil, and was she now annihilated? Or was she a spirit, with a heavenly essence, but which might have been tamed down to human bliss, had Theodore been brave and true enough to claim her? Hearken, my sweet friends,—and hearken, dear Priscilla,—and you shall learn the little more that Zenobia can tell you.

Just at the moment, so far as can be ascertained, when the Veiled Lady vanished, a maiden, pale and shadowy, rose up amid a knot of visionary people, who were seeking for the better life. She was so gentle and so sad,—a nameless melancholy gave her such hold upon their sympathies,—that they never thought of questioning whence she came. She might have heretofore existed, or her thin substance might have been moulded out of air at the very instant when they first beheld her. It was all one to them; they took her to their hearts. Among them was a lady to whom, more than to all the rest, this pale, mysterious girl attached herself.

But one morning the lady was wandering in the woods, and there met her a figure in an Oriental robe, with a dark beard, and holding in his hand a silvery veil. He motioned her to stay. Being a woman of some nerve, she did not shriek, nor run away, nor faint, as many ladies would have been apt to do, but stood quietly, and bade him speak. The truth was, she had seen his face before, but had never feared it, although she knew him to be a terrible magician.

"Lady," said he, with a warning gesture, "you are in peril!" "Peril!" she exclaimed. "And of what nature?"

"There is a certain maiden," replied the magician, "who has come out of the realm of mystery, and made herself your most intimate companion. Now, the fates have so ordained it, that, whether by her own will or no, this stranger is your deadliest enemy. In love, in worldly fortune, in all your pursuit of happiness, she is doomed to fling a blight over your prospects. There is but one possibility of thwarting her disastrous influence."

"Then tell me that one method," said the lady.

"Take this veil," he answered, holding forth the silvery texture. "It is a spell; it is a powerful enchantment, which I wrought for her sake, and beneath which she was once my prisoner. Throw it, at unawares, over the head of this secret foe, stamp your foot, and cry, 'Arise, Magician! Here is the Veiled Lady!' and immediately I will rise up through the earth, and seize her; and from that moment you are safe!"

So the lady took the silvery veil, which was like woven air, or like some substance airier than nothing, and that would float upward and be lost among the clouds, were she once to let it go. Returning homeward, she found the shadowy girl amid the knot of visionary transcendentalists, who were still seeking for the better life. She was joyous now, and had a rose-bloom in her cheeks, and was one of the prettiest creatures, and seemed one of the happiest, that the world could show. But the lady stole noiselessly behind her and threw the veil over her head. As the slight, ethereal texture sank inevitably down over her figure, the poor girl strove to raise it, and met her dear friend's eyes with one glance of mortal terror, and deep, deep reproach. It could not change her purpose.

"Arise, Magician!" she exclaimed, stamping her foot upon the earth. "Here is the Veiled Lady!"

At the word, up rose the bearded man in the Oriental robes,—the beautiful, the dark magician, who had bartered away his soul! He threw his arms around the Veiled Lady, and she was his bond-slave for evermore!

Zenobia, all this while, had been holding the piece of gauze, and so managed it as greatly to increase the dramatic effect of the legend at those points where the magic veil was to be described. Arriving at the catastrophe, and uttering the fatal words, she flung the gauze over Priscilla's head; and for an instant her auditors held their breath, half expecting, I verily believe, that the magician would start up through the floor, and carry off our poor little friend before our eyes.

As for Priscilla, she stood droopingly in the midst of us, making no attempt to remove the veil.

"How do you find yourself, my love?" said Zenobia, lifting a corner of the gauze, and peeping beneath it with a mischievous smile. "Ah, the dear little soul! Why, she is really going to faint! Mr. Coverdale, Mr. Coverdale, pray bring a glass of water!"

Her nerves being none of the strongest, Priscilla hardly recovered her equanimity during the rest of the evening. This, to be sure, was a great pity; but, nevertheless, we thought it a very bright idea of Zenobia's to bring her legend to so effective a conclusion.

XIV. ELIOT'S PULPIT

Our Sundays at Blithedale were not ordinarily kept with such rigid observance as might have befitted the descendants of the Pilgrims, whose high enterprise, as we sometimes flattered ourselves, we had taken up, and were carrying it onward and aloft, to a point which they never dreamed of attaining.

On that hallowed day, it is true, we rested from our labors. Our oxen, relieved from their week-day yoke, roamed at large through the pasture; each yoke-fellow, however, keeping close beside his mate, and continuing to acknowledge, from the force of habit and sluggish sympathy, the union which the taskmaster had imposed for his own hard ends. As for us human yoke-fellows, chosen companions of toil, whose hoes had clinked together throughout the week, we wandered off, in various directions, to enjoy our interval of repose. Some, I believe, went devoutly to the village church. Others, it may be, ascended a city or a country pulpit, wearing the clerical robe with so much dignity that you would scarcely have suspected the yeoman's frock to have been flung off only since milking-time. Others took long rambles among the rustic lanes and by-paths, pausing to look at black old farmhouses, with their sloping roofs; and at the modern cottage, so like a plaything that it seemed as if real joy or sorrow could have no scope within; and at the more pretending villa, with its range of wooden columns supporting the needless insolence of a great portico. Some betook themselves into the wide, dusky barn, and lay there for hours together on the odorous hay; while the sunstreaks and the shadows strove together,—these to make the barn solemn, those to make it cheerful,—and both were conquerors; and the swallows twittered a cheery anthem, flashing into sight, or vanishing as they darted to and fro among the golden rules of sunshine. And others went a little way into the woods, and threw themselves on mother earth, pillowing their heads on a heap of moss, the green decay of an old log; and, dropping asleep, the bumblebees and mosquitoes sung and buzzed about their ears, causing the slumberers to twitch and start, without awaking.

With Hollingsworth, Zenobia, Priscilla, and myself, it grew to be a custom to spend the Sabbath afternoon at a certain rock. It was known to us under the name of Eliot's pulpit, from a tradition that the venerable Apostle Eliot had preached there, two centuries gone by, to an Indian auditory. The old pine forest, through which the Apostle's voice was wont to sound, had fallen an immemorial time ago. But the soil, being of the rudest and most broken surface, had apparently never been brought under tillage; other growths, maple and beech and birch, had succeeded to the primeval trees; so that it was still as wild a tract of woodland as the great-great-great-great grandson of one of Eliot's Indians (had any such posterity been in existence) could have desired for the site and shelter of his wigwam. These after-growths, indeed, lose the stately solemnity of the original forest. If left in due neglect, however, they run into an entanglement of softer wildness, among the rustling leaves of which the sun can scatter cheerfulness as it never could among the dark-browed pines.

The rock itself rose some twenty or thirty feet, a shattered granite bowlder, or heap of bowlders, with an irregular outline and many fissures, out of which sprang shrubs, bushes, and even trees; as if the scanty soil within those crevices were sweeter to their roots than any other earth. At the base of the pulpit, the broken bowlders inclined towards each other, so as to form a shallow cave, within which our little party had sometimes found protection from a summer shower. On the threshold, or just across it, grew a tuft of pale columbines, in their season, and violets, sad and shadowy recluses, such as Priscilla was when we first knew her; children of the sun, who had never seen their father, but dwelt among damp mosses, though not akin to them. At the summit, the rock was overshadowed by the canopy of a birch-tree, which served as a sounding-board for the pulpit. Beneath this shade (with my eyes of sense half shut and those of the imagination widely opened) I used to see the holy Apostle of the Indians, with the sunlight flickering down upon him through the leaves, and glorifying his figure as with the half-perceptible glow of a transfiguration.

I the more minutely describe the rock, and this little Sabbath solitude, because Hollingsworth, at our solicitation, often ascended Eliot's pulpit, and not exactly preached, but talked to us, his few disciples, in a strain that rose and fell as naturally as the wind's breath among the leaves of the birch-tree. No other speech of man has ever moved me like some of those discourses. It seemed most pitiful—a positive calamity to the world—that a treasury of golden thoughts should thus be scattered, by the liberal handful, down among us three, when a thousand hearers might have been the richer for them; and Hollingsworth the richer, likewise, by the sympathy of multitudes. After speaking much or little, as might happen, he would descend from his gray pulpit, and generally fling himself at full length on the ground, face downward. Meanwhile, we talked around him on such topics as were suggested by the discourse.

Since her interview with Westervelt, Zenobia's continual inequalities of temper had been rather difficult for her friends to bear. On the first Sunday after that incident, when Hollingsworth had clambered down from Eliot's pulpit, she declaimed with great earnestness and passion, nothing short of anger, on the injustice which the world did to women, and equally to itself, by not allowing them, in freedom and honor, and with the fullest welcome, their natural utterance in public.

"It shall not always be so!" cried she. "If I live another year, I will lift up my own voice in behalf of woman's wider liberty!"

She perhaps saw me smile.

"What matter of ridicule do you find in this, Miles Coverdale?" exclaimed Zenobia, with a flash of anger in her eyes. "That smile, permit me to say, makes me suspicious of a low tone of feeling and shallow thought. It is my belief—yes, and my prophecy, should I die before it happens—that, when my sex shall achieve its rights, there will be ten eloquent women where there is now one eloquent man. Thus far, no woman in the world has ever once spoken out her whole heart and her whole mind. The mistrust and disapproval of the vast bulk of society throttles us, as with two gigantic hands at our throats! We mumble a few weak words, and leave a thousand better ones unsaid. You let us write a little, it is true, on a limited range of subjects. But the pen is not for woman. Her power is too natural and immediate. It is with the living voice alone that she can compel the world to recognize the light of her intellect and the depth of her heart!"

Now,—though I could not well say so to Zenobia,—I had not smiled from any unworthy estimate of woman, or in denial of the claims which she is beginning to put forth. What amused and puzzled me was the fact, that women, however intellectually superior, so seldom disquiet themselves about the rights or wrongs of their sex, unless their own individual affections chance to lie in idleness, or to be ill at ease. They are not natural reformers, but become such by the pressure of exceptional misfortune. I could measure Zenobia's inward trouble by the animosity with which she now took up the general quarrel of woman against man.

"I will give you leave, Zenobia," replied I, "to fling your utmost scorn upon me, if you ever hear me utter a sentiment unfavorable to the widest liberty which woman has yet dreamed of. I would give her all she asks, and add a great deal more, which she will not be the party to demand, but which men, if they were generous and wise, would grant of their own free motion. For instance, I should love dearly—for the next thousand years, at least—to have all government devolve into the hands of women. I hate to be ruled by my own sex; it excites my jealousy, and wounds my pride. It is the iron sway of bodily force which abases us, in our compelled submission. But how sweet the free, generous courtesy with which I would kneel before a woman-ruler!"

"Yes, if she were young and beautiful," said Zenobia, laughing. "But how if she were sixty, and a fright?"

"Ah! it is you that rate womanhood low," said I. "But let me go on. I have never found it possible to suffer a bearded priest so near my heart and conscience as to do me any spiritual good. I blush at the very thought! Oh, in the better order of things, Heaven grant that the ministry of souls may be left in charge of women! The gates of the Blessed City will be thronged with the multitude that enter in, when that day comes! The task belongs to woman. God meant it for her. He has endowed her with the religious sentiment in its utmost depth and purity, refined from that gross, intellectual alloy with which every masculine theologist—save only One, who merely veiled himself in mortal and masculine shape, but was, in truth, divine—has been prone to mingle it. I have always envied the Catholics their faith in that sweet, sacred Virgin Mother, who stands between them and the

Deity, intercepting somewhat of his awful splendor, but permitting his love to stream upon the worshipper more intelligibly to human comprehension through the medium of a woman's tenderness. Have I not said enough, Zenobia?"

"I cannot think that this is true," observed Priscilla, who had been gazing at me with great, disapproving eyes. "And I am sure I do not wish it to be true!"

"Poor child!" exclaimed Zenobia, rather contemptuously. "She is the type of womanhood, such as man has spent centuries in making it. He is never content unless he can degrade himself by stooping towards what he loves. In denying us our rights, he betrays even more blindness to his own interests than profligate disregard of ours!"

"Is this true?" asked Priscilla with simplicity, turning to Hollingsworth. "Is it all true, that Mr. Coverdale and Zenobia have been saying?"

"No, Priscilla!" answered Hollingsworth with his customary bluntness. "They have neither of them spoken one true word yet."

"Do you despise woman?" said Zenobia.

"Ah, Hollingsworth, that would be most ungrateful!"

"Despise her? No!" cried Hollingsworth, lifting his great shaggy head and shaking it at us, while his eyes glowed almost fiercely. "She is the most admirable handiwork of God, in her true place and character. Her place is at man's side. Her office, that of the sympathizer; the unreserved, unquestioning believer; the recognition, withheld in every other manner, but given, in pity, through woman's heart, lest man should utterly lose faith in himself; the echo of God's own voice, pronouncing, 'It is well done!' All the separate action of woman is, and ever has been, and always shall be, false, foolish, vain, destructive of her own best and holiest qualities, void of every good effect, and productive of intolerable mischiefs! Man is a wretch without woman; but woman is a monster—and, thank Heaven, an almost impossible and hitherto imaginary monster—without man as her acknowledged principal! As true as I had once a mother whom I loved, were there any possible prospect of woman's taking the social stand which some of them,—poor, miserable, abortive creatures, who only dream of such things because they have missed woman's peculiar happiness, or because nature made them really neither man nor woman!—if there were a chance of their attaining the end which these petticoated monstrosities have in view, I would call upon my own sex to use its physical force, that unmistakable evidence of sovereignty, to scourge them back within their proper bounds! But it will not be needful. The heart of time womanhood knows where its own sphere is, and never seeks to stray beyond it!"

Never was mortal blessed—if blessing it were—with a glance of such entire acquiescence and unquestioning faith, happy in its completeness, as our little Priscilla unconsciously bestowed on Hollingsworth. She seemed to take the sentiment from his lips into her heart, and brood over it in perfect content. The very woman whom he pictured—the gentle parasite, the soft reflection of a more powerful existence—sat there at his feet.

I looked at Zenobia, however, fully expecting her to resent—as I felt, by the indignant ebullition of my own blood, that she ought this outrageous affirmation of what struck me as the intensity of masculine egotism. It centred everything in itself, and deprived woman of her very soul, her inexpressible and unfathomable all, to make it a mere incident in the great sum of man. Hollingsworth had boldly uttered what he, and millions of despots like him, really felt. Without intending it, he had disclosed the wellspring of all these troubled waters. Now, if ever, it surely behooved Zenobia to be the champion of her sex.

But, to my surprise, and indignation too, she only looked humbled. Some tears sparkled in her eyes, but they were wholly of grief, not anger.

"Well, be it so," was all she said. "I, at least, have deep cause to think you right. Let man be but manly and godlike, and woman is only too ready to become to him what you say!"

I smiled—somewhat bitterly, it is true—in contemplation of my own ill-luck. How little did these two women care for me, who had freely conceded all their claims, and a great deal more, out of the fulness of my heart; while Hollingsworth, by some necromancy of his horrible injustice, seemed to have brought them both to his feet!

"Women almost invariably behave thus," thought I. "What does the fact mean? Is it their nature? Or is it, at last, the result of ages of compelled degradation? And, in either case, will it be possible ever to redeem them?"

An intuition now appeared to possess all the party, that, for this time, at least, there was no more to be said. With one accord, we arose from the ground, and made our way through the tangled undergrowth towards one of those pleasant wood-paths that wound among the overarching trees. Some of the branches hung so low as partly to conceal the figures that went before from those who followed. Priscilla had leaped up more lightly than the rest of us, and ran along in advance, with as much airy activity of spirit as was typified in the motion of a bird, which chanced to be flitting from tree to tree, in the same direction as herself. Never did she seem so happy as that afternoon. She skipt, and could not help it, from very playfulness of heart.

Zenobia and Hollingsworth went next, in close contiguity, but not with arm in arm. Now, just when they had passed the impending bough of a birch-tree, I plainly saw Zenobia take the hand of Hollingsworth in both her own, press it to her bosom, and let it fall again!

The gesture was sudden, and full of passion; the impulse had evidently taken her by surprise; it expressed all! Had Zenobia knelt before him, or flung herself upon his breast, and gasped out, "I love you, Hollingsworth!" I could not have been more certain of what it meant. They then walked onward, as before. But, methought, as the declining sun threw Zenobia's magnified shadow along the path, I beheld it tremulous; and the delicate stem of the flower which she wore in her hair was likewise responsive to her agitation.

Priscilla—through the medium of her eyes, at least could not possibly have been aware of the gesture above described. Yet, at that instant, I saw her droop.

The buoyancy, which just before had been so bird-like, was utterly departed; the life seemed to pass out of her, and even the substance of her figure to grow thin and gray. I almost imagined her a shadow, tiding gradually into the dimness of the wood. Her pace became so slow that Hollingsworth and Zenobia passed by, and I, without hastening my footsteps, overtook her.

"Come, Priscilla," said I, looking her intently in the face, which was very pale and sorrowful, "we must make haste after our friends. Do you feel suddenly ill? A moment ago, you flitted along so lightly that I was comparing you to a bird. Now, on the contrary, it is as if you had a heavy heart, and a very little strength to bear it with. Pray take my arm!"

"No," said Priscilla, "I do not think it would help me. It is my heart, as you say, that makes me heavy; and I know not why. Just now, I felt very happy."

No doubt it was a kind of sacrilege in me to attempt to come within her maidenly mystery; but, as she appeared to be tossed aside by her other friends, or carelessly let fall, like a flower which they had done with, I could not resist the impulse to take just one peep beneath her folded petals.

"Zenobia and yourself are dear friends of late," I remarked. "At first,—that first evening when you came to us,—she did not receive you quite so warmly as might have been wished."

"I remember it," said Priscilla. "No wonder she hesitated to love me, who was then a stranger to her, and a girl of no grace or beauty,—she being herself so beautiful!"

"But she loves you now, of course?" suggested I. "And at this very instant you feel her to be your dearest friend?"

"Why do you ask me that question?" exclaimed Priscilla, as if frightened at the scrutiny into her feelings which I compelled her to make. "It somehow puts strange thoughts into my mind. But I do love Zenobia dearly! If she only loves me half as well, I shall be happy!"

"How is it possible to doubt that, Priscilla?" I rejoined. "But observe how pleasantly and happily Zenobia and Hollingsworth are walking together. I call it a delightful spectacle. It truly rejoices me that Hollingsworth has found so fit and affectionate a friend! So many people in the world mistrust him,—so many disbelieve and ridicule, while hardly any do him justice, or acknowledge him for the wonderful man he is,—that it is really a blessed thing for him to have won the sympathy of such a woman as Zenobia. Any man might be proud of that. Any man, even if he be as great as Hollingsworth, might love so magnificent a woman. How very beautiful Zenobia is! And Hollingsworth knows it, too."

There may have been some petty malice in what I said. Generosity is a very fine thing, at a proper time and within due limits. But it is an insufferable bore to see one man engrossing every thought of all the women, and leaving his friend to shiver in outer seclusion, without even the alternative of solacing himself with what the more fortunate individual has rejected. Yes, it was out of a foolish bitterness of heart that I had spoken.

"Go on before," said Priscilla abruptly, and with true feminine imperiousness, which heretofore I had never seen her exercise. "It pleases me best to loiter along by myself. I do not walk so fast as you."

With her hand she made a little gesture of dismissal. It provoked me; yet, on the whole, was the most bewitching thing that Priscilla had ever done. I obeyed her, and strolled moodily homeward, wondering—as I had wondered a thousand times already—how Hollingsworth meant to dispose of these two hearts, which (plainly to my perception, and, as I could not but now suppose, to his) he had engrossed into his own huge egotism.

There was likewise another subject hardly less fruitful of speculation. In what attitude did Zenobia present herself to Hollingsworth? Was it in that of a free woman, with no mortgage on her affections nor claimant to her hand, but fully at liberty to surrender both, in exchange for the heart and hand which she apparently expected to receive? But was it a vision that I had witnessed in the wood? Was Westervelt a goblin? Were those words of passion and agony, which Zenobia had uttered in my hearing, a mere stage declamation? Were they formed of a material lighter than common air? Or, supposing them to bear sterling weight, was it a perilous and dreadful wrong which she was meditating towards herself and Hollingsworth?

Arriving nearly at the farmhouse, I looked back over the long slope of pasture land, and beheld them standing together, in the light of sunset, just on the spot where, according to the gossip of the Community, they meant to build their cottage. Priscilla, alone and forgotten, was lingering in the shadow of the wood.

XV. A CRISIS

Thus the summer was passing away,—a summer of toil, of interest, of something that was not pleasure, but which went deep into my heart, and there became a rich experience. I found myself looking forward to years, if not to a lifetime, to be spent on the same system. The Community were now beginning to form their permanent plans. One of our purposes was to erect a Phalanstery (as I think we called it, after Fourier; but the phraseology of those days is not very fresh in my remembrance), where the great and general family should have its abiding-place. Individual members, too, who made it a point of religion to preserve the sanctity of an exclusive home, were selecting sites for their cottages, by the wood-side, or on the breezy swells, or in the sheltered nook of some little valley, according as their taste might lean towards snugness or the picturesque. Altogether, by projecting our minds outward, we had imparted a show of novelty to existence, and contemplated it as hopefully as if the soil beneath our feet had not been fathom-deep with the dust of deluded generations, on every one of which, as on ourselves, the world had imposed itself as a hitherto unwedded bride.

Hollingsworth and myself had often discussed these prospects. It was easy to perceive, however, that he spoke with little or no fervor, but either as questioning the fulfilment of our anticipations, or, at any rate, with a quiet consciousness that it was no personal concern of his. Shortly after the scene at Eliot's pulpit, while he and I were repairing an old stone fence, I amused myself with sallying forward into the future time.

"When we come to be old men," I said, "they will call us uncles, or fathers,—Father Hollingsworth and Uncle Coverdale,—and we will look back cheerfully to these early days, and make a romantic story for the young People (and if a little more romantic than truth may warrant, it will be no harm) out of our severe trials and hardships. In a century or two, we shall, every one of us, be mythical personages, or exceedingly picturesque and poetical ones, at all events. They will have a great public hall, in which your portrait, and mine, and twenty other faces that are living now, shall be hung up; and as for me, I will be painted in my shirtsleeves, and with the sleeves rolled up, to show my muscular development. What stories will be rife among them about our mighty strength!" continued I, lifting a big stone and putting it into its place, "though our posterity will really be far stronger than ourselves, after several generations of a simple, natural, and active life.

What legends of Zenobia's beauty, and Priscilla's slender and shadowy grace, and those mysterious qualities which make her seem diaphanous with spiritual light! In due course of ages, we must all figure heroically in an epic poem; and we will ourselves—at least, I will—bend unseen over the future poet, and lend him inspiration while he writes it."

"You seem," said Hollingsworth, "to be trying how much nonsense you can pour out in a breath."

"I wish you would see fit to comprehend," retorted I, "that the profoundest wisdom must be mingled with nine tenths of nonsense, else it is not worth the breath that utters it. But I do long for the cottages to be built, that the creeping plants may begin to run over them, and the moss to gather on the walls, and the trees—which we will set out—to cover them with a breadth of shadow. This spick-and-span novelty does not quite suit my taste. It is time, too, for children to be born among us. The first-born child is still to come. And I shall never feel as if this were a real, practical, as well as poetical system of human life, until somebody has sanctified it by death."

"A pretty occasion for martyrdom, truly!" said Hollingsworth.

"As good as any other," I replied. "I wonder, Hollingsworth, who, of all these strong men, and fair women and maidens, is doomed the first to die. Would it not be well, even before we have absolute need of it, to fix upon a spot for a cemetery? Let us choose the rudest, roughest, most uncultivable spot, for Death's garden ground; and Death shall teach us to beautify it, grave by grave. By our sweet, calm way of dying, and the airy elegance out of which we will shape our funeral rites, and the cheerful allegories which we will model into tombstones, the final scene shall lose its terrors; so that hereafter it may be happiness to live, and bliss to die. None of us must die young. Yet, should Providence ordain it so, the event shall not be sorrowful, but affect us with a tender, delicious, only half-melancholy, and almost smiling pathos!"

"That is to say," muttered Hollingsworth, "you will die like a heathen, as you certainly live like one. But, listen to me, Coverdale. Your fantastic anticipations make me discern all the more forcibly what a wretched, unsubstantial scheme is this, on which we have wasted a precious summer of our lives. Do you seriously imagine that any such realities as you, and many others here, have dreamed of, will ever be brought to pass?"

"Certainly I do," said I. "Of course, when the reality comes, it will wear the every-day, commonplace, dusty, and rather homely garb that reality always does put on. But, setting aside the ideal charm, I hold that our highest anticipations have a solid footing on common sense."

"You only half believe what you say," rejoined Hollingsworth; "and as for me, I neither have faith in your dream, nor would care the value of this pebble for its realization, were that possible. And what more do you want of it? It has given you a theme for poetry. Let that content you. But now I ask you to be, at last, a man of sobriety and earnestness, and aid me in an enterprise which is worth all our strength, and the strength of a thousand mightier than we."

There can be no need of giving in detail the conversation that ensued. It is enough to say that Hollingsworth once more brought forward his rigid and unconquerable idea,—a scheme for the reformation of the wicked by methods moral, intellectual, and industrial, by the sympathy of pure, humble, and yet exalted minds, and by opening to his pupils the possibility of a worthier life than that which had become their fate. It appeared, unless he overestimated his own means, that Hollingsworth held it at his choice (and he did so choose) to obtain possession of the very ground on which we had planted our Community, and which had not yet been made irrevocably ours, by purchase. It was just the foundation that he desired. Our beginnings might readily be adapted to his great end. The arrangements already completed would work quietly into his system. So plausible looked his theory, and, more than that, so practical,—such an air of reasonableness had he, by patient thought, thrown over it,—each segment of it was contrived to dovetail into all the rest with such a complicated applicability, and so ready was he with a response for every objection, that, really, so far as logic and argument went, he had the matter all his own way.

"But," said I, "whence can you, having no means of your own, derive the enormous capital which is essential to this experiment? State Street, I imagine, would not draw its purser strings very liberally in aid of such a speculation."

"I have the funds—as much, at least, as is needed for a commencement—at command," he answered. "They can be produced within a month, if necessary."

My thoughts reverted to Zenobia. It could only be her wealth which Hollingsworth was appropriating so lavishly. And on what conditions was it to be had? Did she fling it into the scheme with the uncalculating generosity that characterizes a woman when it is her impulse to be generous at all? And did she fling herself along with it? But Hollingsworth did not volunteer an explanation.

"And have you no regrets," I inquired, "in overthrowing this fair system of our new life, which has been planned so deeply, and is now beginning to flourish so hopefully around us? How beautiful it is, and, so far as we can yet see, how practicable! The ages have waited for us, and here we are, the very first that have essayed to carry on our mortal existence in love and mutual help! Hollingsworth, I would be loath to take the ruin of this enterprise upon my conscience."

"Then let it rest wholly upon mine!" he answered, knitting his black brows. "I see through the system. It is full of defects,—irremediable and damning ones!—from first to last, there is nothing else! I grasp it in my hand, and find no substance whatever. There is not human nature in it."

"Why are you so secret in your operations?" I asked. "God forbid that I should accuse you of intentional wrong; but the besetting sin of a philanthropist, it appears to me, is apt to be a moral obliquity. His sense of honor ceases to be the sense of other honorable men. At some point of his course—I know not exactly when or where—he is tempted to palter with the right, and can scarcely forbear persuading himself that the importance of his public ends renders it allowable to throw aside his private conscience. Oh, my dear friend, beware this error! If you meditate the overthrow of this establishment, call together our companions, state your design, support it with all your eloquence, but allow them an opportunity of defending themselves."

"It does not suit me," said Hollingsworth. "Nor is it my duty to do so."

"I think it is," replied I.

Hollingsworth frowned; not in passion, but, like fate, inexorably.

"I will not argue the point," said he. "What I desire to know of you is,—and you can tell me in one word,—whether I am to look for your cooperation in this great scheme of good? Take it up with me! Be my brother in it! It offers you (what you have told me, over and over again, that you most need) a purpose in life, worthy of the extremest self-devotion,—worthy of martyrdom, should God so order it! In this view, I present it to you. You can greatly benefit mankind. Your peculiar faculties, as I shall direct them, are capable of being so wrought into this enterprise that not one of them need lie idle. Strike hands with me, and from this moment you shall never again feel the languor and vague wretchedness of an indolent or half-occupied man. There may be no more aimless beauty in your life; but, in its stead, there shall be strength, courage, immitigable will,—everything that a manly and generous nature should desire! We shall succeed! We shall have done our best for this miserable world; and happiness (which never comes but incidentally) will come to us unawares."

It seemed his intention to say no more. But, after he had quite broken off, his deep eyes filled with tears, and he held out both his hands to me.

"Coverdale," he murmured, "there is not the man in this wide world whom I can love as I could you. Do not forsake me!"

As I look back upon this scene, through the coldness and dimness of so many years, there is still a sensation as if Hollingsworth had caught hold of my heart, and were pulling it towards him with an almost irresistible force. It is a mystery to me how I withstood it. But, in truth, I saw in his scheme of philanthropy nothing but what was odious. A loathsomeness that was to be forever in my daily work! A great black ugliness of sin, which he proposed to collect out of a thousand human hearts, and that we should spend our lives in an experiment of transmuting it into virtue! Had I but touched his extended hand, Hollingsworth's magnetism would perhaps have penetrated me with his own conception of all these matters. But I stood aloof. I fortified myself with doubts whether his strength of purpose had not been too gigantic for his integrity, impelling him to trample on considerations that should have been paramount to every other.

"Is Zenobia to take a part in your enterprise?" I asked.

"She is," said Hollingsworth.

"She!—the beautiful!—the gorgeous!" I exclaimed. "And how have you prevailed with such a woman to work in this squalid element?"

"Through no base methods, as you seem to suspect," he answered; "but by addressing whatever is best and noblest in her."

Hollingsworth was looking on the ground. But, as he often did so,—generally, indeed, in his habitual moods of thought,—I could not judge whether it was from any special unwillingness now to meet my eyes. What it was that dictated my next question, I cannot precisely say. Nevertheless, it rose so inevitably into my mouth, and, as it were, asked itself so involuntarily, that there must needs have been an aptness in it.

"What is to become of Priscilla?"

Hollingsworth looked at me fiercely, and with glowing eyes. He could not have shown any other kind of expression than that, had he meant to strike me with a sword.

"Why do you bring in the names of these women?" said he, after a moment of pregnant silence. "What have they to do with the proposal which I make you? I must have your answer! Will you devote yourself, and sacrifice all to this great end, and be my friend of friends forever?"

"In Heaven's name, Hollingsworth," cried I, getting angry, and glad to be angry, because so only was it possible to oppose his tremendous concentrativeness and indomitable will, "cannot you conceive that a man may wish well to the world, and struggle for its good, on some other plan than precisely that which you have laid down? And will you cast off a friend for no unworthiness, but merely because he stands upon his right as an individual being, and looks at matters through his own optics, instead of yours?"

"Be with me," said Hollingsworth, "or be against me! There is no third choice for you."

"Take this, then, as my decision," I answered. "I doubt the wisdom of your scheme. Furthermore, I greatly fear that the methods by which you allow yourself to pursue it are such as cannot stand the scrutiny of an unbiassed conscience."

"And you will not join me?"

"No!"

I never said the word—and certainly can never have it to say hereafter—that cost me a thousandth part so hard an effort as did that one syllable. The heart-pang was not merely figurative, but an absolute torture of the breast. I was gazing steadfastly at Hollingsworth. It seemed to me that it struck him, too, like a bullet. A ghastly paleness—always so terrific on a swarthy face—overspread his features. There was a convulsive movement of his throat, as if he were forcing down some words that struggled and fought for utterance. Whether words of anger, or words of grief, I cannot tell; although many and many a time I have vainly tormented myself with conjecturing which of the two they were. One other appeal to my friendship,—such as once, already, Hollingsworth had made,—taking me in the revulsion that followed a strenuous exercise of opposing will, would completely have subdued me. But he left the matter there. "Well!" said he.

And that was all! I should have been thankful for one word more, even had it shot me through the heart, as mine did him. But he did not speak it; and, after a few moments, with one accord, we set to work again, repairing the stone fence. Hollingsworth, I observed, wrought like a Titan; and, for my own part, I lifted stones which at this day—or, in a calmer mood, at that one—I should no more have thought it possible to stir than to carry off the gates of Gaza on my back.

XVI. LEAVE-TAKINGS

A few days after the tragic passage-at-arms between Hollingsworth and me, I appeared at the dinner-table actually dressed in a coat, instead of my customary blouse; with a satin cravat, too, a white vest, and several other things that made me seem strange and outlandish to myself. As for my companions, this unwonted spectacle caused a great stir upon the wooden benches that bordered either side of our homely board.

"What's in the wind now, Miles?" asked one of them. "Are you deserting us?"

"Yes, for a week or two," said I. "It strikes me that my health demands a little relaxation of labor, and a short visit to the seaside, during the dog-days."

"You look like it!" grumbled Silas Foster, not greatly pleased with the idea of losing an efficient laborer before the stress of the season was well over. "Now, here's a pretty fellow! His shoulders have broadened a matter of six inches since he came among us; he can do his day's work, if he likes, with any man or ox on the farm; and yet he talks about going to the seashore for his health! Well, well, old woman," added he to his wife, "let me have a plateful of that pork and cabbage! I begin to feel in a very weakly way. When the others have had their turn, you and I will take a jaunt to Newport or Saratoga!"

"Well, but, Mr. Foster," said I, "you must allow me to take a little breath."

"Breath!" retorted the old yeoman. "Your lungs have the play of a pair of blacksmith's bellows already. What on earth do you want more? But go along! I understand the business. We shall never see your face here again. Here ends the reformation of the world, so far as Miles Coverdale has a hand in it!"

"By no means," I replied. "I am resolute to die in the last ditch, for the good of the cause."

"Die in a ditch!" muttered gruff Silas, with genuine Yankee intolerance of any intermission of toil, except on Sunday, the Fourth of July, the autumnal cattle-show, Thanksgiving, or the annual Fast,—"die in a ditch! I believe, in my conscience, you would, if there were no steadier means than your own labor to keep you out of it!"

The truth was, that an intolerable discontent and irksomeness had come over me. Blithedale was no longer what it had been. Everything was suddenly faded. The sunburnt and arid aspect of our woods and pastures, beneath the August sky, did but imperfectly symbolize the lack of dew and moisture, that, since yesterday, as it were, had blighted my fields of thought, and penetrated to the innermost and shadiest of my contemplative recesses. The change will be recognized by many, who, after a period of happiness, have endeavored to go on with the same kind of life, in the same scene, in spite of the alteration or withdrawal of some principal circumstance. They discover (what heretofore, perhaps, they had not known) that it was this which gave the bright color and vivid reality to the whole affair.

I stood on other terms than before, not only with Hollingsworth, but with Zenobia 'and Priscilla. As regarded the two latter, it was that dreamlike and miserable sort of change that denies you the privilege to complain, because you can assert no positive injury, nor lay your finger on anything tangible. It is a matter which you do not see, but feel, and which, when you try to analyze it, seems to lose its very existence, and resolve itself into a sickly humor of your own. Your understanding, possibly, may put faith in this denial. But your heart will not so easily rest satisfied. It incessantly remonstrates, though, most of the time, in a bass-note, which you do not separately distinguish; but, now and then, with a sharp cry, importunate to be heard, and resolute to claim belief. "Things are not as they were!" it keeps saying. "You shall not impose on me! I will never be quiet! I will throb painfully! I will be heavy, and desolate, and shiver with cold! For I, your deep heart, know when to be miserable, as once I knew when to be happy! All is changed for us! You are beloved no more!" And were my life to be spent over again, I would invariably lend my ear to this Cassandra of the inward depths, however clamorous the music and the merriment of a more superficial region.

My outbreak with Hollingsworth, though never definitely known to our associates, had really an effect upon the moral atmosphere of the Community. It was incidental to the closeness of relationship into which we had brought ourselves, that an unfriendly state of feeling could not occur between any two members without the whole society being more or less commoted and made uncomfortable thereby. This species of nervous sympathy (though a pretty characteristic enough, sentimentally considered, and apparently betokening an actual bond of love among us) was yet found rather inconvenient in its practical operation, mortal tempers being so infirm and variable as they are. If one of us happened to give his neighbor a box on the ear, the tingle was immediately felt on the same side of everybody's head. Thus, even on the supposition that we were far less quarrelsome than the rest of the world, a great deal of time was necessarily wasted in rubbing our ears.

Musing on all these matters, I felt an inexpressible longing for at least a temporary novelty. I thought of going across the Rocky Mountains, or to Europe, or up the Nile; of offering myself a volunteer on the Exploring Expedition; of taking a ramble of years, no matter in what direction, and coming back on the other side of the world. Then, should the colonists of Blithedale have established their enterprise on a permanent basis, I might fling aside my pilgrim staff and dusty shoon, and rest as peacefully here as elsewhere. Or, in case Hollingsworth should occupy the ground with his School of Reform, as he now purposed, I might plead earthly guilt enough, by that time, to give me what I was inclined to think the only trustworthy hold on his affections. Meanwhile, before deciding on any ultimate plan, I determined to remove myself to a little distance, and take an exterior view of what we had all been about.

In truth, it was dizzy work, amid such fermentation of opinions as was going on in the general brain of the Community. It was a kind of Bedlam, for the time being, although out of the very thoughts that were wildest and most destructive might grow a wisdom, holy, calm, and pure, and that should incarnate itself with the substance of a noble and happy life. But, as matters now were, I felt myself (and, having a decided tendency towards the actual, I never liked to feel it) getting quite out of my reckoning, with regard to the existing state of the world. I was beginning to lose the sense of what kind of a world it was, among innumerable schemes of what it might or ought to be. It was impossible, situated as we were, not to imbibe the idea that everything in nature and human existence was fluid, or fast becoming so; that the crust of the earth in many places was broken, and its whole surface portentously upheaving; that it was a day of crisis, and that we ourselves were in the critical vortex. Our great globe floated in the atmosphere of infinite space like an unsubstantial bubble. No sagacious man will long retain his sagacity, if he live exclusively among reformers and progressive people, without periodically returning into the settled system of things, to correct himself by a new observation from that old standpoint.

It was now time for me, therefore, to go and hold a little talk with the conservatives, the writers of "The North American Review," the merchants, the politicians, the Cambridge men, and all those respectable old blockheads who still, in this intangibility and mistiness of affairs, kept a death-grip on one or two ideas which had not come into vogue since yesterday morning.

The brethren took leave of me with cordial kindness; and as for the sisterhood, I had serious thoughts of kissing them all round, but forbore to do so, because, in all such general salutations, the penance is fully equal to the pleasure. So I kissed none of them; and nobody, to say the truth, seemed to expect it.

"Do you wish me," I said to Zenobia, "to announce in town, and at the watering-places, your purpose to deliver a course of lectures on the rights of women?"

"Women possess no rights," said Zenobia, with a half-melancholy smile; "or, at all events, only little girls and grandmothers would have the force to exercise them."

She gave me her hand freely and kindly, and looked at me, I thought, with a pitying expression in her eyes; nor was there any settled light of joy in them on her own behalf, but a troubled and passionate flame, flickering and fitful.

"I regret, on the whole, that you are leaving us," she said; "and all the more, since I feel that this phase of our life is finished, and can never be lived over again. Do you know, Mr. Coverdale, that I have been several times on the point of making you my confidant, for lack of a better and wiser one? But you are too young to be my father confessor; and you would not thank me for treating you like one of those good little handmaidens who share the bosom secrets of a tragedy-queen."

"I would, at least, be loyal and faithful," answered I; "and would counsel you with an honest purpose, if not wisely."

"Yes," said Zenobia, "you would be only too wise, too honest. Honesty and wisdom are such a delightful pastime, at another person's expense!"

"Ah, Zenobia," I exclaimed, "if you would but let me speak!"

"By no means," she replied, "especially when you have just resumed the whole series of social conventionalisms, together with that strait-bodied coat. I would as lief open my heart to a lawyer or a clergyman! No, no, Mr. Coverdale; if I choose a counsellor, in the present aspect of my affairs, it must be either an angel or a madman; and I rather apprehend that the latter would be likeliest of the two to speak the fitting word. It needs a wild steersman when we voyage through chaos! The anchor is up,—farewell!"

Priscilla, as soon as dinner was over, had betaken herself into a corner, and set to work on a little purse. As I approached her, she let her eyes rest on me with a calm, serious look; for, with all her delicacy of nerves, there was a singular self-possession in Priscilla, and her sensibilities seemed to lie sheltered from ordinary commotion, like the water in a deep well.

"Will you give me that purse, Priscilla," said I, "as a parting keepsake?"

"Yes," she answered, "if you will wait till it is finished."

"I must not wait, even for that," I replied. "Shall I find you here, on my return?"

"I never wish to go away," said she.

"I have sometimes thought," observed I, smiling, "that you, Priscilla, are a little prophetess, or, at least, that you have spiritual intimations respecting matters which are dark to us grosser people. If that be the case, I should like to ask you what is about to happen; for I am tormented with a strong foreboding that, were I to return even so soon as to-morrow morning, I should find everything changed. Have you any impressions of this nature?"

"Ah, no," said Priscilla, looking at me apprehensively. "If any such misfortune is coming, the shadow has not reached me yet. Heaven forbid! I should be glad if there might never be any change, but one summer follow another, and all just like this."

"No summer ever came back, and no two summers ever were alike," said I, with a degree of Orphic wisdom that astonished myself. "Times change, and people change; and if our hearts do not change as readily, so much the worse for us. Good-by, Priscilla!"

I gave her hand a pressure, which, I think, she neither resisted nor returned. Priscilla's heart was deep, but of small compass; it had room but for a very few dearest ones, among whom she never reckoned me.

On the doorstep I met Hollingsworth. I had a momentary impulse to hold out my hand, or at least to give a parting nod, but resisted both. When a real and strong affection has come to an end, it is not well to mock the sacred past with any show of those commonplace civilities that belong to ordinary intercourse. Being dead henceforth to him, and he to me, there could be no propriety in our chilling one another with the touch of two corpse-like hands, or playing at looks of courtesy with eyes that were impenetrable beneath the glaze and the film. We passed, therefore, as if mutually invisible.

I can nowise explain what sort of whim, prank, or perversity it was, that, after all these leave-takings, induced me to go to the pigsty, and take leave of the swine! There they lay, buried as deeply among the straw as they could burrow, four huge black grunters, the very symbols of slothful ease and sensual comfort. They were asleep, drawing short and heavy breaths, which heaved their big sides up and down. Unclosing their eyes, however, at my approach, they looked dimly forth at the outer world, and simultaneously uttered a gentle grunt; not putting themselves to the trouble of an additional breath for that particular purpose, but grunting with their ordinary inhalation. They were involved, and almost stifled and buried alive, in their own corporeal substance. The very unreadiness and oppression wherewith these greasy citizens gained breath enough to keep their life-machinery in sluggish movement appeared to make them only the more sensible of the ponderous and fat satisfaction of their existence. Peeping at me an instant out of their small, red, hardly perceptible eyes, they dropt asleep again; yet not so far asleep but that their unctuous bliss was still present to them, betwixt dream and reality.

"You must come back in season to eat part of a spare-rib," said Silas Foster, giving my hand a mighty squeeze. "I shall have these fat fellows hanging up by the heels, heads downward, pretty soon, I tell you!"

"O cruel Silas, what a horrible idea!" cried I. "All the rest of us, men, women, and livestock, save only these four porkers, are bedevilled with one grief or another; they alone are happy,—and you mean to cut their throats and eat them! It would be more for the general comfort to let them eat us; and bitter and sour morsels we should be!"

XVII. THE HOTEL

Arriving in town (where my bachelor-rooms, long before this time, had received some other occupant), I established myself, for a day or two, in a certain, respectable hotel. It was situated somewhat aloof from my former track in life; my present mood inclining me to avoid most of my old companions, from whom I was now sundered by other interests, and who would have been likely enough to amuse themselves at the expense of the amateur workingman. The hotel-keeper put me into a back room of the third story of his spacious establishment. The day was lowering, with occasional gusts of rain, and an ugly tempered east wind, which seemed to come right off the chill and melancholy sea, hardly mitigated by sweeping over the roofs, and amalgamating itself with the dusky element of city smoke. All the effeminacy of past days had returned upon me at once. Summer as it still was, I ordered a coal fire in the rusty grate, and was glad to find myself growing a little too warm with an artificial temperature.

My sensations were those of a traveller, long sojourning in remote regions, and at length sitting down again amid customs once familiar. There was a newness and an oldness oddly combining themselves into one impression. It made me acutely sensible how strange a piece of mosaic-work had lately been wrought into my life. True, if you look at it in one way, it had been only a summer in the country. But, considered in a profounder relation, it was part of another age, a different state of society, a segment of an existence peculiar in its aims and methods, a leaf of some mysterious volume interpolated into the current history which time was writing off. At one moment, the very circumstances now surrounding me—my coal fire and the dingy room in the bustling hotel—appeared far off and intangible; the next instant Blithedale looked vague, as if it were at a distance both in time and space, and so shadowy that a question might be raised whether the whole affair had been anything more than the thoughts of a speculative man. I had never before experienced a mood that so robbed the actual world of its solidity. It nevertheless involved a charm, on which—a devoted epicure of my own emotions—I resolved to pause, and enjoy the moral sillabub until quite dissolved away.

Whatever had been my taste for solitude and natural scenery, yet the thick, foggy, stifled element of cities, the entangled life of many men together, sordid as it was, and empty of the beautiful, took quite as strenuous a hold upon my mind.

I felt as if there could never be enough of it. Each characteristic sound was too suggestive to be passed over unnoticed. Beneath and around me, I heard the stir of the hotel; the loud voices of guests, landlord, or bar-keeper; steps echoing on the staircase; the ringing of a bell, announcing arrivals or departures; the porter lumbering past my door with baggage, which he thumped down upon the floors of neighboring chambers; the lighter feet of chambermaids scudding along the passages;—it is ridiculous to think what an interest they had for me! From the street came the tumult of the pavements, pervading the whole house with a continual uproar, so broad and deep that only an unaccustomed ear would dwell upon it. A company of the city soldiery, with a full military band, marched in front of the hotel, invisible to me, but stirringly audible both by its foot-tramp and the clangor of its instruments. Once or twice all the city bells jangled together, announcing a fire, which brought out the engine-men and their machines, like an army with its artillery rushing to battle. Hour by hour the clocks in many steeples responded one to another.

In some public hall, not a great way off, there seemed to be an exhibition of a mechanical diorama; for three times during the day occurred a repetition of obstreperous music, winding up with the rattle of imitative cannon and musketry, and a huge final explosion. Then ensued the applause of the spectators, with clap of hands and thump of sticks, and the energetic pounding of their heels. All this was just as valuable, in its way, as the sighing of the breeze among the birch-trees that overshadowed Eliot's pulpit.

Yet I felt a hesitation about plunging into this muddy tide of human activity and pastime. It suited me better, for the present, to linger on the brink, or hover in the air above it. So I spent the first day, and the greater part of the second, in the laziest manner possible, in a rocking-chair, inhaling the fragrance of a series of cigars, with my legs and slippered feet horizontally disposed, and in my hand a novel purchased of a railroad bibliopolist. The gradual waste of my cigar accomplished itself with an easy and gentle expenditure of breath. My book was of the dullest, yet had a sort of sluggish flow, like that of a stream in which your boat is as often aground as afloat. Had there been a more impetuous rush, a more absorbing passion of the narrative, I should the sooner have struggled out of its uneasy current, and have given myself up to the swell and subsidence of my thoughts. But, as it was, the torpid life of the book served as an unobtrusive accompaniment to the life within me and about me. At intervals, however, when its effect grew a little too soporific,—not for my patience, but for the possibility of keeping my eyes open, I bestirred myself, started from the rocking-chair, and looked out of the window.

A gray sky; the weathercock of a steeple that rose beyond the opposite range of buildings, pointing from the eastward; a sprinkle of small, spiteful-looking raindrops on the window-pane. In that ebb-tide of my energies, had I thought of venturing abroad, these tokens would have checked the abortive purpose.

After several such visits to the window, I found myself getting pretty well acquainted with that little portion of the backside of the universe which it presented to my view. Over against the hotel and its adjacent houses, at the distance of forty or fifty yards, was the rear of a range of buildings which appeared to be spacious, modern, and calculated for fashionable residences. The interval between was apportioned into grass-plots, and here and there an apology for a garden, pertaining severally to these dwellings. There were apple-trees, and pear and peach trees, too, the fruit on which looked singularly large, luxuriant, and abundant, as well it might, in a situation so warm and sheltered, and where the soil had doubtless been enriched to a more than natural fertility. In two or three places grapevines clambered upon trellises, and bore clusters already purple, and promising the richness of Malta or Madeira in their ripened juice. The blighting winds of our rigid climate could not molest these trees and vines; the sunshine, though descending late into this area, and too early intercepted by the height of the surrounding houses, yet lay tropically there, even when less than temperate in every other region. Dreary as was the day, the scene was illuminated by not a few sparrows and other birds, which spread their wings, and flitted and fluttered, and alighted now here, now there, and busily scratched their food out of the wormy earth. Most of these winged people seemed to have their domicile in a robust and healthy buttonwood-tree. It aspired upward, high above the roofs of the houses, and spread a dense head of foliage half across the area.

There was a cat—as there invariably is in such places—who evidently thought herself entitled to the privileges of forest life in this close heart of city conventionalisms. I watched her creeping along the low, flat roofs of the offices, descending a flight of wooden steps, gliding among the grass, and besieging the buttonwood-tree, with murderous purpose against its feathered citizens. But, after all, they were birds of city breeding, and doubtless knew how to guard themselves against the peculiar perils of their position.

Bewitching to my fancy are all those nooks and crannies where Nature, like a stray partridge, hides her head among the long-established haunts of men! It is likewise to be remarked, as a general rule, that there is far more of the picturesque, more truth to native and characteristic tendencies, and vastly greater suggestiveness in the back view of a residence, whether in town or country, than in its front. The latter is always artificial; it is meant for the world's eye, and is therefore a veil and a concealment. Realities keep in the rear, and put forward an advance guard of show and humbug. The posterior aspect of any old farmhouse, behind which a railroad has unexpectedly been opened, is so different from that looking upon the immemorial highway, that the spectator gets new ideas of rural life and individuality in the puff or two of steam-breath which shoots him past the premises. In a city, the distinction between what is offered to the public and what is kept for the family is certainly not less striking.

But, to return to my window at the back of the hotel. Together with a due contemplation of the fruit-trees, the grapevines, the buttonwood-tree, the cat, the birds, and many other particulars, I failed not to study the row of fashionable dwellings to which all these appertained. Here, it must be confessed, there was a general sameness. From the upper story to the first floor, they were so much alike, that I could only conceive of the inhabitants as cut out on one identical pattern, like little wooden toy-people of German manufacture. One long, united roof, with its thousands of slates glittering in the rain, extended over the whole. After the distinctness of separate characters to which I had recently been accustomed, it perplexed and annoyed me not to be able to resolve this combination of human interests into well-defined elements. It seemed hardly worth while for more than one of those families to be in existence, since they all had the same glimpse of the sky, all looked into the same area, all received just their equal share of sunshine through the front windows, and all listened to precisely the same noises of the street on which they boarded. Men are so much alike in their nature, that they grow intolerable unless varied by their circumstances.

Just about this time a waiter entered my room. The truth was, I had rung the bell and ordered a sherry-cobbler.

"Can you tell me," I inquired, "what families reside in any of those houses opposite?"

"The one right opposite is a rather stylish boarding-house," said the waiter. "Two of the gentlemen boarders keep horses at the stable of our establishment. They do things in very good style, sir, the people that live there."

I might have found out nearly as much for myself, on examining the house a little more closely, in one of the upper chambers I saw a young man in a dressing-gown, standing before the glass and brushing his hair for a quarter of an hour together. He then spent an equal space of time in the elaborate arrangement of his cravat, and finally made his appearance in a dress-coat, which I suspected to be newly come from the tailor's, and now first put on for a dinner-party. At a window of the next story below, two children, prettily dressed, were looking out. By and by a middle-aged gentleman came softly behind them, kissed the little girl, and playfully pulled the little boy's ear. It was a papa, no doubt, just come in from his counting-room or office; and anon appeared mamma, stealing as softly behind papa as he had stolen behind the children, and laying her hand on his shoulder to surprise him. Then followed a kiss between papa and mamma; but a noiseless one, for the children did not turn their heads.

"I bless God for these good folks!" thought I to myself. "I have not seen a prettier bit of nature, in all my summer in the country, than they have shown me here, in a rather stylish boarding-house. I will pay them a little more attention by and by."

On the first floor, an iron balustrade ran along in front of the tall and spacious windows, evidently belonging to a back drawing-room; and far into the interior, through the arch of the sliding-doors, I could discern a gleam from the windows of the front apartment. There were no signs of present occupancy in this suite of rooms; the curtains being enveloped in a protective covering, which allowed but a small portion of their crimson material to be seen. But two housemaids were industriously at work; so that there was good prospect that the boarding-house might not long suffer from the absence of its most expensive and profitable guests. Meanwhile, until they should appear, I cast my eyes downward to the lower regions. There, in the dusk that so early settles into such places, I saw the red glow of the kitchen range. The hot cook, or one of her subordinates, with a ladle in her hand, came to draw a cool breath at the back door. As soon as she disappeared, an Irish man-servant, in a white jacket, crept slyly forth, and threw away the fragments of a china dish, which, unquestionably, he had just broken. Soon afterwards, a lady, showily dressed, with a curling front of what must have been false hair, and reddish-brown, I suppose, in hue,—though my remoteness allowed me only to guess at such particulars,—this respectable mistress of the boarding-house made a momentary transit across the kitchen window, and appeared no more. It was her final, comprehensive glance, in order to make sure that soup, fish, and flesh were in a proper state of readiness, before the serving up of dinner.

There was nothing else worth noticing about the house, unless it be that on the peak of one of the dormer windows which opened out of the roof sat a dove, looking very dreary and forlorn; insomuch that I wondered why she chose to sit there, in the chilly rain, while her kindred were doubtless nestling in a warm and comfortable dove-cote. All at once this dove spread her wings, and, launching herself in the air, came flying so straight across the intervening space, that I fully expected her to alight directly on my window-sill. In the latter part of her course, however, she swerved aside, flew upward, and vanished, as did, likewise, the slight, fantastic pathos with which I had invested her.

XVIII. THE BOARDING-HOUSE

The next day, as soon as I thought of looking again towards the opposite house, there sat the dove again, on the peak of the same dormer window! It was by no means an early hour, for the preceding evening I had ultimately mustered enterprise enough to visit the theatre, had gone late to bed, and slept beyond all limit, in my remoteness from Silas Foster's awakening horn. Dreams had tormented me throughout the night. The train of thoughts which, for months past, had worn a track through my mind, and to escape which was one of my chief objects in leaving Blithedale, kept treading remorselessly to and fro in their old footsteps, while slumber left me impotent to regulate them. It was not till I had quitted my three friends that they first began to encroach upon my dreams. In those of the last night, Hollingsworth and Zenobia, standing on either side of my bed, had bent across it to exchange a kiss of passion. Priscilla, beholding this,—for she seemed to be peeping in at the chamber window,—had melted gradually away, and left only the sadness of her expression in my heart. There it still lingered, after I awoke; one of those unreasonable sadnesses that you know not how to deal with, because it involves nothing for common-sense to clutch.

It was a gray and dripping forenoon; gloomy enough in town, and still gloomier in the haunts to which my recollections persisted in transporting me. For, in spite of my efforts to think of something else, I thought how the gusty rain was drifting over the slopes and valleys of our farm; how wet must be the foliage that overshadowed the pulpit rock; how cheerless, in such a day, my hermitage—the tree-solitude of my owl-like humors—in the vine-encircled heart of the tall pine! It was a phase of homesickness. I had wrenched myself too suddenly out of an accustomed sphere. There was no choice, now, but to bear the pang of whatever heartstrings were snapt asunder, and that illusive torment (like the ache of a limb long ago cut off) by which a past mode of life prolongs itself into the succeeding one. I was full of idle and shapeless regrets. The thought impressed itself upon me that I had left duties unperformed. With the power, perhaps, to act in the place of destiny and avert misfortune from my friends, I had resigned them to their fate. That cold tendency, between instinct and intellect, which made me pry with a speculative interest into people's passions and impulses, appeared to have gone far towards unhumanizing my heart.

But a man cannot always decide for himself whether his own heart is cold or warm. It now impresses me that, if I erred at all in regard to Hollingsworth, Zenobia, and Priscilla, it was through too much sympathy, rather than too little.

To escape the irksomeness of these meditations, I resumed my post at the window. At first sight, there was nothing new to be noticed. The general aspect of affairs was the same as yesterday, except that the more decided inclemency of today had driven the sparrows to shelter, and kept the cat within doors; whence, however, she soon emerged, pursued by the cook, and with what looked like the better half of a roast chicken in her mouth. The young man in the dress-coat was invisible; the two children, in the story below, seemed to be romping about the room, under the superintendence of a nursery-maid. The damask curtains of the drawing-room, on the first floor, were now fully displayed, festooned gracefully from top to bottom of the windows, which extended from the ceiling to the carpet. A narrower window, at the left of the drawing-room, gave light to what was probably a small boudoir, within which I caught the faintest imaginable glimpse of a girl's figure, in airy drapery. Her arm was in regular movement, as if she were busy with her German worsted, or some other such pretty and unprofitable handiwork.

While intent upon making out this girlish shape, I became sensible that a figure had appeared at one of the windows of the drawing-room. There was a presentiment in my mind; or perhaps my first glance, imperfect and sidelong as it was, had sufficed to convey subtile information of the truth. At any rate, it was with no positive surprise, but as if I had all along expected the incident, that, directing my eyes thitherward, I beheld—like a full-length picture, in the space between the heavy festoons of the window curtains—no other than Zenobia! At the same instant, my thoughts made sure of the identity of the figure in the boudoir. It could only be Priscilla.

Zenobia was attired, not in the almost rustic costume which she had heretofore worn, but in a fashionable morning-dress. There was, nevertheless, one familiar point. She had, as usual, a flower in her hair, brilliant and of a rare variety, else it had not been Zenobia. After a brief pause at the window, she turned away, exemplifying, in the few steps that removed her out of sight, that noble and beautiful motion which characterized her as much as any other personal charm. Not one woman in a thousand could move so admirably as Zenobia. Many women can sit gracefully; some can stand gracefully; and a few, perhaps, can assume a series of graceful positions. But natural movement is the result and expression of the whole being, and cannot be well and nobly performed unless responsive to something in the character. I often used to think that music—light and airy, wild and passionate, or the full harmony of stately marches, in accordance with her varying mood—should have attended Zenobia's footsteps.

I waited for her reappearance. It was one peculiarity, distinguishing Zenobia from most of her sex, that she needed for her moral well-being, and never would forego, a large amount of physical exercise. At Blithedale, no inclemency of sky or muddiness of earth had ever impeded her daily walks. Here in town, she probably preferred to tread the extent of the two drawing-rooms, and measure out the miles by spaces of forty feet, rather than bedraggle her skirts over the sloppy pavements. Accordingly, in about the time requisite to pass through the arch of the sliding-doors to the front window, and to return upon her steps, there she stood again, between the festoons of the crimson curtains. But another personage was now added to the scene. Behind Zenobia appeared that face which I had first encountered in the wood-path; the man who had passed, side by side with her, in such mysterious familiarity and estrangement, beneath my vine curtained hermitage in the tall pine-tree. It was Westervelt. And though he was looking closely over her shoulder, it still seemed to me, as on the former occasion, that Zenobia repelled him,—that, perchance, they mutually repelled each other, by some incompatibility of their spheres.

This impression, however, might have been altogether the result of fancy and prejudice in me. The distance was so great as to obliterate any play of feature by which I might otherwise have been made a partaker of their counsels.

There now needed only Hollingsworth and old Moodie to complete the knot of characters, whom a real intricacy of events, greatly assisted by my method of insulating them from other relations, had kept so long upon my mental stage, as actors in a drama. In itself, perhaps, it was no very remarkable event that they should thus come across me, at the moment when I imagined myself free. Zenobia, as I well knew, had retained an establishment in town, and had not unfrequently withdrawn herself from Blithedale during brief intervals, on one of which occasions she had taken Priscilla along with her. Nevertheless, there seemed something fatal in the coincidence that had borne me to this one spot, of all others in a great city, and transfixed me there, and compelled me again to waste my already wearied sympathies on affairs which were none of mine, and persons who cared little for me. It irritated my nerves; it affected me with a kind of heart-sickness. After the effort which it cost me to fling them off,—after consummating my escape, as I thought, from these goblins of flesh and blood, and pausing to revive myself with a breath or two of an atmosphere in which they should have no share,—it was a positive despair to find the same figures arraying themselves before me, and presenting their old problem in a shape that made it more insoluble than ever.

I began to long for a catastrophe. If the noble temper of Hollingsworth's soul were doomed to be utterly corrupted by the too powerful purpose which had grown out of what was noblest in him; if the rich and generous qualities of Zenobia's womanhood might not save her; if Priscilla must perish by her tenderness and faith, so simple and so devout, then be it so! Let it all come! As for me, I would look on, as it seemed my part to do, understandingly, if my intellect could fathom the meaning and the moral, and, at all events, reverently and sadly. The curtain fallen, I would pass onward with my poor individual life, which was now attenuated of much of its proper substance, and diffused among many alien interests.

Meanwhile, Zenobia and her companion had retreated from the window. Then followed an interval, during which I directed my eves towards the figure in the boudoir. Most certainly it was Priscilla, although dressed with a novel and fanciful elegance. The vague perception of it, as viewed so far off, impressed me as if she had suddenly passed out of a chrysalis state and put forth wings. Her hands were not now in motion. She had dropt her work, and sat with her head thrown back, in the same attitude that I had seen several times before, when she seemed to be listening to an imperfectly distinguished sound.

Again the two figures in the drawing-room became visible. They were now a little withdrawn from the window, face to face, and, as I could see by Zenobia's emphatic gestures, were discussing some subject in which she, at least, felt a passionate concern. By and by she broke away, and vanished beyond my ken. Westervelt approached the window, and leaned his forehead against a pane of glass, displaying the sort of smile on his handsome features which, when I before met him, had let me into the secret of his gold-bordered teeth. Every human being, when given over to the Devil, is sure to have the wizard mark upon him, in one form or another. I fancied that this smile, with its peculiar revelation, was the Devil's signet on the Professor.

This man, as I had soon reason to know, was endowed with a cat-like circumspection; and though precisely the most unspiritual quality in the world, it was almost as effective as spiritual insight in making him acquainted with whatever it suited him to discover. He now proved it, considerably to my discomfiture, by detecting and recognizing me, at my post of observation. Perhaps I ought to have blushed at being caught in such an evident scrutiny of Professor Westervelt and his affairs. Perhaps I did blush. Be that as it might, I retained presence of mind enough not to make my position yet more irksome by the poltroonery of drawing back.

Westervelt looked into the depths of the drawing-room, and beckoned. Immediately afterwards Zenobia appeared at the window, with color much heightened, and eyes which, as my conscience whispered me, were shooting bright arrows, barbed with scorn, across the intervening space, directed full at my sensibilities as a gentleman. If the truth must be told, far as her flight-shot was, those arrows hit the mark. She signified her recognition of me by a gesture with her head and hand, comprising at once a salutation and dismissal. The next moment she administered one of those pitiless rebukes which a woman always has at hand, ready for any offence (and which she so seldom spares on due occasion), by letting down a white linen curtain between the festoons of the damask ones. It fell like the drop-curtain of a theatre, in the interval between the acts.

Priscilla had disappeared from the boudoir. But the dove still kept her desolate perch on the peak of the attic window.

XIX. ZENOBIA'S DRAWING-ROOM

The remainder of the day, so far as I was concerned, was spent in meditating on these recent incidents. I contrived, and alternately rejected, innumerable methods of accounting for the presence of Zenobia and Priscilla, and the connection of Westervelt with both. It must be owned, too, that I had a keen, revengeful sense of the insult inflicted by Zenobia's scornful recognition, and more particularly by her letting down the curtain; as if such were the proper barrier to be interposed between a character like hers and a perceptive faculty like mine. For, was mine a mere vulgar curiosity? Zenobia should have known me better than to suppose it. She should have been able to appreciate that quality of the intellect and the heart which impelled me (often against my own will, and to the detriment of my own comfort) to live in other lives, and to endeavor—by generous sympathies, by delicate intuitions, by taking note of things too slight for record, and by bringing my human spirit into manifold accordance with the companions whom God assigned me—to learn the secret which was hidden even from themselves.

Of all possible observers, methought a woman like Zenobia and a man like Hollingsworth should have selected me. And now when the event has long been past, I retain the same opinion of my fitness for the office. True, I might have condemned them. Had I been judge as well as witness, my sentence might have been stern as that of destiny itself. But, still, no trait of original nobility of character, no struggle against temptation,—no iron necessity of will, on the one hand, nor extenuating circumstance to be derived from passion and despair, on the other,—no remorse that might coexist with error, even if powerless to prevent it,—no proud repentance that should claim retribution as a meed,—would go unappreciated. True, again, I might give my full assent to the punishment which was sure to follow. But it would be given mournfully, and with undiminished love. And, after all was finished, I would come as if to gather up the white ashes of those who had perished at the stake, and to tell the world—the wrong being now atoned for—how much had perished there which it had never yet known how to praise.

I sat in my rocking-chair, too far withdrawn from the window to expose myself to another rebuke like that already inflicted. My eyes still wandered towards the opposite house, but without effecting any new discoveries. Late in the afternoon, the weathercock on the church spire indicated a change of wind; the sun shone dimly out, as if the golden wine of its beams were mingled half-and-half with water. Nevertheless, they kindled up the whole range of edifices, threw a glow over the windows, glistened on the wet roofs, and, slowly withdrawing upward, perched upon the chimney-tops; thence they took a higher flight, and lingered an instant on the tip of the spire, making it the final point of more cheerful light in the whole sombre scene. The next moment, it was all gone. The twilight fell into the area like a shower of dusky snow, and before it was quite dark, the gong of the hotel summoned me to tea.

When I returned to my chamber, the glow of an astral lamp was penetrating mistily through the white curtain of Zenobia's drawing-room. The shadow of a passing figure was now and then cast upon this medium, but with too vague an outline for even my adventurous conjectures to read the hieroglyphic that it presented.

All at once, it occurred to me how very absurd was my behavior in thus tormenting myself with crazy hypotheses as to what was going on within that drawing-room, when it was at my option to be personally present there, My relations with Zenobia, as yet unchanged,—as a familiar friend, and associated in the same life-long enterprise,—gave me the right, and made it no more than kindly courtesy demanded, to call on her. Nothing, except our habitual independence of conventional rules at Blithedale, could have kept me from sooner recognizing this duty. At all events, it should now be performed.

In compliance with this sudden impulse, I soon found myself actually within the house, the rear of which, for two days past, I had been so sedulously watching. A servant took my card, and, immediately returning, ushered me upstairs. On the way, I heard a rich, and, as it were, triumphant burst of music from a piano, in which I felt Zenobia's character, although heretofore I had known nothing of her skill upon the instrument. Two or three canary-birds, excited by this gush of sound, sang piercingly, and did their utmost to produce a kindred melody. A bright illumination streamed through, the door of the front drawing-room; and I had barely stept across the threshold before Zenobia came forward to meet me, laughing, and with an extended hand.

"Ah, Mr. Coverdale," said she, still smiling, but, as I thought, with a good deal of scornful anger underneath, "it has gratified me to see the interest which you continue to take in my affairs! I have long recognized you as a sort of transcendental Yankee, with all the native propensity of your countrymen to investigate matters that come within their range, but rendered almost poetical, in your case, by the refined methods which you adopt for its gratification. After all, it was an unjustifiable stroke, on my part,—was it not?—to let down the window curtain!"

"I cannot call it a very wise one," returned I, with a secret bitterness, which, no doubt, Zenobia appreciated. "It is really impossible to hide anything in this world, to say nothing of the next. All that we ought to ask, therefore, is, that the witnesses of our conduct, and the speculators on our motives, should be capable of taking the highest view which the circumstances of the case may admit. So much being secured, I, for one, would be most happy in feeling myself followed everywhere by an indefatigable human sympathy."

"We must trust for intelligent sympathy to our guardian angels, if any there be," said Zenobia. "As long as the only spectator of my poor tragedy is a young man at the window of his hotel, I must still claim the liberty to drop the curtain."

While this passed, as Zenobia's hand was extended, I had applied the very slightest touch of my fingers to her own. In spite of an external freedom, her manner made me sensible that we stood upon no real terms of confidence. The thought came sadly across me, how great was the contrast betwixt this interview and our first meeting. Then, in the warm light of the country fireside, Zenobia had greeted me cheerily and hopefully, with a full sisterly grasp of the hand, conveying as much kindness in it as other women could have evinced by the pressure of both arms around my neck, or by yielding a cheek to the brotherly salute. The difference was as complete as between her appearance at that time—so simply attired, and with only the one superb flower in her hair—and now, when her beauty was set off by all that dress and ornament could do for it. And they did much. Not, indeed, that they created or added anything to what Nature had lavishly done for Zenobia. But, those costly robes which she had on, those flaming jewels on her neck, served as lamps to display the personal advantages which required nothing less than such an illumination to be fully seen. Even her characteristic flower, though it seemed to be still there, had undergone a cold and bright transfiguration; it was a flower exquisitely imitated in jeweller's work, and imparting the last touch that transformed Zenobia into a work of art.

"I scarcely feel," I could not forbear saying, "as if we had ever met before. How many years ago it seems since we last sat beneath Eliot's pulpit, with Hollingsworth extended on the fallen leaves, and Priscilla at his feet! Can it be, Zenobia, that you ever really numbered yourself with our little band of earnest, thoughtful, philanthropic laborers?"

"Those ideas have their time and place," she answered coldly. "But I fancy it must be a very circumscribed mind that can find room for no other."

Her manner bewildered me. Literally, moreover, I was dazzled by the brilliancy of the room. A chandelier hung down in the centre, glowing with I know not how many lights; there were separate lamps, also, on two or three tables, and on marble brackets, adding their white radiance to that of the chandelier. The furniture was exceedingly rich. Fresh from our old farmhouse, with its homely board and benches in the dining-room, and a few wicker chairs in the best parlor, it struck me that here was the fulfilment of every fantasy of an imagination revelling in various methods of costly self-indulgence and splendid ease. Pictures, marbles, vases,—in brief, more shapes of luxury than there could be any object in enumerating, except for an auctioneer's advertisement,—and the whole repeated and doubled by the reflection of a great mirror, which showed me Zenobia's proud figure, likewise, and my own. It cost me, I acknowledge, a bitter sense of shame, to perceive in myself a positive effort to bear up against the effect which Zenobia sought to impose on me. I reasoned against her, in my secret mind, and strove so to keep my footing. In the gorgeousness with which she had surrounded herself,—in the redundance of personal ornament, which the largeness of her physical nature and the rich type of her beauty caused to seem so suitable,—I malevolently beheld the true character of the woman, passionate, luxurious, lacking simplicity, not deeply refined, incapable of pure and perfect taste. But, the next instant, she was too powerful for all my opposing struggles. I saw how fit it was that she should make herself as gorgeous as she pleased, and should do a thousand things that would have been ridiculous in the poor, thin, weakly characters of other women. To this day, however, I hardly know whether I then beheld Zenobia in her truest attitude, or whether that were the truer one in which she had presented herself at Blithedale. In both, there was something like the illusion which a great actress flings around her.

"Have you given up Blithedale forever?" I inquired.

"Why should you think so?" asked she.

"I cannot tell," answered I; "except that it appears all like a dream that we were ever there together."

"It is not so to me," said Zenobia. "I should think it a poor and meagre nature that is capable of but one set of forms, and must convert all the past into a dream merely because the present happens to be unlike it. Why should we be content with our homely life of a few months past, to the exclusion of all other modes? It was good; but there are other lives as good, or better. Not, you will understand, that I condemn those who give themselves up to it more entirely than I, for myself, should deem it wise to do."

It irritated me, this self-complacent, condescending, qualified approval and criticism of a system to which many individuals—perhaps as highly endowed as our gorgeous Zenobia—had contributed their all of earthly endeavor, and their loftiest aspirations. I determined to make proof if there were any spell that would exorcise her out of the part which she seemed to be acting. She should be compelled to give me a glimpse of something true; some nature, some passion, no matter whether right or wrong, provided it were real.

"Your allusion to that class of circumscribed characters who can live only in one mode of life," remarked I coolly, "reminds me of our poor friend Hollingsworth. Possibly he was in your thoughts when you spoke thus. Poor fellow! It is a pity that, by the fault of a narrow education, he should have so completely immolated himself to that one idea of his, especially as the slightest modicum of common-sense would teach him its utter impracticability. Now that I have returned into the world, and can look at his project from a distance, it requires quite all my real regard for this respectable and well-intentioned man to prevent me laughing at him,—as I find society at large does."

Zenobia's eyes darted lightning, her cheeks flushed, the vividness of her expression was like the effect of a powerful light flaming up suddenly within her. My experiment had fully succeeded. She had shown me the true flesh and blood of her heart, by thus involuntarily resenting my slight, pitying, half-kind, half-scornful mention of the man who was all in all with her. She herself probably felt this; for it was hardly a moment before she tranquillized her uneven breath, and seemed as proud and self-possessed as ever.

"I rather imagine," said she quietly, "that your appreciation falls short of Mr. Hollingsworth's just claims. Blind enthusiasm, absorption in one idea, I grant, is generally ridiculous, and must be fatal to the respectability of an ordinary man; it requires a very high and powerful character to make it otherwise. But a great man—as, perhaps, you do not know—attains his normal condition only through the inspiration of one great idea. As a friend of Mr. Hollingsworth, and, at the same time, a calm observer, I must tell you that he seems to me such a man. But you are very pardonable for fancying him ridiculous. Doubtless, he is so—to you! There can be no truer test of the noble and heroic, in any individual, than the degree in which he possesses the faculty of distinguishing heroism from absurdity."

I dared make no retort to Zenobia's concluding apothegm. In truth, I admired her fidelity. It gave me a new sense of Hollingsworth's native power, to discover that his influence was no less potent with this beautiful woman here, in the midst of artificial life, than it had been at the foot of the gray rock, and among the wild birch-trees of the wood-path, when she so passionately pressed his hand against her heart. The great, rude, shaggy, swarthy man! And Zenobia loved him!

"Did you bring Priscilla with you?" I resumed. "Do you know I have sometimes fancied it not quite safe, considering the susceptibility of her temperament, that she should be so constantly within the sphere of a man like Hollingsworth. Such tender and delicate natures, among your sex, have often, I believe, a very adequate appreciation of the heroic element in men. But then, again, I should suppose them as likely as any other women to make a reciprocal impression. Hollingsworth could hardly give his affections to a person capable of taking an independent stand, but only to one whom he might absorb into himself. He has certainly shown great tenderness for Priscilla."

Zenobia had turned aside. But I caught the reflection of her face in the mirror, and saw that it was very pale,—as pale, in her rich attire, as if a shroud were round her.

"Priscilla is here," said she, her voice a little lower than usual. "Have not you learnt as much from your chamber window? Would you like to see her?"

She made a step or two into the back drawing-room, and called,—"Priscilla! Dear Priscilla!"

XX. THEY VANISH

Priscilla immediately answered the summons, and made her appearance through the door of the boudoir. I had conceived the idea, which I now recognized as a very foolish one, that Zenobia would have taken measures to debar me from an interview with this girl, between whom and herself there was so utter an opposition of their dearest interests, that, on one part or the other, a great grief, if not likewise a great wrong, seemed a matter of necessity. But, as Priscilla was only a leaf floating on the dark current of events, without influencing them by her own choice or plan, as she probably guessed not whither the stream was bearing her, nor perhaps even felt its inevitable movement,—there could be no peril of her communicating to me any intelligence with regard to Zenobia's purposes.

On perceiving me, she came forward with great quietude of manner; and when I held out my hand, her own moved slightly towards it, as if attracted by a feeble degree of magnetism.

"I am glad to see you, my dear Priscilla," said I, still holding her hand; "but everything that I meet with nowadays makes me wonder whether I am awake. You, especially, have always seemed like a figure in a dream, and now more than ever."

"Oh, there is substance in these fingers of mine," she answered, giving my hand the faintest possible pressure, and then taking away her own. "Why do you call me a dream? Zenobia is much more like one than I; she is so very, very beautiful! And, I suppose," added Priscilla, as if thinking aloud, "everybody sees it, as I do."

But, for my part, it was Priscilla's beauty, not Zenobia's, of which I was thinking at that moment. She was a person who could be quite obliterated, so far as beauty went, by anything unsuitable in her attire; her charm was not positive and material enough to bear up against a mistaken choice of color, for instance, or fashion. It was safest, in her case, to attempt no art of dress; for it demanded the most perfect taste, or else the happiest accident in the world, to give her precisely the adornment which she needed. She was now dressed in pure white, set off with some kind of a gauzy fabric, which—as I bring up her figure in my memory, with a faint gleam on her shadowy hair, and her dark eyes bent shyly on mine, through all the vanished years—seems to be floating about her like a mist. I wondered what Zenobia meant by evolving so much loveliness out of this poor girl. It was what few women could afford to do; for, as I looked from one to the other, the sheen and splendor of Zenobia's presence took nothing from Priscilla's softer spell, if it might not rather be thought to add to it.

"What do you think of her?" asked Zenobia.

I could not understand the look of melancholy kindness with which Zenobia regarded her. She advanced a step, and beckoning Priscilla near her, kissed her cheek; then, with a slight gesture of repulse, she moved to the other side of the room. I followed.

"She is a wonderful creature," I said. "Ever since she came among us, I have been dimly sensible of just this charm which you have brought out. But it was never absolutely visible till now. She is as lovely as a flower!"

"Well, say so if you like," answered Zenobia. "You are a poet,—at least, as poets go nowadays,—and must be allowed to make an opera-glass of your imagination, when you look at women. I wonder, in such Arcadian freedom of falling in love as we have lately enjoyed, it never occurred to you to fall in love with Priscilla. In society, indeed, a genuine American never dreams of stepping across the inappreciable air-line which separates one class from another. But what was rank to the colonists of Blithedale?"

"There were other reasons," I replied, "why I should have demonstrated myself an ass, had I fallen in love with Priscilla. By the bye, has Hollingsworth ever seen her in this dress?"

"Why do you bring up his name at every turn?" asked Zenobia in an undertone, and with a malign look which wandered from my face to Priscilla's. "You know not what you do! It is dangerous, sir, believe me, to tamper thus with earnest human passions, out of your own mere idleness, and for your sport. I will endure it no longer! Take care that it does not happen again! I warn you!"

"You partly wrong me, if not wholly," I responded. "It is an uncertain sense of some duty to perform, that brings my thoughts, and therefore my words, continually to that one point."

"Oh, this stale excuse of duty!" said Zenobia, in a whisper so full of scorn that it penetrated me like the hiss of a serpent. "I have often heard it before, from those who sought to interfere with me, and I know precisely what it signifies. Bigotry; self-conceit; an insolent curiosity; a meddlesome temper; a cold-blooded criticism, founded on a shallow interpretation of half-perceptions; a monstrous scepticism in regard to any conscience or any wisdom, except one's own; a most irreverent propensity to thrust Providence aside, and substitute one's self in its awful place,—out of these, and other motives as miserable as these, comes your idea of duty! But, beware, sir! With all your fancied acuteness, you step blindfold into these affairs. For any mischief that may follow your interference, I hold you responsible!"

It was evident that, with but a little further provocation, the lioness would turn to bay; if, indeed, such were not her attitude already. I bowed, and not very well knowing what else to do, was about to withdraw. But, glancing again towards Priscilla, who had retreated into a corner, there fell upon my heart an intolerable burden of despondency, the purport of which I could not tell, but only felt it to bear reference to her. I approached and held out my hand; a gesture, however, to which she made no response. It was always one of her peculiarities that she seemed to shrink from even the most friendly touch, unless it were Zenobia's or Hollingsworth's. Zenobia, all this while, stood watching us, but with a careless expression, as if it mattered very little what might pass.

"Priscilla," I inquired, lowering my voice, "when do you go back to Blithedale?"

"Whenever they please to take me," said she.

"Did you come away of your own free will?" I asked.

"I am blown about like a leaf," she replied. "I never have any free will."

"Does Hollingsworth know that you are here?" said I.

"He bade me come," answered Priscilla.

She looked at me, I thought, with an air of surprise, as if the idea were incomprehensible that she should have taken this step without his agency.

"What a gripe this man has laid upon her whole being!" muttered I between my teeth.

"Well, as Zenobia so kindly intimates, I have no more business here. I wash my hands of it all. On Hollingsworth's head be the consequences! Priscilla," I added aloud, "I know not that ever we may meet again. Farewell!"

As I spoke the word, a carriage had rumbled along the street, and stopt before the house. The doorbell rang, and steps were immediately afterwards heard on the staircase. Zenobia had thrown a shawl over her dress.

"Mr. Coverdale," said she, with cool courtesy, "you will perhaps excuse us. We have an engagement, and are going out."

"Whither?" I demanded.

"Is not that a little more than you are entitled to inquire?" said she, with a smile. "At all events, it does not suit me to tell you."

The door of the drawing-room opened, and Westervelt appeared. I observed that he was elaborately dressed, as if for some grand entertainment. My dislike for this man was infinite. At that moment it amounted to nothing less than a creeping of the flesh, as when, feeling about in a dark place, one touches something cold and slimy, and questions what the secret hatefulness may be. And still I could not but acknowledge that, for personal beauty, for polish of manner, for all that externally befits a gentleman, there was hardly another like him. After bowing to Zenobia, and graciously saluting Priscilla in her corner, he recognized me by a slight but courteous inclination.

"Come, Priscilla," said Zenobia; "it is time. Mr. Coverdale, good-evening."

As Priscilla moved slowly forward, I met her in the middle of the drawing-room.

"Priscilla," said I, in the hearing of them all, "do you know whither you are going?"

"I do not know," she answered.

"Is it wise to go, and is it your choice to go?" I asked. "If not, I am your friend, and Hollingsworth's friend. Tell me so, at once."

"Possibly," observed Westervelt, smiling, "Priscilla sees in me an older friend than either Mr. Coverdale or Mr. Hollingsworth. I shall willingly leave the matter at her option."

While thus speaking, he made a gesture of kindly invitation, and Priscilla passed me, with the gliding movement of a sprite, and took his offered arm. He offered the other to Zenobia; but she turned her proud and beautiful face upon him with a look which—judging from what I caught of it in profile—would undoubtedly have smitten the man dead, had he possessed any heart, or had this glance attained to it. It seemed to rebound, however, from his courteous visage, like an arrow from polished steel. They all three descended the stairs; and when I likewise reached the street door, the carriage was already rolling away.

XXI. AN OLD ACQUAINTANCE

Thus excluded from everybody's confidence, and attaining no further, by my most earnest study, than to an uncertain sense of something hidden from me, it would appear reasonable that I should have flung off all these alien perplexities. Obviously, my best course was to betake myself to new scenes. Here I was only an intruder. Elsewhere there might be circumstances in which I could establish a personal interest, and people who would respond, with a portion of their sympathies, for so much as I should bestow of mine.

Nevertheless, there occurred to me one other thing to be done. Remembering old Moodie, and his relationship with Priscilla, I determined to seek an interview, for the purpose of ascertaining whether the knot of affairs was as inextricable on that side as I found it on all others. Being tolerably well acquainted with the old man's haunts, I went, the next day, to the saloon of a certain establishment about which he often lurked. It was a reputable place enough, affording good entertainment in the way of meat, drink, and fumigation; and there, in my young and idle days and nights, when I was neither nice nor wise, I had often amused myself with watching the staid humors and sober jollities of the thirsty souls around me.

At my first entrance, old Moodie was not there. The more patiently to await him, I lighted a cigar, and establishing myself in a corner, took a quiet, and, by sympathy, a boozy kind of pleasure in the customary life that was going forward. The saloon was fitted up with a good deal of taste. There were pictures on the walls, and among them an oil-painting of a beefsteak, with such an admirable show of juicy tenderness, that the beholder sighed to think it merely visionary, and incapable of ever being put upon a gridiron. Another work of high art was the lifelike representation of a noble sirloin; another, the hindquarters of a deer, retaining the hoofs and tawny fur; another, the head and shoulders of a salmon; and, still more exquisitely finished, a brace of canvasback ducks, in which the mottled feathers were depicted with the accuracy of a daguerreotype. Some very hungry painter, I suppose, had wrought these subjects of still-life, heightening his imagination with his appetite, and earning, it is to be hoped, the privilege of a daily dinner off whichever of his pictorial viands he liked best.

Then there was a fine old cheese, in which you could almost discern the mites; and some sardines, on a small plate, very richly done, and looking as if oozy with the oil in which they had been smothered. All these things were so perfectly imitated, that you seemed to have the genuine article before you, and yet with an indescribable, ideal charm; it took away the grossness from what was fleshiest and fattest, and thus helped the life of man, even in its earthliest relations, to appear rich and noble, as well as warm, cheerful, and substantial. There were pictures, too, of gallant revellers, those of the old time, Flemish, apparently, with doublets and slashed sleeves, drinking their wine out of fantastic, long-stemmed glasses; quaffing joyously, quaffing forever, with inaudible laughter and song; while the champagne bubbled immortally against their moustaches, or the purple tide of Burgundy ran inexhaustibly down their throats.

But, in an obscure corner of the saloon, there was a little Picture excellently done, moreover of a ragged, bloated, New England toper, stretched out on a bench, in the heavy, apoplectic sleep of drunkenness. The death-in-life was too well portrayed. You smelt the fumy liquor that had brought on this syncope. Your only comfort lay in the forced reflection, that, real as he looked, the poor caitiff was but imaginary, a bit of painted canvass, whom no delirium tremens, nor so much as a retributive headache, awaited, on the morrow.

By this time, it being past eleven o'clock, the two bar-keepers of the saloon were in pretty constant activity. One of these young men had a rare faculty in the concoction of gin-cocktails. It was a spectacle to behold, how, with a tumbler in each hand, he tossed the contents from one to the other. Never conveying it awry, nor spilling the least drop, he compelled the frothy liquor, as it seemed to me, to spout forth from one glass and descend into the other, in a great parabolic curve, as well-defined and calculable as a planet's orbit. He had a good forehead, with a particularly large development just above the eyebrows; fine intellectual gifts, no doubt, which he had educated to this profitable end; being famous for nothing but gin-cocktails, and commanding a fair salary by his one accomplishment. These cocktails, and other artificial combinations of liquor, (of which there were at least a score, though mostly, I suspect, fantastic in their differences,) were much in favor with the younger class of customers, who, at farthest, had only reached the second stage of potatory life. The staunch, old soakers, on the other hand men who, if put on tap, would have yielded a red alcoholic liquor, by way of blood usually confined themselves to plain brandy-and-water, gin, or West India rum; and, oftentimes, they prefaced their dram with some medicinal remark as to the wholesomeness and stomachic qualities of that particular drink. Two or three appeared to have bottles of their own behind the counter; and, winking one red eye to the bar-keeper, he forthwith produced these choicest and peculiar cordials, which it was a matter of great interest and favor, among their acquaintances, to obtain a sip of.

Agreeably to the Yankee habit, under whatever circumstances, the deportment of all these good fellows, old or young, was decorous and thoroughly correct. They grew only the more sober in their cups; there was no confused babble nor boisterous laughter. They sucked in the joyous fire of the decanters and kept it smouldering in their inmost recesses, with a bliss known only to the heart which it warmed and comforted. Their eyes twinkled a little, to be sure; they hemmed vigorously after each glass, and laid a hand upon the pit of the stomach, as if the pleasant titillation there was what constituted the tangible part of their enjoyment. In that spot, unquestionably, and not in the brain, was the acme of the whole affair. But the true purpose of their drinking—and one that will induce men to drink, or do something equivalent, as long as this weary world shall endure—was the renewed youth and vigor, the brisk, cheerful sense of things present and to come, with which, for about a quarter of an hour, the dram permeated their systems. And when such quarters of an hour can be obtained in some mode less baneful to the great sum of a man's life,—but, nevertheless, with a little spice of impropriety, to give it a wild flavor,—we temperance people may ring out our bells for victory!

The prettiest object in the saloon was a tiny fountain, which threw up its feathery jet through the counter, and sparkled down again into an oval basin, or lakelet, containing several goldfishes. There was a bed of bright sand at the bottom, strewn with coral and rock-work; and the fishes went gleaming about, now turning up the sheen of a golden side, and now vanishing into the shadows of the water, like the fanciful thoughts that coquet with a poet in his dream. Never before, I imagine, did a company of water-drinkers remain so entirely uncontaminated by the bad example around them; nor could I help wondering that it had not occurred to any freakish inebriate to empty a glass of liquor into their lakelet. What a delightful idea! Who would not be a fish, if he could inhale jollity with the essential element of his existence!

I had begun to despair of meeting old Moodie, when, all at once, I recognized his hand and arm protruding from behind a screen that was set up for the accommodation of bashful topers. As a matter of course, he had one of Priscilla's little purses, and was quietly insinuating it under the notice of a person who stood near. This was always old Moodie's way. You hardly ever saw him advancing towards you, but became aware of his proximity without being able to guess how he had come thither. He glided about like a spirit, assuming visibility close to your elbow, offering his petty trifles of merchandise, remaining long enough for you to purchase, if so disposed, and then taking himself off, between two breaths, while you happened to be thinking of something else.

By a sort of sympathetic impulse that often controlled me in those more impressible days of my life, I was induced to approach this old man in a mode as undemonstrative as his own. Thus, when, according to his custom, he was probably just about to vanish, he found me at his elbow.

"Ah!" said he, with more emphasis than was usual with him. "It is Mr. Coverdale!"

"Yes, Mr. Moodie, your old acquaintance," answered I. "It is some time now since we ate luncheon together at Blithedale, and a good deal longer since our little talk together at the street corner."

"That was a good while ago," said the old man.

And he seemed inclined to say not a word more. His existence looked so colorless and torpid,—so very faintly shadowed on the canvas of reality,—that I was half afraid lest he should altogether disappear, even while my eyes were fixed full upon his figure. He was certainly the wretchedest old ghost in the world, with his crazy hat, the dingy handkerchief about his throat, his suit of threadbare gray, and especially that patch over his right eye, behind which he always seemed to be hiding himself. There was one method, however, of bringing him out into somewhat stronger relief. A glass of brandy would effect it. Perhaps the gentler influence of a bottle of claret might do the same. Nor could I think it a matter for the recording angel to write down against me, if—with my painful consciousness of the frost in this old man's blood, and the positive ice that had congealed about his heart—I should thaw him out, were it only for an hour, with the summer warmth of a little wine. What else could possibly be done for him? How else could he be imbued with energy enough to hope for a happier state hereafter? How else be inspired to say his prayers? For there are states of our spiritual system when the throb of the soul's life is too faint and weak to render us capable of religious aspiration.

"Mr. Moodie," said I, "shall we lunch together? And would you like to drink a glass of wine?"

His one eye gleamed. He bowed; and it impressed me that he grew to be more of a man at once, either in anticipation of the wine, or as a grateful response to my good fellowship in offering it.

"With pleasure," he replied.

The bar-keeper, at my request, showed us into a private room, and soon afterwards set some fried oysters and a bottle of claret on the table; and I saw the old man glance curiously at the label of the bottle, as if to learn the brand.

"It should be good wine," I remarked, "if it have any right to its label."

"You cannot suppose, sir," said Moodie, with a sigh, "that a poor old fellow like me knows any difference in wines."

And yet, in his way of handling the glass, in his preliminary snuff at the aroma, in his first cautious sip of the wine, and the gustatory skill with which he gave his palate the full advantage of it, it was impossible not to recognize the connoisseur.

"I fancy, Mr. Moodie," said I, "you are a much better judge of wines than I have yet learned to be. Tell me fairly,—did you never drink it where the grape grows?"

"How should that have been, Mr. Coverdale?" answered old Moodie shyly; but then he took courage, as it were, and uttered a feeble little laugh. "The flavor of this wine," added he, "and its perfume still more than its taste, makes me remember that I was once a young man."

"I wish, Mr. Moodie," suggested I,—not that I greatly cared about it, however, but was only anxious to draw him into some talk about Priscilla and Zenobia,—"I wish, while we sit over our wine, you would favor me with a few of those youthful reminiscences."

"Ah," said he, shaking his head, "they might interest you more than you suppose. But I had better be silent, Mr. Coverdale. If this good wine,—though claret, I suppose, is not apt to play such a trick,—but if it should make my tongue run too freely, I could never look you in the face again."

"You never did look me in the face, Mr. Moodie," I replied, "until this very moment."

"Ah!" sighed old Moodie.

It was wonderful, however, what an effect the mild grape-juice wrought upon him. It was not in the wine, but in the associations which it seemed to bring up. Instead of the mean, slouching, furtive, painfully depressed air of an old city vagabond, more like a gray kennel-rat than any other living thing, he began to take the aspect of a decayed gentleman. Even his garments—especially after I had myself quaffed a glass or two—looked less shabby than when we first sat down. There was, by and by, a certain exuberance and elaborateness of gesture and manner, oddly in contrast with all that I had hitherto seen of him. Anon, with hardly any impulse from me, old Moodie began to talk. His communications referred exclusively to a long-past and more fortunate period of his life, with only a few unavoidable allusions to the circumstances that had reduced him to his present state. But, having once got the clew, my subsequent researches acquainted me with the main facts of the following narrative; although, in writing it out, my pen has perhaps allowed itself a trifle of romantic and legendary license, worthier of a small poet than of a grave biographer.

XXII. FAUNTLEROY

Five-and-twenty years ago, at the epoch of this story, there dwelt in one of the Middle States a man whom we shall call Fauntleroy; a man of wealth, and magnificent tastes, and prodigal expenditure. His home might almost be styled a palace; his habits, in the ordinary sense, princely. His whole being seemed to have crystallized itself into an external splendor, wherewith he glittered in the eyes of the world, and had no other life than upon this gaudy surface. He had married a lovely woman, whose nature was deeper than his own. But his affection for her, though it showed largely, was superficial, like all his other manifestations and developments; he did not so truly keep this noble creature in his heart, as wear her beauty for the most brilliant ornament of his outward state. And there was born to him a child, a beautiful daughter, whom he took from the beneficent hand of God with no just sense of her immortal value, but as a man already rich in gems would receive another jewel. If he loved her, it was because she shone.

After Fauntleroy had thus spent a few empty years, coruscating continually an unnatural light, the source of it—which was merely his gold—began to grow more shallow, and finally became exhausted. He saw himself in imminent peril of losing all that had heretofore distinguished him; and, conscious of no innate worth to fall back upon, he recoiled from this calamity with the instinct of a soul shrinking from annihilation. To avoid it,—wretched man!—or rather to defer it, if but for a month, a day, or only to procure himself the life of a few breaths more amid the false glitter which was now less his own than ever,—he made himself guilty of a crime. It was just the sort of crime, growing out of its artificial state, which society (unless it should change its entire constitution for this man's unworthy sake) neither could nor ought to pardon. More safely might it pardon murder. Fauntleroy's guilt was discovered. He fled; his wife perished, by the necessity of her innate nobleness, in its alliance with a being so ignoble; and betwixt her mother's death and her father's ignominy, his daughter was left worse than orphaned.

There was no pursuit after Fauntleroy. His family connections, who had great wealth, made such arrangements with those whom he had attempted to wrong as secured him from the retribution that would have overtaken an unfriended criminal. The wreck of his estate was divided among his creditors: His name, in a very brief space, was forgotten by the multitude who had passed it so diligently from mouth to mouth. Seldom, indeed, was it recalled, even by his closest former intimates. Nor could it have been otherwise. The man had laid no real touch on any mortal's heart. Being a mere image, an optical delusion, created by the sunshine of prosperity, it was his law to vanish into the shadow of the first intervening cloud. He seemed to leave no vacancy; a phenomenon which, like many others that attended his brief career, went far to prove the illusiveness of his existence.

Not, however, that the physical substance of Fauntleroy had literally melted into vapor. He had fled northward to the New England metropolis, and had taken up his abode, under another name, in a squalid street or court of the older portion of the city. There he dwelt among poverty-stricken wretches, sinners, and forlorn good people, Irish, and whomsoever else were neediest. Many families were clustered in each house together, above stairs and below, in the little peaked garrets, and even in the dusky cellars. The house where Fauntleroy paid weekly rent for a chamber and a closet had been a stately habitation in its day. An old colonial governor had built it, and lived there, long ago, and held his levees in a great room where now slept twenty Irish bedfellows; and died in Fauntleroy's chamber, which his embroidered and white-wigged ghost still haunted. Tattered hangings, a marble hearth, traversed with many cracks and fissures, a richly carved oaken mantelpiece, partly hacked away for kindling-stuff, a stuccoed ceiling, defaced with great, unsightly patches of the naked laths,—such was the chamber's aspect, as if, with its splinters and rags of dirty splendor, it were a kind of practical gibe at this poor, ruined man of show.

At first, and at irregular intervals, his relatives allowed Fauntleroy a little pittance to sustain life; not from any love, perhaps, but lest poverty should compel him, by new offences, to add more shame to that with which he had already stained them. But he showed no tendency to further guilt. His character appeared to have been radically changed (as, indeed, from its shallowness, it well might) by his miserable fate; or, it may be, the traits now seen in him were portions of the same character, presenting itself in another phase. Instead of any longer seeking to live in the sight of the world, his impulse was to shrink into the nearest obscurity, and to be unseen of men, were it possible, even while standing before their eyes. He had no pride; it was all trodden in the dust. No ostentation; for how could it survive, when there was nothing left of Fauntleroy, save penury and shame! His very gait demonstrated that he would gladly have faded out of view, and have crept about invisibly, for the sake of sheltering himself from the irksomeness of a human glance. Hardly, it was averred, within the memory of those who knew him now, had he the hardihood to show his full front to the world. He skulked in corners, and crept about in a sort of noonday twilight, making himself gray and misty, at all hours, with his morbid intolerance of sunshine.

In his torpid despair, however, he had done an act which that condition of the spirit seems to prompt almost as often as prosperity and hope. Fauntleroy was again married. He had taken to wife a forlorn, meek-spirited, feeble young woman, a seamstress, whom he found dwelling with her mother in a contiguous chamber of the old gubernatorial residence. This poor phantom—as the beautiful and noble companion of his former life had done brought him a daughter. And sometimes, as from one dream into another, Fauntleroy looked forth out of his present grimy environment into that past magnificence, and wondered whether the grandee of yesterday or the pauper of to-day were real. But, in my mind, the one and the other were alike impalpable. In truth, it was Fauntleroy's fatality to behold whatever he touched dissolve. After a few years, his second wife (dim shadow that she had always been) faded finally out of the world, and left Fauntleroy to deal as he might with their pale and nervous child. And, by this time, among his distant relatives,—with whom he had grown a weary thought, linked with contagious infamy, and which they were only too willing to get rid of,—he was himself supposed to be no more.

The younger child, like his elder one, might be considered as the true offspring of both parents, and as the reflection of their state. She was a tremulous little creature, shrinking involuntarily from all mankind, but in timidity, and no sour repugnance. There was a lack of human substance in her; it seemed as if, were she to stand up in a sunbeam, it would pass right through her figure, and trace out the cracked and dusty window-panes upon the naked floor. But, nevertheless, the poor child had a heart; and from her mother's gentle character she had inherited a profound and still capacity of affection. And so her life was one of love. She bestowed it partly on her father, but in greater part on an idea.

For Fauntleroy, as they sat by their cheerless fireside,—which was no fireside, in truth, but only a rusty stove,—had often talked to the little girl about his former wealth, the noble loveliness of his first wife, and the beautiful child whom she had given him. Instead of the fairy tales which other parents tell, he told Priscilla this. And, out of the loneliness of her sad little existence, Priscilla's love grew, and tended upward, and twined itself perseveringly around this unseen sister; as a grapevine might strive to clamber out of a gloomy hollow among the rocks, and embrace a young tree standing in the sunny warmth above. It was almost like worship, both in its earnestness and its humility; nor was it the less humble—though the more earnest—because Priscilla could claim human kindred with the being whom she, so devoutly loved. As with worship, too, it gave her soul the refreshment of a purer atmosphere. Save for this singular, this melancholy, and yet beautiful affection, the child could hardly have lived; or, had she lived, with a heart shrunken for lack of any sentiment to fill it, she must have yielded to the barren miseries of her position, and have grown to womanhood characterless and worthless. But now, amid all the sombre coarseness of her father's outward life, and of her own, Priscilla had a higher and imaginative life within. Some faint gleam thereof was often visible upon her face. It was as if, in her spiritual visits to her brilliant sister, a portion of the latter's brightness had permeated our dim Priscilla, and still lingered, shedding a faint illumination through the cheerless chamber, after she came back.

As the child grew up, so pallid and so slender, and with much unaccountable nervousness, and all the weaknesses of neglected infancy still haunting her, the gross and simple neighbors whispered strange things about Priscilla. The big, red, Irish matrons, whose innumerable progeny swarmed out of the adjacent doors, used to mock at the pale Western child. They fancied—or, at least, affirmed it, between jest and earnest—that she was not so solid flesh and blood as other children, but mixed largely with a thinner element. They called her ghost-child, and said that she could indeed vanish when she pleased, but could never, in her densest moments, make herself quite visible. The sun at midday would shine through her; in the first gray of the twilight, she lost all the distinctness of her outline; and, if you followed the dim thing into a dark corner, behold! she was not there. And it was true that Priscilla had strange ways; strange ways, and stranger words, when she uttered any words at all. Never stirring out of the old governor's dusky house, she sometimes talked of distant places and splendid rooms, as if she had just left them. Hidden things were visible to her (at least so the people inferred from obscure hints escaping unawares out of her mouth), and silence was audible. And in all the world there was nothing so difficult to be endured, by those who had any dark secret to conceal, as the glance of Priscilla's timid and melancholy eyes.

Her peculiarities were the theme of continual gossip among the other inhabitants of the gubernatorial mansion. The rumor spread thence into a wider circle. Those who knew old Moodie, as he was now called, used often to jeer him, at the very street-corners, about his daughter's gift of second-sight and prophecy. It was a period when science (though mostly through its empirical professors) was bringing forward, anew, a hoard of facts and imperfect theories, that had partially won credence in elder times, but which modern scepticism had swept away as rubbish. These things were now tossed up again, out of the surging ocean of human thought and experience. The story of Priscilla's preternatural manifestations, therefore, attracted a kind of notice of which it would have been deemed wholly unworthy a few years earlier. One day a gentleman ascended the creaking staircase, and inquired which was old Moodie's chamber door. And, several times, he came again. He was a marvellously handsome man,—still youthful, too, and fashionably dressed. Except that Priscilla, in those days, had no beauty, and, in the languor of her existence, had not yet blossomed into womanhood, there would have been rich food for scandal in these visits; for the girl was unquestionably their sole object, although her father was supposed always to be present. But, it must likewise be added, there was something about Priscilla that calumny could not meddle with; and thus far was she privileged, either by the preponderance of what was spiritual, or the thin and watery blood that left her cheek so pallid.

Yet, if the busy tongues of the neighborhood spared Priscilla in one way, they made themselves amends by renewed and wilder babble on another score. They averred that the strange gentleman was a wizard, and that he had taken advantage of Priscilla's lack of earthly substance to subject her to himself, as his familiar spirit, through whose medium he gained cognizance of whatever happened, in regions near or remote. The boundaries of his power were defined by the verge of the pit of Tartarus on the one hand, and the third sphere of the celestial world on the other. Again, they declared their suspicion that the wizard, with all his show of manly beauty, was really an aged and wizened figure, or else that his semblance of a human body was only a necromantic, or perhaps a mechanical contrivance, in which a demon walked about. In proof of it, however, they could merely instance a gold band around his upper teeth, which had once been visible to several old women, when he smiled at them from the top of the governor's staircase. Of course this was all absurdity, or mostly so. But, after every possible deduction, there remained certain very mysterious points about the stranger's character, as well as the connection that he established with Priscilla. Its nature at that period was even less understood than now, when miracles of this kind have grown so absolutely stale, that I would gladly, if the truth allowed, dismiss the whole matter from my narrative.

We must now glance backward, in quest of the beautiful daughter of Fauntleroy's prosperity. What had become of her? Fauntleroy's only brother, a bachelor, and with no other relative so near, had adopted the forsaken child. She grew up in affluence, with native graces clustering luxuriantly about her. In her triumphant progress towards womanhood, she was adorned with every variety of feminine accomplishment. But she lacked a mother's care. With no adequate control, on any hand (for a man, however stern, however wise, can never sway and guide a female child), her character was left to shape itself. There was good in it, and evil. Passionate, self-willed, and imperious, she had a warm and generous nature; showing the richness of the soil, however, chiefly by the weeds that flourished in it, and choked up the herbs of grace. In her girlhood her uncle died. As Fauntleroy was supposed to be likewise dead, and no other heir was known to exist, his wealth devolved on her, although, dying suddenly, the uncle left no will. After his death there were obscure passages in Zenobia's history. There were whispers of an attachment, and even a secret marriage, with a fascinating and accomplished but unprincipled young man. The incidents and appearances, however, which led to this surmise soon passed away, and were forgotten.

Nor was her reputation seriously affected by the report. In fact, so great was her native power and influence, and such seemed the careless purity of her nature, that whatever Zenobia did was generally acknowledged as right for her to do. The world never criticised her so harshly as it does most women who transcend its rules. It almost yielded its assent, when it beheld her stepping out of the common path, and asserting the more extensive privileges of her sex, both theoretically and by her practice. The sphere of ordinary womanhood was felt to be narrower than her development required.

A portion of Zenobia's more recent life is told in the foregoing pages. Partly in earnest,—and, I imagine, as was her disposition, half in a proud jest, or in a kind of recklessness that had grown upon her, out of some hidden grief,—she had given her countenance, and promised liberal pecuniary aid, to our experiment of a better social state. And Priscilla followed her to Blithedale. The sole bliss of her life had been a dream of this beautiful sister, who had never so much as known of her existence. By this time, too, the poor girl was enthralled in an intolerable bondage, from which she must either free herself or perish. She deemed herself safest near Zenobia, into whose large heart she hoped to nestle.

One evening, months after Priscilla's departure, when Moodie (or shall we call him Fauntleroy?) was sitting alone in the state-chamber of the old governor, there came footsteps up the staircase. There was a pause on the landing-place. A lady's musical yet haughty accents were heard making an inquiry from some denizen of the house, who had thrust a head out of a contiguous chamber. There was then a knock at Moodie's door. "Come in!" said he.

And Zenobia entered. The details of the interview that followed being unknown to me,—while, notwithstanding, it would be a pity quite to lose the picturesqueness of the situation,—I shall attempt to sketch it, mainly from fancy, although with some general grounds of surmise in regard to the old man's feelings.

She gazed wonderingly at the dismal chamber. Dismal to her, who beheld it only for an instant; and how much more so to him, into whose brain each bare spot on the ceiling, every tatter of the paper-hangings, and all the splintered carvings of the mantelpiece, seen wearily through long years, had worn their several prints! Inexpressibly miserable is this familiarity with objects that have been from the first disgustful.

"I have received a strange message," said Zenobia, after a moment's silence, "requesting, or rather enjoining it upon me, to come hither. Rather from curiosity than any other motive,—and because, though a woman, I have not all the timidity of one,—I have complied. Can it be you, sir, who thus summoned me?"

"It was," answered Moodie.

"And what was your purpose?" she continued. "You require charity, perhaps? In that case, the message might have been more fitly worded. But you are old and poor, and age and poverty should be allowed their privileges. Tell me, therefore, to what extent you need my aid."

"Put up your purse," said the supposed mendicant, with an inexplicable smile. "Keep it,—keep all your wealth,—until I demand it all, or none! My message had no such end in view. You are beautiful, they tell me; and I desired to look at you."

He took the one lamp that showed the discomfort and sordidness of his abode, and approaching Zenobia held it up, so as to gain the more perfect view of her, from top to toe. So obscure was the chamber, that you could see the reflection of her diamonds thrown upon the dingy wall, and flickering with the rise and fall of Zenobia's breath. It was the splendor of those jewels on her neck, like lamps that burn before some fair temple, and the jewelled flower in her hair, more than the murky, yellow light, that helped him to see her beauty. But he beheld it, and grew proud at heart; his own figure, in spite of his mean habiliments, assumed an air of state and grandeur.

"It is well," cried old Moodie. "Keep your wealth. You are right worthy of it. Keep it, therefore, but with one condition only."

Zenobia thought the old man beside himself, and was moved with pity.

"Have you none to care for you?" asked she. "No daughter?—no kind-hearted neighbor?—no means of procuring the attendance which you need? Tell me once again, can I do nothing for you?"

"Nothing," he replied. "I have beheld what I wished. Now leave me. Linger not a moment longer, or I may be tempted to say what would bring a cloud over that queenly brow. Keep all your wealth, but with only this one condition: Be kind—be no less kind than sisters are—to my poor Priscilla!"

And, it may be, after Zenobia withdrew, Fauntleroy paced his gloomy chamber, and communed with himself as follows,—or, at all events, it is the only solution which I can offer of the enigma presented in his character:—"I am unchanged,—the same man as of yore!" said he. "True, my brother's wealth—he dying intestate—is legally my own. I know it; yet of my own choice, I live a beggar, and go meanly clad, and hide myself behind a forgotten ignominy. Looks this like ostentation? Ah! but in Zenobia I live again! Beholding her, so beautiful,—so fit to be adorned with all imaginable splendor of outward state,—the cursed vanity, which, half a lifetime since, dropt off like tatters of once gaudy apparel from my debased and ruined person, is all renewed for her sake. Were I to reappear, my shame would go with me from darkness into daylight. Zenobia has the splendor, and not the shame. Let the world admire her, and be dazzled by her, the brilliant child of my prosperity! It is Fauntleroy that still shines through her!" But then, perhaps, another thought occurred to him.

"My poor Priscilla! And am I just to her, in surrendering all to this beautiful Zenobia? Priscilla! I love her best,—I love her only!—but with shame, not pride. So dim, so pallid, so shrinking,—the daughter of my long calamity! Wealth were but a mockery in Priscilla's hands. What is its use, except to fling a golden radiance around those who grasp it? Yet let Zenobia take heed! Priscilla shall have no wrong!" But, while the man of show thus meditated,—that very evening, so far as I can adjust the dates of these strange incidents,—Priscilla poor, pallid flower!—was either snatched from Zenobia's hand, or flung wilfully away!

XXIII. A VILLAGE HALL

Well, I betook myself away, and wandered up and down, like an exorcised spirit that had been driven from its old haunts after a mighty struggle. It takes down the solitary pride of man, beyond most other things, to find the impracticability of flinging aside affections that have grown irksome. The bands that were silken once are apt to become iron fetters when we desire to shake them off. Our souls, after all, are not our own. We convey a property in them to those with whom we associate; but to what extent can never be known, until we feel the tug, the agony, of our abortive effort to resume an exclusive sway over ourselves. Thus, in all the weeks of my absence, my thoughts continually reverted back, brooding over the bygone months, and bringing up incidents that seemed hardly to have left a trace of themselves in their passage. I spent painful hours in recalling these trifles, and rendering them more misty and unsubstantial than at first by the quantity of speculative musing thus kneaded in with them. Hollingsworth, Zenobia, Priscilla! These three had absorbed my life into themselves. Together with an inexpressible longing to know their fortunes, there was likewise a morbid resentment of my own pain, and a stubborn reluctance to come again within their sphere.

All that I learned of them, therefore, was comprised in a few brief and pungent squibs, such as the newspapers were then in the habit of bestowing on our socialist enterprise. There was one paragraph, which if I rightly guessed its purport bore reference to Zenobia, but was too darkly hinted to convey even thus much of certainty. Hollingsworth, too, with his philanthropic project, afforded the penny-a-liners a theme for some savage and bloody minded jokes; and, considerably to my surprise, they affected me with as much indignation as if we had still been friends.

Thus passed several weeks; time long enough for my brown and toil-hardened hands to reaccustom themselves to gloves. Old habits, such as were merely external, returned upon me with wonderful promptitude. My superficial talk, too, assumed altogether a worldly tone. Meeting former acquaintances, who showed themselves inclined to ridicule my heroic devotion to the cause of human welfare, I spoke of the recent phase of my life as indeed fair matter for a jest. But, I also gave them to understand that it was, at most, only an experiment, on which I had staked no valuable amount of hope or fear. It had enabled me to pass the summer in a novel and agreeable way, had afforded me some grotesque specimens of artificial simplicity, and could not, therefore, so far as I was concerned, be reckoned a failure. In no one instance, however, did I voluntarily speak of my three friends. They dwelt in a profounder region. The more I consider myself as I then was, the more do I recognize how deeply my connection with those three had affected all my being.

As it was already the epoch of annihilated space, I might in the time I was away from Blithedale have snatched a glimpse at England, and been back again. But my wanderings were confined within a very limited sphere. I hopped and fluttered, like a bird with a string about its leg, gyrating round a small circumference, and keeping up a restless activity to no purpose. Thus it was still in our familiar Massachusetts—in one of its white country villages—that I must next particularize an incident.

The scene was one of those lyceum halls, of which almost every village has now its own, dedicated to that sober and pallid, or rather drab-colored, mode of winter-evening entertainment, the lecture. Of late years this has come strangely into vogue, when the natural tendency of things would seem to be to substitute lettered for oral methods of addressing the public. But, in halls like this, besides the winter course of lectures, there is a rich and varied series of other exhibitions. Hither comes the ventriloquist, with all his mysterious tongues; the thaumaturgist, too, with his miraculous transformations of plates, doves, and rings, his pancakes smoking in your hat, and his cellar of choice liquors represented in one small bottle. Here, also, the itinerant professor instructs separate classes of ladies and gentlemen in physiology, and demonstrates his lessons by the aid of real skeletons, and manikins in wax, from Paris. Here is to be heard the choir of Ethiopian melodists, and to be seen the diorama of Moscow or Bunker Hill, or the moving panorama of the Chinese wall. Here is displayed the museum of wax figures, illustrating the wide catholicism of earthly renown, by mixing up heroes and statesmen, the pope and the Mormon prophet, kings, queens, murderers, and beautiful ladies; every sort of person, in short, except authors, of whom I never beheld even the most famous done in wax. And here, in this many-purposed hall (unless the selectmen of the village chance to have more than their share of the Puritanism, which, however diversified with later patchwork, still gives its prevailing tint to New England character),—here the company of strolling players sets up its little stage, and claims patronage for the legitimate drama.

But, on the autumnal evening which I speak of, a number of printed handbills—stuck up in the bar-room, and on the sign-post of the hotel, and on the meeting-house porch, and distributed largely through the village—had promised the inhabitants an interview with that celebrated and hitherto inexplicable phenomenon, the Veiled Lady!

The hall was fitted up with an amphitheatrical descent of seats towards a platform, on which stood a desk, two lights, a stool, and a capacious antique chair. The audience was of a generally decent and respectable character: old farmers, in their Sunday black coats, with shrewd, hard, sun-dried faces, and a cynical humor, oftener than any other expression, in their eyes; pretty girls, in many-colored attire; pretty young men,—the schoolmaster, the lawyer, or student at law, the shopkeeper,—all looking rather suburban than rural. In these days, there is absolutely no rusticity, except when the actual labor of the soil leaves its earth-mould on the person. There was likewise a considerable proportion of young and middle-aged women, many of them stern in feature, with marked foreheads, and a very definite line of eyebrow; a type of womanhood in which a bold intellectual development seems to be keeping pace with the progressive delicacy of the physical constitution. Of all these people I took note, at first, according to my custom. But I ceased to do so the moment that my eyes fell on an individual who sat two or three seats below me, immovable, apparently deep in thought, with his back, of course, towards me, and his face turned steadfastly upon the platform.

After sitting awhile in contemplation of this person's familiar contour, I was irresistibly moved to step over the intervening benches, lay my hand on his shoulder, put my mouth close to his ear, and address him in a sepulchral, melodramatic whisper: "Hollingsworth! where have you left Zenobia?"

His nerves, however, were proof against my attack. He turned half around, and looked me in the face with great sad eyes, in which there was neither kindness nor resentment, nor any perceptible surprise.

"Zenobia, when I last saw her," he answered, "was at Blithedale."

He said no more. But there was a great deal of talk going on near me, among a knot of people who might be considered as representing the mysticism, or rather the mystic sensuality, of this singular age. The nature of the exhibition that was about to take place had probably given the turn to their conversation.

I heard, from a pale man in blue spectacles, some stranger stories than ever were written in a romance; told, too, with a simple, unimaginative steadfastness, which was terribly efficacious in compelling the auditor to receive them into the category of established facts. He cited instances of the miraculous power of one human being over the will and passions of another; insomuch that settled grief was but a shadow beneath the influence of a man possessing this potency, and the strong love of years melted away like a vapor. At the bidding of one of these wizards, the maiden, with her lover's kiss still burning on her lips, would turn from him with icy indifference; the newly made widow would dig up her buried heart out of her young husband's grave before the sods had taken root upon it; a mother with her babe's milk in her bosom would thrust away her child. Human character was but soft wax in his hands; and guilt, or virtue, only the forms into which he should see fit to mould it. The religious sentiment was a flame which he could blow up with his breath, or a spark that he could utterly extinguish. It is unutterable, the horror and disgust with which I listened, and saw that, if these things were to be believed, the individual soul was virtually annihilated, and all that is sweet and pure in our present life debased, and that the idea of man's eternal responsibility was made ridiculous, and immortality rendered at once impossible, and not worth acceptance. But I would have perished on the spot sooner than believe it.

The epoch of rapping spirits, and all the wonders that have followed in their train,—such as tables upset by invisible agencies, bells self-tolled at funerals, and ghostly music performed on jew's-harps,—had not yet arrived. Alas, my countrymen, methinks we have fallen on an evil age! If these phenomena have not humbug at the bottom, so much the worse for us. What can they indicate, in a spiritual way, except that the soul of man is descending to a lower point than it has ever before reached while incarnate? We are pursuing a downward course in the eternal march, and thus bring ourselves into the same range with beings whom death, in requital of their gross and evil lives, has degraded below humanity! To hold intercourse with spirits of this order, we must stoop and grovel in some element more vile than earthly dust. These goblins, if they exist at all, are but the shadows of past mortality, outcasts, mere refuse stuff, adjudged unworthy of the eternal world, and, on the most favorable supposition, dwindling gradually into nothingness. The less we have to say to them the better, lest we share their fate!

The audience now began to be impatient; they signified their desire for the entertainment to commence by thump of sticks and stamp of boot-heels. Nor was it a great while longer before, in response to their call, there appeared a bearded personage in Oriental robes, looking like one of the enchanters of the Arabian Nights. He came upon the platform from a side door, saluted the spectators, not with a salaam, but a bow, took his station at the desk, and first blowing his nose with a white handkerchief, prepared to speak. The environment of the homely village hall, and the absence of many ingenious contrivances of stage effect with which the exhibition had heretofore been set off, seemed to bring the artifice of this character more openly upon the surface. No sooner did I behold the bearded enchanter, than, laying my hand again on Hollingsworth's shoulder, I whispered in his ear, "Do you know him?"

"I never saw the man before," he muttered, without turning his head.

But I had seen him three times already.

Once, on occasion of my first visit to the Veiled Lady; a second time, in the wood-path at Blithedale; and lastly, in Zenobia's drawing-room. It was Westervelt. A quick association of ideas made me shudder from head to foot; and again, like an evil spirit, bringing up reminiscences of a man's sins, I whispered a question in Hollingsworth's ear,—"What have you done with Priscilla?"

He gave a convulsive start, as if I had thrust a knife into him, writhed himself round on his seat, glared fiercely into my eyes, but answered not a word.

The Professor began his discourse, explanatory of the psychological phenomena, as he termed them, which it was his purpose to exhibit to the spectators. There remains no very distinct impression of it on my memory. It was eloquent, ingenious, plausible, with a delusive show of spirituality, yet really imbued throughout with a cold and dead materialism. I shivered, as at a current of chill air issuing out of a sepulchral vault, and bringing the smell of corruption along with it. He spoke of a new era that was dawning upon the world; an era that would link soul to soul, and the present life to what we call futurity, with a closeness that should finally convert both worlds into one great, mutually conscious brotherhood. He described (in a strange, philosophical guise, with terms of art, as if it were a matter of chemical discovery) the agency by which this mighty result was to be effected; nor would it have surprised me, had he pretended to hold up a portion of his universally pervasive fluid, as he affirmed it to be, in a glass phial.

At the close of his exordium, the Professor beckoned with his hand,—once, twice, thrice,—and a figure came gliding upon the platform, enveloped in a long veil of silvery whiteness. It fell about her like the texture of a summer cloud, with a kind of vagueness, so that the outline of the form beneath it could not be accurately discerned. But the movement of the Veiled Lady was graceful, free, and unembarrassed, like that of a person accustomed to be the spectacle of thousands; or, possibly, a blindfold prisoner within the sphere with which this dark earthly magician had surrounded her, she was wholly unconscious of being the central object to all those straining eyes.

Pliant to his gesture (which had even an obsequious courtesy, but at the same time a remarkable decisiveness), the figure placed itself in the great chair. Sitting there, in such visible obscurity, it was, perhaps, as much like the actual presence of a disembodied spirit as anything that stage trickery could devise. The hushed breathing of the spectators proved how high-wrought were their anticipations of the wonders to be performed through the medium of this incomprehensible creature. I, too, was in breathless suspense, but with a far different presentiment of some strange event at hand.

"You see before you the Veiled Lady," said the bearded Professor, advancing to the verge of the platform. "By the agency of which I have just spoken, she is at this moment in communion with the spiritual world. That silvery veil is, in one sense, an enchantment, having been dipped, as it were, and essentially imbued, through the potency of my art, with the fluid medium of spirits. Slight and ethereal as it seems, the limitations of time and space have no existence within its folds. This hall—these hundreds of faces, encompassing her within so narrow an amphitheatre—are of thinner substance, in her view, than the airiest vapor that the clouds are made of. She beholds the Absolute!"

As preliminary to other and far more wonderful psychological experiments, the exhibitor suggested that some of his auditors should endeavor to make the Veiled Lady sensible of their presence by such methods—provided only no touch were laid upon her person—as they might deem best adapted to that end. Accordingly, several deep-lunged country fellows, who looked as if they might have blown the apparition away with a breath, ascended the platform. Mutually encouraging one another, they shouted so close to her ear that the veil stirred like a wreath of vanishing mist; they smote upon the floor with bludgeons; they perpetrated so hideous a clamor, that methought it might have reached, at least, a little way into the eternal sphere. Finally, with the assent of the Professor, they laid hold of the great chair, and were startled, apparently, to find it soar upward, as if lighter than the air through which it rose. But the Veiled Lady remained seated and motionless, with a composure that was hardly less than awful, because implying so immeasurable a distance betwixt her and these rude persecutors.

"These efforts are wholly without avail," observed the Professor, who had been looking on with an aspect of serene indifference. "The roar of a battery of cannon would be inaudible to the Veiled Lady. And yet, were I to will it, sitting in this very hall, she could hear the desert wind sweeping over the sands as far off as Arabia; the icebergs grinding one against the other in the polar seas; the rustle of a leaf in an East Indian forest; the lowest whispered breath of the bashfullest maiden in the world, uttering the first confession of her love. Nor does there exist the moral inducement, apart from my own behest, that could persuade her to lift the silvery veil, or arise out of that chair."

Greatly to the Professor's discomposure, however, just as he spoke these words, the Veiled Lady arose. There was a mysterious tremor that shook the magic veil. The spectators, it may be, imagined that she was about to take flight into that invisible sphere, and to the society of those purely spiritual beings with whom they reckoned her so near akin. Hollingsworth, a moment ago, had mounted the platform, and now stood gazing at the figure, with a sad intentness that brought the whole power of his great, stern, yet tender soul into his glance.

"Come," said he, waving his hand towards her. "You are safe!"

She threw off the veil, and stood before that multitude of people pale, tremulous, shrinking, as if only then had she discovered that a thousand eyes were gazing at her. Poor maiden! How strangely had she been betrayed! Blazoned abroad as a wonder of the world, and performing what were adjudged as miracles,—in the faith of many, a seeress and a prophetess; in the harsher judgment of others, a mountebank,—she had kept, as I religiously believe, her virgin reserve and sanctity of soul throughout it all. Within that encircling veil, though an evil hand had flung it over her, there was as deep a seclusion as if this forsaken girl had, all the while, been sitting under the shadow of Eliot's pulpit, in the Blithedale woods, at the feet of him who now summoned her to the shelter of his arms. And the true heart-throb of a woman's affection was too powerful for the jugglery that had hitherto environed her. She uttered a shriek, and fled to Hollingsworth, like one escaping from her deadliest enemy, and was safe forever.

XXIV. THE MASQUERADERS

Two nights had passed since the foregoing occurrences, when, in a breezy September forenoon, I set forth from town, on foot, towards Blithedale. It was the most delightful of all days for a walk, with a dash of invigorating ice-temper in the air, but a coolness that soon gave place to the brisk glow of exercise, while the vigor remained as elastic as before. The atmosphere had a spirit and sparkle in it. Each breath was like a sip of ethereal wine, tempered, as I said, with a crystal lump of ice. I had started on this expedition in an exceedingly sombre mood, as well befitted one who found himself tending towards home, but was conscious that nobody would be quite overjoyed to greet him there. My feet were hardly off the pavement, however, when this morbid sensation began to yield to the lively influences of air and motion. Nor had I gone far, with fields yet green on either side, before my step became as swift and light as if Hollingsworth were waiting to exchange a friendly hand-grip, and Zenobia's and Priscilla's open arms would welcome the wanderer's reappearance. It has happened to me on other occasions, as well as this, to prove how a state of physical well-being can create a kind of joy, in spite of the profoundest anxiety of mind.

The pathway of that walk still runs along, with sunny freshness, through my memory. I know not why it should be so. But my mental eye can even now discern the September grass, bordering the pleasant roadside with a brighter verdure than while the summer heats were scorching it; the trees, too, mostly green, although here and there a branch or shrub has donned its vesture of crimson and gold a week or two before its fellows. I see the tufted barberry-bushes, with their small clusters of scarlet fruit; the toadstools, likewise,—some spotlessly white, others yellow or red,—mysterious growths, springing suddenly from no root or seed, and growing nobody can tell how or wherefore. In this respect they resembled many of the emotions in my breast. And I still see the little rivulets, chill, clear, and bright, that murmured beneath the road, through subterranean rocks, and deepened into mossy pools, where tiny fish were darting to and fro, and within which lurked the hermit frog. But no,—I never can account for it, that, with a yearning interest to learn the upshot of all my story, and returning to Blithedale for that sole purpose, I should examine these things so like a peaceful-bosomed naturalist. Nor why, amid all my sympathies and fears, there shot, at times, a wild exhilaration through my frame.

Thus I pursued my way along the line of the ancient stone wall that Paul Dudley built, and through white villages, and past orchards of ruddy apples, and fields of ripening maize, and patches of woodland, and all such sweet rural scenery as looks the fairest, a little beyond the suburbs of a town. Hollingsworth, Zenobia, Priscilla! They glided mistily before me, as I walked. Sometimes, in my solitude, I laughed with the bitterness of self-scorn, remembering how unreservedly I had given up my heart and soul to interests that were not mine. What had I ever had to do with them? And why, being now free, should I take this thraldom on me once again? It was both sad and dangerous, I whispered to myself, to be in too close affinity with the passions, the errors, and the misfortunes of individuals who stood within a circle of their own, into which, if I stept at all, it must be as an intruder, and at a peril that I could not estimate.

Drawing nearer to Blithedale, a sickness of the spirits kept alternating with my flights of causeless buoyancy. I indulged in a hundred odd and extravagant conjectures. Either there was no such place as Blithedale, nor ever had been, nor any brotherhood of thoughtful laborers, like what I seemed to recollect there, or else it was all changed during my absence. It had been nothing but dream work and enchantment. I should seek in vain for the old farmhouse, and for the greensward, the potato-fields, the root-crops, and acres of Indian corn, and for all that configuration of the land which I had imagined. It would be another spot, and an utter strangeness.

These vagaries were of the spectral throng so apt to steal out of an unquiet heart. They partly ceased to haunt me, on my arriving at a point whence, through the trees, I began to catch glimpses of the Blithedale farm. That surely was something real. There was hardly a square foot of all those acres on which I had not trodden heavily, in one or another kind of toil. The curse of Adam's posterity—and, curse or blessing be it, it gives substance to the life around us—had first come upon me there. In the sweat of my brow I had there earned bread and eaten it, and so established my claim to be on earth, and my fellowship with all the sons of labor. I could have knelt down, and have laid my breast against that soil. The red clay of which my frame was moulded seemed nearer akin to those crumbling furrows than to any other portion of the world's dust. There was my home, and there might be my grave.

I felt an invincible reluctance, nevertheless, at the idea of presenting myself before my old associates, without first ascertaining the state in which they were. A nameless foreboding weighed upon me. Perhaps, should I know all the circumstances that had occurred, I might find it my wisest course to turn back, unrecognized, unseen, and never look at Blithedale more. Had it been evening, I would have stolen softly to some lighted window of the old farmhouse, and peeped darkling in, to see all their well-known faces round the supper-board. Then, were there a vacant seat, I might noiselessly unclose the door, glide in, and take my place among them, without a word. My entrance might be so quiet, my aspect so familiar, that they would forget how long I had been away, and suffer me to melt into the scene, as a wreath of vapor melts into a larger cloud. I dreaded a boisterous greeting. Beholding me at table, Zenobia, as a matter of course, would send me a cup of tea, and Hollingsworth fill my plate from the great dish of pandowdy, and Priscilla, in her quiet way, would hand the cream, and others help me to the bread and butter. Being one of them again, the knowledge of what had happened would come to me without a shock. For still, at every turn of my shifting fantasies, the thought stared me in the face that some evil thing had befallen us, or was ready to befall.

Yielding to this ominous impression, I now turned aside into the woods, resolving to spy out the posture of the Community as craftily as the wild Indian before he makes his onset. I would go wandering about the outskirts of the farm, and, perhaps, catching sight of a solitary acquaintance, would approach him amid the brown shadows of the trees (a kind of medium fit for spirits departed and revisitant, like myself), and entreat him to tell me how all things were.

The first living creature that I met was a partridge, which sprung up beneath my feet, and whirred away; the next was a squirrel, who chattered angrily at me from an overhanging bough. I trod along by the dark, sluggish river, and remember pausing on the bank, above one of its blackest and most placid pools (the very spot, with the barkless stump of a tree aslantwise over the water, is depicting itself to my fancy at this instant), and wondering how deep it was, and if any overladen soul had ever flung its weight of mortality in thither, and if it thus escaped the burden, or only made it heavier. And perhaps the skeleton of the drowned wretch still lay beneath the inscrutable depth, clinging to some sunken log at the bottom with the gripe of its old despair. So slight, however, was the track of these gloomy ideas, that I soon forgot them in the contemplation of a brood of wild ducks, which were floating on the river, and anon took flight, leaving each a bright streak over the black surface. By and by, I came to my hermitage, in the heart of the white-pine tree, and clambering up into it, sat down to rest. The grapes, which I had watched throughout the summer, now dangled around me in abundant clusters of the deepest purple, deliciously sweet to the taste, and, though wild, yet free from that ungentle flavor which distinguishes nearly all our native and uncultivated grapes. Methought a wine might be pressed out of them possessing a passionate zest, and endowed with a new kind of intoxicating quality, attended with such bacchanalian ecstasies as the tamer grapes of Madeira, France, and the Rhine are inadequate to produce. And I longed to quaff a great goblet of it that moment!

While devouring the grapes, I looked on all sides out of the peep-holes of my hermitage, and saw the farmhouse, the fields, and almost every part of our domain, but not a single human figure in the landscape. Some of the windows of the house were open, but with no more signs of life than in a dead man's unshut eyes. The barn-door was ajar, and swinging in the breeze. The big old dog,—he was a relic of the former dynasty of the farm,—that hardly ever stirred out of the yard, was nowhere to be seen. What, then, had become of all the fraternity and sisterhood? Curious to ascertain this point, I let myself down out of the tree, and going to the edge of the wood, was glad to perceive our herd of cows chewing the cud or grazing not far off. I fancied, by their manner, that two or three of them recognized me (as, indeed, they ought, for I had milked them and been their chamberlain times without number); but, after staring me in the face a little while, they phlegmatically began grazing and chewing their cuds again. Then I grew foolishly angry at so cold a reception, and flung some rotten fragments of an old stump at these unsentimental cows.

Skirting farther round the pasture, I heard voices and much laughter proceeding from the interior of the wood. Voices, male and feminine; laughter, not only of fresh young throats, but the bass of grown people, as if solemn organ-pipes should pour out airs of merriment. Not a voice spoke, but I knew it better than my own; not a laugh, but its cadences were familiar. The wood, in this portion of it, seemed as full of jollity as if Comus and his crew were holding their revels in one of its usually lonesome glades. Stealing onward as far as I durst, without hazard of discovery, I saw a concourse of strange figures beneath the overshadowing branches. They appeared, and vanished, and came again, confusedly with the streaks of sunlight glimmering down upon them.

Among them was an Indian chief, with blanket, feathers, and war-paint, and uplifted tomahawk; and near him, looking fit to be his woodland bride, the goddess Diana, with the crescent on her head, and attended by our big lazy dog, in lack of any fleeter hound. Drawing an arrow from her quiver, she let it fly at a venture, and hit the very tree behind which I happened to be lurking. Another group consisted of a Bavarian broom-girl, a negro of the Jim Crow order, one or two foresters of the Middle Ages, a Kentucky woodsman in his trimmed hunting-shirt and deerskin leggings, and a Shaker elder, quaint, demure, broad-brimmed, and square-skirted. Shepherds of Arcadia, and allegoric figures from the "Faerie Queen," were oddly mixed up with these. Arm in arm, or otherwise huddled together in strange discrepancy, stood grim Puritans, gay Cavaliers, and Revolutionary officers with three-cornered cocked hats, and queues longer than their swords. A bright-complexioned, dark-haired, vivacious little gypsy, with a red shawl over her head, went from one group to another, telling fortunes by palmistry; and Moll Pitcher, the renowned old witch of Lynn, broomstick in hand, showed herself prominently in the midst, as if announcing all these apparitions to be the offspring of her necromantic art. But Silas Foster, who leaned against a tree near by, in his customary blue frock and smoking a short pipe, did more to disenchant the scene, with his look of shrewd, acrid, Yankee observation, than twenty witches and necromancers could have done in the way of rendering it weird and fantastic.

A little farther off, some old-fashioned skinkers and drawers, all with portentously red noses, were spreading a banquet on the leaf-strewn earth; while a horned and long-tailed gentleman (in whom I recognized the fiendish musician erst seen by Tam O'Shanter) tuned his fiddle, and summoned the whole motley rout to a dance, before partaking of the festal cheer. So they joined hands in a circle, whirling round so swiftly, so madly, and so merrily, in time and tune with the Satanic music, that their separate incongruities were blended all together, and they became a kind of entanglement that went nigh to turn one's brain with merely looking at it. Anon they stopt all of a sudden, and staring at one another's figures, set up a roar of laughter; whereat a shower of the September leaves (which, all day long, had been hesitating whether to fall or no) were shaken off by the movement of the air, and came eddying down upon the revellers.

Then, for lack of breath, ensued a silence, at the deepest point of which, tickled by the oddity of surprising my grave associates in this masquerading trim, I could not possibly refrain from a burst of laughter on my own separate account.

"Hush!" I heard the pretty gypsy fortuneteller say. "Who is that laughing?"

"Some profane intruder!" said the goddess Diana. "I shall send an arrow through his heart, or change him into a stag, as I did Actaeon, if he peeps from behind the trees!"

"Me take his scalp!" cried the Indian chief, brandishing his tomahawk, and cutting a great caper in the air.

"I'll root him in the earth with a spell that I have at my tongue's end!" squeaked Moll Pitcher. "And the green moss shall grow all over him, before he gets free again!"

"The voice was Miles Coverdale's," said the fiendish fiddler, with a whisk of his tail and a toss of his horns. "My music has brought him hither. He is always ready to dance to the Devil's tune!"

Thus put on the right track, they all recognized the voice at once, and set up a simultaneous shout.

"Miles! Miles! Miles Coverdale, where are you?" they cried. "Zenobia! Queen Zenobia! here is one of your vassals lurking in the wood. Command him to approach and pay his duty!"

The whole fantastic rabble forthwith streamed off in pursuit of me, so that I was like a mad poet hunted by chimeras. Having fairly the start of them, however, I succeeded in making my escape, and soon left their merriment and riot at a good distance in the rear. Its fainter tones assumed a kind of mournfulness, and were finally lost in the hush and solemnity of the wood. In my haste, I stumbled over a heap of logs and sticks that had been cut for firewood, a great while ago, by some former possessor of the soil, and piled up square, in order to be carted or sledded away to the farmhouse. But, being forgotten, they had lain there perhaps fifty years, and possibly much longer; until, by the accumulation of moss, and the leaves falling over them, and decaying there, from autumn to autumn, a green mound was formed, in which the softened outline of the woodpile was still perceptible. In the fitful mood that then swayed my mind, I found something strangely affecting in this simple circumstance. I imagined the long-dead woodman, and his long dead wife and children, coming out of their chill graves, and essaying to make a fire with this heap of mossy fuel!

From this spot I strayed onward, quite lost in reverie, and neither knew nor cared whither I was going, until a low, soft, well-remembered voice spoke, at a little distance.

"There is Mr. Coverdale!"

"Miles Coverdale!" said another voice,—and its tones were very stern. "Let him come forward, then!"

"Yes, Mr. Coverdale," cried a woman's voice,—clear and melodious, but, just then, with something unnatural in its chord,—"you are welcome! But you come half an hour too late, and have missed a scene which you would have enjoyed!"

I looked up and found myself nigh Eliot's pulpit, at the base of which sat Hollingsworth, with Priscilla at his feet and Zenobia standing before them.

XXV. THE THREE TOGETHER

Hollingsworth was in his ordinary working-dress. Priscilla wore a pretty and simple gown, with a kerchief about her neck, and a calash, which she had flung back from her head, leaving it suspended by the strings. But Zenobia (whose part among the maskers, as may be supposed, was no inferior one) appeared in a costume of fanciful magnificence, with her jewelled flower as the central ornament of what resembled a leafy crown, or coronet. She represented the Oriental princess by whose name we were accustomed to know her. Her attitude was free and noble; yet, if a queen's, it was not that of a queen triumphant, but dethroned, on trial for her life, or, perchance, condemned already. The spirit of the conflict seemed, nevertheless, to be alive in her. Her eyes were on fire; her cheeks had each a crimson spot, so exceedingly vivid, and marked with so definite an outline, that I at first doubted whether it were not artificial. In a very brief space, however, this idea was shamed by the paleness that ensued, as the blood sunk suddenly away. Zenobia now looked like marble.

One always feels the fact, in an instant, when he has intruded on those who love, or those who hate, at some acme of their passion that puts them into a sphere of their own, where no other spirit can pretend to stand on equal ground with them. I was confused,—affected even with a species of terror,—and wished myself away. The intenseness of their feelings gave them the exclusive property of the soil and atmosphere, and left me no right to be or breathe there.

"Hollingsworth,—Zenobia,—I have just returned to Blithedale," said I, "and had no thought of finding you here. We shall meet again at the house. I will retire."

"This place is free to you," answered Hollingsworth.

"As free as to ourselves," added Zenobia. "This long while past, you have been following up your game, groping for human emotions in the dark corners of the heart. Had you been here a little sooner, you might have seen them dragged into the daylight. I could even wish to have my trial over again, with you standing by to see fair play! Do you know, Mr. Coverdale, I have been on trial for my life?"

She laughed, while speaking thus. But, in truth, as my eyes wandered from one of the group to another, I saw in Hollingsworth all that an artist could desire for the grim portrait of a Puritan magistrate holding inquest of life and death in a case of witchcraft; in Zenobia, the sorceress herself, not aged, wrinkled, and decrepit, but fair enough to tempt Satan with a force reciprocal to his own; and, in Priscilla, the pale victim, whose soul and body had been wasted by her spells. Had a pile of fagots been heaped against the rock, this hint of impending doom would have completed the suggestive picture.

"It was too hard upon me," continued Zenobia, addressing Hollingsworth, "that judge, jury, and accuser should all be comprehended in one man! I demur, as I think the lawyers say, to the jurisdiction. But let the learned Judge Coverdale seat himself on the top of the rock, and you and me stand at its base, side by side, pleading our cause before him! There might, at least, be two criminals instead of one."

"You forced this on me," replied Hollingsworth, looking her sternly in the face. "Did I call you hither from among the masqueraders yonder? Do I assume to be your judge? No; except so far as I have an unquestionable right of judgment, in order to settle my own line of behavior towards those with whom the events of life bring me in contact. True, I have already judged you, but not on the world's part,—neither do I pretend to pass a sentence!"

"Ah, this is very good!" cried Zenobia with a smile. "What strange beings you men are, Mr. Coverdale!—is it not so? It is the simplest thing in the world with you to bring a woman before your secret tribunals, and judge and condemn her unheard, and then tell her to go free without a sentence. The misfortune is, that this same secret tribunal chances to be the only judgment-seat that a true woman stands in awe of, and that any verdict short of acquittal is equivalent to a death sentence!"

The more I looked at them, and the more I heard, the stronger grew my impression that a crisis had just come and gone. On Hollingsworth's brow it had left a stamp like that of irrevocable doom, of which his own will was the instrument. In Zenobia's whole person, beholding her more closely, I saw a riotous agitation; the almost delirious disquietude of a great struggle, at the close of which the vanquished one felt her strength and courage still mighty within her, and longed to renew the contest. My sensations were as if I had come upon a battlefield before the smoke was as yet cleared away.

And what subjects had been discussed here? All, no doubt, that for so many months past had kept my heart and my imagination idly feverish. Zenobia's whole character and history; the true nature of her mysterious connection with Westervelt; her later purposes towards Hollingsworth, and, reciprocally, his in reference to her; and, finally, the degree in which Zenobia had been cognizant of the plot against Priscilla, and what, at last, had been the real object of that scheme. On these points, as before, I was left to my own conjectures. One thing, only, was certain. Zenobia and Hollingsworth were friends no longer. If their heartstrings were ever intertwined, the knot had been adjudged an entanglement, and was now violently broken.

But Zenobia seemed unable to rest content with the matter in the posture which it had assumed.

"Ah! do we part so?" exclaimed she, seeing Hollingsworth about to retire.

"And why not?" said he, with almost rude abruptness. "What is there further to be said between us?"

"Well, perhaps nothing," answered Zenobia, looking him in the face, and smiling. "But we have come many times before to this gray rock, and we have talked very softly among the whisperings of the birch-trees. They were pleasant hours! I love to make the latest of them, though not altogether so delightful, loiter away as slowly as may be. And, besides, you have put many queries to me at this, which you design to be our last interview; and being driven, as I must acknowledge, into a corner, I have responded with reasonable frankness. But now, with your free consent, I desire the privilege of asking a few questions, in my turn."

"I have no concealments," said Hollingsworth.

"We shall see," answered Zenobia. "I would first inquire whether you have supposed me to be wealthy?"

"On that point," observed Hollingsworth, "I have had the opinion which the world holds."

"And I held it likewise," said Zenobia. "Had I not, Heaven is my witness the knowledge should have been as free to you as me. It is only three days since I knew the strange fact that threatens to make me poor; and your own acquaintance with it, I suspect, is of at least as old a date. I fancied myself affluent. You are aware, too, of the disposition which I purposed making of the larger portion of my imaginary opulence,—nay, were it all, I had not hesitated. Let me ask you, further, did I ever propose or intimate any terms of compact, on which depended this—as the world would consider it—so important sacrifice?"

"You certainly spoke of none," said Hollingsworth.

"Nor meant any," she responded. "I was willing to realize your dream freely,—generously, as some might think,—but, at all events, fully, and heedless though it should prove the ruin of my fortune. If, in your own thoughts, you have imposed any conditions of this expenditure, it is you that must be held responsible for whatever is sordid and unworthy in them. And now one other question. Do you love this girl?"

"O Zenobia!" exclaimed Priscilla, shrinking back, as if longing for the rock to topple over and hide her.

"Do you love her?" repeated Zenobia.

"Had you asked me that question a short time since," replied Hollingsworth, after a pause, during which, it seemed to me, even the birch-trees held their whispering breath, "I should have told you—'No!' My feelings for Priscilla differed little from those of an elder brother, watching tenderly over the gentle sister whom God has given him to protect."

"And what is your answer now?" persisted Zenobia.

"I do love her!" said Hollingsworth, uttering the words with a deep inward breath, instead of speaking them outright. "As well declare it thus as in any other way. I do love her!"

"Now, God be judge between us," cried Zenobia, breaking into sudden passion, "which of us two has most mortally offended Him! At least, I am a woman, with every fault, it may be, that a woman ever had,—weak, vain, unprincipled (like most of my sex; for our virtues, when we have any, are merely impulsive and intuitive), passionate, too, and pursuing my foolish and unattainable ends by indirect and cunning, though absurdly chosen means, as an hereditary bond-slave must; false, moreover, to the whole circle of good, in my reckless truth to the little good I saw before me,—but still a woman! A creature whom only a little change of earthly fortune, a little kinder smile of Him who sent me hither, and one true heart to encourage and direct me, might have made all that a woman can be! But how is it with you? Are you a man? No; but a monster! A cold, heartless, self-beginning and self-ending piece of mechanism!"

"With what, then, do you charge me!" asked Hollingsworth, aghast, and greatly disturbed by this attack. "Show me one selfish end, in all I ever aimed at, and you may cut it out of my bosom with a knife!"

"It is all self!" answered Zenobia with still intenser bitterness. "Nothing else; nothing but self, self, self! The fiend, I doubt not, has made his choicest mirth of you these seven years past, and especially in the mad summer which we have spent together. I see it now! I am awake, disenchanted, disinthralled! Self, self, self! You have embodied yourself in a project. You are a better masquerader than the witches and gypsies yonder; for your disguise is a self-deception. See whither it has brought you! First, you aimed a death-blow, and a treacherous one, at this scheme of a purer and higher life, which so many noble spirits had wrought out. Then, because Coverdale could not be quite your slave, you threw him ruthlessly away. And you took me, too, into your plan, as long as there was hope of my being available, and now fling me aside again, a broken tool! But, foremost and blackest of your sins, you stifled down your inmost consciousness!—you did a deadly wrong to your own heart!—you were ready to sacrifice this girl, whom, if God ever visibly showed a purpose, He put into your charge, and through whom He was striving to redeem you!"

"This is a woman's view," said Hollingsworth, growing deadly pale,—"a woman's, whose whole sphere of action is in the heart, and who can conceive of no higher nor wider one!"

"Be silent!" cried Zenobia imperiously. "You know neither man nor woman! The utmost that can be said in your behalf—and because I would not be wholly despicable in my own eyes, but would fain excuse my wasted feelings, nor own it wholly a delusion, therefore I say it—is, that a great and rich heart has been ruined in your breast. Leave me, now. You have done with me, and I with you. Farewell!"

"Priscilla," said Hollingsworth, "come." Zenobia smiled; possibly I did so too. Not often, in human life, has a gnawing sense of injury found a sweeter morsel of revenge than was conveyed in the tone with which Hollingsworth spoke those two words. It was the abased and tremulous tone of a man whose faith in himself was shaken, and who sought, at last, to lean on an affection. Yes; the strong man bowed himself and rested on this poor Priscilla! Oh, could she have failed him, what a triumph for the lookers-on!

And, at first, I half imagined that she was about to fail him. She rose up, stood shivering like the birch leaves that trembled over her head, and then slowly tottered, rather than walked, towards Zenobia. Arriving at her feet, she sank down there, in the very same attitude which she had assumed on their first meeting, in the kitchen of the old farmhouse. Zenobia remembered it.

"Ah, Priscilla!" said she, shaking her head, "how much is changed since then! You kneel to a dethroned princess. You, the victorious one! But he is waiting for you. Say what you wish, and leave me."

"We are sisters!" gasped Priscilla.

I fancied that I understood the word and action. It meant the offering of herself, and all she had, to be at Zenobia's disposal. But the latter would not take it thus.

"True, we are sisters!" she replied; and, moved by the sweet word, she stooped down and kissed Priscilla; but not lovingly, for a sense of fatal harm received through her seemed to be lurking in Zenobia's heart. "We had one father! You knew it from the first; I, but a little while,—else some things that have chanced might have been spared you. But I never wished you harm. You stood between me and an end which I desired. I wanted a clear path. No matter what I meant. It is over now. Do you forgive me?"

"O Zenobia," sobbed Priscilla, "it is I that feel like the guilty one!"

"No, no, poor little thing!" said Zenobia, with a sort of contempt. "You have been my evil fate, but there never was a babe with less strength or will to do an injury. Poor child! Methinks you have but a melancholy lot before you, sitting all alone in that wide, cheerless heart, where, for aught you know,—and as I, alas! believe,—the fire which you have kindled may soon go out. Ah, the thought makes me shiver for you! What will you do, Priscilla, when you find no spark among the ashes?"

"Die!" she answered.

"That was well said!" responded Zenobia, with an approving smile. "There is all a woman in your little compass, my poor sister. Meanwhile, go with him, and live!"

She waved her away with a queenly gesture, and turned her own face to the rock. I watched Priscilla, wondering what judgment she would pass between Zenobia and Hollingsworth; how interpret his behavior, so as to reconcile it with true faith both towards her sister and herself; how compel her love for him to keep any terms whatever with her sisterly affection! But, in truth, there was no such difficulty as I imagined. Her engrossing love made it all clear. Hollingsworth could have no fault. That was the one principle at the centre of the universe. And the doubtful guilt or possible integrity of other people, appearances, self-evident facts, the testimony of her own senses,—even Hollingsworth's self-accusation, had he volunteered it,—would have weighed not the value of a mote of thistledown on the other side. So secure was she of his right, that she never thought of comparing it with another's wrong, but left the latter to itself.

Hollingsworth drew her arm within his, and soon disappeared with her among the trees. I cannot imagine how Zenobia knew when they were out of sight; she never glanced again towards them. But, retaining a proud attitude so long as they might have thrown back a retiring look, they were no sooner departed,—utterly departed,—than she began slowly to sink down. It was as if a great, invisible, irresistible weight were pressing her to the earth. Settling upon her knees, she leaned her forehead against the rock, and sobbed convulsively; dry sobs they seemed to be, such as have nothing to do with tears.

XXVI. ZENOBIA AND COVERDALE

Zenobia had entirely forgotten me. She fancied herself alone with her great grief. And had it been only a common pity that I felt for her,—the pity that her proud nature would have repelled, as the one worst wrong which the world yet held in reserve,—the sacredness and awfulness of the crisis might have impelled me to steal away silently, so that not a dry leaf should rustle under my feet. I would have left her to struggle, in that solitude, with only the eye of God upon her. But, so it happened, I never once dreamed of questioning my right to be there now, as I had questioned it just before, when I came so suddenly upon Hollingsworth and herself, in the passion of their recent debate. It suits me not to explain what was the analogy that I saw or imagined between Zenobia's situation and mine; nor, I believe, will the reader detect this one secret, hidden beneath many a revelation which perhaps concerned me less. In simple truth, however, as Zenobia leaned her forehead against the rock, shaken with that tearless agony, it seemed to me that the self-same pang, with hardly mitigated torment, leaped thrilling from her heartstrings to my own. Was it wrong, therefore, if I felt myself consecrated to the priesthood by sympathy like this, and called upon to minister to this woman's affliction, so far as mortal could?

But, indeed, what could mortal do for her? Nothing! The attempt would be a mockery and an anguish. Time, it is true, would steal away her grief, and bury it and the best of her heart in the same grave. But Destiny itself, methought, in its kindliest mood, could do no better for Zenobia, in the way of quick relief; than to cause the impending rock to impend a little farther, and fall upon her head. So I leaned against a tree, and listened to her sobs, in unbroken silence. She was half prostrate, half kneeling, with her forehead still pressed against the rock. Her sobs were the only sound; she did not groan, nor give any other utterance to her distress. It was all involuntary.

At length she sat up, put back her hair, and stared about her with a bewildered aspect, as if not distinctly recollecting the scene through which she had passed, nor cognizant of the situation in which it left her. Her face and brow were almost purple with the rush of blood. They whitened, however, by and by, and for some time retained this deathlike hue. She put her hand to her forehead, with a gesture that made me forcibly conscious of an intense and living pain there.

Her glance, wandering wildly to and fro, passed over me several times, without appearing to inform her of my presence. But, finally, a look of recognition gleamed from her eyes into mine.

"Is it you, Miles Coverdale?" said she, smiling. "Ah, I perceive what you are about! You are turning this whole affair into a ballad. Pray let me hear as many stanzas as you happen to have ready."

"Oh, hush, Zenobia!" I answered. "Heaven knows what an ache is in my soul!"

"It is genuine tragedy, is it not?" rejoined Zenobia, with a sharp, light laugh. "And you are willing to allow, perhaps, that I have had hard measure. But it is a woman's doom, and I have deserved it like a woman; so let there be no pity, as, on my part, there shall be no complaint. It is all right, now, or will shortly be so. But, Mr. Coverdale, by all means write this ballad, and put your soul's ache into it, and turn your sympathy to good account, as other poets do, and as poets must, unless they choose to give us glittering icicles instead of lines of fire. As for the moral, it shall be distilled into the final stanza, in a drop of bitter honey."

"What shall it be, Zenobia?" I inquired, endeavoring to fall in with her mood.

"Oh, a very old one will serve the purpose," she replied. "There are no new truths, much as we have prided ourselves on finding some. A moral? Why, this: That, in the battlefield of life, the downright stroke, that would fall only on a man's steel headpiece, is sure to light on a woman's heart, over which she wears no breastplate, and whose wisdom it is, therefore, to keep out of the conflict. Or, this: That the whole universe, her own sex and yours, and Providence, or Destiny, to boot, make common cause against the woman who swerves one hair's-breadth out of the beaten track. Yes; and add (for I may as well own it, now) that, with that one hair's-breadth, she goes all astray, and never sees the world in its true aspect afterwards."

"This last is too stern a moral," I observed. "Cannot we soften it a little?"

"Do it if you like, at your own peril, not on my responsibility," she answered. Then, with a sudden change of subject, she went on: "After all, he has flung away what would have served him better than the poor, pale flower he kept. What can Priscilla do for him? Put passionate warmth into his heart, when it shall be chilled with frozen hopes? Strengthen his hands, when they are weary with much doing and no performance? No! but only tend towards him with a blind, instinctive love, and hang her little, puny weakness for a clog upon his arm! She cannot even give him such sympathy as is worth the name. For will he never, in many an hour of darkness, need that proud intellectual sympathy which he might have had from me?—the sympathy that would flash light along his course, and guide, as well as cheer him? Poor Hollingsworth! Where will he find it now?"

"Hollingsworth has a heart of ice!" said I bitterly. "He is a wretch!"

"Do him no wrong," interrupted Zenobia, turning haughtily upon me. "Presume not to estimate a man like Hollingsworth. It was my fault, all along, and none of his. I see it now! He never sought me. Why should he seek me? What had I to offer him? A miserable, bruised, and battered heart, spoilt long before he met me. A life, too, hopelessly entangled with a villain's! He did well to cast me off. God be praised, he did it! And yet, had he trusted me, and borne with me a little longer, I would have saved him all this trouble."

She was silent for a time, and stood with her eyes fixed on the ground. Again raising them, her look was more mild and calm.

"Miles Coverdale!" said she.

"Well, Zenobia," I responded. "Can I do you any service?"

"Very little," she replied. "But it is my purpose, as you may well imagine, to remove from Blithedale; and, most likely, I may not see Hollingsworth again. A woman in my position, you understand, feels scarcely at her ease among former friends. New faces,—unaccustomed looks,—those only can she tolerate. She would pine among familiar scenes; she would be apt to blush, too, under the eyes that knew her secret; her heart might throb uncomfortably; she would mortify herself, I suppose, with foolish notions of having sacrificed the honor of her sex at the foot of proud, contumacious man. Poor womanhood, with its rights and wrongs! Here will be new matter for my course of lectures, at the idea of which you smiled, Mr. Coverdale, a month or two ago. But, as you have really a heart and sympathies, as far as they go, and as I shall depart without seeing Hollingsworth, I must entreat you to be a messenger between him and me."

"Willingly," said I, wondering at the strange way in which her mind seemed to vibrate from the deepest earnest to mere levity. "What is the message?"

"True,—what is it?" exclaimed Zenobia. "After all, I hardly know. On better consideration, I have no message. Tell him,—tell him something pretty and pathetic, that will come nicely and sweetly into your ballad,—anything you please, so it be tender and submissive enough. Tell him he has murdered me! Tell him that I'll haunt him! "—She spoke these words with the wildest energy.—"And give him—no, give Priscilla—this!"

Thus saying, she took the jewelled flower out of her hair; and it struck me as the act of a queen, when worsted in a combat, discrowning herself, as if she found a sort of relief in abasing all her pride.

"Bid her wear this for Zenobia's sake," she continued. "She is a pretty little creature, and will make as soft and gentle a wife as the veriest Bluebeard could desire. Pity that she must fade so soon! These delicate and puny maidens always do. Ten years hence, let Hollingsworth look at my face and Priscilla's, and then choose betwixt them. Or, if he pleases, let him do it now."

How magnificently Zenobia looked as she said this! The effect of her beauty was even heightened by the over-consciousness and self-recognition of it, into which, I suppose, Hollingsworth's scorn had driven her. She understood the look of admiration in my face; and—Zenobia to the last—it gave her pleasure.

"It is an endless pity," said she, "that I had not bethought myself of winning your heart, Mr. Coverdale, instead of Hollingsworth's. I think I should have succeeded, and many women would have deemed you the worthier conquest of the two. You are certainly much the handsomest man. But there is a fate in these things. And beauty, in a man, has been of little account with me since my earliest girlhood, when, for once, it turned my head. Now, farewell!"

"Zenobia, whither are you going?" I asked.

"No matter where," said she. "But I am weary of this place, and sick to death of playing at philanthropy and progress. Of all varieties of mock-life, we have surely blundered into the very emptiest mockery in our effort to establish the one true system. I have done with it; and Blithedale must find another woman to superintend the laundry, and you, Mr. Coverdale, another nurse to make your gruel, the next time you fall ill. It was, indeed, a foolish dream! Yet it gave us some pleasant summer days, and bright hopes, while they lasted. It can do no more; nor will it avail us to shed tears over a broken bubble. Here is my hand! Adieu!"

She gave me her hand with the same free, whole-souled gesture as on the first afternoon of our acquaintance, and, being greatly moved, I bethought me of no better method of expressing my deep sympathy than to carry it to my lips. In so doing, I perceived that this white hand—so hospitably warm when I first touched it, five months since—was now cold as a veritable piece of snow.

"How very cold!" I exclaimed, holding it between both my own, with the vain idea of warming it. "What can be the reason? It is really deathlike!"

"The extremities die first, they say," answered Zenobia, laughing. "And so you kiss this poor, despised, rejected hand! Well, my dear friend, I thank you. You have reserved your homage for the fallen. Lip of man will never touch my hand again. I intend to become a Catholic, for the sake of going into a nunnery. When you next hear of Zenobia, her face will be behind the black veil; so look your last at it now,—for all is over. Once more, farewell!"

She withdrew her hand, yet left a lingering pressure, which I felt long afterwards. So intimately connected as I had been with perhaps the only man in whom she was ever truly interested, Zenobia looked on me as the representative of all the past, and was conscious that, in bidding me adieu, she likewise took final leave of Hollingsworth, and of this whole epoch of her life. Never did her beauty shine out more lustrously than in the last glimpse that I had of her. She departed, and was soon hidden among the trees. But, whether it was the strong impression of the foregoing scene, or whatever else the cause, I was affected with a fantasy that Zenobia had not actually gone, but was still hovering about the spot and haunting it. I seemed to feel her eyes upon me. It was as if the vivid coloring of her character had left a brilliant stain upon the air. By degrees, however, the impression grew less distinct. I flung myself upon the fallen leaves at the base of Eliot's pulpit. The sunshine withdrew up the tree trunks and flickered on the topmost boughs; gray twilight made the wood obscure; the stars brightened out; the pendent boughs became wet with chill autumnal dews. But I was listless, worn out with emotion on my own behalf and sympathy for others, and had no heart to leave my comfortless lair beneath the rock.

I must have fallen asleep, and had a dream, all the circumstances of which utterly vanished at the moment when they converged to some tragical catastrophe, and thus grew too powerful for the thin sphere of slumber that enveloped them.

Starting from the ground, I found the risen moon shining upon the rugged face of the rock, and myself all in a tremble.

XXVII. MIDNIGHT

It could not have been far from midnight when I came beneath Hollingsworth's window, and, finding it open, flung in a tuft of grass with earth at the roots, and heard it fall upon the floor. He was either awake or sleeping very lightly; for scarcely a moment had gone by before he looked out and discerned me standing in the moonlight.

"Is it you, Coverdale?" he asked. "What is the matter?"

"Come down to me, Hollingsworth!" I answered. "I am anxious to speak with you."

The strange tone of my own voice startled me, and him, probably, no less. He lost no time, and soon issued from the house-door, with his dress half arranged.

"Again, what is the matter?" he asked impatiently.

"Have you seen Zenobia," said I, "since you parted from her at Eliot's pulpit?"

"No," answered Hollingsworth; "nor did I expect it."

His voice was deep, but had a tremor in it,

Hardly had he spoken, when Silas Foster thrust his head, done up in a cotton handkerchief, out of another window, and took what he called as it literally was—a squint at us.

"Well, folks, what are ye about here?" he demanded. "Aha! are you there, Miles Coverdale? You have been turning night into day since you left us, I reckon; and so you find it quite natural to come prowling about the house at this time o' night, frightening my old woman out of her wits, and making her disturb a tired man out of his best nap. In with you, you vagabond, and to bed!"

"Dress yourself quickly, Foster," said I. "We want your assistance."

I could not, for the life of me, keep that strange tone out of my voice. Silas Foster, obtuse as were his sensibilities, seemed to feel the ghastly earnestness that was conveyed in it as well as Hollingsworth did. He immediately withdrew his head, and I heard him yawning, muttering to his wife, and again yawning heavily, while he hurried on his clothes. Meanwhile I showed Hollingsworth a delicate handkerchief, marked with a well-known cipher, and told where I had found it, and other circumstances, which had filled me with a suspicion so terrible that I left him, if he dared, to shape it out for himself. By the time my brief explanation was finished, we were joined by Silas Foster in his blue woollen frock.

"Well, boys," cried he peevishly, "what is to pay now?"

"Tell him, Hollingsworth," said I.

Hollingsworth shivered perceptibly, and drew in a hard breath betwixt his teeth. He steadied himself, however, and, looking the matter more firmly in the face than I had done, explained to Foster my suspicions, and the grounds of them, with a distinctness from which, in spite of my utmost efforts, my words had swerved aside. The tough-nerved yeoman, in his comment, put a finish on the business, and brought out the hideous idea in its full terror, as if he were removing the napkin from the face of a corpse.

"And so you think she's drowned herself?" he cried. I turned away my face.

"What on earth should the young woman do that for?" exclaimed Silas, his eyes half out of his head with mere surprise. "Why, she has more means than she can use or waste, and lacks nothing to make her comfortable, but a husband, and that's an article she could have, any day. There's some mistake about this, I tell you!"

"Come," said I, shuddering; "let us go and ascertain the truth."

"Well, well," answered Silas Foster; "just as you say. We'll take the long pole, with the hook at the end, that serves to get the bucket out of the draw-well when the rope is broken. With that, and a couple of long-handled hay-rakes, I'll answer for finding her, if she's anywhere to be found. Strange enough! Zenobia drown herself! No, no; I don't believe it. She had too much sense, and too much means, and enjoyed life a great deal too well."

When our few preparations were completed, we hastened, by a shorter than the customary route, through fields and pastures, and across a portion of the meadow, to the particular spot on the river-bank which I had paused to contemplate in the course of my afternoon's ramble. A nameless presentiment had again drawn me thither, after leaving Eliot's pulpit. I showed my companions where I had found the handkerchief, and pointed to two or three footsteps, impressed into the clayey margin, and tending towards the water. Beneath its shallow verge, among the water-weeds, there were further traces, as yet unobliterated by the sluggish current, which was there almost at a standstill. Silas Foster thrust his face down close to these footsteps, and picked up a shoe that had escaped my observation, being half imbedded in the mud.

"There's a kid shoe that never was made on a Yankee last," observed he. "I know enough of shoemaker's craft to tell that. French manufacture; and see what a high instep! and how evenly she trod in it! There never was a woman that stept handsomer in her shoes than Zenobia did. Here," he added, addressing Hollingsworth, "would you like to keep the shoe?"

Hollingsworth started back.

"Give it to me, Foster," said I.

I dabbled it in the water, to rinse off the mud, and have kept it ever since. Not far from this spot lay an old, leaky punt, drawn up on the oozy river-side, and generally half full of water. It served the angler to go in quest of pickerel, or the sportsman to pick up his wild ducks. Setting this crazy bark afloat, I seated myself in the stern with the paddle, while Hollingsworth sat in the bows with the hooked pole, and Silas Foster amidships with a hay-rake.

"It puts me in mind of my young days," remarked Silas, "when I used to steal out of bed to go bobbing for hornpouts and eels. Heigh-ho!—well, life and death together make sad work for us all! Then I was a boy, bobbing for fish; and now I am getting to be an old fellow, and here I be, groping for a dead body! I tell you what, lads; if I thought anything had really happened to Zenobia, I should feel kind o' sorrowful."

"I wish, at least, you would hold your tongue," muttered I.

The moon, that night, though past the full, was still large and oval, and having risen between eight and nine o'clock, now shone aslantwise over the river, throwing the high, opposite bank, with its woods, into deep shadow, but lighting up the hither shore pretty effectually. Not a ray appeared to fall on the river itself. It lapsed imperceptibly away, a broad, black, inscrutable depth, keeping its own secrets from the eye of man, as impenetrably as mid-ocean could.

"Well, Miles Coverdale," said Foster, "you are the helmsman. How do you mean to manage this business?"

"I shall let the boat drift, broadside foremost, past that stump," I replied. "I know the bottom, having sounded it in fishing. The shore, on this side, after the first step or two, goes off very abruptly; and there is a pool, just by the stump, twelve or fifteen feet deep. The current could not have force enough to sweep any sunken object, even if partially buoyant, out of that hollow."

"Come, then," said Silas; "but I doubt whether I can touch bottom with this hay-rake, if it's as deep as you say. Mr. Hollingsworth, I think you'll be the lucky man to-night, such luck as it is."

We floated past the stump. Silas Foster plied his rake manfully, poking it as far as he could into the water, and immersing the whole length of his arm besides. Hollingsworth at first sat motionless, with the hooked pole elevated in the air. But, by and by, with a nervous and jerky movement, he began to plunge it into the blackness that upbore us, setting his teeth, and making precisely such thrusts, methought, as if he were stabbing at a deadly enemy. I bent over the side of the boat. So obscure, however, so awfully mysterious, was that dark stream, that—and the thought made me shiver like a leaf—I might as well have tried to look into the enigma of the eternal world, to discover what had become of Zenobia's soul, as into the river's depths, to find her body. And there, perhaps, she lay, with her face upward, while the shadow of the boat, and my own pale face peering downward, passed slowly betwixt her and the sky!

Once, twice, thrice, I paddled the boat upstream, and again suffered it to glide, with the river's slow, funereal motion, downward. Silas Foster had raked up a large mass of stuff, which, as it came towards the surface, looked somewhat like a flowing garment, but proved to be a monstrous tuft of water-weeds. Hollingsworth, with a gigantic effort, upheaved a sunken log. When once free of the bottom, it rose partly out of water,—all weedy and slimy, a devilish-looking object, which the moon had not shone upon for half a hundred years,—then plunged again, and sullenly returned to its old resting-place, for the remnant of the century.

"That looked ugly!" quoth Silas. "I half thought it was the Evil One, on the same errand as ourselves,—searching for Zenobia."

"He shall never get her," said I, giving the boat a strong impulse.

"That's not for you to say, my boy," retorted the yeoman. "Pray God he never has, and never may. Slow work this, however! I should really be glad to find something! Pshaw! What a notion that is, when the only good luck would be to paddle, and drift, and poke, and grope, hereabouts, till morning, and have our labor for our pains! For my part, I shouldn't wonder if the creature had only lost her shoe in the mud, and saved her soul alive, after all. My stars! how she will laugh at us, to-morrow morning!"

It is indescribable what an image of Zenobia—at the breakfast-table, full of warm and mirthful life—this surmise of Silas Foster's brought before my mind. The terrible phantasm of her death was thrown by it into the remotest and dimmest background, where it seemed to grow as improbable as a myth.

"Yes, Silas, it may be as you say," cried I. The drift of the stream had again borne us a little below the stump, when I felt—yes, felt, for it was as if the iron hook had smote my breast—felt Hollingsworth's pole strike some object at the bottom of the river!

He started up, and almost overset the boat.

"Hold on!" cried Foster; "you have her!"

Putting a fury of strength into the effort, Hollingsworth heaved amain, and up came a white swash to the surface of the river. It was the flow of a woman's garments. A little higher, and we saw her dark hair streaming down the current. Black River of Death, thou hadst yielded up thy victim! Zenobia was found!

Silas Foster laid hold of the body; Hollingsworth likewise grappled with it; and I steered towards the bank, gazing all the while at Zenobia, whose limbs were swaying in the current close at the boat's side. Arriving near the shore, we all three stept into the water, bore her out, and laid her on the ground beneath a tree.

"Poor child!" said Foster,—and his dry old heart, I verily believe, vouchsafed a tear, "I'm sorry for her!"

Were I to describe the perfect horror of the spectacle, the reader might justly reckon it to me for a sin and shame. For more than twelve long years I have borne it in my memory, and could now reproduce it as freshly as if it were still before my eyes. Of all modes of death, methinks it is the ugliest. Her wet garments swathed limbs of terrible inflexibility. She was the marble image of a death-agony. Her arms had grown rigid in the act of struggling, and were bent before her with clenched hands; her knees, too, were bent, and—thank God for it!—in the attitude of prayer. Ah, that rigidity! It is impossible to bear the terror of it. It seemed,—I must needs impart so much of my own miserable idea,—it seemed as if her body must keep the same position in the coffin, and that her skeleton would keep it in the grave; and that when Zenobia rose at the day of judgment, it would be in just the same attitude as now!

One hope I had, and that too was mingled half with fear. She knelt as if in prayer. With the last, choking consciousness, her soul, bubbling out through her lips, it may be, had given itself up to the Father, reconciled and penitent. But her arms! They were bent before her, as if she struggled against Providence in never-ending hostility. Her hands! They were clenched in immitigable defiance. Away with the hideous thought. The flitting moment after Zenobia sank into the dark pool—when her breath was gone, and her soul at her lips was as long, in its capacity of God's infinite forgiveness, as the lifetime of the world!

Foster bent over the body, and carefully examined it.

"You have wounded the poor thing's breast," said he to Hollingsworth, "close by her heart, too!"

"Ha!" cried Hollingsworth with a start.

And so he had, indeed, both before and after death!

"See!" said Foster. "That's the place where the iron struck her. It looks cruelly, but she never felt it!"

He endeavored to arrange the arms of the corpse decently by its side. His utmost strength, however, scarcely sufficed to bring them down; and rising again, the next instant, they bade him defiance, exactly as before. He made another effort, with the same result.

"In God's name, Silas Foster," cried I with bitter indignation, "let that dead woman alone!"

"Why, man, it's not decent!" answered he, staring at me in amazement. "I can't bear to see her looking so! Well, well," added he, after a third effort, "'tis of no use, sure enough; and we must leave the women to do their best with her, after we get to the house. The sooner that's done, the better."

We took two rails from a neighboring fence, and formed a bier by laying across some boards from the bottom of the boat. And thus we bore Zenobia homeward. Six hours before, how beautiful! At midnight, what a horror! A reflection occurs to me that will show ludicrously, I doubt not, on my page, but must come in for its sterling truth. Being the woman that she was, could Zenobia have foreseen all these ugly circumstances of death,—how ill it would become her, the altogether unseemly aspect which she must put on, and especially old Silas Foster's efforts to improve the matter,—she would no more have committed the dreadful act than have exhibited herself to a public assembly in a badly fitting garment! Zenobia, I have often thought, was not quite simple in her death. She had seen pictures, I suppose, of drowned persons in lithe and graceful attitudes. And she deemed it well and decorous to die as so many village maidens have, wronged in their first love, and seeking peace in the bosom of the old familiar stream,—so familiar that they could not dread it,—where, in childhood, they used to bathe their little feet, wading mid-leg deep, unmindful of wet skirts. But in Zenobia's case there was some tint of the Arcadian affectation that had been visible enough in all our lives for a few months past.

This, however, to my conception, takes nothing from the tragedy. For, has not the world come to an awfully sophisticated pass, when, after a certain degree of acquaintance with it, we cannot even put ourselves to death in whole-hearted simplicity? Slowly, slowly, with many a dreary pause,—resting the bier often on some rock or balancing it across a mossy log, to take fresh hold,—we bore our burden onward through the moonlight, and at last laid Zenobia on the floor of the old farmhouse. By and by came three or four withered women and stood whispering around the corpse, peering at it through their spectacles, holding up their skinny hands, shaking their night-capped heads, and taking counsel of one another's experience what was to be done.

With those tire-women we left Zenobia.

XXVIII. BLITHEDALE PASTURE

Blithedale, thus far in its progress, had never found the necessity of a burial-ground. There was some consultation among us in what spot Zenobia might most fitly be laid. It was my own wish that she should sleep at the base of Eliot's pulpit, and that on the rugged front of the rock the name by which we familiarly knew her, Zenobia,—and not another word, should be deeply cut, and left for the moss and lichens to fill up at their long leisure. But Hollingsworth (to whose ideas on this point great deference was due) made it his request that her grave might be dug on the gently sloping hillside, in the wide pasture, where, as we once supposed, Zenobia and he had planned to build their cottage. And thus it was done, accordingly.

She was buried very much as other people have been for hundreds of years gone by. In anticipation of a death, we Blithedale colonists had sometimes set our fancies at work to arrange a funereal ceremony, which should be the proper symbolic expression of our spiritual faith and eternal hopes; and this we meant to substitute for those customary rites which were moulded originally out of the Gothic gloom, and by long use, like an old velvet pall, have so much more than their first death-smell in them. But when the occasion came we found it the simplest and truest thing, after all, to content ourselves with the old fashion, taking away what we could, but interpolating no novelties, and particularly avoiding all frippery of flowers and cheerful emblems. The procession moved from the farm-house. Nearest the dead walked an old man in deep mourning, his face mostly concealed in a white handkerchief, and with Priscilla leaning on his arm. Hollingsworth and myself came next. We all stood around the narrow niche in the cold earth; all saw the coffin lowered in; all heard the rattle of the crumbly soil upon its lid,—that final sound, which mortality awakens on the utmost verge of sense, as if in the vain hope of bringing an echo from the spiritual world.

I noticed a stranger,—a stranger to most of those present, though known to me,—who, after the coffin had descended, took up a handful of earth and flung it first into the grave. I had given up Hollingsworth's arm, and now found myself near this man.

"It was an idle thing—a foolish thing—for Zenobia to do," said he. "She was the last woman in the world to whom death could have been necessary. It was too absurd! I have no patience with her."

"Why so?" I inquired, smothering my horror at his cold comment, in my eager curiosity to discover some tangible truth as to his relation with Zenobia. "If any crisis could justify the sad wrong she offered to herself, it was surely that in which she stood. Everything had failed her; prosperity in the world's sense, for her opulence was gone,—the heart's prosperity, in love. And there was a secret burden on her, the nature of which is best known to you. Young as she was, she had tried life fully, had no more to hope, and something, perhaps, to fear. Had Providence taken her away in its own holy hand, I should have thought it the kindest dispensation that could be awarded to one so wrecked."

"You mistake the matter completely," rejoined Westervelt.

"What, then, is your own view of it?" I asked.

"Her mind was active, and various in its powers," said he. "Her heart had a manifold adaptation; her constitution an infinite buoyancy, which (had she possessed only a little patience to await the reflux of her troubles) would have borne her upward triumphantly for twenty years to come. Her beauty would not have waned—or scarcely so, and surely not beyond the reach of art to restore it—in all that time. She had life's summer all before her, and a hundred varieties of brilliant success. What an actress Zenobia might have been! It was one of her least valuable capabilities. How forcibly she might have wrought upon the world, either directly in her own person, or by her influence upon some man, or a series of men, of controlling genius! Every prize that could be worth a woman's having—and many prizes which other women are too timid to desire—lay within Zenobia's reach."

"In all this," I observed, "there would have been nothing to satisfy her heart."

"Her heart!" answered Westervelt contemptuously. "That troublesome organ (as she had hitherto found it) would have been kept in its due place and degree, and have had all the gratification it could fairly claim. She would soon have established a control over it. Love had failed her, you say. Had it never failed her before? Yet she survived it, and loved again,—possibly not once alone, nor twice either. And now to drown herself for yonder dreamy philanthropist!"

"Who are you," I exclaimed indignantly, "that dare to speak thus of the dead? You seem to intend a eulogy, yet leave out whatever was noblest in her, and blacken while you mean to praise. I have long considered you as Zenobia's evil fate. Your sentiments confirm me in the idea, but leave me still ignorant as to the mode in which you have influenced her life. The connection may have been indissoluble, except by death. Then, indeed,—always in the hope of God's infinite mercy,—I cannot deem it a misfortune that she sleeps in yonder grave!"

"No matter what I was to her," he answered gloomily, yet without actual emotion. "She is now beyond my reach. Had she lived, and hearkened to my counsels, we might have served each other well. But there Zenobia lies in yonder pit, with the dull earth over her. Twenty years of a brilliant lifetime thrown away for a mere woman's whim!"

Heaven deal with Westervelt according to his nature and deserts!—that is to say, annihilate him. He was altogether earthy, worldly, made for time and its gross objects, and incapable—except by a sort of dim reflection caught from other minds—of so much as one spiritual idea. Whatever stain Zenobia had was caught from him; nor does it seldom happen that a character of admirable qualities loses its better life because the atmosphere that should sustain it is rendered poisonous by such breath as this man mingled with Zenobia's. Yet his reflections possessed their share of truth. It was a woeful thought, that a woman of Zenobia's diversified capacity should have fancied herself irretrievably defeated on the broad battlefield of life, and with no refuge, save to fall on her own sword, merely because Love had gone against her. It is nonsense, and a miserable wrong,—the result, like so many others, of masculine egotism,—that the success or failure of woman's existence should be made to depend wholly on the affections, and on one species of affection, while man has such a multitude of other chances, that this seems but an incident. For its own sake, if it will do no more, the world should throw open all its avenues to the passport of a woman's bleeding heart.

As we stood around the grave, I looked often towards Priscilla, dreading to see her wholly overcome with grief. And deeply grieved, in truth, she was. But a character so simply constituted as hers has room only for a single predominant affection. No other feeling can touch the heart's inmost core, nor do it any deadly mischief. Thus, while we see that such a being responds to every breeze with tremulous vibration, and imagine that she must be shattered by the first rude blast, we find her retaining her equilibrium amid shocks that might have overthrown many a sturdier frame. So with Priscilla; her one possible misfortune was Hollingsworth's unkindness; and that was destined never to befall her, never yet, at least, for Priscilla has not died.

But Hollingsworth! After all the evil that he did, are we to leave him thus, blest with the entire devotion of this one true heart, and with wealth at his disposal to execute the long-contemplated project that had led him so far astray? What retribution is there here? My mind being vexed with precisely this query, I made a journey, some years since, for the sole purpose of catching a last glimpse of Hollingsworth, and judging for myself whether he were a happy man or no. I learned that he inhabited a small cottage, that his way of life was exceedingly retired, and that my only chance of encountering him or Priscilla was to meet them in a secluded lane, where, in the latter part of the afternoon, they were accustomed to walk. I did meet them, accordingly. As they approached me, I observed in Hollingsworth's face a depressed and melancholy look, that seemed habitual; the powerfully built man showed a self-distrustful weakness, and a childlike or childish tendency to press close, and closer still, to the side of the slender woman whose arm was within his. In Priscilla's manner there was a protective and watchful quality, as if she felt herself the guardian of her companion; but, likewise, a deep, submissive, unquestioning reverence, and also a veiled happiness in her fair and quiet countenance.

Drawing nearer, Priscilla recognized me, and gave me a kind and friendly smile, but with a slight gesture, which I could not help interpreting as an entreaty not to make myself known to Hollingsworth. Nevertheless, an impulse took possession of me, and compelled me to address him.

"I have come, Hollingsworth," said I, "to view your grand edifice for the reformation of criminals. Is it finished yet?"

"No, nor begun," answered he, without raising his eyes. "A very small one answers all my purposes."

Priscilla threw me an upbraiding glance. But I spoke again, with a bitter and revengeful emotion, as if flinging a poisoned arrow at Hollingsworth's heart.

"Up to this moment," I inquired, "how many criminals have you reformed?"

"Not one," said Hollingsworth, with his eyes still fixed on the ground. "Ever since we parted, I have been busy with a single murderer."

Then the tears gushed into my eyes, and I forgave him; for I remembered the wild energy, the passionate shriek, with which Zenobia had spoken those words, "Tell him he has murdered me! Tell him that I'll haunt him!"—and I knew what murderer he meant, and whose vindictive shadow dogged the side where Priscilla was not.

The moral which presents itself to my reflections, as drawn from Hollingsworth's character and errors, is simply this, that, admitting what is called philanthropy, when adopted as a profession, to be often useful by its energetic impulse to society at large, it is perilous to the individual whose ruling passion, in one exclusive channel, it thus becomes. It ruins, or is fearfully apt to ruin, the heart, the rich juices of which God never meant should be pressed violently out and distilled into alcoholic liquor by an unnatural process, but should render life sweet, bland, and gently beneficent, and insensibly influence other hearts and other lives to the same blessed end. I see in Hollingsworth an exemplification of the most awful truth in Bunyan's book of such, from the very gate of heaven there is a by-way to the pit!

But, all this while, we have been standing by Zenobia's grave. I have never since beheld it, but make no question that the grass grew all the better, on that little parallelogram of pasture land, for the decay of the beautiful woman who slept beneath. How Nature seems to love us! And how readily, nevertheless, without a sigh or a complaint, she converts us to a meaner purpose, when her highest one—that of a conscious intellectual life and sensibility has been untimely balked! While Zenobia lived, Nature was proud of her, and directed all eyes upon that radiant presence, as her fairest handiwork. Zenobia perished. Will not Nature shed a tear? Ah, no!—she adopts the calamity at once into her system, and is just as well pleased, for aught we can see, with the tuft of ranker vegetation that grew out of Zenobia's heart, as with all the beauty which has bequeathed us no earthly representative except in this crop of weeds. It is because the spirit is inestimable that the lifeless body is so little valued.

XXIX. MILES COVERDALE'S CONFESSION

It remains only to say a few words about myself. Not improbably, the reader might be willing to spare me the trouble; for I have made but a poor and dim figure in my own narrative, establishing no separate interest, and suffering my colorless life to take its hue from other lives. But one still retains some little consideration for one's self; so I keep these last two or three pages for my individual and sole behoof.

But what, after all, have I to tell? Nothing, nothing, nothing! I left Blithedale within the week after Zenobia's death, and went back thither no more. The whole soil of our farm, for a long time afterwards, seemed but the sodded earth over her grave. I could not toil there, nor live upon its products. Often, however, in these years that are darkening around me, I remember our beautiful scheme of a noble and unselfish life; and how fair, in that first summer, appeared the prospect that it might endure for generations, and be perfected, as the ages rolled away, into the system of a people and a world! Were my former associates now there,—were there only three or four of those true-hearted men still laboring in the sun,—I sometimes fancy that I should direct my world-weary footsteps thitherward, and entreat them to receive me, for old friendship's sake. More and more I feel that we had struck upon what ought to be a truth. Posterity may dig it up, and profit by it. The experiment, so far as its original projectors were concerned, proved, long ago, a failure; first lapsing into Fourierism, and dying, as it well deserved, for this infidelity to its own higher spirit. Where once we toiled with our whole hopeful hearts, the town paupers, aged, nerveless, and disconsolate, creep sluggishly afield. Alas, what faith is requisite to bear up against such results of generous effort!

My subsequent life has passed,—I was going to say happily, but, at all events, tolerably enough. I am now at middle age, well, well, a step or two beyond the midmost point, and I care not a fig who knows it!—a bachelor, with no very decided purpose of ever being otherwise. I have been twice to Europe, and spent a year or two rather agreeably at each visit. Being well to do in the world, and having nobody but myself to care for, I live very much at my ease, and fare sumptuously every day. As for poetry, I have given it up, notwithstanding that Dr. Griswold—as the reader, of course, knows—has placed me at a fair elevation among our minor minstrelsy, on the strength of my pretty little volume, published ten years ago. As regards human progress (in spite of my irrepressible yearnings over the Blithedale reminiscences), let them believe in it who can, and aid in it who choose. If I could earnestly do either, it might be all the better for my comfort. As Hollingsworth once told me, I lack a purpose. How strange! He was ruined, morally, by an overplus of the very same ingredient, the want of which, I occasionally suspect, has rendered my own life all an emptiness. I by no means wish to die. Yet, were there any cause, in this whole chaos of human struggle, worth a sane man's dying for, and which my death would benefit, then—provided, however, the effort did not involve an unreasonable amount of trouble—methinks I might be bold to offer up my life. If Kossuth, for example, would pitch the battlefield of Hungarian rights within an easy ride of my abode, and choose a mild, sunny morning, after breakfast, for the conflict, Miles Coverdale would gladly be his man, for one brave rush upon the levelled bayonets. Further than that, I should be loath to pledge myself.

I exaggerate my own defects. The reader must not take my own word for it, nor believe me altogether changed from the young man who once hoped strenuously, and struggled not so much amiss. Frostier heads than mine have gained honor in the world; frostier hearts have imbibed new warmth, and been newly happy. Life, however, it must be owned, has come to rather an idle pass with me. Would my friends like to know what brought it thither? There is one secret,—I have concealed it all along, and never meant to let the least whisper of it escape,—one foolish little secret, which possibly may have had something to do with these inactive years of meridian manhood, with my bachelorship, with the unsatisfied retrospect that I fling back on life, and my listless glance towards the future. Shall I reveal it? It is an absurd thing for a man in his afternoon,—a man of the world, moreover, with these three white hairs in his brown mustache and that deepening track of a crow's-foot on each temple,—an absurd thing ever to have happened, and quite the absurdest for an old bachelor, like me, to talk about. But it rises to my throat; so let it come.

I perceive, moreover, that the confession, brief as it shall be, will throw a gleam of light over my behavior throughout the foregoing incidents, and is, indeed, essential to the full understanding of my story. The reader, therefore, since I have disclosed so much, is entitled to this one word more. As I write it, he will charitably suppose me to blush, and turn away my face:

I—I myself—was in love—with—Priscilla!

MOSSES FROM AN OLD MANSE AND OTHER STORIES

THE BIRTHMARK

In the latter part of the last century there lived a man of science, an eminent proficient in every branch of natural philosophy, who not long before our story opens had made experience of a spiritual affinity more attractive than any chemical one. He had left his laboratory to the care of an assistant, cleared his fine countenance from the furnace smoke, washed the stain of acids from his fingers, and persuaded a beautiful woman to become his wife. In those days when the comparatively recent discovery of electricity and other kindred mysteries of Nature seemed to open paths into the region of miracle, it was not unusual for the love of science to rival the love of woman in its depth and absorbing energy. The higher intellect, the imagination, the spirit, and even the heart might all find their congenial aliment in pursuits which, as some of their ardent votaries believed, would ascend from one step of powerful intelligence to another, until the philosopher should lay his hand on the secret of creative force and perhaps make new worlds for himself. We know not whether Aylmer possessed this degree of faith in man's ultimate control over Nature. He had devoted himself, however, too unreservedly to scientific studies ever to be weaned from them by any second passion. His love for his young wife might prove the stronger of the two; but it could only be by intertwining itself with his love of science, and uniting the strength of the latter to his own.

Such a union accordingly took place, and was attended with truly remarkable consequences and a deeply impressive moral. One day, very soon after their marriage, Aylmer sat gazing at his wife with a trouble in his countenance that grew stronger until he spoke.

"Georgiana," said he, "has it never occurred to you that the mark upon your cheek might be removed?"

"No, indeed," said she, smiling; but perceiving the seriousness of his manner, she blushed deeply. "To tell you the truth it has been so often called a charm that I was simple enough to imagine it might be so."

"Ah, upon another face perhaps it might," replied her husband; "but never on yours. No, dearest Georgiana, you came so nearly perfect from the hand of Nature that this slightest possible defect, which we hesitate whether to term a defect or a beauty, shocks me, as being the visible mark of earthly imperfection."

"Shocks you, my husband!" cried Georgiana, deeply hurt; at first reddening with momentary anger, but then bursting into tears. "Then why did you take me from my mother's side? You cannot love what shocks you!"

To explain this conversation it must be mentioned that in the centre of Georgiana's left cheek there was a singular mark, deeply interwoven, as it were, with the texture and substance of her face. In the usual state of her complexion—a healthy though delicate bloom—the mark wore a tint of deeper crimson, which imperfectly defined its shape amid the surrounding rosiness. When she blushed it gradually became more indistinct, and finally vanished amid the triumphant rush of blood that bathed the whole cheek with its brilliant glow. But if any shifting motion caused her to turn pale there was the mark again, a crimson stain upon the snow, in what Aylmer sometimes deemed an almost fearful distinctness. Its shape bore not a little similarity to the human hand, though of the smallest pygmy size. Georgiana's lovers were wont to say that some fairy at her birth hour had laid her tiny hand upon the infant's cheek, and left this impress there in token of the magic endowments that were to give her such sway over all hearts. Many a desperate swain would have risked life for the privilege of pressing his lips to the mysterious hand. It must not be concealed, however, that the impression wrought by this fairy sign manual varied exceedingly, according to the difference of temperament in the beholders. Some fastidious persons—but they were exclusively of her own sex—affirmed that the bloody hand, as they chose to call it, quite destroyed the effect of Georgiana's beauty, and rendered her countenance even hideous. But it would be as reasonable to say that one of those small blue stains which sometimes occur in the purest statuary marble would convert the Eve of Powers to a monster. Masculine observers, if the birthmark did not heighten their admiration, contented themselves with wishing it away, that the world might possess one living specimen of ideal loveliness without the semblance of a flaw. After his marriage,—for he thought little or nothing of the matter before,—Aylmer discovered that this was the case with himself.

Had she been less beautiful,—if Envy's self could have found aught else to sneer at,—he might have felt his affection heightened by the prettiness of this mimic hand, now vaguely portrayed, now lost, now stealing forth again and glimmering to and fro with every pulse of emotion that throbbed within her heart; but seeing her otherwise so perfect, he found this one defect grow more and more intolerable with every moment of their united lives. It was the fatal flaw of humanity which Nature, in one shape or another, stamps ineffaceably on all her productions, either to imply that they are temporary and finite, or that their perfection must be wrought by toil and pain. The crimson hand expressed the ineludible gripe in which mortality clutches the highest and purest of earthly mould, degrading them into kindred with the lowest, and even with the very brutes, like whom their visible frames return to dust. In this manner, selecting it as the symbol of his wife's liability to sin, sorrow, decay, and death, Aylmer's sombre imagination was not long in rendering the birthmark a frightful object, causing him more trouble and horror than ever Georgiana's beauty, whether of soul or sense, had given him delight.

At all the seasons which should have been their happiest, he invariably and without intending it, nay, in spite of a purpose to the contrary, reverted to this one disastrous topic. Trifling as it at first appeared, it so connected itself with innumerable trains of thought and modes of feeling that it became the central point of all. With the morning twilight Aylmer opened his eyes upon his wife's face and recognized the symbol of imperfection; and when they sat together at the evening hearth his eyes wandered stealthily to her cheek, and beheld, flickering with the blaze of the wood fire, the spectral hand that wrote mortality where he would fain have worshipped. Georgiana soon learned to shudder at his gaze. It needed but a glance with the peculiar expression that his face often wore to change the roses of her cheek into a deathlike paleness, amid which the crimson hand was brought strongly out, like a bass-relief of ruby on the whitest marble.

Late one night when the lights were growing dim, so as hardly to betray the stain on the poor wife's cheek, she herself, for the first time, voluntarily took up the subject.

"Do you remember, my dear Aylmer," said she, with a feeble attempt at a smile, "have you any recollection of a dream last night about this odious hand?"

"None! none whatever!" replied Aylmer, starting; but then he added, in a dry, cold tone, affected for the sake of concealing the real depth of his emotion, "I might well dream of it; for before I fell asleep it had taken a pretty firm hold of my fancy."

"And you did dream of it?" continued Georgiana, hastily; for she dreaded lest a gush of tears should interrupt what she had to say. "A terrible dream! I wonder that you can forget it. Is it possible to forget this one expression?—'It is in her heart now; we must have it out!' Reflect, my husband; for by all means I would have you recall that dream."

The mind is in a sad state when Sleep, the all-involving, cannot confine her spectres within the dim region of her sway, but suffers them to break forth, affrighting this actual life with secrets that perchance belong to a deeper one. Aylmer now remembered his dream. He had fancied himself with his servant Aminadab, attempting an operation for the removal of the birthmark; but the deeper went the knife, the deeper sank the hand, until at length its tiny grasp appeared to have caught hold of Georgiana's heart; whence, however, her husband was inexorably resolved to cut or wrench it away.

When the dream had shaped itself perfectly in his memory, Aylmer sat in his wife's presence with a guilty feeling. Truth often finds its way to the mind close muffled in robes of sleep, and then speaks with uncompromising directness of matters in regard to which we practise an unconscious self-deception during our waking moments. Until now he had not been aware of the tyrannizing influence acquired by one idea over his mind, and of the lengths which he might find in his heart to go for the sake of giving himself peace.

"Aylmer," resumed Georgiana, solemnly, "I know not what may be the cost to both of us to rid me of this fatal birthmark. Perhaps its removal may cause cureless deformity; or it may be the stain goes as deep as life itself. Again: do we know that there is a possibility, on any terms, of unclasping the firm gripe of this little hand which was laid upon me before I came into the world?"

"Dearest Georgiana, I have spent much thought upon the subject," hastily interrupted Aylmer. "I am convinced of the perfect practicability of its removal."

"If there be the remotest possibility of it," continued Georgiana, "let the attempt be made at whatever risk. Danger is nothing to me; for life, while this hateful mark makes me the object of your horror and disgust,—life is a burden which I would fling down with joy. Either remove this dreadful hand, or take my wretched life! You have deep science. All the world bears witness of it. You have achieved great wonders. Cannot you remove this little, little mark, which I cover with the tips of two small fingers? Is this beyond your power, for the sake of your own peace, and to save your poor wife from madness?"

"Noblest, dearest, tenderest wife," cried Aylmer, rapturously, "doubt not my power. I have already given this matter the deepest thought—thought which might almost have enlightened me to create a being less perfect than yourself. Georgiana, you have led me deeper than ever into the heart of science. I feel myself fully competent to render this dear cheek as faultless as its fellow; and then, most beloved, what will be my triumph when I shall have corrected what Nature left imperfect in her fairest work! Even Pygmalion, when his sculptured woman assumed life, felt not greater ecstasy than mine will be."

"It is resolved, then," said Georgiana, faintly smiling. "And, Aylmer, spare me not, though you should find the birthmark take refuge in my heart at last."

Her husband tenderly kissed her cheek—her right cheek—not that which bore the impress of the crimson hand.

The next day Aylmer apprised his wife of a plan that he had formed whereby he might have opportunity for the intense thought and constant watchfulness which the proposed operation would require; while Georgiana, likewise, would enjoy the perfect repose essential to its success. They were to seclude themselves in the extensive apartments occupied by Aylmer as a laboratory, and where, during his toilsome youth, he had made discoveries in the elemental powers of Nature that had roused the admiration of all the learned societies in Europe. Seated calmly in this laboratory, the pale philosopher had investigated the secrets of the highest cloud region and of the profoundest mines; he had satisfied himself of the causes that kindled and kept alive the fires of the volcano; and had explained the mystery of fountains, and how it is that they gush forth, some so bright and pure, and others with such rich medicinal virtues, from the dark bosom of the earth. Here, too, at an earlier period, he had studied the wonders of the human frame, and attempted to fathom the very process by which Nature assimilates all her precious influences from earth and air, and from the spiritual world, to create and foster man, her masterpiece. The latter pursuit, however, Aylmer had long laid aside in unwilling recognition of the truth—against which all seekers sooner or later stumble—that our great creative Mother, while she amuses us with apparently working in the broadest sunshine, is yet severely careful to keep her own secrets, and, in spite of her pretended openness, shows us nothing but results. She permits us, indeed, to mar, but seldom to mend, and, like a jealous patentee, on no account to make. Now, however, Aylmer resumed these half-forgotten investigations; not, of course, with such hopes or wishes as first suggested them; but because they involved much physiological truth and lay in the path of his proposed scheme for the treatment of Georgiana.

As he led her over the threshold of the laboratory, Georgiana was cold and tremulous. Aylmer looked cheerfully into her face, with intent to reassure her, but was so startled with the intense glow of the birthmark upon the whiteness of her cheek that he could not restrain a strong convulsive shudder. His wife fainted.

"Aminadab! Aminadab!" shouted Aylmer, stamping violently on the floor.

Forthwith there issued from an inner apartment a man of low stature, but bulky frame, with shaggy hair hanging about his visage, which was grimed with the vapors of the furnace. This personage had been Aylmer's underworker during his whole scientific career, and was admirably fitted for that office by his great mechanical readiness, and the skill with which, while incapable of comprehending a single principle, he executed all the details of his master's experiments. With his vast strength, his shaggy hair, his smoky aspect, and the indescribable earthiness that incrusted him, he seemed to represent man's physical nature; while Aylmer's slender figure, and pale, intellectual face, were no less apt a type of the spiritual element.

"Throw open the door of the boudoir, Aminadab," said Aylmer, "and burn a pastil."

"Yes, master," answered Aminadab, looking intently at the lifeless form of Georgiana; and then he muttered to himself, "If she were my wife, I'd never part with that birthmark."

When Georgiana recovered consciousness she found herself breathing an atmosphere of penetrating fragrance, the gentle potency of which had recalled her from her deathlike faintness. The scene around her looked like enchantment. Aylmer had converted those smoky, dingy, sombre rooms, where he had spent his brightest years in recondite pursuits, into a series of beautiful apartments not unfit to be the secluded abode of a lovely woman. The walls were hung with gorgeous curtains, which imparted the combination of grandeur and grace that no other species of adornment can achieve; and as they fell from the ceiling to the floor, their rich and ponderous folds, concealing all angles and straight lines, appeared to shut in the scene from infinite space. For aught Georgiana knew, it might be a pavilion among the clouds. And Aylmer, excluding the sunshine, which would have interfered with his chemical processes, had supplied its place with perfumed lamps, emitting flames of various hue, but all uniting in a soft, impurpled radiance. He now knelt by his wife's side, watching her earnestly, but without alarm; for he was confident in his science, and felt that he could draw a magic circle round her within which no evil might intrude.

"Where am I? Ah, I remember," said Georgiana, faintly; and she placed her hand over her cheek to hide the terrible mark from her husband's eyes.

"Fear not, dearest!" exclaimed he. "Do not shrink from me! Believe me, Georgiana, I even rejoice in this single imperfection, since it will be such a rapture to remove it."

"Oh, spare me!" sadly replied his wife. "Pray do not look at it again. I never can forget that convulsive shudder."

In order to soothe Georgiana, and, as it were, to release her mind from the burden of actual things, Aylmer now put in practice some of the light and playful secrets which science had taught him among its profounder lore. Airy figures, absolutely bodiless ideas, and forms of unsubstantial beauty came and danced before her, imprinting their momentary footsteps on beams of light. Though she had some indistinct idea of the method of these optical phenomena, still the illusion was almost perfect enough to warrant the belief that her husband possessed sway over the spiritual world. Then again, when she felt a wish to look forth from her seclusion, immediately, as if her thoughts were answered, the procession of external existence flitted across a screen. The scenery and the figures of actual life were perfectly represented, but with that bewitching, yet indescribable difference which always makes a picture, an image, or a shadow so much more attractive than the original. When wearied of this, Aylmer bade her cast her eyes upon a vessel containing a quantity of earth. She did so, with little interest at first; but was soon startled to perceive the germ of a plant shooting upward from the soil. Then came the slender stalk; the leaves gradually unfolded themselves; and amid them was a perfect and lovely flower.

"It is magical!" cried Georgiana. "I dare not touch it."

"Nay, pluck it," answered Aylmer,—"pluck it, and inhale its brief perfume while you may. The flower will wither in a few moments and leave nothing save its brown seed vessels; but thence may be perpetuated a race as ephemeral as itself."

But Georgiana had no sooner touched the flower than the whole plant suffered a blight, its leaves turning coal-black as if by the agency of fire.

"There was too powerful a stimulus," said Aylmer, thoughtfully.

To make up for this abortive experiment, he proposed to take her portrait by a scientific process of his own invention. It was to be effected by rays of light striking upon a polished plate of metal. Georgiana assented; but, on looking at the result, was affrighted to find the features of the portrait blurred and indefinable; while the minute figure of a hand appeared where the cheek should have been. Aylmer snatched the metallic plate and threw it into a jar of corrosive acid.

Soon, however, he forgot these mortifying failures. In the intervals of study and chemical experiment he came to her flushed and exhausted, but seemed invigorated by her presence, and spoke in glowing language of the resources of his art. He gave a history of the long dynasty of the alchemists, who spent so many ages in quest of the universal solvent by which the golden principle might be elicited from all things vile and base. Aylmer appeared to believe that, by the plainest scientific logic, it was altogether within the limits of possibility to discover this long-sought medium; "but," he added, "a philosopher who should go deep enough to acquire the power would attain too lofty a wisdom to stoop to the exercise of it." Not less singular were his opinions in regard to the elixir vitae. He more than intimated that it was at his option to concoct a liquid that should prolong life for years, perhaps interminably; but that it would produce a discord in Nature which all the world, and chiefly the quaffer of the immortal nostrum, would find cause to curse.

"Aylmer, are you in earnest?" asked Georgiana, looking at him with amazement and fear. "It is terrible to possess such power, or even to dream of possessing it."

"Oh, do not tremble, my love," said her husband. "I would not wrong either you or myself by working such inharmonious effects upon our lives; but I would have you consider how trifling, in comparison, is the skill requisite to remove this little hand."

At the mention of the birthmark, Georgiana, as usual, shrank as if a redhot iron had touched her cheek.

Again Aylmer applied himself to his labors. She could hear his voice in the distant furnace room giving directions to Aminadab, whose harsh, uncouth, misshapen tones were audible in response, more like the grunt or growl of a brute than human speech. After hours of absence, Aylmer reappeared and proposed that she should now examine his cabinet of chemical products and natural treasures of the earth. Among the former he showed her a small vial, in which, he remarked, was contained a gentle yet most powerful fragrance, capable of impregnating all the breezes that blow across a kingdom. They were of inestimable value, the contents of that little vial; and, as he said so, he threw some of the perfume into the air and filled the room with piercing and invigorating delight.

"And what is this?" asked Georgiana, pointing to a small crystal globe containing a gold-colored liquid. "It is so beautiful to the eye that I could imagine it the elixir of life."

"In one sense it is," replied Aylmer; "or, rather, the elixir of immortality. It is the most precious poison that ever was concocted in this world. By its aid I could apportion the lifetime of any mortal at whom you might point your finger. The strength of the dose would determine whether he were to linger out years, or drop dead in the midst of a breath. No king on his guarded throne could keep his life if I, in my private station, should deem that the welfare of millions justified me in depriving him of it."

"Why do you keep such a terrific drug?" inquired Georgiana in horror.

"Do not mistrust me, dearest," said her husband, smiling; "its virtuous potency is yet greater than its harmful one. But see! here is a powerful cosmetic. With a few drops of this in a vase of water, freckles may be washed away as easily as the hands are cleansed. A stronger infusion would take the blood out of the cheek, and leave the rosiest beauty a pale ghost."

"Is it with this lotion that you intend to bathe my cheek?" asked Georgiana, anxiously.

"Oh, no," hastily replied her husband; "this is merely superficial. Your case demands a remedy that shall go deeper."

In his interviews with Georgiana, Aylmer generally made minute inquiries as to her sensations and whether the confinement of the rooms and the temperature of the atmosphere agreed with her. These questions had such a particular drift that Georgiana began to conjecture that she was already subjected to certain physical influences, either breathed in with the fragrant air or taken with her food. She fancied likewise, but it might be altogether fancy, that there was a stirring up of her system—a strange, indefinite sensation creeping through her veins, and tingling, half painfully, half pleasurably, at her heart. Still, whenever she dared to look into the mirror, there she beheld herself pale as a white rose and with the crimson birthmark stamped upon her cheek. Not even Aylmer now hated it so much as she.

To dispel the tedium of the hours which her husband found it necessary to devote to the processes of combination and analysis, Georgiana turned over the volumes of his scientific library. In many dark old tomes she met with chapters full of romance and poetry. They were the works of philosophers of the middle ages, such as Albertus Magnus, Cornelius Agrippa, Paracelsus, and the famous friar who created the prophetic Brazen Head. All these antique naturalists stood in advance of their centuries, yet were imbued with some of their credulity, and therefore were believed, and perhaps imagined themselves to have acquired from the investigation of Nature a power above Nature, and from physics a sway over the spiritual world. Hardly less curious and imaginative were the early volumes of the Transactions of the Royal Society, in which the members, knowing little of the limits of natural possibility, were continually recording wonders or proposing methods whereby wonders might be wrought.

But to Georgiana the most engrossing volume was a large folio from her husband's own hand, in which he had recorded every experiment of his scientific career, its original aim, the methods adopted for its development, and its final success or failure, with the circumstances to which either event was attributable. The book, in truth, was both the history and emblem of his ardent, ambitious, imaginative, yet practical and laborious life. He handled physical details as if there were nothing beyond them; yet spiritualized them all, and redeemed himself from materialism by his strong and eager aspiration towards the infinite. In his grasp the veriest clod of earth assumed a soul. Georgiana, as she read, reverenced Aylmer and loved him more profoundly than ever, but with a less entire dependence on his judgment than heretofore. Much as he had accomplished, she could not but observe that his most splendid successes were almost invariably failures, if compared with the ideal at which he aimed. His brightest diamonds were the merest pebbles, and felt to be so by himself, in comparison with the inestimable gems which lay hidden beyond his reach. The volume, rich with achievements that had won renown for its author, was yet as melancholy a record as ever mortal hand had penned. It was the sad confession and continual exemplification of the shortcomings of the composite man, the spirit burdened with clay and working in matter, and of the despair that assails the higher nature at finding itself so miserably thwarted by the earthly part. Perhaps every man of genius in whatever sphere might recognize the image of his own experience in Aylmer's journal.

So deeply did these reflections affect Georgiana that she laid her face upon the open volume and burst into tears. In this situation she was found by her husband.

"It is dangerous to read in a sorcerer's books," said he with a smile, though his countenance was uneasy and displeased. "Georgiana, there are pages in that volume which I can scarcely glance over and keep my senses. Take heed lest it prove as detrimental to you."

"It has made me worship you more than ever," said she.

"Ah, wait for this one success," rejoined he, "then worship me if you will. I shall deem myself hardly unworthy of it. But come, I have sought you for the luxury of your voice. Sing to me, dearest."

So she poured out the liquid music of her voice to quench the thirst of his spirit. He then took his leave with a boyish exuberance of gayety, assuring her that her seclusion would endure but a little longer, and that the result was already certain. Scarcely had he departed when Georgiana felt irresistibly impelled to follow him. She had forgotten to inform Aylmer of a symptom which for two or three hours past had begun to excite her attention. It was a sensation in the fatal birthmark, not painful, but which induced a restlessness throughout her system. Hastening after her husband, she intruded for the first time into the laboratory.

The first thing that struck her eye was the furnace, that hot and feverish worker, with the intense glow of its fire, which by the quantities of soot clustered above it seemed to have been burning for ages. There was a distilling apparatus in full operation. Around the room were retorts, tubes, cylinders, crucibles, and other apparatus of chemical research. An electrical machine stood ready for immediate use. The atmosphere felt oppressively close, and was tainted with gaseous odors which had been tormented forth by the processes of science. The severe and homely simplicity of the apartment, with its naked walls and brick pavement, looked strange, accustomed as Georgiana had become to the fantastic elegance of her boudoir. But what chiefly, indeed almost solely, drew her attention, was the aspect of Aylmer himself.

He was pale as death, anxious and absorbed, and hung over the furnace as if it depended upon his utmost watchfulness whether the liquid which it was distilling should be the draught of immortal happiness or misery. How different from the sanguine and joyous mien that he had assumed for Georgiana's encouragement!

"Carefully now, Aminadab; carefully, thou human machine; carefully, thou man of clay!" muttered Aylmer, more to himself than his assistant. "Now, if there be a thought too much or too little, it is all over."

"Ho! ho!" mumbled Aminadab. "Look, master! look!"

Aylmer raised his eyes hastily, and at first reddened, then grew paler than ever, on beholding Georgiana. He rushed towards her and seized her arm with a gripe that left the print of his fingers upon it.

"Why do you come hither? Have you no trust in your husband?" cried he, impetuously. "Would you throw the blight of that fatal birthmark over my labors? It is not well done. Go, prying woman, go!"

"Nay, Aylmer," said Georgiana with the firmness of which she possessed no stinted endowment, "it is not you that have a right to complain. You mistrust your wife; you have concealed the anxiety with which you watch the development of this experiment. Think not so unworthily of me, my husband. Tell me all the risk we run, and fear not that I shall shrink; for my share in it is far less than your own."

"No, no, Georgiana!" said Aylmer, impatiently; "it must not be."

"I submit," replied she calmly. "And, Aylmer, I shall quaff whatever draught you bring me; but it will be on the same principle that would induce me to take a dose of poison if offered by your hand."

"My noble wife," said Aylmer, deeply moved, "I knew not the height and depth of your nature until now. Nothing shall be concealed. Know, then, that this crimson hand, superficial as it seems, has clutched its grasp into your being with a strength of which I had no previous conception. I have already administered agents powerful enough to do aught except to change your entire physical system. Only one thing remains to be tried. If that fail us we are ruined."

"Why did you hesitate to tell me this?" asked she.

"Because, Georgiana," said Aylmer, in a low voice, "there is danger."

"Danger? There is but one danger—that this horrible stigma shall be left upon my cheek!" cried Georgiana. "Remove it, remove it, whatever be the cost, or we shall both go mad!"

"Heaven knows your words are too true," said Aylmer, sadly. "And now, dearest, return to your boudoir. In a little while all will be tested."

He conducted her back and took leave of her with a solemn tenderness which spoke far more than his words how much was now at stake. After his departure Georgiana became rapt in musings. She considered the character of Aylmer, and did it completer justice than at any previous moment. Her heart exulted, while it trembled, at his honorable love—so pure and lofty that it would accept nothing less than perfection nor miserably make itself contented with an earthlier nature than he had dreamed of. She felt how much more precious was such a sentiment than that meaner kind which would have borne with the imperfection for her sake, and have been guilty of treason to holy love by degrading its perfect idea to the level of the actual; and with her whole spirit she prayed that, for a single moment, she might satisfy his highest and deepest conception. Longer than one moment she well knew it could not be; for his spirit was ever on the march, ever ascending, and each instant required something that was beyond the scope of the instant before.

The sound of her husband's footsteps aroused her. He bore a crystal goblet containing a liquor colorless as water, but bright enough to be the draught of immortality. Aylmer was pale; but it seemed rather the consequence of a highly-wrought state of mind and tension of spirit than of fear or doubt.

"The concoction of the draught has been perfect," said he, in answer to Georgiana's look. "Unless all my science have deceived me, it cannot fail."

"Save on your account, my dearest Aylmer," observed his wife, "I might wish to put off this birthmark of mortality by relinquishing mortality itself in preference to any other mode. Life is but a sad possession to those who have attained precisely the degree of moral advancement at which I stand. Were I weaker and blinder it might be happiness. Were I stronger, it might be endured hopefully. But, being what I find myself, methinks I am of all mortals the most fit to die."

"You are fit for heaven without tasting death!" replied her husband "But why do we speak of dying? The draught cannot fail. Behold its effect upon this plant."

On the window seat there stood a geranium diseased with yellow blotches, which had overspread all its leaves. Aylmer poured a small quantity of the liquid upon the soil in which it grew. In a little time, when the roots of the plant had taken up the moisture, the unsightly blotches began to be extinguished in a living verdure.

"There needed no proof," said Georgiana, quietly. "Give me the goblet I joyfully stake all upon your word."

"Drink, then, thou lofty creature!" exclaimed Aylmer, with fervid admiration. "There is no taint of imperfection on thy spirit. Thy sensible frame, too, shall soon be all perfect."

She quaffed the liquid and returned the goblet to his hand.

"It is grateful," said she with a placid smile. "Methinks it is like water from a heavenly fountain; for it contains I know not what of unobtrusive fragrance and deliciousness. It allays a feverish thirst that had parched me for many days. Now, dearest, let me sleep. My earthly senses are closing over my spirit like the leaves around the heart of a rose at sunset."

She spoke the last words with a gentle reluctance, as if it required almost more energy than she could command to pronounce the faint and lingering syllables. Scarcely had they loitered through her lips ere she was lost in slumber. Aylmer sat by her side, watching her aspect with the emotions proper to a man the whole value of whose existence was involved in the process now to be tested. Mingled with this mood, however, was the philosophic investigation characteristic of the man of science. Not the minutest symptom escaped him. A heightened flush of the cheek, a slight irregularity of breath, a quiver of the eyelid, a hardly perceptible tremor through the frame,—such were the details which, as the moments passed, he wrote down in his folio volume. Intense thought had set its stamp upon every previous page of that volume, but the thoughts of years were all concentrated upon the last.

While thus employed, he failed not to gaze often at the fatal hand, and not without a shudder. Yet once, by a strange and unaccountable impulse he pressed it with his lips. His spirit recoiled, however, in the very act, and Georgiana, out of the midst of her deep sleep, moved uneasily and murmured as if in remonstrance. Again Aylmer resumed his watch. Nor was it without avail. The crimson hand, which at first had been strongly visible upon the marble paleness of Georgiana's cheek, now grew more faintly outlined. She remained not less pale than ever; but the birthmark with every breath that came and went, lost somewhat of its former distinctness. Its presence had been awful; its departure was more awful still. Watch the stain of the rainbow fading out the sky, and you will know how that mysterious symbol passed away.

"By Heaven! it is well-nigh gone!" said Aylmer to himself, in almost irrepressible ecstasy. "I can scarcely trace it now. Success! success! And now it is like the faintest rose color. The lightest flush of blood across her cheek would overcome it. But she is so pale!"

He drew aside the window curtain and suffered the light of natural day to fall into the room and rest upon her cheek. At the same time he heard a gross, hoarse chuckle, which he had long known as his servant Aminadab's expression of delight.

"Ah, clod! ah, earthly mass!" cried Aylmer, laughing in a sort of frenzy, "you have served me well! Matter and spirit—earth and heaven—have both done their part in this! Laugh, thing of the senses! You have earned the right to laugh."

These exclamations broke Georgiana's sleep. She slowly unclosed her eyes and gazed into the mirror which her husband had arranged for that purpose. A faint smile flitted over her lips when she recognized how barely perceptible was now that crimson hand which had once blazed forth with such disastrous brilliancy as to scare away all their happiness. But then her eyes sought Aylmer's face with a trouble and anxiety that he could by no means account for.

"My poor Aylmer!" murmured she.

"Poor? Nay, richest, happiest, most favored!" exclaimed he. "My peerless bride, it is successful! You are perfect!"

"My poor Aylmer," she repeated, with a more than human tenderness, "you have aimed loftily; you have done nobly. Do not repent that with so high and pure a feeling, you have rejected the best the earth could offer. Aylmer, dearest Aylmer, I am dying!"

Alas! it was too true! The fatal hand had grappled with the mystery of life, and was the bond by which an angelic spirit kept itself in union with a mortal frame. As the last crimson tint of the birthmark—that sole token of human imperfection—faded from her cheek, the parting breath of the now perfect woman passed into the atmosphere, and her soul, lingering a moment near her husband, took its heavenward flight. Then a hoarse, chuckling laugh was heard again! Thus ever does the gross fatality of earth exult in its invariable triumph over the immortal essence which, in this dim sphere of half development, demands the completeness of a higher state. Yet, had Alymer reached a profounder wisdom, he need not thus have flung away the happiness which would have woven his mortal life of the selfsame texture with the celestial. The momentary circumstance was too strong for him; he failed to look beyond the shadowy scope of time, and, living once for all in eternity, to find the perfect future in the present.

YOUNG GOODMAN BROWN

Young Goodman Brown came forth at sunset into the street at Salem village; but put his head back, after crossing the threshold, to exchange a parting kiss with his young wife. And Faith, as the wife was aptly named, thrust her own pretty head into the street, letting the wind play with the pink ribbons of her cap while she called to Goodman Brown.

"Dearest heart," whispered she, softly and rather sadly, when her lips were close to his ear, "prithee put off your journey until sunrise and sleep in your own bed to-night. A lone woman is troubled with such dreams and such thoughts that she's afeard of herself sometimes. Pray tarry with me this night, dear husband, of all nights in the year."

"My love and my Faith," replied young Goodman Brown, "of all nights in the year, this one night must I tarry away from thee. My journey, as thou callest it, forth and back again, must needs be done 'twixt now and sunrise. What, my sweet, pretty wife, dost thou doubt me already, and we but three months married?"

"Then God bless you!" said Faith, with the pink ribbons; "and may you find all well when you come back."

"Amen!" cried Goodman Brown. "Say thy prayers, dear Faith, and go to bed at dusk, and no harm will come to thee."

So they parted; and the young man pursued his way until, being about to turn the corner by the meeting-house, he looked back and saw the head of Faith still peeping after him with a melancholy air, in spite of her pink ribbons.

"Poor little Faith!" thought he, for his heart smote him. "What a wretch am I to leave her on such an errand! She talks of dreams, too. Methought as she spoke there was trouble in her face, as if a dream had warned her what work is to be done tonight. But no, no; 't would kill her to think it. Well, she's a blessed angel on earth; and after this one night I'll cling to her skirts and follow her to heaven."

With this excellent resolve for the future, Goodman Brown felt himself justified in making more haste on his present evil purpose. He had taken a dreary road, darkened by all the gloomiest trees of the forest, which barely stood aside to let the narrow path creep through, and closed immediately behind. It was all as lonely as could be; and there is this peculiarity in such a solitude, that the traveller knows not who may be concealed by the innumerable trunks and the thick boughs overhead; so that with lonely footsteps he may yet be passing through an unseen multitude.

"There may be a devilish Indian behind every tree," said Goodman Brown to himself; and he glanced fearfully behind him as he added, "What if the devil himself should be at my very elbow!"

His head being turned back, he passed a crook of the road, and, looking forward again, beheld the figure of a man, in grave and decent attire, seated at the foot of an old tree. He arose at Goodman Brown's approach and walked onward side by side with him.

"You are late, Goodman Brown," said he. "The clock of the Old South was striking as I came through Boston, and that is full fifteen minutes agone."

"Faith kept me back a while," replied the young man, with a tremor in his voice, caused by the sudden appearance of his companion, though not wholly unexpected.

It was now deep dusk in the forest, and deepest in that part of it where these two were journeying. As nearly as could be discerned, the second traveller was about fifty years old, apparently in the same rank of life as Goodman Brown, and bearing a considerable resemblance to him, though perhaps more in expression than features. Still they might have been taken for father and son. And yet, though the elder person was as simply clad as the younger, and as simple in manner too, he had an indescribable air of one who knew the world, and who would not have felt abashed at the governor's dinner table or in King William's court, were it possible that his affairs should call him thither. But the only thing about him that could be fixed upon as remarkable was his staff, which bore the likeness of a great black snake, so curiously wrought that it might almost be seen to twist and wriggle itself like a living serpent. This, of course, must have been an ocular deception, assisted by the uncertain light.

"Come, Goodman Brown," cried his fellow-traveller, "this is a dull pace for the beginning of a journey. Take my staff, if you are so soon weary."

"Friend," said the other, exchanging his slow pace for a full stop, "having kept covenant by meeting thee here, it is my purpose now to return whence I came. I have scruples touching the matter thou wot'st of."

"Sayest thou so?" replied he of the serpent, smiling apart. "Let us walk on, nevertheless, reasoning as we go; and if I convince thee not thou shalt turn back. We are but a little way in the forest yet."

"Too far! too far!" exclaimed the goodman, unconsciously resuming his walk. "My father never went into the woods on such an errand, nor his father before him. We have been a race of honest men and good Christians since the days of the martyrs; and shall I be the first of the name of Brown that ever took this path and kept—"

"Such company, thou wouldst say," observed the elder person, interpreting his pause. "Well said, Goodman Brown! I have been as well acquainted with your family as with ever a one among the Puritans; and that's no trifle to say. I helped your grandfather, the constable, when he lashed the Quaker woman so smartly through the streets of Salem; and it was I that brought your father a pitch-pine knot, kindled at my own hearth, to set fire to an Indian village, in King Philip's war. They were my good friends, both; and many a pleasant walk have we had along this path, and returned merrily after midnight. I would fain be friends with you for their sake."

"If it be as thou sayest," replied Goodman Brown, "I marvel they never spoke of these matters; or, verily, I marvel not, seeing that the least rumor of the sort would have driven them from New England. We are a people of prayer, and good works to boot, and abide no such wickedness."

"Wickedness or not," said the traveller with the twisted staff, "I have a very general acquaintance here in New England. The deacons of many a church have drunk the communion wine with me; the selectmen of divers towns make me their chairman; and a majority of the Great and General Court are firm supporters of my interest. The governor and I, too—But these are state secrets."

"Can this be so?" cried Goodman Brown, with a stare of amazement at his undisturbed companion. "Howbeit, I have nothing to do with the governor and council; they have their own ways, and are no rule for a simple husbandman like me. But, were I to go on with thee, how should I meet the eye of that good old man, our minister, at Salem village? Oh, his voice would make me tremble both Sabbath day and lecture day."

Thus far the elder traveller had listened with due gravity; but now burst into a fit of irrepressible mirth, shaking himself so violently that his snake-like staff actually seemed to wriggle in sympathy.

"Ha! ha! ha!" shouted he again and again; then composing himself, "Well, go on, Goodman Brown, go on; but, prithee, don't kill me with laughing."

"Well, then, to end the matter at once," said Goodman Brown, considerably nettled, "there is my wife, Faith. It would break her dear little heart; and I'd rather break my own."

"Nay, if that be the case," answered the other, "e'en go thy ways, Goodman Brown. I would not for twenty old women like the one hobbling before us that Faith should come to any harm."

As he spoke he pointed his staff at a female figure on the path, in whom Goodman Brown recognized a very pious and exemplary dame, who had taught him his catechism in youth, and was still his moral and spiritual adviser, jointly with the minister and Deacon Gookin.

"A marvel, truly, that Goody Cloyse should be so far in the wilderness at nightfall," said he. "But with your leave, friend, I shall take a cut through the woods until we have left this Christian woman behind. Being a stranger to you, she might ask whom I was consorting with and whither I was going."

"Be it so," said his fellow-traveller. "Betake you to the woods, and let me keep the path."

Accordingly the young man turned aside, but took care to watch his companion, who advanced softly along the road until he had come within a staff's length of the old dame. She, meanwhile, was making the best of her way, with singular speed for so aged a woman, and mumbling some indistinct words—a prayer, doubtless—as she went. The traveller put forth his staff and touched her withered neck with what seemed the serpent's tail.

"The devil!" screamed the pious old lady.

"Then Goody Cloyse knows her old friend?" observed the traveller, confronting her and leaning on his writhing stick.

"Ah, forsooth, and is it your worship indeed?" cried the good dame. "Yea, truly is it, and in the very image of my old gossip, Goodman Brown, the grandfather of the silly fellow that now is. But—would your worship believe it?—my broomstick hath strangely disappeared, stolen, as I suspect, by that unhanged witch, Goody Cory, and that, too, when I was all anointed with the juice of smallage, and cinquefoil, and wolf's bane."

"Mingled with fine wheat and the fat of a new-born babe," said the shape of old Goodman Brown.

"Ah, your worship knows the recipe," cried the old lady, cackling aloud. "So, as I was saying, being all ready for the meeting, and no horse to ride on, I made up my mind to foot it; for they tell me there is a nice young man to be taken into communion to-night. But now your good worship will lend me your arm, and we shall be there in a twinkling."

"That can hardly be," answered her friend. "I may not spare you my arm, Goody Cloyse; but here is my staff, if you will."

So saying, he threw it down at her feet, where, perhaps, it assumed life, being one of the rods which its owner had formerly lent to the Egyptian magi. Of this fact, however, Goodman Brown could not take cognizance. He had cast up his eyes in astonishment, and, looking down again, beheld neither Goody Cloyse nor the serpentine staff, but his fellow-traveller alone, who waited for him as calmly as if nothing had happened.

"That old woman taught me my catechism," said the young man; and there was a world of meaning in this simple comment.

They continued to walk onward, while the elder traveller exhorted his companion to make good speed and persevere in the path, discoursing so aptly that his arguments seemed rather to spring up in the bosom of his auditor than to be suggested by himself. As they went, he plucked a branch of maple to serve for a walking stick, and began to strip it of the twigs and little boughs, which were wet with evening dew. The moment his fingers touched them they became strangely withered and dried up as with a week's sunshine. Thus the pair proceeded, at a good free pace, until suddenly, in a gloomy hollow of the road, Goodman Brown sat himself down on the stump of a tree and refused to go any farther.

"Friend," said he, stubbornly, "my mind is made up. Not another step will I budge on this errand. What if a wretched old woman do choose to go to the devil when I thought she was going to heaven: is that any reason why I should quit my dear Faith and go after her?"

"You will think better of this by and by," said his acquaintance, composedly. "Sit here and rest yourself a while; and when you feel like moving again, there is my staff to help you along."

Without more words, he threw his companion the maple stick, and was as speedily out of sight as if he had vanished into the deepening gloom. The young man sat a few moments by the roadside, applauding himself greatly, and thinking with how clear a conscience he should meet the minister in his morning walk, nor shrink from the eye of good old Deacon Gookin. And what calm sleep would be his that very night, which was to have been spent so wickedly, but so purely and sweetly now, in the arms of Faith! Amidst these pleasant and praiseworthy meditations, Goodman Brown heard the tramp of horses along the road, and deemed it advisable to conceal himself within the verge of the forest, conscious of the guilty purpose that had brought him thither, though now so happily turned from it.

On came the hoof tramps and the voices of the riders, two grave old voices, conversing soberly as they drew near. These mingled sounds appeared to pass along the road, within a few yards of the young man's hiding-place; but, owing doubtless to the depth of the gloom at that particular spot, neither the travellers nor their steeds were visible. Though their figures brushed the small boughs by the wayside, it could not be seen that they intercepted, even for a moment, the faint gleam from the strip of bright sky athwart which they must have passed. Goodman Brown alternately crouched and stood on tiptoe, pulling aside the branches and thrusting forth his head as far as he durst without discerning so much as a shadow. It vexed him the more, because he could have sworn, were such a thing possible, that he recognized the voices of the minister and Deacon Gookin, jogging along quietly, as they were wont to do, when bound to some ordination or ecclesiastical council. While yet within hearing, one of the riders stopped to pluck a switch.

"Of the two, reverend sir," said the voice like the deacon's, "I had rather miss an ordination dinner than to-night's meeting. They tell me that some of our community are to be here from Falmouth and beyond, and others from Connecticut and Rhode Island, besides several of the Indian powwows, who, after their fashion, know almost as much deviltry as the best of us. Moreover, there is a goodly young woman to be taken into communion."

"Mighty well, Deacon Gookin!" replied the solemn old tones of the minister. "Spur up, or we shall be late. Nothing can be done, you know, until I get on the ground."

The hoofs clattered again; and the voices, talking so strangely in the empty air, passed on through the forest, where no church had ever been gathered or solitary Christian prayed. Whither, then, could these holy men be journeying so deep into the heathen wilderness? Young Goodman Brown caught hold of a tree for support, being ready to sink down on the ground, faint and overburdened with the heavy sickness of his heart. He looked up to the sky, doubting whether there really was a heaven above him. Yet there was the blue arch, and the stars brightening in it.

"With heaven above and Faith below, I will yet stand firm against the devil!" cried Goodman Brown.

While he still gazed upward into the deep arch of the firmament and had lifted his hands to pray, a cloud, though no wind was stirring, hurried across the zenith and hid the brightening stars. The blue sky was still visible, except directly overhead, where this black mass of cloud was sweeping swiftly northward. Aloft in the air, as if from the depths of the cloud, came a confused and doubtful sound of voices. Once the listener fancied that he could distinguish the accents of townspeople of his own, men and women, both pious and ungodly, many of whom he had met at the communion table, and had seen others rioting at the tavern. The next moment, so indistinct were the sounds, he doubted whether he had heard aught but the murmur of the old forest, whispering without a wind. Then came a stronger swell of those familiar tones, heard daily in the sunshine at Salem village, but never until now from a cloud of night There was one voice of a young woman, uttering lamentations, yet with an uncertain sorrow, and entreating for some favor, which, perhaps, it would grieve her to obtain; and all the unseen multitude, both saints and sinners, seemed to encourage her onward.

"Faith!" shouted Goodman Brown, in a voice of agony and desperation; and the echoes of the forest mocked him, crying, "Faith! Faith!" as if bewildered wretches were seeking her all through the wilderness.

The cry of grief, rage, and terror was yet piercing the night, when the unhappy husband held his breath for a response. There was a scream, drowned immediately in a louder murmur of voices, fading into far-off laughter, as the dark cloud swept away, leaving the clear and silent sky above Goodman Brown. But something fluttered lightly down through the air and caught on the branch of a tree. The young man seized it, and beheld a pink ribbon.

"My Faith is gone!" cried he, after one stupefied moment. "There is no good on earth; and sin is but a name. Come, devil; for to thee is this world given."

And, maddened with despair, so that he laughed loud and long, did Goodman Brown grasp his staff and set forth again, at such a rate that he seemed to fly along the forest path rather than to walk or run. The road grew wilder and drearier and more faintly traced, and vanished at length, leaving him in the heart of the dark wilderness, still rushing onward with the instinct that guides mortal man to evil. The whole forest was peopled with frightful sounds—the creaking of the trees, the howling of wild beasts, and the yell of Indians; while sometimes the wind tolled like a distant church bell, and sometimes gave a broad roar around the traveller, as if all Nature were laughing him to scorn. But he was himself the chief horror of the scene, and shrank not from its other horrors.

"Ha! ha! ha!" roared Goodman Brown when the wind laughed at him.

"Let us hear which will laugh loudest. Think not to frighten me with your deviltry. Come witch, come wizard, come Indian powwow, come devil himself, and here comes Goodman Brown. You may as well fear him as he fear you."

In truth, all through the haunted forest there could be nothing more frightful than the figure of Goodman Brown. On he flew among the black pines, brandishing his staff with frenzied gestures, now giving vent to an inspiration of horrid blasphemy, and now shouting forth such laughter as set all the echoes of the forest laughing like demons around him. The fiend in his own shape is less hideous than when he rages in the breast of man. Thus sped the demoniac on his course, until, quivering among the trees, he saw a red light before him, as when the felled trunks and branches of a clearing have been set on fire, and throw up their lurid blaze against the sky, at the hour of midnight. He paused, in a lull of the tempest that had driven him onward, and heard the swell of what seemed a hymn, rolling solemnly from a distance with the weight of many voices. He knew the tune; it was a familiar one in the choir of the village meeting-house. The verse died heavily away, and was lengthened by a chorus, not of human voices, but of all the sounds of the benighted wilderness pealing in awful harmony together. Goodman Brown cried out, and his cry was lost to his own ear by its unison with the cry of the desert.

In the interval of silence he stole forward until the light glared full upon his eyes. At one extremity of an open space, hemmed in by the dark wall of the forest, arose a rock, bearing some rude, natural resemblance either to an altar or a pulpit, and surrounded by four blazing pines, their tops aflame, their stems untouched, like candles at an evening meeting. The mass of foliage that had overgrown the summit of the rock was all on fire, blazing high into the night and fitfully illuminating the whole field. Each pendent twig and leafy festoon was in a blaze. As the red light arose and fell, a numerous congregation alternately shone forth, then disappeared in shadow, and again grew, as it were, out of the darkness, peopling the heart of the solitary woods at once.

"A grave and dark-clad company," quoth Goodman Brown.

In truth they were such. Among them, quivering to and fro between gloom and splendor, appeared faces that would be seen next day at the council board of the province, and others which, Sabbath after Sabbath, looked devoutly heavenward, and benignantly over the crowded pews, from the holiest pulpits in the land. Some affirm that the lady of the governor was there. At least there were high dames well known to her, and wives of honored husbands, and widows, a great multitude, and ancient maidens, all of excellent repute, and fair young girls, who trembled lest their mothers should espy them. Either the sudden gleams of light flashing over the obscure field bedazzled Goodman Brown, or he recognized a score of the church members of Salem village famous for their especial sanctity. Good old Deacon Gookin had arrived, and waited at the skirts of that venerable saint, his revered pastor. But, irreverently consorting with these grave, reputable, and pious people, these elders of the church, these chaste dames and dewy virgins, there were men of dissolute lives and women of spotted fame, wretches given over to all mean and filthy vice, and suspected even of horrid crimes. It was strange to see that the good shrank not from the wicked, nor were the sinners abashed by the saints. Scattered also among their pale-faced enemies were the Indian priests, or powwows, who had often scared their native forest with more hideous incantations than any known to English witchcraft.

"But where is Faith?" thought Goodman Brown; and, as hope came into his heart, he trembled.

Another verse of the hymn arose, a slow and mournful strain, such as the pious love, but joined to words which expressed all that our nature can conceive of sin, and darkly hinted at far more. Unfathomable to mere mortals is the lore of fiends. Verse after verse was sung; and still the chorus of the desert swelled between like the deepest tone of a mighty organ; and with the final peal of that dreadful anthem there came a sound, as if the roaring wind, the rushing streams, the howling beasts, and every other voice of the unconcerted wilderness were mingling and according with the voice of guilty man in homage to the prince of all. The four blazing pines threw up a loftier flame, and obscurely discovered shapes and visages of horror on the smoke wreaths above the impious assembly. At the same moment the fire on the rock shot redly forth and formed a glowing arch above its base, where now appeared a figure. With reverence be it spoken, the figure bore no slight similitude, both in garb and manner, to some grave divine of the New England churches.

"Bring forth the converts!" cried a voice that echoed through the field and rolled into the forest.

At the word, Goodman Brown stepped forth from the shadow of the trees and approached the congregation, with whom he felt a loathful brotherhood by the sympathy of all that was wicked in his heart. He could have well-nigh sworn that the shape of his own dead father beckoned him to advance, looking downward from a smoke wreath, while a woman, with dim features of despair, threw out her hand to warn him back. Was it his mother? But he had no power to retreat one step, nor to resist, even in thought, when the minister and good old Deacon Gookin seized his arms and led him to the blazing rock. Thither came also the slender form of a veiled female, led between Goody Cloyse, that pious teacher of the catechism, and Martha Carrier, who had received the devil's promise to be queen of hell. A rampant hag was she. And there stood the proselytes beneath the canopy of fire.

"Welcome, my children," said the dark figure, "to the communion of your race. Ye have found thus young your nature and your destiny. My children, look behind you!"

They turned; and flashing forth, as it were, in a sheet of flame, the fiend worshippers were seen; the smile of welcome gleamed darkly on every visage.

"There," resumed the sable form, "are all whom ye have reverenced from youth. Ye deemed them holier than yourselves, and shrank from your own sin, contrasting it with their lives of righteousness and prayerful aspirations heavenward. Yet here are they all in my worshipping assembly. This night it shall be granted you to know their secret deeds: how hoary-bearded elders of the church have whispered wanton words to the young maids of their households; how many a woman, eager for widows' weeds, has given her husband a drink at bedtime and let him sleep his last sleep in her bosom; how beardless youths have made haste to inherit their fathers' wealth; and how fair damsels—blush not, sweet ones—have dug little graves in the garden, and bidden me, the sole guest to an infant's funeral. By the sympathy of your human hearts for sin ye shall scent out all the places—whether in church, bedchamber, street, field, or forest—where crime has been committed, and shall exult to behold the whole earth one stain of guilt, one mighty blood spot. Far more than this. It shall be yours to penetrate, in every bosom, the deep mystery of sin, the fountain of all wicked arts, and which inexhaustibly supplies more evil impulses than human power—than my power at its utmost—can make manifest in deeds. And now, my children, look upon each other."

They did so; and, by the blaze of the hell-kindled torches, the wretched man beheld his Faith, and the wife her husband, trembling before that unhallowed altar.

"Lo, there ye stand, my children," said the figure, in a deep and solemn tone, almost sad with its despairing awfulness, as if his once angelic nature could yet mourn for our miserable race. "Depending upon one another's hearts, ye had still hoped that virtue were not all a dream. Now are ye undeceived. Evil is the nature of mankind. Evil must be your only happiness. Welcome again, my children, to the communion of your race."

"Welcome," repeated the fiend worshippers, in one cry of despair and triumph.

And there they stood, the only pair, as it seemed, who were yet hesitating on the verge of wickedness in this dark world. A basin was hollowed, naturally, in the rock. Did it contain water, reddened by the lurid light? or was it blood? or, perchance, a liquid flame? Herein did the shape of evil dip his hand and prepare to lay the mark of baptism upon their foreheads, that they might be partakers of the mystery of sin, more conscious of the secret guilt of others, both in deed and thought, than they could now be of their own. The husband cast one look at his pale wife, and Faith at him. What polluted wretches would the next glance show them to each other, shuddering alike at what they disclosed and what they saw!

"Faith! Faith!" cried the husband, "look up to heaven, and resist the wicked one."

Whether Faith obeyed he knew not. Hardly had he spoken when he found himself amid calm night and solitude, listening to a roar of the wind which died heavily away through the forest. He staggered against the rock, and felt it chill and damp; while a hanging twig, that had been all on fire, besprinkled his cheek with the coldest dew.

The next morning young Goodman Brown came slowly into the street of Salem village, staring around him like a bewildered man. The good old minister was taking a walk along the graveyard to get an appetite for breakfast and meditate his sermon, and bestowed a blessing, as he passed, on Goodman Brown. He shrank from the venerable saint as if to avoid an anathema. Old Deacon Gookin was at domestic worship, and the holy words of his prayer were heard through the open window. "What God doth the wizard pray to?" quoth Goodman Brown. Goody Cloyse, that excellent old Christian, stood in the early sunshine at her own lattice, catechizing a little girl who had brought her a pint of morning's milk. Goodman

Brown snatched away the child as from the grasp of the fiend himself. Turning the corner by the meeting-house, he spied the head of Faith, with the pink ribbons, gazing anxiously forth, and bursting into such joy at sight of him that she skipped along the street and almost kissed her husband before the whole village. But Goodman Brown looked sternly and sadly into her face, and passed on without a greeting.

Had Goodman Brown fallen asleep in the forest and only dreamed a wild dream of a witch-meeting?

Be it so if you will; but, alas! it was a dream of evil omen for young Goodman Brown. A stern, a sad, a darkly meditative, a distrustful, if not a desperate man did he become from the night of that fearful dream. On the Sabbath day, when the congregation were singing a holy psalm, he could not listen because an anthem of sin rushed loudly upon his ear and drowned all the blessed strain. When the minister spoke from the pulpit with power and fervid eloquence, and, with his hand on the open Bible, of the sacred truths of our religion, and of saint-like lives and triumphant deaths, and of future bliss or misery unutterable, then did Goodman Brown turn pale, dreading lest the roof should thunder down upon the gray blasphemer and his hearers. Often, waking suddenly at midnight, he shrank from the bosom of Faith; and at morning or eventide, when the family knelt down at prayer, he scowled and muttered to himself, and gazed sternly at his wife, and turned away. And when he had lived long, and was borne to his grave a hoary corpse, followed by Faith, an aged woman, and children and grandchildren, a goodly procession, besides neighbors not a few, they carved no hopeful verse upon his tombstone, for his dying hour was gloom.

RAPPACCINI'S DAUGHTER [From the Writings of Aubepine.]

We do not remember to have seen any translated specimens of the productions of M. de l'Aubepine—a fact the less to be wondered at, as his very name is unknown to many of his own countrymen as well as to the student of foreign literature. As a writer, he seems to occupy an unfortunate position between the Transcendentalists (who, under one name or another, have their share in all the current literature of the world) and the great body of pen-and-ink men who address the intellect and sympathies of the multitude. If not too refined, at all events too remote, too shadowy, and unsubstantial in his modes of development to suit the taste of the latter class, and yet too popular to satisfy the spiritual or metaphysical requisitions of the former, he must necessarily find himself without an audience, except here and there an individual or possibly an isolated clique. His writings, to do them justice, are not altogether destitute of fancy and originality; they might have won him greater reputation but for an inveterate love of allegory, which is apt to invest his plots and characters with the aspect of scenery and people in the clouds, and to steal away the human warmth out of his conceptions. His fictions are sometimes historical, sometimes of the present day, and sometimes, so far as can be discovered, have little or no reference either to time or space. In any case, he generally contents himself with a very slight embroidery of outward manners,—the faintest possible counterfeit of real life,—and endeavors to create an interest by some less obvious peculiarity of the subject. Occasionally a breath of Nature, a raindrop of pathos and tenderness, or a gleam of humor, will find its way into the midst of his fantastic imagery, and make us feel as if, after all, we were yet within the limits of our native earth. We will only add to this very cursory notice that M. de l'Aubepine's productions, if the reader chance to take them in precisely the proper point of view, may amuse a leisure hour as well as those of a brighter man; if otherwise, they can hardly fail to look excessively like nonsense.

Our author is voluminous; he continues to write and publish with as much praiseworthy and indefatigable prolixity as if his efforts were crowned with the brilliant success that so justly attends those of Eugene Sue. His first appearance was by a collection of stories in a long series of volumes entitled "Contes deux fois racontees." The titles of some of his more recent works (we quote from memory) are as follows: "Le Voyage Celeste a Chemin de Fer," 3 tom., 1838; "Le nouveau Pere Adam et la nouvelle Mere Eve," 2 tom., 1839; "Roderic; ou le Serpent a l'estomac," 2 tom., 1840; "Le Culte du Feu," a folio volume of ponderous research into the religion and ritual of the old Persian Ghebers, published in 1841; "La Soiree du Chateau en Espagne," 1 tom., 8vo, 1842; and "L'Artiste du Beau; ou le Papillon Mecanique," 5 tom., 4to, 1843. Our somewhat wearisome perusal of this startling catalogue of volumes has left behind it a certain personal affection and sympathy, though by no means admiration, for M. de l'Aubepine; and we would fain do the little in our power towards introducing him favorably to the American public. The ensuing tale is a translation of his "Beatrice; ou la Belle Empoisonneuse," recently published in "La Revue Anti-Aristocratique." This journal, edited by the Comte de Bearhaven, has for some years past led the defence of liberal principles and popular rights with a faithfulness and ability worthy of all praise.

A young man, named Giovanni Guasconti, came, very long ago, from the more southern region of Italy, to pursue his studies at the University of Padua. Giovanni, who had but a scanty supply of gold ducats in his pocket, took lodgings in a high and gloomy chamber of an old edifice which looked not unworthy to have been the palace of a Paduan noble, and which, in fact, exhibited over its entrance the armorial bearings of a family long since extinct. The young stranger, who was not unstudied in the great poem of his country, recollected that one of the ancestors of this family, and perhaps an occupant of this very mansion, had been pictured by Dante as a partaker of the immortal agonies of his Inferno. These reminiscences and associations, together with the tendency to heartbreak natural to a young man for the first time out of his native sphere, caused Giovanni to sigh heavily as he looked around the desolate and ill-furnished apartment.

"Holy Virgin, signor!" cried old Dame Lisabetta, who, won by the youth's remarkable beauty of person, was kindly endeavoring to give the chamber a habitable air, "what a sigh was that to come out of a young man's heart! Do you find this old mansion gloomy? For the love of Heaven, then, put your head out of the window, and you will see as bright sunshine as you have left in Naples."

Guasconti mechanically did as the old woman advised, but could not quite agree with her that the Paduan sunshine was as cheerful as that of southern Italy. Such as it was, however, it fell upon a garden beneath the window and expended its fostering influences on a variety of plants, which seemed to have been cultivated with exceeding care.

"Does this garden belong to the house?" asked Giovanni.

"Heaven forbid, signor, unless it were fruitful of better pot herbs than any that grow there now," answered old Lisabetta. "No; that garden is cultivated by the own hands of Signor Giacomo Rappaccini, the famous doctor, who, I warrant him, has been heard of as far as Naples. It is said that he distils these plants into medicines that are as potent as a charm. Oftentimes you may see the signor doctor at work, and perchance the signora, his daughter, too, gathering the strange flowers that grow in the garden."

The old woman had now done what she could for the aspect of the chamber; and, commending the young man to the protection of the saints, took her departure.

Giovanni still found no better occupation than to look down into the garden beneath his window. From its appearance, he judged it to be one of those botanic gardens which were of earlier date in Padua than elsewhere in Italy or in the world. Or, not improbably, it might once have been the pleasure-place of an opulent family; for there was the ruin of a marble fountain in the centre, sculptured with rare art, but so wofully shattered that it was impossible to trace the original design from the chaos of remaining fragments. The water, however, continued to gush and sparkle into the sunbeams as cheerfully as ever. A little gurgling sound ascended to the young man's window, and made him feel as if the fountain were an immortal spirit that sung its song unceasingly and without heeding the vicissitudes around it, while one century imbodied it in marble and another scattered the perishable garniture on the soil. All about the pool into which the water subsided grew various plants, that seemed to require a plentiful supply of moisture for the nourishment of gigantic leaves, and in some instances, flowers gorgeously magnificent. There was one shrub in particular, set in a marble vase in the midst of the pool, that bore a profusion of purple blossoms, each of which had the lustre and richness of a gem; and the whole together made a show so resplendent that it seemed enough to illuminate the garden, even had there been no sunshine. Every portion of the soil was peopled with plants and herbs, which, if less beautiful, still bore tokens of assiduous care, as if all had their individual virtues, known to the scientific mind that fostered them. Some were placed in urns, rich with old carving, and others in common garden pots; some crept serpent-like along the ground or climbed on high, using whatever means of ascent was offered them. One plant had wreathed itself round a statue of Vertumnus, which was thus quite veiled and shrouded in a drapery of hanging foliage, so happily arranged that it might have served a sculptor for a study.

While Giovanni stood at the window he heard a rustling behind a screen of leaves, and became aware that a person was at work in the garden. His figure soon emerged into view, and showed itself to be that of no common laborer, but a tall, emaciated, sallow, and sickly-looking man, dressed in a scholar's garb of black. He was beyond the middle term of life, with gray hair, a thin, gray beard, and a face singularly marked with intellect and cultivation, but which could never, even in his more youthful days, have expressed much warmth of heart.

Nothing could exceed the intentness with which this scientific gardener examined every shrub which grew in his path: it seemed as if he was looking into their inmost nature, making observations in regard to their creative essence, and discovering why one leaf grew in this shape and another in that, and wherefore such and such flowers differed among themselves in hue and perfume. Nevertheless, in spite of this deep intelligence on his part, there was no approach to intimacy between himself and these vegetable existences. On the contrary, he avoided their actual touch or the direct inhaling of their odors with a caution that impressed

Giovanni most disagreeably; for the man's demeanor was that of one walking among malignant influences, such as savage beasts, or deadly snakes, or evil spirits, which, should he allow them one moment of license, would wreak upon him some terrible fatality. It was strangely frightful to the young man's imagination to see this air of insecurity in a person cultivating a garden, that most simple and innocent of human toils, and which had been alike the joy and labor of the unfallen parents of the race. Was this garden, then, the Eden of the present world? And this man, with such a perception of harm in what his own hands caused to grow,—was he the Adam?

The distrustful gardener, while plucking away the dead leaves or pruning the too luxuriant growth of the shrubs, defended his hands with a pair of thick gloves. Nor were these his only armor. When, in his walk through the garden, he came to the magnificent plant that hung its purple gems beside the marble fountain, he placed a kind of mask over his mouth and nostrils, as if all this beauty did but conceal a deadlier malice; but, finding his task still too dangerous, he drew back, removed the mask, and called loudly, but in the infirm voice of a person affected with inward disease, "Beatrice! Beatrice!"

"Here am I, my father. What would you?" cried a rich and youthful voice from the window of the opposite house—a voice as rich as a tropical sunset, and which made Giovanni, though he knew not why, think of deep hues of purple or crimson and of perfumes heavily delectable. "Are you in the garden?"

"Yes, Beatrice," answered the gardener, "and I need your help."

Soon there emerged from under a sculptured portal the figure of a young girl, arrayed with as much richness of taste as the most splendid of the flowers, beautiful as the day, and with a bloom so deep and vivid that one shade more would have been too much. She looked redundant with life, health, and energy; all of which attributes were bound down and compressed, as it were and girdled tensely, in their luxuriance, by her virgin zone. Yet Giovanni's fancy must have grown morbid while he looked down into the garden; for the impression which the fair stranger made upon him was as if here were another flower, the human sister of those vegetable ones, as beautiful as they, more beautiful than the richest of them, but still to be touched only with a glove, nor to be approached without a mask. As Beatrice came down the garden path, it was observable that she handled and inhaled the odor of several of the plants which her father had most sedulously avoided.

"Here, Beatrice," said the latter, "see how many needful offices require to be done to our chief treasure. Yet, shattered as I am, my life might pay the penalty of approaching it so closely as circumstances demand. Henceforth, I fear, this plant must be consigned to your sole charge."

"And gladly will I undertake it," cried again the rich tones of the young lady, as she bent towards the magnificent plant and opened her arms as if to embrace it. "Yes, my sister, my splendour, it shall be Beatrice's task to nurse and serve thee; and thou shalt reward her with thy kisses and perfumed breath, which to her is as the breath of life."

Then, with all the tenderness in her manner that was so strikingly expressed in her words, she busied herself with such attentions as the plant seemed to require; and Giovanni, at his lofty window, rubbed his eyes and almost doubted whether it were a girl tending her favorite flower, or one sister performing the duties of affection to another. The scene soon terminated. Whether Dr. Rappaccini had finished his labors in the garden, or that his watchful eye had caught the stranger's face, he now took his daughter's arm and retired. Night was already closing in; oppressive exhalations seemed to proceed from the plants and steal upward past the open window; and Giovanni, closing the lattice, went to his couch and dreamed of a rich flower and beautiful girl. Flower and maiden were different, and yet the same, and fraught with some strange peril in either shape.

But there is an influence in the light of morning that tends to rectify whatever errors of fancy, or even of judgment, we may have incurred during the sun's decline, or among the shadows of the night, or in the less wholesome glow of moonshine. Giovanni's first movement, on starting from sleep, was to throw open the window and gaze down into the garden which his dreams had made so fertile of mysteries. He was surprised and a little ashamed to find how real and matter-of-fact an affair it proved to be, in the first rays of the sun which gilded the dew-drops that hung upon leaf and blossom, and, while giving a brighter beauty to each rare flower, brought everything within the limits of ordinary experience. The young man rejoiced that, in the heart of the barren city, he had the privilege of overlooking this spot of lovely and luxuriant vegetation. It would serve, he said to himself, as a symbolic language to keep him in communion with Nature. Neither the sickly and thoughtworn Dr. Giacomo Rappaccini, it is true, nor his brilliant daughter, were now visible; so that Giovanni could not determine how much of the singularity which he attributed to both was due to their own qualities and how much to his wonder-working fancy; but he was inclined to take a most rational view of the whole matter.

In the course of the day he paid his respects to Signor Pietro Baglioni, professor of medicine in the university, a physician of eminent repute to whom Giovanni had brought a letter of introduction. The professor was an elderly personage, apparently of genial nature, and habits that might almost be called jovial. He kept the young man to dinner, and made himself very agreeable by the freedom and liveliness of his conversation, especially when warmed by a flask or two of Tuscan wine. Giovanni, conceiving that men of science, inhabitants of the same city, must needs be on familiar terms with one another, took an opportunity to mention the name of Dr. Rappaccini. But the professor did not respond with so much cordiality as he had anticipated.

"Ill would it become a teacher of the divine art of medicine," said Professor Pietro Baglioni, in answer to a question of Giovanni, "to withhold due and well-considered praise of a physician so eminently skilled as Rappaccini; but, on the other hand, I should answer it but scantily to my conscience were I to permit a worthy youth like yourself, Signor Giovanni, the son of an ancient friend, to imbibe erroneous ideas respecting a man who might hereafter chance to hold your life and death in his hands. The truth is, our worshipful Dr. Rappaccini has as much science as any member of the faculty—with perhaps one single exception—in Padua, or all Italy; but there are certain grave objections to his professional character."

"And what are they?" asked the young man.

"Has my friend Giovanni any disease of body or heart, that he is so inquisitive about physicians?" said the professor, with a smile. "But as for Rappaccini, it is said of him—and I, who know the man well, can answer for its truth—that he cares infinitely more for science than for mankind. His patients are interesting to him only as subjects for some new experiment. He would sacrifice human life, his own among the rest, or whatever else was dearest to him, for the sake of adding so much as a grain of mustard seed to the great heap of his accumulated knowledge."

"Methinks he is an awful man indeed," remarked Guasconti, mentally recalling the cold and purely intellectual aspect of Rappaccini. "And yet, worshipful professor, is it not a noble spirit? Are there many men capable of so spiritual a love of science?"

"God forbid," answered the professor, somewhat testily; "at least, unless they take sounder views of the healing art than those adopted by Rappaccini. It is his theory that all medicinal virtues are comprised within those substances which we term vegetable poisons. These he cultivates with his own hands, and is said even to have produced new varieties of poison, more horribly deleterious than Nature, without the assistance of this learned person, would ever have plagued the world withal. That the signor doctor does less mischief than might be expected with such dangerous substances is undeniable. Now and then, it must be owned, he has effected, or seemed to effect, a marvellous cure; but, to tell you my private mind, Signor Giovanni, he should receive little credit for such instances of success,—they being probably the work of chance,—but should be held strictly accountable for his failures, which may justly be considered his own work."

The youth might have taken Baglioni's opinions with many grains of allowance had he known that there was a professional warfare of long continuance between him and Dr. Rappaccini, in which the latter was generally thought to have gained the advantage. If the reader be inclined to judge for himself, we refer him to certain black-letter tracts on both sides, preserved in the medical department of the University of Padua.

"I know not, most learned professor," returned Giovanni, after musing on what had been said of Rappaccini's exclusive zeal for science,—"I know not how dearly this physician may love his art; but surely there is one object more dear to him. He has a daughter."

"Aha!" cried the professor, with a laugh. "So now our friend Giovanni's secret is out. You have heard of this daughter, whom all the young men in Padua are wild about, though not half a dozen have ever had the good hap to see her face. I know little of the Signora Beatrice save that Rappaccini is said to have instructed her deeply in his science, and that, young and beautiful as fame reports her, she is already qualified to fill a professor's chair. Perchance her father destines her for mine! Other absurd rumors there be, not worth talking about or listening to. So now, Signor Giovanni, drink off your glass of lachryma."

Guasconti returned to his lodgings somewhat heated with the wine he had quaffed, and which caused his brain to swim with strange fantasies in reference to Dr. Rappaccini and the beautiful Beatrice. On his way, happening to pass by a florist's, he bought a fresh bouquet of flowers.

Ascending to his chamber, he seated himself near the window, but within the shadow thrown by the depth of the wall, so that he could look down into the garden with little risk of being discovered. All beneath his eye was a solitude. The strange plants were basking in the sunshine, and now and then nodding gently to one another, as if in acknowledgment of sympathy and kindred. In the midst, by the shattered fountain, grew the magnificent shrub, with its purple gems clustering all over it; they glowed in the air, and gleamed back again out of the depths of the pool, which thus seemed to overflow with colored radiance from the rich reflection that was steeped in it. At first, as we have said, the garden was a solitude. Soon, however,—as Giovanni had half hoped, half feared, would be the case,—a figure appeared beneath the antique sculptured portal, and came down between the rows of plants, inhaling their various perfumes as if she were one of those beings of old classic fable that lived upon sweet odors. On again beholding Beatrice, the young man was even startled to perceive how much her beauty exceeded his recollection of it; so brilliant, so vivid, was its character, that she glowed amid the sunlight, and, as Giovanni whispered to himself, positively illuminated the more shadowy intervals of the garden path. Her face being now more revealed than on the former occasion, he was struck by its expression of simplicity and sweetness,—qualities that had not entered into his idea of her character, and which made him ask anew what manner of mortal she might be. Nor did he fail again to observe, or imagine, an analogy between the beautiful girl and the gorgeous shrub that hung its gemlike flowers over the fountain,—a resemblance which Beatrice seemed to have indulged a fantastic humor in heightening, both by the arrangement of her dress and the selection of its hues.

Approaching the shrub, she threw open her arms, as with a passionate ardor, and drew its branches into an intimate embrace—so intimate that her features were hidden in its leafy bosom and her glistening ringlets all intermingled with the flowers.

"Give me thy breath, my sister," exclaimed Beatrice; "for I am faint with common air. And give me this flower of thine, which I separate with gentlest fingers from the stem and place it close beside my heart."

With these words the beautiful daughter of Rappaccini plucked one of the richest blossoms of the shrub, and was about to fasten it in her bosom. But now, unless Giovanni's draughts of wine had bewildered his senses, a singular incident occurred. A small orange-colored reptile, of the lizard or chameleon species, chanced to be creeping along the path, just at the feet of Beatrice. It appeared to Giovanni,—but, at the distance from which he gazed, he could scarcely have seen anything so minute,—it appeared to him, however, that a drop or two of moisture from the broken stem of the flower descended upon the lizard's head. For an instant the reptile contorted itself violently, and then lay motionless in the sunshine. Beatrice observed this remarkable phenomenon and crossed herself, sadly, but without surprise; nor did she therefore hesitate to arrange the fatal flower in her bosom. There it blushed, and almost glimmered with the dazzling effect of a precious stone, adding to her dress and aspect the one appropriate charm which nothing else in the world could have supplied. But Giovanni, out of the shadow of his window, bent forward and shrank back, and murmured and trembled.

"Am I awake? Have I my senses?" said he to himself. "What is this being? Beautiful shall I call her, or inexpressibly terrible?"

Beatrice now strayed carelessly through the garden, approaching closer beneath Giovanni's window, so that he was compelled to thrust his head quite out of its concealment in order to gratify the intense and painful curiosity which she excited. At this moment there came a beautiful insect over the garden wall; it had, perhaps, wandered through the city, and found no flowers or verdure among those antique haunts of men until the heavy perfumes of Dr. Rappaccini's shrubs had lured it from afar. Without alighting on the flowers, this winged brightness seemed to be attracted by Beatrice, and lingered in the air and fluttered about her head. Now, here it could not be but that Giovanni Guasconti's eyes deceived him. Be that as it might, he fancied that, while Beatrice was gazing at the insect with childish delight, it grew faint and fell at her feet; its bright wings shivered; it was dead—from no cause that he could discern, unless it were the atmosphere of her breath. Again Beatrice crossed herself and sighed heavily as she bent over the dead insect.

An impulsive movement of Giovanni drew her eyes to the window. There she beheld the beautiful head of the young man—rather a Grecian than an Italian head, with fair, regular features, and a glistening of gold among his ringlets—gazing down upon her like a being that hovered in mid air. Scarcely knowing what he did, Giovanni threw down the bouquet which he had hitherto held in his hand.

"Signora," said he, "there are pure and healthful flowers. Wear them for the sake of Giovanni Guasconti."

"Thanks, signor," replied Beatrice, with her rich voice, that came forth as it were like a gush of music, and with a mirthful expression half childish and half woman-like. "I accept your gift, and would fain recompense it with this precious purple flower; but if I toss it into the air it will not reach you. So Signor Guasconti must even content himself with my thanks."

She lifted the bouquet from the ground, and then, as if inwardly ashamed at having stepped aside from her maidenly reserve to respond to a stranger's greeting, passed swiftly homeward through the garden. But few as the moments were, it seemed to Giovanni, when she was on the point of vanishing beneath the sculptured portal, that his beautiful bouquet was already beginning to wither in her grasp. It was an idle thought; there could be no possibility of distinguishing a faded flower from a fresh one at so great a distance.

For many days after this incident the young man avoided the window that looked into Dr. Rappaccini's garden, as if something ugly and monstrous would have blasted his eyesight had he been betrayed into a glance. He felt conscious of having put himself, to a certain extent, within the influence of an unintelligible power by the communication which he had opened with Beatrice. The wisest course would have been, if his heart were in any real danger, to quit his lodgings and Padua itself at once; the next wiser, to have accustomed himself, as far as possible, to the familiar and daylight view of Beatrice—thus bringing her rigidly and systematically within the limits of ordinary experience. Least of all, while avoiding her sight, ought Giovanni to have remained so near this extraordinary being that the proximity and possibility even of intercourse should give a kind of substance and reality to the wild vagaries which his imagination ran riot continually in producing. Guasconti had not a deep heart—or, at all events, its depths were not sounded now; but he had a quick fancy, and an ardent southern temperament, which rose every instant to a higher fever pitch. Whether or no Beatrice possessed those terrible attributes, that fatal breath, the affinity with those so beautiful and deadly flowers which were indicated by what Giovanni had witnessed, she had at least instilled a fierce and subtle poison into his system. It was not love, although her rich beauty was a madness to him; nor horror, even while he fancied her spirit to be imbued with the same baneful essence that seemed to pervade her physical frame; but a wild offspring of both love and horror that had each parent in it, and burned like one and shivered like the other. Giovanni knew not what to dread; still less did he know what to hope; yet hope and dread kept a continual warfare in his breast, alternately vanquishing one another and starting up afresh to renew the contest. Blessed are all simple emotions, be they dark or bright! It is the lurid intermixture of the two that produces the illuminating blaze of the infernal regions.

Sometimes he endeavored to assuage the fever of his spirit by a rapid walk through the streets of Padua or beyond its gates: his footsteps kept time with the throbbings of his brain, so that the walk was apt to accelerate itself to a race. One day he found himself arrested; his arm was seized by a portly personage, who had turned back on recognizing the young man and expended much breath in overtaking him.

"Signor Giovanni! Stay, my young friend!" cried he. "Have you forgotten me? That might well be the case if I were as much altered as yourself."

It was Baglioni, whom Giovanni had avoided ever since their first meeting, from a doubt that the professor's sagacity would look too deeply into his secrets. Endeavoring to recover himself, he stared forth wildly from his inner world into the outer one and spoke like a man in a dream.

"Yes; I am Giovanni Guasconti. You are Professor Pietro Baglioni. Now let me pass!"

"Not yet, not yet, Signor Giovanni Guasconti," said the professor, smiling, but at the same time scrutinizing the youth with an earnest glance. "What! did I grow up side by side with your father? and shall his son pass me like a stranger in these old streets of Padua? Stand still, Signor Giovanni; for we must have a word or two before we part."

"Speedily, then, most worshipful professor, speedily," said Giovanni, with feverish impatience. "Does not your worship see that I am in haste?"

Now, while he was speaking there came a man in black along the street, stooping and moving feebly like a person in inferior health. His face was all overspread with a most sickly and sallow hue, but yet so pervaded with an expression of piercing and active intellect that an observer might easily have overlooked the merely physical attributes and have seen only this wonderful energy. As he passed, this person exchanged a cold and distant salutation with Baglioni, but fixed his eyes upon Giovanni with an intentness that seemed to bring out whatever was within him worthy of notice. Nevertheless, there was a peculiar quietness in the look, as if taking merely a speculative, not a human interest, in the young man.

"It is Dr. Rappaccini!" whispered the professor when the stranger had passed. "Has he ever seen your face before?"

"Not that I know," answered Giovanni, starting at the name.

"He HAS seen you! he must have seen you!" said Baglioni, hastily. "For some purpose or other, this man of science is making a study of you. I know that look of his! It is the same that coldly illuminates his face as he bends over a bird, a mouse, or a butterfly, which, in pursuance of some experiment, he has killed by the perfume of a flower; a look as deep as Nature itself, but without Nature's warmth of love. Signor Giovanni, I will stake my life upon it, you are the subject of one of Rappaccini's experiments!"

"Will you make a fool of me?" cried Giovanni, passionately. "THAT, signor professor, were an untoward experiment."

"Patience! patience!" replied the imperturbable professor. "I tell thee, my poor Giovanni, that Rappaccini has a scientific interest in thee. Thou hast fallen into fearful hands! And the Signora Beatrice,—what part does she act in this mystery?"

But Guasconti, finding Baglioni's pertinacity intolerable, here broke away, and was gone before the professor could again seize his arm. He looked after the young man intently and shook his head.

"This must not be," said Baglioni to himself. "The youth is the son of my old friend, and shall not come to any harm from which the arcana of medical science can preserve him. Besides, it is too insufferable an impertinence in Rappaccini, thus to snatch the lad out of my own hands, as I may say, and make use of him for his infernal experiments. This daughter of his! It shall be looked to. Perchance, most learned Rappaccini, I may foil you where you little dream of it!"

Meanwhile Giovanni had pursued a circuitous route, and at length found himself at the door of his lodgings. As he crossed the threshold he was met by old

Lisabetta, who smirked and smiled, and was evidently desirous to attract his attention; vainly, however, as the ebullition of his feelings had momentarily subsided into a cold and dull vacuity. He turned his eyes full upon the withered face that was puckering itself into a smile, but seemed to behold it not. The old dame, therefore, laid her grasp upon his cloak.

"Signor! signor!" whispered she, still with a smile over the whole breadth of her visage, so that it looked not unlike a grotesque carving in wood, darkened by centuries. "Listen, signor! There is a private entrance into the garden!"

"What do you say?" exclaimed Giovanni, turning quickly about, as if an inanimate thing should start into feverish life. "A private entrance into Dr. Rappaccini's garden?"

"Hush! hush! not so loud!" whispered Lisabetta, putting her hand over his mouth. "Yes; into the worshipful doctor's garden, where you may see all his fine shrubbery. Many a young man in Padua would give gold to be admitted among those flowers."

Giovanni put a piece of gold into her hand.

"Show me the way," said he.

A surmise, probably excited by his conversation with Baglioni, crossed his mind, that this interposition of old Lisabetta might perchance be connected with the intrigue, whatever were its nature, in which the professor seemed to suppose that Dr. Rappaccini was involving him. But such a suspicion, though it disturbed Giovanni, was inadequate to restrain him. The instant that he was aware of the possibility of approaching Beatrice, it seemed an absolute necessity of his existence to do so. It mattered not whether she were angel or demon; he was irrevocably within her sphere, and must obey the law that whirled him onward, in ever-lessening circles, towards a result which he did not attempt to foreshadow; and yet, strange to say, there came across him a sudden doubt whether this intense interest on his part were not delusory; whether it were really of so deep and positive a nature as to justify him in now thrusting himself into an incalculable position; whether it were not merely the fantasy of a young man's brain, only slightly or not at all connected with his heart.

He paused, hesitated, turned half about, but again went on. His withered guide led him along several obscure passages, and finally undid a door, through which, as it was opened, there came the sight and sound of rustling leaves, with the broken sunshine glimmering among them. Giovanni stepped forth, and, forcing himself through the entanglement of a shrub that wreathed its tendrils over the hidden entrance, stood beneath his own window in the open area of Dr. Rappaccini's garden.

How often is it the case that, when impossibilities have come to pass and dreams have condensed their misty substance into tangible realities, we find ourselves calm, and even coldly self-possessed, amid circumstances which it would have been a delirium of joy or agony to anticipate! Fate delights to thwart us thus. Passion will choose his own time to rush upon the scene, and lingers sluggishly behind when an appropriate adjustment of events would seem to summon his appearance. So was it now with Giovanni. Day after day his pulses had throbbed with feverish blood at the improbable idea of an interview with Beatrice, and of standing with her, face to face, in this very garden, basking in the Oriental sunshine of her beauty, and snatching from her full gaze the mystery which he deemed the riddle of his own existence. But now there was a singular and untimely equanimity within his breast. He threw a glance around the garden to discover if Beatrice or her father were present, and, perceiving that he was alone, began a critical observation of the plants.

The aspect of one and all of them dissatisfied him; their gorgeousness seemed fierce, passionate, and even unnatural. There was hardly an individual shrub which a wanderer, straying by himself through a forest, would not have been startled to find growing wild, as if an unearthly face had glared at him out of the thicket. Several also would have shocked a delicate instinct by an appearance of artificialness indicating that there had been such commixture, and, as it were, adultery, of various vegetable species, that the production was no longer of God's making, but the monstrous offspring of man's depraved fancy, glowing with only an evil mockery of beauty. They were probably the result of experiment, which in one or two cases had succeeded in mingling plants individually lovely into a compound possessing the questionable and ominous character that distinguished the whole growth of the garden. In fine, Giovanni recognized but two or three plants in the collection, and those of a kind that he well knew to be poisonous. While busy with these contemplations he heard the rustling of a silken garment, and, turning, beheld Beatrice emerging from beneath the sculptured portal.

Giovanni had not considered with himself what should be his deportment; whether he should apologize for his intrusion into the garden, or assume that he was there with the privity at least, if not by the desire, of Dr. Rappaccini or his daughter; but Beatrice's manner placed him at his ease, though leaving him still in doubt by what agency he had gained admittance. She came lightly along the path and met him near the broken fountain. There was surprise in her face, but brightened by a simple and kind expression of pleasure.

"You are a connoisseur in flowers, signor," said Beatrice, with a smile, alluding to the bouquet which he had flung her from the window. "It is no marvel, therefore, if the sight of my father's rare collection has tempted you to take a nearer view. If he were here, he could tell you many strange and interesting facts as to the nature and habits of these shrubs; for he has spent a lifetime in such studies, and this garden is his world."

"And yourself, lady," observed Giovanni, "if fame says true,—you likewise are deeply skilled in the virtues indicated by these rich blossoms and these spicy perfumes. Would you deign to be my instructress, I should prove an apter scholar than if taught by Signor Rappaccini himself."

"Are there such idle rumors?" asked Beatrice, with the music of a pleasant laugh. "Do people say that I am skilled in my father's science of plants? What a jest is there! No; though I have grown up among these flowers, I know no more of them than their hues and perfume; and sometimes methinks I would fain rid myself of even that small knowledge. There are many flowers here, and those not the least brilliant, that shock and offend me when they meet my eye. But pray, signor, do not believe these stories about my science. Believe nothing of me save what you see with your own eyes."

"And must I believe all that I have seen with my own eyes?" asked Giovanni, pointedly, while the recollection of former scenes made him shrink. "No, signora; you demand too little of me. Bid me believe nothing save what comes from your own lips."

It would appear that Beatrice understood him. There came a deep flush to her cheek; but she looked full into Giovanni's eyes, and responded to his gaze of uneasy suspicion with a queenlike haughtiness.

"I do so bid you, signor," she replied. "Forget whatever you may have fancied in regard to me. If true to the outward senses, still it may be false in its essence; but the words of Beatrice Rappaccini's lips are true from the depths of the heart outward. Those you may believe."

A fervor glowed in her whole aspect and beamed upon Giovanni's consciousness like the light of truth itself; but while she spoke there was a fragrance in the atmosphere around her, rich and delightful, though evanescent, yet which the young man, from an indefinable reluctance, scarcely dared to draw into his lungs. It might be the odor of the flowers. Could it be Beatrice's breath which thus embalmed her words with a strange richness, as if by steeping them in her heart? A faintness passed like a shadow over Giovanni and flitted away; he seemed to gaze through the beautiful girl's eyes into her transparent soul, and felt no more doubt or fear.

The tinge of passion that had colored Beatrice's manner vanished; she became gay, and appeared to derive a pure delight from her communion with the youth not unlike what the maiden of a lonely island might have felt conversing with a voyager from the civilized world. Evidently her experience of life had been confined within the limits of that garden. She talked now about matters as simple as the daylight or summer clouds, and now asked questions in reference to the city, or Giovanni's distant home, his friends, his mother, and his sisters—questions indicating such seclusion, and such lack of familiarity with modes and forms, that Giovanni responded as if to an infant. Her spirit gushed out before him like a fresh rill that was just catching its first glimpse of the sunlight and wondering at the reflections of earth and sky which were flung into its bosom. There came thoughts, too, from a deep source, and fantasies of a gemlike brilliancy, as if diamonds and rubies sparkled upward among the bubbles of the fountain. Ever and anon there gleamed across the young man's mind a sense of wonder that he should be walking side by side with the being who had so wrought upon his imagination, whom he had idealized in such hues of terror, in whom he had positively witnessed such manifestations of dreadful attributes,—that he should be conversing with Beatrice like a brother, and should find her so human and so maidenlike. But such reflections were only momentary; the effect of her character was too real not to make itself familiar at once.

In this free intercourse they had strayed through the garden, and now, after many turns among its avenues, were come to the shattered fountain, beside which grew the magnificent shrub, with its treasury of glowing blossoms. A fragrance was diffused from it which Giovanni recognized as identical with that which he had attributed to Beatrice's breath, but incomparably more powerful. As her eyes fell upon it, Giovanni beheld her press her hand to her bosom as if her heart were throbbing suddenly and painfully.

"For the first time in my life," murmured she, addressing the shrub, "I had forgotten thee."

"I remember, signora," said Giovanni, "that you once promised to reward me with one of these living gems for the bouquet which I had the happy boldness to fling to your feet. Permit me now to pluck it as a memorial of this interview."

He made a step towards the shrub with extended hand; but Beatrice darted forward, uttering a shriek that went through his heart like a dagger. She caught his hand and drew it back with the whole force of her slender figure. Giovanni felt her touch thrilling through his fibres.

"Touch it not!" exclaimed she, in a voice of agony. "Not for thy life! It is fatal!"

Then, hiding her face, she fled from him and vanished beneath the sculptured portal. As Giovanni followed her with his eyes, he beheld the emaciated figure and pale intelligence of Dr. Rappaccini, who had been watching the scene, he knew not how long, within the shadow of the entrance.

No sooner was Guasconti alone in his chamber than the image of Beatrice came back to his passionate musings, invested with all the witchery that had been gathering around it ever since his first glimpse of her, and now likewise imbued with a tender warmth of girlish womanhood. She was human; her nature was endowed with all gentle and feminine qualities; she was worthiest to be worshipped; she was capable, surely, on her part, of the height and heroism of love. Those tokens which he had hitherto considered as proofs of a frightful peculiarity in her physical and moral system were now either forgotten, or, by the subtle sophistry of passion transmitted into a golden crown of enchantment, rendering Beatrice the more admirable by so much as she was the more unique. Whatever had looked ugly was now beautiful; or, if incapable of such a change, it stole away and hid itself among those shapeless half ideas which throng the dim region beyond the daylight of our perfect consciousness. Thus did he spend the night, nor fell asleep until the dawn had begun to awake the slumbering flowers in Dr. Rappaccini's garden, whither Giovanni's dreams doubtless led him. Up rose the sun in his due season, and, flinging his beams upon the young man's eyelids, awoke him to a sense of pain. When thoroughly aroused, he became sensible of a burning and tingling agony in his hand—in his right hand—the very hand which Beatrice had grasped in her own when he was on the point of plucking one of the gemlike flowers. On the back of that hand there was now a purple print like that of four small fingers, and the likeness of a slender thumb upon his wrist.

Oh, how stubbornly does love,—or even that cunning semblance of love which flourishes in the imagination, but strikes no depth of root into the heart,—how stubbornly does it hold its faith until the moment comes when it is doomed to vanish into thin mist! Giovanni wrapped a handkerchief about his hand and wondered what evil thing had stung him, and soon forgot his pain in a reverie of Beatrice.

After the first interview, a second was in the inevitable course of what we call fate. A third; a fourth; and a meeting with Beatrice in the garden was no longer an incident in Giovanni's daily life, but the whole space in which he might be said to live; for the anticipation and memory of that ecstatic hour made up the remainder. Nor was it otherwise with the daughter of Rappaccini. She watched for the youth's appearance, and flew to his side with confidence as unreserved as if they had been playmates from early infancy—as if they were such playmates still. If, by any unwonted chance, he failed to come at the appointed moment, she stood beneath the window and sent up the rich sweetness of her tones to float around him in his chamber and echo and reverberate throughout his heart: "Giovanni! Giovanni! Why tarriest thou? Come down!" And down he hastened into that Eden of poisonous flowers.

But, with all this intimate familiarity, there was still a reserve in Beatrice's demeanor, so rigidly and invariably sustained that the idea of infringing it scarcely occurred to his imagination. By all appreciable signs, they loved; they had looked love with eyes that conveyed the holy secret from the depths of one soul into the depths of the other, as if it were too sacred to be whispered by the way; they had even spoken love in those gushes of passion when their spirits darted forth in articulated breath like tongues of long-hidden flame; and yet there had been no seal of lips, no clasp of hands, nor any slightest caress such as love claims and hallows. He had never touched one of the gleaming ringlets of her hair; her garment—so marked was the physical barrier between them—had never been waved against him by a breeze. On the few occasions when Giovanni had seemed tempted to overstep the limit, Beatrice grew so sad, so stern, and withal wore such a look of desolate separation, shuddering at itself, that not a spoken word was requisite to repel him. At such times he was startled at the horrible suspicions that rose, monster-like, out of the caverns of his heart and stared him in the face; his love grew thin and faint as the morning mist, his doubts alone had substance. But, when Beatrice's face brightened again after the momentary shadow, she was transformed at once from the mysterious, questionable being whom he had watched with so much awe and horror; she was now the beautiful and unsophisticated girl whom he felt that his spirit knew with a certainty beyond all other knowledge.

A considerable time had now passed since Giovanni's last meeting with Baglioni. One morning, however, he was disagreeably surprised by a visit from the professor, whom he had scarcely thought of for whole weeks, and would willingly have forgotten still longer. Given up as he had long been to a pervading excitement, he could tolerate no companions except upon condition of their perfect sympathy with his present state of feeling. Such sympathy was not to be expected from Professor Baglioni.

The visitor chatted carelessly for a few moments about the gossip of the city and the university, and then took up another topic.

"I have been reading an old classic author lately," said he, "and met with a story that strangely interested me. Possibly you may remember it. It is of an Indian prince, who sent a beautiful woman as a present to Alexander the Great. She was as lovely as the dawn and gorgeous as the sunset; but what especially distinguished her was a certain rich perfume in her breath—richer than a garden of Persian roses. Alexander, as was natural to a youthful conqueror, fell in love at first sight with this magnificent stranger; but a certain sage physician, happening to be present, discovered a terrible secret in regard to her."

"And what was that?" asked Giovanni, turning his eyes downward to avoid those of the professor.

"That this lovely woman," continued Baglioni, with emphasis, "had been nourished with poisons from her birth upward, until her whole nature was so imbued with them that she herself had become the deadliest poison in existence. Poison was her element of life. With that rich perfume of her breath she blasted the very air. Her love would have been poison—her embrace death. Is not this a marvellous tale?"

"A childish fable," answered Giovanni, nervously starting from his chair. "I marvel how your worship finds time to read such nonsense among your graver studies."

"By the by," said the professor, looking uneasily about him, "what singular fragrance is this in your apartment? Is it the perfume of your gloves? It is faint, but delicious; and yet, after all, by no means agreeable. Were I to breathe it long, methinks it would make me ill. It is like the breath of a flower; but I see no flowers in the chamber."

"Nor are there any," replied Giovanni, who had turned pale as the professor spoke; "nor, I think, is there any fragrance except in your worship's imagination. Odors, being a sort of element combined of the sensual and the spiritual, are apt to deceive us in this manner. The recollection of a perfume, the bare idea of it, may easily be mistaken for a present reality."

"Ay; but my sober imagination does not often play such tricks," said Baglioni; "and, were I to fancy any kind of odor, it would be that of some vile apothecary drug, wherewith my fingers are likely enough to be imbued. Our worshipful friend Rappaccini, as I have heard, tinctures his medicaments with odors richer than those of Araby. Doubtless, likewise, the fair and learned Signora Beatrice would minister to her patients with draughts as sweet as a maiden's breath; but woe to him that sips them!"

Giovanni's face evinced many contending emotions. The tone in which the professor alluded to the pure and lovely daughter of Rappaccini was a torture to his soul; and yet the intimation of a view of her character opposite to his own, gave instantaneous distinctness to a thousand dim suspicions, which now grinned at him like so many demons. But he strove hard to quell them and to respond to Baglioni with a true lover's perfect faith.

"Signor professor," said he, "you were my father's friend; perchance, too, it is your purpose to act a friendly part towards his son. I would fain feel nothing towards you save respect and deference; but I pray you to observe, signor, that there is one subject on which we must not speak. You know not the Signora Beatrice. You cannot, therefore, estimate the wrong—the blasphemy, I may even say—that is offered to her character by a light or injurious word."

"Giovanni! my poor Giovanni!" answered the professor, with a calm expression of pity, "I know this wretched girl far better than yourself. You shall hear the truth in respect to the poisoner Rappaccini and his poisonous daughter; yes, poisonous as she is beautiful. Listen; for, even should you do violence to my gray hairs, it shall not silence me. That old fable of the Indian woman has become a truth by the deep and deadly science of Rappaccini and in the person of the lovely Beatrice."

Giovanni groaned and hid his face

"Her father," continued Baglioni, "was not restrained by natural affection from offering up his child in this horrible manner as the victim of his insane zeal for science; for, let us do him justice, he is as true a man of science as ever distilled his own heart in an alembic. What, then, will be your fate? Beyond a doubt you are selected as the material of some new experiment. Perhaps the result is to be death; perhaps a fate more awful still. Rappaccini, with what he calls the interest of science before his eyes, will hesitate at nothing."

"It is a dream," muttered Giovanni to himself; "surely it is a dream."

"But," resumed the professor, "be of good cheer, son of my friend. It is not yet too late for the rescue. Possibly we may even succeed in bringing back this miserable child within the limits of ordinary nature, from which her father's madness has estranged her. Behold this little silver vase! It was wrought by the hands of the renowned Benvenuto Cellini, and is well worthy to be a love gift to the fairest dame in Italy. But its contents are invaluable. One little sip of this antidote would have rendered the most virulent poisons of the Borgias innocuous. Doubt not that it will be as efficacious against those of Rappaccini. Bestow the vase, and the precious liquid within it, on your Beatrice, and hopefully await the result."

Baglioni laid a small, exquisitely wrought silver vial on the table and withdrew, leaving what he had said to produce its effect upon the young man's mind.

"We will thwart Rappaccini yet," thought he, chuckling to himself, as he descended the stairs; "but, let us confess the truth of him, he is a wonderful man—a wonderful man indeed; a vile empiric, however, in his practice, and therefore not to be tolerated by those who respect the good old rules of the medical profession."

Throughout Giovanni's whole acquaintance with Beatrice, he had occasionally, as we have said, been haunted by dark surmises as to her character; yet so thoroughly had she made herself felt by him as a simple, natural, most affectionate, and guileless creature, that the image now held up by Professor Baglioni looked as strange and incredible as if it were not in accordance with his own original conception. True, there were ugly recollections connected with his first glimpses of the beautiful girl; he could not quite forget the bouquet that withered in her grasp, and the insect that perished amid the sunny air, by no ostensible agency save the fragrance of her breath. These incidents, however, dissolving in the pure light of her character, had no longer the efficacy of facts, but were acknowledged as mistaken fantasies, by whatever testimony of the senses they might appear to be substantiated. There is something truer and more real than what we can see with the eyes and touch with the finger. On such better evidence had Giovanni founded his confidence in Beatrice, though rather by the necessary force of her high attributes than by any deep and generous faith on his part. But now his spirit was incapable of sustaining itself at the height to which the early enthusiasm of passion had exalted it; he fell down, grovelling among earthly doubts, and defiled therewith the pure whiteness of Beatrice's image. Not that he gave her up; he did but distrust. He resolved to institute some decisive test that should satisfy him, once for all, whether there were those dreadful peculiarities in her physical nature which could not be supposed to exist without some corresponding monstrosity of soul. His eyes, gazing down afar, might have deceived him as to the lizard, the insect, and the flowers; but if he could witness, at the distance of a few paces, the sudden blight of one fresh and healthful flower in Beatrice's hand, there would be room for no further question. With this idea he hastened to the florist's and purchased a bouquet that was still gemmed with the morning dew-drops.

It was now the customary hour of his daily interview with Beatrice. Before descending into the garden, Giovanni failed not to look at his figure in the mirror,—a vanity to be expected in a beautiful young man, yet, as displaying itself at that troubled and feverish moment, the token of a certain shallowness of feeling and insincerity of character. He did gaze, however, and said to himself that his features had never before possessed so rich a grace, nor his eyes such vivacity, nor his cheeks so warm a hue of superabundant life.

"At least," thought he, "her poison has not yet insinuated itself into my system. I am no flower to perish in her grasp."

With that thought he turned his eyes on the bouquet, which he had never once laid aside from his hand. A thrill of indefinable horror shot through his frame on perceiving that those dewy flowers were already beginning to droop; they wore the aspect of things that had been fresh and lovely yesterday. Giovanni grew white as marble, and stood motionless before the mirror, staring at his own reflection there as at the likeness of something frightful. He remembered Baglioni's remark about the fragrance that seemed to pervade the chamber. It must have been the poison in his breath! Then he shuddered—shuddered at himself. Recovering from his stupor, he began to watch with curious eye a spider that was busily at work hanging its web from the antique cornice of the apartment, crossing and recrossing the artful system of interwoven lines—as vigorous and active a spider as ever dangled from an old ceiling. Giovanni bent towards the insect, and emitted a deep, long breath. The spider suddenly ceased its toil; the web vibrated with a tremor originating in the body of the small artisan. Again Giovanni sent forth a breath, deeper, longer, and imbued with a venomous feeling out of his heart: he knew not whether he were wicked, or only desperate. The spider made a convulsive gripe with his limbs and hung dead across the window.

"Accursed! accursed!" muttered Giovanni, addressing himself. "Hast thou grown so poisonous that this deadly insect perishes by thy breath?"

At that moment a rich, sweet voice came floating up from the garden.

"Giovanni! Giovanni! It is past the hour! Why tarriest thou? Come down!"

"Yes," muttered Giovanni again. "She is the only being whom my breath may not slay! Would that it might!"

He rushed down, and in an instant was standing before the bright and loving eyes of Beatrice. A moment ago his wrath and despair had been so fierce that he could have desired nothing so much as to wither her by a glance; but with her actual presence there came influences which had too real an existence to be at once shaken off: recollections of the delicate and benign power of her feminine nature, which had so often enveloped him in a religious calm; recollections of many a holy and passionate outgush of her heart, when the pure fountain had been unsealed from its depths and made visible in its transparency to his mental eye; recollections which, had Giovanni known how to estimate them, would have assured him that all this ugly mystery was but an earthly illusion, and that, whatever mist of evil might seem to have gathered over her, the real Beatrice was a heavenly angel. Incapable as he was of such high faith, still her presence had not utterly lost its magic. Giovanni's rage was quelled into an aspect of sullen insensibility. Beatrice, with a quick spiritual sense, immediately felt that there was a gulf of blackness between them which neither he nor she could pass. They walked on together, sad and silent, and came thus to the marble fountain and to its pool of water on the ground, in the midst of which grew the shrub that bore gem-like blossoms. Giovanni was affrighted at the eager enjoyment—the appetite, as it were—with which he found himself inhaling the fragrance of the flowers.

"Beatrice," asked he, abruptly, "whence came this shrub?"

"My father created it," answered she, with simplicity.

"Created it! created it!" repeated Giovanni. "What mean you, Beatrice?"

"He is a man fearfully acquainted with the secrets of Nature," replied Beatrice; "and, at the hour when I first drew breath, this plant sprang from the soil, the offspring of his science, of his intellect, while I was but his earthly child. Approach it not!" continued she, observing with terror that Giovanni was drawing nearer to the shrub. "It has qualities that you little dream of. But I, dearest Giovanni,—I grew up and blossomed with the plant and was nourished with its breath. It was my sister, and I loved it with a human affection; for, alas!—hast thou not suspected it?—there was an awful doom."

Here Giovanni frowned so darkly upon her that Beatrice paused and trembled. But her faith in his tenderness reassured her, and made her blush that she had doubted for an instant.

"There was an awful doom," she continued, "the effect of my father's fatal love of science, which estranged me from all society of my kind. Until Heaven sent thee, dearest Giovanni, oh, how lonely was thy poor Beatrice!"

"Was it a hard doom?" asked Giovanni, fixing his eyes upon her.

"Only of late have I known how hard it was," answered she, tenderly. "Oh, yes; but my heart was torpid, and therefore quiet."

Giovanni's rage broke forth from his sullen gloom like a lightning flash out of a dark cloud.

"Accursed one!" cried he, with venomous scorn and anger. "And, finding thy solitude wearisome, thou hast severed me likewise from all the warmth of life and enticed me into thy region of unspeakable horror!"

"Giovanni!" exclaimed Beatrice, turning her large bright eyes upon his face. The force of his words had not found its way into her mind; she was merely thunderstruck.

"Yes, poisonous thing!" repeated Giovanni, beside himself with passion. "Thou hast done it! Thou hast blasted me! Thou hast filled my veins with poison! Thou hast made me as hateful, as ugly, as loathsome and deadly a creature as thyself—a world's wonder of hideous monstrosity! Now, if our breath be happily as fatal to ourselves as to all others, let us join our lips in one kiss of unutterable hatred, and so die!"

"What has befallen me?" murmured Beatrice, with a low moan out of her heart. "Holy Virgin, pity me, a poor heart-broken child!"

"Thou,—dost thou pray?" cried Giovanni, still with the same fiendish scorn. "Thy very prayers, as they come from thy lips, taint the atmosphere with death. Yes, yes; let us pray! Let us to church and dip our fingers in the holy water at the portal! They that come after us will perish as by a pestilence! Let us sign crosses in the air! It will be scattering curses abroad in the likeness of holy symbols!"

"Giovanni," said Beatrice, calmly, for her grief was beyond passion, "why dost thou join thyself with me thus in those terrible words? I, it is true, am the horrible thing thou namest me. But thou,—what hast thou to do, save with one other shudder at my hideous misery to go forth out of the garden and mingle with thy race, and forget there ever crawled on earth such a monster as poor Beatrice?"

"Dost thou pretend ignorance?" asked Giovanni, scowling upon her. "Behold! this power have I gained from the pure daughter of Rappaccini."

There was a swarm of summer insects flitting through the air in search of the food promised by the flower odors of the fatal garden. They circled round Giovanni's head, and were evidently attracted towards him by the same influence which had drawn them for an instant within the sphere of several of the shrubs. He sent forth a breath among them, and smiled bitterly at Beatrice as at least a score of the insects fell dead upon the ground.

"I see it! I see it!" shrieked Beatrice. "It is my father's fatal science! No, no, Giovanni; it was not I! Never! never! I dreamed only to love thee and be with thee a little time, and so to let thee pass away, leaving but thine image in mine heart; for, Giovanni, believe it, though my body be nourished with poison, my spirit is

God's creature, and craves love as its daily food. But my father,—he has united us in this fearful sympathy. Yes; spurn me, tread upon me, kill me! Oh, what is death after such words as thine? But it was not I. Not for a world of bliss would I have done it."

Giovanni's passion had exhausted itself in its outburst from his lips. There now came across him a sense, mournful, and not without tenderness, of the intimate and peculiar relationship between Beatrice and himself. They stood, as it were, in an utter solitude, which would be made none the less solitary by the densest throng of human life. Ought not, then, the desert of humanity around them to press this insulated pair closer together? If they should be cruel to one another, who was there to be kind to them? Besides, thought Giovanni, might there not still be a hope of his returning within the limits of ordinary nature, and leading Beatrice, the redeemed Beatrice, by the hand? O, weak, and selfish, and unworthy spirit, that could dream of an earthly union and earthly happiness as possible, after such deep love had been so bitterly wronged as was Beatrice's love by Giovanni's blighting words! No, no; there could be no such hope. She must pass heavily, with that broken heart, across the borders of Time—she must bathe her hurts in some fount of paradise, and forget her grief in the light of immortality, and THERE be well.

But Giovanni did not know it.

"Dear Beatrice," said he, approaching her, while she shrank away as always at his approach, but now with a different impulse, "dearest Beatrice, our fate is not yet so desperate. Behold! there is a medicine, potent, as a wise physician has assured me, and almost divine in its efficacy. It is composed of ingredients the most opposite to those by which thy awful father has brought this calamity upon thee and me. It is distilled of blessed herbs. Shall we not quaff it together, and thus be purified from evil?"

"Give it me!" said Beatrice, extending her hand to receive the little silver vial which Giovanni took from his bosom. She added, with a peculiar emphasis, "I will drink; but do thou await the result."

She put Baglioni's antidote to her lips; and, at the same moment, the figure of Rappaccini emerged from the portal and came slowly towards the marble fountain. As he drew near, the pale man of science seemed to gaze with a triumphant expression at the beautiful youth and maiden, as might an artist who should spend his life in achieving a picture or a group of statuary and finally be satisfied with his success. He paused; his bent form grew erect with conscious power; he spread out his hands over them in the attitude of a father imploring a blessing upon his children; but those were the same hands that had thrown poison into the stream of their lives. Giovanni trembled. Beatrice shuddered nervously, and pressed her hand upon her heart.

"My daughter," said Rappaccini, "thou art no longer lonely in the world. Pluck one of those precious gems from thy sister shrub and bid thy bridegroom wear it in his bosom. It will not harm him now. My science and the sympathy between thee and him have so wrought within his system that he now stands apart from common men, as thou dost, daughter of my pride and triumph, from ordinary women. Pass on, then, through the world, most dear to one another and dreadful to all besides!"

"My father," said Beatrice, feebly,—and still as she spoke she kept her hand upon her heart,—"wherefore didst thou inflict this miserable doom upon thy child?"

"Miserable!" exclaimed Rappaccini. "What mean you, foolish girl? Dost thou deem it misery to be endowed with marvellous gifts against which no power nor strength could avail an enemy—misery, to be able to quell the mightiest with a breath—misery, to be as terrible as thou art beautiful? Wouldst thou, then, have preferred the condition of a weak woman, exposed to all evil and capable of none?"

"I would fain have been loved, not feared," murmured Beatrice, sinking down upon the ground. "But now it matters not. I am going, father, where the evil which thou hast striven to mingle with my being will pass away like a dream-like the fragrance of these poisonous flowers, which will no longer taint my breath among the flowers of Eden. Farewell, Giovanni! Thy words of hatred are like lead within my heart; but they, too, will fall away as I ascend. Oh, was there not, from the first, more poison in thy nature than in mine?"

To Beatrice,—so radically had her earthly part been wrought upon by Rappaccini's skill,—as poison had been life, so the powerful antidote was death; and thus the poor victim of man's ingenuity and of thwarted nature, and of the fatality that attends all such efforts of perverted wisdom, perished there, at the feet of her father and Giovanni. Just at that moment Professor Pietro Baglioni looked forth from the window, and called loudly, in a tone of triumph mixed with horror, to the thunderstricken man of science, "Rappaccini! Rappaccini! and is THIS the upshot of your experiment!"

MRS. BULLFROG

It makes me melancholy to see how like fools some very sensible people act in the matter of choosing wives. They perplex their judgments by a most undue attention to little niceties of personal appearance, habits, disposition, and other trifles which concern nobody but the lady herself. An unhappy gentleman, resolving to wed nothing short of perfection, keeps his heart and hand till both get so old and withered that no tolerable woman will accept them. Now this is the very height of absurdity. A kind Providence has so skilfully adapted sex to sex and the mass of individuals to each other, that, with certain obvious exceptions, any male and female may be moderately happy in the married state. The true rule is to ascertain that the match is fundamentally a good one, and then to take it for granted that all minor objections, should there be such, will vanish, if you let them alone. Only put yourself beyond hazard as to the real basis of matrimonial bliss, and it is scarcely to be imagined what miracles, in the way of recognizing smaller incongruities, connubial love will effect.

For my own part I freely confess that, in my bachelorship, I was precisely such an over-curious simpleton as I now advise the reader not to be. My early habits had gifted me with a feminine sensibility and too exquisite refinement. I was the accomplished graduate of a dry goods store, where, by dint of ministering to the whims of fine ladies, and suiting silken hose to delicate limbs, and handling satins, ribbons, chintzes calicoes, tapes, gauze, and cambric needles, I grew up a very ladylike sort of a gentleman. It is not assuming too much to affirm that the ladies themselves were hardly so ladylike as Thomas Bullfrog. So painfully acute was my sense of female imperfection, and such varied excellence did I require in the woman whom I could love, that there was an awful risk of my getting no wife at all, or of being driven to perpetrate matrimony with my own image in the looking-glass. Besides the fundamental principle already hinted at, I demanded the fresh bloom of youth, pearly teeth, glossy ringlets, and the whole list of lovely items, with the utmost delicacy of habits and sentiments, a silken texture of mind, and, above all, a virgin heart. In a word, if a young angel just from paradise, yet dressed in earthly fashion, had come and offered me her hand, it is by no means certain that I should have taken it. There was every chance of my becoming a most miserable old bachelor, when, by the best luck in the world, I made a journey into another state, and was smitten by, and smote again, and wooed, won, and married, the present Mrs. Bullfrog, all in the space of a fortnight. Owing to these extempore measures, I not only gave my bride credit for certain perfections which have not as yet come to light, but also overlooked a few trifling defects, which, however, glimmered on my perception long before the close of the honeymoon. Yet, as there was no mistake about the fundamental principle aforesaid, I soon learned, as will be seen, to estimate Mrs. Bullfrog's deficiencies and superfluities at exactly their proper value.

The same morning that Mrs. Bullfrog and I came together as a unit, we took two seats in the stage-coach and began our journey towards my place of business. There being no other passengers, we were as much alone and as free to give vent to our raptures as if I had hired a hack for the matrimonial jaunt. My bride looked charmingly in a green silk calash and riding habit of pellsse cloth; and whenever her red lips parted with a smile, each tooth appeared like an inestimable pearl. Such was my passionate warmth that—we had rattled out of the village, gentle reader, and were lonely as Adam and Eve in paradise—I plead guilty to no less freedom than a kiss. The gentle eye of Mrs. Bullfrog scarcely rebuked me for the profanation. Emboldened by her indulgence, I threw back the calash from her polished brow, and suffered my fingers, white and delicate as her own, to stray among those dark and glossy curls which realized my daydreams of rich hair.

"My love," said Mrs. Bullfrog tenderly, "you will disarrange my curls."

"Oh, no, my sweet Laura!" replied I, still playing with the glossy ringlet. "Even your fair hand could not manage a curl more delicately than mine. I propose myself the pleasure of doing up your hair in papers every evening at the same time with my own."

"Mr. Bullfrog," repeated she, "you must not disarrange my curls."

This was spoken in a more decided tone than I had happened to hear, until then, from my gentlest of all gentle brides. At the same time she put up her hand and took mine prisoner; but merely drew it away from the forbidden ringlet, and then immediately released it. Now, I am a fidgety little man, and always love to have something in my fingers; so that, being debarred from my wife's curls, I looked about me for any other plaything. On the front seat of the coach there was one of those small baskets in which travelling ladies who are too delicate to appear at a public table generally carry a supply of gingerbread, biscuits and cheese, cold ham, and other light refreshments, merely to sustain nature to the journey's end. Such airy diet will sometimes keep them in pretty good flesh for a week together. Laying hold of this same little basket, I thrust my hand under the newspaper with which it was carefully covered.

"What's this, my dear?" cried I; for the black neck of a bottle had popped out of the basket.

"A bottle of Kalydor, Mr. Bullfrog," said my wife, coolly taking the basket from my hands and replacing it on the front seat.

There was no possibility of doubting my wife's word; but I never knew genuine Kalydor, such as I use for my own complexion, to smell so much like cherry brandy. I was about to express my fears that the lotion would injure her skin, when an accident occurred which threatened more than a skin-deep injury. Our Jehu had carelessly driven over a heap of gravel and fairly capsized the coach, with the wheels in the air and our heels where our heads should have been. What became of my wits I cannot imagine; they have always had a perverse trick of deserting me just when they were most needed; but so it chanced, that in the confusion of our overthrow I quite forgot that there was a Mrs. Bullfrog in the world. Like many men's wives, the good lady served her husband as a steppingstone. I had scrambled out of the coach and was instinctively settling my cravat, when somebody brushed roughly by me, and I heard a smart thwack upon the coachman's ear.

"Take that, you villain!" cried a strange, hoarse voice. "You have ruined me, you blackguard! I shall never be the woman I have been!"

And then came a second thwack, aimed at the driver's other ear; but which missed it, and hit him on the nose, causing a terrible effusion of blood. Now, who or what fearful apparition was inflicting this punishment on the poor fellow remained an impenetrable mystery to me. The blows were given by a person of grisly aspect, with a head almost bald, and sunken cheeks, apparently of the feminine gender, though hardly to be classed in the gentler sex. There being no teeth to modulate the voice, it had a mumbled fierceness, not passionate, but stern, which absolutely made me quiver like calf's-foot jelly. Who could the phantom be? The most awful circumstance of the affair is yet to be told: for this ogre, or whatever it was, had a riding habit like Mrs. Bullfrog's, and also a green silk calash dangling down her back by the strings. In my terror and turmoil of mind I could imagine nothing less than that the Old Nick, at the moment of our overturn, had annihilated my wife and jumped into her petticoats. This idea seemed the most probable, since I could nowhere perceive Mrs. Bullfrog alive, nor, though I looked very sharply about the coach, could I detect any traces of that beloved woman's dead body. There would have been a comfort in giving her Christian burial.

"Come, sir, bestir yourself! Help this rascal to set up the coach," said the hobgoblin to me; then, with a terrific screech at three countrymen at a distance, "Here, you fellows, ain't you ashamed to stand off when a poor woman is in distress?"

The countrymen, instead of fleeing for their lives, came running at full speed, and laid hold of the topsy-turvy coach. I, also, though a small-sized man, went to work like a son of Anak. The coachman, too, with the blood still streaming from his nose, tugged and toiled most manfully, dreading, doubtless, that the next blow might break his head. And yet, bemauled as the poor fellow had been, he seemed to glance at me with an eye of pity, as if my case were more deplorable than his. But I cherished a hope that all would turn out a dream, and seized the opportunity, as we raised the coach, to jam two of my fingers under the wheel, trusting that the pain would awaken me.

"Why, here we are, all to rights again!" exclaimed a sweet voice behind. "Thank you for your assistance, gentlemen. My dear Mr. Bullfrog, how you perspire! Do let me wipe your face. Don't take this little accident too much to heart, good driver. We ought to be thankful that none of our necks are broken."

"We might have spared one neck out of the three," muttered the driver, rubbing his ear and pulling his nose, to ascertain whether he had been cuffed or not. "Why, the woman's a witch!"

I fear that the reader will not believe, yet it is positively a fact, that there stood Mrs. Bullfrog, with her glossy ringlets curling on her brow, and two rows of orient pearls gleaming between her parted lips, which wore a most angelic smile. She had regained her riding habit and calash from the grisly phantom, and was, in all respects, the lovely woman who had been sitting by my side at the instant of our overturn. How she had happened to disappear, and who had supplied her place, and whence she did now return, were problems too knotty for me to solve. There stood my wife. That was the one thing certain among a heap of mysteries. Nothing remained but to help her into the coach, and plod on, through the journey of the day and the journey of life, as comfortably as we could. As the driver closed the door upon us, I heard him whisper to the three countrymen, "How do you suppose a fellow feels shut up in the cage with a she tiger?"

Of course this query could have no reference to my situation. Yet, unreasonable as it may appear, I confess that my feelings were not altogether so ecstatic as when I first called Mrs. Bullfrog mine. True, she was a sweet woman and an angel of a wife; but what if a Gorgon should return, amid the transports of our connubial bliss, and take the angel's place. I recollected the tale of a fairy, who half the time was a beautiful woman and half the time a hideous monster. Had I taken that very fairy to be the wife of my bosom? While such whims and chimeras were flitting across my fancy I began to look askance at Mrs. Bullfrog, almost expecting that the transformation would be wrought before my eyes.

To divert my mind, I took up the newspaper which had covered the little basket of refreshments, and which now lay at the bottom of the coach, blushing with a deep-red stain and emitting a potent spirituous fume from the contents of the broken bottle of Kalydor. The paper was two or three years old, but contained an article of several columns, in which I soon grew wonderfully interested. It was the report of a trial for breach of promise of marriage, giving the testimony in full, with fervid extracts from both the gentleman's and lady's amatory correspondence. The deserted damsel had personally appeared in court, and had borne energetic evidence to her lover's perfidy and the strength of her blighted affections. On the defendant's part there had been an attempt, though insufficiently sustained, to blast the plaintiff's character, and a plea, in mitigation of damages, on account of her unamiable temper. A horrible idea was suggested by the lady's name.

"Madam," said I, holding the newspaper before Mrs. Bullfrog's eyes,—and, though a small, delicate, and thin-visaged man, I feel assured that I looked very terrific,—"madam," repeated I, through my shut teeth, "were you the plaintiff in this cause?"

"Oh, my dear Mr. Bullfrog," replied my wife, sweetly, "I thought all the world knew that!"

"Horror! horror!" exclaimed I, sinking back on the seat.

Covering my face with both hands, I emitted a deep and deathlike groan, as if my tormented soul were rending me asunder—I, the most exquisitely fastidious of men, and whose wife was to have been the most delicate and refined of women, with all the fresh dew-drops glittering on her virgin rosebud of a heart!

I thought of the glossy ringlets and pearly teeth; I thought of the Kalydor; I thought of the coachman's bruised ear and bloody nose; I thought of the tender love secrets which she had whispered to the judge and jury and a thousand tittering auditors,—and gave another groan!

"Mr. Bullfrog," said my wife.

As I made no reply, she gently took my hands within her own, removed them from my face, and fixed her eyes steadfastly on mine.

"Mr. Bullfrog," said she, not unkindly, yet with all the decision of her strong character, "let me advise you to overcome this foolish weakness, and prove yourself, to the best of your ability, as good a husband as I will be a wife. You have discovered, perhaps, some little imperfections in your bride. Well, what did you expect? Women are not angels. If they were, they would go to heaven for husbands; or, at least, be more difficult in their choice on earth."

"But why conceal those imperfections?" interposed I, tremulously.

"Now, my love, are not you a most unreasonable little man?" said Mrs. Bullfrog, patting me on the cheek. "Ought a woman to disclose her frailties earlier than the wedding day? Few husbands, I assure you, make the discovery in such good season, and still fewer complain that these trifles are concealed too long. Well, what a strange man you are! Poh! you are joking."

"But the suit for breach of promise!" groaned I.

"Ah, and is that the rub?" exclaimed my wife. "Is it possible that you view that affair in an objectionable light? Mr. Bullfrog, I never could have dreamed it! Is it an objection that I have triumphantly defended myself against slander and vindicated my purity in a court of justice? Or do you complain because your wife has shown the proper spirit of a woman, and punished the villain who trifled with her affections?"

"But," persisted I, shrinking into a corner of the coach, however,—for I did not know precisely how much contradiction the proper spirit of a woman would endure,—"but, my love, would it not have been more dignified to treat the villain with the silent contempt he merited?"

"That is all very well, Mr. Bullfrog," said my wife, slyly; "but, in that case, where would have been the five thousand dollars which are to stock your dry goods store?"

"Mrs. Bullfrog, upon your honor," demanded I, as if my life hung upon her words, "is there no mistake about those five thousand dollars?"

"Upon my word and honor there is none," replied she. "The jury gave me every cent the rascal had; and I have kept it all for my dear Bullfrog."

"Then, thou dear woman," cried I, with an overwhelming gush of tenderness, "let me fold thee to my heart. The basis of matrimonial bliss is secure, and all thy little defects and frailties are forgiven. Nay, since the result has been so fortunate, I rejoice at the wrongs which drove thee to this blessed lawsuit. Happy Bullfrog that I am!"

THE CELESTIAL RAILROAD

Not a great while ago, passing through the gate of dreams, I visited that region of the earth in which lies the famous City of Destruction. It interested me much to learn that by the public spirit of some of the inhabitants a railroad has recently been established between this populous and flourishing town and the Celestial City. Having a little time upon my hands, I resolved to gratify a liberal curiosity by making a trip thither. Accordingly, one fine morning after paying my bill at the hotel, and directing the porter to stow my luggage behind a coach, I took my seat in the vehicle and set out for the station-house. It was my good fortune to enjoy the company of a gentleman—one Mr. Smooth-it-away—who, though he had never actually visited the Celestial City, yet seemed as well acquainted with its laws, customs, policy, and statistics, as with those of the City of Destruction, of which he was a native townsman. Being, moreover, a director of the railroad corporation and one of its largest stockholders, he had it in his power to give me all desirable information respecting that praiseworthy enterprise.

Our coach rattled out of the city, and at a short distance from its outskirts passed over a bridge of elegant construction, but somewhat too slight, as I imagined, to sustain any considerable weight. On both sides lay an extensive quagmire, which could not have been more disagreeable either to sight or smell, had all the kennels of the earth emptied their pollution there.

"This," remarked Mr. Smooth-it-away, "is the famous Slough of Despond—a disgrace to all the neighborhood; and the greater that it might so easily be converted into firm ground."

"I have understood," said I, "that efforts have been made for that purpose from time immemorial. Bunyan mentions that above twenty thousand cartloads of wholesome instructions had been thrown in here without effect."

"Very probably! And what effect could be anticipated from such unsubstantial stuff?" cried Mr. Smooth-it-away. "You observe this convenient bridge. We obtained a sufficient foundation for it by throwing into the slough some editions of books of morality, volumes of French philosophy and German rationalism; tracts, sermons, and essays of modern clergymen; extracts from Plato, Confucius, and various Hindoo sages together with a few ingenious commentaries upon texts of Scripture,—all of which by some scientific process, have been converted into a mass like granite. The whole bog might be filled up with similar matter."

It really seemed to me, however, that the bridge vibrated and heaved up and down in a very formidable manner; and, in spite of Mr. Smooth-it-away's testimony to the solidity of its foundation, I should be loath to cross it in a crowded omnibus, especially if each passenger were encumbered with as heavy luggage as that gentleman and myself. Nevertheless we got over without accident, and soon found ourselves at the stationhouse. This very neat and spacious edifice is erected on the site of the little wicket gate, which formerly, as all old pilgrims will recollect, stood directly across the highway, and, by its inconvenient narrowness, was a great obstruction to the traveller of liberal mind and expansive stomach The reader of John Bunyan will be glad to know that Christian's old friend Evangelist, who was accustomed to supply each pilgrim with a mystic roll, now presides at the ticket office. Some malicious persons it is true deny the identity of this reputable character with the Evangelist of old times, and even pretend to bring competent evidence of an imposture. Without involving myself in a dispute I shall merely observe that, so far as my experience goes, the square pieces of pasteboard now delivered to passengers are much more convenient and useful along the road than the antique roll of parchment. Whether they will be as readily received at the gate of the Celestial City I decline giving an opinion.

A large number of passengers were already at the station-house awaiting the departure of the cars. By the aspect and demeanor of these persons it was easy to judge that the feelings of the community had undergone a very favorable change in reference to the celestial pilgrimage. It would have done Bunyan's heart good to see it. Instead of a lonely and ragged man with a huge burden on his back, plodding along sorrowfully on foot while the whole city hooted after him, here were parties of the first gentry and most respectable people in the neighborhood setting forth towards the Celestial City as cheerfully as if the pilgrimage were merely a summer tour. Among the gentlemen were characters of deserved eminence—magistrates, politicians, and men of wealth, by whose example religion could not but be greatly recommended to their meaner brethren. In the ladies' apartment, too, I rejoiced to distinguish some of those flowers of fashionable society who are so well fitted to adorn the most elevated circles of the Celestial City. There was much pleasant conversation about the news of the day, topics of business and politics, or the lighter matters of amusement; while religion, though indubitably the main thing at heart, was thrown tastefully into the background. Even an infidel would have heard little or nothing to shock his sensibility.

One great convenience of the new method of going on pilgrimage I must not forget to mention. Our enormous burdens, instead of being carried on our shoulders as had been the custom of old, were all snugly deposited in the baggage car, and, as I was assured, would be delivered to their respective owners at the journey's end. Another thing, likewise, the benevolent reader will be delighted to understand. It may be remembered that there was an ancient feud between Prince Beelzebub and the keeper of the wicket gate, and that the adherents of the former distinguished personage were accustomed to shoot deadly arrows at honest pilgrims while knocking at the door. This dispute, much to the credit as well of the illustrious potentate above mentioned as of the worthy and enlightened directors of the railroad, has been pacifically arranged on the principle of mutual compromise. The prince's subjects are now pretty numerously employed about the station-house, some in taking care of the baggage, others in collecting fuel, feeding the engines, and such congenial occupations; and I can conscientiously affirm that persons more attentive to their business, more willing to accommodate, or more generally agreeable to the passengers, are not to be found on any railroad. Every good heart must surely exult at so satisfactory an arrangement of an immemorial difficulty.

"Where is Mr. Greatheart?" inquired I. "Beyond a doubt the directors have engaged that famous old champion to be chief conductor on the railroad?"

"Why, no," said Mr. Smooth-it-away, with a dry cough. "He was offered the situation of brakeman; but, to tell you the truth, our friend Greatheart has grown preposterously stiff and narrow in his old age. He has so often guided pilgrims over the road on foot that he considers it a sin to travel in any other fashion. Besides, the old fellow had entered so heartily into the ancient feud with Prince Beelzebub that he would have been perpetually at blows or ill language with some of the prince's subjects, and thus have embroiled us anew. So, on the whole, we were not sorry when honest Greatheart went off to the Celestial City in a huff and left us at liberty to choose a more suitable and accommodating man. Yonder comes the engineer of the train. You will probably recognize him at once."

The engine at this moment took its station in advance of the cars, looking, I must confess, much more like a sort of mechanical demon that would hurry us to the infernal regions than a laudable contrivance for smoothing our way to the Celestial City. On its top sat a personage almost enveloped in smoke and flame, which, not to startle the reader, appeared to gush from his own mouth and stomach as well as from the engine's brazen abdomen.

"Do my eyes deceive me?" cried I. "What on earth is this! A living creature? If so, he is own brother to the engine he rides upon!"

"Poh, poh, you are obtuse!" said Mr. Smooth-it-away, with a hearty laugh. "Don't you know Apollyon, Christian's old enemy, with whom he fought so fierce a battle in the Valley of Humiliation? He was the very fellow to manage the engine; and so we have reconciled him to the custom of going on pilgrimage, and engaged him as chief engineer."

"Bravo, bravo!" exclaimed I, with irrepressible enthusiasm; "this shows the liberality of the age; this proves, if anything can, that all musty prejudices are in a fair way to be obliterated. And how will Christian rejoice to hear of this happy transformation of his old antagonist! I promise myself great pleasure in informing him of it when we reach the Celestial City."

The passengers being all comfortably seated, we now rattled away merrily, accomplishing a greater distance in ten minutes than Christian probably trudged over in a day. It was laughable, while we glanced along, as it were, at the tail of a thunderbolt, to observe two dusty foot travellers in the old pilgrim guise, with cockle shell and staff, their mystic rolls of parchment in their hands and their intolerable burdens on their backs. The preposterous obstinacy of these honest people in persisting to groan and stumble along the difficult pathway rather than take advantage of modern improvements, excited great mirth among our wiser brotherhood. We greeted the two pilgrims with many pleasant gibes and a roar of laughter; whereupon they gazed at us with such woful and absurdly compassionate visages that our merriment grew tenfold more obstreperous. Apollyon also entered heartily into the fun, and contrived to flirt the smoke and flame of the engine, or of his own breath, into their faces, and envelop them in an atmosphere of scalding steam. These little practical jokes amused us mightily, and doubtless afforded the pilgrims the gratification of considering themselves martyrs.

At some distance from the railroad Mr. Smooth-it-away pointed to a large, antique edifice, which, he observed, was a tavern of long standing, and had formerly been a noted stopping-place for pilgrims. In Bunyan's road-book it is mentioned as the Interpreter's House.

"I have long had a curiosity to visit that old mansion," remarked I.

"It is not one of our stations, as you perceive," said my companion "The keeper was violently opposed to the railroad; and well he might be, as the track left his house of entertainment on one side, and thus was pretty certain to deprive him of all his reputable customers. But the footpath still passes his door, and the old gentleman now and then receives a call from some simple traveller, and entertains him with fare as old-fashioned as himself."

Before our talk on this subject came to a conclusion we were rushing by the place where Christian's burden fell from his shoulders at the sight of the Cross. This served as a theme for Mr. Smooth-it-away, Mr. Livefor-the-world, Mr. Hide-sin-in-the-heart, Mr. Scaly-conscience, and a knot of gentlemen from the town of Shun-repentance, to descant upon the inestimable advantages resulting from the safety of our baggage. Myself, and all the passengers indeed, joined with great unanimity in this view of the matter; for our burdens were rich in many things esteemed precious throughout the world; and, especially, we each of us possessed a great variety of favorite Habits, which we trusted would not be out of fashion even in the polite circles of the Celestial City. It would have been a sad spectacle to see such an assortment of valuable articles tumbling into the sepulchre. Thus pleasantly conversing on the favorable circumstances of our position as compared with those of past pilgrims and of narrow-minded ones at the present day, we soon found ourselves at the foot of the Hill Difficulty. Through the very heart of this rocky mountain a tunnel has been constructed of most admirable architecture, with a lofty arch and a spacious double track; so that, unless the earth and rocks should chance to crumble down, it will remain an eternal monument of the builder's skill and enterprise. It is a great though incidental advantage that the materials from the heart of the Hill Difficulty have been employed in filling up the Valley of Humiliation, thus obviating the necessity of descending into that disagreeable and unwholesome hollow.

"This is a wonderful improvement, indeed," said I. "Yet I should have been glad of an opportunity to visit the Palace Beautiful and be introduced to the charming young ladies—Miss Prudence, Miss Piety, Miss Charity, and the rest—who have the kindness to entertain pilgrims there."

"Young ladies!" cried Mr. Smooth-it-away, as soon as he could speak for laughing. "And charming young ladies! Why, my dear fellow, they are old maids, every soul of them—prim, starched, dry, and angular; and not one of them, I will venture to say, has altered so much as the fashion of her gown since the days of Christian's pilgrimage."

"Ah, well," said I, much comforted, "then I can very readily dispense with their acquaintance."

The respectable Apollyon was now putting on the steam at a prodigious rate, anxious, perhaps, to get rid of the unpleasant reminiscences connected with the spot where he had so disastrously encountered Christian. Consulting Mr. Bunyan's road-book, I perceived that we must now be within a few miles of the Valley of the Shadow of Death, into which doleful region, at our present speed, we should plunge much sooner than seemed at all desirable. In truth, I expected nothing better than to find myself in the ditch on one side or the Quag on the other; but on communicating my apprehensions to Mr. Smooth-it-away, he assured me that the difficulties of this passage, even in its worst condition, had been vastly exaggerated, and that, in its present state of improvement, I might consider myself as safe as on any railroad in Christendom.

Even while we were speaking the train shot into the entrance of this dreaded Valley. Though I plead guilty to some foolish palpitations of the heart during our headlong rush over the causeway here constructed, yet it were unjust to withhold the highest encomiums on the boldness of its original conception and the ingenuity of those who executed it. It was gratifying, likewise, to observe how much care had been taken to dispel the everlasting gloom and supply the defect of cheerful sunshine, not a ray of which has ever penetrated among these awful shadows. For this purpose, the inflammable gas which exudes plentifully from the soil is collected by means of pipes, and thence communicated to a quadruple row of lamps along the whole extent of the passage. Thus a radiance has been created even out of the fiery and sulphurous curse that rests forever upon the valley—a radiance hurtful, however, to the eyes, and somewhat bewildering, as I discovered by the changes which it wrought in the visages of my companions. In this respect, as compared with natural daylight, there is the same difference as between truth and falsehood, but if the reader have ever travelled through the dark Valley, he will have learned to be thankful for any light that he could get—if not from the sky above, then from the blasted soil beneath. Such was the red brilliancy of these lamps that they appeared to build walls of fire on both sides of the track, between which we held our course at lightning speed, while a reverberating thunder filled the Valley with its echoes. Had the engine run off the track,—a catastrophe, it is whispered, by no means unprecedented,—the bottomless pit, if there be any such place, would undoubtedly have received us. Just as some dismal fooleries of this nature had made my heart quake there came a tremendous shriek, careering along the valley as if a thousand devils had burst their lungs to utter it, but which proved to be merely the whistle of the engine on arriving at a stopping-place.

The spot where we had now paused is the same that our friend Bunyan—a truthful man, but infected with many fantastic notions—has designated, in terms plainer than I like to repeat, as the mouth of the infernal region. This, however, must be a mistake, inasmuch as Mr. Smooth-it-away, while we remained in the smoky and lurid cavern, took occasion to prove that Tophet has not even a metaphorical existence. The place, he assured us, is no other than the crater of a half-extinct volcano, in which the directors had caused forges to be set up for the manufacture of railroad iron. Hence, also, is obtained a plentiful supply of fuel for the use of the engines. Whoever had gazed into the dismal obscurity of the broad cavern mouth, whence ever and anon darted huge tongues of dusky flame, and had seen the strange, half-shaped monsters, and visions of faces horribly grotesque, into which the smoke seemed to wreathe itself, and had heard the awful murmurs, and shrieks, and deep, shuddering whispers of the blast, sometimes forming themselves into words almost articulate, would have seized upon Mr. Smooth-it-away's comfortable explanation as greedily as we did. The inhabitants of the cavern, moreover, were unlovely personages, dark, smoke-begrimed, generally deformed, with misshapen feet, and a glow of dusky redness in their eyes as if their hearts had caught fire and were blazing out of the upper windows. It struck me as a peculiarity that the laborers at the forge and those who brought fuel to the engine, when they began to draw short breath, positively emitted smoke from their mouth and nostrils.

Among the idlers about the train, most of whom were puffing cigars which they had lighted at the flame of the crater, I was perplexed to notice several who, to my certain knowledge, had heretofore set forth by railroad for the Celestial City. They looked dark, wild, and smoky, with a singular resemblance, indeed, to the native inhabitants, like whom, also, they had a disagreeable propensity to ill-natured gibes and sneers, the habit of which had wrought a settled contortion of their visages. Having been on speaking terms with one of these persons,—an indolent, good-for-nothing fellow, who went by the name of Take-it-easy,—I called him, and inquired what was his business there.

"Did you not start," said I, "for the Celestial City?"

"That's a fact," said Mr. Take-it-easy, carelessly puffing some smoke into my eyes. "But I heard such bad accounts that I never took pains to climb the hill on which the city stands. No business doing, no fun going on, nothing to drink, and no smoking allowed, and a thrumming of church music from morning till night. I would not stay in such a place if they offered me house room and living free."

"But, my good Mr. Take-it-easy," cried I, "why take up your residence here, of all places in the world?"

"Oh," said the loafer, with a grin, "it is very warm hereabouts, and I meet with plenty of old acquaintances, and altogether the place suits me. I hope to see you back again some day soon. A pleasant journey to you."

While he was speaking the bell of the engine rang, and we dashed away after dropping a few passengers, but receiving no new ones. Rattling onward through the Valley, we were dazzled with the fiercely gleaming gas lamps, as before. But sometimes, in the dark of intense brightness, grim faces, that bore the aspect and expression of individual sins, or evil passions, seemed to thrust themselves through the veil of light, glaring upon us, and stretching forth a great, dusky hand, as if to impede our progress. I almost thought that they were my own sins that appalled me there. These were freaks of imagination—nothing more, certainly-mere delusions, which I ought to be heartily ashamed of; but all through the Dark Valley I was tormented, and pestered, and dolefully bewildered with the same kind of waking dreams. The mephitic gases of that region intoxicate the brain. As the light of natural day, however, began to struggle with the glow of the lanterns, these vain imaginations lost their vividness, and finally vanished from the first ray of sunshine that greeted our escape from the Valley of the Shadow of Death. Ere we had gone a mile beyond it I could well-nigh have taken my oath that this whole gloomy passage was a dream.

At the end of the valley, as John Bunyan mentions, is a cavern, where, in his days, dwelt two cruel giants, Pope and Pagan, who had strown the ground about their residence with the bones of slaughtered pilgrims. These vile old troglodytes are no longer there; but into their deserted cave another terrible giant has thrust himself, and makes it his business to seize upon honest travellers and fatten them for his table with plentiful meals of smoke, mist, moonshine, raw potatoes, and sawdust. He is a German by birth, and is called Giant Transcendentalist; but as to his form, his features, his substance, and his nature generally, it is the chief peculiarity of this huge miscreant that neither he for himself, nor anybody for him, has ever been able to describe them. As we rushed by the cavern's mouth we caught a hasty glimpse of him, looking somewhat like an ill-proportioned figure, but considerably more like a heap of fog and duskiness. He shouted after us, but in so strange a phraseology that we knew not what he meant, nor whether to be encouraged or affrighted.

It was late in the day when the train thundered into the ancient city of Vanity, where Vanity Fair is still at the height of prosperity, and exhibits an epitome of whatever is brilliant, gay, and fascinating beneath the sun. As I purposed to make a considerable stay here, it gratified me to learn that there is no longer the want of harmony between the town's-people and pilgrims, which impelled the former to such lamentably mistaken measures as the persecution of Christian and the fiery martyrdom of Faithful. On the contrary, as the new railroad brings with it great trade and a constant influx of strangers, the lord of Vanity Fair is its chief patron, and the capitalists of the city are among the largest stockholders. Many passengers stop to take their pleasure or make their profit in the Fair, instead of going onward to the Celestial City. Indeed, such are the charms of the place that people often affirm it to be the true and only heaven; stoutly contending that there is no other, that those who seek further are mere dreamers, and that, if the fabled brightness of the Celestial City lay but a bare mile beyond the gates of Vanity, they would not be fools enough to go thither. Without subscribing to these perhaps exaggerated encomiums, I can truly say that my abode in the city was mainly agreeable, and my intercourse with the inhabitants productive of much amusement and instruction.

Being naturally of a serious turn, my attention was directed to the solid advantages derivable from a residence here, rather than to the effervescent pleasures which are the grand object with too many visitants. The Christian reader, if he have had no accounts of the city later than Bunyan's time, will be surprised to hear that almost every street has its church, and that the reverend clergy are nowhere held in higher respect than at Vanity Fair. And well do they deserve such honorable estimation; for the maxims of wisdom and virtue which fall from their lips come from as deep a spiritual source, and tend to as lofty a religious aim, as those of the sagest philosophers of old. In justification of this high praise I need only mention the names of the Rev. Mr. Shallow-deep, the Rev. Mr. Stumble-at-truth, that fine old clerical character the Rev. Mr. This-today, who expects shortly to resign his pulpit to the Rev. Mr. That-tomorrow; together with the Rev. Mr. Bewilderment, the Rev. Mr. Clog-the-spirit, and, last and greatest, the Rev. Dr. Wind-of-doctrine. The labors of these eminent divines are aided by those of innumerable lecturers, who diffuse such a various profundity, in all subjects of human or celestial science, that any man may acquire an omnigenous erudition without the trouble of even learning to read. Thus literature is etherealized by assuming for its medium the human voice; and knowledge, depositing all its heavier particles, except, doubtless, its gold becomes exhaled into a sound, which forthwith steals into the ever-open ear of the community. These ingenious methods constitute a sort of machinery, by which thought and study are done to every person's hand without his putting himself to the slightest inconvenience in the matter. There is another species of machine for the wholesale manufacture of individual morality. This excellent result is effected by societies for all manner of virtuous purposes, with which a man has merely to connect himself, throwing, as it were, his quota of virtue into the common stock, and the president and directors will take care that the aggregate amount be well applied. All these, and other wonderful improvements in ethics, religion, and literature, being made plain to my comprehension by the ingenious Mr. Smooth-it-away, inspired me with a vast admiration of Vanity Fair.

It would fill a volume, in an age of pamphlets, were I to record all my observations in this great capital of human business and pleasure. There was an unlimited range of society—the powerful, the wise, the witty, and the famous in every walk of life; princes, presidents, poets, generals, artists, actors, and philanthropists,—all making their own market at the fair, and deeming no price too exorbitant for such commodities as hit their fancy. It was well worth one's while, even if he had no idea of buying or selling, to loiter through the bazaars and observe the various sorts of traffic that were going forward.

Some of the purchasers, I thought, made very foolish bargains. For instance, a young man having inherited a splendid fortune, laid out a considerable portion of it in the purchase of diseases, and finally spent all the rest for a heavy lot of repentance and a suit of rags. A very pretty girl bartered a heart as clear as crystal, and which seemed her most valuable possession, for another jewel of the same kind, but so worn and defaced as to be utterly worthless. In one shop there were a great many crowns of laurel and myrtle, which soldiers, authors, statesmen, and various other people pressed eagerly to buy; some purchased these paltry wreaths with their lives, others by a toilsome servitude of years, and many sacrificed whatever was most valuable, yet finally slunk away without the crown. There was a sort of stock or scrip, called Conscience, which seemed to be in great demand, and would purchase almost anything. Indeed, few rich commodities were to be obtained without paying a heavy sum in this particular stock, and a man's business was seldom very lucrative unless he knew precisely when and how to throw his hoard of conscience into the market. Yet as this stock was the only thing of permanent value, whoever parted with it was sure to find himself a loser in the long run. Several of the speculations were of a questionable character. Occasionally a member of Congress recruited his pocket by the sale of his constituents; and I was assured that public officers have often sold their country at very moderate prices. Thousands sold their happiness for a whim. Gilded chains were in great demand, and purchased with almost any sacrifice. In truth, those who desired, according to the old adage, to sell anything valuable for a song, might find customers all over the Fair; and there were innumerable messes of pottage, piping hot, for such as chose to buy them with their birthrights. A few articles, however, could not be found genuine at Vanity Fair. If a customer wished to renew his stock of youth the dealers offered him a set of false teeth and an auburn wig; if he demanded peace of mind, they recommended opium or a brandy bottle.

Tracts of land and golden mansions, situate in the Celestial City, were often exchanged, at very disadvantageous rates, for a few years' lease of small, dismal, inconvenient tenements in Vanity Fair. Prince Beelzebub himself took great interest in this sort of traffic, and sometimes condescended to meddle with smaller matters. I once had the pleasure to see him bargaining with a miser for his soul, which, after much ingenious skirmishing on both sides, his highness succeeded in obtaining at about the value of sixpence. The prince remarked with a smile, that he was a loser by the transaction.

Day after day, as I walked the streets of Vanity, my manners and deportment became more and more like those of the inhabitants. The place began to seem like home; the idea of pursuing my travels to the Celestial City was almost obliterated from my mind. I was reminded of it, however, by the sight of the same pair of simple pilgrims at whom we had laughed so heartily when Apollyon puffed smoke and steam into their faces at the commencement of our journey. There they stood amidst the densest bustle of Vanity; the dealers offering them their purple and fine linen and jewels, the men of wit and humor gibing at them, a pair of buxom ladies ogling them askance, while the benevolent Mr. Smooth-it-away whispered some of his wisdom at their elbows, and pointed to a newly-erected temple; but there were these worthy simpletons, making the scene look wild and monstrous, merely by their sturdy repudiation of all part in its business or pleasures.

One of them—his name was Stick-to-the-right—perceived in my face, I suppose, a species of sympathy and almost admiration, which, to my own great surprise, I could not help feeling for this pragmatic couple. It prompted him to address me.

"Sir," inquired he, with a sad, yet mild and kindly voice, "do you call yourself a pilgrim?"

"Yes," I replied, "my right to that appellation is indubitable. I am merely a sojourner here in Vanity Fair, being bound to the Celestial City by the new railroad."

"Alas, friend," rejoined Mr. Stick-to-the-truth, "I do assure you, and beseech you to receive the truth of my words, that that whole concern is a bubble. You may travel on it all your lifetime, were you to live thousands of years, and yet never get beyond the limits of Vanity Fair. Yea, though you should deem yourself entering the gates of the blessed city, it will be nothing but a miserable delusion."

"The Lord of the Celestial City," began the other pilgrim, whose name was Mr. Foot-it-to-heaven, "has refused, and will ever refuse, to grant an act of incorporation for this railroad; and unless that be obtained, no passenger can ever hope to enter his dominions. Wherefore every man who buys a ticket must lay his account with losing the purchase money, which is the value of his own soul."

"Poh, nonsense!" said Mr. Smooth-it-away, taking my arm and leading me off, "these fellows ought to be indicted for a libel. If the law stood as it once did in Vanity Fair we should see them grinning through the iron bars of the prison window."

This incident made a considerable impression on my mind, and contributed with other circumstances to indispose me to a permanent residence in the city of Vanity; although, of course, I was not simple enough to give up my original plan of gliding along easily and commodiously by railroad. Still, I grew anxious to be gone. There was one strange thing that troubled me. Amid the occupations or amusements of the Fair, nothing was more common than for a person—whether at feast, theatre, or church, or trafficking for wealth and honors, or whatever he might be doing, to vanish like a soap bubble, and be never more seen of his fellows; and so accustomed were the latter to such little accidents that they went on with their business as quietly as if nothing had happened. But it was otherwise with me.

Finally, after a pretty long residence at the Fair, I resumed my journey towards the Celestial City, still with Mr. Smooth-it-away at my side. At a short distance beyond the suburbs of Vanity we passed the ancient silver mine, of which Demas was the first discoverer, and which is now wrought to great advantage, supplying nearly all the coined currency of the world. A little further onward was the spot where Lot's wife had stood forever under the semblance of a pillar of salt. Curious travellers have long since carried it away piecemeal. Had all regrets been punished as rigorously as this poor dame's were, my yearning for the relinquished delights of Vanity Fair might have produced a similar change in my own corporeal substance, and left me a warning to future pilgrims.

The next remarkable object was a large edifice, constructed of moss-grown stone, but in a modern and airy style of architecture. The engine came to a pause in its vicinity, with the usual tremendous shriek.

"This was formerly the castle of the redoubted giant Despair," observed Mr. Smooth-it-away; "but since his death Mr. Flimsy-faith has repaired it, and keeps an excellent house of entertainment here. It is one of our stopping-places."

"It seems but slightly put together," remarked I, looking at the frail yet ponderous walls. "I do not envy Mr. Flimsy-faith his habitation. Some day it will thunder down upon the heads of the occupants."

"We shall escape at all events," said Mr. Smooth-it-away, "for Apollyon is putting on the steam again."

The road now plunged into a gorge of the Delectable Mountains, and traversed the field where in former ages the blind men wandered and stumbled among the tombs. One of these ancient tombstones had been thrust across the track by some malicious person, and gave the train of cars a terrible jolt. Far up the rugged side of a mountain I perceived a rusty iron door, half overgrown with bushes and creeping plants, but with smoke issuing from its crevices.

"Is that," inquired I, "the very door in the hill-side which the shepherds assured Christian was a by-way to hell?"

"That was a joke on the part of the shepherds," said Mr. Smooth-itaway, with a smile. "It is neither more nor less than the door of a cavern which they use as a smoke-house for the preparation of mutton hams."

My recollections of the journey are now, for a little space, dim and confused, inasmuch as a singular drowsiness here overcame me, owing to the fact that we were passing over the enchanted ground, the air of which encourages a disposition to sleep. I awoke, however, as soon as we crossed the borders of the pleasant land of Beulah. All the passengers were rubbing their eyes, comparing watches, and congratulating one another on the prospect of arriving so seasonably at the journey's end. The sweet breezes of this happy clime came refreshingly to our nostrils; we beheld the glimmering gush of silver fountains, overhung by trees of beautiful foliage and delicious fruit, which were propagated by grafts from the celestial gardens. Once, as we dashed onward like a hurricane, there was a flutter of wings and the bright appearance of an angel in the air, speeding forth on some heavenly mission. The engine now announced the close vicinity of the final station-house by one last and horrible scream, in which there seemed to be distinguishable every kind of wailing and woe, and bitter fierceness of wrath, all mixed up with the wild laughter of a devil or a madman. Throughout our journey, at every stopping-place, Apollyon had exercised his ingenuity in screwing the most abominable sounds out of the whistle of the steam-engine; but in this closing effort he outdid himself and created an infernal uproar, which, besides disturbing the peaceful inhabitants of Beulah, must have sent its discord even through the celestial gates.

While the horrid clamor was still ringing in our ears we heard an exulting strain, as if a thousand instruments of music, with height and depth and sweetness in their tones, at once tender and triumphant, were struck in unison, to greet the approach of some illustrious hero, who had fought the good fight and won a glorious victory, and was come to lay aside his battered arms forever. Looking to ascertain what might be the occasion of this glad harmony, I perceived, on alighting from the cars, that a multitude of shining ones had assembled on the other side of the river, to welcome two poor pilgrims, who were just emerging from its depths. They were the same whom Apollyon and ourselves had persecuted with taunts, and gibes, and scalding steam, at the commencement of our journey—the same whose unworldly aspect and impressive words had stirred my conscience amid the wild revellers of Vanity Fair.

"How amazingly well those men have got on," cried I to Mr. Smoothit—away. "I wish we were secure of as good a reception."

"Never fear, never fear!" answered my friend. "Come, make haste; the ferry boat will be off directly, and in three minutes you will be on the other side of the river. No doubt you will find coaches to carry you up to the city gates."

A steam ferry boat, the last improvement on this important route, lay at the river side, puffing, snorting, and emitting all those other disagreeable utterances which betoken the departure to be immediate. I hurried on board with the rest of the passengers, most of whom were in great perturbation: some bawling out for their baggage; some tearing their hair and exclaiming that the boat would explode or sink; some already pale with the heaving of the stream; some gazing affrighted at the ugly aspect of the steersman; and some still dizzy with the slumberous influences of the Enchanted Ground. Looking back to the shore, I was amazed to discern Mr. Smooth-it-away waving his hand in token of farewell.

"Don't you go over to the Celestial City?" exclaimed I.

"Oh, no!" answered he with a queer smile, and that same disagreeable contortion of visage which I had remarked in the inhabitants of the Dark Valley. "Oh, no! I have come thus far only for the sake of your pleasant company. Good-by! We shall meet again."

And then did my excellent friend Mr. Smooth-it-away laugh outright, in the midst of which cachinnation a smoke-wreath issued from his mouth and nostrils, while a twinkle of lurid flame darted out of either eye, proving indubitably that his heart was all of a red blaze. The impudent fiend! To deny the existence of Tophet, when he felt its fiery tortures raging within his breast. I rushed to the side of the boat, intending to fling myself on shore; but the wheels, as they began their revolutions, threw a dash of spray over me so cold—so deadly cold, with the chill that will never leave those waters until Death be drowned in his own river—that with a shiver and a heartquake I awoke. Thank Heaven it was a Dream!

THE PROCESSION OF LIFE

Life figures itself to me as a festal or funereal procession. All of us have our places, and are to move onward under the direction of the Chief Marshal. The grand difficulty results from the invariably mistaken principles on which the deputy marshals seek to arrange this immense concourse of people, so much more numerous than those that train their interminable length through streets and highways in times of political excitement. Their scheme is ancient, far beyond the memory of man or even the record of history, and has hitherto been very little modified by the innate sense of something wrong, and the dim perception of better methods, that have disquieted all the ages through which the procession has taken its march. Its members are classified by the merest external circumstances, and thus are more certain to be thrown out of their true positions than if no principle of arrangement were attempted. In one part of the procession we see men of landed estate or moneyed capital gravely keeping each other company, for the preposterous reason that they chance to have a similar standing in the tax-gatherer's book. Trades and professions march together with scarcely a more real bond of union. In this manner, it cannot be denied, people are disentangled from the mass and separated into various classes according to certain apparent relations; all have some artificial badge which the world, and themselves among the first, learn to consider as a genuine characteristic. Fixing our attention on such outside shows of similarity or difference, we lose sight of those realities by which nature, fortune, fate, or Providence has constituted for every man a brotherhood, wherein it is one great office of human wisdom to classify him. When the mind has once accustomed itself to a proper arrangement of the Procession of Life, or a true classification of society, even though merely speculative, there is thenceforth a satisfaction which pretty well suffices for itself without the aid of any actual reformation in the order of march.

For instance, assuming to myself the power of marshalling the aforesaid procession, I direct a trumpeter to send forth a blast loud enough to be heard from hence to China; and a herald, with world-pervading voice, to make proclamation for a certain class of mortals to take their places. What shall be their principle of union? After all, an external one, in comparison with many that might be found, yet far more real than those which the world has selected for a similar purpose. Let all who are afflicted with like physical diseases form themselves into ranks.

Our first attempt at classification is not very successful. It may gratify the pride of aristocracy to reflect that disease, more than any other circumstance of human life, pays due observance to the distinctions which rank and wealth, and poverty and lowliness, have established among mankind. Some maladies are rich and precious, and only to be acquired by the right of inheritance or purchased with gold. Of this kind is the gout, which serves as a bond of brotherhood to the purple-visaged gentry, who obey the herald's voice, and painfully hobble from all civilized regions of the globe to take their post in the grand procession. In mercy to their toes, let us hope that the march may not be long. The Dyspeptics, too, are people of good standing in the world. For them the earliest salmon is caught in our eastern rivers, and the shy woodcock stains the dry leaves with his blood in his remotest haunts, and the turtle comes from the far Pacific Islands to be gobbled up in soup. They can afford to flavor all their dishes with indolence, which, in spite of the general opinion, is a sauce more exquisitely piquant than appetite won by exercise. Apoplexy is another highly respectable disease. We will rank together all who have the symptom of dizziness in the brain, and as fast as any drop by the way supply their places with new members of the board of aldermen.

On the other hand, here come whole tribes of people whose physical lives are but a deteriorated variety of life, and themselves a meaner species of mankind; so sad an effect has been wrought by the tainted breath of cities, scanty and unwholesome food, destructive modes of labor, and the lack of those moral supports that might partially have counteracted such bad influences. Behold here a train of house painters, all afflicted with a peculiar sort of colic. Next in place we will marshal those workmen in cutlery, who have breathed a fatal disorder into their lungs with the impalpable dust of steel. Tailors and shoemakers, being sedentary men, will chiefly congregate into one part of the procession and march under similar banners of disease; but among them we may observe here and there a sickly student, who has left his health between the leaves of classic volumes; and clerks, likewise, who have caught their deaths on high official stools; and men of genius too, who have written sheet after sheet with pens dipped in their heart's blood. These are a wretched quaking, short-breathed set. But what is this cloud of pale-cheeked, slender girls, who disturb the ear with the multiplicity of their short, dry coughs? They are seamstresses, who have plied the daily and nightly needle in the service of master tailors and close-fisted contractors, until now it is almost time for each to hem the borders of her own shroud. Consumption points their place in the procession. With their sad sisterhood are intermingled many youthful maidens who have sickened in aristocratic mansions, and for whose aid science has unavailingly searched its volumes, and whom breathless love has watched. In our ranks the rich maiden and the poor seamstress may walk arm in arm. We might find innumerable other instances, where the bond of mutual disease—not to speak of nation-sweeping pestilence—embraces high and low, and makes the king a brother of the clown. But it is not hard to own that disease is the natural aristocrat. Let him keep his state, and have his established orders of rank, and wear his royal mantle of the color of a fever flush and let the noble and wealthy boast their own physical infirmities, and display their symptoms as the badges of high station. All things considered, these are as proper subjects of human pride as any relations of human rank that men can fix upon.

Sound again, thou deep-breathed trumpeter! and herald, with thy voice of might, shout forth another summons that shall reach the old baronial castles of Europe, and the rudest cabin of our western wilderness! What class is next to take its place in the procession of mortal life? Let it be those whom the gifts of intellect have united in a noble brotherhood.

Ay, this is a reality, before which the conventional distinctions of society melt away like a vapor when we would grasp it with the hand. Were Byron now alive, and Burns, the first would come from his ancestral abbey, flinging aside, although unwillingly, the inherited honors of a thousand years, to take the arm of the mighty peasant who grew immortal while he stooped behind his plough. These are gone; but the hall, the farmer's fireside, the hut, perhaps the palace, the counting-room, the workshop, the village, the city, life's high places and low ones, may all produce their poets, whom a common temperament pervades like an electric sympathy. Peer or ploughman, we will muster them pair by pair and shoulder to shoulder. Even society, in its most artificial state, consents to this arrangement. These factory girls from Lowell shall mate themselves with the pride of drawing-rooms and literary circles, the bluebells in fashion's nosegay, the Sapphos, and Montagues, and Nortons of the age. Other modes of intellect bring together as strange companies. Silk-gowned professor of languages, give your arm to this sturdy blacksmith, and deem yourself honored by the conjunction, though you behold him grimy from the anvil. All varieties of human speech are like his mother tongue to this rare man. Indiscriminately let those take their places, of whatever rank they come, who possess the kingly gifts to lead armies or to sway a people—Nature's generals, her lawgivers, her kings, and with them also the deep philosophers who think the thought in one generation that is to revolutionize society in the next. With the hereditary legislator in whom eloquence is a far-descended attainment—a rich echo repeated by powerful voices from Cicero downward—we will match some wondrous backwoodsman, who has caught a wild power of language from the breeze among his native forest boughs. But we may safely leave these brethren and sisterhood to settle their own congenialities. Our ordinary distinctions become so trifling, so impalpable, so ridiculously visionary, in comparison with a classification founded on truth, that all talk about the matter is immediately a common place.

Yet the longer I reflect the less am I satisfied with the idea of forming a separate class of mankind on the basis of high intellectual power. At best it is but a higher development of innate gifts common to all. Perhaps, moreover, he whose genius appears deepest and truest excels his fellows in nothing save the knack of expression; he throws out occasionally a lucky hint at truths of which every human soul is profoundly, though unutterably, conscious. Therefore, though we suffer the brotherhood of intellect to march onward together, it may be doubted whether their peculiar relation will not begin to vanish as soon as the procession shall have passed beyond the circle of this present world. But we do not classify for eternity.

And next, let the trumpet pour forth a funereal wail, and the herald's voice give breath in one vast cry to all the groans and grievous utterances that are audible throughout the earth. We appeal now to the sacred bond of sorrow, and summon the great multitude who labor under similar afflictions to take their places in the march.

How many a heart that would have been insensible to any other call has responded to the doleful accents of that voice! It has gone far and wide, and high and low, and left scarcely a mortal roof unvisited. Indeed, the principle is only too universal for our purpose, and, unless we limit it, will quite break up our classification of mankind, and convert the whole procession into a funeral train. We will therefore be at some pains to discriminate. Here comes a lonely rich man: he has built a noble fabric for his dwelling-house, with a front of stately architecture and marble floors and doors of precious woods; the whole structure is as beautiful as a dream and as substantial as the native rock. But the visionary shapes of a long posterity, for whose home this mansion was intended, have faded into nothingness since the death of the founder's only son. The rich man gives a glance at his sable garb in one of the splendid mirrors of his drawing-room, and descending a flight of lofty steps instinctively offers his arm to yonder poverty stricken widow in the rusty black bonnet, and with a check apron over her patched gown. The sailor boy, who was her sole earthly stay, was washed overboard in a late tempest. This couple from the palace and the almshouse are but the types of thousands more who represent the dark tragedy of life and seldom quarrel for the upper parts. Grief is such a leveller, with its own dignity and its own humility, that the noble and the peasant, the beggar and the monarch, will waive their pretensions to external rank without the officiousness of interference on our part. If pride—the influence of the world's false distinctions—remain in the heart, then sorrow lacks the earnestness which makes it holy and reverend. It loses its reality and becomes a miserable shadow. On this ground we have an opportunity to assign over multitudes who would willingly claim places here to other parts of the procession. If the mourner have anything dearer than his grief he must seek his true position elsewhere. There are so many unsubstantial sorrows which the necessity of our mortal state begets on idleness, that an observer, casting aside sentiment, is sometimes led to question whether there be any real woe, except absolute physical suffering and the loss of closest friends. A crowd who exhibit what they deem to be broken hearts—and among them many lovelorn maids and bachelors, and men of disappointed ambition in arts or politics, and the poor who were once rich, or who have sought to be rich in vain—the great majority of these may ask admittance into some other fraternity. There is no room here. Perhaps we may institute a separate class where such unfortunates will naturally fall into the procession. Meanwhile let them stand aside and patiently await their time.

If our trumpeter can borrow a note from the doomsday trumpet blast, let him sound it now. The dread alarum should make the earth quake to its centre, for the herald is about to address mankind with a summons to which even the purest mortal may be sensible of some faint responding echo in his breast. In many bosoms it will awaken a still small voice more terrible than its own reverberating uproar.

The hideous appeal has swept around the globe. Come, all ye guilty ones, and rank yourselves in accordance with the brotherhood of crime. This, indeed, is an awful summons. I almost tremble to look at the strange partnerships that begin to be formed, reluctantly, but by the in vincible necessity of like to like in this part of the procession. A forger from the state prison seizes the arm of a distinguished financier. How indignantly does the latter plead his fair reputation upon 'Change, and insist that his operations, by their magnificence of scope, were removed into quite another sphere of morality than those of his pitiful companion! But let him cut the connection if he can. Here comes a murderer with his clanking chains, and pairs himself—horrible to tell—with as pure and upright a man, in all observable respects, as ever partook of the consecrated bread and wine. He is one of those, perchance the most hopeless of all sinners, who practise such an exemplary system of outward duties, that even a deadly crime may be hidden from their own sight and remembrance, under this unreal frostwork. Yet he now finds his place. Why do that pair of flaunting girls, with the pert, affected laugh and the sly leer at the by-standers, intrude themselves into the same rank with yonder decorous matron, and that somewhat prudish maiden? Surely these poor creatures, born to vice as their sole and natural inheritance, can be no fit associates for women who have been guarded round about by all the proprieties of domestic life, and who could not err unless they first created the opportunity. Oh no; it must be merely the impertinence of those unblushing hussies; and we can only wonder how such respectable ladies should have responded to a summons that was not meant for them.

We shall make short work of this miserable class, each member of which is entitled to grasp any other member's hand, by that vile degradation wherein guilty error has buried all alike. The foul fiend to whom it properly belongs must relieve us of our loathsome task. Let the bond servants of sin pass on. But neither man nor woman, in whom good predominates, will smile or sneer, nor bid the Rogues' March be played, in derision of their array. Feeling within their breasts a shuddering sympathy, which at least gives token of the sin that might have been, they will thank God for any place in the grand procession of human existence, save among those most wretched ones. Many, however, will be astonished at the fatal impulse that drags them thitherward. Nothing is more remarkable than the various deceptions by which guilt conceals itself from the perpetrator's conscience, and oftenest, perhaps, by the splendor of its garments. Statesmen, rulers, generals, and all men who act over an extensive sphere, are most liable to be deluded in this way; they commit wrong, devastation, and murder, on so grand a scale, that it impresses them as speculative rather than actual; but in our procession we find them linked in detestable conjunction with the meanest criminals whose deeds have the vulgarity of petty details. Here the effect of circumstance and accident is done away, and a man finds his rank according to the spirit of his crime, in whatever shape it may have been developed.

We have called the Evil; now let us call the Good. The trumpet's brazen throat should pour heavenly music over the earth, and the herald's voice go forth with the sweetness of an angel's accents, as if to summon each upright man to his reward. But how is this? Does none answer to the call? Not one: for the just, the pure, the true, and an who might most worthily obey it, shrink sadly back, as most conscious of error and imperfection. Then let the summons be to those whose pervading principle is Love. This classification will embrace all the truly good, and none in whose souls there exists not something that may expand itself into a heaven, both of well-doing and felicity.

The first that presents himself is a man of wealth, who has bequeathed the bulk of his property to a hospital; his ghost, methinks, would have a better right here than his living body. But here they come, the genuine benefactors of their race. Some have wandered about the earth with pictures of bliss in their imagination, and with hearts that shrank sensitively from the idea of pain and woe, yet have studied all varieties of misery that human nature can endure. The prison, the insane asylum, the squalid chamber of the almshouse, the manufactory where the demon of machinery annihilates the human soul, and the cotton field where God's image becomes a beast of burden; to these and every other scene where man wrongs or neglects his brother, the apostles of humanity have penetrated. This missionary, black with India's burning sunshine, shall give his arm to a pale-faced brother who has made himself familiar with the infected alleys and loathsome haunts of vice in one of our own cities. The generous founder of a college shall be the partner of a maiden lady of narrow substance, one of whose good deeds it has been to gather a little school of orphan children. If the mighty merchant whose benefactions are reckoned by thousands of dollars deem himself worthy, let him join the procession with her whose love has proved itself by watchings at the sick-bed, and all those lowly offices which bring her into actual contact with disease and wretchedness. And with those whose impulses have guided them to benevolent actions, we will rank others to whom Providence has assigned a different tendency and different powers. Men who have spent their lives in generous and holy contemplation for the human race; those who, by a certain heavenliness of spirit, have purified the atmosphere around them, and thus supplied a medium in which good and high things may be projected and performed—give to these a lofty place among the benefactors of mankind, although no deed, such as the world calls deeds, may be recorded of them. There are some individuals of whom we cannot conceive it proper that they should apply their hands to any earthly instrument, or work out any definite act; and others, perhaps not less high, to whom it is an essential attribute to labor in body as well as spirit for the welfare of their brethren. Thus, if we find a spiritual sage whose unseen, inestimable influence has exalted the moral standard of mankind, we will choose for his companion some poor laborer who has wrought for love in the potato field of a neighbor poorer than himself.

We have summoned this various multitude—and, to the credit of our nature, it is a large one—on the principle of Love. It is singular, nevertheless, to remark the shyness that exists among many members of the present class, all of whom we might expect to recognize one another by the freemasonry of mutual goodness, and to embrace like brethren, giving God thanks for such various specimens of human excellence. But it is far otherwise. Each sect surrounds its own righteousness with a hedge of thorns. It is difficult for the good Christian to acknowledge the good Pagan; almost impossible for the good Orthodox to grasp the hand of the good Unitarian, leaving to their Creator to settle the matters in dispute, and giving their mutual efforts strongly and trustingly to whatever right thing is too evident to be mistaken. Then again, though the heart be large, yet the mind is often of such moderate dimensions as to be exclusively filled up with one idea. When a good man has long devoted himself to a particular kind of beneficence—to one species of reform—he is apt to become narrowed into the limits of the path wherein he treads, and to fancy that there is no other good to be done on earth but that self-same good to which he has put his hand, and in the very mode that best suits his own conceptions. All else is worthless. His scheme must be wrought out by the united strength of the whole world's stock of love, or the world is no longer worthy of a position in the universe. Moreover, powerful Truth, being the rich grape juice expressed from the vineyard of the ages, has an intoxicating quality, when imbibed by any save a powerful intellect, and often, as it were, impels the quaffer to quarrel in his cups. For such reasons, strange to say, it is harder to contrive a friendly arrangement of these brethren of love and righteousness, in the procession of life, than to unite even the wicked, who, indeed, are chained together by their crimes. The fact is too preposterous for tears, too lugubrious for laughter.

But, let good men push and elbow one another as they may during their earthly march, all will be peace among them when the honorable array or their procession shall tread on heavenly ground. There they will doubtless find that they have been working each for the other's cause, and that every well-delivered stroke, which, with an honest purpose any mortal struck, even for a narrow object, was indeed stricken for the universal cause of good. Their own view may be bounded by country, creed, profession, the diversities of individual character—but above them all is the breadth of Providence. How many who have deemed themselves antagonists will smile hereafter, when they look back upon the world's wide harvest field, and perceive that, in unconscious brotherhood, they were helping to bind the selfsame sheaf!

But, come! The sun is hastening westward, while the march of human life, that never paused before, is delayed by our attempt to rearrange its order. It is desirable to find some comprehensive principle, that shall render our task easier by bringing thousands into the ranks where hitherto we have brought one. Therefore let the trumpet, if possible, split its brazen throat with a louder note than ever, and the herald summon all mortals, who, from whatever cause, have lost, or never found, their proper places in the wold.

Obedient to this call, a great multitude come together, most of them with a listless gait, betokening weariness of soul, yet with a gleam of satisfaction in their faces, at a prospect of at length reaching those positions which, hitherto, they have vainly sought. But here will be another disappointment; for we can attempt no more than merely to associate in one fraternity all who are afflicted with the same vague trouble. Some great mistake in life is the chief condition of admittance into this class. Here are members of the learned professions, whom Providence endowed with special gifts for the plough, the forge, and the wheelbarrow, or for the routine of unintellectual business. We will assign to them, as partners in the march, those lowly laborers and handicraftsmen, who have pined, as with a dying thirst, after the unattainable fountains of knowledge. The latter have lost less than their companions; yet more, because they deem it infinite. Perchance the two species of unfortunates may comfort one another. Here are Quakers with the instinct of battle in them; and men of war who should have worn the broad brim. Authors shall be ranked here whom some freak of Nature, making game of her poor children, had imbued with the confidence of genius and strong desire of fame, but has favored with no corresponding power; and others, whose lofty gifts were unaccompanied with the faculty of expression, or any of that earthly machinery by which ethereal endowments must be manifested to mankind. All these, therefore, are melancholy laughing-stocks. Next, here are honest and well intentioned persons, who by a want of tact—by inaccurate perceptions—by a distorting imagination—have been kept continually at cross purposes with the world and bewildered upon the path of life. Let us see if they can confine themselves within the line of our procession. In this class, likewise, we must assign places to those who have encountered that worst of ill success, a higher fortune than their abilities could vindicate; writers, actors, painters, the pets of a day, but whose laurels wither unrenewed amid their hoary hair; politicians, whom some malicious contingency of affairs has thrust into conspicuous station, where, while the world stands gazing at them, the dreary consciousness of imbecility makes them curse their birth hour. To such men, we give for a companion him whose rare talents, which perhaps require a Revolution for their exercise, are buried in the tomb of sluggish circumstances.

Not far from these, we must find room for one whose success has been of the wrong kind; the man who should have lingered in the cloisters of a university, digging new treasures out of the Herculaneum of antique lore, diffusing depth and accuracy of literature throughout his country, and thus making for himself a great and quiet fame. But the outward tendencies around him have proved too powerful for his inward nature, and have drawn him into the arena of political tumult, there to contend at disadvantage, whether front to front, or side by side, with the brawny giants of actual life. He becomes, it may be, a name for brawling parties to bandy to and fro, a legislator of the Union; a governor of his native state; an ambassador to the courts of kings or queens; and the world may deem him a man of happy stars. But not so the wise; and not so himself, when he looks through his experience, and sighs to miss that fitness, the one invaluable touch which makes all things true and real. So much achieved, yet how abortive is his life! Whom shall we choose for his companion? Some weak framed blacksmith, perhaps, whose delicacy of muscle might have suited a tailor's shopboard better than the anvil.

Shall we bid the trumpet sound again? It is hardly worth the while. There remain a few idle men of fortune, tavern and grog-shop loungers, lazzaroni, old bachelors, decaying maidens, and people of crooked intellect or temper, all of whom may find their like, or some tolerable approach to it, in the plentiful diversity of our latter class. There too, as his ultimate destiny, must we rank the dreamer, who, all his life long, has cherished the idea that he was peculiarly apt for something, but never could determine what it was; and there the most unfortunate of men, whose purpose it has been to enjoy life's pleasures, but to avoid a manful struggle with its toil and sorrow. The remainder, if any, may connect themselves with whatever rank of the procession they shall find best adapted to their tastes and consciences. The worst possible fate would be to remain behind, shivering in the solitude of time, while all the world is on the move towards eternity. Our attempt to classify society is now complete. The result may be anything but perfect; yet better—to give it the very lowest praise—than the antique rule of the herald's office, or the modern one of the tax-gatherer, whereby the accidents and superficial attributes with which the real nature of individuals has least to do, are acted upon as the deepest characteristics of mankind. Our task is done! Now let the grand procession move!

Yet pause a while! We had forgotten the Chief Marshal.

Hark! That world-wide swell of solemn music, with the clang of a mighty bell breaking forth through its regulated uproar, announces his approach. He comes; a severe, sedate, immovable, dark rider, waving his truncheon of universal sway, as he passes along the lengthened line, on the pale horse of the Revelation. It is Death! Who else could assume the guidance of a procession that comprehends all humanity? And if some, among these many millions, should deem themselves classed amiss, yet let them take to their hearts the comfortable truth that Death levels us all into one great brotherhood, and that another state of being will surely rectify the wrong of this. Then breathe thy wail upon the earth's wailing wind, thou band of melancholy music, made up of every sigh that the human heart, unsatisfied, has uttered! There is yet triumph in thy tones. And now we move! Beggars in their rags, and Kings trailing the regal purple in the dust; the Warrior's gleaming helmet; the Priest in his sable robe; the hoary Grandsire, who has run life's circle and come back to childhood; the ruddy School-boy with his golden curls, frisking along the march; the Artisan's stuff jacket; the Noble's star-decorated coat;—the whole presenting a motley spectacle, yet with a dusky grandeur brooding over it. Onward, onward, into that dimness where the lights of Time which have blazed along the procession, are flickering in their sockets! And whither! We know not; and Death, hitherto our leader, deserts us by the wayside, as the tramp of our innumerable footsteps echoes beyond his sphere. He knows not, more than we, our destined goal. But God, who made us, knows, and will not leave us on our toilsome and doubtful march, either to wander in infinite uncertainty, or perish by the way!

FEATHERTOP: A MORALIZED LEGEND

"Dickon," cried Mother Rigby, "a coal for my pipe!"

The pipe was in the old dame's mouth when she said these words. She had thrust it there after filling it with tobacco, but without stooping to light it at the hearth, where indeed there was no appearance of a fire having been kindled that morning. Forthwith, however, as soon as the order was given, there was an intense red glow out of the bowl of the pipe, and a whiff of smoke came from Mother Rigby's lips. Whence the coal came, and how brought thither by an invisible hand, I have never been able to discover.

"Good!" quoth Mother Rigby, with a nod of her head. "Thank ye, Dickon! And now for making this scarecrow. Be within call, Dickon, in case I need you again."

The good woman had risen thus early (for as yet it was scarcely sunrise) in order to set about making a scarecrow, which she intended to put in the middle of her corn-patch. It was now the latter week of May, and the crows and blackbirds had already discovered the little, green, rolledup leaf of the Indian corn just peeping out of the soil. She was determined, therefore, to contrive as lifelike a scarecrow as ever was seen, and to finish it immediately, from top to toe, so that it should begin its sentinel's duty that very morning. Now Mother Rigby (as everybody must have heard) was one of the most cunning and potent witches in New England, and might, with very little trouble, have made a scarecrow ugly enough to frighten the minister himself. But on this occasion, as she had awakened in an uncommonly pleasant humor, and was further dulcified by her pipe tobacco, she resolved to produce something fine, beautiful, and splendid, rather than hideous and horrible.

"I don't want to set up a hobgoblin in my own corn-patch, and almost at my own doorstep," said Mother Rigby to herself, puffing out a whiff of smoke; "I could do it if I pleased, but I'm tired of doing marvellous things, and so I'll keep within the bounds of every-day business just for variety's sake. Besides, there is no use in scaring the little children for a mile roundabout, though 't is true I'm a witch."

It was settled, therefore, in her own mind, that the scarecrow should represent a fine gentleman of the period, so far as the materials at hand would allow. Perhaps it may be as well to enumerate the chief of the articles that went to the composition of this figure.

The most important item of all, probably, although it made so little show, was a certain broomstick, on which Mother Rigby had taken many an airy gallop at midnight, and which now served the scarecrow by way of a spinal column, or, as the unlearned phrase it, a backbone. One of its arms was a disabled flail which used to be wielded by Goodman Rigby, before his spouse worried him out of this troublesome world; the other, if I mistake not, was composed of the pudding stick and a broken rung of a chair, tied loosely together at the elbow. As for its legs, the right was a hoe handle, and the left an undistinguished and miscellaneous stick from the woodpile. Its lungs, stomach, and other affairs of that kind were nothing better than a meal bag stuffed with straw. Thus we have made out the skeleton and entire corporosity of the scarecrow, with the exception of its head; and this was admirably supplied by a somewhat withered and shrivelled pumpkin, in which Mother Rigby cut two holes for the eyes and a slit for the mouth, leaving a bluish-colored knob in the middle to pass for a nose. It was really quite a respectable face.

"I've seen worse ones on human shoulders, at any rate," said Mother Rigby. "And many a fine gentleman has a pumpkin head, as well as my scarecrow."

But the clothes, in this case, were to be the making of the man. So the good old woman took down from a peg an ancient plum-colored coat of London make, and with relics of embroidery on its seams, cuffs, pocket-flaps, and button-holes, but lamentably worn and faded, patched at the elbows, tattered at the skirts, and threadbare all over. On the left breast was a round hole, whence either a star of nobility had been rent away, or else the hot heart of some former wearer had scorched it through and through. The neighbors said that this rich garment belonged to the Black Man's wardrobe, and that he kept it at Mother Rigby's cottage for the convenience of slipping it on whenever he wished to make a grand appearance at the governor's table. To match the coat there was a velvet waistcoat of very ample size, and formerly embroidered with foliage that had been as brightly golden as the maple leaves in October, but which had now quite vanished out of the substance of the velvet. Next came a pair of scarlet breeches, once worn by the French governor of Louisbourg, and the knees of which had touched the lower step of the throne of Louis le Grand. The Frenchman had given these small-clothes to an Indian powwow, who parted with them to the old witch for a gill of strong waters, at one of their dances in the forest. Furthermore, Mother Rigby produced a pair of silk stockings and put them on the figure's legs, where they showed as unsubstantial as a dream, with the wooden reality of the two sticks making itself miserably apparent through the holes. Lastly, she put her dead husband's wig on the bare scalp of the pumpkin, and surmounted the whole with a dusty three-cornered hat, in which was stuck the longest tail feather of a rooster.

Then the old dame stood the figure up in a corner of her cottage and chuckled to behold its yellow semblance of a visage, with its nobby little nose thrust into the air. It had a strangely self-satisfied aspect, and seemed to say, "Come look at me!"

"And you are well worth looking at, that's a fact!" quoth Mother Rigby, in admiration at her own handiwork. "I've made many a puppet since I've been a witch, but methinks this is the finest of them all. 'Tis almost too good for a scarecrow. And, by the by, I'll just fill a fresh pipe of tobacco and then take him out to the corn-patch."

While filling her pipe the old woman continued to gaze with almost motherly affection at the figure in the corner. To say the truth, whether it were chance, or skill, or downright witchcraft, there was something wonderfully human in this ridiculous shape, bedizened with its tattered finery; and as for the countenance, it appeared to shrivel its yellow surface into a grin—a funny kind of expression betwixt scorn and merriment, as if it understood itself to be a jest at mankind. The more Mother Rigby looked the better she was pleased.

"Dickon," cried she sharply, "another coal for my pipe!"

Hardly had she spoken, than, just as before, there was a red-glowing coal on the top of the tobacco. She drew in a long whiff and puffed it forth again into the bar of morning sunshine which struggled through the one dusty pane of her cottage window. Mother Rigby always liked to flavor her pipe with a coal of fire from the particular chimney corner whence this had been brought. But where that chimney corner might be, or who brought the coal from it,—further than that the invisible messenger seemed to respond to the name of Dickon,—I cannot tell.

"That puppet yonder," thought Mother Rigby, still with her eyes fixed on the scarecrow, "is too good a piece of work to stand all summer in a corn-patch, frightening away the crows and blackbirds. He's capable of better things. Why, I've danced with a worse one, when partners happened to be scarce, at our witch meetings in the forest! What if I should let him take his chance among the other men of straw and empty fellows who go bustling about the world?"

The old witch took three or four more whiffs of her pipe and smiled.

"He'll meet plenty of his brethren at every street corner!" continued she. "Well; I didn't mean to dabble in witchcraft to-day, further than the lighting of my pipe, but a witch I am, and a witch I'm likely to be, and there's no use trying to shirk it. I'll make a man of my scarecrow, were it only for the joke's sake!"

While muttering these words, Mother Rigby took the pipe from her own mouth and thrust it into the crevice which represented the same feature in the pumpkin visage of the scarecrow.

"Puff, darling, puff!" said she. "Puff away, my fine fellow! your life depends on it!"

This was a strange exhortation, undoubtedly, to be addressed to a mere thing of sticks, straw, and old clothes, with nothing better than a shrivelled pumpkin for a head,—as we know to have been the scarecrow's case. Nevertheless, as we must carefully hold in remembrance, Mother Rigby was a witch of singular power and dexterity; and, keeping this fact duly before our minds, we shall see nothing beyond credibility in the remarkable incidents of our story. Indeed, the great difficulty will be at once got over, if we can only bring ourselves to believe that, as soon as the old dame bade him puff, there came a whiff of smoke from the scarecrow's mouth. It was the very feeblest of whiffs, to be sure; but it was followed by another and another, each more decided than the preceding one.

"Puff away, my pet! puff away, my pretty one!" Mother Rigby kept repeating, with her pleasantest smile. "It is the breath of life to ye; and that you may take my word for."

Beyond all question the pipe was bewitched. There must have been a spell either in the tobacco or in the fiercely-glowing coal that so mysteriously burned on top of it, or in the pungently-aromatic smoke which exhaled from the kindled weed. The figure, after a few doubtful attempts at length blew forth a volley of smoke extending all the way from the obscure corner into the bar of sunshine. There it eddied and melted away among the motes of dust. It seemed a convulsive effort; for the two or three next whiffs were fainter, although the coal still glowed and threw a gleam over the scarecrow's visage. The old witch clapped her skinny hands together, and smiled encouragingly upon her handiwork. She saw that the charm worked well. The shrivelled, yellow face, which heretofore had been no face at all, had already a thin, fantastic haze, as it were of human likeness, shifting to and fro across it; sometimes vanishing entirely, but growing more perceptible than ever with the next whiff from the pipe. The whole figure, in like manner, assumed a show of life, such as we impart to ill-defined shapes among the clouds, and half deceive ourselves with the pastime of our own fancy.

If we must needs pry closely into the matter, it may be doubted whether there was any real change, after all, in the sordid, wornout worthless, and ill-jointed substance of the scarecrow; but merely a spectral illusion, and a cunning effect of light and shade so colored and contrived as to delude the eyes of most men. The miracles of witchcraft seem always to have had a very shallow subtlety; and, at least, if the above explanation do not hit the truth of the process, I can suggest no better.

"Well puffed, my pretty lad!" still cried old Mother Rigby. "Come, another good stout whiff, and let it be with might and main. Puff for thy life, I tell thee! Puff out of the very bottom of thy heart, if any heart thou hast, or any bottom to it! Well done, again! Thou didst suck in that mouthful as if for the pure love of it."

And then the witch beckoned to the scarecrow, throwing so much magnetic potency into her gesture that it seemed as if it must inevitably be obeyed, like the mystic call of the loadstone when it summons the iron.

"Why lurkest thou in the corner, lazy one?" said she. "Step forth! Thou hast the world before thee!"

Upon my word, if the legend were not one which I heard on my grandmother's knee, and which had established its place among things credible before my childish judgment could analyze its probability, I question whether I should have the face to tell it now.

In obedience to Mother Rigby's word, and extending its arm as if to reach her outstretched hand, the figure made a step forward—a kind of hitch and jerk, however, rather than a step—then tottered and almost lost its balance. What could the witch expect? It was nothing, after all, but a scarecrow stuck upon two sticks. But the strong-willed old beldam scowled, and beckoned, and flung the energy of her purpose so forcibly at this poor combination of rotten wood, and musty straw, and ragged garments, that it was compelled to show itself a man, in spite of the reality of things. So it stepped into the bar of sunshine. There it stood, poor devil of a contrivance that it was!—with only the thinnest vesture of human similitude about it, through which was evident the stiff, rickety, incongruous, faded, tattered, good-for-nothing patchwork of its substance, ready to sink in a heap upon the floor, as conscious of its own unworthiness to be erect. Shall I confess the truth? At its present point of vivification, the scarecrow reminds me of some of the lukewarm and abortive characters, composed of heterogeneous materials, used for the thousandth time, and never worth using, with which romance writers (and myself, no doubt, among the rest) have so overpeopled the world of fiction.

But the fierce old hag began to get angry and show a glimpse of her diabolic nature (like a snake's head, peeping with a hiss out of her bosom), at this pusillanimous behavior of the thing which she had taken the trouble to put together.

"Puff away, wretch!" cried she, wrathfully. "Puff, puff, puff, thou thing of straw and emptiness! thou rag or two! thou meal bag! thou pumpkin head! thou nothing! Where shall I find a name vile enough to call thee by? Puff, I say, and suck in thy fantastic life with the smoke! else I snatch the pipe from thy mouth and hurl thee where that red coal came from."

Thus threatened, the unhappy scarecrow had nothing for it but to puff away for dear life. As need was, therefore, it applied itself lustily to the pipe, and sent forth such abundant volleys of tobacco smoke that the small cottage kitchen became all vaporous. The one sunbeam struggled mistily through, and could but imperfectly define the image of the cracked and dusty window pane on the opposite wall. Mother Rigby, meanwhile, with one brown arm akimbo and the other stretched towards the figure, loomed grimly amid the obscurity with such port and expression as when she was wont to heave a ponderous nightmare on her victims and stand at the bedside to enjoy their agony. In fear and trembling did this poor scarecrow puff. But its efforts, it must be acknowledged, served an excellent purpose; for, with each successive whiff, the figure lost more and more of its dizzy and perplexing tenuity and seemed to take denser substance. Its very garments, moreover, partook of the magical change, and shone with the gloss of novelty and glistened with the skilfully embroidered gold that had long ago been rent away. And, half revealed among the smoke, a yellow visage bent its lustreless eyes on Mother Rigby.

At last the old witch clinched her fist and shook it at the figure. Not that she was positively angry, but merely acting on the principle—perhaps untrue, or not the only truth, though as high a one as Mother Rigby could be expected to attain—that feeble and torpid natures, being incapable of better inspiration, must be stirred up by fear. But here was the crisis. Should she fail in what she now sought to effect, it was her ruthless purpose to scatter the miserable simulacre into its original elements.

"Thou hast a man's aspect," said she, sternly. "Have also the echo and mockery of a voice! I bid thee speak!"

The scarecrow gasped, struggled, and at length emitted a murmur, which was so incorporated with its smoky breath that you could scarcely tell whether it were indeed a voice or only a whiff of tobacco. Some narrators of this legend hold the opinion that Mother Rigby's conjurations and the fierceness of her will had compelled a familiar spirit into the figure, and that the voice was his.

"Mother," mumbled the poor stifled voice, "be not so awful with me! I would fain speak; but being without wits, what can I say?"

"Thou canst speak, darling, canst thou?" cried Mother Rigby, relaxing her grim countenance into a smile. "And what shalt thou say, quoth-a! Say, indeed! Art thou of the brotherhood of the empty skull, and demandest of me what thou shalt say? Thou shalt say a thousand things, and saying them a thousand times over, thou shalt still have said nothing! Be not afraid, I tell thee! When thou comest into the world (whither I purpose sending thee forthwith) thou shalt not lack the wherewithal to talk. Talk! Why, thou shall babble like a mill-stream, if thou wilt. Thou hast brains enough for that, I trow!"

"At your service, mother," responded the figure.

"And that was well said, my pretty one," answered Mother Rigby. "Then thou speakest like thyself, and meant nothing. Thou shalt have a hundred such set phrases, and five hundred to the boot of them. And now, darling, I have taken so much pains with thee and thou art so beautiful, that, by my troth, I love thee better than any witch's puppet in the world; and I've made them of all sorts—clay, wax, straw, sticks, night fog, morning mist, sea foam, and chimney smoke. But thou art the very best. So give heed to what I say."

"Yes, kind mother," said the figure, "with all my heart!"

"With all thy heart!" cried the old witch, setting her hands to her sides and laughing loudly. "Thou hast such a pretty way of speaking. With all thy heart! And thou didst put thy hand to the left side of thy waistcoat as if thou really hadst one!"

So now, in high good humor with this fantastic contrivance of hers, Mother Rigby told the scarecrow that it must go and play its part in the great world, where not one man in a hundred, she affirmed, was gifted with more real substance than itself. And, that he might hold up his head with the best of them, she endowed him, on the spot, with an unreckonable amount of wealth. It consisted partly of a gold mine in Eldorado, and of ten thousand shares in a broken bubble, and of half a million acres of vineyard at the North Pole, and of a castle in the air, and a chateau in Spain, together with all the rents and income therefrom accruing. She further made over to him the cargo of a certain ship, laden with salt of Cadiz, which she herself, by her necromantic arts, had caused to founder, ten years before, in the deepest part of mid-ocean. If the salt were not dissolved, and could be brought to market, it would fetch a pretty penny among the fishermen. That he might not lack ready money, she gave him a copper farthing of Birmingham manufacture, being all the coin she had about her, and likewise a great deal of brass, which she applied to his forehead, thus making it yellower than ever.

"With that brass alone," quoth Mother Rigby, "thou canst pay thy way all over the earth. Kiss me, pretty darling! I have done my best for thee."

Furthermore, that the adventurer might lack no possible advantage towards a fair start in life, this excellent old dame gave him a token by which he was to introduce himself to a certain magistrate, member of the council, merchant, and elder of the church (the four capacities constituting but one man), who stood at the head of society in the neighboring metropolis. The token was neither more nor less than a single word, which Mother Rigby whispered to the scarecrow, and which the scarecrow was to whisper to the merchant.

"Gouty as the old fellow is, he'll run thy errands for thee, when once thou hast given him that word in his ear," said the old witch. "Mother Rigby knows the worshipful Justice Gookin, and the worshipful Justice knows Mother Rigby!"

Here the witch thrust her wrinkled face close to the puppet's, chuckling irrepressibly, and fidgeting all through her system, with delight at the idea which she meant to communicate.

"The worshipful Master Gookin," whispered she, "hath a comely maiden to his daughter. And hark ye, my pet! Thou hast a fair outside, and a pretty wit enough of thine own. Yea, a pretty wit enough! Thou wilt think better of it when thou hast seen more of other people's wits. Now, with thy outside and thy inside, thou art the very man to win a young girl's heart. Never doubt it! I tell thee it shall be so. Put but a bold face on the matter, sigh, smile, flourish thy hat, thrust forth thy leg like a dancing-master, put thy right hand to the left side of thy waistcoat, and pretty Polly Gookin is thine own!"

All this while the new creature had been sucking in and exhaling the vapory fragrance of his pipe, and seemed now to continue this occupation as much for the enjoyment it afforded as because it was an essential condition of his existence. It was wonderful to see how exceedingly like a human being it behaved. Its eyes (for it appeared to possess a pair) were bent on Mother Rigby, and at suitable junctures it nodded or shook its head. Neither did it lack words proper for the occasion: "Really! Indeed! Pray tell me! Is it possible! Upon my word! By no means! Oh! Ah! Hem!" and other such weighty utterances as imply attention, inquiry, acquiescence, or dissent on the part of the auditor. Even had you stood by and seen the scarecrow made, you could scarcely have resisted the conviction that it perfectly understood the cunning counsels which the old witch poured into its counterfeit of an ear. The more earnestly it applied its lips to the pipe, the more distinctly was its human likeness stamped among visible realities, the more sagacious grew its expression, the more lifelike its gestures and movements, and the more intelligibly audible its voice. Its garments, too, glistened so much the brighter with an illusory magnificence. The very pipe, in which burned the spell of all this wonderwork, ceased to appear as a smoke-blackened earthen stump, and became a meerschaum, with painted bowl and amber mouthpiece.

It might be apprehended, however, that as the life of the illusion seemed identical with the vapor of the pipe, it would terminate simultaneously with the reduction of the tobacco to ashes. But the beldam foresaw the difficulty.

"Hold thou the pipe, my precious one," said she, "while I fill it for thee again."

It was sorrowful to behold how the fine gentleman began to fade back into a scarecrow while Mother Rigby shook the ashes out of the pipe and proceeded to replenish it from her tobacco-box.

"Dickon," cried she, in her high, sharp tone, "another coal for this pipe!"

No sooner said than the intensely red speck of fire was glowing within the pipe-bowl; and the scarecrow, without waiting for the witch's bidding, applied the tube to his lips and drew in a few short, convulsive whiffs, which soon, however, became regular and equable.

"Now, mine own heart's darling," quoth Mother Rigby, "whatever may happen to thee, thou must stick to thy pipe. Thy life is in it; and that, at least, thou knowest well, if thou knowest nought besides. Stick to thy pipe, I say! Smoke, puff, blow thy cloud; and tell the people, if any question be made, that it is for thy health, and that so the physician orders thee to do. And, sweet one, when thou shalt find thy pipe getting low, go apart into some corner, and (first filling thyself with smoke) cry sharply, 'Dickon, a fresh pipe of tobacco!' and, 'Dickon, another coal for my pipe!' and have it into thy pretty mouth as speedily as may be. Else, instead of a gallant gentleman in a gold-laced coat, thou wilt be but a jumble of sticks and tattered clothes, and a bag of straw, and a withered pumpkin! Now depart, my treasure, and good luck go with thee!"

"Never fear, mother!" said the figure, in a stout voice, and sending forth a courageous whiff of smoke, "I will thrive, if an honest man and a gentleman may!"

"Oh, thou wilt be the death of me!" cried the old witch, convulsed with laughter. "That was well said. If an honest man and a gentleman may! Thou playest thy part to perfection. Get along with thee for a smart fellow; and I will wager on thy head, as a man of pith and substance, with a brain and what they call a heart, and all else that a man should have, against any other thing on two legs. I hold myself a better witch than yesterday, for thy sake. Did not I make thee? And I defy any witch in New England to make such another! Here; take my staff along with thee!"

The staff, though it was but a plain oaken stick, immediately took the aspect of a gold-headed cane.

"That gold head has as much sense in it as thine own," said Mother Rigby, "and it will guide thee straight to worshipful Master Gookin's door. Get thee gone, my pretty pet, my darling, my precious one, my treasure; and if any ask thy name, it is Feathertop. For thou hast a feather in thy hat, and I have thrust a handful of feathers into the hollow of thy head, and thy wig, too, is of the fashion they call Feathertop,—so be Feathertop thy name!"

And, issuing from the cottage, Feathertop strode manfully towards town. Mother Rigby stood at the threshold, well pleased to see how the sunbeams glistened on him, as if all his magnificence were real, and how diligently and lovingly he smoked his pipe, and how handsomely he walked, in spite of a little stiffness of his legs. She watched him until out of sight, and threw a witch benediction after her darling, when a turn of the road snatched him from her view.

Betimes in the forenoon, when the principal street of the neighboring town was just at its acme of life and bustle, a stranger of very distinguished figure was seen on the sidewalk. His port as well as his garments betokened nothing short of nobility. He wore a richly-embroidered plum-colored coat, a waistcoat of costly velvet, magnificently adorned with golden foliage, a pair of splendid scarlet breeches, and the finest and glossiest of white silk stockings. His head was covered with a peruke, so daintily powdered and adjusted that it would have been sacrilege to disorder it with a hat; which, therefore (and it was a gold-laced hat, set off with a snowy feather), he carried beneath his arm. On the breast of his coat glistened a star. He managed his gold-headed cane with an airy grace, peculiar to the fine gentlemen of the period; and, to give the highest possible finish to his equipment, he had lace ruffles at his wrist, of a most ethereal delicacy, sufficiently avouching how idle and aristocratic must be the hands which they half concealed.

It was a remarkable point in the accoutrement of this brilliant personage that he held in his left hand a fantastic kind of a pipe, with an exquisitely painted bowl and an amber mouthpiece. This he applied to his lips as often as every five or six paces, and inhaled a deep whiff of smoke, which, after being retained a moment in his lungs, might be seen to eddy gracefully from his mouth and nostrils.

As may well be supposed, the street was all astir to find out the stranger's name.

"It is some great nobleman, beyond question," said one of the townspeople. "Do you see the star at his breast?"

"Nay; it is too bright to be seen," said another. "Yes; he must needs be a nobleman, as you say. But by what conveyance, think you, can his lordship have voyaged or travelled hither? There has been no vessel from the old country for a month past; and if he have arrived overland from the southward, pray where are his attendants and equipage?"

"He needs no equipage to set off his rank," remarked a third. "If he came among us in rags, nobility would shine through a hole in his elbow. I never saw such dignity of aspect. He has the old Norman blood in his veins, I warrant him."

"I rather take him to be a Dutchman, or one of your high Germans," said another citizen. "The men of those countries have always the pipe at their mouths."

"And so has a Turk," answered his companion. "But, in my judgment, this stranger hath been bred at the French court, and hath there learned politeness and grace of manner, which none understand so well as the nobility of France. That gait, now! A vulgar spectator might deem it stiff—he might call it a hitch and jerk—but, to my eye, it hath an unspeakable majesty, and must have been acquired by constant observation of the deportment of the Grand Monarque. The stranger's character and office are evident enough. He is a French ambassador, come to treat with our rulers about the cession of Canada."

"More probably a Spaniard," said another, "and hence his yellow complexion; or, most likely, he is from the Havana, or from some port on the Spanish main, and comes to make investigation about the piracies which our government is thought to connive at. Those settlers in Peru and Mexico have skins as yellow as the gold which they dig out of their mines."

"Yellow or not," cried a lady, "he is a beautiful man!—so tall, so slender! such a fine, noble face, with so well-shaped a nose, and all that delicacy of expression about the mouth! And, bless me, how bright his star is! It positively shoots out flames!"

"So do your eyes, fair lady," said the stranger, with a bow and a flourish of his pipe; for he was just passing at the instant. "Upon my honor, they have quite dazzled me."

"Was ever so original and exquisite a compliment?" murmured the lady, in an ecstasy of delight.

Amid the general admiration excited by the stranger's appearance, there were only two dissenting voices. One was that of an impertinent cur, which, after snuffing at the heels of the glistening figure, put its tail between its legs and skulked into its master's back yard, vociferating an execrable howl. The other dissentient was a young child, who squalled at the fullest stretch of his lungs, and babbled some unintelligible nonsense about a pumpkin.

Feathertop meanwhile pursued his way along the street. Except for the few complimentary words to the lady, and now and then a slight inclination of the head in requital of the profound reverences of the bystanders, he seemed wholly absorbed in his pipe. There needed no other proof of his rank and consequence than the perfect equanimity with which he comported himself, while the curiosity and admiration of the town swelled almost into clamor around him. With a crowd gathering behind his footsteps, he finally reached the mansion-house of the worshipful Justice Gookin, entered the gate, ascended the steps of the front door, and knocked. In the interim, before his summons was answered, the stranger was observed to shake the ashes out of his pipe.

"What did he say in that sharp voice?" inquired one of the spectators.

"Nay, I know not," answered his friend. "But the sun dazzles my eyes strangely. How dim and faded his lordship looks all of a sudden! Bless my wits, what is the matter with me?"

"The wonder is," said the other, "that his pipe, which was out only an instant ago, should be all alight again, and with the reddest coal I ever saw. There is something mysterious about this stranger. What a whiff of smoke was that! Dim and faded did you call him? Why, as he turns about the star on his breast is all ablaze."

"It is, indeed," said his companion; "and it will go near to dazzle pretty Polly Gookin, whom I see peeping at it out of the chamber window."

The door being now opened, Feathertop turned to the crowd, made a stately bend of his body like a great man acknowledging the reverence of the meaner sort, and vanished into the house. There was a mysterious kind of a smile, if it might not better be called a grin or grimace, upon his visage; but, of all the throng that beheld him, not an individual appears to have possessed insight enough to detect the illusive character of the stranger except a little child and a cur dog.

Our legend here loses somewhat of its continuity, and, passing over the preliminary explanation between Feathertop and the merchant, goes in quest of the pretty Polly Gookin. She was a damsel of a soft, round figure, with light hair and blue eyes, and a fair, rosy face, which seemed neither very shrewd nor very simple. This young lady had caught a glimpse of the glistening stranger while standing on the threshold, and had forthwith put on a laced cap, a string of beads, her finest kerchief, and her stiffest damask petticoat in preparation for the interview. Hurrying from her chamber to the parlor, she had ever since been viewing herself in the large looking-glass and practising pretty airs-now a smile, now a ceremonious dignity of aspect, and now a softer smile than the former, kissing her hand likewise, tossing her head, and managing her fan; while within the mirror an unsubstantial little maid repeated every gesture and did all the foolish things that Polly did, but without making her ashamed of them. In short, it was the fault of pretty Polly's ability rather than her will if she failed to be as complete an artifice as the illustrious Feathertop himself; and, when she thus tampered with her own simplicity, the witch's phantom might well hope to win her.

No sooner did Polly hear her father's gouty footsteps approaching the parlor door, accompanied with the stiff clatter of Feathertop's high-heeled shoes, than she seated herself bolt upright and innocently began warbling a song.

"Polly! daughter Polly!" cried the old merchant. "Come hither, child."

Master Gookin's aspect, as he opened the door, was doubtful and troubled.

"This gentleman," continued he, presenting the stranger, "is the Chevalier Feathertop,—nay, I beg his pardon, my Lord Feathertop,—who hath brought me a token of remembrance from an ancient friend of mine. Pay your duty to his lordship, child, and honor him as his quality deserves."

After these few words of introduction, the worshipful magistrate immediately quitted the room. But, even in that brief moment, had the fair Polly glanced aside at her father instead of devoting herself wholly to the brilliant guest, she might have taken warning of some mischief nigh at hand. The old man was nervous, fidgety, and very pale. Purposing a smile of courtesy, he had deformed his face with a sort of galvanic grin, which, when Feathertop's back was turned, he exchanged for a scowl, at the same time shaking his fist and stamping his gouty foot—an incivility which brought its retribution along with it. The truth appears to have been that Mother Rigby's word of introduction, whatever it might be, had operated far more on the rich merchant's fears than on his good will. Moreover, being a man of wonderfully acute observation, he had noticed that these painted figures on the bowl of Feathertop's pipe were in motion. Looking more closely he became convinced that these figures were a party of little demons, each duly provided with horns and a tail, and dancing hand in hand, with gestures of diabolical merriment, round the circumference of the pipe bowl. As if to confirm his suspicions, while Master Gookin ushered his guest along a dusky passage from his private room to the parlor, the star on Feathertop's breast had scintillated actual flames, and threw a flickering gleam upon the wall, the ceiling, and the floor.

With such sinister prognostics manifesting themselves on all hands, it is not to be marvelled at that the merchant should have felt that he was committing his daughter to a very questionable acquaintance. He cursed, in his secret soul, the insinuating elegance of Feathertop's manners, as this brilliant personage bowed, smiled, put his hand on his heart, inhaled a long whiff from his pipe, and enriched the atmosphere with the smoky vapor of a fragrant and visible sigh. Gladly would poor Master Gookin have thrust his dangerous guest into the street; but there was a constraint and terror within him. This respectable old gentleman, we fear, at an earlier period of life, had given some pledge or other to the evil principle, and perhaps was now to redeem it by the sacrifice of his daughter.

It so happened that the parlor door was partly of glass, shaded by a silken curtain, the folds of which hung a little awry. So strong was the merchant's interest in witnessing what was to ensue between the fair Polly and the gallant Feathertop that, after quitting the room, he could by no means refrain from peeping through the crevice of the curtain.

But there was nothing very miraculous to be seen; nothing—except the trifles previously noticed—to confirm the idea of a supernatural peril environing the pretty Polly. The stranger it is true was evidently a thorough and practised man of the world, systematic and self-possessed, and therefore the sort of a person to whom a parent ought not to confide a simple, young girl without due watchfulness for the result. The worthy magistrate who had been conversant with all degrees and qualities of mankind, could not but perceive every motion and gesture of the distinguished Feathertop came in its proper place; nothing had been left rude or native in him; a well-digested conventionalism had incorporated itself thoroughly with his substance and transformed him into a work of art. Perhaps it was this peculiarity that invested him with a species of ghastliness and awe. It is the effect of anything completely and consummately artificial, in human shape, that the person impresses us as an unreality and as having hardly pith enough to cast a shadow upon the floor. As regarded Feathertop, all this resulted in a wild, extravagant, and fantastical impression, as if his life and being were akin to the smoke that curled upward from his pipe.

But pretty Polly Gookin felt not thus. The pair were now promenading the room: Feathertop with his dainty stride and no less dainty grimace, the girl with a native maidenly grace, just touched, not spoiled, by a slightly affected manner, which seemed caught from the perfect artifice of her companion. The longer the interview continued, the more charmed was pretty Polly, until, within the first quarter of an hour (as the old magistrate noted by his watch), she was evidently beginning to be in love. Nor need it have been witchcraft that subdued her in such a hurry; the poor child's heart, it may be, was so very fervent that it melted her with its own warmth as reflected from the hollow semblance of a lover. No matter what Feathertop said, his words found depth and reverberation in her ear; no matter what he did, his action was heroic to her eye. And by this time it is to be supposed there was a blush on Polly's cheek, a tender smile about her mouth and a liquid softness in her glance; while the star kept coruscating on Feathertop's breast, and the little demons careered with more frantic merriment than ever about the circumference of his pipe bowl. O pretty Polly Gookin, why should these imps rejoice so madly that a silly maiden's heart was about to be given to a shadow! Is it so unusual a misfortune, so rare a triumph?

By and by Feathertop paused, and throwing himself into an imposing attitude, seemed to summon the fair girl to survey his figure and resist him longer if she could. His star, his embroidery, his buckles glowed at that instant with unutterable splendor; the picturesque hues of his attire took a richer depth of coloring; there was a gleam and polish over his whole presence betokening the perfect witchery of well-ordered manners. The maiden raised her eyes and suffered them to linger upon her companion with a bashful and admiring gaze. Then, as if desirous of judging what value her own simple comeliness might have side by side with so much brilliancy, she cast a glance towards the full-length looking-glass in front of which they happened to be standing. It was one of the truest plates in the world and incapable of flattery. No sooner did the images therein reflected meet Polly's eye than she shrieked, shrank from the stranger's side, gazed at him for a moment in the wildest dismay, and sank insensible upon the floor. Feathertop likewise had looked towards the mirror, and there beheld, not the glittering mockery of his outside show, but a picture of the sordid patchwork of his real composition stripped of all witchcraft.

The wretched simulacrum! We almost pity him. He threw up his arms with an expression of despair that went further than any of his previous manifestations towards vindicating his claims to be reckoned human, for perchance the only time since this so often empty and deceptive life of mortals began its course, an illusion had seen and fully recognized itself.

Mother Rigby was seated by her kitchen hearth in the twilight of this eventful day, and had just shaken the ashes out of a new pipe, when she heard a hurried tramp along the road. Yet it did not seem so much the tramp of human footsteps as the clatter of sticks or the rattling of dry bones.

"Ha!" thought the old witch, "what step is that? Whose skeleton is out of its grave now, I wonder?"

A figure burst headlong into the cottage door. It was Feathertop! His pipe was still alight; the star still flamed upon his breast; the embroidery still glowed upon his garments; nor had he lost, in any degree or manner that could be estimated, the aspect that assimilated him with our mortal brotherhood. But yet, in some indescribable way (as is the case with all that has deluded us when once found out), the poor reality was felt beneath the cunning artifice.

"What has gone wrong?" demanded the witch. "Did yonder sniffling hypocrite thrust my darling from his door? The villain! I'll set twenty fiends to torment him till he offer thee his daughter on his bended knees!"

"No, mother," said Feathertop despondingly; "it was not that."

"Did the girl scorn my precious one?" asked Mother Rigby, her fierce eyes glowing like two coals of Tophet. "I'll cover her face with pimples! Her nose shall be as red as the coal in thy pipe! Her front teeth shall drop out! In a week hence she shall not be worth thy having!"

"Let her alone, mother," answered poor Feathertop; "the girl was half won; and methinks a kiss from her sweet lips might have made me altogether human. But," he added, after a brief pause and then a howl of self-contempt, "I've seen myself, mother! I've seen myself for the wretched, ragged, empty thing I am! I'll exist no longer!"

Snatching the pipe from his mouth, he flung it with all his might against the chimney, and at the same instant sank upon the floor, a medley of straw and tattered garments, with some sticks protruding from the heap, and a shrivelled pumpkin in the midst. The eyeholes were now lustreless; but the rudely-carved gap, that just before had been a mouth still seemed to twist itself into a despairing grin, and was so far human.

"Poor fellow!" quoth Mother Rigby, with a rueful glance at the relics of her ill-fated contrivance. "My poor, dear, pretty Feathertop! There are thousands upon thousands of coxcombs and charlatans in the world, made up of just such a jumble of wornout, forgotten, and good-for-nothing trash as he was! Yet they live in fair repute, and never see themselves for what they are. And why should my poor puppet be the only one to know himself and perish for it?"

While thus muttering, the witch had filled a fresh pipe of tobacco, and held the stem between her fingers, as doubtful whether to thrust it into her own mouth or Feathertop's.

"Poor Feathertop!" she continued. "I could easily give him another chance and send him forth again tomorrow. But no; his feelings are too tender, his sensibilities too deep. He seems to have too much heart to bustle for his own advantage in such an empty and heartless world. Well! well! I'll make a scarecrow of him after all. 'Tis an innocent and useful vocation, and will suit my darling well; and, if each of his human brethren had as fit a one, 't would be the better for mankind; and as for this pipe of tobacco, I need it more than he."

So saying Mother Rigby put the stem between her lips. "Dickon!" cried she, in her high, sharp tone, "another coal for my pipe!"

EGOTISM[1]; OR, THE BOSOM SERPENT

[From the Unpublished "Allegories of the Heart."]

"Here he comes!" shouted the boys along the street. "Here comes the man with a snake in his bosom!"

This outcry, saluting Herkimer's ears as he was about to enter the iron gate of the Elliston mansion, made him pause. It was not without a shudder that he found himself on the point of meeting his former acquaintance, whom he had known in the glory of youth, and whom now after an interval of five years, he was to find the victim either of a diseased fancy or a horrible physical misfortune.

"A snake in his bosom!" repeated the young sculptor to himself. "It must be he. No second man on earth has such a bosom friend. And now, my poor Rosina, Heaven grant me wisdom to discharge my errand aright! Woman's faith must be strong indeed since thine has not yet failed."

Thus musing, he took his stand at the entrance of the gate and waited until the personage so singularly announced should make his appearance. After an instant or two he beheld the figure of a lean man, of unwholesome look, with glittering eyes and long black hair, who seemed to imitate the motion of a snake; for, instead of walking straight forward with open front, he undulated along the pavement in a curved line. It may be too fanciful to say that something, either in his moral or material aspect, suggested the idea that a miracle had been wrought by transforming a serpent into a man, but so imperfectly that the snaky nature was yet hidden, and scarcely hidden, under the mere outward guise of humanity. Herkimer remarked that his complexion had a greenish tinge over its sickly white, reminding him of a species of marble out of which he had once wrought a head of Envy, with her snaky locks.

The wretched being approached the gate, but, instead of entering, stopped short and fixed the glitter of his eye full upon the compassionate yet steady countenance of the sculptor.

"It gnaws me! It gnaws me!" he exclaimed.

---

[1] The physical fact, to which it is here attempted to give a moral signification, has been known to occur in more than one instance.

And then there was an audible hiss, but whether it came from the apparent lunatic's own lips, or was the real hiss of a serpent, might admit of a discussion. At all events, it made Herkimer shudder to his heart's core.

"Do you know me, George Herkimer?" asked the snake-possessed.

Herkimer did know him; but it demanded all the intimate and practical acquaintance with the human face, acquired by modelling actual likenesses in clay, to recognize the features of Roderick Elliston in the visage that now met the sculptor's gaze. Yet it was he. It added nothing to the wonder to reflect that the once brilliant young man had undergone this odious and fearful change during the no more than five brief years of Herkimer's abode at Florence. The possibility of such a transformation being granted, it was as easy to conceive it effected in a moment as in an age. Inexpressibly shocked and startled, it was still the keenest pang when Herkimer remembered that the fate of his cousin Rosina, the ideal of gentle womanhood, was indissolubly interwoven with that of a being whom Providence seemed to have unhumanized.

"Elliston! Roderick!" cried he, "I had heard of this; but my conception came far short of the truth. What has befallen you? Why do I find you thus?"

"Oh, 'tis a mere nothing! A snake! A snake! The commonest thing in the world. A snake in the bosom—that's all," answered Roderick Elliston. "But how is your own breast?" continued he, looking the sculptor in the eye with the most acute and penetrating glance that it had ever been his fortune to encounter. "All pure and wholesome? No reptile there? By my faith and conscience, and by the devil within me, here is a wonder! A man without a serpent in his bosom!"

"Be calm, Elliston," whispered George Herkimer, laying his hand upon the shoulder of the snake-possessed. "I have crossed the ocean to meet you. Listen! Let us be private. I bring a message from Rosina—from your wife!"

"It gnaws me! It gnaws me!" muttered Roderick.

With this exclamation, the most frequent in his mouth, the unfortunate man clutched both hands upon his breast as if an intolerable sting or torture impelled him to rend it open and let out the living mischief, even should it be intertwined with his own life. He then freed himself from Herkimer's grasp by a subtle motion, and, gliding through the gate, took refuge in his antiquated family residence. The sculptor did not pursue him. He saw that no available intercourse could be expected at such a moment, and was desirous, before another meeting, to inquire closely into the nature of Roderick's disease and the circumstances that had reduced him to so lamentable a condition. He succeeded in obtaining the necessary information from an eminent medical gentleman.

Shortly after Elliston's separation from his wife—now nearly four years ago—his associates had observed a singular gloom spreading over his daily life, like those chill, gray mists that sometimes steal away the sunshine from a summer's morning. The symptoms caused them endless perplexity. They knew not whether ill health were robbing his spirits of elasticity, or whether a canker of the mind was gradually eating, as such cankers do, from his moral system into the physical frame, which is but the shadow of the former. They looked for the root of this trouble in his shattered schemes of domestic bliss,—wilfully shattered by himself,—but could not be satisfied of its existence there. Some thought that their once brilliant friend was in an incipient stage of insanity, of which his passionate impulses had perhaps been the forerunners; others prognosticated a general blight and gradual decline. From Roderick's own lips they could learn nothing. More than once, it is true, he had been heard to say, clutching his hands convulsively upon his breast,—"It gnaws me! It gnaws me!"—but, by different auditors, a great diversity of explanation was assigned to this ominous expression. What could it be that gnawed the breast of Roderick Elliston? Was it sorrow? Was it merely the tooth of physical disease? Or, in his reckless course, often verging upon profligacy, if not plunging into its depths, had he been guilty of some deed which made his bosom a prey to the deadlier fangs of remorse? There was plausible ground for each of these conjectures; but it must not be concealed that more than one elderly gentleman, the victim of good cheer and slothful habits, magisterially pronounced the secret of the whole matter to be Dyspepsia!

Meanwhile, Roderick seemed aware how generally he had become the subject of curiosity and conjecture, and, with a morbid repugnance to such notice, or to any notice whatsoever, estranged himself from all companionship. Not merely the eye of man was a horror to him; not merely the light of a friend's countenance; but even the blessed sunshine, likewise, which in its universal beneficence typifies the radiance of the Creator's face, expressing his love for all the creatures of his hand. The dusky twilight was now too transparent for Roderick Elliston; the blackest midnight was his chosen hour to steal abroad; and if ever he were seen, it was when the watchman's lantern gleamed upon his figure, gliding along the street, with his hands clutched upon his bosom, still muttering, "It gnaws me! It gnaws me!" What could it be that gnawed him?

After a time, it became known that Elliston was in the habit of resorting to all the noted quacks that infested the city, or whom money would tempt to journey thither from a distance. By one of these persons, in the exultation of a supposed cure, it was proclaimed far and wide, by dint of handbills and little pamphlets on dingy paper, that a distinguished gentleman, Roderick Elliston, Esq., had been relieved of a SNAKE in his stomach! So here was the monstrous secret, ejected from its lurking place into public view, in all its horrible deformity. The mystery was out; but not so the bosom serpent. He, if it were anything but a delusion, still lay coiled in his living den. The empiric's cure had been a sham, the effect, it was supposed, of some stupefying drug which more nearly caused the death of the patient than of the odious reptile that possessed him. When Roderick Elliston regained entire sensibility, it was to find his misfortune the town talk—the more than nine days' wonder and horror—while, at his bosom, he felt the sickening motion of a thing alive, and the gnawing of that restless fang which seemed to gratify at once a physical appetite and a fiendish spite.

He summoned the old black servant, who had been bred up in his father's house, and was a middle-aged man while Roderick lay in his cradle.

"Scipio!" he began; and then paused, with his arms folded over his heart. "What do people say of me, Scipio."

"Sir! my poor master! that you had a serpent in your bosom," answered the servant with hesitation.

"And what else?" asked Roderick, with a ghastly look at the man.

"Nothing else, dear master," replied Scipio, "only that the doctor gave you a powder, and that the snake leaped out upon the floor."

"No, no!" muttered Roderick to himself, as he shook his head, and pressed his hands with a more convulsive force upon his breast, "I feel him still. It gnaws me! It gnaws me!"

From this time the miserable sufferer ceased to shun the world, but rather solicited and forced himself upon the notice of acquaintances and strangers. It was partly the result of desperation on finding that the cavern of his own bosom had not proved deep and dark enough to hide the secret, even while it was so secure a fortress for the loathsome fiend that had crept into it. But still more, this craving for notoriety was a symptom of the intense morbidness which now pervaded his nature. All persons chronically diseased are egotists, whether the disease be of the mind or body; whether it be sin, sorrow, or merely the more tolerable calamity of some endless pain, or mischief among the cords of mortal life. Such individuals are made acutely conscious of a self, by the torture in which it dwells. Self, therefore, grows to be so prominent an object with them that they cannot but present it to the face of every casual passer-by. There is a pleasure—perhaps the greatest of which the sufferer is susceptible—in displaying the wasted or ulcerated limb, or the cancer in the breast; and the fouler the crime, with so much the more difficulty does the perpetrator prevent it from thrusting up its snake-like head to frighten the world; for it is that cancer, or that crime, which constitutes their respective individuality. Roderick Elliston, who, a little while before, had held himself so scornfully above the common lot of men, now paid full allegiance to this humiliating law. The snake in his bosom seemed the symbol of a monstrous egotism to which everything was referred, and which he pampered, night and day, with a continual and exclusive sacrifice of devil worship.

He soon exhibited what most people considered indubitable tokens of insanity. In some of his moods, strange to say, he prided and gloried himself on being marked out from the ordinary experience of mankind, by the possession of a double nature, and a life within a life. He appeared to imagine that the snake was a divinity,—not celestial, it is true, but darkly infernal,—and that he thence derived an eminence and a sanctity, horrid, indeed, yet more desirable than whatever ambition aims at. Thus he drew his misery around him like a regal mantle, and looked down triumphantly upon those whose vitals nourished no deadly monster. Oftener, however, his human nature asserted its empire over him in the shape of a yearning for fellowship. It grew to be his custom to spend the whole day in wandering about the streets, aimlessly, unless it might be called an aim to establish a species of brotherhood between himself and the world. With cankered ingenuity, he sought out his own disease in every breast. Whether insane or not, he showed so keen a perception of frailty, error, and vice, that many persons gave him credit for being possessed not merely with a serpent, but with an actual fiend, who imparted this evil faculty of recognizing whatever was ugliest in man's heart.

For instance, he met an individual, who, for thirty years, had cherished a hatred against his own brother. Roderick, amidst the throng of the street, laid his hand on this man's chest, and looking full into his forbidding face, "How is the snake to-day?" he inquired, with a mock expression of sympathy.

"The snake!" exclaimed the brother hater—"what do you mean?"

"The snake! The snake! Does it gnaw you?" persisted Roderick. "Did you take counsel with him this morning when you should have been saying your prayers? Did he sting, when you thought of your brother's health, wealth, and good repute? Did he caper for joy, when you remembered the profligacy of his only son? And whether he stung, or whether he frolicked, did you feel his poison throughout your body and soul, converting everything to sourness and bitterness? That is the way of such serpents. I have learned the whole nature of them from my own!"

"Where is the police?" roared the object of Roderick's persecution, at the same time giving an instinctive clutch to his breast. "Why is this lunatic allowed to go at large?"

"Ha, ha!" chuckled Roderick, releasing his grasp of the man.— "His bosom serpent has stung him then!"

Often it pleased the unfortunate young man to vex people with a lighter satire, yet still characterized by somewhat of snake-like virulence. One day he encountered an ambitious statesman, and gravely inquired after the welfare of his boa constrictor; for of that species, Roderick affirmed, this gentleman's serpent must needs be, since its appetite was enormous enough to devour the whole country and constitution. At another time, he stopped a close-fisted old fellow, of great wealth, but who skulked about the city in the guise of a scarecrow, with a patched blue surtout, brown hat, and mouldy boots, scraping pence together, and picking up rusty nails. Pretending to look earnestly at this respectable person's stomach, Roderick assured him that his snake was a copper-head and had been generated by the immense quantities of that base metal with which he daily defiled his fingers. Again, he assaulted a man of rubicund visage, and told him that few bosom serpents had more of the devil in them than those that breed in the vats of a distillery. The next whom Roderick honored with his attention was a distinguished clergyman, who happened just then to be engaged in a theological controversy, where human wrath was more perceptible than divine inspiration.

"You have swallowed a snake in a cup of sacramental wine," quoth he.

"Profane wretch!" exclaimed the divine; but, nevertheless, his hand stole to his breast.

He met a person of sickly sensibility, who, on some early disappointment, had retired from the world, and thereafter held no intercourse with his fellow-men, but brooded sullenly or passionately over the irrevocable past. This man's very heart, if Roderick might be believed, had been changed into a serpent, which would finally torment both him and itself to death. Observing a married couple, whose domestic troubles were matter of notoriety, he condoled with both on having mutually taken a house adder to their bosoms. To an envious author, who depreciated works which he could never equal, he said that his snake was the slimiest and filthiest of all the reptile tribe, but was fortunately without a sting. A man of impure life, and a brazen face, asking Roderick if there were any serpent in his breast, he told him that there was, and of the same species that once tortured Don Rodrigo, the Goth. He took a fair young girl by the hand, and gazing sadly into her eyes, warned her that she cherished a serpent of the deadliest kind within her gentle breast; and the world found the truth of those ominous words, when, a few months afterwards, the poor girl died of love and shame. Two ladies, rivals in fashionable life who tormented one another with a thousand little stings of womanish spite, were given to understand that each of their hearts was a nest of diminutive snakes, which did quite as much mischief as one great one.

But nothing seemed to please Roderick better than to lay hold of a person infected with jealousy, which he represented as an enormous green reptile, with an ice-cold length of body, and the sharpest sting of any snake save one.

"And what one is that?" asked a by-stander, overhearing him.

It was a dark-browed man who put the question; he had an evasive eye, which in the course of a dozen years had looked no mortal directly in the face. There was an ambiguity about this person's character,—a stain upon his reputation,—yet none could tell precisely of what nature, although the city gossips, male and female, whispered the most atrocious surmises. Until a recent period he had followed the sea, and was, in fact, the very shipmaster whom George Herkimer had encountered, under such singular circumstances, in the Grecian Archipelago.

"What bosom serpent has the sharpest sting?" repeated this man; but he put the question as if by a reluctant necessity, and grew pale while he was uttering it.

"Why need you ask?" replied Roderick, with a look of dark intelligence. "Look into your own breast. Hark! my serpent bestirs himself! He acknowledges the presence of a master fiend!"

And then, as the by-standers afterwards affirmed, a hissing sound was heard, apparently in Roderick Elliston's breast. It was said, too, that an answering hiss came from the vitals of the shipmaster, as if a snake were actually lurking there and had been aroused by the call of its brother reptile. If there were in fact any such sound, it might have been caused by a malicious exercise of ventriloquism on the part of Roderick.

Thus making his own actual serpent—if a serpent there actually was in his bosom—the type of each man's fatal error, or hoarded sin, or unquiet conscience, and striking his sting so unremorsefully into the sorest spot, we may well imagine that Roderick became the pest of the city. Nobody could elude him—none could withstand him. He grappled with the ugliest truth that he could lay his hand on, and compelled his adversary to do the same. Strange spectacle in human life where it is the instinctive effort of one and all to hide those sad realities, and leave them undisturbed beneath a heap of superficial topics which constitute the materials of intercourse between man and man! It was not to be tolerated that Roderick

Elliston should break through the tacit compact by which the world has done its best to secure repose without relinquishing evil. The victims of his malicious remarks, it is true, had brothers enough to keep them in countenance; for, by Roder-Roderick's theory, every mortal bosom harbored either a brood of small serpents or one overgrown monster that had devoured all the rest. Still the city could not bear this new apostle. It was demanded by nearly all, and particularly by the most respectable inhabitants, that Roderick should no longer be permitted to violate the received rules of decorum by obtruding his own bosom serpent to the public gaze, and dragging those of decent people from their lurking places.

Accordingly, his relatives interfered and placed him in a private asylum for the insane. When the news was noised abroad, it was observed that many persons walked the streets with freer countenances and covered their breasts less carefully with their hands.

His confinement, however, although it contributed not a little to the peace of the town, operated unfavorably upon Roderick himself. In solitude his melancholy grew more black and sullen. He spent whole days—indeed, it was his sole occupation—in communing with the serpent. A conversation was sustained, in which, as it seemed, the hidden monster bore a part, though unintelligibly to the listeners, and inaudible except in a hiss. Singular as it may appear, the sufferer had now contracted a sort of affection for his tormentor, mingled, however, with the intensest loathing and horror. Nor were such discordant emotions incompatible. Each, on the contrary, imparted strength and poignancy to its opposite. Horrible love—horrible antipathy—embracing one another in his bosom, and both concentrating themselves upon a being that had crept into his vitals or been engendered there, and which was nourished with his food, and lived upon his life, and was as intimate with him as his own heart, and yet was the foulest of all created things! But not the less was it the true type of a morbid nature.

Sometimes, in his moments of rage and bitter hatred against the snake and himself, Roderick determined to be the death of him, even at the expense of his own life. Once he attempted it by starvation; but, while the wretched man was on the point of famishing, the monster seemed to feed upon his heart, and to thrive and wax gamesome, as if it were his sweetest and most congenial diet. Then he privily took a dose of active poison, imagining that it would not fail to kill either himself or the devil that possessed him, or both together. Another mistake; for if Roderick had not yet been destroyed by his own poisoned heart nor the snake by gnawing it, they had little to fear from arsenic or corrosive sublimate. Indeed, the venomous pest appeared to operate as an antidote against all other poisons. The physicians tried to suffocate the fiend with tobacco smoke. He breathed it as freely as if it were his native atmosphere. Again, they drugged their patient with opium and drenched him with intoxicating liquors, hoping that the snake might thus be reduced to stupor and perhaps be ejected from the stomach. They succeeded in rendering Roderick insensible; but, placing their hands upon his breast, they were inexpressibly horror stricken to feel the monster wriggling, twining, and darting to and fro within his narrow limits, evidently enlivened by the opium or alcohol, and incited to unusual feats of activity. Thenceforth they gave up all attempts at cure or palliation. The doomed sufferer submitted to his fate, resumed his former loathsome affection for the bosom fiend, and spent whole miserable days before a looking-glass, with his mouth wide open, watching, in hope and horror, to catch a glimpse of the snake's head far down within his throat. It is supposed that he succeeded; for the attendants once heard a frenzied shout, and, rushing into the room, found Roderick lifeless upon the floor.

He was kept but little longer under restraint. After minute investigation, the medical directors of the asylum decided that his mental disease did not amount to insanity, nor would warrant his confinement, especially as its influence upon his spirits was unfavorable, and might produce the evil which it was meant to remedy. His eccentricities were doubtless great; he had habitually violated many of the customs and prejudices of society; but the world was not, without surer ground, entitled to treat him as a madman. On this decision of such competent authority Roderick was released, and had returned to his native city the very day before his encounter with George Herkimer.

As soon as possible after learning these particulars the sculptor, together with a sad and tremulous companion, sought Elliston at his own house. It was a large, sombre edifice of wood, with pilasters and a balcony, and was divided from one of the principal streets by a terrace of three elevations, which was ascended by successive flights of stone steps. Some immense old elms almost concealed the front of the mansion. This spacious and once magnificent family residence was built by a grandee of the race early in the past century, at which epoch, land being of small comparative value, the garden and other grounds had formed quite an extensive domain. Although a portion of the ancestral heritage had been alienated, there was still a shadowy enclosure in the rear of the mansion where a student, or a dreamer, or a man of stricken heart might lie all day upon the grass, amid the solitude of murmuring boughs, and forget that a city had grown up around him.

Into this retirement the sculptor and his companion were ushered by Scipio, the old black servant, whose wrinkled visage grew almost sunny with intelligence and joy as he paid his humble greetings to one of the two visitors.

"Remain in the arbor," whispered the sculptor to the figure that leaned upon his arm. "You will know whether, and when, to make your appearance."

"God will teach me," was the reply. "May He support me too!"

Roderick was reclining on the margin of a fountain which gushed into the fleckered sunshine with the same clear sparkle and the same voice of airy quietude as when trees of primeval growth flung their shadows cross its bosom. How strange is the life of a fountain!—born at every moment, yet of an age coeval with the rocks, and far surpassing the venerable antiquity of a forest.

"You are come! I have expected you," said Elliston, when he became aware of the sculptor's presence.

His manner was very different from that of the preceding day—quiet, courteous, and, as Herkimer thought, watchful both over his guest and himself. This unnatural restraint was almost the only trait that betokened anything amiss. He had just thrown a book upon the grass, where it lay half opened, thus disclosing itself to be a natural history of the serpent tribe, illustrated by lifelike plates. Near it lay that bulky volume, the Ductor Dubitantium of Jeremy Taylor, full of cases of conscience, and in which most men, possessed of a conscience, may find something applicable to their purpose.

"You see," observed Elliston, pointing to the book of serpents, while a smile gleamed upon his lips, "I am making an effort to become better acquainted with my bosom friend; but I find nothing satisfactory in this volume. If I mistake not, he will prove to be sui generis, and akin to no other reptile in creation."

"Whence came this strange calamity?" inquired the sculptor.

"My sable friend Scipio has a story," replied Roderick, "of a snake that had lurked in this fountain—pure and innocent as it looks—ever since it was known to the first settlers. This insinuating personage once crept into the vitals of my great grandfather and dwelt there many years, tormenting the old gentleman beyond mortal endurance. In short it is a family peculiarity. But, to tell you the truth, I have no faith in this idea of the snake's being an heirloom. He is my own snake, and no'man's else."

"But what was his origin?" demanded Herkimer.

"Oh, there is poisonous stuff in any man's heart sufficient to generate a brood of serpents," said Elliston with a hollow laugh. "You should have heard my homilies to the good town's-people. Positively, I deem myself fortunate in having bred but a single serpent. You, however, have none in your bosom, and therefore cannot sympathize with the rest of the world. It gnaws me! It gnaws me!"

With this exclamation Roderick lost his self-control and threw himself upon the grass, testifying his agony by intricate writhings, in which Herkimer could not but fancy a resemblance to the motions of a snake. Then, likewise, was heard that frightful hiss, which often ran through the sufferer's speech, and crept between the words and syllables without interrupting their succession.

"This is awful indeed!" exclaimed the sculptor—"an awful infliction, whether it be actual or imaginary. Tell me, Roderick Elliston, is there any remedy for this loathsome evil?"

"Yes, but an impossible one," muttered Roderick, as he lay wallowing with his face in the grass. "Could I for one moment forget myself, the serpent might not abide within me. It is my diseased self-contemplation that has engendered and nourished him."

"Then forget yourself, my husband," said a gentle voice above him; "forget yourself in the idea of another!"

Rosina had emerged from the arbor, and was bending over him with the shadow of his anguish reflected in her countenance, yet so mingled with hope and unselfish love that all anguish seemed but an earthly shadow and a dream. She touched Roderick with her hand. A tremor shivered through his frame. At that moment, if report be trustworthy, the sculptor beheld a waving motion through the grass, and heard a tinkling sound, as if something had plunged into the fountain. Be the truth as it might, it is certain that Roderick Elliston sat up like a man renewed, restored to his right mind, and rescued from the fiend which had so miserably overcome him in the battle-field of his own breast.

"Rosina!" cried he, in broken and passionate tones, but with nothing of the wild wail that had haunted his voice so long, "forgive! forgive!"

Her happy tears bedewed his face.

"The punishment has been severe," observed the sculptor. "Even Justice might now forgive; how much more a woman's tenderness! Roderick Elliston, whether the serpent was a physical reptile, or whether the morbidness of your nature suggested that symbol to your fancy, the moral of the story is not the less true and strong. A tremendous Egotism, manifesting itself in your case in the form of jealousy, is as fearful a fiend as ever stole into the human heart. Can a breast, where it has dwelt so long, be purified?"

"Oh yes," said Rosina with a heavenly smile. "The serpent was but a dark fantasy, and what it typified was as shadowy as itself. The past, dismal as it seems, shall fling no gloom upon the future. To give it its due importance we must think of it but as an anecdote in our Eternity."

DROWNE'S WOODEN IMAGE

One sunshiny morning, in the good old times of the town of Boston, a young carver in wood, well known by the name of Drowne, stood contemplating a large oaken log, which it was his purpose to convert into the figure-head of a vessel. And while he discussed within his own mind what sort of shape or similitude it were well to bestow upon this excellent piece of timber, there came into Drowne's workshop a certain Captain Hunnewell, owner and commander of the good brig called the Cynosure, which had just returned from her first voyage to Fayal.

"Ah! that will do, Drowne, that will do!" cried the jolly captain, tapping the log with his rattan. "I bespeak this very piece of oak for the figure-head of the Cynosure. She has shown herself the sweetest craft that ever floated, and I mean to decorate her prow with the handsomest image that the skill of man can cut out of timber. And, Drowne, you are the fellow to execute it."

"You give me more credit than I deserve, Captain Hunnewell," said the carver, modestly, yet as one conscious of eminence in his art. "But, for the sake of the good brig, I stand ready to do my best. And which of these designs do you prefer? Here,"—pointing to a staring, half-length figure, in a white wig and scarlet coat,—"here is an excellent model, the likeness of our gracious king. Here is the valiant Admiral Vernon. Or, if you prefer a female figure, what say you to Britannia with the trident?"

"All very fine, Drowne; all very fine," answered the mariner. "But as nothing like the brig ever swam the ocean, so I am determined she shall have such a figure-head as old Neptune never saw in his life. And what is more, as there is a secret in the matter, you must pledge your credit not to betray it."

"Certainly," said Drowne, marvelling, however, what possible mystery there could be in reference to an affair so open, of necessity, to the inspection of all the world as the figure-head of a vessel. "You may depend, captain, on my being as secret as the nature of the case will permit."

Captain Hunnewell then took Drowne by the button, and communicated his wishes in so low a tone that it would be unmannerly to repeat what was evidently intended for the carver's private ear. We shall, therefore, take the opportunity to give the reader a few desirable particulars about Drowne himself.

He was the first American who is known to have attempted—in a very humble line, it is true—that art in which we can now reckon so many names already distinguished, or rising to distinction. From his earliest boyhood he had exhibited a knack—for it would be too proud a word to call it genius—a knack, therefore, for the imitation of the human figure in whatever material came most readily to hand. The snows of a New England winter had often supplied him with a species of marble as dazzingly white, at least, as the Parian or the Carrara, and if less durable, yet sufficiently so to correspond with any claims to permanent existence possessed by the boy's frozen statues. Yet they won admiration from maturer judges than his school-fellows, and were indeed, remarkably clever, though destitute of the native warmth that might have made the snow melt beneath his hand. As he advanced in life, the young man adopted pine and oak as eligible materials for the display of his skill, which now began to bring him a return of solid silver as well as the empty praise that had been an apt reward enough for his productions of evanescent snow. He became noted for carving ornamental pump heads, and wooden urns for gate posts, and decorations, more grotesque than fanciful, for mantelpieces. No apothecary would have deemed himself in the way of obtaining custom without setting up a gilded mortar, if not a head of Galen or Hippocrates, from the skilful hand of Drowne.

But the great scope of his business lay in the manufacture of figure-heads for vessels. Whether it were the monarch himself, or some famous British admiral or general, or the governor of the province, or perchance the favorite daughter of the ship-owner, there the image stood above the prow, decked out in gorgeous colors, magnificently gilded, and staring the whole world out of countenance, as if from an innate consciousness of its own superiority. These specimens of native sculpture had crossed the sea in all directions, and been not ignobly noticed among the crowded shipping of the Thames and wherever else the hardy mariners of New England had pushed their adventures. It must be confessed that a family likeness pervaded these respectable progeny of Drowne's skill; that the benign countenance of the king resembled those of his subjects, and that Miss Peggy Hobart, the merchant's daughter, bore a remarkable similitude to Britannia, Victory, and other ladies of the allegoric sisterhood; and, finally, that they all had a kind of wooden aspect which proved an intimate relationship with the unshaped blocks of timber in the carver's workshop. But at least there was no inconsiderable skill of hand, nor a deficiency of any attribute to render them really works of art, except that deep quality, be it of soul or intellect, which bestows life upon the lifeless and warmth upon the cold, and which, had it been present, would have made Drowne's wooden image instinct with spirit.

The captain of the Cynosure had now finished his instructions.

"And Drowne," said he, impressively, "you must lay aside all other business and set about this forthwith. And as to the price, only do the job in first-rate style, and you shall settle that point yourself."

"Very well, captain," answered the carver, who looked grave and somewhat perplexed, yet had a sort of smile upon his visage; "depend upon it, I'll do my utmost to satisfy you."

From that moment the men of taste about Long Wharf and the Town Dock who were wont to show their love for the arts by frequent visits to Drowne's workshop, and admiration of his wooden images, began to be sensible of a mystery in the carver's conduct. Often he was absent in the daytime. Sometimes, as might be judged by gleams of light from the shop windows, he was at work until a late hour of the evening; although neither knock nor voice, on such occasions, could gain admittance for a visitor, or elicit any word of response. Nothing remarkable, however, was observed in the shop at those late hours when it was thrown open. A fine piece of timber, indeed, which Drowne was known to have reserved for some work of especial dignity, was seen to be gradually assuming shape. What shape it was destined ultimately to take was a problem to his friends and a point on which the carver himself preserved a rigid silence. But day after day, though Drowne was seldom noticed in the act of working upon it, this rude form began to be developed until it became evident to all observers that a female figure was growing into mimic life. At each new visit they beheld a larger pile of wooden chips and a nearer approximation to something beautiful. It seemed as if the hamadryad of the oak had sheltered herself from the unimaginative world within the heart of her native tree, and that it was only necessary to remove the strange shapelessness that had incrusted her, and reveal the grace and loveliness of a divinity. Imperfect as the design, the attitude, the costume, and especially the face of the image still remained, there was already an effect that drew the eye from the wooden cleverness of Drowne's earlier productions and fixed it upon the tantalizing mystery of this new project.

Copley, the celebrated painter, then a young man and a resident of Boston, came one day to visit Drowne; for he had recognized so much of moderate ability in the carver as to induce him, in the dearth of professional sympathy, to cultivate his acquaintance. On entering the shop, the artist glanced at the inflexible image of king, commander, dame, and allegory, that stood around, on the best of which might have been bestowed the questionable praise that it looked as if a living man had here been changed to wood, and that not only the physical, but the intellectual and spiritual part, partook of the stolid transformation. But in not a single instance did it seem as if the wood were imbibing the ethereal essence of humanity. What a wide distinction is here! and how far the slightest portion of the latter merit have outvalued the utmost degree of the former!

"My friend Drowne;" said Copley, smiling to himself, but alluding to the mechanical and wooden cleverness that so invariably distinguished the images, "you are really a remarkable person! I have seldom met with a man in your line of business that could do so much; for one other touch might make this figure of General Wolfe, for instance, a breathing and intelligent human creature."

"You would have me think that you are praising me highly, Mr. Copley," answered Drowne, turning his back upon Wolfe's image in apparent disgust. "But there has come a light into my mind. I know what you know as well, that the one touch which you speak of as deficient is the only one that would be truly valuable, and that without it these works of mine are no better than worthless abortions.

There is the same difference between them and the works of an inspired artist as between a sign-post daub and one of your best pictures."

"This is strange," cried Copley, looking him in the face, which now, as the painter fancied, had a singular depth of intelligence, though hitherto it had not given him greatly the advantage over his own family of wooden images. "What has come over you? How is it that, possessing the idea which you have now uttered, you should produce only such works as these?"

The carver smiled, but made no reply. Copley turned again to the images, conceiving that the sense of deficiency which Drowne had just expressed, and which is so rare in a merely mechanical character, must surely imply a genius, the tokens of which had heretofore been overlooked. But no; there was not a trace of it. He was about to withdraw when his eyes chanced to fall upon a half-developed figure which lay in a corner of the workshop, surrounded by scattered chips of oak. It arrested him at once.

"What is here? Who has done this?" he broke out, after contemplating it in speechless astonishment for an instant. "Here is the divine, the lifegiving touch. What inspired hand is beckoning this wood to arise and live? Whose work is this?"

"No man's work," replied Drowne. "The figure lies within that block of oak, and it is my business to find it."

"Drowne," said the true artist, grasping the carver fervently by the hand, "you are a man of genius!"

As Copley departed, happening to glance backward from the threshold, he beheld Drowne bending over the half-created shape, and stretching forth his arms as if he would have embraced and drawn it to his heart; while, had such a miracle been possible, his countenance expressed passion enough to communicate warmth and sensibility to the lifeless oak.

"Strange enough!" said the artist to himself. "Who would have looked for a modern Pygmalion in the person of a Yankee mechanic!"

As yet, the image was but vague in its outward presentment; so that, as in the cloud shapes around the western sun, the observer rather felt, or was led to imagine, than really saw what was intended by it. Day by day, however, the work assumed greater precision, and settled its irregular and misty outline into distincter grace and beauty. The general design was now obvious to the common eye. It was a female figure, in what appeared to be a foreign dress; the gown being laced over the bosom, and opening in front so as to disclose a skirt or petticoat, the folds and inequalities of which were admirably represented in the oaken substance. She wore a hat of singular gracefulness, and abundantly laden with flowers, such as never grew in the rude soil of New England, but which, with all their fanciful luxuriance, had a natural truth that it seemed impossible for the most fertile imagination to have attained without copying from real prototypes. There were several little appendages to this dress, such as a fan, a pair of earrings, a chain about the neck, a watch in the bosom, and a ring upon the finger, all of which would have been deemed beneath the dignity of sculpture. They were put on, however, with as much taste as a lovely woman might have shown in her attire, and could therefore have shocked none but a judgment spoiled by artistic rules.

The face was still imperfect; but gradually, by a magic touch, intelligence and sensibility brightened through the features, with all the effect of light gleaming forth from within the solid oak. The face became alive. It was a beautiful, though not precisely regular and somewhat haughty aspect, but with a certain piquancy about the eyes and mouth, which, of all expressions, would have seemed the most impossible to throw over a wooden countenance. And now, so far as carving went, this wonderful production was complete.

"Drowne," said Copley, who had hardly missed a single day in his visits to the carver's workshop, "if this work were in marble it would make you famous at once; nay, I would almost affirm that it would make an era in the art. It is as ideal as an antique statue, and yet as real as any lovely woman whom one meets at a fireside or in the street. But I trust you do not mean to desecrate this exquisite creature with paint, like those staring kings and admirals yonder?"

"Not paint her!" exclaimed Captain Hunnewell, who stood by; "not paint the figure-head of the Cynosure! And what sort of a figure should I cut in a foreign port with such an unpainted oaken stick as this over my prow! She must, and she shall, be painted to the life, from the topmost flower in her hat down to the silver spangles on her slippers."

"Mr. Copley," said Drowne, quietly, "I know nothing of marble statuary, and nothing of the sculptor's rules of art; but of this wooden image, this work of my hands, this creature of my heart,"—and here his voice faltered and choked in a very singular manner,—"of this—of her—I may say that I know something. A well-spring of inward wisdom gushed within me as I wrought upon the oak with my whole strength, and soul, and faith. Let others do what they may with marble, and adopt what rules they choose. If I can produce my desired effect by painted wood, those rules are not for me, and I have a right to disregard them."

"The very spirit of genius," muttered Copley to himself. "How otherwise should this carver feel himself entitled to transcend all rules, and make me ashamed of quoting them?"

He looked earnestly at Drowne, and again saw that expression of human love which, in a spiritual sense, as the artist could not help imagining, was the secret of the life that had been breathed into this block of wood.

The carver, still in the same secrecy that marked all his operations upon this mysterious image, proceeded to paint the habiliments in their proper colors, and the countenance with Nature's red and white. When all was finished he threw open his workshop, and admitted the towns people to behold what he had done. Most persons, at their first entrance, felt impelled to remove their hats, and pay such reverence as was due to the richly-dressed and beautiful young lady who seemed to stand in a corner of the room, with oaken chips and shavings scattered at her feet. Then came a sensation of fear; as if, not being actually human, yet so like humanity, she must therefore be something preternatural. There was, in truth, an indefinable air and expression that might reasonably induce the query, Who and from what sphere this daughter of the oak should be? The strange, rich flowers of Eden on her head; the complexion, so much deeper and more brilliant than those of our native beauties; the foreign, as it seemed, and fantastic garb, yet not too fantastic to be worn decorously in the street; the delicately-wrought embroidery of the skirt; the broad gold chain about her neck; the curious ring upon her finger; the fan, so exquisitely sculptured in open work, and painted to resemble pearl and ebony;—where could Drowne, in his sober walk of life, have beheld the vision here so matchlessly embodied! And then her face! In the dark eyes, and around the voluptuous mouth, there played a look made up of pride, coquetry, and a gleam of mirthfulness, which impressed Copley with the idea that the image was secretly enjoying the perplexing admiration of himself and other beholders.

"And will you," said he to the carver, "permit this masterpiece to become the figure-head of a vessel? Give the honest captain yonder figure of Britannia—it will answer his purpose far better—and send this fairy queen to England, where, for aught I know, it may bring you a thousand pounds."

"I have not wrought it for money," said Drowne.

"What sort of a fellow is this!" thought Copley. "A Yankee, and throw away the chance of making his fortune! He has gone mad; and thence has come this gleam of genius."

There was still further proof of Drowne's lunacy, if credit were due to the rumor that he had been seen kneeling at the feet of the oaken lady, and gazing with a lover's passionate ardor into the face that his own hands had created. The bigots of the day hinted that it would be no matter of surprise if an evil spirit were allowed to enter this beautiful form, and seduce the carver to destruction.

The fame of the image spread far and wide. The inhabitants visited it so universally, that after a few days of exhibition there was hardly an old man or a child who had not become minutely familiar with its aspect. Even had the story of Drowne's wooden image ended here, its celebrity might have been prolonged for many years by the reminiscences of those who looked upon it in their childhood, and saw nothing else so beautiful in after life. But the town was now astounded by an event, the narrative of which has formed itself into one of the most singular legends that are yet to be met with in the traditionary chimney corners of the New England metropolis, where old men and women sit dreaming of the past, and wag their heads at the dreamers of the present and the future.

One fine morning, just before the departure of the Cynosure on her second voyage to Fayal, the commander of that gallant vessel was seen to issue from his residence in Hanover Street. He was stylishly dressed in a blue broadcloth coat, with gold lace at the seams and button-holes, an embroidered scarlet waistcoat, a triangular hat, with a loop and broad binding of gold, and wore a silver-hilted hanger at his side. But the good captain might have been arrayed in the robes of a prince or the rags of a beggar, without in either case attracting notice, while obscured by such a companion as now leaned on his arm. The people in the street started, rubbed their eyes, and either leaped aside from their path, or stood as if transfixed to wood or marble in astonishment.

"Do you see it?—do you see it?" cried one, with tremulous eagerness. "It is the very same!"

"The same?" answered another, who had arrived in town only the night before. "Who do you mean? I see only a sea-captain in his shoregoing clothes, and a young lady in a foreign habit, with a bunch of beautiful flowers in her hat. On my word, she is as fair and bright a damsel as my eyes have looked on this many a day!"

"Yes; the same!—the very same!" repeated the other. "Drowne's wooden image has come to life!"

Here was a miracle indeed! Yet, illuminated by the sunshine, or darkened by the alternate shade of the houses, and with its garments fluttering lightly in the morning breeze, there passed the image along the street. It was exactly and minutely the shape, the garb, and the face which the towns-people had so recently thronged to see and admire. Not a rich flower upon her head, not a single leaf, but had had its prototype in Drowne's wooden workmanship, although now their fragile grace had become flexible, and was shaken by every footstep that the wearer made. The broad gold chain upon the neck was identical with the one represented on the image, and glistened with the motion imparted by the rise and fall of the bosom which it decorated. A real diamond sparkled on her finger. In her right hand she bore a pearl and ebony fan, which she flourished with a fantastic and bewitching coquetry, that was likewise expressed in all her movements as well as in the style of her beauty and the attire that so well harmonized with it. The face with its brilliant depth of complexion had the same piquancy of mirthful mischief that was fixed upon the countenance of the image, but which was here varied and continually shifting, yet always essentially the same, like the sunny gleam upon a bubbling fountain. On the whole, there was something so airy and yet so real in the figure, and withal so perfectly did it represent Drowne's image, that people knew not whether to suppose the magic wood etherealized into a spirit or warmed and softened into an actual woman.

"One thing is certain," muttered a Puritan of the old stamp, "Drowne has sold himself to the devil; and doubtless this gay Captain Hunnewell is a party to the bargain."

"And I," said a young man who overheard him, "would almost consent to be the third victim, for the liberty of saluting those lovely lips."

"And so would I," said Copley, the painter, "for the privilege of taking her picture."

The image, or the apparition, whichever it might be, still escorted by the bold captain, proceeded from Hanover Street through some of the cross lanes that make this portion of the town so intricate, to Ann Street, thence into Dock Square, and so downward to Drowne's shop, which stood just on the water's edge. The crowd still followed, gathering volume as it rolled along. Never had a modern miracle occurred in such broad daylight, nor in the presence of such a multitude of witnesses. The airy image, as if conscious that she was the object of the murmurs and disturbance that swelled behind her, appeared slightly vexed and flustered, yet still in a manner consistent with the light vivacity and sportive mischief that were written in her countenance. She was observed to flutter her fan with such vehement rapidity that the elaborate delicacy of its workmanship gave way, and it remained broken in her hand.

Arriving at Drowne's door, while the captain threw it open, the marvellous apparition paused an instant on the threshold, assuming the very attitude of the image, and casting over the crowd that glance of sunny coquetry which all remembered on the face of the oaken lady. She and her cavalier then disappeared.

"Ah!" murmured the crowd, drawing a deep breath, as with one vast pair of lungs.

"The world looks darker now that she has vanished," said some of the young men.

But the aged, whose recollections dated as far back as witch times, shook their heads, and hinted that our forefathers would have thought it a pious deed to burn the daughter of the oak with fire.

"If she be other than a bubble of the elements," exclaimed Copley, "I must look upon her face again."

He accordingly entered the shop; and there, in her usual corner, stood the image, gazing at him, as it might seem, with the very same expression of mirthful mischief that had been the farewell look of the apparition when, but a moment before, she turned her face towards the crowd. The carver stood beside his creation mending the beautiful fan, which by some accident was broken in her hand. But there was no longer any motion in the lifelike image, nor any real woman in the workshop, nor even the witchcraft of a sunny shadow, that might have deluded people's eyes as it flitted along the street. Captain Hunnewell, too, had vanished. His hoarse sea-breezy tones, however, were audible on the other side of a door that opened upon the water.

"Sit down in the stern sheets, my lady," said the gallant captain. "Come, bear a hand, you lubbers, and set us on board in the turning of a minute-glass."

And then was heard the stroke of oars.

"Drowne," said Copley with a smile of intelligence, "you have been a truly fortunate man. What painter or statuary ever had such a subject! No wonder that she inspired a genius into you, and first created the artist who afterwards created her image."

Drowne looked at him with a visage that bore the traces of tears, but from which the light of imagination and sensibility, so recently illuminating it, had departed. He was again the mechanical carver that he had been known to be all his lifetime.

"I hardly understand what you mean, Mr. Copley," said he, putting his hand to his brow. "This image! Can it have been my work? Well, I have wrought it in a kind of dream; and now that I am broad awake I must set about finishing yonder figure of Admiral Vernon."

And forthwith he employed himself on the stolid countenance of one of his wooden progeny, and completed it in his own mechanical style, from which he was never known afterwards to deviate. He followed his business industriously for many years, acquired a competence, and in the latter part of his life attained to a dignified station in the church, being remembered in records and traditions as Deacon Drowne, the carver. One of his productions, an Indian chief, gilded all over, stood during the better part of a century on the cupola of the Province House, bedazzling the eyes of those who looked upward, like an angel of the sun. Another work of the good deacon's hand—a reduced likeness of his friend Captain Hunnewell, holding a telescope and quadrant—may be seen to this day, at the corner of Broad and State streets, serving in the useful capacity of sign to the shop of a nautical instrument maker. We know not how to account for the inferiority of this quaint old figure, as compared with the recorded excellence of the Oaken Lady, unless on the supposition that in every human spirit there is imagination, sensibility, creative power, genius, which, according to circumstances, may either be developed in this world, or shrouded in a mask of dulness until another state of being. To our friend Drowne there came a brief season of excitement, kindled by love. It rendered him a genius for that one occasion, but, quenched in disappointment, left him again the mechanical carver in wood, without the power even of appreciating the work that his own hands had wrought. Yet who can doubt that the very highest state to which a human spirit can attain, in its loftiest aspirations, is its truest and most natural state, and that Drowne was more consistent with himself when he wrought the admirable figure of the mysterious lady, than when he perpetrated a whole progeny of blockheads?

There was a rumor in Boston, about this period, that a young Portuguese lady of rank, on some occasion of political or domestic disquietude, had fled from her home in Fayal and put herself under the protection of Captain Hunnewell, on board of whose vessel, and at whose residence, she was sheltered until a change of affairs. This fair stranger must have been the original of Drowne's Wooden Image.

ROGER MALVIN'S BURIAL

One of the few incidents of Indian warfare naturally susceptible of the moonlight of romance was that expedition undertaken for the defence of the frontiers in the year 1725, which resulted in the well-remembered "Lovell's Fight." Imagination, by casting certain circumstances judicially into the shade, may see much to admire in the heroism of a little band who gave battle to twice their number in the heart of the enemy's country. The open bravery displayed by both parties was in accordance with civilized ideas of valor; and chivalry itself might not blush to record the deeds of one or two individuals. The battle, though so fatal to those who fought, was not unfortunate in its consequences to the country; for it broke the strength of a tribe and conduced to the peace which subsisted during several ensuing years. History and tradition are unusually minute in their memorials of their affair; and the captain of a scouting party of frontier men has acquired as actual a military renown as many a victorious leader of thousands. Some of the incidents contained in the following pages will be recognized, notwithstanding the substitution of fictitious names, by such as have heard, from old men's lips, the fate of the few combatants who were in a condition to retreat after "Lovell's Fight."

The early sunbeams hovered cheerfully upon the tree-tops, beneath which two weary and wounded men had stretched their limbs the night before. Their bed of withered oak leaves was strewn upon the small level space, at the foot of a rock, situated near the summit of one of the gentle swells by which the face of the country is there diversified. The mass of granite, rearing its smooth, flat surface fifteen or twenty feet above their heads, was not unlike a gigantic gravestone, upon which the veins seemed to form an inscription in forgotten characters. On a tract of several acres around this rock, oaks and other hard-wood trees had supplied the place of the pines, which were the usual growth of the land; and a young and vigorous sapling stood close beside the travellers.

The severe wound of the elder man had probably deprived him of sleep; for, so soon as the first ray of sunshine rested on the top of the highest tree, he reared himself painfully from his recumbent posture and sat erect. The deep lines of his countenance and the scattered gray of his hair marked him as past the middle age; but his muscular frame would, but for the effect of his wound, have been as capable of sustaining fatigue as in the early vigor of life. Languor and exhaustion now sat upon his haggard features; and the despairing glance which he sent forward through the depths of the forest proved his own conviction that his pilgrimage was at an end. He next turned his eyes to the companion who reclined by his side. The youth—for he had scarcely attained the years of manhood—lay, with his head upon his arm, in the embrace of an unquiet sleep, which a thrill of pain from his wounds seemed each moment on the point of breaking. His right hand grasped a musket; and, to judge from the violent action of his features, his slumbers were bringing back a vision of the conflict of which he was one of the few survivors. A shout deep and loud in his dreaming fancy—found its way in an imperfect murmur to his lips; and, starting even at the slight sound of his own voice, he suddenly awoke. The first act of reviving recollection was to make anxious inquiries respecting the condition of his wounded fellow-traveller. The latter shook his head.

"Reuben, my boy," said he, "this rock beneath which we sit will serve for an old hunter's gravestone. There is many and many a long mile of howling wilderness before us yet; nor would it avail me anything if the smoke of my own chimney were but on the other side of that swell of land. The Indian bullet was deadlier than I thought."

"You are weary with our three days' travel," replied the youth, "and a little longer rest will recruit you. Sit you here while I search the woods for the herbs and roots that must be our sustenance; and, having eaten, you shall lean on me, and we will turn our faces homeward. I doubt not that, with my help, you can attain to some one of the frontier garrisons."

"There is not two days' life in me, Reuben," said the other, calmly, "and I will no longer burden you with my useless body, when you can scarcely support your own. Your wounds are deep and your strength is failing fast; yet, if you hasten onward alone, you may be preserved. For me there is no hope, and I will await death here."

"If it must be so, I will remain and watch by you," said Reuben, resolutely.

"No, my son, no," rejoined his companion. "Let the wish of a dying man have weight with you; give me one grasp of your hand, and get you hence. Think you that my last moments will be eased by the thought that I leave you to die a more lingering death? I have loved you like a father, Reuben; and at a time like this I should have something of a father's authority. I charge you to be gone that I may die in peace."

"And because you have been a father to me, should I therefore leave you to perish and to lie unburied in the wilderness?" exclaimed the youth. "No; if your end be in truth approaching, I will watch by you and receive your parting words. I will dig a grave here by the rock, in which, if my weakness overcome me, we will rest together; or, if Heaven gives me strength, I will seek my way home."

"In the cities and wherever men dwell," replied the other, "they bury their dead in the earth; they hide them from the sight of the living; but here, where no step may pass perhaps for a hundred years, wherefore should I not rest beneath the open sky, covered only by the oak leaves when the autumn winds shall strew them? And for a monument, here is this gray rock, on which my dying hand shall carve the name of Roger Malvin, and the traveller in days to come will know that here sleeps a hunter and a warrior. Tarry not, then, for a folly like this, but hasten away, if not for your own sake, for hers who will else be desolate."

Malvin spoke the last few words in a faltering voice, and their effect upon his companion was strongly visible. They reminded him that there were other and less questionable duties than that of sharing the fate of a man whom his death could not benefit. Nor can it be affirmed that no selfish feeling strove to enter Reuben's heart, though the consciousness made him more earnestly resist his companion's entreaties.

"How terrible to wait the slow approach of death in this solitude!" exclaimed he. "A brave man does not shrink in the battle; and, when friends stand round the bed, even women may die composedly; but here—"

"I shall not shrink even here, Reuben Bourne," interrupted Malvin. "I am a man of no weak heart, and, if I were, there is a surer support than that of earthly friends. You are young, and life is dear to you. Your last moments will need comfort far more than mine; and when you have laid me in the earth, and are alone, and night is settling on the forest, you will feel all the bitterness of the death that may now be escaped. But I will urge no selfish motive to your generous nature. Leave me for my sake, that, having said a prayer for your safety, I may have space to settle my account undisturbed by worldly sorrows."

"And your daughter,—how shall I dare to meet her eye?" exclaimed Reuben. "She will ask the fate of her father, whose life I vowed to defend with my own. Must I tell her that he travelled three days' march with me from the field of battle and that then I left him to perish in the wilderness? Were it not better to lie down and die by your side than to return safe and say this to Dorcas?"

"Tell my daughter," said Roger Malvin, "that, though yourself sore wounded, and weak, and weary, you led my tottering footsteps many a mile, and left me only at my earnest entreaty, because I would not have your blood upon my soul. Tell her that through pain and danger you were faithful, and that, if your lifeblood could have saved me, it would have flowed to its last drop; and tell her that you will be something dearer than a father, and that my blessing is with you both, and that my dying eyes can see a long and pleasant path in which you will journey together."

As Malvin spoke he almost raised himself from the ground, and the energy of his concluding words seemed to fill the wild and lonely forest with a vision of happiness; but, when he sank exhausted upon his bed of oak leaves, the light which had kindled in Reuben's eye was quenched. He felt as if it were both sin and folly to think of happiness at such a moment. His companion watched his changing countenance, and sought with generous art to wile him to his own good.

"Perhaps I deceive myself in regard to the time I have to live," he resumed. "It may be that, with speedy assistance, I might recover of my wound. The foremost fugitives must, ere this, have carried tidings of our fatal battle to the frontiers, and parties will be out to succor those in like condition with ourselves. Should you meet one of these and guide them hither, who can tell but that I may sit by my own fireside again?"

A mournful smile strayed across the features of the dying man as he insinuated that unfounded hope,—which, however, was not without its effect on Reuben. No merely selfish motive, nor even the desolate condition of Dorcas, could have induced him to desert his companion at such a moment—but his wishes seized on the thought that Malvin's life might be preserved, and his sanguine nature heightened almost to certainty the remote possibility of procuring human aid.

"Surely there is reason, weighty reason, to hope that friends are not far distant," he said, half aloud. "There fled one coward, unwounded, in the beginning of the fight, and most probably he made good speed. Every true man on the frontier would shoulder his musket at the news; and, though no party may range so far into the woods as this, I shall perhaps encounter them in one day's march. Counsel me faithfully," he added, turning to Malvin, in distrust of his own motives. "Were your situation mine, would you desert me while life remained?"

"It is now twenty years," replied Roger Malvin,—sighing, however, as he secretly acknowledged the wide dissimilarity between the two cases,-"it is now twenty years since I escaped with one dear friend from Indian captivity near Montreal. We journeyed many days through the woods, till at length overcome with hunger and weariness, my friend lay down and besought me to leave him; for he knew that, if I remained, we both must perish; and, with but little hope of obtaining succor, I heaped a pillow of dry leaves beneath his head and hastened on."

"And did you return in time to save him?" asked Reuben, hanging on Malvin's words as if they were to be prophetic of his own success.

"I did," answered the other. "I came upon the camp of a hunting party before sunset of the same day. I guided them to the spot where my comrade was expecting death; and he is now a hale and hearty man upon his own farm, far within the frontiers, while I lie wounded here in the depths of the wilderness."

This example, powerful in affecting Reuben's decision, was aided, unconsciously to himself, by the hidden strength of many another motive. Roger Malvin perceived that the victory was nearly won.

"Now, go, my son, and Heaven prosper you!" he said. "Turn not back with your friends when you meet them, lest your wounds and weariness overcome you; but send hitherward two or three, that may be spared, to search for me; and believe me, Reuben, my heart will be lighter with every step you take towards home." Yet there was, perhaps, a change both in his countenance and voice as he spoke thus; for, after all, it was a ghastly fate to be left expiring in the wilderness.

Reuben Bourne, but half convinced that he was acting rightly, at length raised himself from the ground and prepared himself for his departure. And first, though contrary to Malvin's wishes, he collected a stock of roots and herbs, which had been their only food during the last two days. This useless supply he placed within reach of the dying man, for whom, also, he swept together a bed of dry oak leaves. Then climbing to the summit of the rock, which on one side was rough and broken, he bent the oak sapling downward, and bound his handkerchief to the topmost branch. This precaution was not unnecessary to direct any who might come in search of Malvin; for every part of the rock, except its broad, smooth front, was concealed at a little distance by the dense undergrowth of the forest. The handkerchief had been the bandage of a wound upon Reuben's arm; and, as he bound it to the tree, he vowed by the blood that stained it that he would return, either to save his companion's life or to lay his body in the grave. He then descended, and stood, with downcast eyes, to receive Roger Malvin's parting words.

The experience of the latter suggested much and minute advice respecting the youth's journey through the trackless forest. Upon this subject he spoke with calm earnestness, as if he were sending Reuben to the battle or the chase while he himself remained secure at home, and not as if the human countenance that was about to leave him were the last he would ever behold. But his firmness was shaken before he concluded.

"Carry my blessing to Dorcas, and say that my last prayer shall be for her and you. Bid her to have no hard thoughts because you left me here,"—Reuben's heart smote him,—"for that your life would not have weighed with you if its sacrifice could have done me good. She will marry you after she has mourned a little while for her father; and Heaven grant you long and happy days, and may your children's children stand round your death bed! And, Reuben," added he, as the weakness of mortality made its way at last, "return, when your wounds are healed and your weariness refreshed,—return to this wild rock, and lay my bones in the grave, and say a prayer over them."

An almost superstitious regard, arising perhaps from the customs of the Indians, whose war was with the dead as well as the living, was paid by the frontier inhabitants to the rites of sepulture; and there are many instances of the sacrifice of life in the attempt to bury those who had fallen by the "sword of the wilderness." Reuben, therefore, felt the full importance of the promise which he most solemnly made to return and perform Roger Malvin's obsequies. It was remarkable that the latter, speaking his whole heart in his parting words, no longer endeavored to persuade the youth that even the speediest succor might avail to the preservation of his life. Reuben was internally convinced that he should see Malvin's living face no more. His generous nature would fain have delayed him, at whatever risk, till the dying scene were past; but the desire of existence and the hope of happiness had strengthened in his heart, and he was unable to resist them.

"It is enough," said Roger Malvin, having listened to Reuben's promise. "Go, and God speed you!"

The youth pressed his hand in silence, turned, and was departing. His slow and faltering steps, however, had borne him but a little way before Malvin's voice recalled him.

"Reuben, Reuben," said he, faintly; and Reuben returned and knelt down by the dying man.

"Raise me, and let me lean against the rock," was his last request. "My face will be turned towards home, and I shall see you a moment longer as you pass among the trees."

Reuben, having made the desired alteration in his companion's posture, again began his solitary pilgrimage. He walked more hastily at first than was consistent with his strength; for a sort of guilty feeling, which sometimes torments men in their most justifiable acts, caused him to seek concealment from Malvin's eyes; but after he had trodden far upon the rustling forest leaves he crept back, impelled by a wild and painful curiosity, and, sheltered by the earthy roots of an uptorn tree, gazed earnestly at the desolate man. The morning sun was unclouded, and the trees and shrubs imbibed the sweet air of the month of May; yet there seemed a gloom on Nature's face, as if she sympathized with mortal pain and sorrow Roger Malvin's hands were uplifted in a fervent prayer, some of the words of which stole through the stillness of the woods and entered Reuben's heart, torturing it with an unutterable pang. They were the broken accents of a petition for his own happiness and that of Dorcas; and, as the youth listened, conscience, or something in its similitude, pleaded strongly with him to return and lie down again by the rock. He felt how hard was the doom of the kind and generous being whom he had deserted in his extremity. Death would come like the slow approach of a corpse, stealing gradually towards him through the forest, and showing its ghastly and motionless features from behind a nearer and yet a nearer tree. But such must have been Reuben's own fate had he tarried another sunset; and who shall impute blame to him if he shrink from so useless a sacrifice? As he gave a parting look, a breeze waved the little banner upon the sapling oak and reminded Reuben of his vow.

Many circumstances combined to retard the wounded traveller in his way to the frontiers. On the second day the clouds, gathering densely over the sky, precluded the possibility of regulating his course by the position of the sun; and he knew not but that every effort of his almost exhausted strength was removing him farther from the home he sought. His scanty sustenance was supplied by the berries and other spontaneous products of the forest. Herds of deer, it is true, sometimes bounded past him, and partridges frequently whirred up before his footsteps; but his ammunition had been expended in the fight, and he had no means of slaying them. His wounds, irritated by the constant exertion in which lay the only hope of life, wore away his strength and at intervals confused his reason. But, even in the wanderings of intellect, Reuben's young heart clung strongly to existence; and it was only through absolute incapacity of motion that he at last sank down beneath a tree, compelled there to await death.

In this situation he was discovered by a party who, upon the first intelligence of the fight, had been despatched to the relief of the survivors. They conveyed him to the nearest settlement, which chanced to be that of his own residence.

Dorcas, in the simplicity of the olden time, watched by the bedside of her wounded lover, and administered all those comforts that are in the sole gift of woman's heart and hand. During several days Reuben's recollection strayed drowsily among the perils and hardships through which he had passed, and he was incapable of returning definite answers to the inquiries with which many were eager to harass him. No authentic particulars of the battle had yet been circulated; nor could mothers, wives, and children tell whether their loved ones were detained by captivity or by the stronger chain of death. Dorcas nourished her apprehensions in silence till one afternoon when Reuben awoke from an unquiet sleep, and seemed to recognize her more perfectly than at any previous time. She saw that his intellect had become composed, and she could no longer restrain her filial anxiety.

"My father, Reuben?" she began; but the change in her lover's countenance made her pause.

The youth shrank as if with a bitter pain, and the blood gushed vividly into his wan and hollow cheeks. His first impulse was to cover his face; but, apparently with a desperate effort, he half raised himself and spoke vehemently, defending himself against an imaginary accusation.

"Your father was sore wounded in the battle, Dorcas; and he bade me not burden myself with him, but only to lead him to the lakeside, that he might quench his thirst and die. But I would not desert the old man in his extremity, and, though bleeding myself, I supported him; I gave him half my strength, and led him away with me. For three days we journeyed on together, and your father was sustained beyond my hopes, but, awaking at sunrise on the fourth day, I found him faint and exhausted; he was unable to proceed; his life had ebbed away fast; and—"

"He died!" exclaimed Dorcas, faintly.

Reuben felt it impossible to acknowledge that his selfish love of life had hurried him away before her father's fate was decided. He spoke not; he only bowed his head; and, between shame and exhaustion, sank back and hid his face in the pillow. Dorcas wept when her fears were thus confirmed; but the shock, as it had been long anticipated, was on that account the less violent.

"You dug a grave for my poor father in the wilderness, Reuben?" was the question by which her filial piety manifested itself.

"My hands were weak; but I did what I could," replied the youth in a smothered tone. "There stands a noble tombstone above his head; and I would to Heaven I slept as soundly as he!"

Dorcas, perceiving the wildness of his latter words, inquired no further at the time; but her heart found ease in the thought that Roger Malvin had not lacked such funeral rites as it was possible to bestow. The tale of Reuben's courage and fidelity lost nothing when she communicated it to her friends; and the poor youth, tottering from his sick chamber to breathe the sunny air, experienced from every tongue the miserable and humiliating torture of unmerited praise. All acknowledged that he might worthily demand the hand of the fair maiden to whose father he had been "faithful unto death;" and, as my tale is not of love, it shall suffice to say that in the space of a few months Reuben became the husband of Dorcas Malvin. During the marriage ceremony the bride was covered with blushes, but the bridegroom's face was pale.

There was now in the breast of Reuben Bourne an incommunicable thought—something which he was to conceal most heedfully from her whom he most loved and trusted. He regretted, deeply and bitterly, the moral cowardice that had restrained his words when he was about to disclose the truth to Dorcas; but pride, the fear of losing her affection, the dread of universal scorn, forbade him to rectify this falsehood. He felt that for leaving Roger Malvin he deserved no censure. His presence, the gratuitous sacrifice of his own life, would have added only another and a needless agony to the last moments of the dying man; but concealment had imparted to a justifiable act much of the secret effect of guilt; and Reuben, while reason told him that he had done right, experienced in no small degree the mental horrors which punish the perpetrator of undiscovered crime. By a certain association of ideas, he at times almost imagined himself a murderer. For years, also, a thought would occasionally recur, which, though he perceived all its folly and extravagance, he had not power to banish from his mind. It was a haunting and torturing fancy that his father-in-law was yet sitting at the foot of the rock, on the withered forest leaves, alive, and awaiting his pledged assistance. These mental deceptions, however, came and went, nor did he ever mistake them for realities: but in the calmest and clearest moods of his mind he was conscious that he had a deep vow unredeemed, and that an unburied corpse was calling to him out of the wilderness. Yet such was the consequence of his prevarication that he could not obey the call. It was now too late to require the assistance of Roger Malvin's friends in performing his long-deferred sepulture; and superstitious fears, of which none were more susceptible than the people of the outward settlements, forbade Reuben to go alone. Neither did he know where in the pathless and illimitable forest to seek that smooth and lettered rock at the base of which the body lay: his remembrance of every portion of his travel thence was indistinct, and the latter part had left no impression upon his mind. There was, however, a continual impulse, a voice audible only to himself, commanding him to go forth and redeem his vow; and he had a strange impression that, were he to make the trial, he would be led straight to Malvin's bones. But year after year that summons, unheard but felt, was disobeyed. His one secret thought became like a chain binding down his spirit and like a serpent gnawing into his heart; and he was transformed into a sad and downcast yet irritable man.

In the course of a few years after their marriage changes began to be visible in the external prosperity of Reuben and Dorcas. The only riches of the former had been his stout heart and strong arm; but the latter, her father's sole heiress, had made her husband master of a farm, under older cultivation, larger, and better stocked than most of the frontier establishments. Reuben Bourne, however, was a neglectful husbandman; and, while the lands of the other settlers became annually more fruitful, his deteriorated in the same proportion. The discouragements to agriculture were greatly lessened by the cessation of Indian war, during which men held the plough in one hand and the musket in the other, and were fortunate if the products of their dangerous labor were not destroyed, either in the field or in the barn, by the savage enemy. But Reuben did not profit by the altered condition of the country; nor can it be denied that his intervals of industrious attention to his affairs were but scantily rewarded with success. The irritability by which he had recently become distinguished was another cause of his declining prosperity, as it occasioned frequent quarrels in his unavoidable intercourse with the neighboring settlers. The results of these were innumerable lawsuits; for the people of New England, in the earliest stages and wildest circumstances of the country, adopted, whenever attainable, the legal mode of deciding their differences. To be brief, the world did not go well with Reuben Bourne; and, though not till many years after his marriage, he was finally a ruined man, with but one remaining expedient against the evil fate that had pursued him. He was to throw sunlight into some deep recess of the forest, and seek subsistence from the virgin bosom of the wilderness.

The only child of Reuben and Dorcas was a son, now arrived at the age of fifteen years, beautiful in youth, and giving promise of a glorious manhood. He was peculiarly qualified for, and already began to excel in, the wild accomplishments of frontier life. His foot was fleet, his aim true, his apprehension quick, his heart glad and high; and all who anticipated the return of Indian war spoke of Cyrus Bourne as a future leader in the land. The boy was loved by his father with a deep and silent strength, as if whatever was good and happy in his own nature had been transferred to his child, carrying his affections with it. Even Dorcas, though loving and beloved, was far less dear to him; for Reuben's secret thoughts and insulated emotions had gradually made him a selfish man, and he could no longer love deeply except where he saw or imagined some reflection or likeness of his own mind. In Cyrus he recognized what he had himself been in other days; and at intervals he seemed to partake of the boy's spirit, and to be revived with a fresh and happy life. Reuben was accompanied by his son in the expedition, for the purpose of selecting a tract of land and felling and burning the timber, which necessarily preceded the removal of the household gods. Two months of autumn were thus occupied, after which Reuben Bourne and his young hunter returned to spend their last winter in the settlements.

It was early in the month of May that the little family snapped asunder whatever tendrils of affections had clung to inanimate objects, and bade farewell to the few who, in the blight of fortune, called themselves their friends. The sadness of the parting moment had, to each of the pilgrims, its peculiar alleviations. Reuben, a moody man, and misanthropic because unhappy, strode onward with his usual stern brow and downcast eye, feeling few regrets and disdaining to acknowledge any. Dorcas, while she wept abundantly over the broken ties by which her simple and affectionate nature had bound itself to everything, felt that the inhabitants of her inmost heart moved on with her, and that all else would be supplied wherever she might go. And the boy dashed one tear-drop from his eye, and thought of the adventurous pleasures of the untrodden forest.

Oh, who, in the enthusiasm of a daydream, has not wished that he were a wanderer in a world of summer wilderness, with one fair and gentle being hanging lightly on his arm? In youth his free and exulting step would know no barrier but the rolling ocean or the snow-topped mountains; calmer manhood would choose a home where Nature had strewn a double wealth in the vale of some transparent stream; and when hoary age, after long, long years of that pure life, stole on and found him there, it would find him the father of a race, the patriarch of a people, the founder of a mighty nation yet to be. When death, like the sweet sleep which we welcome after a day of happiness, came over him, his far descendants would mourn over the venerated dust. Enveloped by tradition in mysterious attributes, the men of future generations would call him godlike; and remote posterity would see him standing, dimly glorious, far up the valley of a hundred centuries.

The tangled and gloomy forest through which the personages of my tale were wandering differed widely from the dreamer's land of fantasy; yet there was something in their way of life that Nature asserted as her own, and the gnawing cares which went with them from the world were all that now obstructed their happiness. One stout and shaggy steed, the bearer of all their wealth, did not shrink from the added weight of Dorcas; although her hardy breeding sustained her, during the latter part of each day's journey, by her husband's side. Reuben and his son, their muskets on their shoulders and their axes slung behind them, kept an unwearied pace, each watching with a hunter's eye for the game that supplied their food. When hunger bade, they halted and prepared their meal on the bank of some unpolluted forest brook, which, as they knelt down with thirsty lips to drink, murmured a sweet unwillingness, like a maiden at love's first kiss. They slept beneath a hut of branches, and awoke at peep of light refreshed for the toils of another day. Dorcas and the boy went on joyously, and even Reuben's spirit shone at intervals with an outward gladness; but inwardly there was a cold cold sorrow, which he compared to the snowdrifts lying deep in the glens and hollows of the rivulets while the leaves were brightly green above.

Cyrus Bourne was sufficiently skilled in the travel of the woods to observe that his father did not adhere to the course they had pursued in their expedition of the preceding autumn. They were now keeping farther to the north, striking out more directly from the settlements, and into a region of which savage beasts and savage men were as yet the sole possessors. The boy sometimes hinted his opinions upon the subject, and Reuben listened attentively, and once or twice altered the direction of their march in accordance with his son's counsel; but, having so done, he seemed ill at ease. His quick and wandering glances were sent forward apparently in search of enemies lurking behind the tree trunks, and, seeing nothing there, he would cast his eyes backwards as if in fear of some pursuer. Cyrus, perceiving that his father gradually resumed the old direction, forbore to interfere; nor, though something began to weigh upon his heart, did his adventurous nature permit him to regret the increased length and the mystery of their way.

On the afternoon of the fifth day they halted, and made their simple encampment nearly an hour before sunset. The face of the country, for the last few miles, had been diversified by swells of land resembling huge waves of a petrified sea; and in one of the corresponding hollows, a wild and romantic spot, had the family reared their hut and kindled their fire. There is something chilling, and yet heart-warming, in the thought of these three, united by strong bands of love and insulated from all that breathe beside. The dark and gloomy pines looked down upon them, and, as the wind swept through their tops, a pitying sound was heard in the forest; or did those old trees groan in fear that men were come to lay the axe to their roots at last? Reuben and his son, while Dorcas made ready their meal, proposed to wander out in search of game, of which that day's march had afforded no supply. The boy, promising not to quit the vicinity of the encampment, bounded off with a step as light and elastic as that of the deer he hoped to slay; while his father, feeling a transient happiness as he gazed after him, was about to pursue an opposite direction. Dorcas in the meanwhile, had seated herself near their fire of fallen branches upon the mossgrown and mouldering trunk of a tree uprooted years before. Her employment, diversified by an occasional glance at the pot, now beginning to simmer over the blaze, was the perusal of the current year's Massachusetts Almanac, which, with the exception of an old black-letter Bible, comprised all the literary wealth of the family. None pay a greater regard to arbitrary divisions of time than those who are excluded from society; and Dorcas mentioned, as if the information were of importance, that it was now the twelfth of May. Her husband started.

"The twelfth of May! I should remember it well," muttered he, while many thoughts occasioned a momentary confusion in his mind. "Where am I? Whither am I wandering? Where did I leave him?"

Dorcas, too well accustomed to her husband's wayward moods to note any peculiarity of demeanor, now laid aside the almanac and addressed him in that mournful tone which the tender hearted appropriate to griefs long cold and dead.

"It was near this time of the month, eighteen years ago, that my poor father left this world for a better. He had a kind arm to hold his head and a kind voice to cheer him, Reuben, in his last moments; and the thought of the faithful care you took of him has comforted me many a time since. Oh, death would have been awful to a solitary man in a wild place like this!"

"Pray Heaven, Dorcas," said Reuben, in a broken voice,—"pray Heaven that neither of us three dies solitary and lies unburied in this howling wilderness!" And he hastened away, leaving her to watch the fire beneath the gloomy pines.

Reuben Bourne's rapid pace gradually slackened as the pang, unintentionally inflicted by the words of Dorcas, became less acute. Many strange reflections, however, thronged upon him; and, straying onward rather like a sleep walker than a hunter, it was attributable to no care of his own that his devious course kept him in the vicinity of the encampment. His steps were imperceptibly led almost in a circle; nor did he observe that he was on the verge of a tract of land heavily timbered, but not with pine-trees. The place of the latter was here supplied by oaks and other of the harder woods; and around their roots clustered a dense and bushy under-growth, leaving, however, barren spaces between the trees, thick strewn with withered leaves. Whenever the rustling of the branches or the creaking of the trunks made a sound, as if the forest were waking from slumber, Reuben instinctively raised the musket that rested on his arm, and cast a quick, sharp glance on every side; but, convinced by a partial observation that no animal was near, he would again give himself up to his thoughts. He was musing on the strange influence that had led him away from his premeditated course, and so far into the depths of the wilderness. Unable to penetrate to the secret place of his soul where his motives lay hidden, he believed that a supernatural voice had called him onward, and that a supernatural power had obstructed his retreat. He trusted that it was Heaven's intent to afford him an opportunity of expiating his sin; he hoped that he might find the bones so long unburied; and that, having laid the earth over them, peace would throw its sunlight into the sepulchre of his heart. From these thoughts he was aroused by a rustling in the forest at some distance from the spot to which he had wandered. Perceiving the motion of some object behind a thick veil of undergrowth, he fired, with the instinct of a hunter and the aim of a practised marksman. A low moan, which told his success, and by which even animals cars express their dying agony, was unheeded by Reuben Bourne. What were the recollections now breaking upon him?

The thicket into which Reuben had fired was near the summit of a swell of land, and was clustered around the base of a rock, which, in the shape and smoothness of one of its surfaces, was not unlike a gigantic gravestone. As if reflected in a mirror, its likeness was in Reuben's memory. He even recognized the veins which seemed to form an inscription in forgotten characters: everything remained the same, except that a thick covert of bushes shrouded the lowerpart of the rock, and would have hidden Roger Malvin had he still been sitting there. Yet in the next moment Reuben's eye was caught by another change that time had effected since he last stood where he was now standing again behind the earthy roots of the uptorn tree. The sapling to which he had bound the bloodstained symbol of his vow had increased and strengthened into an oak, far indeed from its maturity, but with no mean spread of shadowy branches. There was one singularity observable in this tree which made Reuben tremble. The middle and lower branches were in luxuriant life, and an excess of vegetation had fringed the trunk almost to the ground; but a blight had apparently stricken the upper part of the oak, and the very topmost bough was withered, sapless, and utterly dead. Reuben remembered how the little banner had fluttered on that topmost bough, when it was green and lovely, eighteen years before. Whose guilt had blasted it?

Dorcas, after the departure of the two hunters, continued her preparations for their evening repast. Her sylvan table was the moss-covered trunk of a large fallen tree, on the broadest part of which she had spread a snow-white cloth and arranged what were left of the bright pewter vessels that had been her pride in the settlements. It had a strange aspect that one little spot of homely comfort in the desolate heart of Nature. The sunshine yet lingered upon the higher branches of the trees that grew on rising ground; but the shadows of evening had deepened into the hollow where the encampment was made, and the firelight began to redden as it gleamed up the tall trunks of the pines or hovered on the dense and obscure mass of foliage that circled round the spot. The heart of Dorcas was not sad; for she felt that it was better to journey in the wilderness with two whom she loved than to be a lonely woman in a crowd that cared not for her. As she busied herself in arranging seats of mouldering wood, covered with leaves, for Reuben and her son, her voice danced through the gloomy forest in the measure of a song that she had learned in youth. The rude melody, the production of a bard who won no name, was descriptive of a winter evening in a frontier cottage, when, secured from savage inroad by the high-piled snow-drifts, the family rejoiced by their own fireside. The whole song possessed the nameless charm peculiar to unborrowed thought, but four continually-recurring lines shone out from the rest like the blaze of the hearth whose joys they celebrated. Into them, working magic with a few simple words, the poet had instilled the very essence of domestic love and household happiness, and they were poetry and picture joined in one. As Dorcas sang, the walls of her forsaken home seemed to encircle her; she no longer saw the gloomy pines, nor heard the wind which still, as she began each verse, sent a heavy breath through the branches, and died away in a hollow moan from the burden of the song. She was aroused by the report of a gun in the vicinity of the encampment; and either the sudden sound, or her loneliness by the glowing fire, caused her to tremble violently. The next moment she laughed in the pride of a mother's heart.

"My beautiful young hunter! My boy has slain a deer!" she exclaimed, recollecting that in the direction whence the shot proceeded Cyrus had gone to the chase.

She waited a reasonable time to hear her son's light step bounding over the rustling leaves to tell of his success. But he did not immediately appear; and she sent her cheerful voice among the trees in search of him.

"Cyrus! Cyrus!"

His coming was still delayed; and she determined, as the report had apparently been very near, to seek for him in person. Her assistance, also, might be necessary in bringing home the venison which she flattered herself he had obtained. She therefore set forward, directing her steps by the long-past sound, and singing as she went, in order that the boy might be aware of her approach and run to meet her. From behind the trunk of every tree, and from every hiding-place in the thick foliage of the undergrowth, she hoped to discover the countenance of her son, laughing with the sportive mischief that is born of affection. The sun was now beneath the horizon, and the light that came down among the leaves was sufficiently dim to create many illusions in her expecting fancy. Several times she seemed indistinctly to see his face gazing out from among the leaves; and once she imagined that he stood beckoning to her at the base of a craggy rock. Keeping her eyes on this object, however, it proved to be no more than the trunk of an oak fringed to the very ground with little branches, one of which, thrust out farther than the rest, was shaken by the breeze. Making her way round the foot of the rock, she suddenly found herself close to her husband, who had approached in another direction. Leaning upon the butt of his gun, the muzzle of which rested upon the withered leaves, he was apparently absorbed in the contemplation of some object at his feet.

"How is this, Reuben? Have you slain the deer and fallen asleep over him?" exclaimed Dorcas, laughing cheerfully, on her first slight observation of his posture and appearance.

He stirred not, neither did he turn his eyes towards her; and a cold, shuddering fear, indefinite in its source and object, began to creep into her blood. She now perceived that her husband's face was ghastly pale, and his features were rigid, as if incapable of assuming any other expression than the strong despair which had hardened upon them. He gave not the slightest evidence that he was aware of her approach.

"For the love of Heaven, Reuben, speak to me!" cried Dorcas; and the strange sound of her own voice affrighted her even more than the dead silence.

Her husband started, stared into her face, drew her to the front of the rock, and pointed with his finger.

Oh, there lay the boy, asleep, but dreamless, upon the fallen forest leaves! His cheek rested upon his arm—his curled locks were thrown back from his brow—his limbs were slightly relaxed. Had a sudden weariness overcome the youthful hunter? Would his mother's voice arouse him? She knew that it was death.

"This broad rock is the gravestone of your near kindred, Dorcas," said her husband. "Your tears will fall at once over your father and your son."

She heard him not. With one wild shriek, that seemed to force its way from the sufferer's inmost soul, she sank insensible by the side of her dead boy. At that moment the withered topmost bough of the oak loosened itself in the stilly air, and fell in soft, light fragments upon the rock, upon the leaves, upon Reuben, upon his wife and child, and upon Roger Malvin's bones. Then Reuben's heart was stricken, and the tears gushed out like water from a rock. The vow that the wounded youth had made the blighted man had come to redeem. His sin was expiated,—the curse was gone from him; and in the hour when he had shed blood dearer to him than his own, a prayer, the first for years, went up to Heaven from the lips of Reuben Bourne.

THE ARTIST OF THE BEAUTIFUL

An elderly man, with his pretty daughter on his arm, was passing along the street, and emerged from the gloom of the cloudy evening into the light that fell across the pavement from the window of a small shop. It was a projecting window; and on the inside were suspended a variety of watches, pinchbeck, silver, and one or two of gold, all with their faces turned from the streets, as if churlishly disinclined to inform the wayfarers what o'clock it was. Seated within the shop, sidelong to the window with his pale face bent earnestly over some delicate piece of mechanism on which was thrown the concentrated lustre of a shade lamp, appeared a young man.

"What can Owen Warland be about?" muttered old Peter Hovenden, himself a retired watchmaker, and the former master of this same young man whose occupation he was now wondering at. "What can the fellow be about? These six months past I have never come by his shop without seeing him just as steadily at work as now. It would be a flight beyond his usual foolery to seek for the perpetual motion; and yet I know enough of my old business to be certain that what he is now so busy with is no part of the machinery of a watch."

"Perhaps, father," said Annie, without showing much interest in the question, "Owen is inventing a new kind of timekeeper. I am sure he has ingenuity enough."

"Poh, child! He has not the sort of ingenuity to invent anything better than a Dutch toy," answered her father, who had formerly been put to much vexation by Owen Warland's irregular genius. "A plague on such ingenuity! All the effect that ever I knew of it was to spoil the accuracy of some of the best watches in my shop. He would turn the sun out of its orbit and derange the whole course of time, if, as I said before, his ingenuity could grasp anything bigger than a child's toy!"

"Hush, father! He hears you!" whispered Annie, pressing the old man's arm. "His ears are as delicate as his feelings; and you know how easily disturbed they are. Do let us move on."

So Peter Hovenden and his daughter Annie plodded on without further conversation, until in a by-street of the town they found themselves passing the open door of a blacksmith's shop. Within was seen the forge, now blazing up and illuminating the high and dusky roof, and now confining its lustre to a narrow precinct of the coal-strewn floor, according as the breath of the bellows was puffed forth or again inhaled into its vast leathern lungs. In the intervals of brightness it was easy to distinguish objects in remote corners of the shop and the horseshoes that hung upon the wall; in the momentary gloom the fire seemed to be glimmering amidst the vagueness of unenclosed space. Moving about in this red glare and alternate dusk was the figure of the blacksmith, well worthy to be viewed in so picturesque an aspect of light and shade, where the bright blaze struggled with the black night, as if each would have snatched his comely strength from the other. Anon he drew a white-hot bar of iron from the coals, laid it on the anvil, uplifted his arm of might, and was soon enveloped in the myriads of sparks which the strokes of his hammer scattered into the surrounding gloom.

"Now, that is a pleasant sight," said the old watchmaker. "I know what it is to work in gold; but give me the worker in iron after all is said and done. He spends his labor upon a reality. What say you, daughter Annie?"

"Pray don't speak so loud, father," whispered Annie, "Robert Danforth will hear you."

"And what if he should hear me?" said Peter Hovenden. "I say again, it is a good and a wholesome thing to depend upon main strength and reality, and to earn one's bread with the bare and brawny arm of a blacksmith. A watchmaker gets his brain puzzled by his wheels within a wheel, or loses his health or the nicety of his eyesight, as was my case, and finds himself at middle age, or a little after, past labor at his own trade and fit for nothing else, yet too poor to live at his ease. So I say once again, give me main strength for my money. And then, how it takes the nonsense out of a man! Did you ever hear of a blacksmith being such a fool as Owen Warland yonder?"

"Well said, uncle Hovenden!" shouted Robert Danforth from the forge, in a full, deep, merry voice, that made the roof re-echo. "And what says Miss Annie to that doctrine? She, I suppose, will think it a genteeler business to tinker up a lady's watch than to forge a horseshoe or make a gridiron."

Annie drew her father onward without giving him time for reply.

But we must return to Owen Warland's shop, and spend more meditation upon his history and character than either Peter Hovenden, or probably his daughter Annie, or Owen's old school-fellow, Robert Danforth, would have thought due to so slight a subject. From the time that his little fingers could grasp a penknife, Owen had been remarkable for a delicate ingenuity, which sometimes produced pretty shapes in wood, principally figures of flowers and birds, and sometimes seemed to aim at the hidden mysteries of mechanism. But it was always for purposes of grace, and never with any mockery of the useful. He did not, like the crowd of school-boy artisans, construct little windmills on the angle of a barn or watermills across the neighboring brook. Those who discovered such peculiarity in the boy as to think it worth their while to observe him closely, sometimes saw reason to suppose that he was attempting to imitate the beautiful movements of Nature as exemplified in the flight of birds or the activity of little animals. It seemed, in fact, a new development of the love of the beautiful, such as might have made him a poet, a painter, or a sculptor, and which was as completely refined from all utilitarian coarseness as it could have been in either of the fine arts. He looked with singular distaste at the stiff and regular processes of ordinary machinery. Being once carried to see a steam-engine, in the expectation that his intu- intuitive comprehension of mechanical principles would be gratified, he turned pale and grew sick, as if something monstrous and unnatural had been presented to him. This horror was partly owing to the size and terrible energy of the iron laborer; for the character of Owen's mind was microscopic, and tended naturally to the minute, in accordance with his diminutive frame and the marvellous smallness and delicate power of his fingers. Not that his sense of beauty was thereby diminished into a sense of prettiness. The beautiful idea has no relation to size, and may be as perfectly developed in a space too minute for any but microscopic investigation as within the ample verge that is measured by the arc of the rainbow. But, at all events, this characteristic minuteness in his objects and accomplishments made the world even more incapable than it might otherwise have been of appreciating Owen Warland's genius. The boy's relatives saw nothing better to be done—as perhaps there was not—than to bind him apprentice to a watchmaker, hoping that his strange ingenuity might thus be regulated and put to utilitarian purposes.

Peter Hovenden's opinion of his apprentice has already been expressed. He could make nothing of the lad. Owen's apprehension of the professional mysteries, it is true, was inconceivably quick; but he altogether forgot or despised the grand object of a watchmaker's business, and cared no more for the measurement of time than if it had been merged into eternity. So long, however, as he remained under his old master's care, Owen's lack of sturdiness made it possible, by strict injunctions and sharp oversight, to restrain his creative eccentricity within bounds; but when his apprenticeship was served out, and he had taken the little shop which Peter Hovenden's failing eyesight compelled him to relinquish, then did people recognize how unfit a person was Owen Warland to lead old blind Father Time along his daily course. One of his most rational projects was to connect a musical operation with the machinery of his watches, so that all the harsh dissonances of life might be rendered tuneful, and each flitting moment fall into the abyss of the past in golden drops of harmony. If a family clock was intrusted to him for repair,—one of those tall, ancient clocks that have grown nearly allied to human nature by measuring out the lifetime of many generations,—he would take upon himself to arrange a dance or funeral procession of figures across its venerable face, representing twelve mirthful or melancholy hours. Several freaks of this kind quite destroyed the young watchmaker's credit with that steady and matter-of-fact class of people who hold the opinion that time is not to be trifled with, whether considered as the medium of advancement and prosperity in this world or preparation for the next. His custom rapidly diminished—a misfortune, however, that was probably reckoned among his better accidents by Owen Warland, who was becoming more and more absorbed in a secret occupation which drew all his science and manual dexterity into itself, and likewise gave full employment to the characteristic tendencies of his genius. This pursuit had already consumed many months.

After the old watchmaker and his pretty daughter had gazed at him out of the obscurity of the street, Owen Warland was seized with a fluttering of the nerves, which made his hand tremble too violently to proceed with such delicate labor as he was now engaged upon.

"It was Annie herself!" murmured he. "I should have known it, by this throbbing of my heart, before I heard her father's voice. Ah, how it throbs! I shall scarcely be able to work again on this exquisite mechanism to-night. Annie! dearest Annie! thou shouldst give firmness to my heart and hand, and not shake them thus; for if I strive to put the very spirit of beauty into form and give it motion, it is for thy sake alone. O throbbing heart, be quiet! If my labor be thus thwarted, there will come vague and unsatisfied dreams which will leave me spiritless to-morrow."

As he was endeavoring to settle himself again to his task, the shop door opened and gave admittance to no other than the stalwart figure which Peter Hovenden had paused to admire, as seen amid the light and shadow of the blacksmith's shop. Robert Danforth had brought a little anvil of his own manufacture, and peculiarly constructed, which the young artist had recently bespoken. Owen examined the article and pronounced it fashioned according to his wish.

"Why, yes," said Robert Danforth, his strong voice filling the shop as with the sound of a bass viol, "I consider myself equal to anything in the way of my own trade; though I should have made but a poor figure at yours with such a fist as this," added he, laughing, as he laid his vast hand beside the delicate one of Owen. "But what then? I put more main strength into one blow of my sledge hammer than all that you have expended since you were a 'prentice. Is not that the truth?"

"Very probably," answered the low and slender voice of Owen. "Strength is an earthly monster. I make no pretensions to it. My force, whatever there may be of it, is altogether spiritual."

"Well, but, Owen, what are you about?" asked his old school-fellow, still in such a hearty volume of tone that it made the artist shrink, especially as the question related to a subject so sacred as the absorbing dream of his imagination. "Folks do say that you are trying to discover the perpetual motion."

"The perpetual motion? Nonsense!" replied Owen Warland, with a movement of disgust; for he was full of little petulances. "It can never be discovered. It is a dream that may delude men whose brains are mystified with matter, but not me. Besides, if such a discovery were possible, it would not be worth my while to make it only to have the secret turned to such purposes as are now effected by steam and water power. I am not ambitious to be honored with the paternity of a new kind of cotton machine."

"That would be droll enough!" cried the blacksmith, breaking out into such an uproar of laughter that Owen himself and the bell glasses on his work-board quivered in unison. "No, no, Owen! No child of yours will have iron joints and sinews. Well, I won't hinder you any more. Good night, Owen, and success, and if you need any assistance, so far as a downright blow of hammer upon anvil will answer the purpose, I'm your man."

And with another laugh the man of main strength left the shop.

"How strange it is," whispered Owen Warland to himself, leaning his head upon his hand, "that all my musings, my purposes, my passion for the beautiful, my consciousness of power to create it,—a finer, more ethereal power, of which this earthly giant can have no conception,—all, all, look so vain and idle whenever my path is crossed by Robert Danforth! He would drive me mad were I to meet him often. His hard, brute force darkens and confuses the spiritual element within me; but I, too, will be strong in my own way. I will not yield to him."

He took from beneath a glass a piece of minute machinery, which he set in the condensed light of his lamp, and, looking intently at it through a magnifying glass, proceeded to operate with a delicate instrument of steel. In an instant, however, he fell back in his chair and clasped his hands, with a look of horror on his face that made its small features as impressive as those of a giant would have been.

"Heaven! What have I done?" exclaimed he. "The vapor, the influence of that brute force,—it has bewildered me and obscured my perception. I have made the very stroke—the fatal stroke—that I have dreaded from the first. It is all over—the toil of months, the object of my life. I am ruined!"

And there he sat, in strange despair, until his lamp flickered in the socket and left the Artist of the Beautiful in darkness.

Thus it is that ideas, which grow up within the imagination and appear so lovely to it and of a value beyond whatever men call valuable, are exposed to be shattered and annihilated by contact with the practical. It is requisite for the ideal artist to possess a force of character that seems hardly compatible with its delicacy; he must keep his faith in himself while the incredulous world assails him with its utter disbelief; he must stand up against mankind and be his own sole disciple, both as respects his genius and the objects to which it is directed.

For a time Owen Warland succumbed to this severe but inevitable test. He spent a few sluggish weeks with his head so continually resting in his hands that the towns-people had scarcely an opportunity to see his countenance. When at last it was again uplifted to the light of day, a cold, dull, nameless change was perceptible upon it. In the opinion of Peter Hovenden, however, and that order of sagacious understandings who think that life should be regulated, like clockwork, with leaden weights, the alteration was entirely for the better. Owen now, indeed, applied himself to business with dogged industry. It was marvellous to witness the obtuse gravity with which he would inspect the wheels of a great old silver watch thereby delighting the owner, in whose fob it had been worn till he deemed it a portion of his own life, and was accordingly jealous of its treatment. In consequence of the good report thus acquired, Owen Warland was invited by the proper authorities to regulate the clock in the church steeple. He succeeded so admirably in this matter of public interest that the merchants gruffly acknowledged his merits on 'Change; the nurse whispered his praises as she gave the potion in the sick-chamber; the lover blessed him at the hour of appointed interview; and the town in general thanked Owen for the punctuality of dinner time. In a word, the heavy weight upon his spirits kept everything in order, not merely within his own system, but wheresoever the iron accents of the church clock were audible. It was a circumstance, though minute, yet characteristic of his present state, that, when employed to engrave names or initials on silver spoons, he now wrote the requisite letters in the plainest possible style, omitting a variety of fanciful flourishes that had heretofore distinguished his work in this kind.

One day, during the era of this happy transformation, old Peter Hovenden came to visit his former apprentice.

"Well, Owen," said he, "I am glad to hear such good accounts of you from all quarters, and especially from the town clock yonder, which speaks in your commendation every hour of the twenty-four. Only get rid altogether of your nonsensical trash about the beautiful, which I nor nobody else, nor yourself to boot, could ever understand,—only free yourself of that, and your success in life is as sure as daylight. Why, if you go on in this way, I should even venture to let you doctor this precious old watch of mine; though, except my daughter Annie, I have nothing else so valuable in the world."

"I should hardly dare touch it, sir," replied Owen, in a depressed tone; for he was weighed down by his old master's presence.

"In time," said the latter,—"In time, you will be capable of it."

The old watchmaker, with the freedom naturally consequent on his former authority, went on inspecting the work which Owen had in hand at the moment, together with other matters that were in progress. The artist, meanwhile, could scarcely lift his head. There was nothing so antipodal to his nature as this man's cold, unimaginative sagacity, by contact with which everything was converted into a dream except the densest matter of the physical world. Owen groaned in spirit and prayed fervently to be delivered from him.

"But what is this?" cried Peter Hovenden abruptly, taking up a dusty bell glass, beneath which appeared a mechanical something, as delicate and minute as the system of a butterfly's anatomy. "What have we here? Owen! Owen! there is witchcraft in these little chains, and wheels, and paddles. See! with one pinch of my finger and thumb I am going to deliver you from all future peril."

"For Heaven's sake," screamed Owen Warland, springing up with wonderful energy, "as you would not drive me mad, do not touch it! The slightest pressure of your finger would ruin me forever."

"Aha, young man! And is it so?" said the old watchmaker, looking at him with just enough penetration to torture Owen's soul with the bitterness of worldly criticism. "Well, take your own course; but I warn you again that in this small piece of mechanism lives your evil spirit. Shall I exorcise him?"

"You are my evil spirit," answered Owen, much excited,—"you and the hard, coarse world! The leaden thoughts and the despondency that you fling upon me are my clogs, else I should long ago have achieved the task that I was created for."

Peter Hovenden shook his head, with the mixture of contempt and indignation which mankind, of whom he was partly a representative, deem themselves entitled to feel towards all simpletons who seek other prizes than the dusty one along the highway. He then took his leave, with an uplifted finger and a sneer upon his face that haunted the artist's dreams for many a night afterwards. At the time of his old master's visit, Owen was probably on the point of taking up the relinquished task; but, by this sinister event, he was thrown back into the state whence he had been slowly emerging.

But the innate tendency of his soul had only been accumulating fresh vigor during its apparent sluggishness. As the summer advanced he almost totally relinquished his business, and permitted Father Time, so far as the old gentleman was represented by the clocks and watches under his control, to stray at random through human life, making infinite confusion among the train of bewildered hours. He wasted the sunshine, as people said, in wandering through the woods and fields and along the banks of streams. There, like a child, he found amusement in chasing butterflies or watching the motions of water insects. There was something truly mysterious in the intentness with which he contemplated these living playthings as they sported on the breeze or examined the structure of an imperial insect whom he had imprisoned. The chase of butterflies was an apt emblem of the ideal pursuit in which he had spent so many golden hours; but would the beautiful idea ever be yielded to his hand like the butterfly that symbolized it? Sweet, doubtless, were these days, and congenial to the artist's soul. They were full of bright conceptions, which gleamed through his intellectual world as the butterflies gleamed through the outward atmosphere, and were real to him, for the instant, without the toil, and perplexity, and many disappointments of attempting to make them visible to the sensual eye. Alas that the artist, whether in poetry, or whatever other material, may not content himself with the inward enjoyment of the beautiful, but must chase the flitting mystery beyond the verge of his ethereal domain, and crush its frail being in seizing it with a material grasp. Owen Warland felt the impulse to give external reality to his ideas as irresistibly as any of the poets or painters who have arrayed the world in a dimmer and fainter beauty, imperfectly copied from the richness of their visions.

The night was now his time for the slow progress of re-creating the one idea to which all his intellectual activity referred itself. Always at the approach of dusk he stole into the town, locked himself within his shop, and wrought with patient delicacy of touch for many hours. Sometimes he was startled by the rap of the watchman, who, when all the world should be asleep, had caught the gleam of lamplight through the crevices of Owen Warland's shutters. Daylight, to the morbid sensibility of his mind, seemed to have an intrusiveness that interfered with his pursuits. On cloudy and inclement days, therefore, he sat with his head upon his hands, muffling, as it were, his sensitive brain in a mist of indefinite musings, for it was a relief to escape from the sharp distinctness with which he was compelled to shape out his thoughts during his nightly toil.

From one of these fits of torpor he was aroused by the entrance of Annie Hovenden, who came into the shop with the freedom of a customer, and also with something of the familiarity of a childish friend. She had worn a hole through her silver thimble, and wanted Owen to repair it.

"But I don't know whether you will condescend to such a task," said she, laughing, "now that you are so taken up with the notion of putting spirit into machinery."

"Where did you get that idea, Annie?" said Owen, starting in surprise.

"Oh, out of my own head," answered she, "and from something that I heard you say, long ago, when you were but a boy and I a little child. But come, will you mend this poor thimble of mine?"

"Anything for your sake, Annie," said Owen Warland,—"anything, even were it to work at Robert Danforth's forge."

"And that would be a pretty sight!" retorted Annie, glancing with imperceptible slightness at the artist's small and slender frame. "Well; here is the thimble."

"But that is a strange idea of yours," said Owen, "about the spiritualization of matter."

And then the thought stole into his mind that this young girl possessed the gift to comprehend him better than all the world besides. And what a help and strength would it be to him in his lonely toil if he could gain the sympathy of the only being whom he loved! To persons whose pursuits are insulated from the common business of life—who are either in advance of mankind or apart from it—there often comes a sensation of moral cold that makes the spirit shiver as if it had reached the frozen solitudes around the pole. What the prophet, the poet, the reformer, the criminal, or any other man with human yearnings, but separated from the multitude by a peculiar lot, might feel, poor Owen felt.

"Annie," cried he, growing pale as death at the thought, "how gladly would I tell you the secret of my pursuit! You, methinks, would estimate it rightly. You, I know, would hear it with a reverence that I must not expect from the harsh, material world."

"Would I not? to be sure I would!" replied Annie Hovenden, lightly laughing. "Come; explain to me quickly what is the meaning of this little whirligig, so delicately wrought that it might be a plaything for Queen Mab. See! I will put it in motion."

"Hold!" exclaimed Owen, "hold!"

Annie had but given the slightest possible touch, with the point of a needle, to the same minute portion of complicated machinery which has been more than once mentioned, when the artist seized her by the wrist with a force that made her scream aloud. She was affrighted at the convulsion of intense rage and anguish that writhed across his features. The next instant he let his head sink upon his hands.

"Go, Annie," murmured he; "I have deceived myself, and must suffer for it. I yearned for sympathy, and thought, and fancied, and dreamed that you might give it me; but you lack the talisman, Annie, that should admit you into my secrets.

That touch has undone the toil of months and the thought of a lifetime! It was not your fault, Annie; but you have ruined me!"

Poor Owen Warland! He had indeed erred, yet pardonably; for if any human spirit could have sufficiently reverenced the processes so sacred in his eyes, it must have been a woman's. Even Annie Hovenden, possibly might not have disappointed him had she been enlightened by the deep intelligence of love.

The artist spent the ensuing winter in a way that satisfied any persons who had hitherto retained a hopeful opinion of him that he was, in truth, irrevocably doomed to unutility as regarded the world, and to an evil destiny on his own part. The decease of a relative had put him in possession of a small inheritance. Thus freed from the necessity of toil, and having lost the steadfast influence of a great purpose, great, at least, to him,—he abandoned himself to habits from which it might have been supposed the mere delicacy of his organization would have availed to secure him. But when the ethereal portion of a man of genius is obscured the earthly part assumes an influence the more uncontrollable, because the character is now thrown off the balance to which Providence had so nicely adjusted it, and which, in coarser natures, is adjusted by some other method. Owen Warland made proof of whatever show of bliss may be found in riot. He looked at the world through the golden medium of wine, and contemplated the visions that bubble up so gayly around the brim of the glass, and that people the air with shapes of pleasant madness, which so soon grow ghostly and forlorn. Even when this dismal and inevitable change had taken place, the young man might still have continued to quaff the cup of enchantments, though its vapor did but shroud life in gloom and fill the gloom with spectres that mocked at him. There was a certain irksomeness of spirit, which, being real, and the deepest sensation of which the artist was now conscious, was more intolerable than any fantastic miseries and horrors that the abuse of wine could summon up. In the latter case he could remember, even out of the midst of his trouble, that all was but a delusion; in the former, the heavy anguish was his actual life.

From this perilous state he was redeemed by an incident which more than one person witnessed, but of which the shrewdest could not explain or conjecture the operation on Owen Warland's mind. It was very simple. On a warm afternoon of spring, as the artist sat among his riotous companions with a glass of wine before him, a splendid butterfly flew in at the open window and fluttered about his head.

"Ah," exclaimed Owen, who had drank freely, "are you alive again, child of the sun and playmate of the summer breeze, after your dismal winter's nap? Then it is time for me to be at work!"

And, leaving his unemptied glass upon the table, he departed and was never known to sip another drop of wine.

And now, again, he resumed his wanderings in the woods and fields. It might be fancied that the bright butterfly, which had come so spirit-like into the window as Owen sat with the rude revellers, was indeed a spirit commissioned to recall him to the pure, ideal life that had so etheralized him among men. It might be fancied that he went forth to seek this spirit in its sunny haunts; for still, as in the summer time gone by, he was seen to steal gently up wherever a butterfly had alighted, and lose himself in contemplation of it. When it took flight his eyes followed the winged vision, as if its airy track would show the path to heaven. But what could be the purpose of the unseasonable toil, which was again resumed, as the watchman knew by the lines of lamplight through the crevices of Owen Warland's shutters? The towns-people had one comprehensive explanation of all these singularities. Owen Warland had gone mad! How universally efficacious—how satisfactory, too, and soothing to the injured sensibility of narrowness and dulness—is this easy method of accounting for whatever lies beyond the world's most ordinary scope! From St. Paul's days down to our poor little Artist of the Beautiful, the same talisman had been applied to the elucidation of all mysteries in the words or deeds of men who spoke or acted too wisely or too well. In Owen Warland's case the judgment of his towns-people may have been correct. Perhaps he was mad. The lack of sympathy—that contrast between himself and his neighbors which took away the restraint of example—was enough to make him so. Or possibly he had caught just so much of ethereal radiance as served to bewilder him, in an earthly sense, by its intermixture with the common daylight.

One evening, when the artist had returned from a customary ramble and had just thrown the lustre of his lamp on the delicate piece of work so often interrupted, but still taken up again, as if his fate were embodied in its mechanism, he was surprised by the entrance of old Peter Hovenden. Owen never met this man without a shrinking of the heart. Of all the world he was most terrible, by reason of a keen understanding which saw so distinctly what it did see, and disbelieved so uncompromisingly in what it could not see. On this occasion the old watchmaker had merely a gracious word or two to say.

"Owen, my lad," said he, "we must see you at my house to-morrow night."

The artist began to mutter some excuse.

"Oh, but it must be so," quoth Peter Hovenden, "for the sake of the days when you were one of the household. What, my boy! don't you know that my daughter Annie is engaged to Robert Danforth? We are making an entertainment, in our humble way, to celebrate the event."

That little monosyllable was all he uttered; its tone seemed cold and unconcerned to an ear like Peter Hovenden's; and yet there was in it the stifled outcry of the poor artist's heart, which he compressed within him like a man holding down an evil spirit. One slight outbreak, however, imperceptible to the old watchmaker, he allowed himself. Raising the instrument with which he was about to begin his work, he let it fall upon the little system of machinery that had, anew, cost him months of thought and toil. It was shattered by the stroke!

Owen Warland's story would have been no tolerable representation of the troubled life of those who strive to create the beautiful, if, amid all other thwarting influences, love had not interposed to steal the cunning from his hand. Outwardly he had been no ardent or enterprising lover; the career of his passion had confined its tumults and vicissitudes so entirely within the artist's imagination that Annie herself had scarcely more than a woman's intuitive perception of it;

but, in Owen's view, it covered the whole field of his life. Forgetful of the time when she had shown herself incapable of any deep response, he had persisted in connecting all his dreams of artistical success with Annie's image; she was the visible shape in which the spiritual power that he worshipped, and on whose altar he hoped to lay a not unworthy offering, was made manifest to him. Of course he had deceived himself; there were no such attributes in Annie Hovenden as his imagination had endowed her with. She, in the aspect which she wore to his inward vision, was as much a creature of his own as the mysterious piece of mechanism would be were it ever realized. Had he become convinced of his mistake through the medium of successful love,—had he won Annie to his bosom, and there beheld her fade from angel into ordinary woman,—the disappointment might have driven him back, with concentrated energy, upon his sole remaining object. On the other hand, had he found Annie what he fancied, his lot would have been so rich in beauty that out of its mere redundancy he might have wrought the beautiful into many a worthier type than he had toiled for; but the guise in which his sorrow came to him, the sense that the angel of his life had been snatched away and given to a rude man of earth and iron, who could neither need nor appreciate her ministrations,—this was the very perversity of fate that makes human existence appear too absurd and contradictory to be the scene of one other hope or one other fear. There was nothing left for Owen Warland but to sit down like a man that had been stunned.

He went through a fit of illness. After his recovery his small and slender frame assumed an obtuser garniture of flesh than it had ever before worn. His thin cheeks became round; his delicate little hand, so spiritually fashioned to achieve fairy task-work, grew plumper than the hand of a thriving infant. His aspect had a childishness such as might have induced a stranger to pat him on the head—pausing, however, in the act, to wonder what manner of child was here. It was as if the spirit had gone out of him, leaving the body to flourish in a sort of vegetable existence. Not that Owen Warland was idiotic. He could talk, and not irrationally. Somewhat of a babbler, indeed, did people begin to think him; for he was apt to discourse at wearisome length of marvels of mechanism that he had read about in books, but which he had learned to consider as absolutely fabulous. Among them he enumerated the Man of Brass, constructed by Albertus Magnus, and the Brazen Head of Friar Bacon; and, coming down to later times, the automata of a little coach and horses, which it was pretended had been manufactured for the Dauphin of France; together with an insect that buzzed about the ear like a living fly, and yet was but a contrivance of minute steel springs. There was a story, too, of a duck that waddled, and quacked, and ate; though, had any honest citizen purchased it for dinner, he would have found himself cheated with the mere mechanical apparition of a duck.

"But all these accounts," said Owen Warland, "I am now satisfied are mere impositions."

Then, in a mysterious way, he would confess that he once thought differently. In his idle and dreamy days he had considered it possible, in a certain sense, to spiritualize machinery, and to combine with the new species of life and motion thus produced a beauty that should attain to the ideal which Nature has proposed to herself in all her creatures, but has never taken pains to realize. He seemed, however, to retain no very distinct perception either of the process of achieving this object or of the design itself.

"I have thrown it all aside now," he would say. "It was a dream such as young men are always mystifying themselves with. Now that I have acquired a little common sense, it makes me laugh to think of it."

Poor, poor and fallen Owen Warland! These were the symptoms that he had ceased to be an inhabitant of the better sphere that lies unseen around us. He had lost his faith in the invisible, and now prided himself, as such unfortunates invariably do, in the wisdom which rejected much that even his eye could see, and trusted confidently in nothing but what his hand could touch. This is the calamity of men whose spiritual part dies out of them and leaves the grosser understanding to assimilate them more and more to the things of which alone it can take cognizance; but in Owen Warland the spirit was not dead nor passed away; it only slept.

How it awoke again is not recorded. Perhaps the torpid slumber was broken by a convulsive pain. Perhaps, as in a former instance, the butterfly came and hovered about his head and reinspired him,—as indeed this creature of the sunshine had always a mysterious mission for the artist,—reinspired him with the former purpose of his life. Whether it were pain or happiness that thrilled through his veins, his first impulse was to thank Heaven for rendering him again the being of thought, imagination, and keenest sensibility that he had long ceased to be.

"Now for my task," said he. "Never did I feel such strength for it as now."

Yet, strong as he felt himself, he was incited to toil the more diligently by an anxiety lest death should surprise him in the midst of his labors. This anxiety, perhaps, is common to all men who set their hearts upon anything so high, in their own view of it, that life becomes of importance only as conditional to its accomplishment. So long as we love life for itself, we seldom dread the losing it. When we desire life for the attainment of an object, we recognize the frailty of its texture. But, side by side with this sense of insecurity, there is a vital faith in our invulnerability to the shaft of death while engaged in any task that seems assigned by Providence as our proper thing to do, and which the world would have cause to mourn for should we leave it unaccomplished. Can the philosopher, big with the inspiration of an idea that is to reform mankind, believe that he is to be beckoned from this sensible existence at the very instant when he is mustering his breath to speak the word of light? Should he perish so, the weary ages may pass away—the world's, whose life sand may fall, drop by drop—before another intellect is prepared to develop the truth that might have been uttered then. But history affords many an example where the most precious spirit, at any particular epoch manifested in human shape, has gone hence untimely, without space allowed him, so far as mortal judgment could discern, to perform his mission on the earth. The prophet dies, and the man of torpid heart and sluggish brain lives on. The poet leaves his song half sung, or finishes it, beyond the scope of mortal ears, in a celestial choir. The painter—as Allston did—leaves half his conception on the canvas to sadden us with its imperfect beauty, and goes to picture forth the whole, if it be no irreverence to say so, in the hues of heaven. But rather such incomplete designs of this life will be perfected nowhere. This so frequent abortion of man's dearest projects must be taken as a proof that the deeds of earth, however etherealized by piety or genius, are without value, except as exercises and manifestations of the spirit. In heaven, all ordinary thought is higher and more melodious than Milton's song. Then, would he add another verse to any strain that he had left unfinished here?

But to return to Owen Warland. It was his fortune, good or ill, to achieve the purpose of his life. Pass we over a long space of intense thought, yearning effort, minute toil, and wasting anxiety, succeeded by an instant of solitary triumph: let all this be imagined; and then behold the artist, on a winter evening, seeking admittance to Robert Danforth's fireside circle. There he found the man of iron, with his massive substance thoroughly warmed and attempered by domestic influences. And there was Annie, too, now transformed into a matron, with much of her husband's plain and sturdy nature, but imbued, as Owen Warland still believed, with a finer grace, that might enable her to be the interpreter between strength and beauty. It happened, likewise, that old Peter Hovenden was a guest this evening at his daughter's fireside, and it was his well-remembered expression of keen, cold criticism that first encountered the artist's glance.

"My old friend Owen!" cried Robert Danforth, starting up, and compressing the artist's delicate fingers within a hand that was accustomed to gripe bars of iron. "This is kind and neighborly to come to us at last. I was afraid your perpetual motion had bewitched you out of the remembrance of old times."

"We are glad to see you," said Annie, while a blush reddened her matronly cheek. "It was not like a friend to stay from us so long."

"Well, Owen," inquired the old watchmaker, as his first greeting, "how comes on the beautiful? Have you created it at last?"

The artist did not immediately reply, being startled by the apparition of a young child of strength that was tumbling about on the carpet,—a little personage who had come mysteriously out of the infinite, but with something so sturdy and real in his composition that he seemed moulded out of the densest substance which earth could supply. This hopeful infant crawled towards the new-comer, and setting himself on end, as Robert Danforth expressed the posture, stared at Owen with a look of such sagacious observation that the mother could not help exchanging a proud glance with her husband. But the artist was disturbed by the child's look, as imagining a resemblance between it and Peter Hovenden's habitual expression. He could have fancied that the old watchmaker was compressed into this baby shape, and looking out of those baby eyes, and repeating, as he now did, the malicious question: "The beautiful, Owen! How comes on the beautiful? Have you succeeded in creating the beautiful?"

"I have succeeded," replied the artist, with a momentary light of triumph in his eyes and a smile of sunshine, yet steeped in such depth of thought that it was almost sadness. "Yes, my friends, it is the truth. I have succeeded."

"Indeed!" cried Annie, a look of maiden mirthfulness peeping out of her face again. "And is it lawful, now, to inquire what the secret is?"

"Surely; it is to disclose it that I have come," answered Owen Warland. "You shall know, and see, and touch, and possess the secret! For, Annie,—if by that name I may still address the friend of my boyish years,—Annie, it is for your bridal gift that I have wrought this spiritualized mechanism, this harmony of motion, this mystery of beauty. It comes late, indeed; but it is as we go onward in life, when objects begin to lose their freshness of hue and our souls their delicacy of perception, that the spirit of beauty is most needed. If,—forgive me, Annie,—if you know how—to value this gift, it can never come too late."

He produced, as he spoke, what seemed a jewel box. It was carved richly out of ebony by his own hand, and inlaid with a fanciful tracery of pearl, representing a boy in pursuit of a butterfly, which, elsewhere, had become a winged spirit, and was flying heavenward; while the boy, or youth, had found such efficacy in his strong desire that he ascended from earth to cloud, and from cloud to celestial atmosphere, to win the beautiful. This case of ebony the artist opened, and bade Annie place her fingers on its edge. She did so, but almost screamed as a butterfly fluttered forth, and, alighting on her finger's tip, sat waving the ample magnificence of its purple and gold-speckled wings, as if in prelude to a flight. It is impossible to express by words the glory, the splendor, the delicate gorgeousness which were softened into the beauty of this object. Nature's ideal butterfly was here realized in all its perfection; not in the pattern of such faded insects as flit among earthly flowers, but of those which hover across the meads of paradise for child-angels and the spirits of departed infants to disport themselves with. The rich down was visible upon its wings; the lustre of its eyes seemed instinct with spirit. The firelight glimmered around this wonder—the candles gleamed upon it; but it glistened apparently by its own radiance, and illuminated the finger and outstretched hand on which it rested with a white gleam like that of precious stones. In its perfect beauty, the consideration of size was entirely lost. Had its wings overreached the firmament, the mind could not have been more filled or satisfied.

"Beautiful! beautiful!" exclaimed Annie. "Is it alive? Is it alive?"

"Alive? To be sure it is," answered her husband. "Do you suppose any mortal has skill enough to make a butterfly, or would put himself to the trouble of making one, when any child may catch a score of them in a summer's afternoon? Alive? Certainly! But this pretty box is undoubtedly of our friend Owen's manufacture; and really it does him credit."

At this moment the butterfly waved its wings anew, with a motion so absolutely lifelike that Annie was startled, and even awestricken; for, in spite of her husband's opinion, she could not satisfy herself whether it was indeed a living creature or a piece of wondrous mechanism.

"Is it alive?" she repeated, more earnestly than before.

"Judge for yourself," said Owen Warland, who stood gazing in her face with fixed attention.

The butterfly now flung itself upon the air, fluttered round Annie's head, and soared into a distant region of the parlor, still making itself perceptible to sight by the starry gleam in which the motion of its wings enveloped it. The infant on the floor followed its course with his sagacious little eyes. After flying about the room, it returned in a spiral curve and settled again on Annie's finger.

"But is it alive?" exclaimed she again; and the finger on which the gorgeous mystery had alighted was so tremulous that the butterfly was forced to balance himself with his wings. "Tell me if it be alive, or whether you created it."

"Wherefore ask who created it, so it be beautiful?" replied Owen Warland. "Alive? Yes, Annie; it may well be said to possess life, for it has absorbed my own being into itself; and in the secret of that butterfly, and in its beauty,—which is not merely outward, but deep as its whole system,—is represented the intellect, the imagination, the sensibility, the soul of an Artist of the Beautiful! Yes; I created it. But"—and here his countenance somewhat changed—"this butterfly is not now to me what it was when I beheld it afar off in the daydreams of my youth."

"Be it what it may, it is a pretty plaything," said the blacksmith, grinning with childlike delight. "I wonder whether it would condescend to alight on such a great clumsy finger as mine? Hold it hither, Annie."

By the artist's direction, Annie touched her finger's tip to that of her husband; and, after a momentary delay, the butterfly fluttered from one to the other. It preluded a second flight by a similar, yet not precisely the same, waving of wings as in the first experiment; then, ascending from the blacksmith's stalwart finger, it rose in a gradually enlarging curve to the ceiling, made one wide sweep around the room, and returned with an undulating movement to the point whence it had started.

"Well, that does beat all nature!" cried Robert Danforth, bestowing the heartiest praise that he could find expression for; and, indeed, had he paused there, a man of finer words and nicer perception could not easily have said more. "That goes beyond me, I confess. But what then? There is more real use in one downright blow of my sledge hammer than in the whole five years' labor that our friend Owen has wasted on this butterfly."

Here the child clapped his hands and made a great babble of indistinct utterance, apparently demanding that the butterfly should be given him for a plaything.

Owen Warland, meanwhile, glanced sidelong at Annie, to discover whether she sympathized in her husband's estimate of the comparative value of the beautiful and the practical. There was, amid all her kindness towards himself, amid all the wonder and admiration with which she contemplated the marvellous work of his hands and incarnation of his idea, a secret scorn—too secret, perhaps, for her own consciousness, and perceptible only to such intuitive discernment as that of the artist. But Owen, in the latter stages of his pursuit, had risen out of the region in which such a discovery might have been torture. He knew that the world, and Annie as the representative of the world, whatever praise might be bestowed, could never say the fitting word nor feel the fitting sentiment which should be the perfect recompense of an artist who, symbolizing a lofty moral by a material trifle,—converting what was earthly to spiritual gold,—had won the beautiful into his handiwork. Not at this latest moment was he to learn that the reward of all high performance must be sought within itself, or sought in vain. There was, however, a view of the matter which Annie and her husband, and even Peter Hovenden, might fully have understood, and which would have satisfied them that the toil of years had here been worthily bestowed. Owen Warland might have told them that this butterfly, this plaything, this bridal gift of a poor watchmaker to a blacksmith's wife, was, in truth, a gem of art that a monarch would have purchased with honors and abundant wealth, and have treasured it among the jewels of his kingdom as the most unique and wondrous of them all. But the artist smiled and kept the secret to himself.

"Father," said Annie, thinking that a word of praise from the old watchmaker might gratify his former apprentice, "do come and admire this pretty butterfly."

"Let us see," said Peter Hovenden, rising from his chair, with a sneer upon his face that always made people doubt, as he himself did, in everything but a material existence. "Here is my finger for it to alight upon. I shall understand it better when once I have touched it."

But, to the increased astonishment of Annie, when the tip of her father's finger was pressed against that of her husband, on which the butterfly still rested, the insect drooped its wings and seemed on the point of falling to the floor. Even the bright spots of gold upon its wings and body, unless her eyes deceived her, grew dim, and the glowing purple took a dusky hue, and the starry lustre that gleamed around the blacksmith's hand became faint and vanished.

"It is dying! it is dying!" cried Annie, in alarm.

"It has been delicately wrought," said the artist, calmly. "As I told you, it has imbibed a spiritual essence—call it magnetism, or what you will. In an atmosphere of doubt and mockery its exquisite susceptibility suffers torture, as does the soul of him who instilled his own life into it. It has already lost its beauty; in a few moments more its mechanism would be irreparably injured."

"Take away your hand, father!" entreated Annie, turning pale. "Here is my child; let it rest on his innocent hand. There, perhaps, its life will revive and its colors grow brighter than ever."

Her father, with an acrid smile, withdrew his finger. The butterfly then appeared to recover the power of voluntary motion, while its hues assumed much of their original lustre, and the gleam of starlight, which was its most ethereal attribute, again formed a halo round about it. At first, when transferred from Robert Danforth's hand to the small finger of the child, this radiance grew so powerful that it positively threw the little fellow's shadow back against the wall. He, meanwhile, extended his plump hand as he had seen his father and mother do, and watched the waving of the insect's wings with infantine delight. Nevertheless, there was a certain odd expression of sagacity that made Owen Warland feel as if here were old Pete Hovenden, partially, and but partially, redeemed from his hard scepticism into childish faith.

"How wise the little monkey looks!" whispered Robert Danforth to his wife.

"I never saw such a look on a child's face," answered Annie, admiring her own infant, and with good reason, far more than the artistic butterfly. "The darling knows more of the mystery than we do."

As if the butterfly, like the artist, were conscious of something not entirely congenial in the child's nature, it alternately sparkled and grew dim. At length it arose from the small hand of the infant with an airy motion that seemed to bear it upward without an effort, as if the ethereal instincts with which its master's spirit had endowed it impelled this fair vision involuntarily to a higher sphere. Had there been no obstruction, it might have soared into the sky and grown immortal. But its lustre gleamed upon the ceiling; the exquisite texture of its wings brushed against that earthly medium; and a sparkle or two, as of stardust, floated downward and lay glimmering on the carpet. Then the butterfly came fluttering down, and, instead of returning to the infant, was apparently attracted towards the artist's hand.

"Not so! not so!" murmured Owen Warland, as if his handiwork could have understood him. "Thou has gone forth out of thy master's heart. There is no return for thee."

With a wavering movement, and emitting a tremulous radiance, the butterfly struggled, as it were, towards the infant, and was about to alight upon his finger; but while it still hovered in the air, the little child of strength, with his grandsire's sharp and shrewd expression in his face, made a snatch at the marvellous insect and compressed it in his hand. Annie screamed. Old Peter Hovenden burst into a cold and scornful laugh. The blacksmith, by main force, unclosed the infant's hand, and found within the palm a small heap of glittering fragments, whence the mystery of beauty had fled forever. And as for Owen Warland, he looked placidly at what seemed the ruin of his life's labor, and which was yet no ruin. He had caught a far other butterfly than this. When the artist rose high enough to achieve the beautiful, the symbol by which he made it perceptible to mortal senses became of little value in his eyes while his spirit possessed itself in the enjoyment of the reality.

TWICE-TOLD TALES.

THE GRAY CHAMPION.

There was once a time when New England groaned under the actual pressure of heavier wrongs than those threatened ones which brought on the Revolution. James II., the bigoted successor of Charles the Voluptuous, had annulled the charters of all the colonies and sent a harsh and unprincipled soldier to take away our liberties and endanger our religion. The administration of Sir Edmund Andros lacked scarcely a single characteristic of tyranny—a governor and council holding office from the king and wholly independent of the country; laws made and taxes levied without concurrence of the people, immediate or by their representatives; the rights of private citizens violated and the titles of all landed property declared void; the voice of complaint stifled by restrictions on the press; and finally, disaffection overawed by the first band of mercenary troops that ever marched on our free soil. For two years our ancestors were kept in sullen submission by that filial love which had invariably secured their allegiance to the mother-country, whether its head chanced to be a Parliament, Protector or popish monarch. Till these evil times, however, such allegiance had been merely nominal, and the colonists had ruled themselves, enjoying far more freedom than is even yet the privilege of the native subjects of Great Britain.

At length a rumor reached our shores that the prince of Orange had ventured on an enterprise the success of which would be the triumph of civil and religious rights and the salvation of New England. It was but a doubtful whisper; it might be false or the attempt might fail, and in either case the man that stirred against King James would lose his head. Still, the intelligence produced a marked effect. The people smiled mysteriously in the streets and threw bold glances at their op pressors, while far and wide there was a subdued and silent agitation, as if the slightest signal would rouse the whole land from its sluggish despondency. Aware of their danger, the rulers resolved to avert it by an imposing display of strength, and perhaps to confirm their despotism by yet harsher measures.

One afternoon in April, 1689, Sir Edmund Andros and his favorite councillors, being warm with wine, assembled the red-coats of the governor's guard and made their appearance in the streets of Boston. The sun was near setting when the march commenced. The roll of the drum at that unquiet crisis seemed to go through the streets less as the martial music of the soldiers than as a muster-call to the inhabitants themselves. A multitude by various avenues assembled in King street, which was destined to be the scene, nearly a century afterward, of another encounter between the troops of Britain and a people struggling against her tyranny.

Though more than sixty years had elapsed since the Pilgrims came, this crowd of their descendants still showed the strong and sombre features of their character perhaps more strikingly in such a stern emergency than on happier occasions. There was the sober garb, the general severity of mien, the gloomy but undismayed expression, the scriptural forms of speech and the confidence in Heaven's blessing on a righteous cause which would have marked a band of the original Puritans when threatened by some peril of the wilderness. Indeed, it was not yet time for the old spirit to be extinct, since there were men in the street that day who had worshipped there beneath the trees before a house was reared to the God for whom they had become exiles. Old soldiers of the Parliament were here, too, smiling grimly at the thought that their aged arms might strike another blow against the house of Stuart. Here, also, were the veterans of King Philip's war, who had burned villages and slaughtered young and old with pious fierceness while the godly souls throughout the land were helping them with prayer. Several ministers were scattered among the crowd, which, unlike all other mobs, regarded them with such reverence as if there were sanctity in their very garments. These holy men exerted their influence to quiet the people, but not to disperse them.

Meantime, the purpose of the governor in disturbing the peace of the town at a period when the slightest commotion might throw the country into a ferment was almost the Universal subject of inquiry, and variously explained.

"Satan will strike his master-stroke presently," cried some, "because he knoweth that his time is short. All our godly pastors are to be dragged to prison. We shall see them at a Smithfield fire in King street."

Hereupon the people of each parish gathered closer round their minister, who looked calmly upward and assumed a more apostolic dignity, as well befitted a candidate for the highest honor of his profession—a crown of martyrdom. It was actually fancied at that period that New England might have a John Rogers of her own to take the place of that worthy in the *Primer.*

"The pope of Rome has given orders for a new St. Bartholomew," cried others. "We are to be massacred, man and male-child."

Neither was this rumor wholly discredited; although the wiser class believed the governor's object somewhat less atrocious. His predecessor under the old charter, Bradstreet, a venerable companion of the first settlers, was known to be in town. There were grounds for conjecturing that Sir Edmund Andros intended at once to strike terror by a parade of military force and to confound the opposite faction by possessing himself of their chief.

"Stand firm for the old charter-governor!" shouted the crowd, seizing upon the idea—"the good old Governor Bradstreet!"

While this cry was at the loudest the people were surprised by the well-known figure of Governor Bradstreet himself, a patriarch of nearly ninety, who appeared on the elevated steps of a door and with characteristic mildness besought them to submit to the constituted authorities.

"My children," concluded this venerable person, "do nothing rashly. Cry not aloud, but pray for the welfare of New England and expect patiently what the Lord will do in this matter."

The event was soon to be decided. All this time the roll of the drum had been approaching through Cornhill, louder and deeper, till with reverberations from house to house and the regular tramp of martial footsteps it burst into the street. A double rank of soldiers made their appearance, occupying the whole breadth of the passage, with shouldered matchlocks and matches burning, so as to present a row of fires in the dusk. Their steady march was like the progress of a machine that would roll irresistibly over everything in its way. Next, moving slowly, with a confused clatter of hoofs on the pavement, rode a party of mounted gentlemen, the central figure being Sir Edmund Andros, elderly, but erect and soldier-like. Those around him were his favorite councillors and the bitterest foes of New England. At his right hand rode Edward Randolph, our arch-enemy, that "blasted wretch," as Cotton Mather calls him, who achieved the downfall of our ancient government and was followed with a sensible curse-through life and to his grave. On the other side was Bullivant, scattering jests and mockery as he rode along. Dudley came behind with a downcast look, dreading, as well he might, to meet the indignant gaze of the people, who beheld him, their only countryman by birth, among the oppressors of his native land. The captain of a frigate in the harbor and two or three civil officers under the Crown were also there. But the figure which most attracted the public eye and stirred up the deepest feeling was the Episcopal clergyman of King's Chapel riding haughtily among the magistrates in his priestly vestments, the fitting representative of prelacy and persecution, the union of Church and State, and all those abominations which had driven the Puritans to the wilderness. Another guard of soldiers, in double rank, brought up the rear.

The whole scene was a picture of the condition of New England, and its moral, the deformity of any government that does not grow out of the nature of things and the character of the people—on one side the religious multitude with their sad visages and dark attire, and on the other the group of despotic rulers with the high churchman in the midst and here and there a crucifix at their bosoms, all magnificently clad, flushed with wine, proud of unjust authority and scoffing at the universal groan. And the mercenary soldiers, waiting but the word to deluge the street with blood, showed the only means by which obedience could be secured.

"O Lord of hosts," cried a voice among the crowd, "provide a champion for thy people!"

This ejaculation was loudly uttered, and served as a herald's cry to introduce a remarkable personage. The crowd had rolled back, and were now huddled together nearly at the extremity of the street, while the soldiers had advanced no more than a third of its length. The intervening space was empty—a paved solitude between lofty edifices which threw almost a twilight shadow over it. Suddenly there was seen the figure of an ancient man who seemed to have emerged from among the people and was walking by himself along the centre of the street to confront the armed band. He wore the old Puritan dress—a dark cloak and a steeple-crowned hat in the fashion of at least fifty years before, with a heavy sword upon his thigh, but a staff in his hand to assist the tremulous gait of age.

When at some distance from the multitude, the old man turned slowly round, displaying a face of antique majesty rendered doubly venerable by the hoary beard that descended on his breast. He made a gesture at once of encouragement and warning, then turned again and resumed his way.

"Who is this gray patriarch?" asked the young men of their sires.

"Who is this venerable brother?" asked the old men among themselves.

But none could make reply. The fathers of the people, those of fourscore years and upward, were disturbed, deeming it strange that they should forget one of such evident authority whom they must have known in their early days, the associate of Winthrop and all the old councillors, giving laws and making prayers and leading them against the savage. The elderly men ought to have remembered him, too, with locks as gray in their youth as their own were now. And the young! How could he have passed so utterly from their memories—that hoary sire, the relic of long-departed times, whose awful benediction had surely been bestowed on their uncovered heads in childhood?

"Whence did he come? What is his purpose? Who can this old man be?" whispered the wondering crowd.

Meanwhile, the venerable stranger, staff in hand, was pursuing his solitary walk along the centre of the street. As he drew near the advancing soldiers, and as the roll of their drum came full upon his ear, the old man raised himself to a loftier mien, while the decrepitude of age seemed to fall from his shoulders, leaving him in gray but unbroken dignity. Now he marched onward with a warrior's step, keeping time to the military music. Thus the aged form advanced on one side and the whole parade of soldiers and magistrates on the other, till, when scarcely twenty yards remained between, the old man grasped his staff by the middle and held it before him like a leader's truncheon.

"Stand!" cried he.

The eye, the face and attitude of command, the solemn yet warlike peal of that voice—fit either to rule a host in the battle-field or be raised to God in prayer—were irresistible. At the old man's word and outstretched arm the roll of the drum was hushed at once and the advancing line stood still. A tremulous enthusiasm seized upon the multitude. That stately form, combining the leader and the saint, so gray, so dimly seen, in such an ancient garb, could only belong to some old champion of the righteous cause whom the oppressor's drum had summoned from his grave. They raised a shout of awe and exultation, and looked for the deliverance of New England.

The governor and the gentlemen of his party, perceiving themselves brought to an unexpected stand, rode hastily forward, as if they would have pressed their snorting and affrighted horses right against the hoary apparition. He, however, blenched not a step, but, glancing his severe eye round the group, which half encompassed him, at last bent it sternly on Sir Edmund Andros. One would have thought that the dark old man was chief ruler there, and that the governor and council with soldiers at their back, representing the whole power and authority of the Crown, had no alternative but obedience.

"What does this old fellow here?" cried Edward Randolph, fiercely.—"On, Sir Edmund! Bid the soldiers forward, and give the dotard the same choice that you give all his countrymen—to stand aside or be trampled on."

"Nay, nay! Let us show respect to the good grandsire," said Bullivant, laughing. "See you not he is some old round-headed dignitary who hath lain asleep these thirty years and knows nothing of the change of times? Doubtless he thinks to put us down with a proclamation in Old Noll's name."

"Are you mad, old man?" demanded Sir Edmund Andros, in loud and harsh tones. "How dare you stay the march of King James's governor?"

"I have stayed the march of a king himself ere now," replied the gray figure, with stern composure. "I am here, Sir Governor, because the cry of an oppressed people hath disturbed me in my secret place, and, beseeching this favor earnestly of the Lord, it was vouchsafed me to appear once again on earth in the good old cause of his saints. And what speak ye of James? There is no longer a popish tyrant on the throne of England, and by to-morrow noon his name shall be a byword in this very street, where ye would make it a word of terror. Back, thou that wast a governor, back! With this night thy power is ended. To-morrow, the prison! Back, lest I foretell the scaffold!"

The people had been drawing nearer and nearer and drinking in the words of their champion, who spoke in accents long disused, like one unaccustomed to converse except with the dead of many years ago. But his voice stirred their souls. They confronted the soldiers, not wholly without arms and ready to convert the very stones of the street into deadly weapons. Sir Edmund Andros looked at the old man; then he cast his hard and cruel eye over the multitude and beheld them burning with that lurid wrath so difficult to kindle or to quench, and again he fixed his gaze on the aged form which stood obscurely in an open space where neither friend nor foe had thrust himself. What were his thoughts he uttered no word which might discover, but, whether the oppressor were overawed by the Gray Champion's look or perceived his peril in the threatening attitude of the people, it is certain that he gave back and ordered his soldiers to commence a slow and guarded retreat. Before another sunset the governor and all that rode so proudly with him were prisoners, and long ere it was known that James had abdicated King William was proclaimed throughout New England.

But where was the Gray Champion? Some reported that when the troops had gone from King street and the people were thronging tumultuously in their rear, Bradstreet, the aged governor, was seen to embrace a form more aged than his own. Others soberly affirmed that while they marvelled at the venerable grandeur of his aspect the old man had faded from their eyes, melting slowly into the hues of twilight, till where he stood there was an empty space. But all agreed that the hoary shape was gone. The men of that generation watched for his reappearance in sunshine and in twilight, but never saw him more, nor knew when his funeral passed nor where his gravestone was.

And who was the Gray Champion? Perhaps his name might be found in the records of that stern court of justice which passed a sentence too mighty for the age, but glorious in all after-times for its humbling lesson to the monarch and its high example to the subject. I have heard that whenever the descendants of the Puritans are to show the spirit of their sires the old man appears again. When eighty years had passed, he walked once more in King street. Five years later, in the twilight of an April morning, he stood on the green beside the meeting-house at Lexington where now the obelisk of granite with a slab of slate inlaid commemorates the first-fallen of the Revolution. And when our fathers were toiling at the breastwork on Bunker's Hill, all through that night the old warrior walked his rounds. Long, long may it be ere he comes again! His hour is one of darkness and adversity and peril. But should domestic tyranny oppress us or the invader's step pollute our soil, still may the Gray Champion come! for he is the type of New England's hereditary spirit, and his shadowy march on the eve of danger must ever be the pledge that New England's sons will vindicate their ancestry.

SUNDAY AT HOME.

Every Sabbath morning in the summer-time I thrust back the curtain to watch the sunrise stealing down a steeple which stands opposite my chamber window. First the weathercock begins to flash; then a fainter lustre gives the spire an airy aspect; next it encroaches on the tower and causes the index of the dial to glisten like gold as it points to the gilded figure of the hour. Now the loftiest window gleams, and now the lower. The carved framework of the portal is marked strongly out. At length the morning glory in its descent from heaven comes down the stone steps one by one, and there stands the steeple glowing with fresh radiance, while the shades of twilight still hide themselves among the nooks of the adjacent buildings. Methinks though the same sun brightens it every fair morning, yet the steeple has a peculiar robe of brightness for the Sabbath.

By dwelling near a church a person soon contracts an attachment for the edifice. We naturally personify it, and conceive its massy walls and its dim emptiness to be instinct with a calm and meditative and somewhat melancholy spirit. But the steeple stands foremost in our thoughts, as well as locally. It impresses us as a giant with a mind comprehensive and discriminating enough to care for the great and small concerns of all the town. Hourly, while it speaks a moral to the few that think, it reminds thousands of busy individuals of their separate and most secret affairs. It is the steeple, too, that flings abroad the hurried and irregular accents of general alarm; neither have gladness and festivity found a better utterance than by its tongue; and when the dead are slowly passing to their home, the steeple has a melancholy voice to bid them welcome. Yet, in spite of this connection with human interests, what a moral loneliness on week-days broods round about its stately height! It has no kindred with the houses above which it towers; it looks down into the narrow thoroughfare—the lonelier because the crowd are elbowing their passage at its base. A glance at the body of the church deepens this impression. Within, by the light of distant windows, amid refracted shadows we discern the vacant pews and empty galleries, the silent organ, the voiceless pulpit and the clock which tells to solitude how time is passing. Time—where man lives not—what is it but eternity? And in the church, we might suppose, are garnered up throughout the week all thoughts and feelings that have reference to eternity, until the holy day comes round again to let them forth. Might not, then, its more appropriate site be in the outskirts of the town, with space for old trees to wave around it and throw their solemn shadows over a quiet green? We will say more of this hereafter.

But on the Sabbath I watch the earliest sunshine and fancy that a holier brightness marks the day when there shall be no buzz of voices on the Exchange nor traffic in the shops, nor crowd nor business anywhere but at church. Many have fancied so. For my own part, whether I see it scattered down among tangled woods, or beaming broad across the fields, or hemmed in between brick buildings, or tracing out the figure of the casement on my chamber floor, still I recognize the Sabbath sunshine. And ever let me recognize it! Some illusions—and this among them—are the shadows of great truths. Doubts may flit around me or seem to close their evil wings and settle down, but so long as I imagine that the earth is hallowed and the light of heaven retains its sanctity on the Sabbath—while that blessed sunshine lives within me—never can my soul have lost the instinct of its faith. If it have gone astray, it will return again.

I love to spend such pleasant Sabbaths from morning till night behind the curtain of my open window. Are they spent amiss? Every spot so near the church as to be visited by the circling shadow of the steeple should be deemed consecrated ground to-day. With stronger truth be it said that a devout heart may consecrate a den of thieves, as an evil one may convert a temple to the same. My heart, perhaps, has no such holy, nor, I would fain trust, such impious, potency. It must suffice that, though my form be absent, my inner man goes constantly to church, while many whose bodily presence fills the accustomed seats have left their souls at home. But I am there even before my friend the sexton. At length he comes—a man of kindly but sombre aspect, in dark gray clothes, and hair of the same mixture. He comes and applies his key to the wide portal. Now my thoughts may go in among the dusty pews or ascend the pulpit without sacrilege, but soon come forth again to enjoy the music of the bell. How glad, yet solemn too! All the steeples in town are talking together aloft in the sunny air and rejoicing among themselves while their spires point heavenward. Meantime, here are the children assembling to the Sabbath-school, which is kept somewhere within the church. Often, while looking at the arched portal, I have been gladdened by the sight of a score of these little girls and boys in pink, blue, yellow and crimson frocks bursting suddenly forth into the sunshine like a swarm of gay butterflies that had been shut up in the solemn gloom. Or I might compare them to cherubs haunting that holy place.

About a quarter of an hour before the second ringing of the bell individuals of the congregation begin to appear. The earliest is invariably an old woman in black whose bent frame and rounded shoulders are evidently laden with some heavy affliction which she is eager to rest upon the altar. Would that the Sabbath came twice as often, for the sake of that sorrowful old soul! There is an elderly man, also, who arrives in good season and leans against the corner of the tower, just within the line of its shadow, looking downward with a darksome brow. I sometimes fancy that the old woman is the happier of the two. After these, others drop in singly and by twos and threes, either disappearing through the doorway or taking their stand in its vicinity. At last, and always with an unexpected sensation, the bell turns in the steeple overhead and throws out an irregular clangor, jarring the tower to its foundation. As if there were magic in the sound, the sidewalks of the street, both up and down along, are immediately thronged with two long lines of people, all converging hitherward and streaming into the church. Perhaps the far-off roar of a coach draws nearer—a deeper thunder by its contrast with the surrounding stillness—until it sets down the wealthy worshippers at the portal among their humblest brethren. Beyond that entrance—in theory, at least—there are no distinctions of earthly rank; nor, indeed, by the goodly apparel which is flaunting in the sun would there seem to be such on the hither side. Those pretty girls! Why will they disturb my pious meditations? Of all days in the week, they should strive to look least fascinating on the Sabbath, instead of heightening their mortal loveliness, as if to rival the blessed angels and keep our thoughts from heaven. Were I the minister himself, I must needs look. One girl is white muslin from the waist upward and black silk downward to her slippers; a second blushes from top-knot to shoe-tie, one universal scarlet; another shines of a pervading yellow, as if she had made a garment of the sunshine. The greater part, however, have adopted a milder cheerfulness of hue. Their veils, especially when the wind raises them, give a lightness to the general effect and make them appear like airy phantoms as they flit up the steps and vanish into the sombre doorway. Nearly all—though it is very strange that I should know it—wear white stockings, white as snow, and neat slippers laced crosswise with black ribbon pretty high above the ankles. A white stocking is infinitely more effective than a black one.

Here comes the clergyman, slow and solemn, in severe simplicity, needing no black silk gown to denote his office. His aspect claims my reverence, but cannot win my love. Were I to picture Saint Peter keeping fast the gate of Heaven and frowning, more stern than pitiful, on the wretched applicants, that face should be my study. By middle age, or sooner, the creed has generally wrought upon the heart or been attempered by it. As the minister passes into the church the bell holds its iron tongue and all the low murmur of the congregation dies away. The gray sexton looks up and down the street and then at my window-curtain, where through the small peephole I half fancy that he has caught my eye. Now every loiterer has gone in and the street lies asleep in the quiet sun, while a feeling of loneliness comes over me, and brings also an uneasy sense of neglected privileges and duties. Oh, I ought to have gone to church! The bustle of the rising congregation reaches my ears. They are standing up to pray. Could I bring my heart into unison with those who are praying in yonder church and lift it heavenward with a fervor of supplication, but no distinct request, would not that be the safest kind of prayer?—"Lord, look down upon me in mercy!" With that sentiment gushing from my soul, might I not leave all the rest to him?

Hark! the hymn! This, at least, is a portion of the service which I can enjoy better than if I sat within the walls, where the full choir and the massive melody of the organ would fall with a weight upon me. At this distance it thrills through my frame and plays upon my heart-strings with a pleasure both of the sense and spirit. Heaven be praised! I know nothing of music as a science, and the most elaborate harmonies, if they please me, please as simply as a nurse's lullaby. The strain has ceased, but prolongs itself in my mind with fanciful echoes till I start from my reverie and find that the sermon has commenced. It is my misfortune seldom to fructify in a regular way by any but printed sermons. The first strong idea which the preacher utters gives birth to a train of thought and leads me onward step by step quite out of hearing of the good man's voice unless he be indeed a son of thunder. At my open window, catching now and then a sentence of the "parson's saw," I am as well situated as at the foot of the pulpit stairs. The broken and scattered fragments of this one discourse will be the texts of many sermons preached by those colleague pastors—colleagues, but often disputants—my Mind and Heart. The former pretends to be a scholar and perplexes me with doctrinal points; the latter takes me on the score of feeling; and both, like several other preachers, spend their strength to very little purpose. I, their sole auditor, cannot always understand them.

Suppose that a few hours have passed, and behold me still behind my curtain just before the close of the afternoon service. The hour-hand on the dial has passed beyond four o'clock. The declining sun is hidden behind the steeple and throws its shadow straight across the street; so that my chamber is darkened as with a cloud. Around the church door all is solitude, and an impenetrable obscurity beyond the threshold. A commotion is heard. The seats are slammed down and the pew doors thrown back; a multitude of feet are trampling along the unseen aisles, and the congregation bursts suddenly through the portal. Foremost scampers a rabble of boys, behind whom moves a dense and dark phalanx of grown men, and lastly a crowd of females with young children and a few scattered husbands. This instantaneous outbreak of life into loneliness is one of the pleasantest scenes of the day. Some of the good people are rubbing their eyes, thereby intimating that they have been wrapped, as it were, in a sort of holy trance by the fervor of their devotion. There is a young man, a third-rate coxcomb, whose first care is always to flourish a white handkerchief and brush the seat of a tight pair of black silk pantaloons which shine as if varnished. They must have been made of the stuff called "everlasting," or perhaps of the same piece as Christian's garments in the *Pilgrim's Progress*, for he put them on two summers ago and has not yet worn the gloss off. I have taken a great liking to those black silk pantaloons. But now, with nods and greetings among friends, each matron takes her husband's arm and paces gravely homeward, while the girls also flutter away after arranging sunset walks with their favored bachelors. The Sabbath eve is the eve of love. At length the whole congregation is dispersed. No; here, with faces as glossy as black satin, come two sable ladies and a sable gentleman, and close in their rear the minister, who softens his severe visage and bestows a kind word on each. Poor souls! To them the most captivating picture of bliss in heaven is "There we shall be white!"

All is solitude again. But hark! A broken warbling of voices, and now, attuning its grandeur to their sweetness, a stately peal of the organ. Who are the choristers? Let me dream that the angels who came down from heaven this blessed morn to blend themselves with the worship of the truly good are playing and singing their farewell to the earth. On the wings of that rich melody they were borne upward.

This, gentle reader, is merely a flight of poetry. A few of the singing-men and singing-women had lingered behind their fellows and raised their voices fitfully and blew a careless note upon the organ. Yet it lifted my soul higher than all their former strains. They are gone—the sons and daughters of Music—and the gray sexton is just closing the portal. For six days more there will be no face of man in the pews and aisles and galleries, nor a voice in the pulpit, nor music in the choir. Was it worth while to rear this massive edifice to be a desert in the heart of the town and populous only for a few hours of each seventh day? Oh, but the church is a symbol of religion. May its site, which was consecrated on the day when the first tree was felled, be kept holy for ever, a spot of solitude and peace amid the trouble and vanity of our week-day world! There is a moral, and a religion too, even in the silent walls. And may the steeple still point heavenward and be decked with the hallowed sunshine of the Sabbath morn!

THE WEDDING-KNELL.

There is a certain church, in the city of New York which I have always regarded with peculiar interest on account of a marriage there solemnized under very singular circumstances in my grandmother's girlhood. That venerable lady chanced to be a spectator of the scene, and ever after made it her favorite narrative. Whether the edifice now standing on the same site be the identical one to which she referred I am not antiquarian enough to know, nor would it be worth while to correct myself, perhaps, of an agreeable error by reading the date of its erection on the tablet over the door. It is a stately church surrounded by an enclosure of the loveliest green, within which appear urns, pillars, obelisks, and other forms of monumental marble, the tributes of private affection or more splendid memorials of historic dust. With such a place, though the tumult of the city rolls beneath its tower, one would be willing to connect some legendary interest.

The marriage might be considered as the result of an early engagement, though there had been two intermediate weddings on the lady's part and forty years of celibacy on that of the gentleman. At sixty-five Mr. Ellenwood was a shy but not quite a secluded man; selfish, like all men who brood over their own hearts, yet manifesting on rare occasions a vein of generous sentiment; a scholar throughout life, though always an indolent one, because his studies had no definite object either of public advantage or personal ambition; a gentleman, high-bred and fastidiously delicate, yet sometimes requiring a considerable relaxation in his behalf of the common rules of society. In truth, there were so many anomalies in his character, and, though shrinking with diseased sensibility from public notice, it had been his fatality so often to become the topic of the day by some wild eccentricity of conduct, that people searched his lineage for a hereditary taint of insanity. But there was no need of this. His caprices had their origin in a mind that lacked the support of an engrossing purpose, and in feelings that preyed upon themselves for want of other food. If he were mad, it was the consequence, and not the cause, of an aimless and abortive life.

The widow was as complete a contrast to her third bridegroom in everything but age as can well be conceived. Compelled to relinquish her first engagement, she had been united to a man of twice her own years, to whom she became an exemplary wife, and by whose death she was left in possession of a splendid fortune. A Southern gentleman considerably younger than herself succeeded to her hand and carried her to Charleston, where after many uncomfortable years she found herself again a widow. It would have been singular if any uncommon delicacy of feeling had survived through such a life as Mrs. Dabney's; it could not but be crushed and killed by her early disappointment, the cold duty of her first marriage, the dislocation of the heart's principles consequent on a second union, and the unkindness of her Southern husband, which had inevitably driven her to connect the idea of his death with that of her comfort. To be brief, she was that wisest but unloveliest variety of woman, a philosopher, bearing troubles of the heart with equanimity, dispensing with all that should have been her happiness and making the best of what remained. Sage in most matters, the widow was perhaps the more amiable for the one frailty that made her ridiculous. Being childless, she could not remain beautiful by proxy in the person of a daughter, she therefore refused to grow old and ugly on any consideration; she struggled with Time, and held fast her roses in spite of him, till the venerable thief appeared to have relinquished the spoil as not worth the trouble of acquiring it.

The approaching marriage of this woman of the world with such an unworldly man as Mr. Ellenwood was announced soon after Mrs. Dabney's return to her native city. Superficial observers, and deeper ones, seemed to concur in supposing that the lady must have borne no inactive part in arranging the affair; there were considerations of expediency which she would be far more likely to appreciate than Mr. Ellenwood, and there was just the specious phantom of sentiment and romance in this late union of two early lovers which sometimes makes a fool of a woman who has lost her true feelings among the accidents of life. All the wonder was how the gentleman, with his lack of worldly wisdom and agonizing consciousness of ridicule, could have been induced to take a measure at once so prudent and so laughable. But while people talked the wedding-day arrived. The ceremony was to be solemnized according to the Episcopalian forms and in open church, with a degree of publicity that attracted many spectators, who occupied the front seats of the galleries and the pews near the altar and along the broad aisle. It had been arranged, or possibly it was the custom of the day, that the parties should proceed separately to church. By some accident the bridegroom was a little less punctual than the widow and her bridal attendants, with whose arrival, after this tedious but necessary preface, the action of our tale may be said to commence.

The clumsy wheels of several old-fashioned coaches were heard, and the gentlemen and ladies composing the bridal-party came through the church door with the sudden and gladsome effect of a burst of sunshine. The whole group, except the principal figure, was made up of youth and gayety. As they streamed up the broad aisle, while the pews and pillars seemed to brighten on either side, their steps were as buoyant as if they mistook the church for a ball-room and were ready to dance hand in hand to the altar. So brilliant was the spectacle that few took notice of a singular phenomenon that had marked its entrance. At the moment when the bride's foot touched the threshold the bell swung heavily in the tower above her and sent forth its deepest knell. The vibrations died away, and returned with prolonged solemnity as she entered the body of the church.

"Good heavens! What an omen!" whispered a young lady to her lover.

"On my honor," replied the gentleman, "I believe the bell has the good taste to toll of its own accord. What has she to do with weddings? If you, dearest Julia, were approaching the altar, the bell would ring out its merriest peal. It has only a funeral-knell for her."

The bride and most of her company had been too much occupied with the bustle of entrance to hear the first boding stroke of the bell—or, at least, to reflect on the singularity of such a welcome to the altar. They therefore continued to advance with undiminished gayety. The gorgeous dresses of the time—the crimson velvet coats, the gold-laced hats, the hoop-petticoats, the silk, satin, brocade and embroidery, the buckles, canes and swords, all displayed to the best advantage on persons suited to such finery—made the group appear more like a bright-colored picture than anything real. But by what perversity of taste had the artist represented his principal figure as so wrinkled and decayed, while yet he had decked her out in the brightest splendor of attire, as if the loveliest maiden had suddenly withered into age and become a moral to the beautiful around her? On they went, however, and had glittered along about a third of the aisle, when another stroke of the bell seemed to fill the church with a visible gloom, dimming and obscuring the bright-pageant till it shone forth again as from a mist.

This time the party wavered, stopped and huddled closer together, while a slight scream was heard from some of the ladies and a confused whispering among the gentlemen. Thus tossing to and fro, they might have been fancifully compared to a splendid bunch of flowers suddenly shaken by a puff of wind which threatened to scatter the leaves of an old brown, withered rose on the same stalk with two dewy buds, such being the emblem of the widow between her fair young bridemaids. But her heroism was admirable. She had started with an irrepressible shudder, as if the stroke of the bell had fallen directly on her heart; then, recovering herself, while her attendants were yet in dismay, she took the lead and paced calmly up the aisle. The bell continued to swing, strike and vibrate with the same doleful regularity as when a corpse is on its way to the tomb.

"My young friends here have their nerves a little shaken," said the widow, with a smile, to the clergyman at the altar. "But so many weddings have been ushered in with the merriest peal of the bells, and yet turned out unhappily, that I shall hope for better fortune under such different auspices."

"Madam," answered the rector, in great perplexity, "this strange occurrence brings to my mind a marriage-sermon of the famous Bishop Taylor wherein he mingles so many thoughts of mortality and future woe that, to speak somewhat after his own rich style, he seems to hang the bridal-chamber in black and cut the wedding-garment out of a coffin-pall. And it has been the custom of divers nations to infuse something of sadness into their marriage ceremonies, so to keep death in mind while contracting that engagement which is life's chiefest business. Thus we may draw a sad but profitable moral from this funeral-knell."

But, though the clergyman might have given his moral even a keener point, he did not fail to despatch an attendant to inquire into the mystery and stop those sounds so dismally appropriate to such a marriage. A brief space elapsed, during which the silence was broken only by whispers and a few suppressed titterings among the wedding-party and the spectators, who after the first shock were disposed to draw an ill-natured merriment from the affair. The young have less charity for aged follies than the old for those of youth. The widow's glance was observed to wander for an instant toward a window of the church, as if searching for the time-worn marble that she had dedicated to her first husband; then her eyelids dropped over their faded orbs and her thoughts were drawn irresistibly to another grave. Two buried men with a voice at her ear and a cry afar off were calling her to lie down beside them. Perhaps, with momentary truth of feeling, she thought how much happier had been her fate if, after years of bliss, the bell were now tolling for her funeral and she were followed to the grave by the old affection of her earliest lover, long her husband. But why had she returned to him when their cold hearts shrank from each other's embrace?

Still the death-bell tolled so mournfully that the sunshine seemed to fade in the air. A whisper, communicated from those who stood nearest the windows, now spread through the church: a hearse with a train of several coaches was creeping along the street, conveying some dead man to the churchyard, while the bride awaited a living one at the altar. Immediately after, the footsteps of the bridegroom and his friends were heard at the door. The widow looked down the aisle and clenched the arm of one of her bridemaids in her bony hand with such unconscious violence that the fair girl trembled.

"You frighten me, my dear madam," cried she. "For heaven's sake, what is the matter?"

"Nothing, my dear—nothing," said the widow; then, whispering close to her ear, "There is a foolish fancy that I cannot get rid of. I am expecting my bridegroom to come into the church with my two first husbands for groomsmen."

"Look! look!" screamed the bridemaid. "What is here? The funeral!"

As she spoke a dark procession paced into the church. First came an old man and woman, like chief mourners at a funeral, attired from head to foot in the deepest black, all but their pale features and hoary hair, he leaning on a staff and supporting her decrepit form with his nerveless arm. Behind appeared another and another pair, as aged, as black and mournful as the first. As they drew near the widow recognized in every face some trait of former friends long forgotten, but now returning as if from their old graves to warn her to prepare a shroud, or, with purpose almost as unwelcome, to exhibit their wrinkles and infirmity and claim her as their companion by the tokens of her own decay. Many a merry night had she danced with them in youth, and now in joyless age she felt that some withered partner should request her hand and all unite in a dance of death to the music of the funeral-bell.

While these aged mourners were passing up the aisle it was observed that from pew to pew the spectators shuddered with irrepressible awe as some object hitherto concealed by the intervening figures came full in sight. Many turned away their faces; others kept a fixed and rigid stare, and a young girl giggled hysterically and fainted with the laughter on her lips. When the spectral procession approached the altar, each couple separated and slowly diverged, till in the centre appeared a form that had been worthily ushered in with all this gloomy pomp, the death-knell and the funeral. It was the bridegroom in his shroud.

No garb but that of the grave could have befitted such a death-like aspect. The eyes, indeed, had the wild gleam of a sepulchral lamp; all else was fixed in the stern calmness which old men wear in the coffin. The corpse stood motionless, but addressed the widow in accents that seemed to melt into the clang of the bell, which fell heavily on the air while he spoke.

"Come, my bride!" said those pale lips. "The hearse is ready; the sexton stands waiting for us at the door of the tomb. Let us be married, and then to our coffins!"

How shall the widow's horror be represented? It gave her the ghastliness of a dead man's bride. Her youthful friends stood apart, shuddering at the mourners, the shrouded bridegroom and herself; the whole scene expressed by the strongest imagery the vain struggle of the gilded vanities of this world when opposed to age, infirmity, sorrow and death.

The awestruck silence was first broken by the clergyman.

"Mr. Ellenwood," said he, soothingly, yet with somewhat of authority, "you are not well. Your mind has been agitated by the unusual circumstances in which you are placed. The ceremony must be deferred. As an old friend, let me entreat you to return home."

"Home—yes; but not without my bride," answered he, in the same hollow accents. "You deem this mockery—perhaps madness. Had I bedizened my aged and broken frame with scarlet and embroidery, had I forced my withered lips to smile at my dead heart, that might have been mockery or madness; but now let young and old declare which of us has come hither without a wedding-garment—the bridegroom or the bride."

He stepped forward at a ghostly pace and stood beside the widow, contrasting the awful simplicity of his shroud with the glare and glitter in which she had arrayed herself for this unhappy scene. None that beheld them could deny the terrible strength of the moral which his disordered intellect had contrived to draw.

"Cruel! cruel!" groaned the heartstricken bride.

"Cruel?" repeated he; then, losing his deathlike composure in a wild bitterness, "Heaven judge which of us has been cruel to the other! In youth you deprived me of my happiness, my hopes, my aims; you took away all the substance of my life and made it a dream without reality enough even to grieve at—with only a pervading gloom, through which I walked wearily and cared not whither. But after forty years, when I have built my tomb and would not give up the thought of resting there—no, not for such a life as we once pictured—you call me to the altar. At your summons I am here. But other husbands have enjoyed your youth, your beauty, your warmth of heart and all that could be termed your life. What is there for me but your decay and death? And therefore I have bidden these funeral-friends, and bespoken the sexton's deepest knell, and am come in my shroud to wed you as with a burial-service, that we may join our hands at the door of the sepulchre and enter it together."

It was not frenzy, it was not merely the drunkenness of strong emotion in a heart unused to it, that now wrought upon the bride. The stern lesson of the day had done its work; her worldliness was gone. She seized the bridegroom's hand.

"Yes!" cried she; "let us wed even at the door of the sepulchre. My life is gone in vanity and emptiness, but at its close there is one true feeling. It has made me what I was in youth: it makes me worthy of you. Time is no more for both of us. Let us wed for eternity."

With a long and deep regard the bridegroom looked into her eyes, while a tear was gathering in his own. How strange that gush of human feeling from the frozen bosom of a corpse! He wiped away the tear, even with his shroud.

"Beloved of my youth," said he, "I have been wild. The despair of my whole lifetime had returned at once and maddened me. Forgive and be forgiven. Yes; it is evening with us now, and we have realized none of our morning dreams of happiness. But let us join our hands before the altar as lovers whom adverse circumstances have separated through life, yet who meet again as they are leaving it and find their earthly affection changed into something holy as religion. And what is time to the married of eternity?"

Amid the tears of many and a swell of exalted sentiment in those who felt aright was solemnized the union of two immortal souls. The train of withered mourners, the hoary bridegroom in his shroud, the pale features of the aged bride and the death-bell tolling through the whole till its deep voice overpowered the marriage-words,—all marked the funeral of earthly hopes. But as the ceremony proceeded, the organ, as if stirred by the sympathies of this impressive scene, poured forth an anthem, first mingling with the dismal knell, then rising to a loftier strain, till the soul looked down upon its woe. And when the awful rite was finished and with cold hand in cold hand the married of eternity withdrew, the organ's peal of solemn triumph drowned the wedding-knell.

THE MINISTER'S BLACK VEIL.

A PARABLE.[1]

The sexton stood in the porch of Milford meeting-house pulling lustily at the bell-rope. The old people of the village came stooping along the street. Children with bright faces tripped merrily beside their parents or mimicked a graver gait in the conscious dignity of their Sunday clothes. Spruce bachelors looked sidelong at the pretty maidens, and fancied that the Sabbath sunshine made them prettier than on week-days. When the throng had mostly streamed into the porch, the sexton began to toll the bell, keeping his eye on the Reverend Mr. Hooper's door. The first glimpse of the clergyman's figure was the signal for the bell to cease its summons.

"But what has good Parson Hooper got upon his face?" cried the sexton, in astonishment.

All within hearing immediately turned about and beheld the semblance of Mr. Hooper pacing slowly his meditative way toward the meeting-house. With one accord they started, expressing more wonder than if some strange minister were coming to dust the cushions of Mr. Hooper's pulpit.

"Are you sure it is our parson?" inquired Goodman Gray of the sexton.

"Of a certainty it is good Mr. Hooper," replied the sexton. "He was to have exchanged pulpits with Parson Shute of Westbury, but Parson Shute sent to excuse himself yesterday, being to preach a funeral sermon."

The cause of so much amazement may appear sufficiently slight. Mr. Hooper, a gentlemanly person of about thirty, though still a bachelor, was dressed with due clerical neatness, as if a careful wife had starched his band and brushed the weekly dust from his Sunday's garb. There was but one thing remarkable in his appearance. Swathed about his forehead and hanging down over his face, so low

---

[1] Another clergyman in New England, Mr. Joseph Moody, of York, Maine, who died about eighty years since, made himself remarkable by the same eccentricity that is here related of the Reverend Mr. Hooper. In his case, however, the symbol had a different import. In early life he had accidentally killed a beloved friend, and from that day till the hour of his own death he hid his face from men.

as to be shaken by his breath, Mr. Hooper had on a black veil. On a nearer view it seemed to consist of two folds of crape, which entirely concealed his features except the mouth and chin, but probably did not intercept his sight further than to give a darkened aspect to all living and inanimate things. With this gloomy shade before him good Mr. Hooper walked onward at a slow and quiet pace, stooping somewhat and looking on the ground, as is customary with abstracted men, yet nodding kindly to those of his parishioners who still waited on the meeting-house steps. But so wonder-struck were they that his greeting hardly met with a return.

"I can't really feel as if good Mr. Hooper's face was behind that piece of crape," said the sexton.

"I don't like it," muttered an old woman as she hobbled into the meeting-house. "He has changed himself into something awful only by hiding his face."

"Our parson has gone mad!" cried Goodman Gray, following him across the threshold.

A rumor of some unaccountable phenomenon had preceded Mr. Hooper into the meeting-house and set all the congregation astir. Few could refrain from twisting their heads toward the door; many stood upright and turned directly about; while several little boys clambered upon the seats, and came down again with a terrible racket. There was a general bustle, a rustling of the women's gowns and shuffling of the men's feet, greatly at variance with that hushed repose which should attend the entrance of the minister. But Mr. Hooper appeared not to notice the perturbation of his people. He entered with an almost noiseless step, bent his head mildly to the pews on each side and bowed as he passed his oldest parishioner, a white-haired great-grandsire, who occupied an arm-chair in the centre of the aisle. It was strange to observe how slowly this venerable man became conscious of something singular in the appearance of his pastor. He seemed not fully to partake of the prevailing wonder till Mr. Hooper had ascended the stairs and showed himself in the pulpit, face to face with his congregation except for the black veil. That mysterious emblem was never once withdrawn. It shook with his measured breath as he gave out the psalm, it threw its obscurity between him and the holy page as he read the Scriptures, and while he prayed the veil lay heavily on his uplifted countenance. Did he seek to hide it from the dread Being whom he was addressing?

Such was the effect of this simple piece of crape that more than one woman of delicate nerves was forced to leave the meeting-house. Yet perhaps the pale-faced congregation was almost as fearful a sight to the minister as his black veil to them.

Mr. Hooper had the reputation of a good preacher, but not an energetic one: he strove to win his people heavenward by mild, persuasive influences rather than to drive them thither by the thunders of the word. The sermon which he now delivered was marked by the same characteristics of style and manner as the general series of his pulpit oratory, but there was something either in the sentiment of the discourse itself or in the imagination of the auditors which made it greatly the most powerful effort that they had ever heard from their pastor's lips. It was tinged rather more darkly than usual with the gentle gloom of Mr. Hooper's temperament. The subject had reference to secret sin and those sad mysteries which we hide from our nearest and dearest, and would fain conceal from our own consciousness, even forgetting that the Omniscient can detect them. A subtle power was breathed into his words. Each member of the congregation, the most innocent girl and the man of hardened breast, felt as if the preacher had crept upon them behind his awful veil and discovered their hoarded iniquity of deed or thought. Many spread their clasped hands on their bosoms. There was nothing terrible in what Mr. Hooper said—at least, no violence; and yet with every tremor of his melancholy voice the hearers quaked. An unsought pathos came hand in hand with awe. So sensible were the audience of some unwonted attribute in their minister that they longed for a breath of wind to blow aside the veil, almost believing that a stranger's visage would be discovered, though the form, gesture and voice were those of Mr. Hooper.

At the close of the services the people hurried out with indecorous confusion, eager to communicate their pent-up amazement, and conscious of lighter spirits the moment they lost sight of the black veil. Some gathered in little circles, huddled closely together, with their mouths all whispering in the centre; some went homeward alone, wrapped in silent meditation; some talked loudly and profaned the Sabbath-day with ostentatious laughter. A few shook their sagacious heads, intimating that they could penetrate the mystery, while one or two affirmed that there was no mystery at all, but only that Mr. Hooper's eyes were so weakened by the midnight lamp as to require a shade.

After a brief interval forth came good Mr. Hooper also, in the rear of his flock. Turning his veiled face from one group to another, he paid due reverence to the hoary heads, saluted the middle-aged with kind dignity as their friend and spiritual guide, greeted the young with mingled authority and love, and laid his hands on the little children's heads to bless them. Such was always his custom on the Sabbath-day. Strange and bewildered looks repaid him for his courtesy. None, as on former occasions, aspired to the honor of walking by their pastor's side. Old Squire Saunders—doubtless by an accidental lapse of memory—neglected to invite Mr. Hooper to his table, where the good clergyman had been wont to bless the food almost every Sunday since his settlement. He returned, therefore, to the parsonage, and at the moment of closing the door was observed to look back upon the people, all of whom had their eyes fixed upon the minister. A sad smile gleamed faintly from beneath the black veil and flickered about his mouth, glimmering as he disappeared.

"How strange," said a lady, "that a simple black veil, such as any woman might wear on her bonnet, should become such a terrible thing on Mr. Hooper's face!"

"Something must surely be amiss with Mr. Hooper's intellects," observed her husband, the physician of the village. "But the strangest part of the affair is the effect of this vagary even on a sober-minded man like myself. The black veil, though it covers only our pastor's face, throws its influence over his whole person and makes him ghost-like from head to foot. Do you not feel it so?"

"Truly do I," replied the lady; "and I would not be alone with him for the world. I wonder he is not afraid to be alone with himself."

"Men sometimes are so," said her husband.

The afternoon service was attended with similar circumstances. At its conclusion the bell tolled for the funeral of a young lady. The relatives and friends were assembled in the house and the more distant acquaintances stood about the door, speaking of the good qualities of the deceased, when their talk was interrupted by the appearance of Mr. Hooper, still covered with his black veil. It was now an appropriate emblem. The clergyman stepped into the room where the corpse was laid, and bent over the coffin to take a last farewell of his deceased parishioner. As he stooped the veil hung straight down from his forehead, so that, if her eyelids had not been closed for ever, the dead maiden might have seen his face. Could Mr. Hooper be fearful of her glance, that he so hastily caught back the black veil? A person who watched the interview between the dead and living scrupled not to affirm that at the instant when the clergyman's features were disclosed the corpse had slightly shuddered, rustling the shroud and muslin cap, though the countenance retained the composure of death. A superstitious old woman was the only witness of this prodigy.

From the coffin Mr. Hooper passed into the chamber of the mourners, and thence to the head of the staircase, to make the funeral prayer. It was a tender and heart-dissolving prayer, full of sorrow, yet so imbued with celestial hopes that the music of a heavenly harp swept by the fingers of the dead seemed faintly to be heard among the saddest accents of the minister. The people trembled, though they but darkly understood him, when he prayed that they and himself, and all of mortal race, might be ready, as he trusted this young maiden had been, for the dreadful hour that should snatch the veil from their faces. The bearers went heavily forth and the mourners followed, saddening all the street, with the dead before them and Mr. Hooper in his black veil behind.

"Why do you look back?" said one in the procession to his partner.

"I had a fancy," replied she, "that the minister and the maiden's spirit were walking hand in hand."

"And so had I at the same moment," said the other.

That night the handsomest couple in Milford village were to be joined in wedlock. Though reckoned a melancholy man, Mr. Hooper had a placid cheerfulness for such occasions which often excited a sympathetic smile where livelier merriment would have been thrown away. There was no quality of his disposition which made him more beloved than this. The company at the wedding awaited his arrival with impatience, trusting that the strange awe which had gathered over him throughout the day would now be dispelled. But such was not the result. When Mr. Hooper came, the first thing that their eyes rested on was the same horrible black veil which had added deeper gloom to the funeral and could portend nothing but evil to the wedding. Such was its immediate effect on the guests that a cloud seemed to have rolled duskily from beneath the black crape and dimmed the light of the candles. The bridal pair stood up before the minister, but the bride's cold fingers quivered in the tremulous hand of the bridegroom, and her death-like paleness caused a whisper that the maiden who had been buried a few hours before was come from her grave to be married. If ever another wedding were so dismal, it was that famous one where they tolled the wedding-knell.

After performing the ceremony Mr. Hooper raised a glass of wine to his lips, wishing happiness to the new-married couple in a strain of mild pleasantry that ought to have brightened the features of the guests like a cheerful gleam from the hearth. At that instant, catching a glimpse of his figure in the looking-glass, the black veil involved his own spirit in the horror with which it overwhelmed all others. His frame shuddered, his lips grew white, he spilt the untasted wine upon the carpet and rushed forth into the darkness, for the Earth too had on her black veil.

The next day the whole village of Milford talked of little else than Parson Hooper's black veil. That, and the mystery concealed behind it, supplied a topic for discussion between acquaintances meeting in the street and good women gossipping at their open windows. It was the first item of news that the tavernkeeper told to his guests. The children babbled of it on their way to school. One imitative little imp covered his face with an old black handkerchief, thereby so affrighting his playmates that the panic seized himself and he wellnigh lost his wits by his own waggery.

It was remarkable that, of all the busybodies and impertinent people in the parish, not one ventured to put the plain question to Mr. Hooper wherefore he did this thing. Hitherto, whenever there appeared the slightest call for such interference, he had never lacked advisers nor shown himself averse to be guided by their judgment. If he erred at all, it was by so painful a degree of self-distrust that even the mildest censure would lead him to consider an indifferent action as a crime. Yet, though so well acquainted with this amiable weakness, no individual among his parishioners chose to make the black veil a subject of friendly remonstrance. There was a feeling of dread, neither plainly confessed nor carefully concealed, which caused each to shift the responsibility upon another, till at length it was found expedient to send a deputation of the church, in order to deal with Mr. Hooper about the mystery before it should grow into a scandal. Never did an embassy so ill discharge its duties. The minister received them with friendly courtesy, but became silent after they were seated, leaving to his visitors the whole burden of introducing their important business. The topic, it might be supposed, was obvious enough. There was the black veil swathed round Mr. Hooper's forehead and concealing every feature above his placid mouth, on which, at times, they could perceive the glimmering of a melancholy smile. But that piece of crape, to their imagination, seemed to hang down before his heart, the symbol of a fearful secret between him and them. Were the veil but cast aside, they might speak freely of it, but not till then. Thus they sat a considerable time, speechless, confused and shrinking uneasily from Mr. Hooper's eye, which they felt to be fixed upon them with an invisible glance. Finally, the deputies returned abashed to their constituents, pronouncing the matter too weighty to be handled except by a council of the churches, if, indeed, it might not require a General Synod.

But there was one person in the village unappalled by the awe with which the black veil had impressed all besides herself. When the deputies returned without an explanation, or even venturing to demand one, she with the calm energy of her character determined to chase away the strange cloud that appeared to be settling round Mr. Hooper every moment more darkly than before. As his plighted wife it should be her privilege to know what the black veil concealed. At the minister's first visit, therefore, she entered upon the subject with a direct simplicity which made the task easier both for him and her. After he had seated himself she fixed her eyes steadfastly upon the veil, but could discern nothing of the dreadful gloom that had so overawed the multitude; it was but a double fold of crape hanging down from his forehead to his mouth and slightly stirring with his breath.

"No," said she, aloud, and smiling, "there is nothing terrible in this piece of crape, except that it hides a face which I am always glad to look upon. Come, good sir; let the sun shine from behind the cloud. First lay aside your black veil, then tell me why you put it on."

Mr. Hooper's smile glimmered faintly.

"There is an hour to come," said he, "when all of us shall cast aside our veils. Take it not amiss, beloved friend, if I wear this piece of crape till then."

"Your words are a mystery too," returned the young lady. "Take away the veil from them, at least."

"Elizabeth, I will," said he, "so far as my vow may suffer me. Know, then, this veil is a type and a symbol, and I am bound to wear it ever, both in light and darkness, in solitude and before the gaze of multitudes, and as with strangers, so with my familiar friends. No mortal eye will see it withdrawn. This dismal shade must separate me from the world; even you, Elizabeth, can never come behind it."

"What grievous affliction hath befallen you," she earnestly inquired, "that you should thus darken your eyes for ever?"

"If it be a sign of mourning," replied Mr. Hooper, "I, perhaps, like most other mortals, have sorrows dark enough to be typified by a black veil."

"But what if the world will not believe that it is the type of an innocent sorrow?" urged Elizabeth. "Beloved and respected as you are, there may be whispers that you hide your face under the consciousness of secret sin. For the sake of your holy office do away this scandal."

The color rose into her cheeks as she intimated the nature of the rumors that were already abroad in the village. But Mr. Hooper's mildness did not forsake him. He even smiled again—that same sad smile which always appeared like a faint glimmering of light proceeding from the obscurity beneath the veil.

"If I hide my face for sorrow, there is cause enough," he merely replied; "and if I cover it for secret sin, what mortal might not do the same?" And with this gentle but unconquerable obstinacy did he resist all her entreaties.

At length Elizabeth sat silent. For a few moments she appeared lost in thought, considering, probably, what new methods might be tried to withdraw her lover from so dark a fantasy, which, if it had no other meaning, was perhaps a symptom of mental disease. Though of a firmer character than his own, the tears rolled down her cheeks. But in an instant, as it were, a new feeling took the place of sorrow: her eyes were fixed insensibly on the black veil, when like a sudden twilight in the air its terrors fell around her. She arose and stood trembling before him.

"And do you feel it, then, at last?" said he, mournfully.

She made no reply, but covered her eyes with her hand and turned to leave the room. He rushed forward and caught her arm.

"Have patience with me, Elizabeth!" cried he, passionately. "Do not desert me though this veil must be between us here on earth. Be mine, and hereafter there shall be no veil over my face, no darkness between our souls. It is but a mortal veil; it is not for eternity. Oh, you know not how lonely I am, and how frightened to be alone behind my black veil! Do not leave me in this miserable obscurity for ever."

"Lift the veil but once and look me in the face," said she.

"Never! It cannot be!" replied Mr. Hooper.

"Then farewell!" said Elizabeth.

She withdrew her arm from his grasp and slowly departed, pausing at the door to give one long, shuddering gaze that seemed almost to penetrate the mystery of the black veil. But even amid his grief Mr. Hooper smiled to think that only a material emblem had separated him from happiness, though the horrors which it shadowed forth must be drawn darkly between the fondest of lovers.

From that time no attempts were made to remove Mr. Hooper's black veil or by a direct appeal to discover the secret which it was supposed to hide. By persons who claimed a superiority to popular prejudice it was reckoned merely an eccentric whim, such as often mingles with the sober actions of men otherwise rational and tinges them all with its own semblance of insanity. But with the multitude good Mr. Hooper was irreparably a bugbear. He could not walk the street with any peace of mind, so conscious was he that the gentle and timid would turn aside to avoid him, and that others would make it a point of hardihood to throw themselves in his way. The impertinence of the latter class compelled him to give up his customary walk at sunset to the burial-ground; for when he leaned pensively over the gate, there would always be faces behind the gravestones peeping at his black veil. A fable went the rounds that the stare of the dead people drove him thence. It grieved him to the very depth of his kind heart to observe how the children fled from his approach, breaking up their merriest sports while his melancholy figure was yet afar off. Their instinctive dread caused him to feel more strongly than aught else that a preternatural horror was interwoven with the threads of the black crape. In truth, his own antipathy to the veil was known to be so great that he never willingly passed before a mirror nor stooped to drink at a still fountain lest in its peaceful bosom he should be affrighted by himself. This was what gave plausibility to the whispers that Mr. Hooper's conscience tortured him for some great crime too horrible to be entirely concealed or otherwise than so obscurely intimated. Thus from beneath the black veil there rolled a cloud into the sunshine, an ambiguity of sin or sorrow, which enveloped the poor minister, so that love or sympathy could never reach him. It was said that ghost and fiend consorted with him there. With self-shudderings and outward terrors he walked continually in its shadow, groping darkly within his own soul or gazing through a medium that saddened the whole world. Even the lawless wind, it was believed, respected his dreadful secret and never blew aside the veil. But still good Mr. Hooper sadly smiled at the pale visages of the worldly throng as he passed by.

Among all its bad influences, the black veil had the one desirable effect of making its wearer a very efficient clergyman. By the aid of his mysterious emblem—for there was no other apparent cause—he became a man of awful power over souls that were in agony for sin. His converts always regarded him with a dread peculiar to themselves, affirming, though but figuratively, that before he brought them to celestial light they had been with him behind the black veil. Its gloom, indeed, enabled him to sympathize with all dark affections. Dying sinners cried aloud for Mr. Hooper and would not yield their breath till he appeared, though ever, as he stooped to whisper consolation, they shuddered at the veiled face so near their own. Such were the terrors of the black veil even when Death had bared his visage. Strangers came long distances to attend service at his church with the mere idle purpose of gazing at his figure because it was forbidden them to behold his face. But many were made to quake ere they departed. Once, during Governor Belcher's administration, Mr. Hooper was appointed to preach the election sermon. Covered with his black veil, he stood before the chief magistrate, the council and the representatives, and wrought so deep an impression that the legislative measures of that year were characterized by all the gloom and piety of our earliest ancestral sway.

In this manner Mr. Hooper spent a long life, irreproachable in outward act, yet shrouded in dismal suspicions; kind and loving, though unloved and dimly feared; a man apart from men, shunned in their health and joy, but ever summoned to their aid in mortal anguish. As years wore on, shedding their snows above his sable veil, he acquired a name throughout the New England churches, and they called him Father Hooper. Nearly all his parishioners who were of mature age when he was settled had been borne away by many a funeral: he had one congregation in the church and a more crowded one in the churchyard; and, having wrought so late into the evening and done his work so well, it was now good Father Hooper's turn to rest.

Several persons were visible by the shaded candlelight in the death-chamber of the old clergyman. Natural connections he had none. But there was the decorously grave though unmoved physician, seeking only to mitigate the last pangs of the patient whom he could not save. There were the deacons and other eminently pious members of his church. There, also, was the Reverend Mr. Clark of Westbury, a young and zealous divine who had ridden in haste to pray by the bedside of the expiring minister. There was the nurse—no hired handmaiden of

Death, but one whose calm affection had endured thus long in secrecy, in solitude, amid the chill of age, and would not perish even at the dying-hour. Who but Elizabeth! And there lay the hoary head of good Father Hooper upon the death-pillow with the black veil still swathed about his brow and reaching down over his face, so that each more difficult gasp of his faint breath caused it to stir. All through life that piece of crape had hung between him and the world; it had separated him from cheerful brotherhood and woman's love and kept him in that saddest of all prisons his own heart; and still it lay upon his face, as if to deepen the gloom of his darksome chamber and shade him from the sunshine of eternity.

For some time previous his mind had been confused, wavering doubtfully between the past and the present, and hovering forward, as it were, at intervals, into the indistinctness of the world to come. There had been feverish turns which tossed him from side to side and wore away what little strength he had. But in his most convulsive struggles and in the wildest vagaries of his intellect, when no other thought retained its sober influence, he still showed an awful solicitude lest the black veil should slip aside. Even if his bewildered soul could have forgotten, there was a faithful woman at his pillow who with averted eyes would have covered that aged face which she had last beheld in the comeliness of manhood.

At length the death-stricken old man lay quietly in the torpor of mental and bodily exhaustion, with an imperceptible pulse and breath that grew fainter and fainter except when a long, deep and irregular inspiration seemed to prelude the flight of his spirit.

The minister of Westbury approached the bedside.

"Venerable Father Hooper," said he, "the moment of your release is at hand. Are you ready for the lifting of the veil that shuts in time from eternity?"

Father Hooper at first replied merely by a feeble motion of his head; then—apprehensive, perhaps, that his meaning might be doubtful—he exerted himself to speak.

"Yea," said he, in faint accents; "my soul hath a patient weariness until that veil be lifted."

"And is it fitting," resumed the Reverend Mr. Clark, "that a man so given to prayer, of such a blameless example, holy in deed and thought, so far as mortal judgment may pronounce,—is it fitting that a father in the Church should leave a shadow on his memory that may seem to blacken a life so pure? I pray you, my venerable brother, let not this thing be! Suffer us to be gladdened by your triumphant aspect as you go to your reward. Before the veil of eternity be lifted let me cast aside this black veil from your face;" and, thus speaking, the Reverend Mr. Clark bent forward to reveal the mystery of so many years.

But, exerting a sudden energy that made all the beholders stand aghast, Father Hooper snatched both his hands from beneath the bedclothes and pressed them strongly on the black veil, resolute to struggle if the minister of Westbury would contend with a dying man.

"Never!" cried the veiled clergyman. "On earth, never!"

"Dark old man," exclaimed the affrighted minister, "with what horrible crime upon your soul are you now passing to the judgment?"

Father Hooper's breath heaved: it rattled in his throat; but, with a mighty effort grasping forward with his hands, he caught hold of life and held it back till he should speak. He even raised himself in bed, and there he sat shivering with the arms of Death around him, while the black veil hung down, awful at that last moment in the gathered terrors of a lifetime. And yet the faint, sad smile so often there now seemed to glimmer from its obscurity and linger on Father Hooper's lips.

"Why do you tremble at me alone?" cried he, turning his veiled face round the circle of pale spectators. "Tremble also at each other. Have men avoided me and women shown no pity and children screamed and fled only for my black veil? What but the mystery which it obscurely typifies has made this piece of crape so awful? When the friend shows his inmost heart to his friend, the lover to his best-beloved; when man does not vainly shrink from the eye of his Creator, loathsomely treasuring up the secret of his sin,—then deem me a monster for the symbol beneath which I have lived and die. I look around me, and, lo! on every visage a black veil!"

While his auditors shrank from one another in mutual affright, Father Hooper fell back upon his pillow, a veiled corpse with a faint smile lingering on the lips. Still veiled, they laid him in his coffin, and a veiled corpse they bore him to the grave. The grass of many years has sprung up and withered on that grave, the burial-stone is moss-grown, and good Mr. Hooper's face is dust; but awful is still the thought that it mouldered beneath the black veil.

THE MAYPOLE OF MERRY MOUNT.

There is an admirable foundation for a philosophic romance in the curious history of the early settlement of Mount Wollaston, or Merry Mount. In the slight sketch here attempted the facts recorded on the grave pages of our New England annalists have wrought themselves almost spontaneously into a sort of allegory. The masques, mummeries and festive customs described in the text are in accordance with the manners of the age. Authority on these points may be found in Strutt's *Book of English Sports and Pastimes*.

Bright were the days at Merry Mount when the Maypole was the banner-staff of that gay colony. They who reared it, should their banner be triumphant, were to pour sunshine over New England's rugged hills and scatter flower-seeds throughout the soil. Jollity and gloom were contending for an empire. Midsummer eve had come, bringing deep verdure to the forest, and roses in her lap of a more vivid hue than the tender buds of spring. But May, or her mirthful spirit, dwelt all the year round at Merry Mount, sporting with the summer months and revelling with autumn and basking in the glow of winter's fireside. Through a world of toil and care she flitted with a dream-like smile, and came hither to find a home among the lightsome hearts of Merry Mount.

Never had the Maypole been so gayly decked as at sunset on Midsummer eve. This venerated emblem was a pine tree which had preserved the slender grace of youth, while it equalled the loftiest height of the old wood-monarchs. From its top streamed a silken banner colored like the rainbow. Down nearly to the ground the pole was dressed with birchen boughs, and others of the liveliest green, and some with silvery leaves fastened by ribbons that fluttered in fantastic knots of twenty different colors, but no sad ones. Garden-flowers and blossoms of the wilderness laughed gladly forth amid the verdure, so fresh and dewy that they must have grown by magic on that happy pine tree. Where this green and flowery splendor terminated the shaft of the Maypole was stained with the seven brilliant hues of the banner at its top. On the lowest green bough hung an abundant wreath of roses—some that had been gathered in the sunniest spots of the forest, and others, of still richer blush, which the colonists had reared from English seed. O people of the Golden Age, the chief of your husbandry was to raise flowers!

But what was the wild throng that stood hand in hand about the Maypole? It could not be that the fauns and nymphs, when driven from their classic groves and homes of ancient fable, had sought refuge, as all the persecuted did, in the fresh woods of the West. These were Gothic monsters, though perhaps of Grecian ancestry. On the shoulders of a comely youth uprose the head and branching antlers of a stag; a second, human in all other points, had the grim visage of a wolf; a third, still with the trunk and limbs of a mortal man, showed the beard and horns of a venerable he-goat. There was the likeness of a bear erect, brute in all but his hind legs, which were adorned with pink silk stockings. And here, again, almost as wondrous, stood a real bear of the dark forest, lending each of his forepaws to the grasp of a human hand and as ready for the dance as any in that circle. His inferior nature rose halfway to meet his companions as they stooped. Other faces wore the similitude of man or woman, but distorted or extravagant, with red noses pendulous before their mouths, which seemed of awful depth and stretched from ear to ear in an eternal fit of laughter. Here might be seen the salvage man—well known in heraldry—hairy as a baboon and girdled with green leaves. By his side—a nobler figure, but still a counterfeit—appeared an Indian hunter with feathery crest and wampum-belt. Many of this strange company wore foolscaps and had little bells appended to their garments, tinkling with a silvery sound responsive to the inaudible music of their gleesome spirits. Some youths and maidens were of soberer garb, yet well maintained their places in the irregular throng by the expression of wild revelry upon their features.

Such were the colonists of Merry Mount as they stood in the broad smile of sunset round their venerated Maypole. Had a wanderer bewildered in the melancholy forest heard their mirth and stolen a half-affrighted glance, he might have fancied them the crew of Comus, some already transformed to brutes, some midway between man and beast, and the others rioting in the flow of tipsy jollity that foreran the change; but a band of Puritans who watched the scene, invisible themselves, compared the masques to those devils and ruined souls with whom their superstition peopled the black wilderness.

Within the ring of monsters appeared the two airiest forms that had ever trodden on any more solid footing than a purple-and-golden cloud. One was a youth in glistening apparel with a scarf of the rainbow pattern crosswise on his breast. His right hand held a gilded staff—the ensign of high dignity among the revellers—and his left grasped the slender fingers of a fair maiden not less gayly decorated than himself. Bright roses glowed in contrast with the dark and glossy curls of each, and were scattered round their feet or had sprung up spontaneously there. Behind this lightsome couple, so close to the Maypole that its boughs shaded his jovial face, stood the figure of an English priest, canonically dressed, yet decked with flowers, in heathen fashion, and wearing a chaplet of the native vine leaves. By the riot of his rolling eye and the pagan decorations of his holy garb, he seemed the wildest monster there, and the very Comus of the crew.

"Votaries of the Maypole," cried the flower-decked priest, "merrily all day long have the woods echoed to your mirth. But be this your merriest hour, my hearts! Lo! here stand the Lord and Lady of the May, whom I, a clerk of Oxford and high priest of Merry Mount, am presently to join in holy matrimony.—Up with your nimble spirits, ye morrice-dancers, green men and glee-maidens, bears and wolves and horned gentlemen! Come! a chorus now rich with the old mirth of Merry England and the wilder glee of this fresh forest, and then a dance, to show the youthful pair what life is made of and how airily they should go through it!—All ye that love the Maypole, lend your voices to the nuptial song of the Lord and Lady of the May!"

This wedlock was more serious than most affairs of Merry Mount, where jest and delusion, trick and fantasy, kept up a continual carnival. The Lord and Lady of the May, though their titles must be laid down at sunset, were really and truly to be partners for the dance of life, beginning the measure that same bright eve. The wreath of roses that hung from the lowest green bough of the Maypole had been twined for them, and would be thrown over both their heads in symbol of their flowery union. When the priest had spoken, therefore, a riotous uproar burst from the rout of monstrous figures.

"Begin you the stave, reverend sir," cried they all, "and never did the woods ring to such a merry peal as we of the Maypole shall send up."

Immediately a prelude of pipe, cittern and viol, touched with practised minstrelsy, began to play from a neighboring thicket in such a mirthful cadence that the boughs of the Maypole quivered to the sound. But the May-lord—he of the gilded staff—chancing to look into his lady's eyes, was wonder-struck at the almost pensive glance that met his own.

"Edith, sweet Lady of the May," whispered he, reproachfully, "is yon wreath of roses a garland to hang above our graves that you look so sad? Oh, Edith, this is our golden time. Tarnish it not by any pensive shadow of the mind, for it may be that nothing of futurity will be brighter than the mere remembrance of what is now passing."

"That was the very thought that saddened me. How came it in your mind too?" said Edith, in a still lower tone than he; for it was high treason to be sad at Merry Mount. "Therefore do I sigh amid this festive music. And besides, dear Edgar, I struggle as with a dream, and fancy that these shapes of our jovial friends are visionary and their mirth unreal, and that we are no true lord and lady of the May. What is the mystery in my heart?"

Just then, as if a spell had loosened them, down came a little shower of withering rose-leaves from the Maypole. Alas for the young lovers! No sooner had their hearts glowed with real passion than they were sensible of something vague and unsubstantial in their former pleasures, and felt a dreary presentiment of inevitable change. From the moment that they truly loved they had subjected themselves to earth's doom of care and sorrow and troubled joy, and had no more a home at Merry Mount. That was Edith's mystery. Now leave we the priest to marry them, and the masquers to sport round the Maypole till the last sunbeam be withdrawn from its summit and the shadows of the forest mingle gloomily in the dance. Meanwhile, we may discover who these gay people were.

Two hundred years ago, and more, the Old World and its inhabitants became mutually weary of each other. Men voyaged by thousands to the West—some to barter glass and such like jewels for the furs of the Indian hunter, some to conquer virgin empires, and one stern band to pray. But none of these motives had much weight with the striving to communicate their mirth to the grave Indian, or masquerading in the skins of deer and wolves which they had hunted for that especial purpose. Often the whole colony were playing at Blindman's Buff, magistrates and all with their eyes bandaged, except a single scapegoat, whom the blinded sinners pursued by the tinkling of the bells at his garments. Once, it is said, they were seen following a flower-decked corpse with merriment and festive music to his grave. But did the dead man laugh? In their quietest times they sang ballads and told tales for the edification of their pious visitors, or perplexed them with juggling tricks, or grinned at them through horse-collars; and when sport itself grew wearisome, they made game of their own stupidity and began a yawning-match. At the very least of these enormities the men of iron shook their heads and frowned so darkly that the revellers looked up, imagining that a momentary cloud had overcast the sunshine which was to be perpetual there. On the other hand, the Puritans affirmed that when a psalm was pealing from their place of worship the echo which the forest sent them back seemed often like the chorus of a jolly catch, closing with a roar of laughter. Who but the fiend and his bond-slaves the crew of Merry Mount had thus disturbed them? In due time a feud arose, stern and bitter on one side, and as serious on the other as anything could be among such light spirits as had sworn allegiance to the Maypole. The future complexion of New England was involved in this important quarrel. Should the grisly saints establish their jurisdiction over the gay sinners, then would their spirits darken all the clime and make it a land of clouded visages, of hard toil, of sermon and psalm for ever; but should the banner-staff of Merry Mount be fortunate, sunshine would break upon the hills, and flowers would beautify the forest and late posterity do homage to the Maypole.

After these authentic passages from history we return to the nuptials of the Lord and Lady of the May. Alas! we have delayed too long, and must darken our tale too suddenly. As we glance again at the Maypole a solitary sunbeam is fading from the summit, and leaves only a faint golden tinge blended with the hues of the rainbow banner. Even that dim light is now withdrawn, relinquishing the whole domain of Merry Mount to the evening gloom which has rushed so instantaneously from the black surrounding woods. But some of these black shadows have rushed forth in human shape.

Yes, with the setting sun the last day of mirth had passed from Merry Mount. The ring of gay masquers was disordered and broken; the stag lowered his antlers in dismay; the wolf grew weaker than a lamb; the bells of the morrice-dancers tinkled with tremulous affright. The Puritans had played a characteristic part in the Maypole mummeries. Their darksome figures were intermixed with the wild shapes of their foes, and made the scene a picture of the moment when waking thoughts start up amid the scattered fantasies of a dream. The leader of the hostile party stood in the centre of the circle, while the rout of monsters cowered around him like evil spirits in the presence of a dread magician. No fantastic foolery could look him in the face. So stern was the energy of his aspect that the whole man, visage, frame and soul, seemed wrought of iron gifted with life and thought, yet all of one substance with his headpiece and breastplate. It was the Puritan of Puritans: it was Endicott himself.

"Stand off, priest of Baal!" said he, with a grim frown and laying no reverent hand upon the surplice. "I know thee, Blackstone![1] Thou art the man who couldst not abide the rule even of thine own corrupted Church, and hast come hither to preach iniquity and to give example of it in thy life. But now shall it be seen that the Lord hath sanctified this wilderness for his peculiar people. Woe unto them that would defile it! And first for this flower-decked abomination, the altar of thy worship!"

And with his keen sword Endicott assaulted the hallowed Maypole. Nor long did it resist his arm. It groaned with a dismal sound, it showered leaves and rose-buds upon the remorseless enthusiast, and finally, with all its green boughs and ribbons and flowers, symbolic of departed pleasures, down fell the banner-staff of Merry Mount. As it sank, tradition says, the evening sky grew darker and the woods threw forth a more sombre shadow.

"There!" cried Endicott, looking triumphantly on his work; "there lies the only Maypole in New England. The thought is strong within me that by its fall is shadowed forth the fate of light and idle mirthmakers amongst us and our posterity. Amen, saith John Endicott!"

"Amen!" echoed his followers.

But the votaries of the Maypole gave one groan for their idol. At the sound the Puritan leader glanced at the crew of Comus, each a figure of broad mirth, yet at this moment strangely expressive of sorrow and dismay.

"Valiant captain," quoth Peter Palfrey, the ancient of the band, "what order shall be taken with the prisoners?"

"I thought not to repent me of cutting down a Maypole," replied Endicott, "yet now I could find in my heart to plant it again and give each of these bestial pagans one other dance round their idol. It would have served rarely for a whipping-post."

"But there are pine trees enow," suggested the lieutenant.

"True, good ancient," said the leader. "Wherefore bind the heathen crew and bestow on them a small matter of stripes apiece as earnest of our future justice. Set some of the rogues in the stocks to rest themselves so soon as Providence shall bring us to one of our own well-ordered settlements where such accommodations may be found. Further penalties, such as branding and cropping of ears, shall be thought of hereafter."

"How many stripes for the priest?" inquired Ancient Palfrey.

---

[1] Did Governor Endicott speak less positively, we should suspect a mistake here. The Rev. Mr. Blackstone, though an eccentric, is not known to have been an immoral man. We rather doubt his identity with the priest of Merry Mount.

"None as yet," answered Endicott, bending his iron frown upon the culprit. "It must be for the Great and General Court to determine whether stripes and long imprisonment, and other grievous penalty, may atone for his transgressions. Let him look to himself. For such as violate our civil order it may be permitted us to show mercy, but woe to the wretch that troubleth our religion!"

"And this dancing bear?" resumed the officer. "Must he share the stripes of his fellows?"

"Shoot him through the head!" said the energetic Puritan. "I suspect witchcraft in the beast."

"Here be a couple of shining ones," continued Peter Palfrey, pointing his weapon at the Lord and Lady of the May. "They seem to be of high station among these misdoers. Methinks their dignity will not be fitted with less than a double share of stripes."

Endicott rested on his sword and closely surveyed the dress and aspect of the hapless pair. There they stood, pale, downcast and apprehensive, yet there was an air of mutual support and of pure affection seeking aid and giving it that showed them to be man and wife with the sanction of a priest upon their love. The youth in the peril of the moment, had dropped his gilded staff and thrown his arm about the Lady of the May, who leaned against his breast too lightly to burden him, but with weight enough to express that their destinies were linked together for good or evil. They looked first at each other and then into the grim captain's face. There they stood in the first hour of wedlock, while the idle pleasures of which their companions were the emblems had given place to the sternest cares of life, personified by the dark Puritans. But never had their youthful beauty seemed so pure and high as when its glow was chastened by adversity.

"Youth," said Endicott, "ye stand in an evil case—thou and thy maiden-wife. Make ready presently, for I am minded that ye shall both have a token to remember your wedding-day."

"Stern man," cried the May-lord, "how can I move thee? Were the means at hand, I would resist to the death; being powerless, I entreat. Do with me as thou wilt, but let Edith go untouched."

"Not so," replied the immitigable zealot. "We are not wont to show an idle courtesy to that sex which requireth the stricter discipline.—What sayest thou, maid? Shall thy silken bridegroom suffer thy share of the penalty besides his own?"

"Be it death," said Edith, "and lay it all on me."

Truly, as Endicott had said, the poor lovers stood in a woeful case. Their foes were triumphant, their friends captive and abased, their home desolate, the benighted wilderness around them, and a rigorous destiny in the shape of the Puritan leader their only guide. Yet the deepening twilight could not altogether conceal that the iron man was softened. He smiled at the fair spectacle of early love; he almost sighed for the inevitable blight of early hopes.

"The troubles of life have come hastily on this young couple," observed Endicott. "We will see how they comport themselves under their present trials ere we burden them with greater. If among the spoil there be any garments of a more decent fashion, let them be put upon this May-lord and his Lady instead of their glistening vanities. Look to it, some of you."

"And shall not the youth's hair be cut?" asked Peter Palfrey, looking with abhorrence at the lovelock and long glossy curls of the young man.

"Crop it forthwith, and that in the true pumpkin-shell fashion," answered the captain. "Then bring them along with us, but more gently than their fellows. There be qualities in the youth which may make him valiant to fight and sober to toil and pious to pray, and in the maiden that may fit her to become a mother in our Israel, bringing up babes in better nurture than her own hath been.—Nor think ye, young ones, that they are the happiest, even in our lifetime of a moment, who misspend it in dancing round a Maypole."

And Endicott, the severest Puritan of all who laid the rock-foundation of New England, lifted the wreath of roses from the ruin of the Maypole and threw it with his own gauntleted hand over the heads of the Lord and Lady of the May. It was a deed of prophecy. As the moral gloom of the world overpowers all systematic gayety, even so was their home of wild mirth made desolate amid the sad forest. They returned to it no more. But as their flowery garland was wreathed of the brightest roses that had grown there, so in the tie that united them were intertwined all the purest and best of their early joys. They went heavenward supporting each other along the difficult path which it was their lot to tread, and never wasted one regretful thought on the vanities of Merry Mount.

THE GENTLE BOY.

In the course of the year 1656 several of the people called Quakers—led, as they professed, by the inward movement of the spirit—made their appearance in New England. Their reputation as holders of mystic and pernicious principles having spread before them, the Puritans early endeavored to banish and to prevent the further intrusion of the rising sect. But the measures by which it was intended to purge the land of heresy, though more than sufficiently vigorous, were entirely unsuccessful. The Quakers, esteeming persecution as a divine call to the post of danger, laid claim to a holy courage unknown to the Puritans themselves, who had shunned the cross by providing for the peaceable exercise of their religion in a distant wilderness. Though it was the singular fact that every nation of the earth rejected the wandering enthusiasts who practised peace toward all men, the place of greatest uneasiness and peril, and therefore in their eyes the most eligible, was the province of Massachusetts Bay.

The fines, imprisonments and stripes liberally distributed by our pious forefathers, the popular antipathy, so strong that it endured nearly a hundred years after actual persecution had ceased, were attractions as powerful for the Quakers as peace, honor and reward would have been for the worldly-minded. Every European vessel brought new cargoes of the sect, eager to testify against the oppression which they hoped to share; and when shipmasters were restrained by heavy fines from affording them passage, they made long and circuitous journeys through the Indian country, and appeared in the province as if conveyed by a supernatural power. Their enthusiasm, heightened almost to madness by the treatment which they received, produced actions contrary to the rules of decency as well as of rational religion, and presented a singular contrast to the calm and staid deportment of their sectarian successors of the present day. The command of the Spirit, inaudible except to the soul and not to be controverted on grounds of human wisdom, was made a plea for most indecorous exhibitions which, abstractedly considered, well deserved the moderate chastisement of the rod. These extravagances, and the persecution which was at once their cause and consequence, continued to increase, till in the year 1659 the government of Massachusetts Bay indulged two members of the Quaker sect with the crown of martyrdom.

An indelible stain of blood is upon the hands of all who consented to this act, but a large share of the awful responsibility must rest upon the person then at the head of the government. He was a man of narrow mind and imperfect education, and his uncompromising bigotry was made hot and mischievous by violent and hasty passions; he exerted his influence indecorously and unjustifiably to compass the death of the enthusiasts, and his whole conduct in respect to them was marked by brutal cruelty. The Quakers, whose revengeful feelings were not less deep because they were inactive, remembered this man and his associates in after-times. The historian of the sect affirms that by the wrath of Heaven a blight fell upon the land in the vicinity of the "bloody town" of Boston, so that no wheat would grow there; and he takes his stand, as it were, among the graves of the ancient persecutors, and triumphantly recounts the judgments that overtook them in old age or at the parting-hour. He tells us that they died suddenly and violently and in madness, but nothing can exceed the bitter mockery with which he records the loathsome disease and "death by rottenness" of the fierce and cruel governor.

On the evening of the autumn day that had witnessed the martyrdom of two men of the Quaker persuasion, a Puritan settler was returning from the metropolis to the neighboring country-town in which he resided. The air was cool, the sky clear, and the lingering twilight was made brighter by the rays of a young moon which had now nearly reached the verge of the horizon. The traveller, a man of middle age, wrapped in a gray frieze cloak, quickened his pace when he had reached the outskirts of the town, for a gloomy extent of nearly four miles lay between him and his home. The low straw-thatched houses were scattered at considerable intervals along the road, and, the country having been settled but about thirty years, the tracts of original forest still bore no small proportion to the cultivated ground. The autumn wind wandered among the branches, whirling away the leaves from all except the pine trees and moaning as if it lamented the desolation of which it was the instrument. The road had penetrated the mass of woods that lay nearest to the town, and was just emerging into an open space, when the traveller's ears were saluted by a sound more mournful than even that of the wind. It was like the wailing of some one in distress, and it seemed to proceed from beneath a tall and lonely fir tree in the centre of a cleared but unenclosed and uncultivated field. The Puritan could not but remember that this was the very spot which had been made accursed a few hours before by the execution of the Quakers, whose bodies had been thrown together into one hasty grave beneath the tree on which they suffered. He struggled, however, against the superstitious fears which belonged to the age, and compelled himself to pause and listen.

"The voice is most likely mortal, nor have I cause to tremble if it be otherwise," thought he, straining his eyes through the dim moonlight. "Methinks it is like the wailing of a child—some infant, it may be, which has strayed from its mother and chanced upon this place of death. For the ease of mine own conscience I must search this matter out." He therefore left the path and walked somewhat fearfully across the field. Though now so desolate, its soil was pressed down and trampled by the thousand footsteps of those who had witnessed the spectacle of that day, all of whom had now retired, leaving the dead to their loneliness.

The traveller at length reached the fir tree, which from the middle upward was covered with living branches, although a scaffold had been erected beneath, and other preparations made for the work of death. Under this unhappy tree—which in after-times was believed to drop poison with its dew—sat the one solitary mourner for innocent blood. It was a slender and light-clad little boy who leaned his face upon a hillock of fresh-turned and half-frozen earth and wailed bitterly, yet in a suppressed tone, as if his grief might receive the punishment of crime. The Puritan, whose approach had been unperceived, laid his hand upon the child's shoulder and addressed him compassionately.

"You have chosen a dreary lodging, my poor boy, and no wonder that you weep," said he. "But dry your eyes and tell me where your mother dwells; I promise you, if the journey be not too far, I will leave you in her arms tonight."

The boy had hushed his wailing at once, and turned his face upward to the stranger. It was a pale, bright-eyed countenance, certainly not more than six years old, but sorrow, fear and want had destroyed much of its infantile expression. The Puritan, seeing the boy's frightened gaze and feeling that he trembled under his hand, endeavored to reassure him:

"Nay, if I intended to do you harm, little lad, the readiest way were to leave you here. What! you do not fear to sit beneath the gallows on a new-made grave, and yet you tremble at a friend's touch? Take heart, child, and tell me what is your name and where is your home."

"Friend," replied the little boy, in a sweet though faltering voice, "they call me Ilbrahim, and my home is here."

The pale, spiritual face, the eyes that seemed to mingle with the moonlight, the sweet, airy voice and the outlandish name almost made the Puritan believe that the boy was in truth a being which had sprung up out of the grave on which he sat; but perceiving that the apparition stood the test of a short mental prayer, and remembering that the arm which he had touched was lifelike, he adopted a more rational supposition. "The poor child is stricken in his intellect," thought he, "but verily his words are fearful in a place like this." He then spoke soothingly, intending to humor the boy's fantasy:

"Your home will scarce be comfortable, Ilbrahim, this cold autumn night, and I fear you are ill-provided with food. I am hastening to a warm supper and bed; and if you will go with me, you shall share them."

"I thank thee, friend, but, though I be hungry and shivering with cold, thou wilt not give me food nor lodging," replied the boy, in the quiet tone which despair had taught him even so young. "My father was of the people whom all men hate; they have laid him under this heap of earth, and here is my home."

The Puritan, who had laid hold of little Ilbrahim's hand, relinquished it as if he were touching a loathsome reptile. But he possessed a compassionate heart which not even religious prejudice could harden into stone. "God forbid that I should leave this child to perish, though he comes of the accursed sect," said he to himself. "Do we not all spring from an evil root? Are we not all in darkness till the light doth shine upon us? He shall not perish, neither in body nor, if prayer and instruction may avail for him, in soul." He then spoke aloud and kindly to Ilbrahim, who had again hid his face in the cold earth of the grave:

"Was every door in the land shut against you, my child, that you have wandered to this unhallowed spot?"

"They drove me forth from the prison when they took my father thence," said the boy, "and I stood afar off watching the crowd of people; and when they were gone, I came hither, and found only this grave. I knew that my father was sleeping here, and I said, 'This shall be my home.'"

"No, child, no, not while I have a roof over my head or a morsel to share with you," exclaimed the Puritan, whose sympathies were now fully excited. "Rise up and come with me, and fear not any harm."

The boy wept afresh, and clung to the heap of earth as if the cold heart beneath it were warmer to him than any in a living breast. The traveller, however, continued to entreat him tenderly, and, seeming to acquire some degree of confidence, he at length arose; but his slender limbs tottered with weakness, his little head grew dizzy, and he leaned against the tree of death for support.

"My poor boy, are you so feeble?" said the Puritan. "When did you taste food last?"

"I ate of bread and water with my father in the prison," replied Ilbrahim, "but they brought him none neither yesterday nor to-day, saying that he had eaten enough to bear him to his journey's end. Trouble not thyself for my hunger, kind friend, for I have lacked food many times ere now."

The traveller took the child in his arms and wrapped his cloak about him, while his heart stirred with shame and anger against the gratuitous cruelty of the instruments in this persecution. In the awakened warmth of his feelings he resolved that at whatever risk he would not forsake the poor little defenceless being whom Heaven had confided to his care. With this determination he left the accursed field and resumed the homeward path from which the wailing of the boy had called him. The light and motionless burden scarcely impeded his progress, and he soon beheld the fire-rays from the windows of the cottage which he, a native of a distant clime, had built in the Western wilderness. It was surrounded by a considerable extent of cultivated ground, and the dwelling was situated in the nook of a wood-covered hill, whither it seemed to have crept for protection.

"Look up, child," said the Puritan to Ilbrahim, whose faint head had sunk upon his shoulder; "there is our home."

At the word "home" a thrill passed through the child's frame, but he continued silent. A few moments brought them to the cottage door, at which the owner knocked; for at that early period, when savages were wandering everywhere among the settlers, bolt and bar were indispensable to the security of a dwelling. The summons was answered by a bond-servant, a coarse-clad and dull-featured piece of humanity, who, after ascertaining that his master was the applicant, undid the door and held a flaring pine-knot torch to light him in. Farther back in the passageway the red blaze discovered a matronly woman, but no little crowd of children came bounding forth to greet their father's return.

As the Puritan entered he thrust aside his cloak and displayed Ilbrahim's face to the female.

"Dorothy, here is a little outcast whom Providence hath put into our hands," observed he. "Be kind to him, even as if he were of those dear ones who have departed from us."

"What pale and bright-eyed little boy is this, Tobias?" she inquired. "Is he one whom the wilderness-folk have ravished from some Christian mother?"

"No, Dorothy; this poor child is no captive from the wilderness," he replied. "The heathen savage would have given him to eat of his scanty morsel and to drink of his birchen cup, but Christian men, alas! had cast him out to die." Then he told her how he had found him beneath the gallows, upon his father's grave, and how his heart had prompted him like the speaking of an inward voice to take the little outcast home and be kind unto him. He acknowledged his resolution to feed and clothe him as if he were his own child, and to afford him the instruction which should counteract the pernicious errors hitherto instilled into his infant mind.

Dorothy was gifted with even a quicker tenderness than her husband, and she approved of all his doings and intentions.

"Have you a mother, dear child?" she inquired.

The tears burst forth from his full heart as he attempted to reply, but Dorothy at length understood that he had a mother, who like the rest of her sect was a persecuted wanderer. She had been taken from the prison a short time before, carried into the uninhabited wilderness and left to perish there by hunger or wild beasts. This was no uncommon method of disposing of the Quakers, and they were accustomed to boast that the inhabitants of the desert were more hospitable to them than civilized man.

"Fear not, little boy; you shall not need a mother, and a kind one," said Dorothy, when she had gathered this information. "Dry your tears, Ilbrahim, and be my child, as I will be your mother."

The good woman prepared the little bed from which her own children had successively been borne to another resting-place. Before Ilbrahim would consent to occupy it he knelt down, and as Dorothy listed to his simple and affecting prayer she marvelled how the parents that had taught it to him could have been judged worthy of death. When the boy had fallen asleep, she bent over his pale and spiritual countenance, pressed a kiss upon his white brow, drew the bedclothes up about his neck, and went away with a pensive gladness in her heart.

Tobias Pearson was not among the earliest emigrants from the old country. He had remained in England during the first years of the Civil War, in which he had borne some share as a cornet of dragoons under Cromwell. But when the ambitious designs of his leader began to develop themselves, he quitted the army of the Parliament and sought a refuge from the strife which was no longer holy among the people of his persuasion in the colony of Massachusetts. A more worldly consideration had perhaps an influence in drawing him thither, for New England offered advantages to men of unprosperous fortunes as well as to dissatisfied religionists, and Pearson had hitherto found it difficult to provide for a wife and increasing family. To this supposed impurity of motive the more bigoted Puritans were inclined to impute the removal by death of all the children for whose earthly good the father had been over-thoughtful. They had left their native country blooming like roses, and like roses they had perished in a foreign soil. Those expounders of the ways of Providence, who had thus judged their brother and attributed his domestic sorrows to his sin, were not more charitable when they saw him and Dorothy endeavoring to fill up the void in their hearts by the adoption of an infant of the accursed sect. Nor did they fail to communicate their disapprobation to Tobias, but the latter in reply merely pointed at the little quiet, lovely boy, whose appearance and deportment were indeed as powerful arguments as could possibly have been adduced in his own favor. Even his beauty, however, and his winning manners sometimes produced an effect ultimately unfavorable; for the bigots, when the outer surfaces of their iron hearts had been softened and again grew hard, affirmed that no merely natural cause could have so worked upon them. Their antipathy to the poor infant was also increased by the ill-success of divers theological discussions in which it was attempted to convince him of the errors of his sect. Ilbrahim, it is true, was not a skilful controversialist, but the feeling of his religion was strong as instinct in him, and he could neither be enticed nor driven from the faith which his father had died for.

The odium of this stubbornness was shared in a great measure by the child's protectors, insomuch that Tobias and Dorothy very shortly began to experience a most bitter species of persecution in the cold regards of many a friend whom they had valued. The common people manifested their opinions more openly. Pearson was a man of some consideration, being a representative to the General Court and an approved lieutenant in the train-bands, yet within a week after his adoption of Ilbrahim he had been both hissed and hooted. Once, also, when walking through a solitary piece of woods, he heard a loud voice from some invisible speaker, and it cried, "What shall be done to the backslider? Lo! the scourge is knotted for him, even the whip of nine cords, and every cord three knots." These insults irritated Pearson's temper for the moment; they entered also into his heart, and became imperceptible but powerful workers toward an end which his most secret thought had not yet whispered.

On the second Sabbath after Ilbrahim became a member of their family, Pearson and his wife deemed it proper that he should appear with them at public worship. They had anticipated some opposition to this measure from the boy, but he prepared himself in silence, and at the appointed hour was clad in the new mourning-suit which Dorothy had wrought for him. As the parish was then, and during many subsequent years, unprovided with a bell, the signal for the commencement of religious exercises was the beat of a drum. At the first sound of that martial call to the place of holy and quiet thoughts Tobias and Dorothy set forth, each holding a hand of little Ilbrahim, like two parents linked together by the infant of their love. On their path through the leafless woods they were overtaken by many persons of their acquaintance, all of whom avoided them and passed by on the other side; but a severer trial awaited their constancy when they had descended the hill and drew near the pine-built and undecorated house of prayer. Around the door, from which the drummer still sent forth his thundering summons, was drawn up a formidable phalanx, including several of the oldest members of the congregation, many of the middle-aged and nearly all the younger males. Pearson found it difficult to sustain their united and disapproving gaze, but Dorothy, whose mind was differently circumstanced, merely drew the boy closer to her and faltered not in her approach. As they entered the door they overheard the muttered sentiments of the assemblage; and when the reviling voices of the little children smote Ilbrahim's ear, he wept.

The interior aspect of the meeting-house was rude. The low ceiling, the unplastered walls, the naked woodwork and the undraperied pulpit offered nothing to excite the devotion which without such external aids often remains latent in the heart. The floor of the building was occupied by rows of long cushionless benches, supplying the place of pews, and the broad aisle formed a sexual division impassable except by children beneath a certain age.

Pearson and Dorothy separated at the door of the meeting-house, and Ilbrahim, being within the years of infancy, was retained under the care of the latter. The wrinkled beldams involved themselves in their rusty cloaks as he passed by; even the mild-featured maidens seemed to dread contamination; and many a stern old man arose and turned his repulsive and unheavenly countenance upon the gentle boy, as if the sanctuary were polluted by his presence. He was a sweet infant of the skies that had strayed away from his home, and all the inhabitants of this miserable world closed up their impure hearts against him, drew back their earth-soiled garments from his touch and said, "We are holier than thou."

Ilbrahim, seated by the side of his adopted mother and retaining fast hold of her hand, assumed a grave and decorous demeanor such as might befit a person of matured taste and understanding who should find himself in a temple dedicated to some worship which he did not recognize, but felt himself bound to respect. The exercises had not yet commenced, however, when the boy's attention was arrested by an event apparently of trifling interest. A woman having her face muffled in a hood and a cloak drawn completely about her form advanced slowly up the broad aisle and took place upon the foremost bench. Ilbrahim's faint color varied, his nerves fluttered; he was unable to turn his eyes from the muffled female.

When the preliminary prayer and hymn were over, the minister arose, and, having turned the hour-glass which stood by the great Bible, commenced his discourse. He was now well stricken in years, a man of pale, thin countenance, and his gray hairs were closely covered by a black velvet skull-cap. In his younger days he had practically learned the meaning of persecution from Archbishop Laud, and he was not now disposed to forget the lesson against which he had murmured then. Introducing the often-discussed subject of the Quakers, he gave a history of that sect and a description of their tenets in which error predominated and prejudice distorted the aspect of what was true. He adverted to the recent measures in the province, and cautioned his hearers of weaker parts against calling in question the just severity which God-fearing magistrates had at length been compelled to exercise. He spoke of the danger of pity—in some cases a commendable and Christian virtue, but inapplicable to this pernicious sect. He observed that such was their devilish obstinacy in error that even the little children, the sucking babes, were hardened and desperate heretics. He affirmed that no man without Heaven's especial warrant should attempt their conversion lest while he lent his hand to draw them from the slough he should himself be precipitated into its lowest depths.

The sands of the second hour were principally in the lower half of the glass when the sermon concluded. An approving murmur followed, and the clergyman, having given out a hymn, took his seat with much self-congratulation, and endeavored to read the effect of his eloquence in the visages of the people. But while voices from all parts of the house were tuning themselves to sing a scene occurred which, though not very unusual at that period in the province, happened to be without precedent in this parish.

The muffled female, who had hitherto sat motionless in the front rank of the audience, now arose and with slow, stately and unwavering step ascended the pulpit stairs. The quaverings of incipient harmony were hushed and the divine sat in speechless and almost terrified astonishment while she undid the door and stood up in the sacred desk from which his maledictions had just been thundered. She then divested herself of the cloak and hood, and appeared in a most singular array. A shapeless robe of sackcloth was girded about her waist with a knotted cord; her raven hair fell down upon her shoulders, and its blackness was defiled by pale streaks of ashes, which she had strewn upon her head. Her eyebrows, dark and strongly defined, added to the deathly whiteness of a countenance which, emaciated with want and wild with enthusiasm and strange sorrows, retained no trace of earlier beauty. This figure stood gazing earnestly on the audience, and there was no sound nor any movement except a faint shuddering which every man observed in his neighbor, but was scarcely conscious of in himself. At length, when her fit of inspiration came, she spoke for the first few moments in a low voice and not invariably distinct utterance. Her discourse gave evidence of an imagination hopelessly entangled with her reason; it was a vague and incomprehensible rhapsody, which, however, seemed to spread its own atmosphere round the hearer's soul, and to move his feelings by some influence unconnected with the words. As she proceeded beautiful but shadowy images would sometimes be seen like bright things moving in a turbid river, or a strong and singularly shaped idea leapt forth and seized at once on the understanding or the heart. But the course of her unearthly eloquence soon led her to the persecutions of her sect, and from thence the step was short to her own peculiar sorrows. She was naturally a woman of mighty passions, and hatred and revenge now wrapped themselves in the garb of piety. The character of her speech was changed; her images became distinct though wild, and her denunciations had an almost hellish bitterness.

"The governor and his mighty men," she said, "have gathered together, taking counsel among themselves and saying, 'What shall we do unto this people—even unto the people that have come into this land to put our iniquity to the blush?' And, lo! the devil entereth into the council-chamber like a lame man of low stature and gravely apparelled, with a dark and twisted countenance and a bright, downcast eye. And he standeth up among the rulers; yea, he goeth to and fro, whispering to each; and every man lends his ear, for his word is 'Slay! Slay!' But I say unto ye, Woe to them that slay! Woe to them that shed the blood of saints! Woe to them that have slain the husband and cast forth the child, the tender infant, to wander homeless and hungry and cold till he die, and have saved the mother alive in the cruelty of their tender mercies! Woe to them in their lifetime! Cursed are they in the delight and pleasure of their hearts! Woe to them in their death-hour, whether it come swiftly with blood and violence or after long and lingering pain! Woe in the dark house, in the rottenness of the grave, when the children's children shall revile the ashes of the fathers! Woe, woe, woe, at the judgment, when all the persecuted and all the slain in this bloody land, and the father, the mother and the child, shall await them in a day that they cannot escape! Seed of the faith, seed of the faith, ye whose hearts are moving with a power that ye know not, arise, wash your hands of this innocent blood! Lift your voices, chosen ones, cry aloud, and call down a woe and a judgment with me!"

Having thus given vent to the flood of malignity which she mistook for inspiration, the speaker was silent. Her voice was succeeded by the hysteric shrieks of several women, but the feelings of the audience generally had not been drawn onward in the current with her own. They remained stupefied, stranded, as it were, in the midst of a torrent which deafened them by its roaring, but might not move them by its violence. The clergyman, who could not hitherto have ejected the usurper of his pulpit otherwise than by bodily force, now addressed her in the tone of just indignation and legitimate authority.

"Get you down, woman, from the holy place which you profane," he said, "Is it to the Lord's house that you come to pour forth the foulness of your heart and the inspiration of the devil? Get you down, and remember that the sentence of death is on you—yea, and shall be executed, were it but for this day's work."

"I go, friend, I go, for the voice hath had its utterance," replied she, in a depressed, and even mild, tone. "I have done my mission unto thee and to thy people; reward me with stripes, imprisonment or death, as ye shall be permitted." The weakness of exhausted passion caused her steps to totter as she descended the pulpit stairs.

The people, in the mean while, were stirring to and fro on the floor of the house, whispering among themselves and glancing toward the intruder. Many of them now recognized her as the woman who had assaulted the governor with frightful language as he passed by the window of her prison; they knew, also, that she was adjudged to suffer death, and had been preserved only by an involuntary banishment into the wilderness. The new outrage by which she had provoked her fate seemed to render further lenity impossible, and a gentleman in military dress, with a stout man of inferior rank, drew toward the door of the meetinghouse and awaited her approach. Scarcely did her feet press the floor, however, when an unexpected scene occurred. In that moment of her peril, when every eye frowned with death, a little timid boy threw his arms round his mother.

"I am here, mother; it is I, and I will go with thee to prison," he exclaimed.

She gazed at him with a doubtful and almost frightened expression, for she knew that the boy had been cast out to perish, and she had not hoped to see his face again. She feared, perhaps, that it was but one of the happy visions with which her excited fancy had often deceived her in the solitude of the desert or in prison; but when she felt his hand warm within her own and heard his little eloquence of childish love, she began to know that she was yet a mother.

"Blessed art thou, my son!" she sobbed. "My heart was withered—yea, dead with thee and with thy father—and now it leaps as in the first moment when I pressed thee to my bosom."

She knelt down and embraced him again and again, while the joy that could find no words expressed itself in broken accents, like the bubbles gushing up to vanish at the surface of a deep fountain. The sorrows of past years and the darker peril that was nigh cast not a shadow on the brightness of that fleeting moment. Soon, however, the spectators saw a change upon her face as the consciousness of her sad estate returned, and grief supplied the fount of tears which joy had opened. By the words she uttered it would seem that the indulgence of natural love had given her mind a momentary sense of its errors, and made her know how far she had strayed from duty in following the dictates of a wild fanaticism.

"In a doleful hour art thou returned to me, poor boy," she said, "for thy mother's path has gone darkening onward, till now the end is death. Son, son, I have borne thee in my arms when my limbs were tottering, and I have fed thee with the food that I was fainting for; yet I have ill-performed a mother's part by thee in life, and now I leave thee no inheritance but woe and shame. Thou wilt go seeking through the world, and find all hearts closed against thee and their sweet affections turned to bitterness for my sake. My child, my child, how many a pang awaits thy gentle spirit, and I the cause of all!"

She hid her face on Ilbrahim's head, and her long raven hair, discolored with the ashes of her mourning, fell down about him like a veil. A low and interrupted moan was the voice of her heart's anguish, and it did not fail to move the sympathies of many who mistook their involuntary virtue for a sin. Sobs were audible in the female section of the house, and every man who was a father drew his hand across his eyes.

Tobias Pearson was agitated and uneasy, but a certain feeling like the consciousness of guilt oppressed him; so that he could not go forth and offer himself as the protector of the child. Dorothy, however, had watched her husband's eye. Her mind was free from the influence that had begun to work on his, and she drew near the Quaker woman and addressed her in the hearing of all the congregation.

"Stranger, trust this boy to me, and I will be his mother," she said, taking Ilbrahim's hand. "Providence has signally marked out my husband to protect him, and he has fed at our table and lodged under our roof now many days, till our hearts have grown very strongly unto him. Leave the tender child with us, and be at ease concerning his welfare."

The Quaker rose from the ground, but drew the boy closer to her, while she gazed earnestly in Dorothy's face. Her mild but saddened features and neat matronly attire harmonized together and were like a verse of fireside poetry. Her very aspect proved that she was blameless, so far as mortal could be so, in respect to God and man, while the enthusiast, in her robe of sackcloth and girdle of knotted cord, had as evidently violated the duties of the present life and the future by fixing her attention wholly on the latter. The two females, as they held each a hand of Ilbrahim, formed a practical allegory: it was rational piety and unbridled fanaticism contending for the empire of a young heart.

"Thou art not of our people," said the Quaker, mournfully.

"No, we are not of your people," replied Dorothy, with mildness, "but we are Christians looking upward to the same heaven with you. Doubt not that your boy shall meet you there, if there be a blessing on our tender and prayerful guidance of him. Thither, I trust, my own children have gone before me, for I also have been a mother. I am no longer so," she added, in a faltering tone, "and your son will have all my care."

"But will ye lead him in the path which his parents have trodden?" demanded the Quaker. "Can ye teach him the enlightened faith which his father has died for, and for which I—even I—am soon to become an unworthy martyr? The boy has been baptized in blood; will ye keep the mark fresh and ruddy upon his forehead?"

"I will not deceive you," answered Dorothy. "If your child become our child, we must breed him up in the instruction which Heaven has imparted to us; we must pray for him the prayers of our own faith; we must do toward him according to the dictates of our own consciences, and not of yours. Were we to act otherwise, we should abuse your trust, even in complying with your wishes."

The mother looked down upon her boy with a troubled countenance, and then turned her eyes upward to heaven. She seemed to pray internally, and the contention of her soul was evident.

"Friend," she said, at length, to Dorothy, "I doubt not that my son shall receive all earthly tenderness at thy hands. Nay, I will believe that even thy imperfect lights may guide him to a better world, for surely thou art on the path thither. But thou hast spoken of a husband. Doth he stand here among this multitude of people? Let him come forth, for I must know to whom I commit this most precious trust."

She turned her face upon the male auditors, and after a momentary delay Tobias Pearson came forth from among them. The Quaker saw the dress which marked his military rank, and shook her head; but then she noted the hesitating air, the eyes that struggled with her own and were vanquished, the color that went and came and could find no resting-place. As she gazed an unmirthful smile spread over her features, like sunshine that grows melancholy in some desolate spot. Her lips moved inaudibly, but at length she spake:

"I hear it, I hear it! The voice speaketh within me and saith, 'Leave thy child, Catharine, for his place is here, and go hence, for I have other work for thee. Break the bonds of natural affection, martyr thy love, and know that in all these things eternal wisdom hath its ends.' I go, friends, I go. Take ye my boy, my precious jewel. I go hence trusting that all shall be well, and that even for his infant hands there is a labor in the vineyard."

She knelt down and whispered to Ilbrahim, who at first struggled and clung to his mother with sobs and tears, but remained passive when she had kissed his cheek and arisen from the ground. Having held her hands over his head in mental prayer, she was ready to depart.

"Farewell, friends in mine extremity," she said to Pearson and his wife; "the good deed ye have done me is a treasure laid up in heaven, to be returned a thousandfold hereafter.—And farewell, ye mine enemies, to whom it is not permitted to harm so much as a hair of my head, nor to stay my footsteps even for a moment. The day is coming when ye shall call upon me to witness for ye to this one sin uncommitted, and I will rise up and answer."

She turned her steps toward the door, and the men who had stationed themselves to guard it withdrew and suffered her to pass. A general sentiment of pity overcame the virulence of religious hatred. Sanctified by her love and her affliction, she went forth, and all the people gazed after her till she had journeyed up the hill and was lost behind its brow. She went, the apostle of her own unquiet heart, to renew the wanderings of past years. For her voice had been already heard in many lands of Christendom, and she had pined in the cells of a Catholic Inquisition before she felt the lash and lay in the dungeons of the Puritans. Her mission had extended also to the followers of the Prophet, and from them she had received the courtesy and kindness which all the contending sects of our purer religion united to deny her. Her husband and herself had resided many months in Turkey, where even the sultan's countenance was gracious to them; in that pagan land, too, was Ilbrahim's birthplace, and his Oriental name was a mark of gratitude for the good deeds of an unbeliever.

When Pearson and his wife had thus acquired all the rights over Ilbrahim that could be delegated, their affection for him became, like the memory of their native land or their mild sorrow for the dead, a piece of the immovable furniture of their hearts. The boy, also, after a week or two of mental disquiet, began to gratify his protectors by many inadvertent proofs that he considered them as parents and their house as home. Before the winter snows were melted the persecuted infant, the little wanderer from a remote and heathen country, seemed native in the New England cottage and inseparable from the warmth and security of its hearth. Under the influence of kind treatment, and in the consciousness that he was loved, Ilbrahim's demeanor lost a premature manliness which had resulted from his earlier situation; he became more childlike and his natural character displayed itself with freedom. It was in many respects a beautiful one, yet the disordered imaginations of both his father and mother had perhaps propagated a certain unhealthiness in the mind of the boy. In his general state Ilbrahim would derive enjoyment from the most trifling events and from every object about him; he seemed to discover rich treasures of happiness by a faculty analogous to that of the witch-hazel, which points to hidden gold where all is barren to the eye. His airy gayety, coming to him from a thousand sources, communicated itself to the family, and Ilbrahim was like a domesticated sunbeam, brightening moody countenances and chasing away the gloom from the dark corners of the cottage.

On the other hand, as the susceptibility of pleasure is also that of pain, the exuberant cheerfulness of the boy's prevailing temper sometimes yielded to moments of deep depression. His sorrows could not always be followed up to their original source, but most frequently they appeared to flow—though Ilbrahim was young to be sad for such a cause—from wounded love. The flightiness of his mirth rendered him often guilty of offences against the decorum of a Puritan household, and on these occasions he did not invariably escape rebuke. But the slightest word of real bitterness, which he was infallible in distinguishing from pretended anger, seemed to sink into his heart and poison all his enjoyments till he became sensible that he was entirely forgiven. Of the malice which generally accompanies a superfluity of sensitiveness Ilbrahim was altogether destitute. When trodden upon, he would not turn; when wounded, he could but die. His mind was wanting in the stamina of self-support. It was a plant that would twine beautifully round something stronger than itself; but if repulsed or torn away, it had no choice but to wither on the ground. Dorothy's acuteness taught her that severity would crush the spirit of the child, and she nurtured him with the gentle care of one who handles a butterfly. Her husband manifested an equal affection, although it grew daily less productive of familiar caresses.

The feelings of the neighboring people in regard to the Quaker infant and his protectors had not undergone a favorable change, in spite of the momentary triumph which the desolate mother had obtained over their sympathies. The scorn and bitterness of which he was the object were very grievous to Ilbrahim, especially when any circumstance made him sensible that the children his equals in age partook of the enmity of their parents. His tender and social nature had already overflowed in attachments to everything about him, and still there was a residue of unappropriated love which he yearned to bestow upon the little ones who were taught to hate him. As the warm days of spring came on Ilbrahim was accustomed to remain for hours silent and inactive within hearing of the children's voices at their play, yet with his usual delicacy of feeling he avoided their notice, and would flee and hide himself from the smallest individual among them. Chance, however, at length seemed to open a medium of communication between his heart and theirs; it was by means of a boy about two years older than Ilbrahim, who was injured by a fall from a tree in the vicinity of Pearson's habitation. As the sufferer's own home was at some distance, Dorothy willingly received him under her roof and became his tender and careful nurse.

Ilbrahim was the unconscious possessor of much skill in physiognomy, and it would have deterred him in other circumstances from attempting to make a friend of this boy. The countenance of the latter immediately impressed a beholder disagreeably, but it required some examination to discover that the cause was a very slight distortion of the mouth and the irregular, broken line and near approach of the eyebrows. Analogous, perhaps, to these trifling deformities was an almost imperceptible twist of every joint and the uneven prominence of the breast, forming a body regular in its general outline, but faulty in almost all its details. The disposition of the boy was sullen and reserved, and the village schoolmaster stigmatized him as obtuse in intellect, although at a later period of life he evinced ambition and very peculiar talents. But, whatever might be his personal or moral irregularities, Ilbrahim's heart seized upon and clung to him from the moment that he was brought wounded into the cottage; the child of persecution seemed to compare his own fate with that of the sufferer, and to feel that even different modes of misfortune had created a sort of relationship between them. Food, rest and the fresh air for which he languished were neglected; he nestled continually by the bedside of the little stranger and with a fond jealousy endeavored to be the medium of all the cares that were bestowed upon him. As the boy became convalescent Ilbrahim contrived games suitable to his situation or amused him by a faculty which he had perhaps breathed in with the air of his barbaric birthplace. It was that of reciting imaginary adventures on the spur of the moment, and apparently in inexhaustible succession. His tales were, of course, monstrous, disjointed and without aim, but they were curious on account of a vein of human tenderness which ran through them all and was like a sweet familiar face encountered in the midst of wild and unearthly scenery. The auditor paid much attention to these romances and sometimes interrupted them by brief remarks upon the incidents, displaying shrewdness above his years, mingled with a moral obliquity which grated very harshly against Ilbrahim's instinctive rectitude. Nothing, however, could arrest the progress of the latter's affection, and there were many proofs that it met with a response from the dark and stubborn nature on which it was lavished. The boy's parents at length removed him to complete his cure under their own roof.

Ilbrahim did not visit his new friend after his departure, but he made anxious and continual inquiries respecting him and informed himself of the day when he was to reappear among his playmates. On a pleasant summer afternoon the children of the neighborhood had assembled in the little forest-crowned amphitheatre behind the meeting-house, and the recovering invalid was there, leaning on a staff. The glee of a score of untainted bosoms was heard in light and airy voices, which danced among the trees like sunshine become audible; the grown men of this weary world as they journeyed by the spot marvelled why life, beginning in such brightness, should proceed in gloom, and their hearts or their imaginations answered them and said that the bliss of childhood gushes from its innocence. But it happened that an unexpected addition was made to the heavenly little band. It was Ilbrahim, who came toward the children with a look of sweet confidence on his fair and spiritual face, as if, having manifested his love to one of them, he had no longer to fear a repulse from their society. A hush came over their mirth the moment they beheld him, and they stood whispering to each other while he drew nigh; but all at once the devil of their fathers entered into the unbreeched fanatics, and, sending up a fierce, shrill cry, they rushed upon the poor Quaker child. In an instant he was the centre of a brood of baby-fiends, who lifted sticks against him, pelted him with stones and displayed an instinct of destruction far more loathsome than the bloodthirstiness of manhood.

The invalid, in the mean while, stood apart from the tumult, crying out with a loud voice, "Fear not, Ilbrahim; come hither and take my hand," and his unhappy friend endeavored to obey him. After watching the victim's struggling approach with a calm smile and unabashed eye, the foul-hearted little villain lifted his staff and struck Ilbrahim on the mouth so forcibly that the blood issued in a stream. The poor child's arms had been raised to guard his head from the storm of blows, but now he dropped them at once. His persecutors beat him down, trampled upon him, dragged him by his long fair locks, and Ilbrahim was on the point of becoming as veritable a martyr as ever entered bleeding into heaven. The uproar, however, attracted the notice of a few neighbors, who put themselves to the trouble of rescuing the little heretic, and of conveying him to Pearson's door.

Ilbrahim's bodily harm was severe, but long and careful nursing accomplished his recovery; the injury done to his sensitive spirit was more serious, though not so visible. Its signs were principally of a negative character, and to be discovered only by those who had previously known him. His gait was thenceforth slow, even and unvaried by the sudden bursts of sprightlier motion which had once corresponded to his overflowing gladness; his countenance was heavier, and its former play of expression—the dance of sunshine reflected from moving water—was destroyed by the cloud over his existence; his notice was attracted in a far less degree by passing events, and he appeared to find greater difficulty in comprehending what was new to him than at a happier period. A stranger founding his judgment upon these circumstances would have said that the dulness of the child's intellect widely contradicted the promise of his features, but the secret was in the direction of Ilbrahim's thoughts, which were brooding within him when they should naturally have been wandering abroad. An attempt of Dorothy to revive his former sportiveness was the single occasion on which his quiet demeanor yielded to a violent display of grief; he burst into passionate weeping and ran and hid himself, for his heart had become so miserably sore that even the hand of kindness tortured it like fire. Sometimes at night, and probably in his dreams, he was heard to cry, "Mother! Mother!" as if her place, which a stranger had supplied while Ilbrahim was happy, admitted of no substitute in his extreme affliction. Perhaps among the many life-weary wretches then upon the earth there was not one who combined innocence and misery like this poor broken-hearted infant so soon the victim of his own heavenly nature.

While this melancholy change had taken place in Ilbrahim, one of an earlier origin and of different character had come to its perfection in his adopted father.

The incident with which this tale commences found Pearson in a state of religious dulness, yet mentally disquieted and longing for a more fervid faith than he possessed. The first effect of his kindness to Ilbrahim was to produce a softened feeling, an incipient love for the child's whole sect, but joined to this, and resulting, perhaps, from self-suspicion, was a proud and ostentatious contempt of their tenets and practical extravagances. In the course of much thought, however—for the subject struggled irresistibly into his mind—the foolishness of the doctrine began to be less evident, and the points which had particularly offended his reason assumed another aspect or vanished entirely away. The work within him appeared to go on even while he slept, and that which had been a doubt when he laid down to rest would often hold the place of a truth confirmed by some forgotten demonstration when he recalled his thoughts in the morning. But, while he was thus becoming assimilated to the enthusiasts, his contempt, in nowise decreasing toward them, grew very fierce against himself; he imagined, also, that every face of his acquaintance wore a sneer, and that every word addressed to him was a gibe. Such was his state of mind at the period of Ilbrahim's misfortune, and the emotions consequent upon that event completed the change of which the child had been the original instrument.

In the mean time, neither the fierceness of the persecutors nor the infatuation of their victims had decreased. The dungeons were never empty; the streets of almost every village echoed daily with the lash; the life of a woman whose mild and Christian spirit no cruelty could embitter had been sacrificed, and more innocent blood was yet to pollute the hands that were so often raised in prayer. Early after the Restoration the English Quakers represented to Charles II. that a "vein of blood was open in his dominions," but, though the displeasure of the voluptuous king was roused, his interference was not prompt. And now the tale must stride forward over many months, leaving Pearson to encounter ignominy and misfortune; his wife, to a firm endurance of a thousand sorrows; poor Ilbrahim, to pine and droop like a cankered rose-bud; his mother, to wander on a mistaken errand, neglectful of the holiest trust which can be committed to a woman.

A winter evening, a night of storm, had darkened over Pearson's habitation, and there were no cheerful faces to drive the gloom from his broad hearth. The fire, it is true, sent forth a glowing heat and a ruddy light, and large logs dripping with half-melted snow lay ready to cast upon the embers. But the apartment was saddened in its aspect by the absence of much of the homely wealth which had once adorned it, for the exaction of repeated fines and his own neglect of temporal affairs had greatly impoverished the owner. And with the furniture of peace the implements of war had likewise disappeared; the sword was broken, the helm and cuirass were cast away for ever: the soldier had done with battles, and might not lift so much as his naked hand to guard his head. But the Holy Book remained, and the table on which it rested was drawn before the fire, while two of the persecuted sect sought comfort from its pages.

He who listened while the other read was the master of the house, now emaciated in form and altered as to the expression and healthiness of his countenance, for his mind had dwelt too long among visionary thoughts and his body had been worn by imprisonment and stripes. The hale and weatherbeaten old man who sat beside him had sustained less injury from a far longer course of the same mode of life. In person he was tall and dignified, and, which alone would have made him hateful to the Puritans, his gray locks fell from beneath the broad-brimmed hat and rested on his shoulders. As the old man read the sacred page the snow drifted against the windows or eddied in at the crevices of the door, while a blast kept laughing in the chimney and the blaze leaped fiercely up to seek it. And sometimes, when the wind struck the hill at a certain angle and swept down by the cottage across the wintry plain, its voice was the most doleful that can be conceived; it came as if the past were speaking, as if the dead had contributed each a whisper, as if the desolation of ages were breathed in that one lamenting sound.

The Quaker at length closed the book, retaining, however, his hand between the pages which he had been reading, while he looked steadfastly at Pearson. The attitude and features of the latter might have indicated the endurance of bodily pain; he leaned his forehead on his hands, his teeth were firmly closed and his frame was tremulous at intervals with a nervous agitation.

"Friend Tobias," inquired the old man, compassionately, "hast thou found no comfort in these many blessed passages of Scripture?"

"Thy voice has fallen on my ear like a sound afar off and indistinct," replied Pearson, without lifting his eyes. "Yea; and when I have hearkened carefully, the words seemed cold and lifeless and intended for another and a lesser grief than mine. Remove the book," he added, in a tone of sullen bitterness; "I have no part in its consolations, and they do but fret my sorrow the more."

"Nay, feeble brother; be not as one who hath never known the light," said the elder Quaker, earnestly, but with mildness. "Art thou he that wouldst be content to give all and endure all for conscience' sake, desiring even peculiar trials that thy faith might be purified and thy heart weaned from worldly desires? And wilt thou sink beneath an affliction which happens alike to them that have their portion here below and to them that lay up treasure in heaven? Faint not, for thy burden is yet light."

"It is heavy! It is heavier than I can bear!" exclaimed Pearson, with the impatience of a variable spirit. "From my youth upward I have been a man marked out for wrath, and year by year—yea, day after day—I have endured sorrows such as others know not in their lifetime. And now I speak not of the love that has been turned to hatred, the honor to ignominy, the ease and plentifulness of all things to danger, want and nakedness. All this I could have borne and counted myself blessed. But when my heart was desolate with many losses, I fixed it upon the child of a stranger, and he became dearer to me than all my buried ones; and now he too must die as if my love were poison. Verily, I am an accursed man, and I will lay me down in the dust and lift up my head no more."

"Thou sinnest, brother, but it is not for me to rebuke thee, for I also have had my hours of darkness wherein I have murmured against the cross," said the old Quaker. He continued, perhaps in the hope of distracting his companion's thoughts from his own sorrows: "Even of late was the light obscured within me, when the men of blood had banished me on pain of death and the constables led me onward from village to village toward the wilderness. A strong and cruel hand was wielding the knotted cords; they sunk deep into the flesh, and thou mightst have tracked every reel and totter of my footsteps by the blood that followed. As we went on—"

"Have I not borne all this, and have I murmured?" interrupted Pearson, impatiently.

"Nay, friend, but hear me," continued the other. "As we journeyed on night darkened on our path, so that no man could see the rage of the persecutors or the constancy of my endurance, though Heaven forbid that I should glory therein. The lights began to glimmer in the cottage windows, and I could discern the inmates as they gathered in comfort and security, every man with his wife and children by their own evening hearth. At length we came to a tract of fertile land. In the dim light the forest was not visible around it, and, behold, there was a straw-thatched dwelling which bore the very aspect of my home far over the wild ocean—far in our own England. Then came bitter thoughts upon me—yea, remembrances that were like death to my soul. The happiness of my early days was painted to me, the disquiet of my manhood, the altered faith of my declining years. I remembered how I had been moved to go forth a wanderer when my daughter, the youngest, the dearest of my flock, lay on her dying-bed, and—"

"Couldst thou obey the command at such a moment?" exclaimed Pearson, shuddering.

"Yea! yea!" replied the old man, hurriedly. "I was kneeling by her bedside when the voice spoke loud within me, but immediately I rose and took my staff and gat me gone. Oh that it were permitted me to forget her woeful look when I thus withdrew my arm and left her journeying through the dark valley alone! for her soul was faint and she had leaned upon my prayers. Now in that night of horror I was assailed by the thought that I had been an erring Christian and a cruel parent; yea, even my daughter with her pale dying features seemed to stand by me and whisper, 'Father, you are deceived; go home and shelter your gray head.'—O Thou to whom I have looked in my furthest wanderings," continued the Quaker, raising his agitated eyes to heaven, "inflict not upon the bloodiest of our persecutors the unmitigated agony of my soul when I believed that all I had done and suffered for thee was at the instigation of a mocking fiend!—But I yielded not; I knelt down and wrestled with the tempter, while the scourge bit more fiercely into the flesh. My prayer was heard, and I went on in peace and joy toward the wilderness."

The old man, though his fanaticism had generally all the calmness of reason, was deeply moved while reciting this tale, and his unwonted emotion seemed to rebuke and keep down that of his companion. They sat in silence, with their faces to the fire, imagining, perhaps, in its red embers new scenes of persecution yet to be encountered. The snow still drifted hard against the windows, and sometimes, as the blaze of the logs had gradually sunk, came down the spacious chimney and hissed upon the hearth. A cautious footstep might now and then be heard in a neighboring apartment, and the sound invariably drew the eyes of both Quakers to the door which led thither. When a fierce and riotous gust of wind had led his thoughts by a natural association to homeless travellers on such a night, Pearson resumed the conversation.

"I have wellnigh sunk under my own share of this trial," observed he, sighing heavily; "yet I would that it might be doubled to me, if so the child's mother could be spared. Her wounds have been deep and many, but this will be the sorest of all."

"Fear not for Catharine," replied the old Quaker, "for I know that valiant woman and have seen how she can bear the cross. A mother's heart, indeed, is strong in her, and may seem to contend mightily with her faith, but soon she will stand up and give thanks that her son has been thus early an accepted sacrifice. The boy hath done his work, and she will feel that he is taken hence in kindness both to him and her. Blessed, blessed are they that with so little suffering can enter into peace!"

The fitful rush of the wind was now disturbed by a portentous sound: it was a quick and heavy knocking at the outer door. Pearson's wan countenance grew paler, for many a visit of persecution had taught him what to dread; the old man, on the other hand, stood up erect, and his glance was firm as that of the tried soldier who awaits his enemy.

"The men of blood have come to seek me," he observed, with calmness. "They have heard how I was moved to return from banishment, and now am I to be led to prison, and thence to death. It is an end I have long looked for. I will open unto them lest they say, 'Lo, he feareth!'"

"Nay; I will present myself before them," said Pearson, with recovered fortitude. "It may be that they seek me alone and know not that thou abidest with me."

"Let us go boldly, both one and the other," rejoined his companion. "It is not fitting that thou or I should shrink."

They therefore proceeded through the entry to the door, which they opened, bidding the applicant "Come in, in God's name!" A furious blast of wind drove the storm into their faces and extinguished the lamp; they had barely time to discern a figure so white from head to foot with the drifted snow that it seemed like Winter's self come in human shape to seek refuge from its own desolation.

"Enter, friend, and do thy errand, be it what it may," said Pearson. "It must needs be pressing, since thou comest on such a bitter night."

"Peace be with this household!" said the stranger, when they stood on the floor of the inner apartment.

Pearson started; the elder Quaker stirred the slumbering embers of the fire till they sent up a clear and lofty blaze. It was a female voice that had spoken; it was a female form that shone out, cold and wintry, in that comfortable light.

"Catharine, blessed woman," exclaimed the old man, "art thou come to this darkened land again? Art thou come to bear a valiant testimony as in former years? The scourge hath not prevailed against thee, and from the dungeon hast thou come forth triumphant, but strengthen, strengthen now thy heart, Catharine, for Heaven will prove thee yet this once ere thou go to thy reward."

"Rejoice, friends!" she replied. "Thou who hast long been of our people, and thou whom a little child hath led to us, rejoice! Lo, I come, the messenger of glad tidings, for the day of persecution is over-past. The heart of the king, even Charles, hath been moved in gentleness toward us, and he hath sent forth his letters to stay the hands of the men of blood. A ship's company of our friends hath arrived at yonder town, and I also sailed joyfully among them."

As Catharine spoke her eyes were roaming about the room in search of him for whose sake security was dear to her. Pearson made a silent appeal to the old man, nor did the latter shrink from the painful task assigned him.

"Sister," he began, in a softened yet perfectly calm tone, "thou tellest us of his love manifested in temporal good, and now must we speak to thee of that self-same love displayed in chastenings. Hitherto, Catharine, thou hast been as one journeying in a darksome and difficult path and leading an infant by the hand; fain wouldst thou have looked heavenward continually, but still the cares of that little child have drawn thine eyes and thy affections to the earth. Sister, go on rejoicing, for his tottering footsteps shall impede thine own no more."

But the unhappy mother was not thus to be consoled. She shook like a leaf; she turned white as the very snow that hung drifted into her hair. The firm old man extended his hand and held her up, keeping his eye upon hers as if to repress any outbreak of passion.

"I am a woman—I am but a woman; will He try me above my strength?" said Catharine, very quickly and almost in a whisper. "I have been wounded sore; I have suffered much—many things in the body, many in the mind; crucified in myself and in them that were dearest to me. Surely," added she, with a long shudder, "he hath spared me in this one thing." She broke forth with sudden and irrepressible violence: "Tell me, man of cold heart, what has God done to me? Hath he cast me down never to rise again? Hath he crushed my very heart in his hand?—And thou to whom I committed my child, how hast thou fulfilled thy trust? Give me back the boy well, sound, alive—alive—or earth and heaven shall avenge me!"

The agonized shriek of Catharine was answered by the faint—the very faint—voice of a child.

On this day it had become evident to Pearson, to his aged guest and to Dorothy that Ilbrahim's brief and troubled pilgrimage drew near its close. The two former would willingly have remained by him to make use of the prayers and pious discourses which they deemed appropriate to the time, and which, if they be impotent as to the departing traveller's reception in the world whither he goes, may at least sustain him in bidding adieu to earth. But, though Ilbrahim uttered no complaint, he was disturbed by the faces that looked upon him; so that Dorothy's entreaties and their own conviction that the child's feet might tread heaven's pavement and not soil it had induced the two Quakers to remove. Ilbrahim then closed his eyes and grew calm, and, except for now and then a kind and low word to his nurse, might have been thought to slumber. As nightfall came on, however, and the storm began to rise, something seemed to trouble the repose of the boy's mind and to render his sense of hearing active and acute. If a passing wind lingered to shake the casement, he strove to turn his head toward it; if the door jarred to and fro upon its hinges, he looked long and anxiously thitherward; if the heavy voice of the old man as he read the Scriptures rose but a little higher, the child almost held his dying-breath to listen; if a snowdrift swept by the cottage with a sound like the trailing of a garment, Ilbrahim seemed to watch that some visitant should enter. But after a little time he relinquished whatever secret hope had agitated him and with one low complaining whisper turned his cheek upon the pillow. He then addressed Dorothy with his usual sweetness and besought her to draw near him; she did so, and Ilbrahim took her hand in both of his, grasping it with a gentle pressure, as if to assure himself that he retained it. At intervals, and without disturbing the repose of his countenance, a very faint trembling passed over him from head to foot, as if a mild but somewhat cool wind had breathed upon him and made him shiver.

As the boy thus led her by the hand in his quiet progress over the borders of eternity, Dorothy almost imagined that she could discern the near though dim delightfulness of the home he was about to reach; she would not have enticed the little wanderer back, though she bemoaned herself that she must leave him and return. But just when Ilbrahim's feet were pressing on the soil of Paradise he heard a voice behind him, and it recalled him a few, few paces of the weary path which he had travelled. As Dorothy looked upon his features she perceived that their placid expression was again disturbed. Her own thoughts had been so wrapped in him that all sounds of the storm and of human speech were lost to her; but when Catharine's shriek pierced through the room, the boy strove to raise himself.

"Friend, she is come! Open unto her!" cried he.

In a moment his mother was kneeling by the bedside; she drew Ilbrahim to her bosom, and he nestled there with no violence of joy, but contentedly as if he were hushing himself to sleep. He looked into her face, and, reading its agony, said with feeble earnestness,

"Mourn not, dearest mother. I am happy now;" and with these words the gentle boy was dead.

The king's mandate to stay the New England persecutors was effectual in preventing further martyrdoms, but the colonial authorities, trusting in the remoteness of their situation, and perhaps in the supposed instability of the royal government, shortly renewed their severities in all other respects. Catharine's fanaticism had become wilder by the sundering of all human ties; and wherever a scourge was lifted, there was she to receive the blow; and whenever a dungeon was unbarred, thither she came to cast herself upon the floor. But in process of time a more Christian spirit—a spirit of forbearance, though not of cordiality or approbation—began to pervade the land in regard to the persecuted sect. And then, when the rigid old Pilgrims eyed her rather in pity than in wrath, when the matrons fed her with the fragments of their children's food and offered her a lodging on a hard and lowly bed, when no little crowd of schoolboys left their sports to cast stones after the roving enthusiast,—then did Catharine return to Pearson's dwelling, and made that her home.

As if Ilbrahim's sweetness yet lingered round his ashes, as if his gentle spirit came down from heaven to teach his parent a true religion, her fierce and vindictive nature was softened by the same griefs which had once irritated it. When the course of years had made the features of the unobtrusive mourner familiar in the settlement, she became a subject of not deep but general interest—a being on whom the otherwise superfluous sympathies of all might be bestowed. Every one spoke of her with that degree of pity which it is pleasant to experience; every one was ready to do her the little kindnesses which are not costly, yet manifest good-will; and when at last she died, a long train of her once bitter persecutors followed her with decent sadness and tears that were not painful to her place by Ilbrahim's green and sunken grave.

MR. HIGGINBOTHAM'S CATASTROPHE.

A young fellow, a tobacco-pedler by trade, was on his way from Morristown, where he had dealt largely with the deacon of the Shaker settlement, to the village of Parker's Falls, on Salmon River. He had a neat little cart painted green, with a box of cigars depicted on each side-panel, and an Indian chief holding a pipe and a golden tobacco-stalk on the rear. The pedler drove a smart little mare and was a young man of excellent character, keen at a bargain, but none the worse liked by the Yankees, who, as I have heard them say, would rather be shaved with a sharp razor than a dull one. Especially was he beloved by the pretty girls along the Connecticut, whose favor he used to court by presents of the best smoking-tobacco in his stock, knowing well that the country-lasses of New England are generally great performers on pipes. Moreover, as will be seen in the course of my story, the pedler was inquisitive and something of a tattler, always itching to hear the news and anxious to tell it again.

After an early breakfast at Morristown the tobacco-pedler—whose name was Dominicus Pike—had travelled seven miles through a solitary piece of woods without speaking a word to anybody but himself and his little gray mare. It being nearly seven o'clock, he was as eager to hold a morning gossip as a city shop-keeper to read the morning paper. An opportunity seemed at hand when, after lighting a cigar with a sun-glass, he looked up and perceived a man coming over the brow of the hill at the foot of which the pedler had stopped his green cart. Dominicus watched him as he descended, and noticed that he carried a bundle over his shoulder on the end of a stick and travelled with a weary yet determined pace. He did not look as if he had started in the freshness of the morning, but had footed it all night, and meant to do the same all day.

"Good-morning, mister," said Dominicus, when within speaking-distance. "You go a pretty good jog. What's the latest news at Parker's Falls?"

The man pulled the broad brim of a gray hat over his eyes, and answered, rather sullenly, that he did not come from Parker's Falls, which, as being the limit of his own day's journey, the pedler had naturally mentioned in his inquiry.

"Well, then," rejoined Dominicus Pike, "let's have the latest news where you did come from. I'm not particular about Parker's Falls. Any place will answer."

Being thus importuned, the traveller—who was as ill-looking a fellow as one would desire to meet in a solitary piece of woods—appeared to hesitate a little, as if he was either searching his memory for news or weighing the expediency of telling it. At last, mounting on the step of the cart, he whispered in the ear of Dominicus, though he might have shouted aloud and no other mortal would have heard him.

"I do remember one little trifle of news," said he. "Old Mr. Higginbotham of Kimballton was murdered in his orchard at eight o'clock last night by an Irishman and a nigger. They strung him up to the branch of a St. Michael's pear tree where nobody would find him till the morning."

As soon as this horrible intelligence was communicated the stranger betook himself to his journey again with more speed than ever, not even turning his head when Dominicus invited him to smoke a Spanish cigar and relate all the particulars. The pedler whistled to his mare and went up the hill, pondering on the doleful fate of Mr. Higginbotham, whom he had known in the way of trade, having sold him many a bunch of long nines and a great deal of pig-tail, lady's twist and fig tobacco. He was rather astonished at the rapidity with which the news had spread. Kimballton was nearly sixty miles distant in a straight line; the murder had been perpetrated only at eight o'clock the preceding night, yet Dominicus had heard of it at seven in the morning, when, in all probability, poor Mr. Higginbotham's own family had but just discovered his corpse hanging on the St. Michael's pear tree. The stranger on foot must have worn seven-league boots, to travel at such a rate.

"Ill-news flies fast, they say," thought Dominicus Pike, "but this beats railroads. The fellow ought to be hired to go express with the President's message."

The difficulty was solved by supposing that the narrator had made a mistake of one day in the date of the occurrence; so that our friend did not hesitate to introduce the story at every tavern and country-store along the road, expending a whole bunch of Spanish wrappers among at least twenty horrified audiences. He found himself invariably the first bearer of the intelligence, and was so pestered with questions that he could not avoid filling up the outline till it became quite a respectable narrative. He met with one piece of corroborative evidence. Mr. Higginbotham was a trader, and a former clerk of his to whom Dominicus related the facts testified that the old gentleman was accustomed to return home through the orchard about nightfall with the money and valuable papers of the store in his pocket. The clerk manifested but little grief at Mr. Higginbotham's catastrophe, hinting—what the pedler had discovered in his own dealings with him—that he was a crusty old fellow as close as a vise. His property would descend to a pretty niece who was now keeping school in Kimballton.

What with telling the news for the public good and driving bargains for his own, Dominicus was so much delayed on the road that he chose to put up at a tavern about five miles short of Parker's Falls. After supper, lighting one of his prime cigars, he seated himself in the bar-room and went through the story of the murder, which had grown so fast that it took him half an hour to tell. There were as many as twenty people in the room, nineteen of whom received it all for gospel. But the twentieth was an elderly farmer who had arrived on horseback a short time before and was now seated in a corner, smoking his pipe. When the story was concluded, he rose up very deliberately, brought his chair right in front of Dominicus and stared him full in the face, puffing out the vilest tobacco-smoke the pedler had ever smelt.

"Will you make affidavit," demanded he, in the tone of a country-justice taking an examination, "that old Squire Higginbotham of Kimballton was murdered in his orchard the night before last and found hanging on his great pear tree yesterday morning?"

"I tell the story as I heard it, mister," answered Dominicus, dropping his half-burnt cigar. "I don't say that I saw the thing done, so I can't take my oath that he was murdered exactly in that way."

"But I can take mine," said the farmer, "that if Squire Higginbotham was murdered night before last I drank a glass of bitters with his ghost this morning. Being a neighbor of mine, he called me into his store as I was riding by, and treated me, and then asked me to do a little business for him on the road. He didn't seem to know any more about his own murder than I did."

"Why, then it can't be a fact!" exclaimed Dominicus Pike.

"I guess he'd have mentioned, if it was," said the old farmer; and he removed his chair back to the corner, leaving Dominicus quite down in the mouth.

Here was a sad resurrection of old Mr. Higginbotham! The pedler had no heart to mingle in the conversation any more, but comforted himself with a glass of gin and water and went to bed, where all night long he dreamed of hanging on the St. Michael's pear tree.

To avoid the old farmer (whom he so detested that his suspension would have pleased him better than Mr. Higginbotham's), Dominicus rose in the gray of the morning, put the little mare into the green cart and trotted swiftly away toward Parker's Falls. The fresh breeze, the dewy road and the pleasant summer dawn revived his spirits, and might have encouraged him to repeat the old story had there been anybody awake to bear it, but he met neither ox-team, light wagon, chaise, horseman nor foot-traveller till, just as he crossed Salmon River, a man came trudging down to the bridge with a bundle over his shoulder, on the end of a stick.

"Good-morning, mister," said the pedler, reining in his mare. "If you come from Kimballton or that neighborhood, maybe you can tell me the real fact about this affair of old Mr. Higginbotham. Was the old fellow actually murdered two or three nights ago by an Irishman and a nigger?"

Dominicus had spoken in too great a hurry to observe at first that the stranger himself had a deep tinge of negro blood. On hearing this sudden question the Ethiopian appeared to change his skin, its yellow hue becoming a ghastly white, while, shaking and stammering, he thus replied:

"No, no! There was no colored man. It was an Irishman that hanged him last night at eight o'clock; I came away at seven. His folks can't have looked for him in the orchard yet."

Scarcely had the yellow man spoken, when he interrupted himself and, though he seemed weary enough before, continued his journey at a pace which would have kept the pedler's mare on a smart trot. Dominicus stared after him in great perplexity. If the murder had not been committed till Tuesday night, who was the prophet that had foretold it in all its circumstances on Tuesday morning? If Mr. Higginbotham's corpse were not yet discovered by his own family, how came the mulatto, at above thirty miles' distance, to know that he was hanging in the orchard, especially as he had left Kimballton before the unfortunate man was hanged at all? These ambiguous circumstances, with the stranger's surprise and terror, made Dominicus think of raising a hue-and-cry after him as an accomplice in the murder, since a murder, it seemed, had really been perpetrated.

"But let the poor devil go," thought the pedler. "I don't want his black blood on my head, and hanging the nigger wouldn't unhang Mr. Higginbotham. Unhang the old gentleman? It's a sin, I know, but I should hate to have him come to life a second time and give me the lie."

With these meditations Dominicus Pike drove into the street of Parker's Falls, which, as everybody knows, is as thriving a village as three cotton-factories and a slitting-mill can make it. The machinery was not in motion and but a few of the shop doors unbarred when he alighted in the stable-yard of the tavern and made it his first business to order the mare four quarts of oats. His second duty, of course, was to impart Mr. Higginbotham's catastrophe to the hostler. He deemed it advisable, however, not to be too positive as to the date of the direful fact, and also to be uncertain whether it were perpetrated by an Irishman and a mulatto or by the son of Erin alone. Neither did he profess to relate it on his own authority or that of any one person, but mentioned it as a report generally diffused.

The story ran through the town like fire among girdled trees, and became so much the universal talk that nobody could tell whence it had originated. Mr. Higginbotham was as well known at Parker's Falls as any citizen of the place, being part-owner of the slitting-mill and a considerable stockholder in the cotton-factories. The inhabitants felt their own prosperity interested in his fate. Such was the excitement that the Parker's Falls *Gazette* anticipated its regular day of publication, and came out with half a form of blank paper and a column of double pica emphasized with capitals and headed "HORRID MURDER OF MR. HIGGINBOTHAM!" Among other dreadful details, the printed account described the mark of the cord round the dead man's neck and stated the number of thousand dollars of which he had been robbed; there was much pathos, also, about the affliction of his niece, who had gone from one fainting-fit to another ever since her uncle was found hanging on the St. Michael's pear tree with his pockets inside out. The village poet likewise commemorated the young lady's grief in seventeen stanzas of a ballad. The selectmen held a meeting, and in consideration of Mr. Higginbotham's claims on the town determined to issue handbills offering a reward of five hundred dollars for the apprehension of his murderers and the recovery of the stolen property.

Meanwhile, the whole population of Parker's Falls, consisting of shopkeepers, mistresses of boarding-houses, factory-girls, mill-men and schoolboys, rushed into the street and kept up such a terrible loquacity as more than compensated for the silence of the cotton-machines, which refrained from their usual din out of respect to the deceased. Had Mr. Higginbotham cared about posthumous renown, his untimely ghost would have exulted in this tumult.

Our friend Dominicus in his vanity of heart forgot his intended precautions, and, mounting on the town-pump, announced himself as the bearer of the authentic intelligence which had caused so wonderful a sensation. He immediately became the great man of the moment, and had just begun a new edition of the narrative with a voice like a field-preacher when the mail-stage drove into the village street. It had travelled all night, and must have shifted horses at Kimballton at three in the morning.

"Now we shall hear all the particulars!" shouted the crowd.

The coach rumbled up to the piazza of the tavern followed by a thousand people; for if any man had been minding his own business till then, he now left it at sixes and sevens to hear the news. The pedler, foremost in the race, discovered two passengers, both of whom had been startled from a comfortable nap to find themselves in the centre of a mob. Every man assailing them with separate questions, all propounded at once, the couple were struck speechless, though one was a lawyer and the other a young lady.

"Mr. Higginbotham! Mr. Higginbotham! Tell us the particulars about old Mr. Higginbotham!" bawled the mob. "What is the coroner's verdict? Are the murderers apprehended? Is Mr. Higginbotham's niece come out of her fainting-fits? Mr. Higginbotham! Mr. Higginbotham!"

The coachman said not a word except to swear awfully at the hostler for not bringing him a fresh team of horses. The lawyer inside had generally his wits about him even when asleep; the first thing he did after learning the cause of the excitement was to produce a large red pocketbook. Meantime, Dominicus Pike, being an extremely polite young man, and also suspecting that a female tongue would tell the story as glibly as a lawyer's, had handed the lady out of the coach. She was a fine, smart girl, now wide awake and bright as a button, and had such a sweet, pretty mouth that Dominicus would almost as lief have heard a love-tale from it as a tale of murder.

"Gentlemen and ladies," said the lawyer to the shopkeepers, the mill-men and the factory-girls, "I can assure you that some unaccountable mistake—or, more probably, a wilful falsehood maliciously contrived to injure Mr. Higginbotham's credit—has excited this singular uproar. We passed through Kimballton at three o'clock this morning, and most certainly should have been informed of the murder had any been perpetrated. But I have proof nearly as strong as Mr. Higginbotham's own oral testimony in the negative. Here is a note relating to a suit of his in the Connecticut courts which was delivered me from that gentleman himself. I find it dated at ten o'clock last evening."

So saying, the lawyer, exhibited the date and signature of the note, which irrefragably proved either that this perverse Mr. Higginbotham was alive when he wrote it, or, as some deemed the more probable case of two doubtful ones, that he was so absorbed in worldly business as to continue to transact it even after his death. But unexpected evidence was forthcoming. The young lady, after listening to the pedler's explanation, merely seized a moment to smooth her gown and put her curls in order, and then appeared at the tavern door, making a modest signal to be heard.

"Good people," said she, "I am Mr. Higginbotham's niece."

A wondering murmur passed through the crowd on beholding her so rosy and bright—that same unhappy niece whom they had supposed, on the authority of the Parker's Falls *Gazette*, to be lying at death's door in a fainting-fit. But some shrewd fellows had doubted all along whether a young lady would be quite so desperate at the hanging of a rich old uncle.

"You see," continued Miss Higginbotham, with a smile, "that this strange story is quite unfounded as to myself, and I believe I may affirm it to be equally so in regard to my dear uncle Higginbotham. He has the kindness to give me a home in his house, though I contribute to my own support by teaching a school. I left Kimballton this morning to spend the vacation of commencement-week with a friend about five miles from Parker's Falls. My generous uncle, when he heard me on the stairs, called me to his bedside and gave me two dollars and fifty cents to pay my stage-fare, and another dollar for my extra expenses. He then laid his pocketbook under his pillow, shook hands with me, and advised me to take some biscuit in my bag instead of breakfasting on the road. I feel confident, therefore, that I left my beloved relative alive, and trust that I shall find him so on my return."

The young lady courtesied at the close of her speech, which was so sensible and well worded, and delivered with such grace and propriety, that everybody thought her fit to be preceptress of the best academy in the State. But a stranger would have supposed that Mr. Higginbotham was an object of abhorrence at Parker's Falls and that a thanksgiving had been proclaimed for his murder, so excessive was the wrath of the inhabitants on learning their mistake. The mill-men resolved to bestow public honors on Dominicus Pike, only hesitating whether to tar and feather him, ride him on a rail or refresh him with an ablution at the town-pump, on the top of which he had declared himself the bearer of the news. The selectmen, by advice of the lawyer, spoke of prosecuting him for a misdemeanor in circulating unfounded reports, to the great disturbance of the peace of the commonwealth. Nothing saved Dominicus either from mob-law or a court of justice but an eloquent appeal made by the young lady in his behalf. Addressing a few words of heartfelt gratitude to his benefactress, he mounted the green cart and rode out of town under a discharge of artillery from the schoolboys, who found plenty of ammunition in the neighboring clay-pits and mud-holes. As he turned his head to exchange a farewell glance with Mr. Higginbotham's niece a ball of the consistence of hasty-pudding hit him slap in the mouth, giving him a most grim aspect. His whole person was so bespattered with the like filthy missiles that he had almost a mind to ride back and supplicate for the threatened ablution at the town-pump; for, though not meant in kindness, it would now have been a deed of charity.

However, the sun shone bright on poor Dominicus, and the mud—an emblem of all stains of undeserved opprobrium—was easily brushed off when dry. Being a funny rogue, his heart soon cheered up; nor could he refrain from a hearty laugh at the uproar which his story had excited. The handbills of the selectmen would cause the commitment of all the vagabonds in the State, the paragraph in the Parker's Falls *Gazette* would be reprinted from Maine to Florida, and perhaps form an item in the London newspapers, and many a miser would tremble for his moneybags and life on learning the catastrophe of Mr. Higginbotham. The pedler meditated with much fervor on the charms of the young schoolmistress, and swore that Daniel Webster never spoke nor looked so like an angel as Miss Higginbotham while defending him from the wrathful populace at Parker's Falls.

Dominicus was now on the Kimballton turnpike, having all along determined to visit that place, though business had drawn, him out of the most direct road from Morristown. As he approached the scene of the supposed murder he continued to revolve the circumstances in his mind, and was astonished at the aspect which the whole case assumed. Had nothing occurred to corroborate the story of the first traveller, it might now have been considered as a hoax; but the yellow man was evidently acquainted either with the report or the fact, and there was a mystery in his dismayed and guilty look on being abruptly questioned. When to this singular combination of incidents it was added that the rumor tallied exactly with Mr. Higginbotham's character and habits of life, and that he had an orchard and a St. Michael's pear tree, near which he always passed at nightfall, the circumstantial evidence appeared so strong that Dominicus doubted whether the autograph produced by the lawyer, or even the niece's direct testimony, ought to be equivalent. Making cautious inquiries along the road, the pedler further learned that Mr. Higginbotham had in his service an Irishman of doubtful character whom he had hired without a recommendation, on the score of economy.

"May I be hanged myself," exclaimed Dominicus Pike, aloud, on reaching the top of a lonely hill, "if I'll believe old Higginbotham is unhanged till I see him with my own eyes and hear it from his own mouth. And, as he's a real shaver, I'll have the minister, or some other responsible man, for an endorser."

It was growing dusk when he reached the toll-house on Kimballton turnpike, about a quarter of a mile from the village of this name. His little mare was fast bringing him up with a man on horseback who trotted through the gate a few rods in advance of him, nodded to the toll-gatherer and kept on towards the village. Dominicus was acquainted with the toll-man, and while making change the usual remarks on the weather passed between them.

"I suppose," said the pedler, throwing back his whiplash to bring it down like a feather on the mare's flank, "you have not seen anything of old Mr. Higginbotham within a day or two?"

"Yes," answered the toll-gatherer; "he passed the gate just before you drove up, and yonder he rides now, if you can see him through the dusk. He's been to Woodfield this afternoon, attending a sheriff's sale there. The old man generally shakes hands and has a little chat with me, but to-night he nodded, as if to say, 'Charge my toll,' and jogged on; for, wherever he goes, he must always be at home by eight o'clock."

"So they tell me," said Dominicus.

"I never saw a man look so yellow and thin as the squire does," continued the toll-gatherer. "Says I to myself tonight, 'He's more like a ghost or an old mummy than good flesh and blood.'"

The pedler strained his eyes through the twilight, and could just discern the horseman now far ahead on the village road. He seemed to recognize the rear of Mr. Higginbotham, but through the evening shadows and amid the dust from the horse's feet the figure appeared dim and unsubstantial, as if the shape of the mysterious old man were faintly moulded of darkness and gray light.

Dominicus shivered. "Mr. Higginbotham has come back from the other world by way of the Kimballton turnpike," thought he. He shook the reins and rode forward, keeping about the same distance in the rear of the gray old shadow till the latter was concealed by a bend of the road. On reaching this point the pedler no longer saw the man on horseback, but found himself at the head of the village street, not far from a number of stores and two taverns clustered round the meeting-house steeple. On his left was a stone wall and a gate, the boundary of a wood-lot beyond which lay an orchard, farther still a mowing-field, and last of all a house. These were the premises of Mr. Higginbotham, whose dwelling stood beside the old highway, but had been left in the background by the Kimballton turnpike.

Dominicus knew the place, and the little mare stopped short by instinct, for he was not conscious of tightening the reins. "For the soul of me, I cannot get by this gate!" said he, trembling. "I never shall be my own man again till I see whether Mr. Higginbotham is hanging on the St. Michael's pear tree." He leaped from the cart, gave the rein a turn round the gate-post, and ran along the green path of the wood-lot as if Old Nick were chasing behind. Just then the village clock tolled eight, and as each deep stroke fell Dominicus gave a fresh bound and flew faster than before, till, dim in the solitary centre of the orchard, he saw the fated pear tree. One great branch stretched from the old contorted trunk across the path and threw the darkest shadow on that one spot. But something seemed to struggle beneath the branch.

The pedler had never pretended to more courage than befits a man of peaceable occupation, nor could he account for his valor on this awful emergency. Certain it is, however, that he rushed forward, prostrated a sturdy Irishman with the butt-end of his whip, and found—not, indeed, hanging on the St. Michael's pear tree, but trembling beneath it with a halter round his neck—the old identical Mr. Higginbotham.

"Mr. Higginbotham," said Dominicus, tremulously, "you're an honest man, and I'll take your word for it. Have you been hanged, or not?"

If the riddle be not already guessed, a few words will explain the simple machinery by which this "coming event" was made to cast its "shadow before." Three men had plotted the robbery and murder of Mr. Higginbotham; two of them successively lost courage and fled, each delaying the crime one night by their disappearance; the third was in the act of perpetration, when a champion, blindly obeying the call of fate, like the heroes of old romance, appeared in the person of Dominicus Pike.

It only remains to say that Mr. Higginbotham took the pedler into high favor, sanctioned his addresses to the pretty schoolmistress and settled his whole property on their children, allowing themselves the interest. In due time the old gentleman capped the climax of his favors by dying a Christian death in bed; since which melancholy event, Dominicus Pike has removed from Kimballton and established a large tobacco-manufactory in my native village.

LITTLE ANNIE'S RAMBLE.

Ding-dong! Ding-dong! Ding-dong!

The town-crier has rung his bell at a distant corner, and little Annie stands on her father's doorsteps trying to hear what the man with the loud voice is talking about. Let me listen too. Oh, he is telling the people that an elephant and a lion and a royal tiger and a horse with horns, and other strange beasts from foreign countries, have come to town and will receive all visitors who choose to wait upon them. Perhaps little Annie would like to go? Yes, and I can see that the pretty child is weary of this wide and pleasant street with the green trees flinging their shade across the quiet sunshine and the pavements and the sidewalks all as clean as if the housemaid had just swept them with her broom. She feels that impulse to go strolling away—that longing after the mystery of the great world—which many children feel, and which I felt in my childhood. Little Annie shall take a ramble with me. See! I do but hold out my hand, and like some bright bird in the sunny air, with her blue silk frock fluttering upward from her white pantalets, she comes bounding on tiptoe across the street.

Smooth back your brown curls, Annie, and let me tie on your bonnet, and we will set forth. What a strange couple to go on their rambles together! One walks in black attire, with a measured step and a heavy brow and his thoughtful eyes bent down, while the gay little girl trips lightly along as if she were forced to keep hold of my hand lest her feet should dance away from the earth. Yet there is sympathy between us. If I pride myself on anything, it is because I have a smile that children love; and, on the other hand, there are few grown ladies that could entice me from the side of little Annie, for I delight to let my mind go hand in hand with the mind of a sinless child. So come, Annie; but if I moralize as we go, do not listen to me: only look about you and be merry.

Now we turn the corner. Here are hacks with two horses and stage-coaches with four thundering to meet each other, and trucks and carts moving at a slower pace, being heavily laden with barrels from the wharves; and here are rattling gigs which perhaps will be smashed to pieces before our eyes. Hitherward, also, comes a man trundling a wheelbarrow along the pavement. Is not little Annie afraid of such a tumult? No; she does not even shrink closer to my side, but passes on with fearless confidence, a happy child amidst a great throng of grown people who pay the same reverence to her infancy that they would to extreme old age. Nobody jostles her: all turn aside to make way for little Annie; and, what is most singular, she appears conscious of her claim to such respect. Now her eyes brighten with pleasure. A street-musician has seated himself on the steps of yonder church and pours forth his strains to the busy town—a melody that has gone astray among the tramp of footsteps, the buzz of voices and the war of passing wheels. Who heeds the poor organ-grinder? None but myself and little Annie, whose feet begin to move in unison with the lively tune, as if she were loth that music should be wasted without a dance. But where would Annie find a partner? Some have the gout in their toes or the rheumatism in their joints; some are stiff with age, some feeble with disease; some are so lean that their bones would rattle, and others of such ponderous size that their agility would crack the flagstones; but many, many have leaden feet because their hearts are far heavier than lead. It is a sad thought that I have chanced upon. What a company of dancers should we be! For I too am a gentleman of sober footsteps, and therefore, little Annie, let us walk sedately on.

It is a question with me whether this giddy child or my sage self have most pleasure in looking at the shop-windows. We love the silks of sunny hue that glow within the darkened premises of the spruce dry-goods men; we are pleasantly dazzled by the burnished silver and the chased gold, the rings of wedlock and the costly love-ornaments, glistening at the window of the jeweller; but Annie, more than I, seeks for a glimpse of her passing figure in the dusty looking-glasses at the hardware-stores. All that is bright and gay attracts us both.

Here is a shop to which the recollections of my boyhood as well as present partialities give a peculiar magic. How delightful to let the fancy revel on the dainties of a confectioner—those pies with such white and flaky paste, their contents being a mystery, whether rich mince with whole plums intermixed, or piquant apple delicately rose-flavored; those cakes, heart-shaped or round, piled in a lofty pyramid; those sweet little circlets sweetly named kisses; those dark majestic masses fit to be bridal-loaves at the wedding of an heiress, mountains in size, their summits deeply snow-covered with sugar! Then the mighty treasures of sugarplums, white and crimson and yellow, in large glass vases, and candy of all varieties, and those little cockles—or whatever they are called—much prized by children for their sweetness, and more for the mottoes which they enclose, by love-sick maids and bachelors! Oh, my mouth waters, little Annie, and so doth yours, but we will not be tempted except to an imaginary feast; so let us hasten onward devouring the vision of a plum-cake.

Here are pleasures, as some people would say, of a more exalted kind, in the window of a bookseller. Is Annie a literary lady? Yes; she is deeply read in Peter Parley's tomes and has an increasing love for fairy-tales, though seldom met with nowadays, and she will subscribe next year to the *Juvenile Miscellany*. But, truth to tell, she is apt to turn away from the printed page and keep gazing at the pretty pictures, such as the gay-colored ones which make this shop-window the continual loitering-place of children. What would Annie think if, in the book which I mean to send her on New Year's day, she should find her sweet little self bound up in silk or morocco with gilt edges, there to remain till she become a woman grown with children of her own to read about their mother's childhood? That would be very queer.

Little Annie is weary of pictures and pulls me onward by the hand, till suddenly we pause at the most wondrous shop in all the town. Oh, my stars! Is this a toyshop, or is it fairy-land? For here are gilded chariots in which the king and queen of the fairies might ride side by side, while their courtiers on these small horses should gallop in triumphal procession before and behind the royal pair. Here, too, are dishes of chinaware fit to be the dining-set of those same princely personages when they make a regal banquet in the stateliest hall of their palace—full five feet high—and behold their nobles feasting adown the long perspective of the table. Betwixt the king and queen should sit my little Annie, the prettiest fairy of them all. Here stands a turbaned Turk threatening us with his sabre, like an ugly heathen as he is, and next a Chinese mandarin who nods his head at Annie and myself. Here we may review a whole army of horse and foot in red-and-blue uniforms, with drums, fifes, trumpets, and all kinds of noiseless music; they have halted on the shelf of this window after their weary march from Liliput. But what cares Annie for soldiers? No conquering queen is she—neither a Semiramis nor a Catharine; her whole heart is set upon that doll who gazes at us with such a fashionable stare. This is the little girl's true plaything. Though made of wood, a doll is a visionary and ethereal personage endowed by childish fancy with a peculiar life; the mimic lady is a heroine of romance, an actor and a sufferer in a thousand shadowy scenes, the chief inhabitant of that wild world with which children ape the real one. Little Annie does not understand what I am saying, but looks wishfully at the proud lady in the window. We will invite her home with us as we return.—Meantime, good-bye, Dame Doll! A toy yourself, you look forth from your window upon many ladies that are also toys, though they walk and speak, and upon a crowd in pursuit of toys, though they wear grave visages. Oh, with your never-closing eyes, had you but an intellect to moralize on all that flits before them, what a wise doll would you be!—Come, little Annie, we shall find toys enough, go where we may.

Now we elbow our way among the throng again. It is curious in the most crowded part of a town to meet with living creatures that had their birthplace in some far solitude, but have acquired a second nature in the wilderness of men. Look up, Annie, at that canary-bird hanging out of the window in his cage. Poor little fellow! His golden feathers are all tarnished in this smoky sunshine; he would have glistened twice as brightly among the summer islands, but still he has become a citizen in all his tastes and habits, and would not sing half so well without the uproar that drowns his music. What a pity that he does not know how miserable he is! There is a parrot, too, calling out, "Pretty Poll! Pretty Poll!" as we pass by. Foolish bird, to be talking about her prettiness to strangers, especially as she is not a pretty Poll, though gaudily dressed in green and yellow! If she had said "Pretty Annie!" there would have been some sense in it. See that gray squirrel at the door of the fruit-shop whirling round and round so merrily within his wire wheel! Being condemned to the treadmill, he makes it an amusement. Admirable philosophy!

Here comes a big, rough dog—a countryman's dog—in search of his master, smelling at everybody's heels and touching little Annie's hand with his cold nose, but hurrying away, though she would fain have patted him.—Success to your search, Fidelity!—And there sits a great yellow cat upon a window-sill, a very corpulent and comfortable cat, gazing at this transitory world with owl's eyes, and making pithy comments, doubtless, or what appear such, to the silly beast.—Oh, sage puss, make room for me beside you, and we will be a pair of philosophers.

Here we see something to remind us of the town-crier and his ding-dong-bell. Look! look at that great cloth spread out in the air, pictured all over with wild beasts, as if they had met together to choose a king, according to their custom in the days of Æsop. But they are choosing neither a king nor a President, else we should hear a most horrible snarling! They have come from the deep woods and the wild mountains and the desert sands and the polar snows only to do homage to my little Annie. As we enter among them the great elephant makes us a bow in the best style of elephantine courtesy, bending lowly down his mountain bulk, with trunk abased and leg thrust out behind. Annie returns the salute, much to the gratification of the elephant, who is certainly the best-bred monster in the caravan. The lion and the lioness are busy with two beef-bones. The royal tiger, the beautiful, the untamable, keeps pacing his narrow cage with a haughty step, unmindful of the spectators or recalling the fierce deeds of his former life, when he was wont to leap forth upon such inferior animals from the jungles of Bengal.

Here we see the very same wolf—do not go near him, Annie!—the selfsame wolf that devoured little Red Riding-Hood and her grandmother. In the next cage a hyena from Egypt who has doubtless howled around the pyramids and a black bear from our own forests are fellow-prisoners and most excellent friends. Are there any two living creatures who have so few sympathies that they cannot possibly be friends? Here sits a great white bear whom common observers would call a very stupid beast, though I perceive him to be only absorbed in contemplation; he is thinking of his voyages on an iceberg, and of his comfortable home in the vicinity of the north pole, and of the little cubs whom he left rolling in the eternal snows. In fact, he is a bear of sentiment. But oh those unsentimental monkeys! The ugly, grinning, aping, chattering, ill-natured, mischievous and queer little brutes! Annie does not love the monkeys; their ugliness shocks her pure, instinctive delicacy of taste and makes her mind unquiet because it bears a wild and dark resemblance to humanity. But here is a little pony just big enough for Annie to ride, and round and round he gallops in a circle, keeping time with his trampling hoofs to a band of music. And here, with a laced coat and a cocked hat, and a riding-whip in his hand—here comes a little gentleman small enough to be king of the fairies and ugly enough to be king of the gnomes, and takes a flying leap into the saddle. Merrily, merrily plays the music, and merrily gallops the pony, and merrily rides the little old gentleman.—Come, Annie, into the street again; perchance we may see monkeys on horseback there.

Mercy on us! What a noisy world we quiet people live in! Did Annie ever read the cries of London city? With what lusty lungs doth yonder man proclaim that his wheelbarrow is full of lobsters! Here comes another, mounted on a cart and blowing a hoarse and dreadful blast from a tin horn, as much as to say, "Fresh fish!" And hark! a voice on high, like that of a muezzin from the summit of a mosque, announcing that some chimney-sweeper has emerged from smoke and soot and darksome caverns into the upper air. What cares the world for that? But, well-a-day, we hear a shrill voice of affliction—the scream of a little child, rising louder with every repetition of that smart, sharp, slapping sound produced by an open hand on tender flesh. Annie sympathizes, though without experience of such direful woe.

Lo! the town-crier again, with some new secret for the public ear. Will he tell us of an auction, or of a lost pocket-book or a show of beautiful wax figures, or of some monstrous beast more horrible than any in the caravan? I guess the latter. See how he uplifts the bell in his right hand and shakes it slowly at first, then with a hurried motion, till the clapper seems to strike both sides at once, and the sounds are scattered forth in quick succession far and near.

Ding-dong! Ding-dong! Ding-dong!

Now he raises his clear loud voice above all the din of the town. It drowns the buzzing talk of many tongues and draws each man's mind from his own business; it rolls up and down the echoing street, and ascends to the hushed chamber of the sick, and penetrates downward to the cellar kitchen where the hot cook turns from the fire to listen. Who of all that address the public ear, whether in church or court-house or hall of state, has such an attentive audience as the town-crier! What saith the people's orator?

"Strayed from her home, a LITTLE GIRL of five years old, in a blue silk frock and white pantalets, with brown curling hair and hazel eyes. Whoever will bring her back to her afflicted mother—"

Stop, stop, town-crier! The lost is found.—Oh, my pretty Annie, we forgot to tell your mother of our ramble, and she is in despair and has sent the town-crier to bellow up and down the streets, affrighting old and young, for the loss of a little girl who has not once let go my hand? Well, let us hasten homeward; and as we go forget not to thank Heaven, my Annie, that after wandering a little way into the world you may return at the first summons with an untainted and unwearied heart, and be a happy child again. But I have gone too far astray for the town-crier to call me back.

Sweet has been the charm of childhood on my spirit throughout my ramble with little Annie. Say not that it has been a waste of precious moments, an idle matter, a babble of childish talk and a reverie of childish imaginations about topics unworthy of a grown man's notice. Has it been merely this? Not so—not so. They are not truly wise who would affirm it. As the pure breath of children revives the life of aged men, so is our moral nature revived by their free and simple thoughts, their native feeling, their airy mirth for little cause or none, their grief soon roused and soon allayed. Their influence on us is at least reciprocal with ours on them. When our infancy is almost forgotten and our boyhood long departed, though it seems but as yesterday, when life settles darkly down upon us and we doubt whether to call ourselves young any more,—then it is good to steal away from the society of bearded men, and even of gentler woman, and spend an hour or two with children. After drinking from those fountains of still fresh existence we shall return into the crowd, as I do now, to struggle onward and do our part in life—perhaps as fervently as ever, but for a time with a kinder and purer heart and a spirit more lightly wise. All this by thy sweet magic, dear little Annie!

WAKEFIELD.

In some old magazine or newspaper I recollect a story, told as truth, of a man—let us call him Wakefield—who absented himself for a long time from his wife. The fact, thus abstractedly stated, is not very uncommon, nor, without a proper distinction of circumstances, to be condemned either as naughty or nonsensical. Howbeit, this, though far from the most aggravated, is perhaps the strangest instance on record of marital delinquency, and, moreover, as remarkable a freak as may be found in the whole list of human oddities. The wedded couple lived in London. The man, under pretence of going a journey, took lodgings in the next street to his own house, and there, unheard of by his wife or friends and without the shadow of a reason for such self-banishment, dwelt upward of twenty years. During that period he beheld his home every day, and frequently the forlorn Mrs. Wakefield. And after so great a gap in his matrimonial felicity—when his death was reckoned certain, his estate settled, his name dismissed from memory and his wife long, long ago resigned to her autumnal widowhood—he entered the door one evening quietly as from a day's absence, and became a loving spouse till death.

This outline is all that I remember. But the incident, though of the purest originality, unexampled, and probably never to be repeated, is one, I think, which appeals to the general sympathies of mankind. We know, each for himself, that none of us would perpetrate such a folly, yet feel as if some other might. To my own contemplations, at least, it has often recurred, always exciting wonder, but with a sense that the story must be true and a conception of its hero's character. Whenever any subject so forcibly affects the mind, time is well spent in thinking of it. If the reader choose, let him do his own meditation; or if he prefer to ramble with me through the twenty years of Wakefield's vagary, I bid him welcome, trusting that there will be a pervading spirit and a moral, even should we fail to find them, done up neatly and condensed into the final sentence. Thought has always its efficacy and every striking incident its moral.

What sort of a man was Wakefield? We are free to shape out our own idea and call it by his name. He was now in the meridian of life; his matrimonial affections, never violent, were sobered into a calm, habitual sentiment; of all husbands, he was likely to be the most constant, because a certain sluggishness would keep his heart at rest wherever it might be placed. He was intellectual, but not actively so; his mind occupied itself in long and lazy musings that tended to no purpose or had not vigor to attain it; his thoughts were seldom so energetic as to seize hold of words. Imagination, in the proper meaning of the term, made no part of Wakefield's gifts. With a cold but not depraved nor wandering heart, and a mind never feverish with riotous thoughts nor perplexed with originality, who could have anticipated that our friend would entitle himself to a foremost place among the doers of eccentric deeds? Had his acquaintances been asked who was the man in London the surest to perform nothing to-day which should be remembered on the morrow, they would have thought of Wakefield. Only the wife of his bosom might have hesitated. She, without having analyzed his character, was partly aware of a quiet selfishness that had rusted into his inactive mind; of a peculiar sort of vanity, the most uneasy attribute about him; of a disposition to craft which had seldom produced more positive effects than the keeping of petty secrets hardly worth revealing; and, lastly, of what she called a little strangeness sometimes in the good man. This latter quality is indefinable, and perhaps non-existent.

Let us now imagine Wakefield bidding adieu to his wife. It is the dusk of an October evening. His equipment is a drab greatcoat, a hat covered with an oilcloth, top-boots, an umbrella in one hand and a small portmanteau in the other. He has informed Mrs. Wakefield that he is to take the night-coach into the country. She would fain inquire the length of his journey, its object and the probable time of his return, but, indulgent to his harmless love of mystery, interrogates him only by a look. He tells her not to expect him positively by the return-coach nor to be alarmed should he tarry three or four days, but, at all events, to look for him at supper on Friday evening. Wakefield, himself, be it considered, has no suspicion of what is before him. He holds out his hand; she gives her own and meets his parting kiss in the matter-of-course way of a ten years' matrimony, and forth goes the middle-aged Mr. Wakefield, almost resolved to perplex his good lady by a whole week's absence. After the door has closed behind him, she perceives it thrust partly open and a vision of her husband's face through the aperture, smiling on her and gone in a moment. For the time this little incident is dismissed without a thought, but long afterward, when she has been more years a widow than a wife, that smile recurs and flickers across all her reminiscences of Wakefield's visage. In her many musings she surrounds the original smile with a multitude of fantasies which make it strange and awful; as, for instance, if she imagines him in a coffin, that parting look is frozen on his pale features; or if she dreams of him in heaven, still his blessed spirit wears a quiet and crafty smile. Yet for its sake, when all others have given him up for dead, she sometimes doubts whether she is a widow.

But our business is with the husband. We must hurry after him along the street ere he lose his individuality and melt into the great mass of London life. It would be vain searching for him there. Let us follow close at his heels, therefore, until, after several superfluous turns and doublings, we find him comfortably established by the fireside of a small apartment previously bespoken. He is in the next street to his own and at his journey's end. He can scarcely trust his good-fortune in having got thither unperceived, recollecting that at one time he was delayed by the throng in the very focus of a lighted lantern, and again there were footsteps that seemed to tread behind his own, distinct from the multitudinous tramp around him, and anon he heard a voice shouting afar and fancied that it called his name. Doubtless a dozen busybodies had been watching him and told his wife the whole affair.

Poor Wakefield! little knowest thou thine own insignificance in this great world. No mortal eye but mine has traced thee. Go quietly to thy bed, foolish man, and on the morrow, if thou wilt be wise, get thee home to good Mrs. Wakefield and tell her the truth. Remove not thyself even for a little week from thy place in her chaste bosom. Were she for a single moment to deem thee dead or lost or lastingly divided from her, thou wouldst be woefully conscious of a change in thy true wife for ever after. It is perilous to make a chasm in human affections—not that they gape so long and wide, but so quickly close again.

Almost repenting of his frolic, or whatever it may be termed, Wakefield lies down betimes, and, starting from his first nap, spreads forth his arms into the wide and solitary waste of the unaccustomed bed, "No," thinks he, gathering the bedclothes about him; "I will not sleep alone another night." In the morning he rises earlier than usual and sets himself to consider what he really means to do. Such are his loose and rambling modes of thought that he has taken this very singular step with the consciousness of a purpose, indeed, but without being able to define it sufficiently for his own contemplation. The vagueness of the project and the convulsive effort with which he plunges into the execution of it are equally characteristic of a feeble-minded man. Wakefield sifts his ideas, however, as minutely as he may, and finds himself curious to know the progress of matters at home—how his exemplary wife will endure her widowhood of a week, and, briefly, how the little sphere of creatures and circumstances in which he was a central object will be affected by his removal. A morbid vanity, therefore, lies nearest the bottom of the affair. But how is he to attain his ends? Not, certainly, by keeping close in this comfortable lodging, where, though he slept and awoke in the next street to his home, he is as effectually abroad as if the stage-coach had been whirling him away all night. Yet should he reappear, the whole project is knocked in the head. His poor brains being hopelessly puzzled with this dilemma, he at length ventures out, partly resolving to cross the head of the street and send one hasty glance toward his forsaken domicile. Habit—for he is a man of habits—takes him by the hand and guides him, wholly unaware, to his own door, where, just at the critical moment, he is aroused by the scraping of his foot upon the step.—Wakefield, whither are you going?

At that instant his fate was turning on the pivot. Little dreaming of the doom to which his first backward step devotes him, he hurries away, breathless with agitation hitherto unfelt, and hardly dares turn his head at the distant corner. Can it be that nobody caught sight of him? Will not the whole household—the decent Mrs. Wakefield, the smart maid-servant and the dirty little footboy—raise a hue-and-cry through London streets in pursuit of their fugitive lord and master? Wonderful escape! He gathers courage to pause and look homeward, but is perplexed with a sense of change about the familiar edifice such as affects us all when, after a separation of months or years, we again see some hill or lake or work of art with which we were friends of old. In ordinary cases this indescribable impression is caused by the comparison and contrast between our imperfect reminiscences and the reality. In Wakefield the magic of a single night has wrought a similar transformation, because in that brief period a great moral change has been effected. But this is a secret from himself. Before leaving the spot he catches a far and momentary glimpse of his wife passing athwart the front window with her face turned toward the head of the street. The crafty nincompoop takes to his heels, scared with the idea that among a thousand such atoms of mortality her eye must have detected him. Right glad is his heart, though his brain be somewhat dizzy, when he finds himself by the coal-fire of his lodgings.

So much for the commencement of this long whim-wham. After the initial conception and the stirring up of the man's sluggish temperament to put it in practice, the whole matter evolves itself in a natural train. We may suppose him, as the result of deep deliberation, buying a new wig of reddish hair and selecting sundry garments, in a fashion unlike his customary suit of brown, from a Jew's old-clothes bag. It is accomplished: Wakefield is another man. The new system being now established, a retrograde movement to the old would be almost as difficult as the step that placed him in his unparalleled position. Furthermore, he is rendered obstinate by a sulkiness occasionally incident to his temper and brought on at present by the inadequate sensation which he conceives to have been produced in the bosom of Mrs. Wakefield. He will not go back until she be frightened half to death. Well, twice or thrice has she passed before his sight, each time with a heavier step, a paler cheek and more anxious brow, and in the third week of his non-appearance he detects a portent of evil entering the house in the guise of an apothecary. Next day the knocker is muffled. Toward nightfall comes the chariot of a physician and deposits its big-wigged and solemn burden at Wakefield's door, whence after a quarter of an hour's visit he emerges, perchance the herald of a funeral. Dear woman! will she die?

By this time Wakefield is excited to something like energy of feeling, but still lingers away from his wife's bedside, pleading with his conscience that she must not be disturbed at such a juncture. If aught else restrains him, he does not know it. In the course of a few weeks she gradually recovers. The crisis is over; her heart is sad, perhaps, but quiet, and, let him return soon or late, it will never be feverish for him again. Such ideas glimmer through the mist of Wakefield's mind and render him indistinctly conscious that an almost impassable gulf divides his hired apartment from his former home. "It is but in the next street," he sometimes says. Fool! it is in another world. Hitherto he has put off his return from one particular day to another; henceforward he leaves the precise time undetermined—not to-morrow; probably next week; pretty soon. Poor man! The dead have nearly as much chance of revisiting their earthly homes as the self-banished Wakefield.

Would that I had a folio to write, instead of an article of a dozen pages! Then might I exemplify how an influence beyond our control lays its strong hand on every deed which we do and weaves its consequences into an iron tissue of necessity.

Wakefield is spellbound. We must leave him for ten years or so to haunt around his house without once crossing the threshold, and to be faithful to his wife with all the affection of which his heart is capable, while he is slowly fading out of hers. Long since, it must be remarked, he has lost the perception of singularity in his conduct.

Now for a scene. Amid the throng of a London street we distinguish a man, now waxing elderly, with few characteristics to attract careless observers, yet bearing in his whole aspect the handwriting of no common fate for such as have the skill to read it. He is meagre; his low and narrow forehead is deeply wrinkled; his eyes, small and lustreless, sometimes wander apprehensively about him, but oftener seem to look inward. He bends his head and moves with an indescribable obliquity of gait, as if unwilling to display his full front to the world. Watch him long enough to see what we have described, and you will allow that circumstances—which often produce remarkable men from Nature's ordinary handiwork—have produced one such here. Next, leaving him to sidle along the footwalk, cast your eyes in the opposite direction, where a portly female considerably in the wane of life, with a prayer-book in her hand, is proceeding to yonder church. She has the placid mien of settled widowhood. Her regrets have either died away or have become so essential to her heart that they would be poorly exchanged for joy. Just as the lean man and well-conditioned woman are passing a slight obstruction occurs and brings these two figures directly in contact. Their hands touch; the pressure of the crowd forces her bosom against his shoulder; they stand face to face, staring into each other's eyes. After a ten years' separation thus Wakefield meets his wife. The throng eddies away and carries them asunder. The sober widow, resuming her former pace, proceeds to church, but pauses in the portal and throws a perplexed glance along the street. She passes in, however, opening her prayer-book as she goes.

And the man? With so wild a face that busy and selfish London stands to gaze after him he hurries to his lodgings, bolts the door and throws himself upon the bed. The latent feelings of years break out; his feeble mind acquires a brief energy from their strength; all the miserable strangeness of his life is revealed to him at a glance, and he cries out passionately, "Wakefield, Wakefield! You are mad!" Perhaps he was so. The singularity of his situation must have so moulded him to itself that, considered in regard to his fellow-creatures and the business of life, he could not be said to possess his right mind. He had contrived—or, rather, he had happened—to dissever himself from the world, to vanish, to give up his place and privileges with living men without being admitted among the dead. The life of a hermit is nowise parallel to his. He was in the bustle of the city as of old, but the crowd swept by and saw him not; he was, we may figuratively say, always beside his wife and at his hearth, yet must never feel the warmth of the one nor the affection of the other. It was Wakefield's unprecedented fate to retain his original share of human sympathies and to be still involved in human interests, while he had lost his reciprocal influence on them. It would be a most curious speculation to trace out the effect of such circumstances on his heart and intellect separately and in unison. Yet, changed as he was, he would seldom be conscious of it, but deem himself the same man as ever; glimpses of the truth, indeed, would come, but only for the moment, and still he would keep saying, "I shall soon go back," nor reflect that he had been saying so for twenty years.

I conceive, also, that these twenty years would appear in the retrospect scarcely longer than the week to which Wakefield had at first limited his absence. He would look on the affair as no more than an interlude in the main business of his life. When, after a little while more, he should deem it time to re-enter his parlor, his wife would clap her hands for joy on beholding the middle-aged Mr. Wakefield. Alas, what a mistake! Would Time but await the close of our favorite follies, we should be young men—all of us—and till Doomsday.

One evening, in the twentieth year since he vanished, Wakefield is taking his customary walk toward the dwelling which he still calls his own. It is a gusty night of autumn, with frequent showers that patter down upon the pavement and are gone before a man can put up his umbrella. Pausing near the house, Wakefield discerns through the parlor-windows of the second floor the red glow and the glimmer and fitful flash of a comfortable fire. On the ceiling appears a grotesque shadow of good Mrs. Wakefield. The cap, the nose and chin and the broad waist form an admirable caricature, which dances, moreover, with the up-flickering and down-sinking blaze almost too merrily for the shade of an elderly widow. At this instant a shower chances to fall, and is driven by the unmannerly gust full into Wakefield's face and bosom. He is quite penetrated with its autumnal chill. Shall he stand wet and shivering here, when his own hearth has a good fire to warm him and his own wife will run to fetch the gray coat and small-clothes which doubtless she has kept carefully in the closet of their bedchamber? No; Wakefield is no such fool. He ascends the steps—heavily, for twenty years have stiffened his legs since he came down, but he knows it not.—Stay, Wakefield! Would you go to the sole home that is left you? Then step into your grave.—The door opens. As he passes in we have a parting glimpse of his visage, and recognize the crafty smile which was the precursor of the little joke that he has ever since been playing off at his wife's expense. How unmercifully has he quizzed the poor woman! Well, a good night's rest to Wakefield!

This happy event—supposing it to be such—could only have occurred at an unpremeditated moment. We will not follow our friend across the threshold. He has left us much food for thought, a portion of which shall lend its wisdom to a moral and be shaped into a figure. Amid the seeming confusion of our mysterious world individuals are so nicely adjusted to a system, and systems to one another and to a whole, that by stepping aside for a moment a man exposes himself to a fearful risk of losing his place for ever. Like Wakefield, he may become, as it were, the outcast of the universe.

A RILL FROM THE TOWN-PUMP.

(SCENE, *the corner of two principal streets,*[1] *the* TOWN-PUMP *talking through its nose.*)

Noon by the north clock! Noon by the east! High noon, too, by these hot sunbeams, which full, scarcely aslope, upon my head and almost make the water bubble and smoke in the trough under my nose. Truly, we public characters have a tough time of it! And among all the town-officers chosen at March meeting, where is he that sustains for a single year the burden of such manifold duties as are imposed in perpetuity upon the town-pump? The title of "town-treasurer" is rightfully mine, as guardian of the best treasure that the town has. The overseers of the poor ought to make me their chairman, since I provide bountifully for the pauper without expense to him that pays taxes. I am at the head of the fire department and one of the physicians to the board of health. As a keeper of the peace all water-drinkers will confess me equal to the constable. I perform some of the duties of the town-clerk by promulgating public notices when they are posted on my front. To speak within bounds, I am the chief person of the municipality, and exhibit, moreover, an admirable pattern to my brother-officers by the cool, steady, upright, downright and impartial discharge of my business and the constancy with which I stand to my post. Summer or winter, nobody seeks me in vain, for all day long I am seen at the busiest corner, just above the market, stretching out my arms to rich and poor alike, and at night I hold a lantern over my head both to show where I am and keep people out of the gutters. At this sultry noontide I am cupbearer to the parched populace, for whose benefit an iron goblet is chained to my waist. Like a dramseller on the mall at muster-day, I cry aloud to all and sundry in my plainest accents and at the very tiptop of my voice.

Here it is, gentlemen! Here is the good liquor! Walk up, walk up, gentlemen! Walk up, walk up! Here is the superior stuff! Here is the unadulterated ale of Father Adam—better than Cognac, Hollands, Jamaica, strong beer or wine of any price; here it is by the hogshead or the single glass, and not a cent to pay! Walk up, gentlemen, walk up, and help yourselves!

---

[1] Essex and Washington streets, Salem.

It were a pity if all this outcry should draw no customers. Here they come.—A hot day, gentlemen! Quaff and away again, so as to keep yourselves in a nice cool sweat.—You, my friend, will need another cupful to wash the dust out of your throat, if it be as thick there as it is on your cowhide shoes. I see that you have trudged half a score of miles to-day, and like a wise man have passed by the taverns and stopped at the running brooks and well-curbs. Otherwise, betwixt heat without and fire within, you would have been burnt to a cinder or melted down to nothing at all, in the fashion of a jelly-fish. Drink and make room for that other fellow, who seeks my aid to quench the fiery fever of last night's potations, which he drained from no cup of mine.—Welcome, most rubicund sir! You and I have been great strangers hitherto; nor, to confess the truth, will my nose be anxious for a closer intimacy till the fumes of your breath be a little less potent. Mercy on you, man! the water absolutely hisses down your red-hot gullet and is converted quite to steam in the miniature Tophet which you mistake for a stomach. Fill again, and tell me, on the word of an honest toper, did you ever, in cellar, tavern, or any kind of a dram-shop, spend the price of your children's food for a swig half so delicious? Now, for the first time these ten years, you know the flavor of cold water. Good-bye; and whenever you are thirsty, remember that I keep a constant supply at the old stand.—Who next?—Oh, my little friend, you are let loose from school and come hither to scrub your blooming face and drown the memory of certain taps of the ferule, and other schoolboy troubles, in a draught from the town-pump? Take it, pure as the current of your young life. Take it, and may your heart and tongue never be scorched with a fiercer thirst than now! There, my dear child! put down the cup and yield your place to this elderly gentleman who treads so tenderly over the paving-stones that I suspect he is afraid of breaking them. What! he limps by without so much as thanking me, as if my hospitable offers were meant only for people who have no wine-cellars.—Well, well, sir, no harm done, I hope? Go draw the cork, tip the decanter; but when your great toe shall set you a-roaring, it will be no affair of mine. If gentlemen love the pleasant titillation of the gout, it is all one to the town-pump. This thirsty dog with his red tongue lolling out does not scorn my hospitality, but stands on his hind legs and laps eagerly out of the trough. See how lightly he capers away again!—Jowler, did your worship ever have the gout?

Are you all satisfied? Then wipe your mouths, my good friends, and while my spout has a moment's leisure I will delight the town with a few historical remniscences. In far antiquity, beneath a darksome shadow of venerable boughs, a spring bubbled out of the leaf-strewn earth in the very spot where you now behold me on the sunny pavement. The water was as bright and clear and deemed as precious as liquid diamonds. The Indian sagamores drank of it from time immemorial till the fatal deluge of the firewater burst upon the red men and swept their whole race away from the cold fountains. Endicott and his followers came next, and often knelt down to drink, dipping their long beards in the spring. The richest goblet then was of birch-bark. Governor Winthrop, after a journey afoot from Boston, drank here out of the hollow of his hand. The elder Higginson here wet his palm and laid it on the brow of the first town-born child. For many years it was the watering-place, and, as it were, the washbowl, of the vicinity, whither all decent folks resorted to purify their visages and gaze at them afterward—at least, the pretty maidens did—in the mirror which it made. On Sabbath-days, whenever a babe was to be baptized, the sexton filled his basin here and placed it on the communion-table of the humble meeting-house, which partly covered the site of yonder stately brick one. Thus one generation after another was consecrated to Heaven by its waters, and cast their waxing and waning shadows into its glassy bosom, and vanished from the earth, as if mortal life were but a flitting image in a fountain. Finally the fountain vanished also. Cellars were dug on all sides and cart-loads of gravel flung upon its source, whence oozed a turbid stream, forming a mud-puddle at the corner of two streets. In the hot months, when its refreshment was most needed, the dust flew in clouds over the forgotten birthplace of the waters, now their grave. But in the course of time a town-pump was sunk into the source of the ancient spring; and when the first decayed, another took its place, and then another, and still another, till here stand I, gentlemen and ladies, to serve you with my iron goblet. Drink and be refreshed. The water is as pure and cold as that which slaked the thirst of the red sagamore beneath the aged boughs, though now the gem of the wilderness is treasured under these hot stones, where no shadow falls but from the brick buildings. And be it the moral of my story that, as this wasted and long-lost fountain is now known and prized again, so shall the virtues of cold water—too little valued since your fathers' days—be recognized by all.

Your pardon, good people! I must interrupt my stream of eloquence and spout forth a stream of water to replenish the trough for this teamster and his two yoke of oxen, who have come from Topsfield, or somewhere along that way. No part of my business is pleasanter than the watering of cattle. Look! how rapidly they lower the water-mark on the sides of the trough, till their capacious stomachs are moistened with a gallon or two apiece and they can afford time to breathe it in with sighs of calm enjoyment. Now they roll their quiet eyes around the brim of their monstrous drinking-vessel. An ox is your true toper.

But I perceive, my dear auditors, that you are impatient for the remainder of my discourse. Impute it, I beseech you, to no defect of modesty if I insist a little longer on so fruitful a topic as my own multifarious merits. It is altogether for your good. The better you think of me, the better men and women you will find yourselves. I shall say nothing of my all-important aid on washing-days, though on that account alone I might call myself the household god of a hundred families. Far be it from me, also, to hint, my respectable friends, at the show of dirty faces which you would present without my pains to keep you clean. Nor will I remind you how often, when the midnight bells make you tremble for your combustible town, you have fled to the town-pump and found me always at my post firm amid the confusion and ready to drain my vital current in your behalf. Neither is it worth while to lay much stress on my claims to a medical diploma as the physician whose simple rule of practice is preferable to all the nauseous lore which has found men sick, or left them so, since the days of Hippocrates. Let us take a broader view of my beneficial influence on mankind.

No; these are trifles, compared with the merits which wise men concede to me—if not in my single self, yet as the representative of a class—of being the grand reformer of the age. From my spout, and such spouts as mine, must flow the stream that shall cleanse our earth of the vast portion of its crime and anguish which has gushed from the fiery fountains of the still. In this mighty enterprise the cow shall be my great confederate. Milk and water—the TOWN-PUMP and the Cow! Such is the glorious copartnership that shall tear down the distilleries and brewhouses, uproot the vineyards, shatter the cider-presses, ruin the tea and coffee trade, and finally monopolize the whole business of quenching thirst. Blessed consummation! Then Poverty shall pass away from the land, finding no hovel so wretched where her squalid form may shelter herself. Then Disease, for lack of other victims, shall gnaw its own heart and die. Then Sin, if she do not die, shall lose half her strength. Until now the frenzy of hereditary fever has raged in the human blood, transmitted from sire to son and rekindled in every generation by fresh draughts of liquid flame. When that inward fire shall be extinguished, the heat of passion cannot but grow cool, and war—the drunkenness of nations—perhaps will cease. At least, there will be no war of households. The husband and wife, drinking deep of peaceful joy—a calm bliss of temperate affections—shall pass hand in hand through life and lie down not reluctantly at its protracted close. To them the past will be no turmoil of mad dreams, nor the future an eternity of such moments as follow the delirium of the drunkard. Their dead faces shall express what their spirits were and are to be by a lingering smile of memory and hope.

Ahem! Dry work, this speechifying, especially to an unpractised orator. I never conceived till now what toil the temperance lecturers undergo for my sake; hereafter they shall have the business to themselves.—Do, some kind Christian, pump a stroke or two, just to wet my whistle.—Thank you, sir!—My dear hearers, when the world shall have been regenerated by my instrumentality, you will collect your useless vats and liquor-casks into one great pile and make a bonfire in honor of the town-pump. And when I shall have decayed like my predecessors, then, if you revere my memory, let a marble fountain richly sculptured take my place upon this spot. Such monuments should be erected everywhere and inscribed with the names of the distinguished champions of my cause. Now, listen, for something very important is to come next.

There are two or three honest friends of mine—and true friends I know they are—who nevertheless by their fiery pugnacity in my behalf do put me in fearful hazard of a broken nose, or even a total overthrow upon the pavement and the loss of the treasure which I guard.—I pray you, gentlemen, let this fault be amended. Is it decent, think you, to get tipsy with zeal for temperance and take up the honorable cause of the town-pump in the style of a toper fighting for his brandy-bottle? Or can the excellent qualities of cold water be no otherwise exemplified than by plunging slapdash into hot water and woefully scalding yourselves and other people? Trust me, they may. In the moral warfare which you are to wage—and, indeed, in the whole conduct of your lives—you cannot choose a better example than myself, who have never permitted the dust and sultry atmosphere, the turbulence and manifold disquietudes, of the world around me to reach that deep, calm well of purity which may be called my soul. And whenever I pour out that soul, it is to cool earth's fever or cleanse its stains.

One o'clock! Nay, then, if the dinner-bell begins to speak, I may as well hold my peace. Here comes a pretty young girl of my acquaintance with a large stone pitcher for me to fill. May she draw a husband while drawing her water, as Rachel did of old!—Hold out your vessel, my dear! There it is, full to the brim; so now run home, peeping at your sweet image in the pitcher as you go, and forget not in a glass of my own liquor to drink "SUCCESS TO THE TOWN-PUMP."

THE GREAT CARBUNCLE.[1]

A MYSTERY OF THE WHITE MOUNTAINS.

At nightfall once in the olden time, on the rugged side of one of the Crystal Hills, a party of adventurers were refreshing themselves after a toilsome and fruitless quest for the Great Carbuncle. They had come thither, not as friends nor partners in the enterprise, but each, save one youthful pair, impelled by his own selfish and solitary longing for this wondrous gem. Their feeling of brotherhood, however, was strong enough to induce them to contribute a mutual aid in building a rude hut of branches and kindling a great fire of shattered pines that had drifted down the headlong current of the Amonoosuck, on the lower bank of which they were to pass the night. There was but one of their number, perhaps, who had become so estranged from natural sympathies by the absorbing spell of the pursuit as to acknowledge no satisfaction at the sight of human faces in the remote and solitary region whither they had ascended. A vast extent of wilderness lay between them and the nearest settlement, while scant a mile above their heads was that bleak verge where the hills throw off their shaggy mantle of forest-trees and either robe themselves in clouds or tower naked into the sky. The roar of the Amonoosuck would have been too awful for endurance if only a solitary man had listened while the mountain-stream talked with the wind.

The adventurers, therefore, exchanged hospitable greetings and welcomed one another to the hut where each man was the host and all were the guests of the whole company. They spread their individual supplies of food on the flat surface of a rock and partook of a general repast; at the close of which a sentiment of good-fellowship was perceptible among the party, though repressed by the idea that the renewed search for the Great Carbuncle must make them strangers again in the morning. Seven men and one young woman, they warmed themselves together at the fire, which extended its bright wall along the whole front of their

---

[1] The Indian tradition on which this somewhat extravagant tale is founded is both too wild and too beautiful to be adequately wrought up in prose. Sullivan, in his history of Maine, written since the Revolution, remarks that even then the existence of the Great Carbuncle was not entirely discredited.

wigwam. As they observed the various and contrasted figures that made up the assemblage, each man looking like a caricature of himself in the unsteady light that flickered over him, they came mutually to the conclusion that an odder society had never met in city or wilderness, on mountain or plain.

The eldest of the group—a tall, lean, weatherbeaten man some sixty years of age—was clad in the skins of wild animals whose fashion of dress he did well to imitate, since the deer, the wolf and the bear had long been his most intimate companions. He was one of those ill-fated mortals, such as the Indians told of, whom in their early youth the Great Carbuncle smote with a peculiar madness and became the passionate dream of their existence. All who visited that region knew him as "the Seeker," and by no other name. As none could remember when he first took up the search, there went a fable in the valley of the Saco that for his inordinate lust after the Great Carbuncle he had been condemned to wander among the mountains till the end of time, still with the same feverish hopes at sunrise, the same despair at eve. Near this miserable Seeker sat a little elderly personage wearing a high-crowned hat shaped somewhat like a crucible. He was from beyond the sea—a Doctor Cacaphodel, who had wilted and dried himself into a mummy by continually stooping over charcoal-furnaces and inhaling unwholesome fumes during his researches in chemistry and alchemy. It was told of him—whether truly or not—that at the commencement of his studies he had drained his body of all its richest blood and wasted it, with other inestimable ingredients, in an unsuccessful experiment, and had never been a well man since. Another of the adventurers was Master Ichabod Pigsnort, a weighty merchant and selectman of Boston, and an elder of the famous Mr. Norton's church. His enemies had a ridiculous story that Master Pigsnort was accustomed to spend a whole hour after prayer-time every morning and evening in wallowing naked among an immense quantity of pine-tree shillings, which were the earliest silver coinage of Massachusetts. The fourth whom we shall notice had no name that his companions knew of, and was chiefly distinguished by a sneer that always contorted his thin visage, and by a prodigious pair of spectacles which were supposed to deform and discolor the whole face of nature to this gentleman's perception. The fifth adventurer likewise lacked a name, which was the greater pity, as he appeared to be a poet. He was a bright-eyed man, but woefully pined away, which was no more than natural if, as some people affirmed, his ordinary diet was fog, morning mist and a slice of the densest cloud within his reach, sauced with moonshine whenever he could get it. Certain it is that the poetry which flowed from him had a smack of all these dainties. The sixth of the party was a young man of haughty mien and sat somewhat apart from the rest, wearing his plumed hat loftily among his elders, while the fire glittered on the rich embroidery of his dress and gleamed intensely on the jewelled pommel of his sword. This was the lord De Vere, who when at home was said to spend much of his time in the burial-vault of his dead progenitors rummaging their mouldy coffins in search of all the earthly pride and vainglory that was hidden among bones and dust; so that, besides his own share, he had the collected haughtiness of his whole line of ancestry. Lastly, there was a handsome youth in rustic garb, and by his side a blooming little person in whom a delicate shade of maiden reserve was just melting into the rich glow of a young wife's affection. Her name was Hannah, and her husband's Matthew—two homely names, yet well enough adapted to the simple pair who seemed strangely out of place among the whimsical fraternity whose wits had been set agog by the Great Carbuncle.

Beneath the shelter of one hut, in the bright blaze of the same fire, sat this varied group of adventurers, all so intent upon a single object that of whatever else they began to speak their closing words were sure to be illuminated with the Great Carbuncle. Several related the circumstances that brought them thither. One had listened to a traveller's tale of this marvellous stone in his own distant country, and had immediately been seized with such a thirst for beholding it as could only be quenched in its intensest lustre. Another, so long ago as when the famous Captain Smith visited these coasts, had seen it blazing far at sea, and had felt no rest in all the intervening years till now that he took up the search. A third, being encamped on a hunting-expedition full forty miles south of the White Mountains, awoke at midnight and beheld the Great Carbuncle gleaming like a meteor, so that the shadows of the trees fell backward from it. They spoke of the innumerable attempts which had been made to reach the spot, and of the singular fatality which had hitherto withheld success from all adventurers, though it might seem so easy to follow to its source a light that overpowered the moon and almost matched the sun. It was observable that each smiled scornfully at the madness of every other in anticipating better fortune than the past, yet nourished a scarcely-hidden conviction that he would himself be the favored one. As if to allay their too sanguine hopes, they recurred to the Indian traditions that a spirit kept watch about the gem and bewildered those who sought it either by removing it from peak to peak of the higher hills or by calling up a mist from the enchanted lake over which it hung. But these tales were deemed unworthy of credit, all professing to believe that the search had been baffled by want of sagacity or perseverance in the adventurers, or such other causes as might naturally obstruct the passage to any given point among the intricacies of forest, valley and mountain.

In a pause of the conversation the wearer of the prodigious spectacles looked round upon the party, making each individual in turn the object of the sneer which invariably dwelt upon his countenance.

"So, fellow-pilgrims," said he, "here we are, seven wise men and one fair damsel, who doubtless is as wise as any graybeard of the company. Here we are, I say, all bound on the same goodly enterprise. Methinks, now, it were not amiss that each of us declare what he proposes to do with the Great Carbuncle, provided he have the good hap to clutch it.—What says our friend in the bearskin? How mean you, good sir, to enjoy the prize which you have been seeking the Lord knows how long among the Crystal Hills?"

"How enjoy it!" exclaimed the aged Seeker, bitterly. "I hope for no enjoyment from it: that folly has past long ago. I keep up the search for this accursed stone because the vain ambition of my youth has become a fate upon me in old age. The pursuit alone is my strength, the energy of my soul, the warmth of my blood and the pith and marrow of my bones. Were I to turn my back upon it, I should fall down dead on the hither side of the notch which is the gateway of this mountain-region. Yet not to have my wasted lifetime back again would I give up my hopes of is deemed little better than a traffic with the evil one. Now, think ye that I would have done this grievous wrong to my soul, body, reputation and estate without a reasonable chance of profit?"

"Not I, pious Master Pigsnort," said the man with the spectacles. "I never laid such a great folly to thy charge."

"Truly, I hope not," said the merchant. "Now, as touching this Great Carbuncle, I am free to own that I have never had a glimpse of it, but, be it only the hundredth part so bright as people tell, it will surely outvalue the Great Mogul's best diamond, which he holds at an incalculable sum; wherefore I am minded to put the Great Carbuncle on shipboard and voyage with it to England, France, Spain, Italy, or into heathendom if Providence should send me thither, and, in a word, dispose of the gem to the best bidder among the potentates of the earth, that he may place it among his crown-jewels. If any of ye have a wiser plan, let him expound it."

"That have I, thou sordid man!" exclaimed the poet. "Dost thou desire nothing brighter than gold, that thou wouldst transmute all this ethereal lustre into such dross as thou wallowest in already? For myself, hiding the jewel under my cloak, I shall hie me back to my attic-chamber in one of the darksome alleys of London. There night and day will I gaze upon it. My soul shall drink its radiance; it shall be diffused throughout my intellectual powers and gleam brightly in every line of poesy that I indite. Thus long ages after I am gone the splendor of the Great Carbuncle will blaze around my name."

"Well said, Master Poet!" cried he of the spectacles. "Hide it under thy cloak, sayest thou? Why, it will gleam through the holes and make thee look like a jack-o'-lantern!"

"To think," ejaculated the lord De Vere, rather to himself than his companions, the best of whom he held utterly unworthy of his intercourse—"to think that a fellow in a tattered cloak should talk of conveying the Great Carbuncle to a garret in Grubb street! Have not I resolved within myself that the whole earth contains no fitter ornament for the great hall of my ancestral castle? There shall it flame for ages, making a noonday of midnight, glittering on the suits of armor, the banners and escutcheons, that hang around the wall, and keeping bright the memory of heroes. Wherefore have all other adventurers sought the prize in vain but that I might win it and make it a symbol of the glories of our lofty line? And never on the diadem of the White Mountains did the Great Carbuncle hold a place half so honored as is reserved for it in the hall of the De Veres."

"It is a noble thought," said the cynic, with an obsequious sneer. "Yet, might I presume to say so, the gem would make a rare sepulchral lamp, and would display the glories of Your Lordship's progenitors more truly in the ancestral vault than in the castle-hall."

"Nay, forsooth," observed Matthew, the young rustic, who sat hand in hand with his bride, "the gentleman has bethought himself of a profitable use for this bright stone. Hannah here and I are seeking it for a like purpose."

"How, fellow?" exclaimed His Lordship, in surprise. "What castle-hall hast thou to hang it in?"

"No castle," replied Matthew, "but as neat a cottage as any within sight of the Crystal Hills. Ye must know, friends, that Hannah and I, being wedded the last week, have taken up the search of the Great Carbuncle because we shall need its light in the long winter evenings and it will be such a pretty thing to show the neighbors when they visit us! It will shine through the house, so that we may pick up a pin in any corner, and will set all the windows a-glowing as if there were a great fire of pine-knots in the chimney. And then how pleasant, when we awake in the night, to be able to see one another's faces!"

There was a general smile among the adventurers at the simplicity of the young couple's project in regard to this wondrous and invaluable stone, with which the greatest monarch on earth might have been proud to adorn his palace. Especially the man with spectacles, who had sneered at all the company in turn, now twisted his visage into such an expression of ill-natured mirth that Matthew asked him rather peevishly what he himself meant to do with the Great Carbuncle.

"The Great Carbuncle!" answered the cynic, with ineffable scorn. "Why, you blockhead, there is no such thing in *rerum naturâ*. I have come three thousand miles, and am resolved to set my foot on every peak of these mountains and poke my head into every chasm for the sole purpose of demonstrating to the satisfaction of any man one whit less an ass than thyself that the Great Carbuncle is all a humbug."

Vain and foolish were the motives that had brought most of the adventurers to the Crystal Hills, but none so vain, so foolish, and so impious too, as that of the scoffer with the prodigious spectacles. He was one of those wretched and evil men whose yearnings are downward to the darkness instead of heavenward, and who, could they but extinguish the lights which God hath kindled for us, would count the midnight gloom their chiefest glory.

As the cynic spoke several of the party were startled by a gleam of red splendor that showed the huge shapes of the surrounding mountains and the rock-bestrewn bed of the turbulent river, with an illumination unlike that of their fire, on the trunks and black boughs of the forest-trees. They listened for the roll of thunder, but heard nothing, and were glad that the tempest came not near them. The stars—those dial-points of heaven—now warned the adventurers to close their eyes on the blazing logs and open them in dreams to the glow of the Great Carbuncle.

The young married couple had taken their lodgings in the farthest corner of the wigwam, and were separated from the rest of the party by a curtain of curiously-woven twigs such as might have hung in deep festoons around the bridal-bower of Eve. The modest little wife had wrought this piece of tapestry while the other guests were talking. She and her husband fell asleep with hands tenderly clasped, and awoke from visions of unearthly radiance to meet the more blessed light of one another's eyes. They awoke at the same instant and with one happy smile beaming over their two faces, which grew brighter with their consciousness of the reality of life and love. But no sooner did she recollect where they were than the bride peeped through the interstices of the leafy curtain and saw that the outer room of the hut was deserted.

"Up, dear Matthew!" cried she, in haste. "The strange folk are all gone. Up this very minute, or we shall lose the Great Carbuncle!"

In truth, so little did these poor young people deserve the mighty prize which had lured them thither that they had slept peacefully all night and till the summits of the hills were glittering with sunshine, while the other adventurers had tossed their limbs in feverish wakefulness or dreamed of climbing precipices, and set off to realize their dreams with the curliest peep of dawn. But Matthew and Hannah after their calm rest were as light as two young deer, and merely stopped to say their prayers and wash themselves in a cold pool of the Amonoosuck, and then to taste a morsel of food ere they turned their faces to the mountain-side. It was a sweet emblem of conjugal affection as they toiled up the difficult ascent gathering strength from the mutual aid which they afforded.

After several little accidents, such as a torn robe, a lost shoe and the entanglement of Hannah's hair in a bough, they reached the upper verge of the forest and were now to pursue a more adventurous course. The innumerable trunks and heavy foliage of the trees had hitherto shut in their thoughts, which now shrank affrighted from the region of wind and cloud and naked rocks and desolate sunshine that rose immeasurably above them. They gazed back at the obscure wilderness which they had traversed, and longed to be buried again in its depths rather than trust themselves to so vast and visible a solitude.

"Shall we go on?" said Matthew, throwing his arm round Hannah's waist both to protect her and to comfort his heart by drawing her close to it.

But the little bride, simple as she was, had a woman's love of jewels, and could not forego the hope of possessing the very brightest in the world, in spite of the perils with which it must be won.

"Let us climb a little higher," whispered she, yet tremulously, as she turned her face upward to the lonely sky.

"Come, then," said Matthew, mustering his manly courage and drawing her along with him; for she became timid again the moment that he grew bold.

And upward, accordingly, went the pilgrims of the Great Carbuncle, now treading upon the tops and thickly-interwoven branches of dwarf pines which by the growth of centuries, though mossy with age, had barely reached three feet in altitude. Next they came to masses and fragments of naked rock heaped confusedly together like a cairn reared by giants in memory of a giant chief. In this bleak realm of upper air nothing breathed, nothing grew; there was no life but what was concentred in their two hearts; they had climbed so high that Nature herself seemed no longer to keep them company. She lingered beneath them within the verge of the forest-trees, and sent a farewell glance after her children as they strayed where her own green footprints had never been. But soon they were to be hidden from her eye. Densely and dark the mists began to gather below, casting black spots of shadow on the vast landscape and sailing heavily to one centre, as if the loftiest mountain-peak had summoned a council of its kindred clouds. Finally the vapors welded themselves, as it were, into a mass, presenting the appearance of a pavement over which the wanderers might have trodden, but where they would vainly have sought an avenue to the blessed earth which they had lost. And the lovers yearned to behold that green earth again—more intensely, alas! than beneath a clouded sky they had ever desired a glimpse of heaven. They even felt it a relief to their desolation when the mists, creeping gradually up the mountain, concealed its lonely peak, and thus annihilated—at least, for them—the whole region of visible space. But they drew closer together with a fond and melancholy gaze, dreading lest the universal cloud should snatch them from each other's sight. Still, perhaps, they would have been resolute to climb as far and as high between earth and heaven as they could find foothold if Hannah's strength had not begun to fail, and with that her courage also. Her breath grew short. She refused to burden her husband with her weight, but often tottered against his side, and recovered herself each time by a feebler effort. At last she sank down on one of the rocky steps of the acclivity.

"We are lost, dear Matthew," said she, mournfully; "we shall never find our way to the earth again. And oh how happy we might have been in our cottage!"

"Dear heart, we will yet be happy there," answered Matthew. "Look! In this direction the sunshine penetrates the dismal mist; by its aid I can direct our course to the passage of the Notch. Let us go back, love, and dream no more of the Great Carbuncle."

"The sun cannot be yonder," said Hannah, with despondence. "By this time it must be noon; if there could ever be any sunshine here, it would come from above our heads."

"But look!" repeated Matthew, in a somewhat altered tone. "It is brightening every moment. If not sunshine, what can it be?"

Nor could the young bride any longer deny that a radiance was breaking through the mist and changing its dim hue to a dusky red, which continually grew more vivid, as if brilliant particles were interfused with the gloom. Now, also, the cloud began to roll away from the mountain, while, as it heavily withdrew, one object after another started out of its impenetrable obscurity into sight with precisely the effect of a new creation before the indistinctness of the old chaos had been completely swallowed up. As the process went on they saw the gleaming of water close at their feet, and found themselves on the very border of a mountain-lake, deep, bright, clear and calmly beautiful, spreading from brim to brim of a basin that had been scooped out of the solid rock. A ray of glory flashed across its surface. The pilgrims looked whence it should proceed, but closed their eyes, with a thrill of awful admiration, to exclude the fervid splendor that glowed from the brow of a cliff impending over the enchanted lake.

For the simple pair had reached that lake of mystery and found the long-sought shrine of the Great Carbuncle. They threw their arms around each other and trembled at their own success, for as the legends of this wondrous gem rushed thick upon their memory they felt themselves marked out by fate, and the consciousness was fearful. Often from childhood upward they had seen it shining like a distant star, and now that star was throwing its intensest lustre on their hearts. They seemed changed to one another's eyes in the red brilliancy that flamed upon their cheeks, while it lent the same fire to the lake, the rocks and sky, and to the mists which had rolled back before its power. But with their next glance they beheld an object that drew their attention even from the mighty stone. At the base of the cliff, directly beneath the Great Carbuncle, appeared the figure of a man with his arms extended in the act of climbing and his face turned upward as if to drink the full gush of splendor. But he stirred not, no more than if changed to marble.

"It is the Seeker," whispered Hannah, convulsively grasping her husband's arm. "Matthew, he is dead."

"The joy of success has killed him," replied Matthew, trembling violently. "Or perhaps the very light of the Great Carbuncle was death."

"'The Great Carbuncle'!" cried a peevish voice behind them. "The great humbug! If you have found it, prithee point it out to me."

They turned their heads, and there was the cynic with his prodigious spectacles set carefully on his nose, staring now at the lake, now at the rocks, now at the distant masses of vapor, now right at the Great Carbuncle itself, yet seemingly as unconscious of its light as if all the scattered clouds were condensed about his person. Though its radiance actually threw the shadow of the unbeliever at his own feet as he turned his back upon the glorious jewel, he would not be convinced that there was the least glimmer there.

"Where is your great humbug?" he repeated. "I challenge you to make me see it."

"There!" said Matthew, incensed at such perverse blindness, and turning the cynic round toward the illuminated cliff. "Take off those abominable spectacles, and you cannot help seeing it."

Now, these colored spectacles probably darkened the cynic's sight in at least as great a degree as the smoked glasses through which people gaze at an eclipse. With resolute bravado, however, he snatched them from his nose and fixed a bold stare full upon the ruddy blaze of the Great Carbuncle. But scarcely had he encountered it when, with a deep, shuddering groan, he dropped his head and pressed both hands across his miserable eyes. Thenceforth there was in very truth no light of the Great Carbuncle, nor any other light on earth, nor light of heaven itself, for the poor cynic. So long accustomed to view all objects through a medium that deprived them of every glimpse of brightness, a single flash of so glorious a phenomenon, striking upon his naked vision, had blinded him for ever.

"Matthew," said Hannah, clinging to him, "let us go hence."

Matthew saw that she was faint, and, kneeling down, supported her in his arms while he threw some of the thrillingly-cold water of the enchanted lake upon her face and bosom. It revived her, but could not renovate her courage.

"Yes, dearest," cried Matthew, pressing her tremulous form to his breast; "we will go hence and return to our humble cottage. The blessed sunshine and the quiet moonlight shall come through our window. We will kindle the cheerful glow of our hearth at eventide and be happy in its light. But never again will we desire more light than all the world may share with us."

"No," said his bride, "for how could we live by day or sleep by night in this awful blaze of the Great Carbuncle?"

Out of the hollow of their hands they drank each a draught from the lake, which presented them its waters uncontaminated by an earthly lip. Then, lending their guidance to the blinded cynic, who uttered not a word, and even stifled his groans in his own most wretched heart, they began to descend the mountain. Yet as they left the shore, till then untrodden, of the spirit's lake, they threw a farewell glance toward the cliff and beheld the vapors gathering in dense volumes, through which the gem burned duskily.

As touching the other pilgrims of the Great Carbuncle, the legend goes on to tell that the worshipful Master Ichabod Pigsnort soon gave up the quest as a desperate speculation, and wisely resolved to betake himself again to his warehouse, near the town-dock, in Boston. But as he passed through the Notch of the mountains a war-party of Indians captured our unlucky merchant and carried him to Montreal, there holding him in bondage till by the payment of a heavy ransom he had woefully subtracted from his hoard of pine-tree shillings. By his long absence, moreover, his affairs had become so disordered that for the rest of his life, instead of wallowing in silver, he had seldom a sixpence-worth of copper. Doctor Cacaphodel, the alchemist, returned to his laboratory with a prodigious fragment of granite, which he ground to powder, dissolved in acids, melted in the crucible and burnt with the blowpipe, and published the result of his experiments in one of the heaviest folios of the day. And for all these purposes the gem itself could not have answered better than the granite. The poet, by a somewhat similar mistake, made prize of a great piece of ice which he found in a sunless chasm of the mountains, and swore that it corresponded in all points with his idea of the Great Carbuncle. The critics say that, if his poetry lacked the splendor of the gem, it retained all the coldness of the ice. The lord De Vere went back to his ancestral hall, where he contented himself with a wax-lighted chandelier, and filled in due course of time another coffin in the ancestral vault. As the funeral torches gleamed within that dark receptacle, there was no need of the Great Carbuncle to show the vanity of earthly pomp.

The cynic, having cast aside his spectacles, wandered about the world a miserable object, and was punished with an agonizing desire of light for the wilful blindness of his former life. The whole night long he would lift his splendor-blasted orbs to the moon and stars; he turned his face eastward at sunrise as duly as a Persian idolater; he made a pilgrimage to Rome to witness the magnificent illumination of Saint Peter's church, and finally perished in the Great Fire of London, into the midst of which he had thrust himself with the desperate idea of catching one feeble ray from the blaze that was kindling earth and heaven.

Matthew and his bride spent many peaceful years and were fond of telling the legend of the Great Carbuncle. The tale, however, toward the close of their lengthened lives, did not meet with the full credence that had been accorded to it by those who remembered the ancient lustre of the gem. For it is affirmed that from the hour when two mortals had shown themselves so simply wise as to reject a jewel which would have dimmed all earthly things its splendor waned. When our pilgrims reached the cliff, they found only an opaque stone with particles of mica glittering on its surface. There is also a tradition that as the youthful pair departed the gem was loosened from the forehead of the cliff and fell into the enchanted lake, and that at noontide the Seeker's form may still be seen to bend over its quenchless gleam.

Some few believe that this inestimable stone is blazing as of old, and say that they have caught its radiance, like a flash of summer lightning, far down the valley of the Saco. And be it owned that many a mile from the Crystal Hills I saw a wondrous light around their summits, and was lured by the faith of poesy to be the latest pilgrim of the Great Carbuncle.

THE PROPHETIC PICTURES.[1]

"But this painter!" cried Walter Ludlow, with animation. "He not only excels in his peculiar art, but possesses vast acquirements in all other learning and science. He talks Hebrew with Dr. Mather and gives lectures in anatomy to Dr. Boylston. In a word, he will meet the best-instructed man among us on his own ground. Moreover, he is a polished gentleman, a citizen of the world—yes, a true cosmopolite; for he will speak like a native of each clime and country on the globe, except our own forests, whither he is now going. Nor is all this what I most admire in him."

"Indeed!" said Elinor, who had listened with a women's interest to the description of such a man. "Yet this is admirable enough."

"Surely it is," replied her lover, "but far less so than his natural gift of adapting himself to every variety of character, insomuch that all men—and all women too, Elinor—shall find a mirror of themselves in this wonderful painter. But the greatest wonder is yet to be told."

"Nay, if he have more wonderful attributes than these," said Elinor, laughing, "Boston is a perilous abode for the poor gentleman. Are you telling me of a painter, or a wizard?"

"In truth," answered he, "that question might be asked much more seriously than you suppose. They say that he paints not merely a man's features, but his mind and heart. He catches the secret sentiments and passions and throws them upon the canvas like sunshine, or perhaps, in the portraits of dark-souled men, like a gleam of infernal fire. It is an awful gift," added Walter, lowering his voice from its tone of enthusiasm. "I shall be almost afraid to sit to him."

"Walter, are you in earnest?" exclaimed Elinor.

"For Heaven's sake, dearest Elinor, do not let him paint the look which you now wear," said her lover, smiling, though rather perplexed. "There! it is passing away now; but when you spoke, you seemed frightened to death, and very sad besides. What were you thinking of?"

---

[1] This story was suggested by an anecdote of Stuart related in Dunlap's History of the Arts of Designs—a most entertaining book to the general reader, and a deeply-interesting one, we should think, to the artist.

"Nothing, nothing!" answered Elinor, hastily. "You paint my face with your own fantasies. Well, come for me tomorrow, and we will visit this wonderful artist."

But when the young man had departed, it cannot be denied that a remarkable expression was again visible on the fair and youthful face of his mistress. It was a sad and anxious look, little in accordance with what should have been the feelings of a maiden on the eve of wedlock. Yet Walter Ludlow was the chosen of her heart.

"A look!" said Elinor to herself. "No wonder that it startled him if it expressed what I sometimes feel. I know by my own experience how frightful a look may be. But it was all fancy. I thought nothing of it at the time; I have seen nothing of it since; I did but dream it," and she busied herself about the embroidery of a ruff in which she meant that her portrait should be taken.

The painter of whom they had been speaking was not one of those native artists who at a later period than this borrowed their colors from the Indians and manufactured their pencils of the furs of wild beasts. Perhaps, if he could have revoked his life and prearranged his destiny, he might have chosen to belong to that school without a master in the hope of being at least original, since there were no works of art to imitate nor rules to follow. But he had been born and educated in Europe. People said that he had studied the grandeur or beauty of conception and every touch of the master-hand in all the most famous pictures in cabinets and galleries and on the walls of churches till there was nothing more for his powerful mind to learn. Art could add nothing to its lessons, but Nature might. He had, therefore, visited a world whither none of his professional brethren had preceded him, to feast his eyes on visible images that were noble and picturesque, yet had never been transferred to canvas. America was too poor to afford other temptations to an artist of eminence, though many of the colonial gentry on the painter's arrival had expressed a wish to transmit their lineaments to posterity by moans of his skill. Whenever such proposals were made, he fixed his piercing eyes on the applicant and seemed to look him through and through. If he beheld only a sleek and comfortable visage, though there were a gold-laced coat to adorn the picture and golden guineas to pay for it, he civilly rejected the task and the reward; but if the face were the index of anything uncommon in thought, sentiment or experience, or if he met a beggar in the street with a white beard and a furrowed brow, or if sometimes a child happened to look up and smile, he would exhaust all the art on them that he denied to wealth.

Pictorial skill being so rare in the colonies, the painter became an object of general curiosity. If few or none could appreciate the technical merit of his productions, yet there were points in regard to which the opinion of the crowd was as valuable as the refined judgment of the amateur. He watched the effect that each picture produced on such untutored beholders, and derived profit from their remarks, while they would as soon have thought of instructing Nature herself as him who seemed to rival her. Their admiration, it must be owned, was tinctured with the prejudices of the age and country. Some deemed it an offence against the

Mosaic law, and even a presumptuous mockery of the Creator, to bring into existence such lively images of his creatures. Others, frightened at the art which could raise phantoms at will and keep the form of the dead among the living, were inclined to consider the painter as a magician, or perhaps the famous Black Man of old witch-times plotting mischief in a new guise. These foolish fancies were more, than half believed among the mob. Even in superior circles his character was invested with a vague awe, partly rising like smoke-wreaths from the popular superstitions, but chiefly caused by the varied knowledge and talents which he made subservient to his profession.

Being on the eve of marriage, Walter Ludlow and Elinor were eager to obtain their portraits as the first of what, they doubtless hoped, would be a long series of family pictures. The day after the conversation above recorded they visited the painter's rooms. A servant ushered them into an apartment where, though the artist himself was not visible, there were personages whom they could hardly forbear greeting with reverence. They knew, indeed, that the whole assembly were but pictures, yet felt it impossible to separate the idea of life and intellect from such striking counterfeits. Several of the portraits were known to them either as distinguished characters of the day or their private acquaintances. There was Governor Burnett, looking as if he had just received an undutiful communication from the House of Representatives and were inditing a most sharp response. Mr. Cooke hung beside the ruler whom he opposed, sturdy and somewhat puritanical, as befitted a popular leader. The ancient lady of Sir William Phipps eyed them from the wall in ruff and farthingale, an imperious old dame not unsuspected of witchcraft. John Winslow, then a very young man, wore the expression of warlike enterprise which long afterward made him a distinguished general. Their personal friends were recognized at a glance. In most of the pictures the whole mind and character were brought out on the countenance and concentrated into a single look; so that, to speak paradoxically, the originals hardly resembled themselves so strikingly as the portraits did.

Among these modern worthies there were two old bearded saints who had almost vanished into the darkening canvas. There was also a pale but unfaded Madonna who had perhaps been worshipped in Rome, and now regarded the lovers with such a mild and holy look that they longed to worship too.

"How singular a thought," observed Walter Ludlow, "that this beautiful face has been beautiful for above two hundred years! Oh, if all beauty would endure so well! Do you not envy her, Elinor?"

"If earth were heaven, I might," she replied. "But, where all things fade, how miserable to be the one that could not fade!"

"This dark old St. Peter has a fierce and ugly scowl, saint though he be," continued Walter; "he troubles me. But the Virgin looks kindly at us."

"Yes, but very sorrowfully, methinks," said Elinor.

The easel stood beneath these three old pictures, sustaining one that had been recently commenced. After a little inspection they began to recognize the features of their own minister, the Rev. Dr. Colman, growing into shape and life, as it were, out of a cloud.

"Kind old man!" exclaimed Elinor. "He gazes at me as if he were about to utter a word of paternal advice."

"And at me," said Walter, "as if he were about to shake his head and rebuke me for some suspected iniquity. But so does the original. I shall never feel quite comfortable under his eye till we stand before him to be married."

They now heard a footstep on the floor, and, turning, beheld the painter, who had been some moments in the room and had listened to a few of their remarks. He was a middle-aged man with a countenance well worthy of his own pencil. Indeed, by the picturesque though careless arrangement of his rich dress, and perhaps because his soul dwelt always among painted shapes, he looked somewhat like a portrait himself. His visitors were sensible of a kindred between the artist and his works, and felt as if one of the pictures had stepped from the canvas to salute them.

Walter Ludlow, who was slightly known to the painter, explained the object of their visit. While he spoke a sunbeam was falling athwart his figure and Elinor's with so happy an effect that they also seemed living pictures of youth and beauty gladdened by bright fortune. The artist was evidently struck.

"My easel is occupied for several ensuing days, and my stay in Boston must be brief," said he, thoughtfully; then, after an observant glance, he added, "But your wishes shall be gratified though I disappoint the chief-justice and Madame Oliver. I must not lose this opportunity for the sake of painting a few ells of broadcloth and brocade."

The painter expressed a desire to introduce both their portraits into one picture and represent them engaged in some appropriate action. This plan would have delighted the lovers, but was necessarily rejected because so large a space of canvas would have been unfit for the room which it was intended to decorate. Two half-length portraits were therefore fixed upon. After they had taken leave, Walter Ludlow asked Elinor, with a smile, whether she knew what an influence over their fates the painter was about to acquire.

"The old women of Boston affirm," continued he, "that after he has once got possession of a person's face and figure he may paint him in any act or situation whatever, and the picture will be prophetic. Do you believe it?"

"Not quite," said Elinor, smiling. "Yet if he has such magic, there is something so gentle in his manner that I am sure he will use it well."

It was the painter's choice to proceed with both the portraits at the same time, assigning as a reason, in the mystical language which he sometimes used, that the faces threw light upon each other. Accordingly, he gave now a touch to Walter and now to Elinor, and the features of one and the other began to start forth so vividly that it appeared as if his triumphant art would actually disengage them from the canvas. Amid the rich light and deep shade they beheld their phantom selves, but, though the likeness promised to be perfect, they were not quite satisfied with the expression: it seemed more vague than in most of the painter's works. He, however, was satisfied with the prospect of success, and, being much interested in the lovers, employed his leisure moments, unknown to them, in making a crayon sketch of their two figures. During their sittings he engaged them in conversation and kindled up their faces with characteristic traits, which, though continually varying, it was his purpose to combine and fix. At length he announced that at their next visit both the portraits would be ready for delivery.

"If my pencil will but be true to my conception in the few last touches which I meditate," observed he, "these two pictures will be my very best performances. Seldom indeed has an artist such subjects." While speaking he still bent his penetrative eye upon them, nor withdrew it till they had reached the bottom of the stairs.

Nothing in the whole circle of human vanities takes stronger hold of the imagination than this affair of having a portrait painted. Yet why should it be so? The looking-glass, the polished globes of the andirons, the mirror-like water, and all other reflecting surfaces, continually present us with portraits—or, rather, ghosts—of ourselves which we glance at and straightway forget them. But we forget them only because they vanish. It is the idea of duration—of earthly immortality—that gives such a mysterious interest to our own portraits.

Walter and Elinor were not insensible to this feeling, and hastened to the painter's room punctually at the appointed hour to meet those pictured shapes which were to be their representatives with posterity. The sunshine flashed after them into the apartment, but left it somewhat gloomy as they closed the door. Their eyes were immediately attracted to their portraits, which rested against the farthest wall of the room. At the first glance through the dim light and the distance, seeing themselves in precisely their natural attitudes and with all the air that they recognized so well, they uttered a simultaneous exclamation of delight.

"There we stand," cried Walter, enthusiastically, "fixed in sunshine for ever. No dark passions can gather on our faces."

"No," said Elinor, more calmly; "no dreary change can sadden us."

This was said while they were approaching and had yet gained only an imperfect view of the pictures. The painter, after saluting them, busied himself at a table in completing a crayon sketch, leaving his visitors to form their own judgment as to his perfected labors. At intervals he sent a glance from beneath his deep eyebrows, watching their countenances in profile with his pencil suspended over the sketch. They had now stood some moments, each in front of the other's picture, contemplating it with entranced attention, but without uttering a word. At length Walter stepped forward, then back, viewing Elinor's portrait in various lights, and finally spoke.

"Is there not a change?" said he, in a doubtful and meditative tone. "Yes; the perception of it grows more vivid the longer I look. It is certainly the same picture that I saw yesterday; the dress, the features, all are the same, and yet something is altered."

"Is, then, the picture less like than it was yesterday?" inquired the painter, now drawing near with irrepressible interest.

"The features are perfect Elinor," answered Walter, "and at the first glance the expression seemed also hers; but I could fancy that the portrait has changed countenance while I have been looking at it. The eyes are fixed on mine with a strangely sad and anxious expression. Nay, it is grief and terror. Is this like Elinor?"

"Compare the living face with the pictured one," said the painter.

Walter glanced sidelong at his mistress, and started. Motionless and absorbed, fascinated, as it were, in contemplation of Walter's portrait, Elinor's face had assumed precisely the expression of which he had just been complaining. Had she practised for whole hours before a mirror, she could not have caught the look so successfully. Had the picture itself been a mirror, it could not have thrown back her present aspect with stronger and more melancholy truth. She appeared quite unconscious of the dialogue between the artist and her lover.

"Elinor," exclaimed Walter, in amazement, "what change has come over you?"

She did not hear him nor desist from her fixed gaze till he seized her hand, and thus attracted her notice; then with a sudden tremor she looked from the picture to the face of the original.

"Do you see no change in your portrait?" asked she.

"In mine? None," replied Walter, examining it. "But let me see. Yes; there is a slight change—an improvement, I think, in the picture, though none in the likeness. It has a livelier expression than yesterday, as if some bright thought were flashing from the eyes and about to be uttered from the lips. Now that I have caught the look, it becomes very decided."

While he was intent on these observations Elinor turned to the painter. She regarded him with grief and awe, and felt that he repaid her with sympathy and commiseration, though wherefore she could but vaguely guess.

"That look!" whispered she, and shuddered. "How came it there?"

"Madam," said the painter, sadly, taking her hand and leading her apart, "in both these pictures I have painted what I saw. The artist—the true artist—must look beneath the exterior. It is his gift—his proudest, but often a melancholy one—to see the inmost soul, and by a power indefinable even to himself to make it glow or darken upon the canvas in glances that express the thought and sentiment of years. Would that I might convince myself of error in the present instance!"

They had now approached the table, on which were heads in chalk, hands almost as expressive as ordinary faces, ivied church-towers, thatched cottages, old thunder-stricken trees, Oriental and antique costume, and all such picturesque vagaries of an artist's idle moments. Turning them over with seeming carelessness, a crayon sketch of two figures was disclosed.

"If I have failed," continued he—"if your heart does not see itself reflected in your own portrait, if you have no secret cause to trust my delineation of the other—it is not yet too late to alter them. I might change the action of these figures too. But would it influence the event?" He directed her notice to the sketch.

A thrill ran through Elinor's frame; a shriek was upon her lips, but she stifled it with the self-command that becomes habitual to all who hide thoughts of fear and anguish within their bosoms. Turning from the table, she perceived that Walter had advanced near enough to have seen the sketch, though she could not determine whether it had caught his eye.

"We will not have the pictures altered," said she, hastily. "If mine is sad, I shall but look the gayer for the contrast."

"Be it so," answered the painter, bowing. "May your griefs be such fanciful ones that only your pictures may mourn for them! For your joys, may they be true and deep, and paint themselves upon this lovely face till it quite belie my art!"

After the marriage of Walter and Elinor the pictures formed the two most splendid ornaments of their abode. They hung side by side, separated by a narrow panel, appearing to eye each other constantly, yet always returning the gaze of the spectator. Travelled gentlemen who professed a knowledge of such subjects reckoned these among the most admirable specimens of modern portraiture, while common observers compared them with the originals, feature by feature, and were rapturous in praise of the likeness. But it was on a third class—neither travelled connoisseurs nor common observers, but people of natural sensibility—that the pictures wrought their strongest effect. Such persons might gaze carelessly at first, but, becoming interested, would return day after day and study these painted faces like the pages of a mystic volume. Walter Ludlow's portrait attracted their earliest notice. In the absence of himself and his bride they sometimes disputed as to the expression which the painter had intended to throw upon the features, all agreeing that there was a look of earnest import, though no two explained it alike. There was less diversity of opinion in regard to Elinor's picture. They differed, indeed, in their attempts to estimate the nature and depth of the gloom that dwelt upon her face, but agreed that it was gloom and alien from the natural temperament of their youthful friend. A certain fanciful person announced as the result of much scrutiny that both these pictures were parts of one design, and that the melancholy strength of feeling in Elinor's countenance bore reference to the more vivid emotion—or, as he termed it, the wild passion—in that of Walter. Though unskilled in the art, he even began a sketch in which the action of the two figures was to correspond with their mutual expression.

It was whispered among friends that day by day Elinor's face was assuming a deeper shade of pensiveness which threatened soon to render her too true a counterpart of her melancholy picture. Walter, on the other hand, instead of acquiring the vivid look which the painter had given him on the canvas, became reserved and downcast, with no outward flashes of emotion, however it might be smouldering within. In course of time Elinor hung a gorgeous curtain of purple silk wrought with flowers and fringed with heavy golden tassels before the pictures, under pretence that the dust would tarnish their hues or the light dim them. It was enough. Her visitors felt that the massive folds of the silk must never be withdrawn nor the portraits mentioned in her presence.

Time wore on, and the painter came again. He had been far enough to the north to see the silver cascade of the Crystal Hills, and to look over the vast round of cloud and forest from the summit of New England's loftiest mountain. But he did not profane that scene by the mockery of his art. He had also lain in a canoe on the bosom of Lake George, making his soul the mirror of its loveliness and grandeur till not a picture in the Vatican was more vivid than his recollection. He had gone with the Indian hunters to Niagara, and there, again, had flung his hopeless pencil down the precipice, feeling that he could as soon paint the roar as aught else that goes to make up the wondrous cataract. In truth, it was seldom his impulse to copy natural scenery except as a framework for the delineations of the human form and face instinct with thought, passion or suffering. With store of such his adventurous ramble had enriched him. The stern dignity of Indian chiefs, the dusky loveliness of Indian girls, the domestic life of wigwams, the stealthy march, the battle beneath gloomy pine trees, the frontier fortress with its garrison, the anomaly of the old French partisan bred in courts, but grown gray in shaggy deserts,—such were the scenes and portraits that he had sketched. The glow of perilous moments, flashes of wild feeling, struggles of fierce power, love, hate, grief, frenzy—in a word, all the worn-out heart of the old earth—had been revealed to him under a new form. His portfolio was filled with graphic illustrations of the volume of his memory which genius would transmute into its own substance and imbue with immortality. He felt that the deep wisdom in his art which he had sought so far was found.

But amid stern or lovely nature, in the perils of the forest or its overwhelming peacefulness, still there had been two phantoms, the companions of his way. Like all other men around whom an engrossing purpose wreathes itself, he was insulated from the mass of humankind. He had no aim, no pleasure, no sympathies, but what were ultimately connected with his art. Though gentle in manner and upright in intent and action, he did not possess kindly feelings; his heart was cold: no living creature could be brought near enough to keep him warm. For these two beings, however, he had felt in its greatest intensity the sort of interest which always allied him to the subjects of his pencil. He had pried into their souls with his keenest insight and pictured the result upon their features with his utmost skill, so as barely to fall short of that standard which no genius ever reached, his own severe conception. He had caught from the duskiness of the future—at least, so he fancied—a fearful secret, and had obscurely revealed it on the portraits. So much of himself—of his imagination and all other powers—had been lavished on the study of Walter and Elinor that he almost regarded them as creations of his own, like the thousands with which he had peopled the realms of Picture. Therefore did they flit through the twilight of the woods, hover on the mist of waterfalls, look forth from the mirror of the lake, nor melt away in the noontide sun. They haunted his pictorial fancy, not as mockeries of life nor pale goblins of the dead, but in the guise of portraits, each with an unalterable expression which his magic had evoked from the caverns of the soul. He could not recross the Atlantic till he had again beheld the originals of those airy pictures.

"O glorious Art!" Thus mused the enthusiastic painter as he trod the street. "Thou art the image of the Creator's own. The innumerable forms that wander in nothingness start into being at thy beck. The dead live again; thou recallest them to their old scenes and givest their gray shadows the lustre of a better life, at once earthly and immortal. Thou snatchest back the fleeting moments of history. With then there is no past, for at thy touch all that is great becomes for ever present, and illustrious men live through long ages in the visible performance of the very deeds which made them what they are. O potent Art! as thou bringest the faintly-revealed past to stand in that narrow strip of sunlight which we call 'now,' canst thou summon the shrouded future to meet her there? Have I not achieved it? Am I not thy prophet?"

Thus with a proud yet melancholy fervor did he almost cry aloud as he passed through the toilsome street among people that knew not of his reveries nor could understand nor care for them. It is not good for man to cherish a solitary ambition. Unless there be those around him by whose example he may regulate himself, his thoughts, desires and hopes will become extravagant and he the semblance—perhaps the reality—of a madman. Reading other bosoms with an acuteness almost preternatural, the painter failed to see the disorder of his own.

"And this should be the house," said he, looking up and down the front before he knocked. "Heaven help my brains! That picture! Methinks it will never vanish. Whether I look at the windows or the door, there it is framed within them, painted strongly and glowing in the richest tints—the faces of the portraits, the figures and action of the sketch!"

He knocked.

"The portraits—are they within?" inquired he of the domestic; then, recollecting himself, "Your master and mistress—are they at home?"

"They are, sir," said the servant, adding, as he noticed that picturesque aspect of which the painter could never divest himself, "and the portraits too."

The guest was admitted into a parlor communicating by a central door with an interior room of the same size. As the first apartment was empty, he passed to the entrance of the second, within which his eyes were greeted by those living personages, as well as their pictured representatives, who had long been the objects of so singular an interest. He involuntarily paused on the threshold.

They had not perceived his approach. Walter and Elinor were standing before the portraits, whence the former had just flung back the rich and voluminous folds of the silken curtain, holding its golden tassel with one hand, while the other grasped that of his bride. The pictures, concealed for months, gleamed forth again in undiminished splendor, appearing to throw a sombre light across the room rather than to be disclosed by a borrowed radiance. That of Elinor had been almost prophetic. A pensiveness, and next a gentle sorrow, had successively dwelt upon her countenance, deepening with the lapse of time into a quiet anguish. A mixture of affright would now have made it the very expression of the portrait. Walter's face was moody and dull or animated only by fitful flashes which left a heavier darkness for their momentary illumination. He looked from Elinor to her portrait, and thence to his own, in the contemplation of which he finally stood absorbed.

The painter seemed to hear the step of Destiny approaching behind him on its progress toward its victims. A strange thought darted into his mind. Was not his own the form in which that Destiny had embodied itself, and he a chief agent of the coming evil which he had foreshadowed?

Still, Walter remained silent before the picture, communing with it as with his own heart and abandoning himself to the spell of evil influence that the painter had cast upon the features. Gradually his eyes kindled, while as Elinor watched the increasing wildness of his face her own assumed a look of terror; and when, at last, he turned upon her, the resemblance of both to their portraits was complete.

"Our fate is upon us!" howled Walter. "Die!"

Drawing a knife, he sustained her as she was sinking to the ground, and aimed it at her bosom. In the action and in the look and attitude of each the painter beheld the figures of his sketch. The picture, with all its tremendous coloring, was finished.

"Hold, madman!" cried he, sternly.

He had advanced from the door and interposed himself between the wretched beings with the same sense of power to regulate their destiny as to alter a scene upon the canvas. He stood like a magician controlling the phantoms which he had evoked.

"What!" muttered Walter Ludlow as he relapsed from fierce excitement into sullen gloom. "Does Fate impede its own decree?"

"Wretched lady," said the painter, "did I not warn you?"

"You did," replied Elinor, calmly, as her terror gave place to the quiet grief which it had disturbed. "But I loved him."

Is there not a deep moral in the tale? Could the result of one or all our deeds be shadowed forth and set before us, some would call it fate and hurry onward, others be swept along by their passionate desires, and none be turned aside by the prophetic pictures.

DAVID SWAN.

A FANTASY.

We can be but partially acquainted even with the events which actually influence our course through life and our final destiny. There are innumerable other events, if such they may be called, which come close upon us, yet pass away without actual results or even betraying their near approach by the reflection of any light or shadow across our minds. Could we know all the vicissitudes of our fortunes, life would be too full of hope and fear, exultation or disappointment, to afford us a single hour of true serenity. This idea may be illustrated by a page from the secret history of David Swan.

We have nothing to do with David until we find him, at the age of twenty, on the high road from his native place to the city of Boston, where his uncle, a small dealer in the grocery line, was to take him behind the counter. Be it enough to say that he was a native of New Hampshire, born of respectable parents, and had received an ordinary school education with a classic finish by a year at Gilmanton Academy. After journeying on foot from sunrise till nearly noon of a summer's day, his weariness and the increasing heat determined him to sit down in the first convenient shade and await the coming up of the stage-coach. As if planted on purpose for him, there soon appeared a little tuft of maples with a delightful recess in the midst, and such a fresh bubbling spring that it seemed never to have sparkled for any wayfarer but David Swan. Virgin or not, he kissed it with his thirsty lips and then flung himself along the brink, pillowing his head upon some shirts and a pair of pantaloons tied up in a striped cotton handkerchief. The sunbeams could not reach him; the dust did not yet rise from the road after the heavy rain of yesterday, and his grassy lair suited the young man better than a bed of down. The spring murmured drowsily beside him; the branches waved dreamily across the blue sky overhead, and a deep sleep, perchance hiding dreams within its depths, fell upon David Swan. But we are to relate events which he did not dream of.

While he lay sound asleep in the shade other people were wide awake, and passed to and fro, afoot, on horseback and in all sorts of vehicles, along the sunny road by his bedchamber. Some looked neither to the right hand nor the left and knew not that he was there; some merely glanced that way without admitting the slumberer among their busy thoughts; some laughed to see how soundly he slept, and several whose hearts were brimming full of scorn ejected their venomous superfluity on David Swan. A middle-aged widow, when nobody else was near, thrust her head a little way into the recess, and vowed that the young fellow looked charming in his sleep. A temperance lecturer saw him, and wrought poor David into the texture of his evening's discourse as an awful instance of dead drunkenness by the roadside.

But censure, praise, merriment, scorn and indifference were all one—or, rather, all nothing—to David Swan. He had slept only a few moments when a brown carriage drawn by a handsome pair of horses bowled easily along and was brought to a standstill nearly in front of David's resting-place. A linch-pin had fallen out and permitted one of the wheels to slide off. The damage was slight and occasioned merely a momentary alarm to an elderly merchant and his wife, who were returning to Boston in the carriage. While the coachman and a servant were replacing the wheel the lady and gentleman sheltered themselves beneath the maple trees, and there espied the bubbling fountain and David Swan asleep beside it. Impressed with the awe which the humblest sleeper usually sheds around him, the merchant trod as lightly as the gout would allow, and his spouse took good heed not to rustle her silk gown lest David should start up all of a sudden.

"How soundly he sleeps!" whispered the old gentleman. "From what a depth he draws that easy breath! Such sleep as that, brought on without an opiate, would be worth more to me than half my income, for it would suppose health and an untroubled mind."

"And youth besides," said the lady. "Healthy and quiet age does not sleep thus. Our slumber is no more like his than our wakefulness."

The longer they looked, the more did this elderly couple feel interested in the unknown youth to whom the wayside and the maple shade were as a secret chamber with the rich gloom of damask curtains brooding over him. Perceiving that a stray sunbeam glimmered down upon his face, the lady contrived to twist a branch aside so as to intercept it, and, having done this little act of kindness, she began to feel like a mother to him.

"Providence seems to have laid him here," whispered she to her husband, "and to have brought us hither to find him, after our disappointment in our cousin's son. Methinks I can see a likeness to our departed Henry. Shall we waken him?"

"To what purpose?" said the merchant, hesitating. "We know nothing of the youth's character."

"That open countenance!" replied his wife, in the same hushed voice, yet earnestly. "This innocent sleep!"

While these whispers were passing, the sleeper's heart did not throb, nor his breath become agitated, nor his features betray the least token of interest. Yet Fortune was bending over him, just ready to let fall a burden of gold. The old merchant had lost his only son, and had no heir to his wealth except a distant relative with whose conduct he was dissatisfied. In such cases people sometimes do stranger things than to act the magician and awaken a young man to splendor who fell asleep in poverty.

"Shall we not waken him?" repeated the lady, persuasively.

"The coach is ready, sir," said the servant, behind.

The old couple started, reddened and hurried away, mutually wondering that they should ever have dreamed of doing anything so very ridiculous. The merchant threw himself back in the carriage and occupied his mind with the plan of a magnificent asylum for unfortunate men of business. Meanwhile, David Swan enjoyed his nap.

The carriage could not have gone above a mile or two when a pretty young girl came along with a tripping pace which showed precisely how her little heart was dancing in her bosom. Perhaps it was this merry kind of motion that caused—is there any harm in saying it?—her garter to slip its knot. Conscious that the silken girth—if silk it were—was relaxing its hold, she turned aside into the shelter of the maple trees, and there found a young man asleep by the spring. Blushing as red as any rose that she should have intruded into a gentleman's bedchamber, and for such a purpose too, she was about to make her escape on tiptoe. But there was peril near the sleeper. A monster of a bee had been wandering overhead—buzz, buzz, buzz—now among the leaves, now flashing through the strips of sunshine, and now lost in the dark shade, till finally he appeared to be settling on the eyelid of David Swan. The sting of a bee is sometimes deadly. As free-hearted as she was innocent, the girl attacked the intruder with her handkerchief, brushed him soundly and drove him from beneath the maple shade. How sweet a picture! This good deed accomplished, with quickened breath and a deeper blush she stole a glance at the youthful stranger for whom she had been battling with a dragon in the air.

"He is handsome!" thought she, and blushed redder yet.

How could it be that no dream of bliss grew so strong within him that, shattered by its very strength, it should part asunder and allow him to perceive the girl among its phantoms? Why, at least, did no smile of welcome brighten upon his face? She was come, the maid whose soul, according to the old and beautiful idea, had been severed from his own, and whom in all his vague but passionate desires he yearned to meet. Her only could he love with a perfect love, him only could she receive into the depths of her heart, and now her image was faintly blushing in the fountain by his side; should it pass away, its happy lustre would never gleam upon his life again.

"How sound he sleeps!" murmured the girl. She departed, but did not trip along the road so lightly as when she came.

Now, this girl's father was a thriving country merchant in the neighborhood, and happened at that identical time to be looking out for just such a young man as David Swan. Had David formed a wayside acquaintance with the daughter, he would have become the father's clerk, and all else in natural succession. So here, again, had good fortune—the best of fortunes—stolen so near that her garments brushed against him, and he knew nothing of the matter.

The girl was hardly out of sight when two men turned aside beneath the maple shade. Both had dark faces set off by cloth caps, which were drawn down aslant over their brows. Their dresses were shabby, yet had a certain smartness. These were a couple of rascals who got their living by whatever the devil sent them, and now, in the interim of other business, had staked the joint profits of their next piece of villainy on a game of cards which was to have been decided here under the trees. But, finding David asleep by the spring, one of the rogues whispered to his fellow:

"Hist! Do you see that bundle under his head?"

The other villain nodded, winked and leered.

"I'll bet you a horn of brandy," said the first, "that the chap has either a pocket-book or a snug little hoard of small change stowed away amongst his shirts. And if not there, we will find it in his pantaloons pocket."

"But how if he wakes?" said the other.

His companion thrust aside his waistcoat, pointed to the handle of a dirk and nodded.

"So be it!" muttered the second villain.

They approached the unconscious David, and, while one pointed the dagger toward his heart, the other began to search the bundle beneath his head. Their two faces, grim, wrinkled and ghastly with guilt and fear, bent over their victim, looking horrible enough to be mistaken for fiends should he suddenly awake. Nay, had the villains glanced aside into the spring, even they would hardly have known themselves as reflected there. But David Swan had never worn a more tranquil aspect, even when asleep on his mother's breast.

"I must take away the bundle," whispered one.

"If he stirs, I'll strike," muttered the other.

But at this moment a dog scenting along the ground came in beneath the maple trees and gazed alternately at each of these wicked men and then at the quiet sleeper. He then lapped out of the fountain.

"Pshaw!" said one villain. "We can do nothing now. The dog's master must be close behind."

"Let's take a drink and be off," said the other.

The man with the dagger thrust back the weapon into his bosom and drew forth a pocket-pistol, but not of that kind which kills by a single discharge. It was a flask of liquor with a block-tin tumbler screwed upon the mouth. Each drank a comfortable dram, and left the spot with so many jests and such laughter at their unaccomplished wickedness that they might be said to have gone on their way rejoicing. In a few hours they had forgotten the whole affair, nor once imagined that the recording angel had written down the crime of murder against their souls in letters as durable as eternity. As for David Swan, he still slept quietly, neither conscious of the shadow of death when it hung over him nor of the glow of renewed life when that shadow was withdrawn. He slept, but no longer so quietly as at first. An hour's repose had snatched from his elastic frame the weariness with which many hours of toil had burdened it. Now he stirred, now moved his lips without a sound, now talked in an inward tone to the noonday spectres of his dream. But a noise of wheels came rattling louder and louder along the road, until it dashed through the dispersing mist of David's slumber; and there was the stage-coach. He started up with all his ideas about him.

"Halloo, driver! Take a passenger?" shouted he.

"Room on top!" answered the driver.

Up mounted David, and bowled away merrily toward Boston without so much as a parting glance at that fountain of dreamlike vicissitude. He knew not that a phantom of Wealth had thrown a golden hue upon its waters, nor that one of Love had sighed softly to their murmur, nor that one of Death had threatened to crimson them with his blood, all in the brief hour since he lay down to sleep. Sleeping or waking, we hear not the airy footsteps of the strange things that almost happen. Does it not argue a superintending Providence that, while viewless and unexpected events thrust themselves continually athwart our path, there should still be regularity enough in mortal life to render foresight even partially available?

SIGHTS FROM A STEEPLE.

So! I have climbed high, and my reward is small. Here I stand with wearied knees—earth, indeed, at a dizzy depth below, but heaven far, far beyond me still. Oh that I could soar up into the very zenith, where man never breathed nor eagle ever flew, and where the ethereal azure melts away from the eye and appears only a deepened shade of nothingness! And yet I shiver at that cold and solitary thought. What clouds are gathering in the golden west with direful intent against the brightness and the warmth of this summer afternoon? They are ponderous air-ships, black as death and freighted with the tempest, and at intervals their thunder—the signal-guns of that unearthly squadron—rolls distant along the deep of heaven. These nearer heaps of fleecy vapor—methinks I could roll and toss upon them the whole day long—seem scattered here and there for the repose of tired pilgrims through the sky. Perhaps—for who can tell?—beautiful spirits are disporting themselves there, and will bless my mortal eye with the brief appearance of their curly locks of golden light and laughing faces fair and faint as the people of a rosy dream. Or where the floating mass so imperfectly obstructs the color of the firmament a slender foot and fairy limb resting too heavily upon the frail support may be thrust through and suddenly withdrawn, while longing fancy follows them in vain. Yonder, again, is an airy archipelago where the sunbeams love to linger in their journeyings through space. Every one of those little clouds has been dipped and steeped in radiance which the slightest pressure might disengage in silvery profusion like water wrung from a sea-maid's hair. Bright they are as a young man's visions, and, like them, would be realized in dullness, obscurity and tears. I will look on them no more.

In three parts of the visible circle whose centre is this spire I discern cultivated fields, villages, white country-seats, the waving lines of rivulets, little placid lakes, and here and there a rising ground that would fain be termed a hill. On the fourth side is the sea, stretching away toward a viewless boundary, blue and calm except where the passing anger of a shadow flits across its surface and is gone. Hitherward a broad inlet penetrates far into the land; on the verge of the harbor formed by its extremity is a town, and over it am I, a watchman, all-heeding and unheeded. Oh that the multitude of chimneys could speak, like those of Madrid, and betray in smoky whispers the secrets of all who since their first foundation have assembled at the hearths within! Oh that the Limping Devil of Le Sage would perch beside me here, extend his wand over this contiguity of roofs, uncover every chamber and make me familiar with their inhabitants! The most desirable mode of existence might be that of a spiritualized Paul Pry hovering invisible round man and woman, witnessing their deeds, searching into their hearts, borrowing brightness from their felicity and shade from their sorrow, and retaining no emotion peculiar to himself. But none of these things are possible; and if I would know the interior of brick walls or the mystery of human bosoms, I can but guess.

Yonder is a fair street extending north and south. The stately mansions are placed each on its carpet of verdant grass, and a long flight of steps descends from every door to the pavement. Ornamental trees—the broadleafed horse-chestnut, the elm so lofty and bending, the graceful but infrequent willow, and others whereof I know not the names—grow thrivingly among brick and stone. The oblique rays of the sun are intercepted by these green citizens and by the houses, so that one side of the street is a shaded and pleasant walk. On its whole extent there is now but a single passenger, advancing from the upper end, and he, unless distance and the medium of a pocket spyglass do him more than justice, is a fine young man of twenty. He saunters slowly forward, slapping his left hand with his folded gloves, bending his eyes upon the pavement, and sometimes raising them to throw a glance before him. Certainly he has a pensive air. Is he in doubt or in debt? Is he—if the question be allowable—in love? Does he strive to be melancholy and gentlemanlike, or is he merely overcome by the heat? But I bid him farewell for the present. The door of one of the houses—an aristocratic edifice with curtains of purple and gold waving from the windows—is now opened, and down the steps come two ladies swinging their parasols and lightly arrayed for a summer ramble. Both are young, both are pretty; but methinks the left-hand lass is the fairer of the twain, and, though she be so serious at this moment, I could swear that there is a treasure of gentle fun within her. They stand talking a little while upon the steps, and finally proceed up the street. Meantime, as their faces are now turned from me, I may look elsewhere.

Upon that wharf and down the corresponding street is a busy contrast to the quiet scene which I have just noticed. Business evidently has its centre there, and many a man is wasting the summer afternoon in labor and anxiety, in losing riches or in gaining them, when he would be wiser to flee away to some pleasant country village or shaded lake in the forest or wild and cool sea-beach. I see vessels unlading at the wharf and precious merchandise strown upon the ground abundantly as at the bottom of the sea—that market whence no goods return, and where there is no captain nor supercargo to render an account of sales. Here the clerks are diligent with their paper and pencils and sailors ply the block and tackle that hang over the hold, accompanying their toil with cries long-drawn and roughly melodious till the bales and puncheons ascend to upper air. At a little distance a group of gentlemen are assembled round the door of a warehouse. Grave seniors be they, and I would wager—if it were safe, in these times, to be responsible for any one—that the least eminent among them might vie with old Vincentio, that incomparable trafficker of Pisa. I can even select the wealthiest of the company. It is the elderly personage in somewhat rusty black, with powdered hair the superfluous whiteness of which is visible upon the cape of his coat. His twenty ships are wafted on some of their many courses by every breeze that blows, and his name, I will venture to say, though I know it not, is a familiar sound among the far-separated merchants of Europe and the Indies.

But I bestow too much of my attention in this quarter. On looking again to the long and shady walk I perceive that the two fair girls have encountered the young man. After a sort of shyness in the recognition, he turns back with them. Moreover, he has sanctioned my taste in regard to his companions by placing himself on the inner side of the pavement, nearest the Venus to whom I, enacting on a steeple top the part of Paris on the top of Ida, adjudged the golden apple.

In two streets converging at right angles toward my watch-tower I distinguish three different processions. One is a proud array of voluntary soldiers in bright uniform, resembling, from the height whence I look down, the painted veterans that garrison the windows of a toy-shop. And yet it stirs my heart. Their regular advance, their nodding plumes, the sun-flash on their bayonets and musket-barrels, the roll of their drums ascending past me, and the fife ever and anon piercing through,—these things have wakened a warlike fire, peaceful though I be. Close to their rear marches a battalion of schoolboys ranged in crooked and irregular platoons, shouldering sticks, thumping a harsh and unripe clatter from an instrument of tin and ridiculously aping the intricate manoeuvres of the foremost band. Nevertheless, as slight differences are scarcely perceptible from a church-spire, one might be tempted to ask, "Which are the boys?" or, rather, "Which the men?" But, leaving these, let us turn to the third procession, which, though sadder in outward show, may excite identical reflections in the thoughtful mind. It is a funeral—a hearse drawn by a black and bony steed and covered by a dusty pall, two or three coaches rumbling over the stones, their drivers half asleep, a dozen couple of careless mourners in their every-day attire. Such was not the fashion of our fathers when they carried a friend to his grave. There is now no doleful clang of the bell to proclaim sorrow to the town. Was the King of Terrors more awful in those days than in our own, that wisdom and philosophy have been able to produce this change? Not so. Here is a proof that he retains his proper majesty. The military men and the military boys are wheeling round the corner, and meet the funeral full in the face. Immediately the drum is silent, all but the tap that regulates each simultaneous footfall. The soldiers yield the path to the dusty hearse and unpretending train, and the children quit their ranks and cluster on the side-walks with timorous and instinctive curiosity. The mourners enter the churchyard at the base of the steeple and pause by an open grave among the burial-stones; the lightning glimmers on them as they lower down the coffin, and the thunder rattles heavily while they throw the earth upon its lid. Verily, the shower is near, and I tremble for the young man and the girls, who have now disappeared from the long and shady street.

How various are the situations of the people covered by the roofs beneath me, and how diversified are the events at this moment befalling them! The new-born, the aged, the dying, the strong in life and the recent dead are in the chambers of these many mansions. The full of hope, the happy, the miserable and the desperate dwell together within the circle of my glance. In some of the houses over which my eyes roam so coldly guilt is entering into hearts that are still tenanted by a debased and trodden virtue; guilt is on the very edge of commission, and the impending deed might be averted; guilt is done, and the criminal wonders if it be irrevocable. There are broad thoughts struggling in my mind, and, were I able to give them distinctness, they would make their way in eloquence. Lo! the raindrops are descending.

The clouds within a little time have gathered over all the sky, hanging heavily, as if about to drop in one unbroken mass upon the earth. At intervals the lightning flashes from their brooding hearts, quivers, disappears, and then comes the thunder, travelling slowly after its twin-born flame. A strong wind has sprung up, howls through the darkened streets, and raises the dust in dense bodies to rebel against the approaching storm. The disbanded soldiers fly, the funeral has already vanished like its dead, and all people hurry homeward—all that have a home—while a few lounge by the corners or trudge on desperately at their leisure. In a narrow lane which communicates with the shady street I discern the rich old merchant putting himself to the top of his speed lest the rain should convert his hair-powder to a paste. Unhappy gentleman! By the slow vehemence and painful moderation wherewith he journeys, it is but too evident that Podagra has left its thrilling tenderness in his great toe. But yonder, at a far more rapid pace, come three other of my acquaintance, the two pretty girls and the young man unseasonably interrupted in their walk. Their footsteps are supported by the risen dust, the wind lends them its velocity, they fly like three sea-birds driven landward by the tempestuous breeze. The ladies would not thus rival Atalanta if they but knew that any one were at leisure to observe them. Ah! as they hasten onward, laughing in the angry face of nature, a sudden catastrophe has chanced. At the corner where the narrow lane enters into the street they come plump against the old merchant, whose tortoise-motion has just brought him to that point. He likes not the sweet encounter; the darkness of the whole air gathers speedily upon his visage, and there is a pause on both sides. Finally he thrusts aside the youth with little courtesy, seizes an arm of each of the two girls, and plods onward like a magician with a prize of captive fairies. All this is easy to be understood. How disconsolate the poor lover stands, regardless of the rain that threatens an exceeding damage to his well-fashioned habiliments, till he catches a backward glance of mirth from a bright eye, and turns away with whatever comfort it conveys!

The old man and his daughters are safely housed, and now the storm lets loose its fury. In every dwelling I perceive the faces of the chambermaids as they shut down the windows, excluding the impetuous shower and shrinking away from the quick fiery glare. The large drops descend with force upon the slated roofs and rise again in smoke. There is a rush and roar as of a river through the air, and muddy streams bubble majestically along the pavement, whirl their dusky foam into the kennel, and disappear beneath iron grates. Thus did Arethusa sink. I love not my station here aloft in the midst of the tumult which I am powerless to direct or quell, with the blue lightning wrinkling on my brow and the thunder muttering its first awful syllables in my ear. I will descend. Yet let me give another glance to the sea, where the foam breaks out in long white lines upon a broad expanse of blackness or boils up in far-distant points like snowy mountain-tops in the eddies of a flood; and let me look once more at the green plain and little hills of the country, over which the giant of the storm is striding in robes of mist, and at the town whose obscured and desolate streets might beseem a city of the dead; and, turning a single moment to the sky, now gloomy as an author's prospects, I prepare to resume my station on lower earth. But stay! A little speck of azure has widened in the western heavens; the sunbeams find a passage and go rejoicing through the tempest, and on yonder darkest cloud, born like hallowed hopes of the glory of another world and the trouble and tears of this, brightens forth the rainbow.

THE HOLLOW OF THE THREE HILLS.

In those strange old times when fantastic dreams and madmen's reveries were realized among the actual circumstances of life, two persons met together at an appointed hour and place. One was a lady graceful in form and fair of feature, though pale and troubled and smitten with an untimely blight in what should have been the fullest bloom of her years; the other was an ancient and meanly-dressed woman of ill-favored aspect, and so withered, shrunken and decrepit that even the space since she began to decay must have exceeded the ordinary term of human existence. In the spot where they encountered no mortal could observe them. Three little hills stood near each other, and down in the midst of them sunk a hollow basin almost mathematically circular, two or three hundred feet in breadth and of such depth that a stately cedar might but just be visible above the sides. Dwarf pines were numerous upon the hills and partly fringed the outer verge of the intermediate hollow, within which there was nothing but the brown grass of October and here and there a tree-trunk that had fallen long ago and lay mouldering with no green successor from its roots. One of these masses of decaying wood, formerly a majestic oak, rested close beside a pool of green and sluggish water at the bottom of the basin. Such scenes as this (so gray tradition tells) were once the resort of a power of evil and his plighted subjects, and here at midnight or on the dim verge of evening they were said to stand round the mantling pool disturbing its putrid waters in the performance of an impious baptismal rite. The chill beauty of an autumnal sunset was now gilding the three hill-tops, whence a paler tint stole down their sides into the hollow.

"Here is our pleasant meeting come to pass," said the aged crone, "according as thou hast desired. Say quickly what thou wouldst have of me, for there is but a short hour that we may tarry here."

As the old withered woman spoke a smile glimmered on her countenance like lamplight on the wall of a sepulchre. The lady trembled and cast her eyes upward to the verge of the basin, as if meditating to return with her purpose unaccomplished. But it was not so ordained.

"I am stranger in this land, as you know," said she, at length. "Whence I come it matters not, but I have left those behind me with whom my fate was intimately bound, and from whom I am cut off for ever. There is a weight in my bosom that I cannot away with, and I have come hither to inquire of their welfare."

"And who is there by this green pool that can bring thee news from the ends of the earth?" cried the old woman, peering into the lady's face. "Not from my lips mayst thou hear these tidings; yet be thou bold, and the daylight shall not pass away from yonder hilltop before thy wish be granted."

"I will do your bidding though I die," replied the lady, desperately.

The old woman seated herself on the trunk of the fallen tree, threw aside the hood that shrouded her gray locks and beckoned her companion to draw near.

"Kneel down," she said, "and lay your forehead on my knees."

She hesitated a moment, but the anxiety that had long been kindling burned fiercely up within her. As she knelt down the border of her garment was dipped into the pool; she laid her forehead on the old woman's knees, and the latter drew a cloak about the lady's face, so that she was in darkness. Then she heard the muttered words of prayer, in the midst of which she started and would have arisen.

"Let me flee! Let me flee and hide myself, that they may not look upon me!" she cried. But, with returning recollection, she hushed herself and was still as death, for it seemed as if other voices, familiar in infancy and unforgotten through many wanderings and in all the vicissitudes of her heart and fortune, were mingling with the accents of the prayer. At first the words were faint and indistinct—not rendered so by distance, but rather resembling the dim pages of a book which we strive to read by an imperfect and gradually brightening light. In such a manner, as the prayer proceeded, did those voices strengthen upon the ear, till at length the petition ended, and the conversation of an aged man and of a woman broken and decayed like himself became distinctly audible to the lady as she knelt. But those strangers appeared not to stand in the hollow depth between the three hills. Their voices were encompassed and re-echoed by the walls of a chamber the windows of which were rattling in the breeze; the regular vibration of a clock, the crackling of a fire and the tinkling of the embers as they fell among the ashes rendered the scene almost as vivid as if painted to the eye. By a melancholy hearth sat these two old people, the man calmly despondent, the woman querulous and tearful, and their words were all of sorrow. They spoke of a daughter, a wanderer they knew not where, bearing dishonor along with her and leaving shame and affliction to bring their gray heads to the grave. They alluded also to other and more recent woe, but in the midst of their talk their voices seemed to melt into the sound of the wind sweeping mournfully among the autumn leaves; and when the lady lifted her eyes, there was she kneeling in the hollow between three hills.

"A weary and lonesome time yonder old couple have of it," remarked the old woman, smiling in the lady's face.

"And did you also hear them?" exclaimed she, a sense of intolerable humiliation triumphing over her agony and fear.

"Yea, and we have yet more to hear," replied the old woman, "wherefore cover thy face quickly."

Again the withered hag poured forth the monotonous words of a prayer that was not meant to be acceptable in heaven, and soon in the pauses of her breath strange murmurings began to thicken, gradually increasing, so as to drown and overpower the charm by which they grew. Shrieks pierced through the obscurity of sound and were succeeded by the singing of sweet female voices, which in their turn gave way to a wild roar of laughter broken suddenly by groanings and sobs, forming altogether a ghastly confusion of terror and mourning and mirth. Chains were rattling, fierce and stern voices uttered threats and the scourge resounded at their command. All these noises deepened and became substantial to the listener's ear, till she could distinguish every soft and dreamy accent of the love-songs that died causelessly into funeral-hymns. She shuddered at the unprovoked wrath which blazed up like the spontaneous kindling of flume, and she grew faint at the fearful merriment raging miserably around her. In the midst of this wild scene, where unbound passions jostled each other in a drunken career, there was one solemn voice of a man, and a manly and melodious voice it might once have been. He went to and fro continually, and his feet sounded upon the floor. In each member of that frenzied company whose own burning thoughts had become their exclusive world he sought an auditor for the story of his individual wrong, and interpreted their laughter and tears as his reward of scorn or pity. He spoke of woman's perfidy, of a wife who had broken her holiest vows, of a home and heart made desolate. Even as he went on, the shout, the laugh, the shriek, the sob, rose up in unison, till they changed into the hollow, fitful and uneven sound of the wind as it fought among the pine trees on those three lonely hills.

The lady looked up, and there was the withered woman smiling in her face.

"Couldst thou have thought there were such merry times in a mad-house?" inquired the latter.

"True, true!" said the lady to herself; "there is mirth within its walls, but misery, misery without."

"Wouldst thou hear more?" demanded the old woman.

"There is one other voice I would fain listen to again," replied the lady, faintly.

"Then lay down thy head speedily upon my knees, that thou mayst get thee hence before the hour be past."

The golden skirts of day were yet lingering upon the hills, but deep shades obscured the hollow and the pool, as if sombre night wore rising thence to overspread the world. Again that evil woman began to weave her spell. Long did it proceed unanswered, till the knolling of a bell stole in among the intervals of her words like a clang that had travelled far over valley and rising ground and was just ready to die in the air. The lady shook upon her companion's knees as she heard that boding sound. Stronger it grew, and sadder, and deepened into the tone of a death-bell, knolling dolefully from some ivy-mantled tower and bearing tidings of mortality and woe to the cottage, to the hall and to the solitary wayfarer, that all might weep for the doom appointed in turn to them. Then came a measured tread, passing slowly, slowly on, as of mourners with a coffin, their garments trailing on the ground, so that the ear could measure the length of their melancholy array. Before them went the priest, reading the burial-service, while the leaves of his book were rustling in the breeze. And though no voice but his was heard to speak aloud, still there were revilings and anathemas, whispered but distinct, from women and from men, breathed against the daughter who had wrung the aged hearts of her parents, the wife who had betrayed the trusting fondness of her husband, the mother who had sinned against natural affection and left her child to die. The sweeping sound of the funeral train faded away like a thin vapor, and the wind, that just before had seemed to shake the coffin-pall, moaned sadly round the verge of the hollow between three hills. But when the old woman stirred the kneeling lady, she lifted not her head.

"Here has been a sweet hour's sport!" said the withered crone, chuckling to herself.

THE TOLL-GATHERER'S DAY.

A SKETCH OF TRANSITORY LIFE.

Methinks, for a person whose instinct bids him rather to pore over the current of life than to plunge into its tumultuous waves, no undesirable retreat were a toll-house beside some thronged thoroughfare of the land. In youth, perhaps, it is good for the observer to run about the earth, to leave the track of his footsteps far and wide, to mingle himself with the action of numberless vicissitudes, and, finally, in some calm solitude to feed a musing spirit on all that he has seen and felt. But there are natures too indolent or too sensitive to endure the dust, the sunshine or the rain, the turmoil of moral and physical elements, to which all the wayfarers of the world expose themselves. For such a man how pleasant a miracle could life be made to roll its variegated length by the threshold of his own hermitage, and the great globe, as it were, perform its revolutions and shift its thousand scenes before his eyes without whirling him onward in its course! If any mortal be favored with a lot analogous to this, it is the toll-gatherer. So, at least, have I often fancied while lounging on a bench at the door of a small square edifice which stands between shore and shore in the midst of a long bridge. Beneath the timbers ebbs and flows an arm of the sea, while above, like the life-blood through a great artery, the travel of the north and east is continually throbbing. Sitting on the aforesaid bench, I amuse myself with a conception, illustrated by numerous pencil-sketches in the air, of the toll-gatherer's day.

In the morning—dim, gray, dewy summer's morn—the distant roll of ponderous wheels begins to mingle with my old friend's slumbers, creaking more and more harshly through the midst of his dream and gradually replacing it with realities. Hardly conscious of the change from sleep to wakefulness, he finds himself partly clad and throwing wide the toll-gates for the passage of a fragrant load of hay. The timbers groan beneath the slow-revolving wheels; one sturdy yeoman stalks beside the oxen, and, peering from the summit of the hay, by the glimmer of the half-extinguished lantern over the toll-house is seen the drowsy visage of his comrade, who has enjoyed a nap some ten miles long. The toll is paid; creak, creak, again go the wheels, and the huge hay-mow vanishes into the morning mist. As yet nature is but half awake, and familiar objects appear visionary. But yonder, dashing from the shore with a rattling thunder of the wheels and a confused clatter of hoofs, comes the never-tiring mail, which has hurried onward at the same headlong, restless rate all through the quiet night. The bridge resounds in one continued peal as the coach rolls on without a pause, merely affording the toll-gatherer a glimpse at the sleepy passengers, who now bestir their torpid limbs and snuff a cordial in the briny air. The morn breathes upon them and blushes, and they forget how wearily the darkness toiled away. And behold now the fervid day in his bright chariot, glittering aslant over the waves, nor scorning to throw a tribute of his golden beams on the toll-gatherer's little hermitage. The old man looks eastward, and (for he is a moralizer) frames a simile of the stage-coach and the sun.

While the world is rousing itself we may glance slightly at the scene of our sketch. It sits above the bosom of the broad flood—a spot not of earth, but in the midst of waters which rush with a murmuring sound among the massive beams beneath. Over the door is a weatherbeaten board inscribed with the rates of toll in letters so nearly effaced that the gilding of the sunshine can hardly make them legible. Beneath the window is a wooden bench on which a long succession of weary wayfarers have reposed themselves. Peeping within-doors, we perceive the whitewashed walls bedecked with sundry lithographic prints and advertisements of various import and the immense show-bill of a wandering caravan. And there sits our good old toll-gatherer, glorified by the early sunbeams. He is a man, as his aspect may announce, of quiet soul and thoughtful, shrewd, yet simple mind, who of the wisdom which the passing world scatters along the wayside has gathered a reasonable store.

Now the sun smiles upon the landscape and earth smiles back again upon the sky. Frequent now are the travellers. The toll-gatherer's practised ear can distinguish the weight of every vehicle, the number of its wheels and how many horses beat the resounding timbers with their iron tramp. Here, in a substantial family chaise, setting forth betimes to take advantage of the dewy road, come a gentleman and his wife with their rosy-cheeked little girl sitting gladsomely between them. The bottom of the chaise is heaped with multifarious bandboxes and carpet-bags, and beneath the axle swings a leathern trunk dusty with yesterday's journey. Next appears a four-wheeled carryall peopled with a round half dozen of pretty girls, all drawn by a single horse and driven by a single gentleman. Luckless wight doomed through a whole summer day to be the butt of mirth and mischief among the frolicsome maidens! Bolt upright in a sulky rides a thin, sour-visaged man who as he pays his toll hands the toll-gatherer a printed card to stick upon the wall. The vinegar-faced traveller proves to be a manufacturer of pickles. Now paces slowly from timber to timber a horseman clad in black, with a meditative brow, as of one who, whithersoever his steed might bear him, would still journey through a mist of brooding thought. He is a country preacher going to labor at a protracted meeting. The next object passing townward is a butcher's cart canopied with its arch of snow-white cotton. Behind comes a "sauceman" driving a wagon full of new potatoes, green ears of corn, beets, carrots, turnips and summer squashes, and next two wrinkled, withered witch-looking old gossips in an antediluvian chaise drawn by a horse of former generations and going to peddle out a lot of huckleberries. See, there, a man trundling a wheelbarrow-load of lobsters. And now a milk-cart rattles briskly onward, covered with green canvas and conveying the contributions of a whole herd of cows, in large tin canisters.

But let all these pay their toll and pass. Here comes a spectacle that causes the old toll-gatherer to smile benignantly, as if the travellers brought sunshine with them and lavished its gladsome influence all along the road. It is a barouche of the newest style, the varnished panels of which reflect the whole moving panorama of the landscape, and show a picture, likewise, of our friend with his visage broadened, so that his meditative smile is transformed to grotesque merriment. Within sits a youth fresh as the summer morn, and beside him a young lady in white with white gloves upon her slender hands and a white veil flowing down over her face. But methinks her blushing cheek burns through the snowy veil. Another white-robed virgin sits in front. And who are these on whom, and on all that appertains to them, the dust of earth seems never to have settled? Two lovers whom the priest has blessed this blessed morn and sent them forth, with one of the bride-maids, on the matrimonial tour.—Take my blessing too, ye happy ones! May the sky not frown upon you nor clouds bedew you with their chill and sullen rain! May the hot sun kindle no fever in your hearts! May your whole life's pilgrimage be as blissful as this first day's journey, and its close be gladdened with even brighter anticipations than those which hallow your bridal-night! They pass, and ere the reflection of their joy has faded from his face another spectacle throws a melancholy shadow over the spirit of the observing man. In a close carriage sits a fragile figure muffled carefully and shrinking even from the mild breath of summer. She leans against a manly form, and his arm enfolds her as if to guard his treasure from some enemy. Let but a few weeks pass, and when he shall strive to embrace that loved one, he will press only desolation to his heart.

And now has Morning gathered up her dewy pearls and fled away. The sun rolls blazing through the sky, and cannot find a cloud to cool his face with. The horses toil sluggishly along the bridge, and heave their glistening sides in short quick pantings when the reins are tightened at the toll-house. Glisten, too, the faces of the travellers. Their garments are thickly bestrewn with dust; their whiskers and hair look hoary; their throats are choked with the dusty atmosphere which they have left behind them. No air is stirring on the road. Nature dares draw no breath lest she should inhale a stifling cloud of dust. "A hot and dusty day!" cry the poor pilgrims as they wipe their begrimed foreheads and woo the doubtful breeze which the river bears along with it.—"Awful hot! Dreadful dusty!" answers the sympathetic toll-gatherer. They start again to pass through the fiery furnace, while he re-enters his cool hermitage and besprinkles it with a pail of briny water from the stream beneath. He thinks within himself that the sun is not so fierce here as elsewhere, and that the gentle air doth not forget him in these sultry days. Yes, old friend, and a quiet heart will make a dog-day temperate. He hears a weary footstep, and perceives a traveller with pack and staff, who sits down upon the hospitable bench and removes the hat from his wet brow. The toll-gatherer administers a cup of cold water, and, discovering his guest to be a man of homely sense, he engages him in profitable talk, uttering the maxims of a philosophy which he has found in his own soul, but knows not how it came there. And as the wayfarer makes ready to resume his journey he tells him a sovereign remedy for blistered feet.

Now comes the noontide hour—of all the hours, nearest akin to midnight, for each has its own calmness and repose. Soon, however, the world begins to turn again upon its axis, and it seems the busiest epoch of the day, when an accident impedes the march of sublunary things. The draw being lifted to permit the passage of a schooner laden with wood from the Eastern forests, she sticks immovably right athwart the bridge. Meanwhile, on both sides of the chasm a throng of impatient travellers fret and fume. Here are two sailors in a gig with the top thrown back, both puffing cigars and swearing all sorts of forecastle oaths; there, in a smart chaise, a dashingly-dressed gentleman and lady, he from a tailor's shop-board and she from a milliner's back room—the aristocrats of a summer afternoon. And what are the haughtiest of us but the ephemeral aristocrats of a summer's day? Here is a tin-pedler whose glittering ware bedazzles all beholders like a travelling meteor or opposition sun, and on the other side a seller of spruce beer, which brisk liquor is confined in several dozen of stone bottles. Here conic a party of ladies on horseback, in green ridings habits, and gentlemen attendant, and there a flock of sheep for the market, pattering over the bridge with a multitude nous clatter of their little hoofs; here a Frenchman with a hand-organ on his shoulder, and there an itinerant Swiss jeweller. On this side, heralded by a blast of clarions and bugles, appears a train of wagons conveying all the wild beasts of a caravan; and on that a company of summer soldiers marching from village to village on a festival campaign, attended by the "brass band." Now look at the scene, and it presents an emblem of the mysterious confusion, the apparently insolvable riddle, in which individuals, or the great world itself, seem often to be involved. What miracle shall set all things right again?

But see! the schooner has thrust her bulky carcase through the chasm; the draw descends; horse and foot pass onward and leave the bridge vacant from end to end. "And thus," muses the toll-gatherer, "have I found it with all stoppages, even though the universe seemed to be at a stand." The sage old man!

Far westward now the reddening sun throws a broad sheet of splendor across the flood, and to the eyes of distant boatmen gleams brightly among the timbers of the bridge. Strollers come from the town to quaff the freshening breeze. One or two let down long lines and haul up flapping flounders or cunners or small cod, or perhaps an eel. Others, and fair girls among them, with the flush of the hot day still on their cheeks, bend over the railing and watch the heaps of seaweed floating upward with the flowing tide. The horses now tramp heavily along the bridge and wistfully bethink them of their stables.—Rest, rest, thou weary world! for to-morrow's round of toil and pleasure will be as wearisome as to-day's has been, yet both shall bear thee onward a day's march of eternity.—Now the old toll-gatherer looks seaward and discerns the lighthouse kindling on a far island, and the stars, too, kindling in the sky, as if but a little way beyond; and, mingling reveries of heaven with remembrances of earth, the whole procession of mortal travellers, all the dusty pilgrimage which he has witnessed, seems like a flitting show of phantoms for his thoughtful soul to muse upon.

THE VISION OF THE FOUNTAIN.

At fifteen I became a resident in a country village more than a hundred miles from home. The morning after my arrival—a September morning, but warm and bright as any in July—I rambled into a wood of oaks with a few walnut trees intermixed, forming the closest shade above my head. The ground was rocky, uneven, overgrown with bushes and clumps of young saplings and traversed only by cattle-paths. The track which I chanced to follow led me to a crystal spring with a border of grass as freshly green as on May morning, and overshadowed by the limb of a great oak. One solitary sunbeam found its way down and played like a goldfish in the water.

From my childhood I have loved to gaze into a spring. The water filled a circular basin, small but deep and set round with stones, some of which were covered with slimy moss, the others naked and of variegated hue—reddish, white and brown. The bottom was covered with coarse sand, which sparkled in the lonely sunbeam and seemed to illuminate the spring with an unborrowed light. In one spot the gush of the water violently agitated the sand, but without obscuring the fountain or breaking the glassiness of its surface. It appeared as if some living creature were about to emerge—the naiad of the spring, perhaps, in the shape of a beautiful young woman with a gown of filmy water-moss, a belt of rainbow-drops and a cold, pure, passionless countenance. How would the beholder shiver, pleasantly yet fearfully, to see her sitting on one of the stones, paddling her white feet in the ripples and throwing up water to sparkle in the sun! Wherever she laid her hands on grass and flowers, they would immediately be moist, as with morning dew. Then would she set about her labors, like a careful housewife, to clear the fountain of withered leaves, and bits of slimy wood, and old acorns from the oaks above, and grains of corn left by cattle in drinking, till the bright sand in the bright water were like a treasury of diamonds. But, should the intruder approach too near, he would find only the drops of a summer shower glistening about the spot where he had seen her.

Reclining on the border of grass where the dewy goddess should have been, I bent forward, and a pair of eyes met mine within the watery mirror. They were the reflection of my own. I looked again, and, lo! another face, deeper in the fountain than my own image, more distinct in all the features, yet faint as thought. The vision had the aspect of a fair young girl with locks of paly gold. A mirthful expression laughed in the eyes and dimpled over the whole shadowy countenance, till it seemed just what a fountain would be if, while dancing merrily into the sunshine, it should assume the shape of woman. Through the dim rosiness of the cheeks I could see the brown leaves, the slimy twigs, the acorns and the sparkling sand. The solitary sunbeam was diffused among the golden hair, which melted into its faint brightness and became a glory round that head so beautiful.

My description can give no idea how suddenly the fountain was thus tenanted and how soon it was left desolate. I breathed, and there was the face; I held my breath, and it was gone. Had it passed away or faded into nothing? I doubted whether it had ever been.

My sweet readers, what a dreamy and delicious hour did I spend where that vision found and left me! For a long time I sat perfectly still, waiting till it should reappear, and fearful that the slightest motion, or even the flutter of my breath, might frighten it away. Thus have I often started from a pleasant dream, and then kept quiet in hopes to wile it back. Deep were my musings as to the race and attributes of that ethereal being. Had I created her? Was she the daughter of my fancy, akin to those strange shapes which peep under the lids of children's eyes? And did her beauty gladden me for that one moment and then die? Or was she a water-nymph within the fountain, or fairy or woodland goddess peeping over my shoulder, or the ghost of some forsaken maid who had drowned herself for love? Or, in good truth, had a lovely girl with a warm heart and lips that would bear pressure stolen softly behind me and thrown her image into the spring?

I watched and waited, but no vision came again. I departed, but with a spell upon me which drew me back that same afternoon to the haunted spring. There was the water gushing, the sand sparkling and the sunbeam glimmering. There the vision was not, but only a great frog, the hermit of that solitude, who immediately withdrew his speckled snout and made himself invisible—all except a pair of long legs—beneath a stone. Methought he had a devilish look. I could have slain him as an enchanter who kept the mysterious beauty imprisoned in the fountain.

Sad and heavy, I was returning to the village. Between me and the church-spire rose a little hill, and on its summit a group of trees insulated from all the rest of the wood, with their own share of radiance hovering on them from the west and their own solitary shadow falling to the east. The afternoon being far declined, the sunshine was almost pensive and the shade almost cheerful; glory and gloom were mingled in the placid light, as if the spirits of the Day and Evening had met in friendship under those trees and found themselves akin. I was admiring the picture when the shape of a young girl emerged from behind the clump of oaks. My heart knew her: it was the vision, but so distant and ethereal did she seem, so unmixed with earth, so imbued with the pensive glory of the spot where she was standing, that my spirit sunk within me, sadder than before. How could I ever reach her?

While I gazed a sudden shower came pattering down upon the leaves. In a moment the air was full of brightness, each raindrop catching a portion of sunlight as it fell, and the whole gentle shower appearing like a mist, just substantial enough to bear the burden of radiance. A rainbow vivid as Niagara's was painted in the air. Its southern limb came down before the group of trees and enveloped the fair vision as if the hues of heaven were the only garment for her beauty. When the rainbow vanished, she who had seemed a part of it was no longer there. Was her existence absorbed in nature's loveliest phenomenon, and did her pure frame dissolve away in the varied light? Yet I would not despair of her return, for, robed in the rainbow, she was the emblem of Hope.

Thus did the vision leave me, and many a doleful day succeeded to the parting moment. By the spring and in the wood and on the hill and through the village, at dewy sunrise, burning noon, and at that magic hour of sunset, when she had vanished from my sight, I sought her, but in vain. Weeks came and went, months rolled away, and she appeared not in them. I imparted my mystery to none, but wandered to and fro or sat in solitude like one that had caught a glimpse of heaven and could take no more joy on earth. I withdrew into an inner world where my thoughts lived and breathed, and the vision in the midst of them. Without intending it, I became at once the author and hero of a romance, conjuring up rivals, imagining events, the actions of others and my own, and experiencing every change of passion, till jealousy and despair had their end in bliss. Oh, had I the burning fancy of my early youth with manhood's colder gift, the power of expression, your hearts, sweet ladies, should flutter at my tale.

In the middle of January I was summoned home. The day before my departure, visiting the spots which had been hallowed by the vision, I found that the spring had a frozen bosom, and nothing but the snow and a glare of winter sunshine on the hill of the rainbow. "Let me hope," thought I, "or my heart will be as icy as the fountain and the whole world as desolate as this snowy hill." Most of the day was spent in preparing for the journey, which was to commence at four o'clock the next morning. About an hour after supper, when all was in readiness, I descended from my chamber to the sitting-room to take leave of the old clergyman and his family with whom I had been an inmate. A gust of wind blew out my lamp as I passed through the entry.

According to their invariable custom—so pleasant a one when the fire blazes cheerfully—the family were sitting in the parlor with no other light than what came from the hearth. As the good clergyman's scanty stipend compelled him to use all sorts of economy, the foundation of his fires was always a large heap of tan, or ground bark, which would smoulder away from morning till night with a dull warmth and no flame. This evening the heap of tan was newly put on and surmounted with three sticks of red oak full of moisture, and a few pieces of dry pine that had not yet kindled. There was no light except the little that came sullenly from two half-burnt brands, without even glimmering on the andirons. But I knew the position of the old minister's arm-chair, and also where his wife sat with her knitting-work, and how to avoid his two daughters—one a stout country lass, and the other a consumptive girl. Groping through the gloom, I found my own place next to that of the son, a learned collegian who had come home to keep school in the village during the winter vacation. I noticed that there was less room than usual to-night between the collegian's chair and mine.

As people are always taciturn in the dark, not a word was said for some time after my entrance. Nothing broke the stillness but the regular click of the matron's knitting-needles. At times the fire threw out a brief and dusky gleam which twinkled on the old man's glasses and hovered doubtfully round our circle, but was far too faint to portray the individuals who composed it. Were we not like ghosts? Dreamy as the scene was, might it not be a type of the mode in which departed people who had known and loved each other here would hold communion in eternity? We were aware of each other's presence, not by sight nor sound nor touch, but by an inward consciousness. Would it not be so among the dead?

The silence was interrupted by the consumptive daughter addressing a remark to some one in the circle whom she called Rachel. Her tremulous and decayed accents were answered by a single word, but in a voice that made me start and bend toward the spot whence it had proceeded. Had I ever heard that sweet, low tone? If not, why did it rouse up so many old recollections, or mockeries of such, the shadows of things familiar yet unknown, and fill my mind with confused images of her features who had spoken, though buried in the gloom of the parlor? Whom had my heart recognized, that it throbbed so? I listened to catch her gentle breathing, and strove by the intensity of my gaze to picture forth a shape where none was visible.

Suddenly the dry pine caught; the fire blazed up with a ruddy glow, and where the darkness had been, there was she—the vision of the fountain. A spirit of radiance only, she had vanished with the rainbow and appeared again in the firelight, perhaps to flicker with the blaze and be gone. Vet her cheek was rosy and lifelike, and her features, in the bright warmth of the room, were even sweeter and tenderer than my recollection of them. She knew me. The mirthful expression that had laughed in her eyes and dimpled over her countenance when I beheld her faint beauty in the fountain was laughing and dimpling there now. One moment our glance mingled; the next, down rolled the heap of tan upon the kindled wood, and darkness snatched away that daughter of the light, and gave her back to me no more!

Fair ladies, there is nothing more to tell. Must the simple mystery be revealed, then, that Rachel was the daughter of the village squire and had left home for a boarding-school the morning after I arrived and returned the day before my departure? If I transformed her to an angel, it is what every youthful lover does for his mistress. Therein consists the essence of my story. But slight the change, sweet maids, to make angels of yourselves.

FANCY'S SHOW-BOX.

A MORALITY.

What is guilt? A stain upon the soul. And it is a point of vast interest whether the soul may contract such stains in all their depth and flagrancy from deeds which may have been plotted and resolved upon, but which physically have never had existence. Must the fleshly hand and visible frame of man set its seal to the evil designs of the soul, in order to give them their entire validity against the sinner? Or, while none but crimes perpetrated are cognizable before an earthly tribunal, will guilty thoughts—of which guilty deeds are no more than shadows,—will these draw down the full weight of a condemning sentence in the supreme court of eternity? In the solitude of a midnight chamber or in a desert afar from men or in a church while the body is kneeling the soul may pollute itself even with those crimes which we are accustomed to deem altogether carnal. If this be true, it is a fearful truth.

Let us illustrate the subject by an imaginary example. A venerable gentleman—one Mr. Smith—who had long been regarded as a pattern of moral excellence was warming his aged blood with a glass or two of generous wine. His children being gone forth about their worldly business and his grandchildren at school, he sat alone in a deep luxurious arm-chair with his feet beneath a richly-carved mahogany table. Some old people have a dread of solitude, and when better company may not be had rejoice even to hear the quiet breathing of a babe asleep upon the carpet. But Mr. Smith, whose silver hair was the bright symbol of a life unstained except by such spots as are inseparable from human nature—he had no need of a babe to protect him by its purity, nor of a grown person to stand between him and his own soul. Nevertheless, either manhood must converse with age, or womanhood must soothe him with gentle cares, or infancy must sport around his chair, or his thoughts will stray into the misty region of the past and the old man be chill and sad. Wine will not always cheer him.

Such might have been the case with Mr. Smith, when, through the brilliant medium of his glass of old Madeira, he beheld three figures entering the room. These were Fancy, who had assumed the garb and aspect of an itinerant showman, with a box of pictures on her back; and Memory, in the likeness of a clerk, with a pen behind her ear, an inkhorn at her buttonhole and a huge manuscript volume beneath her arm; and lastly, behind the other two, a person shrouded in a dusky mantle which concealed both face and form. But Mr. Smith had a shrewd idea that it was Conscience. How kind of Fancy, Memory and Conscience to visit the old gentleman just as he was beginning to imagine that the wine had neither so bright a sparkle nor so excellent a flavor as when himself and the liquor were less aged! Through the dim length of the apartment, where crimson curtains muffled the glare of sunshine and created a rich obscurity, the three guests drew near the silver-haired old man. Memory, with a finger between the leaves of her huge volume, placed herself at his right hand; Conscience, with her face still hidden in the dusky mantle, took her station on the left, so as to be next his heart; while Fancy set down her picture-box upon the table with the magnifying-glass convenient to his eye.

We can sketch merely the outlines of two or three out of the many pictures which at the pulling of a string successively peopled the box with the semblances of living scenes. One was a moonlight picture, in the background a lowly dwelling, and in front, partly shadowed by a tree, yet besprinkled with flakes of radiance, two youthful figures, male and female. The young man stood with folded arms, a haughty smile upon his lip and a gleam of triumph in his eye as he glanced downward at the kneeling girl. She was almost prostrate at his feet, evidently sinking under a weight of shame and anguish which hardly allowed her to lift her clasped hands in supplication. Her eyes she could not lift. But neither her agony, nor the lovely features on which it was depicted, nor the slender grace of the form which it convulsed, appeared to soften the obduracy of the young man. He was the personification of triumphant scorn.

Now, strange to say, as old Mr. Smith peeped through the magnifying-glass, which made the objects start out from the canvas with magical deception, he began to recognize the farmhouse, the tree and both the figures of the picture. The young man in times long past had often met his gaze within the looking-glass; the girl was the very image of his first love—his cottage-love, his Martha Burroughs. Mr. Smith was scandalized. "Oh, vile and slanderous picture!" he exclaims. "When have I triumphed over ruined innocence? Was not Martha wedded in her teens to David Tomkins, who won her girlish love and long enjoyed her affection as a wife? And ever since his death she has lived a reputable widow!"

Meantime, Memory was turning over the leaves of her volume, rustling them to and fro with uncertain fingers, until among the earlier pages she found one which had reference to this picture. She reads it close to the old gentleman's ear: it is a record merely of sinful thought which never was embodied in an act, but, while Memory is reading, Conscience unveils her face and strikes a dagger to the heart of Mr. Smith. Though not a death-blow, the torture was extreme.

The exhibition proceeded. One after another Fancy displayed her pictures, all of which appeared to have been painted by some malicious artist on purpose to vex Mr. Smith. Not a shadow of proof could have been adduced in any earthly court that he was guilty of the slightest of those sins which were thus made to stare him in the face. In one scene there was a table set out, with several bottles and glasses half filled with wine, which threw back the dull ray of an expiring lamp. There had been mirth and revelry until the hand of the clock stood just at midnight, when Murder stepped between the boon-companions. A young man had fallen on the floor, and lay stone dead with a ghastly wound crushed into his temple, while over him, with a delirium of mingled rage and horror in his countenance, stood the youthful likeness of Mr. Smith. The murdered youth wore the features of Edward Spencer. "What does this rascal of a painter mean?" cries Mr. Smith, provoked beyond all patience. "Edward Spencer was my earliest and dearest friend, true to me as I to him through more than half a century. Neither I nor any other ever murdered him. Was he not alive within five years, and did he not, in token of our long friendship, bequeath me his gold-headed cane and a mourning-ring?"

Again had Memory been turning over her volume, and fixed at length upon so confused a page that she surely must have scribbled it when she was tipsy. The purport was, however, that while Mr. Smith and Edward Spencer were heating their young blood with wine a quarrel had flashed up between them, and Mr. Smith, in deadly wrath, had flung a bottle at Spencer's head. True, it missed its aim and merely smashed a looking-glass; and the next morning, when the incident was imperfectly remembered, they had shaken hands with a hearty laugh. Yet, again, while Memory was reading, Conscience unveiled her face, struck a dagger to the heart of Mr. Smith and quelled his remonstrance with her iron frown. The pain was quite excruciating.

Some of the pictures had been painted with so doubtful a touch, and in colors so faint and pale, that the subjects could barely be conjectured. A dull, semi-transparent mist had been thrown over the surface of the canvas, into which the figures seemed to vanish while the eye sought most earnestly to fix them. But in every scene, however dubiously portrayed, Mr. Smith was invariably haunted by his own lineaments at various ages as in a dusty mirror. After poring several minutes over one of these blurred and almost indistinguishable pictures, he began to see that the painter had intended to represent him, now in the decline of life, as stripping the clothes from the backs of three half-starved children. "Really, this puzzles me!" quoth Mr. Smith, with the irony of conscious rectitude. "Asking pardon of the painter, I pronounce him a fool as well as a scandalous knave. A man of my standing in the world to be robbing little children of their clothes! Ridiculous!"

But while he spoke Memory had searched her fatal volume and found a page which with her sad calm voice she poured into his ear. It was not altogether inapplicable to the misty scene. It told how Mr. Smith had been grievously tempted by many devilish sophistries, on the ground of a legal quibble, to commence a law-suit against three orphan-children, joint-heirs to a considerable estate. Fortunately, before he was quite decided, his claims had turned out nearly as devoid of law as justice. As Memory ceased to read Conscience again thrust aside her mantle, and would have struck her victim with the envenomed dagger only that he struggled and clasped his hands before his heart. Even then, however, he sustained an ugly gash.

Why should we follow Fancy through the whole series of those awful pictures? Painted by an artist of wondrous power and terrible acquaintance with the secret soul, they embodied the ghosts of all the never-perpetrated sins that had glided through the lifetime of Mr. Smith. And could such beings of cloudy fantasy, so near akin to nothingness, give valid evidence against him at the day of judgment? Be that the case or not, there is reason to believe that one truly penitential tear would have washed away each hateful picture and left the canvas white as snow. But Mr. Smith, at a prick of Conscience too keen to be endured, bellowed aloud with impatient agony, and suddenly discovered that his three guests were gone. There he sat alone, a silver-haired and highly-venerated old man, in the rich gloom of the crimsoned-curtained room, with no box of pictures on the table, but only a decanter of most excellent Madeira. Yet his heart still seemed to fester with the venom of the dagger.

Nevertheless, the unfortunate old gentleman might have argued the matter with Conscience and alleged many reasons wherefore she should not smite him so pitilessly. Were we to take up his cause, it should be somewhat in the following fashion. A scheme of guilt, till it be put in execution, greatly resembles a train of incidents in a projected tale. The latter, in order to produce a sense of reality in the reader's mind, must be conceived with such proportionate strength by the author as to seem in the glow of fancy more like truth, past, present or to come, than purely fiction. The prospective sinner, on the other hand, weaves his plot of crime, but seldom or never feels a perfect certainty that it will be executed. There is a dreaminess diffused about his thoughts; in a dream, as it were, he strikes the death-blow into his victim's heart and starts to find an indelible blood-stain on his hand. Thus a novel-writer or a dramatist, in creating a villain of romance and fitting him with evil deeds, and the villain of actual life in projecting crimes that will be perpetrated, may almost meet each other halfway between reality and fancy. It is not until the crime is accomplished that Guilt clenches its gripe upon the guilty heart and claims it for his own. Then, and not before, sin is actually felt and acknowledged, and, if unaccompanied by repentance, grows a thousandfold more virulent by its self-consciousness. Be it considered, also, that men often overestimate their capacity for evil. At a distance, while its attendant circumstances do not press upon their notice and its results are dimly seen, they can bear to contemplate it. They may take the steps which lead to crime, impelled by the same sort of mental action as in working out a mathematical problem, yet be powerless with compunction at the final moment. They knew not what deed it was that they deemed themselves resolved to do. In truth, there is no such thing in man's nature as a settled and full resolve, either for good or evil, except at the very moment of execution. Let us hope, therefore, that all the dreadful consequences of sin will not be incurred unless the act have set its seal upon the thought.

Yet, with the slight fancy-work which we have framed, some sad and awful truths are interwoven. Man must not disclaim his brotherhood even with the guiltiest, since, though his hand be clean, his heart has surely been polluted by the flitting phantoms of iniquity. He must feel that when he shall knock at the gate of heaven no semblance of an unspotted life can entitle him to entrance there. Penitence must kneel and Mercy come from the footstool of the throne, or that golden gate will never open.

DR. HEIDEGGER'S EXPERIMENT.

That very singular man old Dr. Heidegger once invited four venerable friends to meet him in his study. There were three white-bearded gentlemen—Mr. Medbourne, Colonel Killigrew and Mr. Gascoigne—and a withered gentlewoman whose name was the widow Wycherly. They were all melancholy old creatures who had been unfortunate in life, and whose greatest misfortune it was that they were not long ago in their graves. Mr. Medbourne, in the vigor of his age, had been a prosperous merchant, but had lost his all by a frantic speculation, and was now little better than a mendicant. Colonel Killigrew had wasted his best years and his health and substance in the pursuit of sinful pleasures which had given birth to a brood of pains, such as the gout and divers other torments of soul and body. Mr. Gascoigne was a ruined politician, a man of evil fame—or, at least, had been so till time had buried him from the knowledge of the present generation and made him obscure instead of infamous. As for the widow Wycherly, tradition tells us that she was a great beauty in her day, but for a long while past she had lived in deep seclusion on account of certain scandalous stories which had prejudiced the gentry of the town against her. It is a circumstance worth mentioning that each of these three old gentlemen—Mr. Medbourne, Colonel Killigrew and Mr. Gascoigne—were early lovers of the widow Wycherly, and had once been on the point of cutting each other's throats for her sake. And before proceeding farther I will merely hint that Dr. Heidegger and all his four guests were sometimes thought to be a little beside themselves, as is not infrequently the case with old people when worried either by present troubles or woeful recollections.

"My dear old friends," said Dr. Heidegger, motioning them to be seated, "I am desirous of your assistance in one of those little experiments with which I amuse myself here in my study."

If all stories were true, Dr. Heidegger's study must have been a very curious place. It was a dim, old-fashioned chamber festooned with cobwebs and besprinkled with antique dust. Around the walls stood several oaken bookcases, the lower shelves of which were filled with rows of gigantic folios and black-letter quartos, and the upper with little parchment-covered duodecimos. Over the central bookcase was a bronze bust of Hippocrates, with which, according to some authorities, Dr. Heidegger was accustomed to hold consultations in all difficult cases of his practice. In the obscurest corner of the room stood a tall and narrow oaken closet with its door ajar, within which doubtfully appeared a skeleton. Between two of the bookcases hung a looking-glass, presenting its high and dusty plate within a tarnished gilt frame. Among many wonderful stories related of this mirror, it was fabled that the spirits of all the doctor's deceased patients dwelt within its verge and would stare him in the face whenever he looked thitherward. The opposite side of the chamber was ornamented with the full-length portrait of a young lady arrayed in the faded magnificence of silk, satin and brocade, and with a visage as faded as her dress. Above half a century ago Dr. Heidegger had been on the point of marriage with this young lady, but, being affected with some slight disorder, she had swallowed one of her lover's prescriptions and died on the bridal-evening. The greatest curiosity of the study remains to be mentioned: it was a ponderous folio volume bound in black leather, with massive silver clasps. There were no letters on the back, and nobody could tell the title of the book. But it was well known to be a book of magic, and once, when a chambermaid had lifted it merely to brush away the dust, the skeleton had rattled in its closet, the picture of the young lady had stepped one foot upon the floor and several ghastly faces had peeped forth from the mirror, while the brazen head of Hippocrates frowned and said, "Forbear!"

Such was Dr. Heidegger's study. On the summer afternoon of our tale a small round table as black as ebony stood in the centre of the room, sustaining a cut-glass vase of beautiful form and elaborate workmanship. The sunshine came through the window between the heavy festoons of two faded damask curtains and fell directly across this vase, so that a mild splendor was reflected from it on the ashen visages of the five old people who sat around. Four champagne-glasses were also on the table.

"My dear old friends," repeated Dr. Heidegger, "may I reckon on your aid in performing an exceedingly curious experiment?"

Now, Dr. Heidegger was a very strange old gentleman whose eccentricity had become the nucleus for a thousand fantastic stories. Some of these fables—to my shame be it spoken—might possibly be traced back to mine own veracious self; and if any passages of the present tale should startle the reader's faith, I must be content to bear the stigma of a fiction-monger.

When the doctor's four guests heard him talk of his proposed experiment, they anticipated nothing more wonderful than the murder of a mouse in an air-pump or the examination of a cobweb by the microscope, or some similar nonsense with which he was constantly in the habit of pestering his intimates. But without waiting for a reply Dr. Heidegger hobbled across the chamber and returned with the same ponderous folio bound in black leather which common report affirmed to be a book of magic. Undoing the silver clasps, he opened the volume and took from among its black-letter pages a rose, or what was once a rose, though now the green leaves and crimson petals had assumed one brownish hue and the ancient flower seemed ready to crumble to dust in the doctor's hands.

"This rose," said Dr. Heidegger, with a sigh—"this same withered and crumbling flower—blossomed five and fifty years ago. It was given me by Sylvia

Ward, whose portrait hangs yonder, and I meant to wear it in my bosom at our wedding. Five and fifty years it has been treasured between the leaves of this old volume. Now, would you deem it possible that this rose of half a century could ever bloom again?"

"Nonsense!" said the widow Wycherly, with a peevish toss of her head. "You might as well ask whether an old woman's wrinkled face could ever bloom again."

"See!" answered Dr. Heidegger. He uncovered the vase and threw the faded rose into the water which it contained. At first it lay lightly on the surface of the fluid, appearing to imbibe none of its moisture. Soon, however, a singular change began to be visible. The crushed and dried petals stirred and assumed a deepening tinge of crimson, as if the flower were reviving from a deathlike slumber, the slender stalk and twigs of foliage became green, and there was the rose of half a century, looking as fresh as when Sylvia Ward had first given it to her lover. It was scarcely full-blown, for some of its delicate red leaves curled modestly around its moist bosom, within which two or three dewdrops were sparkling.

"That is certainly a very pretty deception," said the doctor's friends—carelessly, however, for they had witnessed greater miracles at a conjurer's show. "Pray, how was it effected?"

"Did you never hear of the Fountain of Youth?" asked Dr. Heidegger, "which Ponce de Leon, the Spanish adventurer, went in search of two or three centuries ago?"

"But did Ponce de Leon ever find it?" said the widow Wycherly.

"No," answered Dr. Heidegger, "for he never sought it in the right place. The famous Fountain of Youth, if I am rightly informed, is situated in the southern part of the Floridian peninsula, not far from Lake Macaco. Its source is overshadowed by several gigantic magnolias which, though numberless centuries old, have been kept as fresh as violets by the virtues of this wonderful water. An acquaintance of mine, knowing my curiosity in such matters, has sent me what you see in the vase."

"Ahem!" said Colonel Killigrew, who believed not a word of the doctor's story; "and what may be the effect of this fluid on the human frame?"

"You shall judge for yourself, my dear colonel," replied Dr. Heidegger.—"And all of you, my respected friends, are welcome to so much of this admirable fluid as may restore to you the bloom of youth. For my own part, having had much trouble in growing old, I am in no hurry to grow young again. With your permission, therefore, I will merely watch the progress of the experiment."

While he spoke Dr. Heidegger had been filling the four champagne-glasses with the water of the Fountain of Youth. It was apparently impregnated with an effervescent gas, for little bubbles were continually ascending from the depths of the glasses and bursting in silvery spray at the surface. As the liquor diffused a pleasant perfume, the old people doubted not that it possessed cordial and comfortable properties, and, though utter sceptics as to its rejuvenescent power, they were inclined to swallow it at once. But Dr. Heidegger besought them to stay a moment.

"Before you drink, my respectable old friends," said he, "it would be well that, with the experience of a lifetime to direct you, you should draw up a few general rules for your guidance in passing a second time through the perils of youth. Think what a sin and shame it would be if, with your peculiar advantages, you should not become patterns of virtue and wisdom to all the young people of the age!"

The doctor's four venerable friends made him no answer except by a feeble and tremulous laugh, so very ridiculous was the idea that, knowing how closely Repentance treads behind the steps of Error, they should ever go astray again.

"Drink, then," said the doctor, bowing; "I rejoice that I have so well selected the subjects of my experiment."

With palsied hands they raised the glasses to their lips. The liquor, if it really possessed such virtues as Dr. Heidegger imputed to it, could not have been bestowed on four human beings who needed it more woefully. They looked as if they had never known what youth or pleasure was, but had been the offspring of Nature's dotage, and always the gray, decrepit, sapless, miserable creatures who now sat stooping round the doctor's table without life enough in their souls or bodies to be animated even by the prospect of growing young again. They drank off the water and replaced their glasses on the table.

Assuredly, there was an almost immediate improvement in the aspect of the party—not unlike what might have been produced by a glass of generous wine—together with a sudden glow of cheerful sunshine, brightening over all their visages at once. There was a healthful suffusion on their cheeks instead of the ashen hue that had made them look so corpse-like. They gazed at one another, and fancied that some magic power had really begun to smooth away the deep and sad inscriptions which Father Time had been so long engraving on their brows. The widow Wycherly adjusted her cap, for she felt almost like a woman again.

"Give us more of this wondrous water," cried they, eagerly. "We are younger, but we are still too old. Quick! give us more!"

"Patience, patience!" quoth Dr. Heidegger, who sat, watching the experiment with philosophic coolness. "You have been a long time growing old; surely you might be content to grow young in half an hour. But the water is at your service." Again he filled their glasses with the liquor of youth, enough of which still remained in the vase to turn half the old people in the city to the age of their own grandchildren.

While the bubbles were yet sparkling on the brim the doctor's four guests snatched their glasses from the table and swallowed the contents at a single gulp. Was it delusion? Even while the draught was passing down their throats it seemed to have wrought a change on their whole systems. Their eyes grew clear and bright; a dark shade deepened among their silvery locks: they sat around the table three gentlemen of middle age and a woman hardly beyond her buxom prime.

"My dear widow, you are charming!" cried Colonel Killigrew, whose eyes had been fixed upon her face while the shadows of age were flitting from it like darkness from the crimson daybreak.

The fair widow knew of old that Colonel Killigrew's compliments were not always measured by sober truth; so she started up and ran to the mirror, still dreading that the ugly visage of an old woman would meet her gaze.

Meanwhile, the three gentlemen behaved in such a manner as proved that the water of the Fountain of Youth possessed some intoxicating qualities—unless, indeed, their exhilaration of spirits were merely a lightsome dizziness caused by the sudden removal of the weight of years. Mr. Gascoigne's mind seemed to run on political topics, but whether relating to the past, present or future could not easily be determined, since the same ideas and phrases have been in vogue these fifty years. Now he rattled forth full-throated sentences about patriotism, national glory and the people's right; now he muttered some perilous stuff or other in a sly and doubtful whisper, so cautiously that even his own conscience could scarcely catch the secret; and now, again, he spoke in measured accents and a deeply-deferential tone, as if a royal ear were listening to his well-turned periods. Colonel Killigrew all this time had been trolling forth a jolly bottle-song and ringing his glass in symphony with the chorus, while his eyes wandered toward the buxom figure of the widow Wycherly. On the other side of the table, Mr. Medbourne was involved in a calculation of dollars and cents with which was strangely intermingled a project for supplying the East Indies with ice by harnessing a team of whales to the polar icebergs. As for the widow Wycherly, she stood before the mirror courtesying and simpering to her own image and greeting it as the friend whom she loved better than all the world besides. She thrust her face close to the glass to see whether some long-remembered wrinkle or crow's-foot had indeed vanished; she examined whether the snow had so entirely melted from her hair that the venerable cap could be safely thrown aside. At last, turning briskly away, she came with a sort of dancing step to the table.

"My dear old doctor," cried she, "pray favor me with another glass."

"Certainly, my dear madam—certainly," replied the complaisant doctor. "See! I have already filled the glasses."

There, in fact, stood the four glasses brimful of this wonderful water, the delicate spray of which, as it effervesced from the surface, resembled the tremulous glitter of diamonds.

It was now so nearly sunset that the chamber had grown duskier than ever, but a mild and moonlike splendor gleamed from within the vase and rested alike on the four guests and on the doctor's venerable figure. He sat in a high-backed, elaborately-carved oaken arm-chair with a gray dignity of aspect that might have well befitted that very Father Time whose power had never been disputed save by this fortunate company. Even while quaffing the third draught of the Fountain of Youth, they were almost awed by the expression of his mysterious visage. But the next moment the exhilarating gush of young life shot through their veins. They were now in the happy prime of youth. Age, with its miserable train of cares and sorrows and diseases, was remembered only as the trouble of a dream from which they had joyously awoke. The fresh gloss of the soul, so early lost and without which the world's successive scenes had been but a gallery of faded pictures, again threw its enchantment over all their prospects. They felt like new-created beings in a new-created universe.

"We are young! We are young!" they cried, exultingly.

Youth, like the extremity of age, had effaced the strongly-marked characteristics of middle life and mutually assimilated them all. They were a group of merry youngsters almost maddened with the exuberant frolicsomeness of their years. The most singular effect of their gayety was an impulse to mock the infirmity and decrepitude of which they had so lately been the victims. They laughed loudly at their old-fashioned attire—the wide-skirted coats and flapped waistcoats of the young men and the ancient cap and gown of the blooming girl. One limped across the floor like a gouty grandfather; one set a pair of spectacles astride of his nose and pretended to pore over the black-letter pages of the book of magic; a third seated himself in an arm-chair and strove to imitate the venerable dignity of Dr. Heidegger. Then all shouted mirthfully and leaped about the room.

The widow Wycherly—if so fresh a damsel could be called a widow—tripped up to the doctor's chair with a mischievous merriment in her rosy face.

"Doctor, you dear old soul," cried she, "get up and dance with me;" and then the four young people laughed louder than ever to think what a queer figure the poor old doctor would cut.

"Pray excuse me," answered the doctor, quietly. "I am old and rheumatic, and my dancing-days were over long ago. But either of these gay young gentlemen will be glad of so pretty a partner."

"Dance with me, Clara," cried Colonel Killigrew.

"No, no! I will be her partner," shouted Mr. Gascoigne.

"She promised me her hand fifty years ago," exclaimed Mr. Medbourne.

They all gathered round her. One caught both her hands in his passionate grasp, another threw his arm about her waist, the third buried his hand among the glossy curls that clustered beneath the widow's cap. Blushing, panting, struggling, chiding, laughing, her warm breath fanning each of their faces by turns, she strove to disengage herself, yet still remained in their triple embrace. Never was there a livelier picture of youthful rivalship, with bewitching beauty for the prize. Yet, by a strange deception, owing to the duskiness of the chamber and the antique dresses which they still wore, the tall mirror is said to have reflected the figures of the three old, gray, withered grand-sires ridiculously contending for the skinny ugliness of a shrivelled grandam. But they were young: their burning passions proved them so.

Inflamed to madness by the coquetry of the girl-widow, who neither granted nor quite withheld her favors, the three rivals began to interchange threatening glances. Still keeping hold of the fair prize, they grappled fiercely at one another's throats. As they struggled to and fro the table was overturned and the vase dashed into a thousand fragments. The precious Water of Youth flowed in a bright stream across the floor, moistening the wings of a butterfly which, grown old in the decline of summer, had alighted there to die. The insect fluttered lightly through the chamber and settled on the snowy head of Dr. Heidegger.

"Come, come, gentlemen! Come, Madam Wycherly!" exclaimed the doctor. "I really must protest against this riot."

They stood still and shivered, for it seemed as if gray Time were calling them back from their sunny youth far down into the chill and darksome vale of years. They looked at old Dr. Heidegger, who sat in his carved armchair holding the rose of half a century, which he had rescued from among the fragments of the shattered vase. At the motion of his hand the four rioters resumed their seats—the more readily because their violent exertions had wearied them, youthful though they were.

"My poor Sylvia's rose!" ejaculated Dr. Heidegger, holding it in the light of the sunset clouds. "It appears to be fading again."

And so it was. Even while the party were looking at it the flower continued to shrivel up, till it became as dry and fragile as when the doctor had first thrown it into the vase. He shook off the few drops of moisture which clung to its petals.

"I love it as well thus as in its dewy freshness," observed he, pressing the withered rose to his withered lips.

While he spoke the butterfly fluttered down from the doctor's snowy head and fell upon the floor. His guests shivered again. A strange dullness—whether of the body or spirit they could not tell—was creeping gradually over them all. They gazed at one another, and fancied that each fleeting moment snatched away a charm and left a deepening furrow where none had been before. Was it an illusion? Had the changes of a lifetime been crowded into so brief a space, and were they now four aged people sitting with their old friend Dr. Heidegger?

"Are we grown old again so soon?" cried they, dolefully.

In truth, they had. The Water of Youth possessed merely a virtue more transient than that of wine; the delirium which it created had effervesced away. Yes, they were old again. With a shuddering impulse that showed her a woman still, the widow clasped her skinny hands before her face and wished that the coffin-lid were over it, since it could be no longer beautiful.

"Yes, friends, ye are old again," said Dr. Heidegger, "and, lo! the Water of Youth is all lavished on the ground. Well, I bemoan it not; for if the fountain gushed at my very doorstep, I would not stoop to bathe my lips in it—no, though its delirium were for years instead of moments. Such is the lesson ye have taught me."

But the doctor's four friends had taught no such lesson to themselves. They resolved forthwith to make a pilgrimage to Florida and quaff at morning, noon and night from the Fountain of Youth.

LEGENDS OF THE PROVINCE-HOUSE.

I. HOWE'S MASQUERADE.

One afternoon last summer, while walking along Washington street, my eye was attracted by a sign-board protruding over a narrow archway nearly opposite the Old South Church. The sign represented the front of a stately edifice which was designated as the "OLD PROVINCE HOUSE, kept by Thomas Waite." I was glad to be thus reminded of a purpose, long entertained, of visiting and rambling over the mansion of the old royal governors of Massachusetts, and, entering the arched passage which penetrated through the middle of a brick row of shops, a few steps transported me from the busy heart of modern Boston into a small and secluded court-yard. One side of this space was occupied by the square front of the Province House, three stories high and surmounted by a cupola, on the top of which a gilded Indian was discernible, with his bow bent and his arrow on the string, as if aiming at the weathercock on the spire of the Old South. The figure has kept this attitude for seventy years or more, ever since good Deacon Drowne, a cunning carver of wood, first stationed him on his long sentinel's watch over the city.

The Province House is constructed of brick, which seems recently to have been overlaid with a coat of light-colored paint. A flight of red freestone steps fenced in by a balustrade of curiously wrought iron ascends from the court-yard to the spacious porch, over which is a balcony with an iron balustrade of similar pattern and workmanship to that beneath. These letters and figures—"16 P.S. 79"—are wrought into the ironwork of the balcony, and probably express the date of the edifice, with the initials of its founder's name.

A wide door with double leaves admitted me into the hall or entry, on the right of which is the entrance to the bar-room. It was in this apartment, I presume, that the ancient governors held their levees with vice-regal pomp, surrounded by the military men, the counsellors, the judges, and other officers of the Crown, while all the loyalty of the province thronged to do them honor. But the room in its present condition cannot boast even of faded magnificence. The panelled wainscot is covered with dingy paint and acquires a duskier hue from the deep shadow into which the Province House is thrown by the brick block that shuts it in from Washington street. A ray of sunshine never visits this apartment any more than the glare of the festal torches which have been extinguished from the era of the Revolution. The most venerable and ornamental object is a chimney-piece set round with Dutch tiles of blue-figured china, representing scenes from Scripture, and, for aught I know, the lady of Pownall or Bernard may have sat beside this fireplace and told her children the story of each blue tile. A bar in modern style, well replenished with decanters, bottles, cigar-boxes and network bags of lemons, and provided with a beer-pump and a soda-fount, extends along one side of the room.

At my entrance an elderly person was smacking his lips with a zest which satisfied me that the cellars of the Province House still hold good liquor, though doubtless of other vintages than were quaffed by the old governors. After sipping a glass of port-sangaree prepared by the skilful hands of Mr. Thomas Waite, I besought that worthy successor and representative of so many historic personages to conduct me over their time-honored mansion. He readily complied, but, to confess the truth, I was forced to draw strenuously upon my imagination in order to find aught that was interesting in a house which, without its historic associations, would have seemed merely such a tavern as is usually favored by the custom of decent city boarders and old-fashioned country gentlemen. The chambers, which were probably spacious in former times, are now cut up by partitions and subdivided into little nooks, each affording scanty room for the narrow bed and chair and dressing-table of a single lodger: The great staircase, however, may be termed, without much hyperbole, a feature of grandeur and magnificence. It winds through the midst of the house by flights of broad steps, each flight terminating in a square landing-place, whence the ascent is continued toward the cupola. A carved balustrade, freshly painted in the lower stories, but growing dingier as we ascend, borders the staircase with its quaintly twisted and intertwined pillars, from top to bottom. Up these stairs the military boots, or perchance the gouty shoes, of many a governor have trodden as the wearers mounted to the cupola which afforded them so wide a view over their metropolis and the surrounding country. The cupola is an octagon with several windows, and a door opening upon the roof. From this station, as I pleased myself with imagining, Gage may have beheld his disastrous victory on Bunker Hill (unless one of the trimountains intervened), and Howe have marked the approaches of Washington's besieging army, although the buildings since erected in the vicinity have shut out almost every object save the steeple of the Old South, which seems almost within arm's length. Descending from the cupola, I paused in the garret to observe the ponderous white-oak framework, so much more massive than the frames of modern houses, and thereby resembling an antique skeleton. The brick walls, the materials of which were imported from Holland, and the timbers of the mansion, are still as sound as ever, but, the floors and other interior parts being greatly decayed, it is contemplated to gut the whole and build a new house within the ancient frame-and brickwork. Among other inconveniences of the present edifice, mine host mentioned that any jar or motion was apt to shake down the dust of ages out of the ceiling of one chamber upon the floor of that beneath it.

We stepped forth from the great front window into the balcony where in old times it was doubtless the custom of the king's representative to show himself to a loyal populace, requiting their huzzas and tossed-up hats with stately bendings of his dignified person. In those days the front of the Province House looked upon the street, and the whole site now occupied by the brick range of stores, as well as the present court-yard, was laid out in grass-plats overshadowed by trees and bordered by a wrought-iron fence. Now the old aristocratic edifice hides its time-worn visage behind an upstart modern building; at one of the back windows I observed some pretty tailoresses sewing and chatting and laughing, with now and then a careless glance toward the balcony. Descending thence, we again entered the bar-room, where the elderly gentleman above mentioned—the smack of whose lips had spoken so favorably for Mr. Waite's good liquor—was still lounging in his chair. He seemed to be, if not a lodger, at least a familiar visitor of the house who might be supposed to have his regular score at the bar, his summer seat at the open window and his prescriptive corner at the winter's fireside. Being of a sociable aspect, I ventured to address him with a remark calculated to draw forth his historical reminiscences, if any such were in his mind, and it gratified me to discover that, between memory and tradition, the old gentleman was really possessed of some very pleasant gossip about the Province House. The portion of his talk which chiefly interested me was the outline of the following legend. He professed to have received it at one or two removes from an eye-witness, but this derivation, together with the lapse of time, must have afforded opportunities for many variations of the narrative; so that, despairing of literal and absolute truth, I have not scrupled to make such further changes as seemed conducive to the reader's profit and delight.

At one of the entertainments given at the province-house during the latter part of the siege of Boston there passed a scene which has never yet been satisfactorily explained. The officers of the British army and the loyal gentry of the province, most of whom were collected within the beleaguered town, had been invited to a masqued ball, for it was the policy for Sir William Howe to hide the distress and danger of the period and the desperate aspect of the siege under an ostentation of festivity. The spectacle of this evening, if the oldest members of the provincial court circle might be believed, was the most gay and gorgeous affair that had occurred in the annals of the government. The brilliantly-lighted apartments were thronged with figures that seemed to have stepped from the dark canvas of historic portraits or to have flitted forth from the magic pages of romance, or at least to have flown hither from one of the London theatres without a change of garments. Steeled knights of the Conquest, bearded statesmen of Queen Elizabeth and high-ruffed ladies of her court were mingled with characters of comedy, such as a parti-colored Merry Andrew jingling his cap and bells, a Falstaff almost as provocative of laughter as his prototype, and a Don Quixote with a bean-pole for a lance and a pot-lid for a shield.

But the broadest merriment was excited by a group of figures ridiculously dressed in old regimentals which seemed to have been purchased at a military rag-fair or pilfered from some receptacle of the cast-off clothes of both the French and British armies. Portions of their attire had probably been worn at the siege of Louisburg, and the coats of most recent cut might have been rent and tattered by sword, ball or bayonet as long ago as Wolfe's victory. One of these worthies—a tall, lank figure brandishing a rusty sword of immense longitude—purported to be no less a personage than General George Washington, and the other principal officers of the American army, such as Gates, Lee, Putnam, Schuyler, Ward and Heath, were represented by similar scarecrows. An interview in the mock-heroic style between the rebel warriors and the British commander-in-chief was received with immense applause, which came loudest of all from the loyalists of the colony.

There was one of the guests, however, who stood apart, eying these antics sternly and scornfully at once with a frown and a bitter smile. It was an old man formerly of high station and great repute in the province, and who had been a very famous soldier in his day. Some surprise had been expressed that a person of Colonel Joliffe's known Whig principles, though now too old to take an active part in the contest, should have remained in Boston during the siege, and especially that he should consent to show himself in the mansion of Sir William Howe. But thither he had come with a fair granddaughter under his arm, and there, amid all the mirth and buffoonery, stood this stern old figure, the best-sustained character in the masquerade, because so well representing the antique spirit of his native land. The other guests affirmed that Colonel Joliffe's black puritanical scowl threw a shadow round about him, although, in spite of his sombre influence, their gayety continued to blaze higher, like—an ominous comparison—the flickering brilliancy of a lamp which has but a little while to burn.

Eleven strokes full half an hour ago had pealed from the clock of the Old South, when a rumor was circulated among the company that some new spectacle or pageant was about to be exhibited which should put a fitting close to the splendid festivities of the night.

"What new jest has Your Excellency in hand?" asked the Reverend Mather Byles, whose Presbyterian scruples had not kept him from the entertainment. "Trust me, sir, I have already laughed more than beseems my cloth at your Homeric confabulation with yonder ragamuffin general of the rebels. One other such fit of merriment, and I must throw off my clerical wig and band."

"Not so, good Dr. Byles," answered Sir William Howe; "if mirth were a crime, you had never gained your doctorate in divinity. As to this new foolery, I know no more about it than yourself—perhaps not so much. Honestly, now, doctor, have you not stirred up the sober brains of some of your countrymen to enact a scene in our masquerade?"

"Perhaps," slyly remarked the granddaughter of Colonel Joliffe, whose high spirit had been stung by many taunts against New England—"perhaps we are to have a masque of allegorical figures—Victory with trophies from Lexington and Bunker Hill, Plenty with her overflowing horn to typify the present abundance in this good town, and Glory with a wreath for His Excellency's brow."

Sir William Howe smiled at words which he would have answered with one of his darkest frowns had they been uttered by lips that wore a beard. He was spared the necessity of a retort by a singular interruption. A sound of music was heard without the house, as if proceeding from a full band of military instruments stationed in the street, playing, not such a festal strain as was suited to the occasion, but a slow funeral-march. The drums appeared to be muffled, and the trumpets poured forth a wailing breath which at once hushed the merriment of the auditors, filling all with wonder and some with apprehension. The idea occurred to many that either the funeral procession of some great personage had halted in front of the province-house, or that a corpse in a velvet-covered and gorgeously-decorated coffin was about to be borne from the portal. After listening a moment, Sir William Howe called in a stern voice to the leader of the musicians, who had hitherto enlivened the entertainment with gay and lightsome melodies. The man was drum-major to one of the British regiments.

"Dighton," demanded the general, "what means this foolery? Bid your band silence that dead march, or, by my word, they shall have sufficient cause for their lugubrious strains. Silence it, sirrah!"

"Please, Your Honor," answered the drum-major, whose rubicund visage had lost all its color, "the fault is none of mine. I and my band are all here together, and I question whether there be a man of us that could play that march without book. I never heard it but once before, and that was at the funeral of his late Majesty, King George II."

"Well, well!" said Sir William Howe, recovering his composure; "it is the prelude to some masquerading antic. Let it pass."

A figure now presented itself, but among the many fantastic masks that were dispersed through the apartments none could tell precisely from whence it came. It was a man in an old-fashioned dress of black serge and having the aspect of a steward or principal domestic in the household of a nobleman or great English landholder. This figure advanced to the outer door of the mansion, and, throwing both its leaves wide open, withdrew a little to one side and looked back toward the grand staircase, as if expecting some person to descend. At the same time, the music in the street sounded a loud and doleful summons. The eyes of Sir William Howe and his guests being directed to the staircase, there appeared on the uppermost landing-place, that was discernible from the bottom, several personages descending toward the door. The foremost was a man of stern visage, wearing a steeple-crowned hat and a skull-cap beneath it, a dark cloak and huge wrinkled boots that came halfway up his legs. Under his arm was a rolled-up banner which seemed to be the banner of England, but strangely rent and torn; he had a sword in his right hand and grasped a Bible in his left. The next figure was of milder aspect, yet full of dignity, wearing a broad ruff, over which descended a beard, a gown of wrought velvet and a doublet and hose of black satin; he carried a roll of manuscript in his hand. Close behind these two came a young man of very striking countenance and demeanor with deep thought and contemplation on his brow, and perhaps a flash of enthusiasm in his eye; his garb, like that of his predecessors, was of an antique fashion, and there was a stain of blood upon his ruff. In the same group with these were three or four others, all men of dignity and evident command, and bearing themselves like personages who were accustomed to the gaze of the multitude. It was the idea of the beholders that these figures went to join the mysterious funeral that had halted in front of the province-house, yet that supposition seemed to be contradicted by the air of triumph with which they waved their hands as they crossed the threshold and vanished through the portal.

"In the devil's name, what is this?" muttered Sir William Howe to a gentleman beside him. "A procession of the regicide judges of King Charles the martyr?"

"These," said Colonel Joliffe, breaking silence almost for the first time that evening—"these, if I interpret them aright, are the Puritan governors, the rulers of the old original democracy of Massachusetts—Endicott with the banner from which he had torn the symbol of subjection, and Winthrop and Sir Henry Vane and Dudley, Haynes, Bellingham and Leverett."

"Why had that young man a stain of blood upon his ruff?" asked Miss Joliffe.

"Because in after-years," answered her grandfather, "he laid down the wisest head in England upon the block for the principles of liberty."

"Will not Your Excellency order out the guard?" whispered Lord Percy, who, with other British officers, had now assembled round the general. "There may be a plot under this mummery."

"Tush! we have nothing to fear," carelessly replied Sir William Howe. "There can be no worse treason in the matter than a jest, and that somewhat of the dullest. Even were it a sharp and bitter one, our best policy would be to laugh it off. See! here come more of these gentry."

Another group of characters had now partly descended the staircase. The first was a venerable and white-bearded patriarch who cautiously felt his way downward with a staff. Treading hastily behind him, and stretching forth his gauntleted hand as if to grasp the old man's shoulder, came a tall soldier-like figure equipped with a plumed cap of steel, a bright breastplate and a long sword, which rattled against the stairs. Next was seen a stout man dressed in rich and courtly attire, but not of courtly demeanor; his gait had the swinging motion of a seaman's walk, and, chancing to stumble on the staircase, he suddenly grew wrathful and was heard to mutter an oath. He was followed by a noble-looking personage in a curled wig such as are represented in the portraits of Queen Anne's time and earlier, and the breast of his coat was decorated with an embroidered star. While advancing to the door he bowed to the right hand and to the left in a very gracious and insinuating style, but as he crossed the threshold, unlike the early Puritan governors, he seemed to wring his hands with sorrow.

"Prithee, play the part of a chorus, good Dr. Byles," said Sir William Howe. "What worthies are these?"

"If it please Your Excellency, they lived somewhat before my day," answered the doctor; "but doubtless our friend the colonel has been hand and glove with them."

"Their living faces I never looked upon," said Colonel Joliffe, gravely; "although I have spoken face to face with many rulers of this land, and shall greet yet another with an old man's blessing ere I die. But we talk of these figures. I take the venerable patriarch to be Bradstreet, the last of the Puritans, who was governor at ninety or thereabouts. The next is Sir Edmund Andros, a tyrant, as any New England schoolboy will tell you, and therefore the people cast him down from his high seat into a dungeon. Then comes Sir William Phipps, shepherd, cooper, sea-captain and governor. May many of his countrymen rise as high from as low an origin! Lastly, you saw the gracious earl of Bellamont, who ruled us under King William."

"But what is the meaning of it all?" asked Lord Percy.

"Now, were I a rebel," said Miss Joliffe, half aloud, "I might fancy that the ghosts of these ancient governors had been summoned to form the funeral procession of royal authority in New England."

Several other figures were now seen at the turn of the staircase. The one in advance had a thoughtful, anxious and somewhat crafty expression of face, and in spite of his loftiness of manner, which was evidently the result both of an ambitious spirit and of long continuance in high stations, he seemed not incapable of cringing to a greater than himself. A few steps behind came an officer in a scarlet and embroidered uniform cut in a fashion old enough to have been worn by the duke of Marlborough. His nose had a rubicund tinge, which, together with the twinkle of his eye, might have marked him as a lover of the wine-cup and good-fellowship; notwithstanding which tokens, he appeared ill at ease, and often glanced around him as if apprehensive of some secret mischief. Next came a portly gentleman wearing a coat of shaggy cloth lined with silken velvet; he had sense, shrewdness and humor in his face and a folio volume under his arm, but his aspect was that of a man vexed and tormented beyond all patience and harassed almost to death. He went hastily down, and was followed by a dignified person dressed in a purple velvet suit with very rich embroidery; his demeanor would have possessed much stateliness, only that a grievous fit of the gout compelled him to hobble from stair to stair with contortions of face and body. When Dr. Byles beheld this figure on the staircase, he shivered as with an ague, but continued to watch him steadfastly until the gouty gentleman had reached the threshold, made a gesture of anguish and despair and vanished into the outer gloom, whither the funeral music summoned him.

"Governor Belcher—my old patron—in his very shape and dress!" gasped Dr. Byles. "This is an awful mockery."

"A tedious foolery, rather," said Sir William Howe, with an air of indifference. "But who were the three that preceded him?"

"Governor Dudley, a cunning politician; yet his craft once brought him to a prison," replied Colonel Joliffe. "Governor Shute, formerly a colonel under Marlborough, and whom the people frightened out of the province, and learned Governor Burnett, whom the legislature tormented into a mortal fever."

"Methinks they were miserable men—these royal governors of Massachusetts," observed Miss Joliffe. "Heavens! how dim the light grows!"

It was certainly a fact that the large lamp which illuminated the staircase now burned dim and duskily; so that several figures which passed hastily down the stairs and went forth from the porch appeared rather like shadows than persons of fleshly substance.

Sir William Howe and his guests stood at the doors of the contiguous apartments watching the progress of this singular pageant with various emotions of anger, contempt or half-acknowledged fear, but still with an anxious curiosity. The shapes which now seemed hastening to join the mysterious procession were recognized rather by striking peculiarities of dress or broad characteristics of manner than by any perceptible resemblance of features to their prototypes. Their faces, indeed, were invariably kept in deep shadow, but Dr. Byles and other gentlemen who had long been familiar with the successive rulers of the province were heard to whisper the names of Shirley, of Pownall, of Sir Francis Bernard and of the well-remembered Hutchinson, thereby confessing that the actors, whoever they might be, in this spectral march of governors had succeeded in putting on some distant portraiture of the real personages. As they vanished from the door, still did these shadows toss their arms into the gloom of night with a dread expression of woe. Following the mimic representative of Hutchinson came a military figure holding before his face the cocked hat which he had taken from his powdered head, but his epaulettes and other insignia of rank were those of a general officer, and something in his mien reminded the beholders of one who had recently been master of the province-house and chief of all the land.

"The shape of Gage, as true as in a looking-glass!" exclaimed Lord Percy, turning pale.

"No, surely," cried Miss Joliffe, laughing hysterically; "it could not be Gage, or Sir William would have greeted his old comrade in arms. Perhaps he will not suffer the next to pass unchallenged."

"Of that be assured, young lady," answered Sir William Howe, fixing his eyes with a very marked expression upon the immovable visage of her grandfather. "I have long enough delayed to pay the ceremonies of a host to these departing guests; the next that takes his leave shall receive due courtesy."

A wild and dreary burst of music came through the open door. It seemed as it the procession, which had been gradually filling up its ranks, were now about to move, and that this loud peal of the wailing trumpets and roll of the muffled drums were a call to some loiterer to make haste. Many eyes, by an irresistible impulse, were turned upon Sir William Howe, as if it were he whom the dreary music summoned to the funeral of departed power.

"See! here comes the last," whispered Miss Joliffe, pointing her tremulous finger to the staircase.

A figure had come into view as if descending the stairs, although so dusky was the region whence it emerged some of the spectators fancied that they had seen this human shape suddenly moulding itself amid the gloom. Downward the figure came with a stately and martial tread, and, reaching the lowest stair, was observed to be a tall man booted and wrapped in a military cloak, which was drawn up around the face so as to meet the napped brim of a laced hat; the features, therefore, were completely hidden. But the British officers deemed that they had seen that military cloak before, and even recognized the frayed embroidery on the collar, as well as the gilded scabbard of a sword which protruded from the folds of the cloak and glittered in a vivid gleam of light. Apart from these trifling particulars there were characteristics of gait and bearing which impelled the wondering guests to glance from the shrouded figure to Sir William Howe, as if to satisfy themselves that their host had not suddenly vanished from the midst of them. With a dark flush of wrath upon his brow, they saw the general draw his sword and advance to meet the figure in the cloak before the latter had stepped one pace upon the floor.

"Villain, unmuffle yourself!" cried he. "You pass no farther."

The figure, without blenching a hair's-breadth from the sword which was pointed at his breast, made a solemn pause and lowered the cape of the cloak from about his face, yet not sufficiently for the spectators to catch a glimpse of it. But Sir William Howe had evidently seen enough. The sternness of his countenance gave place to a look of wild amazement, if not horror, while he recoiled several steps from the figure and let fall his sword upon the floor. The martial shape again drew the cloak about his features and passed on, but, reaching the threshold with his back toward the spectators, he was seen to stamp his foot and shake his clenched hands in the air. It was afterward affirmed that Sir William Howe had repeated that selfsame gesture of rage and sorrow when for the last time, and as the last royal governor, he passed through the portal of the province-house.

"Hark! The procession moves," said Miss Joliffe.

The music was dying away along the street, and its dismal strains were mingled with the knell of midnight from the steeple of the Old South and with the roar of artillery which announced that the beleaguered army of Washington had intrenched itself upon a nearer height than before. As the deep boom of the cannon smote upon his ear Colonel Joliffe raised himself to the full height of his aged form and smiled sternly on the British general.

"Would Your Excellency inquire further into the mystery of the pageant?" said he.

"Take care of your gray head!" cried Sir William Howe, fiercely, though with a quivering lip. "It has stood too long on a traitor's shoulders."

"You must make haste to chop it off, then," calmly replied the colonel, "for a few hours longer, and not all the power of Sir William Howe, nor of his master, shall cause one of these gray hairs to fall. The empire of Britain in this ancient province is at its last gasp to-night; almost while I speak it is a dead corpse, and methinks the shadows of the old governors are fit mourners at its funeral."

With these words Colonel Joliffe threw on his cloak, and, drawing his granddaughter's arm within his own, retired from the last festival that a British ruler ever held in the old province of Massachusetts Bay. It was supposed that the colonel and the young lady possessed some secret intelligence in regard to the mysterious pageant of that night. However this might be, such knowledge has never become general. The actors in the scene have vanished into deeper obscurity than even that wild Indian hand who scattered the cargoes of the tea-ships on the waves and gained a place in history, yet left no names. But superstition, among other legends of this mansion, repeats the wondrous tale that on the anniversary night of Britain's discomfiture the ghosts of the ancient governors of Massachusetts still glide through the portal of the Province House. And last of all comes a figure shrouded in a military cloak, tossing his clenched hands into the air and stamping his iron-shod boots upon the broad freestone steps with a semblance of feverish despair, but without the sound of a foot-tramp.

When the truth-telling accents of the elderly gentleman were hushed, I drew a long breath and looked round the room, striving with the best energy of my imagination to throw a tinge of romance and historic grandeur over the realities of the scene. But my nostrils snuffed up a scent of cigar-smoke, clouds of which the narrator had emitted by way of visible emblem, I suppose, of the nebulous obscurity of his tale. Moreover, my gorgeous fantasies were woefully disturbed by the rattling of the spoon in a tumbler of whiskey-punch which Mr. Thomas Waite was mingling for a customer. Nor did it add to the picturesque appearance of the panelled walls that the slate of the Brookline stage was suspended against them, instead of the armorial escutcheon of some far-descended governor. A stage-driver sat at one of the windows reading a penny paper of the day—the Boston *Times*—and presenting a figure which could nowise be brought into any picture of "Times in Boston" seventy or a hundred years ago. On the window-seat lay a bundle neatly done up in brown paper, the direction of which I had the idle curiosity to read: "MISS SUSAN HUGGINS, at the PROVINCE HOUSE." A pretty chambermaid, no doubt. In truth, it is desperately hard work when we attempt to throw the spell of hoar antiquity over localities with which the living world and the day that is passing over us have aught to do. Yet, as I glanced at the stately staircase down which the procession of the old governors had descended, and as I emerged through the venerable portal whence their figures had preceded me, it gladdened me to be conscious of a thrill of awe. Then, diving through the narrow archway, a few strides transported me into the densest throng of Washington street.

II. EDWARD RANDOLPH'S PORTRAIT.

The old legendary guest of the Province House abode in my remembrance from midsummer till January. One idle evening last winter, confident that he would be found in the snuggest corner of the bar-room, I resolved to pay him another visit, hoping to deserve well of my country by snatching from oblivion some else unheard-of fact of history. The night was chill and raw, and rendered boisterous by almost a gale of wind which whistled along Washington street, causing the gaslights to flare and flicker within the lamps.

As I hurried onward my fancy was busy with a comparison between the present aspect of the street and that which it probably wore when the British governors inhabited the mansion whither I was now going. Brick edifices in those times were few till a succession of destructive fires had swept, and swept again, the wooden dwellings and warehouses from the most populous quarters of the town. The buildings stood insulated and independent, not, as now, merging their separate existences into connected ranges with a front of tiresome identity, but each possessing features of its own, as if the owner's individual taste had shaped it, and the whole presenting a picturesque irregularity the absence of which is hardly compensated by any beauties of our modern architecture. Such a scene, dimly vanishing from the eye by the ray of here and there a tallow candle glimmering through the small panes of scattered windows, would form a sombre contrast to the street as I beheld it with the gaslights blazing from corner to corner, flaming within the shops and throwing a noonday brightness through the huge plates of glass. But the black, lowering sky, as I turned my eyes upward, wore, doubtless, the same visage as when it frowned upon the ante-Revolutionary New Englanders. The wintry blast had the same shriek that was familiar to their ears. The Old South Church, too, still pointed its antique spire into the darkness and was lost between earth and heaven, and, as I passed, its clock, which had warned so many generations how transitory was their lifetime, spoke heavily and slow the same unregarded moral to myself. "Only seven o'clock!" thought I. "My old friend's legends will scarcely kill the hours 'twixt this and bedtime."

Passing through the narrow arch, I crossed the courtyard, the confined precincts of which were made visible by a lantern over the portal of the Province House. On entering the bar-room, I found, as I expected, the old tradition-monger seated by a special good fire of anthracite, compelling clouds of smoke from a corpulent cigar. He recognized me with evident pleasure, for my rare properties as a patient listener invariably make me a favorite with elderly gentlemen and ladies of narrative propensites. Drawing a chair to the fire, I desired mine host to favor us with a glass apiece of whiskey-punch, which was speedily prepared, steaming hot, with a slice of lemon at the bottom, a dark-red stratum of port wine upon the surface and a sprinkling of nutmeg strewn over all. As we touched our glasses together, my legendary friend made himself known to me as Mr. Bela Tiffany, and I rejoiced at the oddity of the name, because it gave his image and character a sort of individuality in my conception. The old gentleman's draught acted as a solvent upon his memory, so that it overflowed with tales, traditions, anecdotes of famous dead people and traits of ancient manners, some of which were childish as a nurse's lullaby, while others might have been worth the notice of the grave historian. Nothing impressed me more than a story of a black mysterious picture which used to hang in one of the chambers of the Province House, directly above the room where we were now sitting. The following is as correct a version of the fact as the reader would be likely to obtain from any other source, although, assuredly, it has a tinge of romance approaching to the marvellous.

In one of the apartments of the province-house there was long preserved an ancient picture the frame of which was as black as ebony, and the canvas itself so dark with age, damp and smoke that not a touch of the painter's art could be discerned. Time had thrown an impenetrable veil over it and left to tradition and fable and conjecture to say what had once been there portrayed. During the rule of many successive governors it had hung, by prescriptive and undisputed right, over the mantel piece of the same chamber, and it still kept its place when Lieutenant-governor Hutchinson assumed the administration of the province on the departure of Sir Francis Bernard.

The lieutenant-governor sat one afternoon resting his head against the carved back of his stately arm-chair and gazing up thoughtfully at the void blackness of the picture. It was scarcely a time for such inactive musing, when affairs of the deepest moment required the ruler's decision; for within that very hour Hutchinson had received intelligence of the arrival of a British fleet bringing three regiments from Halifax to overawe the insubordination of the people. These troops awaited his permission to occupy the fortress of Castle William and the town itself, yet, instead of affixing his signature to an official order, there sat the lieutenant-governor so carefully scrutinizing the black waste of canvas that his demeanor attracted the notice of two young persons who attended him. One, wearing a military dress of buff, was his kinsman, Francis Lincoln, the provincial captain of Castle William; the other, who sat on a low stool beside his chair, was Alice Vane, his favorite niece. She was clad entirely in white—a pale, ethereal creature who, though a native of New England, had been educated abroad and seemed not merely a stranger from another clime, but almost a being from another world. For several years, until left an orphan, she had dwelt with her father in sunny Italy, and there had acquired a taste and enthusiasm for sculpture and painting which she found few opportunities of gratifying in the undecorated dwellings of the colonial gentry. It was said that the early productions of her own pencil exhibited no inferior genius, though perhaps the rude atmosphere of New England had cramped her hand and dimmed the glowing colors of her fancy. But, observing her uncle's steadfast gaze, which appeared to search through the mist of years to discover the subject of the picture, her curiosity was excited.

"Is it known, my dear uncle," inquired she, "what this old picture once represented? Possibly, could it be made visible, it might prove a masterpiece of some great artist; else why has it so long held such a conspicuous place?"

As her uncle, contrary to his usual custom—for he was as attentive to all the humors and caprices of Alice as if she had been his own best-beloved child—did not immediately reply, the young captain of Castle William took that office upon himself.

"This dark old square of canvas, my fair cousin," said he, "has been an heirloom in the province-house from time immemorial. As to the painter, I can tell you nothing; but if half the stories told of it be true, not one of the great Italian masters has ever produced so marvellous a piece of work as that before you."

Captain Lincoln proceeded to relate some of the strange fables and fantasies which, as it was impossible to refute them by ocular demonstration, had grown to be articles of popular belief in reference to this old picture. One of the wildest, and at the same time the best-accredited, accounts stated it to be an original and authentic portrait of the evil one, taken at a witch-meeting near Salem, and that its strong and terrible resemblance had been confirmed by several of the confessing wizards and witches at their trial in open court. It was likewise affirmed that a familiar spirit or demon abode behind the blackness of the picture, and had shown himself at seasons of public calamity to more than one of the royal governors. Shirley, for instance, had beheld this ominous apparition on the eve of General Abercrombie's shameful and bloody defeat under the walls of Ticonderoga. Many of the servants of the province-house had caught glimpses of a visage frowning down upon them at morning or evening twilight, or in the depths of night while raking up the fire that glimmered on the hearth beneath, although, if any were, bold enough to hold a torch before the picture, it would appear as black and undistinguishable as ever. The oldest inhabitant of Boston recollected that his father—in whose days the portrait had not wholly faded out of sight—had once looked upon it, but would never suffer himself to be questioned as to the face which was there represented. In connection with such stories, it was remarkable that over the top of the frame there were some ragged remnants of black silk, indicating that a veil had formerly hung down before the picture until the duskiness of time had so effectually concealed it. But, after all, it was the most singular part of the affair that so many of the pompous governors of Massachusetts had allowed the obliterated picture to remain in the state-chamber of the province-house.

"Some of these fables are really awful," observed Alice Vane, who had occasionally shuddered as well as smiled while her cousin spoke. "It would be almost worth while to wipe away the black surface of the canvas, since the original picture can hardly be so formidable as those which fancy paints instead of it."

"But would it be possible," inquired her cousin," to restore this dark picture to its pristine hues?"

"Such arts are known in Italy," said Alice.

The lieutenant-governor had roused himself from his abstracted mood, and listened with a smile to the conversation of his young relatives. Yet his voice had something peculiar in its tones when he undertook the explanation of the mystery.

"I am sorry, Alice, to destroy your faith in the legends of which you are so fond," remarked he, "but my antiquarian researches have long since made me acquainted with the subject of this picture—if picture it can be called—which is no more visible, nor ever will be, than the face of the long-buried man whom it once represented. It was the portrait of Edward Randolph, the founder of this house, a person famous in the history of New England."

"Of that Edward Randolph," exclaimed Captain Lincoln, "who obtained the repeal of the first provincial charter, under which our forefathers had enjoyed almost democratic privileges—he that was styled the arch-enemy of New England, and whose memory is still held in detestation as the destroyer of our liberties?"

"It was the same Randolph," answered Hutchinson, moving uneasily in his chair. "It was his lot to taste the bitterness of popular odium."

"Our annals tell us," continued the captain of Castle William, "that the curse of the people followed this Randolph where he went and wrought evil in all the subsequent events of his life, and that its effect was seen, likewise, in the manner of his death. They say, too, that the inward misery of that curse worked itself outward and was visible on the wretched man's countenance, making it too horrible to be looked upon. If so, and if this picture truly represented his aspect, it was in mercy that the cloud of blackness has gathered over it."

"These traditions are folly to one who has proved, as I have, how little of historic truth lies at the bottom," said the lieutenant-governor. "As regards the life and character of Edward Randolph, too implicit credence has been given to Dr. Cotton Mather, who—I must say it, though some of his blood runs in my veins—has filled our early history with old women's tales as fanciful and extravagant as those of Greece or Rome."

"And yet," whispered Alice Vane, "may not such fables have a moral? And methinks, if the visage of this portrait be so dreadful, it is not without a cause that it has hung so long in a chamber of the province-house. When the rulers feel themselves irresponsible, it were well that they should be reminded of the awful weight of a people's curse."

The lieutenant-governor started and gazed for a moment at his niece, as if her girlish fantasies had struck upon some feeling in his own breast which all his policy or principles could not entirely subdue. He knew, indeed, that Alice, in spite of her foreign education, retained the native sympathies of a New England girl.

"Peace, silly child!" cried he, at last, more harshly than he had ever before addressed the gentle Alice. "The rebuke of a king; is more to be dreaded than the clamor of a wild, misguided multitude.—Captain Lincoln, it is decided: the fortress of Castle William must be occupied by the royal troops. The two remaining regiments shall be billeted in the town or encamped upon the Common. It is time, after years of tumult, and almost rebellion, that His Majesty's government should have a wall of strength about it."

"Trust, sir—trust yet a while to the loyalty of the people," said Captain Lincoln, "nor teach them that they can ever be on other terms with British soldiers than those of brotherhood, as when they fought side by side through the French war. Do not convert the streets of your native town into a camp. Think twice before you give up old Castle William, the key of the province, into other keeping than that of true-born New Englanders."

"Young man, it is decided," repeated Hutchinson, rising from his chair. "A British officer will be in attendance this evening to receive the necessary instructions for the disposal of the troops. Your presence also will be required. Till then, farewell."

With these words the lieutenant-governor hastily left the room, while Alice and her cousin more slowly followed, whispering together, and once pausing to glance back at the mysterious picture. The captain of Castle William fancied that the girl's air and mien were such as might have belonged to one of those spirits of fable—fairies or creatures of a more antique mythology—who sometimes mingled their agency with mortal affairs, half in caprice, yet with a sensibility to human weal or woe. As he held the door for her to pass Alice beckoned to the picture and smiled.

"Come forth, dark and evil shape!" cried she. "It is thine hour."

In the evening Lieutenant-governor Hutchinson sat in the same chamber where the foregoing scene had occurred, surrounded by several persons whose various interests had summoned them together. There were the selectmen of Boston—plain patriarchal fathers of the people, excellent representatives of the old puritanical founders whose sombre strength had stamped so deep an impress upon the New England character. Contrasting with these were one or two members of council, richly dressed in the white wigs, the embroidered waistcoats and other magnificence of the time, and making a somewhat ostentatious display of courtier-like ceremonial. In attendance, likewise, was a major of the British army, awaiting the lieutenant-governor's orders for the landing of the troops, which still remained on board the transports. The captain of Castle William stood beside Hutchinson's chair, with folded arms, glancing rather haughtily at the British officer by whom he was soon to be superseded in his command. On a table in the centre of the chamber stood a branched silver candlestick, throwing down the glow of half a dozen waxlights upon a paper apparently ready for the lieutenant-governor's signature.

Partly shrouded in the voluminous folds of one of the window-curtains, which fell from the ceiling to the floor, was seen the white drapery of a lady's robe. It may appear strange that Alice Vane should have been there at such a time, but there was something so childlike, so wayward, in her singular character, so apart from ordinary rules, that her presence did not surprise the few who noticed it. Meantime, the chairman of the selectmen was addressing to the lieutenant-governor a long and solemn protest against the reception of the British troops into the town.

"And if Your Honor," concluded this excellent but somewhat prosy old gentleman, "shall see fit to persist in bringing these mercenary sworders and musketeers into our quiet streets, not on our heads be the responsibility. Think, sir, while there is yet time, that if one drop of blood be shed, that blood shall be an eternal stain upon Your Honor's memory. You, sir, have written with an able pen the deeds of our forefathers; the more to be desired is it, therefore, that yourself should deserve honorable mention as a true patriot and upright ruler when your own doings shall be written down in history."

"I am not insensible, my good sir, to the natural desire to stand well in the annals of my country," replied Hutchinson, controlling his impatience into courtesy, "nor know I any better method of attaining that end than by withstanding the merely temporary spirit of mischief which, with your pardon, seems to have infected older men than myself. Would you have me wait till the mob shall sack the province-house as they did my private mansion? Trust me, sir, the time may come when you will be glad to flee for protection to the king's banner, the raising of which is now so distasteful to you."

"Yes," said the British major, who was impatiently expecting the lieutenant-governor's orders. "The demagogues of this province have raised the devil, and cannot lay him again. We will exorcise him in God's name and the king's."

"If you meddle with the devil, take care of his claws," answered the captain of Castle William, stirred by the taunt against his countrymen.

"Craving your pardon, young sir," said the venerable selectman, "let not an evil spirit enter into your words. We will strive against the oppressor with prayer and fasting, as our forefathers would have done. Like them, moreover, we will submit to whatever lot a wise Providence may send us—always after our own best exertions to amend it."

"And there peep forth the devil's claws!" muttered Hutchinson, who well understood the nature of Puritan submission. "This matter shall be expedited forthwith. When there shall be a sentinel at every corner and a court of guard before the town-house, a loyal gentleman may venture to walk abroad. What to me is the outcry of a mob in this remote province of the realm? The king is my master, and England is my country; upheld by their armed strength, I set my foot upon the rabble and defy them."

He snatched a pen and was about to affix his signature to the paper that lay on the table, when the captain of Castle William placed his hand upon his shoulder. The freedom of the action, so contrary to the ceremonious respect which was then considered due to rank and dignity, awakened general surprise, and in none more than in the lieutenant-governor himself. Looking angrily up, he perceived that his young relative was pointing his finger to the opposite wall. Hutchinson's eye followed the signal, and he saw what had hitherto been unobserved—that a black silk curtain was suspended before the mysterious picture, so as completely to conceal it. His thoughts immediately recurred to the scene of the preceding afternoon, and in his surprise, confused by indistinct emotions, yet sensible that his niece must have had an agency in this phenomenon, he called loudly upon her:

"Alice! Come hither, Alice!"

No sooner had he spoken than Alice Vane glided from her station, and, pressing one hand across her eyes, with the other snatched away the sable curtain that concealed the portrait. An exclamation of surprise burst from every beholder, but the lieutenant-governor's voice had a tone of horror.

"By Heaven!" said he, in a low inward murmur, speaking rather to himself than to those around him; "if the spirit of Edward Randolph were to appear among us from the place of torment, he could not wear more of the terrors of hell upon his face."

"For some wise end," said the aged selectman, solemnly, "hath Providence scattered away the mist of years that had so long hid this dreadful effigy. Until this hour no living man hath seen what we behold."

Within the antique frame which so recently had enclosed a sable waste of canvas now appeared a visible picture-still dark, indeed, in its hues and shadings, but thrown forward in strong relief. It was a half-length figure of a gentleman in a rich but very old-fashioned dress of embroidered velvet, with a broad ruff and a beard, and wearing a hat the brim of which overshadowed his forehead. Beneath this cloud the eyes had a peculiar glare which was almost lifelike. The whole portrait started so distinctly out of the background that it had the effect of a person looking down from the wall at the astonished and awe-stricken spectators. The expression of the face, if any words can convey an idea of it, was that of a wretch detected in some hideous guilt and exposed to the bitter hatred and laughter and withering scorn of a vast surrounding multitude. There was the struggle of defiance, beaten down and overwhelmed by the crushing weight of ignominy. The torture of the soul had come forth upon the countenance. It seemed as if the picture, while hidden behind the cloud of immemorial years, had been all the time acquiring an intenser depth and darkness of expression, till now it gloomed forth again and threw its evil omen over the present hour. Such, if the wild legend may be credited, was the portrait of Edward Randolph as he appeared when a people's curse had wrought its influence upon his nature.

"'Twould drive me mad, that awful face," said Hutchinson, who seemed fascinated by the contemplation of it.

"Be warned, then," whispered Alice. "He trampled on a people's rights. Behold his punishment, and avoid a crime like his."

The lieutenant-governor actually trembled for an instant, but, exerting his energy—which was not, however, his most characteristic feature—he strove to shake off the spell of Randolph's countenance.

"Girl," cried he, laughing bitterly, as he turned to Alice, "have you brought hither your painter's art, your Italian spirit of intrigue, your tricks of stage-effect, and think to influence the councils of rulers and the affairs of nations by such shallow contrivances? See here!"

"Stay yet a while," said the selectman as Hutchinson again snatched the pen; "for if ever mortal man received a warning from a tormented soul, Your Honor is that man."

"Away!" answered Hutchinson, fiercely. "Though yonder senseless picture cried 'Forbear!' it should not move me!"

Casting a scowl of defiance at the pictured face—which seemed at that moment to intensify the horror of its miserable and wicked look—he scrawled on the paper, in characters that betokened it a deed of desperation, the name of Thomas Hutchinson. Then, it is said, he shuddered, as if that signature had granted away his salvation.

"It is done," said he, and placed his hand upon his brow.

"May Heaven forgive the deed!" said the soft, sad accents of Alice Vane, like the voice of a good spirit flitting away.

When morning came, there was a stifled whisper through the household, and spreading thence about the town, that the dark mysterious picture had started from the wall and spoken face to face with Lieutenant-governor Hutchinson. If such a miracle had been wrought, however, no traces of it remained behind; for within the antique frame nothing could be discerned save the impenetrable cloud which had covered the canvas since the memory of man. If the figure had, indeed, stepped forth, it had fled back, spirit-like, at the day-dawn, and hidden itself behind a century's obscurity. The truth probably was that Alice Vane's secret for restoring the hues of the picture had merely effected a temporary renovation. But those who in that brief interval had beheld the awful visage of Edward Randolph desired no second glance, and ever afterward trembled at the recollection of the scene, as if an evil spirit had appeared visibly among them. And, as for Hutchinson, when, far over the ocean, his dying-hour drew on, he gasped for breath and complained that he was choking with the blood of the Boston Massacre, and Francis Lincoln, the former captain of Castle William, who was standing at his bedside, perceived a likeness in his frenzied look to that of Edward Randolph. Did his broken spirit feel at that dread hour the tremendous burden of a people's curse?

At the conclusion of this miraculous legend I inquired of mine host whether the picture still remained in the chamber over our heads, but Mr. Tiffany informed me that it had long since been removed, and was supposed to be hidden in some out-of-the-way corner of the New England Museum. Perchance some curious antiquary may light upon it there, and, with the assistance of Mr. Howorth, the picture-cleaner, may supply a not unnecessary proof of the authenticity of the facts here set down.

During the progress of the story a storm had been gathering abroad and raging and rattling so loudly in the upper regions of the Province House that it seemed as if all the old governors and great men were running riot above stairs while Mr. Bela Tiffany babbled of them below. In the course of generations, when many people have lived and died in an ancient house, the whistling of the wind through its crannies and the creaking of its beams and rafters become strangely like the tones of the human voice, or thundering laughter, or heavy footsteps treading the deserted chambers. It is as if the echoes of half a century were revived. Such were the ghostly sounds that roared and murmured in our ears when I took leave of the circle round the fireside of the Province House and, plunging down the doorsteps, fought my way homeward against a drifting snow-storm.

III. LADY ELEANORE'S MANTLE.

Mine excellent friend the landlord of the Province House was pleased the other evening to invite Mr. Tiffany and myself to an oyster-supper. This slight mark of respect and gratitude, as he handsomely observed, was far less than the ingenious tale-teller, and I, the humble note-taker of his narratives, had fairly earned by the public notice which our joint lucubrations had attracted to his establishment. Many a cigar had been smoked within his premises, many a glass of wine or more potent *aqua vitæ* had been quaffed, many a dinner had been eaten, by curious strangers who, save for the fortunate conjunction of Mr. Tiffany and me, would never have ventured through that darksome avenue which gives access to the historic precincts of the Province House. In short, if any credit be due to the courteous assurances of Mr. Thomas Waite, we had brought his forgotten mansion almost as effectually into public view as if we had thrown down the vulgar range of shoe-shops and dry-good stores which hides its aristocratic front from Washington street. It may be unadvisable, however, to speak too loudly of the increased custom of the house, lest Mr. Waite should find it difficult to renew the lease on so favorable terms as heretofore.

Being thus welcomed as benefactors, neither Mr. Tiffany nor myself felt any scruple in doing full justice to the good things that were set before us. If the feast were less magnificent than those same panelled walls had witnessed in a bygone century; if mine host presided with somewhat less of state than might have befitted a successor of the royal governors; if the guests made a less imposing show than the bewigged and powdered and embroidered dignitaries who erst banqueted at the gubernatorial table and now sleep within their armorial tombs on Copp's Hill or round King's Chapel,—yet never, I may boldly say, did a more comfortable little party assemble in the province-house from Queen Anne's days to the Revolution. The occasion was rendered more interesting by the presence of a venerable personage whose own actual reminiscences went back to the epoch of Gage and Howe, and even supplied him with a doubtful anecdote or two of Hutchinson. He was one of that small, and now all but extinguished, class whose attachment to royalty, and to the colonial institutions and customs that were connected with it, had never yielded to the democratic heresies of after-times. The young queen of Britain has not a more loyal subject in her realm—perhaps not one who would kneel before her throne with such reverential love—as this old grandsire whose head has whitened beneath the mild sway of the republic which still in his mellower moments he terms a usurpation. Yet prejudices so obstinate have not made him an ungentle or impracticable companion. If the truth must be told, the life of the aged loyalist has been of such a scrambling and unsettled character—he has had so little choice of friends and been so often destitute of any—that I doubt whether he would refuse a cup of kindness with either Oliver Cromwell or John Hancock, to say nothing of any democrat now upon the stage. In another paper of this series I may perhaps give the reader a closer glimpse of his portrait.

Our host in due season uncorked a bottle of Madeira of such exquisite perfume and admirable flavor that he surely must have discovered it in an ancient bin down deep beneath the deepest cellar where some jolly old butler stored away the governor's choicest wine and forgot to reveal the secret on his death-bed. Peace to his red-nosed ghost and a libation to his memory! This precious liquor was imbibed by Mr. Tiffany with peculiar zest, and after sipping the third glass it was his pleasure to give us one of the oddest legends which he had yet raked from the storehouse where he keeps such matters. With some suitable adornments from my own fancy, it ran pretty much as follows.

Not long after Colonel Shute had assumed the government of Massachusetts Bay—now nearly a hundred and twenty years ago—a young lady of rank and fortune arrived from England to claim his protection as her guardian. He was her distant relative, but the nearest who had survived the gradual extinction of her family; so that no more eligible shelter could be found for the rich and high-born Lady Eleanore Rochcliffe than within the province-house of a Transatlantic colony. The consort of Governor Shute, moreover, had been as a mother to her childhood, and was now anxious to receive her in the hope that a beautiful young woman would be exposed to infinitely less peril from the primitive society of New England than amid the artifices and corruptions of a court. If either the governor or his lady had especially consulted their own comfort, they would probably have sought to devolve the responsibility on other hands, since with some noble and splendid traits of character Lady Eleanore was remarkable for a harsh, unyielding pride, a haughty consciousness of her hereditary and personal advantages, which made her almost incapable of control. Judging from many traditionary anecdotes, this peculiar temper was hardly less than a monomania; or if the acts which it inspired were those of a sane person, it seemed due from Providence that pride so sinful should be followed by as severe a retribution. That tinge of the marvellous which is thrown over so many of these half-forgotten legends has probably imparted an additional wildness to the strange story of Lady Eleanore Rochcliffe.

The ship in which she came passenger had arrived at Newport, whence Lady Eleanore was conveyed to Boston in the governor's coach, attended by a small escort of gentlemen on horseback. The ponderous equipage, with its four black horses, attracted much notice as it rumbled through Cornhill surrounded by the prancing steeds of half a dozen cavaliers with swords dangling to their stirrups and pistols at their holsters. Through the large glass windows of the coach, as it rolled along, the people could discern the figure of Lady Eleanore, strangely combining an almost queenly stateliness with the grace and beauty of a maiden in her teens. A singular tale had gone abroad among the ladies of the province that their fair rival was indebted for much of the irresistible charm of her appearance to a certain article of dress—an embroidered mantle—which had been wrought by the most skilful artist in London, and possessed even magical properties of adornment. On the present occasion, however, she owed nothing to the witchery of dress, being clad in a riding-habit of velvet which would have appeared stiff and ungraceful on any other form.

The coachman reined in his four black steeds, and the whole cavalcade came to a pause in front of the contorted iron balustrade that fenced the province-house from the public street. It was an awkward coincidence that the bell of the Old South was just then tolling for a funeral; so that, instead of a gladsome peal with which it was customary to announce the arrival of distinguished strangers, Lady Eleanore Rochcliffe was ushered by a doleful clang, as if calamity had come embodied in her beautiful person.

"A very great disrespect!" exclaimed Captain Langford, an English officer who had recently brought despatches to Governor Shute. "The funeral should have been deferred lest Lady Eleanore's spirits be affected by such a dismal welcome."

"With your pardon, sir," replied Dr. Clarke, a physician and a famous champion of the popular party, "whatever the heralds may pretend, a dead beggar must have precedence of a living queen. King Death confers high privileges."

These remarks-were interchanged while the speakers waited a passage through the crowd which had gathered on each side of the gateway, leaving an open avenue to the portal of the province-house. A black slave in livery now leaped from behind the coach and threw open the door, while at the same moment Governor Shute descended the flight of steps from his mansion to assist Lady Eleanore in alighting. But the governor's stately approach was anticipated in a manner that excited general astonishment. A pale young man with his black hair all in disorder rushed from the throng and prostrated himself beside the coach, thus offering his person as a footstool for Lady Eleanore Rochcliffe to tread upon. She held back an instant, yet with an expression as if doubting whether the young man were worthy to bear the weight of her footstep rather than dissatisfied to receive such awful reverence from a fellow-mortal.

"Up, sir!" said the governor, sternly, at the same time lifting his cane over the intruder. "What means the Bedlamite by this freak?"

"Nay," answered Lady Eleanore, playfully, but with more scorn than pity in her tone; "Your Excellency shall not strike him. When men seek only to be trampled upon, it were a pity to deny them a favor so easily granted—and so well deserved!" Then, though as lightly as a sunbeam on a cloud, she placed her foot upon the cowering form and extended her hand to meet that of the governor.

There was a brief interval during which Lady Eleanore retained this attitude, and never, surely, was there an apter emblem of aristocracy and hereditary pride trampling on human sympathies and the kindred of nature than these two figures presented at that moment. Yet the spectators were so smitten with her beauty, and so essential did pride seem to the existence of such a creature, that they gave a simultaneous acclamation of applause.

"Who is this insolent young fellow?" inquired Captain Langford, who still remained beside Dr. Clarke. "If he be in his senses, his impertinence demands the bastinado; if mad, Lady Eleanore should be secured from further inconvenience by his confinement."

"His name is Jervase Helwyse," answered the doctor—"a youth of no birth or fortune, or other advantages save the mind and soul that nature gave him; and, being secretary to our colonial agent in London, it was his misfortune to meet this Lady Eleanore Rochcliffe. He loved her, and her scorn has driven him mad."

"He was mad so to aspire," observed the English officer.

"It may be so," said Dr. Clarke, frowning as he spoke; "but I tell you, sir, I could wellnigh doubt the justice of the Heaven above us if no signal humiliation overtake this lady who now treads so haughtily into yonder mansion. She seeks to place herself above the sympathies of our common nature, which envelops all human souls; see if that nature do not assert its claim over her in some mode that shall bring her level with the lowest."

"Never!" cried Captain Langford, indignantly—"neither in life nor when they lay her with her ancestors."

Not many days afterward the governor gave a ball in honor of Lady Eleanore Rochcliffe. The principal gentry of the colony received invitations, which were distributed to their residences far and near by messengers on horseback bearing missives sealed with all the formality of official despatches. In obedience to the summons, there was a general gathering of rank, wealth and beauty, and the wide door of the province-house had seldom given admittance to more numerous and honorable guests than on the evening of Lady Eleanore's ball. Without much extravagance of eulogy, the spectacle might even be termed splendid, for, according to the fashion of the times, the ladies shone in rich silks and satins outspread over wide-projecting hoops, and the gentlemen glittered in gold embroidery laid unsparingly upon the purple or scarlet or sky-blue velvet which was the material of their coats and waistcoats. The latter article of dress was of great importance, since it enveloped the wearer's body nearly to the knees and was perhaps bedizened with the amount of his whole year's income in golden flowers and foliage. The altered taste of the present day—a taste symbolic of a deep change in the whole system of society—would look upon almost any of those gorgeous figures as ridiculous, although that evening the guests sought their reflections in the pier-glasses and rejoiced to catch their own glitter amid the glittering crowd. What a pity that one of the stately mirrors has not preserved a picture of the scene which by the very traits that were so transitory might have taught us much that would be worth knowing and remembering!

Would, at least, that either painter or mirror could convey to us some faint idea of a garment already noticed in this legend—the Lady Eleanore's embroidered mantle, which the gossips whispered was invested with magic properties, so as to lend a new and untried grace to her figure each time that she put it on! Idle fancy as it is, this mysterious mantle has thrown an awe around my image of her, partly from its fabled virtues and partly because it was the handiwork of a dying woman, and perchance owed the fantastic grace of its conception to the delirium of approaching death.

After the ceremonial greetings had been paid, Lady Eleanore Rochcliffe stood apart from the mob of guests, insulating herself within a small and distinguished circle to whom she accorded a more cordial favor than to the general throng. The waxen torches threw their radiance vividly over the scene, bringing out its brilliant points in strong relief, but she gazed carelessly, and with now and then an expression of weariness or scorn tempered with such feminine grace that her auditors scarcely perceived the moral deformity of which it was the utterance. She beheld the spectacle not with vulgar ridicule, as disdaining to be pleased with the provincial mockery of a court-festival, but with the deeper scorn of one whose spirit held itself too high to participate in the enjoyment of other human souls. Whether or no the recollections of those who saw her that evening were influenced by the strange events with which she was subsequently connected, so it was that her figure ever after recurred to them as marked by something wild and unnatural, although at the time the general whisper was of her exceeding beauty and of the indescribable charm which her mantle threw around her. Some close observers, indeed, detected a feverish flush and alternate paleness of countenance, with a corresponding flow and revulsion of spirits, and once or twice a painful and helpless betrayal of lassitude, as if she were on the point of sinking to the ground. Then, with a nervous shudder, she seemed to arouse her energies, and threw some bright and playful yet half-wicked sarcasm into the conversation. There was so strange a characteristic in her manners and sentiments that it astonished every right-minded listener, till, looking in her face, a lurking and incomprehensible glance and smile perplexed them with doubts both as to her seriousness and sanity. Gradually, Lady Eleanore Rochcliffe's circle grew smaller, till only four gentlemen remained in it. These were Captain Langford, the English officer before mentioned; a Virginian planter who had come to Massachusetts on some political errand; a young Episcopal clergyman, the grandson of a British earl; and, lastly, the private secretary of Governor Shute, whose obsequiousness had won a sort of tolerance from Lady Eleanore.

At different periods of the evening the liveried servants of the province-house passed among the guests bearing huge trays of refreshments and French and Spanish wines. Lady Eleanore Rochcliffe, who refused to wet her beautiful lips even with a bubble of champagne, had sunk back into a large damask chair, apparently overwearied either with the excitement of the scene or its tedium; and while, for an instant, she was unconscious of voices, laughter and music, a young man stole forward and knelt down at her feet. He bore a salver in his hand on which was a chased silver goblet filled to the brim with wine, which he offered as reverentially as to a crowned queen—or, rather, with the awful devotion of a priest doing sacrifice to his idol. Conscious that some one touched her robe, Lady Eleanore started, and unclosed her eyes upon the pale, wild features and dishevelled hair of Jervase Helwyse.

"Why do you haunt me thus?" said she, in a languid tone, but with a kindlier feeling than she ordinarily permitted herself to express. "They tell me that I have done you harm."

"Heaven knows if that be so," replied the young man, solemnly. "But, Lady Eleanore, in requital of that harm, if such there be, and for your own earthly and heavenly welfare, I pray you to take one sip of this holy wine and then to pass the goblet round among the guests. And this shall be a symbol that you have not sought to withdraw yourself from the chain of human sympathies, which whoso would shake off must keep company with fallen angels."

"Where has this mad fellow stolen that sacramental vessel?" exclaimed the Episcopal clergyman.

This question drew the notice of the guests to the silver cup, which was recognized as appertaining to the communion-plate of the Old South Church, and, for aught that could be known, it was brimming over with the consecrated wine.

"Perhaps it is poisoned," half whispered the governor's secretary.

"Pour it down the villain's throat!" cried the Virginian, fiercely.

"Turn him out of the house!" cried Captain Langford, seizing Jervase Helwyse so roughly by the shoulder that the sacramental cup was overturned and its contents sprinkled upon Lady Eleanore's mantle. "Whether knave, fool or Bedlamite, it is intolerable that the fellow should go at large."

"Pray, gentlemen, do my poor admirer no harm," said Lady Eleanore, with a faint and weary smile. "Take him out of my sight, if such be your pleasure, for I can find in my heart to do nothing but laugh at him, whereas, in all decency and conscience, it would become me to weep for the mischief I have wrought."

But while the bystanders were attempting to lead away the unfortunate young man he broke from them and with a wild, impassioned earnestness offered a new and equally strange petition to Lady Eleanore. It was no other than that she should throw off the mantle, which while he pressed the silver cup of wine upon her she had drawn more closely around her form, so as almost to shroud herself within it.

"Cast it from you," exclaimed Jervase Helwyse, clasping his hands in an agony of entreaty. "It may not yet be too late. Give the accursed garment to the flames."

But Lady Eleanore, with a laugh of scorn, drew the rich folds of the embroidered mantle over her head in such a fashion as to give a completely new aspect to her beautiful face, which, half hidden, half revealed, seemed to belong to some being of mysterious character and purposes.

"Farewell, Jervase Helwyse!" said she. "Keep my image in your remembrance as you behold it now."

"Alas, lady!" he replied, in a tone no longer wild, but sad as a funeral-bell; "we must meet shortly when your face may wear another aspect, and that shall be the image that must abide within me." He made no more resistance to the violent efforts of the gentlemen and servants who almost dragged him out of the apartment and dismissed him roughly from the iron gate of the province-house.

Captain Langford, who had been very active in this affair, was returning to the presence of Lady Eleanore Rochcliffe, when he encountered the physician, Dr. Clarke, with whom he had held some casual talk on the day of her arrival. The doctor stood apart, separated from Lady Eleanore by the width of the room, but eying her with such keen sagacity that Captain Langford involuntarily gave him credit for the discovery of some deep secret.

"You appear to be smitten, after all, with the charms of this queenly maiden," said he, hoping thus to draw forth the physician's hidden knowledge.

"God forbid!" answered Dr. Clarke, with a grave smile; "and if you be wise, you will put up the same prayer for yourself. Woe to those who shall be smitten by this beautiful Lady Eleanore! But yonder stands the governor, and I have a word or two for his private ear. Good-night!" He accordingly advanced to Governor Shute and addressed him in so low a tone that none of the bystanders could catch a word of what he said, although the sudden change of His Excellency's hitherto cheerful visage betokened that the communication could be of no agreeable import. A very few moments afterward it was announced to the guests that an unforeseen circumstance rendered it necessary to put a premature close to the festival.

The ball at the province-house supplied a topic of conversation for the colonial metropolis for some days after its occurrence, and might still longer have been the general theme, only that a subject of all-engrossing interest thrust it for a time from the public recollection. This was the appearance of a dreadful epidemic which in that age, and long before and afterward, was wont to slay its hundreds and thousands on both sides of the Atlantic. On the occasion of which we speak it was distinguished by a peculiar virulence, insomuch that it has left its traces—its pitmarks, to use an appropriate figure—on the history of the country, the affairs of which were thrown into confusion by its ravages. At first, unlike its ordinary course, the disease seemed to confine itself to the higher circles of society, selecting its victims from among the proud, the well-born and the wealthy, entering unabashed into stately chambers and lying down with the slumberers in silken beds. Some of the most distinguished guests of the province-house—even those whom the haughty Lady Eleanore Rochcliffe had deemed not unworthy of her favor—were stricken by this fatal scourge. It was noticed with an ungenerous bitterness of feeling that the four gentlemen—the Virginian, the British officer, the young clergyman and the governor's secretary—who had been her most devoted attendants on the evening of the ball were the foremost on whom the plague-stroke fell. But the disease, pursuing its onward progress, soon ceased to be exclusively a prerogative of aristocracy. Its red brand was no longer conferred like a noble's star or an order of knighthood. It threaded its way through the narrow and crooked streets, and entered the low, mean, darksome dwellings and laid its hand of death upon the artisans and laboring classes of the town. It compelled rich and poor to feel themselves brethren then, and stalking to and fro across the Three Hills with a fierceness which made it almost a new pestilence, there was that mighty conqueror—that scourge and horror of our forefathers—the small-pox.

We cannot estimate the affright which this plague inspired of yore by contemplating it as the fangless monster of the present day. We must remember, rather, with what awe we watched the gigantic footsteps of the Asiatic cholera striding from shore to shore of the Atlantic and marching like Destiny upon cities far remote which flight had already half depopulated. There is no other fear so horrible and unhumanizing as that which makes man dread to breathe heaven's vital air lest it be poison, or to grasp the hand of a brother or friend lest the grip of the pestilence should clutch him. Such was the dismay that now followed in the track of the disease or ran before it throughout the town. Graves were hastily dug and the pestilential relics as hastily covered, because the dead were enemies of the living and strove to draw them headlong, as it were, into their own dismal pit. The public councils were suspended, as if mortal wisdom might relinquish its devices now that an unearthly usurper had found his way into the ruler's mansion. Had an enemy's fleet been hovering on the coast or his armies trampling on our soil, the people would probably have committed their defence to that same direful conqueror who had wrought their own calamity and would permit no interference with his sway. This conqueror had a symbol of his triumphs: it was a blood-red flag that fluttered in the tainted air over the door of every dwelling into which the small-pox had entered.

Such a banner was long since waving over the portal of the province-house, for thence, as was proved by tracking its footsteps back, had all this dreadful mischief issued. It had been traced back to a lady's luxurious chamber, to the proudest of the proud, to her that was so delicate and hardly owned herself of earthly mould, to the haughty one who took her stand above human sympathies—to Lady Eleanore. There remained no room for doubt that the contagion had lurked in that gorgeous mantle which threw so strange a grace around her at the festival. Its fantastic splendor had been conceived in the delirious brain of a woman on her death-bed and was the last toil of her stiffening fingers, which had interwoven fate and misery with its golden threads. This dark tale, whispered at first, was now bruited far and wide. The people raved against the Lady Eleanore and cried out that her pride and scorn had evoked a fiend, and that between them both this monstrous evil had been born. At times their rage and despair took the semblance of grinning mirth; and whenever the red flag of the pestilence was hoisted over another and yet another door, they clapped their hands and shouted through the streets in bitter mockery: "Behold a new triumph for the Lady Eleanore!"

One day in the midst of these dismal times a wild figure approached the portal of the province-house, and, folding his arms, stood contemplating the scarlet banner, which a passing breeze shook fitfully, as if to fling abroad the contagion that it typified. At length, climbing one of the pillars by means of the iron balustrade, he took down the flag, and entered the mansion waving it above his head. At the foot of the staircase he met the governor, booted and spurred, with his cloak drawn around him, evidently on the point of setting forth upon a journey.

"Wretched lunatic, what do you seek here?" exclaimed Shute, extending his cane to guard himself from contact. "There is nothing here but Death; back, or you will meet him."

"Death will not touch me, the banner-bearer of the pestilence," cried Jervase Helwyse, shaking the red flag aloft. "Death and the pestilence, who wears the aspect of the Lady Eleanore, will walk through the streets to-night, and I must march before them with this banner."

"Why do I waste words on the fellow?" muttered the governor, drawing his cloak across his mouth. "What matters his miserable life, when none of us are sure of twelve hours' breath?—On, fool, to your own destruction!"

He made way for Jervase Helwyse, who immediately ascended the staircase, but on the first landing-place was arrested by the firm grasp of a hand upon his shoulder. Looking fiercely up with a madman's impulse to struggle with and rend asunder his opponent, he found himself powerless beneath a calm, stern eye which possessed the mysterious property of quelling frenzy at its height. The person whom he had now encountered was the physician, Dr. Clarke, the duties of whose sad profession had led him to the province-house, where he was an infrequent guest in more prosperous times.

"Young man, what is your purpose?" demanded he.

"I seek the Lady Eleanore," answered Jervase Helwyse, submissively.

"All have fled from her," said the physician. "Why do you seek her now? I tell you, youth, her nurse fell death-stricken on the threshold of that fatal chamber. Know ye not that never came such a curse to our shores as this lovely Lady Eleanore, that her breath has filled the air with poison, that she has shaken pestilence and death upon the land from the folds of her accursed mantle?"

"Let me look upon her," rejoined the mad youth, more wildly. "Let me behold her in her awful beauty, clad in the regal garments of the pestilence. She and Death sit on a throne together; let me kneel down before them."

"Poor youth!" said Dr. Clarke, and, moved by a deep sense of human weakness, a smile of caustic humor curled his lip even then. "Wilt thou still worship the destroyer and surround her image with fantasies the more magnificent the more evil she has wrought? Thus man doth ever to his tyrants. Approach, then. Madness, as I have noted, has that good efficacy that it will guard you from contagion, and perhaps its own cure may be found in yonder chamber." Ascending another flight of stairs, he threw open a door and signed to Jervase Helwyse that he should enter.

The poor lunatic, it seems probable, had cherished a delusion that his haughty mistress sat in state, unharmed herself by the pestilential influence which as by enchantment she scattered round about her. He dreamed, no doubt, that her beauty was not dimmed, but brightened into superhuman splendor. With such anticipations he stole reverentially to the door at which the physician stood, but paused upon the threshold, gazing fearfully into the gloom of the darkened chamber.

"Where is the Lady Eleanore?" whispered he.

"Call her," replied the physician.

"Lady Eleanore! princess! queen of Death!" cried Jervase Helwyse, advancing three steps into the chamber. "She is not here. There, on yonder table, I behold the sparkle of a diamond which once she wore upon her bosom. There"—and he shuddered—"there hangs her mantle, on which a dead woman embroidered a spell of dreadful potency. But where is the Lady Eleanore?"

Something stirred within the silken curtains of a canopied bed and a low moan was uttered, which, listening intently, Jervase Helwyse began to distinguish as a woman's voice complaining dolefully of thirst. He fancied, even, that he recognized its tones.

"My throat! My throat is scorched," murmured the voice. "A drop of water!"

"What thing art thou?" said the brain-stricken youth, drawing near the bed and tearing asunder its curtains. "Whose voice hast thou stolen for thy murmurs and miserable petitions, as if Lady Eleanore could be conscious of mortal infirmity? Fie! Heap of diseased mortality, why lurkest thou in my lady's chamber?"

"Oh, Jervase Helwyse," said the voice—and as it spoke the figure contorted itself, struggling to hide its blasted face—"look not now on the woman you once loved. The curse of Heaven hath stricken me because I would not call man my brother nor woman sister. I wrapped myself in pride as in a mantle and scorned the sympathies of nature, and therefore has Nature made this wretched body the medium of a dreadful sympathy. You are avenged, they are all avenged, Nature is avenged; for I am Eleanore Rochcliffe."

The malice of his mental disease, the bitterness lurking at the bottom of his heart, mad as he was, for a blighted and ruined life and love that had been paid with cruel scorn, awoke within the breast of Jervase Helwyse. He shook his finger at the wretched girl, and the chamber echoed, the curtains of the bed were shaken, with his outburst of insane merriment.

"Another triumph for the Lady Eleanore!" he cried. "All have been her victims; who so worthy to be the final victim as herself?" Impelled by some new fantasy of his crazed intellect, he snatched the fatal mantle and rushed from the chamber and the house.

That night a procession passed by torchlight through the streets, bearing in the midst the figure of a woman enveloped with a richly-embroidered mantle, while in advance stalked Jervase Helwyse waving the red flag of the pestilence. Arriving opposite the province-house, the mob burned the effigy, and a strong wind came and swept away the ashes. It was said that from that very hour the pestilence abated, as if its sway had some mysterious connection, from the first plague-stroke to the last, with Lady Elcanore's mantle. A remarkable uncertainty broods over that unhappy lady's fate. There is a belief, however, that in a certain chamber of this mansion a female form may sometimes be duskily discerned shrinking into the darkest corner and muffling her face within an embroidered mantle. Supposing the legend true, can this be other than the once proud Lady Eleanore?

Mine host and the old loyalist and I bestowed no little Warmth of applause upon this narrative, in which we had all been deeply interested; for the reader can scarcely conceive how unspeakably the effect of such a tale is heightened when, as in the present case, we may repose perfect confidence in the veracity of him who tells it. For my own part, knowing how scrupulous is Mr. Tiffany to settle the foundation of his facts, I could not have believed him one whit the more faithfully had he professed himself an eyewitness of the doings and sufferings of poor Lady Eleanore. Some sceptics, it is true, might demand documentary evidence, or even require him to produce the embroidered mantle, forgetting that—Heaven be praised!—it was consumed to ashes.

But now the old loyalist, whose blood was warmed by the good cheer, began to talk, in his turn, about the traditions of the Province House, and hinted that he, if it were agreeable, might add a few reminiscences to our legendary stock. Mr. Tiffany, having no cause to dread a rival, immediately besought him to favor us with a specimen; my own entreaties, of course, were urged to the same effect; and our venerable guest, well pleased to find willing auditors, awaited only the return of Mr. Thomas Waite, who had been summoned forth to provide accommodations for several new arrivals. Perchance the public—but be this as its own caprice and ours shall settle the matter—may read the result in another tale of the Province House.

IV. OLD ESTHER DUDLEY.

Our host having resumed the chair, he as well as Mr. Tiffany and myself expressed much eagerness to be made acquainted with the story to which the loyalist had alluded. That venerable man first of all saw lit to moisten his throat with another glass of wine, and then, turning his face toward our coal-fire, looked steadfastly for a few moments into the depths of its cheerful glow. Finally he poured forth a great fluency of speech. The generous liquid that he had imbibed, while it warmed his age-chilled blood, likewise took off the chill from his heart and mind, and gave him an energy to think and feel which we could hardly have expected to find beneath the snows of fourscore winters. His feelings, indeed, appeared to me more excitable than those of a younger man—or, at least, the same degree of feeling manifested itself by more visible effects than if his judgment and will had possessed the potency of meridian life. At the pathetic passages of his narrative he readily melted into tears. When a breath of indignation swept across his spirit, the blood flushed his withered visage even to the roots of his white hair, and he shook his clinched fist at the trio of peaceful auditors, seeming to fancy enemies in those who felt very kindly toward the desolate old soul. But ever and anon, sometimes in the midst of his most earnest talk, this ancient person's intellect would wander vaguely, losing its hold of the matter in hand and groping for it amid misty shadows. Then would he cackle forth a feeble laugh and express a doubt whether his wits—for by that phrase it pleased our ancient friend to signify his mental powers—were not getting a little the worse for wear.

Under these disadvantages, the old loyalist's story required more revision to render it fit for the public eye than those of the series which have preceded it; nor should it be concealed that the sentiment and tone of the affair may have undergone some slight—or perchance more than slight—metamorphosis in its transmission to the reader through the medium of a thoroughgoing democrat. The tale itself is a mere sketch with no involution of plot nor any great interest of events, yet possessing, if I have rehearsed it aright, that pensive influence over the mind which the shadow of the old Province House flings upon the loiterer in its court-yard.

The hour had come—the hour of defeat and humiliation—when Sir William Howe was to pass over the threshold of the province-house and embark, with no such triumphal ceremonies as he once promised himself, on board the British fleet. He bade his servants and military attendants go before him, and lingered a moment in the loneliness of the mansion to quell the fierce emotions that struggled in his bosom as with a death-throb. Preferable then would he have deemed his fate had a warrior's death left him a claim to the narrow territory of a grave within the soil which the king had given him to defend. With an ominous perception that as his departing footsteps echoed adown the staircase the sway of Britain was passing for ever from New England, he smote his clenched hand on his brow and cursed the destiny that had flung the shame of a dismembered empire upon him.

"Would to God," cried he, hardly repressing his tears of rage, "that the rebels were even now at the doorstep! A blood-stain upon the floor should then bear testimony that the last British ruler was faithful to his trust."

The tremulous voice of a woman replied to his exclamation.

"Heaven's cause and the king's are one," it said. "Go forth, Sir William Howe, and trust in Heaven to bring back a royal governor in triumph."

Subduing at once the passion to which he had yielded only in the faith that it was unwitnessed, Sir William Howe became conscious that an aged woman leaning on a gold-headed staff was standing betwixt him and the door. It was old Esther Dudley, who had dwelt almost immemorial years in this mansion, until her presence seemed as inseparable from it as the recollections of its history. She was the daughter of an ancient and once eminent family which had fallen into poverty and decay and left its last descendant no resource save the bounty of the king, nor any shelter except within the walls of the province-house. An office in the household with merely nominal duties had been assigned to her as a pretext for the payment of a small pension, the greater part of which she expended in adorning herself with an antique magnificence of attire. The claims of Esther Dudley's gentle blood were acknowledged by all the successive governors, and they treated her with the punctilious courtesy which it was her foible to demand, not always with success, from a neglectful world. The only actual share which she assumed in the business of the mansion was to glide through its passages and public chambers late at night to see that the servants had dropped no fire from their flaring torches nor left embers crackling and blazing on the hearths. Perhaps it was this invariable custom of walking her rounds in the hush of midnight that caused the superstition of the times to invest the old woman with attributes of awe and mystery, fabling that she had entered the portal of the province-house—none knew whence—in the train of the first royal governor, and that it was her fate to dwell there till the last should have departed.

But Sir William Howe, if he ever heard this legend, had forgotten it.

"Mistress Dudley, why are you loitering here?" asked he, with some severity of tone. "It is my pleasure to be the last in this mansion of the king."

"Not so, if it please Your Excellency," answered the time-stricken woman. "This roof has sheltered me long; I will not pass from it until they bear me to the tomb of my forefathers. What other shelter is there for old Esther Dudley save the province-house or the grave?"

"Now, Heaven forgive me!" said Sir William Howe to himself. "I was about to leave this wretched old creature to starve or beg.—Take this, good Mistress Dudley," he added, putting a purse into her hands. "King George's head on these golden guineas is sterling yet, and will continue so, I warrant you, even should the rebels crown John Hancock their king. That purse will buy a better shelter than the province-house can now afford."

"While the burden of life remains upon me I will have no other shelter than this roof," persisted Esther Dudley, striking her stuff upon the floor with a gesture that expressed immovable resolve; "and when Your Excellency returns in triumph, I will totter into the porch to welcome you."

"My poor old friend!" answered the British general, and all his manly and martial pride could no longer restrain a gush of bitter tears. "This is an evil hour for you and me. The province which the king entrusted to my charge is lost. I go hence in misfortune—perchance in disgrace—to return no more. And you, whose present being is incorporated with the past, who have seen governor after governor in stately pageantry ascend these steps, whose whole life has been an observance of majestic ceremonies and a worship of the king,—how will you endure the change? Come with us; bid farewell to a land that has shaken off its allegiance, and live still under a royal government at Halifax."

"Never! never!" said the pertinacious old dame. "Here will I abide, and King George shall still have one true subject in his disloyal province."

"Beshrew the old fool!" muttered Sir William Howe, growing impatient of her obstinacy and ashamed of the emotion into which he had been betrayed. "She is the very moral of old-fashioned prejudice, and could exist nowhere but in this musty edifice.—Well, then, Mistress Dudley, since you will needs tarry, I give the province-house in charge to you. Take this key, and keep it safe until myself or some other royal governor shall demand it of you." Smiling bitterly at himself and her, he took the heavy key of the province-house, and, delivering it into the old lady's hands, drew his clonk around him for departure.

As the general glanced back at Esther Dudley's antique figure he deemed her well fitted for such a charge, as being so perfect a representative of the decayed past—of an age gone by, with its manners, opinions, faith and feelings all fallen into oblivion or scorn, of what had once been a reality, but was now merely a vision of faded magnificence. Then Sir William Howe strode forth, smiting his clenched hands together in the fierce anguish of his spirit, and old Esther Dudley was left to keep watch in the lonely province-house, dwelling there with Memory; and if Hope ever seemed to flit around her, still it was Memory in disguise.

The total change of affairs that ensued on the departure of the British troops did not drive the venerable lady from her stronghold. There was not for many years afterward a governor of Massachusetts, and the magistrates who had charge of such matters saw no objection to Esther Dudley's residence in the province-house, especially as they must otherwise have paid a hireling for taking care of the premises, which with her was a labor of love; and so they left her the undisturbed mistress of the old historic edifice. Many and strange were the fables which the gossips whispered about her in all the chimney-corners of the town.

Among the time-worn articles of furniture that had been left in the mansion, there was a tall antique mirror which was well worthy of a tale by itself, and perhaps may hereafter be the theme of one. The gold of its heavily-wrought frame was tarnished, and its surface so blurred that the old woman's figure, whenever she paused before it, looked indistinct and ghostlike. But it was the general belief that Esther could cause the governors of the overthrown dynasty, with the beautiful ladies who had once adorned their festivals, the Indian chiefs who had come up to the province-house to hold council or swear allegiance, the grim provincial warriors, the severe clergymen—in short, all the pageantry of gone days, all the figures that ever swept across the broad-plate of glass in former times,—she could cause the whole to reappear and people the inner world of the mirror with shadows of old life. Such legends as these, together with the singularity of her isolated existence, her age and the infirmity that each added winter flung upon her, made Mistress Dudley the object both of fear and pity, and it was partly the result of either sentiment that, amid all the angry license of the times, neither wrong nor insult ever fell upon her unprotected head. Indeed, there was so much haughtiness in her demeanor toward intruders—among whom she reckoned all persons acting under the new authorities—that it was really an affair of no small nerve to look her in the face. And, to do the people justice, stern republicans as they had now become, they were well content that the old gentlewoman, in her hoop-petticoat and faded embroidery, should still haunt the palace of ruined pride and overthrown power, the symbol of a departed system, embodying a history in her person. So Esther Dudley dwelt year after year in the province-house, still reverencing all that others had flung aside, still faithful to her king, who, so long as the venerable dame yet held her post, might be said to retain one true subject in New England and one spot of the empire that had been wrested from him.

And did she dwell there in utter loneliness? Rumor said, "Not so." Whenever her chill and withered heart desired warmth, she was wont to summon a black slave of Governor Shirley's from the blurred mirror and send him in search of guests who had long ago been familiar in those deserted chambers. Forth went the sable messenger, with the starlight or the moonshine gleaming through him, and did his errand in the burial-grounds, knocking at the iron doors of tombs or upon the marble slabs that covered them, and whispering to those within, "My mistress, old Esther Dudley, bids you to the province-house at midnight;" and punctually as the clock of the Old South told twelve came the shadows of the Olivers, the Hutchinsons, the Dudleys—all the grandees of a bygone generation—gliding beneath the portal into the well-known mansion, where Esther mingled with them as if she likewise were a shade. Without vouching for the truth of such traditions, it is certain that Mistress Dudley sometimes assembled a few of the stanch though crestfallen old Tories who had lingered in the rebel town during those days of wrath and tribulation. Out of a cobwebbed bottle containing liquor that a royal governor might have smacked his lips over they quaffed healths to the king and babbled treason to the republic, feeling as if the protecting shadow of the throne were still flung around them. But, draining the last drops of their liquor, they stole timorously homeward, and answered not again if the rude mob reviled them in the street.

Yet Esther Dudley's most frequent and favored guests were the children of the town. Toward them she was never stern. A kindly and loving nature hindered elsewhere from its free course by a thousand rocky prejudices lavished itself upon these little ones. By bribes of gingerbread of her own making, stamped with a royal crown, she tempted their sunny sportiveness beneath the gloomy portal of the province-house, and would often beguile them to spend a whole play-day there, sitting in a circle round the verge of her hoop-petticoat, greedily attentive to her stories of a dead world. And when these little boys and girls stole forth again from the dark, mysterious mansion, they went bewildered, full of old feelings that graver people had long ago forgotten, rubbing their eyes at the world around them as if they had gone astray into ancient times and become children of the past. At home, when their parents asked where they had loitered such a weary while and with whom they had been at play, the children would talk of all the departed worthies of the province as far back as Governor Belcher and the haughty dame of Sir William Phipps. It would seem as though they had been sitting on the knees of these famous personages, whom the grave had hidden for half a century, and had toyed with the embroidery of their rich waistcoats or roguishly pulled the long curls of their flowing wigs. "But Governor Belcher has been dead this many a year," would the mother say to her little boy. "And did you really see him at the province-house?"—"Oh yes, dear mother—yes!" the half-dreaming child would answer. "But when old Esther had done speaking about him, he faded away out of his chair." Thus, without affrighting her little guests, she led them by the hand into the chambers of her own desolate heart and made childhood's fancy discern the ghosts that haunted there.

Living so continually in her own circle of ideas, and never regulating her mind by a proper reference to present things, Esther Dudley appears to have grown partially crazed. It was found that she had no right sense of the progress and true state of the Revolutionary war, but held a constant faith that the armies of Britain were victorious on every field and destined to be ultimately triumphant. Whenever the town rejoiced for a battle won by Washington or Gates or Morgan or Greene, the news, in passing through the door of the province-house as through the ivory gate of dreams, became metamorphosed into a strange tale of the prowess of Howe, Clinton or Cornwallis. Sooner or later, it was her invincible belief, the colonies would be prostrate at the footstool of the king. Sometimes she seemed to take for granted that such was already the case. On one occasion she startled the townspeople by a brilliant illumination of the province-house with candles at every pane of glass and a transparency of the king's initials and a crown of light in the great balcony-window. The figure of the aged woman in the most gorgeous of her mildewed velvets and brocades was seen passing from casement to casement, until she paused before the balcony and flourished a huge key above her head. Her wrinkled visage actually gleamed with triumph, as if the soul within her were a festal lamp.

"What means this blaze of light? What does old Esther's joy portend?" whispered a spectator. "It is frightful to, see her gliding about the chambers and rejoicing there without a soul to bear her company."

"It is as if she were making merry in a tomb," said another.

"Pshaw! It is no such mystery," observed an old man, after some brief exercise of memory. "Mistress Dudley is keeping jubilee for the king of England's birthday."

Then the people laughed aloud, and would have thrown mud against the blazing transparency of the king's crown and initials, only that they pitied the poor old dame who was so dismally triumphant amid the wreck and ruin of the system to which she appertained.

Oftentimes it was her custom to climb the weary staircase that wound upward to the cupola, and thence strain her dimmed eyesight seaward and countryward, watching for a British fleet or for the march of a grand procession with the king's banner floating over it. The passengers in the street below would discern her anxious visage and send up a shout: "When the golden Indian on the province-house shall shoot his arrow, and when the cock on the Old South spire shall crow, then look for a royal governor again!" for this had grown a by-word through the town. And at last, after long, long years, old Esther Dudley knew—or perchance she only dreamed—that a royal governor was on the eve of returning to the province-house to receive the heavy key which Sir William Howe had committed to her charge. Now, it was the fact that intelligence bearing some faint analogy to Esther's version of it was current among the townspeople. She set the mansion in the best order that her means allowed, and, arraying herself in silks and tarnished gold, stood long before the blurred mirror to admire her own magnificence. As she gazed the gray and withered lady moved her ashen lips, murmuring half aloud, talking to shapes that she saw within the mirror, to shadows of her own fantasies, to the household friends of memory, and bidding them rejoice with her and come forth to meet the governor. And while absorbed in this communion Mistress Dudley heard the tramp of many footsteps in the street, and, looking out at the window, beheld what she construed as the royal governor's arrival.

"Oh, happy day! Oh, blessed, blessed hour!" she exclaimed. "Let me but bid him welcome within the portal, and my task in the province-house and on earth is done." Then, with tottering feet which age and tremulous joy caused to tread amiss, she hurried down the grand staircase, her silks sweeping and rustling as she went; so that the sound was as if a train of special courtiers were thronging from the dim mirror.

And Esther Dudley fancied that as soon as the wide door should be flung open all the pomp and splendor of bygone times would pace majestically into the province-house and the gilded tapestry of the past would be brightened by the sunshine of the present. She turned the key, withdrew it from the lock, unclosed the door and stepped across the threshold. Advancing up the court-yard appeared a person of most dignified mien, with tokens, as Esther interpreted them, of gentle blood, high rank and long-accustomed authority even in his walk and every gesture. He was richly dressed, but wore a gouty shoe, which, however, did not lessen the stateliness of his gait. Around and behind him were people in plain civic dresses and two or three war-worn veterans—evidently officers of rank—arrayed in a uniform of blue and buff. But Esther Dudley, firm in the belief that had fastened its roots about her heart, beheld only the principal personage, and never doubted that this was the long-looked-for governor to whom she was to surrender up her charge. As he approached she involuntarily sank down on her knees and tremblingly held forth the heavy key.

"Receive my trust! Take it quickly," cried she, "for methinks Death is striving to snatch away my triumph. But he conies too late. Thank Heaven for this blessed hour! God save King George!"

"That, madam, is a strange prayer to be offered up at such a moment," replied the unknown guest of the province-house, and, courteously removing his hat, he offered his arm to raise the aged woman. "Yet, in reverence for your gray hairs and long-kept faith, Heaven forbid that any here should say you nay. Over the realms which still acknowledge his sceptre, God save King George!"

Esther Dudley started to her feet, and, hastily clutching back the key, gazed with fearful earnestness at the stranger, and dimly and doubtfully, as if suddenly awakened from a dream, her bewildered eyes half recognized his face. Years ago she had known him among the gentry of the province, but the ban of the king had fallen upon him. How, then, came the doomed victim here? Proscribed, excluded from mercy, the monarch's most dreaded and hated foe, this New England merchant had stood triumphantly against a kingdom's strength, and his foot now trod upon humbled royalty as he ascended the steps of the province-house, the people's chosen governor of Massachusetts.

"Wretch, wretch that I am!" muttered the old woman, with such a heartbroken expression that the tears gushed from the stranger's eyes. "Have I bidden a traitor welcome?—Come, Death! come quickly!"

"Alas, venerable lady!" said Governor Hancock, lending her his support with all the reverence that a courtier would have shown to a queen, "your life has been prolonged until the world has changed around you. You have treasured up all that time has rendered worthless—the principles, feelings, manners, modes of being and acting which another generation has flung aside—and you are a symbol of the past. And I and these around me—we represent a new race of men, living no longer in the past, scarcely in the present, but projecting our lives forward into the future. Ceasing to model ourselves on ancestral superstitions, it is our faith and principle to press onward—onward.—Yet," continued he, turning to his attendants, "let us reverence for the last time the stately and gorgeous prejudices of the tottering past."

While the republican governor spoke he had continued to support the helpless form of Esther Dudley; her weight grew heavier against his arm, but at last, with a sudden effort to free herself, the ancient woman sank down beside one of the pillars of the portal. The key of the province-house fell from her grasp and clanked against the stone.

"I have been faithful unto death," murmured she. "God save the king!"

"She hath done her office," said Hancock, solemnly. "We will follow her reverently to the tomb of her ancestors, and then, my fellow-citizens, onward—onward. We are no longer children of the past."

As the old loyalist concluded his narrative the enthusiasm which had been fitfully flashing within his sunken eyes and quivering across his wrinkled visage faded away, as if all the lingering fire of his soul were extinguished. Just then, too, a lamp upon the mantelpiece threw out a dying gleam, which vanished as speedily as it shot upward, compelling our eyes to grope for one another's features by the dim glow of the hearth. With such a lingering fire, methought, with such a dying gleam, had the glory of the ancient system vanished from the province-house when the spirit of old Esther Dudley took its flight. And now, again, the clock of the Old South threw its voice of ages on the breeze, knolling the hourly knell of the past, crying out far and wide through the multitudinous city, and filling our ears, as we sat in the dusky chamber, with its reverberating depth of tone. In that same mansion—in that very chamber—what a volume of history had been told off into hours by the same voice that was now trembling in the air! Many a governor had heard those midnight accents and longed to exchange his stately cares for slumber. And, as for mine host and Mr. Bela Tiffany and the old loyalist and me, we had babbled about dreams of the past until we almost fancied that the clock was still striking in a bygone century. Neither of us would have wondered had a hoop-petticoated phantom of Esther Dudley tottered into the chamber, walking her rounds in the hush of midnight as of yore, and motioned us to quench the fading embers of the fire and leave the historic precincts to herself and her kindred shades. But, as no such vision was vouchsafed, I retired unbidden, and would advise Mr. Tiffany to lay hold of another auditor, being resolved not to show my face in the Province House for a good while hence—if ever.

THE HAUNTED MIND.

What a singular moment is the first one, when you have hardly begun to recollect yourself, after starting from midnight slumber! By unclosing your eyes so suddenly you seem to have surprised the personages of your dream in full convocation round your bed, and catch one broad glance at them before they can flit into obscurity. Or, to vary the metaphor, you find yourself for a single instant wide awake in that realm of illusions whither sleep has been the passport, and behold its ghostly inhabitants and wondrous scenery with a perception of their strangeness such as you never attain while the dream is undisturbed. The distant sound of a church-clock is borne faintly on the wind. You question with yourself, half seriously, whether it has stolen to your waking ear from some gray tower that stood within the precincts of your dream. While yet in suspense another clock flings its heavy clang over the slumbering town with so full and distinct a sound, and such a long murmur in the neighboring air, that you are certain it must proceed from the steeple at the nearest corner; You count the strokes—one, two; and there they cease with a booming sound like the gathering of a third stroke within the bell.

If you could choose an hour of wakefulness out of the whole night, it would be this. Since your sober bedtime, at eleven, you have had rest enough to take off the pressure of yesterday's fatigue, while before you, till the sun comes from "Far Cathay" to brighten your window, there is almost the space of a summer night—one hour to be spent in thought with the mind's eye half shut, and two in pleasant dreams, and two in that strangest of enjoyments the forgetfulness alike of joy and woe. The moment of rising belongs to another period of time, and appears so distant that the plunge out of a warm bed into the frosty air cannot yet be anticipated with dismay. Yesterday has already vanished among the shadows of the past; tomorrow has not yet emerged from the future. You have found an intermediate space where the business of life does not intrude, where the passing moment lingers and becomes truly the present; a spot where Father Time, when he thinks nobody is watching him, sits down by the wayside to take breath. Oh that he would fall asleep and let mortals live on without growing older!

Hitherto you have lain perfectly still, because the slightest motion would dissipate the fragments of your slumber. Now, being irrevocably awake, you peep through the half-drawn window-curtain, and observe that the glass is ornamented with fanciful devices in frost-work, and that each pane presents something like a frozen dream. There will be time enough to trace out the analogy while waiting the summons to breakfast. Seen through the clear portion of the glass where the silvery mountain-peaks of the frost-scenery do not ascend, the most conspicuous object is the steeple, the white spire of which directs you to the wintry lustre of the firmament. You may almost distinguish the figures on the clock that has just told the hour. Such a frosty sky and the snow-covered roofs and the long vista of the frozen street, all white, and the distant water hardened into rock, might make you shiver even under four blankets and a woollen comforter. Yet look at that one glorious star! Its beams are distinguishable from all the rest, and actually cast the shadow of the casement on the bed with a radiance of deeper hue than moonlight, though not so accurate an outline.

You sink down and muffle your head in the clothes, shivering all the while, but less from bodily chill than the bare idea of a polar atmosphere. It is too cold even for the thoughts to venture abroad. You speculate on the luxury of wearing out a whole existence in bed like an oyster in its shell, content with the sluggish ecstasy of inaction, and drowsily conscious of nothing but delicious warmth such as you now feel again. Ah! that idea has brought a hideous one in its train. You think how the dead are lying in their cold shrouds and narrow coffins through the drear winter of the grave, and cannot persuade your fancy that they neither shrink nor shiver when the snow is drifting over their little hillocks and the bitter blast howls against the door of the tomb. That gloomy thought will collect a gloomy multitude and throw its complexion over your wakeful hour.

In the depths of every heart there is a tomb and a dungeon, though the lights, the music and revelry, above may cause us to forget their existence and the buried ones or prisoners whom they hide. But sometimes, and oftenest at midnight, those dark receptacles are flung wide open. In an hour like this, when the mind has a passive sensibility, but no active strength—when the imagination is a mirror imparting vividness to all ideas without the power of selecting or controlling them—then pray that your griefs may slumber and the brotherhood of remorse not break their chain. It is too late. A funeral train comes gliding by your bed in which passion and feeling assume bodily shape and things of the mind become dim spectres to the eye. There is your earliest sorrow, a pale young mourner wearing a sister's likeness to first love, sadly beautiful, with a hallowed sweetness in her melancholy features and grace in the flow of her sable robe. Next appears a shade of ruined loveliness with dust among her golden hair and her bright garments all faded and defaced, stealing from your glance with drooping head, as fearful of reproach: she was your fondest hope, but a delusive one; so call her Disappointment now. A sterner form succeeds, with a brow of wrinkles, a look and gesture of iron authority; there is no name for him unless it be Fatality—an emblem of the evil influence that rules your fortunes, a demon to whom you subjected yourself by some error at the outset of life, and were bound his slave for ever by once obeying him. See those fiendish lineaments graven on the darkness, the writhed lip of scorn, the mockery of that living eye, the pointed finger touching the sore place in your heart! Do you remember any act of enormous folly at which you would blush even in the remotest cavern of the earth? Then recognize your shame.

Pass, wretched band! Well for the wakeful one if, riotously miserable, a fiercer tribe do not surround him—the devils of a guilty heart that holds its hell within itself. What if Remorse should assume the features of an injured friend? What if the fiend should come in woman's garments with a pale beauty amid sin and desolation, and lie down by your side? What if he should stand at your bed's foot in the likeness of a corpse with a bloody stain upon the shroud? Sufficient without such guilt is this nightmare of the soul, this heavy, heavy sinking of the spirits, this wintry gloom about the heart, this indistinct horror of the mind blending itself with the darkness of the chamber.

By a desperate effort you start upright, breaking from a sort of conscious sleep and gazing wildly round the bed, as if the fiends were anywhere but in your haunted mind. At the same moment the slumbering embers on the hearth send forth a gleam which palely illuminates the whole outer room and flickers through the door of the bedchamber, but cannot quite dispel its obscurity. Your eye searches for whatever may remind you of the living world. With eager minuteness you take note of the table near the fireplace, the book with an ivory knife between its leaves, the unfolded letter, the hat and the fallen glove. Soon the flame vanishes, and with it the whole scene is gone, though its image remains an instant in your mind's eye when darkness has swallowed the reality. Throughout the chamber there is the same obscurity as before, but not the same gloom within your breast.

As your head falls back upon the pillow you think—in a whisper be it spoken—how pleasant in these night solitudes would be the rise and fall of a softer breathing than your own, the slight pressure of a tenderer bosom, the quiet throb of a purer heart, imparting its peacefulness to your troubled one, as if the fond sleeper were involving you in her dream. Her influence is over you, though she have no existence but in that momentary image. You sink down in a flowery spot on the borders of sleep and wakefulness, while your thoughts rise before you in pictures, all disconnected, yet all assimilated by a pervading gladsomeness and beauty. The wheeling of gorgeous squadrons that glitter in the sun is succeeded by the merriment of children round the door of a schoolhouse beneath the glimmering shadow of old trees at the corner of a rustic lane. You stand in the sunny rain of a summer shower, and wander among the sunny trees of an autumnal wood, and look upward at the brightest of all rainbows overarching the unbroken sheet of snow on the American side of Niagara. Your mind struggles pleasantly between the dancing radiance round the hearth of a young man and his recent bride and the twittering flight of birds in spring about their new-made nest. You feel the merry bounding of a ship before the breeze, and watch the tuneful feet of rosy girls as they twine their last and merriest dance in a splendid ball-room, and find yourself in the brilliant circle of a crowded theatre as the curtain falls over a light and airy scene.

With an involuntary start you seize hold on consciousness, and prove yourself but half awake by running a doubtful parallel between human life and the hour which has now elapsed. In both you emerge from mystery, pass through a vicissitude that you can but imperfectly control, and are borne onward to another mystery. Now comes the peal of the distant clock with fainter and fainter strokes as you plunge farther into the wilderness of sleep. It is the knell of a temporary death. Your spirit has departed, and strays like a free citizen among the people of a shadowy world, beholding strange sights, yet without wonder or dismay. So calm, perhaps, will be the final change—so undisturbed, as if among familiar things, the entrance of the soul to its eternal home.

THE VILLAGE UNCLE.

AN IMAGINARY RETROSPECT.

Come! another log upon the hearth. True, our little parlor is comfortable, especially here where the old man sits in his old arm-chair; but on Thanksgiving-night the blaze should dance higher up the chimney and send a shower of sparks into the outer darkness. Toss on an armful of those dry oak chips, the last relicts of the Mermaid's knee-timbers—the bones of your namesake, Susan. Higher yet, and clearer, be the blaze, till our cottage windows glow the ruddiest in the village and the light of our household mirth flash far across the bay to Nahant.

And now come, Susan; come, my children. Draw your chairs round me, all of you. There is a dimness over your figures. You sit quivering indistinctly with each motion of the blaze, which eddies about you like a flood; so that you all have the look of visions or people that dwell only in the firelight, and will vanish from existence as completely as your own shadows when the flame shall sink among the embers.

Hark! let me listen for the swell of the surf; it should be audible a mile inland on a night like this. Yes; there I catch the sound, but only an uncertain murmur, as if a good way down over the beach, though by the almanac it is high tide at eight o'clock, and the billows must now be dashing within thirty yards of our door. Ah! the old man's ears are failing him, and so is his eyesight, and perhaps his mind, else you would not all be so shadowy in the blaze of his Thanksgiving fire.

How strangely the past is peeping over the shoulders of the present! To judge by my recollections, it is but a few moments since I sat in another room. Yonder model of a vessel was not there, nor the old chest of drawers, nor Susan's profile and mine in that gilt frame—nothing, in short, except this same fire, which glimmered on books, papers and a picture, and half discovered my solitary figure in a looking-glass. But it was paler than my rugged old self, and younger, too, by almost half a century.

Speak to me, Susan; speak, my beloved ones; for the scene is glimmering on my sight again, and as it brightens you fade away. Oh, I should be loth to lose my treasure of past happiness and become once more what I was then—a hermit in the depths of my own mind, sometimes yawning over drowsy volumes and anon a scribbler of wearier trash than what I read; a man who had wandered out of the real world and got into its shadow, where his troubles, joys and vicissitudes were of such slight stuff that he hardly knew whether he lived or only dreamed of living. Thank Heaven I am an old man now and have done with all such vanities!

Still this dimness of mine eyes!—Come nearer, Susan, and stand before the fullest blaze of the hearth. Now I behold you illuminated from head to foot, in your clean cap and decent gown, with the dear lock of gray hair across your forehead and a quiet smile about your mouth, while the eyes alone are concealed by the red gleam of the fire upon your spectacles. There! you made me tremble again. When the flame quivered, my sweet Susan, you quivered with it and grew indistinct, as if melting into the warm light, that my last glimpse of you might be as visionary as the first was, full many a year since. Do you remember it? You stood on the little bridge over the brook that runs across King's Beach into the sea. It was twilight, the waves rolling in, the wind sweeping by, the crimson clouds fading in the west and the silver moon brightening above the hill; and on the bridge were you, fluttering in the breeze like a sea-bird that might skim away at your pleasure. You seemed a daughter of the viewless wind, a creature of the ocean-foam and the crimson light, whose merry life was spent in dancing on the crests of the billows that threw up their spray to support your footsteps. As I drew nearer I fancied you akin to the race of mermaids, and thought how pleasant it would be to dwell with you among the quiet coves in the shadow of the cliffs, and to roam along secluded beaches of the purest sand, and, when our Northern shores grew bleak, to haunt the islands, green and lonely, far amid summer seas. And yet it gladdened me, after all this nonsense, to find you nothing but a pretty young girl sadly perplexed with the rude behavior of the wind about your petticoats. Thus I did with Susan as with most other things in my earlier days, dipping her image into my mind and coloring it of a thousand fantastic hues before I could see her as she really was.

Now, Susan, for a sober picture of our village. It was a small collection of dwellings that seemed to have been cast up by the sea with the rock-weed and marine plants that it vomits after a storm, or to have come ashore among the pipe-staves and other lumber which had been washed from the deck of an Eastern schooner. There was just space for the narrow and sandy street between the beach in front and a precipitous hill that lifted its rocky forehead in the rear among a waste of juniper-bushes and the wild growth of a broken pasture. The village was picturesque in the variety of its edifices, though all were rude. Here stood a little old hovel, built, perhaps, of driftwood, there a row of boat-houses, and beyond them a two-story dwelling of dark and weatherbeaten aspect, the whole intermixed with one or two snug cottages painted white, a sufficiency of pig-styes and a shoemaker's shop. Two grocery stores stood opposite each other in the centre of the village. These were the places of resort at their idle hours of a hardy throng of fishermen in red baize shirts, oilcloth trousers and boots of brown leather covering the whole leg—true seven-league boots, but fitter to wade the ocean than walk the earth. The wearers seemed amphibious, as if they did but creep out of salt water to sun themselves; nor would it have been wonderful to see their lower limbs covered with clusters of little shellfish such as cling to rocks and old ship-timber over which the tide ebbs and flows. When their fleet of boats was weather-bound, the butchers raised their price, and the spit was busier than the frying-pan; for this was a place of fish, and known as such to all the country round about. The very air was fishy, being perfumed with dead sculpins, hard-heads and dogfish strewn plentifully on the beach.—You see, children, the village is but little changed since your mother and I were young.

How like a dream it was when I bent over a pool of water one pleasant morning and saw that the ocean had dashed its spray over me and made me a fisherman! There was the tarpaulin, the baize shirt, the oilcloth trousers and seven-league boots, and there my own features, but so reddened with sunburn and sea-breezes that methought I had another face, and on other shoulders too. The seagulls and the loons and I had now all one trade: we skimmed the crested waves and sought our prey beneath them, the man with as keen enjoyment as the birds. Always when the east grew purple I launched my dory, my little flat-bottomed skiff, and rowed cross-handed to Point Ledge, the Middle Ledge, or perhaps beyond Egg Rock; often, too, did I anchor off Dread Ledge—a spot of peril to ships unpiloted—and sometimes spread an adventurous sail and tracked across the bay to South Shore, casting my lines in sight of Scituate. Ere nightfall I hauled my skiff high and dry on the beach, laden with red rock-cod or the white-bellied ones of deep water, haddock bearing the black marks of St. Peter's fingers near the gills, the long-bearded hake whose liver holds oil enough for a midnight lamp, and now and then a mighty halibut with a back broad as my boat. In the autumn I toled and caught those lovely fish the mackerel. When the wind was high, when the whale-boats anchored off the Point nodded their slender masts at each other and the dories pitched and tossed in the surf, when Nahant Beach was thundering three miles off and the spray broke a hundred feet in the air round the distant base of Egg Rock, when the brimful and boisterous sea threatened to tumble over the street of our village,—then I made a holiday on shore.

Many such a day did I sit snugly in Mr. Bartlett's store, attentive to the yarns of Uncle Parker—uncle to the whole village by right of seniority, but of Southern blood, with no kindred in New England. His figure is before me now enthroned upon a mackerel-barrel—a lean old man of great height, but bent with years and twisted into an uncouth shape by seven broken limbs; furrowed, also, and weatherworn, as if every gale for the better part of a century had caught him somewhere on the sea. He looked like a harbinger of tempest—a shipmate of the Flying Dutchman. After innumerable voyages aboard men-of-war and merchantmen, fishing-schooners and chebacco-boats, the old salt had become master of a hand-cart, which he daily trundled about the vicinity, and sometimes blew his fish-horn through the streets of Salem. One of Uncle Parker's eyes had been blown out with gunpowder, and the other did but glimmer in its socket. Turning it upward as he spoke, it was his delight to tell of cruises against the French and battles with his own shipmates, when he and an antagonist used to be seated astride of a sailor's chest, each fastened down by a spike-nail through his trousers, and there to fight it out. Sometimes he expatiated on the delicious flavor of the hagden, a greasy and goose-like fowl which the sailors catch with hook and line on the Grand Banks. He dwelt with rapture on an interminable winter at the Isle of Sables, where he had gladdened himself amid polar snows with the rum and sugar saved from the wreck of a West India schooner. And wrathfully did he shake his fist as he related how a party of Cape Cod men had robbed him and his companions of their lawful spoils and sailed away with every keg of old Jamaica, leaving him not a drop to drown his sorrow. Villains they were, and of that wicked brotherhood who are said to tie lanterns to horses' tails to mislead the mariner along the dangerous shores of the Cape.

Even now I seem to see the group of fishermen with that old salt in the midst. One fellow sits on the counter, a second bestrides an oil-barrel, a third lolls at his length on a parcel of new cod-lines, and another has planted the tarry seat of his trousers on a heap of salt which will shortly be sprinkled over a lot of fish. They are a likely set of men. Some have voyaged to the East Indies or the Pacific, and most of them have sailed in Marblehead schooners to Newfoundland; a few have been no farther than the Middle Banks, and one or two have always fished along the shore; but, as Uncle Parker used to say, they have all been christened in salt water and know more than men ever learn in the bushes. A curious figure, by way of contrast, is a fish-dealer from far up-country listening with eyes wide open to narratives that might startle Sinbad the Sailor.—Be it well with you, my brethren! Ye are all gone—some to your graves ashore and others to the depths of ocean—but my faith is strong that ye are happy; for whenever I behold your forms, whether in dream or vision, each departed friend is puffing his long nine, and a mug of the right blackstrap goes round from lip to lip.

But where was the mermaid in those delightful times? At a certain window near the centre of the village appeared a pretty display of gingerbread men and horses, picture-books and ballads, small fish-hooks, pins, needles, sugarplums and brass thimbles—articles on which the young fishermen used to expend their money from pure gallantry. What a picture was Susan behind the counter! A slender maiden, though the child of rugged parents, she had the slimmest of all waists, brown hair curling on her neck, and a complexion rather pale except when the sea-breeze flushed it. A few freckles became beauty-spots beneath her eyelids.—How was it, Susan, that you talked and acted so carelessly, yet always for the best, doing whatever was right in your own eyes, and never once doing wrong in mine, nor shocked a taste that had been morbidly sensitive till now? And whence had you that happiest gift of brightening every topic with an unsought gayety, quiet but irresistible, so that even gloomy spirits felt your sunshine and did not shrink from it? Nature wrought the charm. She made you a frank, simple, kind-hearted, sensible and mirthful girl. Obeying Nature, you did free things without indelicacy, displayed a maiden's thoughts to every eye, and proved yourself as innocent as naked Eve.—It was beautiful to observe how her simple and happy nature mingled itself with mine. She kindled a domestic fire within my heart and took up her dwelling there, even in that chill and lonesome cavern hung round with glittering icicles of fancy. She gave me warmth of feeling, while the influence of my mind made her contemplative. I taught her to love the moonlight hour, when the expanse of the encircled bay was smooth as a great mirror and slept in a transparent shadow, while beyond Nahant the wind rippled the dim ocean into a dreamy brightness which grew faint afar off without becoming gloomier. I held her hand and pointed to the long surf-wave as it rolled calmly on the beach in an unbroken line of silver; we were silent together till its deep and peaceful murmur had swept by us. When the Sabbath sun shone down into the recesses of the cliffs, I led the mermaid thither and told her that those huge gray, shattered rocks, and her native sea that raged for ever like a storm against them, and her own slender beauty in so stern a scene, were all combined into a strain of poetry. But on the Sabbath-eve, when her mother had gone early to bed and her gentle sister had smiled and left us, as we sat alone by the quiet hearth with household things around, it was her turn to make me feel that here was a deeper poetry, and that this was the dearest hour of all. Thus went on our wooing, till I had shot wild-fowl enough to feather our bridal-bed, and the daughter of the sea was mine.

I built a cottage for Susan and myself, and made a gateway in the form of a Gothic arch by setting up a whale's jaw-bones. We bought a heifer with her first calf, and had a little garden on the hillside to supply us with potatoes and green sauce for our fish. Our parlor, small and neat, was ornamented with our two profiles in one gilt frame, and with shells and pretty pebbles on the mantelpiece, selected from the sea's treasury of such things on Nahant Beach. On the desk, beneath the looking-glass, lay the Bible, which I had begun to read aloud at the book of Genesis, and the singing-book that Susan used for her evening psalm. Except the almanac, we had no other literature. All that I heard of books was when an Indian history or tale of shipwreck was sold by a pedler or wandering subscription-man to some one in the village, and read through its owner's nose to a slumbrous auditory.

Like my brother-fishermen, I grew into the belief that all human erudition was collected in our pedagogue, whose green spectacles and solemn phiz as he passed to his little schoolhouse amid a waste of sand might have gained him a diploma from any college in New England. In truth, I dreaded him.—When our children were old enough to claim his care, you remember, Susan, how I frowned, though you were pleased at this learned man's encomiums on their proficiency. I feared to trust them even with the alphabet: it was the key to a fatal treasure. But I loved to lead them by their little hands along the beach and point to nature in the vast and the minute—the sky, the sea, the green earth, the pebbles and the shells. Then did I discourse of the mighty works and coextensive goodness of the Deity with the simple wisdom of a man whose mind had profited by lonely days upon the deep and his heart by the strong and pure affections of his evening home. Sometimes my voice lost itself in a tremulous depth, for I felt his eye upon me as I spoke. Once, while my wife and all of us were gazing at ourselves in the mirror left by the tide in a hollow of the sand, I pointed to the pictured heaven below and bade her observe how religion was strewn everywhere in our path, since even a casual pool of water recalled the idea of that home whither we were travelling to rest for ever with our children. Suddenly your image, Susan, and all the little faces made up of yours and mine, seemed to fade away and vanish around me, leaving a pale visage like my own of former days within the frame of a large looking-glass. Strange illusion!

My life glided on, the past appearing to mingle with the present and absorb the future, till the whole lies before me at a glance. My manhood has long been waning with a stanch decay; my earlier contemporaries, after lives of unbroken health, are all at rest without having known the weariness of later age; and now with a wrinkled forehead and thin white hair as badges of my dignity I have become the patriarch—the uncle—of the village. I love that name: it widens the circle of my sympathies; it joins all the youthful to my household in the kindred of affection.

Like Uncle Parker, whose rheumatic bones were dashed against Egg Rock full forty years ago, I am a spinner of long yarns. Seated on the gunnel of a dory or on the sunny side of a boat-house, where the warmth is grateful to my limbs, or by my own hearth when a friend or two are there, I overflow with talk, and yet am never tedious. With a broken voice I give utterance to much wisdom. Such, Heaven be praised! is the vigor of my faculties that many a forgotten usage, and traditions ancient in my youth, and early adventures of myself or others hitherto effaced by things more recent, acquire new distinctness in my memory. I remember the happy days when the haddock were more numerous on all the fishing-grounds than sculpins in the surf—when the deep-water cod swam close in-shore, and the dogfish, with his poisonous horn, had not learnt to take the hook. I can number every equinoctial storm in which the sea has overwhelmed the street, flooded the cellars of the village and hissed upon our kitchen hearth. I give the history of the great whale that was landed on Whale Beach, and whose jaws, being now my gateway, will last for ages after my coffin shall have passed beneath them. Thence it is an easy digression to the halibut—scarcely smaller than the whale—which ran out six codlines and hauled my dory to the mouth of Boston harbor before I could touch him with the gaff.

If melancholy accidents be the theme of conversation, I tell how a friend of mine was taken out of his boat by an enormous shark, and the sad, true tale of a young man on the eve of marriage who had been nine days missing, when his drowned body floated into the very pathway on Marble-head Neck that had often led him to the dwelling of his bride, as if the dripping corpse would have come where the mourner was. With such awful fidelity did that lover return to fulfil his vows! Another favorite story is of a crazy maiden who conversed with angels and had the gift of prophecy, and whom all the village loved and pitied, though she went from door to door accusing us of sin, exhorting to repentance and foretelling our destruction by flood or earthquake. If the young men boast their knowledge of the ledges and sunken rocks, I speak of pilots who knew the wind by its scent and the wave by its taste, and could have steered blindfold to any port between Boston and Mount Desert guided only by the rote of the shore—the peculiar sound of the surf on each island, beach and line of rocks along the coast. Thus do I talk, and all my auditors grow wise while they deem it pastime.

I recollect no happier portion of my life than this my calm old age. It is like the sunny and sheltered slope of a valley where late in the autumn the grass is greener than in August, and intermixed with golden dandelions that had not been seen till now since the first warmth of the year. But with me the verdure and the flowers are not frost-bitten in the midst of winter. A playfulness has revisited my mind—a sympathy with the young and gay, an unpainful interest in the business of others, a light and wandering curiosity—arising, perhaps, from the sense that my toil on earth is ended and the brief hour till bedtime may be spent in play. Still, I have fancied that there is a depth of feeling and reflection under this superficial levity peculiar to one who has lived long and is soon to die.

Show me anything that would make an infant smile, and you shall behold a gleam of mirth over the hoary ruin of my visage. I can spend a pleasant hour in the sun watching the sports of the village children on the edge of the surf. Now they chase the retreating wave far down over the wet sand; now it steals softly up to kiss their naked feet; now it comes onward with threatening front, and roars after the laughing crew as they scamper beyond its reach. Why should not an old man be merry too, when the great sea is at play with those little children? I delight, also, to follow in the wake of a pleasure-party of young men and girls strolling along the beach after an early supper at the Point. Here, with handkerchiefs at nose, they bend over a heap of eel-grass entangled in which is a dead skate so oddly accoutred with two legs and a long tail that they mistake him for a drowned animal. A few steps farther the ladies scream, and the gentlemen make ready to protect them against a young shark of the dogfish kind rolling with a lifelike motion in the tide that has thrown him up. Next they are smit with wonder at the black shells of a wagon-load of live lobsters packed in rock-weed for the country-market. And when they reach the fleet of dories just hauled ashore after the day's fishing, how do I laugh in my sleeve, and sometimes roar outright, at the simplicity of these young folks and the sly humor of the fishermen! In winter, when our village is thrown into a bustle by the arrival of perhaps a score of country dealers bargaining for frozen fish to be transported hundreds of miles and eaten fresh in Vermont or Canada, I am a pleased but idle spectator in the throng. For I launch my boat no more.

When the shore was solitary, I have found a pleasure that seemed even to exalt my mind in observing the sports or contentions of two gulls as they wheeled and hovered about each other with hoarse screams, one moment flapping on the foam of the wave, and then soaring aloft till their white bosoms melted into the upper sunshine. In the calm of the summer sunset I drag my aged limbs with a little ostentation of activity, because I am so old, up to the rocky brow of the hill. There I see the white sails of many a vessel outward bound or homeward from afar, and the black trail of a vapor behind the Eastern steamboat; there, too, is the sun, going down, but not in gloom, and there the illimitable ocean mingling with the sky, to remind me of eternity.

But sweetest of all is the hour of cheerful musing and pleasant talk that comes between the dusk and the lighted candle by my glowing fireside. And never, even on the first Thanksgiving-night, when Susan and I sat alone with our hopes, nor the second, when a stranger had been sent to gladden us and be the visible image of our affection, did I feel such joy as now. All that belongs to me are here: Death has taken none, nor Disease kept them away, nor Strife divided them from their parents or each other; with neither poverty nor riches to disturb them, nor the misery of desires beyond their lot, they have kept New England's festival round the patriarch's board. For I am a patriarch. Here I sit among my descendants, in my old arm-chair and immemorial corner, while the firelight throws an appropriate glory round my venerable frame.—Susan! My children! Something whispers me that this happiest hour must be the final one, and that nothing remains but to bless you all and depart with a treasure of recollected joys to heaven. Will you meet me there? Alas! your figures grow indistinct, fading into pictures on the air, and now to fainter outlines, while the fire is glimmering on the walls of a familiar room, and shows the book that I flung down and the sheet that I left half written some fifty years ago. I lift my eyes to the looking-glass, and perceive myself alone, unless those be the mermaid's features retiring into the depths of the mirror with a tender and melancholy smile.

Ah! One feels a chilliness—not bodily, but about the heart—and, moreover, a foolish dread of looking behind him, after these pastimes. I can imagine precisely how a magician would sit down in gloom and terror after dismissing the shadows that had personated dead or distant people and stripping his cavern of the unreal splendor which had changed it to a palace.

And now for a moral to my reverie. Shall it be that, since fancy can create so bright a dream of happiness, it were better to dream on from youth to age than to awake and strive doubtfully for something real? Oh, the slight tissue of a dream can no more preserve us from the stern reality of misfortune than a robe of cobweb could repel the wintry blast. Be this the moral, then: In chaste and warm affections, humble wishes and honest toil for some useful end there is health for the mind and quiet for the heart, the prospect of a happy life and the fairest hope of heaven.

THE AMBITIOUS GUEST.

One September night a family had gathered round their hearth and piled it high with the driftwood of mountain-streams, the dry cones of the pine, and the splintered ruins of great trees that had come crashing down the precipice. Up the chimney roared the fire, and brightened the room with its broad blaze. The faces of the father and mother had a sober gladness; the children laughed. The eldest daughter was the image of Happiness at seventeen, and the aged grandmother, who sat knitting in the warmest place, was the image of Happiness grown old. They had found the "herb heart's-ease" in the bleakest spot of all New England. This family were situated in the Notch of the White Hills, where the wind was sharp throughout the year and pitilessly cold in the winter, giving their cottage all its fresh inclemency before it descended on the valley of the Saco. They dwelt in a cold spot and a dangerous one, for a mountain towered above their heads so steep that the stones would often rumble down its sides and startle them at midnight.

The daughter had just uttered some simple jest that filled them all with mirth, when the wind came through the Notch and seemed to pause before their cottage, rattling the door with a sound of wailing and lamentation before it passed into the valley. For a moment it saddened them, though there was nothing unusual in the tones. But the family were glad again when they perceived that the latch was lifted by some traveller whose footsteps had been unheard amid the dreary blast which heralded his approach and wailed as he was entering and went moaning away from the door.

Though they dwelt in such a solitude, these people held daily converse with the world. The romantic pass of the Notch is a great artery through which the lifeblood of internal commerce is continually throbbing between Maine on one side and the Green Mountains and the shores of the St. Lawrence on the other. The stage-coach always drew up before the door of the cottage. The wayfarer with no companion but his staff paused here to exchange a word, that the sense of loneliness might not utterly overcome him ere he could pass through the cleft of the mountain or reach the first house in the valley. And here the teamster on his way to Portland market would put up for the night, and, if a bachelor, might sit an hour beyond the usual bedtime and steal a kiss from the mountain-maid at parting. It was one of those primitive taverns where the traveller pays only for food and lodging, but meets with a homely kindness beyond all price. When the footsteps were heard, therefore, between the outer door and the inner one, the whole family rose up, grandmother, children and all, as if about to welcome some one who belonged to them, and whose fate was linked with theirs.

The door was opened by a young man. His face at first wore the melancholy expression, almost despondency, of one who travels a wild and bleak road at nightfall and alone, but soon brightened up when he saw the kindly warmth of his reception. He felt his heart spring forward to meet them all, from the old woman who wiped a chair with her apron to the little child that held out its arms to him. One glance and smile placed the stranger on a footing of innocent familiarity with the eldest daughter.

"Ah! this fire is the right thing," cried he, "especially when there is such a pleasant circle round it. I am quite benumbed, for the Notch is just like the pipe of a great pair of bellows; it has blown a terrible blast in my face all the way from Bartlett."

"Then you are going toward Vermont?" said the master of the house as he helped to take a light knapsack off the young man's shoulders.

"Yes, to Burlington, and far enough beyond," replied he. "I meant to have been at Ethan Crawford's to-night, but a pedestrian lingers along such a road as this. It is no matter; for when I saw this good fire and all your cheerful faces, I felt as if you had kindled it on purpose for me and were waiting my arrival. So I shall sit down among you and make myself at home."

The frank-hearted stranger had just drawn his chair to the fire when something like a heavy footstep was heard without, rushing down the steep side of the mountain as with long and rapid strides, and taking such a leap in passing the cottage as to strike the opposite precipice. The family held their breath, because they knew the sound, and their guest held his by instinct.

"The old mountain has thrown a stone at us for fear we should forget him," said the landlord, recovering himself. "He sometimes nods his head and threatens to come down, but we are old neighbors, and agree together pretty well, upon the whole. Besides, we have a sure place of refuge hard by if he should be coming in good earnest."

Let us now suppose the stranger to have finished his supper of bear's meat, and by his natural felicity of manner to have placed himself on a footing of kindness with the whole family; so that they talked as freely together as if he belonged to their mountain-brood. He was of a proud yet gentle spirit, haughty and reserved among the rich and great, but ever ready to stoop his head to the lowly cottage door and be like a brother or a son at the poor man's fireside. In the household of the Notch he found warmth and simplicity of feeling, the pervading intelligence of New England, and a poetry of native growth which they had gathered when they little thought of it from the mountain-peaks and chasms, and at the very threshold of their romantic and dangerous abode. He had travelled far and alone; his whole life, indeed, had been a solitary path, for, with the lofty caution of his nature, he had kept himself apart from those who might otherwise have been his companions. The family, too, though so kind and hospitable, had that consciousness of unity among themselves and separation from the world at large which in every domestic circle should still keep a holy place where no stranger may intrude. But this evening a prophetic sympathy impelled the refined and educated youth to pour out his heart before the simple mountaineers, and constrained them to answer him with the same free confidence. And thus it should have been. Is not the kindred of a common fate a closer tie than that of birth?

The secret of the young man's character was a high and abstracted ambition. He could have borne to live an undistinguished life, but not to be forgotten in the grave. Yearning desire had been transformed to hope, and hope, long cherished, had become like certainty that, obscurely as he journeyed now, a glory was to beam on all his pathway, though not, perhaps, while he was treading it. But when posterity should gaze back into the gloom of what was now the present, they would trace the brightness of his footsteps, brightening as meaner glories faded, and confess that a gifted one had passed from his cradle to his tomb with none to recognize him.

"As yet," cried the stranger, his cheek glowing and his eye flashing with enthusiasm—"as yet I have done nothing. Were I to vanish from the earth tomorrow, none would know so much of me as you—that a nameless youth came up at nightfall from the valley of the Saco, and opened his heart to you in the evening, and passed through the Notch by sunrise, and was seen no more. Not a soul would ask, 'Who was he? Whither did the wanderer go?' But I cannot die till I have achieved my destiny. Then let Death come: I shall have built my monument."

There was a continual flow of natural emotion gushing forth amid abstracted reverie which enabled the family to understand this young man's sentiments, though so foreign from their own. With quick sensibility of the ludicrous, he blushed at the ardor into which he had been betrayed.

"You laugh at me," said he, taking the eldest daughter's hand and laughing himself. "You think my ambition as nonsensical as if I were to freeze myself to death on the top of Mount Washington only that people might spy at me from the country roundabout. And truly that would be a noble pedestal for a man's statue."

"It is better to sit here by this fire," answered the girl, blushing, "and be comfortable and contented, though nobody thinks about us."

"I suppose," said her father, after a fit of musing, "there is something natural in what the young man says; and if my mind had been turned that way, I might have felt just the same.—It is strange, wife, how his talk has set my head running on things that are pretty certain never to come to pass."

"Perhaps they may," observed the wife. "Is the man thinking what he will do when he is a widower?"

"No, no!" cried he, repelling the idea with reproachful kindness. "When I think of your death, Esther, I think of mine too. But I was wishing we had a good farm in Bartlett or Bethlehem or Littleton, or some other township round the White Mountains, but not where they could tumble on our heads. I should want to stand well with my neighbors and be called squire and sent to General Court for a term or two; for a plain, honest man may do as much good there as a lawyer. And when I should be grown quite an old man, and you an old woman, so as not to be long apart, I might die happy enough in my bed, and leave you all crying around me. A slate gravestone would suit me as well as a marble one, with just my name and age, and a verse of a hymn, and something to let people know that I lived an honest man and died a Christian."

"There, now!" exclaimed the stranger; "it is our nature to desire a monument, be it slate or marble, or a pillar of granite, or a glorious memory in the universal heart of man."

"We're in a strange way to-night," said the wife, with tears in her eyes. "They say it's a sign of something when folks' minds go a-wandering so. Hark to the children!"

They listened accordingly. The younger children had been put to bed in another room, but with an open door between; so that they could be heard talking busily among themselves. One and all seemed to have caught the infection from the fireside circle, and were outvying each other in wild wishes and childish projects of what they would do when they came to be men and women. At length a little boy, instead of addressing his brothers and sisters, called out to his mother.

"I'll tell you what I wish, mother," cried he: "I want you and father and grandma'm, and all of us, and the stranger too, to start right away and go and take a drink out of the basin of the Flume."

Nobody could help laughing at the child's notion of leaving a warm bed and dragging them from a cheerful fire to visit the basin of the Flume—a brook which tumbles over the precipice deep within the Notch.

The boy had hardly spoken, when a wagon rattled along the road and stopped a moment before the door. It appeared to contain two or three men who were cheering their hearts with the rough chorus of a song which resounded in broken notes between the cliffs, while the singers hesitated whether to continue their journey or put up here for the night.

"Father," said the girl, "they are calling you by name."

But the good man doubted whether they had really called him, and was unwilling to show himself too solicitous of gain by inviting people to patronize his house. He therefore did not hurry to the door, and, the lash being soon applied, the travellers plunged into the Notch, still singing and laughing, though their music and mirth came back drearily from the heart of the mountain.

"There, mother!" cried the boy, again; "they'd have given us a ride to the Flume."

Again they laughed at the child's pertinacious fancy for a night-ramble. But it happened that a light cloud passed over the daughter's spirit; she looked gravely into the fire and drew a breath that was almost a sigh. It forced its way, in spite of a little struggle to repress it. Then, starting and blushing, she looked quickly around the circle, as if they had caught a glimpse into her bosom. The stranger asked what she had been thinking of.

"Nothing," answered she, with a downcast smile; "only I felt lonesome just then."

"Oh, I have always had a gift of feeling what is in other people's hearts," said he, half seriously. "Shall I tell the secrets of yours? For I know what to think when a young girl shivers by a warm hearth and complains of lonesomeness at her mother's side. Shall I put these feelings into words?"

"They would not be a girl's feelings any longer if they could be put into words," replied the mountain-nymph, laughing, but avoiding his eye.

All this was said apart. Perhaps a germ of love was springing in their hearts so pure that it might blossom in Paradise, since it could not be matured on earth; for women worship such gentle dignity as his, and the proud, contemplative, yet kindly, soul is oftenest captivated by simplicity like hers. But while they spoke softly, and he was watching the happy sadness, the lightsome shadows, the shy yearnings, of a maiden's nature, the wind through the Notch took a deeper and drearier sound. It seemed, as the fanciful stranger said, like the choral strain of the spirits of the blast who in old Indian times had their dwelling among these mountains and made their heights and recesses a sacred region. There was a wail along the road as if a funeral were passing. To chase away the gloom, the family threw pine-branches on their fire till the dry leaves crackled and the flame arose, discovering once again a scene of peace and humble happiness. The light hovered about them fondly and caressed them all. There were the little faces of the children peeping from their bed apart, and here the father's frame of strength, the mother's subdued and careful mien, the high-browed youth, the budding girl and the good old grandam, still knitting in the warmest place.

The aged woman looked up from her task, and with fingers ever busy was the next to speak.

"Old folks have their notions," said she, "as well as young ones. You've been wishing and planning and letting your heads run on one thing and another till you've set my mind a-wandering too. Now, what should an old woman wish for, when she can go but a step or two before she comes to her grave? Children, it will haunt me night and day till I tell you."

"What is it, mother?" cried the husband and wife at once.

Then the old woman, with an air of mystery which drew the circle closer round the fire, informed them that she had provided her grave-clothes some years before—a nice linen shroud, a cap with a muslin ruff, and everything of a finer sort than she had worn since her wedding-day. But this evening an old superstition had strangely recurred to her. It used to be said in her younger days that if anything were amiss with a corpse—if only the ruff were not smooth or the cap did not set right—the corpse, in the coffin and beneath the clods, would strive to put up its cold hands and arrange it. The bare thought made her nervous.

"Don't talk so, grandmother," said the girl, shuddering.

"Now," continued the old woman, with singular earnestness, yet smiling strangely at her own folly, "I want one of you, my children, when your mother is dressed and in the coffin,—I want one of you to hold a looking-glass over my face. Who knows but I may take a glimpse at myself and see whether all's right?"

"Old and young, we dream of graves and monuments," murmured the stranger-youth. "I wonder how mariners feel when the ship is sinking and they, unknown and undistinguished, are to be buried together in the ocean, that wide and nameless sepulchre?"

For a moment the old woman's ghastly conception so engrossed the minds of her hearers that a sound abroad in the night, rising like the roar of a blast, had grown broad, deep and terrible before the fated group were conscious of it. The house and all within it trembled; the foundations of the earth seemed to be shaken, as if this awful sound were the peal of the last trump. Young and old exchanged one wild glance and remained an instant pale, affrighted, without utterance or power to move. Then the same shriek burst simultaneously from all their lips:

"The slide! The slide!"

The simplest words must intimate, but not portray, the unutterable horror of the catastrophe. The victims rushed from their cottage and sought refuge in what they deemed a safer spot, where, in contemplation of such an emergency, a sort of barrier had been reared. Alas! they had quitted their security and fled right into the pathway of destruction. Down came the whole side of the mountain in a cataract of ruin. Just before it reached the house the stream broke into two branches, shivered not a window there, but overwhelmed the whole vicinity, blocked up the road and annihilated everything in its dreadful course. Long ere the thunder of that great slide had ceased to roar among the mountains the mortal agony had been endured and the victims were at peace. Their bodies were never found.

The next morning the light smoke was seen stealing from the cottage chimney up the mountain-side. Within, the fire was yet smouldering on the hearth, and the chairs in a circle round it, as if the inhabitants had but gone forth to view the devastation of the slide and would shortly return to thank Heaven for their miraculous escape. All had left separate tokens by which those who had known the family were made to shed a tear for each. Who has not heard their name? The story has been told far and wide, and will for ever be a legend of these mountains. Poets have sung their fate.

There were circumstances which led some to suppose that a stranger had been received into the cottage on this awful night, and had shared the catastrophe of all its inmates; others denied that there were sufficient grounds for such a conjecture. Woe for the high-souled youth with his dream of earthly immortality! His name and person utterly unknown, his history, his way of life, his plans, a mystery never to be solved, his death and his existence equally a doubt,—whose was the agony of that death-moment?

THE SISTER-YEARS.

Last night, between eleven and twelve o'clock, when the Old Year was leaving her final footprints on the borders of Time's empire, she found herself in possession of a few spare moments, and sat down—of all places in the world—on the steps of our new city-hall. The wintry moonlight showed that she looked weary of body and sad of heart, like many another wayfarer of earth. Her garments, having been exposed to much foul weather and rough usage, were in very ill condition, and, as the hurry of her journey had never before allowed her to take an instant's rest, her shoes were so worn as to be scarcely worth the mending. But after trudging only a little distance farther this poor Old Year was destined to enjoy a long, long sleep. I forgot to mention that when she seated herself on the steps she deposited by her side a very capacious bandbox in which, as is the custom among travellers of her sex, she carried a great deal of valuable property. Besides this luggage, there was a folio book under her arm very much resembling the annual volume of a newspaper. Placing this volume across her knees and resting her elbows upon it, with her forehead in her hands, the weary, bedraggled, world-worn Old Year heaved a heavy sigh and appeared to be taking no very pleasant retrospect of her past existence.

While she thus awaited the midnight knell that was to summon her to the innumerable sisterhood of departed years, there came a young maiden treading lightsomely on tip-toe along the street from the direction of the railroad dépôt. She was evidently a stranger, and perhaps had come to town by the evening train of cars. There was a smiling cheerfulness in this fair maiden's face which bespoke her fully confident of a kind reception from the multitude of people with whom she was soon to form acquaintance. Her dress was rather too airy for the season, and was bedizened with fluttering ribbons and other vanities which were likely soon to be rent away by the fierce storms or to fade in the hot sunshine amid which she was to pursue her changeful course. But still she was a wonderfully pleasant-looking figure, and had so much promise and such an indescribable hopefulness in her aspect that hardly anybody could meet her without anticipating some very desirable thing—the consummation of some long-sought good—from her kind offices. A few dismal characters there may be here and there about the world who have so often been trifled with by young maidens as promising as she that they have now ceased to pin any faith upon the skirts of the New Year. But, for my own part, I have great faith in her, and, should I live to see fifty more such, still from each of those successive sisters I shall reckon upon receiving something that will be worth living for.

The New Year—for this young maiden was no less a personage—carried all her goods and chattels in a basket of no great size or weight, which hung upon her arm. She greeted the disconsolate Old Year with great affection, and sat down beside her on the steps of the city-hall, waiting for the signal to begin her rambles through the world. The two were own sisters, being both granddaughters of Time, and, though one looked so much older than the other, it was rather owing to hardships and trouble than to age, since there was but a twelvemonth's difference between them.

"Well, my dear sister," said the New Year, after the first salutations, "you look almost tired to death. What have you been about during your sojourn in this part of infinite space?"

"Oh, I have it all recorded here in my book of chronicles," answered the Old Year, in a heavy tone. "There is nothing that would amuse you, and you will soon get sufficient knowledge of such matters from your own personal experience. It is but tiresome reading."

Nevertheless, she turned over the leaves of the folio and glanced at them by the light of the moon, feeling an irresistible spell of interest in her own biography, although its incidents were remembered without pleasure. The volume, though she termed it her book of chronicles, seemed to be neither more nor less than the Salem *Gazette* for 1838; in the accuracy of which journal this sagacious Old Year had so much confidence that she deemed it needless to record her history with her own pen.

"What have you been doing in the political way?" asked the New Year.

"Why, my course here in the United States," said the Old Year—"though perhaps I ought to blush at the confession—my political course, I must acknowledge, has been rather vacillatory, sometimes inclining toward the Whigs, then causing the administration party to shout for triumph, and now again uplifting what seemed the almost prostrate banner of the opposition; so that historians will hardly know what to make of me in this respect. But the Loco-Focos—"

"I do not like these party nicknames," interrupted her sister, who seemed remarkably touchy about some points. "Perhaps we shall part in better humor if we avoid any political discussion."

"With all my heart," replied the Old Year, who had already been tormented half to death with squabbles of this kind. "I care not if the name of Whig or Tory, with their interminable brawls about banks and the sub-treasury, abolition, Texas, the Florida war, and a million of other topics which you will learn soon enough for your own comfort,—I care not, I say, if no whisper of these matters ever reaches my ears again. Yet they have occupied so large a share of my attention that I scarcely know what else to tell you. There has, indeed been a curious sort of war on the Canada border, where blood has streamed in the names of liberty and patriotism; but it must remain for some future, perhaps far-distant, year to tell whether or no those holy names have been rightfully invoked. Nothing so much depresses me in my view of mortal affairs as to see high energies wasted and human life and happiness thrown away for ends that appear oftentimes unwise, and still oftener remain unaccomplished. But the wisest people and the best keep a steadfast faith that the progress of mankind is onward and upward, and that the toil and anguish of the path serve to wear away the imperfections of the immortal pilgrim, and will be felt no more when they have done their office."

"Perhaps," cried the hopeful New Year—"perhaps I shall see that happy day."

"I doubt whether it be so close at hand," answered the Old Year, gravely smiling. "You will soon grow weary of looking for that blessed consummation, and will turn for amusement—as has frequently been my own practice—to the affairs of some sober little city like this of Salem. Here we sit on the steps of the new city-hall which has been completed under my administration, and it would make you laugh to see how the game of politics of which the Capitol at Washington is the great chess-board is here played in miniature. Burning Ambition finds its fuel here; here patriotism speaks boldly in the people's behalf and virtuous economy demands retrenchment in the emoluments of a lamplighter; here the aldermen range their senatorial dignity around the mayor's chair of state and the common council feel that they have liberty in charge. In short, human weakness and strength, passion and policy, man's tendencies, his aims and modes of pursuing them, his individual character and his character in the mass, may be studied almost as well here as on the theatre of nations, and with this great advantage—that, be the lesson ever so disastrous, its Liliputian scope still makes the beholder smile."

"Have you done much for the improvement of the city?" asked the New Year. "Judging from what little I have seen, it appears to be ancient and time-worn."

"I have opened the railroad," said the elder Year, "and half a dozen times a day you will hear the bell which once summoned the monks of a Spanish convent to their devotions announcing the arrival or departure of the cars. Old Salem now wears a much livelier expression than when I first beheld her. Strangers rumble down from Boston by hundreds at a time. New faces throng in Essex street. Railroad-hacks and omnibuses rattle over the pavements. There is a perceptible increase of oyster-shops and other establishments for the accommodation of a transitory diurnal multitude. But a more important change awaits the venerable town. An immense accumulation of musty prejudices will be carried off by the free circulation of society. A peculiarity of character of which the inhabitants themselves are hardly sensible will be rubbed down and worn away by the attrition of foreign substances. Much of the result will be good; there will likewise be a few things not so good. Whether for better or worse, there will be a probable diminution of the moral influence of wealth, and the sway of an aristocratic class which from an era far beyond my memory has held firmer dominion here than in any other New England town."

The Old Year, having talked away nearly all of her little remaining breath, now closed her book of chronicles, and was about to take her departure, but her sister detained her a while longer by inquiring the contents of the huge bandbox which she was so painfully lugging along with her.

"These are merely a few trifles," replied the Old Year, "which I have picked up in my rambles and am going to deposit in the receptacle of things past and forgotten. We sisterhood of years never carry anything really valuable out of the world with us. Here are patterns of most of the fashions which I brought into vogue, and which have already lived out their allotted term; you will supply their place with others equally ephemeral. Here, put up in little china pots, like rouge, is a considerable lot of beautiful women's bloom which the disconsolate fair ones owe me a bitter grudge for stealing. I have likewise a quantity of men's dark hair, instead of which I have left gray locks or none at all. The tears of widows and other afflicted mortals who have received comfort during the last twelve months are preserved in some dozens of essence-bottles well corked and sealed. I have several bundles of love-letters eloquently breathing an eternity of burning passion which grew cold and perished almost before the ink was dry. Moreover, here is an assortment of many thousand broken promises and other broken ware, all very light and packed into little space. The heaviest articles in my possession are a large parcel of disappointed hopes which a little while ago were buoyant enough to have inflated Mr. Lauriat's balloon."

"I have a fine lot of hopes here in my basket," remarked the New Year. "They are a sweet-smelling flower—a species of rose."

"They soon lose their perfume," replied the sombre Old Year. "What else have you brought to insure a welcome from the discontented race of mortals?"

"Why, to say the truth, little or nothing else," said her sister, with a smile, "save a few new *Annuals* and almanacs, and some New Year's gifts for the children. But I heartily wish well to poor mortals, and mean to do all I can for their improvement and happiness."

"It is a good resolution," rejoined the Old Year. "And, by the way, I have a plentiful assortment of good resolutions which have now grown so stale and musty that I am ashamed to carry them any farther. Only for fear that the city authorities would send Constable Mansfield with a warrant after me, I should toss them into the street at once. Many other matters go to make up the contents of my bandbox, but the whole lot would not fetch a single bid even at an auction of worn-out furniture; and as they are worth nothing either to you or anybody else, I need not trouble you with a longer catalogue."

"And must I also pick up such worthless luggage in my travels?" asked the New Year.

"Most certainly, and well if you have no heavier load to bear," replied the other. "And now, my dear sister, I must bid you farewell, earnestly advising and exhorting you to expect no gratitude nor good-will from this peevish, unreasonable, inconsiderate, ill-intending and worse-behaving world. However warmly its inhabitants may seem to welcome you, yet, do what you may and lavish on them what means of happiness you please, they will still be complaining, still craving what it is not in your power to give, still looking forward to some other year for the accomplishment of projects which ought never to have been formed, and which, if successful, would only provide new occasions of discontent. If these ridiculous people ever see anything tolerable in you, it will be after you are gone for ever."

"But I," cried the fresh-hearted New Year—"I shall try to leave men wiser than I find them. I will offer them freely whatever good gifts Providence permits me to distribute, and will tell them to be thankful for what they have and humbly hopeful for more; and surely, if they are not absolute fools, they will condescend to be happy, and will allow me to be a happy year. For my happiness must depend on them."

"Alas for you, then, my poor sister!" said the Old Year, sighing, as she uplifted her burden. "We grandchildren of Time are born to trouble. Happiness, they say, dwells in the mansions of eternity, but we can only lead mortals thither step by step with reluctant murmurings, and ourselves must perish on the threshold. But hark! my task is done."

The clock in the tall steeple of Dr. Emerson's church struck twelve; there was a response from Dr. Flint's, in the opposite quarter of the city; and while the strokes were yet dropping into the air the Old Year either flitted or faded away, and not the wisdom and might of angels, to say nothing of the remorseful yearnings of the millions who had used her ill, could have prevailed with that departed year to return one step. But she, in the company of Time and all her kindred, must hereafter hold a reckoning with mankind. So shall it be, likewise, with the maidenly New Year, who, as the clock ceased to strike, arose from the steps of the city-hall and set out rather timorously on her earthly course.

"A happy New Year!" cried a watchman, eying her figure very questionably, but without the least suspicion that he was addressing the New Year in person.

"Thank you kindly," said the New Year; and she gave the watchman one of the roses of hope from her basket. "May this flower keep a sweet smell long after I have bidden you good-bye!"

Then she stepped on more briskly through the silent streets, and such as were awake at the moment heard her footfall and said, "The New Year is come!" Wherever there was a knot of midnight roisterers, they quaffed her health. She sighed, however, to perceive that the air was tainted—as the atmosphere of this world must continually be—with the dying breaths of mortals who had lingered just long enough for her to bury them. But there were millions left alive to rejoice at her coming, and so she pursued her way with confidence, strewing emblematic flowers on the doorstep of almost every dwelling, which some persons will gather up and wear in their bosoms, and others will trample under foot. The carrier-boy can only say further that early this morning she filled his basket with New Year's addresses, assuring him that the whole city, with our new mayor and the aldermen and common council at its head, would make a general rush to secure copies. Kind patrons, will not you redeem the pledge of the New Year?

SNOWFLAKES.

There is snow in yonder cold gray sky of the morning, and through the partially-frosted window-panes I love to watch the gradual beginning of the storm. A few feathery flakes are scattered widely through the air and hover downward with uncertain flight, now almost alighting on the earth, now whirled again aloft into remote regions of the atmosphere. These are not the big flakes heavy with moisture which melt as they touch the ground and are portentous of a soaking rain. It is to be in good earnest a wintry storm. The two or three people visible on the sidewalks have an aspect of endurance, a blue-nosed, frosty fortitude, which is evidently assumed in anticipation of a comfortless and blustering day. By nightfall—or, at least, before the sun sheds another glimmering smile upon us—the street and our little garden will be heaped with mountain snowdrifts. The soil, already frozen for weeks past, is prepared to sustain whatever burden may be laid upon it, and to a Northern eye the landscape will lose its melancholy bleakness and acquire a beauty of its own when Mother Earth, like her children, shall have put on the fleecy garb of her winter's wear. The cloud-spirits are slowly weaving her white mantle. As yet, indeed, there is barely a rime like hoar-frost over the brown surface of the street; the withered green of the grass-plat is still discernible, and the slated roofs of the houses do but begin to look gray instead of black. All the snow that has yet fallen within the circumference of my view, were it heaped up together, would hardly equal the hillock of a grave. Thus gradually by silent and stealthy influences are great changes wrought. These little snow-particles which the storm-spirit flings by handfuls through the air will bury the great Earth under their accumulated mass, nor permit her to behold her sister Sky again for dreary months. We likewise shall lose sight of our mother's familiar visage, and must content ourselves with looking heavenward the oftener.

Now, leaving the Storm to do his appointed office, let us sit down, pen in hand, by our fireside. Gloomy as it may seem, there is an influence productive of cheerfulness and favorable to imaginative thought in the atmosphere of a snowy day. The native of a Southern clime may woo the Muse beneath the heavy shade of summer foliage reclining on banks of turf, while the sound of singing-birds and warbling rivulets chimes in with the music of his soul. In our brief summer I do not think, but only exist in the vague enjoyment of a dream. My hour of inspiration—if that hour ever comes—is when the green log hisses upon the hearth, and the bright flame, brighter for the gloom of the chamber, rustles high up the chimney, and the coals drop tinkling down among the growing heaps of ashes. When the casement rattles in the gust and the snowflakes or the sleety raindrops pelt hard against the window-panes, then I spread out my sheet of paper with the certainty that thoughts and fancies will gleam forth upon it like stars at twilight or like violets in May, perhaps to fade as soon. However transitory their glow, they at least shine amid the darksome shadow which the clouds of the outward sky fling through the room. Blessed, therefore, and reverently welcomed by me, her true-born son, be New England's winter, which makes us one and all the nurslings of the storm and sings a familiar lullaby even in the wildest shriek of the December blast. Now look we forth again and see how much of his task the storm-spirit has done.

Slow and sure! He has the day—perchance the week—before him, and may take his own time to accomplish Nature's burial in snow. A smooth mantle is scarcely yet thrown over the withered grass-plat, and the dry stalks of annuals still thrust themselves through the white surface in all parts of the garden. The leafless rose-bushes stand shivering in a shallow snowdrift, looking, poor things! as disconsolate as if they possessed a human consciousness of the dreary scene. This is a sad time for the shrubs that do not perish with the summer. They neither live nor die; what they retain of life seems but the chilling sense of death. Very sad are the flower-shrubs in midwinter. The roofs of the houses are now all white, save where the eddying wind has kept them bare at the bleak corners. To discern the real intensity of the storm, we must fix upon some distant object—as yonder spire—and observe how the riotous gust fights with the descending snow throughout the intervening space. Sometimes the entire prospect is obscured; then, again, we have a distinct but transient glimpse of the tall steeple, like a giant's ghost; and now the dense wreaths sweep between, as if demons were flinging snowdrifts at each other in mid-air. Look next into the street, where we have an amusing parallel to the combat of those fancied demons in the upper regions. It is a snow-battle of schoolboys. What a pretty satire on war and military glory might be written in the form of a child's story by describing the snow-ball fights of two rival schools, the alternate defeats and victories of each, and the final triumph of one party, or perhaps of neither! What pitched battles worthy to be chanted in Homeric strains! What storming of fortresses built all of massive snow-blocks! What feats of individual prowess and embodied onsets of martial enthusiasm! And when some well-contested and decisive victory had put a period to the war, both armies should unite to build a lofty monument of snow upon the battlefield and crown it with the victor's statue hewn of the same frozen marble. In a few days or weeks thereafter the passer-by would observe a shapeless mound upon the level common, and, unmindful of the famous victory, would ask, "How came it there? Who reared it? And what means it?" The shattered pedestal of many a battle-monument has provoked these questions when none could answer.

Turn we again to the fireside and sit musing there, lending our ears to the wind till perhaps it shall seem like an articulate voice and dictate wild and airy matter for the pen. Would it might inspire me to sketch out the personification of a New England winter! And that idea, if I can seize the snow-wreathed figures that flit before my fancy, shall be the theme of the next page.

How does Winter herald his approach? By the shrieking blast of latter autumn which is Nature's cry of lamentation as the destroyer rushes among the shivering groves where she has lingered and scatters the sear leaves upon the tempest. When that cry is heard, the people wrap themselves in cloaks and shake their heads disconsolately, saying, "Winter is at hand." Then the axe of the woodcutter echoes sharp and diligently in the forest; then the coal-merchants rejoice because each shriek of Nature in her agony adds something to the price of coal per ton; then the peat-smoke spreads its aromatic fragrance through the atmosphere. A few days more, and at eventide the children look out of the window and dimly perceive the flaunting of a snowy mantle in the air. It is stern Winter's vesture. They crowd around the hearth and cling to their mother's gown or press between their father's knees, affrighted by the hollow roaring voice that bellows adown the wide flue of the chimney.

It is the voice of Winter; and when parents and children hear it, they shudder and exclaim, "Winter is come. Cold Winter has begun his reign already." Now throughout New England each hearth becomes an altar sending up the smoke of a continued sacrifice to the immitigable deity who tyrannizes over forest, country-side and town. Wrapped in his white mantle, his staff a huge icicle, his beard and hair a wind-tossed snowdrift, he travels over the land in the midst of the northern blast, and woe to the homeless wanderer whom he finds upon his path! There he lies stark and stiff, a human shape of ice, on the spot where Winter overtook him. On strides the tyrant over the rushing rivers and broad lakes, which turn to rock beneath his footsteps. His dreary empire is established; all around stretches the desolation of the pole. Yet not ungrateful be his New England children (for Winter is our sire, though a stern and rough one)—not ungrateful even for the severities which have nourished our unyielding strength of character. And let us thank him, too, for the sleigh-rides cheered by the music of merry bells; for the crackling and rustling hearth when the ruddy firelight gleams on hardy manhood and the blooming cheek of woman: for all the home-enjoyments and the kindred virtues which flourish in a frozen soil. Not that we grieve when, after some seven months of storm and bitter frost, Spring, in the guise of a flower-crowned virgin, is seen driving away the hoary despot, pelting him with violets by the handful and strewing green grass on the path behind him. Often ere he will give up his empire old Winter rushes fiercely buck and hurls a snowdrift at the shrinking form of Spring, yet step by step he is compelled to retreat northward, and spends the summer month within the Arctic circle.

Such fantasies, intermixed among graver toils of mind, have made the winter's day pass pleasantly. Meanwhile, the storm has raged without abatement, and now, as the brief afternoon declines, is tossing denser volumes to and fro about the atmosphere. On the window-sill there is a layer of snow reaching halfway up the lowest pane of glass. The garden is one unbroken bed. Along the street are two or three spots of uncovered earth where the gust has whirled away the snow, heaping it elsewhere to the fence-tops or piling huge banks against the doors of houses. A solitary passenger is seen, now striding mid-leg deep across a drift, now scudding over the bare ground, while his cloak is swollen with the wind. And now the jingling of bells—a sluggish sound responsive to the horse's toilsome progress through the unbroken drifts—announces the passage of a sleigh with a boy clinging behind and ducking his head to escape detection by the driver. Next comes a sledge laden with wood for some unthrifty housekeeper whom winter has surprised at a cold hearth. But what dismal equipage now struggles along the uneven street? A sable hearse bestrewn with snow is bearing a dead man through the storm to his frozen bed. Oh how dreary is a burial in winter, when the bosom of Mother Earth has no warmth for her poor child!

Evening—the early eve of December—begins to spread its deepening veil over the comfortless scene. The firelight gradually brightens and throws my flickering shadow upon the walls and ceiling of the chamber, but still the storm rages and rattles against the windows. Alas! I shiver and think it time to be disconsolate, but, taking a farewell glance at dead Nature in her shroud, I perceive a flock of snowbirds skimming lightsomely through the tempest and flitting from drift to drift as sportively as swallows in the delightful prime of summer. Whence come they? Where do they build their nests and seek their food? Why, having airy wings, do they not follow summer around the earth, instead of making themselves the playmates of the storm and fluttering on the dreary verge of the winter's eve? I know not whence they come, nor why; yet my spirit has been cheered by that wandering flock of snow-birds.

THE SEVEN VAGABONDS.

Rambling on foot in the spring of my life and the summer of the year, I came one afternoon to a point which gave me the choice of three directions. Straight before me the main road extended its dusty length to Boston; on the left a branch went toward the sea, and would have lengthened my journey a trifle of twenty or thirty miles, while by the right-hand path I might have gone over hills and lakes to Canada, visiting in my way the celebrated town of Stamford. On a level spot of grass at the foot of the guide-post appeared an object which, though locomotive on a different principle, reminded me of Gulliver's portable mansion among the Brobdignags. It was a huge covered wagon—or, more properly, a small house on wheels—with a door on one side and a window shaded by green blinds on the other. Two horses munching provender out of the baskets which muzzled them were fastened near the vehicle. A delectable sound of music proceeded from the interior, and I immediately conjectured that this was some itinerant show halting at the confluence of the roads to intercept such idle travellers as myself. A shower had long been climbing up the western sky, and now hung so blackly over my onward path that it was a point of wisdom to seek shelter here.

"Halloo! Who stands guard here? Is the doorkeeper asleep?" cried I, approaching a ladder of two or three steps which was let down from the wagon.

The music ceased at my summons, and there appeared at the door, not the sort of figure that I had mentally assigned to the wandering showman, but a most respectable old personage whom I was sorry to have addressed in so free a style. He wore a snuff-colored coat and small-clothes, with white top-boots, and exhibited the mild dignity of aspect and manner which may often be noticed in aged schoolmasters, and sometimes in deacons, selectmen or other potentates of that kind. A small piece of silver was my passport within his premises, where I found only one other person, hereafter to be described.

"This is a dull day for business," said the old gentleman as he ushered me in; "but I merely tarry here to refresh the cattle, being bound for the camp-meeting at Stamford."

Perhaps the movable scene of this narrative is still peregrinating New England, and may enable the reader to test the accuracy of my description. The spectacle—for I will not use the unworthy term of "puppet-show"—consisted of a multitude of little people assembled on a miniature stage. Among them were artisans of every kind in the attitudes of their toil, and a group of fair ladies and gay gentlemen standing ready for the dance; a company of foot-soldiers formed a line across the stage, looking stern, grim and terrible enough to make it a pleasant consideration that they were but three inches high; and conspicuous above the whole was seen a Merry Andrew in the pointed cap and motley coat of his profession. All the inhabitants of this mimic world were motionless, like the figures in a picture, or like that people who one moment were alive in the midst of their business and delights and the next were transformed to statues, preserving an eternal semblance of labor that was ended and pleasure that could be felt no more. Anon, however, the old gentleman turned the handle of a barrel-organ, the first note of which produced a most enlivening effect upon the figures and awoke them all to their proper occupations and amusements. By the selfsame impulse the tailor plied his needle, the blacksmith's hammer descended upon the anvil and the dancers whirled away on feathery tiptoes; the company of soldiers broke into platoons, retreated from the stage, and were succeeded by a troop of horse, who came prancing onward with such a sound of trumpets and trampling of hoofs as might have startled Don Quixote himself; while an old toper of inveterate ill-habits uplifted his black bottle and took off a hearty swig. Meantime, the Merry Andrew began to caper and turn somersets, shaking his sides, nodding his head and winking his eyes in as lifelike a manner as if he were ridiculing the nonsense of all human affairs and making fun of the whole multitude beneath him. At length the old magician (for I compared the showman to Prospero entertaining his guests with a masque of shadows) paused that I might give utterance to my wonder.

"What an admirable piece of work is this!" exclaimed I, lifting up my hands in astonishment.

Indeed, I liked the spectacle and was tickled with the old man's gravity as he presided at it, for I had none of that foolish wisdom which reproves every occupation that is not useful in this world of vanities. If there be a faculty which I possess more perfectly than most men, it is that of throwing myself mentally into situations foreign to my own and detecting with a cheerful eye the desirable circumstances of each. I could have envied the life of this gray-headed showman, spent as it had been in a course of safe and pleasurable adventure in driving his huge vehicle sometimes through the sands of Cape Cod and sometimes over the rough forest-roads of the north and east, and halting now on the green before a village meeting-house and now in a paved square of the metropolis. How often must his heart have been gladdened by the delight of children as they viewed these animated figures, or his pride indulged by haranguing learnedly to grown men on the mechanical powers which produced such wonderful effects, or his gallantry brought into play—for this is an attribute which such grave men do not lack—by the visits of pretty maidens! And then with how fresh a feeling must he return at intervals to his own peculiar home! "I would I were assured of as happy a life as his," thought I.

Though the showman's wagon might have accommodated fifteen or twenty spectators, it now contained only himself and me and a third person, at whom I threw a glance on entering. He was a neat and trim young man of two or three and twenty; his drab hat and green frock-coat with velvet collar were smart, though no longer new, while a pair of green spectacles that seemed needless to his brisk little eyes gave him something of a scholar-like and literary air. After allowing me a sufficient time to inspect the puppets, he advanced with a bow and drew my attention to some books in a corner of the wagon. These he forthwith began to extol with an amazing volubility of well-sounding words and an ingenuity of praise that won him my heart as being myself one of the most merciful of critics. Indeed, his stock required some considerable powers of commendation in the salesman. There were several ancient friends of mine—the novels of those happy days when my affections wavered between the *Scottish Chiefs* and *Thomas Thumb*—besides a few of later date whose merits had not been acknowledged by the public. I was glad to find that dear little venerable volume the *New England Primer*, looking as antique as ever, though in its thousandth new edition; a bundle of superannuated gilt picture-books made such a child of me that, partly for the glittering covers and partly for the fairy-tales within, I bought the whole, and an assortment of ballads and popular theatrical songs drew largely on my purse. To balance these expenditures, I meddled neither with sermons nor science nor morality, though volumes of each were there, nor with a *Life of Franklin* in the coarsest of paper, but so showily bound that it was emblematical of the doctor himself in the court-dress which he refused to wear at Paris, nor with Webster's spelling-book, nor some of Byron's minor poems, nor half a dozen little Testaments at twenty-five cents each. Thus far the collection might have been swept from some great bookstore or picked up at an evening auction-room, but there was one small blue-covered pamphlet which the pedler handed me with so peculiar an air that I purchased it immediately at his own price; and then for the first time the thought struck me that I had spoken face to face with the veritable author of a printed book.

The literary-man now evinced a great kindness for me, and I ventured to inquire which way he was travelling.

"Oh," said he, "I keep company with this old gentlemen here, and we are moving now toward the camp-meeting at Stamford."

He then explained to me that for the present season he had rented a corner of the wagon as a book-store, which, as he wittily observed, was a true circulating library, since there were few parts of the country where it had not gone its rounds. I approved of the plan exceedingly, and began to sum up within my mind the many uncommon felicities in the life of a book-pedler, especially when his character resembled that of the individual before me. At a high rate was to be reckoned the daily and hourly enjoyment of such interviews as the present, in which he seized upon the admiration of a passing stranger and made him aware that a man of literary taste, and even of literary achievement, was travelling the country in a showman's wagon. A more valuable yet not infrequent triumph might be won in his conversations with some elderly clergyman long vegetating in a rocky, woody, watery back-settlement of New England, who as he recruited his library from the pedler's stock of sermons would exhort him to seek a college education and become the first scholar in his class. Sweeter and prouder yet would be his sensations when, talking poetry while he sold spelling-books, he should charm the mind, and haply touch the heart, of a fair country schoolmistress, herself an unhonored poetess, a wearer of blue stockings which none but himself took pains to look at. But the scene of his completest glory would be when the wagon had halted for the night and his stock of books was transferred to some crowded bar-room. Then would he recommend to the multifarious company, whether traveller from the city, or teamster from the hills, or neighboring squire, or the landlord himself, or his loutish hostler, works suited to each particular taste and capacity, proving, all the while, by acute criticism and profound remark, that the lore in his books was even exceeded by that in his brain. Thus happily would he traverse the land, sometimes a herald before the march of Mind, sometimes walking arm in arm with awful Literature, and reaping everywhere a harvest of real and sensible popularity which the secluded bookworms by whose toil he lived could never hope for.

"If ever I meddle with literature," thought I, fixing myself in adamantine resolution, "it shall be as a travelling bookseller."

Though it was still mid-afternoon, the air had now grown dark about us, and a few drops of rain came down upon the roof of our vehicle, pattering like the feet of birds that had flown thither to rest. A sound of pleasant voices made us listen, and there soon appeared halfway up the ladder the pretty person of a young damsel whose rosy face was so cheerful that even amid the gloomy light it seemed as if the sunbeams were peeping under her bonnet. We next saw the dark and handsome features of a young man who, with easier gallantry than might have been expected in the heart of Yankee-land, was assisting her into the wagon. It became immediately evident to us, when the two strangers stood within the door, that they were of a profession kindred to those of my companions, and I was delighted with the more than hospitable—the even paternal—kindness of the old showman's manner as he welcomed them, while the man of literature hastened to lead the merry-eyed girl to a seat on the long bench.

"You are housed but just in time, my young friends," said the master of the wagon; "the sky would have been down upon you within five minutes."

The young man's reply marked him as a foreigner—not by any variation from the idiom and accent of good English, but because he spoke with more caution and accuracy than if perfectly familiar with the language.

"We knew that a shower was hanging over us," said he, "and consulted whether it were best to enter the house on the top of yonder hill, but, seeing your wagon in the road—"

"We agreed to come hither," interrupted the girl, with a smile, "because we should be more at home in a wandering house like this."

I, meanwhile, with many a wild and undetermined fantasy was narrowly inspecting these two doves that had flown into our ark. The young man, tall, agile and athletic, wore a mass of black shining curls clustering round a dark and vivacious countenance which, if it had not greater expression, was at least more active and attracted readier notice, than the quiet faces of our countrymen. At his first appearance he had been laden with a neat mahogany box of about two feet square, but very light in proportion to its size, which he had immediately unstrapped from his shoulders and deposited on the floor of the wagon.

The girl had nearly as fair a complexion as our own beauties, and a brighter one than most of them; the lightness of her figure, which seemed calculated to traverse the whole world without weariness, suited well with the glowing cheerfulness of her face, and her gay attire, combining the rainbow hues of crimson, green and a deep orange, was as proper to her lightsome aspect as if she had been born in it. This gay stranger was appropriately burdened with that mirth-inspiring instrument the fiddle, which her companion took from her hands, and shortly began the process of tuning. Neither of us the previous company of the wagon needed to inquire their trade, for this could be no mystery to frequenters of brigade-musters, ordinations, cattle-shows, commencements, and other festal meetings in our sober land; and there is a dear friend of mine who will smile when this page recalls to his memory a chivalrous deed performed by us in rescuing the show-box of such a couple from a mob of great double-fisted countrymen.

"Come," said I to the damsel of gay attire; "shall we visit all the wonders of the world together?"

She understood the metaphor at once, though, indeed, it would not much have troubled me if she had assented to the literal meaning of my words. The mahogany box was placed in a proper position, and I peeped in through its small round magnifying-window while the girl sat by my side and gave short descriptive sketches as one after another the pictures were unfolded to my view. We visited together—at least, our imaginations did—full many a famous city in the streets of which I had long yearned to tread. Once, I remember, we were in the harbor of Barcelona, gazing townward; next, she bore me through the air to Sicily and bade me look up at blazing Ætna; then we took wing to Venice and sat in a gondola beneath the arch of the Rialto, and anon she set me down among the thronged spectators at the coronation of Napoleon. But there was one scene—its locality she could not tell—which charmed my attention longer than all those gorgeous palaces and churches, because the fancy haunted me that I myself the preceding summer had beheld just such a humble meeting-house, in just such a pine-surrounded nook, among our own green mountains. All these pictures were tolerably executed, though far inferior to the girl's touches of description; nor was it easy to comprehend how in so few sentences, and these, as I supposed, in a language foreign to her, she contrived to present an airy copy of each varied scene.

When we had travelled through the vast extent of the mahogany box, I looked into my guide's face.

"'Where are you going, my pretty maid?'" inquired I, in the words of an old song.

"Ah!" said the gay damsel; "you might as well ask where the summer wind is going. We are wanderers here and there and everywhere. Wherever there is mirth our merry hearts are drawn to it. To-day, indeed, the people have told us of a great frolic and festival in these parts; so perhaps we may be needed at what you call the camp-meeting at Stamford."

Then, in my happy youth, and while her pleasant voice yet sounded in my ears, I sighed; for none but myself, I thought, should have been her companion in a life which seemed to realize my own wild fancies cherished all through visionary boyhood to that hour. To these two strangers the world was in its Golden Age—not that, indeed, it was less dark and sad than ever, but because its weariness and sorrow had no community with their ethereal nature. Wherever they might appear in their pilgrimage of bliss, Youth would echo back their gladness, care-stricken Maturity would rest a moment from its toil, and Age, tottering among the graves, would smile in withered joy for their sakes. The lonely cot, the narrow and gloomy street, the sombre shade, would catch a passing gleam like that now shining on ourselves as these bright spirits wandered by. Blessed pair, whose happy home was throughout all the earth! I looked at my shoulders, and thought them broad enough to sustain those pictured towns and mountains; mine, too, was an elastic foot as tireless as the wing of the bird of Paradise; mine was then an untroubled heart that would have gone singing on its delightful way.

"Oh, maiden," said I aloud, "why did you not come hither alone?"

While the merry girl and myself were busy with the show-box the unceasing rain had driven another wayfarer into the wagon. He seemed pretty nearly of the old showman's age, but much smaller, leaner and more withered than he, and less respectably clad in a patched suit of gray; withal, he had a thin, shrewd countenance and a pair of diminutive gray eyes, which peeped rather too keenly out of their puckered sockets. This old fellow had been joking with the showman in a manner which intimated previous acquaintance, but, perceiving that the damsel and I had terminated our affairs, he drew forth a folded document and presented it to me. As I had anticipated, it proved to be a circular, written in a very fair and legible hand and signed by several distinguished gentlemen whom I had never heard of, stating that the bearer had encountered every variety of misfortune and recommending him to the notice of all charitable people. Previous disbursements had left me no more than a five-dollar bill, out of which, however, I offered to make the beggar a donation provided he would give me change for it. The object of my beneficence looked keenly in my face, and discerned that I had none of that abominable spirit, characteristic though it be, of a full-blooded Yankee, which takes pleasure in detecting every little harmless piece of knavery.

"Why, perhaps," said the ragged old mendicant, "if the bank is in good standing, I can't say but I may have enough about me to change your bill."

"It is a bill of the Suffolk Bank," said I, "and better than the specie."

As the beggar had nothing to object, he now produced a small buff leather bag tied up carefully with a shoe-string. When this was opened, there appeared a very comfortable treasure of silver coins of all sorts and sizes, and I even fancied that I saw gleaming among them the golden plumage of that rare bird in our currency the American eagle. In this precious heap was my bank-note deposited, the rate of exchange being considerably against me.

His wants being thus relieved, the destitute man pulled out of his pocket an old pack of greasy cards which had probably contributed to fill the buff leather bag in more ways than one.

"Come!" said he; "I spy a rare fortune in your face, and for twenty-five cents more I'll tell you what it is."

I never refuse to take a glimpse into futurity; so, after shuffling the cards and when the fair damsel had cut them, I dealt a portion to the prophetic beggar. Like others of his profession, before predicting the shadowy events that were moving on to meet me he gave proof of his preternatural science by describing scenes through which I had already passed.

Here let me have credit for a sober fact. When the old man had read a page in his book of fate, he bent his keen gray eyes on mine and proceeded to relate in all its minute particulars what was then the most singular event of my life. It was one which I had no purpose to disclose till the general unfolding of all secrets, nor would it be a much stranger instance of inscrutable knowledge or fortunate conjecture if the beggar were to meet me in the street today and repeat word for word the page which I have here written.

The fortune-teller, after predicting a destiny which time seems loth to make good, put up his cards, secreted his treasure-bag and began to converse with the other occupants of the wagon.

"Well, old friend," said the showman, "you have not yet told us which way your face is turned this afternoon."

"I am taking a trip northward this warm weather," replied the conjurer, "across the Connecticut first, and then up through Vermont, and maybe into Canada before the fall. But I must stop and see the breaking up of the camp-meeting at Stamford."

I began to think that all the vagrants in New England were converging to the camp-meeting and had made this wagon, their rendezvous by the way.

The showman now proposed that when the shower was over they should pursue the road to Stamford together, it being sometimes the policy of these people to form a sort of league and confederacy.

"And the young lady too," observed the gallant bibliopolist, bowing to her profoundly, "and this foreign gentleman, as I understand, are on a jaunt of pleasure to the same spot. It would add incalculably to my own enjoyment, and I presume to that of my colleague and his friend, if they could be prevailed upon to join our party."

This arrangement met with approbation on all hands, nor were any of those concerned more sensible of its advantages than myself, who had no title to be in cluded in it.

Having already satisfied myself as to the several modes in which the four others attained felicity, I next set my mind at work to discover what enjoyments were peculiar to the old "straggler," as the people of the country would have termed the wandering mendicant and prophet. As he pretended to familiarity with the devil, so I fancied that he was fitted to pursue and take delight in his way of life by possessing some of the mental and moral characteristics—the lighter and more comic ones—of the devil in popular stories. Among them might be reckoned a love of deception for its own sake, a shrewd eye and keen relish for human weakness and ridiculous infirmity, and the talent of petty fraud. Thus to this old man there would be pleasure even in the consciousness—so insupportable to some minds—that his whole life was a cheat upon the world, and that, so far as he was concerned with the public, his little cunning had the upper hand of its united wisdom. Every day would furnish him with a succession of minute and pungent triumphs—as when, for instance, his importunity wrung a pittance out of the heart of a miser, or when my silly good-nature transferred a part of my slender purse to his plump leather bag, or when some ostentatious gentleman should throw a coin to the ragged beggar who was richer than himself, or when—though he would not always be so decidedly diabolical—his pretended wants should make him a sharer in the scanty living of real indigence. And then what an inexhaustible field of enjoyment, both as enabling him to discern so much folly and achieve such quantities of minor mischief, was opened to his sneering spirit by his pretensions to prophetic knowledge.

All this was a sort of happiness which I could conceive of, though I had little sympathy with it. Perhaps, had I been then inclined to admit it, I might have found that the roving life was more proper to him than to either of his companions; for Satan, to whom I had compared the poor man, has delighted, ever since the time of Job, in "wandering up and down upon the earth," and, indeed, a crafty disposition which operates not in deep-laid plans, but in disconnected tricks, could not have an adequate scope, unless naturally impelled to a continual change of scene and society.

My reflections were here interrupted.

"Another visitor!" exclaimed the old showman.

The door of the wagon had been closed against the tempest, which was roaring and blustering with prodigious fury and commotion and beating violently against our shelter, as if it claimed all those homeless people for its lawful prey, while we, caring little for the displeasure of the elements, sat comfortably talking. There was now an attempt to open the door, succeeded by a voice uttering some strange, unintelligible gibberish which my companions mistook for Greek and I suspected to be thieves' Latin. However, the showman stepped forward and gave admittance to a figure which made me imagine either that our wagon had rolled back two hundred years into past ages or that the forest and its old inhabitants had sprung up around us by enchantment. It was a red Indian armed with his bow and arrow. His dress was a sort of cap adorned with a single feather of some wild bird, and a frock of blue cotton girded tight about him; on his breast, like orders of knighthood, hung a crescent and a circle and other ornaments of silver, while a small crucifix betokened that our father the pope had interposed between the Indian and the Great Spirit whom he had worshipped in his simplicity. This son of the wilderness and pilgrim of the storm took his place silently in the midst of us. When the first surprise was over, I rightly conjectured him to be one of the Penobscot tribe, parties of which I had often seen in their summer excursions down our Eastern rivers. There they paddle their birch canoes among the coasting-schooners, and build their wigwam beside some roaring mill-dam, and drive a little trade in basket-work where their fathers hunted deer. Our new visitor was probably wandering through the country toward Boston, subsisting on the careless charity of the people while he turned his archery to profitable account by shooting at cents which were to be the prize of his successful aim.

The Indian had not long been seated ere our merry damsel sought to draw him into conversation. She, indeed, seemed all made up of sunshine in the month of May, for there was nothing so dark and dismal that her pleasant mind could not cast a glow over it; and the wild man, like a fir tree in his native forest, soon began to brighten into a sort of sombre cheerfulness. At length she inquired whether his journey had any particular end or purpose.

"I go shoot at the camp-meeting at Stamford," replied the Indian.

"And here are five more," said the girl, "all aiming at the camp-meeting too. You shall be one of us, for we travel with light hearts; and, as for me, I sing merry songs and tell merry tales and am full of merry thoughts, and I dance merrily along the road, so that there is never any sadness among them that keep me company. But oh, you would find it very dull indeed to go all the way to Stamford alone."

My ideas of the aboriginal character led me to fear that the Indian would prefer his own solitary musings to the gay society thus offered him; on the contrary, the girl's proposal met with immediate acceptance and seemed to animate him with a misty expectation of enjoyment.

I now gave myself up to a course of thought which, whether it flowed naturally from this combination of events or was drawn forth by a wayward fancy, caused my mind to thrill as if I were listening to deep music. I saw mankind in this weary old age of the world either enduring a sluggish existence amid the smoke and dust of cities, or, if they breathed a purer air, still lying down at night with no hope but to wear out to-morrow, and all the to-morrows which make up life, among the same dull scenes and in the same wretched toil that had darkened the sunshine of today. But there were some full of the primeval instinct who preserved the freshness of youth to their latest years by the continual excitement of new objects, new pursuits and new associates, and cared little, though their birthplace might have been here in New England, if the grave should close over them in Central Asia. Fate was summoning a parliament of these free spirits; unconscious of the impulse which directed them to a common centre, they had come hither from far and near, and last of all appeared the representatives of those mighty vagrants who had chased the deer during thousands of years, and were chasing it now in the spirit-land. Wandering down through the waste of ages, the woods had vanished around his path; his arm had lost somewhat of its strength, his foot of its fleetness, his mien of its wild regality, his heart and mind of their savage virtue and uncultured force, but here, untamable to the routine of artificial life, roving now along the dusty road as of old over the forest-leaves,—here was the Indian still.

"Well," said the old showman, in the midst of my meditations, "here is an honest company of us—one, two, three, four, five, six—all going to the camp-meeting at Stamford. Now, hoping no offence, I should like to know where this young gentleman may be going?"

I started. How came I among these wanderers? The free mind that preferred its own folly to another's wisdom, the open spirit that found companions everywhere—above all, the restless impulse that had so often made me wretched in the midst of enjoyments,—these were my claims to be of their society.

"My friends," cried I, stepping into the centre of the wagon, "I am going with you to the camp-meeting at Stamford."

"But in what capacity?" asked the old showman, after a moment's silence. "All of us here can get our bread in some creditable way. Every honest man should have his livelihood. You, sir, as I take it, are a mere strolling gentleman."

I proceeded to inform the company that when Nature gave me a propensity to their way of life she had not left me altogether destitute of qualifications for it, though I could not deny that my talent was less respectable, and might be less profitable, than the meanest of theirs. My design, in short, was to imitate the story-tellers of whom Oriental travellers have told us, and become an itinerant novelist, reciting my own extemporaneous fictions to such audiences as I could collect.

"Either this," said I, "is my vocation, or I have been born in vain."

The fortune-teller, with a sly wink to the company, proposed to take me as an apprentice to one or other of his professions, either of which undoubtedly would have given full scope to whatever inventive talent I might possess. The bibliopolist spoke a few words in opposition to my plan—influenced partly, I suspect, by the jealousy of authorship, and partly by an apprehension that the *vivâ-voce* practice would become general among novelists, to the infinite detriment of the book trade.

Dreading a rejection, I solicited the interest of the merry damsel.

"'Mirth,'" cried I, most aptly appropriating the words of L'Allegro, "'to thee I sue! Mirth, admit me of thy crew!'"

"Let us indulge the poor youth," said Mirth, with a kindness which made me love her dearly, though I was no such coxcomb as to misinterpret her motives. "I have espied much promise in him. True, a shadow sometimes flits across his brow, but the sunshine is sure to follow in a moment. He is never guilty of a sad thought but a merry one is twin-born with it. We will take him with us, and you shall see that he will set us all a-laughing before we reach the camp-meeting at Stamford." Her voice silenced the scruples of the rest and gained me admittance into the league; according to the terms of which, without a community of goods or profits, we were to lend each other all the aid and avert all the harm that might be in our power.

This affair settled, a marvellous jollity entered into the whole tribe of us, manifesting itself characteristically in each individual. The old showman, sitting down to his barrel-organ, stirred up the souls of the pigmy people with one of the quickest tunes in the music-book; tailors, blacksmiths, gentlemen and ladies all seemed to share in the spirit of the occasion, and the Merry Andrew played his part more facetiously than ever, nodding and winking particularly at me. The young foreigner flourished his fiddle-bow with a master's hand, and gave an inspiring echo to the showman's melody. The bookish man and the merry damsel started up simultaneously to dance, the former enacting the double shuffle in a style which everybody must have witnessed ere election week was blotted out of time, while the girl, setting her arms akimbo with both hands at her slim waist, displayed such light rapidity of foot and harmony of varying attitude and motion that I could not conceive how she ever was to stop, imagining at the moment that Nature had made her, as the old showman had made his puppets, for no earthly purpose but to dance jigs. The Indian bellowed forth a succession of most hideous outcries, somewhat affrighting us till we interpreted them as the war-song with which, in imitation of his ancestors, he was prefacing the assault on Stamford. The conjurer, meanwhile, sat demurely in a corner extracting a sly enjoyment from the whole scene, and, like the facetious Merry Andrew, directing his queer glance particularly at me. As for myself, with great exhilaration of fancy, I began to arrange and color the incidents of a tale wherewith I proposed to amuse an audience that very evening; for I saw that my associates were a little ashamed of me, and that no time was to be lost in obtaining a public acknowledgment of my abilities.

"Come, fellow-laborers," at last said the old showman, whom we had elected president; "the shower is over, and we must be doing our duty by these poor souls at Stamford."

"We'll come among them in procession, with music and dancing," cried the merry damsel.

Accordingly—for it must be understood that our pilgrimage was to be performed on foot—we sallied joyously out of the wagon, each of us, even the old gentleman in his white top-boots, giving a great skip as we came down the ladder. Above our heads there was such a glory of sunshine and splendor of clouds, and such brightness of verdure below, that, as I modestly remarked at the time, Nature seemed to have washed her face and put on the best of her jewelry and a fresh green gown in honor of our confederation. Casting our eyes northward, we beheld a horseman approaching leisurely and splashing through the little puddle on the Stamford road. Onward he came, sticking up in his saddle with rigid perpendicularity, a tall, thin figure in rusty black, whom the showman and the conjurer shortly recognized to be what his aspect sufficiently indicated—a travelling preacher of great fame among the Methodists. What puzzled us was the fact that his face appeared turned from, instead of to, the camp-meeting at Stamford. However, as this new votary of the wandering life drew near the little green space where the guide-post and our wagon were situated, my six fellow-vagabonds and myself rushed forward and surrounded him, crying out with united voices, "What news? What news from the camp-meeting at Stamford?"

The missionary looked down in surprise at as singular a knot of people as could have been selected from all his heterogeneous auditors. Indeed, considering that we might all be classified under the general head of Vagabond, there was great diversity of character among the grave old showman, the sly, prophetic beggar, the fiddling foreigner and his merry damsel, the smart bibliopolist, the sombre Indian and myself, the itinerant novelist, a slender youth of eighteen. I even fancied that a smile was endeavoring to disturb the iron gravity of the preacher's mouth.

"Good people," answered he, "the camp-meeting is broke up."

So saying, the Methodist minister switched his steed and rode westward. Our union being thus nullified by the removal of its object, we were sundered at once to the four winds of heaven. The fortune-teller, giving a nod to all and a peculiar wink to me, departed on his Northern tour, chuckling within himself as he took the Stamford road. The old showman and his literary coadjutor were already tackling their horses to the wagon with a design to peregrinate south-west along the sea-coast. The foreigner and the merry damsel took their laughing leave and pursued the eastern road, which I had that day trodden; as they passed away the young man played a lively strain and the girl's happy spirit broke into a dance, and, thus dissolving, as it were, into sunbeams and gay music, that pleasant pair departed from my view. Finally, with a pensive shadow thrown across my mind, yet emulous of the light philosophy of my late companions, I joined myself to the Penobscot Indian and set forth toward the distant city.

THE WHITE OLD MAID.

The moonbeams came through two deep and narrow windows and showed a spacious chamber richly furnished in an antique fashion. From one lattice the shadow of the diamond panes was thrown upon the floor; the ghostly light through the other slept upon a bed, falling between the heavy silken curtains and illuminating the face of a young man. But how quietly the slumberer lay! how pale his features! And how like a shroud the sheet was wound about his frame! Yes, it was a corpse in its burial-clothes.

Suddenly the fixed features seemed to move with dark emotion. Strange fantasy! It was but the shadow of the fringed curtain waving betwixt the dead face and the moonlight as the door of the chamber opened and a girl stole softly to the bedside. Was there delusion in the moonbeams, or did her gesture and her eye betray a gleam of triumph as she bent over the pale corpse, pale as itself, and pressed her living lips to the cold ones of the dead? As she drew back from that long kiss her features writhed as if a proud heart were fighting with its anguish. Again it seemed that the features of the corpse had moved responsive to her own. Still an illusion. The silken curtains had waved a second time betwixt the dead face and the moonlight as another fair young girl unclosed the door and glided ghostlike to the bedside. There the two maidens stood, both beautiful, with the pale beauty of the dead between them. But she who had first entered was proud and stately, and the other a soft and fragile thing.

"Away!" cried the lofty one. "Thou hadst him living; the dead is mine."

"Thine!" returned the other, shuddering. "Well hast thou spoken; the dead is thine."

The proud girl started and stared into her face with a ghastly look, but a wild- and mournful expression passed across the features of the gentle one, and, weak and helpless, she sank down on the bed, her head pillowed beside that of the corpse and her hair mingling with his dark locks. A creature of hope and joy, the first draught of sorrow had bewildered her.

"Edith!" cried her rival.

Edith groaned as with a sudden compression of the heart, and, removing her cheek from the dead youth's pillow, she stood upright, fearfully encountering the eyes of the lofty girl.

"Wilt thou betray me?" said the latter, calmly.

"Till the dead bid me speak I will be silent," answered Edith. "Leave us alone together. Go and live many years, and then return and tell me of thy life. He too will be here. Then, if thou tellest of sufferings more than death, we will both forgive thee."

"And what shall be the token?" asked the proud girl, as if her heart acknowledged a meaning in these wild words.

"This lock of hair," said Edith, lifting one of the dark clustering curls that lay heavily on the dead man's brow.

The two maidens joined their hands over the bosom of the corpse and appointed a day and hour far, far in time to come for their next meeting in that chamber. The statelier girl gave one deep look at the motionless countenance and departed, yet turned again and trembled ere she closed the door, almost believing that her dead lover frowned upon her. And Edith, too! Was not her white form fading into the moonlight? Scorning her own weakness, she went forth and perceived that a negro slave was waiting in the passage with a waxlight, which he held between her face and his own and regarded her, as she thought, with an ugly expression of merriment. Lifting his torch on high, the slave lighted her down the staircase and undid the portal of the mansion. The young clergyman of the town had just ascended the steps, and, bowing to the lady, passed in without a word.

Years—many years—rolled on. The world seemed new again, so much older was it grown since the night when those pale girls had clasped their hands across the bosom of the corpse. In the interval a lonely woman had passed from youth to extreme age, and was known by all the town as the "Old Maid in the Winding-Sheet." A taint of insanity had affected her whole life, but so quiet, sad and gentle, so utterly free from violence, that she was suffered to pursue her harmless fantasies unmolested by the world with whose business or pleasures she had naught to do. She dwelt alone, and never came into the daylight except to follow funerals. Whenever a corpse was borne along the street, in sunshine, rain or snow, whether a pompous train of the rich and proud thronged after it or few and humble were the mourners, behind them came the lonely woman in a long white garment which the people called her shroud. She took no place among the kindred or the friends, but stood at the door to hear the funeral prayer, and walked in the rear of the procession as one whose earthly charge it was to haunt the house of mourning and be the shadow of affliction and see that the dead were duly buried. So long had this been her custom that the inhabitants of the town deemed her a part of every funeral, as much as the coffin-pall or the very corpse itself, and augured ill of the sinner's destiny unless the Old Maid in the Winding-Sheet came gliding like a ghost behind. Once, it is said, she affrighted a bridal-party with her pale presence, appearing suddenly in the illuminated hall just as the priest was uniting a false maid to a wealthy man before her lover had been dead a year. Evil was the omen to that marriage. Sometimes she stole forth by moonlight and visited the graves of venerable integrity and wedded love and virgin innocence, and every spot where the ashes of a kind and faithful heart were mouldering. Over the hillocks of those favored dead would she stretch out her arms with a gesture as if she were scattering seeds, and many believed that she brought them from the garden of Paradise, for the graves which she had visited were green beneath the snow and covered with sweet flowers from April to November. Her blessing was better than a holy verse upon the tombstone. Thus wore away her long, sad, peaceful and fantastic life till few were so old as she, and the people of later generations wondered how the dead had ever been buried or mourners had endured their grief without the Old Maid in the Winding-Sheet. Still years went on, and still she followed funerals and was not yet summoned to her own festival of death.

One afternoon the great street of the town was all alive with business and bustle, though the sun now gilded only the upper half of the church-spire, having left the housetops and loftiest trees in shadow. The scene was cheerful and animated in spite of the sombre shade between the high brick buildings. Here were pompous merchants in white wigs and laced velvet, the bronzed faces of sea-captains, the foreign garb and air of Spanish Creoles, and the disdainful port of natives of Old England, all contrasted with the rough aspect of one or two back-settlers negotiating sales of timber from forests where axe had never sounded. Sometimes a lady passed, swelling roundly forth in an embroidered petticoat, balancing her steps in high-heeled shoes and courtesying with lofty grace to the punctilious obeisances of the gentlemen. The life of the town seemed to have its very centre not far from an old mansion that stood somewhat back from the pavement, surrounded by neglected grass, with a strange air of loneliness rather deepened than dispelled by the throng so near it. Its site would have been suitably occupied by a magnificent Exchange or a brick block lettered all over with various signs, or the large house itself might have made a noble tavern with the "King's Arms" swinging before it and guests in every chamber, instead of the present solitude. But, owing to some dispute about the right of inheritance, the mansion had been long without a tenant, decaying from year to year and throwing the stately gloom of its shadow over the busiest part of the town.

Such was the scene, and such the time, when a figure unlike any that have been described was observed at a distance down the street.

"I espy a strange sail yonder," remarked a Liverpool captain—"that woman in the long white garment."

The sailor seemed much struck by the object, as were several others who at the same moment caught a glimpse of the figure that had attracted his notice. Almost immediately the various topics of conversation gave place to speculations in an undertone on this unwonted occurrence.

"Can there be a funeral so late this afternoon?" inquired some.

They looked for the signs of death at every door—the sexton, the hearse, the assemblage of black-clad relatives, all that makes up the woeful pomp of funerals. They raised their eyes, also, to the sun-gilt spire of the church, and wondered that no clang proceeded from its bell, which had always tolled till now when this figure appeared in the light of day. But none had heard that a corpse was to be borne to its home that afternoon, nor was there any token of a funeral except the apparition of the Old Maid in the Winding-Sheet.

"What may this portend?" asked each man of his neighbor.

All smiled as they put the question, yet with a certain trouble in their eyes, as if pestilence, or some other wide calamity, were prognosticated by the untimely intrusion among the living of one whose presence had always been associated with death and woe. What a comet is to the earth was that sad woman to the town. Still she moved on, while the hum of surprise was hushed at her approach, and the proud and the humble stood aside that her white garment might not wave against them. It was a long, loose robe of spotless purity. Its wearer appeared very old, pale, emaciated and feeble, yet glided onward without the unsteady pace of extreme age. At one point of her course a little rosy boy burst forth from a door and ran with open arms toward the ghostly woman, seeming to expect a kiss from her bloodless lips. She made a slight pause, fixing her eye upon him with an expression of no earthly sweetness, so that the child shivered and stood awestruck rather than affrighted while the Old Maid passed on. Perhaps her garment might have been polluted even by an infant's touch; perhaps her kiss would have been death to the sweet boy within the year.

"She is but a shadow," whispered the superstitious. "The child put forth his arms and could not grasp her robe."

The wonder was increased when the Old Maid passed beneath the porch of the deserted mansion, ascended the moss-covered steps, lifted the iron knocker and gave three raps. The people could only conjecture that some old remembrance, troubling her bewildered brain, had impelled the poor woman hither to visit the friends of her youth—all gone from their home long since and for ever unless their ghosts still haunted it, fit company for the Old Maid in the Winding-Sheet.

An elderly man approached the steps, and, reverently uncovering his gray locks, essayed to explain the matter.

"None, madam," said he, "have dwelt in this house these fifteen years agone—no, not since the death of old Colonel Fenwicke, whose funeral you may remember to have followed. His heirs, being ill-agreed among themselves, have let the mansion-house go to ruin."

The Old Maid looked slowly round with a slight gesture of one hand and a finger of the other upon her lip, appearing more shadow-like than ever in the obscurity of the porch. But again she lifted the hammer, and gave, this time, a single rap. Could it be that a footstep was now heard coming down the staircase of the old mansion which all conceived to have been so long untenanted? Slowly, feebly, yet heavily, like the pace of an aged and infirm person, the step approached, more distinct on every downward stair, till it reached the portal. The bar fell on the inside; the door was opened. One upward glance toward the church-spire, whence the sunshine had just faded, was the last that the people saw of the Old Maid in the Winding-Sheet.

"Who undid the door?" asked many.

This question, owing to the depth of shadow beneath the porch, no one could satisfactorily answer. Two or three aged men, while protesting against an inference which might be drawn, affirmed that the person within was a negro and bore a singular resemblance to old Cæsar, formerly a slave in the house, but freed by death some thirty years before.

"Her summons has waked up a servant of the old family," said one, half seriously.

"Let us wait here," replied another; "more guests will knock at the door anon. But the gate of the graveyard should be thrown open."

Twilight had overspread the town before the crowd began to separate or the comments on this incident were exhausted. One after another was wending his way homeward, when a coach—no common spectacle in those days—drove slowly into the street. It was an old-fashioned equipage, hanging close to the ground, with arms on the panels, a footman behind and a grave, corpulent coachman seated high in front, the whole giving an idea of solemn state and dignity. There was something awful in the heavy rumbling of the wheels.

The coach rolled down the street, till, coming to the gateway of the deserted mansion, it drew up, and the footman sprang to the ground.

"Whose grand coach is this?" asked a very inquisitive body.

The footman made no reply, but ascended the steps of the old house, gave three taps with the iron hammer, and returned to open the coach door. An old man possessed of the heraldic lore so common in that day examined the shield of arms on the panel.

"Azure, a lion's head erased, between three flowers de luce," said he, then whispered the name of the family to whom these bearings belonged. The last inheritor of its honors was recently dead, after a long residence amid the splendor of the British court, where his birth and wealth had given him no mean station. "He left no child," continued the herald, "and these arms, being in a lozenge, betoken that the coach appertains to his widow."

Further disclosures, perhaps, might have been made had not the speaker been suddenly struck dumb by the stern eye of an ancient lady who thrust forth her head from the coach, preparing to descend. As she emerged the people saw that her dress was magnificent, and her figure dignified in spite of age and infirmity—a stately ruin, but with a look at once of pride and wretchedness. Her strong and rigid features had an awe about them unlike that of the white Old Maid, but as of something evil. She passed up the steps, leaning on a gold-headed cane. The door swung open as she ascended, and the light of a torch glittered on the embroidery of her dress and gleamed on the pillars of the porch. After a momentary pause, a glance backward and then a desperate effort, she went in.

The decipherer of the coat-of-arms had ventured up the lower step, and, shrinking back immediately, pale and tremulous, affirmed that the torch was held by the very image of old Cæsar.

"But such a hideous grin," added he, "was never seen on the face of mortal man, black or white. It will haunt me till my dying-day."

Meantime, the coach had wheeled round with a prodigious clatter on the pavement and rumbled up the street, disappearing in the twilight, while the ear still tracked its course. Scarcely was it gone when the people began to question whether the coach and attendants, the ancient lady, the spectre of old Cæsar and the Old Maid herself were not all a strangely-combined delusion with some dark purport in its mystery. The whole town was astir, so that, instead of dispersing, the crowd continually increased, and stood gazing up at the windows of the mansion, now silvered by the brightening moon. The elders, glad to indulge the narrative propensity of age, told of the long-faded splendor of the family, the entertainments they had given and the guests, the greatest of the land, and even titled and noble ones from abroad, who had passed beneath that portal. These graphic reminiscences seemed to call up the ghosts of those to whom they referred. So strong was the impression on some of the more imaginative hearers that two or three were seized with trembling fits at one and the same moment, protesting that they had distinctly heard three other raps of the iron knocker.

"Impossible!" exclaimed others. "See! The moon shines beneath the porch, and shows every part of it except in the narrow shade of that pillar. There is no one there."

"Did not the door open?" whispered one of these fanciful persons.

"Didst thou see it too?" said his companion, in a startled tone.

But the general sentiment was opposed to the idea that a third visitant had made application at the door of the deserted house. A few, however, adhered to this new marvel, and even declared that a red gleam like that of a torch had shone through the great front window, as if the negro were lighting a guest up the staircase. This too was pronounced a mere fantasy.

But at once the whole multitude started, and each man beheld his own terror painted in the faces of all the rest.

"What an awful thing is this!" cried they.

A shriek too fearfully distinct for doubt had been heard within the mansion, breaking forth suddenly and succeeded by a deep stillness, as if a heart had burst in giving it utterance. The people knew not whether to fly from the very sight of the house or to rush trembling in and search out the strange mystery. Amid their confusion and affright they were somewhat reassured by the appearance of their clergyman, a venerable patriarch, and equally a saint, who had taught them and their fathers the way to heaven for more than the space of an ordinary lifetime. He was a reverend figure with long white hair upon his shoulders, a white beard upon his breast and a back so bent over his staff that he seemed to be looking downward continually, as if to choose a proper grave for his weary frame. It was some time before the good old man, being deaf and of impaired intellect, could be made to comprehend such portions of the affair as were comprehensible at all. But when possessed of the facts, his energies assumed unexpected vigor.

"Verily," said the old gentleman, "it will be fitting that I enter the mansion-house of the worthy Colonel Fenwicke, lest any harm should have befallen that true Christian woman whom ye call the 'Old Maid in the Winding-Sheet.'"

Behold, then, the venerable clergyman ascending the steps of the mansion with a torch-bearer behind him. It was the elderly man who had spoken to the Old Maid, and the same who had afterward explained the shield of arms and recognized the features of the negro. Like their predecessors, they gave three raps with the iron hammer.

"Old Cæsar cometh not," observed the priest. "Well, I wot he no longer doth service in this mansion."

"Assuredly, then, it was something worse in old Cæsar's likeness," said the other adventurer.

"Be it as God wills," answered the clergyman. "See! my strength, though it be much decayed, hath sufficed to open this heavy door. Let us enter and pass up the staircase."

Here occurred a singular exemplification of the dreamy state of a very old man's mind. As they ascended the wide flight of stairs the aged clergyman appeared to move with caution, occasionally standing aside, and oftener bending his head, as it were in salutation, thus practising all the gestures of one who makes his way through a throng. Reaching the head of the staircase, he looked around with sad and solemn benignity, laid aside his staff, bared his hoary locks, and was evidently on the point of commencing a prayer.

"Reverend sir," said his attendant, who conceived this a very suitable prelude to their further search, "would it not be well that the people join with us in prayer?"

"Well-a-day!" cried the old clergyman, staring strangely around him. "Art thou here with me, and none other? Verily, past times were present to me, and I deemed that I was to make a funeral prayer, as many a time heretofore, from the head of this staircase. Of a truth, I saw the shades of many that are gone. Yea, I have prayed at their burials, one after another, and the Old Maid in the Winding-Sheet hath seen them to their graves."

Being now more thoroughly awake to their present purpose, he took his staff and struck forcibly on the floor, till there came an echo from each deserted chamber, but no menial to answer their summons. They therefore walked along the passage, and again paused, opposite to the great front window, through which was seen the crowd in the shadow and partial moonlight of the street beneath. On their right hand was the open door of a chamber, and a closed one on their left.

The clergyman pointed his cane to the carved oak panel of the latter.

"Within that chamber," observed he, "a whole lifetime since, did I sit by the death-bed of a goodly young man who, being now at the last gasp—" Apparently, there was some powerful excitement in the ideas which had now flashed across his mind. He snatched the torch from his companion's hand, and threw open the door with such sudden violence that the flame was extinguished, leaving them no other light than the moonbeams which fell through two windows into the spacious chamber. It was sufficient to discover all that could be known. In a high-backed oaken arm-chair, upright, with her hands clasped across her breast and her head thrown back, sat the Old Maid in the Winding-Sheet. The stately dame had fallen on her knees with her forehead on the holy knees of the Old Maid, one hand upon the floor and the other pressed convulsively against her heart. It clutched a lock of hair—once sable, now discolored with a greenish mould.

As the priest and layman advanced into the chamber the Old Maid's features assumed such a semblance of shifting expression that they trusted to hear the whole mystery explained by a single word. But it was only the shadow of a tattered curtain waving betwixt the dead face and the moonlight.

"Both dead!" said the venerable man. "Then who shall divulge the secret? Methinks it glimmers to and fro in my mind like the light and shadow across the Old Maid's face. And now 'tis gone!"

PETER GOLDTHWAITE'S TREASURE.

"And so, Peter, you won't even consider of the business?" said Mr. John Brown, buttoning his surtout over the snug rotundity of his person and drawing on his gloves. "You positively refuse to let me have this crazy old house, and the land under and adjoining, at the price named?"

"Neither at that, nor treble the sum," responded the gaunt, grizzled and threadbare Peter Goldthwaite. "The fact is, Mr. Brown, you must find another site for your brick block and be content to leave my estate with the present owner. Next summer I intend to put a splendid new mansion over the cellar of the old house."

"Pho, Peter!" cried Mr. Brown as he opened the kitchen door; "content yourself with building castles in the air, where house-lots are cheaper than on earth, to say nothing of the cost of bricks and mortar. Such foundations are solid enough for your edifices, while this underneath us is just the thing for mine; and so we may both be suited. What say you, again?"

"Precisely what I said before, Mr. Brown," answered Peter Goldthwaite. "And, as for castles in the air, mine may not be as magnificent as that sort of architecture, but perhaps as substantial, Mr. Brown, as the very respectable brick block with dry-goods stores, tailors' shops and banking-rooms on the lower floor, and lawyers' offices in the second story, which you are so anxious to substitute."

"And the cost, Peter? Eh?" said Mr. Brown as he withdrew in something of a pet. "That, I suppose, will be provided for off-hand by drawing a check on Bubble Bank?"

John Brown and Peter Goldthwaite had been jointly known to the commercial world between twenty and thirty years before under the firm of Goldthwaite & Brown; which copartnership, however, was speedily dissolved by the natural incongruity of its constituent parts. Since that event, John Brown, with exactly the qualities of a thousand other John Browns, and by just such plodding methods as they used, had prospered wonderfully and become one of the wealthiest John Browns on earth. Peter Goldthwaite, on the contrary, after innumerable schemes which ought to have collected all the coin and paper currency of the country into his coffers, was as needy a gentleman as ever wore a patch upon his elbow. The contrast between him and his former partner may be briefly marked, for Brown never reckoned upon luck, yet always had it, while Peter made luck the main condition of his projects, and always missed it. While the means held out his speculations had been magnificent, but were chiefly confined of late years to such small business as adventures in the lottery. Once he had gone on a gold-gathering expedition somewhere to the South, and ingeniously contrived to empty his pockets more thoroughly than ever, while others, doubtless, were filling theirs with native bullion by the handful. More recently he had expended a legacy of a thousand or two of dollars in purchasing Mexican scrip, and thereby became the proprietor of a province; which, however, so far as Peter could find out, was situated where he might have had an empire for the same money—in the clouds. From a search after this valuable real estate Peter returned so gaunt and threadbare that on reaching New England the scarecrows in the corn-fields beckoned to him as he passed by. "They did but flutter in the wind," quoth Peter Goldthwaite. No, Peter, they beckoned, for the scarecrows knew their brother.

At the period of our story his whole visible income would not have paid the tax of the old mansion in which we find him. It was one of those rusty, moss-grown, many-peaked wooden houses which are scattered about the streets of our elder towns, with a beetle-browed second story projecting over the foundation, as if it frowned at the novelty around it. This old paternal edifice, needy as he was, and though, being centrally situated on the principal street of the town, it would have brought him a handsome sum, the sagacious Peter had his own reasons for never parting with, either by auction or private sale. There seemed, indeed, to be a fatality that connected him with his birthplace; for, often as he had stood on the verge of ruin, and standing there even now, he had not yet taken the step beyond it which would have compelled him to surrender the house to his creditors. So here he dwelt with bad luck till good should come.

Here, then, in his kitchen—the only room where a spark of fire took off the chill of a November evening—poor Peter Goldthwaite had just been visited by his rich old partner. At the close of their interview, Peter, with rather a mortified look, glanced downward at his dress, parts of which appeared as ancient as the days of Goldthwaite & Brown. His upper garment was a mixed surtout, woefully faded, and patched with newer stuff on each elbow; beneath this he wore a threadbare black coat, some of the silk buttons of which had been replaced with others of a different pattern; and, lastly, though he lacked not a pair of gray pantaloons, they were very shabby ones, and had been partially turned brown by the frequent toasting of Peter's shins before a scanty fire. Peter's person was in keeping with his goodly apparel. Gray-headed, hollow-eyed, pale-cheeked and lean-bodied, he was the perfect picture of a man who had fed on windy schemes and empty hopes till he could neither live on such unwholesome trash nor stomach more substantial food. But, withal, this Peter Goldthwaite, crack-brained simpleton as, perhaps, he was, might have cut a very brilliant figure in the world had he employed his imagination in the airy business of poetry instead of making it a demon of mischief in mercantile pursuits. After all, he was no bad fellow, but as harmless as a child, and as honest and honorable, and as much of the gentleman which Nature meant him for, as an irregular life and depressed circumstances will permit any man to be.

As Peter stood on the uneven bricks of his hearth looking round at the disconsolate old kitchen his eyes began to kindle with the illumination of an enthusiasm that never long deserted him. He raised his hand, clenched it and smote it energetically against the smoky panel over the fireplace.

"The time is come," said he; "with such a treasure at command, it were folly to be a poor man any longer. Tomorrow morning I will begin with the garret, nor desist till I have torn the house down."

Deep in the chimney-corner, like a witch in a dark cavern, sat a little old woman mending one of the two pairs of stockings wherewith Peter Goldthwaite kept his toes from being frost-bitten. As the feet were ragged past all darning, she had cut pieces out of a cast-off flannel petticoat to make new soles. Tabitha Porter was an old maid upward of sixty years of age, fifty-five of which she had sat in that same chimney-corner, such being the length of time since Peter's grandfather had taken her from the almshouse. She had no friend but Peter, nor Peter any friend but Tabitha; so long as Peter might have a shelter for his own head, Tabitha would know where to shelter hers, or, being homeless elsewhere, she would take her master by the hand and bring him to her native home, the almshouse. Should it ever be necessary, she loved him well enough to feed him with her last morsel and clothe him with her under-petticoat. But Tabitha was a queer old woman, and, though never infected with Peter's flightiness, had become so accustomed to his freaks and follies that she viewed them all as matters of course. Hearing him threaten to tear the house down, she looked quietly up from her work.

"Best leave the kitchen till the last, Mr. Peter," said she.

"The sooner we have it all down, the better," said Peter Goldthwaite. "I am tired to death of living in this cold, dark, windy, smoky, creaking, groaning, dismal old house. I shall feel like a younger man when we get into my splendid brick mansion, as, please Heaven, we shall by this time next autumn. You shall have a room on the sunny side, old Tabby, finished and furnished as best may suit your own notions."

"I should like it pretty much such a room as this kitchen," answered Tabitha. "It will never be like home to me till the chimney-corner gets as black with smoke as this, and that won't be these hundred years. How much do you mean to lay out on the house, Mr. Peter?"

"What is that to the purpose?" exclaimed Peter, loftily. "Did not my great-grand-uncle, Peter Goldthwaite, who died seventy years ago, and whose namesake I am, leave treasure enough to build twenty such?"

"I can't say but he did, Mr. Peter," said Tabitha, threading her needle.

Tabitha well understood that Peter had reference to an immense hoard of the precious metals which was said to exist somewhere in the cellar or walls, or under the floors, or in some concealed closet or other out-of-the-way nook of the old house. This wealth, according to tradition, had been accumulated by a former Peter Goldthwaite whose character seems to have borne a remarkable similitude to that of the Peter of our story. Like him, he was a wild projector, seeking to heap up gold by the bushel and the cart-load instead of scraping it together coin by coin. Like Peter the second, too, his projects had almost invariably failed, and, but for the magnificent success of the final one, would have left him with hardly a coat and pair of breeches to his gaunt and grizzled person. Reports were various as to the nature of his fortunate speculation, one intimating that the ancient Peter had made the gold by alchemy; another, that he had conjured it out of people's pockets by the black art; and a third—still more unaccountable—that the devil had given him free access to the old provincial treasury. It was affirmed, however, that some secret impediment had debarred him from the enjoyment of his riches, and that he had a motive for concealing them from his heir, or, at any rate, had died without disclosing the place of deposit. The present Peter's father had faith enough in the story to cause the cellar to be dug over. Peter himself chose to consider the legend as an indisputable truth, and amid his many troubles had this one consolation—that, should all other resources fail, he might build up his fortunes by tearing his house down. Yet, unless he felt a lurking distrust of the golden tale, it is difficult to account for his permitting the paternal roof to stand so long, since he had never yet seen the moment when his predecessor's treasure would not have found plenty of room in his own strong-box. But now was the crisis. Should he delay the search a little longer, the house would pass from the lineal heir, and with it the vast heap of gold, to remain in its burial-place till the ruin of the aged walls should discover it to strangers of a future generation.

"Yes," cried Peter Goldthwaite, again; "to-morrow I will set about it."

The deeper he looked at the matter, the more certain of success grew Peter. His spirits were naturally so elastic that even now, in the blasted autumn of his age, he could often compete with the springtime gayety of other people. Enlivened by his brightening prospects, he began to caper about the kitchen like a hobgoblin, with the queerest antics of his lean limbs and gesticulations of his starved features. Nay, in the exuberance of his feelings, he seized both of Tabitha's hands and danced the old lady across the floor till the oddity of her rheumatic motions set him into a roar of laughter, which was echoed back from the rooms and chambers, as if Peter Goldthwaite were laughing in every one. Finally, he bounded upward, almost out of sight, into the smoke that clouded the roof of the kitchen, and, alighting safely on the floor again, endeavored to resume his customary gravity.

"To-morrow, at sunrise," he repeated, taking his lamp to retire to bed, "I'll see whether this treasure be hid in the wall of the garret."

"And, as we're out of wood, Mr. Peter," said Tabitha, puffing and panting with her late gymnastics, "as fast as you tear the house down I'll make a fire with the pieces."

Gorgeous that night were the dreams of Peter Goldthwaite. At one time he was turning a ponderous key in an iron door not unlike the door of a sepulchre, but which, being opened, disclosed a vault heaped up with gold coin as plentifully as golden corn in a granary. There were chased goblets, also, and tureens, salvers, dinner-dishes and dish-covers of gold or silver-gilt, besides chains and other jewels, incalculably rich, though tarnished with the damps of the vault; for, of all the wealth that was irrevocably lost to man, whether buried in the earth or sunken in the sea, Peter Goldthwaite had found it in this one treasure-place. Anon he had returned to the old house as poor as ever, and was received at the door by the gaunt and grizzled figure of a man whom he might have mistaken for himself, only that his garments were of a much elder fashion. But the house, without losing its former aspect, had been changed into a palace of the precious metals. The floors, walls and ceilings were of burnished silver; the doors, the window-frames, the cornices, the balustrades and the steps of the staircase, of pure gold; and silver, with gold bottoms, were the chairs, and gold, standing on silver legs, the high chests of drawers, and silver the bedsteads, with blankets of woven gold and sheets of silver tissue. The house had evidently been transmuted by a single touch, for it retained all the marks that Peter remembered, but in gold or silver instead of wood, and the initials of his name—which when a boy he had cut in the wooden door-post—remained as deep in the pillar of gold. A happy man would have been Peter Goldthwaite except for a certain ocular deception which, whenever he glanced backward, caused the house to darken from its glittering magnificence into the sordid gloom of yesterday.

Up betimes rose Peter, seized an axe, hammer and saw which he had placed by his bedside, and hied him to the garret. It was but scantily lighted up as yet by the frosty fragments of a sunbeam which began to glimmer through the almost opaque bull-eyes of the window. A moralizer might find abundant themes for his speculative and impracticable wisdom in a garret. There is the limbo of departed fashions, aged trifles of a day and whatever was valuable only to one generation of men, and which passed to the garret when that generation passed to the grave—not for safekeeping, but to be out of the way. Peter saw piles of yellow and musty account-books in parchment covers, wherein creditors long dead and buried had written the names of dead and buried debtors in ink now so faded that their moss-grown tombstones were more legible. He found old moth-eaten garments, all in rags and tatters, or Peter would have put them on. Here was a naked and rusty sword—not a sword of service, but a gentleman's small French rapier—which had never left its scabbard till it lost it. Here were canes of twenty different sorts, but no gold-headed ones, and shoebuckles of various pattern and material, but not silver nor set with precious stones. Here was a large box full of shoes with high heels and peaked toes. Here, on a shelf, were a multitude of phials half filled with old apothecary's stuff which, when the other half had done its business on Peter's ancestors, had been brought hither from the death-chamber. Here—not to give a longer inventory of articles that will never be put up at auction—was the fragment of a full-length looking-glass which by the dust and dimness of its surface made the picture of these old things look older than the reality. When Peter, not knowing that there was a mirror there, caught the faint traces of his own figure, he partly imagined that the former Peter Goldthwaite had come back either to assist or impede his search for the hidden wealth. And at that moment a strange notion glimmered through his brain that he was the identical Peter who had concealed the gold, and ought to know whereabout it lay. This, however, he had unaccountably forgotten.

"Well, Mr. Peter!" cried Tabitha, on the garret stairs. "Have you torn the house down enough to heat the teakettle?"

"Not yet, old Tabby," answered Peter, "but that's soon done, as you shall see." With the word in his mouth, he uplifted the axe, and laid about him so vigorously that the dust flew, the boards crashed, and in a twinkling the old woman had an apron full of broken rubbish.

"We shall get our winter's wood cheap," quoth Tabitha.

The good work being thus commenced, Peter beat down all before him, smiting and hewing at the joints and timbers, unclenching spike-nails, ripping and tearing away boards, with a tremendous racket from morning till night. He took care, however, to leave the outside shell of the house untouched, so that the neighbors might not suspect what was going on.

Never, in any of his vagaries, though each had made him happy while it lasted, had Peter been happier than now. Perhaps, after all, there was something in Peter Goldthwaite's turn of mind which brought him an inward recompense for all the external evil that it caused. If he were poor, ill-clad, even hungry and exposed, as it were, to be utterly annihilated by a precipice of impending ruin, yet only his body remained in these miserable circumstances, while his aspiring soul enjoyed the sunshine of a bright futurity. It was his nature to be always young, and the tendency of his mode of life to keep him so. Gray hairs were nothing—no, nor wrinkles nor infirmity; he might look old, indeed, and be somewhat disagreeably connected with a gaunt old figure much the worse for wear, but the true, the essential Peter was a young man of high hopes just entering on the world. At the kindling of each new fire his burnt-out youth rose afresh from the old embers and ashes. It rose exulting now. Having lived thus long—not too long, but just to the right age—a susceptible bachelor with warm and tender dreams, he resolved, so soon as the hidden gold should flash to light, to go a-wooing and win the love of the fairest maid in town. What heart could resist him? Happy Peter Goldthwaite!

Every evening—as Peter had long absented himself from his former lounging-places at insurance offices, news-rooms, and book-stores, and as the honor of his company was seldom requested in private circles—he and Tabitha used to sit down sociably by the kitchen hearth. This was always heaped plentifully with the rubbish of his day's labor. As the foundation of the fire there would be a goodly-sized back-log of red oak, which after being sheltered from rain or damp above a century still hissed with the heat and distilled streams of water from each end, as if the tree had been cut down within a week or two. Next there were large sticks, sound, black and heavy, which had lost the principle of decay and were indestructible except by fire, wherein they glowed like red-hot bars of iron. On this solid basis Tabitha would rear a lighter structure, composed of the splinters of door-panels, ornamented mouldings, and such quick combustibles, which caught like straw and threw a brilliant blaze high up the spacious flue, making its sooty sides visible almost to the chimney-top. Meantime, the gloom of the old kitchen would be chased out of the cobwebbed corners and away from the dusky cross-beams overhead, and driven nobody could tell whither, while Peter smiled like a gladsome man and Tabitha seemed a picture of comfortable age. All this, of course, was but an emblem of the bright fortune which the destruction of the house would shed upon its occupants.

While the dry pine was flaming and crackling like an irregular discharge of fairy-musketry, Peter sat looking and listening in a pleasant state of excitement; but when the brief blaze and uproar were succeeded by the dark-red glow, the substantial heat and the deep singing sound which were to last throughout the evening, his humor became talkative. One night—the hundredth time—he teased Tabitha to tell him something new about his great-granduncle.

"You have been sitting in that chimney-corner fifty-five years, old Tabby, and must have heard many a tradition about him," said Peter. "Did not you tell me that when you first came to the house there was an old woman sitting where you sit now who had been housekeeper to the famous Peter Goldthwaite?"

"So there was, Mr. Peter," answered Tabitha, "and she was near about a hundred years old. She used to say that she and old Peter Goldthwaite had often spent a sociable evening by the kitchen fire—pretty much as you and I are doing now, Mr. Peter."

"The old fellow must have resembled me in more points than one," said Peter, complacently, "or he never would have grown so rich. But methinks he might have invested the money better than he did. No interest! nothing but good security! and the house to be torn down to come at it! What made him hide it so snug, Tabby?"

"Because he could not spend it," said Tabitha, "for as often as he went to unlock the chest the Old Scratch came behind and caught his arm. The money, they say, was paid Peter out of his purse, and he wanted Peter to give him a deed of this house and land, which Peter swore he would not do."

"Just as I swore to John Brown, my old partner," remarked Peter. "But this is all nonsense, Tabby; I don't believe the story."

"Well, it may not be just the truth," said Tabitha, "for some folks say that Peter did make over the house to the Old Scratch, and that's the reason it has always been so unlucky to them that lived in it. And as soon as Peter had given him the deed the chest flew open, and Peter caught up a handful of the gold. But, lo and behold! there was nothing in his fist but a parcel of old rags."

"Hold your tongue, you silly old Tabby!" cried Peter, in great wrath. "They were as good golden guineas as ever bore the effigies of the king of England. It seems as if I could recollect the whole circumstance, and how I, or old Peter, or whoever it was, thrust in my hand, or his hand, and drew it out all of a blaze with gold. Old rags indeed!"

But it was not an old woman's legend that would discourage Peter Goldthwaite. All night long he slept among pleasant dreams, and awoke at daylight with a joyous throb of the heart which few are fortunate enough to feel beyond their boyhood. Day after day he labored hard without wasting a moment except at meal-times, when Tabitha summoned him to the pork and cabbage, or such other sustenance as she had picked up or Providence had sent them. Being a truly pious man, Peter never failed to ask a blessing—if the food were none of the best, then so much the more earnestly, as it was more needed—nor to return thanks, if the dinner had been scanty, yet for the good appetite which was better than a sick stomach at a feast. Then did he hurry back to his toil, and in a moment was lost to sight in a cloud of dust from the old walls, though sufficiently perceptible to the ear by the clatter which he raised in the midst of it.

How enviable is the consciousness of being usefully employed! Nothing troubled Peter, or nothing but those phantoms of the mind which seem like vague recollections, yet have also the aspect of presentiments. He often paused with his axe uplifted in the air, and said to himself, "Peter Goldthwaite, did you never strike this blow before?" or "Peter, what need of tearing the whole house down? Think a little while, and you will remember where the gold is hidden." Days and weeks passed on, however, without any remarkable discovery. Sometimes, indeed, a lean gray rat peeped forth at the lean gray man, wondering what devil had got into the old house, which had always been so peaceable till now. And occasionally Peter sympathized with the sorrows of a female mouse who had brought five or six pretty, little, soft and delicate young ones into the world just in time to see them crushed by its ruin. But as yet no treasure.

By this time, Peter, being as determined as fate and as diligent as time, had made an end with the uppermost regions and got down to the second story, where he was busy in one of the front chambers. It had formerly been the state-bedchamber, and was honored by tradition as the sleeping-apartment of Governor Dudley and many other eminent guests. The furniture was gone. There were remnants of faded and tattered paper-hangings, but larger spaces of bare wall ornamented with charcoal sketches, chiefly of people's heads in profile. These being specimens of Peter's youthful genius, it went more to his heart to obliterate them than if they had been pictures on a church wall by Michael Angelo. One sketch, however, and that the best one, affected him differently. It represented a ragged man partly supporting himself on a spade and bending his lean body over a hole in the earth, with one hand extended to grasp something that he had found. But close behind him, with a fiendish laugh on his features, appeared a figure with horns, a tufted tail and a cloven hoof.

"Avaunt, Satan!" cried Peter. "The man shall have his gold." Uplifting his axe, he hit the horned gentleman such a blow on the head as not only demolished him, but the treasure-seeker also, and caused the whole scene to vanish like magic. Moreover, his axe broke quite through the plaster and laths and discovered a cavity.

"Mercy on us, Mr. Peter! Are you quarrelling with the Old Scratch?" said Tabitha, who was seeking some fuel to put under the dinner-pot.

Without answering the old woman, Peter broke down a further space of the wall, and laid open a small closet or cupboard on one side of the fireplace, about breast-high from the ground. It contained nothing but a brass lamp covered with verdigris, and a dusty piece of parchment. While Peter inspected the latter, Tabitha seized the lamp and began to rub it with her apron.

"There is no use in rubbing it, Tabitha," said Peter. "It is not Aladdin's lamp, though I take it to be a token of as much luck. Look here, Tabby!"

Tabitha took the parchment and held it close to her nose, which was saddled with a pair of iron-bound spectacles. But no sooner had she begun to puzzle over it than she burst into a chuckling laugh, holding both her hands against her sides.

"You can't make a fool of the old woman," cried she. "This is your own handwriting, Mr. Peter, the same as in the letter you sent me from Mexico."

"There is certainly a considerable resemblance," said Peter, again examining the parchment. "But you know yourself, Tabby, that this closet must have been plastered up before you came to the house or I came into the world. No; this is old Peter Goldthwaite's writing. These columns of pounds, shillings and pence are his figures, denoting the amount of the treasure, and this, at the bottom, is doubtless a reference to the place of concealment. But the ink has either faded or peeled off, so that it is absolutely illegible. What a pity!"

"Well, this lamp is as good as new. That's some comfort," said Tabitha.

"A lamp!" thought Peter. "That indicates light on my researches."

For the present Peter felt more inclined to ponder on this discovery than to resume his labors. After Tabitha had gone down stairs he stood poring over the parchment at one of the front windows, which was so obscured with dust that the sun could barely throw an uncertain shadow of the casement across the floor. Peter forced it open and looked out upon the great street of the town, while the sun looked in at his old house. The air, though mild, and even warm, thrilled Peter as with a dash of water.

It was the first day of the January thaw. The snow lay deep upon the housetops, but was rapidly dissolving into millions of water-drops, which sparkled downward through the sunshine with the noise of a summer shower beneath the eaves. Along the street the trodden snow was as hard and solid as a pavement of white marble, and had not yet grown moist in the spring-like temperature. But when Peter thrust forth his head, he saw that the inhabitants, if not the town, were already thawed out by this warm day, after two or three weeks of winter weather. It gladdened him—a gladness with a sigh breathing through it—to see the stream of ladies gliding along the slippery sidewalks with their red cheeks set off by quilted hoods, boas and sable capes like roses amidst a new kind of foliage. The sleigh bells jingled to and fro continually, sometimes announcing the arrival of a sleigh from Vermont laden with the frozen bodies of porkers or sheep, and perhaps a deer or two; sometimes, of a regular marketman with chickens, geese and turkeys, comprising the whole colony of a barn-yard; and sometimes, of a farmer and his dame who had come to town partly for the ride, partly to go a-shopping and partly for the sale of some eggs and butter. This couple rode in an old-fashioned square sleigh which had served them twenty winters and stood twenty summers in the sun beside their door. Now a gentleman and lady skimmed the snow in an elegant car shaped somewhat like a cockle-shell; now a stage-sleigh with its cloth curtains thrust aside to admit the sun dashed rapidly down the street, whirling in and out among the vehicles that obstructed its passage; now came round a corner the similitude of Noah's ark on runners, being an immense open sleigh with seats for fifty people and drawn by a dozen horses. This spacious receptacle was populous with merry maids and merry bachelors, merry girls and boys and merry old folks, all alive with fun and grinning to the full width of their mouths. They kept up a buzz of babbling voices and low laughter, and sometimes burst into a deep, joyous shout which the spectators answered with three cheers, while a gang of roguish boys let drive their snow-balls right among the pleasure-party. The sleigh passed on, and when concealed by a bend of the street was still audible by a distant cry of merriment.

Never had Peter beheld a livelier scene than was constituted by all these accessories—the bright sun, the flashing water-drops, the gleaming snow, the cheerful multitude, the variety of rapid vehicles and the jingle-jangle of merry bells which made the heart dance to their music. Nothing dismal was to be seen except that peaked piece of antiquity Peter Goldthwaite's house, which might well look sad externally, since such a terrible consumption was preying on its insides. And Peter's gaunt figure, half visible in the projecting second story, was worthy of his house.

"Peter! How goes it, friend Peter?" cried a voice across the street as Peter was drawing in his head. "Look out here, Peter!"

Peter looked, and saw his old partner, Mr. John Brown, on the opposite sidewalk, portly and comfortable, with his furred cloak thrown open, disclosing a handsome surtout beneath. His voice had directed the attention of the whole town to Peter Goldthwaite's window, and to the dusty scarecrow which appeared at it.

"I say, Peter!" cried Mr. Brown, again; "what the devil are you about there, that I hear such a racket whenever I pass by? You are repairing the old house, I suppose, making a new one of it? Eh?"

"Too late for that, I am afraid, Mr. Brown," replied Peter. "If I make it new, it will be new inside and out, from the cellar upward."

"Had not you better let me take the job?" said Mr. Brown, significantly.

"Not yet," answered Peter, hastily shutting the window; for ever since he had been in search of the treasure he hated to have people stare at him.

As he drew back, ashamed of his outward poverty, yet proud of the secret wealth within his grasp, a haughty smile shone out on Peter's visage with precisely the effect of the dim sunbeams in the squalid chamber. He endeavored to assume such a mien as his ancestor had probably worn when he gloried in the building of a strong house for a home to many generations of his posterity. But the chamber was very dark to his snow-dazzled eyes, and very dismal, too, in contrast with the living scene that he had just looked upon. His brief glimpse into the street had given him a forcible impression of the manner in which the world kept itself cheerful and prosperous by social pleasures and an intercourse of business, while he in seclusion was pursuing an object that might possibly be a phantasm by a method which most people would call madness. It is one great advantage of a gregarious mode of life that each person rectifies his mind by other minds and squares his conduct to that of his neighbors, so as seldom to be lost in eccentricity. Peter Goldthwaite had exposed himself to this influence by merely looking out of the window. For a while he doubted whether there were any hidden chest of gold, and in that case whether it was so exceedingly wise to tear the house down only to be convinced of its non-existence.

But this was momentary. Peter the Destroyer resumed the task which Fate had assigned him, nor faltered again till it was accomplished. In the course of his search he met with many things that are usually found in the ruins of an old house, and also with some that are not. What seemed most to the purpose was a rusty key which had been thrust into a chink of the wall, with a wooden label appended to the handle, bearing the initials "P.G." Another singular discovery was that of a bottle of wine walled up in an old oven. A tradition ran in the family that Peter's grandfather, a jovial officer in the old French war, had set aside many dozens of the precious liquor for the benefit of topers then unborn. Peter needed no cordial to sustain his hopes, and therefore kept the wine to gladden his success. Many half-pence did he pick up that had been lost through the cracks of the floor, and some few Spanish coins, and the half of a broken sixpence which had doubtless been a love-token. There was likewise a silver coronation medal of George III. But old Peter Goldthwaite's strong-box fled from one dark corner to another, or otherwise eluded the second Peter's clutches till, should he seek much farther, he must burrow into the earth.

We will not follow him in his triumphant progress step by step. Suffice it that Peter worked like a steam-engine and finished in that one winter the job which all the former inhabitants of the house, with time and the elements to aid them, had only half done in a century. Except the kitchen, every room and chamber was now gutted. The house was nothing but a shell, the apparition of a house, as unreal as the painted edifices of a theatre. It was like the perfect rind of a great cheese in which a mouse had dwelt and nibbled till it was a cheese no more. And Peter was the mouse.

What Peter had torn down, Tabitha had burnt up, for she wisely considered that without a house they should need no wood to warm it, and therefore economy was nonsense. Thus the whole house might be said to have dissolved in smoke and flown up among the clouds through the great black flue of the kitchen chimney. It was an admirable parallel to the feat of the man who jumped down his own throat.

On the night between the last day of winter and the first of spring every chink and cranny had been ransacked except within the precincts of the kitchen. This fated evening was an ugly one. A snow-storm had set in some hours before, and was still driven and tossed about the atmosphere by a real hurricane which fought against the house as if the prince of the air in person were putting the final stroke to Peter's labors. The framework being so much weakened and the inward props removed, it would have been no marvel if in some stronger wrestle of the blast the rotten walls of the edifice and all the peaked roofs had come crashing down upon the owner's head. He, however, was careless of the peril, but as wild and restless as the night itself, or as the flame that quivered up the chimney at each roar of the tempestuous wind.

"The wine, Tabitha," he cried—"my grandfather's rich old wine! We will drink it now."

Tabitha arose from her smoke-blackened bench in the chimney-corner and placed the bottle before Peter, close beside the old brass lamp which had likewise been the prize of his researches. Peter held it before his eyes, and, looking through the liquid medium, beheld the kitchen illuminated with a golden glory which also enveloped Tabitha and gilded her silver hair and converted her mean garments into robes of queenly splendor. It reminded him of his golden dream.

"Mr. Peter," remarked Tabitha, "must the wine be drunk before the money is found?"

"The money *is* found!" exclaimed Peter, with a sort of fierceness. "The chest is within my reach; I will not sleep till I have turned this key in the rusty lock. But first of all let us drink."

There being no corkscrew in the house, he smote the neck of the bottle with old Peter Goldthwaite's rusty key, and decapitated the sealed cork at a single blow. He then filled two little china teacups which Tabitha had brought from the cupboard. So clear and brilliant was this aged wine that it shone within the cups and rendered the sprig of scarlet flowers at the bottom of each more distinctly visible than when there had been no wine there. Its rich and delicate perfume wasted itself round the kitchen.

"Drink, Tabitha!" cried Peter. "Blessings on the honest old fellow who set aside this good liquor for you and me! And here's to Peter Goldthwaite's memory!"

"And good cause have we to remember him," quoth Tabitha as she drank.

How many years, and through what changes of fortune and various calamity, had that bottle hoarded up its effervescent joy, to be quaffed at last by two such boon-companions! A portion of the happiness of a former age had been kept for them, and was now set free in a crowd of rejoicing visions to sport amid the storm and desolation of the present time. Until they have finished the bottle we must turn our eyes elsewhere.

It so chanced that on this stormy night Mr. John Brown found himself ill at ease in his wire-cushioned arm-chair by the glowing grate of anthracite which heated his handsome parlor. He was naturally a good sort of a man, and kind and pitiful whenever the misfortunes of others happened to reach his heart through the padded vest of his own prosperity. This evening he had thought much about his old partner, Peter Goldthwaite, his strange vagaries and continual ill-luck, the poverty of his dwelling at Mr. Brown's last visit, and Peter's crazed and haggard aspect when he had talked with him at the window.

"Poor fellow!" thought Mr. John Brown. "Poor crack-brained Peter Goldthwaite! For old acquaintance' sake I ought to have taken care that he was comfortable this rough winter." These feelings grew so powerful that, in spite of the inclement weather, he resolved to visit Peter Goldthwaite immediately.

The strength of the impulse was really singular. Every shriek of the blast seemed a summons, or would have seemed so had Mr. Brown been accustomed to hear the echoes of his own fancy in the wind. Much amazed at such active benevolence, he huddled himself in his cloak, muffled his throat and ears in comforters and handkerchiefs, and, thus fortified, bade defiance to the tempest. But the powers of the air had rather the best of the battle. Mr. Brown was just weathering the corner by Peter Goldthwaite's house when the hurricane caught him off his feet, tossed him face downward into a snow-bank and proceeded to bury his protuberant part beneath fresh drifts. There seemed little hope of his reappearance earlier than the next thaw. At the same moment his hat was snatched away and whirled aloft into some far-distant region whence no tidings have as yet returned.

Nevertheless Mr. Brown contrived to burrow a passage through the snow-drift, and with his bare head bent against the storm floundered onward to Peter's door. There was such a creaking and groaning and rattling, and such an ominous shaking, throughout the crazy edifice that the loudest rap would have been inaudible to those within. He therefore entered without ceremony, and groped his way to the kitchen. His intrusion even there was unnoticed. Peter and Tabitha stood with their backs to the door, stooping over a large chest which apparently they had just dragged from a cavity or concealed closet on the left side of the chimney. By the lamp in the old woman's hand Mr. Brown saw that the chest was barred and clamped with iron, strengthened with iron plates and studded with iron nails, so as to be a fit receptacle in which the wealth of one century might be hoarded up for the wants of another.

Peter Goldthwaite was inserting a key into the lock.

"Oh, Tabitha," cried he, with tremulous rapture, "how shall I endure the effulgence? The gold!—the bright, bright gold! Methinks I can remember my last glance at it just as the iron-plated lid fell down. And ever since, being seventy years, it has been blazing in secret and gathering its splendor against this glorious moment. It will flash upon us like the noonday sun."

"Then shade your eyes, Mr. Peter!" said Tabitha, with somewhat less patience than usual. "But, for mercy's sake, do turn the key!"

And with a strong effort of both hands Peter did force the rusty key through the intricacies of the rusty lock. Mr. Brown, in the mean time, had drawn near and thrust his eager visage between those of the other two at the instant that Peter threw up the lid. No sudden blaze illuminated the kitchen.

"What's here?" exclaimed Tabitha, adjusting her spectacles and holding the lamp over the open chest. "Old Peter Goldthwaite's hoard of old rags!"

"Pretty much so, Tabby," said Mr. Brown, lifting a handful of the treasure.

Oh what a ghost of dead and buried wealth had Peter Goldthwaite raised to scare himself out of his scanty wits withal! Here was the semblance of an incalculable sum, enough to purchase the whole town and build every street anew, but which, vast as it was, no sane man would have given a solid sixpence for. What, then, in sober earnest, were the delusive treasures of the chest? Why, here were old provincial bills of credit and treasury notes and bills of land-banks, and all other bubbles of the sort, from the first issue—above a century and a half ago—down nearly to the Revolution. Bills of a thousand pounds were intermixed with parchment pennies, and worth no more than they.

"And this, then, is old Peter Goldthwaite's treasure!" said John Brown. "Your namesake, Peter, was something like yourself; and when the provincial currency had depreciated fifty or seventy-five per cent, he bought it up in expectation of a rise. I have heard my grandfather say that old Peter gave his father a mortgage of this very house and land to raise cash for his silly project. But the currency kept sinking till nobody would take it as a gift, and there was old Peter Goldthwaite, like Peter the second, with thousands in his strong-box and hardly a coat to his back. He went mad upon the strength of it. But never mind, Peter; it is just the sort of capital for building castles in the air."

"The house will be down about our ears," cried Tabitha as the wind shook it with increasing violence.

"Let it fall," said Peter, folding his arms, as he seated himself upon the chest.

"No, no, my old friend Peter!" said John Brown. "I have house-room for you and Tabby, and a safe vault for the chest of treasure. To-morrow we will try to come to an agreement about the sale of this old house; real estate is well up, and I could afford you a pretty handsome price."

"And I," observed Peter Goldthwaite, with reviving spirits, "have a plan for laying out the cash to great advantage."

"Why, as to that," muttered John Brown to himself, "we must apply to the next court for a guardian to take care of the solid cash; and if Peter insists upon speculating, he may do it to his heart's content with old Peter Goldthwaite's treasure."

CHIPPINGS WITH A CHISEL.

Passing a summer several years since at Edgartown, on the island of Martha's Vineyard, I became acquainted with a certain carver of tombstones who had travelled and voyaged thither from the interior of Massachusetts in search of professional employment. The speculation had turned out so successful that my friend expected to transmute slate and marble into silver and gold to the amount of at least a thousand dollars during the few months of his sojourn at Nantucket and the Vineyard. The secluded life and the simple and primitive spirit which still characterizes the inhabitants of those islands, especially of Martha's Vineyard, insure their dead friends a longer and dearer remembrance than the daily novelty and revolving bustle of the world can elsewhere afford to beings of the past. Yet, while every family is anxious to erect a memorial to its departed members, the untainted breath of Ocean bestows such health and length of days upon the people of the isles as would cause a melancholy dearth of business to a resident artist in that line. His own monument, recording his decease by starvation, would probably be an early specimen of his skill. Gravestones, therefore, have generally been an article of imported merchandise.

In my walks through the burial-ground of Edgartown—where the dead have lain so long that the soil, once enriched by their decay, has returned to its original barrenness—in that ancient burial-ground I noticed much variety of monumental sculpture. The elder stones, dated a century back or more, have borders elaborately carved with flowers and are adorned with a multiplicity of death's-heads, crossbones, scythes, hour-glasses, and other lugubrious emblems of mortality, with here and there a winged cherub to direct the mourner's spirit upward. These productions of Gothic taste must have been quite beyond the colonial skill of the day, and were probably carved in London and brought across the ocean to commemorate the defunct worthies of this lonely isle. The more recent monuments are mere slabs of slate in the ordinary style, without any superfluous flourishes to set off the bald inscriptions. But others—and those far the most impressive both to my taste and feelings—were roughly hewn from the gray rocks of the island, evidently by the unskilled hands of surviving friends and relatives. On some there were merely the initials of a name; some were inscribed with misspelt prose or rhyme, in deep letters which the moss and wintry rain of many years had not been able to obliterate. These, these were graves where loved ones slept. It is an old theme of satire, the falsehood and vanity of monumental eulogies; but when affection and sorrow grave the letters with their own painful labor, then we may be sure that they copy from the record on their hearts.

My acquaintance the sculptor—he may share that title with Greenough, since the dauber of signs is a painter as well as Raphael—had found a ready market for all his blank slabs of marble and full occupation in lettering and ornamenting them. He was an elderly man, a descendant of the old Puritan family of Wigglesworth, with a certain simplicity and singleness both of heart and mind which, methinks, is more rarely found among us Yankees than in any other community of people. In spite of his gray head and wrinkled brow, he was quite like a child in all matters save what had some reference to his own business; he seemed, unless my fancy misled me, to view mankind in no other relation than as people in want of tombstones, and his literary attainments evidently comprehended very little either of prose of poetry which had not at one time or other been inscribed on slate or marble. His sole task and office among the immortal pilgrims of the tomb—the duty for which Providence had sent the old man into the world, as it were with a chisel in his hand—was to label the dead bodies, lest their names should be forgotten at the resurrection. Yet he had not failed, within a narrow scope, to gather a few sprigs of earthly, and more than earthly, wisdom—the harvest of many a grave. And, lugubrious as his calling might appear, he was as cheerful an old soul as health and integrity and lack of care could make him, and used to set to work upon one sorrowful inscription or another with that sort of spirit which impels a man to sing at his labor. On the whole, I found Mr. Wigglesworth an entertaining, and often instructive, if not an interesting, character; and, partly for the charm of his society, and still more because his work has an invariable attraction for "man that is born of woman," I was accustomed to spend some hours a day at his workshop. The quaintness of his remarks and their not infrequent truth—a truth condensed and pointed by the limited sphere of his view—gave a raciness to his talk which mere worldliness and general cultivation would at once have destroyed.

Sometimes we would discuss the respective merits of the various qualities of marble, numerous slabs of which were resting against the walls of the shop, or sometimes an hour or two would pass quietly without a word on either side while I watched how neatly his chisel struck out letter after letter of the names of the Nortons, the Mayhews, the Luces, the Daggets, and other immemorial families of the Vineyard. Often with an artist's pride the good old sculptor would speak of favorite productions of his skill which were scattered throughout the village graveyards of New England. But my chief and most instructive amusement was to witness his interviews with his customers, who held interminable consultations about the form and fashion of the desired monuments, the buried excellence to be commemorated, the anguish to be expressed, and finally the lowest price in dollars and cents for which a marble transcript of their feelings might be obtained. Really, my mind received many fresh ideas which perhaps may remain in it even longer than Mr. Wigglesworth's hardest marble will retain the deepest strokes of his chisel.

An elderly lady came to bespeak a monument for her first love, who had been killed by a whale in the Pacific Ocean no less than forty years before. It was singular that so strong an impression of early feeling should have survived through the changes of her subsequent life, in the course of which she had been a wife and a mother, and, so far as I could judge, a comfortable and happy woman. Reflecting within myself, it appeared to me that this lifelong sorrow—as, in all good faith, she deemed it—was one of the most fortunate circumstances of her history. It had given an ideality to her mind; it had kept her purer and less earthy than she would otherwise have been by drawing a portion of her sympathies apart from earth. Amid the throng of enjoyments and the pressure of worldly care and all the warm materialism of this life she had communed with a vision, and had been the better for such intercourse. Faithful to the husband of her maturity, and loving him with a far more real affection than she ever could have felt for this dream of her girlhood, there had still been an imaginative faith to the ocean-buried; so that an ordinary character had thus been elevated and refined. Her sighs had been the breath of Heaven to her soul. The good lady earnestly desired that the proposed monument should be ornamented with a carved border of marine plants intertwined with twisted sea-shells, such as were probably waving over her lover's skeleton or strewn around it in the far depths of the Pacific. But, Mr. Wigglesworth's chisel being inadequate to the task, she was forced to content herself with a rose hanging its head from a broken stem.

After her departure I remarked that the symbol was none of the most apt.

"And yet," said my friend the sculptor, embodying in this image the thoughts that had been passing through my own mind, "that broken rose has shed its sweet smell through forty years of the good woman's life."

It was seldom that I could find such pleasant food for contemplation as in the above instance. None of the applicants, I think, affected me more disagreeably than an old man who came, with his fourth wife hanging on his arm, to bespeak gravestones for the three former occupants of his marriage-bed. I watched with some anxiety to see whether his remembrance of either were more affectionate than of the other two, but could discover no symptom of the kind. The three monuments were all to be of the same material and form, and each decorated in bas-relief with two weeping willows, one of these sympathetic trees bending over its fellow, which was to be broken in the midst and rest upon a sepulchral urn. This, indeed, was Mr. Wigglesworth's standing emblem of conjugal bereavement. I shuddered at the gray polygamist who had so utterly lost the holy sense of individuality in wedlock that methought he was fain to reckon upon his fingers how many women who had once slept by his side were now sleeping in their graves. There was even—if I wrong him, it is no great matter—a glance sidelong at his living spouse, as if he were inclined to drive a thriftier bargain by bespeaking four gravestones in a lot.

I was better pleased with a rough old whaling-captain who gave directions for a broad marble slab divided into two compartments, one of which was to contain an epitaph on his deceased wife and the other to be left vacant till death should engrave his own name there. As is frequently the case among the whalers of Martha's Vineyard, so much of this storm-beaten widower's life had been tossed away on distant seas that out of twenty years of matrimony he had spent scarce three, and those at scattered intervals, beneath his own roof. Thus the wife of his youth, though she died in his and her declining age, retained the bridal dewdrops fresh around her memory.

My observations gave me the idea, and Mr. Wigglesworth confirmed it, that husbands were more faithful in setting up memorials to their dead wives than widows to their dead husbands. I was not ill-natured enough to fancy that women less than men feel so sure of their own constancy as to be willing to give a pledge of it in marble. It is more probably the fact that, while men are able to reflect upon their lost companions as remembrances apart from themselves, women, on the other hand, are conscious that a portion of their being has gone with the departed whithersoever he has gone. Soul clings to soul, the living dust has a sympathy with the dust of the grave; and by the very strength of that sympathy the wife of the dead shrinks the more sensitively from reminding the world of its existence. The link is already strong enough; it needs no visible symbol. And, though a shadow walks ever by her side and the touch of a chill hand is on her bosom, yet life, and perchance its natural yearnings, may still be warm within her and inspire her with new hopes of happiness. Then would she mark out the grave the scent of which would be perceptible on the pillow of the second bridal? No, but rather level its green mound with the surrounding earth, as if, when she dug up again her buried heart, the spot had ceased to be a grave.

Yet, in spite of these sentimentalities, I was prodigiously amused by an incident of which I had not the good-fortune to be a witness, but which Mr. Wigglesworth related with considerable humor. A gentlewoman of the town, receiving news of her husband's loss at sea, had bespoken a handsome slab of marble, and came daily to watch the progress of my friend's chisel. One afternoon, when the good lady and the sculptor were in the very midst of the epitaph—which the departed spirit might have been greatly comforted to read—who should walk into the workshop but the deceased himself, in substance as well as spirit! He had been picked up at sea, and stood in no present need of tombstone or epitaph.

"And how," inquired I, "did his wife bear the shock of joyful surprise?"

"Why," said the old man, deepening the grin of a death's-head on which his chisel was just then employed, "I really felt for the poor woman; it was one of my best pieces of marble—and to be thrown away on a living man!"

A comely woman with a pretty rosebud of a daughter came to select a gravestone for a twin-daughter, who had died a month before. I was impressed with the different nature of their feelings for the dead. The mother was calm and woefully resigned, fully conscious of her loss, as of a treasure which she had not always possessed, and therefore had been aware that it might be taken from her; but the daughter evidently had no real knowledge of what Death's doings were. Her thoughts knew, but not her heart. It seemed to me that by the print and pressure which the dead sister had left upon the survivor's spirit her feelings were almost the same as if she still stood side by side and arm in arm with the departed, looking at the slabs of marble, and once or twice she glanced around with a sunny smile, which, as its sister-smile had faded for ever, soon grew confusedly overshadowed. Perchance her consciousness was truer than her reflection; perchance her dead sister was a closer companion than in life.

The mother and daughter talked a long while with Mr. Wigglesworth about a suitable epitaph, and finally chose an ordinary verse of ill-matched rhymes which had already been inscribed upon innumerable tombstones. But when we ridicule the triteness of monumental verses, we forget that Sorrow reads far deeper in them than we can, and finds a profound and individual purport in what seems so vague and inexpressive unless interpreted by her. She makes the epitaph anew, though the selfsame words may have served for a thousand graves.

"And yet," said I afterward to Mr. Wigglesworth, "they might have made a better choice than this. While you were discussing the subject I was struck by at least a dozen simple and natural expressions from the lips of both mother and daughter. One of these would have formed an inscription equally original and appropriate."

"No, no!" replied the sculptor, shaking his head; "there is a good deal of comfort to be gathered from these little old scraps of poetry, and so I always recommend them in preference to any new-fangled ones. And somehow they seem to stretch to suit a great grief and shrink to fit a small one."

It was not seldom that ludicrous images were excited by what took place between Mr. Wigglesworth and his customers. A shrewd gentlewoman who kept a tavern in the town was anxious to obtain two or three gravestones for the deceased members of her family, and to pay for these solemn commodities by taking the sculptor to board. Hereupon a fantasy arose in my mind of good Mr. Wigglesworth sitting down to dinner at a broad, flat tombstone carving one of his own plump little marble cherubs, gnawing a pair of crossbones and drinking out of a hollow death's-head or perhaps a lachrymatory vase or sepulchral urn, while his hostess's dead children waited on him at the ghastly banquet. On communicating this nonsensical picture to the old man he laughed heartily and pronounced my humor to be of the right sort.

"I have lived at such a table all my days," said he, "and eaten no small quantity of slate and marble."

"Hard fare," rejoined I, smiling, "but you seemed to have found it excellent of digestion, too."

A man of fifty or thereabouts with a harsh, unpleasant countenance ordered a stone for the grave of his bitter enemy, with whom he had waged warfare half a lifetime, to their mutual misery and ruin. The secret of this phenomenon was that hatred had become the sustenance and enjoyment of the poor wretch's soul; it had supplied the place of all kindly affections; it had been really a bond of sympathy between himself and the man who shared the passion; and when its object died, the unappeasable foe was the only mourner for the dead. He expressed a purpose of being buried side by side with his enemy.

"I doubt whether their dust will mingle," remarked the old sculptor to me; for often there was an earthliness in his conceptions.

"Oh yes," replied I, who had mused long upon the incident; "and when they rise again, these bitter foes may find themselves dear friends. Methinks what they mistook for hatred was but love under a mask."

A gentleman of antiquarian propensities provided a memorial for an Indian of Chabbiquidick—one of the few of untainted blood remaining in that region, and said to be a hereditary chieftain descended from the sachem who welcomed Governor Mayhew to the Vineyard. Mr. Wiggles-worth exerted his best skill to carve a broken bow and scattered sheaf of arrows in memory of the hunters and warriors whose race was ended here, but he likewise sculptured a cherub, to denote that the poor Indian had shared the Christian's hope of immortality.

"Why," observed I, taking a perverse view of the winged boy and the bow and arrows, "it looks more like Cupid's tomb than an Indian chief's."

"You talk nonsense," said the sculptor, with the offended pride of art. He then added with his usual good-nature, "How can Cupid die when there are such pretty maidens in the Vineyard?"

"Very true," answered I; and for the rest of the day I thought of other matters than tombstones.

At our next meeting I found him chiselling an open book upon a marble headstone, and concluded that it was meant to express the erudition of some black-letter clergyman of the Cotton Mather school. It turned out, however, to be emblematical of the scriptural knowledge of an old woman who had never read anything but her Bible, and the monument was a tribute to her piety and good works from the orthodox church of which she had been a member. In strange contrast with this Christian woman's memorial was that of an infidel whose gravestone, by his own direction, bore an avowal of his belief that the spirit within him would be extinguished like a flame, and that the nothingness whence he sprang would receive him again.

Mr. Wigglesworth consulted me as to the propriety of enabling a dead man's dust to utter this dreadful creed.

"If I thought," said he, "that a single mortal would read the inscription without a shudder, my chisel should never cut a letter of it. But when the grave speaks such falsehoods, the soul of man will know the truth by its own horror."

"So it will," said I, struck by the idea. "The poor infidel may strive to preach blasphemies from his grave, but it will be only another method of impressing the soul with a consciousness of immortality."

There was an old man by the name of Norton, noted throughout the island for his great wealth, which he had accumulated by the exercise of strong and shrewd faculties combined with a most penurious disposition. This wretched miser, conscious that he had not a friend to be mindful of him in his grave, had himself taken the needful precautions for posthumous remembrance by bespeaking an immense slab of white marble with a long epitaph in raised letters, the whole to be as magnificent as Mr. Wigglesworth's skill could make it. There was something very characteristic in this contrivance to have his money's worth even from his own tombstone, which, indeed, afforded him more enjoyment in the few months that he lived thereafter than it probably will in a whole century, now that it is laid over his bones.

This incident reminds me of a young girl—a pale, slender, feeble creature most unlike the other rosy and healthful damsels of the Vineyard, amid whose brightness she was fading away. Day after day did the poor maiden come to the sculptor's shop and pass from one piece of marble to another, till at last she pencilled her name upon a slender slab which, I think, was of a more spotless white than all the rest. I saw her no more, but soon afterward found Mr. Wigglesworth cutting her virgin-name into the stone which she had chosen.

"She is dead, poor girl!" said he, interrupting the tune which he was whistling, "and she chose a good piece of stuff for her headstone. Now, which of these slabs would you like best to see your own name upon?"

"Why, to tell you the truth, my good Mr. Wigglesworth," replied I, after a moment's pause, for the abruptness of the question had somewhat startled me—"to be quite sincere with you, I care little or nothing about a stone for my own grave, and am somewhat inclined to scepticism as to the propriety of erecting monuments at all over the dust that once was human. The weight of these heavy marbles, though unfelt by the dead corpse or the enfranchised soul, presses drearily upon the spirit of the survivor and causes him to connect the idea of death with the dungeon-like imprisonment of the tomb, instead of with the freedom of the skies. Every gravestone that you ever made is the visible symbol of a mistaken system. Our thoughts should soar upward with the butterfly, not linger with the exuviæ that confined him. In truth and reason, neither those whom we call the living, and still less the departed, have anything to do with the grave."

"I never heard anything so heathenish," said Mr. Wigglesworth, perplexed and displeased at sentiments which controverted all his notions and feelings and implied the utter waste, and worse, of his whole life's labor. "Would you forget your dead friends the moment they are under the sod?"

"They are not under the sod," I rejoined; "then why should I mark the spot where there is no treasure hidden? Forget them? No; but, to remember them aright, I would forget what they have cast off. And to gain the truer conception of death I would forget the grave."

But still the good old sculptor murmured, and stumbled, as it were, over the gravestones amid which he had walked through life. Whether he were right or wrong, I had grown the wiser from our companionship and from my observations of nature and character as displayed by those who came, with their old griefs or their new ones, to get them recorded upon his slabs of marble. And yet with my gain of wisdom I had likewise gained perplexity; for there was a strange doubt in my mind whether the dark shadowing of this life, the sorrows and regrets, have not as much real comfort in them—leaving religious influences out of the question—as what we term life's joys.

THE SHAKER BRIDAL.

One day, in the sick-chamber of Father Ephraim, who had been forty years the presiding elder over the Shaker settlement at Goshen, there was an assemblage of several of the chief men of the sect. Individuals had come from the rich establishment at Lebanon, from Canterbury, Harvard and Alfred, and from all the other localities where this strange people have fertilized the rugged hills of New England by their systematic industry. An elder was likewise there who had made a pilgrimage of a thousand miles from a village of the faithful in Kentucky to visit his spiritual kindred the children of the sainted Mother Ann. He had partaken of the homely abundance of their tables, had quaffed the far-famed Shaker cider, and had joined in the sacred dance every step of which is believed to alienate the enthusiast from earth and bear him onward to heavenly purity and bliss. His brethren of the North had now courteously invited him to be present on an occasion when the concurrence of every eminent member of their community was peculiarly desirable.

The venerable Father Ephraim sat in his easy-chair, not only hoary-headed and infirm with age, but worn down by a lingering disease which it was evident would very soon transfer his patriarchal staff to other hands. At his footstool stood a man and woman, both clad in the Shaker garb.

"My brethren," said Father Ephraim to the surrounding elders, feebly exerting himself to utter these few words, "here are the son and daughter to whom I would commit the trust of which Providence is about to lighten my weary shoulders. Read their faces, I pray you, and say whether the inward movement of the spirit hath guided my choice aright."

Accordingly, each elder looked at the two candidates with a most scrutinizing gaze. The man—whose name was Adam Colburn—had a face sunburnt with labor in the fields, yet intelligent, thoughtful and traced with cares enough for a whole lifetime, though he had barely reached middle age. There was something severe in his aspect and a rigidity throughout his person—characteristics that caused him generally to be taken for a schoolmaster; which vocation, in fact, he had formerly exercised for several years. The woman, Martha Pierson, was somewhat above thirty, thin and pale, as a Shaker sister almost invariably is, and not entirely free from that corpse-like appearance which the garb of the sisterhood is so well calculated to impart.

"This pair are still in the summer of their years," observed the elder from Harvard, a shrewd old man. "I would like better to see the hoar-frost of autumn on their heads. Methinks, also, they will be exposed to peculiar temptations on account of the carnal desires which have heretofore subsisted between them."

"Nay, brother," said the elder from Canterbury; "the hoar-frost and the black frost hath done its work on Brother Adam and Sister Martha, even as we sometimes discern its traces in our cornfields while they are yet green. And why should we question the wisdom of our venerable Father's purpose, although this pair in their early youth have loved one another as the world's people love? Are there not many brethren and sisters among us who have lived long together in wedlock, yet, adopting our faith, find their hearts purified from all but spiritual affection?"

Whether or no the early loves of Adam and Martha had rendered it inexpedient that they should now preside together over a Shaker village, it was certainly most singular that such should be the final result of many warm and tender hopes. Children of neighboring families, their affection was older even than their school-days; it seemed an innate principle interfused among all their sentiments and feelings, and not so much a distinct remembrance as connected with their whole volume of remembrances. But just as they reached a proper age for their union misfortunes had fallen heavily on both and made it necessary that they should resort to personal labor for a bare subsistence. Even under these circumstances Martha Pierson would probably have consented to unite her fate with Adam Colburn's, and, secure of the bliss of mutual love, would patiently have awaited the less important gifts of Fortune. But Adam, being of a calm and cautious character, was loth to relinquish the advantages which a single man possesses for raising himself in the world. Year after year, therefore, their marriage had been deferred.

Adam Colburn had followed many vocations, had travelled far and seen much of the world and of life. Martha had earned her bread sometimes as a sempstress, sometimes as help to a farmer's wife, sometimes as schoolmistress of the village children, sometimes as a nurse or watcher of the sick, thus acquiring a varied experience the ultimate use of which she little anticipated. But nothing had gone prosperously with either of the lovers; at no subsequent moment would matrimony have been so prudent a measure as when they had first parted, in the opening bloom of life, to seek a better fortune. Still, they had held fast their mutual faith. Martha might have been the wife of a man who sat among the senators of his native State, and Adam could have won the hand, as he had unintentionally won the heart, of a rich and comely widow. But neither of them desired good-fortune save to share it with the other.

At length that calm despair which occurs only in a strong and somewhat stubborn character and yields to no second spring of hope settled down on the spirit of Adam Colburn. He sought an interview with Martha and proposed that they should join the Society of Shakers. The converts of this sect are oftener driven within its hospitable gates by worldly misfortune than drawn thither by fanaticism, and are received without inquisition as to their motives. Martha, faithful still, had placed her hand in that of her lover and accompanied him to the Shaker village. Here the natural capacity of each, cultivated and strengthened by the difficulties of their previous lives, had soon gained them an important rank in the society, whose members are generally below the ordinary standard of intelligence. Their faith and feelings had in some degree become assimilated to those of their fellow-worshippers. Adam Colburn gradually acquired reputation not only in the management of the temporal affairs of the society, but as a clear and efficient preacher of their doctrines. Martha was not less distinguished in the duties proper to her sex. Finally, when the infirmities of Father Ephraim had admonished him to seek a successor in his patriarchal office, he thought of Adam and Martha, and proposed to renew in their persons the primitive form of Shaker government as established by Mother Ann. They were to be the father and mother of the village. The simple ceremony which would constitute them such was now to be performed.

"Son Adam and daughter Martha," said the venerable Father Ephraim, fixing his aged eyes piercingly upon them, "if ye can conscientiously undertake this charge, speak, that the brethren may not doubt of your fitness."

"Father," replied Adam, speaking with the calmness of his character, "I came to your village a disappointed man, weary of the world, worn out with continual trouble, seeking only a security against evil fortune, as I had no hope of good. Even my wishes of worldly success were almost dead within me. I came hither as a man might come to a tomb willing to lie down in its gloom and coldness for the sake of its peace and quiet. There was but one earthly affection in my breast, and it had grown calmer since my youth; so that I was satisfied to bring Martha to be my sister in our new abode. We are brother and sister, nor would I have it otherwise. And in this peaceful village I have found all that I hope for—all that I desire. I will strive with my best strength for the spiritual and temporal good of our community. My conscience is not doubtful in this matter. I am ready to receive the trust."

"Thou hast spoken well, son Adam," said the father. "God will bless thee in the office which I am about to resign."

"But our sister," observed the elder from Harvard. "Hath she not likewise a gift to declare her sentiments?"

Martha started and moved her lips as if she would have made a formal reply to this appeal. But, had she attempted it, perhaps the old recollections, the long-repressed feelings of childhood, youth and womanhood, might have gushed from her heart in words that it would have been profanation to utter there.

"Adam has spoken," said she, hurriedly; "his sentiments are likewise mine."

But while speaking these few words Martha grew so pale that she looked fitter to be laid in her coffin than to stand in the presence of Father Ephraim and the elders; she shuddered, also, as if there were something awful or horrible in her situation and destiny. It required, indeed, a more than feminine strength of nerve to sustain the fixed observance of men so exalted and famous throughout the Beet as these were. They had overcome their natural sympathy with human frailties and affections. One, when he joined the society, had brought with him his wife and children, but never from that hour had spoken a fond word to the former or taken his best-loved child upon his knee. Another, whose family refused to follow him, had been enabled—such was his gift of holy fortitude—to leave them to the mercy of the world. The youngest of the elders, a man of about fifty, had been bred from infancy in a Shaker village, and was said never to have clasped a woman's hand in his own, and to have no conception of a closer tie than the cold fraternal one of the sect. Old Father Ephraim was the most awful character of all. In his youth he had been a dissolute libertine, but was converted by Mother Ann herself, and had partaken of the wild fanaticism of the early Shakers. Tradition whispered at the firesides of the village that Mother Ann had been compelled to sear his heart of flesh with a red-hot iron before it could be purified from earthly passions.

However that might be, poor Martha had a woman's heart, and a tender one, and it quailed within her as she looked round at those strange old men, and from them to the calm features of Adam Colburn. But, perceiving that the elders eyed her doubtfully, she gasped for breath and again spoke.

"With what strength is left me by my many troubles," said she, "I am ready to undertake this charge, and to do my best in it."

"My children, join your hands," said Father Ephraim.

They did so. The elders stood up around, and the father feebly raised himself to a more erect position, but continued sitting in his great chair.

"I have bidden you to join your hands," said he, "not in earthly affection, for ye have cast off its chains for ever, but as brother and sister in spiritual love and helpers of one another in your allotted task. Teach unto others the faith which ye have received. Open wide your gates—I deliver you the keys thereof—open them wide to all who will give up the iniquities of the world and come hither to lead lives of purity and peace. Receive the weary ones who have known the vanity of earth; receive the little children, that they may never learn that miserable lesson. And a blessing be upon your labors; so that the time may hasten on when the mission of Mother Ann shall have wrought its full effect, when children shall no more be born and die, and the last survivor of mortal race—some old and weary man like me—shall see the sun go down nevermore to rise on a world of sin and sorrow."

The aged father sank back exhausted, and the surrounding elders deemed, with good reason, that the hour was come when the new heads of the village must enter on their patriarchal duties. In their attention to Father Ephraim their eyes were turned from Martha Pierson, who grew paler and paler, unnoticed even by Adam Colburn. He, indeed, had withdrawn his hand from hers and folded his arms with a sense of satisfied ambition. But paler and paler grew Martha by his side, till, like a corpse in its burial-clothes, she sank down at the feet of her early lover; for, after many trials firmly borne, her heart could endure the weight of its desolate agony no longer.

NIGHT-SKETCHES,

BENEATH AN UMBRELLA.

Pleasant is a rainy winter's day within-doors. The best study for such a day—or the best amusement: call it what you will—is a book of travels describing scenes the most unlike that sombre one which is mistily presented through the windows. I have experienced that Fancy is then most successful in imparting distinct shapes and vivid colors to the objects which the author has spread upon his page, and that his words become magic spells to summon up a thousand varied pictures. Strange landscapes glimmer through the familiar walls of the room, and outlandish figures thrust themselves almost within the sacred precincts of the hearth. Small as my chamber is, it has space enough to contain the ocean-like circumference of an Arabian desert, its parched sands tracked by the long line of a caravan with the camels patiently journeying through the heavy sunshine. Though my ceiling be not lofty, yet I can pile up the mountains of Central Asia beneath it till their summits shine far above the clouds of the middle atmosphere. And with my humble means—a wealth that is not taxable—I can transport hither the magnificent merchandise of an Oriental bazaar, and call a crowd of purchasers from distant countries to pay a fair profit for the precious articles which are displayed on all sides. True it is, however, that amid the bustle of traffic, or whatever else may seem to be going on around me, the raindrops will occasionally be heard to patter against my window-panes, which look forth upon one of the quietest streets in a New England town. After a time, too, the visions vanish, and will not appear again at my bidding. Then, it being nightfall, a gloomy sense of unreality depresses my spirits, and impels me to venture out before the clock shall strike bedtime to satisfy myself that the world is not entirely made up of such shadowy materials as have busied me throughout the day. A dreamer may dwell so long among fantasies that the things without him will seem as unreal as those within.

When eve has fairly set in, therefore, I sally forth, tightly buttoning my shaggy overcoat and hoisting my umbrella, the silken dome of which immediately resounds with the heavy drumming of the invisible raindrops. Pausing on the lowest doorstep, I contrast the warmth and cheerfulness of my deserted fireside with the drear obscurity and chill discomfort into which I am about to plunge. Now come fearful auguries innumerable as the drops of rain. Did not my manhood cry shame upon me, I should turn back within-doors, resume my elbow-chair, my slippers and my book, pass such an evening of sluggish enjoyment as the day has been, and go to bed inglorious. The same shivering reluctance, no doubt, has quelled for a moment the adventurous spirit of many a traveller when his feet, which were destined to measure the earth around, were leaving their last tracks in the home-paths.

In my own case poor human nature may be allowed a few misgivings. I look upward and discern no sky, not even an unfathomable void, but only a black, impenetrable nothingness, as though heaven and all its lights were blotted from the system of the universe. It is as if Nature were dead and the world had put on black and the clouds were weeping for her. With their tears upon my cheek I turn my eyes earthward, but find little consolation here below. A lamp is burning dimly at the distant corner, and throws just enough of light along the street to show, and exaggerate by so faintly showing, the perils and difficulties which beset my path. Yonder dingily-white remnant of a huge snowbank, which will yet cumber the sidewalk till the latter days of March, over or through that wintry waste must I stride onward. Beyond lies a certain Slough of Despond, a concoction of mud and liquid filth, ankle-deep, leg-deep, neck-deep—in a word, of unknown bottom—on which the lamplight does not even glimmer, but which I have occasionally watched in the gradual growth of its horrors from morn till nightfall. Should I flounder into its depths, farewell to upper earth! And hark! how roughly resounds the roaring of a stream the turbulent career of which is partially reddened by the gleam of the lamp, but elsewhere brawls noisily through the densest gloom! Oh, should I be swept away in fording that impetuous and unclean torrent, the coroner will have a job with an unfortunate gentleman who would fain end his troubles anywhere but in a mud-puddle.

Pshaw! I will linger not another instant at arm's-length from these dim terrors, which grow more obscurely formidable the longer I delay to grapple with them. Now for the onset, and, lo! with little damage save a dash of rain in the face and breast, a splash of mud high up the pantaloons and the left boot full of ice-cold water, behold me at the corner of the street. The lamp throws down a circle of red light around me, and twinkling onward from corner to corner I discern other beacons, marshalling my way to a brighter scene. But this is a lonesome and dreary spot. The tall edifices bid gloomy defiance to the storm with their blinds all closed, even as a man winks when he faces a spattering gust. How loudly tinkles the collected rain down the tin spouts! The puffs of wind are boisterous, and seem to assail me from various quarters at once. I have often observed that this corner is a haunt and loitering-place for those winds which have no work to do upon the deep dashing ships against our iron-bound shores, nor in the forest tearing up the sylvan giants with half a rood of soil at their vast roots. Here they amuse themselves with lesser freaks of mischief. See, at this moment, how they assail yonder poor woman who is passing just within the verge of the lamplight! One blast struggles for her umbrella and turns it wrong side outward, another whisks the cape of her cloak across her eyes, while a third takes most unwarrantable liberties with the lower part of her attire. Happily, the good dame is no gossamer, but a figure of rotundity and fleshly substance; else would these aerial tormentors whirl her aloft like a witch upon a broomstick, and set her down, doubtless, in the filthiest kennel hereabout.

From hence I tread upon firm pavements into the centre of the town. Here there is almost as brilliant an illumination as when some great victory has been won either on the battlefield or at the polls. Two rows of shops with windows down nearly to the ground cast a glow from side to side, while the black night hangs overhead like a canopy, and thus keeps the splendor from diffusing itself away. The wet sidewalks gleam with a broad sheet of red light. The raindrops glitter as if the sky were pouring down rubies. The spouts gush with fire. Methinks the scene is an emblem of the deceptive glare which mortals throw around their footsteps in the moral world, thus bedazzling themselves till they forget the impenetrable obscurity that hems them in, and that can be dispelled only by radiance from above.

And, after all, it is a cheerless scene, and cheerless are the wanderers in it. Here comes one who has so long been familiar with tempestuous weather that he takes the bluster of the storm for a friendly greeting, as if it should say, "How fare ye, brother?" He is a retired sea-captain wrapped in some nameless garment of the pea-jacket order, and is now laying his course toward the marine-insurance office, there to spin yarns of gale and shipwreck with a crew of old seadogs like himself. The blast will put in its word among their hoarse voices, and be understood by all of them. Next I meet an unhappy slipshod gentleman with a cloak flung hastily over his shoulders, running a race with boisterous winds and striving to glide between the drops of rain. Some domestic emergency or other has blown this miserable man from his warm fireside in quest of a doctor. See that little vagabond! How carelessly he has taken his stand right underneath a spout while staring at some object of curiosity in a shop-window! Surely the rain is his native element; he must have fallen with it from the clouds, as frogs are supposed to do.

Here is a picture, and a pretty one—a young man and a girl, both enveloped in cloaks and huddled beneath the scanty protection of a cotton umbrella. She wears rubber overshoes, but he is in his dancing-pumps, and they are on their way no doubt, to some cotillon-party or subscription-ball at a dollar a head, refreshments included. Thus they struggle against the gloomy tempest, lured onward by a vision of festal splendor. But ah! a most lamentable disaster! Bewildered by the red, blue and yellow meteors in an apothecary's window, they have stepped upon a slippery remnant of ice, and are precipitated into a confluence of swollen floods at the corner of two streets. Luckless lovers! Were it my nature to be other than a looker-on in life, I would attempt your rescue. Since that may not be, I vow, should you be drowned, to weave such a pathetic story of your fate as shall call forth tears enough to drown you both anew. Do ye touch bottom, my young friends? Yes; they emerge like a water-nymph and a river-deity, and paddle hand in hand out of the depths of the dark pool. They hurry homeward, dripping, disconsolate, abashed, but with love too warm to be chilled by the cold water. They have stood a test which proves too strong for many. Faithful though over head and ears in trouble!

Onward I go, deriving a sympathetic joy or sorrow from the varied aspect of mortal affairs even as my figure catches a gleam from the lighted windows or is blackened by an interval of darkness. Not that mine is altogether a chameleon spirit with no hue of its own. Now I pass into a more retired street where the dwellings of wealth and poverty are intermingled, presenting a range of strongly-contrasted pictures. Here, too, may be found the golden mean. Through yonder casement I discern a family circle—the grandmother, the parents and the children—all flickering, shadow-like, in the glow of a wood-fire.—Bluster, fierce blast, and beat, thou wintry rain, against the window-panes! Ye cannot damp the enjoyment of that fireside.—Surely my fate is hard that I should be wandering homeless here, taking to my bosom night and storm and solitude instead of wife and children. Peace, murmurer! Doubt not that darker guests are sitting round the hearth, though the warm blaze hides all but blissful images.

Well, here is still a brighter scene—a stately mansion illuminated for a ball, with cut-glass chandeliers and alabaster lamps in every room, and sunny landscapes hanging round the walls. See! a coach has stopped, whence emerges a slender beauty who, canopied by two umbrellas, glides within the portal and vanishes amid lightsome thrills of music. Will she ever feel the night-wind and the rain? Perhaps—perhaps! And will Death and Sorrow ever enter that proud mansion? As surely as the dancers will be gay within its halls to-night. Such thoughts sadden yet satisfy my heart, for they teach me that the poor man in this mean, weatherbeaten hovel, without a fire to cheer him, may call the rich his brother—brethren by Sorrow, who must be an inmate of both their households; brethren by Death, who will lead them both to other homes.

Onward, still onward, I plunge into the night. Now have I reached the utmost limits of the town, where the last lamp struggles feebly with the darkness like the farthest star that stands sentinel on the borders of uncreated space. It is strange what sensations of sublimity may spring from a very humble source. Such are suggested by this hollow roar of a subterranean cataract where the mighty stream of a kennel precipitates itself beneath an iron grate and is seen no more on earth. Listen a while to its voice of mystery, and Fancy will magnify it till you start and smile at the illusion. And now another sound—the rumbling of wheels as the mail-coach, outward bound, rolls heavily off the pavements and splashes through the mud and water of the road. All night long the poor passengers will be tossed to and fro between drowsy watch and troubled sleep, and will dream of their own quiet beds and awake to find themselves still jolting onward. Happier my lot, who will straightway hie me to my familiar room and toast myself comfortably before the fire, musing and fitfully dozing and fancying a strangeness in such sights as all may see. But first let me gaze at this solitary figure who comes hitherward with a tin lantern which throws the circular pattern of its punched holes on the ground about him. He passes fearlessly into the unknown gloom, whither I will not follow him.

This figure shall supply me with a moral wherewith, for lack of a more appropriate one, I may wind up my sketch. He fears not to tread the dreary path before him, because his lantern, which was kindled at the fireside of his home, will light him back to that same fireside again. And thus we, night-wanderers through a stormy and dismal world, if we bear the lamp of Faith enkindled at a celestial fire, it will surely lead us home to that heaven whence its radiance was borrowed.

ENDICOTT AND THE RED CROSS.

At noon of an autumnal day more than two centuries ago the English colors were displayed by the standard bearer of the Salem train-band, which had mustered for martial exercise under the orders of John Endicott. It was a period when the religious exiles were accustomed often to buckle on their armor and practise the handling of their weapons of war. Since the first settlement of New England its prospects had never been so dismal. The dissensions between Charles I. and his subjects were then, and for several years afterward, confined to the floor of Parliament. The measures of the king and ministry were rendered more tyrannically violent by an opposition which had not yet acquired sufficient confidence in its own strength to resist royal injustice with the sword. The bigoted and haughty primate Laud, archbishop of Canterbury, controlled the religious affairs of the realm, and was consequently invested with powers which might have wrought the utter ruin of the two Puritan colonies, Plymouth and Massachusetts. There is evidence on record that our forefathers perceived their danger, but were resolved that their infant country should not fall without a struggle, even beneath the giant strength of the king's right arm.

Such was the aspect of the times when the folds of the English banner with the red cross in its field were flung out over a company of Puritans. Their leader, the famous Endicott, was a man of stern and resolute countenance, the effect of which was heightened by a grizzled beard that swept the upper portion of his breastplate. This piece of armor was so highly polished that the whole surrounding scene had its image in the glittering steel. The central object in the mirrored picture was an edifice of humble architecture with neither steeple nor bell to proclaim it—what, nevertheless, it was—the house of prayer. A token of the perils of the wilderness was seen in the grim head of a wolf which had just been slain within the precincts of the town, and, according to the regular mode of claiming the bounty, was nailed on the porch of the meeting-house. The blood was still plashing on the doorstep. There happened to be visible at the same noontide hour so many other characteristics of the times and manners of the Puritans that we must endeavor to represent them in a sketch, though far less vividly than they were reflected in the polished breastplate of John Endicott.

In close vicinity to the sacred edifice appeared that important engine of Puritanic authority the whipping-post, with the soil around it well trodden by the feet of evil-doers who had there been disciplined. At one corner of the meeting-house was the pillory and at the other the stocks, and, by a singular good fortune for our sketch, the head of an Episcopalian and suspected Catholic was grotesquely encased in the former machine, while a fellow-criminal who had boisterously quaffed a health to the king was confined by the legs in the latter. Side by side on the meeting-house steps stood a male and a female figure. The man was a tall, lean, haggard personification of fanaticism, bearing on his breast this label, "A WANTON GOSPELLER," which betokened that he had dared to give interpretations of Holy Writ unsanctioned by the infallible judgment of the civil and reli-religious rulers. His aspect showed no lack of zeal to maintain his heterodoxies even at the stake. The woman wore a cleft stick on her tongue, in appropriate retribution for having wagged that unruly member against the elders of the church, and her countenance and gestures gave much cause to apprehend that the moment the stick should be removed a repetition of the offence would demand new ingenuity in chastising it.

The above-mentioned individuals had been sentenced to undergo their various modes of ignominy for the space of one hour at noonday. But among the crowd were several whose punishment would be lifelong—some whose ears had been cropped like those of puppy-dogs, others whose cheeks had been branded with the initials of their misdemeanors; one with his nostrils slit and seared, and another with a halter about his neck, which he was forbidden ever to take off or to conceal beneath his garments. Methinks he must have been grievously tempted to affix the other end of the rope to some convenient beam or bough. There was likewise a young woman with no mean share of beauty whose doom it was to wear the letter A on the breast of her gown in the eyes of all the world and her own children. And even her own children knew what that initial signified. Sporting with her infamy, the lost and desperate creature had embroidered the fatal token in scarlet cloth with golden thread and the nicest art of needlework; so that the capital A might have been thought to mean "Admirable," or anything rather than "Adulteress."

Let not the reader argue from any of these evidences of iniquity that the times of the Puritans were more vicious than our own, when as we pass along the very street of this sketch we discern no badge of infamy on man or woman. It was the policy of our ancestors to search out even the most secret sins and expose them to shame, without fear or favor, in the broadest light of the noonday sun. Were such the custom now, perchance we might find materials for a no less piquant sketch than the above.

Except the malefactors whom we have described and the diseased or infirm persons, the whole male population of the town, between sixteen years and sixty were seen in the ranks of the train-band. A few stately savages in all the pomp and dignity of the primeval Indian stood gazing at the spectacle. Their flint-headed arrows were but childish weapons, compared with the matchlocks of the Puritans, and would have rattled harmlessly against the steel caps and hammered iron breastplates which enclosed each soldier in an individual fortress. The valiant

John Endicott glanced with an eye of pride at his sturdy followers, and prepared to renew the martial toils of the day.

"Come, my stout hearts!" quoth he, drawing his sword. "Let us show these poor heathen that we can handle our weapons like men of might. Well for them if they put us not to prove it in earnest!"

The iron-breasted company straightened their line, and each man drew the heavy butt of his matchlock close to his left foot, thus awaiting the orders of the captain. But as Endicott glanced right and left along the front he discovered a personage at some little distance with whom it behoved him to hold a parley. It was an elderly gentleman wearing a black cloak and band and a high-crowned hat beneath which was a velvet skull-cap, the whole being the garb of a Puritan minister. This reverend person bore a staff which seemed to have been recently cut in the forest, and his shoes were bemired, as if he had been travelling on foot through the swamps of the wilderness. His aspect was perfectly that of a pilgrim, heightened also by an apostolic dignity. Just as Endicott perceived him he laid aside his staff and stooped to drink at a bubbling fountain which gushed into the sunshine about a score of yards from the corner of the meeting-house. But ere the good man drank he turned his face heavenward in thankfulness, and then, holding back his gray beard with one hand, he scooped up his simple draught in the hollow of the other.

"What ho, good Mr. Williams!" shouted Endicott. "You are welcome back again to our town of peace. How does our worthy Governor Winthrop? And what news from Boston?"

"The governor hath his health, worshipful sir," answered Roger Williams, now resuming his staff and drawing near. "And, for the news, here is a letter which, knowing I was to travel hitherward to-day, His Excellency committed to my charge. Belike it contains tidings of much import, for a ship arrived yesterday from England."

Mr. Williams, the minister of Salem, and of course known to all the spectators, had now reached the spot where Endicott was standing under the banner of his company, and put the governor's epistle into his hand. The broad seal was impressed with Winthrop's coat-of-arms. Endicott hastily unclosed the letter and began to read, while, as his eye passed down the page, a wrathful change came over his manly countenance. The blood glowed through it till it seemed to be kindling with an internal heat, nor was it unnatural to suppose that his breastplate would likewise become red hot with the angry fire of the bosom which it covered. Arriving at the conclusion, he shook the letter fiercely in his hand, so that it rustled as loud as the flag above his head.

"Black tidings these, Mr. Williams," said he; "blacker never came to New England. Doubtless you know their purport?"

"Yea, truly," replied Roger Williams, "for the governor consulted respecting this matter with my brethren in the ministry at Boston, and my opinion was likewise asked. And His Excellency entreats you by me that the news be not suddenly noised abroad, lest the people be stirred up unto some outbreak, and thereby give the king and the archbishop a handle against us."

"The governor is a wise man—a wise man, and a meek and moderate," said Endicott, setting his teeth grimly. "Nevertheless, I must do according to my own best judgment. There is neither man, woman nor child in New England but has a concern as dear as life in these tidings; and if John Endicott's voice be loud enough, man, woman and child shall hear them.—Soldiers, wheel into a hollow square.—Ho, good people! Here are news for one and all of you."

The soldiers closed in around their captain, and he and Roger Williams stood together under the banner of the red cross, while the women and the aged men pressed forward and the mothers held up their children to look Endicott in the face. A few taps of the drum gave signal for silence and attention.

"Fellow-soldiers, fellow-exiles," began Endicott, speaking under strong excitement, yet powerfully restraining it, "wherefore did ye leave your native country? Wherefore, I say, have we left the green and fertile fields, the cottages, or, perchance, the old gray halls, where we were born and bred, the churchyards where our forefathers lie buried? Wherefore have we come hither to set up our own tombstones in a wilderness? A howling wilderness it is. The wolf and the bear meet us within halloo of our dwellings. The savage lieth in wait for us in the dismal shadow of the woods. The stubborn roots of the trees break our ploughshares when we would till the earth. Our children cry for bread, and we must dig in the sands of the seashore to satisfy them. Wherefore, I say again, have we sought this country of a rugged soil and wintry sky? Was it not for the enjoyment of our civil rights? Was it not for liberty to worship God according to our conscience?"

"Call you this liberty of conscience?" interrupted a voice on the steps of the meeting-house.

It was the wanton gospeller. A sad and quiet smile flitted across the mild visage of Roger Williams, but Endicott, in the excitement of the moment, shook his sword wrathfully at the culprit—an ominous gesture from a man like him.

"What hast thou to do with conscience, thou knave?" cried he. "I said liberty to worship God, not license to profane and ridicule him. Break not in upon my speech, or I will lay thee neck and heels till this time to-morrow.—Hearken to me, friends, nor heed that accursed rhapsodist. As I was saying, we have sacrificed all things, and have come to a land whereof the Old World hath scarcely heard, that we might make a new world unto ourselves and painfully seek a path from hence to heaven. But what think ye now? This son of a Scotch tyrant—this grandson of a papistical and adulterous Scotch woman whose death proved that a golden crown doth not always save an anointed head from the block—"

"Nay, brother, nay," interposed Mr. Williams; "thy words are not meet for a secret chamber, far less for a public street."

"Hold thy peace, Roger Williams!" answered Endicott, imperiously. "My spirit is wiser than thine for the business now in hand.—I tell ye, fellow-exiles, that Charles of England and Laud, our bitterest persecutor, arch-priest of Canterbury, are resolute to pursue us even hither. They are taking counsel, saith this letter, to send over a governor-general in whose breast shall be deposited all the law and equity of the land. They are minded, also, to establish the idolatrous forms of English episcopacy; so that when Laud shall kiss the pope's toe as cardinal of Rome he may deliver New England, bound hand and foot, into the power of his master."

A deep groan from the auditors—a sound of wrath as well as fear and sorrow—responded to this intelligence.

"Look ye to it, brethren," resumed Endicott, with increasing energy. "If this king and this arch-prelate have their will, we shall briefly behold a cross on the spire of this tabernacle which we have builded, and a high altar within its walls, with wax tapers burning round it at noon-day. We shall hear the sacring-bell and the voices of the Romish priests saying the mass. But think ye, Christian men, that these abominations may be suffered without a sword drawn, without a shot fired, without blood spilt—yea, on the very stairs of the pulpit? No! Be ye strong of hand and stout of heart. Here we stand on our own soil, which we have bought with our goods, which we have won with our swords, which we have cleared with our axes, which we have tilled with the sweat of our brows, which we have sanctified with our prayers to the God that brought us hither! Who shall enslave us here? What have we to do with this mitred prelate—with this crowned king? What have we to do with England?"

Endicott gazed round at the excited countenances of the people, now full of his own spirit, and then turned suddenly to the standard-bearer, who stood close behind him.

"Officer, lower your banner," said he.

The officer obeyed, and, brandishing his sword, Endicott thrust it through the cloth and with his left hand rent the red cross completely out of the banner. He then waved the tattered ensign above his head.

"Sacrilegious wretch!" cried the high-churchman in the pillory, unable longer to restrain himself; "thou hast rejected the symbol of our holy religion."

"Treason! treason!" roared the royalist in the stocks. "He hath defaced the king's banner!"

"Before God and man I will avouch the deed," answered Endicott.—"Beat a flourish, drummer—shout, soldiers and people—in honor of the ensign of New England. Neither pope nor tyrant hath part in it now."

With a cry of triumph the people gave their sanction to one of the boldest exploits which our history records. And for ever honored be the name of Endicott! We look back through the mist of ages, and recognize in the rending of the red cross from New England's banner the first omen of that deliverance which our fathers consummated after the bones of the stern Puritan had lain more than a century in the dust.

THE LILY'S QUEST.

AN APOLOGUE.

Two lovers once upon a time had planned a little summer-house in the form of an antique temple which it was their purpose to consecrate to all manner of refined and innocent enjoyments. There they would hold pleasant intercourse with one another and the circle of their familiar friends; there they would give festivals of delicious fruit; there they would hear lightsome music intermingled with the strains of pathos which make joy more sweet; there they would read poetry and fiction and permit their own minds to flit away in day-dreams and romance; there, in short—for why should we shape out the vague sunshine of their hopes?—there all pure delights were to cluster like roses among the pillars of the edifice and blossom ever new and spontaneously.

So one breezy and cloudless afternoon Adam Forrester and Lilias Fay set out upon a ramble over the wide estate which they were to possess together, seeking a proper site for their temple of happiness. They were themselves a fair and happy spectacle, fit priest and priestess for such a shrine, although, making poetry of the pretty name of Lilias, Adam Forrester was wont to call her "Lily" because her form was as fragile and her cheek almost as pale. As they passed hand in hand down the avenue of drooping elms that led from the portal of Lilias Fay's paternal mansion they seemed to glance like winged creatures through the strips of sunshine, and to scatter brightness where the deep shadows fell.

But, setting forth at the same time with this youthful pair, there was a dismal figure wrapped in a black velvet cloak that might have been made of a coffin-pall, and with a sombre hat such as mourners wear drooping its broad brim over his heavy brows. Glancing behind them, the lovers well knew who it was that followed, but wished from their hearts that he had been elsewhere, as being a companion so strangely unsuited to their joyous errand. It was a near relative of Lilias Fay, an old man by the name of Walter Gascoigne, who had long labored under the burden of a melancholy spirit which was sometimes maddened into absolute insanity and always had a tinge of it. What a contrast between the young pilgrims of bliss and their unbidden associate! They looked as if moulded of heaven's sunshine and he of earth's gloomiest shade; they flitted along like Hope and Joy roaming hand in hand through life, while his darksome figure stalked behind, a type of all the woeful influences which life could fling upon them.

But the three had not gone far when they reached a spot that pleased the gentle Lily, and she paused.

"What sweeter place shall we find than this?" said she. "Why should we seek farther for the site of our temple?"

It was indeed a delightful spot of earth, though undistinguished by any very prominent beauties, being merely a nook in the shelter of a hill, with the prospect of a distant lake in one direction and of a church-spire in another. There were vistas and pathways leading onward and onward into the green woodlands and van-vanishing away in the glimmering shade. The temple, if erected here, would look toward the west; so that the lovers could shape all sorts of magnificent dreams out of the purple, violet and gold of the sunset sky, and few of their anticipated pleasures were dearer than this sport of fantasy.

"Yes," said Adam Forrester; "we might seek all day and find no lovelier spot. We will build our temple here."

But their sad old companion, who had taken his stand on the very site which they proposed to cover with a marble floor, shook his head and frowned, and the young man and the Lily deemed it almost enough to blight the spot and desecrate it for their airy temple that his dismal figure had thrown its shadow there. He pointed to some scattered stones, the remnants of a former structure, and to flowers such as young girls delight to nurse in their gardens, but which had now relapsed into the wild simplicity of nature.

"Not here," cried old Walter Gascoigne. "Here, long ago, other mortals built their temple of happiness; seek another site for yours."

"What!" exclaimed Lilias Fay. "Have any ever planned such a temple save ourselves?"

"Poor child!" said her gloomy kinsman. "In one shape or other every mortal has dreamed your dream." Then he told the lovers, how—not, indeed, an antique temple, but a dwelling—had once stood there, and that a dark-clad guest had dwelt among its inmates, sitting for ever at the fireside and poisoning all their household mirth.

Under this type Adam Forrester and Lilias saw that the old man spake of sorrow. He told of nothing that might not be recorded in the history of almost every household, and yet his hearers felt as if no sunshine ought to fall upon a spot where human grief had left so deep a stain—or, at least, that no joyous temple should be built there.

"This is very sad," said the Lily, sighing.

"Well, there are lovelier spots than this," said Adam Forrester, soothingly—"spots which sorrow has not blighted."

So they hastened away, and the melancholy Gascoigne followed them, looking as if he had gathered up all the gloom of the deserted spot and was bearing it as a burden of inestimable treasure. But still they rambled on, and soon found themselves in a rocky dell through the midst of which ran a streamlet with ripple and foam and a continual voice of inarticulate joy. It was a wild retreat walled on either side with gray precipices which would have frowned somewhat too sternly had not a profusion of green shrubbery rooted itself into their crevices and wreathed gladsome foliage around their solemn brows. But the chief joy of the dell was in the little stream which seemed like the presence of a blissful child with nothing earthly to do save to babble merrily and disport itself, and make every living soul its playfellow, and throw the sunny gleams of its spirit upon all.

"Here, here is the spot!" cried the two lovers, with one voice, as they reached a level space on the brink of a small cascade. "This glen was made on purpose for our temple."

"And the glad song of the brook will be always in our ears," said Lilias Fay.

"And its long melody shall sing the bliss of our lifetime," said Adam Forrester.

"Ye must build no temple here," murmured their dismal companion.

And there again was the old lunatic standing just on the spot where they meant to rear their lightsome dome, and looking like the embodied symbol of some great woe that in forgotten days had happened there. And, alas! there had been woe, nor that alone. A young man more than a hundred years before had lured hither a girl that loved him, and on this spot had murdered her and washed his bloody hands in the stream which sang so merrily, and ever since the victim's death-shrieks were often heard to echo between the cliffs.

"And see!" cried old Gascoigne; "is the stream yet pure from the stain of the murderer's hands?"

"Methinks it has a tinge of blood," faintly answered the Lily; and, being as slight as the gossamer, she trembled and clung to her lover's arm, whispering, "Let us flee from this dreadful vale."

"Come, then," said Adam Forrester as cheerily as he could; "we shall soon find a happier spot."

They set forth again, young pilgrims on that quest which millions—which every child of earth—has tried in turn.

And were the Lily and her lover to be more fortunate than all those millions? For a long time it seemed not so. The dismal shape of the old lunatic still glided behind them, and for every spot that looked lovely in their eyes he had some legend of human wrong or suffering so miserably sad that his auditors could never afterward connect the idea of joy with the place where it had happened. Here a heartbroken woman kneeling to her child had been spurned from his feet; here a desolate old creature had prayed to the evil one, and had received a fiendish malignity of soul in answer to her prayer; here a new-born infant, sweet blossom of life, had been found dead with the impress of its mother's fingers round its throat; and here, under a shattered oak, two lovers had been stricken by lightning and fell blackened corpses in each other's arms. The dreary Gascoigne had a gift to know whatever evil and lamentable thing had stained the bosom of Mother Earth; and when his funereal voice had told the tale, it appeared like a prophecy of future woe as well as a tradition of the past. And now, by their sad demeanor, you would have fancied that the pilgrim-lovers were seeking, not a temple of earthly joy, but a tomb for themselves and their posterity.

"Where in this world," exclaimed Adam Forrester, despondingly, "shall we build our temple of happiness?"

"Where in this world, indeed?" repeated Lilias Fay; and, being faint and weary—the more so by the heaviness of her heart—the Lily drooped her head and sat down on the summit of a knoll, repeating, "Where in this world shall we build our temple?"

"Ah! have you already asked yourselves that question?" said their companion, his shaded features growing even gloomier with the smile that dwelt on them. "Yet there is a place even in this world where ye may build it."

While the old man spoke Adam Forrester and Lilias had carelessly thrown their eyes around, and perceived that the spot where they had chanced to pause possessed a quiet charm which was well enough adapted to their present mood of mind. It was a small rise of ground with a certain regularity of shape that had perhaps been bestowed by art, and a group of trees which almost surrounded it threw their pensive shadows across and far beyond, although some softened glory of the sunshine found its way there. The ancestral mansion wherein the lovers would dwell together appeared on one side, and the ivied church where they were to worship on another. Happening to cast their eyes on the ground, they smiled, yet with a sense of wonder, to see that a pale lily was growing at their feet.

"We will build our temple here," said they, simultaneously, and with an indescribable conviction that they had at last found the very spot.

Yet while they uttered this exclamation the young man and the Lily turned an apprehensive glance at their dreary associate, deeming it hardly possible that some tale of earthly affliction should not make those precincts loathsome, as in every former case. The old man stood just behind them, so as to form the chief figure in the group, with his sable cloak muffling the lower part of his visage and his sombre hat overshadowing his brows. But he gave no word of dissent from their purpose, and an inscrutable smile was accepted by the lovers as a token that here had been no footprint of guilt or sorrow to desecrate the site of their temple of happiness.

In a little time longer, while summer was still in its prime, the fairy-structure of the temple arose on the summit of the knoll amid the solemn shadows of the trees, yet often gladdened with bright sunshine. It was built of white marble, with slender and graceful pillars supporting a vaulted dome, and beneath the centre of this dome, upon a pedestal, was a slab of dark-veined marble on which books and music might be strewn. But there was a fantasy among the people of the neighborhood that the edifice was planned after an ancient mausoleum and was intended for a tomb, and that the central slab of dark-veined marble was to be inscribed with the names of buried ones. They doubted, too, whether the form of Lilias Fay could appertain to a creature of this earth, being so very delicate and growing every day more fragile, so that she looked as if the summer breeze should snatch her up and waft her heavenward. But still she watched the daily growth of the temple, and so did old Walter Gascoigne, who now made that spot his continual haunt, leaning whole hours together on his staff and giving as deep attention to the work as though it had been indeed a tomb. In due time it was finished and a day appointed for a simple rite of dedication.

On the preceding evening, after Adam Forrester had taken leave of his mistress, he looked back toward the portal of her dwelling and felt a strange thrill of fear, for he imagined that as the setting sunbeams faded from her figure she was exhaling away, and that something of her ethereal substance was withdrawn with each lessening gleam of light. With his farewell glance a shadow had fallen over the portal, and Lilias was invisible. His foreboding spirit deemed it an omen at the time, and so it proved; for the sweet earthly form by which the Lily had been manifested to the world was found lifeless the next morning in the temple with her head resting on her arms, which were folded upon the slab of dark-veined marble. The chill winds of the earth had long since breathed a blight into this beautiful flower; so that a loving hand had now transplanted it to blossom brightly in the garden of Paradise.

But alas for the temple of happiness! In his unutterable grief Adam Forrester had no purpose more at heart than to convert this temple of many delightful hopes into a tomb and bury his dead mistress there. And, lo! a wonder! Digging a grave beneath the temple's marble floor, the sexton found no virgin earth such as was meet to receive the maiden's dust, but an ancient sepulchre in which were treasured up the bones of generations that had died long ago. Among those forgotten ancestors was the Lily to be laid; and when the funeral procession brought Lilias thither in her coffin, they beheld old Walter Gascoigne standing beneath the dome of the temple with his cloak of pall and face of darkest gloom, and wherever that figure might take its stand the spot would seem a sepulchre. He watched the mourners as they lowered the coffin down.

"And so," said he to Adam Forrester, with the strange smile in which his insanity was wont to gleam forth, "you have found no better foundation for your happiness than on a grave?"

But as the shadow of Affliction spoke a vision of hope and joy had its birth in Adam's mind even from the old man's taunting words, for then he knew what was betokened by the parable in which the Lily and himself had acted, and the mystery of life and death was opened to him.

"Joy! joy!" he cried, throwing his arms toward heaven. "On a grave be the site of our temple, and now our happiness is for eternity."

With those words a ray of sunshine broke through the dismal sky and glimmered down into the sepulchre, while at the same moment the shape of old Walter Gascoigne stalked drearily away, because his gloom, symbolic of all earthly sorrow, might no longer abide there now that the darkest riddle of humanity was read.

FOOTPRINTS ON THE SEASHORE.

It must be a spirit much unlike my own which can keep itself in health and vigor without sometimes stealing from the sultry sunshine of the world to plunge into the cool bath of solitude. At intervals, and not infrequent ones, the forest and the ocean summon me—one with the roar of its waves, the other with the murmur of its boughs—forth from the haunts of men. But I must wander many a mile ere I could stand beneath the shadow of even one primeval tree, much less be lost among the multitude of hoary trunks and hidden from the earth and sky by the mystery of darksome foliage. Nothing is within my daily reach more like a forest than the acre or two of woodland near some suburban farmhouse. When, therefore, the yearning for seclusion becomes a necessity within me, I am drawn to the seashore which extends its line of rude rocks and seldom-trodden sands for leagues around our bay. Setting forth at my last ramble on a September morning, I bound myself with a hermit's vow to interchange no thoughts with man or woman, to share no social pleasure, but to derive all that day's enjoyment from shore and sea and sky, from my soul's communion with these, and from fantasies and recollections or anticipated realities. Surely here is enough to feed a human spirit for a single day.—Farewell, then, busy world! Till your evening lights shall shine along the street—till they gleam upon my sea-flushed face as I tread homeward—free me from your ties and let me be a peaceful outlaw.

Highways and cross-paths are hastily traversed, and, clambering down a crag, I find myself at the extremity of a long beach. How gladly does the spirit leap forth and suddenly enlarge its sense of being to the full extent of the broad blue, sunny deep! A greeting and a homage to the sea! I descend over its margin and dip my hand into the wave that meets me, and bathe my brow. That far-resounding roar is Ocean's voice of welcome. His salt breath brings a blessing along with it. Now let us pace together—the reader's fancy arm in arm with mine—this noble beach, which extends a mile or more from that craggy promontory to yonder rampart of broken rocks. In front, the sea; in the rear, a precipitous bank the grassy verge of which is breaking away year after year, and flings down its tufts of verdure upon the barrenness below. The beach itself is a broad space of sand, brown and sparkling, with hardly any pebbles intermixed. Near the water's edge there is a wet margin which glistens brightly in the sunshine and reflects objects like a mirror, and as we tread along the glistening border a dry spot flashes around each footstep, but grows moist again as we lift our feet. In some spots the sand receives a complete impression of the sole, square toe and all; elsewhere it is of such marble firmness that we must stamp heavily to leave a print even of the iron-shod heel. Along the whole of this extensive beach gambols the surf-wave. Now it makes a feint of dashing onward in a fury, yet dies away with a meek murmur and does but kiss the strand; now, after many such abortive efforts, it rears itself up in an unbroken line, heightening as it advances, without a speck of foam on its green crest. With how fierce a roar it flings itself forward and rushes far up the beach!

As I threw my eyes along the edge of the surf I remember that I was startled, as Robinson Crusoe might have been, by the sense that human life was within the magic circle of my solitude. Afar off in the remote distance of the beach, appearing like sea-nymphs, or some airier things such as might tread upon the feathery spray, was a group of girls. Hardly had I beheld them, when they passed into the shadow of the rocks and vanished. To comfort myself—for truly I would fain have gazed a while longer—I made acquaintance with a flock of beach-birds. These little citizens of the sea and air preceded me by about a stone's-throw along the strand, seeking, I suppose, for food upon its margin. Yet, with a philosophy which mankind would do well to imitate, they drew a continual pleasure from their toil for a subsistence. The sea was each little bird's great playmate. They chased it downward as it swept back, and again ran up swiftly before the impending wave, which sometimes overtook them and bore them off their feet. But they floated as lightly as one of their own feathers on the breaking crest. In their airy flutterings they seemed to rest on the evanescent spray. Their images—long-legged little figures with gray backs and snowy bosoms—were seen as distinctly as the realities in the mirror of the glistening strand. As I advanced they flew a score or two of yards, and, again alighting, recommenced their dalliance with the surf-wave; and thus they bore me company along the beach, the types of pleasant fantasies, till at its extremity they took wing over the ocean and were gone. After forming a friendship with these small surf-spirits, it is really worth a sigh to find no memorial of them save their multitudinous little tracks in the sand.

When we have paced the length of the beach, it is pleasant and not unprofitable to retrace our steps and recall the whole mood and occupation of the mind during the former passage. Our tracks, being all discernible, will guide us with an observing consciousness through every unconscious wandering of thought and fancy. Here we followed the surf in its reflux to pick up a shell which the sea seemed loth to relinquish. Here we found a seaweed with an immense brown leaf, and trailed it behind us by its long snake-like stalk. Here we seized a live horse-shoe by the tail, and counted the many claws of that queer monster. Here we dug into the sand for pebbles, and skipped them upon the surface of the water. Here we wet our feet while examining a jelly-fish which the waves, having just tossed it up, now sought to snatch away again. Here we trod along the brink of a fresh-water brooklet which flows across the beach, becoming shallower and more shallow, till at last it sinks into the sand and perishes in the effort to bear its little tribute to the main. Here some vagary appears to have bewildered us, for our tracks go round and round and are confusedly intermingled, as if we had found a labyrinth upon the level beach. And here amid our idle pastime we sat down upon almost the only stone that breaks the surface of the sand, and were lost in an unlooked-for and overpowering conception of the majesty and awfulness of the great deep. Thus by tracking our footprints in the sand we track our own nature in its wayward course, and steal a glance upon it when it never dreams of being so observed. Such glances always make us wiser.

This extensive beach affords room for another pleasant pastime. With your staff you may write verses—love-verses if they please you best—and consecrate them with a woman's name. Here, too, may be inscribed thoughts, feelings, desires, warm outgushings from the heart's secret places, which you would not pour upon the sand without the certainty that almost ere the sky has looked upon them the sea will wash them out. Stir not hence till the record be effaced. Now (for there is room enough on your canvas) draw huge faces—huge as that of the Sphynx on Egyptian sands—and fit them with bodies of corresponding immensity and legs which might stride halfway to yonder island. Child's-play becomes magnificent on so grand a scale. But, after all, the most fascinating employment is simply to write your name in the sand. Draw the letters gigantic, so that two strides may barely measure them, and three for the long strokes; cut deep, that the record may be permanent. Statesmen and warriors and poets have spent their strength in no better cause than this. Is it accomplished? Return, then, in an hour or two, and seek for this mighty record of a name. The sea will have swept over it, even as time rolls its effacing waves over the names of statesmen and warriors and poets. Hark! the surf-wave laughs at you.

Passing from the beach, I begin to clamber over the crags, making my difficult way among the ruins of a rampart shattered and broken by the assaults of a fierce enemy. The rocks rise in every variety of attitude. Some of them have their feet in the foam and are shagged halfway upward with seaweed; some have been hollowed almost into caverns by the unwearied toil of the sea, which can afford to spend centuries in wearing away a rock, or even polishing a pebble. One huge rock ascends in monumental shape, with a face like a giant's tombstone, on which the veins resemble inscriptions, but in an unknown tongue. We will fancy them the forgotten characters of an antediluvian race, or else that Nature's own hand has here recorded a mystery which, could I read her language, would make mankind the wiser and the happier. How many a thing has troubled me with that same idea! Pass on and leave it unexplained. Here is a narrow avenue which might seem to have been hewn through the very heart of an enormous crag, affording passage for the rising sea to thunder back and forth, filling it with tumultuous foam and then leaving its floor of black pebbles bare and glistening. In this chasm there was once an intersecting vein of softer stone, which the waves have gnawed away piecemeal, while the granite walls remain entire on either side. How sharply and with what harsh clamor does the sea rake back the pebbles as it momentarily withdraws into its own depths! At intervals the floor of the chasm is left nearly dry, but anon, at the outlet, two or three great waves are seen struggling to get in at once; two hit the walls athwart, while one rushes straight through, and all three thunder as if with rage and triumph. They heap the chasm with a snow-drift of foam and spray. While watching this scene I can never rid myself of the idea that a monster endowed with life and fierce energy is striving to burst his way through the narrow pass. And what a contrast to look through the stormy chasm and catch a glimpse of the calm bright sea beyond!

Many interesting discoveries may be made among these broken cliffs. Once, for example, I found a dead seal which a recent tempest had tossed into the nook of the rocks, where his shaggy carcase lay rolled in a heap of eel-grass as if the sea-monster sought to hide himself from my eye. Another time a shark seemed on the point of leaping from the surf to swallow me, nor did I wholly without dread approach near enough to ascertain that the man-eater had already met his own death from some fisherman in the bay. In the same ramble I encountered a bird—a large gray bird—but whether a loon or a wild goose or the identical albatross of the Ancient Mariner was beyond my ornithology to decide. It reposed so naturally on a bed of dry seaweed, with its head beside its wing, that I almost fancied it alive, and trod softly lest it should suddenly spread its wings skyward. But the sea-bird would soar among the clouds no more, nor ride upon its native waves; so I drew near and pulled out one of its mottled tail-feathers for a remembrance. Another day I discovered an immense bone wedged into a chasm of the rocks; it was at least ten feet long, curved like a scymitar, bejewelled with barnacles and small shellfish and partly covered with a growth of seaweed. Some leviathan of former ages had used this ponderous mass as a jaw-bone. Curiosities of a minuter order may be observed in a deep reservoir which is replenished with water at every tide, but becomes a lake among the crags save when the sea is at its height. At the bottom of this rocky basin grow marine plants, some of which tower high beneath the water and cast a shadow in the sunshine. Small fishes dart to and fro and hide themselves among the seaweed; there is also a solitary crab who appears to lead the life of a hermit, communing with none of the other denizens of the place, and likewise several five-fingers; for I know no other name than that which children give them. If your imagination be at all accustomed to such freaks, you may look down into the depths of this pool and fancy it the mysterious depth of ocean. But where are the hulks and scattered timbers of sunken ships? where the treasures that old Ocean hoards? where the corroded cannon? where the corpses and skeletons of seamen who went down in storm and battle?

On the day of my last ramble—it was a September day, yet as warm as summer—what should I behold as I approached the above-described basin but three girls sitting on its margin and—yes, it is veritably so—laving their snowy feet in the sunny water? These, these are the warm realities of those three visionary shapes that flitted from me on the beach. Hark their merry voices as they toss up the water with their feet! They have not seen me. I must shrink behind this rock and steal away again.

In honest truth, vowed to solitude as I am, there is something in this encounter that makes the heart flutter with a strangely pleasant sensation. I know these girls to be realities of flesh and blood, yet, glancing at them so briefly, they mingle like kindred creatures with the ideal beings of my mind. It is pleasant, likewise, to gaze down from some high crag and watch a group of children gathering pebbles and pearly shells and playing with the surf as with old Ocean's hoary beard. Nor does it infringe upon my seclusion to see yonder boat at anchor off the shore swinging dreamily to and fro and rising and sinking with the alternate swell, while the crew—four gentlemen in roundabout jackets—are busy with their fishing-lines. But with an inward antipathy and a headlong flight do I eschew the presence of any meditative stroller like myself, known by his pilgrim-staff, his sauntering step, his shy demeanor, his observant yet abstracted eye.

From such a man as if another self had scared me I scramble hastily over the rocks, and take refuge in a nook which many a secret hour has given me a right to call my own. I would do battle for it even with the churl that should produce the title-deeds. Have not my musings melted into its rocky walls and sandy floor and made them a portion of myself? It is a recess in the line of cliffs, walled round by a rough, high precipice which almost encircles and shuts in a little space of sand. In front the sea appears as between the pillars of a portal; in the rear the precipice is broken and intermixed with earth which gives nourishment not only to clinging and twining shrubs, but to trees that grip the rock with their naked roots and seem to struggle hard for footing and for soil enough to live upon. These are fir trees, but oaks hang their heavy branches from above, and throw down acorns on the beach, and shed their withering foliage upon the waves. At this autumnal season the precipice is decked with variegated splendor. Trailing wreaths of scarlet flaunt from the summit downward; tufts of yellow-flowering shrubs and rose-bushes, with their reddened leaves and glossy seed-berries, sprout from each crevice; at every glance I detect some new light or shade of beauty, all contrasting with the stern gray rock. A rill of water trickles down the cliff and fills a little cistern near the base. I drain it at a draught, and find it fresh and pure. This recess shall be my dining-hall. And what the feast? A few biscuits made savory by soaking them in sea-water, a tuft of samphire gathered from the beach, and an apple for the dessert. By this time the little rill has filled its reservoir again, and as I quaff it I thank God more heartily than for a civic banquet that he gives me the healthful appetite to make a feast of bread and water.

Dinner being over, I throw myself at length upon the sand and, basking in the sunshine, let my mind disport itself at will. The walls of this my hermitage have no tongue to tell my follies, though I sometimes fancy that they have ears to hear them and a soul to sympathize. There is a magic in this spot. Dreams haunt its precincts and flit around me in broad sunlight, nor require that sleep shall blindfold me to real objects ere these be visible. Here can I frame a story of two lovers, and make their shadows live before me and be mirrored in the tranquil water as they tread along the sand, leaving no footprints. Here, should I will it, I can summon up a single shade and be myself her lover.—Yes, dreamer, but your lonely heart will be the colder for such fancies.—Sometimes, too, the Past comes back, and finds me here, and in her train come faces which were gladsome when I knew them, yet seem not gladsome now. Would that my hiding-place were lonelier, so that the Past might not find me!—Get ye all gone, old friends, and let me listen to the murmur of the sea—a melancholy voice, but less sad than yours. Of what mysteries is it telling? Of sunken ships and whereabouts they lie? Of islands afar and undiscovered whose tawny children are unconscious of other islands and of continents, and deem the stars of heaven their nearest neighbors? Nothing of all this. What, then? Has it talked for so many ages and meant nothing all the while? No; for those ages find utterance in the sea's unchanging voice, and warn the listener to withdraw his interest from mortal vicissitudes and let the infinite idea of eternity pervade his soul. This is wisdom, and therefore will I spend the next half-hour in shaping little boats of driftwood and launching them on voyages across the cove, with the feather of a sea-gull for a sail. If the voice of ages tell me true, this is as wise an occupation as to build ships of five hundred tons and launch them forth upon the main, bound to "Far Cathay." Yet how would the merchant sneer at me!

And, after all, can such philosophy be true? Methinks I could find a thousand arguments against it. Well, then, let yonder shaggy rock mid-deep in the surf—see! he is somewhat wrathful: he rages and roars and foams,—let that tall rock be my antagonist, and let me exercise my oratory like him of Athens who bandied words with an angry sea and got the victory. My maiden-speech is a triumphant one, for the gentleman in seaweed has nothing to offer in reply save an immitigable roaring. His voice, indeed, will be heard a long while after mine is hushed. Once more I shout and the cliffs reverberate the sound. Oh what joy for a shy man to feel himself so solitary that he may lift his voice to its highest pitch without hazard of a listener!—But hush! Be silent, my good friend! Whence comes that stifled laughter? It was musical, but how should there be such music in my solitude? Looking upward, I catch a glimpse of three faces peeping from the summit of the cliff like angels between me and their native sky.—Ah, fair girls! you may make yourself merry at my eloquence, but it was my turn to smile when I saw your white feet in the pool. Let us keep each other's secrets.

The sunshine has now passed from my hermitage, except a gleam upon the sand just where it meets the sea. A crowd of gloomy fantasies will come and haunt me if I tarry longer here in the darkening twilight of these gray rocks. This is a dismal place in some moods of the mind. Climb we, therefore, the precipice, and pause a moment on the brink gazing down into that hollow chamber by the deep where we have been what few can be—sufficient to our own pastime. Yes, say the word outright: self-sufficient to our own happiness. How lonesome looks the recess now, and dreary too, like all other spots where happiness has been! There lies my shadow in the departing sunshine with its head upon the sea. I will pelt it with pebbles. A hit! a hit! I clap my hands in triumph, and see my shadow clapping its unreal hands and claiming the triumph for itself. What a simpleton must I have been all day, since my own shadow makes a mock of my fooleries!

Homeward! homeward! It is time to hasten home. It is time—it is time; for as the sun sinks over the western wave the sea grows melancholy and the surf has a saddened tone. The distant sails appear astray and not of earth in their remoteness amid the desolate waste. My spirit wanders forth afar, but finds no resting-place and comes shivering back. It is time that I were hence. But grudge me not the day that has been spent in seclusion which yet was not solitude, since the great sea has been my companion, and the little sea-birds my friends, and the wind has told me his secrets, and airy shapes have flitted around me in my hermitage. Such companionship works an effect upon a man's character as if he had been admitted to the society of creatures that are not mortal. And when, at noontide, I tread the crowded streets, the influence of this day will still be felt; so that I shall walk among men kindly and as a brother, with affection and sympathy, but yet shall not melt into the indistinguishable mass of humankind. I shall think my own thoughts and feel my own emotions and possess my individuality unviolated.

But it is good at the eve of such a day to feel and know that there are men and women in the world. That feeling and that knowledge are mine at this moment, for on the shore, far below me, the fishing-party have landed from their skiff and are cooking their scaly prey by a fire of driftwood kindled in the angle of two rude rocks. The three visionary girls are likewise there. In the deepening twilight, while the surf is dashing near their hearth, the ruddy gleam of the fire throws a strange air of comfort over the wild cove, bestrewn as it is with pebbles and seaweed and exposed to the "melancholy main." Moreover, as the smoke climbs up the precipice, it brings with it a savory smell from a pan of fried fish and a black kettle of chowder, and reminds me that my dinner was nothing but bread and water and a tuft of samphire and an apple. Methinks the party might find room for another guest at that flat rock which serves them for a table; and if spoons be scarce, I could pick up a clam-shell on the beach. They see me now; and—the blessing of a hungry man upon him!—one of them sends up a hospitable shout: "Halloo, Sir Solitary! Come down and sup with us!" The ladies wave their handkerchiefs. Can I decline? No; and be it owned, after all my solitary joys, that this is the sweetest moment of a day by the seashore.

EDWARD FANE'S ROSEBUD.

There is hardly a more difficult exercise of fancy than, while gazing at a figure of melancholy age, to recreate its youth, and without entirely obliterating the identity of form and features to restore those graces which Time has snatched away. Some old people—especially women—so age-worn and woeful are they, seem never to have been young and gay. It is easier to conceive that such gloomy phantoms were sent into the world as withered and decrepit as we behold them now, with sympathies only for pain and grief, to watch at death-beds and weep at funerals. Even the sable garments of their widowhood appear essential to their existence; all their attributes combine to render them darksome shadows creeping strangely amid the sunshine of human life. Yet it is no unprofitable task to take one of these doleful creatures and set Fancy resolutely at work to brighten the dim eye, and darken the silvery locks, and paint the ashen cheek with rose-color, and repair the shrunken and crazy form, till a dewy maiden shall be seen in the old matron's elbow-chair. The miracle being wrought, then let the years roll back again, each sadder than the last, and the whole weight of age and sorrow settle down upon the youthful figure. Wrinkles and furrows, the handwriting of Time, may thus be deciphered and found to contain deep lessons of thought and feeling.

Such profit might be derived by a skilful observer from my much-respected friend the Widow Toothaker, a nurse of great repute who has breathed the atmosphere of sick-chambers and dying-breaths these forty years. See! she sits cowering over her lonesome hearth with her gown and upper petticoat drawn upward, gathering thriftily into her person the whole warmth of the fire which now at nightfall begins to dissipate the autumnal chill of her chamber. The blaze quivers capriciously in front, alternately glimmering into the deepest chasms of her wrinkled visage, and then permitting a ghostly dimness to mar the outlines of her venerable figure. And Nurse Toothaker holds a teaspoon in her right hand with which to stir up the contents of a tumbler in her left, whence steams a vapory fragrance abhorred of temperance societies. Now she sips, now stirs, now sips again. Her sad old heart has need to be revived by the rich infusion of Geneva which is mixed half and half with hot water in the tumbler. All day long she has been sitting by a death-pillow, and quitted it for her home only when the spirit of her patient left the clay and went homeward too. But now are her melancholy meditations cheered and her torpid blood warmed and her shoulders lightened of at least twenty ponderous years by a draught from the true fountain of youth in a case-bottle. It is strange that men should deem that fount a fable, when its liquor fills more bottles than the Congress-water.—Sip it again, good nurse, and see whether a second draught will not take off another score of years, and perhaps ten more, and show us in your high-backed chair the blooming damsel who plighted troths with Edward Fane.—Get you gone, Age and Widowhood!—Come back, unwedded Youth!—But, alas! the charm will not work. In spite of Fancy's most potent spell, I can see only an old dame cowering over the fire, a picture of decay and desolation, while the November blast roars at her in the chimney and fitful showers rush suddenly against the window.

Yet there was a time when Rose Grafton—such was the pretty maiden-name of Nurse Toothaker—possessed beauty that would have gladdened this dim and dismal chamber as with sunshine. It won for her the heart of Edward Fane, who has since made so great a figure in the world and is now a grand old gentleman with powdered hair and as gouty as a lord. These early lovers thought to have walked hand in hand through life. They had wept together for Edward's little sister Mary, whom Rose tended in her sickness—partly because she was the sweetest child that ever lived or died, but more for love of him. She was but three years old. Being such an infant, Death could not embody his terrors in her little corpse; nor did Rose fear to touch the dead child's brow, though chill, as she curled the silken hair around it, nor to take her tiny hand and clasp a flower within its fingers. Afterward, when she looked through the pane of glass in the coffin-lid and beheld Mary's face, it seemed not so much like death or life as like a waxwork wrought into the perfect image of a child asleep and dreaming of its mother's smile. Rose thought her too fair a thing to be hidden in the grave, and wondered that an angel did not snatch up little Mary's coffin and bear the slumbering babe to heaven and bid her wake immortal. But when the sods were laid on little Mary, the heart of Rose was troubled. She shuddered at the fantasy that in grasping the child's cold fingers her virgin hand had exchanged a first greeting with mortality and could never lose the earthy taint. How many a greeting since! But as yet she was a fair young girl with the dewdrops of fresh feeling in her bosom, and, instead of "Rose"—which seemed too mature a name for her half-opened beauty—her lover called her "Rosebud."

The rosebud was destined never to bloom for Edward Fane. His mother was a rich and haughty dame with all the aristocratic prejudices of colonial times. She scorned Rose Grafton's humble parentage and caused her son to break his faith, though, had she let him choose, he would have prized his Rosebud above the richest diamond. The lovers parted, and have seldom met again. Both may have visited the same mansions, but not at the same time, for one was bidden to the festal hall and the other to the sick-chamber; he was the guest of Pleasure and Prosperity, and she of Anguish. Rose, after their separation, was long secluded within the dwelling of Mr. Toothaker, whom she married with the revengeful hope of breaking her false lover's heart. She went to her bridegroom's arms with bitterer tears, they say, than young girls ought to shed at the threshold of the bridal-chamber. Yet, though her husband's head was getting gray and his heart had been chilled with an autumnal frost, Rose soon began to love him, and wondered at her own conjugal affection. He was all she had to love; there were no children.

In a year or two poor Mr. Toothaker was visited with a wearisome infirmity which settled in his joints and made him weaker than a child. He crept forth about his business, and came home at dinner-time and eventide, not with the manly tread that gladdens a wife's heart, but slowly, feebly, jotting down each dull foot-step with a melancholy dub of his staff. We must pardon his pretty wife if she sometimes blushed to own him. Her visitors, when they heard him coming, looked for the appearance of some old, old man, but he dragged his nerveless limbs into the parlor—and there was Mr. Toothaker! The disease increasing, he never went into the sunshine save with a staff in his right hand and his left on his wife's shoulder, bearing heavily downward like a dead man's hand. Thus, a slender woman still looking maiden-like, she supported his tall, broad-chested frame along the pathway of their little garden, and plucked the roses for her gray-haired husband, and spoke soothingly as to an infant. His mind was palsied with his body; its utmost energy was peevishness. In a few months more she helped him up the staircase with a pause at every step, and a longer one upon the landing-place, and a heavy glance behind as he crossed the threshold of his chamber. He knew, poor man! that the precincts of those four walls would thenceforth be his world—his world, his home, his tomb, at once a dwelling-and a burial-place—till he were borne to a darker and a narrower one. But Rose was with him in the tomb. He leaned upon her in his daily passage from the bed to the chair by the fireside, and back again from the weary chair to the joyless bed—his bed and hers, their marriage-bed—till even this short journey ceased and his head lay all day upon the pillow and hers all night beside it. How long poor Mr. Toothaker was kept in misery! Death seemed to draw near the door, and often to lift the latch, and sometimes to thrust his ugly skull into the chamber, nodding to Rose and pointing at her husband, but still delayed to enter. "This bedridden wretch cannot escape me," quoth Death. "I will go forth and run a race with the swift and fight a battle with the strong, and come back for Toothaker at my leisure." Oh, when the deliverer came so near, in the dull anguish of her worn-out sympathies did she never long to cry, "Death, come in"?

But no; we have no right to ascribe such a wish to our friend Rose. She never failed in a wife's duty to her poor sick husband. She murmured not though a glimpse of the sunny sky was as strange to her as him, nor answered peevishly though his complaining accents roused her from sweetest dream only to share his wretchedness. He knew her faith, yet nourished a cankered jealousy; and when the slow disease had chilled all his heart save one lukewarm spot which Death's frozen fingers were searching for, his last words were, "What would my Rose have done for her first love, if she has been so true and kind to a sick old man like me?" And then his poor soul crept away and left the body lifeless, though hardly more so than for years before, and Rose a widow, though in truth it was the wedding-night that widowed her. She felt glad, it must be owned, when Mr.

Toothaker was buried, because his corpse had retained such a likeness to the man half alive that she hearkened for the sad murmur of his voice bidding her shift his pillow. But all through the next winter, though the grave had held him many a month, she fancied him calling from that cold bed, "Rose, Rose! Come put a blanket on my feet!"

So now the Rosebud was the widow Toothaker. Her troubles had come early, and, tedious as they seemed, had passed before all her bloom was fled. She was still fair enough to captivate a bachelor, or with a widow's cheerful gravity she might have won a widower, stealing into his heart in the very guise of his dead wife. But the widow Toothaker had no such projects. By her watchings and continual cares her heart had become knit to her first husband with a constancy which changed its very nature and made her love him for his infirmities, and infirmity for his sake. When the palsied old man was gone, even her early lover could not have supplied his place. She had dwelt in a sick-chamber and been the companion of a half-dead wretch till she could scarcely breathe in a free air and felt ill at ease with the healthy and the happy. She missed the fragrance of the doctor's stuff. She walked the chamber with a noiseless footfall. If visitors came in, she spoke in soft and soothing accents, and was startled and shocked by their loud voices. Often in the lonesome evening she looked timorously from the fireside to the bed, with almost a hope of recognizing a ghastly face upon the pillow. Then went her thoughts sadly to her husband's grave. If one impatient throb had wronged him in his lifetime, if she had secretly repined because her buoyant youth was imprisoned with his torpid age, if ever while slumbering beside him a treacherous dream had admitted another into her heart,—yet the sick man had been preparing a revenge which the dead now claimed. On his painful pillow he had cast a spell around her; his groans and misery had proved more captivating charms than gayety and youthful grace; in his semblance Disease itself had won the Rosebud for a bride, nor could his death dissolve the nuptials. By that indissoluble bond she had gained a home in every sick-chamber, and nowhere else; there were her brethren and sisters; thither her husband summoned her with that voice which had seemed to issue from the grave of Toothaker. At length she recognized her destiny.

We have beheld her as the maid, the wife, the widow; now we see her in a separate and insulated character: she was in all her attributes Nurse Toothaker. And Nurse Toothaker alone, with her own shrivelled lips, could make known her experience in that capacity. What a history might she record of the great sicknesses in which she has gone hand in hand with the exterminating angel! She remembers when the small-pox hoisted a red banner on almost every house along the street. She has witnessed when the typhus fever swept off a whole household, young and old, all but a lonely mother, who vainly shrieked to follow her last loved one. Where would be Death's triumph if none lived to weep? She can speak of strange maladies that have broken out as if spontaneously, but were found to have been imported from foreign lands with rich silks and other merchandise, the costliest portion of the cargo. And once, she recollects, the people died of what was considered a new pestilence, till the doctors traced it to the ancient grave of a young girl who thus caused many deaths a hundred years after her own burial. Strange that such black mischief should lurk in a maiden's grave! She loves to tell how strong men fight with fiery fevers, utterly refusing to give up their breath, and how consumptive virgins fade out of the world, scarcely reluctant, as if their lovers were wooing them to a far country.—Tell us, thou fearful woman; tell us the death-secrets. Fain would I search out the meaning of words faintly gasped with intermingled sobs and broken sentences half-audibly spoken between earth and the judgment-seat.

An awful woman! She is the patron-saint of young physicians and the bosom-friend of old ones. In the mansions where she enters the inmates provide themselves black garments; the coffin-maker follows her, and the bell tolls as she comes away from the threshold. Death himself has met her at so many a bedside that he puts forth his bony hand to greet Nurse Toothaker. She is an awful woman. And oh, is it conceivable that this handmaid of human infirmity and affliction—so darkly stained, so thoroughly imbued with all that is saddest in the doom of mortals—can ever again be bright and gladsome even though bathed in the sunshine of eternity? By her long communion with woe has she not forfeited her inheritance of immortal joy? Does any germ of bliss survive within her?

Hark! an eager knocking st Nurse Toothaker's door. She starts from her drowsy reverie, sets aside the empty tumbler and teaspoon, and lights a lamp at the dim embers of the fire. "Rap, rap, rap!" again, and she hurries adown the staircase, wondering which of her friends can be at death's door now, since there is such an earnest messenger at Nurse Toothaker's. Again the peal resounds just as her hand is on the lock. "Be quick, Nurse Toothaker!" cries a man on the doorstep. "Old General Fane is taken with the gout in his stomach and has sent for you to watch by his death-bed. Make haste, for there is no time to lose."—"Fane! Edward Fane! And has he sent for me at last? I am ready. I will get on my cloak and begone. So," adds the sable-gowned, ashen-visaged, funereal old figure, "Edward Fane remembers his Rosebud."

Our question is answered. There is a germ of bliss within her. Her long-hoarded constancy, her memory of the bliss that was remaining amid the gloom of her after-life like a sweet-smelling flower in a coffin, is a symbol that all may be renewed. In some happier clime the Rosebud may revive again with all the dew-drops in its bosom.

THE THREEFOLD DESTINY.

A FAËRY LEGEND.

I have sometimes produced a singular and not unpleasing effect, so far as my own mind was concerned, by imagining a train of incidents in which the spirit and mechanism of the faëry legend should be combined with the characters and manners of familiar life. In the little tale which follows a subdued tinge of the wild and wonderful is thrown over a sketch of New England personages and scenery, yet, it is hoped, without entirely obliterating the sober hues of nature. Rather than a story of events claiming to be real, it may be considered as an allegory such as the writers of the last century would have expressed in the shape of an Eastern tale, but to which I have endeavored to give a more lifelike warmth than could be infused into those fanciful productions.

In the twilight of a summer eve a tall dark figure over which long and remote travel had thrown an outlandish aspect was entering a village not in "faëry londe," but within our own familiar boundaries. The staff on which this traveller leaned had been his companion from the spot where it grew in the jungles of Hindostan; the hat that overshadowed his sombre brow, had shielded him from the suns of Spain; but his cheek had been blackened by the red-hot wind of an Arabian desert and had felt the frozen breath of an Arctic region. Long sojourning amid wild and dangerous men, he still wore beneath his vest the ataghan which he had once struck into the throat of a Turkish robber. In every foreign clime he had lost something of his New England characteristics, and perhaps from every people he had unconsciously borrowed a new peculiarity; so that when the world-wanderer again trod the street of his native village it is no wonder that he passed unrecognized, though exciting the gaze and curiosity of all. Yet, as his arm casually touched that of a young woman who was wending her way to an evening lecture, she started and almost uttered a cry.

"Ralph Cranfield!" was the name that she half articulated.

"Can that be my old playmate Faith Egerton?" thought the traveller, looking round at her figure, but without pausing.

Ralph Cranfield from his youth upward had felt himself marked out for a high destiny. He had imbibed the idea—we say not whether it were revealed to him by witchcraft or in a dream of prophecy, or that his brooding fancy had palmed its own dictates upon him as the oracles of a sybil, but he had imbibed the idea, and held it firmest among his articles of faith—that three marvellous events of his life were to be confirmed to him by three signs.

The first of these three fatalities, and perhaps the one on which his youthful imagination had dwelt most fondly, was the discovery of the maid who alone of all the maids on earth could make him happy by her love. He was to roam around the world till he should meet a beautiful woman wearing on her bosom a jewel in the shape of a heart—whether of pearl or ruby or emerald or carbuncle or a changeful opal, or perhaps a priceless diamond, Ralph Cranfield little cared, so long as it were a heart of one peculiar shape. On encountering this lovely stranger he was bound to address her thus: "Maiden, I have brought you a heavy heart. May I rest its weight on you?" And if she were his fated bride—if their kindred souls were destined to form a union here below which all eternity should only bind more closely—she would reply, with her finger on the heart-shaped jewel, "This token which I have worn so long is the assurance that you may."

And, secondly, Ralph Cranfield had a firm belief that there was a mighty treasure hidden somewhere in the earth of which the burial-place would be revealed to none but him. When his feet should press upon the mysterious spot, there would be a hand before him pointing downward—whether carved of marble or hewn in gigantic dimensions on the side of a rocky precipice, or perchance a hand of flame in empty air, he could not tell, but at least he would discern a hand, the forefinger pointing downward, and beneath it the Latin word "*Effode*"—"Dig!" And, digging thereabouts, the gold in coin or ingots, the precious stones, or of whatever else the treasure might consist, would be certain to reward his toil.

The third and last of the miraculous events in the life of this high-destined man was to be the attainment of extensive influence and sway over his fellow-creatures. Whether he were to be a king and founder of a hereditary throne, or the victorious leader of a people contending for their freedom, or the apostle of a purified and regenerated faith, was left for futurity to show. As messengers of the sign by which Ralph Cranfield might recognize the summons, three venerable men were to claim audience of him. The chief among them—a dignified and majestic person arrayed, it may be supposed, in the flowing garments of an ancient sage—would be the bearer of a wand or prophet's rod. With this wand or rod or staff the venerable sage would trace a certain figure in the air, and then proceed to make known his Heaven-instructed message, which, if obeyed, must lead to glorious results.

With this proud fate before him, in the flush of his imaginative youth Ralph Cranfield had set forth to seek the maid, the treasure, and the venerable sage with his gift of extended empire. And had he found them? Alas! it was not with the aspect of a triumphant man who had achieved a nobler destiny than all his fellows, but rather with the gloom of one struggling against peculiar and continual adversity, that he now passed homeward to his mother's cottage. He had come back, but only for a time, to lay aside the pilgrim's staff, trusting that his weary manhood would regain somewhat of the elasticity of youth in the spot where his threefold fate had been foreshown him. There had been few changes in the village, for it was not one of those thriving places where a year's prosperity makes more than the havoc of a century's decay, but, like a gray hair in a young man's head, an antiquated little town full of old maids and aged elms and moss-grown dwellings. Few seemed to be the changes here. The drooping elms, indeed, had a more majestic spread, the weather-blackened houses were adorned with a denser thatch of verdant moss, and doubtless there were a few more gravestones in the burial-ground inscribed with names that had once been familiar in the village street; yet, summing up all the mischief that ten years had wrought, it seemed scarcely more than if Ralph Cranfield had gone forth that very morning and dreamed a day-dream till the twilight, and then turned back again. But his heart grew cold because the village did not remember him as he remembered the village.

"Here is the change," sighed he, striking his hand upon his breast. "Who is this man of thought and care, weary with world-wandering and heavy with disappointed hopes? The youth returns not who went forth so joyously."

And now Ralph Cranfield was at his mother's gate, in front of the small house where the old lady, with slender but sufficient means, had kept herself comfortable during her son's long absence. Admitting himself within the enclosure, he leaned against a great old tree, trifling with his own impatience as people often do in those intervals when years are summed into a moment. He took a minute survey of the dwelling—its windows brightened with the sky-gleam, its doorway with the half of a millstone for a step, and the faintly-traced path waving thence to the gate. He made friends again with his childhood's friend—the old tree against which he leaned—and, glancing his eye down its trunk, beheld something that excited a melancholy smile. It was a half-obliterated inscription—the Latin word "*Effode*"—which he remembered to have carved in the bark of the tree with a whole day's toil when he had first begun to muse about his exalted destiny. It might be accounted a rather singular coincidence that the bark just above the inscription had put forth an excrescence shaped not unlike a hand, with the forefinger pointing obliquely at the word of fate. Such, at least, was its appearance in the dusky light.

"Now, a credulous man," said Ralph Cranfield, carelessly, to himself, "might suppose that the treasure which I have sought round the world lies buried, after all, at the very door of my mother's dwelling. That would be a jest indeed."

More he thought not about the matter, for now the door was opened and an elderly woman appeared on the threshold, peering into the dusk to discover who it might be that had intruded on her premises and was standing in the shadow of her tree. It was Ralph Cranfield's mother. Pass we over their greeting, and leave the one to her joy and the other to his rest—if quiet rest he found.

But when morning broke, he arose with a troubled brow, for his sleep and his wakefulness had alike been full of dreams. All the fervor was rekindled with which he had burned of yore to unravel the threefold mystery of his fate. The crowd of his early visions seemed to have awaited him beneath his mother's roof and thronged riotously around to welcome his return. In the well-remembered chamber, on the pillow where his infancy had slumbered, he had passed a wilder night than ever in an Arab tent or when he had reposed his head in the ghastly shades of a haunted forest. A shadowy maid had stolen to his bedside and laid her finger on the scintillating heart; a hand of flame had glowed amid the darkness, pointing downward to a mystery within the earth; a hoary sage had waved his prophetic wand and beckoned the dreamer onward to a chair of state. The same phantoms, though fainter in the daylight, still flitted about, the cottage and mingled among the crowd of familiar faces that were drawn thither by the news of Ralph Cranfield's return to bid him welcome for his mother's sake. There they found him, a tall, dark, stately man of foreign aspect, courteous in demeanor and mild of speech, yet with an abstracted eye which seemed often to snatch a glance at the invisible.

Meantime, the widow Cranfield went bustling about the house full of joy that she again had somebody to love and be careful of, and for whom she might vex and tease herself with the petty troubles of daily life. It was nearly noon when she looked forth from the door and descried three personages of note coming along the street through the hot sunshine and the masses of elm-tree shade. At length they reached her gate and undid the latch.

"See, Ralph!" exclaimed she, with maternal pride; "here is Squire Hawkwood and the two other selectmen coming on purpose to see you. Now, do tell them a good long story about what you have seen in foreign parts."

The foremost of the three visitors, Squire Hawkwood, was a very pompous but excellent old gentleman, the head and prime-mover in all the affairs of the village, and universally acknowledged to be one of the sagest men on earth. He wore, according to a fashion even then becoming antiquated, a three-cornered hat, and carried a silver-headed cane the use of which seemed to be rather for flourishing in the air than for assisting the progress of his legs. His two companions were elderly and respectable yeomen who, retaining an ante-Revolutionary reverence for rank and hereditary wealth, kept a little in the squire's rear.

As they approached along the pathway Ralph Cranfield sat in an oaken elbow-chair half unconsciously gazing at the three visitors and enveloping their homely figures in the misty romance that pervaded his mental world. "Here," thought he, smiling at the conceit—"here come three elderly personages, and the first of the three is a venerable sage with a staff. What if this embassy should bring me the message of my fate?"

While Squire Hawkwood and his colleagues entered, Ralph rose from his seat and advanced a few steps to receive them, and his stately figure and dark countenance as he bent courteously toward his guests had a natural dignity contrasting well with the bustling importance of the squire. The old gentleman, according to invariable custom, gave an elaborate preliminary flourish with his cane in the air, then removed his three-cornered hat in order to wipe his brow, and finally proceeded to make known his errand.

"My colleagues and myself," began the squire, "are burdened with momentous duties, being jointly selectmen of this village. Our minds for the space of three days past have been laboriously bent on the selection of a suitable person to fill a most important office and take upon himself a charge and rule which, wisely considered, may be ranked no lower than those of kings and potentates. And whereas you, our native townsman, are of good natural intellect and well cultivated by foreign travel, and that certain vagaries and fantasies of your youth are doubtless long ago corrected,—taking all these matters, I say, into due consideration, we are of opinion that Providence hath sent you hither at this juncture for our very purpose."

During this harangue Cranfield gazed fixedly at the speaker, as if he beheld something mysterious and unearthly in his pompous little figure, and as if the squire had worn the flowing robes of an ancient sage instead of a square-skirted coat, flapped waistcoat, velvet breeches and silk stockings. Nor was his wonder without sufficient cause, for the flourish of the squire's staff, marvellous to relate, had described precisely the signal in the air which was to ratify the message of the prophetic sage whom Cranfield had sought around the world.

"And what," inquired Ralph Cranfield, with a tremor in his voice—"what may this office be which is to equal me with kings and potentates?"

"No less than instructor of our village school," answered Squire Hawkwood, "the office being now vacant by the death of the venerable Master Whitaker after a fifty years' incumbency."

"I will consider of your proposal," replied Ralph Cranfield, hurriedly, "and will make known my decision within three days."

After a few more words the village dignitary and his companions took their leave. But to Cranfield's fancy their images were still present, and became more and more invested with the dim awfulness of figures which had first appeared to him in a dream, and afterward had shown themselves in his waking moments, assuming homely aspects among familiar things. His mind dwelt upon the features of the squire till they grew confused with those of the visionary sage and one appeared but the shadow of the other. The same visage, he now thought, had looked forth upon him from the Pyramid of Cheops; the same form had beckoned to him among the colonnades of the Alhambra; the same figure had mistily revealed itself through the ascending steam of the Great Geyser. At every effort of his memory he recognized some trait of the dreamy messenger of destiny in this pompous, bustling, self-important, little-great man of the village. Amid such musings Ralph Cranfield sat all day in the cottage, scarcely hearing and vaguely answering his mother's thousand questions about his travels and adventures. At sunset he roused himself to take a stroll, and, passing the aged elm tree, his eye was again caught by the semblance of a hand pointing downward at the half-obliterated inscription.

As Cranfield walked down the street of the village the level sunbeams threw his shadow far before him, and he fancied that, as his shadow walked among distant objects, so had there been a presentiment stalking in advance of him throughout his life. And when he drew near each object over which his tall shadow had preceded him, still it proved to be one of the familiar recollections of his infancy and youth. Every crook in the pathway was remembered. Even the more transitory characteristics of the scene were the same as in by-gone days. A company of cows were grazing on the grassy roadside, and refreshed him with their fragrant breath. "It is sweeter," thought he, "than the perfume which was wafted to our ship from the Spice Islands." The round little figure of a child rolled from a doorway and lay laughing almost beneath Cranfield's feet. The dark and stately man stooped down, and, lifting the infant, restored him to his mother's arms. "The children," said he to himself, and sighed and smiled—"the children are to be my charge." And while a flow of natural feeling gushed like a well-spring in his heart he came to a dwelling which he could nowise forbear to enter. A sweet voice which seemed to come from a deep and tender soul was warbling a plaintive little air within. He bent his head and passed through the lowly door. As his foot sounded upon the threshold a young woman advanced from the dusky interior of the house, at first hastily, and then with a more uncertain step, till they met face to face. There was a singular contrast in their two figures—he dark and picturesque, one who had battled with the world, whom all suns had shone upon and whom all winds had blown on a varied course; she neat, comely and quiet—quiet even in her agitation—as if all her emotions had been subdued to the peaceful tenor of her life. Yet their faces, all unlike as they were, had an expression that seemed not so alien—a glow of kindred feeling flashing upward anew from half-extinguished embers.

"You are welcome home," said Faith Egerton.

But Cranfield did not immediately answer, for his eye had, been caught by an ornament in the shape of a heart which Faith wore as a brooch upon her bosom. The material was the ordinary white quartz, and he recollected having himself shaped it out of one of those Indian arrowheads which are so often found in the ancient haunts of the red men. It was precisely on the pattern of that worn by the visionary maid. When Cranfield departed on his shadowy search, he had bestowed this brooch, in a gold setting, as a parting gift to Faith Egerton.

"So, Faith, you have kept the heart?" said he, at length.

"Yes," said she, blushing deeply; then, more gayly, "And what else have you brought me from beyond the sea?"

"Faith," replied Ralph Cranfield, uttering the fated words by an uncontrollable impulse, "I have brought you nothing but a heavy heart. May I rest its weight on you?"

"This token which I have worn so long," said Faith, laying her tremulous finger on the heart, "is the assurance that you may."

"Faith, Faith!" cried Cranfield, clasping her in his arms; "you have interpreted my wild and weary dream!"

Yes, the wild dreamer was awake at last. To find the mysterious treasure he was to till the earth around his mother's dwelling and reap its products; instead of warlike command or regal or religious sway, he was to rule over the village children; and now the visionary maid had faded from his fancy, and in her place he saw the playmate of his childhood.

Would all who cherish such wild wishes but look around them, they would oftenest find their sphere of duty, of prosperity and happiness, within those precincts and in that station where Providence itself has cast their lot. Happy they who read the riddle without a weary world-search or a lifetime spent in vain!

Footnotes:

TANGLEWOOD TALES

THE WAYSIDE. INTRODUCTORY.

A short time ago, I was favored with a flying visit from my young friend Eustace Bright, whom I had not before met with since quitting the breezy mountains of Berkshire. It being the winter vacation at his college, Eustace was allowing himself a little relaxation, in the hope, he told me, of repairing the inroads which severe application to study had made upon his health; and I was happy to conclude, from the excellent physical condition in which I saw him, that the remedy had already been attended with very desirable success. He had now run up from Boston by the noon train, partly impelled by the friendly regard with which he is pleased to honor me, and partly, as I soon found, on a matter of literary business.

It delighted me to receive Mr. Bright, for the first time, under a roof, though a very humble one, which I could really call my own. Nor did I fail (as is the custom of landed proprietors all about the world) to parade the poor fellow up and down over my half a dozen acres; secretly rejoicing, nevertheless, that the disarray of the inclement season, and particularly the six inches of snow then upon the ground, prevented him from observing the ragged neglect of soil and shrubbery into which the place had lapsed. It was idle, however, to imagine that an airy guest from Monument Mountain, Bald Summit, and old Graylock, shaggy with primeval forests, could see anything to admire in my poor little hillside, with its growth of frail and insect-eaten locust trees. Eustace very frankly called the view from my hill top tame; and so, no doubt, it was, after rough, broken, rugged, headlong Berkshire, and especially the northern parts of the county, with which his college residence had made him familiar. But to me there is a peculiar, quiet charm in these broad meadows and gentle eminences. They are better than mountains, because they do not stamp and stereotype themselves into the brain, and thus grow wearisome with the same strong impression, repeated day after day. A few summer weeks among mountains, a lifetime among green meadows and placid slopes, with outlines forever new, because continually fading out of the memory—such would be my sober choice.

I doubt whether Eustace did not internally pronounce the whole thing a bore, until I led him to my predecessor's little ruined, rustic summer house, midway on the hillside. It is a mere skeleton of slender, decaying tree trunks, with neither walls nor a roof; nothing but a tracery of branches and twigs, which the next wintry blast will be very likely to scatter in fragments along the terrace. It looks, and is, as evanescent as a dream; and yet, in its rustic network of boughs, it has somehow enclosed a hint of spiritual beauty, and has become a true emblem of the subtile and ethereal mind that planned it. I made Eustace Bright sit down on a snow bank, which had heaped itself over the mossy seat, and gazing through the arched windows opposite, he acknowledged that the scene at once grew picturesque.

"Simple as it looks," said he, "this little edifice seems to be the work of magic. It is full of suggestiveness, and, in its way, is as good as a cathedral. Ah, it would be just the spot for one to sit in, of a summer afternoon, and tell the children some more of those wild stories from the classic myths!"

"It would, indeed," answered I. "The summer house itself, so airy and so broken, is like one of those old tales, imperfectly remembered; and these living branches of the Baldwin apple tree, thrusting so rudely in, are like your unwarrantable interpolations. But, by the by, have you added any more legends to the series, since the publication of the 'Wonder-Book'?"

"Many more," said Eustace; "Primrose, Periwinkle, and the rest of them, allow me no comfort of my life unless I tell them a story every day or two. I have run away from home partly to escape the importunity of these little wretches! But I have written out six of the new stories, and have brought them for you to look over."

"Are they as good as the first?" I inquired.

"Better chosen, and better handled," replied Eustace Bright. "You will say so when you read them."

"Possibly not," I remarked. "I know from my own experience, that an author's last work is always his best one, in his own estimate, until it quite loses the red heat of composition. After that, it falls into its true place, quietly enough. But let us adjourn to my study, and examine these new stories. It would hardly be doing yourself justice, were you to bring me acquainted with them, sitting here on this snow bank!"

So we descended the hill to my small, old cottage, and shut ourselves up in the south-eastern room, where the sunshine comes in, warmly and brightly, through the better half of a winter's day. Eustace put his bundle of manuscript into my hands; and I skimmed through it pretty rapidly, trying to find out its merits and demerits by the touch of my fingers, as a veteran story-teller ought to know how to do.

It will be remembered that Mr. Bright condescended to avail himself of my literary experience by constituting me editor of the "Wonder-Book." As he had no reason to complain of the reception of that erudite work by the public, he was now disposed to retain me in a similar position with respect to the present volume, which he entitled TANGLEWOOD TALES. Not, as Eustace hinted, that there was any real necessity for my services as introducer, inasmuch as his own name had become established in some good degree of favor with the literary world. But the connection with myself, he was kind enough to say, had been highly agreeable; nor was he by any means desirous, as most people are, of kicking away the ladder that had perhaps helped him to reach his present elevation. My young friend was willing, in short, that the fresh verdure of his growing reputation should spread over my straggling and half-naked boughs; even as I have sometimes thought of training a vine, with its broad leafiness, and purple fruitage, over the worm-eaten posts and rafters of the rustic summer house. I was not insensible to the advantages of his proposal, and gladly assured him of my acceptance.

Merely from the title of the stories I saw at once that the subjects were not less rich than those of the former volume; nor did I at all doubt that Mr. Bright's audacity (so far as that endowment might avail) had enabled him to take full advantage of whatever capabilities they offered. Yet, in spite of my experience of his free way of handling them, I did not quite see, I confess, how he could have obviated all the difficulties in the way of rendering them presentable to children. These old legends, so brimming over with everything that is most abhorrent to our Christianized moral sense some of them so hideous, others so melancholy and miserable, amid which the Greek tragedians sought their themes, and moulded them into the sternest forms of grief that ever the world saw; was such material the stuff that children's playthings should be made of! How were they to be purified? How was the blessed sunshine to be thrown into them?

But Eustace told me that these myths were the most singular things in the world, and that he was invariably astonished, whenever he began to relate one, by the readiness with which it adapted itself to the childish purity of his auditors. The objectionable characteristics seem to be a parasitical growth, having no essential connection with the original fable. They fall away, and are thought of no more, the instant he puts his imagination in sympathy with the innocent little circle, whose wide-open eyes are fixed so eagerly upon him. Thus the stories (not by any strained effort of the narrator's, but in harmony with their inherent germ) transform themselves, and re-assume the shapes which they might be supposed to possess in the pure childhood of the world. When the first poet or romancer told these marvellous legends (such is Eustace Bright's opinion), it was still the Golden Age. Evil had never yet existed; and sorrow, misfortune, crime, were mere shadows which the mind fancifully created for itself, as a shelter against too sunny realities; or, at most, but prophetic dreams to which the dreamer himself did not yield a waking credence. Children are now the only representatives of the men and women of that happy era; and therefore it is that we must raise the intellect and fancy to the level of childhood, in order to re-create the original myths.

I let the youthful author talk as much and as extravagantly as he pleased, and was glad to see him commencing life with such confidence in himself and his performances. A few years will do all that is necessary towards showing him the truth in both respects. Meanwhile, it is but right to say, he does really appear to have overcome the moral objections against these fables, although at the expense of such liberties with their structure as must be left to plead their own excuse, without any help from me. Indeed, except that there was a necessity for it—and that the inner life of the legends cannot be come at save by making them entirely one's own property—there is no defense to be made.

Eustace informed me that he had told his stories to the children in various situations—in the woods, on the shore of the lake, in the dell of Shadow Brook, in the playroom, at Tanglewood fireside, and in a magnificent palace of snow, with ice windows, which he helped his little friends to build. His auditors were even more delighted with the contents of the present volume than with the specimens which have already been given to the world. The classically learned Mr. Pringle, too, had listened to two or three of the tales, and censured them even more bitterly than he did THE THREE GOLDEN APPLES; so that, what with praise, and what with criticism, Eustace Bright thinks that there is good hope of at least as much success with the public as in the case of the "WonderBook."

I made all sorts of inquiries about the children, not doubting that there would be great eagerness to hear of their welfare, among some good little folks who have written to me, to ask for another volume of myths. They are all, I am happy to say (unless we except Clover), in excellent health and spirits. Primrose is now almost a young lady, and, Eustace tells me, is just as saucy as ever. She pretends to consider herself quite beyond the age to be interested by such idle stories as these; but, for all that, whenever a story is to be told, Primrose never fails to be one of the listeners, and to make fun of it when finished. Periwinkle is very much grown, and is expected to shut up her baby house and throw away her doll in a month or two more. Sweet Fern has learned to read and write, and has put on a jacket and pair of pantaloons—all of which improvements I am sorry for. Squash Blossom, Blue Eye, Plantain, and Buttercup have had the scarlet fever, but came easily through it. Huckleberry, Milkweed, and Dandelion were attacked with the whooping cough, but bore it bravely, and kept out of doors whenever the sun shone. Cowslip, during the autumn, had either the measles, or some eruption that looked very much like it, but was hardly sick a day. Poor Clover has been a good deal troubled with her second teeth, which have made her meagre in aspect and rather fractious in temper; nor, even when she smiles, is the matter much mended, since it discloses a gap just within her lips, almost as wide as the barn door. But all this will pass over, and it is predicted that she will turn out a very pretty girl.

As for Mr. Bright himself, he is now in his senior year at Williams College, and has a prospect of graduating with some degree of honorable distinction at the next Commencement. In his oration for the bachelor's degree, he gives me to understand, he will treat of the classical myths, viewed in the aspect of baby stories, and has a great mind to discuss the expediency of using up the whole of ancient history, for the same purpose. I do not know what he means to do with himself after leaving college, but trust that, by dabbling so early with the dangerous and seductive business of authorship, he will not be tempted to become an author by profession. If so I shall be very sorry for the little that I have had to do with the matter, in encouraging these first beginnings.

I wish there were any likelihood of my soon seeing Primrose, Periwinkle, Dandelion, Sweet Fern, Clover Plantain, Huckleberry, Milkweed, Cowslip, Buttercup, Blue Eye, and Squash Blossom again. But as I do not know when I shall re-visit Tanglewood, and as Eustace Bright probably will not ask me to edit a third "WonderBook," the public of little folks must not expect to hear any more about those dear children from me. Heaven bless them, and everybody else, whether grown people or children!

THE MINOTAUR.

In the old city of Troezene, at the foot of a lofty mountain, there lived, a very long time ago, a little boy named Theseus. His grandfather, King Pittheus, was the sovereign of that country, and was reckoned a very wise man; so that Theseus, being brought up in the royal palace, and being naturally a bright lad, could hardly fail of profiting by the old king's instructions. His mother's name was Aethra. As for his father, the boy had never seen him. But, from his earliest remembrance, Aethra used to go with little Theseus into a wood, and sit down upon a moss-grown rock, which was deeply sunken into the earth. Here she often talked with her son about his father, and said that he was called Aegeus, and that he was a great king, and ruled over Attica, and dwelt at Athens, which was as famous a city as any in the world. Theseus was very fond of hearing about King Aegeus, and often asked his good mother Aethra why he did not come and live with them at Troezene.

"Ah, my dear son," answered Aethra, with a sigh, "a monarch has his people to take care of. The men and women over whom he rules are in the place of children to him; and he can seldom spare time to love his own children as other parents do. Your father will never be able to leave his kingdom for the sake of seeing his little boy."

"Well, but, dear mother," asked the boy, "why cannot I go to this famous city of Athens, and tell King Aegeus that I am his son?"

"That may happen by and by," said Aethra. "Be patient, and we shall see. You are not yet big and strong enough to set out on such an errand."

"And how soon shall I be strong enough?" Theseus persisted in inquiring.

"You are but a tiny boy as yet," replied his mother. "See if you can lift this rock on which we are sitting?"

The little fellow had a great opinion of his own strength. So, grasping the rough protuberances of the rock, he tugged and toiled amain, and got himself quite out of breath, without being able to stir the heavy stone. It seemed to be rooted into the ground. No wonder he could not move it; for it would have taken all the force of a very strong man to lift it out of its earthy bed.

His mother stood looking on, with a sad kind of a smile on her lips and in her eyes, to see the zealous and yet puny efforts of her little boy. She could not help being sorrowful at finding him already so impatient to begin his adventures in the world.

"You see how it is, my dear Theseus," said she. "You must possess far more strength than now before I can trust you to go to Athens, and tell King Aegeus that you are his son. But when you can lift this rock, and show me what is hidden beneath it, I promise you my permission to depart."

Often and often, after this, did Theseus ask his mother whether it was yet time for him to go to Athens; and still his mother pointed to the rock, and told him that, for years to come, he could not be strong enough to move it. And again and again the rosy-checked and curly-headed boy would tug and strain at the huge mass of stone, striving, child as he was, to do what a giant could hardly have done without taking both of his great hands to the task. Meanwhile the rock seemed to be sinking farther and farther into the ground. The moss grew over it thicker and thicker, until at last it looked almost like a soft green seat, with only a few gray knobs of granite peeping out. The overhanging trees, also, shed their brown leaves upon It, as often as the autumn came; and at its base grew ferns and wild flowers, some of which crept quite over its surface. To all appearance, the rock was as firmly fastened as any other portion of the earth's substance.

But, difficult as the matter looked, Theseus was now growing up to be such a vigorous youth, that, in his own opinion, the time would quickly come when he might hope to get the upper hand of this ponderous lump of stone.

"Mother, I do believe it has started!" cried he, after one of his attempts. "The earth around it is certainly a little cracked!"

"No, no, child!" his mother hastily answered. "It is not possible you can have moved it, such a boy as you still are!"

Nor would she be convinced, although Theseus showed her the place where he fancied that the stem of a flower had been partly uprooted by the movement of the rock. But Aethra sighed, and looked disquieted; for, no doubt, she began to be conscious that her son was no longer a child, and that, in a little while hence, she must send him forth among the perils and troubles of the world.

It was not more than a year afterwards when they were again sitting on the moss-covered stone. Aethra had once more told him the oft-repeated story of his father, and how gladly he would receive Theseus at his stately palace, and how he would present him to his courtiers and the people, and tell them that here was the heir of his dominions. The eyes of Theseus glowed with enthusiasm, and he would hardly sit still to hear his mother speak.

"Dear mother Aethra," he exclaimed, "I never felt half so strong as now! I am no longer a child, nor a boy, nor a mere youth! I feel myself a man! It is now time to make one earnest trial to remove the stone."

"Ah, my dearest Theseus," replied his mother "not yet! not yet!"

"Yes, mother," said he, resolutely, "the time has come!"

Then Theseus bent himself in good earnest to the task, and strained every sinew, with manly strength and resolution. He put his whole brave heart into the effort. He wrestled with the big and sluggish stone, as if it had been a living enemy. He heaved, he lifted, he resolved now to succeed, or else to perish there, and let the rock be his monument forever! Aethra stood gazing at him, and clasped her hands, partly with a mother's pride, and partly with a mother's sorrow. The great rock stirred! Yes, it was raised slowly from the bedded moss and earth, uprooting the shrubs and flowers along with it, and was turned upon its side. Theseus had conquered!

While taking breath, he looked joyfully at his mother, and she smiled upon him through her tears.

"Yes, Theseus," she said, "the time has come, and you must stay no longer at my side! See what King Aegeus, your royal father, left for you beneath the stone, when he lifted it in his mighty arms, and laid it on the spot whence you have now removed it."

Theseus looked, and saw that the rock had been placed over another slab of stone, containing a cavity within it; so that it somewhat resembled a roughly-made chest or coffer, of which the upper mass had served as the lid. Within the cavity lay a sword, with a golden hilt, and a pair of sandals.

"That was your father's sword," said Aethra, "and those were his sandals. When he went to be king of Athens, he bade me treat you as a child until you should prove yourself a man by lifting this heavy stone. That task being accomplished, you are to put on his sandals, in order to follow in your father's footsteps, and to gird on his sword, so that you may fight giants and dragons, as King Aegeus did in his youth."

"I will set out for Athens this very day!" cried Theseus.

But his mother persuaded him to stay a day or two longer, while she got ready some necessary articles for his journey. When his grandfather, the wise King Pittheus, heard that Theseus intended to present himself at his father's palace, he earnestly advised him to get on board of a vessel, and go by sea; because he might thus arrive within fifteen miles of Athens, without either fatigue or danger.

"The roads are very bad by land," quoth the venerable king; "and they are terribly infested with robbers and monsters. A mere lad, like Theseus, is not fit to be trusted on such a perilous journey, all by himself. No, no; let him go by sea."

But when Theseus heard of robbers and monsters, he pricked up his ears, and was so much the more eager to take the road along which they were to be met with. On the third day, therefore, he bade a respectful farewell to his grandfather, thanking him for all his kindness; and, after affectionately embracing his mother, he set forth with a good many of her tears glistening on his cheeks, and some, if the truth must be told, that had gushed out of his own eyes. But he let the sun and wind dry them, and walked stoutly on, playing with the golden hilt of his sword, and taking very manly strides in his father's sandals.

I cannot stop to tell you hardly any of the adventures that befell Theseus on the road to Athens. It is enough to say, that he quite cleared that part of the country of the robbers about whom King Pittheus had been so much alarmed. One of these bad people was named Procrustes; and he was indeed a terrible fellow, and had an ugly way of making fun of the poor travelers who happened to fall into his clutches. In his cavern he had a bed, on which, with great pretense of hospitality, he invited his guests to lie down; but, if they happened to be shorter than the bed, this wicked villain stretched them out by main force; or, if they were too tall, he lopped off their heads or feet, and laughed at what he had done, as an excellent joke. Thus, however weary a man might be, he never liked to lie in the bed of Procrustes. Another of these robbers, named Scinis, must likewise have been a very great scoundrel. He was in the habit of flinging his victims off a high cliff into the sea; and, in order to give him exactly his deserts, Theseus tossed him off the very same place. But if you will believe me, the sea would not pollute itself by receiving such a bad person into its bosom; neither would the earth, having once got rid of him, consent to take him back; so that, between the cliff and the sea, Scinis stuck fast in the air, which was forced to bear the burden of his naughtiness.

After these memorable deeds, Theseus heard of an enormous sow, which ran wild, and was the terror of all the farmers round about; and, as he did not consider himself above doing any good thing that came in his way, he killed this monstrous creature, and gave the carcass to the poor people for bacon. The great sow had been an awful beast, while ramping about the woods and fields, but was a pleasant object enough when cut up into joints, and smoking on I know not how many dinner tables.

Thus, by the time he reached his journey's end, Theseus had done many valiant feats with his father's golden-hilted sword, and had gained the renown of being one of the bravest young men of the day. His fame traveled faster than he did, and reached Athens before him. As he entered the city, he heard the inhabitants talking at the street corners, and saying that Hercules was brave, and Jason too, and Castor and Pollux likewise, but that Theseus, the son of their own king, would turn out as great a hero as the best of them. Theseus took longer strides on hearing this, and fancied himself sure of a magnificent reception at his father's court, since he came thither with Fame to blow her trumpet before him, and cry to King Aegeus, "Behold your son!"

He little suspected, innocent youth that he was, that here, in this very Athens, where his father reigned, a greater danger awaited him than any which he had encountered on the road. Yet this was the truth. You must understand that the father of Theseus, though not very old in years, was almost worn out with the cares of government, and had thus grown aged before his time. His nephews, not expecting him to live a very great while, intended to get all the power of the kingdom into their own hands. But when they heard that Theseus had arrived in Athens, and learned what a gallant young man he was, they saw that he would not be at all the kind of a person to let them steal away his father's crown and scepter, which ought to be his own by right of inheritance. Thus these bad-hearted nephews of King Aegeus, who were the own cousins of Theseus, at once became his enemies. A still more dangerous enemy was Medea, the wicked enchantress; for she was now the king's wife, and wanted to give the kingdom to her son Medus, instead of letting it be given to the son of Aethra, whom she hated.

It so happened that the king's nephews met Theseus, and found out who he was, just as he reached the entrance of the royal palace. With all their evil designs against him, they pretended to be their cousin's best friends, and expressed great joy at making his acquaintance. They proposed to him that he should come into the king's presence as a stranger, in order to try whether Aegeus would discover in the young man's features any likeness either to himself or his mother Aethra, and thus recognize him for a son. Theseus consented; for he fancied that his father would know him in a moment, by the love that was in his heart. But, while he waited at the door, the nephews ran and told King Aegeus that a young man had arrived in Athens, who, to their certain knowledge, intended to put him to death, and get possession of his royal crown.

"And he is now waiting for admission to your majesty's presence," added they.

"Aha!" cried the old king, on hearing this. "Why, he must be a very wicked young fellow indeed! Pray, what would you advise me to do with him?"

In reply to this question, the wicked Medea put in her word. As I have already told you, she was a famous enchantress. According to some stories, she was in the habit of boiling old people in a large caldron, under pretense of making them young again; but King Aegeus, I suppose, did not fancy such an uncomfortable way of growing young, or perhaps was contented to be old, and therefore would never let himself be popped into the caldron. If there were time to spare from more important matters, I should be glad to tell you of Medea's fiery chariot, drawn by winged dragons, in which the enchantress used often to take an airing among the clouds. This chariot, in fact, was the vehicle that first brought her to Athens, where she had done nothing but mischief ever since her arrival. But these and many other wonders must be left untold; and it is enough to say, that Medea, amongst a thousand other bad things, knew how to prepare a poison, that was instantly fatal to whomsoever might so much as touch it with his lips.

So, when the king asked what he should do with Theseus, this naughty woman had an answer ready at her tongue's end.

"Leave that to me, please your majesty," she replied. "Only admit this evil-minded young man to your presence, treat him civilly, and invite him to drink a goblet of wine. Your majesty is well aware that I sometimes amuse myself by distilling very powerful medicines. Here is one of them in this small phial. As to what it is made of, that is one of my secrets of state. Do but let me put a single drop into the goblet, and let the young man taste it; and I will answer for it, he shall quite lay aside the bad designs with which he comes hither."

As she said this, Medea smiled; but, for all her smiling face, she meant nothing less than to poison the poor innocent Theseus, before his father's eyes. And King Aegeus, like most other kings, thought any punishment mild enough for a person who was accused of plotting against his life. He therefore made little or no objection to Medea's scheme, and as soon as the poisonous wine was ready, gave orders that the young stranger should be admitted into his presence.

The goblet was set on a table beside the king's throne; and a fly, meaning just to sip a little from the brim, immediately tumbled into it, dead. Observing this, Medea looked round at the nephews, and smiled again.

When Theseus was ushered into the royal apartment, the only object that he seemed to behold was the white-bearded old king. There he sat on his magnificent throne, a dazzling crown on his head, and a scepter in his hand. His aspect was stately and majestic, although his years and infirmities weighed heavily upon him, as if each year were a lump of lead, and each infirmity a ponderous stone, and all were bundled up together, and laid upon his weary shoulders. The tears both of joy and sorrow sprang into the young man's eyes; for he thought how sad it was to see his dear father so infirm, and how sweet it would be to support him with his own youthful strength, and to cheer him up with the alacrity of his loving spirit. When a son takes a father into his warm heart it renews the old man's youth in a better way than by the heat of Medea's magic caldron. And this was what Theseus resolved to do. He could scarcely wait to see whether King Aegeus would recognize him, so eager was he to throw himself into his arms.

Advancing to the foot of the throne, he attempted to make a little speech, which he had been thinking about, as he came up the stairs. But he was almost choked by a great many tender feelings that gushed out of his heart and swelled into his throat, all struggling to find utterance together. And therefore, unless he could have laid his full, over-brimming heart into the king's hand, poor Theseus knew not what to do or say. The cunning Medea observed what was passing in the young man's mind. She was more wicked at that moment than ever she had been before; for (and it makes me tremble to tell you of it) she did her worst to turn all this unspeakable love with which Theseus was agitated to his own ruin and destruction.

"Does your majesty see his confusion?" she whispered in the king's ear. "He is so conscious of guilt, that he trembles and cannot speak. The wretch lives too long! Quick! offer him the wine!"

Now King Aegeus had been gazing earnestly at the young stranger, as he drew near the throne. There was something, he knew not what, either in his white brow, or in the fine expression of his mouth, or in his beautiful and tender eyes, that made him indistinctly feel as if he had seen this youth before; as if, indeed, he had trotted him on his knee when a baby, and had beheld him growing to be a stalwart man, while he himself grew old. But Medea guessed how the king felt, and would not suffer him to yield to these natural sensibilities; although they were the voice of his deepest heart, telling him as plainly as it could speak, that here was our dear son, and Aethra's son, coming to claim him for a father. The enchantress again whispered in the king's ear, and compelled him, by her witchcraft, to see everything under a false aspect.

He made up his mind, therefore, to let Theseus drink off the poisoned wine.

"Young man," said he, "you are welcome! I am proud to show hospitality to so heroic a youth. Do me the favor to drink the contents of this goblet. It is brimming over, as you see, with delicious wine, such as I bestow only on those who are worthy of it! None is more worthy to quaff it than yourself!"

So saying, King Aegeus took the golden goblet from the table, and was about to offer it to Theseus. But, partly through his infirmities, and partly because it seemed so sad a thing to take away this young man's life. however wicked he might be, and partly, no doubt, because his heart was wiser than his head, and quaked within him at the thought of what he was going to do—for all these reasons, the king's hand trembled so much that a great deal of the wine slopped over. In order to strengthen his purpose, and fearing lest the whole of the precious poison should be wasted, one of his nephews now whispered to him:

"Has your Majesty any doubt of this stranger's guilt? This is the very sword with which he meant to slay you. How sharp, and bright, and terrible it is! Quick!—let him taste the wine; or perhaps he may do the deed even yet."

At these words, Aegeus drove every thought and feeling out of his breast, except the one idea of how justly the young man deserved to be put to death. He sat erect on his throne, and held out the goblet of wine with a steady hand, and bent on Theseus a frown of kingly severity; for, after all, he had too noble a spirit to murder even a treacherous enemy with a deceitful smile upon his face.

"Drink!" said he, in the stern tone with which he was wont to condemn a criminal to be beheaded. "You have well deserved of me such wine as this!"

Theseus held out his hand to take the wine. But, before he touched it, King Aegeus trembled again. His eyes had fallen on the gold-hilted sword that hung at the young man's side. He drew back the goblet.

"That sword!" he exclaimed: "how came you by it?"

"It was my father's sword," replied Theseus, with a tremulous voice. "These were his sandals. My dear mother (her name is Aethra) told me his story while I was yet a little child. But it is only a month since I grew strong enough to lift the heavy stone, and take the sword and sandals from beneath it, and come to Athens to seek my father."

"My son! my son!" cried King Aegeus, flinging away the fatal goblet, and tottering down from the throne to fall into the arms of Theseus. "Yes, these are Aethra's eyes. It is my son."

I have quite forgotten what became of the king's nephews. But when the wicked Medea saw this new turn of affairs, she hurried out of the room, and going to her private chamber, lost no time to setting her enchantments to work. In a few moments, she heard a great noise of hissing snakes outside of the chamber window; and behold! there was her fiery chariot, and four huge winged serpents, wriggling and twisting in the air, flourishing their tails higher than the top of the palace, and all ready to set off on an aerial journey. Medea staid only long enough to take her son with her, and to steal the crown jewels, together with the king's best robes, and whatever other valuable things she could lay hands on; and getting into the chariot, she whipped up the snakes, and ascended high over the city.

The king, hearing the hiss of the serpents, scrambled as fast as he could to the window, and bawled out to the abominable enchantress never to come back. The whole people of Athens, too, who had run out of doors to see this wonderful spectacle, set up a shout of joy at the prospect of getting rid of her. Medea, almost bursting with rage, uttered precisely such a hiss as one of her own snakes, only ten times more venomous and spiteful; and glaring fiercely out of the blaze of the chariot, she shook her hands over the multitude below, as if she were scattering a million of curses among them. In so doing, however, she unintentionally let fall about five hundred diamonds of the first water, together with a thousand great pearls, and two thousand emeralds, rubies, sapphires, opals, and topazes, to which she had helped herself out of the king's strong box. All these came pelting down, like a shower of many-colored hailstones, upon the heads of grown people and children, who forthwith gathered them up, and carried them back to the palace. But King Aegeus told them that they were welcome to the whole, and to twice as many more, if he had them, for the sake of his delight at finding his son, and losing the wicked Medea. And, indeed, if you had seen how hateful was her last look, as the flaming chariot flew upward, you would not have wondered that both king and people should think her departure a good riddance.

And now Prince Theseus was taken into great favor by his royal father. The old king was never weary of having him sit beside him on his throne (which was quite wide enough for two), and of hearing him tell about his dear mother, and his childhood, and his many boyish efforts to lift the ponderous stone. Theseus, however, was much too brave and active a young man to be willing to spend all his time in relating things which had already happened. His ambition was to perform other and more heroic deeds, which should be better worth telling in prose and verse. Nor had he been long in Athens before he caught and chained a terrible mad bull, and made a public show of him, greatly to the wonder and admiration of good King Aegeus and his subjects. But pretty soon, he undertook an affair that made all his foregone adventures seem like mere boy's play. The occasion of it was as follows:

One morning, when Prince Theseus awoke, he fancied that he must have had a very sorrowful dream, and that it was still running in his mind, even now that his eyes were opened. For it appeared as if the air was full of a melancholy wail; and when he listened more attentively, he could hear sobs, and groans, and screams of woe, mingled with deep, quiet sighs, which came from the king's palace, and from the streets, and from the temples, and from every habitation in the city. And all these mournful noises, issuing out of thousands of separate hearts, united themselves into one great sound of affliction, which had startled Theseus from slumber. He put on his clothes as quickly as he could (not forgetting his sandals and gold-hilted sword), and, hastening to the king, inquired what it all meant.

"Alas! my son," quoth King Aegeus, heaving a long sigh, "here is a very lamentable matter in hand! This is the wofulest anniversary in the whole year. It is the day when we annually draw lots to see which of the youths and maids of Athens shall go to be devoured by the horrible Minotaur!"

"The Minotaur!" exclaimed Prince Theseus; and like a brave young prince as he was, he put his hand to the hilt of his sword. "What kind of a monster may that be? Is it not possible, at the risk of one's life, to slay him?"

But King Aegeus shook his venerable head, and to convince Theseus that it was quite a hopeless case, he gave him an explanation of the whole affair. It seems that in the island of Crete there lived a certain dreadful monster, called a Minotaur, which was shaped partly like a man and partly like a bull, and was altogether such a hideous sort of a creature that it is really disagreeable to think of him. If he were suffered to exist at all, it should have been on some desert island, or in the duskiness of some deep cavern, where nobody would ever be tormented by his abominable aspect. But King Minos, who reigned over Crete, laid out a vast deal of money in building a habitation for the Minotaur, and took great care of his health and comfort, merely for mischief's sake. A few years before this time, there had been a war between the city of Athens and the island of Crete, in which the Athenians were beaten, and compelled to beg for peace. No peace could they obtain, however, except on condition that they should send seven young men and seven maidens, every year, to be devoured by the pet monster of the cruel King Minos. For three years past, this grievous calamity had been borne. And the sobs, and groans, and shrieks, with which the city was now filled, were caused by the people's woe, because the fatal day had come again, when the fourteen victims were to be chosen by lot; and the old people feared lest their sons or daughters might be taken, and the youths and damsels dreaded lest they themselves might be destined to glut the ravenous maw of that detestable man-brute.

But when Theseus heard the story, he straightened himself up, so that he seemed taller than ever before; and as for his face it was indignant, despiteful, bold, tender, and compassionate, all in one look.

"Let the people of Athens this year draw lots for only six young men, instead of seven," said he, "I will myself be the seventh; and let the Minotaur devour me if he can!"

"O my dear son," cried King Aegeus, "why should you expose yourself to this horrible fate? You are a royal prince, and have a right to hold yourself above the destinies of common men."

"It is because I am a prince, your son, and the rightful heir of your kingdom, that I freely take upon me the calamity of your subjects," answered Theseus, "And you, my father, being king over these people, and answerable to Heaven for their welfare, are bound to sacrifice what is dearest to you, rather than that the son or daughter of the poorest citizen should come to any harm."

The old king shed tears, and besought Theseus not to leave him desolate in his old age, more especially as he had but just begun to know the happiness of possessing a good and valiant son. Theseus, however, felt that he was in the right, and therefore would not give up his resolution. But he assured his father that he did not intend to be eaten up, unresistingly, like a sheep, and that, if the Minotaur devoured him, it should not be without a battle for his dinner. And finally, since he could not help it, King Aegeus consented to let him go. So a vessel was got ready, and rigged with black sails; and Theseus, with six other young men, and seven tender and beautiful damsels, came down to the harbor to embark. A sorrowful multitude accompanied them to the shore. There was the poor old king, too, leaning on his son's arm, and looking as if his single heart held all the grief of Athens.

Just as Prince Theseus was going on board, his father bethought himself of one last word to say.

"My beloved son," said he, grasping the Prince's hand, "you observe that the sails of this vessel are black; as indeed they ought to be, since it goes upon a voyage of sorrow and despair. Now, being weighed down with infirmities, I know not whether I can survive till the vessel shall return. But, as long as I do live, I shall creep daily to the top of yonder cliff, to watch if there be a sail upon the sea. And, dearest Theseus, if by some happy chance, you should escape the jaws of the Minotaur, then tear down those dismal sails, and hoist others that shall be bright as the sunshine. Beholding them on the horizon, myself and all the people will know that you are coming back victorious, and will welcome you with such a festal uproar as Athens never heard before."

Theseus promised that he would do so. Then going on board, the mariners trimmed the vessel's black sails to the wind, which blew faintly off the shore, being pretty much made up of the sighs that everybody kept pouring forth on this melancholy occasion. But by and by, when they had got fairly out to sea, there came a stiff breeze from the north-west, and drove them along as merrily over the white-capped waves as if they had been going on the most delightful errand imaginable. And though it was a sad business enough, I rather question whether fourteen young people, without any old persons to keep them in order, could continue to spend the whole time of the voyage in being miserable. There had been some few dances upon the undulating deck, I suspect, and some hearty bursts of laughter, and other such unseasonable merriment among the victims, before the high blue mountains of Crete began to show themselves among the far-off clouds. That sight, to be sure, made them all very grave again.

Theseus stood among the sailors, gazing eagerly towards the land; although, as yet, it seemed hardly more substantial than the clouds, amidst which the mountains were looming up. Once or twice, he fancied that he saw a glare of some bright object, a long way off, flinging a gleam across the waves.

"Did you see that flash of light?" he inquired of the master of the vessel.

"No, prince; but I have seen it before," answered the master. "It came from Talus, I suppose."

As the breeze came fresher just then, the master was busy with trimming his sails, and had no more time to answer questions. But while the vessel flew faster and faster towards Crete, Theseus was astonished to behold a human figure, gigantic in size, which appeared to be striding, with a measured movement, along the margin of the island. It stepped from cliff to cliff, and sometimes from one headland to another, while the sea foamed and thundered on the shore beneath, and dashed its jets of spray over the giant's feet. What was still more remarkable, whenever the sun shone on this huge figure, it flickered and glimmered; its vast countenance, too, had a metallic lustre, and threw great flashes of splendor through the air. The folds of its garments, moreover, instead of waving in the wind, fell heavily over its limbs, as if woven of some kind of metal.

The nigher the vessel came, the more Theseus wondered what this immense giant could be, and whether it actually had life or no. For, though it walked, and made other lifelike motions, there yet was a kind of jerk in its gait, which, together with its brazen aspect, caused the young prince to suspect that it was no true giant, but only a wonderful piece of machinery. The figure looked all the more terrible because it carried an enormous brass club on its shoulder.

"What is this wonder?" Theseus asked of the master of the vessel, who was now at leisure to answer him.

"It is Talus, the Man of Brass," said the master.

"And is he a live giant, or a brazen image?" asked Theseus.

"That, truly," replied the master, "is the point which has always perplexed me. Some say, indeed, that this Talus was hammered out for King Minos by Vulcan himself, the skilfullest of all workers in metal. But who ever saw a brazen image that had sense enough to walk round an island three times a day, as this giant walks round the island of Crete, challenging every vessel that comes nigh the shore? And, on the other hand, what living thing, unless his sinews were made of brass, would not be weary of marching eighteen hundred miles in the twenty-four hours, as Talus does, without ever sitting down to rest? He is a puzzler, take him how you will."

Still the vessel went bounding onward; and now Theseus could hear the brazen clangor of the giant's footsteps, as he trod heavily upon the sea-beaten rocks, some of which were seen to crack and crumble into the foaming waves beneath his weight. As they approached the entrance of the port, the giant straddled clear across it, with a foot firmly planted on each headland, and uplifting his club to such a height that its butt-end was hidden in the cloud, he stood in that formidable posture, with the sun gleaming all over his metallic surface. There seemed nothing else to be expected but that, the next moment, he would fetch his great club down, slam bang, and smash the vessel into a thousand pieces, without heeding how many innocent people he might destroy; for there is seldom any mercy in a giant, you know, and quite as little in a piece of brass clockwork. But just when Theseus and his companions thought the blow was coming, the brazen lips unclosed themselves, and the figure spoke.

"Whence come you, strangers?"

And when the ringing voice ceased, there was just such a reverberation as you may have heard within a great church bell, for a moment or two after the stroke of the hammer.

"From Athens!" shouted the master in reply.

"On what errand?" thundered the Man of Brass.

And he whirled his club aloft more threateningly than ever, as if he were about to smite them with a thunderstroke right amidships, because Athens, so little while ago, had been at war with Crete.

"We bring the seven youths and the seven maidens," answered the master, "to be devoured by the Minotaur!"

"Pass!" cried the brazen giant.

That one loud word rolled all about the sky, while again there was a booming reverberation within the figure's breast. The vessel glided between the headlands of the port, and the giant resumed his march. In a few moments, this wondrous sentinel was far away, flashing in the distant sunshine, and revolving with immense strides round the island of Crete, as it was his never-ceasing task to do.

No sooner had they entered the harbor than a party of the guards of King Minos came down to the water side, and took charge of the fourteen young men and damsels. Surrounded by these armed warriors, Prince Theseus and his companions were led to the king's palace, and ushered into his presence. Now, Minos was a stern and pitiless king. If the figure that guarded Crete was made of brass, then the monarch, who ruled over it, might be thought to have a still harder metal in his breast, and might have been called a man of iron. He bent his shaggy brows upon the poor Athenian victims. Any other mortal, beholding their fresh and tender beauty, and their innocent looks, would have felt himself sitting on thorns until he had made every soul of them happy by bidding them go free as the summer wind. But this immitigable Minos cared only to examine whether they were plump enough to satisfy the Minotaur's appetite. For my part, I wish he himself had been the only victim; and the monster would have found him a pretty tough one.

One after another, King Minos called these pale, frightened youths and sobbing maidens to his footstool, gave them each a poke in the ribs with his sceptre (to try whether they were in good flesh or no), and dismissed them with a nod to his guards. But when his eyes rested on Theseus, the king looked at him more attentively, because his face was calm and brave.

"Young man," asked he, with his stern voice, "are you not appalled at the certainty of being devoured by this terrible Minotaur?"

"I have offered my life in a good cause," answered Theseus, "and therefore I give it freely and gladly. But thou, King Minos, art thou not thyself appalled, who, year after year, hast perpetrated this dreadful wrong, by giving seven innocent youths and as many maidens to be devoured by a monster? Dost thou not tremble, wicked king, to turn shine eyes inward on shine own heart? Sitting there on thy golden throne, and in thy robes of majesty, I tell thee to thy face, King Minos, thou art a more hideous monster than the Minotaur himself!"

"Aha! do you think me so?" cried the king, laughing in his cruel way. "To-morrow, at breakfast time, you shall have an opportunity of judging which is the greater monster, the Minotaur or the king! Take them away, guards; and let this free-spoken youth be the Minotaur's first morsel."

Near the king's throne (though I had no time to tell you so before) stood his daughter Ariadne. She was a beautiful and tender-hearted maiden, and looked at these poor doomed captives with very different feelings from those of the iron-breasted King Minos. She really wept indeed, at the idea of how much human happiness would be needlessly thrown away, by giving so many young people, in the first bloom and rose blossom of their lives, to be eaten up by a creature who, no doubt, would have preferred a fat ox, or even a large pig, to the plumpest of them. And when she beheld the brave, spirited figure of Prince Theseus bearing himself so calmly in his terrible peril, she grew a hundred times more pitiful than before. As the guards were taking him away, she flung herself at the king's feet, and besought him to set all the captives free, and especially this one young man.

"Peace, foolish girl!" answered King Minos.

"What hast thou to do with an affair like this? It is a matter of state policy, and therefore quite beyond thy weak comprehension. Go water thy flowers, and think no more of these Athenian caitiffs, whom the Minotaur shall as certainly eat up for breakfast as I will eat a partridge for my supper."

So saying, the king looked cruel enough to devour Theseus and all the rest of the captives himself, had there been no Minotaur to save him the trouble. As he would hear not another word in their favor, the prisoners were now led away, and clapped into a dungeon, where the jailer advised them to go to sleep as soon as possible, because the Minotaur was in the habit of calling for breakfast early. The seven maidens and six of the young men soon sobbed themselves to slumber. But Theseus was not like them. He felt conscious that he was wiser, and braver, and stronger than his companions, and that therefore he had the responsibility of all their lives upon him, and must consider whether there was no way to save them, even in this last extremity. So he kept himself awake, and paced to and fro across the gloomy dungeon in which they were shut up.

Just before midnight, the door was softly unbarred, and the gentle Ariadne showed herself, with a torch in her hand.

"Are you awake, Prince Theseus?" she whispered.

"Yes," answered Theseus. "With so little time to live, I do not choose to waste any of it in sleep."

"Then follow me," said Ariadne, "and tread softly."

What had become of the jailer and the guards, Theseus never knew. But, however that might be, Ariadne opened all the doors, and led him forth from the darksome prison into the pleasant moonlight.

"Theseus," said the maiden, "you can now get on board your vessel, and sail away for Athens."

"No," answered the young man; "I will never leave Crete unless I can first slay the Minotaur, and save my poor companions, and deliver Athens from this cruel tribute."

"I knew that this would be your resolution," said Ariadne. "Come, then, with me, brave Theseus. Here is your own sword, which the guards deprived you of. You will need it; and pray Heaven you may use it well."

Then she led Theseus along by the hand until they came to a dark, shadowy grove, where the moonlight wasted itself on the tops of the trees, without shedding hardly so much as a glimmering beam upon their pathway. After going a good way through this obscurity, they reached a high marble wall, which was overgrown with creeping plants, that made it shaggy with their verdure. The wall seemed to have no door, nor any windows, but rose up, lofty, and massive, and mysterious, and was neither to be clambered over, nor, as far as Theseus could perceive, to be passed through. Nevertheless, Ariadne did but press one of her soft little fingers against a particular block of marble and, though it looked as solid as any other part of the wall, it yielded to her touch, disclosing an entrance just wide enough to admit them They crept through, and the marble stone swung back into its place.

"We are now," said Ariadne, "in the famous labyrinth which Daedalus built before he made himself a pair of wings, and flew away from our island like a bird. That Daedalus was a very cunning workman; but of all his artful contrivances, this labyrinth is the most wondrous. Were we to take but a few steps from the doorway, we might wander about all our lifetime, and never find it again. Yet in the very center of this labyrinth is the Minotaur; and, Theseus, you must go thither to seek him."

"But how shall I ever find him," asked Theseus, "if the labyrinth so bewilders me as you say it will?"

Just as he spoke, they heard a rough and very disagreeable roar, which greatly resembled the lowing of a fierce bull, but yet had some sort of sound like the human voice. Theseus even fancied a rude articulation in it, as if the creature that uttered it were trying to shape his hoarse breath into words. It was at some distance, however, and he really could not tell whether it sounded most like a bull's roar or a man's harsh voice.

"That is the Minotaur's noise," whispered Ariadne, closely grasping the hand of Theseus, and pressing one of her own hands to her heart, which was all in a tremble. "You must follow that sound through the windings of the labyrinth, and, by and by, you will find him. Stay! take the end of this silken string; I will hold the other end; and then, if you win the victory, it will lead you again to this spot. Farewell, brave Theseus."

So the young man took the end of the silken string in his left hand, and his gold-hilted sword, ready drawn from its scabbard, in the other, and trod boldly into the inscrutable labyrinth. How this labyrinth was built is more than I can tell you. But so cunningly contrived a mizmaze was never seen in the world, before nor since. There can be nothing else so intricate, unless it were the brain of a man like Daedalus, who planned it, or the heart of any ordinary man; which last, to be sure, is ten times as great a mystery as the labyrinth of Crete. Theseus had not taken five steps before he lost sight of Ariadne; and in five more his head was growing dizzy. But still he went on, now creeping through a low arch, now ascending a flight of steps, now in one crooked passage and now in another, with here a door opening before him, and there one banging behind, until it really seemed as if the walls spun round, and whirled him round along with them. And all the while, through these hollow avenues, now nearer, now farther off again, resounded the cry of the Minotaur; and the sound was so fierce, so cruel, so ugly, so like a bull's roar, and withal so like a human voice, and yet like neither of them, that the brave heart of Theseus grew sterner and angrier at every step; for he felt it an insult to the moon and sky, and to our affectionate and simple Mother Earth, that such a monster should have the audacity to exist.

As he passed onward, the clouds gathered over the moon, and the labyrinth grew so dusky that Theseus could no longer discern the bewilderment through which he was passing. He would have left quite lost, and utterly hopeless of ever again walking in a straight path, if, every little while, he had not been conscious of a gentle twitch at the silken cord. Then he knew that the tender-hearted Ariadne was still holding the other end, and that she was fearing for him, and hoping for him, and giving him just as much of her sympathy as if she were close by his side. O, indeed, I can assure you, there was a vast deal of human sympathy running along that slender thread of silk. But still he followed the dreadful roar of the Minotaur, which now grew louder and louder, and finally so very loud that Theseus fully expected to come close upon him, at every new zizgag and wriggle of the path. And at last, in an open space, at the very center of the labyrinth, he did discern the hideous creature.

Sure enough, what an ugly monster it was! Only his horned head belonged to a bull; and yet, somehow or other, he looked like a bull all over, preposterously waddling on his hind legs; or, if you happened to view him in another way, he seemed wholly a man, and all the more monstrous for being so. And there he was, the wretched thing, with no society, no companion, no kind of a mate, living only to do mischief, and incapable of knowing what affection means. Theseus hated him, and shuddered at him, and yet could not but be sensible of some sort of pity; and all the more, the uglier and more detestable the creature was. For he kept striding to and fro, in a solitary frenzy of rage, continually emitting a hoarse roar, which 'was oddly mixed up with half-shaped words; and, after listening a while, Theseus understood that the Minotaur was saying to himself how miserable he was, and how hungry, and how he hated everybody, and how he longed to eat up the human race alive.

Ah! the bull-headed villain! And O, my good little people, you will perhaps see, one of these days, as I do now, that every human being who suffers any thing evil to get into his nature, or to remain there, is a kind of Minotaur, an enemy of his fellow-creatures, and separated from all good companionship, as this poor monster was.

Was Theseus afraid? By no means, my dear auditors. What! a hero like Theseus afraid, Not had the Minotaur had twenty bull-heads instead of one. Bold as he was, however, I rather fancy that it strengthened his valiant heart, just at this crisis, to feel a tremulous twitch at the silken cord, which he was still holding in his left hand. It was as if Ariadne were giving him all her might and courage; and much as he already had, and little as she had to give, it made his own seem twice as much. And to confess the honest truth, he needed the whole; for now the Minotaur, turning suddenly about, caught sight of Theseus, and instantly lowered his horribly sharp horns, exactly as a mad bull does when he means to rush against an enemy. At the same time, he belched forth a tremendous roar, in which there was something like the words of human language, but all disjointed and shaken to pieces by passing through the gullet of a miserably enraged brute.

Theseus could only guess what the creature intended to say, and that rather by his gestures than his words; for the Minotaur's horns were sharper than his wits, and of a great deal more service to him than his tongue. But probably this was the sense of what he uttered:

"Ah, wretch of a human being! I'll stick my horns through you, and toss you fifty feet high, and eat you up the moment you come down."

"Come on, then, and try it!" was all that Theseus deigned to reply; for he was far too magnanimous to assault his enemy with insolent language.

Without more words on either side, there ensued the most awful fight between Theseus and the Minotaur that ever happened beneath the sun or moon. I really know not how it might have turned out, if the monster, in his first headlong rush against Theseus, had not missed him, by a hair's breadth, and broken one of his horns short off against the stone wall. On this mishap, he bellowed so intolerably that a part of the labyrinth tumbled down, and all the inhabitants of Crete mistook the noise for an uncommonly heavy thunder storm. Smarting with the pain, he galloped around the open space in so ridiculous a way that Theseus laughed at it, long afterwards, though not precisely at the moment. After this, the two antagonists stood valiantly up to one another, and fought, sword to horn, for a long while. At last, the Minotaur made a run at Theseus, grazed his left side with his horn, and flung him down; and thinking that he had stabbed him to the heart, he cut a great caper in the air, opened his bull mouth from ear to ear, and prepared to snap his head off. But Theseus by this time had leaped up, and caught the monster off his guard. Fetching a sword stroke at him with all his force, he hit him fair upon the neck, and made his bull head skip six yards from his human body, which fell down flat upon the ground.

So now the battle was ended. Immediately the moon shone out as brightly as if all the troubles of the world, and all the wickedness and the ugliness that infest human life, were past and gone forever. And Theseus, as he leaned on his sword, taking breath, felt another twitch of the silken cord; for all through the terrible encounter, he had held it fast in his left hand. Eager to let Ariadne know of his success, he followed the guidance of the thread, and soon found himself at the entrance of the labyrinth.

"Thou hast slain the monster," cried Ariadne, clasping her hands.

"Thanks to thee, dear Ariadne," answered Theseus, "I return victorious."

"Then," said Ariadne, "we must quickly summon thy friends, and get them and thyself on board the vessel before dawn. If morning finds thee here, my father will avenge the Minotaur."

To make my story short, the poor captives were awakened, and, hardly knowing whether it was not a joyful dream, were told of what Theseus had done, and that they must set sail for Athens before daybreak. Hastening down to the vessel, they all clambered on board, except Prince Theseus, who lingered behind them on the strand, holding Ariadne's hand clasped in his own.

"Dear maiden," said he, "thou wilt surely go with us. Thou art too gentle and sweet a child for such an iron-hearted father as King Minos. He cares no more for thee than a granite rock cares for the little flower that grows in one of its crevices. But my father, King Aegeus, and my dear mother, Aethra, and all the fathers and mothers in Athens, and all the sons and daughters too, will love and honor thee as their benefactress. Come with us, then; for King Minos will be very angry when he knows what thou hast done."

Now, some low-minded people, who pretend to tell the story of Theseus and Ariadne, have the face to say that this royal and honorable maiden did really flee away, under cover of the night, with the young stranger whose life she had preserved. They say, too, that Prince Theseus (who would have died sooner than wrong the meanest creature in the world) ungratefully deserted Ariadne, on a solitary island, where the vessel touched on its voyage to Athens. But, had the noble Theseus heard these falsehoods, he would have served their slanderous authors as he served the Minotaur! Here is what Ariadne answered, when the brave prince of Athens besought her to accompany him:

"No, Theseus," the maiden said, pressing his hand, and then drawing back a step or two, "I cannot go with you. My father is old, and has nobody but myself to love him. Hard as you think his heart is, it would break to lose me. At first, King Minos will be angry; but he will soon forgive his only child; and, by and by, he will rejoice, I know, that no more youths and maidens must come from Athens to be devoured by the Minotaur. I have saved you, Theseus, as much for my father's sake as for your own. Farewell! Heaven bless you!"

All this was so true, and so maiden-like, and was spoken with so sweet a dignity, that Theseus would have blushed to urge her any longer. Nothing remained for him, therefore, but to bid Ariadne an affectionate farewell, and to go on board the vessel, and set sail.

In a few moments the white foam was boiling up before their prow, as Prince Theseus and his companions sailed out of the harbor, with a whistling breeze behind them. Talus, the brazen giant, on his never-ceasing sentinel's march, happened to be approaching that part of the coast; and they saw him, by the glimmering of the moonbeams on his polished surface, while he was yet a great way off. As the figure moved like clockwork, however, and could neither hasten his enormous strides nor retard them, he arrived at the port when they were just beyond the reach of his club. Nevertheless, straddling from headland to headland, as his custom was, Talus attempted to strike a blow at the vessel, and, overreaching himself, tumbled at full length into the sea, which splashed high over his gigantic shape, as when an iceberg turns a somerset. There he lies yet; and whoever desires to enrich himself by means of brass had better go thither with a diving bell, and fish up Talus.

On the homeward voyage, the fourteen youths and damsels were in excellent spirits, as you will easily suppose. They spent most of their time in dancing, unless when the sidelong breeze made the deck slope too much. In due season, they came within sight of the coast of Attica, which was their native country. But here, I am grieved to tell you, happened a sad misfortune.

You will remember (what Theseus unfortunately forgot) that his father, King Aegeus, had enjoined it upon him to hoist sunshiny sails, instead of black ones, in case he should overcome the Minotaur, and return victorious. In the joy of their success, however, and amidst the sports, dancing, and other merriment, with which these young folks wore away the time, they never once thought whether their sails were black, white, or rainbow colored, and, indeed, left it entirely to the mariners whether they had any sails at all. Thus the vessel returned, like a raven, with the same sable wings that had wafted her away. But poor King Aegeus, day after day, infirm as he was, had clambered to the summit of a cliff that overhung the sea, and there sat watching for Prince Theseus, homeward bound; and no sooner did he behold the fatal blackness of the sails, than he concluded that his dear son, whom he loved so much, and felt so proud of, had been eaten by the Minotaur. He could not bear the thought of living any longer; so, first flinging his crown and sceptre into the sea (useless baubles that they were to him now), King Aegeus merely stooped forward, and fell headlong over the cliff, and was drowned, poor soul, in the waves that foamed at its base!

This was melancholy news for Prince Theseus, who, when he stepped ashore, found himself king of all the country, whether he would or no; and such a turn of fortune was enough to make any young man feel very much out of spirits. However, he sent for his dear mother to Athens, and, by taking her advice in matters of state, became a very excellent monarch, and was greatly beloved by his people.

THE PYGMIES.

A great while ago, when the world was full of wonders, there lived an earth-born Giant, named Antaeus, and a million or more of curious little earth-born people, who were called Pygmies. This Giant and these Pygmies being children of the same mother (that is to say, our good old Grandmother Earth), were all brethren, and dwelt together in a very friendly and affectionate manner, far, far off, in the middle of hot Africa. The Pygmies were so small, and there were so many sandy deserts and such high mountains between them and the rest of mankind, that nobody could get a peep at them oftener than once in a hundred years. As for the Giant, being of a very lofty stature, it was easy enough to see him, but safest to keep out of his sight.

Among the Pygmies, I suppose, if one of them grew to the height of six or eight inches, he was reckoned a prodigiously tall man. It must have been very pretty to behold their little cities, with streets two or three feet wide, paved with the smallest pebbles, and bordered by habitations about as big as a squirrel's cage. The king's palace attained to the stupendous magnitude of Periwinkle's baby house, and stood in the center of a spacious square, which could hardly have been covered by our hearth-rug. Their principal temple, or cathedral, was as lofty as yonder bureau, and was looked upon as a wonderfully sublime and magnificent edifice. All these structures were built neither of stone nor wood. They were neatly plastered together by the Pygmy workmen, pretty much like birds' nests, out of straw, feathers, egg shells, and other small bits of stuff, with stiff clay instead of mortar; and when the hot sun had dried them, they were just as snug and comfortable as a Pygmy could desire.

The country round about was conveniently laid out in fields, the largest of which was nearly of the same extent as one of Sweet Fern's flower beds. Here the Pygmies used to plant wheat and other kinds of grain, which, when it grew up and ripened, overshadowed these tiny people as the pines, and the oaks, and the walnut and chestnut trees overshadow you and me, when we walk in our own tracts of woodland. At harvest time, they were forced to go with their little axes and cut down the grain, exactly as a woodcutter makes a clearing in the forest; and when a stalk of wheat, with its overburdened top, chanced to come crashing down upon an unfortunate Pygmy, it was apt to be a very sad affair. If it did not smash him all to pieces, at least, I am sure, it must have made the poor little fellow's head ache. And O, my stars! if the fathers and mothers were so small, what must the children and babies have been? A whole family of them might have been put to bed in a shoe, or have crept into an old glove, and played at hide-and-seek in its thumb and fingers. You might have hidden a year-old baby under a thimble.

Now these funny Pygmies, as I told you before, had a Giant for their neighbor and brother, who was bigger, if possible, than they were little. He was so very tall that he carried a pine tree, which was eight feet through the butt, for a walking stick. It took a far-sighted Pygmy, I can assure you, to discern his summit without the help of a telescope; and sometimes, in misty weather, they could not see his upper half, but only his long legs, which seemed to be striding about by themselves. But at noonday in a clear atmosphere, when the sun shone brightly over him, the Giant Antaeus presented a very grand spectacle. There he used to stand, a perfect mountain of a man, with his great countenance smiling down upon his little brothers, and his one vast eye (which was as big as a cart wheel, and placed right in the center of his forehead) giving a friendly wink to the whole nation at once.

The Pygmies loved to talk with Antaeus; and fifty times a day, one or another of them would turn up his head, and shout through the hollow of his fists, "Halloo, brother Antaeus! How are you, my good fellow?" And when the small distant squeak of their voices reached his ear, the Giant would make answer, "Pretty well, brother Pygmy, I thank you," in a thunderous roar that would have shaken down the walls of their strongest temple, only that it came from so far aloft.

It was a happy circumstance that Antaeus was the Pygmy people's friend; for there was more strength in his little finger than in ten million of such bodies as this. If he had been as ill-natured to them as he was to everybody else, he might have beaten down their biggest city at one kick, and hardly have known that he did it. With the tornado of his breath, he could have stripped the roofs from a hundred dwellings and sent thousands of the inhabitants whirling through the air. He might have set his immense foot upon a multitude; and when he took it up again, there would have been a pitiful sight, to be sure. But, being the son of Mother Earth, as they likewise were, the Giant gave them his brotherly kindness, and loved them with as big a love as it was possible to feel for creatures so very small. And, on their parts, the Pygmies loved Antaeus with as much affection as their tiny hearts could hold. He was always ready to do them any good offices that lay in his power; as for example, when they wanted a breeze to turn their windmills, the Giant would set all the sails a-going with the mere natural respiration of his lungs. When the sun was too hot, he often sat himself down, and let his shadow fall over the kingdom, from one frontier to the other; and as for matters in general, he was wise enough to let them alone, and leave the Pygmies to manage their own affairs—which, after all, is about the best thing that great people can do for little ones.

In short, as I said before, Antaeus loved the Pygmies, and the Pygmies loved Antaeus. The Giant's life being as long as his body was large, while the lifetime of a Pygmy was but a span, this friendly intercourse had been going on for innumerable generations and ages. It was written about in the Pygmy histories, and talked about in their ancient traditions. The most venerable and white-bearded Pygmy had never heard of a time, even in his greatest of grandfathers' days, when the Giant was not their enormous friend. Once, to be sure (as was recorded on an obelisk, three feet high, erected on the place of the catastrophe), Antaeus sat down upon about five thousand Pygmies, who were assembled at a military review. But this was one of those unlucky accidents for which nobody is to blame; so that the small folks never took it to heart, and only requested the Giant to be careful forever afterwards to examine the acre of ground where he intended to squat himself.

It is a very pleasant picture to imagine Antaeus standing among the Pygmies, like the spire of the tallest cathedral that ever was built, while they ran about like pismires at his feet; and to think that, in spite of their difference in size, there were affection and sympathy between them and him! Indeed, it has always seemed to me that the Giant needed the little people more than the Pygmies needed the Giant. For, unless they had been his neighbors and well wishers, and, as we may say, his playfellows, Antaeus would not have had a single friend in the world. No other being like himself had ever been created. No creature of his own size had ever talked with him, in thunder-like accents, face to face. When he stood with his head among the clouds, he was quite alone, and had been so for hundreds of years, and would be so forever. Even if he had met another Giant, Antaeus would have fancied the world not big enough for two such vast personages, and, instead of being friends with him, would have fought him till one of the two was killed. But with the Pygmies he was the most sportive and humorous, and merry-hearted, and sweet-tempered old Giant that ever washed his face in a wet cloud.

His little friends, like all other small people, had a great opinion of their own importance, and used to assume quite a patronizing air towards the Giant.

"Poor creature!" they said one to another. "He has a very dull time of it, all by himself; and we ought not to grudge wasting a little of our precious time to amuse him. He is not half so bright as we are, to be sure; and, for that reason, he needs us to look after his comfort and happiness. Let us be kind to the old fellow. Why, if Mother Earth had not been very kind to ourselves, we might all have been Giants too."

On all their holidays, the Pygmies had excellent sport with Antaeus. He often stretched himself out at full length on the ground, where he looked like the long ridge of a hill; and it was a good hour's walk, no doubt, for a short-legged Pygmy to journey from head to foot of the Giant. He would lay down his great hand flat on the grass, and challenge the tallest of them to clamber upon it, and straddle from finger to finger. So fearless were they, that they made nothing of creeping in among the folds of his garments. When his head lay sidewise on the earth, they would march boldly up, and peep into the great cavern of his mouth, and take it all as a joke (as indeed it was meant) when Antaeus gave a sudden snap of his jaws, as if he were going to swallow fifty of them at once. You would have laughed to see the children dodging in and out among his hair, or swinging from his beard. It is impossible to tell half of the funny tricks that they played with their huge comrade; but I do not know that anything was more curious than when a party of boys were seen running races on his forehead, to try which of them could get first round the circle of his one great eye. It was another favorite feat with them to march along the bridge of his nose, and jump down upon his upper lip.

If the truth must be told, they were sometimes as troublesome to the Giant as a swarm of ants or mosquitoes, especially as they had a fondness for mischief, and liked to prick his skin with their little swords and lances, to see how thick and tough it was. But Antaeus took it all kindly enough; although, once in a while, when he happened to be sleepy, he would grumble out a peevish word or two, like the muttering of a tempest, and ask them to have done with their nonsense. A great deal oftener, however, he watched their merriment and gambols until his huge, heavy, clumsy wits were completely stirred up by them; and then would he roar out such a tremendous volume of immeasurable laughter, that the whole nation of Pygmies had to put their hands to their ears, else it would certainly have deafened them.

"Ho! ho! ho!" quoth the Giant, shaking his mountainous sides. "What a funny thing it is to be little! If I were not Antaeus, I should like to be a Pygmy, just for the joke's sake."

The Pygmies had but one thing to trouble them in the world. They were constantly at war with the cranes, and had always been so, ever since the long-lived Giant could remember. From time to time, very terrible battles had been fought in which sometimes the little men won the victory, and sometimes the cranes. According to some historians, the Pygmies used to go to the battle, mounted on the backs of goats and rams; but such animals as these must have been far too big for Pygmies to ride upon; so that, I rather suppose, they rode on squirrel-back, or rabbit-back, or rat-back, or perhaps got upon hedgehogs, whose prickly quills would be very terrible to the enemy. However this might be, and whatever creatures the Pygmies rode upon, I do not doubt that they made a formidable appearance, armed with sword and spear, and bow and arrow, blowing their tiny trumpet, and shouting their little war cry. They never failed to exhort one another to fight bravely, and recollect that the world had its eyes upon them; although, in simple truth, the only spectator was the Giant Antaeus, with his one, great, stupid eye in the middle of his forehead.

When the two armies joined battle, the cranes would rush forward, flapping their wings and stretching out their necks, and would perhaps snatch up some of the Pygmies crosswise in their beaks. Whenever this happened, it was truly an awful spectacle to see those little men of might kicking and sprawling in the air, and at last disappearing down the crane's long, crooked throat, swallowed up alive. A hero, you know, must hold himself in readiness for any kind of fate; and doubtless the glory of the thing was a consolation to him, even in the crane's gizzard. If Antaeus observed that the battle was going hard against his little allies, he generally stopped laughing, and ran with mile-long strides to their assistance, flourishing his club aloft and shouting at the cranes, who quacked and croaked, and retreated as fast as they could. Then the Pygmy army would march homeward in triumph, attributing the victory entirely to their own valor, and to the warlike skill and strategy of whomsoever happened to be captain general; and for a tedious while afterwards, nothing would be heard of but grand processions, and public banquets, and brilliant illuminations, and shows of wax-work, with likenesses of the distinguished officers, as small as life.

In the above-described warfare, if a Pygmy chanced to pluck out a crane's tail feather, it proved a very great feather in his cap. Once or twice, if you will believe me, a little man was made chief ruler of the nation for no other merit in the world than bringing home such a feather.

But I have now said enough to let you see what a gallant little people these were, and how happily they and their forefathers, for nobody knows how many generations, had lived with the immeasurable Giant Antaeus. In the remaining part of the story, I shall tell you of a far more astonishing battle than any that was fought between the Pygmies and the cranes.

One day the mighty Antaeus was lolling at full length among his little friends. His pine-tree walking stick lay on the ground, close by his side. His head was in one part of the kingdom, and his feet extended across the boundaries of another part; and he was taking whatever comfort he could get, while the Pygmies scrambled over him, and peeped into his cavernous mouth, and played among his hair. Sometimes, for a minute or two, the Giant dropped asleep, and snored like the rush of a whirlwind. During one of these little bits of slumber, a Pygmy chanced to climb upon his shoulder, and took a view around the horizon, as from the summit of a hill; and he beheld something, a long way off, which made him rub the bright specks of his eyes, and look sharper than before. At first he mistook it for a mountain, and wondered how it had grown up so suddenly out of the earth. But soon he saw the mountain move. As it came nearer and nearer, what should it turn out to be but a human shape, not so big as Antaeus, it is true, although a very enormous figure, in comparison with Pygmies, and a vast deal bigger than the men we see nowadays.

When the Pygmy was quite satisfied that his eyes had not deceived him, he scampered, as fast as his legs would carry him, to the Giant's ear, and stooping over its cavity, shouted lustily into it:

"Halloo, brother Antaeus! Get up this minute, and take your pine-tree walking stick in your hand. Here comes another Giant to have a tussle with you."

"Poh, poh!" grumbled Antaeus, only half awake. "None of your nonsense, my little fellow! Don't you see I'm sleepy? There is not a Giant on earth for whom I would take the trouble to get up."

But the Pygmy looked again, and now perceived that the stranger was coming directly towards the prostrate form of Antaeus. With every step, he looked less like a blue mountain, and more like an immensely large man. He was soon so nigh, that there could be no possible mistake about the matter. There he was, with the sun flaming on his golden helmet, and flashing from his polished breastplate; he had a sword by his side, and a lion's skin over his back, and on his right shoulder he carried a club, which looked bulkier and heavier than the pine-tree walking stick of Antaeus.

By this time, the whole nation of the Pygmies had seen the new wonder, and a million of them set up a shout all together; so that it really made quite an audible squeak.

"Get up, Antaeus! Bestir yourself, you lazy old Giant! Here comes another Giant, as strong as you are, to fight with you."

"Nonsense, nonsense!" growled the sleepy Giant. "I'll have my nap out, come who may."

Still the stranger drew nearer; and now the Pygmies could plainly discern that, if his stature were less lofty than the Giant's, yet his shoulders were even broader. And, in truth, what a pair of shoulders they must have been! As I told you, a long while ago, they once upheld the sky. The Pygmies, being ten times as vivacious as their great numskull of a brother, could not abide the Giant's slow movements, and were determined to have him on his feet. So they kept shouting to him, and even went so far as to prick him with their swords.

"Get up, get up, get up," they cried. "Up with you, lazy bones! The strange Giant's club is bigger than your own, his shoulders are the broadest, and we think him the stronger of the two."

Antaeus could not endure to have it said that any mortal was half so mighty as himself. This latter remark of the Pygmies pricked him deeper than their swords; and, sitting up, in rather a sulky humor, he gave a gape of several yards wide, rubbed his eyes, and finally turned his stupid head in the direction whither his little friends were eagerly pointing.

No sooner did he set eyes on the stranger, than, leaping on his feet, and seizing his walking stick, he strode a mile or two to meet him; all the while brandishing the sturdy pine tree, so that it whistled through the air.

"Who are you?" thundered the Giant. "And what do you want in my dominions?"

There was one strange thing about Antaeus, of which I have not yet told you, lest, hearing of so many wonders all in a lump, you might not believe much more than half of them. You are to know, then, that whenever this redoubtable Giant touched the ground, either with his hand, his foot, or any other part of his body, he grew stronger than ever he had been before. The Earth, you remember, was his mother, and was very fond of him, as being almost the biggest of her children; and so she took this method of keeping him always in full vigor. Some persons affirm that he grew ten times stronger at every touch; others say that it was only twice as strong. But only think of it! Whenever Antaeus took a walk, supposing it were but ten miles, and that he stepped a hundred yards at a stride, you may try to cipher out how much mightier he was, on sitting down again, than when he first started. And whenever he flung himself on the earth to take a little repose, even if he got up the very next instant, he would be as strong as exactly ten just such giants as his former self. It was well for the world that Antaeus happened to be of a sluggish disposition and liked ease better than exercise; for, if he had frisked about like the Pygmies, and touched the earth as often as they did, he would long ago have been strong enough to pull down the sky about people's ears. But these great lubberly fellows resemble mountains, not only in bulk, but in their disinclination to move.

Any other mortal man, except the very one whom Antaeus had now encountered, would have been half frightened to death by the Giant's ferocious aspect and terrible voice. But the stranger did not seem at all disturbed. He carelessly lifted his club, and balanced it in his hand, measuring Antaeus with his eye, from head to foot, not as if wonder-smitten at his stature, but as if he had seen a great many Giants before, and this was by no means the biggest of them. In fact, if the Giant had been no bigger than the Pygmies (who stood pricking up their ears, and looking and listening to what was going forward), the stranger could not have been less afraid of him.

"Who are you, I say?" roared Antaeus again. "What's your name? Why do you come hither? Speak, you vagabond, or I'll try the thickness of your skull with my walking-stick!"

"You are a very discourteous Giant," answered the stranger quietly, "and I shall probably have to teach you a little civility, before we part. As for my name, it is Hercules. I have come hither because this is my most convenient road to the garden of the Hesperides, whither I am going to get three of the golden apples for King Eurystheus."

"Caitiff, you shall go no farther!" bellowed Antaeus, putting on a grimmer look than before; for he had heard of the mighty Hercules, and hated him because he was said to be so strong. "Neither shall you go back whence you came!"

"How will you prevent me," asked Hercules, "from going whither I please?"

"By hitting you a rap with this pine tree here," shouted Antaeus, scowling so that he made himself the ugliest monster in Africa. "I am fifty times stronger than you; and now that I stamp my foot upon the ground, I am five hundred times stronger! I am ashamed to kill such a puny little dwarf as you seem to be. I will make a slave of you, and you shall likewise be the slave of my brethren here, the Pygmies. So throw down your club and your other weapons; and as for that lion's skin, I intend to have a pair of gloves made of it."

"Come and take it off my shoulders, then," answered Hercules, lifting his club.

Then the Giant, grinning with rage, strode tower-like towards the stranger (ten times strengthened at every step), and fetched a monstrous blow at him with his pine tree, which Hercules caught upon his club; and being more skilful than Antaeus, he paid him back such a rap upon the sconce, that down tumbled the great lumbering man-mountain, flat upon the ground. The poor little Pygmies (who really never dreamed that anybody in the world was half so strong as their brother Antaeus) were a good deal dismayed at this. But no sooner was the Giant down, than up he bounced again, with tenfold might, and such a furious visage as was horrible to behold. He aimed another blow at Hercules, but struck awry, being blinded with wrath, and only hit his poor innocent Mother Earth, who groaned and trembled at the stroke. His pine tree went so deep into the ground, and stuck there so fast, that, before Antaeus could get it out, Hercules brought down his club across his shoulders with a mighty thwack, which made the Giant roar as if all sorts of intolerable noises had come screeching and rumbling out of his immeasurable lungs in that one cry. Away it went, over mountains and valleys, and, for aught I know, was heard on the other side of the African deserts.

As for the Pygmies, their capital city was laid in ruins by the concussion and vibration of the air; and, though there was uproar enough without their help, they all set up a shriek out of three millions of little throats, fancying, no doubt, that they swelled the Giant's bellow by at least ten times as much. Meanwhile, Antaeus had scrambled upon his feet again, and pulled his pine tree out of the earth; and, all aflame with fury, and more outrageously strong than ever, he ran at Hercules, and brought down another blow.

"This time, rascal," shouted he, "you shall not escape me."

But once more Hercules warded off the stroke with his club, and the Giant's pine tree was shattered into a thousand splinters, most of which flew among the Pygmies, and did them more mischief than I like to think about. Before Antaeus could get out of the way, Hercules let drive again, and gave him another knock-down blow, which sent him heels over head, but served only to increase his already enormous and insufferable strength. As for his rage, there is no telling what a fiery furnace it had now got to be. His one eye was nothing but a circle of red flame. Having now no weapons but his fists, he doubled them up (each bigger than a hogshead), smote one against the other, and danced up and down with absolute frenzy, flourishing his immense arms about, as if he meant not merely to kill Hercules, but to smash the whole world to pieces.

"Come on!" roared this thundering Giant. "Let me hit you but one box on the ear, and you'll never have the headache again."

Now Hercules (though strong enough, as you already know, to hold the sky up) began to be sensible that he should never win the victory, if he kept on knocking Antaeus down; for, by and by, if he hit him such hard blows, the Giant would inevitably, by the help of his Mother Earth, become stronger than the mighty Hercules himself. So, throwing down his club, with which he had fought so many dreadful battles, the hero stood ready to receive his antagonist with naked arms.

"Step forward," cried he. "Since I've broken your pine tree, we'll try which is the better man at a wrestling match."

"Aha! then I'll soon satisfy you," shouted the Giant; for, if there was one thing on which he prided himself more than another, it was his skill in wrestling. "Villain, I'll fling you where you can never pick yourself up again."

On came Antaeus, hopping and capering with the scorching heat of his rage, and getting new vigor wherewith to wreak his passion, every time he hopped.

But Hercules, you must understand, was wiser than this numskull of a Giant, and had thought of a way to fight him—huge, earth-born monster that he was—and to conquer him too, in spite of all that his Mother Earth could do for him. Watching his opportunity, as the mad Giant made a rush at him, Hercules caught him round the middle with both hands, lifted him high into the air, and held him aloft overhead.

Just imagine it, my dear little friends. What a spectacle it must have been, to see this monstrous fellow sprawling in the air, face downwards, kicking out his long legs and wriggling his whole vast body, like a baby when its father holds it at arm's length towards the ceiling.

But the most wonderful thing was, that, as soon as Antaeus was fairly off the earth, he began to lose the vigor which he had gained by touching it. Hercules very soon perceived that his troublesome enemy was growing weaker, both because he struggled and kicked with less violence, and because the thunder of his big voice subsided into a grumble. The truth was that unless the Giant touched Mother Earth as often as once in five minutes, not only his overgrown strength, but the very breath of his life, would depart from him. Hercules had guessed this secret; and it may be well for us all to remember it, in case we should ever have to fight a battle with a fellow like Antaeus. For these earth-born creatures are only difficult to conquer on their own ground, but may easily be managed if we can contrive to lift them into a loftier and purer region. So it proved with the poor Giant, whom I am really a little sorry for, notwithstanding his uncivil way of treating strangers who came to visit him.

When his strength and breath were quite gone, Hercules gave his huge body a toss, and flung it about a mile off, where it fell heavily, and lay with no more motion than a sand hill. It was too late for the Giant's Mother Earth to help him now; and I should not wonder if his ponderous bones were lying on the same spot to this very day, and were mistaken for those of an uncommonly large elephant.

But, alas me! What a wailing did the poor little Pygmies set up when they saw their enormous brother treated in this terrible manner! If Hercules heard their shrieks, however, he took no notice, and perhaps fancied them only the shrill, plaintive twittering of small birds that had been frightened from their nests by the uproar of the battle between himself and Antaeus. Indeed, his thoughts had been so much taken up with the Giant, that he had never once looked at the Pygmies, nor even knew that there was such a funny little nation in the world. And now, as he had traveled a good way, and was also rather weary with his exertions in the fight, he spread out his lion's skin on the ground, and, reclining himself upon it, fell fast asleep.

As soon as the Pygmies saw Hercules preparing for a nap, they nodded their little heads at one another, and winked with their little eyes. And when his deep, regular breathing gave them notice that he was asleep, they assembled together in an immense crowd, spreading over a space of about twenty-seven feet square. One of their most eloquent orators (and a valiant warrior enough, besides, though hardly so good at any other weapon as he was with his tongue) climbed upon a toadstool, and, from that elevated position, addressed the multitude. His sentiments were pretty much as follows; or, at all events, something like this was probably the upshot of his speech:

"Tall Pygmies and mighty little men! You and all of us have seen what a public calamity has been brought to pass, and what an insult has here been offered to the majesty of our nation. Yonder lies Antaeus, our great friend and brother, slain, within our territory, by a miscreant who took him at disadvantage, and fought him (if fighting it can be called) in a way that neither man, nor Giant, nor Pygmy ever dreamed of fighting, until this hour. And, adding a grievous contumely to the wrong already done us, the miscreant has now fallen asleep as quietly as if nothing were to be dreaded from our wrath! It behooves you, fellow-countrymen, to consider in what aspect we shall stand before the world, and what will be the verdict of impartial history, should we suffer these accumulated outrages to go unavenged.

"Antaeus was our brother, born of that same beloved parent to whom we owe the thews and sinews, as well as the courageous hearts, which made him proud of our relationship. He was our faithful ally, and fell fighting as much for our national rights and immunities as for his own personal ones. We and our forefathers have dwelt in friendship with him, and held affectionate intercourse as man to man, through immemorial generations. You remember how often our entire people have reposed in his great shadow, and how our little ones have played at hide-and-seek in the tangles of his hair, and how his mighty footsteps have familiarly gone to and fro among us, and never trodden upon any of our toes. And there lies this dear brother—this sweet and amiable friend—this brave and faithful ally—this virtuous Giant—this blameless and excellent Antaeus—dead! Dead! Silent! Powerless! A mere mountain of clay! Forgive my tears! Nay, I behold your own. Were we to drown the world with them, could the world blame us?

"But to resume: Shall we, my countrymen, suffer this wicked stranger to depart unharmed, and triumph in his treacherous victory, among distant communities of the earth? Shall we not rather compel him to leave his bones here on our soil, by the side of our slain brother's bones? so that, while one skeleton shall remain as the everlasting monument of our sorrow, the other shall endure as long, exhibiting to the whole human race a terrible example of Pygmy vengeance! Such is the question. I put it to you in full confidence of a response that shall be worthy of our national character, and calculated to increase, rather than diminish, the glory which our ancestors have transmitted to us, and which we ourselves have proudly vindicated in our warfare with the cranes."

The orator was here interrupted by a burst of irrepressible enthusiasm; every individual Pygmy crying out that the national honor must be preserved at all hazards. He bowed, and, making a gesture for silence, wound up his harangue in the following admirable manner:

"It only remains for us, then, to decide whether we shall carry on the war in our national capacity—one united people against a common enemy—or whether some champion, famous in former fights, shall be selected to defy the slayer of our brother Antaeus to single combat. In the latter case, though not unconscious that there may be taller men among you, I hereby offer myself for that enviable duty. And believe me, dear countrymen, whether I live or die, the honor of this great country, and the fame bequeathed us by our heroic progenitors, shall suffer no diminution in my hands. Never, while I can wield this sword, of which I now fling away the scabbard—never, never, never, even if the crimson hand that slew the great Antaeus shall lay me prostrate, like him, on the soil which I give my life to defend."

So saying, this valiant Pygmy drew out his weapon (which was terrible to behold, being as long as the blade of a penknife), and sent the scabbard whirling over the heads of the multitude. His speech was followed by an uproar of applause, as its patriotism and self-devotion unquestionably deserved; and the shouts and clapping of hands would have been greatly prolonged, had they not been rendered quite inaudible by a deep respiration, vulgarly called a snore, from the sleeping Hercules.

It was finally decided that the whole nation of Pygmies should set to work to destroy Hercules; not, be it understood, from any doubt that a single champion would be capable of putting him to the sword, but because he was a public enemy, and all were desirous of sharing in the glory of his defeat. There was a debate whether the national honor did not demand that a herald should be sent with a trumpet, to stand over the ear of Hercules, and after blowing a blast right into it, to defy him to the combat by formal proclamation. But two or three venerable and sagacious Pygmies, well versed in state affairs, gave it as their opinion that war already existed, and that it was their rightful privilege to take the enemy by surprise. Moreover, if awakened, and allowed to get upon his feet, Hercules might happen to do them a mischief before he could be beaten down again. For, as these sage counselors remarked, the stranger's club was really very big, and had rattled like a thunderbolt against the skull of Antaeus. So the Pygmies resolved to set aside all foolish punctilios, and assail their antagonist at once.

Accordingly, all the fighting men of the nation took their weapons, and went boldly up to Hercules, who still lay fast asleep, little dreaming of the harm which the Pygmies meant to do him. A body of twenty thousand archers marched in front, with their little bows all ready, and the arrows on the string. The same number were ordered to clamber upon Hercules, some with spades to dig his eyes out, and others with bundles of hay, and all manner of rubbish with which they intended to plug up his mouth and nostrils, so that he might perish for lack of breath. These last, however, could by no means perform their appointed duty; inasmuch as the enemy's breath rushed out of his nose in an obstreperous hurricane and whirlwind, which blew the Pygmies away as fast as they came nigh. It was found necessary, therefore, to hit upon some other method of carrying on the war.

After holding a council, the captains ordered their troops to collect sticks, straws, dry weeds, and whatever combustible stuff they could find, and make a pile of it, heaping it high around the head of Hercules. As a great many thousand Pygmies were employed in this task, they soon brought together several bushels of inflammatory matter, and raised so tall a heap, that, mounting on its summit, they were quite upon a level with the sleeper's face. The archers, meanwhile, were stationed within bow shot, with orders to let fly at Hercules the instant that he stirred. Everything being in readiness, a torch was applied to the pile, which immediately burst into flames, and soon waxed hot enough to roast the enemy, had he but chosen to lie still. A Pygmy, you know, though so very small, might set the world on fire, just as easily as a Giant could; so that this was certainly the very best way of dealing with their foe, provided they could have kept him quiet while the conflagration was going forward.

But no sooner did Hercules begin to be scorched, than up he started, with his hair in a red blaze.

"What's all this?" he cried, bewildered with sleep, and staring about him as if he expected to see another Giant.

At that moment the twenty thousand archers twanged their bowstrings, and the arrows came whizzing, like so many winged mosquitoes, right into the face of Hercules. But I doubt whether more than half a dozen of them punctured the skin, which was remarkably tough, as you know the skin of a hero has good need to be.

"Villain!" shouted all the Pygmies at once. "You have killed the Giant Antaeus, our great brother, and the ally of our nation. We declare bloody war against you, and will slay you on the spot."

Surprised at the shrill piping of so many little voices, Hercules, after putting out the conflagration of his hair, gazed all round about, but could see nothing. At last, however, looking narrowly on the ground, he espied the innumerable assemblage of Pygmies at his feet. He stooped down, and taking up the nearest one between his thumb and finger, set him on the palm of his left hand, and held him at a proper distance for examination. It chanced to be the very identical Pygmy who had spoken from the top of the toadstool, and had offered himself as a champion to meet Hercules in single combat.

"What in the world, my little fellow," ejaculated Hercules, "may you be?"

"I am your enemy," answered the valiant Pygmy, in his mightiest squeak. "You have slain the enormous Antaeus, our brother by the mother's side, and for ages the faithful ally of our illustrious nation. We are determined to put you to death; and for my own part, I challenge you to instant battle, on equal ground."

Hercules was so tickled with the Pygmy's big words and warlike gestures, that he burst into a great explosion of laughter, and almost dropped the poor little mite of a creature off the palm of his hand, through the ecstasy and convulsion of his merriment.

"Upon my word," cried he, "I thought I had seen wonders before to-day—hydras with nine heads, stags with golden horns, six-legged men, three-headed dogs, giants with furnaces in their stomachs, and nobody knows what besides. But here, on the palm of my hand, stands a wonder that outdoes them all! Your body, my little friend, is about the size of an ordinary man's finger. Pray, how big may your soul be?"

"As big as your own!" said the Pygmy.

Hercules was touched with the little man's dauntless courage, and could not help acknowledging such a brotherhood with him as one hero feels for another.

"My good little people," said he, making a low obeisance to the grand nation, "not for all the world would I do an intentional injury to such brave fellows as you! Your hearts seem to me so exceedingly great, that, upon my honor, I marvel how your small bodies can contain them. I sue for peace, and, as a condition of it, will take five strides, and be out of your kingdom at the sixth. Good-bye. I shall pick my steps carefully, for fear of treading upon some fifty of you, without knowing it. Ha, ha, ha! Ho, ho, ho! For once, Hercules acknowledges himself vanquished."

Some writers say, that Hercules gathered up the whole race of Pygmies in his lion's skin, and carried them home to Greece, for the children of King Eurystheus to play with. But this is a mistake. He left them, one and all, within their own territory, where, for aught I can tell, their descendants are alive to the present day, building their little houses, cultivating their little fields, spanking their little children, waging their little warfare with the cranes, doing their little business, whatever it may be, and reading their little histories of ancient times. In those histories, perhaps, it stands recorded, that, a great many centuries ago, the valiant Pygmies avenged the death of the Giant Antaeus by scaring away the mighty Hercules.

THE DRAGON'S TEETH.

Cadmus, Phoenix, and Cilix, the three sons of King Agenor, and their little sister Europa (who was a very beautiful child), were at play together near the seashore in their father's kingdom of Phoenicia. They had rambled to some distance from the palace where their parents dwelt, and were now in a verdant meadow, on one side of which lay the sea, all sparkling and dimpling in the sunshine, and murmuring gently against the beach. The three boys were very happy, gathering flowers, and twining them into garlands, with which they adorned the little Europa. Seated on the grass, the child was almost hidden under an abundance of buds and blossoms, whence her rosy face peeped merrily out, and, as Cadmus said, was the prettiest of all the flowers.

Just then, there came a splendid butterfly, fluttering along the meadow; and Cadmus, Phoenix, and Cilix set off in pursuit of it, crying out that it was a flower with wings. Europa, who was a little wearied with playing all day long, did not chase the butterfly with her brothers, but sat still where they had left her, and closed her eyes. For a while, she listened to the pleasant murmur of the sea, which was like a voice saying "Hush!" and bidding her go to sleep. But the pretty child, if she slept at all, could not have slept more than a moment, when she heard something trample on the grass, not far from her, and, peeping out from the heap of flowers, beheld a snow-white bull.

And whence could this bull have come? Europa and her brothers had been a long time playing in the meadow, and had seen no cattle, nor other living thing, either there or on the neighboring hills.

"Brother Cadmus!" cried Europa, starting up out of the midst of the roses and lilies. "Phoenix! Cilix! Where are you all? Help! Help! Come and drive away this bull!"

But her brothers were too far off to hear; especially as the fright took away Europa's voice, and hindered her from calling very loudly. So there she stood, with her pretty mouth wide open, as pale as the white lilies that were twisted among the other flowers in her garlands.

Nevertheless, it was the suddenness with which she had perceived the bull, rather than anything frightful in his appearance, that caused Europa so much alarm. On looking at him more attentively, she began to see that he was a beautiful animal, and even fancied a particularly amiable expression in his face. As for his breath—the breath of cattle, you know, is always sweet—it was as fragrant as if he had been grazing on no other food than rosebuds, or at least, the most delicate of clover blossoms. Never before did a bull have such bright and tender eyes, and such smooth horns of ivory, as this one. And the bull ran little races, and capered sportively around the child; so that she quite forgot how big and strong he was, and, from the gentleness and playfulness of his actions, soon came to consider him as innocent a creature as a pet lamb.

Thus, frightened as she at first was, you might by and by have seen Europa stroking the bull's forehead with her small white hand, and taking the garlands off her own head to hang them on his neck and ivory horns. Then she pulled up some blades of grass, and he ate them out of her hand, not as if he were hungry, but because he wanted to be friends with the child, and took pleasure in eating what she had touched. Well, my stars! was there ever such a gentle, sweet, pretty, and amiable creature as this bull, and ever such a nice playmate for a little girl?

When the animal saw (for the bull had so much intelligence that it is really wonderful to think of), when he saw that Europa was no longer afraid of him, he grew overjoyed, and could hardly contain himself for delight. He frisked about the meadow, now here, now there, making sprightly leaps, with as little effort as a bird expends in hopping from twig to twig. Indeed, his motion was as light as if he were flying through the air, and his hoofs seemed hardly to leave their print in the grassy soil over which he trod. With his spotless hue, he resembled a snow drift, wafted along by the wind. Once he galloped so far away that Europa feared lest she might never see him again; so, setting up her childish voice, called him back.

"Come back, pretty creature!" she cried. "Here is a nice clover blossom."

And then it was delightful to witness the gratitude of this amiable bull, and how he was so full of joy and thankfulness that he capered higher than ever. He came running, and bowed his head before Europa, as if he knew her to be a king's daughter, or else recognized the important truth that a little girl is everybody's queen. And not only did the bull bend his neck, he absolutely knelt down at her feet, and made such intelligent nods, and other inviting gestures, that Europa understood what he meant just as well as if he had put it in so many words.

"Come, dear child," was what he wanted to say, "let me give you a ride on my back."

At the first thought of such a thing, Europa drew back. But then she considered in her wise little head that there could be no possible harm in taking just one gallop on the back of this docile and friendly animal, who would certainly set her down the very instant she desired it. And how it would surprise her brothers to see her riding across the green meadow! And what merry times they might have, either taking turns for a gallop, or clambering on the gentle creature, all four children together, and careering round the field with shouts of laughter that would be heard as far off as King Agenor's palace!

"I think I will do it," said the child to herself.

And, indeed, why not? She cast a glance around, and caught a glimpse of Cadmus, Phoenix, and Cilix, who were still in pursuit of the butterfly, almost at the other end of the meadow. It would be the quickest way of rejoining them, to get upon the white bull's back. She came a step nearer to him therefore; and—sociable creature that he was—he showed so much joy at this mark of her confidence, that the child could not find in her heart to hesitate any longer. Making one bound (for this little princess was as active as a squirrel), there sat Europa on the beautiful bull, holding an ivory horn in each hand, lest she should fall off.

"Softly, pretty bull, softly!" she said, rather frightened at what she had done. "Do not gallop too fast."

Having got the child on his back, the animal gave a leap into the air, and came down so like a feather that Europa did not know when his hoofs touched the ground. He then began a race to that part of the flowery plain where her three brothers were, and where they had just caught their splendid butterfly. Europa screamed with delight; and Phoenix, Cilix, and Cadmus stood gaping at the spectacle of their sister mounted on a white bull, not knowing whether to be frightened or to wish the same good luck for themselves. The gentle and innocent creature (for who could possibly doubt that he was so?) pranced round among the children as sportively as a kitten. Europa all the while looked down upon her brothers, nodding and laughing, but yet with a sort of stateliness in her rosy little face. As the bull wheeled about to take another gallop across the meadow, the child waved her hand, and said, "Good-bye," playfully pretending that she was now bound on a distant journey, and might not see her brothers again for nobody could tell how long.

"Good-bye," shouted Cadmus, Phoenix, and Cilix, all in one breath.

But, together with her enjoyment of the sport, there was still a little remnant of fear in the child's heart; so that her last look at the three boys was a troubled one, and made them feel as if their dear sister were really leaving them forever. And what do you think the snowy bull did next? Why, he set off, as swift as the wind, straight down to the seashore, scampered across the sand, took an airy leap, and plunged right in among the foaming billows. The white spray rose in a shower over him and little Europa, and fell spattering down upon the water.

Then what a scream of terror did the poor child send forth! The three brothers screamed manfully, likewise, and ran to the shore as fast as their legs would carry them, with Cadmus at their head. But it was too late. When they reached the margin of the sand, the treacherous animal was already far away in the wide blue sea, with only his snowy head and tail emerging, and poor little Europa between them, stretching out one hand towards her dear brothers, while she grasped the bull's ivory horn with the other. And there stood Cadmus, Phoenix, and Cilix, gazing at this sad spectacle, through their tears, until they could no longer distinguish the bull's snowy head from the white-capped billows that seemed to boil up out of the sea's depths around him. Nothing more was ever seen of the white bull—nothing more of the beautiful child.

This was a mournful story, as you may well think, for the three boys to carry home to their parents. King Agenor, their father, was the ruler of the whole country; but he loved his little daughter Europa better than his kingdom, or than all his other children, or than anything else in the world. Therefore, when Cadmus and his two brothers came crying home, and told him how that a white bull had carried off their sister, and swam with her over the sea, the king was quite beside himself with grief and rage. Although it was now twilight, and fast growing dark, he bade them set out instantly in search of her.

"Never shall you see my face again," he cried, "unless you bring me back my little Europa, to gladden me with her smiles and her pretty ways. Begone, and enter my presence no more, till you come leading her by the hand."

As King Agenor said this, his eyes flashed fire (for he was a very passionate king), and he looked so terribly angry that the poor boys did not even venture to ask for their suppers, but slunk away out of the palace, and only paused on the steps a moment to consult whither they should go first. While they were standing there, all in dismay, their mother, Queen Telephassa (who happened not to be by when they told the story to the king), came hurrying after them, and said that she too would go in quest of her daughter.

"O, no, mother!" cried the boys. "The night is dark, and there is no knowing what troubles and perils we may meet with."

"Alas! my dear children," answered poor Queen Telephassa; weeping bitterly, "that is only another reason why I should go with you. If I should lose you, too, as well as my little Europa, what would become of me!"

"And let me go likewise!" said their playfellow Thasus, who came running to join them.

Thasus was the son of a seafaring person in the neighborhood; he had been brought up with the young princes, and was their intimate friend, and loved Europa very much; so they consented that he should accompany them. The whole party, therefore, set forth together. Cadmus, Phoenix, Cilix, and Thasus clustered round Queen Telephassa, grasping her skirts, and begging her to lean upon their shoulders whenever she felt weary. In this manner they went down the palace steps, and began a journey, which turned out to be a great deal longer than they dreamed of. The last that they saw of King Agenor, he came to the door, with a servant holding a torch beside him, and called after them into the gathering darkness:

"Remember! Never ascend these steps again without the child!"

"Never!" sobbed Queen Telephassa; and the three brothers and Thasus answered, "Never! Never! Never! Never!"

And they kept their word. Year after year, King Agenor sat in the solitude of his beautiful palace, listening in vain for their returning footsteps, hoping to hear the familiar voice of the queen, and the cheerful talk of his sons and their playfellow Thasus, entering the door together, and the sweet, childish accents of little Europa in the midst of them. But so long a time went by, that, at last, if they had really come, the king would not have known that this was the voice of Telephassa, and these the younger voices that used to make such joyful echoes, when the children were playing about the palace. We must now leave King Agenor to sit on his throne, and must go along with Queen Telephassa, and her four youthful companions.

They went on and on, and traveled a long way, and passed over mountains and rivers, and sailed over seas. Here, and there, and everywhere, they made continual inquiry if any person could tell them what had become of Europa. The rustic people, of whom they asked this question, paused a little while from their labors in the field, and looked very much surprised. They thought it strange to behold a woman in the garb of a queen (for Telephassa in her haste had forgotten to take off her crown and her royal robes), roaming about the country, with four lads around her, on such an errand as this seemed to be. But nobody could give them any tidings of Europa; nobody had seen a little girl dressed like a princess, and mounted on a snow-white bull, which galloped as swiftly as the wind.

I cannot tell you how long Queen Telephassa, and Cadmus, Phoenix, and Cilix, her three sons, and Thasus, their playfellow, went wandering along the highways and bypaths, or through the pathless wildernesses of the earth, in this manner. But certain it is, that, before they reached any place of rest, their splendid garments were quite worn out. They all looked very much travel-stained, and would have had the dust of many countries on their shoes, if the streams, through which they waded, had not washed it all away. When they had been gone a year, Telephassa threw away her crown, because it chafed her forehead.

"It has given me many a headache," said the poor queen, "and it cannot cure my heartache."

As fast as their princely robes got torn and tattered, they exchanged them for such mean attire as ordinary people wore. By and by, they come to have a wild and homeless aspect; so that you would much sooner have taken them for a gypsy family than a queen and three princes, and a young nobleman, who had once a palace for a home, and a train of servants to do their bidding. The four boys grew up to be tall young men, with sunburnt faces. Each of them girded on a sword, to defend themselves against the perils of the way. When the husbandmen, at whose farmhouses they sought hospitality, needed their assistance in the harvest field, they gave it willingly; and Queen Telephassa (who had done no work in her palace, save to braid silk threads with golden ones) came behind them to bind the sheaves. If payment was offered, they shook their heads, and only asked for tidings of Europa.

"There are bulls enough in my pasture," the old farmers would reply; "but I never heard of one like this you tell me of. A snow-white bull with a little princess on his back! Ho! ho! I ask your pardon, good folks; but there never such a sight seen hereabouts."

At last, when his upper lip began to have the down on it, Phoenix grew weary of rambling hither and thither to no purpose. So one day, when they happened to be passing through a pleasant and solitary tract of country, he sat himself down on a heap of moss.

"I can go no farther," said Phoenix. "It is a mere foolish waste of life, to spend it as we do, always wandering up and down, and never coming to any home at nightfall. Our sister is lost, and never will be found. She probably perished in the sea; or, to whatever shore the white bull may have carried her, it is now so many years ago, that there would be neither love nor acquaintance between us, should we meet again. My father has forbidden us to return to his palace, so I shall build me a hut of branches, and dwell here."

"Well, son Phoenix," said Telephassa, sorrowfully, "you have grown to be a man, and must do as you judge best. But, for my part, I will still go in quest of my poor child."

"And we three will go along with you!" cried Cadmus and Cilix, and their faithful friend Thasus.

But, before setting out, they all helped Phoenix to build a habitation. When completed, it was a sweet rural bower, roofed overhead with an arch of living boughs. Inside there were two pleasant rooms, one of which had a soft heap of moss for a bed, while the other was furnished with a rustic seat or two, curiously fashioned out of the crooked roots of trees. So comfortable and home-like did it seem, that Telephassa and her three companions could not help sighing, to think that they must still roam about the world, instead of spending the remainder of their lives in some such cheerful abode as they had here built for Phoenix. But, when they bade him farewell, Phoenix shed tears, and probably regretted that he was no longer to keep them company.

However, he had fixed upon an admirable place to dwell in. And by and by there came other people, who chanced to have no homes; and, seeing how pleasant a spot it was, they built themselves huts in the neighborhood of Phoenix's habhabitation. Thus, before many years went by, a city had grown up there, in the center of which was seen a stately palace of marble, wherein dwelt Phoenix, clothed in a purple robe, and wearing a golden crown upon his head. For the inhabitants of the new city, finding that he had royal blood in his veins, had chosen him to be their king. The very first decree of state which King Phoenix issued was, that, if a maiden happened to arrive in the kingdom, mounted on a snow-white bull, and calling herself Europa, his subjects should treat her with the greatest kindness and respect, and immediately bring her to the palace. You may see, by this, that Phoenix's conscience never quite ceased to trouble him, for giving up the quest of his dear sister, and sitting himself down to be comfortable, while his mother and her companions went onward.

But often and often, at the close of a weary day's journey, did Telephassa and Cadmus, Cilix, and Thasus, remember the pleasant spot in which they had left Phoenix. It was a sorrowful prospect for these wanderers, that on the morrow they must again set forth, and that, after many nightfalls, they would perhaps be no nearer the close of their toilsome pilgrimage than now. These thoughts made them all melancholy at times, but appeared to torment Cilix more than the rest of the party. At length, one morning, when they were taking their staffs in hand to set out, he thus addressed them:

"My dear mother, and you, good brother Cadmus, and my friend Thasus, methinks we are like people in a dream. There is no substance in the life which we are leading. It is such a dreary length of time since the white bull carried off my sister Europa, that I have quite forgotten how she looked, and the tones of her voice, and, indeed, almost doubt whether such a little girl ever lived in the world. And whether she once lived or no, I am convinced that she no longer survives, and that therefore it is the merest folly to waste our own lives and happiness in seeking her. Were we to find her, she would now be a woman grown, and would look upon us all as strangers. So, to tell you the truth, I have resolved to take up my abode here; and I entreat you, mother, brother, and friend, to follow my example."

"Not I, for one," said Telephassa; although the poor queen, firmly as she spoke, was so travel-worn that she could hardly put her foot to the ground. "Not I, for one! In the depths of my heart, little Europa is still the rosy child who ran to gather flowers so many years ago. She has not grown to womanhood, nor forgotten me. At noon, at night, journeying onward, sitting down to rest, her childish voice is always in my ears, calling, 'Mother! mother!' Stop here who may, there is no repose for me."

"Nor for me," said Cadmus, "while my dear mother pleases to go onward."

And the faithful Thasus, too, was resolved to bear them company. They remained with Cilix a few days, however, and helped him to build a rustic bower, resembling the one which they had formerly built for Phoenix.

When they were bidding him farewell Cilix burst into tears, and told his mother that it seemed just as melancholy a dream to stay there, in solitude, as to go onward. If she really believed that they would ever find Europa, he was willing to continue the search with them, even now. But Telephassa bade him remain there, and be happy, if his own heart would let him. So the pilgrims took their leave of him, and departed, and were hardly out of sight before some other wandering people came along that way, and saw Cilix's habitation, and were greatly delighted with the appearance of the place. There being abundance of unoccupied ground in the neighborhood, these strangers built huts for themselves, and were soon joined by a multitude of new settlers, who quickly formed a city. In the middle of it was seen a magnificent palace of colored marble, on the balcony of which, every noontide, appeared Cilix, in a long purple robe, and with a jeweled crown upon his head; for the inhabitants, when they found out that he was a king's son, had considered him the fittest of all men to be a king himself.

One of the first acts of King Cilix's government was to send out an expedition, consisting of a grave ambassador, and an escort of bold and hardy young men, with orders to visit the principal kingdoms of the earth, and inquire whether a young maiden had passed through those regions, galloping swiftly on a white bull. It is, therefore, plain to my mind, that Cilix secretly blamed himself for giving up the search for Europa, as long as he was able to put one foot before the other.

As for Telephassa, and Cadmus, and the good Thasus, it grieves me to think of them, still keeping up that weary pilgrimage. The two young men did their best for the poor queen, helping her over the rough places, often carrying her across rivulets in their faithful arms and seeking to shelter her at nightfall, even when they themselves lay on the ground. Sad, sad it was to hear them asking of every passer-by if he had seen Europa, so long after the white bull had carried her away. But, though the gray years thrust themselves between, and made the child's figure dim in their remembrance, neither of these true-hearted three ever dreamed of giving up the search.

One morning, however, poor Thasus found that he had sprained his ankle, and could not possibly go a step farther.

"After a few days, to be sure," said he, mournfully, "I might make shift to hobble along with a stick. But that would only delay you, and perhaps hinder you from finding dear little Europa, after all your pains and trouble. Do you go forward, therefore, my beloved companions, and leave me to follow as I may."

"Thou hast been a true friend, dear Thasus," said Queen Telephassa, kissing his forehead. "Being neither my son, nor the brother of our lost Europa, thou hast shown thyself truer to me and her than Phoenix and Cilix did, whom we have left behind us. Without thy loving help, and that of my son Cadmus, my limbs could not have borne me half so far as this. Now, take thy rest, and be at peace. For—and it is the first time I have owned it to myself—I begin to question whether we shall ever find my beloved daughter in this world."

Saying this, the poor queen shed tears, because it was a grievous trial to the mother's heart to confess that her hopes were growing faint. From that day forward, Cadmus noticed that she never traveled with the same alacrity of spirit that had heretofore supported her. Her weight was heavier upon his arm.

Before setting out, Cadmus helped Thasus build a bower; while Telephassa, being too infirm to give any great assistance, advised them how to fit it up and furnish it, so that it might be as comfortable as a hut of branches could. Thasus, however, did not spend all his days in this green bower. For it happened to him, as to Phoenix and Cilix, that other homeless people visited the spot, and liked it, and built themselves habitations in the neighborhood. So here, in the course of a few years, was another thriving city, with a red freestone palace in the center of it, where Thasus sat upon a throne, doing justice to the people, with a purple robe over his shoulders, a sceptre in his hand, and a crown upon his head. The inhabitants had made him king, not for the sake of any royal blood (for none was in his veins), but because Thasus was an upright, true-hearted, and courageous man, and therefore fit to rule.

But when the affairs of his kingdom were all settled, King Thasus laid aside his purple robe and crown, and sceptre, and bade his worthiest subjects distribute justice to the people in his stead. Then, grasping the pilgrim's staff that had supported him so long, he set forth again, hoping still to discover some hoof-mark of the snow-white bull, some trace of the vanished child. He returned after a lengthened absence, and sat down wearily upon his throne. To his latest hour, nevertheless, King Thasus showed his true-hearted remembrance of Europa, by ordering that a fire should always be kept burning in his palace, and a bath steaming hot, and food ready to be served up, and a bed with snow-white sheets, in case the maiden should arrive, and require immediate refreshment. And, though Europa never came, the good Thasus had the blessings of many a poor traveler, who profited by the food and lodging which were meant for the little playmate of the king's boyhood.

Telephassa and Cadmus were now pursuing their weary way, with no companion but each other. The queen leaned heavily upon her son's arm, and could walk only a few miles a day. But for all her weakness and weariness, she would not be persuaded to give up the search. It was enough to bring tears into the eyes of bearded men to hear the melancholy tone with which she inquired of every stranger whether he could not tell her any news of the lost child.

"Have you seen a little girl—no, no, I mean a young maiden of full growth—passing by this way, mounted on a snow-white bull, which gallops as swiftly as the wind?"

"We have seen no such wondrous sight," the people would reply; and very often, taking Cadmus aside, they whispered to him, "Is this stately and sad-looking woman your mother? Surely she is not in her right mind; and you ought to take her home, and make her comfortable, and do your best to get this dream out of her fancy."

"It is no dream," said Cadmus. "Everything else is a dream, save that."

But, one day, Telephassa seemed feebler than usual, and leaned almost her whole weight on the arm of Cadmus, and walked more slowly than ever before. At last they reached a solitary spot, where she told her son that she must needs lie down, and take a good long rest.

"A good long rest!" she repeated, looking Cadmus tenderly in the face. "A good long rest, thou dearest one!"

"As long as you please, dear mother," answered Cadmus.

Telephassa bade him sit down on the turf beside her, and then she took his hand.

"My son," said she, fixing her dim eyes most lovingly upon him, "this rest that I speak of will be very long indeed! You must not wait till it is finished. Dear Cadmus, you do not comprehend me. You must make a grave here, and lay your mother's weary frame into it. My pilgrimage is over."

Cadmus burst into tears, and, for a long time, refused to believe that his dear mother was now to be taken from him. But Telephassa reasoned with him, and kissed him, and at length made him discern that it was better for her spirit to pass away out of the toil, the weariness, and grief, and disappointment which had burdened her on earth, ever since the child was lost. He therefore repressed his sorrow, and listened to her last words.

"Dearest Cadmus," said she, "thou hast been the truest son that ever mother had, and faithful to the very last. Who else would have borne with my infirmities as thou hast! It is owing to thy care, thou tenderest child, that my grave was not dug long years ago, in some valley, or on some hillside, that lies far, far behind us. It is enough. Thou shalt wander no more on this hopeless search. But, when thou hast laid thy mother in the earth, then go, my son, to Delphi, and inquire of the oracle what thou shalt do next."

"O mother, mother," cried Cadmus, "couldst thou but have seen my sister before this hour!"

"It matters little now," answered Telephassa, and there was a smile upon her face. "I go now to the better world, and, sooner or later, shall find my daughter there."

I will not sadden you, my little hearers, with telling how Telephassa died and was buried, but will only say, that her dying smile grew brighter, instead of vanishing from her dead face; so that Cadmus left convinced that, at her very first step into the better world, she had caught Europa in her arms. He planted some flowers on his mother's grave, and left them to grow there, and make the place beautiful, when he should be far away.

After performing this last sorrowful duty, he set forth alone, and took the road towards the famous oracle of Delphi, as Telephassa had advised him. On his way thither, he still inquired of most people whom he met whether they had seen Europa; for, to say the truth, Cadmus had grown so accustomed to ask the question, that it came to his lips as readily as a remark about the weather. He received various answers. Some told him one thing, and some another. Among the rest, a mariner affirmed, that, many years before, in a distant country, he had heard a rumor about a white bull, which came swimming across the sea with a child on his back, dressed up in flowers that were blighted by the sea water. He did not know what had become of the child or the bull; and Cadmus suspected, indeed, by a queer twinkle in the mariner's eyes, that he was putting a joke upon him, and had never really heard anything about the matter.

Poor Cadmus found it more wearisome to travel alone than to bear all his dear mother's weight, while she had kept him company. His heart, you will understand, was now so heavy that it seemed impossible, sometimes, to carry it any farther. But his limbs were strong and active, and well accustomed to exercise. He walked swiftly along, thinking of King Agenor and Queen Telephassa, and his brothers, and the friendly Thasus, all of whom he had left behind him, at one point of his pilgrimage or another, and never expected to see them any more. Full of these remembrances, he came within sight of a lofty mountain, which the people thereabouts told him was called Parnassus. On the slope of Mount Parnassus was the famous Delphi, whither Cadmus was going.

This Delphi was supposed to be the very midmost spot of the whole world. The place of the oracle was a certain cavity in the mountain side, over which, when Cadmus came thither, he found a rude bower of branches. It reminded him of those which he had helped to build for Phoenix and Cilix, and afterwards for Thasus. In later times, when multitudes of people came from great distances to put questions to the oracle, a spacious temple of marble was erected over the spot. But in the days of Cadmus, as I have told you, there was only this rustic bower, with its abundance of green foliage, and a tuft of shrubbery, that ran wild over the mysterious hole in the hillside.

When Cadmus had thrust a passage through the tangled boughs, and made his way into the bower, he did not at first discern the half-hidden cavity. But soon he felt a cold stream of air rushing out of it, with so much force that it shook the ringlets on his cheek. Pulling away the shrubbery which clustered over the hole, he bent forward, and spoke in a distinct but reverential tone, as if addressing some unseen personage inside of the mountain.

"Sacred oracle of Delphi," said he, "whither shall I go next in quest of my dear sister Europa?"

There was at first a deep silence, and then a rushing sound, or a noise like a long sigh, proceeding out of the interior of the earth. This cavity, you must know, was looked upon as a sort of fountain of truth, which sometimes gushed out in audible words; although, for the most part, these words were such a riddle that they might just as well have staid at the bottom of the hole. But Cadmus was more fortunate than many others who went to Delphi in search of truth. By and by, the rushing noise began to sound like articulate language. It repeated, over and over again, the following sentence, which, after all, was so like the vague whistle of a blast of air, that Cadmus really did not quite know whether it meant anything or not:

"Seek her no more! Seek her no more! Seek her no more!"

"What, then, shall I do?" asked Cadmus.

For, ever since he was a child, you know, it had been the great object of his life to find his sister. From the very hour that he left following the butterfly in the meadow, near his father's palace, he had done his best to follow Europa, over land and sea. And now, if he must give up the search, he seemed to have no more business in the world.

But again the sighing gust of air grew into something like a hoarse voice.

"Follow the cow!" it said. "Follow the cow! Follow the cow!"

And when these words had been repeated until Cadmus was tired of hearing them (especially as he could not imagine what cow it was, or why he was to follow her), the gusty hole gave vent to another sentence.

"Where the stray cow lies down, there is your home."

These words were pronounced but a single time, and died away into a whisper before Cadmus was fully satisfied that he had caught the meaning. He put other questions, but received no answer; only the gust of wind sighed continually out of the cavity, and blew the withered leaves rustling along the ground before it.

"Did there really come any words out of the hole?" thought Cadmus; "or have I been dreaming all this while?"

He turned away from the oracle, and thought himself no wiser than when he came thither. Caring little what might happen to him, he took the first path that offered itself, and went along at a sluggish pace; for, having no object in view, nor any reason to go one way more than another, it would certainly have been foolish to make haste. Whenever he met anybody, the old question was at his tongue's end.

"Have you seen a beautiful maiden, dressed like a king's daughter, and mounted on a snow-white bull, that gallops as swiftly as the wind?"

But, remembering what the oracle had said, he only half uttered the words, and then mumbled the rest indistinctly; and from his confusion, people must have imagined that this handsome young man had lost his wits.

I know not how far Cadmus had gone, nor could he himself have told you, when at no great distance before him, he beheld a brindled cow. She was lying down by the wayside, and quietly chewing her cud; nor did she take any notice of the young man until he had approached pretty nigh. Then, getting leisurely upon her feet, and giving her head a gentle toss, she began to move along at a moderate pace, often pausing just long enough to crop a mouthful of grass. Cadmus loitered behind, whistling idly to himself, and scarcely noticing the cow; until the thought occurred to him, whether this could possibly be the animal which, according to the oracle's response, was to serve him for a guide. But he smiled at himself for fancying such a thing. He could not seriously think that this was the cow, because she went along so quietly, behaving just like any other cow. Evidently she neither knew nor cared so much as a wisp of hay about Cadmus, and was only thinking how to get her living along the wayside, where the herbage was green and fresh. Perhaps she was going home to be milked.

"Cow, cow, cow!" cried Cadmus. "Hey, Brindle, hey! Stop, my good cow!"

He wanted to come up with the cow, so as to examine her, and see if she would appear to know him, or whether there were any peculiarities to distinguish her from a thousand other cows, whose only business is to fill the milk-pail, and sometimes kick it over. But still the brindled cow trudged on, whisking her tail to keep the flies away, and taking as little notice of Cadmus as she well could. If he walked slowly, so did the cow, and seized the opportunity to graze. If he quickened his pace, the cow went just so much the faster; and once, when Cadmus tried to catch her by running, she threw out her heels, stuck her tail straight on end, and set off at a gallop, looking as queerly as cows generally do, while putting themselves to their speed.

When Cadmus saw that it was impossible to come up with her, he walked on moderately, as before. The cow, too, went leisurely on, without looking behind. Wherever the grass was greenest, there she nibbled a mouthful or two. Where a brook glistened brightly across the path, there the cow drank, and breathed a comfortable sigh, and drank again, and trudged onward at the pace that best suited herself and Cadmus.

"I do believe," thought Cadmus, "that this may be the cow that was foretold me. If it be the one, I suppose she will lie down somewhere hereabouts."

Whether it were the oracular cow or some other one, it did not seem reasonable that she should travel a great way farther. So, whenever they reached a particularly pleasant spot on a breezy hillside, or in a sheltered vale, or flowery meadow, on the shore of a calm lake, or along the bank of a clear stream, Cadmus looked eagerly around to see if the situation would suit him for a home. But still, whether he liked the place or no, the brindled cow never offered to lie down. On she went at the quiet pace of a cow going homeward to the barn yard; and, every moment, Cadmus expected to see a milkmaid approaching with a pail, or a herdsman running to head the stray animal, and turn her back towards the pasture. But no milkmaid came; no herdsman drove her back; and Cadmus followed the stray Brindle till he was almost ready to drop down with fatigue.

"O brindled cow," cried he, in a tone of despair, "do you never mean to stop?"

He had now grown too intent on following her to think of lagging behind, however long the way, and whatever might be his fatigue. Indeed, it seemed as if there were something about the animal that bewitched people. Several persons who happened to see the brindled cow, and Cadmus following behind, began to trudge after her, precisely as he did. Cadmus was glad of somebody to converse with, and therefore talked very freely to these good people. He told them all his adventures, and how he had left King Agenor in his palace, and Phoenix at one place, and Cilix at another, and Thasus at a third, and his dear mother, Queen Telephassa, under a flowery sod; so that now he was quite alone, both friendless and homeless. He mentioned, likewise, that the oracle had bidden him be guided by a cow, and inquired of the strangers whether they supposed that this brindled animal could be the one.

"Why, 'tis a very wonderful affair," answered one of his new companions. "I am pretty well acquainted with the ways of cattle, and I never knew a cow, of her own accord, to go so far without stopping. If my legs will let me, I'll never leave following the beast till she lies down."

"Nor I!" said a second.

"Nor I!" cried a third. "If she goes a hundred miles farther, I am determined to see the end of it."

The secret of it was, you must know, that the cow was an enchanted cow, and that, without their being conscious of it, she threw some of her enchantment over everybody that took so much as half a dozen steps behind her. They could not possibly help following her, though all the time they fancied themselves doing it of their own accord. The cow was by no means very nice in choosing her path; so that sometimes they had to scramble over rocks, or wade through mud and mire, and all in a terribly bedraggled condition, and tired to death, and very hungry, into the bargain. What a weary business it was!

But still they kept trudging stoutly forward, and talking as they went. The strangers grew very fond of Cadmus, and resolved never to leave him, but to help him build a city wherever the cow might lie down. In the center of it there should be a noble palace, in which Cadmus might dwell, and be their king, with a throne, a crown, a sceptre, a purple robe, and everything else that a king ought to have; for in him there was the royal blood, and the royal heart, and the head that knew how to rule.

While they were talking of these schemes, and beguiling the tediousness of the way with laying out the plan of the new city, one of the company happened to look at the cow.

"Joy! joy!" cried he, clapping his hands. "Brindle is going to lie down."

They all looked; and, sure enough, the cow had stopped, and was staring leisurely about her, as other cows do when on the point of lying down. And slowly, slowly did she recline herself on the soft grass, first bending her forelegs, and then crouching her hind ones. When Cadmus and his companions came up with her, there was the brindled cow taking her ease, chewing her cud, and looking them quietly in the face; as if this was just the spot she had been seeking for, and as if it were all a matter of course.

"This, then," said Cadmus, gazing around him, "this is to be my home."

It was a fertile and lovely plain, with great trees flinging their sun-speckled shadows over it, and hills fencing it in from the rough weather At no great distance, they beheld a river gleaming in the sunshine. A home feeling stole into the heart of poor Cadmus. He was very glad to know that here he might awake in the morning without the necessity of putting on his dusty sandals to travel farther and farther. The days and the years would pass over him, and find him still in this pleasant spot. If he could have had his brothers with him, and his friend Thasus, and could have seen his dear mother under a roof of his own, he might here have been happy after all their disappointments. Some day or other, too, his sister Europa might have come quietly to the door of his home, and smiled round upon the familiar faces. But, indeed, since there was no hope of regaining the friends of his boyhood, or ever seeing his dear sister again, Cadmus resolved to make himself happy with these new companions, who had grown so fond of him while following the cow.

"Yes, my friends," said he to them, "this is to be our home. Here we will build our habitations. The brindled cow, which has led us hither, will supply us with milk. We will cultivate the neighboring soil and lead an innocent and happy life."

His companions joyfully assented to this plan; and, in the first place, being very hungry and thirsty, they looked about them for the means of providing a comfortable meal. Not far off they saw a tuft of trees, which appeared as if there might be a spring of water beneath them. They went thither to fetch some, leaving Cadmus stretched on the ground along with the brindled cow; for, now that he had found a place of rest, it seemed as if all the weariness of his pilgrimage, ever since he left King Agenor's palace, had fallen upon him at once. But his new friends had not long been gone, when he was suddenly startled by cries, shouts, and screams, and the noise of a terrible struggle, and in the midst of it all, a most awful hissing, which went right through his ears like a rough saw.

Running towards the tuft of trees, he beheld the head and fiery eyes of an immense serpent or dragon, with the widest jaws that ever a dragon had, and a vast many rows of horribly sharp teeth. Before Cadmus could reach the spot, this pitiless reptile had killed his poor companions, and was busily devouring them, making but a mouthful of each man.

It appears that the fountain of water was enchanted, and that the dragon had been set to guard it, so that no mortal might ever quench his thirst there. As the neighboring inhabitants carefully avoided the spot, it was now a long time (not less than a hundred years or thereabouts) since the monster had broken his fast; and, as was natural enough, his appetite had grown to be enormous, and was not half satisfied by the poor people whom he had just eaten up. When he caught sight of Cadmus, therefore, he set up another abominable hiss, and flung back his immense jaws, until his mouth looked like a great red cavern, at the farther end of which were seen the legs of his last victim, whom he had hardly had time to swallow.

But Cadmus was so enraged at the destruction of his friends that he cared neither for the size of the dragon's jaws nor for his hundreds of sharp teeth. Drawing his sword, he rushed at the monster, and flung himself right into his cavernous mouth. This bold method of attacking him took the dragon by surprise; for, in fact, Cadmus had leaped so far down into his throat, that the rows of terrible teeth could not close upon him, nor do him the least harm in the world. Thus, though the struggle was a tremendous one, and though the dragon shattered the tuft of trees into small splinters by the lashing of his tail, yet, as Cadmus was all the while slashing and stabbing at his very vitals, it was not long before the scaly wretch bethought himself of slipping away. He had not gone his length, however, when the brave Cadmus gave him a sword thrust that finished the battle; and creeping out of the gateway of the creature's jaws, there he beheld him still wriggling his vast bulk, although there was no longer life enough in him to harm a little child.

But do not you suppose that it made Cadmus sorrowful to think of the melancholy fate which had befallen those poor, friendly people, who had followed the cow along with him? It seemed as if he were doomed to lose everybody whom he loved, or to see them perish in one way or another. And here he was, after all his toils and troubles, in a solitary place, with not a single human being to help him build a hut.

"What shall I do?" cried he aloud. "It were better for me to have been devoured by the dragon, as my poor companions were."

"Cadmus," said a voice but whether it came from above or below him, or whether it spoke within his own breast, the young man could not tell—"Cadmus, pluck out the dragon's teeth, and plant them in the earth."

This was a strange thing to do; nor was it very easy, I should imagine, to dig out all those deep-rooted fangs from the dead dragon's jaws. But Cadmus toiled and tugged, and after pounding the monstrous head almost to pieces with a great stone, he at last collected as many teeth as might have filled a bushel or two. The next thing was to plant them. This, likewise, was a tedious piece of work, especially as Cadmus was already exhausted with killing the dragon and knocking his head to pieces, and had nothing to dig the earth with, that I know of, unless it were his sword blade. Finally, however, a sufficiently large tract of ground was turned up, and sown with this new kind of seed; although half of the dragon's teeth still remained to be planted some other day.

Cadmus, quite out of breath, stood leaning upon his sword, and wondering what was to happen next. He had waited but a few moments, when he began to see a sight, which was as great a marvel as the most marvelous thing I ever told you about.

The sun was shining slantwise over the field, and showed all the moist, dark soil just like any other newly-planted piece of ground. All at once, Cadmus fancied he saw something glisten very brightly, first at one spot, then at another, and then at a hundred and a thousand spots together. Soon he perceived them to be the steel heads of spears, sprouting up everywhere like so many stalks of grain, and continually growing taller and taller. Next appeared a vast number of bright sword blades, thrusting themselves up in the same way. A moment afterwards, the whole surface of the ground was broken by a multitude of polished brass helmets, coming up like a crop of enormous beans. So rapidly did they grow, that Cadmus now discerned the fierce countenance of a man beneath every one. In short, before he had time to think what a wonderful affair it was, he beheld an abundant harvest of what looked like human beings, armed with helmets and breastplates, shields, swords, and spears; and before they were well out of the earth, they brandished their weapons, and clashed them one against another, seeming to think, little while as they had yet lived, that they had wasted too much of life without a battle. Every tooth of the dragon had produced one of these sons of deadly mischief.

Up sprouted also a great many trumpeters; and with the first breath that they drew, they put their brazen trumpets to their lips, and sounded a tremendous and ear-shattering blast, so that the whole space, just now so quiet and solitary, reverberated with the clash and clang of arms, the bray of warlike music, and the shouts of angry men. So enraged did they all look, that Cadmus fully expected them to put the whole world to the sword. How fortunate would it be for a great conqueror, if he could get a bushel of the dragon's teeth to sow!

"Cadmus," said the same voice which he had before heard, "throw a stone into the midst of the armed men."

So Cadmus seized a large stone, and flinging it into the middle of the earth army, saw it strike the breastplate of a gigantic and fierce-looking warrior. Immediately on feeling the blow, he seemed to take it for granted that somebody had struck him; and, uplifting his weapon, he smote his next neighbor a blow that cleft his helmet asunder, and stretched him on the ground. In an instant, those nearest the fallen warrior began to strike at one another with their swords, and stab with their spears. The confusion spread wider and wider. Each man smote down his brother, and was himself smitten down before he had time to exult in his victory. The trumpeters, all the while, blew their blasts shriller and shriller; each soldier shouted a battle cry, and often fell with it on his lips. It was the strangest spectacle of causeless wrath, and of mischief for no good end, that had ever been witnessed; but, after all, it was neither more foolish nor more wicked than a thousand battles that have since been fought, in which men have slain their brothers with just as little reason as these children of the dragon's teeth. It ought to be considered, too, that the dragon people were made for nothing else; whereas other mortals were born to love and help one another.

Well, this memorable battle continued to rage until the ground was strewn with helmeted heads that had been cut off. Of all the thousands that began the fight, there were only five left standing. These now rushed from different parts of the field, and, meeting in the middle of it, clashed their swords, and struck at each other's hearts as fiercely as ever.

"Cadmus," said the voice again, "bid those five warriors sheathe their swords. They will help you to build the city."

Without hesitating an instant, Cadmus stepped forward, with the aspect of a king and a leader, and extending his drawn sword amongst them, spoke to the warriors in a stern and commanding voice.

"Sheathe your weapons!" said he.

And forthwith, feeling themselves bound to obey him, the five remaining sons of the dragon's teeth made him a military salute with their swords, returned them to the scabbards, and stood before Cadmus in a rank, eyeing him as soldiers eye their captain, while awaiting the word of command.

These five men had probably sprung from the biggest of the dragon's teeth, and were the boldest and strongest of the whole army. They were almost giants indeed, and had good need to be so, else they never could have lived through so terrible a fight. They still had a very furious look, and, if Cadmus happened to glance aside, would glare at one another, with fire flashing out of their eyes. It was strange, too, to observe how the earth, out of which they had so lately grown, was incrusted, here and there, on their bright breastplates, and even, begrimed their faces; just as you may have seen it clinging to beets and carrots, when pulled out of their native soil. Cadmus hardly knew whether to consider them as men, or some odd kind of vegetable; although, on the whole, he concluded that there was human nature in them, because they were so fond of trumpets and weapons, and so ready to shed blood.

They looked him earnestly in the face, waiting for his next order, and evidently desiring no other employment than to follow him from one battlefield to another, all over the wide world. But Cadmus was wiser than these earth-born creatures, with the dragon's fierceness in them, and knew better how to use their strength and hardihood.

"Come!" said he. "You are sturdy fellows. Make yourselves useful! Quarry some stones with those great swords of yours, and help me to build a city."

The five soldiers grumbled a little, and muttered that it was their business to overthrow cities, not to build them up. But Cadmus looked at them with a stern eye, and spoke to them in a tone of authority, so that they knew him for their master, and never again thought of disobeying his commands. They set to work in good earnest, and toiled so diligently, that, in a very short time, a city began to make its appearance. At first, to be sure, the workmen showed a quarrelsome disposition. Like savage beasts, they would doubtless have done one another a mischief, if Cadmus had not kept watch over them, and quelled the fierce old serpent that lurked in their hearts, when he saw it gleaming out of their wild eyes. But, in course of time, they got accustomed to honest labor, and had sense enough to feel that there was more true enjoyment in living at peace, and doing good to one's neighbor, than in striking at him with a two-edged sword. It may not be too much to hope that the rest of mankind will by and by grow as wise and peaceable as these five earth-begrimed warriors, who sprang from the dragon's teeth.

And now the city was built, and there was a home in it for each of the workmen. But the palace of Cadmus was not yet erected, because they had left it till the last, meaning to introduce all the new improvements of architecture, and make it very commodious, as well as stately and beautiful. After finishing the rest of their labors, they all went to bed betimes, in order to rise in the gray of the morning, and get at least the foundation of the edifice laid before nightfall. But, when Cadmus arose, and took his way towards the site where the palace was to be built, followed by his five sturdy workmen marching all in a row, what do you think he saw?

What should it be but the most magnificent palace that had ever been seen in the world. It was built of marble and other beautiful kinds of stone, and rose high into the air, with a splendid dome and a portico along the front, and carved pillars, and everything else that befitted the habitation of a mighty king. It had grown up out of the earth in almost as short a time as it had taken the armed host to spring from the dragon's teeth; and what made the matter more strange, no seed of this stately edifice ever had been planted.

When the five workmen beheld the dome, with the morning sunshine making it look golden and glorious, they gave a great shout.

"Long live King Cadmus," they cried, "in his beautiful palace."

And the new king, with his five faithful followers at his heels, shouldering their pickaxes and marching in a rank (for they still had a soldier-like sort of behavior, as their nature was), ascended the palace steps. Halting at the entrance, they gazed through a long vista of lofty pillars, that were ranged from end to end of a great hall. At the farther extremity of this hall, approaching slowly towards him, Cadmus beheld a female figure, wonderfully beautiful, and adorned with a royal robe, and a crown of diamonds over her golden ringlets, and the richest necklace that ever a queen wore. His heart thrilled with delight. He fancied it his long-lost sister Europa, now grown to womanhood, coming to make him happy, and to repay him with her sweet sisterly affection, for all those weary wonderings in quest of her since he left King Agenor's palace—for the tears that he had shed, on parting with Phoenix, and Cilix, and Thasus—for the heart-breakings that had made the whole world seem dismal to him over his dear mother's grave.

But, as Cadmus advanced to meet the beautiful stranger, he saw that her features were unknown to him, although, in the little time that it required to tread along the hall, he had already felt a sympathy betwixt himself and her.

"No, Cadmus," said the same voice that had spoken to him in the field of the armed men, "this is not that dear sister Europa whom you have sought so faithfully all over the wide world. This is Harmonia, a daughter of the sky, who is given you instead of sister, and brothers, and friend, and mother. You will find all those dear ones in her alone."

So King Cadmus dwelt in the palace, with his new friend Harmonia, and found a great deal of comfort in his magnificent abode, but would doubtless have found as much, if not more, in the humblest cottage by the wayside. Before many years went by, there was a group of rosy little children (but how they came thither has always been a mystery to me) sporting in the great hall, and on the marble steps of the palace, and running joyfully to meet King Cadmus when affairs of state left him at leisure to play with them. They called him father, and Queen Harmonia mother. The five old soldiers of the dragon's teeth grew very fond of these small urchins, and were never weary of showing them how to shoulder sticks, flourish wooden swords, and march in military order, blowing a penny trumpet, or beating an abominable rub-a-dub upon a little drum.

But King Cadmus, lest there should be too much of the dragon's tooth in his children's disposition, used to find time from his kingly duties to teach them their A B C—which he invented for their benefit, and for which many little people, I am afraid, are not half so grateful to him as they ought to be.

CIRCE'S PALACE.

Some of you have heard, no doubt, of the wise King Ulysses, and how he went to the siege of Troy, and how, after that famous city was taken and burned, he spent ten long years in trying to get back again to his own little kingdom of Ithaca. At one time in the course of this weary voyage, he arrived at an island that looked very green and pleasant, but the name of which was unknown to him. For, only a little while before he came thither, he had met with a terrible hurricane, or rather a great many hurricanes at once, which drove his fleet of vessels into a strange part of the sea, where neither himself nor any of his mariners had ever sailed. This misfortune was entirely owing to the foolish curiosity of his shipmates, who, while Ulysses lay asleep, had untied some very bulky leathern bags, in which they supposed a valuable treasure to be concealed. But in each of these stout bags, King Aeolus, the ruler of the winds, had tied up a tempest, and had given it to Ulysses to keep in order that he might be sure of a favorable passage homeward to Ithaca; and when the strings were loosened, forth rushed the whistling blasts, like air out of a blown bladder, whitening the sea with foam, and scattering the vessels nobody could tell whither.

Immediately after escaping from this peril, a still greater one had befallen him. Scudding before the hurricane, he reached a place, which, as he afterwards found, was called Laestrygonia, where some monstrous giants had eaten up many of his companions, and had sunk every one of his vessels, except that in which he himself sailed, by flinging great masses of rock at them, from the cliffs along the shore. After going through such troubles as these, you cannot wonder that King Ulysses was glad to moor his tempest-beaten bark in a quiet cove of the green island, which I began with telling you about. But he had encountered so many dangers from giants, and one-eyed Cyclops, and monsters of the sea and land, that he could not help dreading some mischief, even in this pleasant and seemingly solitary spot. For two days, therefore, the poor weather-worn voyagers kept quiet, and either staid on board of their vessel, or merely crept along under the cliffs that bordered the shore; and to keep themselves alive, they dug shellfish out of the sand, and sought for any little rill of fresh water that might be running towards the sea.

Before the two days were spent, they grew very weary of this kind of life; for the followers of King Ulysses, as you will find it important to remember, were terrible gormandizers, and pretty sure to grumble if they missed their regulars meals, and their irregular ones besides. Their stock of provisions was quite exhausted, and even the shellfish began to get scarce, so that they had now to choose between starving to death or venturing into the interior of the island, where perhaps some huge three-headed dragon, or other horrible monster, had his den. Such misshapen creatures were very numerous in those days; and nobody ever expected to make a voyage, or take a journey, without running more or less risk of being devoured by them.

But King Ulysses was a bold man as well as a prudent one; and on the third morning he determined to discover what sort of a place the island was, and whether it were possible to obtain a supply of food for the hungry mouths of his companions. So, taking a spear in his hand, he clambered to the summit of a cliff, and gazed round about him. At a distance, towards the center of the island, he beheld the stately towers of what seemed to be a palace, built of snow-white marble, and rising in the midst of a grove of lofty trees. The thick branches of these trees stretched across the front of the edifice, and more than half concealed it, although, from the portion which he saw, Ulysses judged it to be spacious and exceedingly beautiful, and probably the residence of some great nobleman or prince. A blue smoke went curling up from the chimney, and was almost the pleasantest part of the spectacle to Ulysses. For, from the abundance of this smoke, it was reasonable to conclude that there was a good fire in the kitchen, and that, at dinner-time, a plentiful banquet would be served up to the inhabitants of the palace, and to whatever guests might happen to drop in.

With so agreeable a prospect before him, Ulysses fancied that he could not do better than go straight to the palace gate, and tell the master of it that there was a crew of poor shipwrecked mariners, not far off, who had eaten nothing for a day or two, save a few clams and oysters, and would therefore be thankful for a little food. And the prince or nobleman must be a very stingy curmudgeon, to be sure, if, at least, when his own dinner was over, he would not bid them welcome to the broken victuals from the table.

Pleasing himself with this idea, King Ulysses had made a few steps in the direction of the palace, when there was a great twittering and chirping from the branch of a neighboring tree. A moment afterwards, a bird came flying towards him, and hovered in the air, so as almost to brush his face with its wings. It was a very pretty little bird, with purple wings and body, and yellow legs, and a circle of golden feathers round its neck, and on its head a golden tuft, which looked like a king's crown in miniature. Ulysses tried to catch the bird. But it fluttered nimbly out of his reach, still chirping in a piteous tone, as if it could have told a lamentable story, had it only been gifted with human language. And when he attempted to drive it away, the bird flew no farther than the bough of the next tree, and again came fluttering about his head, with its doleful chirp, as soon as he showed a purpose of going forward.

"Have you anything to tell me, little bird?" asked Ulysses.

And he was ready to listen attentively to whatever the bird might communicate; for, at the siege of Troy, and elsewhere, he had known such odd things to happen, that he would not have considered it much out of the common run had this little feathered creature talked as plainly as himself.

"Peep!" said the bird, "peep, peep, pe—weep!" And nothing else would it say, but only, "Peep, peep, pe—weep!" in a melancholy cadence, and over and over and over again. As often as Ulysses moved forward, however, the bird showed the greatest alarm, and did its best to drive him back, with the anxious flutter of its purple wings. Its unaccountable behavior made him conclude, at last, that the bird knew of some danger that awaited him, and which must needs be very terrible, beyond all question, since it moved even a little fowl to feel compassion for a human being. So he resolved, for the present, to return to the vessel, and tell his companions what he had seen.

This appeared to satisfy the bird. As soon as Ulysses turned back, it ran up the trunk of a tree, and began to pick insects out of the bark with its long, sharp bill; for it was a kind of woodpecker, you must know, and had to get its living in the same manner as other birds of that species. But every little while, as it pecked at the bark of the tree, the purple bird bethought itself of some secret sorrow, and repeated its plaintive note of "Peep, peep, pe—weep!"

On his way to the shore, Ulysses had the good luck to kill a large stag by thrusting his spear into his back. Taking it on his shoulders (for he was a remarkably strong man), he lugged it along with him, and flung it down before his hungry companions. I have already hinted to you what gormandizers some of the comrades of King Ulysses were. From what is related of them, I reckon that their favorite diet was pork, and that they had lived upon it until a good part of their physical substance was swine's flesh, and their tempers and dispositions were very much akin to the hog. A dish of venison, however, was no unacceptable meal to them, especially after feeding so long on oysters and clams. So, beholding the dead stag, they felt of its ribs, in a knowing way, and lost no time in kindling a fire of driftwood, to cook it. The rest of the day was spent in feasting; and if these enormous eaters got up from table at sunset, it was only because they could not scrape another morsel off the poor animal's bones.

The next morning, their appetites were as sharp as ever. They looked at Ulysses, as if they expected him to clamber up the cliff again, and come back with another fat deer upon his shoulders. Instead of setting out, however, he summoned the whole crew together, and told them it was in vain to hope that he could kill a stag every day for their dinner, and therefore it was advisable to think of some other mode of satisfying their hunger.

"Now," said he, "when I was on the cliff, yesterday, I discovered that this island is inhabited. At a considerable distance from the shore stood a marble palace, which appeared to be very spacious, and had a great deal of smoke curling out of one of its chimneys."

"Aha!" muttered some of his companions, smacking their lips. "That smoke must have come from the kitchen fire. There was a good dinner on the spit; and no doubt there will be as good a one to-day."

"But," continued the wise Ulysses, "you must remember, my good friends, our misadventure in the cavern of one-eyed Polyphemus, the Cyclops! Instead of his ordinary milk diet, did he not eat up two of our comrades for his supper, and a couple more for breakfast, and two at his supper again? Methinks I see him yet, the hideous monster, scanning us with that great red eye, in the middle of his forehead, to single out the fattest. And then, again, only a few days ago, did we not fall into the hands of the king of the Laestrygons, and those other horrible giants, his subjects, who devoured a great many more of us than are now left? To tell you the truth, if we go to yonder palace, there can be no question that we shall make our appearance at the dinner table; but whether seated as guests, or served up as food, is a point to be seriously considered."

"Either way," murmured some of the hungriest of the crew; "it will be better than starvation; particularly if one could be sure of being well fattened beforehand, and daintily cooked afterwards."

"That is a matter of taste," said King Ulysses, "and, for my own part, neither the most careful fattening nor the daintiest of cookery would reconcile me to being dished at last. My proposal is, therefore, that we divide ourselves into two equal parties, and ascertain, by drawing lots, which of the two shall go to the palace, and beg for food and assistance. If these can be obtained, all is well. If not, and if the inhabitants prove as inhospitable as Polyphemus, or the Laestrygons, then there will but half of us perish, and the remainder may set sail and escape."

As nobody objected to this scheme, Ulysses proceeded to count the whole band, and found that there were forty-six men, including himself. He then numbered off twenty-two of them, and put Eurylochus (who was one of his chief officers, and second only to himself in sagacity) at their head. Ulysses took command of the remaining twenty-two men, in person. Then, taking off his helmet, he put two shells into it, on one of which was written, "Go," and on the other "Stay." Another person now held the helmet, while Ulysses and Eurylochus drew out each a shell; and the word "Go" was found written on that which Eurylochus had drawn. In this manner, it was decided that Ulysses and his twenty-two men were to remain at the seaside until the other party should have found out what sort of treatment they might expect at the mysterious palace. As there was no help for it, Eurylochus immediately set forth at the head of his twenty-two followers, who went off in a very melancholy state of mind, leaving their friends in hardly better spirits than themselves.

No sooner had they clambered up the cliff, than they discerned the tall marble towers of the palace, ascending, as white as snow, out of the lovely green shadow of the trees which surrounded it. A gush of smoke came from a chimney in the rear of the edifice. This vapor rose high in the air, and, meeting with a breeze, was wafted seaward, and made to pass over the heads of the hungry mariners. When people's appetites are keen, they have a very quick scent for anything savory in the wind.

"That smoke comes from the kitchen!" cried one of them, turning up his nose as high as he could, and snuffing eagerly. "And, as sure as I'm a half-starved vagabond, I smell roast meat in it."

"Pig, roast pig!" said another. "Ah, the dainty little porker. My mouth waters for him."

"Let us make haste," cried the others, "or we shall be too late for the good cheer!"

But scarcely had they made half a dozen steps from the edge of the cliff, when a bird came fluttering to meet them. It was the same pretty little bird, with the purple wings and body, the yellow legs, the golden collar round its neck, and the crown-like tuft upon its head, whose behavior had so much surprised Ulysses. It hovered about Eurylochus, and almost brushed his face with its wings.

"Peep, peep, pe—weep!" chirped the bird.

So plaintively intelligent was the sound, that it seemed as if the little creature were going to break its heart with some mighty secret that it had to tell, and only this one poor note to tell it with.

"My pretty bird," said Eurylochus—for he was a wary person, and let no token of harm escape his notice—"my pretty bird, who sent you hither? And what is the message which you bring?"

"Peep, peep, pe—weep!" replied the bird, very sorrowfully.

Then it flew towards the edge of the cliff, and looked around at them, as if exceedingly anxious that they should return whence they came. Eurylochus and a few of the others were inclined to turn back. They could not help suspecting that the purple bird must be aware of something mischievous that would befall them at the palace, and the knowledge of which affected its airy spirit with a human sympathy and sorrow. But the rest of the voyagers, snuffing up the smoke from the palace kitchen, ridiculed the idea of returning to the vessel. One of them (more brutal than his fellows, and the most notorious gormandizer in the crew) said such a cruel and wicked thing, that I wonder the mere thought did not turn him into a wild beast, in shape, as he already was in his nature.

"This troublesome and impertinent little fowl," said he, "would make a delicate titbit to begin dinner with. Just one plump morsel, melting away between the teeth. If he comes within my reach, I'll catch him, and give him to the palace cook to be roasted on a skewer."

The words were hardly out of his mouth, before the purple bird flew away, crying, "Peep, peep, pe—weep," more dolorously than ever.

"That bird," remarked Eurylochus, "knows more than we do about what awaits us at the palace."

"Come on, then," cried his comrades, "and we'll soon know as much as he does."

The party, accordingly, went onward through the green and pleasant wood. Every little while they caught new glimpses of the marble palace, which looked more and more beautiful the nearer they approached it. They soon entered a broad pathway, which seemed to be very neatly kept, and which went winding along, with streaks of sunshine falling across it and specks of light quivering among the deepest shadows that fell from the lofty trees. It was bordered, too, with a great many sweet-smelling flowers, such as the mariners had never seen before. So rich and beautiful they were, that, if the shrubs grew wild here, and were native in the soil, then this island was surely the flower garden of the whole earth; or, if transplanted from some other clime, it must have been from the Happy Islands that lay towards the golden sunset.

"There has been a great deal of pains foolishly wasted on these flowers," observed one of the company; and I tell you what he said, that you may keep in mind what gormandizers they were. "For my part, if I were the owner of the palace, I would bid my gardener cultivate nothing but savory pot herbs to make a stuffing for roast meat, or to flavor a stew with."

"Well said!" cried the others. "But I'll warrant you there's a kitchen garden in the rear of the palace."

At one place they came to a crystal spring, and paused to drink at it for want of liquor which they liked better. Looking into its bosom, they beheld their own faces dimly reflected, but so extravagantly distorted by the gush and motion of the water, that each one of them appeared to be laughing at himself and all his companions. So ridiculous were these images of themselves, indeed, that they did really laugh aloud, and could hardly be grave again as soon as they wished. And after they had drank, they grew still merrier than before.

"It has a twang of the wine cask in it," said one, smacking his lips.

"Make haste!" cried his fellows: "we'll find the wine cask itself at the palace, and that will be better than a hundred crystal fountains."

Then they quickened their pace, and capered for joy at the thought of the savory banquet at which they hoped to be guests. But Eurylochus told them that he felt as if he were walking in a dream.

"If I am really awake," continued he, "then, in my opinion, we are on the point of meeting with some stranger adventure than any that befell us in the cave of Polyphemus, or among the gigantic man-eating Laestrygons, or in the windy palace of King Aeolus, which stands on a brazen-walled island. This kind of dreamy feeling always comes over me before any wonderful occurrence. If you take my advice, you will turn back."

"No, no," answered his comrades, snuffing the air, in which the scent from the palace kitchen was now very perceptible. "We would not turn back, though we were certain that the king of the Laestrygons, as big as a mountain, would sit at the head of the table, and huge Polyphemus, the one-eyed Cyclops, at its foot."

At length they came within full sight of the palace, which proved to be very large and lofty, with a great number of airy pinnacles upon its roof. Though it was midday, and the sun shone brightly over the marble front, yet its snowy whiteness, and its fantastic style of architecture, made it look unreal, like the frost work on a window pane, or like the shapes of castles which one sees among the clouds by moonlight. But, just then, a puff of wind brought down the smoke of the kitchen chimney among them, and caused each man to smell the odor of the dish that he liked best; and, after scenting it, they thought everything else moonshine, and nothing real save this palace, and save the banquet that was evidently ready to be served up in it.

So they hastened their steps towards the portal, but had not got half way across the wide lawn, when a pack of lions, tigers, and wolves came bounding to meet them. The terrified mariners started back, expecting no better fate than to be torn to pieces and devoured. To their surprise and joy, however, these wild beasts merely capered around them, wagging their tails, offering their heads to be stroked and patted, and behaving just like so many well-bred house dogs, when they wish to express their delight at meeting their master, or their master's friends. The biggest lion licked the feet of Eurylochus; and every other lion, and every wolf and tiger, singled out one of his two and twenty followers, whom the beast fondled as if he loved him better than a beef bone.

But, for all that, Eurylochus imagined that he saw something fierce and savage in their eyes; nor would he have been surprised, at any moment, to feel the big lion's terrible claws, or to see each of the tigers make a deadly spring, or each wolf leap at the throat of the man whom he had fondled. Their mildness seemed unreal, and a mere freak; but their savage nature was as true as their teeth and claws.

Nevertheless, the men went safely across the lawn with the wild beasts frisking about them, and doing no manner of harm; although, as they mounted the steps of the palace, you might possibly have heard a low growl, particularly from the wolves; as if they thought it a pity, after all, to let the strangers pass without so much as tasting what they were made of.

Eurylochus and his followers now passed under a lofty portal, and looked through the open doorway into the interior of the palace. The first thing that they saw was a spacious hall, and a fountain in the middle of it, gushing up towards the ceiling out of a marble basin, and falling back into it with a continual plash. The water of this fountain, as it spouted upward, was constantly taking new shapes, not very distinctly, but plainly enough for a nimble fancy to recognize what they were. Now it was the shape of a man in a long robe, the fleecy whiteness of which was made out of the fountain's spray; now it was a lion, or a tiger, or a wolf, or an ass, or, as often as anything else, a hog, wallowing in the marble basin as if it were his sty. It was either magic or some very curious machinery that caused the gushing waterspout to assume all these forms. But, before the strangers had time to look closely at this wonderful sight, their attention was drawn off by a very sweet and agreeable sound. A woman's voice was singing melodiously in another room of the palace, and with her voice was mingled the noise of a loom, at which she was probably seated, weaving a rich texture of cloth, and intertwining the high and low sweetness of her voice into a rich tissue of harmony.

By and by, the song came to an end; and then, all at once, there were several feminine voices, talking airily and cheerfully, with now and then a merry burst of laughter, such as you may always hear when three or four young women sit at work together.

"What a sweet song that was!" exclaimed one of the voyagers.

"Too sweet, indeed," answered Eurylochus, shaking his head. "Yet it was not so sweet as the song of the Sirens, those bird-like damsels who wanted to tempt us on the rocks, so that our vessel might be wrecked, and our bones left whitening along the shore."

"But just listen to the pleasant voices of those maidens, and that buzz of the loom, as the shuttle passes to and fro," said another comrade. "What a domestic, household, home-like sound it is! Ah, before that weary siege of Troy, I used to hear the buzzing loom and the women's voices under my own roof. Shall I never hear them again? nor taste those nice little savory dishes which my dearest wife knew how to serve up?"

"Tush! we shall fare better here," said another. "But how innocently those women are babbling together, without guessing that we overhear them! And mark that richest voice of all, so pleasant and so familiar, but which yet seems to have the authority of a mistress among them. Let us show ourselves at once. What harm can the lady of the palace and her maidens do to mariners and warriors like us?"

"Remember," said Eurylochus, "that it was a young maiden who beguiled three of our friends into the palace of the king of the Laestrygons, who ate up one of them in the twinkling of an eye."

No warning or persuasion, however, had any effect on his companions. They went up to a pair of folding doors at the farther end of the hall, and throwing them wide open, passed into the next room. Eurylochus, meanwhile, had stepped behind a pillar. In the short moment while the folding doors opened and closed again, he caught a glimpse of a very beautiful woman rising from the loom, and coming to meet the poor weather-beaten wanderers, with a hospitable smile, and her hand stretched out in welcome. There were four other young women, who joined their hands and danced merrily forward, making gestures of obeisance to the strangers. They were only less beautiful than the lady who seemed to be their mistress. Yet Eurylochus fancied that one of them had sea-green hair, and that the close-fitting bodice of a second looked like the bark of a tree, and that both the others had something odd in their aspect, although he could not quite determine what it was, in the little while that he had to examine them.

The folding doors swung quickly back, and left him standing behind the pillar, in the solitude of the outer hall. There Eurylochus waited until he was quite weary, and listened eagerly to every sound, but without hearing anything that could help him to guess what had become of his friends. Footsteps, it is true, seemed to be passing and repassing, in other parts of the palace. Then there was a clatter of silver dishes, or golden ones, which made him imagine a rich feast in a splendid banqueting hall. But by and by he heard a tremendous grunting and squealing, and then a sudden scampering, like that of small, hard hoofs over a marble floor, while the voices of the mistress and her four handmaidens were screaming all together, in tones of anger and derision. Eurylochus could not conceive what had happened, unless a drove of swine had broken into the palace, attracted by the smell of the feast. Chancing to cast his eyes at the fountain, he saw that it did not shift its shape, as formerly, nor looked either like a long-robed man, or a lion, a tiger, a wolf, or an ass. It looked like nothing but a hog, which lay wallowing in the marble basin, and filled it from brim to brim.

But we must leave the prudent Eurylochus waiting in the outer hall, and follow his friends into the inner secrecy of the palace. As soon as the beautiful woman saw them, she arose from the loom, as I have told you, and came forward, smiling, and stretching out her hand. She took the hand of the foremost among them, and bade him and the whole party welcome.

"You have been long expected, my good friends," said she. "I and my maidens are well acquainted with you, although you do not appear to recognize us. Look at this piece of tapestry, and judge if your faces must not have been familiar to us."

So the voyagers examined the web of cloth which the beautiful woman had been weaving in her loom; and, to their vast astonishment, they saw their own figures perfectly represented in different colored threads. It was a life-like picture of their recent adventures, showing them in the cave of Polyphemus, and how they had put out his one great moony eye; while in another part of the tapestry they were untying the leathern bags, puffed out with contrary winds; and farther on, they beheld themselves scampering away from the gigantic king of the Laestrygons, who had caught one of them by the leg. Lastly, there they were, sitting on the desolate shore of this very island, hungry and downcast, and looking ruefully at the bare bones of the stag which they devoured yesterday. This was as far as the work had yet proceeded; but when the beautiful woman should again sit down at her loom, she would probably make a picture of what had since happened to the strangers, and of what was now going to happen.

"You see," she said, "that I know all about your troubles; and you cannot doubt that I desire to make you happy for as long a time as you may remain with me. For this purpose, my honored guests, I have ordered a banquet to be prepared. Fish, fowl, and flesh, roasted, and in luscious stews, and seasoned, I trust, to all your tastes, are ready to be served up. If your appetites tell you it is dinner time, then come with me to the festal saloon."

At this kind invitation, the hungry mariners were quite overjoyed; and one of them, taking upon himself to be spokesman, assured their hospitable hostess that any hour of the day was dinner time with them, whenever they could get flesh to put in the pot, and fire to boil it with. So the beautiful woman led the way; and the four maidens (one of them had sea-green hair, another a bodice of oak bark, a third sprinkled a shower of water drops from her fingers' ends, and the fourth had some other oddity, which I have forgotten), all these followed behind, and hurried the guests along, until they entered a magnificent saloon. It was built in a perfect oval, and lighted from a crystal dome above. Around the walls were ranged two and twenty thrones, overhung by canopies of crimson and gold, and provided with the softest of cushions, which were tasselled and fringed with gold cord. Each of the strangers was invited to sit down; and there they were, two and twenty storm-beaten mariners, in worn and tattered garb, sitting on two and twenty cushioned and canopied thrones, so rich and gorgeous that the proudest monarch had nothing more splendid in his stateliest hall.

Then you might have seen the guests nodding, winking with one eye, and leaning from one throne to another, to communicate their satisfaction in hoarse whispers.

"Our good hostess has made kings of us all," said one. "Ha! do you smell the feast? I'll engage it will be fit to set before two and twenty kings."

"I hope," said another, "it will be, mainly, good substantial joints, sirloins, spareribs, and hinder quarters, without too many kickshaws. If I thought the good lady would not take it amiss, I should call for a fat slice of fried bacon to begin with."

Ah, the gluttons and gormandizers! You see how it was with them. In the loftiest seats of dignity, on royal thrones, they could think of nothing but their greedy appetite, which was the portion of their nature that they shared with wolves and swine; so that they resembled those vilest of animals far more than they did kings—if, indeed, kings were what they ought to be.

But the beautiful woman now clapped her hands; and immediately there entered a train of two and twenty serving man, bringing dishes of the richest food, all hot from the kitchen fire, and sending up such a steam that it hung like a cloud below the crystal dome of the saloon. An equal number of attendants brought great flagons of wine, of various kinds, some of which sparkled as it was poured out, and went bubbling down the throat; while, of other sorts, the purple liquor was so clear that you could see the wrought figures at the bottom of the goblet. While the servants supplied the two and twenty guests with food and drink, the hostess and her four maidens went from one throne to another, exhorting them to eat their fill, and to quaff wine abundantly, and thus to recompense themselves, at this one banquet, for the many days when they had gone without a dinner. But whenever the mariners were not looking at them (which was pretty often, as they looked chiefly into the basins and platters), the beautiful woman and her damsels turned aside, and laughed. Even the servants, as they knelt down to present the dishes, might be seen to grin and sneer, while the guests were helping themselves to the offered dainties.

And, once in a while, the strangers seemed to taste something that they did not like.

"Here is an odd kind of spice in this dish," said one. "I can't say it quite suits my palate. Down it goes, however."

"Send a good draught of wine down your throat," said his comrade on the next throne. "That is the stuff to make this sort of cookery relish well. Though I must needs say, the wine has a queer taste too. But the more I drink of it, the better I like the flavor."

Whatever little fault they might find with the dishes, they sat at dinner a prodigiously long while; and it would really have made you ashamed to see how they swilled down the liquor and gobbled up the food. They sat on golden thrones, to be sure; but they behaved like pigs in a sty; and, if they had had their wits about them, they might have guessed that this was the opinion of their beautiful hostess and her maidens. It brings a blush into my face to reckon up, in my own mind, what mountains of meat and pudding, and what gallons of wine, these two and twenty guzzlers and gormandizers ate and drank. They forgot all about their homes, and their wives and children, and all about Ulysses, and everything else, except this banquet, at which they wanted to keep feasting forever. But at length they began to give over, from mere incapacity to hold any more.

"That last bit of fat is too much for me," said one.

"And I have not room for another morsel," said his next neighbor, heaving a sigh. "What a pity! My appetite is as sharp as ever."

In short, they all left off eating, and leaned back on their thrones, with such a stupid and helpless aspect as made them ridiculous to behold. When their hostess saw this, she laughed aloud; so did her four damsels; so did the two and twenty serving men that bore the dishes, and their two and twenty fellows that poured out the wine. And the louder they all laughed, the more stupid and helpless did the two and twenty gormandizers look. Then the beautiful woman took her stand in the middle of the saloon, and stretching out a slender rod (it had been all the while in her hand, although they never noticed it till this moment), she turned it from one guest to another, until each had felt it pointed at himself. Beautiful as her face was, and though there was a smile on it, it looked just as wicked and mischievous as the ugliest serpent that ever was seen; and fat-witted as the voyagers had made themselves, they began to suspect that they had fallen into the power of an evil-minded enchantress.

"Wretches," cried she, "you have abused a lady's hospitality; and in this princely saloon your behavior has been suited to a hog-pen. You are already swine in everything but the human form, which you disgrace, and which I myself should be ashamed to keep a moment longer, were you to share it with me. But it will require only the slightest exercise of magic to make the exterior conform to the hoggish disposition. Assume your proper shapes, gormandizers, and begone to the sty!"

Uttering these last words, she waved her wand; and stamping her foot imperiously, each of the guests was struck aghast at beholding, instead of his comrades in human shape, one and twenty hogs sitting on the same number of golden thrones. Each man (as he still supposed himself to be) essayed to give a cry of surprise, but found that he could merely grunt, and that, in a word, he was just such another beast as his companions. It looked so intolerably absurd to see hogs on cushioned thrones, that they made haste to wallow down upon all fours, like other swine. They tried to groan and beg for mercy, but forthwith emitted the most awful grunting and squealing that ever came out of swinish throats. They would have wrung their hands in despair, but, attempting to do so, grew all the more desperate for seeing themselves squatted on their hams, and pawing the air with their fore trotters. Dear me! what pendulous ears they had! what little red eyes, half buried in fat! and what long snouts, instead of Grecian noses!

But brutes as they certainly were, they yet had enough of human nature in them to be shocked at their own hideousness; and still intending to groan, they uttered a viler grunt and squeal than before. So harsh and ear-piercing it was, that you would have fancied a butcher was sticking his knife into each of their throats, or, at the very least, that somebody was pulling every hog by his funny little twist of a tail.

"Begone to your sty!" cried the enchantress, giving them some smart strokes with her wand; and then she turned to the serving men—"Drive out these swine, and throw down some acorns for them to eat."

The door of the saloon being flung open, the drove of hogs ran in all directions save the right one, in accordance with their hoggish perversity, but were finally driven into the back yard of the palace. It was a sight to bring tears into one's eyes (and I hope none of you will be cruel enough to laugh at it), to see the poor creatures go snuffing along, picking up here a cabbage leaf and there a turnip top, and rooting their noses in the earth for whatever they could find. In their sty, moreover, they behaved more piggishly than the pigs that had been born so; for they bit and snorted at one another, put their feet in the trough, and gobbled up their victuals in a ridiculous hurry; and, when there was nothing more to be had, they made a great pile of themselves among some unclean straw, and fell fast asleep. If they had any human reason left, it was just enough to keep them wondering when they should be slaughtered, and what quality of bacon they should make.

Meantime, as I told you before, Eurylochus had waited, and waited, and waited, in the entrance hall of the palace, without being able to comprehend what had befallen his friends. At last, when the swinish uproar resounded through the palace, and when he saw the image of a hog in the marble basin, he thought it best to hasten back to the vessel, and inform the wise Ulysses of these marvelous occurrences. So he ran as fast as he could down the steps, and never stopped to draw breath till he reached the shore.

"Why do you come alone?" asked King Ulysses, as soon as he saw him. "Where are your two and twenty comrades?"

At these questions, Eurylochus burst into tears.

"Alas!" he cried, "I greatly fear that we shall never see one of their faces again."

Then he told Ulysses all that had happened, as far as he knew it, and added that he suspected the beautiful woman to be a vile enchantress, and the marble palace, magnificent as it looked, to be only a dismal cavern in reality. As for his companions, he could not imagine what had become of them, unless they had been given to the swine to be devoured alive. At this intelligence, all the voyagers were greatly affrighted. But Ulysses lost no time in girding on his sword, and hanging his bow and quiver over his shoulders, and taking a spear in his right hand. When his followers saw their wise leader making these preparations, they inquired whither he was going, and earnestly besought him not to leave them.

"You are our king," cried they; "and what is more, you are the wisest man in the whole world, and nothing but your wisdom and courage can get us out of this danger. If you desert us, and go to the enchanted palace, you will suffer the same fate as our poor companions, and not a soul of us will ever see our dear Ithaca again."

"As I am your king," answered Ulysses, "and wiser than any of you, it is therefore the more my duty to see what has befallen our comrades, and whether anything can yet be done to rescue them. Wait for me here until tomorrow. If I do not then return, you must hoist sail, and endeavor to find your way to our native land. For my part, I am answerable for the fate of these poor mariners, who have stood by my side in battle, and been so often drenched to the skin, along with me, by the same tempestuous surges. I will either bring them back with me, or perish."

Had his followers dared, they would have detained him by force. But King Ulysses frowned sternly on them, and shook his spear, and bade them stop him at their peril. Seeing him so determined, they let him go, and sat down on the sand, as disconsolate a set of people as could be, waiting and praying for his return.

It happened to Ulysses, just as before, that, when he had gone a few steps from the edge of the cliff, the purple bird came fluttering towards him, crying, "Peep, peep, pe—weep!" and using all the art it could to persuade him to go no farther.

"What mean you, little bird?" cried Ulysses. "You are arrayed like a king in purple and gold, and wear a golden crown upon your head. Is it because I too am a king, that you desire so earnestly to speak with me? If you can talk in human language, say what you would have me do."

"Peep!" answered the purple bird, very dolorously. "Peep, peep, pe—we—e!"

Certainly there lay some heavy anguish at the little bird's heart; and it was a sorrowful predicament that he could not, at least, have the consolation of telling what it was. But Ulysses had no time to waste in trying to get at the mystery. He therefore quickened his pace, and had gone a good way along the pleasant wood path, when there met him a young man of very brisk and intelligent aspect, and clad in a rather singular garb. He wore a short cloak and a sort of cap that seemed to be furnished with a pair of wings; and from the lightness of his step, you would have supposed that there might likewise be wings on his feet. To enable him to walk still better (for he was always on one journey or another) he carried a winged staff, around which two serpents were wriggling and twisting. In short, I have said enough to make you guess that it was Quicksilver; and Ulysses (who knew him of old, and had learned a great deal of his wisdom from him) recognized him in a moment.

"Whither are you going in such a hurry, wise Ulysses?" asked Quicksilver. "Do you not know that this island is enchanted? The wicked enchantress (whose name is Circe, the sister of King Aetes) dwells in the marble palace which you see yonder among the trees. By her magic arts she changes every human being into the brute, beast, or fowl whom he happens most to resemble."

"That little bird, which met me at the edge of the cliff," exclaimed Ulysses; "was he a human being once?"

"Yes," answered Quicksilver. "He was once a king, named Picus, and a pretty good sort of a king, too, only rather too proud of his purple robe, and his crown, and the golden chain about his neck; so he was forced to take the shape of a gaudy-feathered bird. The lions, and wolves, and tigers, who will come running to meet you, in front of the palace, were formerly fierce and cruel men, resembling in their disposition the wild beasts whose forms they now rightfully wear."

"And my poor companions," said Ulysses. "Have they undergone a similar change, through the arts of this wicked Circe?"

"You well know what gormandizers they were," replied Quicksilver; and rogue that he was, he could not help laughing at the joke. "So you will not be surprised to hear that they have all taken the shapes of swine! If Circe had never done anything worse, I really should not think her so very much to blame."

"But can I do nothing to help them?" inquired Ulysses.

"It will require all your wisdom," said Quicksilver, "and a little of my own into the bargain, to keep your royal and sagacious self from being transformed into a fox. But do as I bid you; and the matter may end better than it has begun."

While he was speaking, Quicksilver seemed to be in search of something; he went stooping along the ground, and soon laid his hand on a little plant with a snow-white flower, which he plucked and smelt of. Ulysses had been looking at that very spot only just before; and it appeared to him that the plant had burst into full flower the instant when Quicksilver touched it with his fingers.

"Take this flower, King Ulysses," said he. "Guard it as you do your eyesight; for I can assure you it is exceedingly rare and precious, and you might seek the whole earth over without ever finding another like it. Keep it in your hand, and smell of it frequently after you enter the palace, and while you are talking with the enchantress. Especially when she offers you food, or a draught of wine out of her goblet, be careful to fill your nostrils with the flower's fragrance. Follow these directions, and you may defy her magic arts to change you into a fox."

Quicksilver then gave him some further advice how to behave, and bidding him be bold and prudent, again assured him that, powerful as Circe was, he would have a fair prospect of coming safely out of her enchanted palace. After listening attentively, Ulysses thanked his good friend, and resumed his way. But he had taken only a few steps, when, recollecting some other questions which he wished to ask, he turned round again, and beheld nobody on the spot where Quicksilver had stood; for that winged cap of his, and those winged shoes, with the help of the winged staff, had carried him quickly out of sight.

When Ulysses reached the lawn, in front of the palace, the lions and other savage animals came bounding to meet him, and would have fawned upon him and licked his feet. But the wise king struck at them with his long spear, and sternly bade them begone out of his path; for he knew that they had once been bloodthirsty men, and would now tear him limb from limb, instead of fawning upon him, could they do the mischief that was in their hearts. The wild beasts yelped and glared at him, and stood at a distance, while he ascended the palace steps.

On entering the hall, Ulysses saw the magic fountain in the center of it. The up-gushing water had now again taken the shape of a man in a long, white, fleecy robe, who appeared to be making gestures of welcome. The king likewise heard the noise of the shuttle in the loom and the sweet melody of the beautiful woman's song, and then the pleasant voices of herself and the four maidens talking together, with peals of merry laughter intermixed. But Ulysses did not waste much time in listening to the laughter or the song. He leaned his spear against one of the pillars of the hall, and then, after loosening his sword in the scabbard, stepped boldly forward, and threw the folding doors wide open. The moment she beheld his stately figure standing in the doorway, the beautiful woman rose from the loom, and ran to meet him with a glad smile throwing its sunshine over her face, and both her hands extended.

"Welcome, brave stranger!" cried she. "We were expecting you."

And the nymph with the sea-green hair made a courtesy down to the ground, and likewise bade him welcome; so did her sister with the bodice of oaken bark, and she that sprinkled dew-drops from her fingers' ends, and the fourth one with some oddity which I cannot remember. And Circe, as the beautiful enchantress was called (who had deluded so many persons that she did not doubt of being able to delude Ulysses, not imagining how wise he was), again addressed him:

"Your companions," said she, "have already been received into my palace, and have enjoyed the hospitable treatment to which the propriety of their behavior so well entitles them. If such be your pleasure, you shall first take some refreshment, and then join them in the elegant apartment which they now occupy. See, I and my maidens have been weaving their figures into this piece of tapestry."

She pointed to the web of beautifully-woven cloth in the loom. Circe and the four nymphs must have been very diligently at work since the arrival of the mariners; for a great many yards of tapestry had now been wrought, in addition to what I before described. In this new part, Ulysses saw his two and twenty friends represented as sitting on cushions and canopied thrones, greedily devouring dainties, and quaffing deep draughts of wine. The work had not yet gone any further. O, no, indeed. The enchantress was far too cunning to let Ulysses see the mischief which her magic arts had since brought upon the gormandizers.

"As for yourself, valiant sir," said Circe, "judging by the dignity of your aspect, I take you to be nothing less than a king. Deign to follow me, and you shall be treated as befits your rank."

So Ulysses followed her into the oval saloon, where his two and twenty comrades had devoured the banquet, which ended so disastrously for themselves. But, all this while, he had held the snow-white flower in his hand, and had constantly smelt of it while Circe was speaking; and as he crossed the threshold of the saloon, he took good care to inhale several long and deep snuffs of its fragrance. Instead of two and twenty thrones, which had before been ranged around the wall, there was now only a single throne, in the center of the apartment. But this was surely the most magnificent seat that ever a king or an emperor reposed himself upon, all made of chased gold, studded with precious stones, with a cushion that looked like a soft heap of living roses, and overhung by a canopy of sunlight which Circe knew how to weave into drapery. The enchantress took Ulysses by the hand, and made him sit down upon this dazzling throne. Then, clapping her hands, she summoned the chief butler.

"Bring hither," said she, "the goblet that is set apart for kings to drink out of. And fill it with the same delicious wine which my royal brother, King Aetes, praised so highly, when he last visited me with my fair daughter Medea. That good and amiable child! Were she now here, it would delight her to see me offering this wine to my honored guest."

But Ulysses, while the butler was gone for the wine, held the snow-white flower to his nose.

"Is it a wholesome wine?" he asked.

At this the four maidens tittered; whereupon the enchantress looked round at them, with an aspect of severity.

"It is the wholesomest juice that ever was squeezed out of the grape," said she; "for, instead of disguising a man, as other liquor is apt to do, it brings him to his true self, and shows him as he ought to be."

The chief butler liked nothing better than to see people turned into swine, or making any kind of a beast of themselves; so he made haste to bring the royal goblet, filled with a liquid as bright as gold, and which kept sparkling upward, and throwing a sunny spray over the brim. But, delightfully as the wine looked, it was mingled with the most potent enchantments that Circe knew how to concoct. For every drop of the pure grape juice there were two drops of the pure mischief; and the danger of the thing was, that the mischief made it taste all the better. The mere smell of the bubbles, which effervesced at the brim, was enough to turn a man's beard into pig's bristles, or make a lion's claws grow out of his fingers, or a fox's brush behind him.

"Drink, my noble guest," said Circe, smiling, as she presented him with the goblet. "You will find in this draught a solace for all your troubles."

King Ulysses took the goblet with his right hand, while with his left he held the snow-white flower to his nostrils, and drew in so long a breath that his lungs were quite filled with its pure and simple fragrance. Then, drinking off all the wine, he looked the enchantress calmly in the face.

"Wretch," cried Circe, giving him a smart stroke with her wand, "how dare you keep your human shape a moment longer! Take the form of the brute whom you most resemble. If a hog, go join your fellow-swine in the sty; if a lion, a wolf, a tiger, go howl with the wild beasts on the lawn; if a fox, go exercise your craft in stealing poultry. Thou hast quaffed off my wine, and canst be man no longer."

But, such was the virtue of the snow-white flower, instead of wallowing down from his throne in swinish shape, or taking any other brutal form, Ulysses looked even more manly and king-like than before. He gave the magic goblet a toss, and sent it clashing over the marble floor to the farthest end of the saloon. Then, drawing his sword, he seized the enchantress by her beautiful ringlets, and made a gesture as if he meant to strike off her head at one blow.

"Wicked Circe," cried he, in a terrible voice, "this sword shall put an end to thy enchant meets. Thou shalt die, vile wretch, and do no more mischief in the world, by tempting human beings into the vices which make beasts of them."

The tone and countenance of Ulysses were so awful, and his sword gleamed so brightly, and seemed to have so intolerably keen an edge, that Circe was almost killed by the mere fright, without waiting for a blow. The chief butler scrambled out of the saloon, picking up the golden goblet as he went; and the enchantress and the four maidens fell on their knees, wringing their hands, and screaming for mercy.

"Spare me!" cried Circe. "Spare me, royal and wise Ulysses. For now I know that thou art he of whom Quicksilver forewarned me, the most prudent of mortals, against whom no enchantments can prevail. Thou only couldst have conquered Circe. Spare me, wisest of men. I will show thee true hospitality, and even give myself to be thy slave, and this magnificent palace to be henceforth thy home."

The four nymphs, meanwhile, were making a most piteous ado; and especially the ocean nymph, with the sea-green hair, wept a great deal of salt water, and the fountain nymph, besides scattering dewdrops from her fingers' ends, nearly melted away into tears. But Ulysses would not be pacified until Circe had taken a solemn oath to change back his companions, and as many others as he should direct, from their present forms of beast or bird into their former shapes of men.

"On these conditions," said he, "I consent to spare your life. Otherwise you must die upon the spot."

With a drawn sword hanging over her, the enchantress would readily have consented to do as much good as she had hitherto done mischief, however little she might like such employment. She therefore led Ulysses out of the back entrance of the palace, and showed him the swine in their sty. There were about fifty of these unclean beasts in the whole herd; and though the greater part were hogs by birth and education, there was wonderfully little difference to be seen betwixt them and their new brethren, who had so recently worn the human shape. To speak critically, indeed, the latter rather carried the thing to excess, and seemed to make it a point to wallow in the miriest part of the sty, and otherwise to outdo the original swine in their own natural vocation. When men once turn to brutes, the trifle of man's wit that remains in them adds tenfold to their brutality.

The comrades of Ulysses, however, had not quite lost the remembrance of having formerly stood erect. When he approached the sty, two and twenty enormous swine separated themselves from the herd, and scampered towards him, with such a chorus of horrible squealing as made him clap both hands to his ears. And yet they did not seem to know what they wanted, nor whether they were merely hungry, or miserable from some other cause. It was curious, in the midst of their distress, to observe them thrusting their noses into the mire, in quest of something to eat. The nymph with the bodice of oaken bark (she was the hamadryad of an oak) threw a handful of acorns among them; and the two and twenty hogs scrambled and fought for the prize, as if they had tasted not so much as a noggin of sour milk for a twelvemonth.

"These must certainly be my comrades," said Ulysses. "I recognize their dispositions. They are hardly worth the trouble of changing them into the human form again. Nevertheless, we will have it done, lest their bad example should corrupt the other hogs. Let them take their original shapes, therefore, Dame Circe, if your skill is equal to the task. It will require greater magic, I trow, than it did to make swine of them."

So Circe waved her wand again, and repeated a few magic words, at the sound of which the two and twenty hogs pricked up their pendulous ears. It was a wonder to behold how their snouts grew shorter and shorter, and their mouths (which they seemed to be sorry for, because they could not gobble so expeditiously) smaller and smaller, and how one and another began to stand upon his hind legs, and scratch his nose with his fore trotters. At first the spectators hardly knew whether to call them hogs or men, but by and by came to the conclusion that they rather resembled the latter. Finally, there stood the twenty-two comrades of Ulysses, looking pretty much the same as when they left the vessel.

You must not imagine, however, that the swinish quality had entirely gone out of them. When once it fastens itself into a person's character, it is very difficult getting rid of it. This was proved by the hamadryad, who, being exceedingly fond of mischief, threw another handful of acorns before the twenty-two newly-restored people; whereupon down they wallowed in a moment, and gobbled them up in a very shameful way. Then, recollecting themselves, they scrambled to their feet, and looked more than commonly foolish.

"Thanks, noble Ulysses!" they cried. "From brute beasts you have restored us to the condition of men again."

"Do not put yourselves to the trouble of thanking me," said the wise king. "I fear I have done but little for you."

To say the truth, there was a suspicious kind of a grunt in their voices, and, for a long time afterwards, they spoke gruffly, and were apt to set up a squeal.

"It must depend on your own future behavior," added Ulysses, "whether you do not find your way back to the sty."

At this moment, the note of a bird sounded from the branch of a neighboring tree.

"Peep, peep, pe—wee—e!"

It was the purple bird, who, all this while, had been sitting over their heads, watching what was going forward, and hoping that Ulysses would remember how he had done his utmost to keep him and his followers out of harm's way. Ulysses ordered Circe instantly to make a king of this good little fowl, and leave him exactly as she found him. Hardly were the words spoken, and before the bird had time to utter another "pe—weep," King Picus leaped down from the bough of a tree, as majestic a sovereign as any in the world, dressed in a long purple robe and gorgeous yellow stockings, with a splendidly wrought collar about his neck, and a golden crown upon his head. He and King Ulysses exchanged with one another the courtesies which belong to their elevated rank. But from that time forth, King Picus was no longer proud of his crown and his trappings of royalty, nor of the fact of his being a king; he felt himself merely the upper servant of his people, and that it must be his life-long labor to make them better and happier.

As for the lions, tigers, and wolves (though Circe would have restored them to their former shapes at his slightest word), Ulysses thought it advisable that they should remain as they now were, and thus give warning of their cruel dispositions, instead of going about under the guise of men, and pretending to human sympathies, while their hearts had the blood-thirstiness of wild beasts. So he let them howl as much as they liked, but never troubled his head about them. And, when everything was settled according to his pleasure, he sent to summon the remainder of his comrades, whom he had left at the sea-shore. These being arrived, with the prudent Eurylochus at their head, they all made themselves comfortable in Circe's enchanted palace, until quite rested and refreshed from the toils and hardships of their voyage.

THE POMEGRANATE SEEDS.

Mother Ceres was exceedingly fond of her daughter Proserpina, and seldom let her go alone into the fields. But, just at the time when my story begins, the good lady was very busy, because she had the care of the wheat, and the Indian corn, and the rye and barley and, in short, of the crops of every kind, all over the earth; and as the season had thus far been uncommonly backward, it was necessary to make the harvest ripen more speedily than usual. So she put on her turban, made of poppies (a kind of flower which she was always noted for wearing), and got into her car drawn by a pair of winged dragons, and was just ready to set off.

"Dear mother," said Proserpina, "I shall be very lonely while you are away. May I not run down to the shore, and ask some of the sea nymphs to come up out of the waves and play with me?"

"Yes, child," answered Mother Ceres. "The sea nymphs are good creatures, and will never lead you into any harm. But you must take care not to stray away from them, nor go wandering about the fields by yourself. Young girls, without their mothers to take care of them, are very apt to get into mischief."

The child promised to be as prudent as if she were a grown-up woman; and, by the time the winged dragons had whirled the car out of sight, she was already on the shore, calling to the sea nymphs to come and play with her. They knew Proserpina's voice, and were not long in showing their glistening faces and sea-green hair above the water, at the bottom of which was their home. They brought along with them a great many beautiful shells; and sitting down on the moist sand, where the surf wave broke over them, they busied themselves in making a necklace, which they hung round Proserpina's neck. By way of showing her gratitude, the child besought them to go with her a little way into the fields, so that they might gather abundance of flowers, with which she would make each of her kind playmates a wreath.

"O no, dear Proserpina," cried the sea nymphs; "we dare not go with you upon the dry land. We are apt to grow faint, unless at every breath we can snuff up the salt breeze of the ocean. And don't you see how careful we are to let the surf wave break over us every moment or two, so as to keep ourselves comfortably moist? If it were not for that, we should look like bunches of uprooted seaweed dried in the sun.

"It is a great pity," said Proserpina. "But do you wait for me here, and I will run and gather my apron full of flowers, and be back again before the surf wave has broken ten times over you. I long to make you some wreaths that shall be as lovely as this necklace of many colored shells."

"We will wait, then," answered the sea nymphs. "But while you are gone, we may as well lie down on a bank of soft sponge under the water. The air to-day is a little too dry for our comfort. But we will pop up our heads every few minutes to see if you are coming."

The young Proserpina ran quickly to a spot where, only the day before, she had seen a great many flowers. These, however, were now a little past their bloom; and wishing to give her friends the freshest and loveliest blossoms, she strayed farther into the fields, and found some that made her scream with delight. Never had she met with such exquisite flowers before—violets so large and fragrant—roses with so rich and delicate a blush—such superb hyacinths and such aromatic pinks—and many others, some of which seemed to be of new shapes and colors. Two or three times, moreover, she could not help thinking that a tuft of most splendid flowers had suddenly sprouted out of the earth before her very eyes, as if on purpose to tempt her a few steps farther. Proserpina's apron was soon filled, and brimming over with delightful blossoms. She was on the point of turning back in order to rejoin the sea nymphs, and sit with them on the moist sands, all twining wreaths together. But, a little farther on, what should she behold? It was a large shrub, completely covered with the most magnificent flowers in the world.

"The darlings!" cried Proserpina; and then she thought to herself, "I was looking at that spot only a moment ago. How strange it is that I did not see the flowers!"

The nearer she approached the shrub, the more attractive it looked, until she came quite close to it; and then, although its beauty was richer than words can tell, she hardly knew whether to like it or not. It bore above a hundred flowers of the most brilliant hues, and each different from the others, but all having a kind of resemblance among themselves, which showed them to be sister blossoms. But there was a deep, glossy luster on the leaves of the shrub, and on the petals of the flowers, that made Proserpina doubt whether they might not be poisonous. To tell you the truth, foolish as it may seem, she was half inclined to turn round and run away.

"What a silly child I am!" thought she, taking courage. "It is really the most beautiful shrub that ever sprang out of the earth. I will pull it up by the roots, and carry it home, and plant it in my mother's garden."

Holding up her apron full of flowers with her left hand, Proserpina seized the large shrub with the other, and pulled, and pulled, but was hardly able to loosen the soil about its roots. What a deep-rooted plant it was! Again the girl pulled with all her might, and observed that the earth began to stir and crack to some distance around the stem. She gave another pull, but relaxed her hold, fancying that there was a rumbling sound right beneath her feet. Did the roots extend down into some enchanted cavern? Then laughing at herself for so childish a notion, she made another effort: up came the shrub, and Proserpina staggered back, holding the stem triumphantly in her hand, and gazing at the deep hole which its roots had left in the soil.

Much to her astonishment, this hole kept spreading wider and wider, and growing deeper and deeper, until it really seemed to have no bottom; and all the while, there came a rumbling noise out of its depths, louder and louder, and nearer and nearer, and sounding like the tramp of horses' hoofs and the rattling of wheels. Too much frightened to run away, she stood straining her eyes into this wonderful cavity, and soon saw a team of four sable horses, snorting smoke out of their nostrils, and tearing their way out of the earth with a splendid golden chariot whirling at their heels. They leaped out of the bottomless hole, chariot and all; and there they were, tossing their black manes, flourishing their black tails, and curvetting with every one of their hoofs off the ground at once, close by the spot where Proserpina stood. In the chariot sat the figure of a man, richly dressed, with a crown on his head, all flaming with diamonds. He was of a noble aspect, and rather handsome, but looked sullen and discontented; and he kept rubbing his eyes and shading them with his hand, as if he did not live enough in the sunshine to be very fond of its light.

As soon as this personage saw the affrighted Proserpina, he beckoned her to come a little nearer.

"Do not be afraid," said he, with as cheerful a smile as he knew how to put on. "Come! Will you not like to ride a little way with me, in my beautiful chariot?"

But Proserpina was so alarmed, that she wished for nothing but to get out of his reach. And no wonder. The stranger did not look remarkably good-natured, in spite of his smile; and as for his voice, its tones were deep and stern, and sounded as much like the rumbling of an earthquake underground than anything else. As is always the case with children in trouble, Proserpina's first thought was to call for her mother.

"Mother, Mother Ceres!" cried she, all in a tremble. "Come quickly and save me."

But her voice was too faint for her mother to hear. Indeed, it is most probable that Ceres was then a thousand miles off, making the corn grow in some far distant country. Nor could it have availed her poor daughter, even had she been within hearing; for no sooner did Proserpina begin to cry out, than the stranger leaped to the ground, caught the child in his arms, and again mounted the chariot, shook the reins, and shouted to the four black horses to set off. They immediately broke into so swift a gallop, that it seemed rather like flying through the air than running along the earth. In a moment, Proserpina lost sight of the pleasant vale of Enna, in which she had always dwelt. Another instant, and even the summit of Mount Aetna had become so blue in the distance, that she could scarcely distinguish it from the smoke that gushed out of its crater. But still the poor child screamed, and scattered her apron full of flowers along the way, and left a long cry trailing behind the chariot; and many mothers, to whose ears it came, ran quickly to see if any mischief had befallen their children. But Mother Ceres was a great way off, and could not hear the cry.

As they rode on, the stranger did his best to soothe her.

"Why should you be so frightened, my pretty child?" said he, trying to soften his rough voice. "I promise not to do you any harm. What! you have been gathering flowers? Wait till we come to my palace, and I will give you a garden full of prettier flowers than those, all made of pearls, and diamonds, and rubies. Can you guess who I am? They call my name Pluto; and I am the king of diamonds and all other precious stones. Every atom of the gold and silver that lies under the earth belongs to me, to say nothing of the copper and iron, and of the coal mines, which supply me with abundance of fuel. Do you see this splendid crown upon my head? You may have it for a plaything. O, we shall be very good friends, and you will find me more agreeable than you expect, when once we get out of this troublesome sunshine."

"Let me go home!" cried Proserpina. "Let me go home!"

"My home is better than your mother's," answered King Pluto. "It is a palace, all made of gold, with crystal windows; and because there is little or no sunshine thereabouts, the apartments are illuminated with diamond lamps. You never saw anything half so magnificent as my throne. If you like, you may sit down on it, and be my little queen, and I will sit on the footstool."

"I don't care for golden palaces and thrones," sobbed Proserpina. "Oh, my mother, my mother! Carry me back to my mother!"

But King Pluto, as he called himself, only shouted to his steeds to go faster.

"Pray do not be foolish, Proserpina," said he, in rather a sullen tone. "I offer you my palace and my crown, and all the riches that are under the earth; and you treat me as if I were doing you an injury. The one thing which my palace needs is a merry little maid, to run upstairs and down, and cheer up the rooms with her smile. And this is what you must do for King Pluto."

"Never!" answered Proserpina, looking as miserable as she could. "I shall never smile again till you set me down at my mother's door."

But she might just as well have talked to the wind that whistled past them, for Pluto urged on his horses, and went faster than ever. Proserpina continued to cry out, and screamed so long and so loudly that her poor little voice was almost screamed away; and when it was nothing but a whisper, she happened to cast her eyes over a great broad field of waving grain—and whom do you think she saw? Who, but Mother Ceres, making the corn grow, and too busy to notice the golden chariot as it went rattling along. The child mustered all her strength, and gave one more scream, but was out of sight before Ceres had time to turn her head.

King Pluto had taken a road which now began to grow excessively gloomy. It was bordered on each side with rocks and precipices, between which the rumbling of the chariot wheels was reverberated with a noise like rolling thunder. The trees and bushes that grew in the crevices of the rocks had very dismal foliage; and by and by, although it was hardly noon, the air became obscured with a gray twilight. The black horses had rushed along so swiftly, that they were already beyond the limits of the sunshine. But the duskier it grew, the more did Pluto's visage assume an air of satisfaction. After all, he was not an ill-looking person, especially when he left off twisting his features into a smile that did not belong to them. Proserpina peeped at his face through the gathering dusk, and hoped that he might not be so very wicked as she at first thought him.

"Ah, this twilight is truly refreshing," said King Pluto, "after being so tormented with that ugly and impertinent glare of the sun. How much more agreeable is lamplight or torchlight, more particularly when reflected from diamonds! It will be a magnificent sight, when we get to my palace."

"Is it much farther?" asked Proserpina. "And will you carry me back when I have seen it?"

"We will talk of that by and by," answered Pluto. "We are just entering my dominions. Do you see that tall gateway before us? When we pass those gates, we are at home. And there lies my faithful mastiff at the threshold. Cerberus! Cerberus! Come hither, my good dog!"

So saying, Pluto pulled at the reins, and stopped the chariot right between the tall, massive pillars of the gateway. The mastiff of which he had spoken got up from the threshold, and stood on his hinder legs, so as to put his fore paws on the chariot wheel. But, my stars, what a strange dog it was! Why, he was a big, rough, ugly-looking monster, with three separate heads, and each of them fiercer than the two others; but fierce as they were, King Pluto patted them all. He seemed as fond of his three-headed dog as if it had been a sweet little spaniel, with silken ears and curly hair. Cerberus, on the other hand, was evidently rejoiced to see his master, and expressed his attachment, as other dogs do, by wagging his tail at a great rate. Proserpina's eyes being drawn to it by its brisk motion, she saw that this tail was neither more nor less than a live dragon, with fiery eyes, and fangs that had a very poisonous aspect. And while the three-headed Cerberus was fawning so lovingly on King Pluto, there was the dragon tail wagging against its will, and looking as cross and ill-natured as you can imagine, on its own separate account.

"Will the dog bite me?" asked Proserpina, shrinking closer to Pluto. "What an ugly creature he is!"

"O, never fear," answered her companion. "He never harms people, unless they try to enter my dominions without being sent for, or to get away when I wish to keep them here. Down, Cerberus! Now, my pretty Proserpina, we will drive on."

On went the chariot, and King Pluto seemed greatly pleased to find himself once more in his own kingdom. He drew Proserpina's attention to the rich veins of gold that were to be seen among the rocks, and pointed to several places where one stroke of a pickaxe would loosen a bushel of diamonds. All along the road, indeed, there were sparkling gems, which would have been of inestimable value above ground, but which here were reckoned of the meaner sort and hardly worth a beggar's stooping for.

Not far from the gateway, they came to a bridge, which seemed to be built of iron. Pluto stopped the chariot, and bade Proserpina look at the stream which was gliding so lazily beneath it. Never in her life had she beheld so torpid, so black, so muddy-looking a stream; its waters reflected no images of anything that was on the banks, and it moved as sluggishly as if it had quite forgotten which way it ought to flow, and had rather stagnate than flow either one way or the other.

"This is the River Lethe," observed King Pluto. "Is it not a very pleasant stream?"

"I think it a very dismal one," answered Proserpina.

"It suits my taste, however," answered Pluto, who was apt to be sullen when anybody disagreed with him. "At all events, its water has one excellent quality; for a single draught of it makes people forget every care and sorrow that has hitherto tormented them. Only sip a little of it, my dear Proserpina, and you will instantly cease to grieve for your mother, and will have nothing in your memory that can prevent your being perfectly happy in my palace. I will send for some, in a golden goblet, the moment we arrive."

"O, no, no, no!" cried Proserpina, weeping afresh. "I had a thousand times rather be miserable with remembering my mother, than be happy in forgetting her. That dear, dear mother! I never, never will forget her."

"We shall see," said King Pluto. "You do not know what fine times we will have in my palace. Here we are just at the portal. These pillars are solid gold, I assure you."

He alighted from the chariot, and taking Proserpina in his arms, carried her up a lofty flight of steps into the great hall of the palace. It was splendidly illuminated by means of large precious stones, of various hues, which seemed to burn like so many lamps, and glowed with a hundred-fold radiance all through the vast apartment. And yet there was a kind of gloom in the midst of this enchanted light; nor was there a single object in the hall that was really agreeable to behold, except the little Proserpina herself, a lovely child, with one earthly flower which she had not let fall from her hand. It is my opinion that even King Pluto had never been happy in his palace, and that this was the true reason why he had stolen away Proserpina, in order that he might have something to love, instead of cheating his heart any longer with this tiresome magnificence. And, though he pretended to dislike the sunshine of the upper world, yet the effect of the child's presence, bedimmed as she was by her tears, was as if a faint and watery sunbeam had somehow or other found its way into the enchanted hall.

Pluto now summoned his domestics, and bade them lose no time in preparing a most sumptuous banquet, and above all things, not to fail of setting a golden beaker of the water of Lethe by Proserpina's plate.

"I will neither drink that nor anything else," said Proserpina. "Nor will I taste a morsel of food, even if you keep me forever in your palace."

"I should be sorry for that," replied King Pluto, patting her cheek; for he really wished to be kind, if he had only known how. "You are a spoiled child, I perceive, my little Proserpina; but when you see the nice things which my cook will make for you, your appetite will quickly come again."

Then, sending for the head cook, he gave strict orders that all sorts of delicacies, such as young people are usually fond of, should be set before Proserpina.

He had a secret motive in this; for, you are to understand, it is a fixed law, that when persons are carried off to the land of magic, if they once taste any food there, they can never get back to their friends. Now, if King Pluto had been cunning enough to offer Proserpina some fruit, or bread and milk (which was the simple fare to which the child had always been accustomed), it is very probable that she would soon have been tempted to eat it. But he left the matter entirely to his cook, who, like all other cooks, considered nothing fit to eat unless it were rich pastry, or highly-seasoned meat, or spiced sweet cakes—things which Proserpina's mother had never given her, and the smell of which quite took away her appetite, instead of sharpening it.

But my story must now clamber out of King Pluto's dominions, and see what Mother Ceres had been about, since she was bereft of her daughter. We had a glimpse of her, as you remember, half hidden among the waving grain, while the four black steeds were swiftly whirling along the chariot, in which her beloved Proserpina was so unwillingly borne away. You recollect, too, the loud scream which Proserpina gave, just when the chariot was out of sight.

Of all the child's outcries, this last shriek was the only one that reached the ears of Mother Ceres. She had mistaken the rumbling of the chariot wheels for a peal of thunder, and imagined that a shower was coming up, and that it would assist her in making the corn grow. But, at the sound of Proserpina's shriek, she started, and looked about in every direction, not knowing whence it came, but feeling almost certain that it was her daughter's voice. It seemed so unaccountable, however, that the girl should have strayed over so many lands and seas (which she herself could not have traversed without the aid of her winged dragons), that the good Ceres tried to believe that it must be the child of some other parent, and not her own darling Proserpina, who had uttered this lamentable cry. Nevertheless, it troubled her with a vast many tender fears, such as are ready to bestir themselves in every mother's heart, when she finds it necessary to go away from her dear children without leaving them under the care of some maiden aunt, or other such faithful guardian. So she quickly left the field in which she had been so busy; and, as her work was not half done, the grain looked, next day, as if it needed both sun and rain, and as if it were blighted in the ear, and had something the matter with its roots.

The pair of dragons must have had very nimble wings; for, in less than an hour, Mother Ceres had alighted at the door of her home, and found it empty. Knowing, however, that the child was fond of sporting on the sea-shore, she hastened thither as fast as she could, and there beheld the wet faces of the poor sea nymphs peeping over a wave. All this while, the good creatures had been waiting on the bank of sponge, and once, every half minute or so, had popped up their four heads above water, to see if their playmate were yet coming back. When they saw Mother Ceres, they sat down on the crest of the surf wave, and let it toss them ashore at her feet.

"Where is Proserpina?" cried Ceres. "Where is my child? Tell me, you naughty sea nymphs, have you enticed her under the sea?"

"O, no, good Mother Ceres," said the innocent sea nymphs, tossing back their green ringlets, and looking her in the face. "We never should dream of such a thing. Proserpina has been at play with us, it is true; but she left us a long while ago, meaning only to run a little way upon the dry land, and gather some flowers for a wreath. This was early in the day, and we have seen nothing of her since."

Ceres scarcely waited to hear what the nymphs had to say, before she hurried off to make inquiries all through the neighborhood. But nobody told her anything that would enable the poor mother to guess what had become of Proserpina. A fisherman, it is true, had noticed her little footprints in the sand, as he went homeward along the beach with a basket of fish; a rustic had seen the child stooping to gather flowers; several persons had heard either the rattling of chariot wheels, or the rumbling of distant thunder; and one old woman, while plucking vervain and catnip, had heard a scream, but supposed it to be some childish nonsense, and therefore did not take the trouble to look up. The stupid people! It took them such a tedious while to tell the nothing that they knew, that it was dark night before Mother Ceres found out that she must seek her daughter elsewhere. So she lighted a torch, and set forth, resolving never to come back until Proserpina was discovered.

In her haste and trouble of mind, she quite forgot her car and the winged dragons; or, it may be, she thought that she could follow up the search more thoroughly on foot. At all events, this was the way in which she began her sorrowful journey, holding her torch before her, and looking carefully at every object along the path. And as it happened, she had not gone far before she found one of the magnificent flowers which grew on the shrub that Proserpina had pulled up.

"Ha!" thought Mother Ceres, examining it by torchlight. "Here is mischief in this flower! The earth did not produce it by any help of mine, nor of its own accord. It is the work of enchantment, and is therefore poisonous; and perhaps it has poisoned my poor child."

But she put the poisonous flower in her bosom, not knowing whether she might ever find any other memorial of Proserpina.

All night long, at the door of every cottage and farm-house, Ceres knocked, and called up the weary laborers to inquire if they had seen her child; and they stood, gaping and half-asleep, at the threshold, and answered her pityingly, and besought her to come in and rest. At the portal of every palace, too, she made so loud a summons that the menials hurried to throw open the gate, thinking that it must be some great king or queen, who would demand a banquet for supper and a stately chamber to repose in. And when they saw only a sad and anxious woman, with a torch in her hand and a wreath of withered poppies on her head, they spoke rudely, and sometimes threatened to set the dogs upon her. But nobody had seen Proserpina, nor could give Mother Ceres the least hint which way to seek her. Thus passed the night; and still she continued her search without sitting down to rest, or stopping to take food, or even remembering to put out the torch although first the rosy dawn, and then the glad light of the morning sun, made its red flame look thin and pale. But I wonder what sort of stuff this torch was made of; for it burned dimly through the day, and, at night, was as bright as ever, and never was extinguished by the rain or wind, in all the weary days and nights while Ceres was seeking for Proserpina.

It was not merely of human beings that she asked tidings of her daughter. In the woods and by the streams, she met creatures of another nature, who used, in those old times, to haunt the pleasant and solitary places, and were very sociable with persons who understood their language and customs, as Mother Ceres did. Sometimes, for instance, she tapped with her finger against the knotted trunk of a majestic oak; and immediately its rude bark would cleave asunder, and forth would step a beautiful maiden, who was the hamadryad of the oak, dwelling inside of it, and sharing its long life, and rejoicing when its green leaves sported with the breeze. But not one of these leafy damsels had seen Proserpina. Then, going a little farther, Ceres would, perhaps, come to a fountain, gushing out of a pebbly hollow in the earth, and would dabble with her hand in the water. Behold, up through its sandy and pebbly bed, along with the fountain's gush, a young woman with dripping hair would arise, and stand gazing at Mother Ceres, half out of the water, and undulating up and down with its ever-restless motion. But when the mother asked whether her poor lost child had stopped to drink out of the fountain, the naiad, with weeping eyes (for these water-nymphs had tears to spare for everybody's grief), would answer "No!" in a murmuring voice, which was just like the murmur of the stream.

Often, likewise, she encountered fauns, who looked like sunburnt country people, except that they had hairy ears, and little horns upon their foreheads, and the hinder legs of goats, on which they gamboled merrily about the woods and fields. They were a frolicsome kind of creature but grew as sad as their cheerful dispositions would allow, when Ceres inquired for her daughter, and they had no good news to tell. But sometimes she same suddenly upon a rude gang of satyrs, who had faces like monkeys, and horses' tails behind them, and who were generally dancing in a very boisterous manner, with shouts of noisy laughter. When she stopped to question them, they would only laugh the louder, and make new merriment out of the lone woman's distress. How unkind of those ugly satyrs! And once, while crossing a solitary sheep pasture, she saw a personage named Pan, seated at the foot of a tall rock, and making music on a shepherd's flute. He, too, had horns, and hairy ears, and goats' feet; but, being acquainted with Mother Ceres, he answered her question as civilly as he knew how, and invited her to taste some milk and honey out of a wooden bowl. But neither could Pan tell her what had become of Proserpina, any better than the rest of these wild people.

And thus Mother Ceres went wandering about for nine long days and nights, finding no trace of Proserpina, unless it were now and then a withered flower; and these she picked up and put in her bosom, because she fancied that they might have fallen from her poor child's hand. All day she traveled onward through the hot sun; and, at night again, the flame of the torch would redden and gleam along the pathway, and she continued her search by its light, without ever sitting down to rest.

On the tenth day, she chanced to espy the mouth of a cavern within which (though it was bright noon everywhere else) there would have been only a dusky twilight; but it so happened that a torch was burning there. It flickered, and struggled with the duskiness, but could not half light up the gloomy cavern with all its melancholy glimmer. Ceres was resolved to leave no spot without a search; so she peeped into the entrance of the cave, and lighted it up a little more, by holding her own torch before her. In so doing, she caught a glimpse of what seemed to be a woman, sitting on the brown leaves of the last autumn, a great heap of which had been swept into the cave by the wind. This woman (if woman it were) was by no means so beautiful as many of her sex; for her head, they tell me, was shaped very much like a dog's, and, by way of ornament, she wore a wreath of snakes around it. But Mother Ceres, the moment she saw her, knew that this was an odd kind of a person, who put all her enjoyment in being miserable, and never would have a word to say to other people, unless they were as melancholy and wretched as she herself delighted to be.

"I am wretched enough now," thought poor Ceres, "to talk with this melancholy Hecate, were she ten times sadder than ever she was yet." So she stepped into the cave, and sat down on the withered leaves by the dog-headed woman's side. In all the world, since her daughter's loss, she had found no other companion.

"O Hecate," said she, "if ever you lose a daughter, you will know what sorrow is. Tell me, for pity's sake, have you seen my poor child Proserpina pass by the mouth of your cavern?"

"No," answered Hecate, in a cracked voice, and sighing betwixt every word or two; "no, Mother Ceres, I have seen nothing of your daughter. But my ears, you must know, are made in such a way, that all cries of distress and affright all over the world are pretty sure to find their way to them; and nine days ago, as I sat in my cave, making myself very miserable, I heard the voice of a young girl, shrieking as if in great distress. Something terrible has happened to the child, you may rest assured. As well as I could judge, a dragon, or some other cruel monster, was carrying her away."

"You kill me by saying so," cried Ceres, almost ready to faint. "Where was the sound, and which way did it seem to go?"

"It passed very swiftly along," said Hecate, "and, at the same time, there was a heavy rumbling of wheels towards the eastward. I can tell you nothing more, except that, in my honest opinion, you will never see your daughter again. The best advice I can give you is, to take up your abode in this cavern, where we will be the two most wretched women in the world."

"Not yet, dark Hecate," replied Ceres. "But do you first come with your torch, and help me to seek for my lost child. And when there shall be no more hope of finding her (if that black day is ordained to come), then, if you will give me room to fling myself down, either on these withered leaves or on the naked rock, I will show what it is to be miserable. But, until I know that she has perished from the face of the earth, I will not allow myself space even to grieve."

The dismal Hecate did not much like the idea of going abroad into the sunny world. But then she reflected that the sorrow of the disconsolate Ceres would be like a gloomy twilight round about them both, let the sun shine ever so brightly, and that therefore she might enjoy her bad spirits quite as well as if she were to stay in the cave. So she finally consented to go, and they set out together, both carrying torches, although it was broad daylight and clear sunshine. The torchlight seemed to make a gloom; so that the people whom they met, along the road, could not very distinctly see their figures; and, indeed, if they once caught a glimpse of Hecate, with the wreath of snakes round her forehead, they generally thought it prudent to run away, without waiting for a second glance.

As the pair traveled along in this woe-begone manner, a thought struck Ceres.

"There is one person," she exclaimed, "who must have seen my poor child, and can doubtless tell what has become of her. Why did not I think of him before? It is Phoebus."

"What," said Hecate, "the young man that always sits in the sunshine? O, pray do not think of going near him. He is a gay, light, frivolous young fellow, and will only smile in your face. And besides, there is such a glare of the sun about him, that he will quite blind my poor eyes, which I have almost wept away already."

"You have promised to be my companion," answered Ceres. "Come, let us make haste, or the sunshine will be gone, and Phoebus along with it."

Accordingly, they went along in quest of Phoebus, both of them sighing grievously, and Hecate, to say the truth, making a great deal worse lamentation than Ceres; for all the pleasure she had, you know, lay in being miserable, and therefore she made the most of it. By and by, after a pretty long journey, they arrived at the sunniest spot in the whole world. There they beheld a beautiful young man, with long, curling ringlets, which seemed to be made of golden sunbeams; his garments were like light summer clouds; and the expression of his face was so exceedingly vivid, that Hecate held her hands before her eyes, muttering that he ought to wear a black veil. Phoebus (for this was the very person whom they were seeking) had a lyre in his hands, and was making its chords tremble with sweet music; at the same time singing a most exquisite song, which he had recently composed. For, beside a great many other accomplishments, this young man was renowned for his admirable poetry.

As Ceres and her dismal companion approached him, Phoebus smiled on them so cheerfully that Hecate's wreath of snakes gave a spiteful hiss, and Hecate heartily wished herself back in her cave. But as for Ceres, she was too earnest in her grief either to know or care whether Phoebus smiled or frowned.

"Phoebus!" exclaimed she, "I am in great trouble, and have come to you for assistance. Can you tell me what has become of my dear child Proserpina?"

"Proserpina! Proserpina, did you call her name?" answered Phoebus, endeavoring to recollect; for there was such a continual flow of pleasant ideas in his mind, that he was apt to forget what had happened no longer ago than yesterday. "Ah, yes, I remember her now. A very lovely child, indeed. I am happy to tell you, my dear madam, that I did see the little Proserpina not many days ago. You may make yourself perfectly easy about her. She is safe, and in excellent hands."

"O, where is my dear child?" cried Ceres, clasping her hands, and flinging herself at his feet.

"Why," said Phoebus—and as he spoke he kept touching his lyre so as to make a thread of music run in and out among his words—"as the little damsel was gathering flowers (and she has really a very exquisite taste for flowers), she was suddenly snatched up by King Pluto, and carried off to his dominions. I have never been in that part of the universe; but the royal palace, I am told, is built in a very noble style of architecture, and of the most splendid and costly materials. Gold, diamonds, pearls, and all manner of precious stones will be your daughter's ordinary playthings. I recommend to you, my dear lady, to give yourself no uneasiness. Proserpina's sense of beauty will be duly gratified, and even in spite of the lack of sunshine, she will lead a very enviable life."

"Hush! Say not such a word!" answered Ceres, indignantly. "What is there to gratify her heart? What are all the splendors you speak of without affection? I must have her back again. Will you go with me you go with me, Phoebus, to demand my daughter of this wicked Pluto?"

"Pray excuse me," replied Phoebus, with an elegant obeisance. "I certainly wish you success, and regret that my own affairs are so immediately pressing that I cannot have the pleasure of attending you. Besides, I am not upon the best of terms with King Pluto. To tell you the truth, his three-headed mastiff would never let me pass the gateway; for I should be compelled to take a sheaf of sunbeams along with me, and those, you know, are forbidden things in Pluto's kingdom."

"Ah, Phoebus," said Ceres, with bitter meaning in her words, "you have a harp instead of a heart. Farewell."

"Will not you stay a moment," asked Phoebus, "and hear me turn the pretty and touching story of Proserpina into extemporary verses?"

But Ceres shook her head, and hastened away, along with Hecate. Phoebus (who, as I have told you, was an exquisite poet) forthwith began to make an ode about the poor mother's grief; and, if we were to judge of his sensibility by this beautiful production, he must have been endowed with a very tender heart. But when a poet gets into the habit of using his heartstrings to make chords for his lyre, he may thrum upon them as much as he will, without any great pain to himself. Accordingly, though Phoebus sang a very sad song, he was as merry all the while as were the sunbeams amid which he dwelt.

Poor Mother Ceres had now found out what had become of her daughter, but was not a whit happier than before. Her case, on the contrary, looked more desperate than ever. As long as Proserpina was above ground, there might have been hopes of regaining her. But now that the poor child was shut up within the iron gates of the king of the mines, at the threshold of which lay the three-headed Cerberus, there seemed no possibility of her ever making her escape. The dismal Hecate, who loved to take the darkest view of things, told Ceres that she had better come with her to the cavern, and spend the rest of her life in being miserable.

Ceres answered, that Hecate was welcome to go back thither herself, but that, for her part, she would wander about the earth in quest of the entrance to King Pluto's dominions. And Hecate took her at her word, and hurried back to her beloved cave, frightening a great many little children with a glimpse of her dog's face as she went.

Poor Mother Ceres! It is melancholy to think of her, pursuing her toilsome way, all alone, and holding up that never-dying torch, the flame of which seemed an emblem of the grief and hope that burned together in her heart.

So much did she suffer, that, though her aspect had been quite youthful when her troubles began, she grew to look like an elderly person in a very brief time. She cared not how she was dressed, nor had she ever thought of flinging away the wreath of withered poppies, which she put on the very morning of Proserpina's disappearance. She roamed about in so wild a way, and with her hair so disheveled, that people took her for some distracted creature, and never dreamed that this was Mother Ceres, who had the oversight of every seed which the husbandman planted. Nowadays, however, she gave herself no trouble about seed time nor harvest, but left the farmers to take care of their own affairs, and the crops to fade or flourish, as the case might be. There was nothing, now, in which Ceres seemed to feel an interest, unless when she saw children at play, or gathering flowers along the wayside. Then, indeed, she would stand and gaze at them with tears in her eyes. The children, too, appeared to have a sympathy with her grief, and would cluster themselves in a little group about her knees, and look up wistfully in her face; and Ceres, after giving them a kiss all round, would lead them to their homes, and advise their mothers never to let them stray out of sight.

"For if they do," said she, "it may happen to you, as it has to me, that the iron-hearted King Pluto will take a liking to your darlings, and snatch them up in his chariot, and carry them away."

One day, during her pilgrimage in quest of the entrance to Pluto's kingdom, she came to the palace of King Cereus, who reigned at Eleusis. Ascending a lofty flight of steps, she entered the portal, and found the royal household in very great alarm about the queen's baby. The infant, it seems, was sickly (being troubled with its teeth, I suppose), and would take no food, and was all the time moaning with pain. The queen—her name was Metanira—was desirous of funding a nurse; and when she beheld a woman of matronly aspect coming up the palace steps, she thought, in her own mind, that here was the very person whom she needed. So Queen Metanira ran to the door, with the poor wailing baby in her arms, and besought Ceres to take charge of it, or, at least, to tell her what would do it good.

"Will you trust the child entirely to me?" asked Ceres.

"Yes, and gladly, too," answered the queen, "if you will devote all your time to him. For I can see that you have been a mother."

"You are right," said Ceres. "I once had a child of my own. Well; I will be the nurse of this poor, sickly boy. But beware, I warn you, that you do not interfere with any kind of treatment which I may judge proper for him. If you do so, the poor infant must suffer for his mother's folly."

Then she kissed the child, and it seemed to do him good; for he smiled and nestled closely into her bosom.

So Mother Ceres set her torch in a corner (where it kept burning all the while), and took up her abode in the palace of King Cereus, as nurse to the little Prince Demophoon. She treated him as if he were her own child, and allowed neither the king nor the queen to say whether he should be bathed in warm or cold water, or what he should eat, or how often he should take the air, or when he should be put to bed. You would hardly believe me, if I were to tell how quickly the baby prince got rid of his ailments, and grew fat, and rosy, and strong, and how he had two rows of ivory teeth in less time than any other little fellow, before or since. Instead of the palest, and wretchedest, and puniest imp in the world (as his own mother confessed him to be, when Ceres first took him in charge), he was now a strapping baby, crowing, laughing, kicking up his heels, and rolling from one end of the room to the other. All the good women of the neighborhood crowded to the palace, and held up their hands, in unutterable amazement, at the beauty and wholesomeness of this darling little prince. Their wonder was the greater, because he was never seen to taste any food; not even so much as a cup of milk.

"Pray, nurse," the queen kept saying, "how is it that you make the child thrive so?"

"I was a mother once," Ceres always replied; "and having nursed my own child, I know what other children need."

But Queen Metanira, as was very natural, had a great curiosity to know precisely what the nurse did to her child. One night, therefore, she hid herself in the chamber where Ceres and the little prince were accustomed to sleep. There was a fire in the chimney, and it had now crumbled into great coals and embers, which lay glowing on the hearth, with a blaze flickering up now and then, and flinging a warm and ruddy light upon the walls. Ceres sat before the hearth with the child in her lap, and the firelight making her shadow dance upon the ceiling overhead. She undressed the little prince, and bathed him all over with some fragrant liquid out of a vase. The next thing she did was to rake back the red embers, and make a hollow place among them, just where the backlog had been. At last, while the baby was crowing, and clapping its fat little hands, and laughing in the nurse's face (just as you may have seen your little brother or sister do before going into its warm bath), Ceres suddenly laid him, all naked as he was, in the hollow among the red-hot embers. She then raked the ashes over him, and turned quietly away.

You may imagine, if you can, how Queen Metanira shrieked, thinking nothing less than that her dear child would be burned to a cinder. She burst forth from her hiding-place, and running to the hearth, raked open the fire, and snatched up poor little Prince Demophoon out of his bed of live coals, one of which he was gripping in each of his fists. He immediately set up a grievous cry, as babies are apt to do, when rudely startled out of a sound sleep. To the queen's astonishment and joy, she could perceive no token of the child's being injured by the hot fire in which he had lain. She now turned to Mother Ceres, and asked her to explain the mystery.

"Foolish woman," answered Ceres, "did you not promise to intrust this poor infant entirely to me? You little know the mischief you have done him. Had you left him to my care, he would have grown up like a child of celestial birth, endowed with superhuman strength and intelligence, and would have lived forever. Do you imagine that earthly children are to become immortal without being tempered to it in the fiercest heat of the fire? But you have ruined your own son. For though he will be a strong man and a hero in his day, yet, on account of your folly, he will grow old, and finally die, like the sons of other women. The weak tenderness of his mother has cost the poor boy an immortality. Farewell."

Saying these words, she kissed the little Prince Demophoon, and sighed to think what he had lost, and took her departure without heeding Queen Metanira, who entreated her to remain, and cover up the child among the hot embers as often as she pleased. Poor baby! He never slept so warmly again.

While she dwelt in the king's palace, Mother Ceres had been so continually occupied with taking care of the young prince, that her heart was a little lightened of its grief for Proserpina. But now, having nothing else to busy herself about, she became just as wretched as before. At length, in her despair, she came to the dreadful resolution that not a stalk of grain, nor a blade of grass, not a potato, nor a turnip, nor any other vegetable that was good for man or beast to eat, should be suffered to grow until her daughter were restored. She even forbade the flowers to bloom, lest somebody's heart should be cheered by their beauty.

Now, as not so much as a head of asparagus ever presumed to poke itself out of the ground, without the especial permission of Ceres, you may conceive what a terrible calamity had here fallen upon the earth. The husbandmen plowed and planted as usual; but there lay the rich black furrows, all as barren as a desert of sand. The pastures looked as brown in the sweet month of June as ever they did in chill November. The rich man's broad acres and the cottager's small garden patch were equally blighted. Every little girl's flower bed showed nothing but dry stalks. The old people shook their white heads, and said that the earth had grown aged like themselves, and was no longer capable of wearing the warm smile of summer on its face. It was really piteous to see the poor, starving cattle and sheep, how they followed behind Ceres, lowing and bleating, as if their instinct taught them to expect help from her; and everybody that was acquainted with her power besought her to have mercy on the human race, and, at all events, to let the grass grow. But Mother Ceres, though naturally of an affectionate disposition, was now inexorable.

"Never," said she. "If the earth is ever again to see any verdure, it must first grow along the path which my daughter will tread in coming back to me."

Finally, as there seemed to be no other remedy, our old friend Quicksilver was sent post-haste to King Pluto, in hopes that he might be persuaded to undo the mischief he had done, and to set everything right again, by giving up Proserpina. Quicksilver accordingly made the best of his way to the great gate, took a flying leap right over the three-headed mastiff, and stood at the door of the palace in an inconceivably short time. The servants knew him both by his face and garb; for his short cloak, and his winged cap and shoes, and his snaky staff had often been seen thereabouts in times gone by. He requested to be shown immediately into the king's presence; and Pluto, who heard his voice from the top of the stairs, and who loved to recreate himself with Quicksilver's merry talk, called out to him to come up. And while they settle their business together, we must inquire what Proserpina had been doing ever since we saw her last.

The child had declared, as you may remember, that she would not taste a mouthful of food as long as she should be compelled to remain in King Pluto's palace. How she contrived to maintain her resolution, and at the same time to keep herself tolerably plump and rosy, is more than I can explain; but some young ladies, I am given to understand, possess the faculty of living on air, and Proserpina seems to have possessed it too. At any rate, it was now six months since she left the outside of the earth; and not a morsel, so far as the attendants were able to testify, had yet passed between her teeth. This was the more creditable to Proserpina, inasmuch as King Pluto had caused her to be tempted day by day, with all manner of sweetmeats, and richly-preserved fruits, and delicacies of every sort, such as young people are generally most fond of. But her good mother had often told her of the hurtfulness of these things; and for that reason alone, if there had been no other, she would have resolutely refused to taste them.

All this time, being of a cheerful and active disposition, the little damsel was not quite so unhappy as you may have supposed. The immense palace had a thousand rooms, and was full of beautiful and wonderful objects. There was a never-ceasing gloom, it is true, which half hid itself among the innumerable pillars, gliding before the child as she wandered among them, and treading stealthily behind her in the echo of her footsteps. Neither was all the dazzle of the precious stones, which flamed with their own light, worth one gleam of natural sunshine; nor could the most brilliant of the many-colored gems, which Proserpina had for playthings, vie with the simple beauty of the flowers she used to gather. But still, whenever the girl went among those gilded halls and chambers, it seemed as if she carried nature and sunshine along with her, and as if she scattered dewy blossoms on her right hand and on her left. After Proserpina came, the palace was no longer the same abode of stately artifice and dismal magnificence that it had before been. The inhabitants all felt this, and King Pluto more than any of them.

"My own little Proserpina," he used to say. "I wish you could like me a little better. We gloomy and cloudy-natured persons have often as warm hearts, at bottom, as those of a more cheerful character. If you would only stay with me of your own accord, it would make me happier than the possession of a hundred such palaces as this."

"Ah," said Proserpina, "you should have tried to make me like you before carrying me off. And the best thing you can now do is, to let me go again. Then I might remember you sometimes, and think that you were as kind as you knew how to be. Perhaps, too, one day or other, I might come back, and pay you a visit."

"No, no," answered Pluto, with his gloomy smile, "I will not trust you for that. You are too fond of living in the broad daylight, and gathering flowers. What an idle and childish taste that is! Are not these gems, which I have ordered to be dug for you, and which are richer than any in my crown—are they not prettier than a violet?"

"Not half so pretty," said Proserpina, snatching the gems from Pluto's hand, and flinging them to the other end of the hall. "O my sweet violets, shall I never see you again?"

And then she burst into tears. But young people's tears have very little saltness or acidity in them, and do not inflame the eyes so much as those of grown persons; so that it is not to be wondered at, if, a few moments afterwards, Proserpina was sporting through the hall almost as merrily as she and the four sea nymphs had sported along the edge of the surf wave. King Pluto gazed after her, and wished that he, too, was a child. And little Proserpina, when she turned about, and beheld this great king standing in his splendid hall, and looking so grand, and so melancholy, and so lonesome, was smitten with a kind of pity. She ran back to him, and, for the first time in all her life, put her small, soft hand in his.

"I love you a little," whispered she, looking up in his face.

"Do you, indeed, my dear child?" cried Pluto, bending his dark face down to kiss her; but Proserpina shrank away from the kiss, for, though his features were noble, they were very dusky and grim. "Well, I have not deserved it of you, after keeping you a prisoner for so many months, and starving you besides. Are you not terribly hungry? Is there nothing which I can get you to eat?"

In asking this question, the king of the mines had a very cunning purpose; for, you will recollect, if Proserpina tasted a morsel of food in his dominions, she would never afterwards be at liberty to quit them.

"No indeed," said Proserpina. "Your head cook is always baking, and stewing, and roasting, and rolling out paste, and contriving one dish or another, which he imagines may be to my liking. But he might just as well save himself the trouble, poor, fat little man that he is. I have no appetite for anything in the world, unless it were a slice of bread, of my mother's own baking, or a little fruit out of her garden."

When Pluto heard this, he began to see that he had mistaken the best method of tempting Proserpina to eat. The cook's made dishes and artificial dainties were not half so delicious, in the good child's opinion, as the simple fare to which Mother Ceres had accustomed her. Wondering that he had never thought of it before, the king now sent one of his trusty attendants with a large basket, to get some of the finest and juiciest pears, peaches, and plums which could anywhere be found in the upper world. Unfortunately, however, this was during the time when Ceres had forbidden any fruits or vegetables to grow; and, after seeking all over the earth, King Pluto's servant found only a single pomegranate, and that so dried up as not to be worth eating. Nevertheless, since there was no better to be had, he brought this dry, old withered pomegranate home to the palace, put it on a magnificent golden salver, and carried it up to Proserpina. Now, it happened, curiously enough, that, just as the servant was bringing the pomegranate into the back door of the palace, our friend Quicksilver had gone up the front steps, on his errand to get Proserpina away from King Pluto.

As soon as Proserpina saw the pomegranate on the golden salver, she told the servant he had better take it away again.

"I shall not touch it, I assure you," said she. "If I were ever so hungry, I should never think of eating such a miserable, dry pomegranate as that."

"It is the only one in the world," said the servant.

He set down the golden salver, with the wizened pomegranate upon it, and left the room. When he was gone, Proserpina could not help coming close to the table, and looking at this poor specimen of dried fruit with a great deal of eagerness; for, to say the truth, on seeing something that suited her taste, she felt all the six months' appetite taking possession of her at once. To be sure, it was a very wretched-looking pomegranate, and seemed to have no more juice in it than an oyster shell. But there was no choice of such things in King Pluto's palace. This was the first fruit she had seen there, and the last she was ever likely to see; and unless she ate it up immediately, it would grow drier than it already was, and be wholly unfit to eat.

"At least, I may smell it," thought Proserpina.

So she took up the pomegranate, and applied it to her nose; and, somehow or other, being in such close neighborhood to her mouth, the fruit found its way into that little red cave. Dear me! what an everlasting pity! Before Proserpina knew what she was about, her teeth had actually bitten it, of their own accord. Just as this fatal deed was done, the door of the apartment opened, and in came King Pluto, followed by Quicksilver, who had been urging him to let his little prisoner go. At the first noise of their entrance, Proserpina withdrew the pomegranate from her mouth. But Quicksilver (whose eyes were very keen, and his wits the sharpest that ever anybody had) perceived that the child was a little confused; and seeing the empty salver, he suspected that she had been taking a sly nibble of something or other. As for honest Pluto, he never guessed at the secret.

"My little Proserpina," said the king, sitting down, and affectionately drawing her between his knees, "here is Quicksilver, who tells me that a great many misfortunes have befallen innocent people on account of my detaining you in my dominions. To confess the truth, I myself had already reflected that it was an unjustifiable act to take you away from your good mother. But, then, you must consider, my dear child, that this vast palace is apt to be gloomy (although the precious stones certainly shine very bright), and that I am not of the most cheerful disposition, and that therefore it was a natural thing enough to seek for the society of some merrier creature than myself. I hoped you would take my crown for a plaything, and me—ah, you laugh, naughty Proserpina—me, grim as I am, for a playmate. It was a silly expectation."

"Not so extremely silly," whispered Proserpina. "You have really amused me very much, sometimes."

"Thank you," said King Pluto, rather dryly. "But I can see plainly enough, that you think my palace a dusky prison, and me the iron-hearted keeper of it. And an iron heart I should surely have, if I could detain you here any longer, my poor child, when it is now six months since you tasted food. I give you your liberty. Go with Quicksilver. Hasten home to your dear mother."

Now, although you may not have supposed it, Proserpina found it impossible to take leave of poor King Pluto without some regrets, and a good deal of compunction for not telling him about the pomegranate. She even shed a tear or two, thinking how lonely and cheerless the great palace would seem to him, with all its ugly glare of artificial light, after she herself—his one little ray of natural sunshine, whom he had stolen, to be sure, but only because he valued her so much—after she should have departed. I know not how many kind things she might have said to the disconsolate king of the mines, had not Quicksilver hurried her way.

"Come along quickly," whispered he in her ear, "or his majesty may change his royal mind. And take care, above all things, that you say nothing of what was brought you on the golden salver."

In a very short time, they had passed the great gateway (leaving the three-headed Cerberus, barking, and yelping, and growling, with threefold din, behind them), and emerged upon the surface of the earth. It was delightful to behold, as Proserpina hastened along, how the path grew verdant behind and on either side of her. Wherever she set her blessed foot, there was at once a dewy flower. The violets gushed up along the wayside. The grass and the grain began to sprout with tenfold vigor and luxuriance, to make up for the dreary months that had been wasted in barrenness. The starved cattle immediately set to work grazing, after their long fast, and ate enormously, all day, and got up at midnight to eat more.

But I can assure you it was a busy time of year with the farmers, when they found the summer coming upon them with such a rush. Nor must I forget to say, that all the birds in the whole world hopped about upon the newly-blossoming trees, and sang together, in a prodigious ecstasy of joy.

Mother Ceres had returned to her deserted home, and was sitting disconsolately on the doorstep, with her torch burning in her hand. She had been idly watching the flame for some moments past, when, all at once, it flickered and went out.

"What does this mean?" thought she. "It was an enchanted torch, and should have kept burning till my child came back."

Lifting her eyes, she was surprised to see a sudden verdure flashing over the brown and barren fields, exactly as you may have observed a golden hue gleaming far and wide across the landscape, from the just risen sun.

"Does the earth disobey me?" exclaimed Mother Ceres, indignantly. "Does it presume to be green, when I have bidden it be barren, until my daughter shall be restored to my arms?"

"Then open your arms, dear mother," cried a well-known voice, "and take your little daughter into them."

And Proserpina came running, and flung herself upon her mother's bosom. Their mutual transport is not to be described. The grief of their separation had caused both of them to shed a great many tears; and now they shed a great many more, because their joy could not so well express itself in any other way.

When their hearts had grown a little more quiet, Mother Ceres looked anxiously at Proserpina.

"My child," said she, "did you taste any food while you were in King Pluto's palace?"

"Dearest mother," exclaimed Proserpina, "I will tell you the whole truth. Until this very morning, not a morsel of food had passed my lips. But to-day, they brought me a pomegranate (a very dry one it was, and all shriveled up, till there was little left of it but seeds and skin), and having seen no fruit for so long a time, and being faint with hunger, I was tempted just to bite it. The instant I tasted it, King Pluto and Quicksilver came into the room. I had not swallowed a morsel; but—dear mother, I hope it was no harm—but six of the pomegranate seeds, I am afraid, remained in my mouth."

"Ah, unfortunate child, and miserable me!" exclaimed Ceres. "For each of those six pomegranate seeds you must spend one month of every year in King Pluto's palace. You are but half restored to your mother. Only six months with me, and six with that good-for-nothing King of Darkness!"

"Do not speak so harshly of poor King Pluto," said Prosperina, kissing her mother. "He has some very good qualities; and I really think I can bear to spend six months in his palace, if he will only let me spend the other six with you. He certainly did very wrong to carry me off; but then, as he says, it was but a dismal sort of life for him, to live in that great gloomy place, all alone; and it has made a wonderful change in his spirits to have a little girl to run up stairs and down. There is some comfort in making him so happy; and so, upon the whole, dearest mother, let us be thankful that he is not to keep me the whole year round."

THE GOLDEN FLEECE.

When Jason, the son of the dethroned King of Iolchos, was a little boy, he was sent away from his parents, and placed under the queerest schoolmaster that ever you heard of. This learned person was one of the people, or quadrupeds, called Centaurs. He lived in a cavern, and had the body and legs of a white horse, with the head and shoulders of a man. His name was Chiron; and, in spite of his odd appearance, he was a very excellent teacher, and had several scholars, who afterwards did him credit by making a great figure in the world. The famous Hercules was one, and so was Achilles, and Philoctetes likewise, and Aesculapius, who acquired immense repute as a doctor. The good Chiron taught his pupils how to play upon the harp, and how to cure diseases, and how to use the sword and shield, together with various other branches of education, in which the lads of those days used to be instructed, instead of writing and arithmetic.

I have sometimes suspected that Master Chiron was not really very different from other people, but that, being a kind-hearted and merry old fellow, he was in the habit of making believe that he was a horse, and scrambling about the schoolroom on all fours, and letting the little boys ride upon his back. And so, when his scholars had grown up, and grown old, and were trotting their grandchildren on their knees, they told them about the sports of their school days; and these young folks took the idea that their grandfathers had been taught their letters by a Centaur, half man and half horse. Little children, not quite understanding what is said to them, often get such absurd notions into their heads, you know.

Be that as it may, it has always been told for a fact (and always will be told, as long as the world lasts), that Chiron, with the head of a schoolmaster, had the body and legs of a horse. Just imagine the grave old gentleman clattering and stamping into the schoolroom on his four hoofs, perhaps treading on some little fellow's toes, flourishing his switch tail instead of a rod, and, now and then, trotting out of doors to eat a mouthful of grass! I wonder what the blacksmith charged him for a set of iron shoes?

So Jason dwelt in the cave, with this four-footed Chiron, from the time that he was an infant, only a few months old, until he had grown to the full height of a man. He became a very good harper, I suppose, and skilful in the use of weapons, and tolerably acquainted with herbs and other doctor's stuff, and, above all, an admirable horseman; for, in teaching young people to ride, the good Chiron must have been without a rival among schoolmasters. At length, being now a tall and athletic youth, Jason resolved to seek his fortune in the world, without asking Chiron's advice, or telling him anything about the matter. This was very unwise, to be sure; and I hope none of you, my little hearers, will ever follow Jason's example.

But, you are to understand, he had heard how that he himself was a prince royal, and how his father, King Jason, had been deprived of the kingdom of Iolchos by a certain Pelias, who would also have killed Jason, had he not been hidden in the Centaur's cave. And, being come to the strength of a man, Jason determined to set all this business to rights, and to punish the wicked Pelias for wronging his dear father, and to cast him down from the throne, and seat himself there instead.

With this intention, he took a spear in each hand, and threw a leopard's skin over his shoulders, to keep off the rain, and set forth on his travels, with his long yellow ringlets waving in the wind. The part of his dress on which he most prided himself was a pair of sandals, that had been his father's. They were handsomely embroidered, and were tied upon his feet with strings of gold. But his whole attire was such as people did not very often see; and as he passed along, the women and children ran to the doors and windows, wondering whither this beautiful youth was journeying, with his leopard's skin and his golden-tied sandals, and what heroic deeds he meant to perform, with a spear in his right hand and another in his left.

I know not how far Jason had traveled, when he came to a turbulent river, which rushed right across his pathway, with specks of white foam among its black eddies, hurrying tumultuously onward, and roaring angrily as it went. Though not a very broad river in the dry seasons of the year, it was now swollen by heavy rains and by the melting of the snow on the sides of Mount Olympus; and it thundered so loudly, and looked so wild and dangerous, that Jason, bold as he was, thought it prudent to pause upon the brink. The bed of the stream seemed to be strewn with sharp and rugged rocks, some of which thrust themselves above the water. By and by, an uprooted tree, with shattered branches, came drifting along the current, and got entangled among the rocks. Now and then, a drowned sheep, and once the carcass of a cow, floated past.

In short, the swollen river had already done a great deal of mischief. It was evidently too deep for Jason to wade, and too boisterous for him to swim; he could see no bridge; and as for a boat, had there been any, the rocks would have broken it to pieces in an instant.

"See the poor lad," said a cracked voice close to his side. "He must have had but a poor education, since he does not know how to cross a little stream like this. Or is he afraid of wetting his fine golden-stringed sandals? It is a pity his four-footed schoolmaster is not here to carry him safely across on his back!"

Jason looked round greatly surprised, for he did not know that anybody was near. But beside him stood an old woman, with a ragged mantle over her head, leaning on a staff, the top of which was carved into the shape of a cuckoo. She looked very aged, and wrinkled, and infirm; and yet her eyes, which were as brown as those of an ox, were so extremely large and beautiful, that, when they were fixed on Jason's eyes, he could see nothing else but them. The old woman had a pomegranate in her hand, although the fruit was then quite out of season.

"Whither are you going, Jason?" she now asked.

She seemed to know his name, you will observe; and, indeed, those great brown eyes looked as if they had a knowledge of everything, whether past or to come. While Jason was gazing at her, a peacock strutted forward, and took his stand at the old woman's side.

"I am going to Iolchos," answered the young man, "to bid the wicked King Pelias come down from my father's throne, and let me reign in his stead."

"Ah, well, then," said the old woman, still with the same cracked voice, "if that is all your business, you need not be in a very great hurry. Just take me on your back, there's a good youth, and carry me across the river. I and my peacock have something to do on the other side, as well as yourself."

"Good mother," replied Jason, "your business can hardly be so important as the pulling down a king from his throne. Besides, as you may see for yourself, the river is very boisterous; and if I should chance to stumble, it would sweep both of us away more easily than it has carried off yonder uprooted tree. I would gladly help you if I could; but I doubt whether I am strong enough to carry you across."

"Then," said she, very scornfully, "neither are you strong enough to pull King Pelias off his throne. And, Jason, unless you will help an old woman at her need, you ought not to be a king. What are kings made for, save to succor the feeble and distressed? But do as you please. Either take me on your back, or with my poor old limbs I shall try my best to struggle across the stream."

Saying this, the old woman poked with her staff in the river, as if to find the safest place in its rocky bed where she might make the first step. But Jason, by this time, had grown ashamed of his reluctance to help her. He felt that he could never forgive himself, if this poor feeble creature should come to any harm in attempting to wrestle against the headlong current. The good Chiron, whether half horse or no, had taught him that the noblest use of his strength was to assist the weak; and also that he must treat every young woman as if she were his sister, and every old one like a mother. Remembering these maxims, the vigorous and beautiful young man knelt down, and requested the good dame to mount upon his back.

"The passage seems to me not very safe," he remarked. "But as your business is so urgent, I will try to carry you across. If the river sweeps you away, it shall take me too."

"That, no doubt, will be a great comfort to both of us," quoth the old woman. "But never fear. We shall get safely across."

So she threw her arms around Jason's neck; and lifting her from the ground, he stepped boldly into the raging and foaming current, and began to stagger away from the shore. As for the peacock, it alighted on the old dame's shoulder. Jason's two spears, one in each hand, kept him from stumbling, and enabled him to feel his way among the hidden rocks; although every instant, he expected that his companion and himself would go down the stream, together with the driftwood of shattered trees, and the carcasses of the sheep and cow. Down came the cold, snowy torrent from the steep side of Olympus, raging and thundering as if it had a real spite against Jason, or, at all events, were determined to snatch off his living burden from his shoulders. When he was half way across, the uprooted tree (which I have already told you about) broke loose from among the rocks, and bore down upon him, with all its splintered branches sticking out like the hundred arms of the giant Briareus. It rushed past, however, without touching him. But the next moment his foot was caught in a crevice between two rocks, and stuck there so fast, that, in the effort to get free, he lost one of his golden-stringed sandals.

At this accident Jason could not help uttering a cry of vexation.

"What is the matter, Jason?" asked the old woman.

"Matter enough," said the young man. "I have lost a sandal here among the rocks. And what sort of a figure shall I cut, at the court of King Pelias, with a golden-stringed sandal on one foot, and the other foot bare!"

"Do not take it to heart," answered his companion cheerily. "You never met with better fortune than in losing that sandal. It satisfies me that you are the very person whom the Speaking Oak has been talking about."

There was no time, just then, to inquire what the Speaking Oak had said. But the briskness of her tone encouraged the young man; and, besides, he had never in his life felt so vigorous and mighty as since taking this old woman on his back. Instead of being exhausted, he gathered strength as he went on; and, struggling up against the torrent, he at last gained the opposite shore, clambered up the bank, and set down the old dame and her peacock safely on the grass. As soon as this was done, however, he could not help looking rather despondently at his bare foot, with only a remnant of the golden string of the sandal clinging round his ankle.

"You will get a handsomer pair of sandals by and by," said the old woman, with a kindly look out of her beautiful brown eyes. "Only let King Pelias get a glimpse of that bare foot, and you shall see him turn as pale as ashes, I promise you. There is your path. Go along, my good Jason, and my blessing go with you. And when you sit on your throne remember the old woman whom you helped over the river."

With these words, she hobbled away, giving him a smile over her shoulder as she departed.

Whether the light of her beautiful brown eyes threw a glory round about her, or whatever the cause might be, Jason fancied that there was something very noble and majestic in her figure, after all, and that, though her gait seemed to be a rheumatic hobble, yet she moved with as much grace and dignity as any queen on earth. Her peacock, which had now fluttered down from her shoulder, strutted behind her in a prodigious pomp, and spread out its magnificent tail on purpose for Jason to admire it.

When the old dame and her peacock were out of sight, Jason set forward on his journey. After traveling a pretty long distance, he came to a town situated at the foot of a mountain, and not a great way from the shore of the sea. On the outside of the town there was an immense crowd of people, not only men and women, but children too, all in their best clothes, and evidently enjoying a holiday. The crowd was thickest towards the sea-shore; and in that direction, over the people's heads, Jason saw a wreath of smoke curling upward to the blue sky. He inquired of one of the multitude what town it was near by, and why so many persons were here assembled together.

"This is the kingdom of Iolchos," answered the man, "and we are the subjects of King Pelias. Our monarch has summoned us together, that we may see him sacrifice a black bull to Neptune, who, they say, is his majesty's father. Yonder is the king, where you see the smoke going up from the altar."

While the man spoke he eyed Jason with great curiosity; for his garb was quite unlike that of the Iolchians, and it looked very odd to see a youth with a leopard's skin over his shoulders, and each hand grasping a spear. Jason perceived, too, that the man stared particularly at his feet, one of which, you remember, was bare, while the other was decorated with his father's golden-stringed sandal.

"Look at him! only look at him!" said the man to his next neighbor. "Do you see? He wears but one sandal!"

Upon this, first one person, and then another, began to stare at Jason, and everybody seemed to be greatly struck with something in his aspect; though they turned their eyes much oftener towards his feet than to any other part of his figure. Besides, he could hear them whispering to one another.

"One sandal! One sandal!" they kept saying. "The man with one sandal! Here he is at last! Whence has he come? What does he mean to do? What will the king say to the one-sandaled man?"

Poor Jason was greatly abashed, and made up his mind that the people of Iolchos were exceedingly ill-bred, to take such public notice of an accidental deficiency in his dress. Meanwhile, whether it were that they hustled him forward, or that Jason, of his own accord, thrust a passage through the crowd, it so happened that he soon found himself close to the smoking altar, where King Pelias was sacrificing the black bull. The murmur and hum of the multitude, in their surprise at the spectacle of Jason with his one bare foot, grew so loud that it disturbed the ceremonies; and the king, holding the great knife with which he was just going to cut the bull's throat, turned angrily about, and fixed his eyes on Jason. The people had now withdrawn from around him, so that the youth stood in an open space, near the smoking altar, front to front with the angry King Pelias.

"Who are you?" cried the king, with a terrible frown. "And how dare you make this disturbance, while I am sacrificing a black bull to my father Neptune?"

"It is no fault of mine," answered Jason. "Your majesty must blame the rudeness of your subjects, who have raised all this tumult because one of my feet happens to be bare."

When Jason said this, the king gave a quick startled glance down at his feet.

"Ha!" muttered he, "here is the one-sandaled fellow, sure enough! What can I do with him?"

And he clutched more closely the great knife in his hand, as if he were half a mind to slay Jason, instead of the black bull. The people round about caught up the king's words, indistinctly as they were uttered; and first there was a murmur amongst them, and then a loud shout.

"The one-sandaled man has come! The prophecy must be fulfilled!"

For you are to know, that, many years before, King Pelias had been told by the Speaking Oak of Dodona, that a man with one sandal should cast him down from his throne. On this account, he had given strict orders that nobody should ever come into his presence, unless both sandals were securely tied upon his feet; and he kept an officer in his palace, whose sole business it was to examine people's sandals, and to supply them with a new pair, at the expense of the royal treasury, as soon as the old ones began to wear out. In the whole course of the king's reign, he had never been thrown into such a fright and agitation as by the spectacle of poor Jason's bare foot. But, as he was naturally a bold and hard-hearted man, he soon took courage, and began to consider in what way he might rid himself of this terrible one-sandaled stranger.

"My good young man," said King Pelias, taking the softest tone imaginable, in order to throw Jason off his guard, "you are excessively welcome to my kingdom. Judging by your dress, you must have traveled a long distance, for it is not the fashion to wear leopard skins in this part of the world. Pray what may I call your name? and where did you receive your education?"

"My name is Jason," answered the young stranger. "Ever since my infancy, I have dwelt in the cave of Chiron the Centaur. He was my instructor, and taught me music, and horsemanship, and how to cure wounds, and likewise how to inflict wounds with my weapons!"

"I have heard of Chiron the schoolmaster," replied King Pelias, "and how that there is an immense deal of learning and wisdom in his head, although it happens to be set on a horse's body. It gives me great delight to see one of his scholars at my court. But to test how much you have profited under so excellent a teacher, will you allow me to ask you a single question?"

"I do not pretend to be very wise," said Jason. "But ask me what you please, and I will answer to the best of my ability."

Now King Pelias meant cunningly to entrap the young man, and to make him say something that should be the cause of mischief and distraction to himself. So, with a crafty and evil smile upon his face, he spoke as follows:

"What would you do, brave Jason," asked he, "if there were a man in the world, by whom, as you had reason to believe, you were doomed to be ruined and slain—what would you do, I say, if that man stood before you, and in your power?"

When Jason saw the malice and wickedness which King Pelias could not prevent from gleaming out of his eyes, he probably guessed that the king had discovered what he came for, and that he intended to turn his own words against himself. Still he scorned to tell a falsehood. Like an upright and honorable prince as he was, he determined to speak out the real truth. Since the king had chosen to ask him the question, and since Jason had promised him an answer, there was no right way save to tell him precisely what would be the most prudent thing to do, if he had his worst enemy in his power.

Therefore, after a moment's consideration, he spoke up, with a firm and manly voice.

"I would send such a man," said he, "in quest of the Golden Fleece!"

This enterprise, you will understand, was, of all others, the most difficult and dangerous in the world. In the first place it would be necessary to make a long voyage through unknown seas. There was hardly a hope, or a possibility, that any young man who should undertake this voyage would either succeed in obtaining the Golden Fleece, or would survive to return home, and tell of the perils he had run. The eyes of King Pelias sparkled with joy, therefore, when he heard Jason's reply.

"Well said, wise man with the one sandal!" cried he. "Go, then, and at the peril of your life, bring me back the Golden Fleece."

"I go," answered Jason, composedly. "If I fail, you need not fear that I will ever come back to trouble you again. But if I return to Iolchos with the prize, then, King Pelias, you must hasten down from your lofty throne, and give me your crown and sceptre."

"That I will," said the king, with a sneer. "Meantime, I will keep them very safely for you."

The first thing that Jason thought of doing, after he left the king's presence, was to go to Dodona, and inquire of the Talking Oak what course it was best to pursue. This wonderful tree stood in the center of an ancient wood. Its stately trunk rose up a hundred feet into the air, and threw a broad and dense shadow over more than an acre of ground. Standing beneath it, Jason looked up among the knotted branches and green leaves, and into the mysterious heart of the old tree, and spoke aloud, as if he were addressing some person who was hidden in the depths of the foliage.

"What shall I do," said he, "in order to win the Golden Fleece?"

At first there was a deep silence, not only within the shadow of the Talking Oak, but all through the solitary wood. In a moment or two, however, the leaves of the oak began to stir and rustle, as if a gentle breeze were wandering amongst them, although the other trees of the wood were perfectly still. The sound grew louder, and became like the roar of a high wind. By and by, Jason imagined that he could distinguish words, but very confusedly, because each separate leaf of the tree seemed to be a tongue, and the whole myriad of tongues were babbling at once. But the noise waxed broader and deeper, until it resembled a tornado sweeping through the oak, and making one great utterance out of the thousand and thousand of little murmurs which each leafy tongue had caused by its rustling. And now, though it still had the tone of a mighty wind roaring among the branches, it was also like a deep bass voice, speaking as distinctly as a tree could be expected to speak, the following words:

"Go to Argus, the shipbuilder, and bid him build a galley with fifty oars."

Then the voice melted again into the indistinct murmur of the rustling leaves, and died gradually away. When it was quite gone, Jason felt inclined to doubt whether he had actually heard the words, or whether his fancy had not shaped them out of the ordinary sound made by a breeze, while passing through the thick foliage of the tree.

But on inquiry among the people of Iolchos, he found that there was really a man in the city, by the name of Argus, who was a very skilful builder of vessels. This showed some intelligence in the oak; else how should it have known that any such person existed? At Jason's request, Argus readily consented to build him a galley so big that it should require fifty strong men to row it; although no vessel of such a size and burden had heretofore been seen in the world. So the head carpenter and all his journeymen and apprentices began their work; and for a good while afterwards, there they were, busily employed, hewing out the timbers, and making a great clatter with their hammers; until the new ship, which was called the Argo, seemed to be quite ready for sea. And, as the Talking Oak had already given him such good advice, Jason thought that it would not be amiss to ask for a little more. He visited it again, therefore, and standing beside its huge, rough trunk, inquired what he should do next.

This time, there was no such universal quivering of the leaves, throughout the whole tree, as there had been before. But after a while, Jason observed that the foliage of a great branch which stretched above his head had begun to rustle, as if the wind were stirring that one bough, while all the other boughs of the oak were at rest.

"Cut me off!" said the branch, as soon as it could speak distinctly; "cut me off! cut me off! and carve me into a figure-head for your galley."

Accordingly, Jason took the branch at its word, and lopped it off the tree. A carver in the neighborhood engaged to make the figurehead. He was a tolerably good workman, and had already carved several figure-heads, in what he intended for feminine shapes, and looking pretty much like those which we see nowadays stuck up under a vessel's bowsprit, with great staring eyes, that never wink at the dash of the spray. But (what was very strange) the carver found that his hand was guided by some unseen power, and by a skill beyond his own, and that his tools shaped out an image which he had never dreamed of. When the work was finished, it turned out to be the figure of a beautiful woman, with a helmet on her head, from beneath which the long ringlets fell down upon her shoulders. On the left arm was a shield, and in its center appeared a lifelike representation of the head of Medusa with the snaky locks. The right arm was extended, as if pointing onward. The face of this wonderful statue, though not angry or forbidding, was so grave and majestic, that perhaps you might call it severe; and as for the mouth, it seemed just ready to unclose its lips, and utter words of the deepest wisdom.

Jason was delighted with the oaken image, and gave the carver no rest until it was completed, and set up where a figure-head has always stood, from that time to this, in the vessel's prow.

"And now," cried he, as he stood gazing at the calm, majestic face of the statue, "I must go to the Talking Oak and inquire what next to do."

"There is no need of that, Jason," said a voice which, though it was far lower, reminded him of the mighty tones of the great oak. "When you desire good advice, you can seek it of me."

Jason had been looking straight into the face of the image when these words were spoken. But he could hardly believe either his ears or his eyes. The truth was, however, that the oaken lips had moved, and, to all appearance, the voice had proceeded from the statue's mouth. Recovering a little from his surprise, Jason bethought himself that the image had been carved out of the wood of the Talking Oak, and that, therefore, it was really no great wonder, but on the contrary, the most natural thing in the world, that it should possess the faculty of speech. It would have been very odd, indeed, if it had not. But certainly it was a great piece of good fortune that he should be able to carry so wise a block of wood along with him in his perilous voyage.

"Tell me, wondrous image," exclaimed Jason,—"since you inherit the wisdom of the Speaking Oak of Dodona, whose daughter you are,—tell me, where shall I find fifty bold youths, who will take each of them an oar of my galley? They must have sturdy arms to row, and brave hearts to encounter perils, or we shall never win the Golden Fleece."

"Go," replied the oaken image, "go, summon all the heroes of Greece."

And, in fact, considering what a great deed was to be done, could any advice be wiser than this which Jason received from the figure-head of his vessel? He lost no time in sending messengers to all the cities, and making known to the whole people of Greece, that Prince Jason, the son of King Jason, was going in quest of the Fleece of Gold, and that he desired the help of forty-nine of the bravest and strongest young men alive, to row his vessel and share his dangers. And Jason himself would be the fiftieth.

At this news, the adventurous youths, all over the country, began to bestir themselves. Some of them had already fought with giants, and slain dragons; and the younger ones, who had not yet met with such good fortune, thought it a shame to have lived so long without getting astride of a flying serpent, or sticking their spears into a Chimaera, or, at least, thrusting their right arms down a monstrous lion's throat. There was a fair prospect that they would meet with plenty of such adventures before finding the Golden Fleece. As soon as they could furbish up their helmets and shields, therefore, and gird on their trusty swords, they came thronging to Iolchos, and clambered on board the new galley. Shaking hands with Jason, they assured him that they did not care a pin for their lives, but would help row the vessel to the remotest edge of the world, and as much farther as he might think it best to go.

Many of these brave fellows had been educated by Chiron, the four-footed pedagogue, and were therefore old schoolmates of Jason, and knew him to be a lad of spirit. The mighty Hercules, whose shoulders afterwards upheld the sky, was one of them. And there were Castor and Pollux, the twin brothers, who were never accused of being chicken-hearted, although they had been hatched out of an egg; and Theseus, who was so renowned for killing the Minotaur, and Lynceus, with his wonderfully sharp eyes, which could see through a millstone, or look right down into the depths of the earth, and discover the treasures that were there; and Orpheus, the very best of harpers, who sang and played upon his lyre so sweetly, that the brute beasts stood upon their hind legs, and capered merrily to the music. Yes, and at some of his more moving tunes, the rocks bestirred their moss-grown bulk out of the ground, and a grove of forest trees uprooted themselves, and, nodding their tops to one another, performed a country dance.

One of the rowers was a beautiful young woman, named Atalanta, who had been nursed among the mountains by a bear. So light of foot was this fair damsel, that she could step from one foamy crest of a wave to the foamy crest of another, without wetting more than the sole of her sandal. She had grown up in a very wild way, and talked much about the rights of women, and loved hunting and war far better than her needle. But in my opinion, the most remarkable of this famous company were two sons of the North Wind (airy youngsters, and of rather a blustering disposition) who had wings on their shoulders, and, in case of a calm, could puff out their cheeks, and blow almost as fresh a breeze as their father. I ought not to forget the prophets and conjurors, of whom there were several in the crew, and who could foretell what would happen to-morrow or the next day, or a hundred years hence, but were generally quite unconscious of what was passing at the moment.

Jason appointed Tiphys to be helmsman because he was a star-gazer, and knew the points of the compass. Lynceus, on account of his sharp sight, was stationed as a look-out in the prow, where he saw a whole day's sail ahead, but was rather apt to overlook things that lay directly under his nose. If the sea only happened to be deep enough, however, Lynceus could tell you exactly what kind of rocks or sands were at the bottom of it; and he often cried out to his companions, that they were sailing over heaps of sunken treasure, which yet he was none the richer for beholding. To confess the truth, few people believed him when he said it.

Well! But when the Argonauts, as these fifty brave adventurers were called, had prepared everything for the voyage, an unforeseen difficulty threatened to end it before it was begun. The vessel, you must understand, was so long, and broad, and ponderous, that the united force of all the fifty was insufficient to shove her into the water. Hercules, I suppose, had not grown to his full strength, else he might have set her afloat as easily as a little boy launches his boat upon a puddle. But here were these fifty heroes, pushing, and straining, and growing red in the face, without making the Argo start an inch. At last, quite wearied out, they sat themselves down on the shore exceedingly disconsolate, and thinking that the vessel must be left to rot and fall in pieces, and that they must either swim across the sea or lose the Golden Fleece.

All at once, Jason bethought himself of the galley's miraculous figure-head.

"O, daughter of the Talking Oak," cried he, "how shall we set to work to get our vessel into the water?"

"Seat yourselves," answered the image (for it had known what had ought to be done from the very first, and was only waiting for the question to be put),—"seat yourselves, and handle your oars, and let Orpheus play upon his harp."

Immediately the fifty heroes got on board, and seizing their oars, held them perpendicularly in the air, while Orpheus (who liked such a task far better than rowing) swept his fingers across the harp. At the first ringing note of the music, they felt the vessel stir. Orpheus thrummed away briskly, and the galley slid at once into the sea, dipping her prow so deeply that the figure-head drank the wave with its marvelous lips, and rising again as buoyant as a swan. The rowers plied their fifty oars; the white foam boiled up before the prow; the water gurgled and bubbled in their wake; while Orpheus continued to play so lively a strain of music, that the vessel seemed to dance over the billows by way of keeping time to it. Thus triumphantly did the Argo sail out of the harbor, amidst the huzzas and good wishes of everybody except the wicked old Pelias, who stood on a promontory, scowling at her, and wishing that he could blow out of his lungs the tempest of wrath that was in his heart, and so sink the galley with all on board. When they had sailed above fifty miles over the sea, Lynceus happened to cast his sharp eyes behind, and said that there was this bad-hearted king, still perched upon the promontory, and scowling so gloomily that it looked like a black thunder-cloud in that quarter of the horizon.

In order to make the time pass away more pleasantly during the voyage, the heroes talked about the Golden Fleece. It originally belonged, it appears, to a Boeotian ram, who had taken on his back two children, when in danger of their lives, and fled with them over land and sea as far as Colchis. One of the children, whose name was Helle, fell into the sea and was drowned. But the other (a little boy, named Phrixus) was brought safe ashore by the faithful ram, who, however, was so exhausted that he immediately lay down and died. In memory of this good deed, and as a token of his true heart, the fleece of the poor dead ram was miraculously changed to gold, and became one of the most beautiful objects ever seen on earth. It was hung upon a tree in a sacred grove, where it had now been kept I know not how many years, and was the envy of mighty kings, who had nothing so magnificent in any of their palaces.

If I were to tell you all the adventures of the Argonauts, it would take me till nightfall, and perhaps a great deal longer. There was no lack of wonderful events, as you may judge from what you have already heard. At a certain island, they were hospitably received by King Cyzicus, its sovereign, who made a feast for them, and treated them like brothers. But the Argonauts saw that this good king looked downcast and very much troubled, and they therefore inquired of him what was the matter. King Cyzicus hereupon informed them that he and his subjects were greatly abused and incommoded by the inhabitants of a neighboring mountain, who made war upon them, and killed many people, and ravaged the country. And while they were talking about it, Cyzicus pointed to the mountain, and asked Jason and his companions what they saw there.

"I see some very tall objects," answered Jason; "but they are at such a distance that I cannot distinctly make out what they are. To tell your majesty the truth, they look so very strangely that I am inclined to think them clouds, which have chanced to take something like human shapes."

"I see them very plainly," remarked Lynceus, whose eyes, you know, were as far-sighted as a telescope. "They are a band of enormous giants, all of whom have six arms apiece, and a club, a sword, or some other weapon in each of their hands."

"You have excellent eyes," said King Cyzicus. "Yes; they are six-armed giants, as you say, and these are the enemies whom I and my subjects have to contend with."

The next day, when the Argonauts were about setting sail, down came these terrible giants, stepping a hundred yards at a stride, brandishing their six arms apiece, and looking formidable, so far aloft in the air. Each of these monsters was able to carry on a whole war by himself, for with one arm he could fling immense stones, and wield a club with another, and a sword with a third, while the fourth was poking a long spear at the enemy, and the fifth and sixth were shooting him with a bow and arrow. But, luckily, though the giants were so huge, and had so many arms, they had each but one heart, and that no bigger nor braver than the heart of an ordinary man. Besides, if they had been like the hundred-armed Briareus, the brave Argonauts would have given them their hands full of fight. Jason and his friends went boldly to meet them, slew a great many, and made the rest take to their heels, so that if the giants had had six legs apiece instead of six arms, it would have served them better to run away with.

Another strange adventure happened when the voyagers came to Thrace, where they found a poor blind king, named Phineus, deserted by his subjects, and living in a very sorrowful way, all by himself: On Jason's inquiring whether they could do him any service, the king answered that he was terribly tormented by three great winged creatures, called Harpies, which had the faces of women, and the wings, bodies, and claws of vultures. These ugly wretches were in the habit of snatching away his dinner, and allowed him no peace of his life. Upon hearing this, the Argonauts spread a plentiful feast on the sea-shore, well knowing, from what the blind king said of their greediness, that the Harpies would snuff up the scent of the victuals, and quickly come to steal them away. And so it turned out; for, hardly was the table set, before the three hideous vulture women came flapping their wings, seized the food in their talons, and flew off as fast as they could. But the two sons of the North Wind drew their swords, spread their pinions, and set off through the air in pursuit of the thieves, whom they at last overtook among some islands, after a chase of hundreds of miles. The two winged youths blustered terribly at the Harpies (for they had the rough temper of their father), and so frightened them with their drawn swords, that they solemnly promised never to trouble King Phineus again.

Then the Argonauts sailed onward and met with many other marvelous incidents, any one of which would make a story by itself. At one time they landed on an island, and were reposing on the grass, when they suddenly found themselves assailed by what seemed a shower of steel-headed arrows. Some of them stuck in the ground, while others hit against their shields, and several penetrated their flesh. The fifty heroes started up, and looked about them for the hidden enemy, but could find none, nor see any spot, on the whole island, where even a single archer could lie concealed. Still, however, the steel-headed arrows came whizzing among them; and, at last, happening to look upward, they beheld a large flock of birds, hovering and wheeling aloft, and shooting their feathers down upon the Argonauts. These feathers were the steel-headed arrows that had so tormented them. There was no possibility of making any resistance; and the fifty heroic Argonauts might all have been killed or wounded by a flock of troublesome birds, without ever setting eyes on the Golden Fleece, if Jason had not thought of asking the advice of the oaken image.

So he ran to the galley as fast as his legs would carry him.

"O, daughter of the Speaking Oak," cried he, all out of breath, "we need your wisdom more than ever before! We are in great peril from a flock of birds, who are shooting us with their steel-pointed feathers. What can we do to drive them away?"

"Make a clatter on your shields," said the image.

On receiving this excellent counsel, Jason hurried back to his companions (who were far more dismayed than when they fought with the six-armed giants), and bade them strike with their swords upon their brazen shields. Forthwith the fifty heroes set heartily to work, banging with might and main, and raised such a terrible clatter, that the birds made what haste they could to get away; and though they had shot half the feathers out of their wings, they were soon seen skimming among the clouds, a long distance off, and looking like a flock of wild geese. Orpheus celebrated this victory by playing a triumphant anthem on his harp, and sang so melodiously that Jason begged him to desist, lest, as the steel-feathered birds had been driven away by an ugly sound, they might be enticed back again by a sweet one.

While the Argonauts remained on this island, they saw a small vessel approaching the shore, in which were two young men of princely demeanor, and exceedingly handsome, as young princes generally were, in those days. Now, who do you imagine these two voyagers turned out to be? Why, if you will believe me, they were the sons of that very Phrixus, who, in his childhood, had been carried to Colchis on the back of the golden-fleeced ram. Since that time, Phrixus had married the king's daughter; and the two young princes had been born and brought up at Colchis, and had spent their play-days in the outskirts of the grove, in the center of which the Golden Fleece was hanging upon a tree. They were now on their way to Greece, in hopes of getting back a kingdom that had been wrongfully taken from their father.

When the princes understood whither the Argonauts were going, they offered to turn back, and guide them to Colchis. At the same time, however, they spoke as if it were very doubtful whether Jason would succeed in getting the Golden

Fleece. According to their account, the tree on which it hung was guarded by a terrible dragon, who never failed to devour, at one mouthful, every person who might venture within his reach.

"There are other difficulties in the way," continued the young princes. "But is not this enough? Ah, brave Jason, turn back before it is too late. It would grieve us to the heart, if you and your nine and forty brave companions should be eaten up, at fifty mouthfuls, by this execrable dragon."

"My young friends," quietly replied Jason, "I do not wonder that you think the dragon very terrible. You have grown up from infancy in the fear of this monster, and therefore still regard him with the awe that children feel for the bugbears and hobgoblins which their nurses have talked to them about. But, in my view of the matter, the dragon is merely a pretty large serpent, who is not half so likely to snap me up at one mouthful as I am to cut off his ugly head, and strip the skin from his body. At all events, turn back who may, I will never see Greece again, unless I carry with me the Golden Fleece."

"We will none of us turn back!" cried his nine and forty brave comrades. "Let us get on board the galley this instant; and if the dragon is to make a breakfast of us, much good may it do him."

And Orpheus (whose custom it was to set everything to music) began to harp and sing most gloriously, and made every mother's son of them feel as if nothing in this world were so delectable as to fight dragons, and nothing so truly honorable as to be eaten up at one mouthful, in case of the worst.

After this (being now under the guidance of the two princes, who were well acquainted with the way), they quickly sailed to Colchis. When the king of the country, whose name was Aetes, heard of their arrival, he instantly summoned Jason to court. The king was a stern and cruel looking potentate; and though he put on as polite and hospitable an expression as he could, Jason did not like his face a whit better than that of the wicked King Pelias, who dethroned his father. "You are welcome, brave Jason," said King Aetes. "Pray, are you on a pleasure voyage?—Or do you meditate the discovery of unknown islands?—or what other cause has procured me the happiness of seeing you at my court?"

"Great sir," replied Jason, with an obeisance—for Chiron had taught him how to behave with propriety, whether to kings or beggars—"I have come hither with a purpose which I now beg your majesty's permission to execute. King Pelias, who sits on my father's throne (to which he has no more right than to the one on which your excellent majesty is now seated), has engaged to come down from it, and to give me his crown and sceptre, provided I bring him the Golden Fleece. This, as your majesty is aware, is now hanging on a tree here at Colchis; and I humbly solicit your gracious leave to take it away." In spite of himself, the king's face twisted itself into an angry frown; for, above all things else in the world, he prized the Golden Fleece, and was even suspected of having done a very wicked act, in order to get it into his own possession. It put him into the worst possible humor, therefore, to hear that the gallant Prince Jason, and forty-nine of the bravest young warriors of Greece, had come to Colchis with the sole purpose of taking away his chief treasure.

"Do you know," asked King Aetes, eyeing Jason very sternly, "what are the conditions which you must fulfill before getting possession of the Golden Fleece?"

"I have heard," rejoined the youth, "that a dragon lies beneath the tree on which the prize hangs, and that whoever approaches him runs the risk of being devoured at a mouthful."

"True," said the king, with a smile that did not look particularly good-natured. "Very true, young man. But there are other things as hard, or perhaps a little harder, to be done before you can even have the privilege of being devoured by the dragon. For example, you must first tame my two brazen-footed and brazen-lunged bulls, which Vulcan, the wonderful blacksmith, made for me. There is a furnace in each of their stomachs; and they breathe such hot fire out of their mouths and nostrils, that nobody has hitherto gone nigh them without being instantly burned to a small, black cinder. What do you think of this, my brave Jason?"

"I must encounter the peril," answered Jason, composedly, "since it stands in the way of my purpose."

"After taming the fiery bulls," continued King Aetes, who was determined to scare Jason if possible, "you must yoke them to a plow, and must plow the sacred earth in the Grove of Mars, and sow some of the same dragon's teeth from which Cadmus raised a crop of armed men. They are an unruly set of reprobates, those sons of the dragon's teeth; and unless you treat them suitably, they will fall upon you sword in hand. You and your nine and forty Argonauts, my bold Jason, are hardly numerous or strong enough to fight with such a host as will spring up."

"My master Chiron," replied Jason, "taught me, long ago, the story of Cadmus. Perhaps I can manage the quarrelsome sons of the dragon's teeth as well as Cadmus did."

"I wish the dragon had him," muttered King Aetes to himself, "and the four-footed pedant, his schoolmaster, into the bargain. Why, what a foolhardy, self-conceited coxcomb he is! We'll see what my fire-breathing bulls will do for him. Well, Prince Jason," he continued, aloud, and as complaisantly as he could, "make yourself comfortable for to-day, and to-morrow morning, since you insist upon it, you shall try your skill at the plow."

While the king talked with Jason, a beautiful young woman was standing behind the throne. She fixed her eyes earnestly upon the youthful stranger, and listened attentively to every word that was spoken; and when Jason withdrew from the king's presence, this young woman followed him out of the room.

"I am the king's daughter," she said to him, "and my name is Medea. I know a great deal of which other young princesses are ignorant, and can do many things which they would be afraid so much as to dream of. If you will trust to me, I can instruct you how to tame the fiery bulls, and sow the dragon's teeth, and get the Golden Fleece."

"Indeed, beautiful princess," answered Jason, "if you will do me this service, I promise to be grateful to you my whole life long.'" Gazing at Medea, he beheld a wonderful intelligence in her face. She was one of those persons whose eyes are full of mystery; so that, while looking into them, you seem to see a very great way, as into a deep well, yet can never be certain whether you see into the farthest depths, or whether there be not something else hidden at the bottom. If Jason had been capable of fearing anything, he would have been afraid of making this young princess his enemy; for, beautiful as she now looked, she might, the very next instant, become as terrible as the dragon that kept watch over the Golden Fleece.

"Princess," he exclaimed, "you seem indeed very wise and very powerful. But how can you help me to do the things of which you speak? Are you an enchantress?"

"Yes, Prince Jason," answered Medea, with a smile, "you have hit upon the truth. I am an enchantress. Circe, my father's sister, taught me to be one, and I could tell you, if I pleased, who was the old woman with the peacock, the pomegranate, and the cuckoo staff, whom you carried over the river; and, likewise, who it is that speaks through the lips of the oaken image, that stands in the prow of your galley. I am acquainted with some of your secrets, you perceive. It is well for you that I am favorably inclined; for, otherwise, you would hardly escape being snapped up by the dragon."

"I should not so much care for the dragon," replied Jason, "if I only knew how to manage the brazen-footed and fiery-lunged bulls."

"If you are as brave as I think you, and as you have need to be," said Medea, "your own bold heart will teach you that there is but one way of dealing with a mad bull. What it is I leave you to find out in the moment of peril. As for the fiery breath of these animals, I have a charmed ointment here, which will prevent you from being burned up, and cure you if you chance to be a little scorched."

So she put a golden box into his hand, and directed him how to apply the perfumed unguent which it contained, and where to meet her at midnight.

"Only be brave," added she, "and before daybreak the brazen bulls shall be tamed."

The young man assured her that his heart would not fail him. He then rejoined his comrades, and told them what had passed between the princess and himself, and warned them to be in readiness in case there might be need of their help. At the appointed hour he met the beautiful Medea on the marble steps of the king's palace. She gave him a basket, in which were the dragon's teeth, just as they had been pulled out of the monster's jaws by Cadmus, long ago. Medea then led Jason down the palace steps, and through the silent streets of the city, and into the royal pasture ground, where the two brazen-footed bulls were kept. It was a starry night, with a bright gleam along the eastern edge of the sky, where the moon was soon going to show herself. After entering the pasture, the princess paused and looked around.

"There they are," said she, "reposing themselves and chewing their fiery cuds in that farthest corner of the field. It will be excellent sport, I assure you, when they catch a glimpse of your figure. My father and all his court delight in nothing so much as to see a stranger trying to yoke them, in order to come at the Golden Fleece. It makes a holiday in Colchis whenever such a thing happens. For my part, I enjoy it immensely. You cannot imagine in what a mere twinkling of an eye their hot breath shrivels a young man into a black cinder."

"Are you sure, beautiful Medea," asked Jason, "quite sure, that the unguent in the gold box will prove a remedy against those terrible burns?"

"If you doubt, if you are in the least afraid," said the princess, looking him in the face by the dim starlight, "you had better never have been born than to go a step nigher to the bulls."

But Jason had set his heart steadfastly on getting the Golden Fleece; and I positively doubt whether he would have gone back without it, even had he been certain of finding himself turned into a red-hot cinder, or a handful of white ashes, the instant he made a step farther. He therefore let go Medea's hand, and walked boldly forward in the direction whither she had pointed. At some distance before him he perceived four streams of fiery vapor, regularly appearing and again vanishing, after dimly lighting up the surrounding obscurity. These, you will understand, were caused by the breath of the brazen bulls, which was quietly stealing out of their four nostrils, as they lay chewing their cuds.

At the first two or three steps which Jason made, the four fiery streams appeared to gush out somewhat more plentifully; for the two brazen bulls had heard his foot tramp, and were lifting up their hot noses to snuff the air. He went a little farther, and by the way in which the red vapor now spouted forth, he judged that the creatures had got upon their feet. Now he could see glowing sparks, and vivid jets of flame. At the next step, each of the bulls made the pasture echo with a terrible roar, while the burning breath, which they thus belched forth, lit up the whole field with a momentary flash. One other stride did bold Jason make; and, suddenly as a streak of lightning, on came these fiery animals, roaring like thunder, and sending out sheets of white flame, which so kindled up the scene that the young man could discern every object more distinctly than by daylight. Most distinctly of all he saw the two horrible creatures galloping right down upon him, their brazen hoofs rattling and ringing over the ground, and their tails sticking up stiffly into the air, as has always been the fashion with angry bulls. Their breath scorched the herbage before them. So intensely hot it was, indeed, that it caught a dry tree under which Jason was now standing, and set it all in a light blaze. But as for Jason himself (thanks to Medea's enchanted ointment), the white flame curled around his body, without injuring him a jot more than if he had been made of asbestos.

Greatly encouraged at finding himself not yet turned into a cinder, the young man awaited the attack of the bulls. Just as the brazen brutes fancied themselves sure of tossing him into the air, he caught one of them by the horn, and the other by his screwed-up tail, and held them in a gripe like that of an iron vice, one with his right hand, the other with his left. Well, he must have been wonderfully strong in his arms, to be sure. But the secret of the matter was, that the brazen bulls were enchanted creatures, and that Jason had broken the spell of their fiery fierceness by his bold way of handling them. And, ever since that time, it has been the favorite method of brave men, when danger assails them, to do what they call "taking the bull by the horns"; and to gripe him by the tail is pretty much the same thing—that is, to throw aside fear, and overcome the peril by despising it. It was now easy to yoke the bulls, and to harness them to the plow, which had lain rusting on the ground for a great many years gone by; so long was it before anybody could be found capable of plowing that piece of land. Jason, I suppose, had been taught how to draw a furrow by the good old Chiron, who, perhaps, used to allow himself to be harnessed to the plow. At any rate, our hero succeeded perfectly well in breaking up the greensward; and, by the time that the moon was a quarter of her journey up the sky, the plowed field lay before him, a large tract of black earth, ready to be sown with the dragon's teeth. So Jason scattered them broadcast, and harrowed them into the soil with a brush-harrow, and took his stand on the edge of the field, anxious to see what would happen next.

"Must we wait long for harvest time?" he inquired of Medea, who was now standing by his side.

"Whether sooner or later, it will be sure to come," answered the princess. "A crop of armed men never fails to spring up, when the dragon's teeth have been sown."

The moon was now high aloft in the heavens, and threw its bright beams over the plowed field, where as yet there was nothing to be seen. Any farmer, on viewing it, would have said that Jason must wait weeks before the green blades would peep from among the clods, and whole months before the yellow grain would be ripened for the sickle. But by and by, all over the field, there was something that glistened in the moonbeams, like sparkling drops of dew. These bright objects sprouted higher, and proved to be the steel heads of spears. Then there was a dazzling gleam from a vast number of polished brass helmets, beneath which, as they grew farther out of the soil, appeared the dark and bearded visages of warriors, struggling to free themselves from the imprisoning earth. The first look that they gave at the upper world was a glare of wrath and defiance. Next were seen their bright breastplates; in every right hand there was a sword or a spear, and on each left arm a shield; and when this strange crop of warriors had but half grown out of the earth, they struggled—such was their impatience of restraint—and, as it were, tore themselves up by the roots. Wherever a dragon's tooth had fallen, there stood a man armed for battle. They made a clangor with their swords against their shields, and eyed one another fiercely; for they had come into this beautiful world, and into the peaceful moonlight, full of rage and stormy passions, and ready to take the life of every human brother, in recompense of the boon of their own existence.

There have been many other armies in the world that seemed to possess the same fierce nature with the one which had now sprouted from the dragon's teeth; but these, in the moonlit field, were the more excusable, because they never had women for their mothers. And how it would have rejoiced any great captain, who was bent on conquering the world, like Alexander or Napoleon, to raise a crop of armed soldiers as easily as Jason did! For a while, the warriors stood flourishing their weapons, clashing their swords against their shields, and boiling over with the red-hot thirst for battle. Then they began to shout—"Show us the enemy! Lead us to the charge! Death or victory!" "Come on, brave comrades! Conquer or die!" and a hundred other outcries, such as men always bellow forth on a battle field, and which these dragon people seemed to have at their tongues' ends. At last, the front rank caught sight of Jason, who, beholding the flash of so many weapons in the moonlight, had thought it best to draw his sword. In a moment all the sons of the dragon's teeth appeared to take Jason for an enemy; and crying with one voice, "Guard the Golden Fleece!" they ran at him with uplifted swords and protruded spears. Jason knew that it would be impossible to withstand this blood-thirsty battalion with his single arm, but determined, since there was nothing better to be done, to die as valiantly as if he himself had sprung from a dragon's tooth.

Medea, however, bade him snatch up a stone from the ground.

"Throw it among them quickly!" cried she. "It is the only way to save yourself."

The armed men were now so nigh that Jason could discern the fire flashing out of their enraged eyes, when he let fly the stone, and saw it strike the helmet of a tall warrior, who was rushing upon him with his blade aloft. The stone glanced from this man's helmet to the shield of his nearest comrade, and thence flew right into the angry face of another, hitting him smartly between the eyes. Each of the three who had been struck by the stone took it for granted that his next neighbor had given him a blow; and instead of running any farther towards Jason, they began to fight among themselves. The confusion spread through the host, so that it seemed scarcely a moment before they were all hacking, hewing, and stabbing at one another, lopping off arms, heads, and legs and doing such memorable deeds that Jason was filled with immense admiration; although, at the same time, he could not help laughing to behold these mighty men punishing each other for an offense which he himself had committed. In an incredibly short space of time (almost as short, indeed, as it had taken them to grow up), all but one of the heroes of the dragon's teeth were stretched lifeless on the field. The last survivor, the bravest and strongest of the whole, had just force enough to wave his crimson sword over his head and give a shout of exultation, crying, "Victory! Victory! Immortal fame!" when he himself fell down, and lay quietly among his slain brethren.

And there was the end of the army that had sprouted from the dragon's teeth. That fierce and feverish fight was the only enjoyment which they had tasted on this beautiful earth.

"Let them sleep in the bed of honor," said the Princess Medea, with a sly smile at Jason. "The world will always have simpletons enough, just like them, fighting and dying for they know not what, and fancying that posterity will take the trouble to put laurel wreaths on their rusty and battered helmets. Could you help smiling, Prince Jason, to see the self-conceit of that last fellow, just as he tumbled down?"

"It made me very sad," answered Jason, gravely. "And, to tell you the truth, princess, the Golden Fleece does not appear so well worth the winning, after what I have here beheld!"

"You will think differently in the morning," said Medea. "True, the Golden Fleece may not be so valuable as you have thought it; but then there is nothing better in the world; and one must needs have an object, you know. Come! Your night's work has been well performed; and to-morrow you can inform King Aetes that the first part of your allotted task is fulfilled."

Agreeably to Medea's advice, Jason went betimes in the morning to the palace of King Aetes. Entering the presence chamber, he stood at the foot of the throne, and made a low obeisance.

"Your eyes look heavy, Prince Jason," observed the king; "you appear to have spent a sleepless night. I hope you have been considering the matter a little more wisely, and have concluded not to get yourself scorched to a cinder, in attempting to tame my brazen-lunged bulls."

"That is already accomplished, may it please your majesty," replied Jason. "The bulls have been tamed and yoked; the field has been plowed; the dragon's teeth have been sown broadcast, and harrowed into the soil; the crop of armed warriors have sprung up, and they have slain one another, to the last man. And now I solicit your majesty's permission to encounter the dragon, that I may take down the Golden Fleece from the tree, and depart, with my nine and forty comrades."

King Aetes scowled, and looked very angry and excessively disturbed; for he knew that, in accordance with his kingly promise, he ought now to permit Jason to win the Fleece, if his courage and skill should enable him to do so. But, since the young man had met with such good luck in the matter of the brazen bulls and the dragon's teeth, the king feared that he would be equally successful in slaying the dragon. And therefore, though he would gladly have seen Jason snapped up at a mouthful, he was resolved (and it was a very wrong thing of this wicked potentate) not to run any further risk of losing his beloved Fleece.

"You never would have succeeded in this business, young man," said he, "if my undutiful daughter Medea had not helped you with her enchantments. Had you acted fairly, you would have been, at this instant, a black cinder, or a handful of white ashes. I forbid you, on pain of death, to make any more attempts to get the Golden Fleece. To speak my mind plainly, you shall never set eyes on so much as one of its glistening locks."

Jason left the king's presence in great sorrow and anger. He could think of nothing better to be done than to summon together his forty-nine brave Argonauts, march at once to the Grove of Mars, slay the dragon, take possession of the Golden Fleece, get on board the Argo, and spread all sail for Iolchos. The success of this scheme depended, it is true, on the doubtful point whether all the fifty heroes might not be snapped up, at so many mouthfuls, by the dragon. But, as Jason was hastening down the palace steps, the Princess Medea called after him, and beckoned him to return. Her black eyes shone upon him with such a keen intelligence, that he felt as if there were a serpent peeping out of them; and, although she had done him so much service only the night before, he was by no means very certain that she would not do him an equally great mischief before sunset. These enchantresses, you must know, are never to be depended upon.

"What says King Aetes, my royal and upright father?" inquired Medea, slightly smiling. "Will he give you the Golden Fleece, without any further risk or trouble?"

"On the contrary," answered Jason, "he is very angry with me for taming the brazen bulls and sowing the dragon's teeth. And he forbids me to make any more attempts, and positively refuses to give up the Golden Fleece, whether I slay the dragon or no."

"Yes, Jason," said the princess, "and I can tell you more. Unless you set sail from Colchis before to-morrow's sunrise, the king means to burn your fifty-oared galley, and put yourself and your forty-nine brave comrades to the sword. But be of good courage. The Golden Fleece you shall have, if it lies within the power of my enchantments to get it for you. Wait for me here an hour before midnight."

At the appointed hour you might again have seen Prince Jason and the Princess Medea, side by side, stealing through the streets of Colchis, on their way to the sacred grove, in the center of which the Golden Fleece was suspended to a tree. While they were crossing the pasture ground, the brazen bulls came towards Jason, lowing, nodding their heads, and thrusting forth their snouts, which, as other cattle do, they loved to have rubbed and caressed by a friendly hand. Their fierce nature was thoroughly tamed; and, with their fierceness, the two furnaces in their stomachs had likewise been extinguished, insomuch that they probably enjoyed far more comfort in grazing and chewing their cuds than ever before. Indeed, it had heretofore been a great inconvenience to these poor animals, that, whenever they wished to eat a mouthful of grass, the fire out of their nostrils had shriveled it up, before they could manage to crop it. How they contrived to keep themselves alive is more than I can imagine. But now, instead of emitting jets of flame and streams of sulphurous vapor, they breathed the very sweetest of cow breath.

After kindly patting the bulls, Jason followed Medea's guidance into the Grove of Mars, where the great oak trees, that had been growing for centuries, threw so thick a shade that the moonbeams struggled vainly to find their way through it. Only here and there a glimmer fell upon the leaf-strewn earth, or now and then a breeze stirred the boughs aside, and gave Jason a glimpse of the sky, lest, in that deep obscurity, he might forget that there was one, overhead. At length, when they had gone farther and farther into the heart of the duskiness, Medea squeezed Jason's hand.

"Look yonder," she whispered. "Do you see it?"

Gleaming among the venerable oaks, there was a radiance, not like the moonbeams, but rather resembling the golden glory of the setting sun. It proceeded from an object, which appeared to be suspended at about a man's height from the ground, a little farther within the wood.

"What is it?" asked Jason.

"Have you come so far to seek it," exclaimed Medea, "and do you not recognize the meed of all your toils and perils, when it glitters before your eyes? It is the Golden Fleece."

Jason went onward a few steps farther, and then stopped to gaze. O, how beautiful it looked, shining with a marvelous light of its own, that inestimable prize which so many heroes had longed to behold, but had perished in the quest of it, either by the perils of their voyage, or by the fiery breath of the brazen-lunged bulls.

"How gloriously it shines!" cried Jason, in a rapture. "It has surely been dipped in the richest gold of sunset. Let me hasten onward, and take it to my bosom."

"Stay," said Medea, holding him back. "Have you forgotten what guards it?"

To say the truth, in the joy of beholding the object of his desires, the terrible dragon had quite slipped out of Jason's memory. Soon, however, something came to pass, that reminded him what perils were still to be encountered. An antelope, that probably mistook the yellow radiance for sunrise, came bounding fleetly through the grove. He was rushing straight towards the Golden Fleece, when suddenly there was a frightful hiss, and the immense head and half the scaly body of the dragon was thrust forth (for he was twisted round the trunk of the tree on which the Fleece hung), and seizing the poor antelope, swallowed him with one snap of his jaws.

After this feat, the dragon seemed sensible that some other living creature was within reach, on which he felt inclined to finish his meal. In various directions he kept poking his ugly snout among the trees, stretching out his neck a terrible long way, now here, now there, and now close to the spot where Jason and the princess were hiding behind an oak. Upon my word, as the head came waving and undulating through the air, and reaching almost within arm's length of Prince Jason, it was a very hideous and uncomfortable sight. The gape of his enormous jaws was nearly as wide as the gateway of the king's palace.

"Well, Jason," whispered Medea (for she was ill natured, as all enchantresses are, and wanted to make the bold youth tremble), "what do you think now of your prospect of winning the Golden Fleece?"

Jason answered only by drawing his sword, and making a step forward.

"Stay, foolish youth," said Medea, grasping his arm. "Do not you see you are lost, without me as your good angel? In this gold box I have a magic potion, which will do the dragon's business far more effectually than your sword."

The dragon had probably heard the voices; for swift as lightning, his black head and forked tongue came hissing among the trees again, darting full forty feet at a stretch. As it approached, Medea tossed the contents of the gold box right down the monster's wide-open throat. Immediately, with an outrageous hiss and a tremendous wriggle—flinging his tail up to the tip-top of the tallest tree, and shattering all its branches as it crashed heavily down again—the dragon fell at full length upon the ground, and lay quite motionless.

"It is only a sleeping potion," said the enchantress to Prince Jason. "One always finds a use for these mischievous creatures, sooner or later; so I did not wish to kill him outright. Quick! Snatch the prize, and let us begone. You have won the Golden Fleece."

Jason caught the fleece from the tree, and hurried through the grove, the deep shadows of which were illuminated as he passed by the golden glory of the precious object that he bore along. A little way before him, he beheld the old woman whom he had helped over the stream, with her peacock beside her. She clapped her hands for joy, and beckoning him to make haste, disappeared among the duskiness of the trees. Espying the two winged sons of the North Wind (who were disporting themselves in the moonlight, a few hundred feet aloft), Jason bade them tell the rest of the Argonauts to embark as speedily as possible. But Lynceus, with his sharp eyes, had already caught a glimpse of him, bringing the Golden Fleece, although several stone walls, a hill, and the black shadows of the Grove of Mars, intervened between. By his advice, the heroes had seated themselves on the benches of the galley, with their oars held perpendicularly, ready to let fall into the water.

As Jason drew near, he heard the Talking Image calling to him with more than ordinary eagerness, in its grave, sweet voice:

"Make haste, Prince Jason! For your life, make haste!"

With one bound, he leaped aboard. At sight of the glorious radiance of the Golden Fleece, the nine and forty heroes gave a mighty shout, and Orpheus, striking his harp, sang a song of triumph, to the cadence of which the galley flew over the water, homeward bound, as if careering along with wings!

The Edith Wharton Collection (complete and unabridged) Including: The Age of Innocence, Ethan Frome, The House of Mirth, Summer, The Custom of the Country and The Reef
Edith Wharton
Benediction Classics, 2012
1188 pages
ISBN: 978-1-78139-340-6

Available from www.amazon.com, www.amazon.co.uk

Edith Wharton (1862 - 1937), was a Pulitzer Prize-winning American novelist and short story writer. She grew up in upper-class pre-WWI society and many of her stories critique this culture, using subtle irony. In this volume are brought together her six most acclaimed works: The Age of Innocence, Ethan Frome, The House of Mirth, Summer, The Custom of the Country and The Reef. Enjoy the beauty of Wharton's writing in this great collection, where the characters are beautifully captured, they struggle between duty and love in a society that dreads scandal more than disease and they wrestle courageously against their sometimes tragic fates. Wharton writes fine and intense narratives and is the greatest critic of her society.

Wilkie Collins Collection (complete and unabridged):The Woman in White, The Moonstone, No Name, Armadale
Wilkie Collins
Benediction Classics, 2012
1136 pages
ISBN: 978-1-78139-328-4

Available from www.amazon.com, www.amazon.co.uk

Wilkie Collins (1824-1889) is best known as the innovator of the detective novel. He was a prolific writer, with 30 novels, more than 60 short stories, 14 plays, and more than 100 non-fiction pieces to his name. He was a close friend of Charles Dickens and one of the best known and loved Victorian Fiction writers. After his death, his popularity diminished as Dickens's grew. Now, Collins is once again becoming popular with most of his books in print and film, television and radio adaptations being made. There is much still to be discovered about this great author and this volume contains his four most popular novels.

F Scott Fitzgerald's Novels - unabridged - This Side of Paradise, The Beautiful and the Damned, The Great Gatsby, Tender is the Night
F Scott Fitzgerald
Benediction Classics, 2012
870 pages
ISBN: 978-1-78139-238-6

Available from www.amazon.com, www.amazon.co.uk

"This Side of Paradise" was published in 1920. The novel explores the lives and morality of post-World War I youth and the theme of love corrupted by greed. "The Beautiful and the Damned" is about a 1920s socialite and his relationship with his wife, his service in the army and his alcoholism. It explores the themes of love, money and decadence. "The Great Gatsby" was first published in 1925 and quickly became a classic novel. The Modern Library named it the second best English-language novel of the 20th Century. Set in 1922 America is enjoying the roaring twenties, however Prohibition has made alcohol an illegal substance and hence the bootleggers are making a killing. "Tender Is the Night" is the final complete novel that F. Scott Fitzgerald wrote, it was published in 1934. It explores complex relationships and mental health issues, it is quite dark at times.

Willa Cather Collection (complete and unabridged) Including: Alexander's Bridge, My Antonia, O Pioneers!, The Song of the Lark, One of Ours, Youth and the Bright Medusa and The Troll Garden and other stories
Willa Cather
Oxford City Press, 2012
1200 pages
ISBN: 978-1-78139-341-3

Available from www.amazon.com, www.amazon.co.uk

Willa Cather was a brilliant American author who wrote evocative novels mainly about frontier life on the Great Plains of Nebraska, in her early works - Alexander's Bridge, O Pioneers!, My Antonia, and The Song of the Lark. However, her next novel, "One of Ours" was set during World War I and she received the Pulitzer Prize for it in 1923. These four Novels are available in this volume, along with two collections of her short stories - "Youth and the Bright Medusa" and "The Troll Garden and other stories".

Also from Benediction Books ...
Wandering Between Two Worlds: Essays on Faith and Art
Anita Mathias
Benediction Books, 2007
152 pages
ISBN: 0955373700

Available from www.amazon.com, www.amazon.co.uk

In these wide-ranging lyrical essays, Anita Mathias writes, in lush, lovely prose, of her naughty Catholic childhood in Jamshedpur, India; her large, eccentric family in Mangalore, a sea-coast town converted by the Portuguese in the sixteenth century; her rebellion and atheism as a teenager in her Himalayan boarding school, run by German missionary nuns, St. Mary's Convent, Nainital; and her abrupt religious conversion after which she entered Mother Teresa's convent in Calcutta as a novice. Later rich, elegant essays explore the dualities of her life as a writer, mother, and Christian in the United States-- Domesticity and Art, Writing and Prayer, and the experience of being "an alien and stranger" as an immigrant in America, sensing the need for roots.

About the Author

Anita Mathias is the author of *Wandering Between Two Worlds: Essays on Faith and Art*. She has a B.A. and M.A. in English from Somerville College, Oxford University, and an M.A. in Creative Writing from the Ohio State University, USA. Anita won a National Endowment of the Arts fellowship in Creative Nonfiction in 1997. She lives in Oxford, England with her husband, Roy, and her daughters, Zoe and Irene.

Anita's website:
http://www.anitamathias.com, and
Anita's blog Dreaming Beneath the Spires:
http://dreamingbeneaththespires.blogspot.com

The Church That Had Too Much
Anita Mathias
Benediction Books, 2010
52 pages
ISBN: 9781849026567

Available from www.amazon.com, www.amazon.co.uk

The Church That Had Too Much was very well-intentioned. She wanted to love God, she wanted to love people, but she was both hampered by her muchness and the abundance of her possessions, and beset by ambition, power struggles and snobbery. Read about the surprising way The Church That Had Too Much began to resolve her problems in this deceptively simple and enchanting fable.

About the Author

Anita Mathias is the author of *Wandering Between Two Worlds: Essays on Faith and Art*. She has a B.A. and M.A. in English from Somerville College, Oxford University, and an M.A. in Creative Writing from the Ohio State University, USA. Anita won a National Endowment of the Arts fellowship in Creative Non-fiction in 1997. She lives in Oxford, England with her husband, Roy, and her daughters, Zoe and Irene.

Anita's website:
http://www.anitamathias.com, and
Anita's blog Dreaming Beneath the Spires:
http://dreamingbeneaththespires.blogspot.com

www.ingramcontent.com/pod-product-compliance
Lightning Source LLC
Chambersburg PA
CBHW080811020826
48982CB00017B/901

* 9 7 8 1 7 8 1 3 9 3 8 0 2 *